A DAY
BEYOND THE SHINING WATER

Audrey Howard's novels in Coronet

The Mallow Years
Shining Threads
A Day Will Come
All the Dear Faces
There Is No Parting
The Woman from Browhead
Echo of Another Time
The Silence of Strangers
A World of Difference
Promises Lost
The Shadowed Hills
Strand of Dreams
Tomorrow's Memories
Not a Bird Will Sing
When Morning Comes
Beyond the Shining Water
Angel Meadow
Rivers of the Heart

About the author

Audrey Howard was born in Liverpool in 1929. Before she began to write she had a variety of jobs, among them hairdresser, model, shop assistant, cleaner and civil servant. In 1981 she wrote the first of her novels when she was out of work and living in Australia. There are now more than twenty.

A Day Will Come

Beyond the
Shining Water

Audrey Howard

CORONET BOOKS
Hodder & Stoughton

First published as two separate volumes:

A Day Will Come Copyright © 1992 by Audrey Howard
First published in Great Britain in 1992
by Hodder and Stoughton
First published in Coronet paperback in 1992
by Hodder and Stoughton
A division of Hodder Headline

Beyond the Shining Water Copyright © 1999 by Audrey Howard
First published in Great Britain in 1999
by Hodder and Stoughton
First published in Coronet paperback in 1999
by Hodder and Stoughton
A division of Hodder Headline

A Coronet Paperback

ISBN 0 340 79376 7

Printed and bound in Great Britain by
Clays Ltd, St Ives plc

Hodder and Stoughton
A division of Hodder Headline
338 Euston Road
London NW1 3BH

A DAY WILL COME

To the only lady of my acquaintance
who has bought all my books
IN HARDBACK!
Thank you, Beryl Mulligan

Part I

1

Daisy watched the gangmaster as he furtively divided out the money on the ale-house counter. His dirt-ingrained fingers were deft, moving so quickly and smoothly they were no more than a blur in the poor light from the candles. The sound of coin striking against coin could scarcely be heard, drowned out as it was by the shrieks of bawdy laughter which came from the women at the far end of the room, and Daisy doubted if any of those who caroused there, and who were about to be paid for the week's work they had just completed, were in any fit state to notice should this man slip away taking their wages with him. The gin they swilled at a penny a quartern was cheap and strong and it took a very small sum of money to become disgustingly intoxicated. 'Drunk for a penny, dead drunk for tuppence,' it was said and the maxim was true, for the women and their male companions were fast becoming wild and unruly. One of them was Daisy's mother.

She rubbed one bare foot on top of the other, fastidiously flicking aside the cockroach which wandered across it. It had come from a crack in the hard earthen floor, looking for the filth its kind thrived on and which was in such abundance here. She was tempted to squash it as she would squash any of the myriad crawling creatures that dwelt not only in her surroundings but on her person, but for a child for whom such circumstances were commonplace she was surprisingly squeamish over certain things. Cockroaches were one of them. She knew its shell would crack quite easily beneath her hard and calloused heel but the mess it would leave on her skin was too disgusting to contemplate. She watched it carefully as it made its way beneath a pile of dirt in the corner of the smoke-filled room and when she was certain that it had gone she resumed her vigilant observation of the gangmaster.

His eyes constantly flickered away from his task, turning again and again to the women who were creating such a drunken clamour. His glance passed over the attentive figure of the child, taking no more interest in her than he would of one of the pots which hung at the back of the bar counter. She was to him merely a tool, as the pots were a tool of the inn's trade, part of his 'gang' and as such had been employed by him since the day she had heaved herself up on to her own two unsteady legs. Picking stones and scaring rooks at a tender age with the other infants – those who survived – born to 'his' women. Earning her keep, for you got 'nowt for nowt' in his world.

With a sleight of hand which none of the brawling women would have noticed sober, let alone drunk, several of the coins were transferred easily from the counter to his pocket and Daisy hissed knowingly through her teeth. She was right! She had been right all along. He was quick, there was no doubt about it, but this time she had clearly seen it. She'd had her suspicions several times over the past few months when the amount her mother had handed over to her – after she had recovered from her drunken stupor – had not added up to what Daisy reckoned it should be. Fourpence a day for herself and eightpence for her Mam. Seven days work at a shilling a day for the pair of them which, in any-body's calculations, came to seven shillings. Her mother had parted with a few pence for gin on the day they were paid, which was always a Saturday, but even so there should have been more than the four shillings and eightpence which had been put into Daisy's hand last week.

The dirty sod! The rotten bastard! It was him. Taking what was not his. Taking what she and her Mam and all the other overworked and underpaid women in the gang had broken their backs to earn in the past week. Pocketing the profits himself, naturally, for it was he who agreed the price with the farmer for his gang's labour but taking a few pence more from the wages of each of his labourers. Whilst they were scarcely able to stand, let alone count what he put into their hands, he was cheating them, relying on the fact that though most of them could recognise and calculate the coins whilst sober, drunk they could not.

Daisy had known no life other than that with the gangmaster. For ten years she and her mother and the rest of the women had roamed the farmlands of Lancashire from Kendal to St Helens, from the coast to the foothills of the great Pennine chain, working the fields of all the great landowners, including the two wealthiest of them all, Lord Derby of Knowsley and Lord Thornley of Thornley Green, and a dozen others. The aristocracy on whose broad acres she and her itinerant companions were employed in stone-picking, hoeing and gleaning, dung-spreading and turnip-cleaning and any other casual work the gangmaster could get for them. Stone-picking was done mainly by the younger children. The fields were raked overnight in order to loosen the stones and in the morning the children moved across the ground, bending over their task for twelve to fourteen hours each day while the light lasted. Each picker carried a two-gallon pail which held a 'peck' of stones and as each pail was filled the stones were dumped in a heap in the furrows ready to be counted by the vigilant gangmaster for it was from these that the farmer reckoned the gangmaster's wages. This was done in January right through until March, also picking 'twitch', roots of couch grass, and preparing the fields for planting. In April, May and June they were set to weeding the growing crops and in July 'singling' turnips and all under the keen supervision of the gangmaster. They never knew his name since from the first they had simply called him 'master' and that was who he was and what he was, their master. In August and September came the harvest. They worked from dawn to dusk then, following the men as the corn was mown, hauling it into rows ready for the cart, binding it into sheaves, raking the stubble, staggering under swathes of barley as they were made ready for pitching on to the waggons. In October and November they gathered turnips and carrots and in December, when the

13

frosts came to turn the ground to iron, stone-picking began again. So it went on, year in, year out, the seasons and the weather ruling the routine of their lives.

Daisy could just remember being placed in the shade between two bundles of corn in an angle of the harvest field, fastened with other unemployable infants to a gatepost with a length of twine and fed from her mother's breast during a brief interval in the gleaning. Well, she said she remembered it but perhaps the reminiscences of her mother and the other women about the fire as they smoked their short black pipes had been absorbed by her child's mind, colouring them into a pleasant picture. Sun-dappled shade and the sweet smell of honeysuckle. Meadows thick with the daisies for which she had been named. Warm breezes on her bare brown legs and her mother's careless embrace before she returned to work. The days of thin drizzle and cold mist when she and the other children too young to work had huddled together beneath the shelter of the dripping leaves of the oak tree were hazy, hidden with other, less pleasant memories in her short life. The smell of the cowpats amongst which they had hurriedly been roped together, the sharpness of the stubble which was their bed and her mother's irritable tongue and hard hand, brought about by the gin she had drunk the night before. These memories were lost, overlaid by the remembrances of better times, for who wanted to dwell on misery? Certainly none of them, for there had been far too much of it in their shifting lives.

Two dozen women and children then, for the gangmaster would employ no men, nor boys. It was only disabled men, brought low by illness or infirmity, who would consider such menial work, since they could get no other, or young lads with no home or parents, escapees from institutions such as the poorhouse or a cotton mill. But the gangmaster would have no truck with them, saying they brought nothing but trouble. They interfered with the women, attachments were formed and his 'gang' became unworkable.

Now it was October. The harvest was in and it was time to move on to wherever their master could find them work.

They had finished the gleaning that day. The last sheaf had been removed from the last field on Abel Dixon's place, a tenant farmer renting Park Farm on Lord Thornley's land. It had been gone over with the hand drag-rake and the last wisp of corn left by the harvesters had been gathered in. Abel Dixon himself had put the bag of coins into the gang-master's hand and Daisy had heard him say that he would see them all next year, God willing. A handshake to seal the bargain, a touch to the brim of his hat from the gangmaster, respectful like, for the man was his employer and he had called them all to him sharply, leading them off like a small flock of sheep in the direction of Primrose Bank and the Last Shift, the only ale-house in the village.

"We'll have us a sup to wet our whistles, my lasses," he had said genially, "and then we'll be on our way. I reckon we can find us some work, picking potatoes and mangold-wurzels fer a week or two but the turnip an' carrot crop's poor this year, I heard tell. So it looks as though it might have to be St Helens if we're to eat this winter."

They had all groaned at the mention of St Helens because of the coal mines there but they moved off amiably enough for had they not a whole day before them in which to do nothing but recover from the gin they had promised themselves tonight? Their wages for the week would be in their hand by the end of the day, the weather was still fine and warm, they were all comparatively healthy and well fed after a summer – a fine summer, at that – working in the fields, and the prospect of the long cold winter ahead was just that. Ahead! In the future, and when had they ever concerned themselves with the future? Their master would fend for them, find them work and a roof of sorts over their heads. They had nowt to think about but the evening's entertainment. Life was grand, wasn't it?

They had laughed and shouted obscenities at each other as they entered the village, shocking the decent villagers with their loud and coarse conversation, not at all ashamed of their great thick boots, nor the tattered and stained petti-coats which they wore tucked up between their bare legs, just as they had in the fields from which they had come.

Grown men blushed as Gertie Wilson winked and made a suggestive movement with her soil-encrusted hand, indicating that what was hidden beneath her drawn-up petticoat was well worth their consideration.

Now they were all as drunk as fiddlers' bitches, hanging about the neck of any man who cared to take them on and there were more than a few, farm labourers and 'navvies' who worked the railway line which was under construction from St Helens to Rainford. Rough men and rough women, fondling one another quite openly in the smoke from a dozen candles and as many long-stemmed pipes. Male figures lounged about in the gathered smock of the countryman, battered hats upon their heads, their arms about one another's shoulders in the last stages of drunkenness before they fell down. Young children, the offspring of the women in the gang, loitered about in the doorway, their eyes hooded and watchful, for men in their cups were careless with their money. Two of them, no more than three or four years of age, were drinking from a jug someone had left on an upturned barrel and a woman with no bonnet, a pair of men's boots on her feet and the most furious black eye Daisy had ever seen, nursed a baby, giving it sips of gin from her glass.

The gangmaster stood up and stretched himself to his considerable height, then turned and the rich golden brown of Daisy's accusing eyes met his. She said nothing. She was ten years old and what could she do against the power and the might of the man who was her owner, her father for all she knew since he had sired many of the children in the gang? He had them all, women and children, in his cruel grasp, a hard master who would not hesitate to rid himself in any careless way he thought fit of anyone who interfered with his self-made way of life. Cross him and he would discard her and her mother as he would any troublesome baggage which no longer gave service. But all the same she'd not be cheated, not by him or any man. She'd let him see she knew his game and if he clouted her one, which wouldn't be the first time by any means, what did it matter as long as she got her full seven bob? She had bruises even now on her fine young flesh, not just put there by him but by her Mam when she was in one of her drunken rages, but she was used to that.

She stepped forward boldly, tossing back the thick matted curtain of her curling hair, meaning to do no more than stare pointedly at the pouch of coins in the gangmaster's hand then let her eyes fall to the pocket in which he had put the stolen coins, but her sense of injustice and resentment at the theft of the few pennies, so hard earned, overcame her caution.

"That weren't right what you just did." The words were out before she knew she was going to say them. Her heart missed a beat in her narrow chest but the surge of anger in her pumped the blood vigorously through her veins and it gave her a strange courage. "I saw yer put that brass in yer pocket and what I want ter know is how much? Me and me Mam earn a shilling a day between us and that's what I want put in me hand right now. Now if them others are too drunk to notice you've fiddled a bit of their wages on the side that's their business and more fool them fer letting yer do it but I'm having me full pay and so's me Mam."

Her face was pink with righteous indignation beneath its coating of dirt and the narrowed gleam of her amber eyes was strangely cat-like. She was a thin child, wiry and small for her age. Dressed as she was in an assortment of women's clothing which had been carelessly tied on to her with lengths of string until it more or less fitted her growing frame, she showed no promise of the beauty which would one day be hers. She was indescribably dirty. Her bare feet and ankles, revealed by the shortness of her roughly hacked-off skirt, were a uniform grey with a thick rim of black on the soles of her feet and between her toes. Her long curling toenails which had never been trimmed had a rim of the same muck beneath them, as had her fingernails. In her ears and in the soft and childish creases of her neck lay a coating of filth which had not been disturbed for what looked like years. Her hair vibrated about her small head, flowing down her back to her waist, a dense mass of close curls, dusty and tangled; caught in it were burrs from the field, grass and, very evident to even the most casual eye, the vermin which was always with the great mass of the unwashed poor.

Slowly, incredulously, the expression on the gangmaster's face changed from one of gloating satisfaction to a venom which boded ill for the child who defied him. His eyes narrowed dangerously and his mouth thinned. He took a step towards her, lowering his head like a bull about to charge, and was surprised when she did not back away. He felt a prick of admiration for it took spunk to stand up to him but by heck he'd have no one speak as she had. A kid of no more than eight or nine telling him to his bloody face he was cheating his workforce – even if he was – and that *she'd* have none of it! He was not unduly concerned that the women in his employ might overhear this exchange for there was not one at this particular moment who knew what time of day it was, let alone what he was up to. They were so drunk they could scarcely stand and were being 'helped' out of the ale-house by their male companions, ready to collapse on the nearest bit of spare ground or cottage garden, like bitches on heat, in their eagerness to be about one another in the customary finish to their Saturday night revelry.

"You better watch yer mouth, my lass, or you might find you're minus a few teeth before long." His voice was soft, not because he did not wish to be overheard but because he had found that a mild tone could often be more menacing when subduing a bit of rebellion. Speak soft before you belted them and they became much more amenable. And this one looked as though she might need one of his lessons in good manners. He'd have to watch her and if she proved awkward show her who was the master. Something she'd not forget in a hurry. He'd overlook this lapse for now but he'd keep an eye on her. Skinny little thing she was, all eyes and hair, but she could cause trouble if she wasn't shown the error of her ways before she got out of hand. He smiled, revealing the blackened and rotting stumps of his teeth.

"You'd best cut along with yer Mam," he continued pleasantly enough. "She's found herself a chap by the look of it but I reckon he'd not mind if you was to join them. Off yer go now and don't let me hear no more about what don't concern yer."

"It do concern me. Me and me Mam. We worked hard last week and we want what's coming to us."

"You'll get more than that if yer don't watch what yer saying, my girl. Kid like you giving me lip. Bugger off back to yer Mam and tell her she'll get her wages later, same as the rest of 'em."

"She's too drunk to know what you're giving her and tomorrow she'll think she spent it on gin." Though her heart was banging badly out of control Daisy stood her ground, her eyes glaring just as savagely as her master's. She'd not be cheated again, not by this beggar and not by anyone. Her mother had gone now, staggering off into the night with some great Irish navvy who would share the bit of sacking Lizzie Brindle called her bed in the barn the gangmaster had begged from Farmer Dixon for the month of harvest. They would all be there. Gertie Wilson, Mary-Kate Barton, her mother and the rest of the women, pushing aside sleeping children to accommodate their lovers, grunting and sweating until drunken sleep overcame them. The night was still mild so Daisy herself would wrap up in her own bit of sacking and sleep under the hedge which bordered Farmer Dixon's field, glad to be away from the adult occupation which was so commonplace in her young life.

The blow nearly lifted her from her feet. Her head snapped to one side on her frail neck and tears spurted from her eyes. She fell heavily against the smoke-blackened wall, disturbing the pile of rubbish which had lain against it for weeks. Scores of cockroaches scrambled from it, running in every direction, but the child did not see them, nor feel them against her skin as her reeling senses almost left her. She could feel the flesh about her left eye begin to swell even as she tried to sit up and from somewhere about her mouth blood was flowing. The patrons of the ale-house looked incuriously in her direction, watching for a moment or two then turning back to their ale or gin. When the migrant workers invaded the village it was not uncommon to see them belabour their own offspring. What was it to them, they asked one another, since the gangs contained nothing but the scum of the earth? They wandered the length and breadth of Lancashire causing nothing but trouble and if this chap felt the need to chastise the girl who probably deserved it anyway, knowing her kind, who were they to interfere?

The gangmaster smiled as he lifted her to her feet. She almost fell again but he put out what might have been a solicitous hand to steady her, pleased when she flinched away from him for it meant she had learned something from the encounter. She trembled in the chimney corner, one eye rapidly closing, the other not yet quite focused. He continued to smile, nis pale eyes as cold as flint, smoothing back the tangle of her hair with a hard and calloused hand.

"You'll have to be more careful with me, lass, if we're to be friends," he said silkily. She shrank further away from him, not because she was afraid – which she was, of course – but because the idea of Daisy Brindle being 'friends' with this man filled her with revulsion. Her head felt as though it was stuffed with rocks, a rock-filled bag which had just been shaken soundly until every part of it ached. Her eye throbbed and she was sure he had dislodged one of her teeth. She was rather proud of her teeth for they were white and even except one to the side of her mouth which, when she laughed, revealed itself to be slightly crooked. The other members of the gang, particularly the older women, had teeth like the gangmaster, black stumps amongst which decaying food festered, with gaping holes and gaps where a tooth had simply fallen out. She didn't know why hers had retained the perfection of her first teeth unless it was her habit of rubbing them and her gums with a bit of twig after she had eaten. She liked milk too, which the others didn't, preferring the small beer the farmer's wife gave them, and she was partial to apples and cheese and any raw vegetable she found growing in a field or a cottage garden and which was edible, instead of the eternal oats and potatoes on which the others survived. The other children jeered at her but what did she care? She had good sound teeth and a smooth, disease-free skin under her habitual filth and she could only put it down to the difference between her own habits and theirs.

"I'd get back to yer Mam if I were you. Tell her she'll get her wages in the morning. I'd not disturb her ... er ... enjoyment tonight if I was you." He grinned wolfishly, revealing amongst his own teeth the remains of the tasty steak and kidney pudding he had taken for his supper. "And one more thing, girl. If yer want to stay with me ... and yer Mam, I should keep yer nose out of my business. Yer Mam and me understand one another. Well, we would, wouldn't we? We've bin together a long time and she knows which side her bread's buttered. She's getting a bit past looking after herself, yer Mam is, and if I was to tell her you didn't suit she'd leave yer high and dry ter fend fer yerself. She'd have no choice. And yer know what'd happen to yer then, don't yer, without my protection? What happens to all females no matter how old or young they are. So you say nowt tonight. *Nowt!* Understand?"

She stared at him with her one good eye and even he, coarsened as he was by the life he had led and what he had seen in it, was made perfectly aware of her hatred of him. Funny that. He'd never really noticed her before. They all looked alike to him. Bundles of tattered rags of varying sizes. Heads bent, backs bent, dirty hands busy picking stones, hoeing turnips or potatoes. Mostly girls, for when a lad born to one of his women lived to be six or so he was put into one of the many textile factories which abounded in Lancashire. And not one, lad or lass, had ever given him 'lip' before and certainly had never recognised that for years now he had been creaming off a small percentage of the already miserable wage he paid them. Half of them were that dim-witted you had to explain to them a dozen times how to chuck a stone in the bloody pail. But not this one. Sharp as a tack, this one, if he guessed right and he usually did.

"D'you understand?" he repeated mildly. "D'you know what I'm telling yer ... er ... what's yer name?"

"Daisy."

"Daisy, is it? Right then, Daisy. Tell me you understand

that I mean it when I say it'll do you no good to interfere wi' me."

She nodded briefly since she understood only too well and she understood something else as well. She'd made a mistake tonight. Her own outrage had led her into a confrontation with someone who was far too important for her to challenge. Her angry resentment at being cheated had made her headstrong. She had spoken without thought and had been punished for her rash and ill-advised opposition to a man who, for the moment, held her in his power. She should have bitten her tongue, considered from every side how to go about getting what was rightfully hers without a direct attack on the authority above her. She'd know better next time.

Her good eye glinted in the candlelight as she turned silently away. Her bare feet rustled on the foul-smelling straw which lay about the floor and she did not even notice when she stepped on a cockroach which skittered across her path. She kept her head high and her back straight, glaring at those who had witnessed what had befallen her since she felt no shame. She had done her best to defend what was hers and she had lost but that was nothing to cry over. She'd get the better of him one day, see if she didn't, and she'd not crawl away from him like some whipped animal. She'd not forget tonight and the wrong done her, not if she lived to be ninety, and she'd not forget who did it to her and one way or another she and her Mam would have their full wage. Seven shillings a week!

They were asleep and snoring when she slipped into the barn. Her head felt several sizes too large for her thin neck to support, banging so furiously it made her feel sick. Her Mam and the navvy lay, naked from the waist down, their limbs still entwined, in the corner of the wall which, when the night was wet, Daisy usually shared with her. Her mother, one flaccid breast exposed to the navvy's fondling hand, had her head turned so that she seemed to stare directly at her daughter though her eyes were closed. Her mouth gaped and in the yellow light from the great harvest moon which shone through a hole in the roof Daisy studied the woman who was her mother. Twenty-four years old, that's what her Mam said she was, and for the past thirteen years she had been on the road with the gangmaster. She had only vague memories, she had told Daisy, of being brought to one of the Lancashire cotton towns with a cartload of other pauper children, of running away with Gertie Wilson one summer night when they were both sick to death of the hardship of the mill they had been put in. She had spoken of a fair which had come to town, promising the two young girls some 'fun', something they had known little of. They had found, not fun, but the gangmaster who had pledged them both a better life as he took each young girl in turn on his pallet bed in the corner of the farmer's barn.

Twenty-four years then, Lizzie Brindle, who had taken her name from some village through which she had passed, looking fifty-four, her hard and dissolute life etched into her once pretty face, and as Daisy stared down at her she swore in that moment that she'd not end up like this. She'd not be taken in her turn by the gangmaster or any other man who fancied he'd get between her legs. She'd seen them herself, watched them coax an unwilling girl, showing her sixpence, or even a shilling, and if she wasn't to be coaxed willingly, they held her down with her skirt over her face whilst a couple of skylarking fellows had their way with her. Field girls, they called them, and nobody gave a damn over the tears they shed as their violation was rewarded with a few coppers. And if the girl reported her grievance it had been known for a farm foreman to dismiss her and threaten she'd not work again in the parish if she continued to make a nuisance of herself.

Shoving with all her strength Daisy jostled her mother to one side. She found a corner of the sacking which was hers and with a great heave pulled it over from beneath the still snoring man and woman.

"I'm sleeping outside," she declared loudly to the assembled company, not one of whom heard her. "Me head hurts and I'll have a lovely shiner in the morning but a fat lot any of you care. Well, just wait until it's your turn and see if I give a damn about you."

It was not until she was curled up in the dry hollow beneath the sweet-smelling hedgerow, her throbbing head laid carefully on a pillow of clover, the sacking pulled up about her shoulders, that she allowed herself to weep. No one saw her tears, nor heard the anguish, childish and desolate, in her voice, only the night creatures who rustled in the undergrowth about her. The next morning, when her mother enquired half-heartedly, her own head thumping, who had given her the 'mouse', her daughter answered abruptly that she had fallen as she walked home in the dark along Pike Brow.

Lizzie Brindle had five shillings and sevenpence in her hand, put there by the gangmaster only a minute since, which, when she had paid him her own and Daisy's 'board', left her sevenpence for gin. The puzzlement of how she could have spent one shilling and fivepence on gin the night before and still be able to stand this morning was a mystery and her ten-year-old daughter's battered face paled into insignificance beside it.

2

The late autumn sunshine turned what had been the green summer beauty of the woodland to a soft and mellow gold. Trees which had carried a great and bountiful burden of leaves of every shade of green from the palest to the deepest emerald were now transformed to amber, copper, rose and flame. Some of the leaves had already begun to fall, spiralling gracefully to the ground where they formed a crisp carpet, coming to rest among the browning bracken and mosses. They drifted over fallen logs and the cut stumps of trees, brightly glowing in the dimness of the quiet glades. The sun was low, shining horizontally through the few shimmering leaves which remained on the branches of the tall trees, trees which had been there when the great House of Tudor had come into being three hundred and fifty years before. Oak, massive and venerable, hornbeam, sycamore, beech – considered the woodland's most elegant tree – holly and buckthorn and dogwood. Ferns clustered thickly about each tree-trunk and hidden almost from sight in the shelter of the great roots were wood sorrel and anemone. In the absolute stillness several rabbits ventured across an open clearing, a hedgehog crept close to the safety of a holly bush and among the undergrowth woodcock and pheasant hid their nests.

But the youth riding the glossy roan saw none of these things as he thundered, at great danger, it seemed, not only to himself but to the animal he rode, along the rough track which led through the wood. He was bent low over the beast's neck. Both were breathing hard but though the roan showed signs of distress in its mad flight, in the wildness of its eye and the mass of foam which flecked back from its tender mouth, the youth did not. In his eyes, which were the brilliant blue of a sapphire, was the intense excitement which comes to those who know they court peril. The thrill of risking one's neck for the hell of it, though it seemed doubtful that he gave his danger more than a passing thought as he careered at breakneck speed towards his home. A good-looking hound ran silently behind, his muzzle no more than six inches from the horse's lethal hooves.

He was a handsome boy. Dark as a gypsy, with hair like the smooth wing of a blackbird. In the darkness of his face his vivid eyes were startling. They were heavily fringed with thick black lashes and his eyebrows swooped fiercely upwards. His mouth was still young, not yet formed into that of a man's, but there was already a hint of hardness, even cruelty, in its well-cut mobility.

Branches hanging low from close-packed trees snatched

at his uncovered head but he dodged them adroitly, steering his roan between the rough-barked trunks with no more than inches to spare on either side. He leapt a small stream, the animal's hooves almost slipping in the stretch of water violets and oozing mud which lined each bank. To his left the deep throbbing autumn voice of a wood pigeon became suddenly silent as the violent crashing of his passage disturbed its tranquillity.

The trees began to thin out somewhat as he neared the edge of the wood and the sunlight fell on a smooth green clearing. On the far side of the clearing an enormous horse chestnut was rooted by an old gate which was let into a long, winding hedge, its wide head leaning towards the track beyond and throwing its shadow over the gate.

The boy gripped the horse with his strong legs, his eyes assessing the height of the gate and though the animal strained to one side, evidently alarmed, its rider urged it on, using a small but stinging crop to emphasise his determination to have his own way.

"Up Samson, up boy. We can do it, you know we can," he shouted triumphantly, impelling the tall roan forward at the full gallop and lifting himself in the saddle in a most perilous fashion. The animal was snorting in panic, wild of eye, his coat steaming with the effort he had made on his mad ride through the wood. His hooves churned up the grass, his body rose in flight and, like the pedigreed thoroughbred he was, he lifted himself and his rider over the gate and into the lane beyond.

The horse was amongst the long, trailing group of women and children before he, his rider, or even the cortège itself were aware that others beside themselves were in the immediate vicinity. Daisy had heard the thunder of the animal's hooves on the turf and had even caught the horseman's shout but she had stopped several yards back from the tail end of the straggling file to remove a stone from her boot. The deep, oak-lined track was dim, like a tunnel, with only a midge-filled haze of sunshine to light it. The branches of a hawthorn tree, laden with a blaze of red berries, formed a rich splash of colour, brightened by the orange and yellow of the autumn leaves, the whole creating a lacy canopy which reached from one side of the lane to the other. It obscured from Daisy's view the exact nature of what was happening ahead.

For several seconds she was thrown into a state of bewildered confusion. It seemed as though Old Scrat himself had been set down amongst the gang, judging by the screams which were ripping apart the quiet afternoon air, though she doubted if the gangmaster would be shouting quite so loudly if he had. There was a dreadful crash. Something heavy went down and above the cries, the cries of the women and the children, the shouts of the gangmaster and another voice she did not recognise, was the haunting sound of an animal in pain.

Picking up her boot, for not even in a drastic circumstance such as this appeared to be would she carelessly leave it lying about since she might not get another, she ran up the shaded lane to the turmoil which lay all about her.

It looked as though a giant hand had reached out and gathered a dozen or so frail humans into its grasp before flinging them heedlessly into a tangled heap about the track. Children sobbed in ditches and women, her own mother among them, lay with their tattered skirts about their waists or over their heads, stunned and ready to break into indignant weeping when they could recover their composure and their voices. The gangmaster, who had been at the head of his slow-moving column of workers as they made their way northward from Park Farm to Chadwick's Farm above Winstanley, was shouting his outrage at the damage done to the human tools of his trade and in the midst of it lay the horse, quivering, and even to Daisy's inexperienced eye, dying on the grassy track. There was a young gentleman kneeling at the animal's side, his head bent, his face hidden from her view, his hand on the neck of the trembling animal which made no attempt to rise; indeed, in Daisy's opinion, by the look of its legs it would never rise again. A dog lay panting by the boy's side.

"You bloody young fool," the gangmaster was shouting savagely. "What the hell were you doing jumping that bloody

27

animal over a gate and on to a path filled with women and children? Have you no sense? Didn't yer think ter look before yer come leaping out of nowhere on a bloody horse that looks damn near wild ter me? Yer could have killed someone and by God..."

"Be quiet, you ignorant bastard. Shut your foul mouth before I shut it for you." The voice was muffled but it was the voice of a gentleman, the voice of the privileged ruling class, and it cut off the flow of invective which poured from the gangmaster's mouth as though a hand had been clamped over it. It was authority speaking and not to be ignored, despite its youth, and the gangmaster knew it. He fell back indecisively amongst his aggrieved band of women as they gathered up their weeping children, soothing them roughly, shaking those who were inclined to grizzle. Daisy stood beside him, her sharp eyes taking in every small detail of the boy's appearance, the expensive cut of his breeches, the splendour of his silk shirt and the glossy quality of his tall top boots.

"What the hell were you doing loitering on private property?" The young gentleman spoke through gritted teeth without raising his head, his hand still soothing the neck of the injured animal. Daisy looked up at her master to see what he would have to say to this but it seemed that for once he was without words. He had indeed been trespassing and well he knew it. Whenever they came this way they always cut through Caleb's Wood which was situated on a piece of land belonging to Lord Thornley. It cut off a corner, saving about three miles' walking. There was never anyone there for it was several miles from his lordship's home, separated from Thornley Green, where he resided, by a deer park and a large natural lake. It was really only a bulge which protruded from Lord Thornley's splendid estate, considered almost common ground by those who walked the long miles from St Helens to Wigan and to all the scattered hamlets between. There was a bit of poaching done there, he had heard, for his lordship's gamekeepers were somewhat slack about guarding these few acres despite the game which lived there. Lord Thornley, his family and guests did not shoot over this way, preferring the richer, better-stocked miles of woodland to the east of his estate.

"Well, sir, how was we to know it was private property," the gangmaster blustered, "there weren't no sign..."

"You'll pay for this, you swine..." Still the young man did not look up.

"Nay, sir, t'weren't my fault, sir." In his fear the gangmaster began to whine and Daisy was most intrigued since she had never known him to be anything other than an oppressive tyrant who exacted reprisals from anyone who so much as looked sideways at him. Now he was almost grovelling and Daisy found the sight most gratifying. "We thought this were a public track, sir. We've a long haul up to Chadwick's Farm, and then there's little 'uns..." indicating with a sweep of his exceedingly dirty hand the children sprawled on the grass verge "... I hadn't the heart to make 'em walk them extra miles round the wood."

Realising that he had just admitted to knowing those extra miles were on the public track and that he should have been on them and not here, he cast about in his mind to worm his way out of this catastrophe and thinking he had found it he continued, "Besides, sir, you did come over that gate like a bat out of hell and..."

"I had a perfect right to, damn your insolence. My father owns the land and be warned I shall make sure you pay the full penalty for breaking the law. You and these ... this mob. Do you know how much this roan cost? Do you? Now it will have to be shot and it's your bloody fault." He bent his dark head over the horse and Daisy watched with interest, convinced he was about to weep and all over a bloody horse! He looked as though he was saying a prayer over the dying animal and she waited, for would he shoot it here, she wondered, or would he send for someone to fetch a cart to carry it back to wherever it was he lived?

"Go up to the house and tell someone to fetch a gun at once," the boy continued jerkily, "and be quick about it," but the gangmaster reared away just as though he was the one who was to have a bullet in his brain. Bloody hell, the sooner he and his lot were away from here the better and even then would he escape the retribution which would undoubtedly fall on the head of the man who had caused the death of one of Lord Thornley's valuable bloodstock? Like as not wherever he went from now on they'd be on the lookout for a man with a gang of women and children. A man wanted by one of the greatest landowners in these parts and not just for the death of his bloody horse but for the risk to the life of his lordship's son. They'd hound him wherever he went and when they found him, which they undoubtedly would for who could hide with this rabble tied to his coat-tails, they would hang him. Jesus, they hung nine-year-old lads for stealing sixpence so the man convicted for the destruction of a fine thoroughbred worth hundreds of guineas would certainly get the same sentence.

He looked about him wildly. He'd have to get rid of them. All of them. Leave the bloody lot of them and run for his life. Manchester way would be the best for anyone could disappear in that teeming city and never be found, not by anyone. He could lie low for a few months. He'd got a tidy sum put by where no one could get their hands on it and with a nubile girl to keep him company, not one of these raddled old bags but someone young and toothsome, he'd have a bit of a holiday.

He was about to make a dash for it while the young lordling was still bent over the dreadful quivering agony of his horse when his eye fell on the still, strangely boneless figure of Bessie Dalton. At least he thought it was Bessie. It was hard to tell since the figure had its face pressed into a clump of grass. The head was at an awkward angle though the rest of the body rested quite naturally just as though it lay sleeping. Was it Bessie? There was a child sitting beside her, doing nothing in particular, not watching the man and his horse with the same interest as the rest of the gang but simply staring blankly into space. It was Bessie's child all right. A pretty little thing with hair like newly minted silver and eyes the colour of pansies, though where she had come by them was a mystery. And by some stroke of good fortune the child's mother, Bessie Dalton, once as pretty as her daughter, appeared to be dead. Killed by the beast which was now breathing its last on the track leading to Wigan.

"Your animal's not the only one to suffer, sir, if you don't mind me interrupting your grieving. It seems as if in its mad gallop across that there wood and on to this track it's killed my wife." He bent his head in apparent pain but not before his pale eyes had shot Daisy a warning glance, a glance which said clearly to the girl who stood with her mouth agape that she had better close it and keep it closed. Strangely, he didn't even bother about the rest of them. It was as though they were nothing but beasts of burden with little between their ears except the knowledge that he was the provider and that from him would come their next meal, which was all that mattered to them. They were none of them capable of understanding what was happening, or even what he was talking about. But she did. Daisy Brindle. And she'd best keep her trap shut.

Turning away, a man in the first stages of shocked sorrow, he sank to his knees beside Bessie Dalton's lifeless body and bowed his head.

The young gentleman raised his eyes from his roan for the first time and Daisy looked into them. Into the bluest, the most beautiful eyes she had ever seen in her life. Cassie Dalton's took a lot of beating in their velvet pansy loveliness but these were a brilliant blue, like a jewel, Daisy thought, though she had never seen one. Or were they the colour of those pretty flowers which grew in the grass verges? Speedwell, she had heard Farmer Dixon call them. And yet they were neither of these. Their colour was unique and so was the face in which they were set, a face which turned for a moment to her before it followed the gangmaster. A face which showed nothing but horror and Daisy would have done anything in the world at that moment to take that look from it. Nothing had prepared her for the thrill of admiration his beauty instilled in her, for the strange warmth which started in the region of her heart and ran through her entire body, for the enchantment the sun-darkened face awoke in her, and she yearned in her ten-year-old heart which had never been stirred to more than an impatient and rough affection for her Mam, to ease that wide-eyed look of fear from him and take it upon herself. He was so bright, so fine, a young and well-bred gentleman who was being deceived by the gangmaster, an evil man who did not deserve to breathe the same air as this god-like being who crouched beside her. But what could she do? How could Daisy Brindle help him? How could she ease his burden of suffering over the agony of his lovely horse and now the death of Bessie Dalton? None of it was his fault really. He was on his father's land. He had every right to jump and gallop wherever he fancied. But the gangmaster's shrewd brain and quick wit had taken advantage of him and what could she do to let him know – without incurring her master's vicious rage – that she was here to help him?

She reached out her dirty hand, meaning to pull on the sleeve of his lovely silken shirt to attract his attention, then, seeing it for the first time in her life with eyes other than her own, withdrew it hastily, hiding it in the folds of her grey skirt.

"I'll fetch someone for yer," she said instead, waiting for those incredible eyes to turn to her again, humble in her love, her childish and yet strangely complete love, for it was her first. When they did they struck her an almost physical blow for they had changed from an expression of dread to one of gratitude, gratitude directed at her.

"I would be extremely obliged if you would," he said thankfully, just as though she was a great lady and not a grubby urchin the likes of which he had never before seen, let alone addressed. His hand, which rested gently on the roan's neck, trembled violently now for he was still only a boy, not yet sixteen, and badly frightened by the death of the man's wife even if she were only one of the intinerant poor who wandered from place to place looking for work.

Daisy watched that hand, longing to take it between her own and reassure him that it would be all right, that she wouldn't let anything happen to him, no, not even if she had to confess to felling Bessie Dalton herself but she merely stood up, shaking out her old skirt in an unconsciously graceful gesture.

"Where to?" she asked abruptly, eager to be off and fetch

help for this magnificent creature who had quite mysteriously stolen her newly budding woman's heart from her child's body.

"Thornley Green," he said simply, just as though everyone knew exactly where it was.

"Where is it?"

"Thornley Green," he said again.

"Where's that?"

"Over there." He pointed across the hedge in the vague direction of the north, his eyes returning fearfully to the gangmaster who had, in a moment of highly imaginative play-acting, clasped his hands together and closed his eyes as though in prayer over the body of Bessie Dalton. Cassie Dalton sat as though transfixed and the other women, fearful now that their master had apparently become deranged, closed in about the group, wondering what to do next, for without him to tell them after all these years they were lost.

"Tell me," the child Daisy said, quite anguished by her own ignorance.

"Go back down the path," he said hastily, "and you will reach Broad Lane. Continue on until you reach the big gates."

Yes, she remembered the big gates. They had passed them only an hour since and she had wondered where they led to. There was a pretty little house beside them and at the back of the house a clean and respectable woman hanging out lovely white things on the bushes to dry. Is that where he lived and was that his mother?

"Tell the gatekeeper ... oh no, don't go that way, it would take too long and Dewhurst is so slow and probably wouldn't believe you. Look, d'you see the gate, that one there?"

She nodded her head, her senses in thrall to the sound of his voice, the shape of his mouth and the soft amber texture of his firm skin.

"... go through it and beyond the bit of woodland on the far side. Skirt the top end of the lake which you'll come to, cross another strip of woodland and you will be in the deer park. You should be able to see the house from there.

Tell my father where I am, and for God's sake hurry..." for I want to be left no longer than is absolutely necessary with this appalling pack of women and children and their keeper, his eyes told her. His shock was beginning to subside somewhat and his natural arrogance, born and bred in the autocratic bones of him, demanded that he be released from his quite terrible promixity to the lower orders at once but his upbringing as a gentleman prevented him from leaving his dying horse in their midst. He, through no fault of his own, had been the cause of its fall and he must dispose of the animal as a gentleman should.

Daisy climbed the gate since his manner told her she had no time to unfasten it. She was like a young rabbit, fleet of foot and with a spring in her heels as she raced through the wood, jumping over fallen logs and even a little singing stream. Then she was out of the trees. A great expanse of smooth and undulating parkland was spread out before her, going on for what seemed miles and to her right, stretching as far as the eye could see, was a lake on which the most beautiful white birds with long, arched necks glided silently across its mirror smoothness. She did not stop to stare at them though she would dearly have loved to, but flew across the smooth grass towards several chimneys which she could just make out above another stand of trees in the far distance. She'd never seen a place with so many bloody trees, she thought, as she ran on, her breath sawing in her throat and cutting through her labouring lungs.

She was severely startled by some animals with long legs and sticks growing out of their heads which they raised from the grass to study her. They were lovely, slender and graceful as they bounded away from her, but she was glad they had gone in the other direction for they might have been ferocious for all she knew. The gentry certainly kept some funny things in their gardens, she said to herself, reducing Lord Thornley's estate of twenty thousand acres to nothing more than a small enclosed plot.

And there was the house. Thornley Green, he had called it, and quite simply, without the slightest hesitation or even wonder at it, she loved it from the moment her awed and

34

dazzled eyes fell on it. Just as she had instantly loved the boy who lived in it. Though she was aware that this was no time to stand and stare, that he would be waiting anxiously for her return with the help he needed so badly, her step faltered until it was no more than a hesitant walk and then to a full stop for the old house seemed to have put a spell on her which, for the moment, she could not break. Thornley Green. Even the name was beautiful, thrilling the senses with pictures of the rolling splendour from which the house appeared to have grown as naturally as the trees.

She had come at it from the back though she was not aware of it, scampering up some steps through a wide, wrought-iron gateway and on to a broad gravel path. On both sides of her was smooth lawn in which were set dozens of clipped privet bushes of every shape and size, square, round, spherical, some like the wide and flounced skirts she had seen on the grand ladies in town. In front of where she stood in rapt and reverent silence, set across the path which divided round it, was a circular pond in which were beautiful flowers, white they were, floating on glossy green leaves, and beyond that, guarded by two enormous trees, was the house, Thornley Green, ancestral home of the Thornley family. Its bricks were a soft and rosy pink, glowing in the late autumn sunshine with a blush as sweet as a young girl's. It was large and square with a dozen round chimneys and a strong guarding tower at each corner. The mullioned windows were set in groups of no particular pattern, oriel windows on the upper floor, some of them square, some tall and deep with a bay. The largest of these had beautiful coloured glass in it with patterns of lions and birds and some writing which Daisy, of course, could not read. The steep roof was battlemented for, centuries ago, an Englishman's house had been his castle with need for defence. There was a sundial clock hewed in stone set above a deep arched window, carved and intricate, with ivy growing about it.

And over the whole was an air of timeless tranquillity, of grace and peace and purpose. It was a house which was deeply loved, she could tell that just by looking at its beauty.

It was a house which needed love and here she was ready to lavish on it the devotion she knew it deserved. She was not awfully sure what her confused mind was telling her; she only knew she had been born to love something, to love someone with every fibre of her being. She had met the boy, now here was the house.

She was so entranced she did not hear the footsteps on the path behind her.

"Who the bloody hell are you and how did you get here?" a voice said in her ear, alarming her already jangling nerves, and a hand fell heavily on her shoulders, but the splendour of her new-found love and his need of her had made her strong and fearless, impatient of any fool who tried to interfere with the duty she had been asked to undertake.

"I have to see the master," she answered haughtily, lifting her verminous head even higher. "I've a message for him an' it's urgent so if you'll just tell me where to find him I'd be obliged." *He'd* said that word and she'd liked it.

Daisy squirmed away from the man's restraining hand, offended by his action in treating her as though she was no more than a common trespasser. She was here on behalf of the young lord, an errand of mercy if ever there was one, and every moment wasted meant more suffering, not only for him but for that poor horse. Not that *that* bothered her unduly since she had no idea in the first place why it had to be shot, poor sod, but it evidently upset the boy and what hurt him, hurt Daisy Brindle. And this man had no right to stop her when she was on such important business and if she had time she'd tell him so an' all.

"You can come along of me an' we'll see what Mr Greenhalgh has to say about this," the man continued and he caught her by the scruff of her neck, almost lifting her off her feet as he began to half carry, half drag her, not in the direction of the house but off to one side. There were other men working, some on their knees weeding, getting ready for winter planting, others sweeping into neat piles the leaves which were spiralling from the branches of the trees shading the wide stretch of lawn.

She had begun to scream her rage when another voice

spoke and in it was the sound of authority, quiet but definitely meant to be obeyed.

"Put that child down, Simpson," it said.

"But, Mr Greenhalgh, sir, I found her wandering about at the .. "

"I wasn't wandering. I was sent ..."

"Wandering she was, sir, where she shouldn't be. Staring up at the house, she were, and no telling what she were up to. Probably sizing the place up for a gang of ..."

"Put her down, Simpson, and let's hear what she has to say."

When she was set on her feet, almost speechless with outrage, Daisy glared up into the face of the second man. He squatted down on his haunches, his face almost on a level with hers.

"Now then, what's all this about?"

3

The shot lifted a flock of ravens high into the paling autumn sky and Daisy watched them wheel about with sharp concentration. Not that the horse's death upset her but she did hate to see the way in which Miles's face jerked as the revolver was put to his roan's head.

Miles! That was his name. Daisy had heard his father call him that with her own ears. Miles. It was a splendid name, one she had not heard before, but then she had never seen anyone like him before, and it suited him exactly.

The past hour had been a confused one. What an uproar there had been when finally Mr Greenhalgh had got the story straight, though why he should have had such trouble in understanding her was beyond her. He kept asking her to repeat things, saying her broad accent was scarcely recognisable as the Queen's English. She hadn't even known she had one, or even what an accent was, but she had to admit the way she spoke seemed very different to his.

They had forgotten her then. She had been left standing in the sunken garden, nobody caring at all whether she stared at the house or not, it seemed. Even the men working in the garden ignored her, nodding their heads together, talking about someone she didn't know who dashed about the countryside on his wild thoroughbred – whatever that was – and who deserved everything that happened to him, reckless young bugger that he was. The man who had finally listened to her, and got the hang of her message, had gone racing off like the wind and seeing there was nothing further to be done here she had set off back the way she had come, eager to be with *him* again.

They had all arrived together. Men on horseback and following behind on foot several workers carrying spades, and herself. But he hadn't noticed her, not even to nod a 'thank you'. She stood with her mother and the other women and children, her eyes on him, waiting for him to turn to her, to tell his father, the great Lord Thornley, that she was the one who had helped him, who had run until her heart had threatened to burst from her chest so that he need wait no longer than she could help for the assistance she had gone for. But he did not. His father was there beside him, keeping a sharp eye on the boy to make sure he showed no sign of ungentlemanly distress in front of the servants who were everywhere. The culture and customs of the English aristocracy had moulded his son into the well-bred, well-polished young gentleman he was, taught him to hide emotion of any sort, but he need not have concerned himself for though the boy did not pull the trigger himself he stood steadfastly beside the gamekeeper who did. His face was pale as the men began to dig an enormous hole beneath the hawthorn tree and when his father called sharply to him he turned away and began to walk towards the spare horse which the groom had tethered to the branch of a tree.

"There is no more to be done here, my boy," she heard his father say.

"No indeed, sir. But he was a fine horse and I am sorry to lose him."

"Naturally, but another can be found just as good. I know you were fond of the animal but you may have the pick of the stable and if there is none to suit I believe Sir Christopher Faulkner knows of some decent bloodstock for sale."

"Thank you, sir."

"Not at all, my boy. Besides, it is time you had a decent hunter with the season about to begin."

His lordship turned as he was about to mount his own tall bay, speaking incisively to his bailiff who was directing the disposal of the horse's body.

"Keep these people here, Greenhalgh, until the constable arrives," and with these words he acknowledged for the first time the presence of the gang of labourers who had caused the death of his son's horse. Acknowledging them but certainly taking no account of them for were they not landless peasants and, as such, of no more importance than the cattle in his pasture or the birds in his trees? Less, for the animals and birds had a worth which this flotsam did not.

He was a tall man, handsome as his son but finely built and with an air of superiority which had come from a long line of privileged aristocracy stretching back to the days of Henry VII. Hugh Charles Thornley had become the Fourteenth Baron ten years previously on the death of his father, a direct line from father to son since the land had been granted to the first Thornley three hundred and fifty years ago for some favour he had done his sovereign. Each heir had married a great heiress. There was land in Cheshire, Yorkshire and Scotland and some said that in Lancashire only the Earl of Derby was wealthier than they. Through the generations the Thornleys of Thornley Green had been distinguished for their military prowess, winning glory at Flodden, at Worcester and lately on the battlefield of Waterloo where a younger brother of his lordship had fought and died for his country. Several had been Parliamentarians, taking an active part in affairs of state, but on the whole it seemed they had preferred to be gentlemen of leisure, leaving public life to others. It was said that the Honourable Miles Thornley had a fancy for the army before he settled down to the running of the great estate which would one day be his and certainly he had the aggression for it by all accounts, but he was young yet, only fifteen and still at school. Besides, he was the only son and it was doubtful his father would allow it.

Lord Thornley had his foot in the stirrup, the matter settled in his opinion, when a coarse voice from behind him turned him sharply about, almost overbalancing him and causing his mount to rear off awkwardly.

"Excuse me, yer lordship, but what about me wife? Is she ter be buried with the horse?"

Lord Thornley allowed his groom to hold his restive animal whilst he glared at the man who had spoken. A tall, thin man, incredibly dirty, who stood in the midst of the huddled group of women and children, all of whom looked as though they had not the least notion of what was happening.

His lordship's eyes narrowed and his crop slashed dangerously against his own high boot as he advanced towards the man who had spoken. The women who stood about him edged even closer, drawing in their children and bending their heads in terror. The man was afraid too, his lordship could sense it, and so he had a right to be for he would be in St Helens Gaol before nightfall, charged with trespass. If he could have been charged with murdering a horse Lord Thornley would have seen to it that he was.

"Did this man speak, Greenhalgh?" he asked his bailiff since it was not his custom to address such a ruffian himself. He stared into the pale eyes of the gangmaster, waiting for them to shift away from his but they did not waver. The gangmaster had nothing to lose and everything to gain if he could keep his head above the floodwater which was already lapping about his chin, his expression said, and he did not want to drown, nor be transported to the colonies for his supposed crime.

"It's his wife, your lordship." Greenhalgh stood quietly by his master's side and Daisy, from her position on the edge of the group where her hand was clutched fearfully by that of seven-year-old Cassie Dalton, knew that of all these men who worked for Lord Thornley, only Mr Greenhalgh was not afraid of him.

"His wife? What is wrong with his wife?"

"She's dead, my lord."

"Dead? What has that to do with me?"

"He claims it was Master Miles' horse which killed her as he jumped the gate. I believe her neck is broken." The bailiff pointed towards the pathetic tumble of torn and stained clothing, the hank of dusty hair which was all that remained of Bessie Dalton.

For the first time Lord Thornley noticed the dead woman and though the steely expression on his face did not alter in any way there was a sense of withdrawing from the strong position of contemptuous authority which he held over these riffraff. He walked over to the body and peered down at it distastefully, then he beckoned to his son and Daisy watched the tall and indolent figure of Miles Thornley move across the shaded lane. The way he walked fascinated her. Every part of him moved in perfect unison and grace. It was quite amazing and if he would only look at her and smile she would go to gaol with the rest of them quite happily. But he did not.

Father and son spoke for several minutes whilst the gangmaster held his breath, his eyes never leaving them. A child began to wail and with a sharp movement of his hand he indicated to its mother that it was to be silenced. How, he did not care. Strangle it if needs be but shut it up.

The horses moved impatiently, nodding their heads up and down and jingling their harness. The men beyond the hedge dug silently, the only sound their spades as they bit into the soft ground, and all the while Daisy watched the young man, her eyes dazzled, her expression soft and tremulous. He would save them. He would not allow her to be put in gaol, not after what she had done for him. She smiled reassuringly at Cassie then turned back to Lord Thornley and his beautiful son, watching as they strode off towards their horses. They mounted and after a word with

Mr Greenhalgh she was not at all surprised when the bailiff told them they could go.

"Oh thank you, thank you, your lordship," the gangmaster whined, almost grovelling in the dusty track in his relief. His face was coated with sweat and his eyes were wild and bloodshot and Daisy knew that they would all be made to pay dearly for what he had suffered this day, despite the fact that it was none of their doing. "I knew yer'd see the justice of it, Lord, and though I've nothing ter say against his young lordship's riding he did come over that gate a mite too fast for safety."

"I am not your lord, nor anybody's," Greenhalgh said sourly, "and my advice to you is to get well clear of Thornley Green as quickly as possible."

"Yer right, sir, yer right, and so we shall and when yer get a chance thank the young lord fer his kindness if yer please. It were good of him ter take the blame . . ."

"Oh it was nothing to do with Master Miles, I do assure you. You caused the death of his favourite horse, or so he believes, and if he had his way you would all swing for it. It was his father's decision to show mercy and let you go."

"Dear sweet Jesus."

"Aye, and it's a good job his lordship believes in Him for his son does not, nor His teachings. Now if you'll be so good as to arrange the removal of your wife's body."

"Who?"

"Your wife. The woman who lies in the ditch yonder."

"Oh her." The gangmaster grinned wolfishly then turned away to follow his gang, including Daisy, who was straggling off in the direction of Chadwick's Farm and well out of earshot. "Chuck her in the hole with the bloody horse."

"Come on, off yer bums and on yer feet, yer lazy sluts. Get yer bundles together, or whatever it is yer cart about with yer and let's be off. There's nowt ter be had round here now them late potatoes are planted and there'll be no more until January at Foot of Hill Farm, that's if the ground's workable for the 'earlies' ter go in. We'll have a scout round between here and St Helens and if we can find nowt then it's the colliery for us all," not meaning himself, of course, which they all understood.

The gangmaster was quite recovered from his frightful ordeal on the Thornley estate a week ago, helped no doubt by his attention to the pubescent young body of the daughter of Mary-Kate Barton who he had been saving for a rainy day such as this and a real comfort she had been to him an' all. A diversion, you might say. She had not been exactly willing but her acceptance of what she knew – or what her mother knew – to be inevitable, had smoothed the strain of the past few days. They had reached the shelter of Chadwick's Farm and the dilapidated barn in which they always slept when working there, not aware, any of them, that they were still on Lord Thornley's broad acres. In fact they were unaware that most of the farms on which they worked were not owned by the men who farmed them and whose families had been there for generations, but by the man from whom they were rented, Lord Thornley himself. Arnold Chadwick and Abel Dixon of Park Farm, from where they had recently come, paid rent to his lordship as had their fathers and their fathers' fathers before them, stretching back almost as far as Lord Thornley's own family's ancestors. Tenant farmers who were as proud of their lineage as their landlord. Their yearly incomes were sometimes as high as £300, their farmhouses sturdily built of brick and stone, and they were hard-working and prudent. Up to three hundred acres many of them had, taking advantage of the new, revolutionary methods of farming. On Lord Thornley's land there were fine, corn-bearing fields, barley and rye and wheat, turnips and potatoes, and cattle for the splendid butter and cheese their milk produced.

The gang had worked for a week at Chadwick's gathering potatoes and mangold-wurzels, bending hour after hour in the grey drizzle which had set in just as they arrived. It was the end of October now and the fine mellow days of autumn had gone. This would be their last farming job until after Christmas and unless they were to apply to the workhouse the gangmaster knew that some employment must be found to feed them during the next few months. They had been fortunate in previous years finding casual labour throughout the winter, drifting as far north as Ingleborough and to the area about Stockport in the south, often cold and hungry for days on end but managing to avoid the work they loathed and feared in the collieries of Wigan and St Helens. Pit-brow lasses, the women who worked at the coal-face were called, and it looked as though for the first time in six years that was what they were to be.

It was not that the gangmaster cared unduly what became of his band of workers since, if he abandoned them, he knew that come the spring another lot could easily be found. There were always destitute women roaming the countryside willing to do anything to feed their starving children but he had become used to the women he had. They were good workers, well known for their tireless experience, earning him a decent sum each week. They knew his ways and what he expected of them and though they were rough, hardened and made coarse by the life they led, they were pliant enough with him. And there were around a dozen children, young girls naturally, who, trained by him, were almost ready to step into the boots of their ageing mothers. Mary-Kate's daughter, Agnes, who currently held his attention, Patsy Wilson, Fanny Holden and Jess Formby who were all coming on eight or nine years old, and of course, Daisy Brindle. Still a bit on the young side and as yet too thin and childlike, but time would remedy that. Unlike some men he could mention, his taste did not run to very young children, but by God he'd enjoy taming that one when the time came.

But daydreaming by the fire which Farmer Chadwick had allowed them to light outside the barn – seeing as how it had turned so cold, he said – was not the way to find work and so they must pack up their bits of things and set off for St Helens and the collieries there.

They did not cross Caleb's Wood this time but cut west beyond Farmer Chadwick's fields until they reached Primrose Bank Brow, the lane which led them south through Primrose Bank, Moss Bank and on to St Helens. Daisy, holding Cassie Dalton by the hand as the child trudged beside her, looked out for Miles every step of the way. They were skirting the Thornley Green estate by no more than a mile or two and perhaps he might be riding out this way on the new horse his father had promised him. She had a picture of their meeting in her head. He would be galloping at full speed across a meadow, his lovely hair swept back by the wind, his blue eyes shining with a smile just meant for her. He would stop and jump from his horse and tell her how sorry he was that he had not thanked her for her help last week. He would explain how upset he had been at the death of his animal but that he wanted her to know how 'obliged' he had been. She would thank him and tell him how 'obliged' she was that he had prevented his father from sending them to gaol, letting him know that though she might only be a member of a labouring gang, she was a quick learner. She had learned the word 'obliged', hadn't she, and she knew what it meant an' all and if she could only be around people like him all the time, not in the same class level, of course, since that was clearly impossible, she knew with an absolute certainty which seemed to be part of her that she could learn a lot more of the things that people like him took for granted. Reading, for instance, and how to write her own name. How to be more than a field girl. She didn't know exactly what she did want to do, not yet, but one day she would find it and when she did she wanted to be ready for it. And if he was all that she knew him to be she felt that somehow he could be the man – for he *was* a man in her child's eye – who might show her the way to do it. And if she kept her eyes peeled on this dismal journey she might just catch a glimpse of him. They would smile and chat in the sunshine – the sun would of course come out with his presence – and he would say that if ever she was this way again he would look out for her. Her dreaming mind took her no further than that. It was all she asked for in her innocence. A chance to see him again. The promise that somewhere, some day, he would greet her kindly, acknowledge her as something other than ... than the field girl she was.

Cassie began to cry silently, the great fat tears brimming from her incredible eyes with the fluency of raindrops slipping down a pane of glass. She did not screw up her eyes, nor open her mouth wide as children do. Her face remained completely passive, without expression, and had it not been for the steady flow of tears it would not have been apparent that she was distressed. Her pansy eyes were like smooth velvet beneath the burden of moisture and Daisy knelt down beside her in exasperation. For some reason, perhaps because Daisy's hand had been the first she had held after her mother's death, Cassie had clung to her with all the fierceness of ivy to the trunk of an oak tree. Or perhaps with that strange instinct of self-preservation children possess she had sensed that of all the females with whom she had lived in her short life Daisy was the one she stood the greatest chance of surviving with.

"What's the matter now?" Daisy was impatient. Hadn't she enough to cope with without being saddled by this scrap of humanity? It took all her ingenuity to make sure she and her Mam got their share from the meagre diet the master provided them with and now, if she could not foist her off on one of the other women, she would have to share what they had with Bessie Dalton's brat. Her Mam didn't like it now, having Cassie Dalton along with them, for every extra penny spent on the child meant one less for her gin when they reached the ale-house in Primrose Bank. Not that Lizzie Brindle knew much about money. As long as she had her wages put in her hand every Saturday which, when she had paid for their board and her gin, was handed over to her daughter she was satisfied to leave all the financial arrangements to Daisy. A good kid, really, who could be relied on to find a penny for her Mam's gin when she was desperate for a sip or two. Lizzie could count to ten for that was how many fingers she had but beyond that was a mystery to her and as for how many pennies there were in a shilling, or shillings in a sovereign, or a guinea, you might as well ask her how many feathers there were on a bird's wing. She'd never seen a guinea in her life, nor studied a bird's wing! No, Daisy would see to it. A sensible lass was Daisy and no trouble to her Mam who lived from one jug of gin to the next. And so she was unaware, as indeed they all were, of the tiny collection of coins, farthings for the most part, which Daisy had hidden about her person. Gleaned over the years, three or four, since she had taken over her mother's money matters and ready when the day came, which she knew it would, when it was her turn and she would be forced to flee from the demands of her master. One day he would look at her and see beneath the filthy tatters of her old bodice and skirt, beneath the dirt which coated her skin, and when he did she would be off. That was why, apart from her teeth, she made no attempt to clean herself though she knew in the end a bit of dirt would not deter the old bugger who exercised a kind of 'droit du seigneur' – though she did not use that phrase, naturally – over his young employees. Still, best to look as puny and filth-covered as she could for it offered some protection.

She scowled at Cassie, wondering if she could get rid of her in the village. She was a fetching little girl and given a bit of a wash there might be some childless woman who would take her in.

"What's up?" she repeated, giving Cassie a shake, but the little girl did not speak, merely looked with huge, tear-filled eyes into Daisy's. Daisy sighed and rose to her feet. Cassie had not spoken since she had seen her Mam flung willy-nilly into the ditch in Caleb's Wood. She had screamed just once, Gertie Wilson had told Daisy, when the horse's hoof had caught her a glancing blow to the head and indeed she had a livid bruise beneath her hairline just at her temple but it had faded now and still Cassie had not uttered a word. She had worked beside Daisy in Chadwick's field, passing her the seed potatoes when instructed to do so, picking stones and placing them neatly in the pail, running obediently wherever she was told but always coming back to huddle against Daisy.

She took hold of the child's hand again. It was no good. She was landed with her, it seemed, for the time being anyway. Her eyes strayed across a field on her right to where a horseman skirted the rows of furrows which were being allowed to lie fallow for the winter in the old-fashioned way, but it was not him. Even from here she could see that the

47

rider had not the dash and brilliance of the young lordling and she settled once more to her daydreaming, following the shabby and ill-fitting – but warm – overcoat of the master as he led them towards St Helens.

They shared the track with many travellers who became more numerous as they drew nearer habitation, countrymen and women of all ages. The men wore short jackets and sleeveless waistcoats in various shades of brown, breeches and short boots. One or two had on an apron and a black hat and Daisy wondered what their trade could be. The women wore what looked like bedgowns belted about their waists, a neckerchief or shawl about their shoulders, lined caps or a bonnet of straw tied beneath their chin with ribbons. There were carters, farm labourers and shepherds, all dressed in smock-frocks of brown or light blue linen. Where were they all going, she wondered as the lane became even more crowded, then suddenly it came to her. It was almost Martinmas and the customary day of the hirings when all those looking for their next year's employment would congregate in the market-place and offer themselves for hire. They would indicate their trade by holding up the implement appropriate to it. She wished she could do that. The trouble was she had no skills other than those she had learned in the fields where she had been put by the gang-master. She could dig and hoe and weed, plant potatoes and turnips, glean and pick stones, but the work inside the farmhouses and cottages she had seen from a distance was an unknown quantity to her. She had never in her life even been inside one. Indeed the only buildings she had ever entered, beside the ale-houses which her mother and the other women frequented, were the often ramshackle barns in which she had slept all her life. She knew that serving wenches and such were hired in the market-places at Martinmas but how could she put herself forward as one of these at her age, even if she had known what one did?

It had begun to rain heavily now and the crowd thinned out somewhat as those who could please themselves took shelter wherever they could but the gangmaster strode on in the direction of Primrose Bank, not even looking back to check that his women were still behind him. They belonged to him, every last one of them and so accustomed to it were they, as was he, it never occurred to him that one might take it into her head to defect. Daisy watched his back and with great stealth, pretending she had a blister on her calloused heel, gradually dropped behind until she and Cassie were at the end of the straggling line. She had no particular plan in mind, only the hazy idea that somehow, if luck was on her side and she could rid herself of Cassie's clinging hand, she might find work which would put her on the road to a better life than this. She didn't even consider what that might be since she had known no other than that in the gang. She didn't even know why this longing had come over her now, at this particular moment in her life, unless it was her encounter with Miles Thornley and the unidentified yearning towards something sweet and clean he had awakened in her. She had lived in filth all her life. Filth of the worst kind, to do not with honest dirt, the sort you met in a good day's work, but the filth which festered in men's minds. She had seen things which she had accepted stoically as part of life but in some strange way she had not allowed them to coat her with their obscenity. She knew things no ten-year-old girl should know and one of them was that if she did not get away soon, not just from *him* and the life he forced her and the others to live, but from her own degraded mother, she would become as her mother was.

And this could be her chance. The hirings in the marketplace. She lifted her head, turning her eyes rapidly from side to side, watching carefully what those on the road were doing and where they were going. The rain pelted on to her matted hair, running from it across her face, washing away the dust and dirt with which it was coated, and slowly the satin-smooth fineness of her skin was revealed. White it was, the perfect creamy white of buttermilk and which often accompanies hair the exact shade of a fox's pelt. There was no hint of colour in her face anywhere. It was completely unblemished except for a small indent in her cheek, just near the corner of her mouth, which appeared when she smiled.

She did not smile now. She had the tense look of a hunted animal. As though she was poised for flight, waiting until the pursuer had gone by, which in a way she was. The rain flattened her springing hair and she pushed a hand through it impatiently, dragging it back from her forehead to reveal the triangle of her pointed face. Broad at the forehead where dark eyebrows winged upwards, and at the cheekbones, but tapering to a small, pugnacious chin. A wide mouth made for laughter, the colour of a ripe peach and just as soft as the rain ran across it. Her golden-brown eyes peered furtively from between long silken lashes, returning again and again to the narrow back of her master but as yet she had seen nothing which told her she should leave him and her slight figure strode on at his back. When the time was right she would know.

They reached the edge of the village just as dusk fell and the women in front of her began to jingle the few coins in their pockets in anticipation of the gin they would consume in the Last Shift.

"We'll stop here for the night," the gangmaster told them over his shoulder. "I suppose yer'll be fancying a little drink, eeh? Well, off yer go then." His tone was avuncular, one might almost have said affectionate if his true character had not been known. In his pocket was the week's wages Farmer Chadwick had paid him for the gang's labour and whilst they had their 'little drink' he would count it out into the appropriate amounts as he usually did. The landlord of the ale-house would let him have the use of an old and reeking stable for the night in which the women might sleep off the excesses of their evening's revelry, whilst he would sample the delights of Aggie Barton in one of the upper rooms of the inn. Tomorrow they would make an early start and if his luck was in he would get every last one of them set on by nightfall at one of the collieries around St Helens. There was Cowley Hill, Green Lane, Gerards Bridge and the Union Colliery and that was only to the north of the town. There were rich coal seams all around the area, and many pits, and his income for the coming winter months would be assured when he had his women employed in one of them.

He carefully counted out the shillings and pence into neat and very small piles, as he did each Saturday night, speculating on how much of his gang's wages he might put in his own pocket this week. He glanced about him to make sure that brat of Lizzie Brindle's was not watching him with her accusing eyes but she was not there and, though her suspicions meant nothing to him since what he did was his own concern, he was glad. The less she knew about his business the better for he wanted no dissension in the camp, so to speak. She might take it into her head to tell the others that he was creaming off a part of their wages for himself and then he'd have trouble on his hands. He could handle it, of course, but things were going smoothly at the moment. He had a good gang and he wanted no troublemakers to disturb the peace. She'd probably be with Bessie Dalton's kid in the stable and best place for her. Keep her nose out of what was nowt to do with her, seeing to Bessie's brat.

It was not until the next morning when he moved amongst the women, kicking them to wakefulness, that it was discovered that Daisy Brindle and Bessie Dalton's brat were missing.

4

She did her best to slip away without Cassie but wherever she went Cassie was there behind her, clinging like a limpet to her skirt, snivelling dolefully, saying nothing but making it quite clear she was not prepared to let Daisy out of her sight. It was as though she sensed that Daisy was up to something, there was an excitement about the girl she had chosen as her protector and she did not trust it. She fell asleep at last. She was only seven years old and she had walked, on and off, for the best part of ten hours that day. But even in sleep her hand clutched Daisy's skirt and when Daisy, judging that her mother and the other women would be so far gone in drink when they returned to the stable they would not miss her, slid cautiously from beneath her sacking, Cassie awoke immediately. When Daisy stood up Cassie rose with her, her eyes deep and unfathomable in the gloom of the stable, pressing herself into the folds of Daisy's skirt.

"You can't come with me. Lie down and go to sleep." Daisy picked the child up and placed her back amongst the nest of foul straw and sacking where they had lain, wishing that the other children were there for it would have been easier to persuade Cassie to lie amongst them and go back to sleep, giving herself the chance to slip away undetected. But, unsupervised in even the most casual fashion, most of the youngsters would be hanging about the ale-house, or indeed anywhere they might find easy pickings amongst the villagers. Wild as any unrestrained animal, they roamed about looking for mischief, anything they might steal, or both. A sip of gin or stout, something to fill their always hungry bellies, apples from the trees or potatoes from the ground.

"Lie down and go to sleep," she hissed at the passive child but the moment she turned away Cassie was up and at her heels, her huge eyes staring up unblinkingly into her own.

"I can't take you with me, for God's sake," she said sharply. "The others'll be back soon and then you can sleep with them. I've got to go out so let go of me skirt and lie down." She shook off the little girl's hands and, turning her back on her, moved purposefully towards the stable door. She had her boots tied by their frayed laces about her neck ready to put on when she reached the road. She only wore them when they were on the march. Many of the rutted tracks were scattered with sharp stones ready to slice the skin of even the most hardened sole but in the fields and when she was sleeping she slung them round her neck for safety. They had belonged to another child who had died in the night next to Daisy and while they all slept Daisy had laid claim to them. They were the first she had ever owned and though they were beginning to pinch a bit she meant to take them with her. She could hardly find employment with no boots to her feet, could she? She must look her best and the boots gave her a sense of being someone for only the poorest of the poor tramped barefoot.

Though Cassie no longer held on to Daisy's skirt, when she reached the road which ran through the village the child was there behind her, a tiny, big-eyed ghost pattering on bare feet across the cobbles of the yard at the back of the inn and through the stone archway. When Daisy stopped, so did she, just waiting, not for orders but to see which way Daisy was going.

Daisy turned on her and pushed her so roughly Cassie fell backwards and sat down on the cobbles. Tears gathered in her eyes and began to slide through the years of grime which had accumulated on her face but she made no sound.

"Let go of me, yer little bugger." Daisy's heart was curiously stirred by the little girl and she had the strangest urge to pick her up and hold her close but she restrained herself. She was not naturally cruel but the world had taught her that there was only one way to survive in it and that was to sacrifice the interests of others and safeguard only what was best for oneself. Deviate a fraction of an inch from this outlook on life and you wouldn't last a week with this lot. Look after yourself for no one else would, she had learned even before she could walk, for the other children who toddled and crawled about her would have taken the crust right out of her mouth if she had not clamped her baby teeth firmly about it. And certainly you did not become attached to another human being in even the most casual way for the chances were they died, or left the gang, or turned nasty on you just when you thought the friendliness they showed was a very pleasant thing to have. Best walk alone, tied to no one, not even the woman who went under the name of 'mother' and certainly not to this pathetic waif who would only hinder her at every step of the way. How could she possible find work with a child hanging on her skirts, thought the girl who was no more than a child herself? It would be difficult enough to claim a corner for Daisy Brindle in the kitchen of one of those 'homes', as they were called, and of which now and again she had caught a glimpse of what seemed heaven as she passed by, without finding one for Cassie Dalton as well.

"Get back to the stable and wait for the others," she whispered furiously, afraid even here that the gangmaster might hear. "They'll be back soon and one of the women'll look after yer. I can't take yer with me. Yer too small ter work." For the child was seriously undersized. Despite herself her voice became apologetic. "I've got ter find a job and they'll not take you an' all. You can't work and I can't earn enough fer two of us. I don't even know if I'll find summat to do or even where it'll be."

Cassie stared up in the dark, the whites of her eyes shimmering beneath their burden of tears.

"It's no good looking at me like that. I can't take yer and that's all there is to it. Now sod off before I land yer one."

Cassie did not move and Daisy groaned softly. It was no good. She'd just have to go on and leave her. She didn't like it. She knew that the brat would only pick herself up and follow her, which is what she would do in Cassie's place, and eventually, when Daisy, who was older and stronger, drew ahead Cassie would be left stranded on the roadside. She should have knocked at one of the cottage doors in the street to see if someone would take the child in but one look at the clean and shining state of them and the unsavoury state of Cassie was enough to tell her that the village women would have shrieked and slammed the door in her face. Besides, the gangmaster would not have taken kindly to one of his future workforce being handed over to someone else and would have been immediately suspicious of Daisy's motives.

She turned away sharply and without waiting to put on her boots began to walk towards the edge of the village, keeping to the shadows. It was about five miles to the next village. She would be there before dawn and with a bit of luck would find a dry place under a hedgerow or in a hayloft to sleep during the day. Chinkham Wood lay just behind it and there would be cover there, or if not she'd just follow the St Helens railway line until she came to the town and the hirings. She'd have a wash in Rainford Brook before she got there, put on her boots and present herself for employment in the market-place.

The frantic patter of the small girl's feet followed her up the street. She walked briskly, closing her ears to the sound and to the laboured breathing which rasped in Cassie's chest. She held her head high for she was away to a new life, a life in which she, Daisy Brindle, was to become the kind of person Lord Thornley's beautiful son would admire. Not for her own beauty, she thought humbly, since she knew she had none, nor for her standing in his world since she did not even exist in it, but for her determination to get away from her own beginnings. To better herself. To rise out of the morass of filth which, until she had looked into his glorious eyes, she had accepted as normal.

The sounds behind her died away and she did not look back. The straggle of cottages fell away and she was out in open country with high hedges on either side of her and the black sky above lit with nothing but the prick of a star as the thin clouds slid by. It was not really cold as yet and her brisk walking set the blood coursing through her veins. She did not put on her boots, deciding to risk the uneven surface, since she wished to move as silently as possible. God only knew what tinker or vagrant might be sleeping in a ditch to the side of the road and she did not want to chance walking into the arms of some villain as evil as the gangmaster. They were all about you, men and women who would slit your throat for the boots on your feet. She patted her small hoard of coins which added up to no more than sevenpence three-farthings but at least she could buy herself a bite to eat when she got to the town. She felt grand, she told herself, with only Daisy Brindle to think about. With only the splendid life ahead of her which she knew one day would be hers. With the job she would find at the hirings and which would set her on the way to a better state than the one she had known for the past ten years. She would have decent work, clean work, if there was such a thing, amongst clean people. Proper boots to her feet and a warm coat for winter. A blazing fire to sit by at the end of the day when her work was done, and a full belly. Survival without the prospect of achieving it only through the attentions of a filthy old man. Cleanliness then, warmth, and her own bed to sleep in. Her young dreams took her no further than this. Oh yes, she felt grand, she told herself again, so why did she entertain the need to look over her shoulder to see if Cassie Dalton was still following her, which was daft because even if the child was there, which was unlikely, she would not be able to see her in the dark.

She kept to the silent road, meeting no one. There were strange sounds, night sounds which she had never noticed before when they had all tramped together at the dark end of a long day. A dog barked across the fields, a frantic bark as though the fox had invaded his territory. There was a whoosh of wings across the lane ahead of her and she heard the sound of an owl as the bird made for the shelter of the trees. A cool wind blew directly into her face, full of the smells that country folk know herald the winter. A hint of the slowing down of nature as she eases from the gentleness of summer into the bleakness of the months to come. It would be November soon, in fact it probably was already. Daisy had no way of knowing. She was tired now. She had walked a long way since the gangmaster had wakened them this morning and she had eaten nothing but the potato mush mixed with some cold-water oats he had doled out at dawn. Her feet were sore and she was tempted to put her boots on but she really did not want to wear them until it was absolutely necessary. When she stopped to wash herself in Rainford Brook she meant to give them a good clean-up so that she presented as pleasing a picture as possible in the market-place. But she really must have a bit of a lie-down. She had no idea of the time but a rest in the shelter of the hedge for a few minutes would not hurt, then she'd be off again towards Moss Bank.

It was almost light when she awoke. It was the birds that did it. Starlings they were, just a handful at first as they swooped about the dawn sky on fluttering wings, then suddenly there were twice as many, sweeping round and round, cracking their wings until the sky was filled with them. The crimson blush of the sunrise was behind them in the east and she watched them, fascinated by their graceful beauty, still scarcely conscious of where she was. The tufty grass on which she lay was damp and she shivered, hitching herself closer to the warmth which was plastered against her shoulder and right side, and it was not until the warmth and softness moved and murmured did she realise that lying in the crook of her arm was Bessie Dalton's brat.

She sat up slowly, careful not to disturb the little girl. She looked down at the small face in which the greyness of exhaustion showed clearly, despite the grime. The eye-sockets were deep pits and the long fine lashes lay without movement on the child's cheek as though in death. Daisy studied her for a moment and for the second time in a week felt her heart stir with warmth towards another human being. She had been enchanted with the splendour of young Miles Thornley. The impact of him had stunned her, made her aware of her own deficiencies and, at the same time, resolute in her determination to mend them. He had stolen her heart right out of her childish breast, making her his captive, his slave, his protector should he ever need it, her worship of him as complete and strong, as endlessly trusting as only that of a child can be. He was without flaw and if she could serve him in some way her life would be whole and lovely because of it. A glorious being then, who stood so far above her it seemed almost a sin to love him so, but this child who had crept into her arms in the black of night was as earth-born as herself and aroused a different kind of love. Hours she had walked, stumbled, run on her little bare feet to catch Daisy up, not complaining or bearing a grudge at being left behind but struggling on until she found what she was after. What a plucky little beggar she was and Daisy admired pluck. It was what got you up on your feet when they still bled from yesterday's walk. It was what kept the tears hidden from others who might take it as a sign of weakness. It was what made you grit your teeth and lift your head when someone had just fetched you a clout which made it ring. Cassie had it and Daisy wouldn't desert her again. Somehow she would manage. Somehow *they* would manage.

They found a sheltered hiding-place between the huge roots of an oak tree in Chinkham Wood. They filled it with dry leaves, making it snug, and when Daisy placed Cassie in it and told her to stay there and sleep, the little girl lay back and closed her eyes trustingly, sinking once again into the exhausted sleep from which Daisy had roused her. Though she could have bought some milk, some bread and cheese from the farmer's wife at the farmhouse across the fields, Daisy decided it would be prudent not to reveal their presence. There was a neat vegetable patch to the side of the farmhouse and a run for hens and, with a stealth and skill born of long practice, Daisy gathered three eggs, half a dozen old potatoes and two wizened carrots, leaving no trace that she had been there. The dog which had barked the previous night had gone, presumably with the farmer, and by nine o'clock she and Cassie had eaten – by their standards – a good breakfast, settling themselves down again in their snug nest as soon as it was gone. They slept all day and when darkness fell set off hand in hand towards the road which would take them in the direction of St Helens. Later they slept for another couple of hours behind a dry-stone wall, huddled close together for warmth, and when she woke again the light was beginning to lay a finger along the peaks of the Pennine foothills in the east and she knew they must move on again.

They reached Rainford Brook as the sun filtered through the bare branches of the white willow trees lining the banks. The two children slithered down the slick grass to the water's edge and walked beside it until they were hidden beneath the bridge which spanned the stream.

"We'll have us a wash here," Daisy told Cassie purposefully, then wondered how one went about such a mysterious business. Water was involved, naturally, but what else? The child stood obediently, her deep violet eyes looking up at Daisy, waiting to be told what to do next, quite willing it seemed to join in whatever it was, if Daisy said so.

Daisy stared doubtfully into the shallow depths of the fast-running stream then looked about her for inspiration. There was some soft vegetation on the bank, green and pretty and sweet-smelling, and tentatively she pulled out a handful and Cassie obligingly did the same, waiting to see what Daisy did with it.

"D'you think we could use it to ... well, to rub some water on us?" Daisy asked her and Cassie studied it curiously, then turned her glance on the sparkling water. It looked quite lovely. Considering it was November the air was surprisingly warm and the sun shone on the flat stones which stuck up out of the water. She waited.

"If we went right under the bridge and on to the far side where no one could see us we could take our clothes off," Daisy continued, her eyes widening at her own daring. "What d'you think?" It really was rather nice to have someone to talk to, even if Cassie didn't talk back. She knew Cassie understood every word she was saying. She seemed to consider, as though she really was thinking about it, then her face broke into the most beautiful smile. Daisy was enchanted. She was an incredibly pretty little girl and surely, if she could get her clean, no one could resist the appeal of her and would not object to Daisy taking her with her on the new job. She'd say Cassie was her sister and that she could do simple tasks and would not be a ha'p'orth of bother to anyone.

"Come on then, take yer things off."

They both gasped in shock and Cassie would have scrambled out of the water again as its icy glitter flowed over them if Daisy had not held on to her. For a second they were both speechless and when Daisy spoke her teeth chattered wildly beneath her trembling lips.

"Hold on ter me. See, it's getting warmer" – which was not true – "now, rub yerself with some of this grass stuff, no, stand still ... all right then, sit on that stone. Feel, it's quite warm. Now start with yer feet and work upwards. Now, isn't that grand?"

The sun shone, warm as June almost, and the two little girls were all alone in their increasing pleasure. The sting had gone from the water as their bodies became accustomed to it. Daisy even took her courage in both hands and dipped her head right under, gasping in delight as the biting cleanliness ran through her hair. She rubbed at it furiously and Cassie, who would now do anything that Daisy told her to do if it meant they could stay together in this lovely world to which she had been introduced, did the same. For half an hour they romped and splashed, oblivious to everything but the joy of being children in a child's world. They rubbed themselves again and again with the green stuff until their skin glowed, marvelling at now lovely they smelled, at the shining whiteness of their own flesh which neither had seen before, and at the ripple of their wet hair, clean and heavy, which hung about them and Daisy wondered at the ability Cassie seemed to have of making herself understood without saying a word.

But the cold drove them out at last and it was then that the worst part began, for they were forced to don the filthy garments they had taken off carelessly only half an hour since and which, then, they had not realised were so dreadful.

"Never mind," Daisy said, as she shuddered her way into the stiff and odious sketch of a skirt and the evil-smelling bodice which was all she possessed. "I'll buy us summat better with me first week's wages." Her innocent trust and optimistic conviction that within the week they would be both in clover was believed absolutely by Cassie.

By ten o'clock they were on the road to St Helens and within the hour they entered the town itself, two small girls almost hidden amongst the crowd which thronged its way along Church Street, turning left into Market Street towards the square and the hirings. Displayed on stalls were gingerbread and lemonade and baked potatoes, onions, pies and muffins, fish and turnips, and because they had not eaten for twenty-four hours Daisy sacrificed several of her precious farthings on a muffin each – which neither of them had ever tasted – and a glass of lemonade. It really was grand. Everywhere you looked there were people, laughing and pushing, pedlars selling everything from bootlaces to tea-trays, from cough drops to corn plasters, tinkers and organ-grinders adding their voices to the cheerful racket. There was a band playing somewhere in the distance and Daisy thought she had never felt so happy in her life. The crowds seemed to overflow with goodwill, smiling and determined to enjoy themselves, and she wondered where the serious business of the hirings was to take place.

There was a woman, roughly dressed but pleasant-faced, standing on a corner as though she was looking for someone and when Daisy pulled her sleeve and asked her politely where the hirings were the woman pointed to several rows of men and women, all waiting with the patience of animals in a field.

"Just stand over there, lass, and they'll come to you."

Daisy wondered who 'they' were but obediently she took a stand at the end of the front row and waited. She had decided that whatever her new master asked of her, that was what her occupation would be. She would tell him she could do anything from setting seedlings to ploughing a furrow. Her experience of life inside a farmhouse was nonexistent and so her mind could not imagine any task beyond those she had performed in the fields. If she had to lie she would do so. She was a quick learner and once she had been shown, she could do anything she was told to do. But she must keep Cassie hidden until she had got the job so, with this in mind, she had instructed the little girl to sit against the wall where Daisy could see her but not to let on to anyone that they were together until Daisy said so. She could see her now, her back against the wall, her little legs stretched out before her, the sunlight turning her pale, newly washed hair to the shimmer of silver. Her soft skin, white as ivory and just as smooth, was quite perfect against the drab greyness of her dress and when she looked up to watch the comings and goings of the crowd her eyes were like flowers in her shy face. Her loveliness struck Daisy an anxious blow and she prayed that no one would notice her and wonder what such a striking child was doing all alone in the market square.

Her own improved image, unseen by herself, was just as

startling, not the least being the heavy and shining mass of her richly burnished hair. Though it was tangled still after its wash and unkempt, it hung to her buttocks in a mass of curls, tipping her small head back until her pale golden eyes stared imperiously about her in a most unservile way. Her skin had a creamy transparent texture and her full apricot mouth parted to show her white teeth. She was not beautiful, nor even pretty in the accepted sense as Cassie was. In repose her face would not attract undue attention for her features were far from perfect. Her mouth was far too wide, for one thing, with a grim determination about it which spoke of an inclination not towards laughter and the frivolous things of life, but of survival, of endurance, of durability in hardship. Not a child who would be likely to draw any eyes to her, besides which those about her were too concerned with their own anxiety to bother about others'. Some had been there since the week of the hirings had begun and were still not 'taken on'. There was apprehension and even resignation on many of the older faces but when some men began to walk along the lines, stopping now and again to speak to one of them, they straightened their backs and lifted their heads and tried to look ten years younger. One or two of the men, masters she took them to be, stopped in front of her, looking her up and down in the most offensive way and she tried not to appear as though she resented it, even if she did. She was here to find a job, wasn't she, and she'd just have to put up with their stares.

She had been there for three hours and the sun had slipped away behind a solid mass of sullen cloud. It had turned colder and she stamped her feet to keep them warm. She had on her boots, of course, but she wondered how Cassie was managing with her bare feet and clothing which was more holes than fabric. She tried to peer round the organ-grinder's barrow which now stood just in front of the child but a crowd had gathered to watch the antics of the sad-eyed monkey and Cassie was hidden from her view.

When the man spoke to her she turned guiltily to face him. This was no time to be worrying about Cassie. She was here to find a job of work, *any* work, and she must keep her attention on that and nothing else. He was a big man, looking a lot like Farmer Chadwick for whom she had last worked. He wore a tall, black hat, thick cord breeches, gaiters and a good ribbed coat. He looked what he was, a prosperous farmer, and when he spoke to her she was reassured by the kindly but puzzled expression in his pale blue eyes, eyes set in a ruddy face which looked as though it had never known a hungry day in its life.

"Good day to you, lass. Is it a skivvy's job you're after?" and he waited, smiling for her answer.

She had not the faintest notion what a 'skivvy' was but if that was what he was after she was quite happy to be one.

"Yes, sir, if you please," and she smiled. As she did so she saw his face relax and an answering smile lift the corners of his mouth. She had no idea what it was that had made her answer so prettily, nor smile so glowingly, but she could see that he liked it. She was completely unaware of the change in her when she smiled and which transformed her from a plain and serious child into a creature so delightful that other men had begun to gather at the farmer's back, though they could not have said why.

"How old are you?" Again instinct led her.

'Twelve, sir."

"You're small for twelve, lass," but what did that matter, his manner said. The missus would be delighted with this engaging young girl.

"But I'm strong, sir."

"Oh aye." His eyes twinkled in the sun-browned creases of his genial face. "And where did you work last?"

"Chadwick's." Not a lie.

"Farmer Chadwick, you mean, up beyond Primrose Bank?"

"Yes, sir."

"And what did you do there?"

"I was skivvy, sir."

"And Mrs Chadwick was pleased with your work?"

"Oh yes, sir."

"Then why did you leave, my girl?" and on his face was a

63

look of reluctant doubt but her quick brain, which was often to stand her in good stead, was a match for his.

"My mother fell ill, sir, and being the only girl I had to go home ter nurse her. Mrs Chadwick had ter take on another skivvy and when I got back ter the farm me job was gone."

"Oh dear me, and your mother?"

"She died, sir." Her great golden eyes were sorrowful as she looked up into the man's face and she saw in it the awkward compassion a big man feels for something small and pitiful. She had struck exactly the right note with him, trusting her instincts, and though he was looking somewhat askance at her filthy garments which no self-respecting lass should be wearing she knew that he was going to give her the job.

"I've been on the road two days, sir," she said apologetically, as though to explain the state of her skirt and bodice, and man-like, the explanation seemed to suit. What his wife would say when he took her home she had no idea but it would be too late then. Give her a bit of decent clothing, which surely any mistress would supply, and something to tie up her abundant hair and she would be just as presentable as any lass here. She'd say nothing about Cassie as yet. If she could catch the child's eye she would signal to her to hang back for a minute or two and then to follow where Daisy and the man went. Cassie would follow in any case, she knew that, but Daisy must get her toe in the door of this new place before she introduced the matter of her little 'sister'.

"Well, the missus said I was to pick a good strong girl of about fourteen and you're none of those..." but he was taken with her, she knew it. She kept her soulful eyes on his, ready to smile if he did, ready to follow him to the ends of the earth if he would only nod in agreement. His face was uncertain and he picked at his lip as he studied her. Several of the men at his back for some strange reason, since she was not the sort of servant one usually hired, waited impatiently for him to make up his mind and it was perhaps this which decided him.

64

He smiled and nodded.

"Righto, lass. Four shillings a week and your board." *Four shillings a week and her board!* She could feel the elation, the triumph well up in her, and her face was like a pale and beautiful candle, the golden flame glowing in her eyes, and the farmer was nonplussed, wondering how his missus would react to this delightful little besom. "I'll bond you for six months," he continued, "and see how you fare. Now get yer things together..." He looked about him, expecting the bundle or box in which most servants carried all they possessed, and was surprised when there was none.

"Have you no things, then?" he asked and stepped to one side as though to search behind her, for surely she would have something.

As he moved, the men at his back were revealed. One of them was the gangmaster and he had Cassie casually slung beneath his arm.

5

She lay for almost a week on the lice-ridden palliasse, not able to move, the skin on her back stripped almost to the bone by the lash he had laid on her. Her own mother, affronted one supposed by what she saw as her daughter's attempted desertion or perhaps through the fear of what might happen to *her* should she show sympathy, came nowhere near her. Had it not been for Cassie Dalton and for Gertie Wilson who, despite her coarseness and a nature hardened by what her life had been, had a warmer and braver heart than the others, it is doubtful she would have lived.

Lodging-houses were not easy to find in the close-packed

tenements which sheltered the homeless of St Helens. Thousands of them slept at twopence a night on a bundle of rags in a bunk, having the use of the fire in the kitchen to cook their food should they be fortunate enough to have any. Labourers, beggars, vagrants, drunkards and prostitutes slept cheek by jowl for a penny on the bare floor. The gangmaster had rented the cellar of a house in Green Lane though if ever there was a thoroughfare which was mis-named this had to be it. The sulphurous smoke which poured from a score of chimneys coated every surface, not just of Green Lane but of the whole of this town in which many industries thrived side by side. Brass foundries, copper-smelting works, chemical manufacturers, glass-makers and of course the collieries which produced the power to serve them all.

The West Lancashire coalfields had developed rapidly as coal replaced wood for fuel. Sand and fireclay were also in plentiful supply and in the seventeenth century glass-making was begun in the area. Glass-works sprang up and it was claimed that St Helens made two-thirds of the country's plate glass and one third of its window glass. There was a flourishing alkali trade supplying the local manufacturers of soap and it was said that almost two million tons of coal were mined annually in the district. The era of canals had begun here when the first to be built in the country was constructed by deepening Sankey Brook from St Helens to the River Mersey linking the town to the sea, and to the rest of the trading world.

With the coming of this great new industrial age the popu-lation which in 1831 had been a mere six thousand, doubled and trebled almost overnight, it seemed, as thousands of starving men, women and children left the fields to work there. And they crowded together as close as grains of sand, filling every corner of every room in houses which tottered, near to collapse, in the narrow, putrid alleys. Rotten warrens of broken roofs, crumbling chimneys, empty window-frames and gaping doorways, built around uncleaned and ill-ventilated courtyards where the hundreds of occupants shared one privy and one water-tap. The town was coated in soot, dust and the stench, noxious and foul-smelling, from the factories. A great yellow pall hung over the rooftops, drifting with the prevailing wind across blackened buildings, and even on its outskirts coal dust from the collieries lay in a fine black film over everything it touched. It was a town of machinery and chimneys, black canals and steam engines, broken-down men and women, stunted children, over-flowing privies and open ashpits. Water from the polluted canals and rivers flooded the cellars where twenty to thirty persons slept each night, excrement rotted in the streets, sewers were unknown and the average age of death amongst the inhabitants was fifteen years. A town of sharp contrasts, as were all the Lancashire industrial towns, in which the most appalling poverty lived in intimate proximity to new and immense wealth, and quietly, amidst it all, Daisy Brindle lay on her face on the damp and fouled palliasse, the spirit and hope and will viciously taken from her, staring into the grim future of her life.

She was aware of the women and children around her, of their comings and goings at all times of the day and night, of the obscenities which were bandied about the foul air in the cellar, of the drink-fuddled fumblings of the men who sought the company of the women, but it seemed to take place in another world, a world which had nothing to do with her and her suffering. She lay in what seemed already to be her coffin. Nothing could touch her again. The worst had happened and she was apart from them and yet one of them now in her shock and pain, for when the worst has happened what is there to be afraid of, or concerned with? She had dared to hope she might escape the fate of the other women. She had flown for two days to the dizzy heights a freed bird would reach but when he had caught her the hunter had clipped her wings cruelly, crippling her so that she would never fly again.

He had raped her first before he flogged her, tearing his way into her child's body until she screamed in agony and the women in the shadows of the room had turned their faces away, remembering perhaps their own initiation into his brutal world. Putting his mark on her he had called it, the foul mark of his ownership, and now she belonged utterly to him, like the rest of them. He forced her to acknowledge it as she lay under him. Now she wanted to die for it was the only way to freedom.

But Gertie Wilson and Cassie Dalton would not let her.

"Get this inside yer," Gertie said roughly, shoving a bowl of cold-water oats beneath her nose and when she turned her head away stiffly, Gertie gripped her long matted hair and hissed into her face.

"Listen here, madam. Yer not the only one this has happened to, yer know. We've all bin through it. I were your age when I were set on and there was three of them. Overlookers in the mill, big lads an' all. Bloody hell, I couldn't walk for a month but I got over it and so will you. Now get this down yer and stop feeling sorry for yerself. He'll not give up on yer, yer know that. He'll not let yer lie there fer much longer so yer'd best get yer strength back. Come on, Daisy lass, fight him, don't let him beat yer."

She ate after that. It seemed less trouble somehow, allowing Cassie to spoon whatever slop was put before her into her torn mouth, but still she lay passively in a corner of the room while the life of the gang flowed about her. They were all working at the collieries which surrounded the town, all but the children under five and they ran wild in the streets and alleys, half naked in the grey drizzle of November, no more than small animals as they foraged for scraps to keep themselves alive. The gangmaster had told them all the previous night that he intended to find them work in one of the cotton towns since little 'piecers' and 'scavengers' were always needed. Small hands and small bodies to clamber beneath the lethally moving machinery. When the spring came and they moved back to their seasonal work on the land they would all be collected, he told their mothers, most of them indifferent but a few in whom the maternal instinct lived, anxious about the fate of their offspring.

He had been in good spirits. He had obtained work for all his gang except the girl and he'd have her down at the coal-face before the week ended, back or no back. She'd learned her lesson like they all did and she'd work without complaining from now on. Not that she'd ever complained before but she must have had the spirit of rebellion in her to take it into her head to run away like that but she'd not do it again. Give her six months down the pit with the rest of them and when she came up in the spring she'd be more than willing to work the fields again. He'd have to let her heal for a day or two since she'd be no good for drawing tubs in her present state but the brat, Bessie Dalton's brat, could see to her while he took the rest of the children to a millowner he had struck a deal with and when he got back he'd dispose of the Dalton kid in the workhouse or some such institution which took in paupers. He could just abandon her, like many men would, to fend for herself on some lonely bit of moorland but he was not like that. No, he looked after those in his care, he did. The irony of this thought did not cross his mind.

It was the absolute quiet which brought her back to her full senses. For days, ever since she had been flung on the palliasse in the corner, there had been noise and movement, screams of laughter, shouts and swearing voices, snoring, coughing, all the sounds made by a score of humanity living in close proximity to one another. Drunkenness, dirt and bad language, violence even. Vermin to the extent where life was unbearable and sleep impossible if she had not been used to the bugs, the fleas, the lice and the rats which shared the cellar with them. Now, though the vermin were still her bedfellows, the room was empty, except for Cassie, and was as quiet as the grave.

The child crouched at Daisy's head, her own on one side in a listening attitude, her eyes fixed attentively on Daisy. She was as filthy as she had been before her wash in Rainford Brook but when Daisy's eyes turned to hers she smiled gravely, revealing her small teeth. She leaned forward to touch Daisy's cheek, then, putting her finger to her lips she slipped to the foot of the bed and from beneath it produced the heal of a loaf of bread. It was almost fresh and when she broke a morsel from it and put it gently between Daisy's lips, Daisy felt the saliva come to her mouth. The bread tasted quite delicious and she sucked it carefully until it was soft enough to swallow. Cassie gave her another piece, then another, taking nothing for herself, her eyes narrowed and watchful, like a mother who is determined her finicky child shall eat every scrap of food on its plate.

Daisy indicated with her eyes that Cassie should have some too but the little girl shook her head and smiled, blithely scattering lice in a shower from her matted hair. She dived again beneath the bed and this time she produced a bottle in which was a pale brown liquid and when she held it to Daisy's lips the smell of cold tea and the taste of it on her parched tongue was the best Daisy had ever known.

When Daisy had finished her meal the child carefully wiped her face with a damp, stinking cloth but did not touch her in any other way. The raw, half-healed abomination of Daisy's back was too much even for her. She had managed in some way to filch the bread and tea without the others knowing, to hide it from them and keep it for her friend, fiercely watching over her as Daisy had watched over herself but she was afraid of the injuries, afraid to look at Daisy's back since it brought into her damaged mind the memory of the horror of what the master had done that night. She had not understood it but Daisy's screams and Daisy's terror lived uneasily on the edge of her mind and she did not want to be forced to confront what was there.

She resumed her patient vigil by Daisy's bed, crouching on her haunches, her eyes unfocused and half closed but when, with a great farrago of harsh voices, bawdy laughter and black coal dust, the women returned from their shift at the pit she became instantly alert. The women did not wash. There were twenty hovels surrounding the court in which they were temporarily housed and there was one tap which was turned on for an hour three times a week and that was at six o'clock in the morning. Those who had an inclination towards cleanliness rose at four and queued perhaps for three hours for their quota of water but as long as the gang women had enough for drinking purposes and to cook their 'spuds' and oatmeal, they did not concern themselves with keeping clean. It was too much trouble. The water was impure and had all kinds of unmentionable things floating in it so for the most part they quenched their thirst with ale or gin.

"How yer feeling?" Gertie asked Daisy, leaning across casually to inspect her back. "I got some spuds and a bit of bacon so get it down yer and no arguing. Yer beginning ter heal nicely by the look of yer but yer'll have a scar or two on that back. The other'll not show," she grinned not unkindly, "so best forget about it. The worst's over for you. D'yer want a sip of gin ter make yer sleep? No? Well, don't say I didn't offer."

She slept anyway, shock and pain drugging her more effectively than any spirits. She dreamed of a tall, engaging boy, beautiful as an angel with wings of dark hair sweeping away from eyes the colour of the sky in spring. They smiled down into hers and a hand smoothed her hair away from her flushed brow. She was hot, so hot, and he bathed her forehead with cool water, then she was cold and a warm body – surely his? – snuggled itself close to hers. He fed her a morsel of food which she didn't really want but to please him she swallowed it and when he placed a lovely glass cup against her lips she drank what was in it gratefully.

When she awoke the dream was gone and she wept bitterly for a while. Her head was completely clear and Cassie was there, watching, waiting as she had done for nearly a week. And behind her was the gangmaster.

"Right, my girl," he said pleasantly enough, "it's time you was up off that bed. I've let yer lay there long enough, I reckon, and that job I've got fer yer won't be kept for ever. They'll be back soon, the rest of them, so how about you and nipper getting something ready fer them to eat. Start earning yer keep. You've had a nice little rest but yer know I won't have no idlers in my gang and I'll not feed them what won't work." He leaned against the wall, his long tattered coat as filthy as his surroundings. He had his arms folded across his chest and his hooded eyes were speculative, though neither Daisy nor Cassie could read the expression in them. He was like a man assessing a bit of property he had acquired, perhaps pondering on its value and the possibility of getting a good price for it should he decide to part with it.

Daisy wondered indifferently where the defiance she had known a week ago had gone to, and the positive conviction that she was to be different from the rest of them. Only a few days since, she had known herself to be youthfully contemptuous of the women who seemed to have no will of their own and were content to do whatever their master demanded of them. She had sneered at them in her childlike naïvety, telling herself that in no way would she ever be as they were. She had despised them and now, in the space of one horrific hour, he had made her one of them. But it didn't seem to matter. Nothing mattered. Her eyes were blank and almost colourless, the lovely golden brightness melted away. As he continued to study her she lifted herself obediently on to her elbows and then turned slightly until she rested on her side. She felt the half-healed welts on her back pull and she winced but swinging her feet round she sat up. The sack which had been flung across her naked body slipped down and she clutched at it, attempting to cover her unformed breasts, keeping her eyes averted from contact with his, not from shame or even fear though she felt both, but from a curious conviction that if she could not see him, she herself would be invisible. Cassie watched her carefully and when Daisy's eyes shifted furtively to hers she seemed to know exactly what she wanted, handing her the skirt and bodice which had been stripped savagely off her a week since. She drew them on beneath his smiling gaze.

She stood up stiffly, her eyes still lowered, looking around her hesitantly, her mind awkward and blank, just as though the horror of what had been done to her had dulled her wits and taken the core of her own identity from her. She couldn't seem to get to grips with what was needed of her, what she was expected to do, and though she found she couldn't really care she supposed she must make some effort.

It was Cassie who directed her, putting into her hands the cooking pot which was the only utensil the women appeared to own, the potatoes and carrots, the mouldy bread and mouldy bacon which Cassie indicated was to be their meal.

"I should look sharp if I were you. They'll be in soon and by the way, don't get too dependent on that kid. Yer'd best begin ter see ter yerself from now on because she's off tomorrow. Pity really. She'd've made a good little worker if she'd bin a bit bigger and had a tongue in her head. She's bin useful this past week what with one thing and another, running errands and seeing to you, though why I should've bothered I don't know. An ungrateful little bitch like you don't deserve the care I've seen yer got but I reckon you'll be a fair return soon enough. A bit on the scrawny side as yet but..." He seemed to be talking to himself now, his head on one side as he considered her, and he did not notice the sudden slight stiffening of her frail, battered body nor the slow lifting of her bruised face until her eyes looked directly into his. The cooking pot hung from one of her limp hands and in the other she held the scrap of bacon. She was about to put one into the other, Cassie sidling close beside her, ready to help, but his words had touched a nerve inside Daisy's empty head, making no sense as yet, but very important, she knew that, when she could get the hang of it.

"...useful this week ... off tomorrow ... see to yerself ... off tomorrow ... off tomorrow..."

She was not awfully sure she had his true meaning at first. It was as though some speech impediment had eradicated every third or fourth word he spoke so that only a few were intelligible.

"...off tomorrow ... useful ... factory in..." and then slowly, like a tap dripping into a bucket, drop by drop, the substance of it began to fill her mind. He was talking about Cassie. Her Cassie. The little scrap of a girl who until ten days ago she had scarcely known existed but who was now, apart from the boy in the wood, the person Daisy cared about more than anyone else in the world. She'd be dead if it wasn't for Cassie, she realised, forgetting that for the past few days she'd had no thought in her mind but to die. Cassie wasn't all there, Daisy knew that, but what *was* there was worth more than the rest of them put together, including her own mother. Stuck like a burr, she had, brave and true and loyal, doing all she could despite being no bigger than a dainty wood violet. And cheerful too. Though she said nowt you could see her good nature shining out of her eyes and now, when her childish usefulness was at an end, she was to be discarded like a bit of unwanted sacking.

Her mouth was swollen and she thought she detected a gap in the teeth she had been so proud of but she formed the words somehow, forcing them out from between curiously unmanageable lips.

"You'll have ter kill me first," she said flatly, and her golden eyes glowed again. She felt the life flow back into her, coursing along limbs which until now had been flaccid and weak. It flooded to her brain, setting it alight with her hatred. She might only be ten years old and she was terrified of him still but what had she got to lose now? What she had suffered had not, as she had thought, weakened her but made her gloriously strong. She would never be weak again, not with him, not with any man since the worst they could do to her had already been done. He could kill her, of course, but what good would that do him? None at all, since she was a valuable commodity to him. Money in his pocket, and anything else he wished to take from her. But he'd not have Cassie, not if Daisy Brindle had anything to do with it. She glared at him, showing him her teeth like a feral cat.

He pushed himself away from the wall, staring in astonishment at this yellow-eyed kitten which was spitting at him as though she was a full-grown lioness. She had dropped the pot and the bacon on to the decaying floor and was standing with her hands curled into claws, defiant and apparently unafraid of him and again, as he had in the village inn weeks ago, he felt a stab of admiration for her bloody nerve. But he'd not have it. He couldn't afford to. He couldn't let her defy him or they'd all be at it. He'd have to show her who was the master here or she'd be forever challenging his authority. He'd have to knock some sense into her or he'd not have a minute's peace ...

He stopped, confused for the first time in his brutish life since it seemed to him she'd already had more than enough to subdue her, to make her submit her will to his, and yet here she was asking for it all over again. She was one of those rare creatures you meet now and then whose spirit, no matter what is done to them, cannot be broken, so what was he to do about it? He hesitated and Daisy's quick brain saw its chance and rushed on before it was lost.

"She can come with me. We can work together."

"There's only a job fer you."

"They don't have to pay her."

"I'm not feeding her, my lass, that's fer sure."

"I'll feed her."

"What? Share your grub with her?" wondering why he was even bothering to argue with her when a clout round the earhole would do just as well and be twice as effective ... wouldn't it? "I helped myself to the few farthings you had about your person when I ... well ... I'm sure you remember..." watching her face spasm in horror, "so there's no need ter think yer can buy food with that. Anyway, they won't take her down. She's too puny. She don't look no more than four or five."

"She can help me. They'll not even know she's there."

"I'm keeping nobody who don't work."

"Then you'll have ter get shut of me an' all because if she doesn't stay I'm not working."

"Yer'll do as I say."

"Try me."

His hands curled into fists and his wide brutish mouth lifted in a cruel smile.

"Don't challenge me, girl, or you may be sorry." She could see his knuckles shining white in the dim light of the cellar and her heart hammered furiously in her thin chest. "You'll do what I tell you, as you always have, an' if I say the brat goes, she will. Nasty things happen ter those who don't do what I tell them, as you should well know, my lass, and I don't like my arrangements upset, d'you understand? Do you understand?" he repeated when she did not answer.

"Yes."

"Well then." He reached forward to touch her and though she recoiled sharply her eyes still blazed in her battered face. He tilted her chin up and his own eyes narrowed even further when he saw the expression in hers. Cassie whimpered in the corner but neither of them heard her. "You'll do as yer told or I swear ter God I'll hurt yer in ways yer've not even imagined."

There was a deep silence, intense, burning and cruel, then the girl lifted her head and he recognised in that moment that this one would be something one day and did he want to lose her? He was a realist in his own strange way, quite rare in that he was patient and ready to wait for the benefit to come, not tomorrow or even next week but in the future, and to *him*.

He watched her and she watched him, the strangest pair of protagonists that would ever face one another in these quarters. His eyes gleamed in anticipation and his furred tongue moved across his lips. She felt her stomach heave as she saw it, remembering, remembering things she wanted desperately to forget, but she did not falter. Her voice was steady.

"If yer take her away you'll get nothing else from me. I know what yer do with the women's wages, me Mam included and if I was ter tell them yer'd get nothing from them neither. D'yer think Gertie Wilson'd take kindly ter knowing you've bin keeping money what rightly belongs ter her? They might be frightened of you but if I was ter speak out and they stuck together you'd be without a team. Now you can go on as yer've been doing and I'll say nowt if yer'll let me keep the kid, or you'll lose not only me but the whole bloody lot of us."

The gangmaster lifted his chin and thrust it forward. In the depths of his cold eyes something stirred. There was an air of dreadful menace about him which entered Daisy's fast-beating heart like a sliver of ice and she felt an urgent desire to take another step backwards and an even more urgent desire to relieve herself down her own legs, then, amazingly, he began to laugh. The expression of peril in his eyes changed to one of amused admiration. She could tell he was not at all displeased by her show of defiance though she could not have said why. He was a strange man. So

76

brutal, so implacably brutal in his dealings with those he would hold in his tyranny. A quiet and yet forceful savagery which would not allow those in his power the slightest departure from the route he planned for them and if they should attempt it his retribution was swift and terrible. Witness her own 'punishment'. And yet he respected it, should anyone have the nerve to try. He was looking at her strangely and the terror ran wild through her. She knew if he were to touch her again in *that* way her hard-won bravery would vanish as quickly as it had come, but though it took every ounce of her strength she kept her head up and her eyes on his. She had a suspicion that she was probably the first of his gang ever to stand up to him and that in an odd way he was enjoying it. If she could just hang on to the 'edge' she had won without showing signs of faltering she might use it to her own and Cassie's advantage.

Suddenly he stepped away from her, his step light and what she could only describe as carefree. There was still something nasty in his expression and she knew she had not heard the last of it but for the moment he appeared to have given in. Perhaps not given in, for he would never do that, but from his attitude as he made his smiling way towards the slimy steps which led up to the street, he was prepared to postpone, at least for the moment, the transfer of Cassie Dalton to other hands which could be worse than his own. Not from benevolence but simply because, at the moment, it suited him. There were men, depraved men, who would pay him well for a little girl as fresh and pretty as Cassie but it seemed it amused him to keep her for now. His purpose in doing so was not revealed to Daisy and as she and Cassie curled up together in their own bit of bedding she did not attempt to analyse it. She would live each day as it came, wary as a sparrow in a hawk's nest, and if the hawk should show signs of turning on her again she would be ready to fly as far and as wide as her fragile wings would take her. The opportunity would come. She would make it come. One day.

6

They were lowered in an iron cage to the dark passages which led to the coal-face, following as fast as they could in the candlelit dimness the rest of the children who had been roughly instructed to show the new girl the way. The roof was so low they were forced to bend their heads and in places drop to their hands and knees, crawling across rough, uneven surfaces and through many stretches where the water was so deep that Daisy was alarmed for Cassie's safety. The air was foul, full of coal dust which clung to every surface it touched, every inch of her uncovered skin, inside her mouth when she opened it to breathe, in her nostrils and beneath her eyelids, and she began at once to cough like the rest.

The roof was supported by pillars of coal which would themselves be demolished when the mine was exhausted, she was later told, but she almost crashed into half a dozen of them, dragging Cassie along by her hand as she hurried after the scampering child who was last in the line. There was refuse and rotting garbage beneath the soles of her bare feet, slimy and evil-smelling, made all the worse because her shrinking eyes could not see it and her shrinking flesh had no way to avoid it. The blackness was almost complete, a blackness she had never before experienced even on the darkest winter's night. Her young mind felt it would spin into madness as this latest horror was forced upon her but her will to survive it clung desperately to her reason and she became steadier as she went along. Bloody hell, she said to herself, she had barely been underground five minutes and she was ready to go off her rocker. If she was to be so easily unnerved she might just as well lie down right here in the mucky water which lapped about her feet, and Cassie with her. She took deep breaths of the noxious air and clung to Cassie's hand, taking courage from the need the smaller girl had of her, and when the first naked man stepped out of the gloom she was so dumbfounded she completely forgot her own predicament.

"This 'un's ter 'hurry' fer yer, Mr Clegg," the sexless child ahead of her shouted, then vanished into the gloom. There were a couple of candles stuck to the wall with clay, their poor light revealing several other men, also naked. One lay on his back, the short, sharp pickaxe he wielded no more than six inches from his nose, picking into the coal seam above him with all the force he could manage in a such a confined space. A third was squatting on his haunches and a fourth chipping out pockets into which he was preparing to drive wedges. There were three or four other shadowy figures no bigger than herself whom Daisy took to be children who were to be employed as she was.

"Right, lass," Mr Clegg said, "yer best get out of them clothes an' put on these breeches if yer ter get about them passages."

He threw some garment at her, breeches so damp and thick with the coal dust and dirt deposited by their previous owner they were stiff and solid in her head. She could see the holes in them even in the gloom. She looked at them, her mouth agape, then back at the small and swinging genitals of the man who was, it appeared, to be her new master and she had an almost hysterical desire to scream with laughter. Was she mad, or were they? It was not that she was prudish. How could she be amidst the bestiality of the life she lived each day, the drunkenness, the debauchery, the lust and nudity of the women in the gang, and the men who fornicated with them? She had seen every act the human body can perform and latterly had suffered some of it personally but the sight of these naked men shocked her deeply.

"What's up, lass? Have yer not seen a man afore?" The speaker grasped his filthy male organ and made some lewd gesture, laughing towards his mate as he did so, but it was a good-natured laugh, letting her know he meant her no harm.

She lifted her head in unconscious regality, aware of the tight cap she had consented to put on to bind her luxurious hair. Though she was as black and dirty as any child in the mine and her hair harboured as much vermin, she had been surprisingly squeamish at the thought of wearing an article of clothing worn by another and there was simply nothing on this earth, or in it, that would make her put on those disgusting breeches. She would tie up her skirt between her legs for easier walking and crawling, as she had always done.

She told him so.

"Is that so? Well, please thissen. See, here's yer basket. The loader'll fill it for yer and then yer pulls it along the passage ter the crane. Put yer basket ont' crane which hauls it up to wheret' pit ponies are. Now I'm yer hewer. I get the coal for yer . . ." he stopped abruptly and peered into the darkness, his eyes picking out the shape of the small child who clung to Daisy's skirt ". . . ay up, who's that with yer?"

"She's me . . . me little sister. I've got no one ter leave her with." Daisy's voice was defiant before she realised that she must not oppose this man who, whilst she was underground, was her owner. He had the right to get rid of not only Cassie, but her. Employable children were ten a penny and if she was to be turned off for giving cheek or disobeying orders, or even for giving this chap a funny look, she could be easily replaced and it would go ill for her with the gangmaster.

The colliery buildings stood on the north edge of the town. They were no more than a sprawl of dark shapes against the darker stretch of the morning sky when she and Cassie, with hundreds of others, had shuffled through the gate for the start of the day shift. There was a wheel turning high above the heads of the colliers and pit-lasses who hastened to their labours, afraid to be late since they would be fined for it. The tall outline of the headgear was lit by half a dozen lamps, picking out the tubs, some empty, others heaped with the gleaming black of coal, and a frenzy of running figures obscured by the shifting smoke and shadowed darkness of an early midwinter dawn.

The gangmaster had watched Cassie and herself slip out from the damp and achingly cold shelter of the cellar that morning into the dark and even colder turmoil of the street, joining all the others who hurried along in the direction of the factories, mines and mills of St Helens. He had stopped her for a moment, smiling down dangerously into her upturned face as though to remind her she had only one chance and she was not to squander it. So she must be polite to Mr Clegg until she had got herself a toehold on the new life she still meant to make for herself and Cassie. Not now, of course, or even next week, but one day. And today was as good as any to begin the preparations for it and if being servile to this man was part of that preparation, then so be it. She meant to survive, did Daisy Brindle, and no naked little monkey with his prick in his hand was going to deter her.

"She's not big enough, girl, she'll have ter go." She had already alienated him with her lofty refusal to dress as the others did. Dozens of women and girls, some only a few years older than herself, had hurried past along the dim passage, all of them wearing nothing but a tight cap to bind their hair and a pair of men's trousers, their breasts exposed, some just formed and perkily bobbing, others drooping, empty of life as were the women on whom they hung. Several of the women were in various stages of child-bearing, their swollen bellies straining against the waistbands of the trousers they wore.

Daisy averted her eyes from them and smiled, the whiteness of her sound teeth shining in the gloom.

"She could help me, mister. She's strong and she don't need no wages."

"And she'll get none, my lass, so yer'd best get shut of her."

"Please, mister, she'll get in no one's way. She's nearly ten ..." which obviously was a lie "... and she'll manage." She added 'sir' just for good measure, smiling ingratiatingly though in her heart she hated him as she hated all men, with the exception of one, and he was still really only a boy.

"She's not strong enough. Yer can see that, surely," but he was weakening, her politeness and use of the word 'sir' pleasing some trampled-on part of him which had been subdued and almost extinguished in his life of servitude. The little lass was looking at him hopefully, her attitude one of guarding the even smaller lass by her side. She appeared to stand over her charge as though daring anyone to lay a hand on her but by the look of her, *she* was the one who could have done with a bit of protection. Even in the poor light from the candles he could make out the swelling about her left eye and the kind of lopsided look to her face. There was a cut in her lower lip, just scabbing over, and though he could not have sworn to it owing to the usual layer of filth which coated all the children who worked in the pit, he was almost certain there were bruises about her thin neck. Someone had given her a hiding by the look of her. Scawny little thing she was with enormous eyes – at least one was – in her pointed face but she had spirit, he could tell that by the lift of her head and the brave squaring of her shoulders.

His face brightened and he put a hand to his chin.

"Tell you what though . . ."

"What?" Daisy stepped forward eagerly, her face smiling up into his, and like the man at the hirings he was startled by the sudden appeal of her.

"She could do the ventilation doors. Opening and shutting them, but it's a responsible job." He looked somewhat doubtful as Cassie turned her face into Daisy's skirt. "D'you reckon she could manage it? She looks a bit cracked ter me."

"Show me what ter do and I'll learn her," and he knew she would.

Daisy herself was to drag or push, along with other girls and boys, the laden baskets of coal to the crane. The ground was uneven and often clogged with clay or swamped with water up to her thighs. There were steep inclines and passages so narrow she had to crawl on all fours to get through them. Hitching her short skirt so that she was still modestly covered she allowed the belt to be fastened about her waist by the hewer and he showed her how to adjust the chain which passed between her legs and was then attached to the basket.

Like some small beast of burden she began her day's labour. At some point in the shift – she was not sure of the time, buried as she was in the stygian dark – she ate some scraps she had brought with her, relieved that, as had happened to one or two of the children, the rats had not eaten them, passing half to Cassie as she went by her. The little girl sat in the dim light of a small lantern, rhythmically opening and closing the ventilation door, her eyes blank and unfocused.

"You all right?" Daisy asked her gruffly, knowing there was nothing to be done if Cassie wasn't, but the little girl nodded, an almost hypnotic response to the only voice she trusted.

Daisy's body was at first ravaged by pain, on fire from head to toe with the need to crouch and strain her stricken flesh in postures to which it was not accustomed, and she told herself numbly that she must bring something to protect the still tender wound of the gangmaster's violation of her child's body. The chain rubbed her unmercifully between her legs and when, at the end of her shift it was apparen' that she was to be allowed to leave she was so tired she was not awfully certain she could make her way to the surface again, let alone stagger through the streets to the cellar which she called home.

Taking the hand of the almost stupefied Cassie, they fumbled their way together through the blackness with the rest of the children, mindless with exhaustion, ready to lay down wherever they fell.

"Loose ... l-o-o-s-e ... l-o-o-s-e." Three times the word had been shouted, echoing to the men, women and children below, going from mouth to mouth, gallery to gallery, until those in even the most remote corners of the pit were aware that it was time to leave the black hell-hole in which they had laboured for so long, some on a double shift of twenty-six hours. Gang after gang winding themselves up the dim and perilous way to freedom, bent and weary, stunted and diseased in lungs and heart, most coughing up the 'black spittle'. It was 1847 and despite the passing of Lord Ashley's Bill five years ago prohibiting the employment of women and small children underground, coal owners continued to give them work, the saving on their wages well worth the fine they might incur. There were 118,000 coal-miners in Britain, a great many of them women, and where a woman would work for two shillings a day, a man demanded three-and-sixpence and it took no great mathematical brain to reckon the profit lost if female labour was discontinued.

All through that long winter they both toiled, Daisy and Cassie Brindle, as the small girl came to be called since the name of her dead mother was soon forgotten, and at the end of each week Daisy put her wages in the gangmaster's hand, keeping her eyes lowered so as not to stir the memory of that day when he had abused her. She prayed he would not notice her, or Cassie, since she did not want to draw attention to the fact that the little girl was still with her, eating whatever Daisy could lay her hands on, but bringing in no wages. And she was terribly afraid that, should he tire of Agnes Barton's charms, he might turn again to herself. She shrank back into dark corners whenever he appeared, glad of the smoke-filled gloom of the cellar which, during the winter months, never knew the light of day. She neither washed nor tended to the long, tangled mat of her hair and was barely recognisable as a girl child beneath the disreputable assortment of garments she hung on her thin frame. She and Cassie were inseparable, seeming almost to be one flesh as they clung together, not only for warmth in the raw bleakness of the short winter days and the long winter nights, but for comfort in the only human contact each had ever really known. Each, as an infant, had known the rough embrace, the friendly nipple of a mother's breast, but once they had gained their feet and were able to perform simple tasks in the fields they had been abandoned as a bitch will abandon her growing pups. Now, craving something they had scarcely known and finding it, wordlessly, in one another, except when Daisy was 'hurrying', they were never apart. Like small grey spirits they moved furtively on the edge of the gang's activities through the winter, doing as they were bid without question. Daisy's eyes would signal to Cassie who seemed to understand implicitly that she was to make as small a target of herself as possible, to draw no one's eye to her, that she was to be no more than a shadow on the wall, and not even that if possible.

Though it could not be said that she became used to the work, or that it became any easier for her, Daisy's unflagging will forced her to accept what could not be changed. She was excessively thin but the work she had done in the fields had made her strong and wiry and though she had gone hungry many times in her ten years of life, the food she had eaten on many occasions at the farmer's kitchen door had been nourishing. It stood her in good stead now. She learned to blot out the beastliness which thrived in the bank below ground. Had she not lived amongst it all her life, the gross depravity of women like her own mother and the rest of the gang? She found she could turn her gaze inwards, away from what went on about her. When she came across a naked man casually covering the young girl who 'hurried' for him, grunting as he took a moment's pleasure, she switched off her conscious thoughts as smoothly as she might blow out a candle. Her brain did not retain the picture of coal-encrusted limbs entwined as naturally as dogs in an alley but looked beyond the hundreds of feet of earth and rock above her to the meadows surrounding the farms in which she would work when spring came. Meadows studded with cow parsley, buttercups and ox-eye daisies, hedged with hawthorn laden with blossom. When some woman gave birth in a shallow cut at the side of the passage, screaming and heaving to relieve herself of her burden, when the newborn infant was carried up the pit-shaft in its mother's skirt, Daisy did not concern herself with thoughts of the child's future, or indeed if it would have any in this vicious world in which she and Cassie only just survived. She herself had been beaten that day by her hewer for not being ready with her basket and her head still rang from the clout she had received. The hewer was paid by results, his wage reckoned on how much coal he got to the surface, and he depended not only on a good seam of coal but a good 'hurrier'. She had been cornered yet again by a lad not much older than herself and had been thrown to the ground as he tried to mount her, but her spitting, cat-like eyes, as dangerous as any wild animal, her fearless, cat-like claws, her language so foul that even he had faltered, had quenched his ardour. He had stood up and shrugged as though to say there were plenty more willing than her. As he sauntered away her mind had grasped desperately at the lifeline which kept her, just, fastened to the dream she had of the future for her and Cassie. The dream which made the days and nights able to be got through.

On Sunday the mines were closed and the men and women who laboured in them for six days took their pleasure on the seventh. First and foremost they liked to drink but to this was added the traditional miners' pastimes such as whippet-racing and cock-fighting. There was a saying that the Lancashire collier's coat of arms should have been a stark-naked child and a gamecock for such were the large sums of money lost gambling on cock-fights there was none left to clothe his children.

But Daisy and Cassie cared for neither of these pursuits and when the day was fine they walked, like two 'fashionable' ladies, out of the maze of alleys and courts where they lived, picking their way daintily in their bare and filthy feet – the boots having now been outgrown though saved for the day when they would fit Cassie – across cesspools, dunghills and middens until they reached the thoroughfare of Liverpool Row. They would saunter along the street well away from the gangmaster's baleful eye, and the rest of the women who were more drawn to cock-fighting, until they reached the King's Head where linnet-singing matches took place. There were grand prizes to be won such as copper kettles or pretty ornaments and though neither Daisy nor Cassie had the entrance fee of a shilling, nor a linnet to enter in the competition, it was lovely to stand on the edge of the more select crowd which gathered there and listen to the chirping of the small brown birds whilst the judges decided which was the sweetest.

There was often a contest known as a 'pastry feast' where young courting couples were invited to parade in front of the assembled drinkers, running the gauntlet of ribald commentary. The customary prize for the bonniest girl was a pint of rum and a sixpenny pasty whilst the most homely received a pound of black pudding. So pleased was the bonny girl to be chosen she sometimes forgot her pasty, leaving it carelessly on a table or windowsill whilst she shared her rum with her suitor and Daisy became adept at slipping the dainty morsel unobserved into the folds of her noisome skirt. The homely girl, incensed at being so named, would often fling her black pudding into the gutter and these also found their way into Daisy's clothing.

She and Cassie ate well on a Sunday.

They did not watch the cruel pastime of 'purring'. It was a favourite of the gang women which was enough to deter Daisy, and they could be seen cheering on their own choice or screaming obscenities at his opponent. The two girls, used as they were to violence and cruelty at its most malevolent, did not care for the harshness of the sport. The sight of two men, naked but for a pair of pit clogs, kicking each other until one fell to the ground and was battered into insensibility by the victor, was distasteful to them both. On the one occasion when Daisy and Cassie had gone along to watch, thinking that 'purring' might have something to do with cats, or better still, kittens, they had hurried away at the first sight of the naked men. It was, of course, done for money and the results were bet on heavily but they were not concerned with that and they saw enough of men and their 'dangly' bits in the mine.

And so at last came the day when, for the first time, it was still light when Daisy, Cassie and the rest of the children staggered out of the cage which had lifted them from the bowels of the earth. Six o'clock on a fine March evening and though the muted spring sun had almost fallen behind the colliery buildings, barely a quarter of it still visible, it seemed to almost blind their eyes which had, for the past four months, come up to darkness and gloom. Daisy could feel the tears of joy start beneath her eyelids and she put up a hand to hide them. Months and months of almost total darkness every night of the week. It must be nearly spring and time for setting potatoes, her country-bred instincts told her though she had no idea what month of the year it was, so would they not soon be off again, striking out into the farmland of north Lancashire in search of summer work again? Out of the deep dungeon of the mine where it was so hot the candle she carried in her mouth melted. Out of the pitchy warrens, the hours of being cold and wet, the sense of having the whole world press down on your head, to where the sun was shining and the fresh wind was blowing. She had mouldered and decayed for months in what she had begun to think of as her own grave, in the silent, unceasing darkness, in the clangour which hurt your brain when an explosion shook the very ground which held you.

Now surely the time had come for what she had dreamed of all winter? She held Cassie's hand tightly with both of hers, looking down into the child's grey face which was lit by the last of the sun's rays. Cassie smiled up at her, displaying her small teeth. In them was the decaying matter of the food she had eaten and around her mouth were sores, some of them nasty and weeping. Daisy clearly remembered her long hair as a pure silver from that day when they had bathed in Rainford Brook. It had been as soft as silk and just as shimmering then, now it was plastered about her small head in greasy, coal-encrusted, vermin-infested hanks.

She was shocked at Cassie's appearance. She had seen the child in daylight every Sunday but she had not really noticed her and now she looked at her with the sharp eye which a prospective employer might cast upon her. Cassie looked awful, like one of those sore-eyed, stunted children who fought and screamed in the gutters about the house in which they now lived. She was foul and verminous, puny as a skinned rabbit but really, could you expect anything else when the pair of them had lived on what was scarcely enough for one belly, let alone two? She supposed she herself looked, and stank, just as nasty though the smell which pervaded the world in which they lived had become so familiar she had not been aware of it.

She shrugged, the light going from her face as she turned towards the cobweb of backstreets in which the cellar lay. She might just as well give over thinking what day it was, or what month it was. Until the gangmaster said it was time to move on she was as much a prisoner in the colliery as any felon convicted and locked up in gaol.

She clenched her jaw and thrust it forward in what was to become a familiar gesture to those who knew her later. Her eyes were still narrowed against the light which shone on the hurrying figures ahead of her. She joined the throng who poured out of the pityard, dividing and parting as they passed into the narrow streets of the town. As she moved deeper into the honeycomb of the district where the labouring class lived she passed small, dirty shops, taverns from which even now bawdy songs and laughter erupted, and pawnbrokers doing brisk business as the week drew nearer to Saturday and payday. Would she ever know the joy of the fields again, the glory of the green meadows, the beauty of the trees and the song of the birds? Would she ever sleep with her head on a pillow of sweet clover and wake to the fresh, crisp air in which there was no smoke, no sulphurous fumes, no particles of grit and acid and coal dust? Would she ever feel the sun's heat on her back as she bent over the neat rows of potatoes and carrots in Farmer Chadwick's field? Would she ever be a field girl again?

She and Cassie were asleep, curled up in their filthy nest of bedding, as close as two kittens in a basket when the gangmaster entered the cellar that night. He had Agnes Barton on his arm. She was seven months gone with his child and her cumbersome body was not quite as much to his taste as once it had been, but that was easily remedied for there were two or three girls who were ripe for taking her place. The thought pleased him as his eyes studied his gang. He was good-humoured and smiling, a sure sign that all was well with the schemes he had planned and the arrangement he had come to with the farmers with whom he regularly did business. The couple of dozen women and their children had brought him in a splendid return during their winter's labour in the pit and he had arranged, for a small price but well worth it, next year's employment for them.

Now it was time for him to inform them of his plans for the next six or seven months, to get them cleaned up as best he could for he doubted that even the farmers in whose fields they worked would take kindly to these coal-veneered, stinking creatures who had been near no water for the best part of six months. Not that they were overzealous in the summer months but at least they had access to plenty of clean, pure water and could be forced to take a wash now and then when the farmer demanded it of them.

He stirred the nearest sleeping figure with his toe and when it failed to respond, gave it a sharp kick.

"Come on, yer lazy sluts. Get yerselves out of them beds and listen ter what I have ter tell yer. See, Fanny Holden, close yer bloody mouth and open yer eyes and try ter take that half-witted look off yer face. Jesus, it don't half stink in here. What have yer got in them beds with yer? A couple of pigs? Or is it half a dozen colliers because I'm not right sure they don't smell even worse."

The women puffed and sighed, rubbing their sleep-filled eyes and cursing softly beneath their breath. They had worked a twelve-hour shift that day. Most had gone to bed sodden with gin and it took a great deal of effort not only to sit up and show an interest in the old sod but to clear their heads sufficiently to understand what he was saying.

"Now listen, the lot of yer. We're ter be off on Sunday up to Foot of Hill Farm so termorrow's yer last day in the pit." They all became instantly alert, even the most stupefied. The promise that they were to get out of the mine in which they had worked all winter, into the open fields of the country, which, though they had grumbled about it often enough in the past, now seemed a magical fairyland after the hell of the pit, was received as though the gangmaster had told them they were off to the seaside taking the new and exciting railway train to get there.

"I thought that'd make yer more lively, sodden lot of old women that you are."

They laughed joyously, not at all offended by his words, their faces turning to one another in anticipation of the summer to come. They forgot the nights they had slept in the open with nothing above their heads to keep off the rain but a hawthorn hedge. They forgot the days in the fields when they could not straighten their aching backs after twelve hours picking stones, the miles they tramped until their feet were blistered and bloody, to get to those fields.

"All right, all right, now yer can get back ter yer beds but tomorrow night when yer come off shift I've arranged fer a couple of tubs of hot water and a bar of soap ter be put int stable at the back of the King's Head. Yer've ter take a bath, the whole bloody lot of yer and that means you an' all, Gertie Wilson. I've got yer some new duds ter put on. Now don't get so bloody excited, fer God's sake," as the women clutched one another in delight. "There's nowt much," which was true for he had bought a job lot from the master of the workhouse where folk died by the shoal and the sale of their few poor possessions brought him in a small but steady income. "Sort 'em out between yer . . ." knowing the strongest would be best dressed ". . . and be ready ter leave before light on Sunday morning."

Daisy hugged Cassie to her, her thin face glowing in the faint light from the candle the gangmaster had lit when he came in.

"Did yer hear that, Cass? Did yer hear that? We're ter be off on Sunday. D'yer know what I'm saying?"

She peered down into the blank eyes of the small girl and her heart throbbed with love and pity and something else which she could only describe as fear. All through the dark days in the depths of the pit Cassie had dutifully done her work as a 'trapper', opening and closing the ventilation doors. It was work well within the scope of a child of her age but the very nature of it and the conditions in which she did it were enough to disorientate the most stable and mature mind. Hour after hour, alone but for the rats and the 'hurriers' who scampered past but who had no time to speak to her, Cassie had steadfastly done what Daisy had told her, but each week as the winter drew on she appeared to have retreated further and further into a state of fixed inertia, her eyes as blank and frosted as the icy pools of stagnant water which lay about the courtyard each wintry morning. The lovely warm violet in them seemed to have drained away, leaving a colourless apathy, and the small, delicately-boned face was quite without expression.

Daisy drew the child closer to her own childish breast, holding her fiercely. Cassie would be all right when she got out into the sun-filled, wind-blown space of the fields again, she told herself. When they could run and stretch their bodies which had been cramped and bent like those of two little old women for so long. When their arms and legs could be used to their full capacity instead of restricted to the confines the pits had forced on them. It was over. The hours and days and weeks in the damp, foul-smelling black-ness which they had endured together was over and the day after tomorrow they would leave it for ever.

She was not to know that it would be another three years before it would finally be over.

7

Lord Thornley of Thornley Green sat at the head of his enormous oval breakfast table which was placed in the exact centre of his breakfast room. The early-morning sun was reflected from its superbly polished surface and glinted on silver cruets, toast racks, muffineers and tea urns. It picked out the braid on the livery of the vigilant footmen who hovered unobtrusively by the oak serving table at the side of the room and seemed to offer a warm and impatient challenge to those who still breakfasted, as though telling them to get a move on or the day would be wasted.

Lord Thornley's butler, Petch, whose duty it was to ensure that his master and his master's guests who were to join the hunt that day, set forth with as much inside them as would feed the entire family of one of his lordship's farm labourers for a whole week, if not a fortnight, was assiduous in his supervision of the footmen and parlourmaids who were there to serve the thirty or forty guests expected to ride to hounds that day. It was nine thirty and the hunt breakfast, a tradition which dated back to the days of the present baron's great-great-grandfather and probably beyond, consisted of, among other things, large joints of sirloin and corned beef, cold roast pheasant and game pie, roast chicken and turkey and a good quantity of cheese. There was an uncut ham, pyramids of muffins, toast and kidneys kept warm beneath the lid of a silver dish on the sideboard.

By way of liquid refreshment, sherry, brandy, cherry brandy and liqueurs were provided and if the occasion warranted it, champagne. It was often a mystery to his lordship, who was a man moderate in all things, how his guests managed to remain in their saddles if one considered the amount of intoxicating beverage most of them consumed before setting forth but it was also an important part of the hunt ritual and his lordship was a stickler for tradition.

Whilst the gentlemen and several of the ladies, those who had the inclination and energy for fox-hunting, discussed and carefully planned their manoeuvres on the field, they broke their fast with an enthusiasm which bordered, in his lordship's opinion, on the wolfish. One would think they had not eaten a square meal for a week the way the gentlemen were shovelling food into their mouths and when one remembered the magnificent and substantial dinner his chef had served only twelve hours since, which had included a boar's head garnished with aspic jelly, fowl, ham, a decorated tongue, pheasant, veal, capon and lobster, followed by a mountain of tipsy cake, trifle and ice-creams of all flavours, one wondered at the state of their digestion.

"I hear you have purchased a pair of matched foxhounds,

Thornley," one of the breakfast guests remarked. "I thought I heard you say you were well satisfied with those you already have. What does your kennelman have to say about it, eh? I know mine would tell me in no uncertain terms if I introduced new blood into the pack, into his pack, as he considers it, without asking him first. It's the very devil when one cannot please oneself in one's own kennel."

The speaker, a well-set-up, florid-faced gentleman who looked as though he had spent half of his life on the hunting field, and the other with a gun across his arm in a walking line of men shooting birds on the wing, brought Lord Thornley from his lounging, contemplative position in the balloon-backed rosewood breakfast chair to the alert and courteous attitude one showed towards a guest in one's home, and he smiled.

"I know the feeling well, Faulkner. My man is a martinet in the care of *his* hounds but I'm afraid your informant was mistaken. I am merely 'walking' two hound puppies for Dick Tennant. Just for a year until they become used to people and can be trusted to behave properly at the meet."

"I see, and where is Tennant this morning?" Sir Christopher Faulkner looked about him cheerfully, at the same time indicating to the respectful footman at his elbow that he would take another muffin, or perhaps two. "He distinctly told me last night, or should I say the early hours of this morning, that he fully intended to be up at dawn to try out his new hunter over a jump or two." He grinned mischievously, like an errant schoolboy, either not seeing, or choosing to ignore, his host's frowning displeasure. It was well-known in the pedigreed class to which he and Lord Thornley both belonged that despite the somewhat lax outlook on the sexual indulgences which prevailed in their society, particularly during weekends such as these, his lordship did not approve of the flirtations, and often more, which took place under his own roof. Dick Tennant, Sir Richard Anthony Tennant, Baronet, of Tennants Hall near Lymm in Cheshire, had been seen to pay a great deal of attention to the Honourable Mrs Stephen Rathmell, an extremely attractive lady whose elderly husband had, for reasons of ill-health, been unable to endure the hunt and had remained at his family seat, near Orrell, to nurse his frail bones. Sir Christopher, retiring somewhat late himself to the room he shared with his own wife, had witnessed, unseen, the stealthy approach of Sir Richard who should, at his age, have known better, to Mrs Rathmell's bedroom door; had seen it open quickly and his lordship slip inside and could you now wonder that he was unable to summon the strength to mount another spirited mare this morning?

Sir Christopher winked at young Miles Thornley who smothered a grin, and said no more, though everyone there from Lord Thornley down to the youngest parlourmaid knew exactly what had been implied.

The guests continued to plough through the hearty breakfast which was expected to see them through the excitement of the day. They would set off, not too early for the fox, being a night feeder, would be somewhat sluggish for an hour or two after dawn, when they had partaken of another hunt tradition, the stirrup cup. There would be a 'lawn' meet on the gravel sweep which led up to the great front door of Thornley Green and dressed as was customary in their vivid scarlet or black coats the riders would receive a short but potent drink, usually punch, from the stirrup cup.

There was silence for several moments and Lord Thornley relaxed somewhat, taking pleasure from the lovely surroundings of his home which never failed to comfort and soothe him whenever he was out of sorts which nowadays, until his son returned to Cambridge, was often. The breakfast room was the least formal of all the public rooms in the great house. It was bright, catching the morning sun which streamed in golden wellbeing through the wide window at his lordship's back. It was placed next to the great dining hall which, if necessary, could easily seat one hundred guests but as this was thought to be too grand for the eating of a simple meal such as breakfast, the smaller room had been designed for just that purpose. It was a quiet room made for the slow and silent process of waking up or, as now, a friendly meeting-place for the hunt breakfast. It faced exactly east-north-east, a perfect direction for the rising sun to fall across the breakfast table which was of glowing rosewood. The curtains were of cream linen, hand-embroidered and delicate so as not to shut out the light or the breathtaking view down to the lake. The carpet was Persian and rich, patterned in shades of cream and apple green. There was little heavy furniture beside the table, the breakfast chairs and the serving sideboard on which hot dishes were kept warm above spirit heaters. The walls were papered in apple-green silk and the woodwork painted white. There was a picture or two above the fireplace in which a fire burned for Lord Thornley, whatever the temperature outside, liked to see a cheerful blaze at breakfast.

In the centre of the table, on the mantelshelf of the fireplace, on the serving sideboard and, or so it appeared, everywhere there was a foot or two of space, were bowls and vases of flowers for Lady Mary Thornley, his lordship's wife, loved them, and her garden, beyond anything else in her life. Next to her son, who was the sum and substance of her entire existence. There were flowers of every season and colour, grown in the hothouses at the back of Thornley Green, providing a constant supply of any bloom her ladyship desired, irrespective of the time of year.

His lordship frowned again as his eye fell on his only son. He was leaning boldly against the black-coated shoulder of the luscious Mrs Sarah Bentham, a widow of some thirty-five years, the sister of Dick Tennant and apparently as free with her favours as her brother, her host thought sourly. She was a handsome woman whose husband, an army captain, had served and died in some crack Lancashire regiment, leaving her not only heart-whole and free to do whatever she pleased, but with more than enough money to ensure she could stay that way. Her brother, not for the sake of propriety since what did he know of that, nor even out of a sense of family duty but simply to get her settled again and off his hands, had brought her to Thornley Green. He was a bachelor and therefore could escort her to numerous balls, supper dances, parties, picnics and weekends such as this one in the hope that she might find a second husband who would suit her exacting standards but so far his efforts had been in vain. The 'splendid Sarah' as she was called somewhat coarsely among the many young gentlemen who sought her company was not yet old enough, in her opinion, nor passé enough, to give up this enchanting freedom. Leaving her two sons in the care of their tutor she did exactly as she pleased and at the moment Lord Thornley was exasperated to see that what pleased her was the enticement of his young son.

His lordship would have been alarmed had he known the true state of their relationship. That his son was not in the least dazzled – he had gone beyond that stage – and had he been privy to the conversation which was taking place between the Honourable Miles Thornley and Mrs Sarah Bentham, who was exactly twice his son's age, he would have been not only alarmed but extremely worried.

"Don't tease me, Miles. You know how easily I am ... wounded."

"My darling Sarah, you have never been wounded in your life and who would be so cold-hearted as to do so? Not I, for you are quite the most delectable creature I have ever had the good fortune to ... admire. Now would I cause a moment's suffering to a lady who has given me such ... joy?"

The words were spoken with a sardonic twist of Miles Thornley's sensual mouth and a lifting of his dark eyebrows.

Sarah Bentham's hand on his knee was as light as the touch of a butterfly and as it made its practised way along his inner thigh he smiled but continued to eat the strip of almost raw beef which was on his plate.

"Yes, you would, you rascal. You swore you would come to my room last night and though I was awake for hours you did not come." She tried to pout prettily as though it was of no particular concern to her but her mouth, which was really past such girlish *moues*, was stiff and the smile became a grimace. Her hand reached its destination beneath the napkin which rested on the young lordling's lap but with a worldly composure unusual in one so young he waited until he had the opportunity then lifted it to the table, resting it gently beside her plate.

"Sarah." His mouth continued to smile but the gleaming azure blue of his eyes was cool. "No matter how delightful it is you really must not do this in full view of my family and guests. I'm sorry about last night, really I am since there is nothing sweeter than your ... embrace and I was heartbroken to forego it but I swear my father, who is, as you know, something of a despot, never took his eyes from me the whole evening and at eleven thirty indicated that it was time, in view of my youth, that I left the diversions of the gaming table and the claret to the more mature gentlemen. Pity, for I was having a good run at cards too, but whatever you do don't let Papa know." The oblique reference to the difference in their ages, aged Mrs Bentham even further.

"You could have come later ..." Her voice was almost desperate and she made a great effort to control it.

"Aah ... no." He smiled, completely unabashed, and at the far end of the table his father's frown deepened. "I meant to, I swear it, but my valet was there and when he finally left I'm afraid I just ... fell asleep." His heavy-lidded gaze was unreadable, though his lips curved in a smile over teeth so white they were a dramatic slash against his sun-browned face. He was quite unbelievably handsome. Though he was only eighteen years of age he had the poise and charm of a man much older. His expression was alert and yet at the same time lazy with a look in his eyes which said that whatever Miles Thornley wanted, he would have. So far in his young and exceptionally enjoyable life this certainty had not let him down. He was the only son, the only child of one of the wealthiest peers of the realm, heir to Thornley Green and its eight hundred acres of surrounding parkland and the twenty thousand acres of farmland in which the house and park were set. Thornley Green, deriving its name from the village and green which in medieval times had sprung up there, had been enlarged from a fourteenth-century stone tower into the late Tudor hall it now was. Constructed from the natural products of the district it was built of red sandstone, a beautifully proportioned house with the typical circular north-country chimneys. Peaceful and dignified in its setting of green parkland and tall trees, its small mullioned windows hid deep recesses which had provided pleasant seats for almost four centuries of Thornleys to dream in. Six wide steps led up to a screened entrance door, moulded and panelled in a linen pattern, huge and heavy and built to keep out all intruders. Above the door was the Thornley coat of arms.

But it was the gardens and surrounding park in which the old house seemed to rest so serenely that gave it, lovely as it was in its own right, the framework which enhanced its perfection. There was a forecourt approached by a drive for carriages which curved for almost three miles from the gatehouse and archway leading into the park. The grounds consisted of wide lawns, woods, two fountains, two lakes before the house and one behind fed by a stream. There was a walled garden of almost ten acres in which grew every vegetable and fruit known to 'Old' Janner, the head gardener, hothouses, greenhouses, and enfolding the whole of it like some plump, brilliantly hued cushion were Lady Mary's flower gardens. There were broad paved sunny terraces, tier upon tier of them around the house, and shady colonnades linked by steps which had been ancient when Miles Thornley's great-great-grandfather had been a boy. The rich perfume of an ancestral orange tree which was said to have been in the family for three hundred years, the bright blossom of Virginia creeper up the side walls of the house, a winter garden – a new endeavour of Lady Mary's – bursting with camellias, magnolias and singing birds in gilt cages, and the formal geometry of well-clipped box hedges.

To the side of the house and some distance away were the stables and coach house, as pleasing to the eye in their symmetry as the house. Shading them were noble yew trees, oak, chestnut and sycamore, part of the great forest through which, it was rumoured, kings of England had once hunted. And all about the park in which deer browsed, were farms, each one consisting of two or three hundred acres which Lord Thornley leased on a yearly basis to farmers, some to the third or fourth generation of the same family, those who were hard-working and punctual with their rent. Fields, half of which were under plough, neatly furrowed and ready for planting, awaiting only the gangs of women the farmers employed to pick the stones, the rest grazing land where well-nourished cattle stood knee-deep in lush grass and clover.

And enlaced with the farms, the well-tended fields and meandering lanes lined with bramble hedges was the blazing autumn glory of Lord Thornley's woods which had stood long before the house was built. His lordship was not, or so he considered, a sentimentalist and he would have scorned the word 'love' to describe the emotion he felt for his vast estate but the passionate interest, the possessiveness, the acute pleasure he knew whenever he rode its splendid acres must surely come near to justifying the term.

He stood up briskly, signifying that it was time to get on with the business of the day. The stirrup cup, which he as Master of Foxhounds would be the first to taste, was already at the entrance porch. After his guests were mounted and he had taken the first sip, the cup would then be passed to the huntsman, the whipper-in, followed in order of nobility by each of his guests. Only the leading hunt officers and followers wore the distinguished scarlet coat with the crested buttons and black velvet hat. The rest of the field must make do with sombre black or grey coats, top hats, dark waistcoats, white stock, white breeches and double-fold boots.

Fifteen minutes later, eager to be away on this crisp autumn morning, the Master commanded the first draw and the hunting party rode out to the covert, unleashing the twenty couples of matched foxhounds which were controlled only by the huntsman's voice. The clear ringing tones of the hunting horn sounded to signal the sight of the fox and as the riders spread out, streaming across Abel Freeman's freshly ploughed field, Lord Thornley noticed that Mrs Bentham, one of the few ladies fearless enough to join the sport which could be vigorous and often fraught with danger, rode knee to knee with his son.

They had been picking stones that day, she and Cassie, and as the sun drifted slowly down the sky towards Thornley

Green wood, Daisy looked back at the acres and acres of furrows she and the rest of the women had picked clean during the last week. On one side of each furrow the light shone in a deep violet hue almost the colour of Cassie's eyes and on the other, where the shadow lay, it had turned to dark chocolate.

She had heard the huntsman's horn earlier in the day and had turned eagerly in the direction of the sound but though she had searched with narrowed eyes the long stream of riders who trampled Farmer Freeman's field, she had not seen him. She had performed the same action every hour or so during the day, as she had done ever since that first spring three years ago when they had come back from the mine. It had become a habit, one bred in her by her yearning to see the tall and graceful horseman who had lived in her dreams ever since that magical day when she had been of service to him. Every rider who went past the fields in which she was working was subjected to the same careful scrutiny, no longer than a second or so for there was no one like the unique, unrepeatable son of Lord Thornley, not in the whole of Lancashire, and it did not take her long to recognise that none were him. Not once in three summers had she seen him and her disappointment had been sharp. What he would do should they meet she had not even thought about. It was enough to fall into a daydream, dwelling on the shape and colour of his eyes, the smooth texture of his tanned cheek which she remembered clearly and the height of his splendid frame, for he would be a man now.

She turned her dreaming gaze back across Farmer Freeman's broad acres. It really was quite lovely and so peaceful, she thought, as she straightened her long, supple back, arching it to ease out the bones of her spine which had been bent double for twelve long hours. She shaded her eyes against the lowering sun but its rays crept beneath her hand and their deep golden brown melted to the colour of clear honey. The same stream of light ignited her tawny hair to a glowing flame so that it resembled nothing less than the pelt of the fox which was at this moment being ripped apart by Lord Thornley's hounds. It was thick and curling, untamed by brush or comb. She had washed it only the night before in the stream which murmured through the spinney at the back of the barn where they slept whilst they worked for Farmer Freeman. She and Cassie had slipped away as dusk fell, holding hands as they crept stealthily beneath the hedge of hawthorn bordering the field and into the little stand of trees. Without speaking they had stood for a moment on the far side, sharing, as they did so many things, the last beauty of the breathless evening. The sky was a vast bowl of the most delicate blue as the sun went down, shading to the palest green, to lemon and peach, to cinnamon and finally a smoky grey where it touched the treetops. They had sighed in unison, turning to smile at one another before hurrying on, for they wanted none of the other children to share this moment of pleasure. They bathed whenever they could, but furtively so as not to draw attention to themselves, rubbing each other's hair and scalp with a sweet-smelling flower which grew at the edge of the water. Cassie's hair had returned to a pale silvery fairness and her own to the rich colour of a copper-beech leaf, she thought, never having seen a fox, and so she had hastily covered both their heads with the old caps they had worn in the mine before dressing again in the torn and filthy clothing they always wore. No use in attracting the attention of the others or of *him*. He appeared to have forgotten Daisy's existence and certainly the night when he had 'marked' her with his own bestiality had long since slipped from his mind, if not from hers, and she meant to keep it that way.

She was thirteen now and still painfully thin, which was perhaps why he did not notice her, she reckoned. She had no breasts to speak of, for which lack she breathed a thankful sigh of relief. She was tall, with an unconscious grace, a way of moving, of holding her back and heavily weighted head which was quite captivating but she kept herself well covered, especially her hair, bending her head and shoulders when *he* was about and adopting an awkward shuffle which revealed nothing of her growing girlhood.

But in a month or two, if she could find no alternative work, if she could find no way to escape the life she and

Cassie shared, they would be all back to St Helens or Wigan to the coal-mines there. Three winters she had spent now in the damp black of the mines, working at the coal-face, harnessed like one of the pit ponies which worked on the surface, a candle between her teeth, chains between her legs, fighting for space and air with the rats and swearing desperately that somehow, this year, she would get herself and Cassie away from the horror of it. Three summers in the open fields, three bad summers when it had been cold and wet for weeks on end. Where some of the women, weakened by age, child-bearing, hard work and poor food, sickened and died of fevers, of aching of the limbs and dreadful attacks which took their breath and put fire in their lungs.

For the last two weeks the sun had shone and everyone's spirit had lightened, the prospect of the winter ahead not weighing too heavily on their gin-soaked minds. That was the gangmaster's responsibility, finding work for them, and shelter. The years with him had conditioned them to accept it as natural and, should he have abandoned them, it is doubtful many of them would have managed to make their own way.

But Daisy knew that Cassie would not survive this life much longer. Each spring when they emerged from the blackness into the light and gentle warmth of the coming season the little girl was like some crumpled snowdrop on which a cruel foot had stamped again and again. Pale and strange, eyes shielded by her long fair lashes, head bent, shoulders bowed, silent and blank-faced, not until they crept from the squalor and stench of the town and into the clean smells of the farmlands did she begin to lift her head. Then, slowly, day by day, week by week, the emptiness, the freshness, the goodness of the land worked its miracle and she began to stretch and recover, opening up the petals of her mind, smiling in pleasure, working willingly at whatever she was put to, not speaking, never speaking, but there somehow, not only in body but in her damaged mind.

Now it was October again and each morning this week, though the days were warm and soft with that strange Indian summer which sometimes lays its goodness over the cooling earth, there had been a ground frost.

Daisy sighed, then taking Cassie by the hand, followed the line of weary women and children around the edge of the field towards the gate which led out of it. It took them almost half an hour to trudge across several more pastures, along a sun-dappled lane and round the back of the farmhouse where Farmer Freeman's wife was just fetching in her washing. It was not a big farm and apart from one man and a girl in the kitchen and dairy there were no other farmhands. Abel Freeman employed casual labour as and when he needed it, paying the gangmasters who roamed about Lancashire the poorest of wages for the hire of his gang. His wife fed them, hardly better than the slops she gave her pigs, and they slept for the week or two they were required – harvest or other seasonal work – in the tumbledown building on the far side of the hayfield.

The gangmaster, strangely, shared their rancid meal with them that night, stretching out his hand wordlessly as Gertie Wilson heaped his plate with the scrag end of mutton, the lumpy 'back-end' potatoes, only half cooked, and the gravy in which a carrot or two floated. Mrs Freeman had described it, snickering, as 'mutton stew' when she handed the bucket in which it was contained to Gertie at the kitchen door, patently thinking it was better than they deserved, filthy creatures.

They were all dozing, some snoring, when Daisy and Cassie slipped quietly through the sagging doorway, making for the hawthorn hedge and the spinney beyond and when the gangmaster stood up and followed them, his eyes gleaming cruelly between his lashless lids, the sliver of moon which hung palely in the silver-blue sky was not bright enough to reveal even his shadow.

He had stripped her down to her ragged underdrawers when the horse knocked him off his feet and the blow to his head from its nervously flailing hoof killed him instantly.

"What the devil's going on here?" The voice, though loud and startled, was cultured, so cultured Daisy did not even understand what it had said, had she been in a fit state of mind to wonder. She stood, like some sacrificial lamb caught in the flame of the lamp, her body white as alabaster but for the tiny pink buds of her nipples. Her hair hung about her, well below her waist, where his hands had dragged at it to restrain her for she had fought him like a wildcat, and her eyes were black with shock and terror. Clinging to her like a burr to a rabbit, as Sir Christopher was to describe it later to his wife, was quite the most delicately lovely child he had seen in his life.

"Sweet Jesus, who the devil are these two children and where are they from?"

"I don't know, Sir Christopher, but if you would care to ride on with Thompkins I'll deal with it."

"Don't talk rot, man. I can't just turn my back on ... Oh damnation, help me down from this confounded animal. Why in hell did my hunter have to fall today of all days? All these years he's served me and just when I thought him too sensible he has to jib at a bloody scrap of paper. And so far from Thornley Green. I feel like some pewling woman having to be brought back on this old hack."

"Indeed, Sir Christopher, but as I explained the mare is old and quiet and there was no alternative other than ..."

"Yes, yes, I know all that, Abbotsley. You have explained it all to me until I am fatigued by it so I would be obliged if you would not utter another word on the subject."

"Very good, Sir Christopher."

"I suppose I should have taken up his lordship's offer of the carriage but my leg seemed capable of allowing me to ride home and now look what we have run into. Dammit, don't just sit there gawping, Abbotsley, help me down and lets see what's amiss here."

"Your leg, sir ..."

"Damn my leg, man. I'm sure I can stand on it for a minute or two, or are you my physician as well as my minder? Now then, Thompkins, go and have a look at that f ow on the ground and for God's sake, cover up that ... th t child."

The three men had dismounted, Sir Christopher a mite lopsided as he favoured his injured leg. He had come off five miles from Thornley Green when his hunter had thrown him and though the animal was unhurt Sir Christopher had fallen awkwardly, turning his foot underneath his heavy body. The ankle had swollen alarmingly inside his boot, hot and aching, and though he had been assured by his host's groom who was well used to such tumbles on the hunting field, that it was not broken, he had been unable to remount his own tall and suddenly skittish old hunter. Refusing the offer of his lordship's carriage, which, he had been told, would take no more than a couple of hours to fetch on the winding lanes from the house to where Sir Christopher had fallen, he had been hoisted on to the back of the patient and extremely slow old mare kept for just such emergencies.

"Now then, child, got a bit rough with you, did he? Tried to take what you weren't prepared to give. Well, you should know better than to hang about in a lonely place like this, my girl, and with a child as young as that as well. You ask for trouble, really you do." Sir Christopher's voice was rough but kindly. He was not unused to the almost animal-like coupling of the lower orders. Girls of thirteen and fourteen, undefended by family or any male protector, were fair game to any man who fancied them and there was nothing much to be done about it but he didn't like to see a slip of a girl such as this being taken, obviously against her will. Though Thompkins had flung his jacket about her she still stood like a trapped rabbit, not moving, nor even blinking those great dark eyes of hers.

"The man's dead, Sir Christopher." Thompkins' voice came from the darkness beyond the lamplight and Sir Christopher distinctly heard a hiss from between the clenched teeth of the girl and she lifted her head then in an uncommonly imperious manner. But he had things to think of other than her sudden and strange awakening from the trance she had appeared to be in. He turned sharply in the direction of Thompkins' voice, wincing visibly as he did so.

"Dead? Good God, are you sure?"

"Yes, sir. His head's kicked in."

"Well I never."

"Yes, sir."

"Now then..." Sir Christopher removed his black top hat and scratched his head. He was clearly dismayed, not at all sure what should be done next and not at all sure he felt like doing it. Now that he was standing, or rather hobbling, on his own two feet the pain of his injury was almost too much to bear. If he did not get this boot off soon he doubted he ever would. As it was, he was sure it would have to be cut off. A damn fine pair of boots ruined and now this pother which he could well do without. He'd a good mind to get back on the patient mare and amble off to Thornley Green, which was not far away, and if he sent Thompkins to fetch help he could be in his bed with a brandy in his hand, his boot off and his wife's ministrations to soothe him, within the hour.

"I'll see to these two, Sir Christopher. There's a gang of women working for one of his lordship's tenant farmers nearby. They'll most likely belong there. I'll make sure they get back."

"And what of the man?" After all, one couldn't leave a dead man just lying about in the wood for anyone to trip over. He noticed that the taller girl had her arm protectively about the small one, a fierce gesture which was strange for after all she was the one who was being molested.

"I'll send for the special constable, sir, but don't you think you had better get back to the house?" Abbotsley, head groom to Lord Thornley for the past five years and before that stable lad and groom since he was ten years old, was conscious that his lordship would not care to have an important guest troubled with such a slight matter as this. "I'll see it's put in the hands of the authorities, Sir Christopher."

Sir Christopher turned awkwardly away from the two girls, relieved to have the whole damned thing taken off his hands.

"Good man, now get me on this bloody horse."

He was about to ride off when the gleam of the lamp picked out the eyes of the older child. They were staring at him in the most curious way just as though they were trying to say something to him and for a moment he was his old self, the one who could not bear to see a hurt child or a puppy kicked, at least not in his presence, and it stopped him momentarily.

"Let me know the outcome of this, Abbotsley," Daisy heard him say as he disappeared into the darkness of the trees.

8

"I can't get rid of them, Mr Greenhalgh. It's been a week now and they're still camped out in my barn. Twenty-three of them, counting the little 'uns, and I can't feed them any more. You said I was to see to them for a couple of days while the dead chap was sorted out, like, and that his lordship would pay me for what they ate but that was a week ago and they're still here."

"Can't you find them some work, Freeman?"

"No, sir, I can't. There's nothing for them to do now the harvest's in and the stone-picking's done. They were to go on somewhere, the gangmaster told me, but they don't know where it was. They went where he told them and no argument and he wasn't the sort to discuss what he were up to with a field woman."

Robert Greenhalgh grimaced distastefully as Abel Freeman spoke. He did not agree with the 'gang' system of farm labouring and he had spoken up about it to Lord Thornley whose bailiff he was. It was as bad as the negro slave labour in the southern states of America, in his opinion, and should be done away with and he had said so but his employer had merely shrugged and said what his tenant farmers did, providing it did no harm to *his* land, was their own affair. Providing they paid their rents, how they made the money to do so did not concern him. The gangs were not to come on to his parkland, naturally, and any found trespassing would be severely dealt with but apart from that he didn't care how they employed themselves.

"And what of the women who are at Abel Freeman's farm, my lord? With the gangmaster dead they seem unable to decide what they should do next," Greenhalgh had said several days ago to his employer.

"They are nothing to do with me, Greenhalgh. They must be moved on. Tell Freeman that."

"Very good, my lord," and Greenhalgh would have left it at that, stepping back politely to allow his employer to leave the office from which he himself ran the great estate of Thornley Green but at that moment Sir Christopher Faulkner limped across threshold.

"Aah, Thornley, I've been looking for you, old chap. You said at breakfast that it would be convenient to ride over and look at the new stallion you were considering buying for young Miles. I believe my ankle would stand the strain of a short jaunt and as I am to be off tomorrow . . ."

"Of course, Faulkner. I shall be but a minute. I was just having a word with Greenhalgh about those damned women left at Freeman's farm."

"Which damned women are those?" Sir Christopher asked courteously, lowering himself gently into a chair.

"The ones who belonged to that blighter who was killed."

"Belonged?"

"Well, I use the term loosely but they were his 'gang' so to speak. He hired out their labour to the farmers."

"Yes, I have heard of the system. But what is the problem?"

"It seems they are all at sixes and sevens and cannot, or will not, be moved on. I shall have to get some of my men to eject them, I suppose. In the meanwhile, Greenhalgh . . ." he turned to his bailiff ". . . tell Freeman to feed them for a couple of days longer and I shall see he is not out of pocket. Attend to it at once, will you? They are to be off my land by the end of the week."

"Hold on a minute, Thornley, old fellow." His lordship turned agreeably to his guest and Greenhalgh turned too, well aware that his employer would not take kindly to having what was, after all, his own business interfered with by another, even a friend of such long standing as Sir Christopher Faulkner.

Lord Thornley smiled and waited for his guest to continue.

"I appreciate that there is nothing to be done for those women. Indeed, having seen some of them pass through my own village I can understand your eagerness to be shut of them. Nasty foul-mouthed creatures, most of them, drunk half the time and lying in the gutter with any man who has a fancy for them."

His lordship lifted his fine head and his lip curled as though he had just tasted something sour. Sir Christopher saw it and smiled. He himself was not as finicky about such things as Hugh Thornley and was prepared to call a spade a spade but he felt somewhat at fault for what had occurred the other night though it had not been the plodding animal he rode which had killed the man. If his own hunter had not shied at that scrap of paper there would have been no accident and he and the Thornley grooms would not have been riding through the spinney when they were. But having thought of this and mentioned it to his wife she had pointed out that, far from causing the death of the man, which was not strictly true, he had saved the little maid, perhaps even two of them, from a dreadful experience. She was right, of course, and perhaps the gods, fate, chance or whatever you cared to call it had put him there for a purpose. A trifle superstitious was Sir Christopher and it seemed that destiny had taken a hand that night and who was he to meddle with it? Abbotsley had not forgotten his injunction to let him know what had become of the two young girls and that was one of his reasons for speaking of it to Thornley.

"It's those two children I'm thinking of, old chap."

"Children? Which children? There must be a dozen or so."

"Aye, so Greenhalgh told me but there's nothing to be done with the rest. No, I was thinking of the two girls. The ones the man was . . . well, not to put too fine a point on it

... interfering with. The smallest can have been no more than seven or eight, I'd say ..." And a picture of the pansy-eyed, silver-haired comeliness of Cassie Brindle which had been revealed in the flickering light from the torch slipped sentimentally into Sir Christopher's mind.

"What are you trying to say, Faulkner? You are surely not proposing that I take these ... these draggle-tails into my home? Put them amongst my own servants. Decent people who would not take kindly to having girls who are no better than vagrants in their midst?"

"Good God, of course not." Sir Christopher laughed and Lord Thornley relaxed. The expression of outrage left his face but the shadow of it remained in his eyes as he waited for his guest to continue. "I was thinking of one of those schools."

"Schools?" His lordship's voice was frosty. In his opinion God had put each man on this earth in his allotted place, where he should remain without question until the end of his days. A god-fearing man, he was, who did not care to alter the course of a man's life by lifting him to a place higher than he was intended to be, and what Sir Christopher seemed to be saying smacked of heresy to him.

"Yes, schools, Thornley. Several of the colliery owners have started them for the girls brought out of the mines by Ashley's Bill of 1842. You know of it, naturally."

"I do," Lord Thornley said stiffly.

"Boys can go into the pit when they reach ten years of age but girls cannot, so Lord and Lady Francis Egerton from over Worsley way ... he owns the Bridgewater Collieries ... have opened what he calls a servants' school to train former pit girls for domestic service. One or two others have followed suit and ... well ... feeling somewhat responsible for taking away the man who – though I do not approve of it – found these two employment, I thought it might be the answer. I'm sure my wife could arrange a place for them. There's one been opened in Denton Green. Jack Pennington, you remember him, he was at Harrow with us, has turned philanthropist. He calls it a School of Industry. He has about sixty poor girls, my wife tells me, and as she is friendly with his wife she is pretty sure room could be found for them there."

"Why in God's name are you doing this, Faulkner? The man was a blackguard and should not have been ... doing what he was, but if he ... well, have you considered that it probably would not have been the first time? The girl was more than likely quite accustomed to accommodating him."

"I doubt it, Thornley. I very much doubt it. From the look on the child's face when we came on them she was being forced."

"That may be so but has it occurred to you that if she was ... that he had ... trifled with her before, she could at this moment be carrying his child?"

Sir Christopher stiffened at the word 'trifled' but he did not give up.

"She was no more than a child herself, Thornley, and as for the other one, if he was one of those perverts ... well ... it hardly bears thinking about."

"But we must think about it." Lord Thornley's voice softened. He was fond of Chris Faulkner. They had been friends for many years, since schooldays in fact, and he had always known him to have a somewhat soft heart. Kind to kittens and all manner of young animals and it was probably this which was influencing him now but one must be practical about these things. The girl might be diseased, let alone pregnant, and if so she would hardly be welcome in a school for girls even if they were of her own class. And would she even want to go? She would more than likely beg to stay with her own kind.

He said so.

"Very well, Thornley." Sir Christopher stood up. "Send your man to fetch her and we'll find out. If she says no, let her stay with the other women and to the devil with her."

So Robert Greenhalgh had been sent, his lordship making it plain he thought the whole affair to be folly and that he had agreed merely to please an old friend, to ask Daisy Brindle if she would like to go to school.

"Anyway I'm not here to argue with you, Freeman," he said now, "nor to reimburse you further. The women are

112

to be put off this land at once and if there is trouble send up to the house for some men. Tell the women they will be forcibly ejected. That will move them."

"But what are they to do, Mr Greenhalgh?"

"Dear God, man, do you care?"

"No, but I don't want them creeping back here."

"Tell them you'll send for his lordship's men if they do and that they will be arrested for trespass. Now that is an end to it, but for one thing more. Fetch the two girls who were involved."

"Involved, sir?"

"Those who were in the wood when the man was killed."

"Nay, I don't know which is which, Mr Greenhalgh. They're all as black as the fire grate."

"Well, bring them all." Robert Greenhalgh was exasperated almost beyond reason and for two pins he would have told Freeman not to bother himself and then informed Lord Thornley that the two children had already left but a strict sense of morality, of what was fair and right, held him back. It was his duty to serve his employer to the best of his ability. He had been told to attend to this matter and so he must see it through to the end.

They stood in a cringing line before him and without being told he picked her out. She was thin and her clothes drifted about her in frail shreds, held together with bits and pieces of thread, all of different fabrics and faded colours. Her face and neck were as dirty as the rest of the band but her white flesh gleamed through the rents and tears of her clothing. She had no shoes to her filthy feet and they squelched with apparent unconcern in the cowdung which was inches deep in Abel Freeman's farmyard. About her head was a binding of some sort so that not a wisp of her hair showed but it only served to emphasise the fine bone-structure of her face. High cheekbones and a pointed chin lifted defiantly and a full creamy-pink mouth. Her eyes were narrowed as though speculating on his motive in gathering herself and her companions about him and in their golden depths there was some expression he could not read. Perhaps his lordship was right after all. She could not have been more than twelve or thirteen but she certainly did not look as though the experience in the wood a week ago in which, so he had heard, she had been found naked with the man who was killed, had frightened her in any way. Could one presume from that, as his lordship seemed to, that she was accustomed to such treatment? It certainly appeared so. A small girl held her hand, just as dirty, just as ragged but with exquisite violet eyes.

He studied them both and the taller girl stared back though the small one lowered her fine silky lashes shyly. He felt his mouth soften as she did so and he wanted to smile.

"Step over here, girl," he said sternly, "and bring the little one with you."

She did as she was told, swinging her tattered skirt and lifting her bound head as though she was conferring some favour on him. My God, she'd better curb that challenging way she had or she'd be forever in trouble where she was going, he thought. She drew closer and it was then he saw the wary expression which lurked in her eyes and he knew that deep within her, though she did her best to hide it, she was hurt and afraid and he could only find it in him to admire the strange strength in her that was determined not to let him see it. The knowledge made him gentle.

"By what name are you known, lass?"

"Daisy Brindle."

"And you are the one who...?"

"Yes."

"You were not ... willing?"

"What?"

"The man ... he was ... forcing you?"

He saw the pupils of her eyes dilate and she swallowed several times. She grimaced as though at remembered horror and he needed no answer from her.

"It's all right. There's no need to ... I take it he was and so we will say no more about it except ... did he ... did he hurt you?" or rather did he get what he was after, his eyes asked her.

"No." Her voice was abrupt, harsh and he wondered ...

well ... perhaps ... but she stared at him, her eyes clear and challenging.

He became brisk. "How old are you?"

She relaxed. "I don't know."

He sighed, then looked about him, suddenly aware that the rest of the children were still standing in a gawking line across the yard. Abel Freeman was all ears, as was his curious wife from her vantage point on her kitchen step. With an impatient gesture he indicated that the farmer, his wife and the children were to disperse. He put out a hand to draw Daisy away to a quiet corner but she recoiled so fiecely he dropped it hastily to his side, then moved towards the gate where his horse was tethered.

"Come with me, Daisy."

"Where to?" Though she remembered him as the man she had given the message to on that splendid day when she had first set eyes on the young Miles Thornley, the day when his horse had fallen and she had helped him, Daisy was still deeply suspicious. Robert Greenhalgh, whose own memory had long forgotten the same incident and certainly did not connect this ragged child with that one, was not surprised. Was there anyone in the world she had found she could trust, he wondered, but still she must be told what his lordship had in mind for her and he had no wish to divulge it to the rest of them.

"First of all, Daisy, I must impress upon you that when you speak to me, or to anyone of a higher rank than yourself," which must be about everyone she would meet in the next few days, "... you must address them as 'sir' or 'madam'. I do not tell you this for my sake, but for yours, you understand? It will make life somewhat easier for you."

Daisy Brindle learned the first lesson of her new life that day and she was to be grateful to Robert Greenhalgh for it.

She nodded.

"Very well. Now can you give me some idea of your age and that of..." He smiled at Cassie, "... and of the small girl. What is her name?"

"Cassie ... sir. Cassie Brindle."

"You are sisters?"

"Yes ... sir." Defiantly.

"You don't look alike. Your colouring is completely different," for by this time he had caught a glimpse of the red tendrils which were escaping from Daisy's headgear.

"She's my sister and I'm hers." She omitted the 'sir'.

"Very well. About your ages, Daisy."

"I'm thirteen. She's ten ... sir."

"Can you read or write?"

She looked at him, startled, and he realised what a foolish question that had been.

"What can you do?"

"Pick spuds, scare rooks, hoe, pick stones, hurry..."

"Hurry?"

"Mmm, in the mine, and Cassie's been a trapper..."

"Trapper?"

"Aye. We both worked in the pits in St Helens."

"Whose ...?" His voice was faint.

"Nay, don't ask me. We went where we were told."

"And will you go where you are told now?"

The wary look of a trapped but defiant young cat came again to her transparent golden eyes.

"Depends," she said shortly, clutching Cassie protectively to her skirt.

"Could you not trust me when I say no one ..., no man ... will hurt you?"

"Depends," she said again.

"In fact there are no men where you're going, that's if you want to go. You will be warm and well fed..." Dear God, he hoped he was speaking the truth, "... and you will both learn a job which is respectable and could lead to an improvement in your circumstances."

Her expression was becoming more and more bewildered and he realised that she had not the slightest idea what he was talking about.

"Do you know what a school is, Daisy?"

"I might."

She had been taught by life to be careful, not only with her own and her 'sister's' person but with her thoughts, her words, and indeed any careless movement which might

116

draw attention to herself. But she had not yet learned to conceal the expression in her eyes. They revealed her bright and excited interest now.

"Tell me." Robert Greenhalgh waited with quite extraordinary curiosity for her answer.

"It's where you go to learn things."

"What kind of things?" and he wondered why he was deriving such satisfaction from the girl's response, or indeed why he was striving to achieve one. All that was needed was a plain, "Do you want to come or stay?" and that would be the end of it but for some strange reason he felt the need to see her come to life, to lose that cautious and unchildlike instinct for self-preservation with which she guarded herself.

She pulled a face, irritated, not with him but with herself for not knowing the answer.

"Would you like to be able to read, Daisy?" he asked and was overwhelmed by the sudden glow in her wide eyes, a glow which grew and brightened, flaring to a brilliance which dazzled him. It was as though a tiny rushlight, wavering behind a dense curtain of smoke had turned into a candle, growing brighter in an ever-widening circle until it then became a torch, a radiance reaching even beyond the light of the sun, bursting forth until it threatened to consume her, to consume them all.

"You know what that means, don't you, Daisy?" he asked quietly and had no need of her answer and did not expect to get one for her eyes told him.

He was about to move away, ready to mount his horse and give her instructions on how to reach the neat lodge where his wife would know what to do with her and the child until his lordship could be informed, when her harsh voice, made so by her terror of losing this miracle, stopped him.

"I'll not go nowhere without Cassie," it said.

"I would not expect you to leave your 'sister', Daisy." The emphasis on the word, and his smile, told her that the lie about her and Cassie did not matter.

Emma Greenhalgh had borne seven children, all girls, three of whom had survived and she had thought herself fortunate to rear those. They were all married now and scattered across Lancashire, farmer's wives two of them, the third, being pretty and brighter than her sisters, wed to a solicitor.

Emma would not have called herself a romantic but perhaps the four little graves in the churchyard in the village accounted for her inability to bring herself to throw away any of their infant garments and several quite good little dresses her three living daughters had once worn. She had told herself a dozen times that there were many poor and deserving children from decent families who would be glad of such things and was it not her Christian duty to distribute the clothing amongst them, but still they lay in lavender in the chest in the room where her girls had once slept.

She could not have said who was the most stunned, herself or the two . . . well, she could really give them no name beyond knowing they were female . . . which her husband deposited on the kitchen doorstep like a couple of badly wrapped parcels. Her cook swore vehemently that if they were brought over her doorstep, *her* doorstep mind, she would not be answerable for the things which might come in with them and the skivvy, a scrawny girl who, though scrupulously clean, of course, herself looked as though she wore another person's cast-off clothing, studied the newcomers with all the hauteur an upper servant gives a lower. And could you blame her, Emma Greenhalgh asked herself hysterically as her husband explained what was expected of her.

". . . bathe them . . ." He might have said truss them up and serve them for dinner, so great was her horror.

"Well, I can hardly present them to his lordship as they are, my dear."

". . . his lordship . . . ?"

". . . and if you could find something to put them in . . ."

". . . put them in . . ."

". . . perhaps do something with their hair. They must have some beneath those cap things . . ."

". . . their hair . . . ?"

". . . that tin bath the maidservants use . . ."

"...Robert...please..."

"I know it is short notice but it's over an hour since his lordship sent me for them and he'll be waiting in his study, he said. Sir Christopher Faulkner is with him..."

"...Sir Christopher ... Dear Lord, Robert, I cannot imagine what you are talking about and if you don't explain to me at once I swear I shall box your ears."

The servants, a cook, a housemaid, the skivvy, a groom who doubled up as a coachman and a man who saw to the outside work and who happened to be bringing in the coals at that moment, were grouped about their mistress. Every eye was upon the two urchins in the doorway who, it appeared, the master proposed to bring into the kitchen and have cleaned up for his lordship at the big house to look over.

The house where Robert and Emma Greenhalgh had lived ever since Robert had taken over the duties of Lord Thornley's land agent, or bailiff as his lordship preferred to call him, had been built over a hundred years ago of the same soft red sandstone as the main house. It was square and solid with deep-set windows and a pleasant half-acre of pretty garden about it. Robert, who was, as his lordship's bailiff, a servant of the most superior kind with a responsible position in his master's household, was, as such, entitled to a household of his own, to servants of his own and to this small but comfortable house on the edge of the wood to the side of Thornley Green. But in his own home, despite his position of authority on the estate, his wife was the ruler and it took several minutes of heated argument, to which the servants were avid spectators, before she would allow the two children to be brought into the kitchen and it was only her husband's insistence that this was a direct order from the great man who ruled all their lives that made her give way.

"Very well, Robert, but should you find some ... some unmentionable creeping thing in your bed or floating in your soup at the dinner table please don't blame me..." this despite the presence of Daisy and Cassie, not to mention Mrs Lewis, the cook, who immediately took offence at the idea of her allowing some 'creeping thing' to be served in a meal *she* had prepared.

"Clear the kitchen, Josie..." to the maid "...and you, Dolly, scoot up to the attic and fetch down the tin bath. You help her, Zack..." to the outside man who had hoped to slip away to his garden unnoticed "...and get some water boiling, Mrs Lewis. Go on, all the men, and that means you too, Robert, out of the kitchen. See, you two..." gesturing to Daisy and Cassie who stood like two graven images on the threshold of this bedlam, clutching at one another for fear they might be dragged into it "...step inside, no, not too far, just behind the door and take off those clothes, and Ted, you get a fire going at the back of the house and Zack will bring these ... these garments out to you. Burn them at once and I want that floor scrubbed, Dolly..."

Cassie began to weep silently, great silver tears of terror slipping down her thin cheeks and leaving tracks through the grime. She obediently did what Daisy whispered despite her distress, tugging off her bodice and what could just about be called a skirt and the tatters she wore beneath. When she was completely naked she tried to hide herself in Daisy's own skirt which Daisy had not yet removed, burying her face in the folds, for though she was a child dragged up in the 'gutters' of her own world and had witnessed nudity in the mine, her childish mind told her it was not nice somehow to stand naked amongst these strangers who all looked at her as though she had two heads. She was not to know that they were quite speechless at the sight of her savagely thin, white, clean body which seemed at such odds with the filth on the rest of her. When the binding was removed her hair fell in pale shining curls about her shoulders and back, and they gasped, all of the women, even Dolly.

"Well...!" Emma Greenhalgh could find no words. She walked slowly across the kitchen until she stood in front of Daisy and Cassie. Daisy held the little girl close into her skirt, her arms about her as Emma knelt before them.

"She's..." Daisy did not know how to explain Cassie's fear, nor the state of her mind. Her voice was rough. "She's

120

not cracked and don't you dare say she is. She's a bit ... slow, that's all."

"How does she come to be so clean?" Emma did not appear to have heard Daisy's words. She could not take her eyes off Cassie's hair which was like spun silver, and that was being fanciful, she knew. "And what is her name?"

"Cassie ... madam and ... well ... me and her go in the river sometimes."

"Will you tell her we won't hurt her. We only want to bathe her and ..." put her in my Janet's little dress, the one with the pretty cornflower-blue ribbons at the waist. The thought darted into her mind though she did not voice it.

"She's frightened." Daisy did not add that so was she.

"Will you ... perhaps if you were to ... come to the bath with her." Emma did not even look up at Daisy but smiled encouragingly into the small portion of face which was all Cassie would allow her to see.

They were all twittering about like birds at nesting-time, their female hearts bursting with compassion for the 'little dear' who was, after all, not as lousy as she had appeared, coaxing her with soft smiles, cooing noises, the offer of one of Mrs Lewis's almond flakes, and none looked at the lanky frame of the 'older one' who had also divested herself of her filthy garments. The kitchen fire was warm and the tub stood before it. Even Dolly, the supercilious young skivvy, had unbent enough to hang over it with a huge bathtowel ready for the little dear when she had been soaped and sponged and it was not until Mrs Greenhalgh turned absently to the older one, indicating that she should now get into the warm water Cassie had just silently vacated, that Daisy was really looked at.

Emma stood up slowly, clumsily, and her hand went to her mouth in horror. Her eyes were enormous in her suddenly ashen face and she took a step back, almost falling into the bath.

"Dear sweet God," she was heard to whisper and they all turned curiously for Mrs Greenhalgh was not one for taking the Lord's name in vain. Dolly, who was towelling Cassie's gleaming white body, begging Josie to look at the loveliness of the colour of Cassie's eyes and had she ever seen hair like it because *she* certainly hadn't, stilled her hands and her own unremarkable blue eyes almost popped out of her head.

"Oh my Gawd..."

Daisy shivered. She stood with her knees clamped together, her hands dragging at her rippling hair in an effort to hide her nakedness. Her breasts were tiny, just forming as she approached womanhood, and in the nest between her thighs a tuft of red-gold pubic hair was beginning to flower but it was not at these the women stared.

"Child ... Dear God ... what has been done to you?" Emma swallowed and blinked to clear her eyes of the tears which had sprung there.

Daisy hung her head, the shame and degradation of the night when the gangmaster had raped her filling her with self-loathing amongst these decent women who seemed to know what had happened to her. How could they tell, she wondered hopelessly? How did they know of the filth which lay, not on the outside of her where it showed, but inside, in her heart and in her soul and all about the very substance of Daisy Brindle? Then she saw where their eyes lingered and she turned her head awkwardly, trying to see what it was they were all staring at in such horror.

"Who did that to you, child?" the lady asked her again, then put a hesitant hand on her shoulder where her hair had parted. "Who ... who whipped you?"

Oh, the whipping! They were talking about the marks on her back and shoulders, and not the other. The relief was enormous. She knew she had a raised ridge or two, the worst across the small of her back where she could feel them with her hand. They were crowding round her, Mrs Lewis, Josie and the lady, tracing gentle fingers across her shoulderblades and lifting her heavy hair to study them more closely.

"Did you ever see anything like it?"

"Dear Lord, she must have been cut to the bone."

"Poor little..." Dolly had almost said 'bugger' in her

distress. She cuddled Cassie closer to her and the child allowed it.

"Who did this ... er ... what is your name, my dear?"

"Daisy, madam," wishing they would leave her alone. She was longing to get into that lovely soapy water ... soapy, that's what they called it ... soap ... it smelled so fresh and sweet and Cassie looked like a little angel now and she wished to be the same. She was a bit worried about what they were both going to wear after the lady had said that about burning their clothes but she'd hardly be likely to let them walk about stark naked, would she, so she must have something in mind. She wondered when the 'school' bit was going to start and whether they'd give her some of that lovely stuff ... almond flake, the fat lady had called it ... because she was very hungry. *Soap. Almond flake*, some new words learned already and her not half an hour into her new life.

"Who did this to your back, Daisy?" the lady asked again very sternly. "He must be punished for I have never, never seen anything like it. Tell me his name and I will have my husband find him at once."

Daisy was still for a moment. She wanted nothing from her old life to spill over into this bright and magical new one. Besides, he was dead now, they had said so, those men in the woods, so there was nothing to be done about it, even if she were to tell them. She had a chance here to make a fresh and wonderful start. She had no idea what it was but by God she was going to grab it with both hands, so what had happened three years ago, even three hours ago, must be erased from her memory, now and for ever. She was to go to school. She was to learn to read and though she could not imagine what that might lead her to she was damn well going to find out.

She lifted her head and flung back her glorious hair and the women were startled by the gesture, wondering for a moment how they could have thought the little dear was the most attractive of the two children.

"He's dead, madam, and now can I get in the bath?"

123

9

"Are these they, Greenhalgh?"

"They are, my lord."

Greenhalgh's expression could only be described as smug, just as if it was he who had produced from his own loins these two delightful little girls standing so meekly before his lordship's desk.

"But I understood them to be vagrants." Lord Thornley was mystified and utterly disbelieving, his manner said so clearly. What the devil was Greenhalgh up to?

"My wife has had them cleaned up, my lord. They were not fit to be brought into the house as they were."

From his chair to one side of Lord Thornley's desk Sir Christopher Faulkner studied the tall, one could almost say, composed, figure of the older child, trying to picture her as he had last seen her. Like a wild woodland creature she had been, with fierce eyes glaring out from the tangle of her bright copper hair. A fox, a fox cornered by a pack of snarling hounds, that was it, with her few bits of clothing torn away from her and her unformed girl's body gleaming palely in the torchlight and but for the tiny breasts and the white, white skin she might not have been human. He had scarcely noticed the little one except to observe her extraordinary prettiness and how fiercely the older one had protected her.

But would you look at them both now. True they were as thin as pipe cleaners, the pair of them, with a frail, ivory look about them which spoke of a poor diet, but it seemed they were strong enough to work in the fields. The little one was almost paralysed with fear, her eyes fixed blankly on the bit of space before her but the older one, the one whom he had saved, he hoped, from the brutish attentions of the man who had died, was devouring the room and its contents with great golden eyes which were on fire with curiosity. They skipped and darted from the sporting prints on the walls, the large leather-topped desk, the fishing-rods and guns, the deep comfortable chairs before the fire, the books, the lamps and the rich rugs which her neatly booted feet surreptitiously rubbed.

His lordship's study, from where he supervised the running of his great estate, was near to the side entrance of the house so that men such as Greenhalgh, his gamekeepers, or any estate tenant needing to speak to him, would not tread the hallowed halls of his home. Greenhalgh and the two girls had therefore moved along only a short, rather dim passage to the door of the study. Daisy Brindle had never in her life seen the inside of any room beyond the cellar in St Helens and the parlours of the various ale-houses her mother and the other women had frequented. Not until today, that is, and now she had been introduced to two within the space of a few hours. But though the kitchen at the Greenhalgh home had been a wondrous sight it could surely not be compared to this?

She was dressed in a dark and serviceable navy-blue dress which had once belonged to Faith Greenhalgh, Emma's eldest and most sensible daughter. It was too short and yet far too big for her. Her feet were just the right size, however, for the black boots she wore and she wriggled her toes inside them, bemused by the sensation and the smoothness of the long black stockings which covered her thin legs. Mrs Greenhalgh had brushed her hair until her eyes smarted, tutting at its thickness, its springing curls and unmanageability, finally braiding it severely into a plait as thick as a man's forearm which hung down her back to below her waist, tying a navy-blue ribbon on its curling end. She looked neat, well scrubbed and eminently suitable for the purpose Lord Thornley intended. She was not pretty in the accepted sense of the word and yet she had an air about her, bright and expectant, inquisitive even, as though she meant to miss nothing. She would do well, Sir Christopher thought.

But the child, Cassie! Could any man, or woman for that matter, resist her? She was a tender young blossom, as delicate as a newly fallen snowflake, as soft and fragile as lacework and as transparent as a bit of gossamer, making one want to pick her up and shelter her from harm, to shield her from the cold, to make her smile, to keep her from life's hardships and he could understand the older lass's devotion to her. It brought out a man's protective instincts, Sir Christopher thought as he looked into the soft, unfocused blankness of Cassie Brindle's deep purple eyes. Mrs Greenhalgh had tricked her up in a pretty white gown of some soft and gauzy stuff, highly unsuitable, of course, for a child of her station, with blue ribbons at the waist. She had brushed the child's hair until it glinted like newly minted silver in the firelight but instead of dragging it back from her face, as she had done with the older one, she had tied it up with a blue ribbon to match the ones on the dress and curling tendrils fell about her neck and ears. Oh, what a beauty she would be one day! For the life of him he could not see her in Jack Pennington's school for destitute girls.

The two aristocratic gentlemen sat back in their chairs and Robert Greenhalgh waited patiently for their verdict. It was pretty obvious to all three of them that the older one, Daisy, was not only suitable to be trained as a servant but eager to be about it. Sir Christopher had been right in that, the bailiff thought. Feed her up a bit and in a year or two she would be an asset to any lady's household. She had an air of bright intelligence about her that said clearly she would do her best to learn, that she was well aware this was her chance to make something of herself, and they all approved of it, and, as far as they were able, since after all, she was of an inferior class to them, of her. Well trained, as she would be at the servants' school, taught to read and write and speak so that she might be understood, the rough edges polished to smoothness, recommended, if she did well and applied herself, by his lordship himself, she would find work easily, perhaps in this very house. But the other

126

one? – the little one – that was another matter and Robert was perfectly sure his lordship would see it, and when he did he and his Emma had the answer.

"You know why you are here, Brindle?" His lordship was of the class which did not call a servant by his or her Christian name. Daisy looked somewhat surprised but answered well enough.

"Yes, sir."

"I am addressed as 'my lord'." His lordship's voice was stern and his eyebrows crested with hauteur.

She turned to look at Mr Greenhalgh who nodded encouragingly. She almost shrugged, for really the ways of the gentry were very odd, but she meant to do well here with these strange folk and she could only manage it by doing as she was told.

"Yes, my lord."

"You wish to go to school?"

At once she lit up like a flaring coal in the fire and his lordship was somewhat startled by the sudden brilliant loveliness of her, then it vanished as she composed herself and she was no more than a neat and tidy young girl again.

"Yes, my lord." Her hand gripped Cassie's in an ecstasy of excitement, trying to convey to her what this meant to them both. She was not to be frightened, it said, because they would be together as they had always been in this great and wonderful experience they were to share.

"The school is at Denton Green so you will board there, naturally."

Yes, she knew Denton Green. She and the gang had gone through it times. Had even worked a farm or two in the area so it was not as if they were to be sent to some far and distant place which would be unfamiliar. But the word . . . what was it . . . . 'board' . . . that was not familiar.

"Board . . . ?"

"Yes. You will stay there. Sleep, one presumes in a dormitory with other . . . girls like yourself. How long will it be, Greenhalgh?" He turned to his bailiff.

"Two years, I believe, my lord."

"Two years, and then work will be found for you."

Work would be found for them! Clean and decent work which would put them both in a different world to the one they had known for so long. They would be with hard-working, honest people who would treat her and Cassie with the regard they deserved, which they would earn, for they would be hard-working and decent themselves. The past would be wiped clean away. She and Cassie would be wiped clean, clean of the filth and degradation, in which they had lived and which they had survived. At last. At last!

My lord turned his gaze to Cassie then and Daisy saw his grim face relax, as all men did when they gazed at her fragile prettiness, relax into what on another might almost have been an indulgent smile. Cassie trembled against her skirt, her eyes enormous in her pinched face. It was plain she had not the slightest idea what went on about her and was longing only to be away from this strange place, these large and, to her, commanding men. Daisy soothed her with a gentle hand on her head, smiling down into her face, and Robert Greenhalgh could see she was doing her best to let the child know that they had fallen on their feet here, that there was nothing to be afraid of and that soon the pair of them would be off to the grand life they, or rather, she, had striven for all these years.

It was going to be difficult to part them. He cleared his throat.

"May I have a word with you, my lord?"

"Speak up, man."

"If the girls could be taken back to my house, my lord. Perhaps one of the servants?"

"Very well," and his lordship rang the bell to the side of the fireplace.

There was a perfunctory knock and the door opened immediately and when they all turned, surprised at the speed with which his lordship's butler had come from the servants' hall, it was not Petch, nor even one of the liveried footmen, who stood there but his only son, the Honourable Miles Thornley.

Daisy was convinced she would fall in that first moment as her mind reeled with the shock. It was as though someone had given her head a sharp clout, making it ring, disturbing its contents so that they whirled round and round inside it. She felt slightly sick as her stomach lurched and her heart gave a great joyful leap in her narrow chest but she clung to her senses tenaciously.

It was him! It was *him*! *Him*, the boy grown into a man, the boy she had never forgotten in the three years since that day when he had entrusted her with the message for his father. She had recognised him, of course, the father, and the man they called Greenhalgh, for they had both been there then. And ever since she had realised that she was to be taken somewhere in the very grounds in which *he* lived she had looked out for him. On the walk from the great arched gateway at the park entrance to Mr Greenhalgh's kitchen door and then from there through a lovely little wood and across grass so smooth and green she had almost been afraid to step on it, to the doorway of this beautiful house. Her eyes had searched out every bit of garden, scanned the distances which might hold his mounted figure in the hope that she might see him.

Now, here he was and could she ever be as happy again as she was at this moment? she asked herself dazedly.

'Oh, I beg your pardon, Papa. I did not realise you were engaged. I was concerned that you and Sir Christopher might have forgotten the stallion. I am most anxious that we should ride over to see him today,' and he grinned infectiously, disarmingly, as though to ask forgiveness for reverting to a boy promised a treat which he is eager to begin.

"Dear Lord, I admit I had forgotten in this domestic turmoil which seems to have sprung up," his father replied, and which is really nothing to do with me, his expression said as he looked testily at Sir Christopher. This was to be the boy's birthday present and how could his own father be so forgetful? He was not even sure how he had become involved with what, surely, could have been dealt with by the housekeeper and Greenhalgh between them, but Chris Faulkner had been insistent, even admitting to the ridiculous fancy of actually looking these two over, for heaven's sake, but he was a guest in his lordship's home and the rules of hospitality would not allow him to refuse.

"See to this, will you, Greenhalgh," indicating the two children, "that is, if Sir Christopher is satisfied," he smiled rather coolly at his guest, "and do whatever you think best for them. The older one, certainly, for the school. She looks as though something might be made of her but the younger one is surely not strong enough, or even old enough. Perhaps she could be lodged with one of the estate workers . . ." His voice rose on the question as he stood up and began to move in the direction of his son who lounged carelessly by the door.

The Honourable Miles Thornley gave no more than a cursory glance at the tall gawky girl with the long plait who was staring at him breathlessly. He was used to admiration, even adoration from the female sex, from his old Nanny in the nursery down to the smallest skivvy in the kitchen, though it is doubtful he would have noticed the latter, and he supposed this girl to be one of those, though what she was doing in his father's study was a mystery. His attention was caught, as were the other gentlemen, by the bewitching little creature beside her.

Daisy, enchanted, speechless, worshipping, devoured him with her eyes. He was so beautiful, with his vigorously curling dark hair, tall and lean and brown-skinned, his startling blue eyes gleaming between heavy black lashes. His teeth were whiter, his shoulders broader, his smile more dazzling than any man's she had ever seen and she loved him utterly, devotedly, with no hope, nor need of ever having her love returned. It was enough simply to exist in the same hallowed space as he did. He was dressed in sleek, dove-grey trousers, a well-cut, beautifully fitting plum-coloured coat, a positive waterfall of white cravat and pleated shirtfront, and she could not tear her eyes away from him. He would turn his gaze on her in a minute, she knew he would. He would smile, remembering her, of course, and when his father, my lord, told him what she was about to do the bond of love which had nailed her to him three years ago would become stronger still.

He did not recognise her. Well, how could he? They had both grown up since then, but in a plethora of love she forgave him at once, for was she not three years older and had she not changed beyond recognition from that filthy brat she had been – only three hours ago – to the elegant young lady she now was? He was blameless, faultless and, despite the fact that he was giving all his attention to Cassie, which was only natural really, she loved him without question.

"What have we here?" he was saying, smiling graciously at Cassie, thinking, no doubt, that this was a child of the gentry in her pretty and obviously expensive little dress, hiding shyly and charmingly in the skirts of some family servant. "Who is this pretty little kitten?" he asked and Daisy prayed that he would say the same to her, not with the 'kitten' bit, of course, but he was smiling, first at Cassie, then at his father, and he did not look at her once.

"Oh, some waif Greenhalgh has taken pity on but that is all taken care of, my boy. Come, let us go and see what Dash has to say about the stallion. He had a look at him a day or two ago so if he is agreed that the animal is worth buying you shall have him. Will you take my arm, Faulkner, or will your ankle support you?" his manner conveying that he had had more than enough of this tarradiddle, which, had it not been for this sentimental old fool, would not have been brought to his notice.

Daisy was still floating, bemused, on a soft cloud of enchantment and they had been back in the lady's kitchen for several minutes before she began to understand what was happening, not to her, but to Cassie.

She protested at once, hysterical and beyond anyone's control, it seemed, when Emma Greenhalgh took Cassie's hand and began to draw her, gently of course, since she was not an unkind woman, away from Daisy.

"... so you see, Daisy, it would be best if you went at once. Mr Greenhalgh will take you in the trap and then Cassie can settle in here before nightfall. She will have a little while to get used to the house and the room where she is to sleep. It is a lovely room, Daisy, belonging once to my youngest daughter..." which I have been getting ready while you have been over at the house. The bed aired and hung with pretty frilled muslin curtains, a doll or two placed in the window-bottom and a picture book which I shall show her whilst we sit together in the lamplight and the firelight before she drops off to sleep in my lap, but naturally she did not say this to Daisy.

"What?" Daisy's mouth dropped open and her heart lurched, just as it had earlier but in a quite appalling way this time.

"I said that it would be better if..."

"What?"

Emma looked uncertain and Mrs Lewis and Josie exchanged glances.

"I thought that if you were to go at once, with no long goodbyes, it would be easier for the child..."

"What child?"

"Why, Cassie, of course. As Mr Greenhalgh has just explained to you..." Really, the girl looked quite demented and yet she had stood, smiling, whilst Robert had told her that in the circumstances they had both thought it best if they kept Cassie whilst Daisy went to the servants' school. After all, it was obvious to anyone that Cassie was far too young for such an experience. How could she learn if she could not talk, or respond to those who would teach her? Robert had asked and the girl had seemed to agree with her quiet, smiling demeanour.

Daisy's eyes narrowed dangerously and she pulled Cassie even closer to her, lashing out at Mrs Greenhalgh's hand which clung to Cassie's. Her mouth, which had been softly dreaming and turned up at the corners in a half-smile, began to snarl like some mother animal protecting its young and an obscenity of such beastliness spat from her mouth they all gasped.

"I'm going nowhere without Cassie," she hissed and she began to back away towards the kitchen door, ready, should it be necessary, to dart out into the lowering sunshine and across the park to freedom.

Emma put out a placatory hand and Robert moved casually towards the same door with the apparent intention of cutting off Daisy's retreat.

"Now, Daisy, you cannot expect to take a small girl with you to a school where they train girls to be servants. The minimum age is twelve..."

"She's twelve."

"How can you say that? She is only half your size."

"She's small for her age but she'll grow. I'll look after her, like I always have."

"That is very commendable of you but she's not strong like you. Do you want to see her scrubbing floors and cleaning grates..."

"She worked in the mine for twelve hours a day. She'll manage," and all the time the child in question was being pulled this way and that like some china doll over which two children are fighting. Emma could not remember when she had last felt so strong an emotion as she now felt for Cassie Brindle and she was resolute that she would keep the child, nurture her, bring her up as she might a grandchild. None of her own daughters had yet reared a girl though Janet, who had once worn the very dress Emma had put on Cassie, had given birth to two. Faith had three sons but it was not the same as a little girl, was it? Emma meant to take the child to her own dressmaker and have half a dozen little winter dresses made for her. Dresses in soft colours, soft materials. And dainty kid slippers, little boots, a mantle of blue wool with fur about the hood, trick her out like a little princess though she was somewhat doubtful Robert would approve. He agreed with her, of course, that it was not suitable for Cassie to go with Daisy to the school. She was too young, too delicate, but he had no idea of the emotion which was growing in Emma's breast, nor of her plans to make her into the granddaughter Emma did not have. A good home until she was able to fend for herself, Robert had agreed, but even his eyes had been soft when they rested on the lovely child and it would not be hard to convince him of the rightness of what Emma planned.

"Daisy, if you love this child you will listen to me."

"Let her go, she's mine," Daisy shrieked, struggling to hold on to Cassie who had gone limp and boneless in her terror. Robert had hold of Daisy's arms now, pulling her backwards, and Emma gathered the almost senseless younger child into her arms, sitting down with her in the rocking chair by the fire and cradling her in her lap. She brushed the feather of curls from Cassie's forehead, crooning to her, soothing her, rocking her, oblivious to the rest of them, and as they watched they distinctly saw Cassie settle, like a fledgling in a nest, against Emma's ample breast. Her eyelids fluttered for a moment and she sighed. She moved her head more comfortably and then was still.

Robert Greenhalgh slowly let go of Daisy's arms, aware that the crisis was over, that she would give no more trouble. She stood there in her plain navy dress, ungainly and awkward, her expression of suffering giving her a sullen look which was not attractive. Her head drooped, her hands hung by her side and every person in the room, except Emma and Cassie, felt the wash of pain which came from her. Each one experienced it in their own pitying heart though they knew Mr and Mrs Greenhalgh were right. The school was no fit place to send a delicate ten-year-old, even if they would have her, which they wouldn't, but it was a grand opportunity for the older one. For *both* of them. It had been apparent from the first that Mrs Greenhalgh had really taken to the little mite and could you blame her? Sweet as an angel in heaven she was and yet, anyone could see, not able to look after herself. Not quite right somehow. Very attached to Daisy, of course, but she'd respond to kindness wherever she was put, like a homeless puppy. It was the older one who'd do the suffering. Would you look at her, poor little beggar, with her heart breaking at the sight of the little dear settled so comfortably on the mistress's lap. She looked as though someone had whipped her – again – and yet anyone with half an eye could see she knew Mrs Greenhalgh was right.

She tried one last time.

"She's my little sister. I've looked after her for a long time. She can't manage without me." Her voice was dull and hopeless. "We've had nobody but each other," and now, without her, I have no one, her voice seemed to add. "She'll fret if I leave her on her own."

Robert stepped forward into the pool of light cast by the lamp which Dolly had just lit. He was a down-to-earth sort of a chap with no time for romantic fiddle-faddle, perhaps the reason his wife felt the need to adopt Cassie, and the purpose in keeping the child, or so he told himself, was simply that there was nowhere else for her to go. She'd make no difference to his life, which he spent out and about the estate from dawn until dusk and in the estate office of an evening, but she'd be a bit of company for Emma and some time in the vague future, he supposed, she and her sister would be reunited and do whatever females of their class did. Cassie could even learn, under the gentle supervision of his wife, the rudiments of a parlourmaid's work, perhaps, or some employment more suited to her fragile disposition, though what that could be was a bit hazy in his mind. There must be something she could be taught so that when the time came for he and Emma to part with her she would be prepared for the life of a working-class woman. Daisy would be trained and educated and able to stand by her but until then he and Emma would give Cassie a decent home. Dear little thing she was, quiet and biddable. He saw her almost as an engaging young puppy or kitten, no trouble to anyone as long as she was fed and warm and treated with kindness. He failed completely to see the obsessive glint in his wife's gloating eyes.

But strangely, despite his blindness, the suffering of the older girl, Daisy, stirred him. He had not realised the strength of feeling which she carried in her for Cassie.

"She'll be all right in a day or two, my dear," he said kindly. "Mrs Greenhalgh will see to her, don't you worry about that. You want her to be well looked after while you are at school, don't you? To know that while you are learning a grand new job she is in good hands. And I promise you this, if she frets and goes into a decline..." he smiled at the absurdity of the notion "...I will come and fetch you and see if something else can be arranged for her. Now, you can't say fairer than that, can you? Can you?" he repeated sharply when she did not answer. He was completely unaware of the hatred of him which had been planted in Daisy Brindle's heart and which was already putting down roots. Hatred of him and every man who, in her short life, had taken something from her she had valued. Only one male person had ever shown her, if not kindness, then gratitude for what she had done for him, asking nothing for it in return. "I'm obliged," he had said, his eyes warm and grateful, and in response she had given him her stalwart heart. The rest had made her suffer, every one of them and now this one, whom she had thought she could trust, was no better than the rest.

"No, sir," she answered and kept the expression in her eyes well hidden.

"So you will leave her in Mrs Greenhalgh's care?"

"Yes, sir."

Pleased that she had become so amenable, for it would make it easier when the time for parting came, he even went on to say that if it could be arranged he would bring Cassie over to see her, or perhaps, if the headmistress allowed it, Daisy might come for the day to visit Cassie.

"Now say goodbye and we will get off. A message has been sent to expect us at the school so best look sharp. It'll be full dark soon and I don't care for driving the trap on those lanes between here and Denton Green. See, give her a ... well ... say goodbye..." He indicated awkwardly that Daisy might bid her sister farewell, but Cassie slept peacefully in her new protector's arms and when Daisy was hurried through the kitchen door and into the trap which Ted Whittaker had brought round, there was only Dolly and Josie to wish her Godspeed.

136

10

It was dark when Mr Greenhalgh led her through the high front door of Denton House, the building Lord Pennington had donated as a school for the colliery lasses, those who had once worked in his mines and who were considered to be capable of learning a new employment. The house was somewhat grim, having been built for the purpose of sheltering what were known as the 'afflicted poor', in other words as a workhouse, no longer used as such since those who fitted into this category in the parish were, quite simply, moved on. Lord Pennington looked after his own elderly estate workers, those no longer fit to be employed, tucking them tidily away in his almshouses, and he expected other landlords to do the same. The rest, the vagrants and itinerant unemployable, must find shelter elsewhere.

The school was set in two acres of what was known as the 'garden', which is what it was but no flower grew there, no tree, no lawn, only a no-nonsense, geometrically neat square of splendid vegetables, everything the headmistress thought suitable for the pupils to consume and what remained, to sell.

But Daisy saw none of this. She had no more than a blurred impression of cold stone floors, achingly clean, sensible walls of well-scrubbed dark green paint, the eye-watering sting of carbolic and a voice murmuring that ". . . they had already eaten and it would not do. Mr Greenhalgh, really it wouldn't, to disturb the girl whose turn it was to cook at this time of night. The new pupil . . . who? . . . yes . . . Daisy Brindle . . . well, Brindle must manage until breakfast."

Daisy's skin prickled, not just with the damp chill which pervaded the hallway, but with the damp chill in the speaker's voice. A tall thin woman carrying a lamp which cast a circle of flickering light on narrow stone steps, a narrow bare corridor and finally a narrow and scrupulously neat bed.

"This is the dormitory in which you will sleep, Brindle," the woman said briskly. "There is a nightgown in the locker and don't forget to say your prayers. The rest are asleep so make no noise if you please. I'll take the lamp. You'll not need it," and then she was gone, closing the door quietly behind her.

The silence, broken by what Daisy took to be the breathing of the girls who slept in the 'dormitory' – another new word, her wounded, bleeding heart whispered consolingly – was deep and black for it was a moonless night and no light penetrated the small, high windows. She stood for perhaps five minutes, it may have been five hours, time had no meaning for her yet, still and scarcely breathing, like a deer hiding from the hunter behind the concealing leaves of the forest. She had done this many times before, turning in on herself for strength and the goodness of her brave young heart when danger threatened. It was a trick she had learned long ago in the savage nights of debauchery and drunkenness which took place in cellar and barn, and she tried to do it now but all she could see was Cassie, her pale face flushed, her hair tumbled, her cheek turned against Mrs Greenhalgh's motherly breast. She knew she should feel gladness that Cassie was safe and not only safe, but evidently to be loved, but she didn't. She felt only loss and the dragging emptiness of her own loveless heart. She had loved Cassie and she had needed Cassie's dependency on her. She was honest enough to accept that she probably needed Cassie more than Cassie needed her. Anyone who was kind to Cassie, and as yet there had been only herself, would win her affection and trust. Be honest, she told herself brutally, but the knowledge didn't help her. She missed her dreadfully since they had never been parted for a moment in the last three years. She was angry with the lady for taking Cassie from her and she hurt from it, she hurt so badly she didn't quite know how she was to survive it.

Daylight was breaking when she came out of her black reverie and it was the sound of a bell which brought her from it. She was to live by that bell for the next two years. It summoned her from her bed in the morning and told her when she should douse her candle last thing at night and in between its clangour informed her exactly where she should be at every minute of the day.

For the first week she faltered through the hours and days, scarcely aware of the other girls, most about her own age, who moved on the fringe of her conscious mind. They paid no regard to her. They had been picked from hundreds of others like them for their diligence and determination to 'get on', girls who had worked in the deep tunnels of the mines and had been thrown out of work by Lord Ashley's Bill. There was room only for sixty in Lord Pennington's enlightened scheme and so only those His Lordship considered worthy, and capable of learning, had been chosen and they certainly had no time to bother with the new girl. They had themselves been thrust into a world which was so different from the one they had known they might have been set down amongst the Hottentots of Africa which they read about in the books they were seeing for the first time in their young lives. They had overcome their stupefying fear and sense of banishment from everything they had ever known, and so must she.

The pupils were maintained, clothed and rewarded by the establishment in which they now found themselves for it was the practice of the school to sell the produce of their work in order that these favoured few might be reminded that they were working for their bread. So Miss Monk, the headmistress, told them daily. They were taught to sew simple garments, to mend, to bake, to wash and iron, dairy work such as milking and churning since who was to know in what part of a household they might find themselves employed? The products of their labour, simple infant garments, cakes, pies, scones, bread, butter, cheese, and vegetables were sold to the local shops and to the kitchens of the middle-class families in the district. The laundry took in the washing of scores of smaller houses, not the gentry, naturally, for they had their own laundrymaids, and it was the task of the more established girls to collect the dirty linen and then deliver baskets of freshly washed and immaculately ironed garments to their customers' back doors each week.

The first bell rang at five o'clock. The immediate duty of the day, supervised by the most senior of the 'assistants', a girl who had almost served her two years at the school, was, Daisy soon learned, to kneel at the foot of one's bed, with the rest of the girls at theirs, and say prayers, slowly, distinctly and in an audible voice. All must say 'amen' and join in the Lord's Prayer. In that first week she had not the faintest conception of what they were about, nor indeed to whom they addressed this singsong plea, nor did she care. She knelt when told, dumbly, bent her head when told, and whilst the rest chanted in one voice to be given their daily bread, she watched the pictures of Cassie and herself which were imprinted on the inside of her eyelids. Her favourite was of that first day when they had played in the icy waters of Rainford Brook, the sun warm on their naked bodies. The next, she decided, was the Sundays when they had listened to the linnets singing, their hands clasped, their bellies rumbling with the juicy meat pasty they had just eaten and which she had filched from the young lady who had won the 'pastry feast'. There had not been many such happy events in their hard lives but she lived on the memories of those they had.

"Brindle, I cannot hear your voice amongst the others," the assistant said tartly on the third morning. "You know the rules for I told you them myself on the first morning you were here."

Had she? Daisy didn't remember. She didn't remember anything which had taken place since she had arrived at Denton House for her mind would keep slipping back to Cassie, wondering how she was managing, was she eating the good food Mrs Greenhalgh would certainly be stuffing into her, was she sleeping without Daisy beside her, was she making herself understood in her voiceless world? She and Daisy had contrived to communicate with one another without words, but would Mrs Greenhalgh and the others in the kitchen know how to 'talk' and 'listen' to Cassie?

"Repeat after me, Brindle, if you please, the Lord's Prayer and tomorrow I wish you to be word-perfect."

She listened then, repeating the words the assistant carefully mouthed and the next day, to the assistant's astonishment, could recite the prayer with the rest of the girls. She was not to know that Daisy had not the slightest knowledge of its meaning.

They dressed then and filed downstairs where they washed their hands and faces and combed their hair, an easy task for most but one Daisy, with her thick, springing curls which seemed during the night to twist themselves into unmanageable and tangled knots, found so defeating she wished apathetically – since it really did not matter – that she could cut it all off.

"We cannot have this, Brindle," the same patient assistant said. "At all times a servant must be clean and tidy and you must find some way of restraining that ... that ..." It was clear she could find no words to describe Daisy's tumbled mass of glowing hair which gave the appearance of having an existence of its own. Indeed, if the assistant had been a person of a fanciful nature, which she was not, she might have considered that the hair was drawing life itself from the new girl for she was certainly a spiritless thing. Drifting about from place to place, going where she was told blindly, doing as she was bid but with a dazed look about her which boded ill for her future as a domestic servant in a 'good' place, which was what most of them aimed for.

A brush was found, one which had been used in the past to comb the mane and tail of a carriage horse, and with the blind obedience and mindlessness which she seemed unable to throw off, Daisy mastered the skill of braiding it neatly and tightly about her head.

She ate her breakfast that first day, plain and nourishing and plentiful, her eyes looking neither to the right nor left, her ears closed to the muted conversation which went on about her, and when the assistant told her sharply to "follow me, Brindle", she followed.

"I shall show you round today and explain what your duties are to be and then tomorrow you can begin. Miss Monk wants to see you in her study at ten o'clock so we'd best look sharp. We'll go to the kitchen first because that's where you'll start and then on to the laundry..."

The assistant stopped speaking and tutted irritably for really the new girl had an almost ... well, she could only call it *simple* ... look about her and if she didn't pull herself together she'd not be kept on, no matter who had vouched for her. The rumour was that it had been a favour from their benefactor to an old friend. That Brindle was not the usual 'pit-brow lassie', that she had no family, and that Miss Monk had made an exception in taking her in. The headmistress always had a say in who came here, after all she had to prepare them for their new life, picking out only those she thought capable of moving up the social structure from colliery girl to housemaid.

"Come on, Brindle. You can't stand about gawking." The truth of it was she was not really gawking. She just stood there, her eyes shuttered, her pale face blank, as though she was interested in nothing. None of those who came here had ever in their lives entered a house of this size, having been born and dragged up in a collier's cottage, and they were all inclined to stand and stare, awestruck, dumbstruck, homesick and overcome by it all, but this one didn't even seem to *be* here. Well, she'd best shape herself or she wouldn't be, not for long.

She stood before Miss Monk who turned out to be the tall, thin lady who had taken her in the night before, and though this room was pleasant, comfortable, with a warm fire glowing in the grate, pictures on the walls and rugs beneath her feet, she barely gave it a glance. She was remembering that other room – was it only yesterday? – when she and Cassie had stood side by side in front of My Lord's desk. She had been filled with excited anticipation, longing to hear about 'school', the place where they, together, would learn all the magical, wondrous things which would take them to a better life than any they had ever known or even imagined. *He* had been there, gloriously handsome, filling her with gladness, a glow of happiness which could not be described, and Cassie, *her* Cassie, had held her hand and it had stretched out before them like the rainbows she had seen after a shower of rain.

It had all been wrenched from her with a speed which stunned her and she knew her heart to be breaking.

"Stand up straight, Brindle, and don't hang your head like that."

She lifted her head and stared obediently over the headmistress's shoulder at a small picture on the wall.

"That's better. I deplore a sloppy posture. Please remember that. If you ever attain the post of housemaid it would not do to slouch about your mistress's drawing room like that, would it?"

"No."

"No, ma'am."

Mr Greenhalgh had warned her but in her misery she had forgotten.

"No, ma'am."

Miss Monk sat up even straighter as though to set an example to her new pupil, clasping her hands on the desk in front of her. She studied Daisy Brindle dispassionately, coldly even. She made no distinction between any of her scholars and she did not intend to start now, despite the girl's look of deep despair. She'd be no good to anyone if she couldn't 'adjust', a word Miss Monk used often, so she'd best start at once. Miss Monk had heard something of her background from Mr Greenhalgh, Lord Thornley's bailiff, but it was no more harrowing than that of the rest of the girls and if she was to learn to make something of herself in the future this was where she must start and the quicker she got rid of that look the better it would be. Miss Monk didn't give a farthing for what had gone before in her girls' lives. She was concerned, as Lord Pennington had trusted her to be, only with their future.

"You wish to be a housemaid, Brindle?"

"Yes, ma'am," not even knowing what that was.

"Then you shall if you apply yourself."

"Yes, ma'am."

"It will mean hard work but then I am sure you are used to that."

"Yes, ma'am."

"But it will be a different kind of hard work, Brindle. I am aware that you, like the rest of the girls, have worked manually with no need to use the brains which God gave you. Now you will have the chance. A girl who thinks, who puts thought into what she is about to do, whatever it is, will always be a step ahead of one who goes at it blindly. Do you understand?"

For a moment she did. She knew exactly what Miss Monk meant. A tiny snap of interest lit her eyes. She had done exactly that in the mine, hadn't she? There had been children who had loaded their tubs so heavily they had almost been unable to draw them through the tunnels, thinking to save themselves a journey. It had taken them twice as long as her for though they had sneered at the lighter loads she had pulled, in the end it had been Daisy Brindle who had drawn more tubs than any one of them. She might have covered twice the distance but the smaller load had allowed her to crawl at incredible speed up and down the long tunnels; she had not exhausted herself quite so drastically as they and she had earned her 'hewer' more wages than any man at the coal-face. That was what Miss Monk meant. Planning, thought, a bit of method . . .

"I see you do, Brindle," the headmistress said, leaning forward, caught by the sudden play of light in Brindle's eyes. This girl had something about her which Miss Monk found she liked, which she recognised, and whom Miss Monk liked, she chastened, and she had the feeling that Daisy Brindle would be well chastened by the end of her training.

But the girl seemed to . . . well . . . to switch herself off and no matter what Miss Monk said to her in an effort to rekindle that spark she was so certain she had seen in her eyes, she remained no more than politely uninterested.

Miss Monk sighed.

"Very well, Brindle, you may go now. I shall no doubt see you in my reading class."

She began the next morning. After prayers and the exhausting task of taming her wild hair, after washing and making herself tidy, eating her breakfast of hot porridge followed by bacon put between thick slices of fresh bread which, two days ago, would have made her think she had died and gone to heaven, she was taken by a first-year assistant to the kitchen.

"Put that apron on, Brindle, and I'll show you how to do the kitchen range. You have to clear away the ashes, light the fire, clean the hearth and polish all them bright parts with this special cleaner. D'you understand? Now it's already been done this morning," the girl said briskly, "as you can see..."

Had it? Daisy stared blankly at the huge black monster, the likes of which she had never before seen, wondering what it was, wishing she was back in the fields with the good damp soil between her toes, with the cheerful song of the blackbird in the trees, the sun hot on her back and Cassie beside her. And *him* waiting for you in the spinney, a small desperate voice said in her head, but she took no notice of that as she allowed her attention to wander from the girl's droning voice.

"... up at five when it's your turn for kitchen duty. Miss Monk is always a bit easy on your first week but tomorrow you'll have to be up alongside me to light the range before we make breakfast. Very particular Miss Monk is that each girl teaches the next one down, if you see what I mean, and I like things done right as you'll find out when you learn how to make bread..."

Without quite knowing how she came to be there, Daisy found herself on her knees before a fireplace in another room. A big room with long tables and benches down the side of each wall and the drifting reminder of the smell of bacon and she realised that this was the room in which she had eaten her breakfast ... wouldn't Cassie have loved that fresh bread ... she'd probably be eating better things than even fresh bread, a nasty voice said inside her, probably sitting on the lady's lap . . .

". . . you have to roll up the rug first, take up the fender and lay this cloth down so that you don't get ash on the . . ."

What would she be doing now? Walking in that pretty garden with the lady, running after one of those mischievous kittens she had spied in the yard, her lovely white dress held up about her knees, her eyes sparkling . . . or would she be crying . . . fretting for Daisy, and she felt shame when she knew that the second picture pleased her more than the first.

". . . the hall has to be swept towards the front door so that the dust . . . Are you listening to me, Brindle?"

"Yes, ma'am."

"You don't have to call me ma'am."

"No, ma'am . . . sorry."

"And so you should be. I'm trying to teach you a job of work here and you'll not learn it daydreaming. I've no time to waste and neither has Miss Monk if you're not willing to put all your mind to it. Now, what have I just said to you . . . ?"

"What . . . ?"

"What did I just tell you was Miss Monk's favourite saying?"

"I . . ."

"Listen here, Brindle, you'd better shape yourself or you'll not last long here. Miss Monk likes everything done proper and if you're not willing to be taught how to do it you might as well walk out of that door right now. So, listen to me. You'd best learn it by heart because she's bound to ask you. 'Cleanliness is next to godliness', but she always says that 'Order' is in the next degree. That means . . ."

"I know what it means."

"Well, you'd better learn some right quick."

Daisy felt a small prick of irritation. Who the hell did this girl think she was, queening it over her as though Daisy was nowt a pound and a bloody idiot into the bargain? She could do this piddling job with one hand tied behind her back, and standing on her head with a bit of practice and if she wasn't missing Cassie so desperately that she couldn't even think straight, if she wasn't worrying about her so savagely she actually ached with it, she'd get stuck into that ... what was it? ... polishing that black monster ... the kitchen range so that you could see your bloody face in it. But somehow she hadn't the heart for it, really she hadn't, and for two pins she'd walk out of that open front door and leg it back to Thornley Green, pick Cassie up, and the two of them would be off, off to ... well ... wherever there was work ...

And where was that, her crisp, practical mind asked her, the mind which had lain dormant ever since she had been led from the Greenhalgh kitchen leaving Cassie behind. There *is* no work for a girl like you. None which will give you and Cassie, one day, the decent life you've always told yourself you'd have. This is it! This is what you've longed for ever since you were old enough to know the difference. This is your chance. You *have* to get to grips with it, this strange life which somehow is overwhelming you even more than the black hellhole of the pit. Stop thinking about the past. Get on with the future.

She felt her heart sigh within her, sad and heavy with longing for something she had lost. In the mine she had been with Cassie whom she had been so busy protecting and comforting she had had no time to think about herself. She had had the dubious but familiar company of the other women and the need to undertake the survival of herself and Cassie amongst them to the exclusion of everything else. Now, for the first time in her life, she was alone.

She lay in her narrow bed that night, staring into the blackness which pressed against her face, and forced herself to recognise that if she and Cassie were to have that life which she had promised them she must pull herself together and learn what Mr Greenhalgh had told her would get it for them. She had let herself go badly these last two days, or was it weeks? it seemed like it, which surely was enough to tell her how childish she had been. She was thirteen, or so her mother's calculations had told her, and almost a grown woman, and she was witless to let herself get into such a low state. But she must manage now. She

147

must pull herself from the mindless stupor her parting from Cassie had caused. She must work and work and soak up every bit of learning that was available to her, learn how to be . . . well, whatever it was they were going to make of her and when her two years were up she and Cassie would start a grand new life, just the two of them. It would be hard. Two years was a long time, but she'd show them, especially that silly cow who had spoken to her so sharply this morning. She was already a bloody sight better off than she had been this time last week, wasn't she? She had this lovely clean bed to lie in, good food in her belly, a grand dress to wear and decent boots on her feet. She was warm and dry and free from the constant fear that the gangmaster would take her, as he had taken Aggie Barton, Emmy Holden and Lily Formby. So stop moping and grizzling, she told herself sternly.

But her last thoughts as she drifted into sleep were of Cassie and the emptiness, not only in her young heart which had known no other affection, but of her arms which had held the little girl as they slept for the last three years.

It was the word *think* that really did it. It was used all the time for Miss Monk held the firm belief that, with a few exceptions, each girl who came into her care, despite her poor beginnings where she had been treated as no better than a dumb animal, was capable of thought.

"We must learn to think, Brindle," she said, commencing the chastening process at once, the word emphasised with a heavy ruler across Daisy's knuckles. "Use our brains, that is if we have any. Our God-given brains, Brindle, and I would be obliged if you would allow me to examine yours. Now what have I just said," she asked, lifting Daisy's chin so that her face was illuminated by a shaft of sunlight which streamed from the high window, and though Daisy had vowed only last night that she would pull herself together and take advantage of what was being offered her she was today again in a misery so deep and black, in a pit of self-pity so thick she had the greatest difficulty in recognising where she was or even who this woman was.

She felt her brain stir sluggishly to life inside her aching head.

"Think," she murmured.

"Think, *ma'am*, if you please."

"Think, ma'am," Daisy mumbled.

"And what must we think *about* when we first come to this school which has so charitably taken us in?"

"I . . . don't know."

"I don't know, *ma'am*." Another sharp crack with the ruler and Daisy's brain twitched, this time, angrily.

"I don't know, ma'am," and really, I don't bloody well care, but she wasn't quite angry enough to say that.

"Rules, Brindle. All life is lived by rules and this school is no exception. Keep to them and you cannot go wrong. Now then, let us learn some of the rules of this establishment. We shall learn one each day and each day you will repeat to me the one you learned the day before. Do you understand?"

"Yes . . . ma'am."

"Very well. Here is the first. When I have said it, you will say it and go on saying it until you are word-perfect. Do you understand?"

"Yes, ma'am."

" 'The duty of each boarder is to take care of her person and her clothes. Any found wanting will be reported to the headmistress.' That is myself, of course. Repeat that phrase."

Daisy did so, and much to Miss Monk's astonishment did not say 'that is myself, of course', which most did.

"Good. I will give you another tomorrow."

And she did.

"Each boarder must spend a week in the dairy, the kitchen, the sewing room, the laundry and the garden in strict rotation. Any infringement of this rule shall be reported to the headmistress," explaining carefully to Daisy, as she had done to every other girl, what the word 'infringement' meant.

'There shall be no talking in class . . .'

'Each boarder shall help to serve at table . . .'

'. . . say her prayers night and morning . . .'

'... learn her catechism ...' What was that?

'... go to chapel each Sunday ...'

'... wear her best dress only for chapel ...' Her best dress? She only had the one!

'... fold her clothes ...'

'... sit straight and not loll at her books ...'

'... not leave the school grounds without permission ...'

'... keep her own housemaid's box neat and tidy ...' and on and on until Daisy thought her head would burst with it. But at least the learning of each rule and the chanting of them, as she scrubbed and polished, swept grates and hearths, shook rugs, black-leaded the stove, cleaned windows and made beds, kept her mind from the ache which was left inside her by Cassie's absence.

The following week she was taken into the laundry which consisted of a washing house, an ironing and drying room, and a drying closet heated by furnaces. In the washing room there was a range of tubs, some round and some oblong, opposite to and sloping towards the windows, narrower at the bottom than the top in order that the girls might more easily bend over them. There were taps from which, to Daisy's awed amazement, real water ran into the tubs. There was a boiler and a furnace. The work of the laundrymaid began each day with the careful scrutiny of the laundry book which was included with each basket of laundry picked up the day before by the girl whose job it was that week. Each item in the basket must correspond with the list in the book. A girl who was in her second year was in charge of this as, naturally, it needed someone who could read. By the end of the week, though she could not, of course, read the laundry book, Daisy had been praised for her light hand with muslins and other delicate fabrics, her meticulous attention to the removal, prior to washing, of any grease spots, wine stains or ink on the garments, the way in which she quickly learned to rub one linen surface against another and not her own skin, saving her hands, and in particular, for the way in which she tackled the most important task of ironing. There was the flat-iron for the work, as the name implied, of ordinary household ironing. The oval iron for more delicate jobs, the box iron, hollow and heated by another, red hot and inserted into the outer box. The smooth outside was used on articles such as frills and pleated fabrics and needed patience and dexterity. By the end of that second week at Denton House they were saying in the laundry, "Oh, give that to Brindle. She has a way with such things."

And in her third week, when a lovely spell of late autumn sunshine lay over the village and surrounding farmland, and she was put to work in the gardens, she was taken back in her mind to her days spent in the fields with her mother and the other women. There were several girls besides herself, all dressed in their 'old' gowns and stout boots, some turning over the ground which had been cleared of the summer's produce, others taking up what looked like old plants and laying them on their sides in a sheltered spot by the wall.

"Cauliflowers," her guide said briefly, "for next year." There were two girls kneeling beside a row of tall plants, pushing the soil up about each one, and again the one who was directing Daisy about the garden was sparing of words.

"Celery. They're earthing it up. It'll be ready for Christmas."

There were potatoes and cabbage, carrots and early Brussels sprouts, all saleable and much of the produce sent to the markets in Wigan and St Helens.

"Need a bit of hoeing, those spuds," Daisy couldn't resist saying, bringing a surprised lift of the eyebrows from her mentor, and the following week, when it was her turn to work in the dairy, she was the talk of the school when, on her first day, she calmly squatted on a stool and began to milk one of the cows.

"Cub, cub, lass . . ." she said soothingly to the beast, just as though she was used to doing such a thing every day of the week.

"I hear you have begun to *think*, Brindle," Miss Monk said to her that evening at prayers and Daisy found herself glowing in a quite splendid flush of self-satisfaction. She slept dreamlessly that night.

It was the afternoon of the next day when Daisy Brindle's

151

mind finally broke through the shell which had encased it ever since, as a small girl, she had first questioned the life she had been born to.

At precisely two o'clock, seated at a bench in the school-room, she was given a small book called – she found out later – *The Only Method To Make Reading Easy or Child's Best Instructor*.

"Page one, if you please," Miss Monk said, fixing a stern eye on Daisy. "That is the first page, Brindle. Now, let us begin at the beginning. Those of you who are able may continue with your Bible."

Daisy turned the book – the first she had ever seen, let alone handled – over in reverent hands, marvelling at its mysterious beauty. This was the key, she knew it, which would open up the whole world to her. When she had mastered this and whatever was inside it she would know what it was she and Cassie were to do. She was ignorant. She knew nothing about the world, about the country in which she lived, beyond the knowledge that it was called England and was bigger than St Helens. She knew nothing about anything apart from farm work and pit work but there must be more than that to life. There *was* more than that to life. She had seen Thornley Green and its park and sensed the splendour which lay within it, but with this book, this magical book, she would find out for herself. She knew there were such things as newspapers. She had seen Farmer Chadwick study one as he sat at the kitchen table and heard him say to his comfortable wife, "I see Her Majesty's had another girl. It says here the little princess is to be called Helena Augusta Victoria." The newspaper told you things, things that happened miles and miles away. And that's what Daisy wanted to do. To find out what was happening not just here, in Denton, or even St Helens, but in the rest of the world and the only way to do it was by reading!

BAD, LAD, MAD, BED, RED, LED, BIB, NIB, FIB.

She was achingly disappointed. Hour after hour, to the accompaniment of Miss Monk's voice exhorting them to follow what she had written on the blackboard, and in the first pages of the book, they chanted these meaningless words.

COT, DOT, GOT, HOT. It made no bloody sense at all. It told you absolutely nothing. She knew what BAD meant, and LAD and HOT and some of the other 'words', as Miss Monk called them, JUG, RUN, SUN, though she could not have said which of the squiggles on the pages actually *said* them, so what the devil had they to do with learning about things? Miss Monk jabbed at the blackboard with a bit of stick called a 'ruler', pointing at the words she had written in chalk, then walked between the rows of benches, putting each girl's finger on the same word in her book, commanding them to notice the shape of the letters and to think, think, *think* how they formed the word.

Daisy tried, she really did. Day in and day out she repeated the words until she could have said them in her sleep, and frequently did. The reason for it all escaped her until one day, bored to distraction and wishing she was out in the garden hoeing the potatoes she had helped to plant, her eyes on the now familiar curves and sticks Miss Monk had put on the blackboard, she suddenly noticed the similarity between two of the letters in the words. BAD and BALD and BLOT all began with the same shape. They all sounded different as Miss Monk mouthed them patiently, pointing to each one as she said its name, but the first shape had the same fat curves held up by a thin stick! BAD was two fat curves joined together with a thin stick ... then ... then ... two thin sticks with a little one holding them together ... then ... Oh Lord ... then a thin stick holding a fat curve. It made sense. It really made sense. All those curves and sticks when you put them together in the right way made a word which *said* something. It was BAD. She could see it. She could see it as plain as she could see Miss Monk's stick calmly pointing at the blackboard.

Wonderingly, her ears and her mind closed to the rest of the droning class of girls, some of whom had almost finished their first year and still could scarcely recognise a letter in the alphabet, she followed the shapes in her book, putting the sounds to the shapes, matching them, not yet fitting them

153

exactly into words, but identifying one here, one there. AT
... IT ... TO ... She turned back to the first page, unaware
that Miss Monk was watching her though her ruler continued to point out the words on the blackboard and her
voice to repeat them.

Daisy's lips moved silently, stretching, pursing together,
stretching again. Her eyes studied the little animal in the
first picture then the curves and sticks which she knew said
its name. The first was two long sticks with a little stick
across it just like the one in the middle of what Miss Monk
had told them was the word BAD. It came then, just inside
her head behind her eyes, just as clear as the water which
came from the tap, and as miraculous. APE. It said APE and
she knew she was right because that was what the picture
was. An APE, for Miss Monk had said so. She couldn't seem
to get the next word, no matter how hard she tried, because
it had four letters in it, but the third word said ... said COW
... then ... then DOG!

She turned the page, utterly absorbed, not understanding
them all but making out those which had only three letters
in them. She turned the page again and began to read,
actually *read* the first line at the top, slowly at first, forming
the words soundlessly.

'WHO ... CAN ... SAY ... HE ... HAS ... NO ... SIN ...'
What did it mean? Bloody hell, what did it mean? She didn't
know. It made no sense at all but by God, she'd read it, and
if she could read that she could read anything.

"Who can say he has no sin," she said out loud triumphantly and the whole class fell silent. Miss Monk walked
slowly towards her and each girl held her breath, waiting
for the retribution which was Brindle's due. She had done
something awful, they were certain, though they were not
sure what it was.

"What did you say, Brindle?" Miss Monk's voice sounded
strange and menacing.

Daisy repeated what she had read, her eyes skipping along
the line quite nimbly now.

"Stand up."

She stood, her head high, her back straight, her eyes

shining like amber in the white excitement of her face. She didn't care what Miss Monk did to her for disturbing the class, which was a dreadful breaking of the rules, because she, Daisy Brindle, could read.

"Read the rest of it, if you please."

" 'The way of man is ill, but not the way of God
My son, go not in the way of bad men,
No man can do as God can do,
Let me not go out of thy way.' "

It had been read haltingly, but it had been read.

"That's enough, Brindle, you may sit down," and Miss Monk's own voice had trembled somewhat.

The next day, under Miss Monk's stern eye, she began her real education, becoming a legend in the school as the first girl who had learned to read in the space of a month.

11

Within six months she was a monitor, and in a year an assistant and at the end of two years Miss Monk begged her, not quite with tears in her eyes but not far off, to reconsider her offer to stay on as a junior teacher. Appalled at the idea of remaining, without Cassie, in this sterile world for the rest of her life, Daisy refused gently.

Of course, if she was honest, it was not just Cassie who drew her back to Thornley Green where a position had been promised her, but the hope, long cherished, that she might see Miles Thornley. Nothing more, naturally, for anything else would be out of the question, but just to see him now and again, perhaps cantering by on his tall hunter though where that might be she could not imagine. He would nod graciously, wherever it was, smile perhaps and wish her a 'good morning' and her day would be brighter for it. Or if fate was especially kind, might she not be allowed to serve him in some way, as she was perfectly certain *he* had served her in helping to send her to this school? Perhaps in the capacity of chambermaid, move about the bedroom in which he slept, to touch and tidy what was his, and therefore precious. It was a bright dream to keep beside the others she had. She had taken the first step on the road to those dreams. Now she was to take the second and though she was uncertain where the road would lead she must go back to Thornley Green·to find out.

She was tall now, tall and exquisitely slim with tiny pointed breasts. She wore black which emphasised the spare boyishness of her figure, a dress she had made herself, plain and serviceable with long sleeves and a high neck and from it her face flowered, creamy white and pointed of chin. Her eyes were a glowing golden brown, her eyebrows delicately arched and her hair, severely restrained into a long, thick braid wound about her head, was the bright colour of copper beech. The black gave her a mature air, severe almost, despite her fifteen years, as though her spirit was kept securely reined for fear it might take wing but it shone from her eyes in bright intelligence.

"I can't, Miss Monk, really I can't. I have my sister to look after." Her voice, though still strong with the vowels of the north, was low and pleasant.

"But she's well settled with Mr and Mrs Greenhalgh. You told me so yourself."

"I have a job to go to, Miss Monk. A fine job."

"A servant's job." Miss Monk's voice was contemptuous. "You are worth more than that, Brindle. You could teach, as I do. Bring forth young minds from their shell of apathy. Oh, I know there aren't many who respond or who are even capable of it, as you are, and that most will get no further than kitchenmaid or dairymaid, but some can do more and that makes it all worth while. You have a good mind, my dear. You have learned to read and write and could easily do the accounts of this school, you are so skilled with numbers. In two years you have learned everything I can teach you and yet you choose to become a servant..."

"I'm sorry, Miss Monk, but I promised myself that my sister and I would be together again one day."

Her disappointment made Miss Monk cruel. She chose to overlook the shining devotion, the loyal and true resolution which had been Daisy Brindle's lodestar for the past five years. Her voice was cutting.

"She is not really your sister, Brindle, and from what Mr Greenhalgh has told me she has become a member of his family now."

"I know that." Though Daisy's heart winced at the sharpness of the words, which she knew to be true, she did not falter. Her head rose a little higher and her expression cooled. "I shall not, as yet, be able to provide a home for Cassie but I shall work hard and save..."

"And then what will you do? You will still be no more than a maidservant earning eight pounds a year and from that you cannot possibly save enough to get together a home for both of you. And if you did, could you leave her in it alone, since you would have your duties at Thornley Green to see to? I am aware that your ... er ... sister is not ... able to ... fend for herself, so would it be kind to take her away from the environment she knows? Be practical, Brindle. Mr Greenhalgh has spoken for a job for you which is more than good of him. Two years ago I would have told you to thank God for it but you were untutored then and would have been considered well suited to it. But now, with what you have learned to be, and from what your 'sister' has become, from all accounts, it seems to me you would be far better served to remain here where..."

"Miss Monk, please..."

"Cassie ... is that her name...?"

"Yes..." Daisy's hands clenched tightly in the folds of her skirt and her creamy skin became even paler but her eyes were mutinous and her small jaw tightened.

"She is ... so Mr Greenhalgh tells me ... settled and it would be unkind to try and uproot her from what has become her home, where she has formed attachments. She is a dearly loved..."

"I love her, Miss Monk. She is my sister, whatever anyone says to the contrary, and I mean to be near her. I appreciate that ... at first ... it will not be easy but I mean to try. It is all that we have ever wanted, Cassie and I ..." ignoring the delicate raising of Miss Monk's expressive eyebrows. "You have been ... more than a teacher to me for which I thank you but I must do what I have always meant to do, for me and Cassie, and that is to make a new life for us. We have been forced to live apart through no fault of our own. Two years it has been, but I know when she sees me again she will want to be with me. Mr and Mrs Greenhalgh have looked after her but she is twelve now and will be strong so ... when the time comes, which it will very soon, we will be together. I'm not sure how but we will. Now, if you will excuse me, I must go and get my things. I want to be at Thornley Green before dark."

She strode out in her sturdy boots, her bright hair completely covered by the large black bonnet Miss Monk had considered suitable for a servant girl. She looked like a widow, her brave spirit quenched and hidden beneath the dark garments but it bubbled inside her, threatening to overflow like champagne from a cork. She would see Cassie by nightfall. What would she be like now? Would she be as quiet and shy? Was she as pretty? Would she remember Daisy? These and a dozen other questions ran through her eager mind as she turned her face away from the school in Denton Green.

The sun shone, mild and mellow, but with a cool hint in the air of the autumn and winter to come. The hawthorn hedge on either side of her was as high as her head and when she came to a gate she stopped for a moment to stare curiously into the empty field. It had been harvested and gleaned and on the far side children were picking stones. A boy sat on a five-barred gate waving a rattle, ready to scare away birds though why he should bother when there was no crop was a mystery. Her eyes became unfocused as she looked back to that child she had once been, the child who had bent just as industriously over her work as these children did. What had happened to all the others? she wondered. Her mother? Gertie Wilson, Mary-Kate Barton and the children they had borne? Where had they gone when she and Cassie had been taken up to Thornley Green? Had they found a new gangmaster, employment, and did they still roam about Lancashire as she had done? Did they still live? She found she could not really seem to care, not even about the woman who had been her mother. Why should she, she asked herself, since not one, apart from Gertie, had cared about her and her pain and terror on the night their master had beaten and raped her.

She turned abruptly and walked on, putting the thoughts from her decisively since they were no longer a part of her life, but almost every step of the way revived memories of those days. So many of these fields she had laboured in, so many of these villages she and the gang had passed through. Primrose Bank, Moss Bank, Potters Hill, Woolfall Heath and Fenny Bank but then as the sun slid towards Caleb's Wood she was on Brook Lane and there were the gates to Thornley Green.

Thornley Green. Thornley Green, her new home, her new life and she could scarcely wait to begin it. She was polite to the gatekeeper, Dewhurst, bidding him good afternoon in the way she had been taught at Denton Green.

Aye, he'd been told to expect her, he said cheerfully. She was to go straight up the drive until she came to a left turn. She'd see the stables on her right and the walled garden and at the back of the house was the door to the kitchens. Mrs Crosby was expecting her and not to dawdle because Mrs Crosby didn't like dawdlers.

The drive was long. Three miles, Dewhurst said, and if she didn't look sharp she wouldn't get there before dark. The trees which lined it were tall and close together and her booted feet crunched on the gravel, so neatly raked each tiny piece seemed to lie next to its neighbour in perfect unison. There was no sound but that of the birds settling for the night and she was glad when she reached the turn

Dewhurst had described. Not that she minded the dark, or the country lanes where she knew what to expect, but here it was different. Those animals she had seen the last time she was here, which she now knew to be deer, might still be about and though she was aware they would not harm her she had no wish to come face to face with them in the twilight.

She turned the corner of a long yew hedge, staring across the parkland towards the wood where she knew Mr Greenhalgh's house lay and for a moment, abandoning all common sense, she almost turned in that direction, overcome by a deep need to see Cassie, not tomorrow, or even later tonight, which was what she hoped for, but now. Right this minute. But reason prevailed. It had been two years so what was another two hours, her practical mind asked.

"Oh, there you are. We almost gave you up, didn't we, Tipping?" The girl who answered her firm knock on what she hoped was the kitchen door, spoke over her shoulder to another. "Best come in then and I'll go and tell Mrs Crosby you're here. Of course, we're right in the middle of preparing dinner..." just as though Daisy could not have called at a more inconvenient time. "Wipe your feet. Chef don't like his kitchen mucked up."

She had never seen so many people in one place in her life. There had been sixty girls at Denton House, with half a dozen staff, and when they had all been together at mealtimes it had seemed a multitude but this ... well, she could hardly get in at the door, or so it seemed, there were so many servants crammed into the place. She later learned that Lord Thornley employed forty-three indoor servants but at that moment, when she first stepped into the enormous main kitchen at Thornley Green, she would have sworn there were at least twice as many and that each and every one of them was in the kitchen that evening.

It was a splendid room, warm and cheerful and so clean and shining each surface gave the appearance of reflecting the light, winking back at her from every corner. There were dozens of copper pots and pans hanging on dazzlingly white walls and the flagged stone floor was lustrous with red polish. All the servants who were engaged in preparing dinner were in white, neat caps, aprons or jackets, even the menservants' trousers. And over it all lay the most delicious smell Daisy had ever encountered. Those whose job it was, and there seemed to be at least a dozen, were bent over enormous ovens, lifting lids and stirring the contents of pans, and all under the dictatorial supervision of one regal gentleman in a tall white hat and sitting in a chair so high he could see above the heads of those who ran to do his bidding!

A hand touched her arm. "Come this way," the girl who had let her in said haughtily. "Mrs Crosby'll see you now."

She followed humbly, grateful to be rescued from the hurly-burly of the kitchen, from the impolite stares, the nudges amongst themselves of several manservants, some in quite magnificent livery, and the jostling from a pert kitchenmaid who told her that if *she* had nothing to do but stand and gawp there were some who were here to work. They moved, she and the girl who had come to fetch her, through a door on the far side of the kitchen, down a short passage and, after a polite knock on a closed door, entered a room which, following the din of the kitchen, seemed a haven of peace and calm. It was large and comfortable, the walls lined with shelves and cupboards, all painted in a practical shade of pale grey. There were several small ornaments on the mantelshelf and a picture on the wall above it but apart from these the room had a curiously impersonal air as though the woman who sat at the table was merely passing through. There was an enormous desk, plain, functional, with a dropleaf writing surface and a great quantity of pigeonholes in which were neatly folded pieces of paper. To the side of the fireplace was a small tripod tea-table on which a silver teapot, sugar basin and milk jug stood beside a fine bone china teacup and saucer. A cheerful fire blazed in the scrupulously black-leaded grate. There were two comfortable chairs before it but most of the centre of the room was taken up by a large cloth-covered table. It was here that the housekeeper, an 'upper' servant in the house and effectively her mistress's representative, ruled those who were under her. It was here that she discussed accounts with the butler, entered items of household expenditure in her enormous ledgers, gave orders to housemaids and laundrymaids and interviewed applicants for jobs.

The housekeeper raised her head as Daisy entered and instantly her pale gaze snapped about Daisy's hesitant figure, holding her without a word to the square foot of carpet on which she stood.

"Thank you, Miller," she said to the girl who had led Daisy here and the girl bobbed a respectful curtsey before quietly leaving the room.

There was silence for twenty seconds, the longest twenty seconds in Daisy's life. Mrs Crosby's small black eyes studied her from head to toe, lingering on her boots, and Daisy's heart sank for though they had been so highly polished this morning she could see her own face in the toecaps, the walk along the dry, rutted lanes had lain a fine film of dust on them. She wished she had given them a surreptitious rub up the back of her stockinged leg as she knocked on the back door but it was too late now. She was clean and neat, and had been ever since the first rule of the school was instilled into her two years ago. 'The duty of each boarder is to take care of her person and her clothes' and that was what she did and she knew that apart from her boots, which she couldn't help, she was as presentable as any servant in this great house.

The thought gave her confidence. She lifted her head a shade higher, not to the point of haughtiness but to let Mrs Crosby know she had a pride in her appearance. Her gaze was clear and steady as she waited for the housekeeper to speak.

"Step forward, Brindle, where I may see you." She did so, quietly and with grace, moving to stand before the large table.

"Remove your bonnet." Daisy did as she was told, releasing unconsciously into the air about her head the sudden eruption of vivid colour her hair created, glowing and so vibrant Mrs Crosby had the distinct impression she could have warmed her hands against it on a cold day. And yet it was severely restrained about the girl's head. Drawn back and tightly braided, the braids themselves twined into a heavy coil on the nape of her neck. But there were tendrils, wayward and springing, which escaped defiantly to lie about her ears and on her brow and Mrs Crosby didn't like them. It put a cutting edge in her voice.

"You have come from the School of Industry, I believe?" She made it sound as though Daisy had this morning been released from the house of correction for wayward girls.

"Yes, ma'am."

"You were there two years?"

"Yes, ma'am."

"And learned the duties of housemaid, I was told?" Her expression said she found it hard to believe.

"Yes, ma'am. I can also do dairy work, laundry work, sewing, some cooking, and have been trained in some of the duties of a lady's maid."

"I see." Mrs Crosby was not impressed. There was not the smallest chance that Daisy would ever become lady's maid, not with her in charge. It was written in her face that she was not only unimpressed, she was not at all pleased. "I would prefer to have had the teaching of you myself, as I do most of my staff unless they come from a household which can be relied on to train up their girls to my standards. Unfortunately I have had no choice in this matter. It appears Mr Greenhalgh was made some promise by his lordship about your future two years ago. An experiment, I was led to believe, and it has been decided to try you out at Thornley Green now that your ... er ... training is completed." Her whole demeanour said exactly what she thought of such radical experiments and the aggravation it was bound to cause. "Naturally you will begin in the lowest position ..."

"I was told housemaid, if you please, ma'am."

It was a mistake and the moment Daisy spoke she knew it. No one interrupted Mrs Crosby and certainly no one contradicted her, particularly when your name was Daisy Brindle and you were the result of one half-witted demonstration of philanthropy on the part of his lordship and his friend Sir Christopher Faulkner who had begun the whole sorry scheme. But Mrs Crosby's expression did not alter at all. Her eyes were just as impassive and yet there was something about her which told Daisy she had now made two mistakes. The first had been to boast, which was how the housekeeper saw it, about her abilities, not as a housemaid but as a lady's maid which was one of the highest positions in the house. The second was to question Mrs Crosby's place in the servants' structure, her power, her authority to put Daisy wherever she pleased in this house, and for as long as she wished her to be there.

She had not made a good start and it was pride which had been her downfall. Pride in her own new skills, pride in the memory of what Miss Monk had said only that morning, pride in herself for what she had overcome, pride in her ability to read, to write, to add long columns of figures and to subtract them again, and in what she knew she could now go on to do if given the chance.

"I beg your pardon, ma'am. I shall, of course, serve in whatever position you choose to give me." Eat humble pie then, if it got her what she wanted in the end. She didn't like it, not one bit, and if there ever came a chance to take the old cow down a peg or two, she'd do it but for now she must smile and bow her head meekly and take anything those above her carelessly flung in her direction. If it opened the door to a bright new life she could take anything.

"Indeed you will, Brindle. Now then, describe to me the duties of a kitchenmaid."

So that was to be it, was it? Bloody kitchenmaid after all she had learned but it could have been worse, she supposed. Scullerymaid, for instance, which consisted of nothing but scrubbing.

Daisy did so.

"And housemaid, if you please. There might come a day when I consider you competent to take on such a position."

Again Daisy did so, explaining in detail all she had been taught at Denton House.

"What would be the correct way to clean marble and the polish to use?"

Daisy told her.

For ten minutes Mrs Crosby questioned her on the cleaning of plate, how to brighten a gilt frame, to preserve bright grates and fire-irons from rust, how to beat a carpet and clean watered silk wallpaper and Daisy answered unhesitatingly but without embellishment, remembering the housekeeper's objection to what she considered to be Daisy's inclination to boast.

"And you can read, I believe."

"Yes, ma'am."

"Hmm!" Maidservants were really getting above themselves, her expression said.

"Turn round."

Daisy turned.

"Show me your hands."

Daisy held out her hands, wishing she had had an opportunity to wash them but they seemed to pass muster.

"You have no clothes other than those you have on."

"No, ma'am."

"Perhaps as well," for God alone knew what gaudy outfit she might take it into her head to wear, the look in her eyes said. "You will be provided with a uniform. Now then, you are to start as scullerymaid..." *Scullerymaid!* After all she had learned, sweated over, worked her fingers to the bone for, she was to be no more than scullerymaid. The old bitch! Pretending she was going to put her on as kitchenmaid and then, perhaps, housemaid and all the while she knew she was going to stick her in the lowest position in the house. She'd be at the beck and call of every other servant, cleaning up everybody else's muck. The first to rise and the last to get to her bed at night, scouring the pans which must all be spotless before she was allowed to leave the scullery. Well, she'd show her. She'd show her what Daisy Brindle was made of and if she thought she was going to get a rise out of her she was mistaken. Not by a flicker of an eyelash would she let her, or anybody, see that she minded. She'd be the best damned scullerymaid this house had ever known and she'd act as though it was the best damned job in this house, see if she didn't. Her face was completely without expression and though she had missed some of what Mrs Crosby had said she gave no indication of it.

". . . and if you shape yourself I might review the situation later. You will rise at five each morning and do anything that is required of you in the kitchen and scullery until dinner has been served in the evening and the kitchen has been cleaned in readiness for the next day. Long hours, but necessary, I am sure you will agree, for a scullerymaid to perform her job properly," and it would be all the same if she didn't.

"Of course, Mrs Crosby."

Mrs Crosby drew back her thin lips in what, for her, passed as a smile.

"I require my girls to be of good behaviour and good character, Brindle. And at no time are you allowed to form . . . attachments with the menservants. Do you take my meaning?" Of course she did, and if Mrs Crosby thought she had the slightest interest in a man, any man, detestable creatures that they were, after what she had suffered at their hands, she was mistaken. True, Mr Greenhalgh had done what he had promised but really, when you considered what Mrs Crosby had said about experiments, had he? It seemed his lordship had had a hand in it and it had not been solely up to the bailiff after all. And she would never, *never* forgive him for taking Cassie away from her, whatever, if anything, he had done for her since.

"Yes, ma'am," she answered, her voice expressionless, her eyes showing no hint of her thoughts.

"Very well then. You will be under the direction of Chef who is in charge of the kitchen, of course, and he will keep me informed of your progress. Now ring the bell, if you please," indicating the brass-handled bellpull beside the fireplace, "and Miller will show you where to go."

Mrs Crosby had at her waist the symbol of her high office, a beautiful silver chatelaine. It had a filigree belt-plate and from it hung keys, a small pin-cushion, scissors in a sheath, a thimble, a silver-covered notebook with ivory leaves, a letter-opener and a fine silver-backed watch. Its workmanship was superb, its value vast for this was a wealthy household. She wore it with evident pride, pride in herself for attaining her high position in this house and in the house itself of which she was the virtual ruler. It was a great house. It was a great family she served and Daisy must be worthy of the honour which was about to be bestowed on her. She rattled the chatelaine as she moved and Daisy knew it was a signal that the interview was over.

There was a discreet knock at the door. "Show Brindle where she will sleep, Miller," she said to the same smart young housemaid who had brought Daisy to her. "See she has the necessary aprons and cap, a working dress, stockings, and then put her in Watson's charge. She will show her what she is to do. That will be all."

"Yes, Mrs Crosby."

They both sketched a curtsey and with scarcely a sound glided from the room. Daisy felt a great desire to let out her breath on a relieved sigh and was ready to turn to Miller and smile, for were they not in the same boat, so to speak, subject to the same strict discipline and condescension, and a friend was always useful . . . but the maid hurried ahead of her, her face quite glacial as she turned impatiently to speak over her shoulder to Daisy.

"Come along, Brindle. I haven't got all day. The family will be down soon and I'm helping in the pantry tonight. I really haven't time for this, you know. Nobody'll do my job while I'm running round after you and if I'm not back in five minutes Mr Petch'll have me on the carpet. Chef's screaming for someone to scrub out the storeroom floor where that half-witted Lewis spilled a jar of treacle and you should see the mess there. She's having hysterics because he slapped her and there's nothing being done."

"Show me where it is and I'll scrub it out." She might as well start right now in her climb to the top which was where she meant to be, and any hand which helped her would be acceptable. And a friend in this overwhelming, even frightening new environment might come in handy one day.

"What . . . ?" Miller stopped so suddenly Daisy almost collided with her.

"Give me an apron and a cap and I'll do it. You can show me my bed later."

Miller's face melted in relief and Daisy thought she was about to embrace her. "Eeh, it wouldn't be fair, not with you only just . . ." but she could not keep the hopeful expression from her face.

"Don't be daft. I've nothing else to do, have I? Unless I'm to sit down to dine with the family."

Miller's somewhat serious face dissolved into laughter, then resumed its solemnity.

"Would you? Would you really? Only Mr Petch is a real tartar and though it's not my fault that Mrs Crosby sent for me . . ."

"No, but it's mine."

"Well, not really, you wasn't to know."

Miller's thankfulness made her ready to forgive Daisy anything. She was herself no more than eighteen or so, a plain, no-nonsense sort of girl who had been tried to the end of her patience by the crisis in the kitchen and the apparent importance of her own participation in the serving of dinner to the family and Daisy's readiness to lend a hand, and her only just over the doorstep, you might say, turned Miller's sharpness to a rare gratitude. They had heard something of the new scullerymaid's history in the servants' hall. Whispers of a man who had died, had been killed actually, in an accident in which this girl had been involved. Shuffled off to a paupers' school she had been then, and her no better than she should be and now they were landed with her. None too pleased Mrs Crosby had been, so it was said, for she liked to engage her own girls and not have them foisted on her as a favour from his lordship to a friend. But here she was, bright and smiling and eager to be about her job within five minutes of taking off her bonnet. Miller liked that. She liked a worker, did Miller.

"Come on then. That's real good of you. I'll show you where everything is and then later, when I've finished, we'll have something to eat. You can sleep next to me if you like."

She got to know them all in the next few days, memorising their faces and their names and which went with which but that first night all she saw was the storeroom floor, the scullery sink and the passage between the two which she had to pass through to empty and refill the bucket. She was on her knees for the best part of two hours, her arms in hot water up to the elbow and she might not have been there at all for all the notice they took of her, those who bustled about, stepping on her clean floor to get this or that from the shelves and cupboards of the vast storeroom. They were all so busy with their own duties, the bent back, the hidden face and the arms which wielded the scrubbing brush might have been any one of half a dozen maids, without identity, without even a name.

"You can start on the stillroom when you've done that," one lofty voice told her. A pair of long black legs stepped over her, took something from a cupboard, then stepped over her again as they hurried from the room.

The stillroom? Where the dickens was that? She stood up and straightened her supple back. She dropped the scrubbing brush into the dirty water, picked up the bucket and moved along the passage to the scullery sink for the twentieth time, emptying the water away, putting the pail beneath the sink and the brush on the ledge amongst the neat row of others. Peeping down the passage and finding it empty she moved along it towards the hum of activity which was coming from the main kitchen. Stepping inside she stood for several moments, her eyes flickering from one corner of the room to the other until she spotted what she thought was the doorway through which she had come earlier. No one took the least notice of her. The chef, or she supposed him to be that, was directing a girl in the garnishing of some dish, and another – could there be two chefs, she thought, astonished – was delicately whisking something in a large bowl. Everyone was completely absorbed with what they were doing and when, just to be on the safe side and so that she might say truthfully that she *did* ask, she took the arm of a passing girl in the uniform of a housemaid and begged to be told where the stillroom might be, the girl tutted impatiently and answered that she was too busy at the moment and to ask her later.

Daisy edged round the perimeter of the kitchen, ready, should someone ask her, to do anything she was told but it almost seemed as though she was invisible. No one even glanced at her. At any other time she would have been fascinated by the activities of those who worked there for though, as she had first thought, it appeared to be chaos and confusion, when she studied those who whirled about she could see that each servant's occupation fitted neatly into one done by another and that the chef, who appeared to do nothing but fling his arms about and screech in a language she could not understand, had it all tidily under his control.

But she had no time now to give more than a cursory glance at what was happening. Just for this moment she was under no one's supervision. She had covered herself by asking where the stillroom was, which would be remembered tomorrow should she be questioned, so now was her chance, perhaps for no more than a few minutes, to slip out and speed across the park to see Cassie.

She found the house without too much difficulty. Country-bred for most of her life, she had a good sense of direction and was not afraid of the dark. The gate opened without a sound and she was crossing Emma Greenhalgh's smooth lawn, a tall, black shadow amongst others, before the gate closed behind her. The dogs in the kennels at the back of the stable, as though sensing an intruder, even so far away, set up a hullabaloo but she was at the front door by then and the sound of her knock made her heart beat faster, joyously faster. It was two years almost to the day since she had been bundled through this very doorway. She had been blind, deaf, almost insensible with loss, with shock for they had caught her off her guard. They had taken Cassie from her just when she had been at the peak of her happiness, whirling her down and down until she had barely known what they were about, but now she was back ready to pick up the threads of that strong bond of love which had tied her and Cassie together, ready to fasten it again so that no one could part them.

It was Dolly the maid who answered the door, her face somewhat apprehensive for who could be knocking at this time of night? Only someone from the house, of course, but even so it was not usual.

Dolly didn't know her. Daisy had grown and was taller than Dolly now. Though she was still slim as a wand, it was no longer the scrawny skin and bone of the half-starved. She was neat, clean, respectable, despite her two hours at the scrub bucket, and her manner was civil.

"I am here to see Cassie," she said, smiling.

"Beg pardon."

"Would you tell Cassie that her sister is here to see her." Daisy might have been visiting gentry as she spoke the words she had rehearsed a hundred times during her training. Not what *she* would ever say in her new employment but what might be said to *her* when she opened her mistress's front door to callers.

Dolly's eyes popped and her face was a picture of consternation but on it was a glimmer, not exactly of recognition for how could this plainly dressed, perfectly decent young woman be that senseless, anguished girl who had left here two years ago? It was more a stirring of memory and really, she had no idea what to do with it, her expression said, now that it had returned, as Daisy had.

There was a flicker of movement behind her. No more than a shadow of white in the lamplit hall, a swirl of some gauzy stuff and the feeling of laughter and wellbeing, of comfort and sanctuary. A man's voice told someone, "...think I left it on my desk, sweetheart..." and a woman's followed saying, "...would misplace his own head if it wasn't fastened to his shoulders."

The drift of white came down the hall and stopped behind Dolly's shoulder and a face, smiling, somewhat vague, but very, very pretty peeped round it. For a second, no more, the face drew back a little, shy, hesitant, then with a silent shout of joy, a mouth widening in delight, eyes glittering with an overflow of tears, Cassie pushed Dolly to one side and flew like a homing bird into Daisy Brindle's arms.

12

She had been at Thornley Green a year before she saw Miles Thornley again and in that time, though she worked just as long and just as hard as she had as a field girl, she was supremely content. She had bettered herself. She had decent, respectable employment. She was under the strict supervision of Mrs Crosby, for within six months she had attained the position of housemaid she had hoped for. Even Mrs Crosby, set against her from the start due to the unconventional way in which she, Daisy, had been engaged, was not blind to the new scullerymaid's capacity to work at twice the speed of the others, the way in which she organised what she did so that it was done efficiently and without getting in the way of anyone else. She had method, skill, was untiring and cheerful but at the same time kept strictly to herself. In other words, the perfect servant and Mrs Crosby, whatever else she might be, was not without the sense to recognise it.

The methodical routine of Daisy's work appealed to something in her which had been repelled by the dirt and disorder of her previous life. She liked the strictly female company since menservants were not allowed, in any way, to mix with the maids except at mealtimes in the servants' hall and then under the watchful eye of Mr Petch, the butler, and Mrs Crosby, the housekeeper. There was no male and lustful eye to fall about her trim figure as she worked, no male hand to interfere with what was not his, no male voice to whisper of what he would do to her when they were alone. Naturally, some of the servants managed to fraternise – though how, she did not know, so strictly watched were they – but she let it be known that Daisy Brindle was concerned only with her duties. A cold fish, they called her, the footmen and grooms, the bootboys and gardeners who intimated that given the chance they would like to be friendly, but after threatening one more bold than the rest with the loss of his job should she report him to Mr Petch, she was never bothered again.

The working offices in which the maids and menservants performed their duties were as considerable and various as their own ranks and though there were servants at Thornley Green who, after six months in service, could still not find their way about the vast house, Daisy knew exactly where everything was within the first month of becoming a housemaid. There were butlers' pantries, linen rooms, knife rooms, plate rooms, lamp rooms, all on the ground floor, naturally, leather rooms, boot rooms, stillrooms, gun rooms, washhouses, mangling rooms, ironing rooms, folding rooms and airing rooms and in every one of these there was a list of strict rules instructing servants in the proper method of carrying out their duties.

But it was *their* part of the house, the family's part of the house, which lifted her to the sublime degree of pleasure to which beauty was always to take her. Beautiful things! The delicacy of Meissen porcelain, which she held in her hands for the first time; of hand-blown, fragile Italian glassware, so clear and ingeniously engraved she could only stare wordlessly at its loveliness. The dainty, beech-framed, silk-upholstered chairs and sofas, piecrust tables of glowing walnut and mahogany, carved giltwood mirrors, elegant white marble fireplaces, silver sugar baskets and tea caddies, ornamental vases of Wedgwood known as Jasper ware and black basaltware. And each and every one to be tended by Daisy Brindle. Put in her care for her to cherish, and love.

There was the conservatory, so filled with beautiful things Miller had to drag her forcibly from the trance into which the sight of it had flung her. White wickerwork furniture heaped with gaily-coloured cushions, white birds in cages singing their heads off, trailing green plants and dazzling flowers like none she had ever seen before, sunshine and warmth in the middle of winter, jardinières overflowing with rare blooms, statuary reclining amongst ferns and a fragrance so heady and sweet it quite took the senses away.

It was almost more than she could bear, the joy of being allowed to care for such wondrous things, and though she understood that she was being fanciful she felt herself to be honoured to do so. She said nothing of this to anyone, of course. They thought her to be odd in any case, with her passion for work, but what did she care, she had never been happier.

There was a more mundane side to her job. A housemaid had her own dustpan and must learn how to hold it, together with a candle, in one hand so that she could brush with the other, but of course Daisy had mastered this at Denton Green and had no need to be shown how to manage it, which was perhaps why she was so swiftly promoted. She knew how to polish the metal fittings on furniture with fine sand, how to clean paintwork with cream dressing, sweep carpets with damp tealeaves, strip off old polish with vinegar and put on new with beeswax and turpentine, wash high ceilings with soda and water while standing on top of a high ladder, dust down brocaded walls and rub them over with tissue paper and a silk duster, take up carpets, whiten corridors with pipeclay and spread French chalk on the ballroom floor, make a bed, black a grate with a mixture of ivory black, treacle, oil, small beer and sulphuric acid, and at what time the sunlight came into each room so that the blinds might be drawn to protect the furniture and carpets against its harmful rays.

And in November, when she had been at Thornley Green thirteen months, she was given a rise from eight pounds to ten a year. She was not liked. The regiment of maids with whom she worked, housemaids, parlourmaids, chambermaids, stillroom, scullery-, kitchen-, laundry- and dairymaids were agreed that she was too quick, too willing, too conscientious, too practical and altogether too hard-working, making their own efforts, though equally carefully performed, appear slow and unhandy. The menservants, from the groom of the chambers, footmen, valets, and chefs, to the kitchenboys and all the outside men, some of whom had been icily rejected by the new and, they admitted, extraordinary new maid – though why they should call her that they were not really sure – soon decided she was not worth the trouble she undoubtedly would cause. You only had to look at that red hair of hers to see she had a quick temper and a sharp tongue and meant every word she said about reporting them to Mr Petch. ·

She had one friend in the house, which surely was enough, she contentedly told herself, and that was Bess Miller, the young housemaid who had taken her to Mrs Crosby's room on the first day she had arrived and who had never forgotten Daisy's offer of help, but even then they were not true friends, merely respecting one another's capabilities and therefore ready to side together against the others in any argument. Daisy had been too long alone in the first ten years of her life to get the hang of friendship. She had always been self-sufficient, needing no one until she had taken Cassie under her wing and every ounce of feeling, of love, she had was directed still in Cassie's direction. As for Miles Thornley, the emotion he had awakened in her was kept soft and secret in a place where no one was allowed, a shining jewel locked away, taken out and held in reverent hands when she was alone.

She had only one sadness and though, in her heart, she admitted to herself that it was what, if she was brutally honest, she had known would happen, it was a bitter test of her firm resolve to realise that the new life she and Cassie were to have together could never take place.

They had both wept that first night, she noisily, harshly, her eyes red and swollen with tears, Cassie with that incredible, quite exquisite spilling of crystal droplets which slipped from her pansy eyes and down her cheeks without effort.

"Cassie ... Cassie ... oh, Cassie ..." She could say no more as she held the slender, newly budding figure of the girl she called her sister in her arms. Cassie's head fitted just beneath Daisy's chin and her soft hair, tied elaborately with a velvet ribbon of apple green to match those on her dress, drifted across Daisy's face. Cassie made no sound but her velvet eyes spoke of her joy and when Emma Green-halgh bustled into the hallway to see what all the fuss was about Cassie would not let go of Daisy, throwing off the restraining arms of the woman who had loved her as her own for two years, clinging to Daisy and trembling with some deep emotion only Daisy understood.

"It's all right, it's all right, Cassie. I'm not going away again, ever," she whispered in Cassie's ear. "I promise you. I'm here now and I'll never leave you again."

"Well, we didn't expect to see you tonight," Mrs Green-halgh said tartly, not afraid exactly, since how could this girl who was, she had heard, to be no more than a skivvy at the big house, take away her darling from her, not now, not after two years, but not liking the passionate show of devotion she herself had never received from Cassandra just the same. "Mrs Crosby is very good in allowing you to come over so soon."

Emma Greenhalgh had been bitterly against having Daisy Brindle back again to disturb the delightful tempo of the life she had created for Cassandra and herself and had told Robert so right from the start, but as he said, it was really nothing to do with him now. Lord Thornley had not been overly concerned with what happened to Daisy Brindle. But Sir Christopher Faulkner was, the silly old buffer. A memory like an elephant, the old fool had, and though no mention had been made of her, at least in Robert's hearing, from the day she left to go to Denton Green, right out of the blue his lordship had said that Sir Christopher had reminded him of her and she was to be given a post in the house. Quite interested, it seemed, at least Sir Christopher was, to see what the pauper child had made of herself and now, here she was, grown into a decent young woman with the child he and Emma considered to be their own, weeping their combined joy at being reunited.

But still, what could Daisy Brindle do now that Cassandra was legally theirs, he asked himself. Lord Thornley's lawyer had arranged it all, since the child, who could never, of course, marry, must be adequately safeguarded after they were both gone.

"She will confuse the child, Robert, and revive memories that are best forgotten. See how happy she is . . ." and they had both watched indulgently as 'Cassandra', as they now called her, the name so much more appropriate than 'Cassie', had hung over a basket of kittens on the safe acre of lawn in which she had only, at first, been allowed to wander.

"Perhaps she will not even remember the girl, Emma," Robert had said soothingly but it was very evident from this . . . this performance in the hallway that she did.

For an hour they had sat together on Emma's plush sofa, hands clasped, smiling at one another, Cassandra nodding delightedly as Daisy reminded her of the 'linnet-singing competition', 'the pastry feast and those lovely black puddings', 'that first bath we took in Rainford Brook', all pleasant memories that could hurt no one, her eyes told the anxious Emma who hovered, ready to snatch her darling away should she show signs of distress, and the devil of it was, Cassandra was . . . well . . . one could only call it more *knowing* than Emma had ever seen her. She never spoke, of course. Emma had given over trying to converse with her long ago, which had, now that she saw her with Daisy, perhaps been a mistake, but she was always happy, loving, ready to laugh, and everyone from Ted Whittaker and Zack in the yard, to Robert himself, absolutely adored her. She was a child, *their* child, and it was mortifying to see the way she responded to Daisy Brindle.

Reluctantly Daisy stood up and immediately Cassie began to cry.

"There, there, darling, come to Grandmother," Emma said, amazingly, holding out her arms, but her 'darling' clung, as she had always done in the past, to Daisy.

It took another ten minutes to soothe her back to reluctant acceptance that Daisy would come again and then it had only been through Daisy that it was managed. She had held the child's lovely face between gentle hands, gazing stead-fastly into Cassie's eyes, forcing her to be calm, to stop that crying, to believe, *believe* because Daisy promised it, that she would be back soon.

"When?" Cassie's eyes asked but only Daisy knew what it was they said.

"I don't know when. I work at the big house now. You know where I mean?"

Cassie nodded that she did, her eyes still brimming.

"I have to stay there until they say I can come but I am only a little way away, and ... look at me, Cassie ..." and Cassie obeyed her "... I will be back soon. Do you believe me?" and Cassie, it seemed, did.

At first, until she had made Cassie understand that she herself was working for a living, as she had in the fields and the pit, and could not simply put aside what she was doing and go out into the park to 'play' with her, whenever Cassie wanted her to, Cassie was constantly at the kitchen door of Thornley Green looking for her. They all knew her, the servants, for in the two years she had been there, with the resilience of the six-year-old child she still mentally was, she had gained the confidence to leave the sanctuary of the cocoon Emma Greenhalgh would have kept her in, escaping from the garden and wandering up to the men who worked in the park, the stableyard, watching what they were doing, smiling in delight when she was allowed to 'help'. She had become a favourite with them all. Though she was still shy, hesitant with those she did not know, they watched out for her, saved sweetmeats to give her, won her trust, captivated by her silent charm and delicate loveliness.

Daisy went as often as she could to the bailiff's house, and that was another thing which separated her from the rest of the servants. She took tea with Mrs Greenhalgh who was, after all, the bailiff's wife, and they did not trust it, those with whom she worked, for who knew what she might be saying to Mrs Greenhalgh who in turn could pass it on to Mr Greenhalgh and so to his lordship? They were not to know that Emma Greenhalgh and Daisy Brindle barely exchanged a word on these awkward occasions nor that the only frail thread which kept pulling Daisy back to the bailiff's house was the thirteen-year-old child whose name was now

Cassandra Greenhalgh, and who, Emma was painfully aware, would not survive another separation from the girl who had been her only comfort and security for three long and appalling years. Emma had seen Daisy Brindle's scarred back. She had heard from Robert of the work the two little girls had been forced to do in the pit at St Helens and her mind had recoiled from it. She would watch the dainty figure of the child she called her granddaughter, so ethereal it seemed she might blow away on the first stray breeze, and she could scarcely bear to think of what she had suffered.

Daisy and Cassie, due more to Cassie's ability to weep brokenheartedly if she was thwarted which Emma Green-halgh could not bear, were allowed to walk alone in the small wood which lay to the side of Robert Greenhalgh's home during that first summer, whenever Daisy had a free hour which was too often in Emma's opinion. She and Robert truly loved their 'granddaughter' but as the months moved on and it became apparent that Daisy was to become no threat to what Emma and Cassandra shared, that Daisy had no intention, now, of trying to entice Cassie away, that she had accepted that Cassandra was better off where she was, an uneasy truce was formed between them. Though Emma did not like it she allowed the loving friendship to blossom again, to continue as it had once done. She was not an unkind woman, merely jealous of the affection she was forced to share with another but if her 'darling' was safe and happy she was prepared to put up with it.

It was Christmas when Miles Thornley came home. Daisy had heard his name mentioned, naturally, for when Mr Petch and Mrs Crosby were absent the servants gossiped amongst themselves about the family and the 'goings-on' of the family guests who came for 'Fridays to Mondays', for the hunting season, the fishing, the grouse in August. They always brought their own valets and ladies' maids, the great ladies and gentlemen who came to stay at Thornley Green, and there would often be titbits of scandal exchanged in the servants' hall and though Daisy would listen idly, not overly concerned with what, after all, could have no bearing on her own advancement in life, when his name was spoken, her heart surged and banged painfully in her chest.

"His young lordship's just arrived." That was the name by which he was known amongst themselves though as the son of a baron he was, of course, only accorded the title 'The Honourable Miles Thornley'. It was Talbot, the under footman, who told them the news, three days before Christmas. "And you've never seen so many boxes in your life. God knows what's in them. You'd best look sharp, Mason," to the second footman who was trimming lamps in the lamp room, just off the kitchen, "and you too, Ogden, because he's in a filthy mood and you know what that means."

Daisy was collecting the damp tealeaves which were saved from the dozens and dozens of pots of tea which were brewed in a day at Thornley Green – for the servants denied themselves nothing they had a fancy for in this wealthy house – putting them to one side in readiness for the cleaning of the carpet in the great drawing room. There was to be a Christmas party with more than fifty guests on Christmas Eve and the whole room to be done tomorrow and she and Bess were to clean it between them. They worked well together, she and Miller, and though Mrs Crosby hated to admit it since she still felt her wishes had been overlooked when Daisy Brindle had been set on without her say-so, she was honest enough to admit that in Brindle and Miller she had two of the most trustworthy and hard-working servants in the household.

Daisy didn't know who they were talking about and didn't much care. She was listening with only half an ear as Mason hurriedly drew on his liveried jacket.

"He's always the same when he comes home. He has to behave himself when his Papa's watching. He managed to escape it last year, being abroad an' all, but he couldn't avoid it again. Master Miles has to toe the line if he wants to continue with the fine life he leads, and the means his lordship allows him to do it . . ."

Master Miles! She heard no more than that and it was as if something vital inside her had slipped. They were talking about Master Miles! *Her* Miles, though she shouldn't really refer to him as that, even to herself, since he was so far above her, but in her innermost heart she always considered that it was because of him that she was here today. He was a kind of talisman, a good-luck piece, *her* good-luck piece because it was through him and what had happened six years ago that she had set herself the challenge of becoming something other than a common field girl. And she had done it, and now after all these years she was to see him again, perhaps be of service to him in some way. Not that he would notice, but *she* would know and be glad that she could repay him.

"... because he wanted to go in the army and of course his lordship wouldn't allow it. Well, he is the heir and the only son and if anything happened to him the line would die out. But I reckon if he'd been allowed it he'd not be the beggar he is."

It was Susan Tipping, the upper housemaid, who was airing her views and Daisy's hands stilled as she edged nearer to the table in the centre of the kitchen where Tipping was setting a tray for her mistress who had just rung for tea. Tipping was a woman of about thirty and had been employed at Thornley Green ever since she had been taken on as a kitchenmaid seventeen years ago. She had her sights on Mrs Crosby's position when the housekeeper retired which surely could not be long now, and of all the servants she was the best informed of the family's history.

"... he's got nothing to do, you see. His lordship has the estate, doesn't he, with Mr Greenhalgh to manage the farms and so Master Miles spends his time gambling and in other pastimes which don't bear mentioning in the presence of ..."

"Tipping!" Mary-Ellen Frost, another upper housemaid and only a year or two behind Tipping in the hierarchy of the servants' hall, spoke warningly.

"It's true. They say the devil finds mischief for idle hands and ever since he left Cambridge he's been junketing around Europe with those fast friends of his and I bet his lordship doesn't know half of what he gets up to."

"And I suppose you do." The words were out of Daisy's

mouth before she could stop them but it was too late even if she had wanted to. "You seem to know a lot more than a housemaid should and most of it your imagination, I'll be bound. Well, you'd better watch what you're saying or you could be in more trouble than you bargained for." She could have bitten her tongue, really she could, but it had already done its damage. It had got her into difficulties as long ago as the incident in the ale-house when she had accused the gangmaster of stealing from the gangwomen's wages, and that had done no good, only drawn her to the gangmaster's attention, which was what was happening now.

They all turned to stare at her, nonplussed, for Brindle was not much of a one for joining in any gossip, or even ordinary, everyday conversation which circulated about the kitchen or servants' hall. She got on with her work, busy from morning till night with her own duties, bothering no one, and they had become used to her. She'd give a hand when asked and though certainly not popular she had become more or less tolerated. Her friendship with the little slip of a thing who'd been taken in by Mr Greenhalgh and his wife – said to be her sister, though that couldn't be true – had caused no real trouble and for the most part they scarcely noticed her. The menservants who had initially eyed her appreciatively and been ready for a bit of 'fun' if she was, often wondered what it was they had seen in her, for more often than not she enveloped herself in a shapeless cleaning apron and a balloon of a cap which covered her bright hair, doing away with any pretence to the looks she might have had. Now, in the strangest way, she had come vitally to life. Her pale skin was flushed with rose at the cheekbone, her brown eyes were hot and fierce and somehow, just as though only escape from the cap would do, her hair seemed to break from beneath it into a dozen curling tendrils.

"Well, I have never heard such insolence in my life and you can be sure this will be reported to Mrs Crosby." Tipping was mortified. She put her hands on her hips and glared at Daisy to let them all know, particularly Brindle, that no one, *no one*, least of all an under housemaid, would go unchallenged in the face of *her* authority. It was not to be flouted in any shape or form, neither was her knowledge, received first-hand from Kitty Green who was Lady Mary's personal maid and Susan Tipping's personal friend, of many of the family's secrets. She knew exactly what was said about the heir to Thornley Green by his father, who had to pay his gambling debts, to his mother, who could not bear to have her boy chastised. He was wild, the Honourable Miles Thornley, but then so were most young men of his age but there was no badness in him, his mother said, and perhaps it was true, but it was known that a pretty maidservant was fair game to the young lordling and only the ferociously keen eye and strong sense of moral duty which Mrs Crosby possessed had kept more than one or two as chaste as they should be.

Daisy could be imperious too when she chose, as now, when she bristled up to Tipping. "Tell Mrs Crosby by all means for if she became aware that you were maligning the name of his lordship's son you would be out of here so fast that whippet Dewhurst keeps wouldn't be able to catch you."

They were stunned, every last one of them. It was not only the way in which Brindle dared to speak to Tipping who was her superior, nor the truth of the words for if Mrs Crosby did know Tipping would be in deep trouble, but the actual words which Brindle had used. None of them could read, nor write. They had come when they were barely more than children, most of them, since their families needed even the small wage they earned, to learn their trade in the kitchens, the dairies, the gardens of Thornley Green and that did not include being taught to read, as Brindle had been.

It was perhaps because she was not awfully sure, not only of her ground since she should not have been gossiping, but of all that had been said to her, except the last part, which was true, that Tipping backed off and Daisy breathed a sigh of relief. Another minute and she might have given away her true feelings for Master Miles Thornley and that would have been disastrous. As it was, they had her named as a double-tongued troublemaker who might run to Mr

Petch or Mrs Crosby with tales of what was said behind their backs. It hadn't done her much good but at least her secret was safe. She was almost ready to strike Tipping for what she had said about Master Miles. Just as if anyone as fine, as splendid, as he could be anything other than the English gentleman he so obviously was, but she must be careful what she said in future.

"I should get back to work if I were you, Brindle," was all Tipping could find to say, "otherwise tales might be told to Mr Petch or Mrs Crosby of certain servants who neglect their duties."

She looked for him wherever she went. She was not one of those who 'saw' to his bedroom and sitting room and even if she had been it was doubtful she would have caught a glimpse of him since all the cleaning was done on the upper floors whilst the family and guests were at breakfast, and should a maid be caught on a corridor, God forbid, she had instructions to vanish into the nearest linen cupboard, or failing that to flatten herself as invisibly as she could manage against the wall. Servants must be as self-effacing as was humanly possible, with no shape or form or substance and certainly no voice unless personally addressed. No more than a pair of hands which served, or cleaned, ironed shirts or polished boots.

She managed to slip across to see Cassie on Christmas Day. She had been paid in October when she had been at Thornley Green for a year, the first money she had ever earned, or at least the first to be put in *her* hand for her to spend as she liked. Though some of it had been spent on a couple of dress lengths for herself, one in a tawny golden wool, soft and glowing, for winter, the other a light sprigged muslin of the palest cream for summer, and a pair of stout leather boots which must do for both, she had bought a length of the prettiest white lawn and made Cassie a petticoat. It was appliquéd with white lace, the cost prohibitive but so lovely she could not resist it and what else had she to spend her small amount of spare money on? She knew Mr and Mrs Greenhalgh bought their 'granddaughter' more dainty and expensive dresses and soft kid boots, ribbons and fans and reticules than any girl of Cassie's age could ever wear but the petticoat was stitched by her own hand in the light of a candle long after the other girls were asleep, and stitched with love.

"Very pretty, I'm sure," Mrs Greenhalgh said, somewhat put out by what she considered Cassandra's unseemly joy and not at all pleased that her granddaughter, who was usually as docile as a nesting dove, had insisted upon giving Daisy a Christmas gift in return. Only a bunch of ribbons but of the loveliest golden velvet which was the perfect colour for Daisy's hair and the perfect match for her new dress. It really was amazing how the child became more ... well ... sharp ... when anything which concerned Daisy Brindle was ventured. It was as though the very sound of the girl's name lit some tiny spark of intelligence in Cassandra's poor mind.

The house was decorated with holly and ivy, with mistletoe and a large 'tree of love', the Christmas tree introduced by Her Majesty's husband, Prince Albert, soon after their marriage. It was covered with small trinkets, tinsel, silver-wrapped chocolates and a hundred candles and Daisy was as enraptured as Cassie since this was the first time she had been so close to such a beautiful thing. Of course there was one twice as big at the house and the servants had been allowed to peep from the minstrels' gallery in the great hall but this moment, shared with Cassie, was as precious to her as any they had ever known. Mrs Greenhalgh had gone to the kitchen, loth to leave her darling alone with the girl she thought of as a rival, but some crisis had called her away and Daisy and Cassie were left by themselves for a moment.

"Did you ever think we'd see the likes of this, Cass?" There was absolutely no way Daisy could call her Cassie 'Cassandra' and she never did so, to Mrs Greenhalgh's chagrin. "When we were working the fields and sleeping rough did we ever imagine this kind of thing existed?" She was the only one who talked to Cassie sensibly, treating her not as a charming child, but as a growing girl.

Cassie stared, mesmerised, into the tiny leaping flames of the candles, then turned to Daisy and shook her head. She

185

took Daisy's hand and leaned against her, her head on Daisy's shoulder. She wore white with a rose-pink velvet sash, rose-pink velvet slippers and ribbons to match in her hair. She looked exquisite but beside her Daisy was just as striking. She had made up the soft tawny wool into a gown which was simple but surprisingly elegant. She had a good eye and a retentive memory and she had paid careful attention to the fashionable gowns worn by the ladies who were guests at Thornley Green. It was close-fitting in the bodice, fastened down the front with two dozen tiny pearl buttons. She had edged the neck and cuffs in satin ribbon of the same shade and made a narrow satin sash for her slender waist, tied at the front in a becoming bow. The skirt was full and graceful, the only jarring note the stout black boots which were all she owned.

"All those years you and me slaved but we came through, didn't we, Cass? And now we're safe and cosy."

Cassie nodded understandingly.

"You *are* happy here, aren't you, Cassie?" Daisy lifted Cassie's chin and looked gravely into the young girl's soft eyes. "You like being here with Mr and Mrs Greenhalgh, because if you don't . . ." If you don't, you've only to give me the nod and you and me'll be off, the unspoken words said, but Cassie smiled then put her arms about Daisy and hugged her. She stood away, letting Daisy see her expression which told Daisy all she needed to know. It said that if Daisy could be with her all the time it would be lovely, but she couldn't so Cassie must be content with what they had. She seemed to know, just at that moment, that she could not really function as she should on her own, that she was really no more than a child who would always need someone to care for her. Daisy had done it once. Now Mr and Mrs Greenhalgh had taken over, accepting the affection she gave them, which she needed to give to someone and though Daisy would always come first she was happy with the man and woman who had taken her in.

Her eyes told Daisy this, hoping for understanding, and as she saw it in Daisy's eyes she lost her seriousness and when Mrs Greenhalgh returned Cassie had unbraided

Daisy's hair and was tying the ribbons which were her own special gift into its thick, rippling curls.

"Oh, Cassandra, darling, don't you know it's not seemly for Daisy to have her hair hanging down her back like that," her doting grandmother cried, and really had there ever been anything quite so beautiful as Daisy Brindle's hair? It had a life of its own, so vivid it was like fire in the dim midwinter afternoon. It swirled to the girl's buttocks, so heavy it tipped her head back, and how she managed it day in and day out with the work she had to do was a mystery to Emma Greenhalgh. But when Daisy would have rebraided it Cassie grew fretful, her eyes telling Daisy she wanted to see her own lovely golden Christmas gift in Daisy's free-flowing tangle of curls.

"But, Cassie, Mrs Crosby would have a fit if I turned up at the kitchen door with my hair like this," not to mention all those leering men who would be bound to think that with her hair all over the place she was anybody's for the taking. She always kept it fastened severely back, mostly under a cap since she was by now well aware of her changed appearance when her hair was loose. She had borrowed Bess Miller's old black cloak to fling over her new dress since there would have been some comment about it otherwise. Having all worked like slaves since five thirty this morning – after only a few hours' sleep for last night's merriment among the guests had kept them up until one thirty this morning – the servants had been allowed a Christmas dinner of their own and a drink or two, which, in some cases, had become more than two. Talbot had pinched a bit of mistletoe which he had hung above the pantry door and there had been more than a few amorous scuffles beneath it whilst Mr Petch and Mrs Crosby had their backs turned. Though the kitchen staff were supposedly under the direction of the chef – a gentleman by the name of Pierre, if you please – he was of a somewhat volatile nature, being French she assumed, contemptuous of those without his skills, and only in control of himself, or so Daisy thought, when he was actually preparing and cooking a meal. He and his assistants, half a dozen of them, were really a class apart from the other servants and providing his ovens and his floor, his pans and pots and spoons were spotless, Pierre kept himself somewhat aloof from the 'common herd'. He spoke in a language no one could understand, bandying words about such as *daubière*, which turned out to be his stewing-pan, for goodness' sake, *croutons*, which were only bits of fried bread, *flamber* and *foncer*, and other such nonsense, but at least he wasn't forever watching you like Mrs Crosby or Mr Petch who would be sure to give her what for if she was not respectably neat and tidy.

But though both she and Mrs Greenhalgh coaxed her, Cassie had set her heart on Daisy leaving her hair hanging free. "She's overexcited," Mrs Greenhalgh mouthed over Cassie's head, just as though Cassie really was the six-year-old she seemed for most of the time still to be, and as Daisy stepped out beyond the gate – 'humouring the child', as Mrs Greenhalgh put it – which led from the Greenhalgh gardens into the small strip of wood beside it, her face still soft, her eyes shining, her cloak swinging back from her shoulders, Miles Thornley, for the first time in his life, was quite speechless as he came face to face with her.

They both stopped and became quite, quite still. He was the first to regain his voice.

"Good God," he said softly, his eyes narrowing in masculine predatory appreciation.

She did not even bob a curtsey. She knew a moment of what she could only call timelessness. In that moment all the small pleasures she had known in the past, all the hopes of those to come in the future filled her mind and fused together. The smell of primroses as she and Cassie had walked the spring lanes, the sound of the cuckoo in the deep wood, the first time she had tasted what Pierre called 'meringue', the colour of the sky over the roofs of Thornley Green, Thornley Green itself. How could she explain it? As his vivid, incredibly blue eyes smiled down into hers, filled with his astonished admiration, it was as though she was a musical instrument and his glance was the passing of a hand over it.

She dare not move in case she broke the spell.

"Where did *you* spring from?" he asked at last, doing her the courtesy of not allowing his eyes to run over her body as he normally would with a pretty girl of her class. She was not of his own, he knew that, for a girl with the same breeding as his would not be out here alone, but she was very different from the servant girls he had known and enjoyed ever since he was fifteen.

At last she found her voice but her eyes still clung to his. She was not to know that he was not really listening to what she said, for what went on in the lives of those who were put on this earth to serve him was no concern of his.

"I came to visit ... Mr and Mrs Greenhalgh." Her voice was no more than a thread of sound in her throat for indeed she felt as though she was in a dream and she wanted no loud noise to wake her from it.

"Did you indeed? Are you related to the family then?" which was possible since Robert Greehalgh, despite his position as Lord Thornley's bailiff, came from humble stock.

"Oh no."

"Then ... ?" His smile was teasing, his manner telling her that she had no need to be afraid, or in awe of him. He was merely charmed by her and as such was longing to know a little more about her even if he had to wheedle it out of her. In fact he would find it delightful to do so. That hair was the most magnificent thing he had ever seen and the thought of getting his hands in it, of finding out if the rest of her was just as glorious, was something he would find extremely enjoyable.

"I have a ... well, I call her my sister though we are not really related. We were brought up together ..." If only she could catch her breath but it kept coming up into her throat then sliding down again in the most sickening – and delightful – manner, making it difficult not only to speak, but to think of the words to say. "Mr Greenhalgh was ... kind ... she lives with him now ... she is thirteen ..."

"And is she as beautiful as you?"

Daisy smiled for the first time and Miles Thornley, for a fraction of a second, felt it in that barely used part of his anatomy, his heart, and he was taken by surprise. Her face was like a fine creamy candle, her skin almost transparent and her eyes so light and clear a brown they had turned to amber. Her mouth, which was the pale colour of an apricot and only a moment ago had been unsure, soft, full, a child's mouth, was now wide and laughing, stretched over teeth which were white and even. Her neck was long and smooth and her tiny breasts peaked against the soft wool of her tawny gown. And peeping from beneath the skirt were the heavy black boots. He pretended not to see them.

"Cassie is the most beautiful girl in the world," she said, pushing back her heavy hair with an impatient hand, wishing she had fastened it back as she left the Greenhalghs' front door. It was then he saw what she was. Her hands gave her away. They were roughened, red, the nails short, some broken. Perfectly clean but the hands of a servant and he knew he would have her then, just as he had any woman he fancied.

But he would play with this one. By God, he would enjoy it. He had to stay at home and do his duty for the next few months. Pretend an interest in the damned estate or his father would refuse to pay the gambling debts he had incurred since he left Cambridge, but this beauty – no, she was not really beautiful, she was more than that – would make those months a little less tedious.

"May I walk a little way with you?" he said gravely. "Wherever you are going," knowing full well where that was but pretending, beginning the game of seduction he knew so well and when Daisy bobbed her head, too full to speak, he gently took her arm and began to lead her into the little wood just as though she was the grandest lady in the land.

13

She was lost, of course, from that first moment. She had loved him for so long in a pure and childlike way, believing him to be the most honourable – was that not what he was called – man to walk the earth and she found no reason to alter her opinion when, against all that was sensible, he chose to make a friend of her.

He was careful with her at first, delighting in her innocence, which, when he was ready, he would take from her. He had never in the past had a fancy for virgin flesh, believing it to be tedious, for how could a woman who had known no man's body, please his? but for the time being Daisy was his pure little dove, his delight, untouched and unsullied, so inexperienced she had no conception of how she affected him, which was, of course, part of her charm.

That first day he walked her no further than the far edge of the stand of trees which lay beside the Greenhalgh home but though he knew she was more than willing to share an hour with him he also knew that should he not get her back to the kitchen within that hour there would be an outcry that would reach not only the old harpy who was his mother's housekeeper, but his mother herself. At Thornley Green the son of the house, or indeed any of his wild and reckless friends of which he had more than a few since his sort always hung together, were not allowed to tamper with his lordship's housemaids. His father was a moral, god-fearing man and how he had ever sired a son such as himself who liked nothing better than to enjoy life to the very fullest, and then beyond, he was never to know but one did one's best to overcome it and so far, though how long it would last was anyone's guess, his father had unwillingly baled him out of a couple of bad scrapes, believing his mother when she told him it was no more than boyish high spirits. Boyish high spirits and himself nearly twenty-two but if the old fool was gullible enough to believe it, who was *he* to argue?

She told him her name that first day, scarcely able to speak she felt so shy, so bewitched, so disbelieving that this was happening to her, that this fascinating, incredibly handsome, god-like creature should find her worthwhile. She could feel the warmth of his hand on the inside of her arm long after they had parted and almost, *almost* forgot to put up her hair as they made their way back to the house, keeping as close to the trees as they could. If he had not courteously indicated – dear God, his manners were impeccable – that it might be wiser to do so she would have run into the kitchen with it swinging about her like a great bloody cloak.

"I shall look out for you tomorrow, Daisy," he said gravely, just before she slipped through the arched gateway which led into the yard at the back of the house. "Now that we are friends..." He did not finish the sentence for the simple reason that the goodness and beauty of her eyes quite bowled him over. He was to wonder why, five minutes after he left her, smiling to himself at his own foolishness, and yet ... pleasure. It was a long time since his jaded senses had been quite so intrigued as this. It was going to be a most enjoyable winter!

The hunt met at Thornley Green the following day but before that the traditional Boxing Day gift was given out to every servant, all appropriate to each man's, or woman's, rank. Daisy and the rest of the lower housemaids received a length of serviceable navy-blue serge, good quality and meant to last a lifetime. She knew the others were not overjoyed, preferring to have something pretty, or frivolous, something they themselves could not afford and therefore would not buy, and besides not many of them could sew as well as she did, but if she could beg a bit of colourful material from Green, her ladyship's maid who was quite often handed down her ladyship's 'old' gowns, she might make an elegantly lined cloak. A bright shade to back the plain navy, or edge the collar and cuffs. It only took a bit of imagination to turn what would be a plain cloak into one with style and then she would have no need to borrow Bess Miller's old one when she went out on her afternoons off – perhaps to meet *him* again – but she did not allow that thought to insinuate itself into her mind for more than a fraction of a second.

He was there in the great hall when the servants were assembled but she kept her eyes down, afraid to look up at him in case he was looking at her, afraid to look up at him in case he was not. Someone would notice her, see the expression on her face, see her eyes warm and soften, see her lips part and become moist with ... She got no further than that as her gift was put into her hands and a voice wished her a Happy New Year in cultured tones. She bobbed her curtsey, conscious of her pretty frilled and fluted cap which she had put on for the first time that morning – for him, of course – though she told herself it was because it was Christmas. She had swept up her hair neatly but the coils were not so severely dragged back and a curl or two strayed engagingly on to the arch of her long white neck.

She was at a bedroom window when the hunt moved off, half a hundred elegant horsemen and women, the ladies sewn into their tight-fitting costumes only half an hour since by their maids, Bess told her, and riding side-saddle. And him! So beautiful she thought she would die of love for him. He was in scarlet, like his father, or hunting pink as it was called, for one day he would be Master of Foxhounds as his lordship now was. The winter sun burnished his hair to the gloss of the dark mahogany of the table she herself polished in the great hall. His teeth gleamed in his brown face as he laughed at something one of the ladies said and Daisy felt the first savage pangs of jealousy tear at her as the lady put her hand on his well-muscled thigh.

Then, strangely, he turned away and looked up to where she hid behind the heavy brocade of the curtains she had been cleaning with tissue and as though he knew she was there he raised his tall hat in a gesture so gallant she almost swept aside the curtains to wave to him.

He made no move to go near her in the house though he knew he could have accosted her in any of the half-dozen rooms she cleaned, all of them empty at the time of day she was there. He had no wish to frighten her into bolting, which his instinct told him she would do if alarmed, so he waited, as 'good as gold now' he heard his mother say to his father, though she certainly meant something entirely different, and when Daisy came back from her next visit to Cassie, he was there, at the edge of the wood, a superb white flower in his hand.

"It's an orchid," he said simply, "out of my mother's conservatory. Smell it," and when she did its fragrance was so delicately lovely it was almost more than she could bear. "I thought of you when I saw it. I thought it was the most beautiful flower I had ever seen so I brought it for you."

She had seen the very same flower herself when she and Bess had scrubbed the conservatory floor and had not particularly cared for it. Its waxy perfection had seemed to her, accustomed to the casual beauty of meadow flowers, to be unnatural and stilted but now, given from his hand, declaring his thoughts of her when they were apart, it took on the pricelessness of the Crown jewels.

"It's . . ." There was nothing she could say to describe how she felt. She gazed at it, the implication of his offering of it endowing the bloom with a quality it had not previously possessed. The white was whiter, surely, and its flesh-pink centre quite exquisite but it was not the flower which overwhelmed her, of course it wasn't, but his gift of it to her, who was no more than a servant girl. She held it in her hands, cupping it reverently between them, her eyes studying its new perfection, no thought in her head of how she was to explain it to the servants, several of whom had seen the inside of Lady Mary's winter garden and would know it had come from there. For the moment it was enough that she held it in her hands, his gift to her, his concern for her pleasure which was the sweetest gift of all.

The silence lasted for almost a minute. He studied the top

of her head, fascinated by the startling white of her parting, the long silken length of her lashes, a shade or two darker than her hair, and which brushed her cheeks, the delicate curl of her mouth which, even when she was unsmiling and serious as she was now, turned up at each corner.

"I don't know what to say. No one has ever given me a flower before," she said at last in a low voice.

"Say nothing, Daisy. It is not needed. I can see you like it and so I am happy and as for the last, every man you have ever met must be blind or a fool."

She blushed charmingly. "It is the ... the first gift I have ... ever had..." then she remembered the ribbons from Cassie and she looked up swiftly, putting her hand to the heavy coil at the back of her neck where they lay "... except for these..."

"The ribbons." He moved a step nearer to her, ready to put out a hand to touch them, to touch her, for really she was the sweetest thing and he knew he couldn't wait another moment to have her long and lovely body stripped of all its wrappings and close to his, her lips opening beneath his, then he stopped himself. No, by God, he mustn't move too quickly or, knowing himself, it would all be over by the end of January and he wanted it to last. He wanted to savour that first time, to look forward to it, for he knew it would be quite splendid. She had a look about her, shy as she was with him, which he recognised, and which said she would be sensual, responsive and would be all the more exciting for the wait. There was a woman in St Helens whom he could pay to satisfy his bodily needs quickly, simply, and without fuss until this enchantress was ripe for the picking and *he* would decide when that was. He would woo her, just as though she was a lady. The thought was so piquant he almost laughed out loud.

"Cassie gave them to me for Christmas." For a moment he couldn't recall what she was talking about and didn't much care, really, for his mind was conjuring with erotic pictures of a most delightful kind. Perhaps the cap ... and the apron he had seen her in ... black stockings or was that being a trifle plebeian? ... something unusual ... he was sure he would think of something...

He shook himself from his daydream.

"Cassie?" he murmured. His eyes had changed colour with his thoughts. They narrowed to an expression which, for a fleeting moment, Daisy recognised but before she could get a good grip on it it was gone and her heart wrenched with love for him as he looked gravely down at her.

"She's the girl I told you about. The one who I think of as my sister."

"Tell me about her, and about yourself. Have you five minutes to spare to walk a little way into the wood?" and again he took her arm so politely, so gently, guiding her away from the bailiff's house, through the little wood, across a small clearing and deeper into what was known as Rough Wood. There were woodcock, partridge and pheasant to be had here, reared by his lordship's gamekeepers. When spring came and birds were mating and rearing young broods the men would walk the estate shooting stoats, weasels, polecats, jays, magpies, hawks and owls, all the creatures which destroy the young birds, but now it was empty and devoid of all animal sounds. Only the birds themselves could be heard and they grew quiet as Daisy Brindle and Miles Thornley walked amongst them.

"I think I came through here six years ago," she said, looking about her. For a moment the lovely flower which she held to her nose and the man who had given it to her became misted and she was again that scruffy urchin, barefoot and breathless, who had darted through the trees and across the parkland to bring help to a young boy who had needed it, needed her. Six years and now they were both full-grown, a man and a woman, and the time between, so much of it scarcely to be thought of without pain, had brought them to this place together again. Not that she thought of Miles Thornley in that way, at least not consciously. Not as a man, to her woman, for such thoughts were not for the likes of her. He was a gentleman and would one day marry a lady but if she could just consider him as

... as a friend, know that he looked on her as one, if she could serve him and his family faithfully in this decent life they had given her, she would be content.

"You came through here?" he prompted, astonished. "Through this wood? What on earth for, and how?" since trespassers were severely dealt with, his expression said.

"You don't remember?" She turned to look at him, a faint look of disappointment on her face. The incident was so important to her. The most important in her life, and yet could she expect him to recall that small, ten-year-old child, covered in filth and, yes, she admitted it, crawling with vermin. He had not changed except to grow taller and more handsome but she had, and she smiled as she thanked God for it. "Of course you don't."

"Tell me, for pity's sake, before I expire in anticipation."

"It was the day your horse broke its leg. You jumped the gate in Caleb's Wood and we were there." She hung her head guiltily.

"We . . . ?"

For a moment she was ashamed of what she had been that day and of what had happened to her because of it. It was not his fault, of course, but it was her meeting with him that had given her the courage to run away and . . . she could feel the hot rush of shame and humiliation burn her body, then the ice-cold sweat of pain and terror follow it as the degrading memory carved her to the bone. How could she bring herself to walk beside this fine man, to talk to him as though she was as clean and untarnished as he was, when what had been done to her later would always set her apart from other women? She would never know the purity of innocence, the simple goodness of a body and mind which were undefiled by man's bestiality and the knowledge of this was unbearable. She turned her head away, then looked down at the immaculate white flower in her hand.

"What is it? Tell me. What has made you . . . turn away?"

"It . . ." she sighed deeply ". . . it was something that happened . . ."

"To my horse, you said? I think I remember. There was a gang of women with a man . . ."

"Yes." Still she would not look up at him and though her hesitancy in another would have irritated him enormously, he found it to be vastly intriguing in her.

"Daisy?"

"Yes."

"Look at me," and when she did he was smiling his lovely, deep-blue smile, humorous and kind, as though to let her know that what had happened six years ago really no longer mattered.

"I was the girl who ran for your father."

The picture, as clear and sharp as though it had happened only that morning, flashed into his fastidious mind of a group of filthy vagrants, women and children, and a man. There had been a great deal of swearing and screaming, confusion, and on his part, savage anger. Then a child had detached itself from the rest, offered to run for help, and had gone he presumed since he had never seen her again.

And now, here she was, smiling shyly and waiting, he supposed, for some sign of recognition and thanks. He pulled himself together swiftly since any advantage he might gain with this one was not to be ignored.

"I remember the day distinctly and I remember the child who helped me," he lied. "She did me a great service." He watched her bob her head, her eyes as radiant as the stars in a clear night sky. "But I must admit that I would not have recognised you. You are a lovely young lady now." He bowed gallantly, bending his head, then, with a gesture which brought a glow to her cheeks, he took her hands in both of his and brought them to his lips. "And not a vestige remains of that sharp imp who not only took in the seriousness of my plight but sprang at once to help me overcome it." He made it sound as though he had not been concerned with her squalid appearance, as if he had not even noticed it. "Now then, you shall tell me everything that has happened to you since and how you came to work in my father's house..."

"I cannot ... really..."

"Cannot? And why is that?" He bent to smile into her face.

"I ... well..."

198

"What is it, Daisy?" His voice was concerned.

"Sir..."

"Sir? My name is Miles and that is what you shall call me."

Miles! He wanted her to call him Miles and yet he knew she was no more than a servant girl in the great house which would one day be his. He wanted her to stroll with him in the weak winter sunshine just as though they were of the same class but he must be made to realise that it could not be so. Surely he knew how impossible this was. His generous nature and kindness seemed to blind him to the fact and she loved and admired him all the more for it but he must be told that ... well ... their friendship, for want of a better word, could be no more than ... than ... She sighed, for really, she didn't know how to describe it, or even if there was anything to describe.

"I must get back to the kitchen, sir," she said firmly. "I am a housemaid and it's ... it's not seemly for you and me to walk about the grounds as though ... as though ... and besides someone might see us..."

He gave a great delighted shout of laughter and she looked about her hastily for surely everyone for miles around must have heard him.

"Seemly! Seemly! What an absolutely wonderful word, Daisy. I have not heard it spoken since my mother chided a female cousin of mine for strolling out of sight in the garden with a gentleman who, though his intentions were honourable, was not a relative. I thought at the time how foolish it was, for the gentleman respected my cousin, as I respect you, and meant her no harm, as I mean you no harm. What can be wrong with talking, in broad daylight, with a person one finds congenial? Tell me that, Daisy brown-eyes?".

She dissolved into laughter for his merriment was infectious and really, what he said was quite reasonable. They were wronging no one with this small interlude, this harmless stroll together, or so she told herself, but she must get back despite the plausibility of what he said. It was not a question of what was right, or wrong, but the simple truth that if she wasn't in the kitchen by four o'clock Mrs Crosby would want to know the reason why and if she ever, *ever* discovered that Daisy Brindle, housemaid, had been chatting, just as though she was as good as he, with the heir to this great and ancient estate, however innocently, she would be in water so hot and so deep, it was doubtful she would ever survive.

She told him so and instantly he was contrite.

"Of course, I do beg your pardon. I find your company so ... so delightful I'm afraid time means nothing. And, Daisy ..." his expression was very serious "... I cannot find it in me to be concerned that you are ... what you are in my father's house and that I am ... well ..." he smiled boyishly "... his son. Does it really matter if we ... enjoy a moment's conversation together?"

He made it sound so unimportant, so simple, so natural, but as she blew out her candle that night, burrowing beneath the ice-cold sheets of her hard, narrow bed under the eaves of the vast house, conscious that *he* was somewhere within the same four walls, she felt a pang of misgiving thrust itself slyly into the delicious daze of joy he had created about her, then his voice whispered softly, 'Daisy brown-eyes ...'

She was smiling as she fell asleep.

They made no plans, no prior arrangements to meet, or rather *he* didn't since, in her humble state, it would not have even occurred to her to consider it, but somehow, during those first wintry weeks of the New Year, when the snow came in on a great raging blizzard so that the house was cut off for three days and nights by a seven-foot wall of snow, when the thaw came to turn the park and woodlands to a soft and squelching morass, when winds blew to dry it out and frost bit so deep the lake froze, he managed to snatch a moment or two with her each week. Never by deliberate intention, or so he would have her think, catching her perhaps between the Greenhalgh house and Thornley Green; once when she was sent to the dairy with a message for the dairymaid, and once, dangerous but immensely exciting to him, on the wide corridor which led from the linen room on the first floor, to his bedroom. There had been no one about at that precise moment since the family were at breakfast and Mason, the chambermaid, was actually sorting linen with the door to the linen room closed. Her heart had plunged like a nervous colt at the sight of him and she had been ready to sketch a curtsey and stand to one side, pressing her back against the wall as she had been instructed, but his eyes had been brimming with mischief and his teeth gleamed in a delighted smile.

"Daisy, what luck," he said softly, ready, if she had but known it, to sweep her into his arms and kiss her panic-stricken face to smiles. He was enchanted with her apprehension, the way she looked about her as if searching for a bolt hole down which to bolt.

"It's all right, there's no one about," he whispered, coming to a stop before her, and when she would have darted round him, stepping to the side to prevent her.

"Oh please, sir..." she whispered back, "let me go..."

"Not *sir*, Daisy. What did I tell you?"

"Please, sir, I'll get the sack."

"Of course you won't. There is no one here. Now then, what is my name?"

"Sir ... please ... Mrs Crosby..."

"Daisy!"

"Miles, then. Now, for God's sake stand aside."

"You have a temper then, Daisy brown-eyes. Always before you have been so demure with your soft brown eyes cast down but now I can see you have kept your spirit hidden. I do admire spirit in a woman, Daisy," but he smiled and stood aside and when she disappeared into some cupboard or other he began to whistle as he walked towards the staircase which led down to the lower floor.

Spring came early. Larks sang in the middle of February and the multitude of birds in Rough Wood began to gather materials for their nests. Willow bushes almost overnight were heavy with downy white balls and beneath the hedgebanks and amongst the roots of the trees snowdrops lifted their delicate heads. Primroses clustered in a sheltered spot beside the stream which fed into the lake at the back of Thornley Green and on such a day Daisy persuaded Mrs Greenhalgh to allow Cassie to walk with her, not across the park and beyond to the smooth lawns and budding flower-beds where Lady Mary's gardeners worked but into the tiny wood where the daffodils grew.

"I don't know, Daisy. It's still very wet underfoot and if she catches a chill I shall never forgive myself."

Cassie pulled on Mrs Greenhalgh's arm, her pansy eyes pleading to be allowed to go, hopping from foot to foot like any child longing for an outing.

"It's not very far, Mrs Greenhalgh, and I promise I won't let her get her feet wet. We'll keep to the path and go no further than the edge of Rough Wood. It's not really cold and I really will take good care of her."

She often smiled ironically to herself at the way in which Mrs Greenhalgh cosseted Cassie, just as though she was made from spun sugar when really the girl, despite her delicate appearance, could stand far more than wet feet. Had she not survived three winters in the black damp of the pits and though she was inclined to cough a little in the winter, probably because of her incarceration there, she ailed nothing much.

"Well..."

"Please, Mrs Greenhalgh. The spring flowers are just coming through..." and Cassie pulled more fiercely on her 'grandmother's' sleeve until the lady had no choice but to give in.

"We'll walk through the wood, Cass," Daisy said as they set off briskly, "then turn right and go over to that little bridge which crosses the stream and do a bit of exploring. Would you like that?" Cassie was not sure what that meant but if she and Daisy were to do it together than she was more than willing. "I've seen it times when I've been this way with ... well, when I came this way before," she continued, "and I've often wondered where it leads to. There's another bit of parkland over there and then some fields. The home farm, they call it up at the house, where all the stuff for the kitchen comes from. Mary-Ellen Frost, she's one of the chambermaids, came from there when she was twelve. I just fancy having a look at a field with something growing in it, though God knows why. You'd think I'd have had enough of fields to last me a lifetime, wouldn't you? We worked in a few, didn't we, Cass? You know, we're very lucky to have ended up the way we have, Cass. I told you we'd live in clover one day, didn't I?"

Cassie nodded agreeably, holding Daisy's hand, skipping along beside her and sticking to the path like Grandmother had told her. She would love to dart across the sodden mass of last year's leaves and pick a bunch of the golden-trumpeted daffodils which clustered thickly beneath the trees but the habit of obedience to Daisy was still strong within her. She wore a soft blue woollen dress tied at the waist and wrist with blue velvet ribbons and over it a snugly lined cloak of a deeper shade of blue. It had a hood edged in swan's-down and from it her small face peeped, flushed and so lovely it stopped the breath to look at it.

"Now we'll keep this a secret, won't we . . . ?" just as if it could be anything else with Cassie, she thought to herself as they crossed the little bridge ". . . and perhaps we can do it again when the summer comes. Have a little picnic. Would you like that?"

Cassie nodded. She knew all about picnics.

"May I come too?" the voice said from behind them and when they both turned, considerably startled, thinking themselves to be quite alone, he raised his hat politely, an engaging smile on his amber-skinned face, his air of boyish charm absolutely irresistible. "I'm sorry, Daisy, I was walking Barney here, thinking how lovely it is at this time of the year. A beginning of something wonderful . . ." his eyes speaking other unspoken words which she only half understood ". . . when I heard your voices and we could not resist coming to investigate, could we, Barney? I thought it to be spirits of the air, fairy-folk, you understand . . . ?" addressing the remark to Cassie who began to smile after her first instinctive wariness, since she did indeed know about fairies. Grandmother read her stories about them and she had looked for them whenever she came to what she was convinced were fairy rings in the meadow at the back of the big house.

Daisy's heart thumped erratically as it always did whenever she saw him. She had been alarmed at first. Cassie would be the only person to see them together, though of course they were not really together. They had only met by chance and even if Cassie could speak and told Mrs Greenhalgh there was nothing wrong in being greeted by Master Miles. He was the future master of Thornley Green, a gentleman and it would have been impolite to have ignored them, she and Cassie, even if Daisy was a servant in his house. And he had a perfect right to walk his dog here and had she not been given permission to take Cassie for a short walk in this direction so where was the harm in it? Nevertheless it had given her a nasty turn.

"Good afternoon, sir," she said demurely.

"Good afternoon, Daisy," and while Cassie bent to stroke the retriever's golden head, he winked at her and it was all she could do not to laugh out loud.

"This must be your pretty sister." He turned to Cassie and bowed again.

"Yes, sir, this is Cassie. She and I were ... walking."

"It is a lovely day for it. Would you mind if Barney and I walked with you?"

"No, sir, of course not," dimpling.

"Fetch a stick, Barney, and perhaps Cassie will throw it for you."

In a moment the girl and the dog were engaged in an enchanting game, enchanting to both of them, and as they ran ahead Miles took Daisy's hand and raised it to his lips.

"I had hoped to see you, you know that, don't you? I walked this way deliberately, knowing you came to see your sister. I couldn't stay away, Daisy. I have tried but when I heard your voice I had to come. Say you are not angry with me. I couldn't bear it if you were angry with me."

His face was very serious, his eyes grave. There was no mischief there, no teasing, only what he beseeched her to recognise as his regard, his respect, and something else which filled her with such joy she almost reeled into his arms.

"Miles..."

"Don't ... don't say anything, Daisy..."

"I cannot believe..."

"Neither can I but it seems it has happened. We must meet somewhere quiet where we can talk. Be alone. Oh dear God, I have tried so hard to keep away from you ... but..."

"Miles..." Her face was bemused with a rapture so rare that strangely, just for a moment, something in him, some feeling of what in another man might have been remorse, stirred his senses. She was looking at him as though he had offered her paradise here on earth and if he had been of a fanciful nature, which he was not, he might have described it as having her soul in her eyes. Almost unearthly really. There was something ... something mystic about her ... she was so innocent ... so bloody naïve to believe ... to believe ... Then, mentally, he shook his head at his own foolishness. She was a lovely girl, one who had caught his bored imagination. He was a man and could any man refuse this which was being so patently offered to him?

"Can you get out?"

"When...?"

"Tonight?"

"Oh no..."

"Try, try my lovely girl. I'll wait by the gateway into the shrubbery garden. The one with the small round pond. Do you know where I mean?"

Of course she did. Was it not in that very garden that she had seen for the first time the beauty of the house called Thornley Green? On the same day that she had first laid eyes on this man whose own male beauty had held her in thrall ever since. It seemed, somehow, as though it was an omen.

He lifted her hands to his lips and his eyes told her all she wanted to know.

14

"I'm here," he whispered and from a shadow beside the stone gatepost a hand touched her arm. She almost screamed, her nerves strung to straining point by the deception she had been forced to act out in the kitchen, then his soothing voice calmed her.

"Ssh, ssh, my lovely girl, it's only me. Good God, you're shaking like an aspen tree. There's no need to be frightened. See, I'm here and we're all alone but for the owls."

"Oh, sir . . ."

"Don't call me that."

"Miles then, but can't we get further away from the house? I'm afraid someone will look out of a window and if I'm caught I'll get the sack. I'm sure Mrs Crosby didn't believe me when I said I felt ill. I even put some flour on my face and rubbed a bit of ash under my eyes to make myself look worse and she said I could go to bed, but if she decides to come up to the maid's bedroom . . ."

All the while she was speaking, her voice exploding from her in nervous gasps, he was leading her down the stone steps, away from the walled shrubbery garden and across the dark parkland towards the small summerhouse which stood among the trees beside the lake. He was not really listening to what she said. He didn't give a damn how she got out, or, at the moment, how she would explain her absence if it was discovered. This was the moment that mattered. Not tomorrow, or the weeks following in which he meant to enjoy her until the time came when he could persuade his father that he had done his duty as a son should and that Freddy Rawstrone, Lord Frederick Rawstrone's house party at his villa in Monte Carlo, really should be attended by himself. The hunting season was almost finished. The last hunt ball was to be on Saturday and from then until the start of the grouse in August the weeks stretched out before him, barren and empty of anything which might be called enjoyable. At least what he considered enjoyable. There was Newmarket, Ascot Heath, but how could a fellow enjoy the racing if his allowance was cut and it was made known that his own father refused to honour any of his promissory notes? He had sworn he would pay no more of his son's gambling debts, as he had last year, unless Miles promised, promised as a gentleman, that he would remain at home and take an interest in the estate which would one day be his. And so he had. For three long bloody months. But the hunt and its attendant parties and balls, all the social round which made the winter months more endurable, was at an end. Now all that was left was the fancy he had taken to this delightful little serving wench. Every one of his friends would soon be off to London for the season. He was not to go, his father had told him bluntly, and a chap must have some diversion and she, now that he had convinced her of his feelings, would do nicely.

He wondered as he raced her across the lawn why he should concern himself with this pretence of emotion. Why had he not just helped himself as he had always done in the past, to whatever bit of woman-flesh he had lusted after? He couldn't answer the question unless it was that this one, for some reason, seemed to offer more than the others. There was this . . . this sexuality about her, unconscious of course, which stirred something in him and he wanted it to last for a while. He had enjoyed the game he had played during the winter months, looking forward immensely to the moment, now in fact, when he would take her innocence from her, show her a trick or two which he would teach her to please him and, hopefully, alleviate the boredom which would plague him until he could get himself over to Freddy's place in France.

Her breath was rasping in her throat when he drew her inside the summerhouse. She still wore her afternoon uniform. Black dress, white apron and white frilled cap. Her hair had come loose from its pins in their wild flight across the park, drooping in heavy coils down her back, and she automatically put up her hands to adjust it but he stopped her.

"No ... please ... don't..." His breath was no more than a sigh in his throat. He removed her cap and plunged both hands into the mass of her hair, gently, and loosened it further, lifting it, smoothing it back from her face, letting it fall across her shoulders and down her back where it rippled to her buttocks. The tension was at fever-pitch and she became still, a huge-eyed fawn captured on the edge of a forest glade in the hunter's sights and her breathing almost stopped. Her heart was leaping in her breast until she was sure he would see the movement of it beneath the bib of her apron but he stepped back from her reverently, his eyes on her face. In the semi-gloom all she could see was the pale blur of his shirtfront and the darker shape of his shoulders, and above them his shining eyes.

"You know how I feel about you, don't you, Daisy?" he said softly.

"No ... I mean ..." She swallowed and her breath was rapid and shallow, fluttering like a trapped bird in her throat. Her brain had ceased to function on any level beyond that which was aware that they were alone, that she loved him and that he seemed to be telling her he felt the same. It was impossible, absolutely absurd, of course. He had said they were to talk, but what about, for God's sake? ... Dear Lord ... she loved him ... what did it matter ...?

"I can think of no one but you, Daisy. You ... you haunt me ... all the time..." That was a good one! "... and I have never felt like this about anyone..." which he supposed was true in a way "... anyone. I won't tell you there has never been ... I am a man, Daisy, and ..."

"I don't care ... It doesn't matter..." She swayed towards him, mesmerised with joy.

"... it meant nothing, not now. Not since I first saw you in the wood in your lovely tawny dress and those golden ribbons in your hair..." Imagine him remembering that

... "and your hair, so beautiful ... so beautiful..." His hands went to her hair again. His fingers combed through it. "...would you let me ... just for a moment, then I promise you I will help you put it up again..." He was babbling, he was aware of it, and hoped to God she wasn't. "We can slip in at the side entrance ... the servants will still be in the kitchen and you can go right up to ... oh Daisy ... Daisy, you are so unutterably sweet ... sweet..."

He cupped her face with his hands, so gently, so tenderly she was quite bewitched. She lifted her mouth to his for the first time, for her first kiss, sixteen years old and as ignorant of seduction, of men, of their desires, as an infant just born. She had known man at his worst. She had been initiated into his beastliness at the age of ten and even before that when she had witnessed the careless coupling of the women in the gang and the men who stumbled after them. Not one had seen the core of goodness in her, the belief in something better to come which lived, not in them, but in herself. None had *given* to her, except perhaps the family of this beloved man when they had sent her to school. In a small, unlistened-to, fraction of her mind was a tiny voice which reminded her that men were creatures who were not to be trusted but she was deaf to it, blinded by her love for the man who, she believed, in her whole life had been the only one to give something to Daisy Brindle. And that something had been the promise of joy, of hope, a dream. Now that dream, that hope, that joy, was here.

"Daisy ... oh my little love ... what are we to do...?"

She was not awfully sure she knew what he meant. Her mouth, now that his had left it, felt curiously defenceless. The softness of his lips, the sweetness of the kiss he had given her was indescribable. She had tasted the wine he had drunk at dinner, and the brandy since, but it was not that which moved her. It was the essence of Miles Thornley himself, his flesh, the moistness of his lips, the flavour of his breath, the sensation of his tongue against hers for a bare second and she thirsted for more. She could feel her arms lifting and her hands move carefully to touch his shoulders, longing to grasp tightly but she dare not. He was so far above her perhaps he might not like it if she was too ... well ... too forward. He still held her face, looking down into her eyes, his no more than a soft glow in the dark, and her pulses leapt, her heart leapt and ... and ... what? What came next? What was to come next?

"You know I want you to belong to me, don't you?"

Merciful Lord, what did he mean? He was looking at her with such longing, with such ... such sadness, just as though whatever it was, was completely out of his reach, as though she was out of his reach, as far away and inaccessible as a star in the heavens when all he had to do was fold her in his arms, next to his heart where she belonged.

"Miles ..."

"Don't speak, my sweet girl. Let me kiss you again ... if I may."

"Miles ..." Even to speak his name was a joy. "Miles, I don't know what you're saying."

"I ... I think I am falling in love with you, Daisy, and I don't know what to do about it. That is why I wanted to have these few moments to talk to you. You see ... oh, my darling ... I may have to go away ..."

"No ... please ... don't go away because of me!"

"You know what I am saying, Daisy. You understand ... being who I am and ..."

"Don't ... I love you, I love you ..."

"Do you, Daisy, really?"

"You know I do ... but ... Oh dear God ... you cannot leave because of me."

Her voice was anguished, and, uncaring now of the niceties of their social position, she flung her arms about his neck and pressed her body close to his.

He felt the triumph surge through him but still he held back. She was his, willingly, he knew it but he wanted to savour it for another moment of excited anticipation. Savour that moment when the hunter has the prey in his sights and the choice to kill, or not. And more than that, he wanted her to be not just willing, but eager, responsive, passionate so that the next time and the next there would be no need for this play-acting. He wanted to turn her into the best little whore this side of St Helens so that, until he got bored with it, until he could persuade his father that he was a reformed character and really did deserve a couple of months with Freddy Rawstrone in the sunshine of France, he would have a surfeit of pleasure so great it would fill every bored moment of his day and night.

"Daisy ... Dear God, don't you know what you are doing to me? I cannot resist you when you ... please, my lovely girl ... I'm only human and you are more than I can resist..."

He put his arms about her then, lifting her against him and his lips sank deeply into hers, parting them, opening her mouth wide, hurting her a little but her senses, her *sense* had gone, the small, sensible nucleus of Daisy Brindle, spiralling away on the delirious pleasure his nearness, his strength, his masculinity aroused in her.

For several minutes, holding back his own desires, he did no more than hold her, kiss her, her mouth, her cheeks, her eyes, the smooth curve of her throat, the hollow beneath her ear. He could hear her breath quicken and she whimpered deep in her throat, her hands had begun to flutter about his face, the back of his neck, grasping his hair, caressing his ears and he knew, at last, that it was time.

"Jesus ... oh ... Jesus ... I cannot let you go," he said harshly.

"No ... oh no ... never ... let ... me ... go..."

Buttons? At the front or the back? He should know, bloody hell, he'd divested enough housemaids of their uniforms in his time and when he found them there were so many he simply tore them apart. Her skirt next and whatever it was she had on underneath and then she was naked in his hands. She was like a boy, she was so slim, so fine, with tiny pointed breasts, the peaks hard and thrusting between his fingers. He ran his hands over her, smoothing her, soothing her for she had begun inexplicably to weep and he knew he must be quick.

"Have you any idea what you mean to me, my little love," he murmured automatically whilst his hands were busy with his own clothing.

"Miles..." and the growing radiance, the aura of lightness and joy which surrounded her blurred her mind to his frantic greed.

"God... I need you," he whispered urgently, his manhood surging demandingly against her. She was barely conscious now, quivering as his hand closed on her breast; began to squeeze and smooth and caress, so lightly it was a delight and yet a pain which she never wanted to end.

His weight was on top of her as he laid her down on the floor and for a moment she knew a sense of panic as though something was wrong... familiar... wrong... not again ... not again ... but this was Miles ... Miles who loved her and she loved him then he pierced her, taking away the last whisper of her conscious mind as he cried out in orgasm. When he fell across her with a harsh and ripping groan her arms clung to him lest she fall into the deep pit her own body had dug for her.

He lay for several minutes until his breathing slowed, heavy and inert across her still body, then, senses returned, he became again what he meant her to believe – for the moment – he was. He drew her to him, light as a snowflake against his dark strength, crooning to her, smoothing her cheek and neck, her fine-boned shoulders, her small, delicate breasts.

"It's all right, my darling. I know it's the first time for you but let me hold you, lie against me, we will rest for a while... I love you..."

"Do you...?"

"You know I do."

His hand caressed her, the curve of her hip, the base of her stomach, moving until it touched the small of her back and the threads of fine ridges which lay across the fine skin. They laced one another like a spider's-web where the gangmaster's lash had cut her and she felt him tense. His fingers investigated them in the dark and inside her something became tight strung and her heart, which had begun to slow, missed a beat before it quickened again.

"What are these, my love?" he asked softly, curiously. "They feel like scars. Have you had some accident?"

212

"No." He will hate me now, her mind agonised, for the scars were closely linked with the other thing which had happened to her that night and would not any man's love turn to loathing when he learned what the woman in his arms had once been to another? When he learned how she had been abused and dragged in the filth of depravity?

"Then what, please tell me." There was no loathing in his voice, only interest and a curious ... excitement?

"I ... I don't know how to."

"Why not? Have you done something wrong?"

She had done no wrong, but a wrong had been done her. Was it the same? Was it? Would *he* think so and would it alter the tender feelings he had for her? She could not bear it if it did.

"I don't know."

"What happened, Daisy?"

Oh God, help me. "I was ... was whipped."

"Whipped? By the man who worked you in the fields?" Again there was that strange expression in his voice and she was afraid of it but he drew her more closely to him, stroking his fingers across her back, tracing each raised ridge carefully.

"I would like to see them." His voice was dreamlike.

"No, oh please, Miles ... no."

"Daisy, I only mean to ... kiss them better." His manner was light, almost as though he was amused by her distress, and something inside her stirred uncomfortably. He crushed her to him then, his passion swamping him again, an excited passion which, for some curious reason, she could not – this time – meet. She wanted just to lie beside him, to be warm and still, to be cocooned in quiet whilst her mind recaptured the beauty of their love. But he would not have it. Sensing her misgivings, his hands, his mouth, his soft voice, wooed her to warmth and then to passion, to the sensuality which he knew she possessed, creating sensations in her which she could not deny and she fell back, filled with the most amazing languor, a feeling that nothing mattered except this exquisite lassitude which built up inside her until it became such an unbearable rapture nothing could ease it but his penetration which, last time, had hurt and troubled her but which now, as he took her again, laughing at her eagerness, thrilled and terrified her with its slashing intensity, and she was possessed by him with a certainty which was unbreakable.

"You're mine now, Daisy brown-eyes," he said triumphantly. "You belong to me. You know it, don't you?" and she did.

She didn't know what time it was when she got back to the safety of her bed. She had been quite amazed to find, when she did get there, that her pillow had been laid down the centre, the sheet and blanket carefully tucked around it so that for a horrified moment she had thought there was someone sleeping in it. Her heart hammered. She was sure the other girls in the attic room must awaken with its deafening noise but they all slept on. Servants who rise at five thirty and work for sixteen or seventeen hours with very few breaks and none of them long, are not easily roused.

Miles had got her in, entering the side-door boldly as he had every right to do, then going ahead of her to see that the way was clear, along corridors, up stairs, other corridors, until she was at the door of the maidservants' quarters.

"Goodnight, sweet girl," he whispered, ready to laugh, to kiss her, to enjoy this danger – not to himself, of course – to the full, his face good-humoured for though she had this first time done nothing beyond allowing him his way, he had enjoyed the unusual slenderness of her body, the smallness of her breasts, the long and willowy fineness that was so different to the fleshly beauties he usually admired. And next time he would begin to show her a few refinements in the art of lovemaking which, when she was proficient, would make her doubly rewarding.

She cowered at last beneath the bedclothes, her torn dress safely hidden in her drawer. She would have to repair it somehow ... thank God she was handy with her needle ... Jesus ... who could have put the pillow in the bed? ... Bess, it must be ... Oh, Miles ... Miles ... I love you ... can this really have happened to me? ... and you love me

... what will happen now and does it matter? ... he loves me ... I'm happy ... could anyone be so happy? ... Miles Thornley loves Daisy Brindle ... how shall I face them all tomorrow? ... surely they'll be able to tell what has happened to me? ... will it show? ... he was ... it was ... She felt herself become warm beneath the blanket and knew it had nothing to do with its softness and weight. Her body ached, felt bruised, almost scraped raw on her shoulder-blades where he had ... how long had it been? ... how many bruises had she...? She burrowed deeper, beginning to smile, her eyes tight shut as she remembered. She wanted to touch herself where his hand had been, to rub her breasts which still tingled from his mouth, his questing fingers, then she felt ashamed. No, she didn't, she thought fiercely, she didn't feel ashamed at all, though perhaps she should, but really could anything so lovely, so *right*, be wicked? She had enjoyed it. After what had happened to her when she was ten years old she had imagined that she would never want to do *it* again, to have it done to her, but then this time it had been with Miles, who loved her. Who had been tender and loving with her. It had been done in love.

"Who is it, Daisy?" Bess asked her accusingly the next morning as they closed the drawing-room door behind them. She put her housemaid's box which contained all her own tools for black-leading grates – though there were none of those in this elegant room – and all the necessary brushes and dusters, polishes and creams on to the sheet of coarse wrapping which she spread before the beautiful white marble fireplace. The room was furnished and decorated in the style of the previous century with dainty gilded chairs upholstered in pale grey damask, silk damask wall-hangings and tall, pier glass mirrors. The high ceiling was vaulted and covered with painted panels set in magnificent plasterwork. Festoon curtains at the window were of the palest rose silk, and marble-topped tables held splendid candelabra with six ornate candle branches. There was a crystal chandelier hanging from a central rosette in the ceiling – to be cleaned only once a month, thank God – and the floor of the large room, actually one of the smallest drawing rooms at Thornley Green, was covered by a square carpet of delicate oriental design.

Bess began immediately to sweep out the ashes from yesterday's fire since they had only so long to clean this room and had no time to stand and chat. Any talking they did must be done as they worked and if Mrs Crosby came in and caught them at it they'd be for it.

"Was it one of the grooms?" she continued.

"Don't be daft." Daisy had started on the carpet, sprinkling it first with tealeaves, then sweeping it towards the fireplace as she had been taught at the School of Industry, going at it as though Mrs Crosby herself was watching.

"There is someone and I mean to find out, Daisy Brindle. I covered for you last night but I'll not do it again. It was a damn good job I went up first or you would have been in trouble. Have you no sense, girl . . . ?"

Daisy chose to ignore the last question. "Thanks, Bess, but . . ."

"There's no 'buts' about it. You know you'll lose your job if anyone finds out and not only that, you'll go without a character. You'll never get another job in a house like this and then where will you be? And then there's him, whoever he is, he'll go too. I'm surprised at you, Daisy. I thought you had more sense . . ." Bess sat back on her heels, so aggrieved by what she saw as Daisy's madness she forgot to get on with her work ". . . and I didn't even know you had your eye on one of them. You're a deep one . . ."

"I haven't. You must be out of your mind if you think I'd chance my job for a groom!" Daisy reached for the cushions on the elegant sofa, tossing each one about with a rare disregard for their cost and spendour, and with such a force of nervous energy Bess stared at her in amazement. She seemed to exude some secret excitement, some explosion of vigour which filled the air, disturbing it, and Bess, with its potency.

"Then if it's not a groom . . . or a . . . gardener, who else is there outside that you'd go to meet? Someone from the village?"

216

Daisy's hand hesitated and she felt her effervescent mind which this morning was like champagne bubbling up forcibly, *unthinkably*, come to its senses. Good God, she had almost given it away. In her contemptuous denial of a dalliance with a groom or any of the outside men she had left Bess with only one alternative and that was that a man from the village had caught Daisy's attention and she must let her go on thinking that because if Bess knew who it really was ... dear Lord ... oh dear Lord ... if she knew ... but she must never know. She must protect him. She must never let it be known that the Honourable Miles Thornley was ... was ...

"Come on, Daisy, tell me who it is. You know I'd never give you away, not if you don't want me to. Although if you're serious about him, and you must be to risk what you did last night, don't you think you'd better tell Mrs Crosby? Get it all out in the open, decent-like? She'll not like you courting but if you're to be respectably wed it doesn't matter. Or is there some reason you don't want her to know, and not just her but me as well?"

Bess, suspicious suddenly, stood up and, taking a chance that Mrs Crosby or Susan Tipping, who was upper housemaid and sometimes took the housekeeper's rounds, was nowhere about, moved slowly across the room to Daisy.

"It's someone ... high up, isn't it, Daisy?"

"I don't know what you mean." Daisy polished a tabletop as though her life depended upon it.

"Yes you do. It's not some village lad, or some farm lad who'd set you up in an estate cottage since you'd not be interested in a chap like that, would you? Not Daisy Brindle who's clawed her way up from nowhere and doesn't mean to give over until she's at the top. Not that I blame you, Daisy. Don't think that. I know what you've been through. Not all of it, since you're not one for talking about the past, but you didn't do it to wind up in some labourer's cottage with a brood of children at your skirts, did you? But ... well, what I mean to say is, don't do anything daft, Daisy. Don't get ... swept off your feet by ... whoever it is you met last night. They're all the same, you know, these ...

these *gentlemen*, for that's what they call themselves though they think nothing of having their way with any maid who happens to take their fancy, willing or not, and there's many a lass ruined by it. In this house an' all. I can remember when his young lordship had a crowd of his friends up from Cambridge. No more than eighteen any of them and when they'd gone poor Jenny Ashton ... you'll not know her ... well, you wouldn't because five months later she was fired, and the child she carried. I'm not saying it was Master Miles who put her in the family way, but one of them did. So don't you get involved..."

"I'm not and I'll thank you to mind your own business." Daisy flung herself across the room to the window and with no thought for the ancient frailness of the curtains began to shake them vigorously, hardly aware of what she was doing in her temper. Her eyes were wild and fierce and the blood ran hotly beneath her smooth creamy skin. How dare she! How dare Bess Miller try to besmirch what was growing between herself and Miles? How dare she imply that he was no better than a seducer, a rogue who would dishonour a simple housemaid with honeyed words and a few kisses? That he was a man who would think nothing of pretending to emotion he did not feel merely to ... to get a girl to open her legs for him. If he was such a man, could he not have led her astray – a stupid word for no one led Daisy Brindle anywhere she did not wish to go – at any time during the last three or four months? They had met week in and week out since Christmas and he had done nothing which could not have been seen by his own mother, and had said not one word that was not completely proper. A gentleman, honourable and good, and despite last night – which really had been as much her fault as his, for at any time she might have stopped it – he was still a gentleman. What they were to do, Miles Thornley, gentleman, and Daisy Brindle, housemaid, with this rare and beautiful gift they had been given she would leave to him to decide. He was a true man, wise and steadfast, and whatever it was she would follow him in it.

But that was for the future. She was sixteen, she was in

love and she was loved in return. They were young, she and Miles, full of joy, health, and with the sweet loveliness of what had happened between them so new and fragile she could not bear another to even consider it let alone talk about it. It was hidden, safe, secret and it must be kept that way. It was hers to gloat over when she was alone and if Bess Miller thought she could wheedle out of her who it was Daisy Brindle loved, she'd better think again.

"Daisy . . . I'm not trying to interfere in your life." Bess's voice was soft but the expression on her face said quite plainly that she believed Daisy to be somewhat artless and in need of a firm hand to guide her. Bess was a few years older and, in her opinion, more experienced in the ways of the gentry and surely it was up to her, as Daisy's friend, to try and make Daisy see the foolishness of her behaviour. "I don't know you all that well, not really," she continued. "We seemed to . . . to like each other when you first came and we've stuck together. We work well together or else Mrs Crosby wouldn't have teamed us, so I feel I can say . . . well . . don't do it, lass . . ."

"Don't do what?" Daisy said sharply, flinging open the window with such force several men working on the lawns below raised their heads to stare.

"Dear God, whatever it is you're doing. You weren't on your own last night, were you?"

"I may have been," Daisy spoke through clenched teeth for really she had had quite enough of this, "and then I may not but whether I was or I wasn't it's got nothing to do with you. Now, if you don't mind I've these candelabra to clean and if *you* don't want to get the sack, which you keep threatening *me* with, you'd best get that hearth finished before Mrs Crosby comes."

"I'll not cover for you again," Bess said wildly.

"I'm not asking you to. I can manage my own life, thanks. I always have and I always will."

15

She firmly believed it right through that soft and lovely spring, that glorious summer when even the weather seemed to smile on their love. Whenever she could get away from the house undetected she would slip stealthily through the side-door – not the one which led to Lord Thornley's estate office – but one seldom used since it led nowhere except to a tiny garden. Lady Mary had, years ago, developed a fancy to grow rare herbs, those not in common usage in the gardens of England. A tall, sheltering wall had been built around the garden she planted but the herbs had not thrived in the cold English climate and so it had been allowed to run wild with lavender and creeping ivy which covered the walls. There was a narrow, half-hidden gate leading out into another garden full of old-fashioned flowers which in itself was bordered by a tall yew hedge. There were trees, abundant and concealing, and shrubs grown wild. An old garden in which one could conceal oneself from inquisitive eyes and from there slip away through the woodland to the summerhouse where a lover awaited.

It seemed as though fate, laughing behind its hand, was determined to do all in its power to make it easy for Daisy Brindle to follow the path she trod so lightly. It was two weeks later, during which time no matter how she twisted and turned, she could not get out of the maids' bedroom to meet Miles, that Maudie Watson, upper housemaid with Susan Tipping, declared that she was to marry Albert Thompkins, one of Lord Thornley's grooms. They had had an understanding for five years with Mrs Crosby's approval, naturally, for Watson was a good sensible girl and

Thompkins well thought of by his lordship. There would be a small estate cottage since married couples were encouraged to set up home together, particularly when they were such good and conscientious workers as Thompkins and Watson. Watson could continue in her employment at the big house but not, unfortunately, as upper housemaid. There was no such thing as a 'married' housemaid, but she might do casual cleaning if she desired it, or until the children started to come, as come they would, but in the meanwhile a replacement must be found for her and who else could possibly be considered but Bess Miller? Young she might be but a more hard-working girl was not to be found anywhere and had she not been trained to the exacting standards expected, nay, demanded by Mrs Crosby, and by Mrs Crosby herself? Susan Tipping, with whom Maudie Watson had shared a room, just the two of them, older than Bess by ten years and in her opinion a higher class of servant altogether due to her experience, set the servants' hall on its ear one day when she declared that it was high time she had her own room.

"I am sure you will agree, Mrs Crosby," she remarked somewhat tearfully, "that I have done my duty all these years and that I deserve to be considered in this case. I have nothing against Miller..." she bowed regally at Bess "...but I really feel that..."

"I think we might continue this conversation in my room, Tipping," Mrs Crosby said, her face quite rigid, her manner implying that Tipping would be lucky to come out of this with her job, never mind her own room, but surprisingly Susan Tipping was all gracious smiles when she returned to the servants' hall, beckoning Bess and Daisy with an imperious finger and an order to get along to the housekeeper's room at once.

Mrs Crosby was gracious enough to tell them that their work was adequate which, from her, was high praise indeed where no words at all was considered a good thing. In view of this, and Tipping's removal to a bedroom of her own, they were to share the one she and Watson had occupied. A rare privilege truly for it was only the upper servants who were allowed the measure of privacy a bedroom for two gave.

"There are two new girls starting next week. One a scullerymaid and the other to go in the laundry so they can have your beds in the dormitory. Watson is to go home for a few days before her marriage so you may move your things on Saturday. Now remember, you are both on probation. If I find either of you abusing the trust I put in you you will be severely dealt with. That will be all."

She saw him on Sunday afternoon when she visited Cassie. He had cornered her – if you could describe it as that – twice on the upstairs landing, frightening her badly with his urgent demand to 'come to the summerhouse tonight, sweetheart', his arms ready to crush her to him, his lips warm and tingling in the hollow of her throat. He did not care, it seemed, who saw them together. "It's been two weeks. Two whole weeks and not even a kiss. I can't go on like this, Daisy. I must see you tonight, d'you hear. Promise me you'll come tonight."

"Dear God, Miles . . ." Her eager body pressed itself sublimely to his for what did *it* care that Mrs Crosby was only a few yards away in the linen room with Frost the chambermaid, both of them ready at any moment, she knew, to emerge with an armful of bedlinen to be mended. But her mind knew and begged her to take care, it begged him to take care but he was insistent, drawing her towards the half-open door of a bedroom.

"Come in here for a moment and let me hold you in my arms . . ."

"I can't . . . I *can't*, Miles. Mrs Crosby is in the linen room," she hissed, doing her best to pull away from him. He was mad, quite mad, and if he didn't let her go at once she knew she would be caught struggling in his arms and it would not be *him* who would get the sack.

"The linen room? What the hell do I care for that, whatever it is. I want to talk to you . . ." which he didn't, of course, but the soft, female, struggling flesh in his arms only made him more determined, now, to have her anywhere he

222

could lay her. His hand cupped her breast and she moaned, half with delight, half with terror.

"Come ..." he whispered and then they were in an empty bedroom with the door closed behind them. God, she was sweet, so sweet and soft and pliant. Tall, yes, as he bent to place his acquisitive mouth on her white throat, but the slightness of her, the delicate smoothness of her white arms and shoulders, her little peaked breasts which quickened in his greedy fingers were the most exciting ...

"Where *has* that girl got to? I told Mason to send her up immediately to take this bedlinen to the seamstress. Slip down the back stairs with this first pile, Frost, and tell Brindle to come at once ..."

"Miles ... please ... oh please let me go. Can't you hear Mrs Crosby? She's only just outside the door. If she should take it into her head to come in ..." Daisy's voice was a harsh urgent whisper deep in her throat.

"Daisy ... just let me ..."

"*No!* For God's sake ... I promise I'll see you tomorrow afternoon when I visit Cassie ..."

"I can't wait ..."

"Please, Miles ..." She was desperate in her effort to push away his strong fingers which were undoing buttons as fast as she was doing them up, her own hands trembling not only with terror, but with desire as strong as his. His hands, his lips, his strong body seemed to have some magic which weakened her own to the point where, if she was not resolute, she wouldn't give a damn if Mrs Crosby and the whole household of servants marched in on them. She could feel the melting joy tremble in the pit of her stomach, spreading hotly to her breasts and inner thighs and she longed simply to sink down with him into the softness, the fierceness of their passion, amazed at her own response in the face of Mrs Crosby's imminent entry into the bedroom.

Reluctantly he let her go.

On another occasion when the family and the majority of the servants – she and Bess were to take the opportunity whilst she was absent to clean Mrs Crosby's sitting room – were at church, he had coaxed her to give in to his not altogether good-humoured blandishments. There had been no one about that day when she ran up to the linen room and on the bedroom landing lay only the hush of empty rooms.

He slipped from nowhere, it seemed, the first intimation that she was not alone, his arms about her waist from behind. "Let me kiss you properly," he said, "that chaste peck you allowed me last Sunday could have been given me by my maiden aunt."

"Have you one?" she asked breathlessly, hoping to keep the situation carelessly light whilst she escaped him but he pulled her into his arms and his lips parted on hers, hard and demanding as his passion for her outstripped caution. "It's been days," he said thickly. His mouth travelled across her cheek, laying itself roughly about her eyes and ears where his tongue probed the delicate pulsing core, sending trembling signals down her neck and shoulders. She lifted herself against him, her soft woman's body ready and searching for the hardness of his and when she found it, surging up against him in need.

"Where ... damnation ... where ... ?" His hands ripped at the buttons of her grey morning dress and when they would not do as they were bid tore them savagely and her back was revealed down to her waist.

"Miles ... please ..." though she really did not know whether she was pleading with him to go on or to stop. He had her backed up to a closed door, ready to pull her dress further down and she wanted it, she wanted it as much as he did but this was lunacy.

"To hell with please," he said roughly, his hands reaching for the roundness and softness and peaked hardness of her breasts as they erupted from the falling dress. They could hear a voice coming from the hallway below and he put a hand to the double doors behind her, opening them quickly, taking her with him into the linen cupboard, each shelf laid out neatly with Mrs Crosby's freshly laundered sheets and blankets.

"Inside," he whispered, pushing her backwards until she fell on a stacked pile of soft, sweet-smelling blankets. He closed the door behind him and in the dim light which came through the crack around the doorjamb she watched him strip himself of his clothes. When he was completely naked he turned to her.

"Now you, madam ... No, I will do it, if you please." When she was as naked as he, he fell heavily on top of her. His body fitted tightly about hers and she felt the fluttering joy he induced in her flood to the nerves and pulses and pores of every surface of her skin. Dear God, what was wrong with her? She was in a cupboard on a Sunday morning, without a stitch to her body, allowing the son of the house to make love to her, *forced* to it and yet she loved it and him. It didn't seem to matter to her that at any moment one of the family – were they all at church? she didn't know, nor care, or so it appeared – or a servant might hear the sounds he was making – or was it her? – and open the linen-cupboard door to investigate! He was trembling with excitement and the depth of his mounting passion. He did not hold back, nor wait for her to catch up to him, concerned only with his own pleasure, but she was too drugged with desire to notice. Dust motes lifted in the shaft of light which fell on them and they lay together, sweat gathering and sliding from them to Mrs Crosby's blankets, causing the housekeeper a great deal of concern several days later when the state of them was discovered.

They dressed rapidly, Miles laughing and ready to forgive her for her initial reluctance. "We'll do that again," he whispered as he drew on his breeches. "It gave it a certain piquancy, don't you think, and this afternoon, perhaps if you could come without Cassie we might do it again."

"I can't come without Cassie, Miles." Her voice was distracted for somehow she must get herself to the maids' dormitory and change her dress since she could hardly go back to the kitchen ... dear God, what was it she had come up for? ... and how long had it been ... but he was not listening.

"I can't talk to you with ... with Cassie there," he hissed, only just preventing himself from saying 'that idiot' instead of Cassie.

"I know . . . I know . . ." Dear Lord, don't let him be contrary now, she anguished, then wondered at her own implied criticism of this man she loved so passionately. She hurried to cover it up. "If you bring Barney and let her play with him . . ."

He grinned in the gloom and an excited smile curved his mouth.

". . . we could perhaps snatch a moment . . ." he finished for her.

"Yes . . . and, Miles . . ."

"Yes, my love?" He was pleased now as anything – such as the last thrilling half-hour – which dispelled the boredom, anything out of the ordinary always pleased him, and the thought of making love to her behind a tree, perhaps, while the 'loony' played nearby was quite splendid.

". . . Bess and I are to have our own room. I shall be able to get out at night." Her breath was sweet and warm against his ear and he swept her into his arms in delight.

"Daisy, what a clever girl you are."

"But you must let me go now."

"I will, I promise you. Just one more kiss to tell me you love me and forgive me for my . . . impetuosity. Say it, my darling."

"I love you, Miles. I always will."

She would not allow him to make love to her again that afternoon as he had hoped and she had her first glimpse of the icy temper which could turn him from a laughing, teasing, attractive, amiable young man into something even the closest of his friends did their best to steer clear of. It was no more than a shadow, a shape seen through fog, scarcely recognisable and gone as soon as it had come, but for that fraction of a second it was as though she was clasped in the arms of a stranger.

Cassie had wandered ahead of them, turning to smile as the dog capered at her side. She had grown used to Miles's presence by now and was enchanted with his good-humoured smile, his small jokes, his gentle teasing. She was like a child who is treated as an adult by another adult, bobbing her head delightedly when he talked to her, smiling her exquisite smile, ready to be friends with him as she was with anyone who was kind to her. The four years she had lived with the Greenhalghs seemed to have wiped clean the slate of her memory and though Daisy had been afraid that Cassie might mistrust him, as a man, it had not been so. The tolerant good humour she met from all the male employees on the estate had built a confidence in her which allowed her to take on trust any man who showed her kindness. And Miles was kind to her, so patient and gentlemanly he would make any woman feel secure. He brought her sweetmeats, bonbons his mother ordered from London, presenting them to her with a bow, just as though Cassie was a ... well ... a real woman, a grown, normal woman. Cassie loved Barney, romping with him and giving Daisy and Miles time to talk, to hold hands and now and then to slip behind a tree to snatch a kiss.

But he was not satisfied with a kiss. It was a long time since Miles Thornley had been refused by a woman. His masculine sexuality and ego needed replenishing every day and it was only just under control. His passion for Daisy was at its highest peak, flaring badly beyond his control, and when they slipped behind the gnarled trunk of a wide oak tree his kisses became deeper, stronger, and his hands more and more unrestrained. Daisy felt as though she had been thrown into a pool, a pool of lovely warm water in which she was drowning; fragrant, soft and from which, though she really didn't want to, she knew she must struggle to escape. Somewhere in the sun-filled air above the water she could hear the excited barking of the dog and Miles's voice, thick and mumbling. Her back was to the broad trunk of the tree and he leaned against her so that she was completely enclosed, their limbs trembling and blending with one another. His eyes were glazed as he pressed closer and closer to her, holding her body with his and his hands moved down to her skirt, pulling it up, easing it between their bodies until it was about her waist. His fingers were at her drawers, pushing them down, caressing the slim curve of her hips as they were revealed and just behind the tree, no more than three feet away, the dog barked again and she came to her senses.

"No..." Dear Lord, she always seemed to be saying 'no' to him and yet she could not allow him, as she had done this very morning, to take her here where Cassie might come upon them even though, God help her, she wanted it as much as he did.

"Oh yes, madam ... oh yes..." His face was expressionless as his hand moved to his own trousers. She turned her head away, moving it frantically from side to side. The dog had come round the tree and was looking at them, its eyes bright, its head on one side, its plumed tail moving lazily. It had the stick in its mouth and where ... dear Lord ... where was Cassie?

"Cassie..."

"Damn Cassie..." His voice was as without expression as his face.

"The dog ... is here ... stop it ... Miles ... please..." and as she dragged herself away, using brute force, only her own fear – for Cassie – giving her the strength for it, Cassie's face peeped round the tree-trunk, brimming with laughter.

Smoothing down her skirt Daisy stepped towards her, trying to smile, trying to put into her voice the usual loving calm with which she always spoke to her, hardly daring to look back at Miles. She put up a trembling hand to her hair, tucking a loose strand behind her ear.

"There you are," she managed to say, then bent a hand to the dog but it backed away. Cassie smiled, her eyes on the animal, then reached to take the stick and whilst she was distracted again Daisy found the courage to turn.

He was leaning with his back to the tree. His face was anguished and when she moved towards him he passed a shaking hand across his sweat-slicked face. It seemed he could not bring himself to look at her.

"Forgive me," he said softly.

At once her loyal heart filled with love and she took his hand in hers, lifting it to her lips, kissing it passionately.

"There's nothing to forgive."

"There is, really there is. And for this morning too. I am

no gentleman, Daisy, I am ashamed to say. I have only one excuse and that is that I love you so much I cannot . . . I cannot seem to think coherently when I am with you. Say you will forgive me."

"Miles . . . really, there is no need . . ." She turned to look at Cassie. The girl was holding the stick high and the dog was jumping for it and Daisy turned back, chancing a kiss, soft and awkward, on Miles's cheek for she was still very aware, even yet, of who she was and who *he* was. In passion, in the fierceness of the ardour he aroused in her she forgot their separate stations in life and they were only man and woman but at other times she was conscious, perhaps only slightly but conscious nevertheless, that she was a house-maid and one day he would be a 'lord'.

"There is nothing to be sorry for," she whispered shyly. "I . . . I want to as much as you but I want it to be when we are alone. Soon . . . next Saturday when Bess and I move . . ."

Bloody Hell! Next Saturday and he was as hot for her as though it had been a month instead of only a few hours since he had last had her. He'd have to force her, here and now, which would be damned awkward but there was no doubt he could do if he wanted to, but it would ruin all the careful work he had put in on her up to now. There was so much she could still give him, this delectable little wench and he knew, somehow, that if he could just curb his own damned eagerness *and* temper since he did like to have his own way, it would be well worth a bit of patience. Next Saturday night and every night after that if he cared to, she was telling him. Besides any other half-hour in which he could entice her out of the clutches of the damned house-keeper who watched over the servants like a bloody gaoler.

He bent his head until it rested on her shoulder, hiding the expression on his face, the picture of abject penitence, and Daisy put up a wondering hand to smooth back his dark tumbled hair. Her heart was too full to speak. They would be together next week. She and Miles. She went no further than that. She sank into the enchanting contemplation of it as her love put his arms about her, only for a second since he was now obedient to her wishes, his contrite face told her, then they stepped apart. Cassie was near and he would respect that. She smiled at him, supremely happy.

He made love to her the following Saturday and the one after that and every night in between until her body was drugged and languorous with it. A long, stretching pleasure as her breasts strained towards his hands, her body arched and lengthened as he demanded, needing him to overpower her with his love which was all she had now in the world and which meant more than life itself to her. There was nothing else. She adored his body and what it did to hers, more and more as his whims and fancies, many of them involving her cap and frilled housemaid's apron, some at first strange and erotic, began to overwhelm her. And she was overwhelmed. By his need of her, for she made him groan and tremble and shudder to helpless esctasy beyond any he had known before, he told her. By her growing need of him as her woman's body submitted to that of his. But not only for that. He had an ability to make her laugh at his often coarse sense of humour. He bemused her with his fancy to suddenly treat her as if she was a queen – though that often had more to do with a sensualism she did not even know the meaning of – and by his absolute belief that everything would come right for them. How, he was not sure, he told her, but she was to trust him to see that they would always be together. Did she not understand how much she meant to him? Did she not know that he could not live without her, without this ... and this ... and this ... and if she would just turn over and bend her knees thus, lifting her delightful little ... yes, yes ... that was just right, and he would soar away to groaning fulfilment taking her with him.

"It can't last, Daisy Brindle, really it can't and all I'm frightened of is that when they find out, as find out they surely will, they'll give me the sack as well as you, for my part in it. It stands to reason. We share a room, which you're rarely in, at least for no more than an hour or two each night and so I must know what you're up to, mustn't I? Why haven't I reported you, they'll ask, seeing as how I'm an upper house-maid and over you ..."

Bess Miller was frightened. She knew now, of course, for how could she not, who it was Daisy crept out most nights to meet. It had begun on the first Saturday she and Daisy had been alone in their new bedroom when Daisy, instead of changing into the plain white nightgown all the maids wore, sat down slowly on her own bed and waited until Bess had slipped between the covers of hers.

"What's the matter?" Bess said, surprised that Daisy was not as eager as herself to get to sleep. There were two dozen weekend guests at Thornley Green for the fishing Lord Thornley offered to his friends during the summer months. He had a well-stocked river, of trout and salmon, which crossed his estate and for those who did not care for the sport there were innumerable games of croquet, cricket for the gentlemen or just the lazy passing away of the hours in tea parties on the sun-dappled wide lawns and the endless gossip the ladies found so fascinating. The servants, from five thirty in the morning until almost midnight, had barely time to drink a cup of tea, let alone have a proper meal, and the maids had taken their supper standing up in between seeing to the needs of the guests. They were exhausted, all of them except, it seemed, Daisy Brindle who sat on her bed as though the last thing in the world she wanted was to get into it.

"Aren't you coming to bed?" Bess had been smiling then. She wasn't smiling ten seconds later.

"I'm going out," Daisy said abruptly.

"Wha ... ?" Bess's face was foolishly comical.

"You heard."

"But ... I don't ..." She did, of course.

"I'm going to slip down the back stairs ..."

"Oh no ..."

"Yes ... I must, Bess."

"There's no must about it. I told you last time I wasn't covering for you and I meant it."

"You don't need to cover for me. If anyone comes here to look for me, which is unlikely, all you have to say is you

231

don't know where I am. That when you went to sleep I was here."

"How can I do that? For God's sake, Daisy, don't do this to me, or yourself." Bess's face was anguished. "Dear God," she moaned, "why was it me who fetched you on that first day you came? Why didn't one of the others get lumbered with you? Mary-Ellen Frost or Katy Mason? Why did it have to be me? And what I want to know is who is it? It can't be one of the guests because the last time you went out there was none here. I know it must be ... gentry ... someone high. Knowing you, you'd not bother with another servant so it must be ... someone in the house..."

It began then. An expression of knowing. A reluctant recognition quickly suppressed since surely no one ... *no one* would be so insane as to carry on ... an intrigue ... was that the word? ... with ... with ... Dear sweet Jesus ... not ... not with *him*?

Daisy watched Bess struggle with her new knowledge, not awfully sure she could cope with it; absolutely sure she didn't want to, and yet what could she, Bess Miller, do to stop Daisy from ruining not only her chance of a decent position in this house, but her life, for how else could this end but in disaster? A housemaid and the heir to the estate, for who else could it be? He'd been home now for almost six months and that was how long – now that Bess recalled – Daisy had been ... well, different. Light and bright with a look about her which had been hard to describe except with the word *radiant*, and now she was off to meet him, as she had done a few weeks ago and with no one but herself to stand in the way now that they had their own room. How thrilled she had been to get out of the dormitory and how pleased that it was Daisy who was to come with her. She had taken a fancy to her on that first day and they had got on together, worked well together and now, dear God, now they were to go down together.

She tried one last time.

"Don't go, Daisy. He's not worth it."

"Who?" Daisy's face was cold and set.

"You know who I mean and so do I. *Him*, Master Miles..."

"Don't, Bess..."

"There's been talk about him ever since he was fifteen, lass. A womaniser they call him, creeping from one bedroom to another and under his own mother's roof..."

Daisy sprang up, her eyes striking sparks of fury in the dim light from the candle. Her face was livid and around her mouth a thin white line had formed. Her fists were clenched and she stood over Bess as though she was no more than a second away from blacking her eyes, both of them. Bess had never seen such snapping rage and instinctively she cowered away from it but she was not yet done. If Daisy hit her that would be the end of their tentative, slowly budding friendship but she'd be no friend if she didn't do her best to stop someone she was ... well, fond of, from taking this ruinous road.

"Daisy, listen to me, even if he was the best creature that walked God's earth, where's it to end? He can't marry you, you know that, so what are you to do? Be his ... his mistress, his fancy woman...?"

"I'm warning you, Bess, if you say one more word to tarnish the name of a man whose boots you're not fit to clean then I swear you and me are finished. He's the finest, dearest..."

"All right, I'll say no more about him, but what about you, Daisy? What about you? What if you should fall for a child?" Bess sat up. Her voice was quiet, her eyes steady.

Daisy stepped back uncertainly, hers wary.

"Fall...?"

"Dear God!" It was almost a snarl which came from Bess's throat for really the girl was a simpleton, as naïve as that child she called her sister over at the Greenhalghs'. "How ... how often have you...?" She could not finish. She was a good girl, plain-spoken but not about matters such as this. A virgin herself with no knowledge of men, and no desire for it since she was the eldest of fifteen children and had seen what it did to her mother, so how could she question Daisy on the ... on the functions of her female body? But she must. In her way she was as fiercely loyal as Daisy. Nearly two years ago she had taken the new girl under her wing and she felt responsible for her, though God alone knew why.

"How often have you been with him?" There, was that blunt enough?

"Been with him?" Apparently not.

"Lain with him then?" Bess was beyond niceties now in her desperation.

"That has nothing to do with you, even if I had, and I'll thank . . ."

"Have you had your monthlies since?"

Daisy was outraged. "How dare you? How dare you question me on such a . . ."

"Have you?"

"Yes, as it happens but . . ."

"Thank God, then it's not too late."

"Too late for what?"

"To stop it now. To give him up. It has occurred to you that you could have a child, I suppose?"

No, it had not. In the enchanted world to which Miles transported her there had been no thoughts of consequence, no attention to tomorrow, of what might happen. No words such as stability, steadiness, balance, gravity. Not in their world which was made up of clear skies and sunshine, laughter and soft kisses, joy in eyes of the bluest blue. A child . . . Miles's child . . . Dear Lord, the thought bewitched her but it could not be so . . . not now . . . not for a while . . . if ever, a small cold voice told her . . . *never!*

But it was of no importance, she told herself as she whirled away from Bess's restraining, compassionate hand. All she cared about was Miles. He was her life, her love and it made no difference what Bess said. She would go to him, now, and for as long as it was . . . as long as she was able . . . for as long as he . . .

"I'm sorry, Bess. I must go." Her voice was unutterably sad. "I . . . love . . . him, you see. There is nothing else for me. No one else who matters. I've cared about him for seven years now, aye, you didn't know that, did you? so it's no fanciful whim. And he loves me. I don't know what's to become of us but I tell you this. Whatever ... gossip has gone before him, he's ... not like that and I will never believe it of him. He loves me, Bess. I trust him and if ... if anything should happen ... well, you will know what I mean, he will take care of me. I'm going now. Mr Petch has bolted the side-door but I oiled the hinges and I can get in and out easily enough. I shall have to leave it unlocked but it will be safe." Her voice was soft and distracted. She had moved on to other things which had nothing to do with Bess Miller. "I shall go through the little side garden and be back before dawn. He's waiting for me."

Her face was lit with the loveliest expression. Soft, yes, marvelling that she should be so loved, sorry for those who were not, loving to the point of worship the man who had awoken these feelings in her and as she slipped through the bedroom door, turning for a moment to smile reassuringly at her, Bess felt the pain of what was to come pierce her own pitying heart.

And so the summer of Daisy Brindle's love moved on through the buds of May, the fairest month of all it was said, through June when the crops ripened and midsummer came and went. July when the dog days began, bees swarmed and butterflies made a dancing cloud above the butterfly bush. There was the mowing of grass and hay, and in the somnolent fields, waggons to bear it away, mayfly, midges and dragonfly dipping in the shafts of hot sunlight and wood birds fluttering and chattering in the bushes that overhung the stream. A dreamtime from which there could be no awakening, Daisy Brindle thought, and Bess Miller watched it, and waited for the sleeper to stir.

16

Daisy watched him go on that warm August morning just as she had watched him go last winter. Then he had been mounted on his splendid hunter surrounded by dozens of others on similar animals; by a pack of milling, excited foxhounds, red and black hunting coats, by the quiet-footed servility of footmen as they passed the stirrup cup amongst those who were to ride to hounds that morning. It had been cold then with vapour whipping away from smiling mouths, a hoar frost beneath the horses' hooves and the magnificent tracery of bare branches against the pale winter sky.

Today it was already warm even though it was only an hour past dawn, with a sky which was a pure summer blue except for a thin brushing of high clouds, featherlike, at the very top of its arc. There was a hint of mist amongst those same trees, thickly foliaged now, and the guests longed to begin, they told one another, since the season was short. They were all in a fever of excitement, the talk of guns, dogs and game which was why they were here, of course, and the noise of it rose up to where Daisy loitered behind the curtain. Snatches of conversation came through the open window, none of it making sense to her but it seemed as clear as daylight to them.

"The hatching season has been finer than I've ever known it," she heard Sir Christopher Faulkner say to his lordship and she smiled for they all liked Sir Christopher, especially Daisy Brindle who had cause to bless him. But for him, God only knew where she and Cassie would be today but the less her thoughts dwelled on that the better since it did no good to look back, she scolded herself.

"The broods are larger and more numerous than my gamekeeper has ever counted," his lordship replied, "and there is no doubt it will be a good day."

They were military men, some of his lordship's guests, and Daisy thought a soldier before battle could not be more anxious nor excited than they. There were dogs everywhere – setters, retrievers, all trained to the gun, she had heard Talbot remark the night before. They were howling and yelping, as mad to get away as the gentlemen, and at the edge of the gravel drive in front of the house were the keepers and beaters, the dogcarts filled with all they might need in the way of guns, gun cases and ammunition. Whips cracked and the march was sounded. The dogs surged, yelping even louder, but just before he strode away Miles looked up at the window and she saw his teeth gleam whitely in the smooth brown of his face. She smiled back, though of course he could not see her.

Only last night he had told her that he might not be able to meet her for the week or ten days of the grouse shoot, begging her to be patient with him because he had promised his father he would give every moment of his time to their guests, which a fellow must do, after all, and assuring her that as soon as they had all gone and the house was quiet again they would resume their loving relationship. He had been hinting lately that there was to be a change soon, smiling mysteriously as he spoke, kissing her anticipation to the passion and eagerness she showed in the vigorous and inventive loveplay he initiated. He had taught her so many things in the name of love, things she had thought strange and somewhat shocking, telling her she would enjoy them as much as he did. Some she had. Some made her uneasy but they loved one another so what did it signify if he hurt her at times, when he could kiss her better, as he put it, so entrancingly. He could be so tender, so gentle, so ... so submissive almost, demanding that she ... well ... do things to him which surely must cause him pain, sharp with her when she refused, saying she did not love him. He could be hard, fierce, alarming but he was a man and men were like that, or so he told her, and if he loved her, which he did, then she was content. He could do no wrong. She loved him. She trusted him. He would know what was right for them both and any change he meant to make could only be for the better.

Bess watched her like a hawk, of course, worse than a mother but then what did Daisy Brindle know about mothers?

"If you should fall," she said shortly after their first conflict over Miles, "let me know at once." Her face had been closed, furtive almost, but her eyes were fixed on Daisy's in a way which said Daisy would know what she meant.

"Fall?"

"Yes. I know of something. My mother had fifteen before she was given this . . . remedy. She had no more."

"I haven't the faintest idea what you're talking about, Bess Miller."

Sometimes Daisy's innocence, despite what she was up to with that bastard, amazed Bess. She went out almost every night, taking risks so great Bess thought she could stand it no longer and to get it over and done with she would report Daisy to Mrs Crosby. Night after night, sometimes until the dawn flushed the eastern sky, her eyes heavy and drugged when she came back, her movements languorous, her face though pale, lit by an exquisite beauty. And yet in the midst of this evident sensuality which surely to God someone would recognise soon, she was like a child who blunders about among a pack of wild animals, unaware of her danger.

Bess gritted her teeth, longing to shake her, or slap her, or lock her up in an asylum for surely she was insane.

"I mean, Daisy Brindle, if you should become pregnant. God love us, girl, it can happen and why it hasn't done so is a mystery to me. If ever you're . . . late with your . . . well, with your monthlies, let me know at once."

But it had not happened.

She walked over to the Greenhalghs the next but one Sunday, taking with her some chocolate ice-cream for Cassie. Pierre had made it, lacing it with some secret ingredient, whipping it up with cream and almonds, and she had helped herself to a bowlful, packed it with ice and meant to tempt

Cassie's appetite with it. Cassie had not been herself for a week or two now, brought low with some childish ailment which caused her 'grandmother' to suffer pangs of anxiety for had she not lost several of her own children through some 'fever', as illnesses of an unknown origin were called. Not of Cassie's age, of course, for these things came usually to young children and Cassie must be fourteen by Emma's reckoning. She had started her 'woman's curse' a year ago but to Emma she was still no more than a child. Lovely, still as fragile and crushable as a wood violet but loved, and precious to Emma and Robert Greenhalgh as their own children.

"How is she today, Mrs Greenhalgh?" Daisy called as she opened the gate which led from the woodland path into the Greenhalgh garden. Emma was cutting roses, laying them in a basket, her face tranquil beneath the large-brimmed straw bonnet she wore to protect her face from the sun.

"See for yourself."

Cassie was playing with the retriever puppy Robert had brought over from the stables for her. Master Miles's dog had been mated with a bitch from Lord Pennington's pack of gundogs and the runt of the litter, due to be put down for really it would never make anything, had been rescued by Robert.

"Well, what else could I do? I was there when Lord Pennington told his lordship the pup was no good and right away I thought of our Cassie. She's been mad for a puppy ever since we met Master Miles that day in Rough Wood when he had his dog with him. Remember how well they got on together, her and Barney, just as though she'd seen him before and even if she can't speak she certainly knows how to make her wishes known."

They called the bitch Feather since she was a real lightweight and though Cassie made no sound it came to her clicking fingers or a clap of the hands and she adored it, and it her.

She lay now on her back, her skirts above her knees, her head thrown back in silent laughter. as the puppy romped all over her, licking any area of bare flesh she could find, her excited yelps disturbing a flock of white doves in the dovecote.

Daisy and Emma Greenhalgh stood for a moment in amicable companionship, the animosity the older woman had once felt for the younger gone now in the sureness of Cassie's love for her 'grandmother'. The sun was warm and golden. The happiness of the child – for what else could you call her – seemed to endow the moment with a special quality which Daisy had never experienced before, a quality of peace and joy which surely must be seized and held firm lest it slip away. They had both found a happiness in the years since they had come to Thornley Green, she and Cassie, which she had never expected to know, had not even been aware existed, but this fraction of time was so perfect, so exquisitely benign that Daisy knew a moment's thrill of sheer terror. It was almost too much to bear. Just like great pain she found great happiness could be a burden, too, for one was so afraid it might be lost.

"She's quite recovered, as you see," Mrs Greenhalgh continued fondly, trying hard to be disapproving for really the child was growing up and should not display such hoydenish ways, but would you look at her, her doting expression said, and could you be cross?

They sat on the lawn and drank tea, the two of them, Mrs Greenhalgh and Daisy, whilst Cassie ate the ice-cream, feeding spoonfuls to the excited puppy. Emma had long since stopped bothering over the fact that Daisy was a servant at the big house. After all, what was Robert, and therefore she, but a servant, and besides, she had become fond of the girl and they shared a common bond in Cassie.

"I'd best be off," Daisy said at last, standing up and shaking out her skirts. "There's the dining-room table to be set up and Frost and Mason running up and down stairs with hot water and warm towels for goodness knows how many. Mrs Bentham always likes a hot bath before dinner and Green told me her ladyship is determined that tonight's entertainment should be extra special seeing as how they're to be off tomorrow. There's to be a musical extravaganza, Green said, whatever that is, with that friend of her ladyship's, you know, the one who sings, giving a performance."

"Lady Shelton?"

"That's the one, and her daughter will play the piano to accompany her. There's to be a violinist, a flute and a harpsichord, though they are to be brought in after dinner. Professional musicians, Mr Petch told us, and they will want feeding later. It's to be a grand evening, Mr Petch said."

Daisy was still smiling as she slipped through the side-door and ran up the servants' stairs to her room to change. Mrs Greenhalgh had been too polite to remark on the quality of Lady Shelton's voice but it was evident they were all to suffer from it, those who would be forced to listen. Poor Miles! How restless he would be. She could see him now moving from one foot to the other, doing his best to seem entranced, as his mother would like him to be, his eyes searching for some means of escape, but he would smile and applaud with the rest and be the courteous gentleman he had been brought up to be.

When she entered the bedroom she was surprised to see Bess sitting, straight-backed and straight-faced on the narrow, white-covered bed which was hers. She had her hands folded in her lap and her expression was strained. It was only a small room, high in the attic under the roof with a sloping ceiling and a dormer window. Besides the two beds there was a washstand, a wooden chair and a simple pine chest of drawers which they were expected to share. It was immaculately clean and tidy with nothing to show that two persons occupied it.

"Bess, what are you doing up here? Shouldn't you be down in the kitchen getting ready for tonight? With three dozen sitting down to dinner they'll be run off their feet. I'd best look lively myself or Mrs Crosby'll be sending out a search party. Come on, Bess, don't just sit there. Hand me my clean apron from the drawer and put me a drop of water in the bowl, there's a dear."

She was still smiling, pulling her pretty muslin 'going-out' dress over her head and throwing it carelessly to the bed. Bess would put it away for her whilst she hurried into her black dress, her white apron and cap, but as she reached for the pretty frilled and starched cap she was suddenly aware that Bess still sat, like one of those craven images she had read about in the Bible when she was at school, on the edge of her bed.

A feather of unease ran down her spine. Her hands, which had been fluffing out the frill on her cap, became still and she turned slowly to face her friend.

"What is it?" she asked, her voice falling to a lower key, more suited to the solemnity of the announcement Bess was going to make and which she knew would be annihilating. Why? Why? she asked herself. How did she know? but she did, even before Bess had spoken a word.

"They . . . don't need me," Bess said hollowly, still looking beyond Daisy's shoulder at something she seemed to find not to her liking but which must be faced.

"Don't need you?" Daisy's voice went up an octave, almost shrill now in her fear . . . Of what? for God's sake, she asked herself desperately.

"No, nor you. Not until . . . later."

"But . . . the table . . . the . . . ?"

"Tipping and Burrows can manage."

"What! With more than three dozen guests . . . ?"

"There's to be only . . . a dozen."

A dozen? A dozen people to sit down to dinner when the shooting party she had watched set out over a week ago had numbered three times that many? What had happened? What drama had been played out at Thornley Green whilst she had been sitting in Mrs Greenhalgh's sunlit garden watching Cassie play with her new puppy?

This time the fear turned to a kind of dead despair as though all along she had really known this – whatever it was – would happen but had not, even in the quietest, most secret core of her mind, faced up to it in her eagerness to believe that 'everything would be all right' as he told her it would.

"It was her who declared, so Frost said, that she couldn't bear to sit through another evening of . . . of boredom with Lady Shelton screeching her head off to the accompaniment of a crowd of third-rate musicians. Not in her ladyship's hearing, of course, but she said she ... thought ... if Frost could help her maid to get her packed she'd leave at once. She called for her carriage ..."

"Who ...?"

"Mrs Bentham. Talbot said ... said they rode off as though they hadn't a minute to spare. As though they were in search of something they seemed to find missing here now the grouse is over."

"They ...?" Daisy's voice was very careful and she held herself still as though to cushion the blow when it fell.

"Yes, they all went, her and that troupe of young men she seems to take with her wherever she goes."

Bess turned away from her contemplation of the bare wall behind Daisy's shoulder and looked directly into her eyes. Her own were infinitely sad as she waited for the question which would surely come.

"Who ...?"

"All of them."

But it had to be said, his name.

"*Who*, for Christ's sake?"

"His young lordship and his friends. It seems Lord Thornley's pleased with him for the way he's 'buckled' down these last nine months to matters of the estate. His conduct has been exemplary, he was heard to say ... *Ha!* ..." Bess lifted her eyes to the ceiling, almost in tears "... and so he has given him permission to go off to France with the Honourable Freddy ..."

"France?"

"He has a villa there ..."

She heard no more after that. A great silence fell about her and when Bess put her arm around her shoulders, clucking soothingly as one would with a child who has been hurt, she allowed herself to be led to the bed, to be placed on its edge, to be told that she mustn't worry, that everything would turn out for the best, though of course she knew, as Bess knew, that it wouldn't. That it would never be all right again.

Strangely, after the initial blow which, she told herself,

had really been no more than a condition of massive shock, she felt absolutely nothing. Though she sat for an hour or more with Bess murmuring beside her, sipped the cup of tea which mysteriously came into her hand, she did not really hear anything of what was said to her. She was dazed, numbed with the realisation that he had gone, not just gone, but gone without telling her, then, without warning like a burst of sunlight which breaks through a dark and uneasy raincloud, she was suddenly struck with the brilliant, life-giving thought that there was nothing else he could have done but simply ride away with his friends. Was he to leave a message with one of the servants?

"Tell Daisy I'm to be away for a week or two and will see her on my return."

Of course not. If, as it seemed, the arrangements for this journey had been made on the spur of the moment then there had been nothing he could do about it. She had gone to see Cassie, been out of the house for two hours so what else could he do but just go? Poor Miles, how he would have fretted to have to leave without a word of goodbye but he would know she would understand. He knew how much she loved him and wanted nothing but his wellbeing and happiness. It would have been splendid to have had a small note perhaps, explaining what was happening, but of course he would not know that he could trust Bess to deliver it and say nothing. He thought that only the two of them knew of their love for one another. She must not blame him and she did not. He was a gentleman, a member of the class which was pedigreed and wealthy and which did this kind of thing all the while. Dashing off to Scotland for the deer-hunting, she'd heard tell, to Leicestershire for the fox-hunting, to London for the season, here and there and everywhere in pursuit of the privileged life they led. And now it was France so was she in any position to deny him the life which was rightfully his? Of course she wasn't. She could not expect him to regulate what he did because of his love for her. He must go wherever his station in life took him and she must wait patiently for him to come home to her. She had been lucky, so lucky. She had had nine months of perfect happiness, his presence in the house, even when she did not see him, a constant joy to her and now she must let him go and not tarnish what they had been given with regrets for what might have been.

She said so to Bess, sitting up straight and squaring her slender shoulders bravely.

"He couldn't help it, Bess, could he? and so I must just be patient and get on with my life until he comes home again. Was there . . . was there anything said about . . . about how long he was to be gone, did you hear?" She tried to keep her voice light, untroubled, the voice of an unconcerned, uninvolved observer questioning the movements of an acquaintance.

"Not that I heard. They were gone so quickly."

"Well, there's no good sitting here moaning about it, is there, Bess? We've . . . jobs to do, haven't we, so we'd best get on with them."

Bess sighed, saying nothing more.

Daisy grew thin and her face became even more pointed, the cheekbones standing out prominently beneath her fine skin. Her eyes were deep and enormous in their bony sockets and the bloom, the serenity, the beauty which comes to a woman when she is loved, left her, returning her to the somewhat plain and quiet housemaid she had been before Miles Thornley had seduced her.

They had news of him from Kitty Green, her ladyship's personal maid. It seemed he wrote now and again to his mother since, as Green put it, you don't ignore the goose which can be coaxed, once in a while to lay a golden egg. Green knew for a fact that when his allowance ran out, long before month-end, it was to his doting mother her son turned to lend him a sovereign or two and a letter kept her sweet and took only a moment or two of his time after all. Well accustomed to his ways Kitty Green appeared to be, which, though they seemed to have changed of late and only God knew why, were now back to normal. Wild he had been since he was a boy, and wild he was again, and his poor mother, just when she thought those days were over, was worrying herself into a decline over him again.

Daisy listened quietly to the exaggerated lies they told about him, the unfair picture that was painted, and was appalled by their malice and by the fact that she could not defend him. She supposed, in a way, he was somewhat wild though she would have called it high-spirited but then, weren't they all, these fast-riding, mettlesome thorough-breds? They had been brought up to be somewhat nervous and highly strung, changeable and enthusiastic and could you expect such men to settle down easily to the responsibilities which would one day be theirs? The ruling classes they were and surely different to the rest of mankind and would she have him any different? That was what she loved about him. She knew by now, of course, that he was not the blameless, perfect man she had thought him to be a year ago but he was not *bad*, not the rogue the other servants, especially Kitty Green, whom Daisy suspected of having an unrequited fancy for him herself, made him out to be. Daisy knew of his faults but she loved him just the same. It was very hard to keep her mouth shut though.

"They're off to Venice next week, he says, so I suppose that means he's got into trouble gambling at Baden-Baden and cannot meet his debts. Not that her ladyship would realise that. She only sees what he tells her . . ."

". . . so it's to be Rome for a week or two, he told her, and he'd be sure to be home for the start of the hunting season, if you can believe him . . ."

And then one magical day . . .

". . . and so he hopes she doesn't mind if he stays with Bertie Millington in Leicestershire. He has bought himself a new hunter and is to hunt with the Quorn . . ."

Leicestershire! Leicestershire, that was in England, wasn't it? Down south somewhere, and whilst Bess kept an eye out for her she looked it up on the map in his lordship's study whilst they were cleaning it, and there it was. Barely six inches on the map from St Helens and with the start of the hunting season he would be home soon, he had said. Ten weeks! Ten long weeks he had been gone but she had got through it. It had been hard at times, keeping faith with him when Green was so spiteful, passing on to them what she had overheard his mother say to his father, and his father to his mother, which seemed to be so harsh. Her ladyship defended his 'young lordship', pleading with his father to give the boy one more chance, or so Green said, preening somewhat for it really was splendid to be the centre of attention once more as she recounted his young lordship's misdoings. He had been a 'good boy' for a while and there had been nothing to tell, but now she could regale the servants' hall with stories of how his lordship had stated plainly he would pay no more of his son's gambling debts; that if he didn't give up the bad company he kept, which meant, for one, the 'splendid Sarah'; if he did not come home and show some interest in his inheritance, he would be disowned for if he went on as he was, there would be nothing to inherit!

"Dear God, if I hear that bloody woman say one more word against Miles I swear I'll strangle her, Bess. I don't know how I stop myself, really I don't. She shouldn't be doing it, you know, talking like that about Miles and repeating what her ladyship says to his lordship and vice versa. She's in a position of trust and she abuses it. I've a good mind to report her to Mrs Crosby or Mr Petch. You notice she doesn't gossip in front of them. Oh no, she knows they wouldn't have it and neither will I for much longer. She's up there with her ladyship, listening to everything they say and then passing it all on to the rest of the servants. It makes my blood boil because I know very well she makes most of it up..."

"Why should she?" Bess's voice was quiet. They were getting ready for bed. For the past ten minutes Bess had been watching Daisy whirl about the small bedroom like the weathervane on the coach-house roof, twisting this way and that as though one of the stiff easterly winds which blew directly over the Pennine moorland had got her. She had unbraided her hair. The brush was in her hand ready to attack the wild and rippling curtain which never failed to catch Bess's breath in admiration. It was so thick, so curling, so springing she wondered why it did not sap the strength of the tall young girl whose slenderness had become even more accentuated during the weeks Miles Thornley had been away.

"What d'you mean?"

"Why should Green make up stories about his young lordship?"

Daisy turned slowly, the hand which held the brush still upraised. Her face assumed the expression of truculence Bess knew so well, an expression which said she'd best not criticise Miles Thornley, not in Daisy's hearing, not unless she was ready to have her ears boxed when suddenly, surprisingly, it slipped away and with a low moan Daisy sank to the bed.

"Bess ... oh God, Bess ... it's hard ... so hard to keep faith with him when none of them have a good word for him. When all the talk is of how he lifts the skirts of any woman he fancies whether she fancies it or not." Her face jerked, the flesh so bloodless as to be almost transparent. "It can't be true, can it, Bess? The gambling debts ... the way they say he treats his mother. I know he's ... reckless sometimes, but whatever he might have done in the past, he loves me ... he does love me, doesn't he, Bess?" Her face was piteous and Bess dropped to her knees before her, her own heart dragging with painful compassion. Ironically, now that Daisy seemed inclined at least to listen to the stories about the man she loved and perhaps wonder *why* they were told, Bess wanted to reassure her that she was to take no notice, that they were all scandal- and gossipmongers in the servants' hall, that they liked nothing better than to stir up trouble for those in higher places than themselves, in fact, to say anything which might take the ghastly expression of agonised doubt from Daisy's face. All these months she had refused to believe that he was anything but an honourable gentleman, had defended him hotly – in Bess's presence only, of course – had waited patiently, trustingly for him to come home, and now, when it seemed he was about to do so, she had begun to waver, to have misgivings, perhaps a sense of uncertainty in her own judgement. It was as if, having defended him loudly, strongly, passionately, she had begun to wonder if it had been to cover her

248

own deeply buried suspicions that *they* might be right. That Daisy Brindle might be wrong.

"Speak to me, Bess. Tell me I'm right." Her voice was a long shuddering moan. "Tell me that he's not what they say."

"I ... can't, lass." She tried to take Daisy's hands in her own but Daisy slapped them away, striking at her with the hairbrush, pushing her until Bess fell back on the floor. Daisy jumped up, flinging herself at the small window, staring out into the darkness, blinking back the tears which blurred the thinning tops of the tall black trees swaying above the coach-house roof. Bess sat back on her hands and waited patiently, there, should she be needed, waiting for what she had known would come sooner or later.

"I won't believe it, Bess." Daisy's voice was low but strong. "None of you know him like I do."

"That's true." The words were spoken with unconscious irony but Daisy appeared not to notice.

"He's never lied to me, Bess. He's never promised me anything ... like marriage, well, he wouldn't, would he, and I never expected it. All we wanted was to be together whenever we could. That's all we asked. I knew it would ... it could not ... go anywhere. He always said he would never harm me..."

"But he has, Daisy, hasn't he?"

"NO!" Daisy whirled to face her, her eyes defiant, struggling hard to stay that way but her look of bewilderment was stronger, a look which said she couldn't understand what had come to separate her from her lovely dream, turning it into this which was happening to her now. Her shoulders slumped as she acceded a measure of defeat. "Yes, I suppose in a way he has but I'm sure when he comes home, when we're together again as we were, he'll explain, Bess, why he went away without saying goodbye ... well, there's no need to explain really, not to me, but when he comes home everything will be as it was..." Her voice trailed away uncertainly and Bess stood up slowly, the fear which prickled her at the back of her neck sliding down her back with an icy-fingered touch.

249

"And then what will happen, Daisy? What will become of you then?"

Daisy did not hear the question, or chose to ignore it.

"He loves me, Bess, so why did he go away and leave me?" It was all slipping away, all the resolute, stiff-necked, tight-lipped determination to believe in him no matter what, all slipping away on a tide of desolation and terror that, though she did her best to cling to her belief and trust, was threatening to drown her in its deepening waves. "What am I to do, Bess? What ... am ... I ... to ... do ... if ... oh, sweet Jesus ... he loves me ... I know he does ... he said he loved me ..."

"And you're determined to hang on to that belief, is that it?" Bess's voice was tired. She sank down on the edge of her bed and sighed deeply.

"It'll be all right, Bess, just you wait and see. When he comes home it'll be fine. We'll be just as we were, I know we will. Don't look like that, Bess. Really, I don't know what's come over me, weeping like a silly girl over something that will be as right as rain as soon as Miles comes home. I should be ashamed of myself for having the smallest doubt in my mind about him. Just because Green talks about him ... makes it all up, I'll be bound, just to get attention, I've allowed myself to ... well, to be dragged.low." She made a brave attempt to smile, moving across the small room towards Bess, lifting the brush to her hair again and sweeping it back from her thin face. "I don't know what's to happen, Bess, but I must keep faith. I mustn't let them in the servants' hall destroy what is so good and lovely between Miles and me."

"And if ... if it doesn't happen, what then?"

"Of course it will." Daisy's voice was bright now, though her eyes would not meet Bess's and her face was strained.

"Don't be daft, Daisy. This is me you're talking to so let's face the truth."

Daisy let out her breath on a long shuddering sigh but still she would not let Bess's incredulity shatter her hard-won belief in the man she loved. They might all be against him, rake his name into the gutter but she would defend him with her last breath, her manner said, since none knew him as she did.

She lifted her head proudly, ashamed of her momentary doubts. "I love him, Bess, and I am privileged to have him love me. That is enough for any woman."

17

They rode in on a great eruption of hoofbeats and shouted laughter, a wild and noisy group of mud-spattered young gentlemen who had ridden through a drenching downpour of heavy winter rain, needing hot water and clean towels, aired beds and champagne, but not strictly in that order.

"He's home, Bess, he's home." Daisy's eyes starred her pale face, brilliant with joy as the kitchen burst into excited confusion. Footmen were throwing on their liveried jackets, ready to move to the front of the house to carry in the dozens of boxes containing the silk shirts and cravats, the doeskin breeches and tailored jackets, the hunting outfits, the evening dress, the fine, polished boots, the sporting jackets, the frock coats, the morning coats, the lounging jackets, the capes and cloaks and gloves the young gentlemen felt necessary for a weekend or two in the country. Chambermaids were everywhere, all under Mrs Crosby's calm guidance, making sure fires which were lit in every bedroom every day were cheerful and blazing, that coals were carried up, that dirty boots were brought down to be cleaned and beds checked and towels were in abundance. Indeed every detail which would ensure that the Honourable Miles Thornley, son of the house, and his guests, including the three ladies who arrived in a carriage an hour later, were as luxuriously and comfortably arranged as their rank demanded.

Daisy and Bess were drawn into the turbulence, which, though it might appear to be orderless, was in reality the smooth initiation of a procedure to which all the servants were well accustomed. The dining hall, though it had been cleaned thoroughly only that morning, must be checked for dust which might have crept in since then, the lamps scrutinised and retrimmed, given a final polish. Lord and Lady Thornley were to have dined simply and alone in the small dining parlour used when only the family were present but now, with two dozen to sit down to dinner, the huge mahogany dining table in the great hall must be repolished, the carpet inspected, the enormous hearth swept, the fire replenished, logs brought in, fresh flowers for the copper bowls, a hundred and one tasks which Mrs Crosby demanded in the name of perfection. Mr Petch checked the wine cellar, consulting with Pierre on the menu for the evening which, naturally, must now be changed. Footmen, when boxes were arranged to their guests' liking in the warm comfort of bedrooms, ran to check silver tureens, sauceboats, platters, trays, mustard pots and salt cellars, wine coolers and epergnes on which fruit, nuts and sweetmeats would be arranged. Table linen, cutlery, the Coalport porcelain dinner service, the fragile, hand-blown Venetian glassware, all perfectly in order, of course, for Mr Petch and Mrs Crosby would not allow it to be anything else since were they not the embodiment of quiet and enduring efficiency, but the verifying that all was as it should be in their master's household was the stuff of life to them.

"Mrs Bentham would like a bath immediately," her personal maid declared, no more than five minutes after the carriage which had deposited the three ladies had been taken round to the coach house, "and could you send up a maid to collect several gowns which have mud about the hems. They need a thorough brushing. She wishes to wear her cream silk tonight so she would be obliged if it could be rubbed with a piece of merino. You have such a thing, I presume?"

"Of course," Mrs Crosby said coolly. "Burrows, go with Mrs Bentham's maid at once. Frost and Mason, you take up the hot water," and instantly the necessary implementation needed to serve the guests swung into action.

It was the same with the other ladies, who turned out to be Lady Felicia and Lady Caroline Woodward, wife and daughter of the baronet Sir Ernest Woodward, both of whom had been in the house party at Freddy Rawstrone's villa in Monte Carlo and were now, it seemed, to join Lord Thornley's hunt the following weekend. Hot water, clean towels, maids up and down the stairs a dozen times an hour with dainty trays of tea and meringues, with ribbons to be cleaned and petticoats to be ironed, and it was not until the guests were seated at the splendid table, glittering with silver and crystal, with candle-flame – which her ladyship perferred to lamps – and flowers, that Daisy and Bess sank down for a moment's rest at the table in the servants' hall.

Daisy felt the pulses at her wrist and throat beat to the rhythm of her excited heart. He was here within these four walls at last. Three months he had been gone and in those three months she had known despair and doubt, and then shame at having these doubts. She had known loneliness and deep unhappiness for the heart that loves cannot be content when it is parted from the target of its loving, but she had accepted long ago that she must be prepared to live on the crumbs of love which fell from Miles Thornley's table. Oh, she had no doubt in her heart that he loved her, make no mistake of that, but she was realist enough to know that he could give her no more, no matter how desperately he wanted to. He was the heir to a great and noble lineage. A great lady would be chosen, would become his wife and the mother of his sons but she would not have what Daisy Brindle had, which was his love, his heart, his devotion. She had not looked to the future during the last year but now it seemed to reveal itself to her, slowly, becoming more vivid with every passing moment. She would stay here at Thornley Green. To the others she would never be more than a servant in this house but to him, to its future master, she would be anything he needed her to be in the years to come. His friend, his helpmeet, his lover, any secret role he deferred upon her and she would be, *must* be content with that. She had no choice. She loved him and, quite simply, that would be her function in life. To be the woman who loved Miles Thornley. That was what she was, who she was. It was enough. It must be enough, for there could be nothing more. Cassie was safe, happy and well guarded. The future was secure now for them both. She had done what she set out to do years ago and that was to find a secure harbour, a decent way of life, and she must get on with it. Take from it what was given to her but have the strength not to ask for more. She would tell him so, explain that she asked no more of him than to be allowed to go on loving him and, when he could, that he continue to love her in return.

"How long will it be before we get to bed, d'you think?" she murmured to Bess, unaware that her friend had been watching her over the rim of the hurried cup of tea she drank. Bess had seen the sweet joy, the darting, exhilarated glow in Daisy's eyes. She had watched them darken from a pale golden amber to the deep bronze of sensual anticipation, had noted the soft flush of apricot on her high cheekbones, the parted, smiling lips, the drawn-in breath, the quick, skimming movements as though the sooner the work was done the sooner she would be released to run like the wind into the arms of her lover. She had seen it and despaired.

"Why?" she said before she could stop herself. "Are you going somewhere?"

Daisy turned quickly, then seeing the scorn in Bess's eyes, lowered her own for a moment before she answered.

"You know I am." Her voice was soft.

"Don't go, Daisy, please."

"I must, Bess, you know that. He will be looking for me."

"Will he?" Bess couldn't keep the contempt from her voice. Already, though they had been in the house no more than four or five hours the gossip had gone round the kitchen, the servants' hall, whispered from ear to ear, that his young lordship was 'involved' – though the actual word used was not as polite – with, not the young Lady Caroline

Woodward as might have been expected, but with her mother. A woman of thirty-eight or nine, it was said, who was offering her rich, plain and still unmarried twenty-year-old daughter in the marriage market. An earl or a viscount preferably but a baron, such as Miles Thornley would one day be, was quite acceptable. But in the meanwhile, providing they were discreet, which meant as long as her host and hostess, and her daughter naturally, were not aware of it, she found it vastly entertaining to sample what she hoped to get for her Caroline.

But how could Bess tell Daisy this? How could she watch the devastation strike down the girl of whom she had become so fond? she asked herself. It would crucify her, probably kill her quite dead, for Bess Miller had never seen such devotion as Daisy Brindle gave to Miles Thornley and when she learned of his true character how was she to get on with her life? She should at least hint at it, Bess knew she should, but she was a coward and though she despised herself for it she said nothing as Daisy slipped stealthily from their bedroom late that night. She had changed from her uniform into her newly cleaned, newly pressed tawny wool dress – ready for weeks now for this very occasion – brushed her hair until it crackled in living russet curls down her back, leaving it loose as he liked it and when she turned to smile at Bess, Bess felt as though she herself was personally about to stab Daisy Brindle in the middle of her unsuspecting back.

She did not sleep. Half a dozen times she rose from her bed, throwing a shawl about her shoulders since it was bitterly cold, crossing the room to stare out into the solid darkness of the November night, trying to pierce it with burning eyes for the sight of a dark caped figure. Their room looked out over the coach house and stableyard and the summerhouse was on the opposite side across the parkland but still she found herself time and time again at the window though there was no hope of seeing Daisy.

"Dear Lord Jesus, watch over her. Keep her safe . . ." Safe! From what? It was too late for that since Daisy Brindle had already been besieged and struck down, but perhaps God could find it in his heart to protect her from further harm, to give her strength and courage to fight her way through what was surely ... *surely* about to engulf her.

She crept in a little before dawn and as Bess sprang from her bed, knowing, even before Daisy spoke that he had not come, she could hear her teeth chattering, her very bones rattling it seemed, the shuddering, chilling shaking of her whole body. She helped her off with her clothes and took her wordlessly into her own warm bed, wrapping her in her shawl, wrapping her in comforting arms, doing her best to still the appalling tremors which seemed as though they would shake Daisy's slender frame into a thousand pieces.

"He did not come," Daisy whispered at last.

"No, lass."

"I should not really have expected him on his first night. He would have his guests to see to and he would be tired..." this from a girl who had just spent eighteen hours on her feet "...so of course ... and he would not know I would be there, Bess..."

"Dear God, Daisy..." Bess was almost beyond speech, "Daisy..."

"Don't, Bess ... don't say anything against him for I won't have it. He wouldn't know but tomorrow ... somehow I must let him know..."

"For God's sake, lass ... don't do this to yourself..." Bess began to weep, the wealth of her pity for this girl who would not give up, would not believe, would not allow herself to desert the man she loved, too much for even her own phlegmatic calm. "He's not worth it, everyone knows he's not worth it so why won't you accept what he really is?"

"... d'you think you could put a note in his hand?"

Bess continued to weep, continued to rock Daisy Brindle in the strength of her despairing arms, knowing that it did no good. Daisy wasn't even listening. She wouldn't believe it whatever Bess said. She'd go on making excuses for him, go on defending him, loving him, believing in him until ... until he flung it in her face, told her in his own brutal way what a fool she had been. Would she believe it then? she wondered hysterically.

Seven days later she believed it.

On the seventh night she crept back a bare thirty minutes after she had left and she knew the truth then.

"Did you ... was he there?" Bess asked her, dreading the answer for surely something dreadful had happened?

"Yes," no more.

"What ... did he say?"

"Nothing to me."

"Then ... ?"

"He ... there was ... someone with him."

"Daisy ... oh, lass ..."

"He was ... they were ... drinking champagne and then he began to ... undress her ..."

"Daisy ... don't ..."

Bess watched her in the tiny glow of the candlestub which she had put a light to. Bess sat at the head of her bed, her shawl draped over her shoulders, her nightdress tucked about her feet, and watched the thin, silent apparition who had once been the hard-working, optimistically good-humoured girl she had come to admire and ... yes ... to love. She was none of these things now. She looked as though she had taken a fatal blow to the heart, a blow which had winded her so that she could not catch a breath. As though there was something she didn't, or couldn't, understand. Her mouth was working convulsively though she said nothing more. Her face was paper-white and blue half-moons had appeared beneath her eyes. But she made no desperate, last-minute attempt to defend him now. She did not even look at Bess. She took off her dress and put on her nightgown. She took up the brush and without a glance at Bess, dragged back her glorious hair, scraping it so severely away from her face it actually pulled the skin taut.

She turned then, piercing Bess with eyes which were as hard and fixed as brown rock. In them was an expression which made Bess flinch away though she was well aware that it was not directed at her. Daisy said nothing, even then, merely blew out the candle and climbed into her own cold and empty bed.

"What's up with Brindle?" The question was asked a dozen times in the following weeks, though not to her face, of course. There was not one who would dare, for she had a look about her which sent those who would have been inclined to a show of goodwill – for were they not all somewhat harassed and overworked at times? – scurrying out of her path. She worked like a demon so Mrs Crosby had no fault to find with her. Her silent withdrawal might have been put down to a chap if it had not been well-known that Brindle had no time for that sort of thing and besides, she was never out of the sight of the other servants except when she was in her bed. The only time she was out of the house was on a Sunday afternoon when she went over to see that 'sister' of hers who lived with the bailiff and his wife, and Mrs Greenhalgh would hardly be likely to encourage a housemaid from the big house to associate with a man on her premises.

They were all agog just after the New Year when Dolly Bradshaw, her that worked as scullerymaid in the Greenhalgh household, knocked on the kitchen door, scarcely waiting until Lizzie Lewis had it open before she was over the doorstep, almost knocking poor Lizzie across the kitchen in her eagerness to be inside.

"Where's Daisy?" she screeched, her plain face as red as the tiles on the kitchen floor with the frantic dash she had made through the little wood, and across the wide lawns which stretched between the two houses. "For God's sake, where is she?"

"What's up, Dolly?" Lizzie ventured, her aggrieved expression at almost being flung to the floor of the kitchen she herself had just scrubbed and on which Dolly had traipsed half a ton of muck with her boots, changing to one of excited anticipation. Life was, for the most part, tedious and unchanging for a scullerymaid who saw nothing but dirty floors and mop-buckets from one year's end to the next, not like a housemaid or chambermaid who at least had the cleaning of something nice to look at. The prospect

258

of a bit of melodrama in her dull routine had Lizzie quite openly burning with curiosity.

"It's Miss Cassie."

"Is she not well then?" How disappointing!

Dolly tried to connect the simple words with the drama of what was happening in the pretty bedroom at the home of Mr and Mrs Greenhalgh but her mind shied away from it. Taking Lizzie by the shoulders she began to shake her, screaming something incomprehensible at the same time, and all about the large room heads turned to stare in amazement. Pierre got down from his high chair since he was just at the most important stage in the preparation and direction of one of his superb dishes and this commotion had completely broken his concentration. There were to be thirty guests for dinner since it was right in the middle of the hunting season but how could he be expected to create a meal worthy of his reputation in the midst of such confusion?

She was there then, quiet, contained, with her black afternoon dress and apron which had somehow become too big for her recently tied tightly about her slender waist. Her white cap covered her hair, her ears and most of her forehead and her great golden eyes, surely too big for such a small pointed face, gazed out coolly from beneath it.

"What is it? Tell me what's wrong, Dolly."

Dolly turned to her, frantic and clutching. "It's Miss Cassie, Daisy. Mrs Greenhalgh says you're to come at once..."

"I can't leave my work, Dolly." Mrs Crosby was at her back, ready to slap Dolly Bradshaw's silly face, should it be needed, since it seemed she was about to succumb to hysteria which Mrs Crosby would not allow.

"Of course you cannot, Brindle. Now get back to the stillroom and I will deal with this."

"Oh no, Mrs Crosby, no ... please, you've got to let her come." Dolly was babbling now, the memory of that pretty bedroom and what it contained allowed no other thought in her head but that she was to get Daisy to it as soon as was humanly possible.

Daisy hesitated. In the heart of the great cold silence, the vacuum of non-existence, of emptiness, which allowed her to get through the days and nights, to contain the agony which never left her, not for a single second, an unease began to gather. She didn't want it. She didn't want to feel anything. She didn't want anything to stir the silence, to shatter the icy calm in which she had managed to function for the past four weeks but ... Cassie ... they were saying there was something wrong with Cassie ... how could that be ...? She had been with her only last Sunday ... she had been healthy and lively then ... in fact, in the tiny portion of Daisy's brain which still continued to function on the level of the basic, everyday matters of life, she had thought, and had even mentioned it to Mrs Greenhalgh in the automatic way the brain commands one to do, that she had never seen Cassie look so well. A blooming which had come on her just lately as she developed from a slender young girl into the beautiful young woman she undoubtedly would be.

Daisy felt the ice which had encased her, which had grown thicker and more solid with every day that passed, begin to thaw. Her brain shifted from the animal-like consideration of dusters and brushes, of polishes and creams which had absorbed her whole attention ever since ... ever since ... no ... no, she must not think of that ... she must not allow that certain picture, the one in which the hard, brown and beautiful male body of Miles Thornley pressed itself ardently against the white curves of Lady ... of ... no ... no ... she must concentrate on this ... on Dolly ... on what Dolly was saying about Cassie.

Mrs Crosby was pushing the weeping figure of Mrs Greenhalgh's scullerymaid towards the kitchen door, her manner not at all pleased, and announcing quite clearly that she would allow none of *her* girls to conduct themselves as this one was doing. Distraught the girl was, but even so could not Mrs Greenhalgh manage the emergencies of her household in a more efficient way than this? Sending a servant to summon one of *hers*, just as though she had the right to order the household staff about as she pleased.

"Tell Mrs Greenhalgh that Brindle is far too busy to run over there whenever she happens to have a fancy for it," she was saying firmly, manhandling the unwilling Dolly through the doorway and out into the yard. "If she has time and I consider it necessary I may give her permission to slip across when the family have dined but until then I'm afraid your mistress will have to manage without her."

"Wait." Daisy began to follow the housekeeper, putting a most insubordinate hand on the door to prevent her from closing it. Her ash-pale face had assumed an expression of anxiety and her eyes, for the first time in weeks, were alive. Emma Greenhalgh wouldn't send across to the big house if all that ailed Cassie was a ... a sniffle, or an upset stomach, or some trivial childish ailment which now and then assailed her beloved 'granddaughter', much as she adored her, indulged her, cosseted her, since she knew the running of Thornley Green and the routine of its servants would not allow the frivolous toing and froing of one of its maids. It must be serious, grave even for her to send Dolly, who was nearly beside herself, to fetch Daisy.

Daisy's mind jerked painfully from its state of fog-like density and began to function in the crisp and disciplined way it had been taught at the School of Industry and which had been its normal process before Miles Thornley had shattered its peace.

"What's wrong with her, Dolly?" she asked, almost pushing the sacrosanct person of Mrs Crosby to one side. "Why does Mrs Greenhalgh need me?"

"Oh, Daisy ... please ..." Dolly scrabbled at her, her face awash with tears, her nose dripping, not bothering to attend to either, not even noticing them. "Mrs Greenhalgh says ..." A look of guile crossed her blubbering face and her eyes slid to Mrs Crosby whose normally well-subdued bosom heaved madly at the impertinence of these two servants who were taking not the slightest notice of her, but Dolly had herself in hand now that she had Daisy's full attention.

"It's ... Mrs Greenhalgh said it was most urgent ... *most* urgent but I was to ... well, it's ... a family matter and I was to tell no one but you ..."

"*Well!*" Mrs Crosby drew herself up to her full height and

bestowed on Daisy and Dolly a look which boded ill for them both. Of course she had no control over Mrs Greenhalgh's servant but she'd have a word or two to say to Brindle when she had got rid of this insolent creature who had come for her. First she must get her own housemaid back to the stillroom where the preparation for dinner was in full swing but before she could utter another word and without even a glance in her direction Brindle had disappeared into the night with Dolly, not even having the decency to close the door behind her.

The door to the Greenhalgh house stood wide open, the light streaming from it across the smooth white lawn. A hoar frost was gathering thickly on every stalk of grass and every twig, lying like spun sugar against tree-trunk and branch. There was a mist drifting in icy waves, clinging and ghostly, but Daisy noticed none of these things nor the lung-biting, flesh-numbing cold as she ran ahead of Dolly who, now that her message was successfully delivered, hung back as though reluctant to return to whatever it was that had sent her.

Robert Greenhalgh sat in a chair in the wide hallway. Just sat there, his hands limp and dangling, his face old beyond his fifty-nine years, and the colour of unbaked bread. The wrinkles in it had deepened to grey seams and his eyes stared out blankly from beneath his thick eyebrows. He looked at nothing, expressionless and totally cut off from everything which went on around him as a weeping maid ran dementedly towards the swinging kitchen door. Amazingly, since he was an outdoor servant, Ted Whittaker hung about at the foot of the stairs. The fire was almost out, just a glow from a half-burned log and a wisp of grey smoke drifting up the wide chimney, and in the air, so thick it could almost be seen was a feeling of desolation, of dread, of misery.

Daisy felt something inside her lurch in terror and her heart pounded so that she could scarcely breathe. Nausea attacked her, rising in her throat and choking her, and her feet seemed rooted to the spot just inside the front door where she had come to rest. Oh sweet Jesus, her mind whispered ... oh dear sweet Jesus ... what is it? ... what in Christ's name has happened? ... Dear God, let it be nothing ... nothing serious, and all the while her mind begged, and her heart begged the faceless, scarcely acknowledged Deity to listen to her prayers, she knew she was grappling with shadows since Robert Greenhalgh's still, grey etched figure, Ted Whittaker's very presence where he had no right to be, the maid's anguish told her quite plainly she was wasting her time.

"Oh, Daisy ... thank God..." Ted Whittaker sprang across the hall and grasped her hand like a man in water too deep for his feeble endeavours. "Let me fetch the doctor, Daisy. Let me go ... I can saddle one of the horses ... a fast horse and go for Doctor Blamire ... she won't have it ..." tossing his head in the direction of the stairs "... but if I was to go now perhaps summat could be done. The master's give up ..." he waved a frantic hand at Mr Greenhalgh "... but there must be summat we can do ... please, Daisy ... please ... the little lass..."

Ted Whittaker began to weep, his weatherbeaten face which Daisy had never seen other than plain-visaged, dour, his manner blunt-spoken and then a few words, telling her as nothing else had done, even Robert Greenhalgh's quiet rigidity, that there was something dreadful waiting for her upstairs.

The bedroom was so hot Daisy felt the sweat break out savagely beneath her dress and across her face the moment she opened the door. The curtains were tight drawn as though to keep out prying eyes. The fire was high, bright and leaping, as were the half a dozen lamps which stood on dresser and table. Shadows moved in golden grace on the white ceiling except for one which was grey and dense and still, the shadow of Emma Greenhalgh who sat like stone in the chair beside the bed. Josie, Mrs Greenhalgh's house-maid, was there, her face pressed to the wall, no movement at all in her back which was all Daisy could see of her, and on the bed, covered by a thick white quilt across which were scattered pink rosebuds and white lace lover's knots, Cassie lay quiet, pale and sleeping. She was neat, tidy, but for her hair all of a snarl upon the pillow which seemed to be stained with something Daisy could not recognise. The same stains marked Mrs Greenhalgh's gown, the large apron she wore, her quietly folded hands and, surprisingly, her cheeks. There was a smell, a hot and dreadful smell which again, though it was familiar, Daisy could put no name to.

She simply stood there, knowing what it was, not acknowledging that she knew, of course, for that would turn a possibility into a truth which she could not stand. The seconds ticked by and then the minutes and still no one moved. Cassie was undoubtedly sleeping and Daisy didn't want to wake her. She had been ill ... feverish perhaps ... and Mrs Greenhalgh ... that's it ... had just got her off to sleep. They were tired, exhausted, she and Josie – who still faced the corner of the room ... how odd! – and that was why they were so silent and if she could bring herself to move, first one foot then the other, until she reached the bed, she would put her hand on Cassie's forehead which would be hot – why was she so pale? – and then send Mrs Greenhalgh away for a rest whilst she herself sat with Cassie.

Someone was moaning and it was a few moments before she realised that it was herself. Josie turned slowly, her face ghastly, all sunken grey hollows and protruding bones. She also wore an apron and there was no mistaking the great and obscene stain which spread from its neckline to its hem, which splattered Josie's arms and face and even her tangled hair. No mistaking now what Daisy could smell. There was a bucket which was revealed as Josie moved, stuffed with towels ... and something ... Oh God ... and all vivid with the scarlet of ... of ...

"Daisy ..." The maid sank slowly, quite gracefully to her knees, her arms about herself, and began to rock backwards and forwards in the age-old manner of a grieving woman. Daisy wanted to scream. To scream and run from what lay under that lovely and immaculate quilt but something in her, something which remained of a ten-year-old girl who had survived rape, pushed her forward until she stood beside the bed. She lifted the quilt and the horror rose up to strike her as her eyes were drawn to what lay beneath it.

It was a mistake, of course, for no one could do to her lovely, sweet-natured, trusting Cassie what *had* been done to her. It was all a ghastly mistake, a nightmare from which she would soon awaken ... oh please God ... There was a punched, gasping feeling in her chest and she felt the terror, the pain, the ... the confusion dominate her. What ... what had ... happened ... what ... where had all the ... blood ... dear God ... *blood* ... could one human body contain so much ... blood ... blood ... She couldn't move. She was struck for ever in the bewildered pose the sight of all the ... blood ... had frozen her in, one arm raised holding up the quilt, her head on one side, the shock so stunning there seemed no way to get loose from it.

Mrs Greenhalgh, her face completely without expression, began to babble then. No movement, no emotion, nothing except the flow of words which poured from her, filling the hot and stinking room as a bucket will fill until it overflows.

"... she was playing with the dog that's all she was doing playing and jumping rolling about in the garden I told her to stop it it was not ladylike and she was laughing like she does but no sound of course and then her face changed and she fell down fell down and the dog jumped on her and she had on her new coat and I couldn't see the blood the blood ran from her and the dog began to howl the blood ran down her legs and into her boots and she lay on the ground I screamed screamed and Josie came and Robert and when we lifted her the blood ran and something else ... something else ... something else and Ted wanted to go for the doctor don't let him go don't let him Josie and I can manage please Robert then no one will know poor baby poor baby why did I not know poor baby she was getting plump but I thought no don't go for the doctor send for Daisy she'll know what to do I cannot bear it we cannot leave here now not after all these years no one must know send for Daisy..."

And as suddenly as it had begun it stopped.

She could not stand the agony. It tore through her, hacking and slashing, drawing *her* blood, she was sure. A blunt knife about her own cringing flesh, raw flesh which

265

screamed in such pain she thought she would lose her senses. She would have to turn away soon. She would have to let go of the quilt and turn away, make a decision about what to do, what to say, how to go about the next minute, hour, day, week, but there was someone whimpering and she was again surprised when it turned out to be herself. It had sounded like an animal with a dreadful wound and that, she supposed, was what it really was, what *she* really was.

But she must get away. Find some means to pull herself into a semblance of order . . .

It began again.

" . . . she loved him you see and when he said could he take her and Feather walking with Barney and himself I saw no harm in it he is a gentleman and Robert is his servant so how could I refuse and I thought she is no more than a child and she would be safe with him he is a gentleman . . ."

Daisy felt the darkness come at her with the speed of a runaway horse and she fell into it gratefully.

18

She was walking through the little wood which lay between the Greenhalgh house and Thornley Green when next she was aware of her surroundings and though everything about her was frozen into a shimmering still-life she did not feel the cold. It was dark but ahead of her she could see the lights of the big house. Every window was lit up and across the paths and sparkling white lawn, about the trunks of the tall bare trees which guarded it, a golden-yellow haze fell, beautiful and unearthly.

She had no awareness of how she had got there. She could not remember coming from the kind and sheltering darkness into which Emma Greehalgh's words had spun her, nor of leaving that stricken, harrowed house in which despair lay, heavy and immovable. They must have picked her up, she supposed, set her on her feet. Someone, perhaps Ted, or Mrs Greenhalgh's cook, for the rest had appeared mindless in their devastation, had told her to go home, to go back to the house in which she worked for here she was, on the path leading to the gate which led into the yard and the kitchen door.

Someone dropped something as Daisy entered the kitchen. Whatever it was fell and shattered into a dozen pieces on the shining red stone of the floor and Pierre's soup, a clear beef essence heavily laced with sherry, just ready for serving and piping hot, splattered all over the black boots of the housemaid who was about to carry it through to Mr Petch. She began to scream from the pain of the scalding soup and from terror, cowering back against the kitchen table and Pierre, his white hat wobbling with rage, ready to strike her, for really, could anyone be so clumsy, allowed his gaze to follow her pointing, trembling finger. Other heads turned in wonder and other girls joined in the housemaid's hysterical cries. They were petrified into strange and graceless poses, struck to the spot in which they had been working and able only to emit horrified noises for surely Daisy Brindle had met with some dreadful disaster on her journey to, or was it from, the bailiff's house? She was already in the direst of trouble, having gone against the housekeeper's express order that she was not to go with Dolly and here she was back again in less than an hour with a face on her like suet, her eyes staring and quite wild, her hair all over the place as though someone had torn it from beneath that unbecoming cap she wore, and which appeared to be missing and her dress every which way. And was that blood on her apron, on her hands and ... yes ... even on her face? Dear God, what had attacked her, for surely something had and where was she going, stalking through the crowd of staring, appalled servants as if she had seen a ghost?

"Daisy..." It was Bess Miller who put a shaking hand on

267

her arm only to have it brushed off as though it was nothing more than a troublesome fly. Daisy continued on her way avoiding sympathetic hands which, now that their owners had got over the first shock, were eager to help poor Daisy for surely she needed it.

Talbot, in his best livery almost fell on his back as he came through the green baize door which separated the kitchen from the passage off which the butler's pantry, the stillroom, the housekeeper's room and many others lay, as Daisy elbowed her way through it, and Bess, at first no more than shocked and alarmed for the safety of her friend, and what had happened to her in the hour since she had left the kitchen, was gripped with a new fear.

Mrs Crosby stood up as Daisy passed her open doorway.

"Brindle, I will see you at once in my room, if you please," she thundered, but her order fell on deaf ears. She hurried round the table towards the door, the first time she had moved so quickly in many years, her face, vermilion with fury, quelling with one livid glance the crowd of servants at Daisy's back, sending them scuttling to the kitchen, all but one, Bess Miller, who continued to call Daisy's name.

"Get back to the kitchen, Miller. I will deal with this," but by this time Daisy was through the second door, the one which led into the softly lit, warm and luxurious hallway, beautifully furnished with deep armchairs and sofas, costly rugs and exquisitely turned tables, with lamps and flowers and pale, watered silk walls. The log fire glowed and flickered in the enormous stone fireplace. There was fragrance in the air of expensive French perfume, expensive Havana cigars and the lovely aroma of burning applewood and there was Mr Petch leading a dozen or so servants, upper housemaids and footmen, all carrying silver soup tureens and other assorted serving dishes to the table in the great dining hall where the guests sat chatting between the first and second course of the splendid meal Pierre and the other chefs had prepared for them.

"Daisy!" Bess's voice was high and frantic and Mr Petch, electrified by the sound where no such sound should be, where no sound of any sort should be except by his orders, turned abruptly, considerably startled. Ogden, the second footman, also startled, walked into him, as did Haigh who was behind Ogden and with the most horrendous clatter, the whole formation deteriorated into congestion and chaos which, at any other time, might have been comical. But not now. Not at this horrifying, unbelievable moment. And in the midst of it Daisy was able to walk directly into the dining hall with no one making the least effort to stop her, should they have thought to try, which they didn't. They were none of them awfully sure what was going on and the two who were, Bess and Mrs Crosby, were too appalled to do more than stand in the doorway and watch Daisy Brindle move like a sleepwalker along the seated row of open-mouthed, slack-jawed, elegantly dressed ladies and gentlemen until she reached the lounging figure of Miles Thornley.

He had been laughing at something Lady Woodward had just whispered in his ear and even now, in the depths of her desolation, Daisy found she still had it in her to admire the pure physical beauty of him. In the midst of her hatred and despair the smooth line of his amber cheek still had the power to move her. The deep and startling blue of his eyes gleaming in the candlelight touched something inside her for the last time and her loathing could not quell it. The burnished gloss of his dark hair, the remembered strength and leanness of his body, burned in agony the heart of her, the heart which would not be told that this man was a liar, a cheat, and a murderer.

"What the devil is going on?" Daisy heard his lordship, seated at the head of the table, cry out and at its foot his wife moaned as though the heart in her mother's breast knew what was in Daisy's.

Miles Thornley got slowly to his feet and Daisy could see the anger in him begin to snarl, fighting like some animal to escape the well-bred chains that bound it, recognising her, of course, believing that she had gone mad, that she had broken in here to upbraid him for his desertion of her, though how she had the gall to do so was beyond him. To humiliate him before his friends for what she thought he had done to her. It was on his handsome face. Not fear, for what could the Honourable Miles Thornley have to fear from a housemaid, but rage that she had been allowed to get as far as she had in her search for revenge. They would not reproach him, his gentlemen friends, for had they not all had their share of serving wenches, but the insult to his mother, to the other ladies about the table was insupportable and by God, this little bitch would be made to pay for it.

The superbly polished table – attended to only that morning by Daisy herself – glowed like silk in the candlelight. It was swathed with ivy and the palest of pink rosebuds set about place cards, place settings and candelabra. It gleamed with rich silver and sparkled with delicate crystal glassware and about it sat the splendid, the well-bred, those with impeccable backgrounds stretching back into the far distances of time. Their customs, their breeding, their good manners which said they should ignore this vicissitude which had unfortunately beset their host, held them rigid in their chairs, their faces blank and expressionless, but if anyone cared to look closely at his neighbour, the avid curiosity was there for all to see. Footmen stood about the room, quiet, unobtrusive. Mr Petch was frozen in the doorway beside Mrs Crosby and Bess and behind them crowded the lesser servants for this amazing spectacle must not be missed. Brindle, of all people, straight-faced, straight-backed Brindle who had put not a foot wrong in the two years or so that she had been at Thornley Green and now she had lost her senses, or was it her mind?

They strained their ears to hear what was said, peeping over the shoulders of those in front of them for a better view, and Bess Miller moaned softly deep in her throat.

Daisy stood before the man she had loved devotedly, passionately, innocently, blindly, she knew that now, of course, since she was ten years old. Seven years she had given to the worship of him, seeing in him the character to which he was the exact opposite. She watched his face alter imperceptibly. It was still incredibly handsome, unbelievably so. His eyes were just as deep an azure blue, his skin as smooth, his teeth as white, but that goodness she had seen there, that humour and kindness she had *put* there simply did not exist. Instead she saw the gnawed-out shell of a man so emotionally void there was nothing to him but this beauty which blinded those who looked at him. There was greed in the sensual curve of his well-cut mouth, and cruelty. There was avarice, there was a pitilessness hidden in the splendid blue of his eyes; self-interest, contempt for those he considered his inferior, an indifference to those he destroyed in his search for relief from the limitless boredom which moved in him like a sickness, a sickness which had struck him young and which drove him from one excess to another.

"She's dead," she said flatly, the strong, bitter, corrosive hating in her so great it bound her limbs and prevented her leaping at his incensed face and tearing the eyes from it with her own curved fingernails. The quiet was eerie. No one moved a muscle nor fluttered an eyelash. No one made a sound, not even Bess now, and those servants who stood just outside the door began to wish they had not been quite so curious. There was something bad here, something awful, something so evil that even their master sat spellbound and speechless in the presence of it. His young lordship put out a hand to the back of his chair as though to steady himself and neither the expression on his face, nor in his eyes, altered. He remained just as he always was, arrogant, insolent, oppressive, his eyes narrowed as he studied Daisy Brindle. They did not waver from hers and somehow, though he made no move towards her, everyone was suddenly aware that he longed to strike her with all the force he could muster.

"Who is?" he asked dangerously, turning his gaze from her for really this was too much to have to endure, not only for himself, but his family and guests, and why had this lunatic slut been allowed to gain access here, his manner asked as he nodded to a footman to remove her at once.

"You know perfectly well who I mean and you know who killed her."

"Dear God, what *is* this?" He snapped his fingers imperiously at the footman who had not moved. "Will you have this ... this person taken away at once and turned over to the proper authorities since she is undoubtedly out of her mind."

Lord Thornley stirred then, his face taking on the expression of a man who has been accosted, amazingly, by some low creature, but who, though momentarily nonplussed, is now ready to dispose of it, but Daisy's next words pushed him back into his seat.

"I have just come from the room where she gave birth to your child, or what there was of it for it was born before its time. A son, the maidservant who was with her told me, but dead, naturally." Daisy's voice was devoid of all expression and she held the assembled company frozen to their chairs, or square foot of floor, more positively than angry words or a loud demonstration of grief might have done. "She was not strong, you see. Completely incapable of bearing a child, both mentally and physically and when the birth pangs struck her she began to bleed. They could not stop it, Mrs Greenhalgh and her maid ..."

Lady Caroline Woodward began to whimper.

"... I have never seen so much blood, Miles, though I daresay an abattoir might ..."

"Hugh ... stop her ... please stop her ..." Lady Mary's scream lifted the hairs on the neck of everyone present except perhaps the two protagonists. His lordship stood up then, his face as old and seamed as Robert Greenhalgh's had been. He put out a hand, a hand used to crisp decision, to curt orders which were always obeyed, and instantly. A hand accustomed to the ruling not only of this estate but of this land in which he was a member of the class which made it great. It was pale and trembling and so was he and when Daisy turned to him so great was her power, fed and strengthened by her hatred of his son, he sat down again. He and his wife knew who she was talking about now, of course, and so did Sir Christopher Faulkner who was one of their guests, but the rest, mystified and mesmerised, sat like expensively dressed statues about the table.

"This is her blood that you see on me. She died in a river of it and you murdered her. I have come here to see justice

272

done for a murderer must pay for his crime. She was no more than..."

"Stop it... *stop it*... please..." Lady Mary was swooning against her chairback but nobody seemed inclined to go to her aid, not yet.

Daisy's voice had sunk to a whisper, but so clear there was not a person in that quiet room who could not hear it. "You must have been making love to her at the same time you were making love to me, though the word 'love' is somewhat misplaced, wouldn't you think..."

"You must be out of your mind, you foul-mouthed bitch..."

"A child of fourteen. That is, her body was fourteen though her mind was that of a six-year-old and would not know what was happening to her. She was that age when your horse struck her the blow which stopped her mind's growth and you took advantage of that, didn't you? How it must have titillated those... those strange whims and fancies you showed to me, to make use of them on a child, a trusting, affectionate child who knew no better. But I did, and that's what is eating me up. I was taken in by you. I believed every foul lie, every sweet word you uttered and I don't know how I am to live the rest of my life knowing I allowed myself to be so... simple. But worse than that is the knowledge that through my naïvety, my blind belief, I led you to that lovely child you violated and killed with your bestiality..."

Miles Thornley lunged for her then and all the ladies in the room began to utter shrill and inhuman cries of distress, his mother's the most piercing and agonised. His hands were about Daisy's throat and he held her, her feet lifting from the floor as he shook her violently, his rage quite uncontrollable. His face was scarlet with pulsing blood and his eyes, drained of their lovely blue, were shot with wild savagery. But even in the roaring greyness, the twisting, circling shadows into which she was fast disappearing, Daisy's hands rose for his face, for his eyes. Her nails raked his flesh, four deep runnels of blood springing to the surface of each smooth cheek and he let her go then, roaring his madness and pain and with it his father became himself again. Became Hugh Charles Thornley, Fourteenth Baron of Thornley Green, who was absolutely appalled at what was taking place in his dining room and who wondered, for one dazed moment, how he could have let it go on for as long as he had.

"Talbot, Ogden, Haigh, get hold of this woman at once and remove her..."

"...he murdered her, the bastard... murdered a child for his own perverted sexual needs..." She was beginning to lose control now as the footmen laid brutal, not altogether decorous hands upon her, the tight and unnatural rein which had been imposed on her by shock, slipping badly. She could see that pathetic, blood-soaked bed, that narrow, blood-soaked body over which Mrs Greenhalgh had laid the immaculate white quilt as though to make her the innocent child she had once been. Obscene and unforgettable, and yet above it was Cassie's pale and peaceful face, as lovely in death as it had been in life. She could not tear it from her mind's eye, and did she ever want to? for this moment was to be the start of the new goal she had set herself some time in the last hour. Where once she had been nothing more than the woman who had loved Miles Thornley, now she was nothing more than the woman who hated him and would do exactly what was needed to grasp the justice she must have. That was who she was. That was what she was and always would be for as long as *he* lived. Her hatred erupted from her in a demented, crazed frenzy of grief and loss. If she could get her hands on him she would kill him. Why had she not taken one of those splendid silver knives from the table when she had the chance and plunged it into his heart ... Oh God ... she hated him ... She had borne her own pain, her own suffering at the realisation of how she had been used by this monster. She had gritted her teeth and told herself that she was not the first woman to be duped by a good-looking, sweet-talking man and she would not be the last. She had suffered her own abandonment, the murder of her own foolish belief in the man she loved, telling herself she had suffered worse blows, from which she had recovered, and she would recover from this but she would never, *never* recover from the agony of what had been done to Cassie. Of the loss of Cassie, whom she herself had introduced to the fate she had suffered. She was well aware in the midst of her torment that nothing could be done to punish Miles Thornley. Gentlemen had ravished women of the lower classes since time began and their own class did not condemn them but she had hoped for redress in some way from his father whom she believed to be a fair man. But she had gone about it in the wrong way. She had shamed him and his family in front of others and now he would never forgive her, nor give her the punishment she sought for his son.

"Take her away and please..." His lordship turned to his guests, his concern for them overshadowing any concern he might have felt for the death of a scarcely known child, "...I beg of you..." What could he say? What could anyone say in the face of what had happened here tonight? His wife was being carried from the room by a footman, her maid in attendance. His son had moved savagely to the window where he glared out into the night, his face awash with his own blood, Freddy Rawstrone at his side for should not one friend comfort another after what had been said, all untrue of course, for were they not gentlemen and though allowed to make free with housemaids certainly, not with children.

The ladies and gentlemen, some of the latter, though they said nothing, half inclined to believe it of Miles Thornley who was known not only to be wild, but unreasonably so, began to murmur amongst themselves, trying not to listen, or watch as the girl was dragged shrieking from the room, presumably in the direction of the lunatic asylum in Wigan.

Mrs Crosby, white-faced and trembling, shattered from her deep-seated belief that everything which went on this house she knew about, found her way to her own sitting room on the arm of Mr Petch since it seemed none of the guests required dinner in the immediate future, where they both drank a stiff brandy to fortify themselves for the ordeal – as ordeal there would be – ahead of them.

It was midnight when she found herself outside the stout, closed gates to Thornley Green and for half an hour she just stood there, staring into the darkness which lay on every side. A black impenetrable darkness, a winter darkness through which she must make her way if she was not to freeze to death where she stood. Which way, she asked herself, shrugging her good cloak which she had been allowed to bring, more closely about her. Should she turn north for Wigan or south to St Helens? Should she just stand here, a small voice inside her asked, lie down here and freeze to death comfortably, or should she live, live to get for herself and for Cassie the retribution she needed so badly? She could just imagine his lordship's gatekeeper having to run up to the house in the morning to inform his master that the servant he had thrown out so dramatically had in fact not gone on her way as she had been ordered but had had the impudence to die on the gravelled pathway outside his fine, wrought-iron gates. She shook her head at her own frivolous thoughts, then raised it to stare into the black sky. No, not Daisy Brindle. That was not what she had in mind at all. She had had a dream, a hope for the future for most of her life, and she had been well on the way to getting it. Now, in the space of a few hours she had another and this, like the first, would keep her alive and fighting until it was realised.

She sighed deeply, feeling nothing now of the violent emotion which had almost torn her into a thousand agonised pieces over the past four or five hours. She supposed the human mind can only suffer so much before it blows itself out into the calmer, more comforting darkness of shock, the inert and merciful languor which it needs to heal itself. It would come back, she knew it would, the primitive need of blood for blood, the desolation of loss, the wrenching up of an emotion she had nurtured for so long, but for now she was glad of the deadness, the stillness which had her in its grip. She must turn soon, in one direction or the other, make some decision, but nevertheless she stood there as though some deep-seated core of her was still working in a practical way and was telling her she must wait a little while longer.

She was not particularly surprised when she heard her name whispered, just at her back.

"Daisy, it's me."

She smiled and lifted her head, knowing who it was. "You shouldn't have come, Bess, though I knew, of course, that you would. I'm glad you did."

"I couldn't let you go, lass, not without saying goodbye. They kept me, asking questions about you, and I couldn't get away but I came as soon as I could. Thank God you waited. I brought you a few things. Your good dresses and your best boots."

Daisy turned and could see nothing but a pale blur hanging just inside the gate, Bess's face pressed desperately against the wrought-iron bars which kept her in and Daisy Brindle forever out. Daisy moved back to her and placed her hands over the ones which gripped the gate.

"Thank you, Bess. I knew I was waiting for something or someone and shouldn't I have known it was you? Have you heard ... anything ... about Cassie?"

"Aye, my lass. She ... died of a fever and is to be buried in Thornley Green churchyard the day after tomorrow."

"Aah ... Cassie ... sweet Jesus, he's to be ... whitewashed then?"

"Yes, the tale is that you were off your head..."

"And ... the others ... will believe it?"

"Oh yes. They hang together, Daisy, the gentry, and the servants have no wish to lose their jobs."

Daisy bowed her head and Bess felt the hot, bitter tears fall on to their clasped hands. She wept silently, tearingly, for five minutes, her face pressed against the bars which separated her from the only friend she had in the world whilst behind the curtained window of the gatehouse one of Dewhurst's innumerable children wept too as his father's hand connected with his ear.

Daisy spoke at last. "You'd best get back, Bess. They'll be

watching you now to see none of my wickedness rubs off on you. Don't get into any more trouble on my account." She was seized by a sudden anxiety. "They've not ... punished you for what I've done, have they? Because we shared a room, I mean. Remember what you used to say about them blaming you ...?"

"Of course not," but Bess spoke far too quickly and Daisy knew that they had.

"What? What have they done?" Her voice was urgent.

"Nothing."

"They have, I know they have. They've not ... sacked you?"

"Would I be here on this side if they had?"

"Then ... what?"

Bess laughed mirthlessly then leaned forward, putting her hand through the bars of the gate to touch Daisy's cheek.

"Lass, all the trouble you're in and you're worrying about me and my ..."

"They've put you down, haven't they? Made you housemaid again? Or even less, I shouldn't wonder." Her voice was fierce and angry and the dormant pain flared up and took hold of her. "Dear God, why must we always be trodden into the muck by these devils? Blamed and punished for what *they* do to *us*? Isn't it enough that they've ... they've broken my heart, Bess ... truly ... killed the only person who loved me ... she was all I had ... allowed *him* to get away with it ... dismissed me because I was reckless enough to speak up, with no character to my name and now you, an innocent ... it's not to be borne, Bess ... *it's not to be borne* ..."

She threw back her head and would have howled into the icy winter night air but Bess gripped her fiercely, putting her arm through the bars and about her neck, drawing Daisy's face to her own against the cold iron.

"Don't Daisy, don't, it does no good. Let it go. I've worked hard to move up in the house and now I'll have to do it again but don't you worry about me. At least I have a pillow to put my head on at night and food in my belly. But what will you do? Where in God's name will you go?"

It was there then, like a lamp which has just been lit, guiding her through the darkness about her and showing her the direction in which she should go. She had nothing. Nothing but a bundle containing a couple of pretty dresses and what she had on her back. She knew nothing but what she had been taught at the School of Industry and at Thornley Green but was that not enough to get her a job of some sort in that great city of opportunity she had read of in the newspapers Mr Petch had retrieved from his lordship's study when they were done with? The centre in the north for arts, science and luxury, she had read, with extensive commercial and maritime connections. Spacious docks where flags of all nations flew gaily in the breeze. Wide streets and noble public buildings, handsome shops and commodious dwelling-houses, or so the newspapers had told her, and surely somewhere there would be a place for Daisy Brindle? It might be difficult to obtain the position of a housemaid in a decent house without a reference but she could damn well try.

"I'm going to Liverpool, Bess. St Helens or Wigan are too close. The Thornley family are well known. I'd never get a job within twenty miles of here but in Liverpool no one will have heard of my ... of what happened here. I should be able to get some work. There are hotels so big and splendid they would make Thornley Green seem like a cottage and they're bound to need experienced maids." Her face brightened, the expression on it invisible in the pitchy black but her eyes gleamed in it as she leaned closer to Bess. Her voice was soft, pleading, for it needed all her courage to set off again, all by herself.

"Come with me, Bess. Climb this bloody gate and come with me."

There was a long silence in which Daisy distinctly heard the hoot of an owl over in Caleb's Wood. She could feel Bess's fear, a fear of the unknown since Bess had been no further than Thornley Green in her life and though she was staunch and loyal and would probably have overcome that fear, to follow where Daisy led, she had half a dozen younger brothers and sisters still at home in her mother's cottage in Primrose Bank and they relied on her for a bob or two each week.

"I can't, lass, you know that."

"Aye, I know, Bess."

There was silence again and Daisy knew she must go. She couldn't hang about here any longer or she'd never tear herself away. She hated them, this bloody family who had brought her down and then flung her out when she had objected, but this was the familiar, the known, shelter, and what she had thought to be hope for the future. All gone now, of course, but it was still hard to step out into the unfamiliar, the unknown, the black cold of the night.

"God bless you, Daisy."

"I don't know about that, Bess."

"Will you ... write? I could ask Mrs Crosby to read it to me."

"Write! To this place? Eeh, Bess, I couldn't. Don't ask me to but I tell you this, it's not seen the last of Daisy Brindle."

"I don't know what you mean. Are you to come back then?"

"There's no doubt about it, Bess. I'll come riding through these bloody gates in a shining carriage lined with velvet, pulled by the finest matched greys you ever saw. I'll wear silk and have golden sovereigns in my purse and the Thornleys will eat the dust my horses scatter in their faces."

"Daisy, you're talking wild, lass."

"Wild is it, Bess Miller? You wait and see. I'll have it all one day. I made a vow when his lordship told me to get off his land. When I stood in front of his desk and saw his contempt for the likes of me. He thought I was nothing, Bess. A nobody who had been rash enough to speak up to her betters and needed teaching a lesson. Oh, he knew I was telling the truth about his son. I could see it in his face but that didn't matter, you see. I had no right to accuse him, to besmirch the family name and try to drag what was fine and ... and sacred through the mud. His family name meant more to him than what had been done to a simple-minded child, more than the violation and destruction, for that was what it was, of a young girl who had no defence against him and I hated him for it as I hate his son. But I promise you this, Bess, you've not heard the last of me, and neither have they. I mean to get on. I don't know how but I will and when I've got the power it needs I'll bring this family to its knees, I swear it."

"Daisy ... dear God..."

"Watch for me, Bess. A day will come when Miles Thornley will curse the moment when he rode over a gang of women in Caleb's Wood, and certainly that moment when he decided to smile in the direction of Daisy Brindle."

The words were spoken without menace, without emotion, in a voice which was cold and expressionless and because of it was all the more frightening, all the more commanding. It came out of the dark, lingering on the air like the last trembling moments of a nightmare and Bess Miller shivered.

PART II

19

It was a cold, bright day in March when he first saw her. She was standing on the Marine Parade as he approached George's Dock from Brunswick Dock where the *Golden Lady* was being unloaded and the first thing he noticed about her was her hair. She was in front of the long, low building of the public baths, dressed in a good-quality dark blue cloak but it seemed she must have just come from the baths for her hair was still damp. It was the colour of a fox's pelt, and, in sharp contrast to her pale, sad face, was vibrant and marvellously alive. She had strained it back from her brow with scant attention to style or even neatness and tied it with a froth of golden ribbons which was in itself unusual, and it hung down the outside of her cloak in a thick tumble of springing curls to just below her waist. He thought he had never seen anything so glorious.

He slowed his long stride, hesitating at the bottom of the wide flight of steps which would take him up to the Goree Piazza where he was about to arrange the warehousing of the cargo of timber he had just brought from Newfoundland. He hesitated a moment or two longer, he could not have said why, and later was to wonder at his own curiosity.

The girl, for she was no more than that, moved slowly towards the parapet which lined the parade, leaning somewhat tiredly, he thought, against the stone, staring out across the waters of the river to the fine views on its far side which today were sharp and clear. The woods of Cheshire were a diaphanous outline of newly greening foliage to the south. To the north was the dancing, shimmering highway of the Irish Channel towards which several packet ships and a brigantine were racing and in between was Bootle Bay, the Rock Perch lighthouse and fort and the whole line of the Cheshire coast from New Brighton to Eastham. Half a dozen pilot boats buffeted through the swell hurrying to catch the tide. They were small, strongly built sloops, painted white with a green stripe along the side. They each had a number on a flag at their masthead, or on one of their sails which were full and cracking as they sped lightly across the water. There were four-masted barques and fast sailing brigs, frigates and schooners and an elegant clipper ship, swift and sleek like his own, and going unconcernedly amongst them, butting their heads into the heaving swell like resolute, black-faced nanny-goats were the ferry boats. They left the landing-stage just below where the girl stood, heading out amongst the busy traffic to Woodside, Birkenhead and Runcorn. A great bustling of craft and passengers arriving and departing every half-hour so that at no time was there a moment's quiet or cessation of movement.

Away from the landing-stage, stretching as far as the eye could see in both directions, were the great docks of Liverpool. The Manchester Basin crowded with flats and barges, small craft employed in inland navigation. Canning Dock, named after a distinguished statesman, Salthouse Dock, so called because of its proximity to the saltworks. The new Albert Dock, Duke's Dock, constructed by the late Duke of Bridgewater, King's Dock adjoining the great 'Tobacco Warehouse' and containing a floating chapel for the use of mariners. Queen's Dock where vessels in the Russian, Baltic and Dutch trade berthed, Union Dock and Brunswick Dock where sailing ships like his own in the timber trade were brought, discharging their cargoes on to the quays from their bows instead of over the ship's sides because of the length of the wood brought from foreign ports. To the north was Waterloo, Victoria, Trafalgar and Clarence Docks and the proposed new dock to be named Strand Dock.

Against a forest of masts, so thick the sky was hidden from view, the clipper bow of the mighty *Dreadnought*, carrying the figurehead of a winged dragon with its tail curling down its stem, dwarfed the men, the horses and waggons on the quay. 'The wild boar of the Atlantic' she was called, so great was her speed. All around her men shouted and whistled and hammered, stopping only for a moment to watch admiringly as a tall frigate swayed gracefully out to sea, bursting into white-sail bloom as she went. The water was turning to a pale grey as evening drew near, with shadows of darkness where the currents lay, its force and speed slowing to stillness as the tide began to turn. One of the new iron steamships, squat and inclined to matronly fussiness, poured smoke in a great swathe from its funnel and hooted irritably and as it did so the girl turned and looked directly at him.

Her eyes were a liquid golden brown, their sadness so deep he felt his breath catch in his throat but when she saw his glance they changed at once from sadness to hostility. Her head lifted imperiously and her shoulders squared and her manner said quite clearly that she had not the time or inclination for the likes of him and should he not take himself off at once he would feel the length of her tongue.

He smiled but made no move towards her, instinct telling him he'd be better served if he kept some distance between them. He was quite bewildered by his own interest in this girl who, but for her hair, was thin, plain and nondescript and he was surprised to hear his own voice as he spoke.

"I shouldn't stand just there if I were you," he said, "or you could find yourself in a situation which might be embarrassing for you. Seamen just back from a long voyage are inclined to be somewhat ... well ... exuberant ... and you are ... forgive me, but they might mistake you for something you are not. I do beg your pardon if I offend you but being a seaman myself I know their ways." His grin was warm and engaging, with no threat in it.

Her expression did not alter. It remained cool, disdainful, but her eyes studied him carefully as though she was trying to make up her mind about something. They moved across his pleasant but quite unremarkable face, then quickly took in the details of his sleeved cloak made of the best Yorkshire wool, his well-cut plaid trousers, the snowy fall of his cravat, his tall top hat which he had removed to speak to her just as though he was addressing a lady.

Then she smiled, at least her mouth did, revealing white and even teeth, and her cheek-muscles twitched though her eyes had become the strangest muddy brown, without light or humour.

"How do you know what I am?" she smirked in the most dreadful parody of coyness and again, for some reason, he felt moved by a strange emotion. "Perhaps it is you who are mistaking me for something I'm not," she went on, still artfully coquettish. "I would hardly stand here amongst all these ... gentlemen if I was not..." she gulped painfully and the tender white skin of her throat revealed the tendons beneath "...if I was not looking for ... for company."

"Company?" He felt amazement, and amusement well up within him for if there was any female less like one of the gaudy, bantering creatures who plied their trade in this lucrative area, it was this one. A man, even a seaman starved of fleshly pleasures, would think twice about accepting what she seemed to say she was offering since she looked as though a summer breeze would have her over.

"D'you know what you're saying?" he asked her, ready to believe she had no idea, ready to tell her to run home to her mother before she got into the kind of trouble she might have difficulty getting out of, for she looked no more than fourteen and, but for that magnificent mane of hair, was not a female to catch the male eye.

"You know what I mean," she said, lifting her head boldly and staring at him as though defying him to challenge her, "and if you don't I can show you." She allowed her cloak to part at the front revealing a black dress beneath. She drew in her breath, raising her tiny breasts so that her nipples thrust against the bodice. She tossed back her hair and bared her teeth again in a mask of smiling, painful seduction.

"Don't do that." The cry was involuntary and he was astounded that it came from him. Why should he care? Girls of this age, and much younger, sold themselves a dozen times a day to any man who had the price. Prostitution was widespread and was accepted as a natural accompaniment of society. It served a useful purpose so why should this one be any different from the rest? "Pull your cloak about you and go home, for God's sake." All the humour had gone from his face now and he was ready to turn away, to stride up the steps to the Goree Piazza and get on with his business but she moved towards him, her stride long and graceful, her carriage tall and proud. Her face was calm and resolute and he saw she was older than he thought. Her smile was real now, the artifice gone, the simpering pretension gone and he wondered why he had thought her plain. She stopped in front of him and her voice was quiet.

"I need money," she said, her mouth curling on the word, still smiling but very serious.

"There are better ways to earn it than this," he answered harshly, not at all sure he liked her nearness or the clean smell of carbolic soap which came from her.

"I have tried them all. I have worked in a pin-heading factory in Banastre Street. Do you know what that is . . . ? . . . no, I didn't think so . . . and in a boot-making works in Great Howard Street, just beside the gaol. In a dye-house in Gradwell Street and a rope-walk in Water Street where I was employed to turn the wheel used to twist the yarn. Severe work in the winter for it means being out of doors but I did it for one must eat. The master was a man of . . . filthy habits . . . as they all were, and did his best to . . . use me, for no extra wage, of course, and when I refused, as I refused them all, like the rest he fired me. So now I have taken up the profession for which they all seem to think I am best suited and for which I shall be paid. I am quite clean, sir . . ." her gaze was sardonic, "since I have just spent my last few pence on a bath . . ."

"When did you start this new profession?" he interrupted.

"I beg your pardon?" since it was nothing to do with him. She raised her head haughtily though her eyes were uncertain.

"When did you take up this fine new post of yours?"

"This morning."

"I see, and I am your first customer?"

"Does that matter? I was led to believe that gentlemen have a taste for . . . for . . ."

"Virgin flesh?" He raised a sardonic eyebrow.

"Yes, so I was told."

"I am not one of them, madam, nor do I care to exploit children who should not..."

"You would sooner see them starve then?"

He had been about to turn away, disgusted somehow, not with her, but with himself though he could not have said why. Perhaps it was with all men who, because of their lust, held cheap young girls such as this, exploiting them to satisfy their own desires. Because he was of the gender which did such things and he felt shame at it. His foot was on the bottom step. His eyes, cool and expressionless, had fixed themselves on the roof of the Custom House which could be seen beyond Canning Dock when he heard her sigh, her breath leaving her lungs on a slow expulsion of air, and he was just in time to catch her as she drifted, light and boneless, towards the ground.

"Damnation," he growled through gritted teeth, hitching her up against his chest, her head hanging limply across his arm, one of her hands floating like a leaf, pale and lifeless. Heads turned as he carried her up the steps and passers-by murmured to one another, asking what was to do with the poor child, but he paid them no heed.

There was a line of hackney coaches and cars at George's Pierhead, the coaches having four wheels and pulled by two horses, the cars having two wheels and drawn by one. The first in line was a coach and he made for it, bundling his burden without a great deal of care on to the seat where she lolled palely, her lovely hair spilling in vivid confusion over her face. The coach driver was inclined to stare but it was none of his business if the well-set-up gentleman had a preference for plainly dressed, drunken whores.

"Where to, sir?" he asked cheerfully, clucking to his horse.

"Duke Street and look lively. The young lady is unwell."

She had not felt so warm and so comfortable for a long time. In fact she could not remember *any* time when she had felt so warm and comfortable for even her bed at Thornley Green had been thin and poorly covered. She could feel soft cushions beneath her head and a light woollen rug laid over her. There was a fire cheerfully crackling close by, the heat of it glowing against her cheek. She could see the light of the flames behind closed eyelids and but for the gnawing, bitter, endless pain in her belly could have drifted off again into the lovely insensibility from which she had just come. But it would not let her sleep, that pain. It had been with her for the best part of three months, assuaged now and again by some morsel of stale bread, a handful of old fruit or vegetables, some green cheese, fish which would not keep another day on the market stall, a rancid pie, whatever was going mouldy and was therefore going cheap.

There was the loveliest aroma drifting inside her head, part of the dream of being warm and cosy, she supposed. The fragrance of hot soup ... chicken, she thought, and fresh, crusty bread and was that pork pie and surely ... apple cheesecake? She knew she was dreaming, or had she died and gone to heaven since only there could such delicacies now be found?

She opened her eyes carefully, looking up into the lamplit shadowed darkness of a high ceiling. She could not make out its colour but she thought it might be a rich burgundy. She moved her head a fraction, anxious not to draw attention to herself for she had a feeling she was not alone in the room. There were luxurious velvet curtains at the long windows, all draped and pelmeted, with fringes and swags. There was a fitted carpet of oriental design in shades of deep plum and the palest blue, a fireplace of ornately carved marble in which an enormous fire burned, a highly polished brass fender before it with shelves on either side crammed with books. Three or four lamps stood on tables. One of the tables was spread with a dainty lace cloth and upon it was a tray with dishes and covered silver platters. There were plum-red velvet, button-back chairs, a glass-fronted cabinet in a corner crammed with ornaments of a very foreign sort, a Coalport clock ticking comfortably on the mantelshelf and across from the sofa on which she lay, a gentleman lounged, reading a newspaper.

He looked up and smiled, his white teeth slashing his

exceedingly brown face. Was he a foreign gentleman, she thought confusedly, not really caring what he was providing she could remain here in this lovely warmth and comfort for ever.

"Ah, there you are," he said. "I was wondering how long you were going to remain asleep. I made you some soup and brought you whatever was in the larder since I'm sure you are hungry. Yes, I thought so. Would you like to sit up to the table or would you like me to spoon-feed you? We might, perhaps, both find it . . . amusing. What d'you say?"

Even in the soft lamplight she could see the humorous glint in his green eyes and recognised the face of the man she had spoken to – how long ago and how had she got here? – on the Marine Parade. His eyes were heavy-lidded, deep and watchful and ever so slightly mocking as though anything their owner said was not always to be believed. They were fringed with thick brown lashes. His hair was the deep burnished brown of a chestnut in which the firelight had placed streaks of gold. It was heavy and straight, falling over his forehead as though he frequently ran a hand through it. His smiling mouth was well cut, curling and sensual. He was not handsome but his face was strong, compelling and completely masculine. The face of a man accustomed to giving orders, she imagined, and to having them obeyed. A man used to his own way and yet there was a warmth in it which said he might have a weakness for defenceless creatures, a tendency to rescue a kitten or a child in distress. But then who was she to judge a man, she thought cynically, for she had placed the same characteristics in the heart of Miles Thornley.

The fragrant smell of the food had set her mouth watering and eagerly she sat up, pushing aside the rug and setting her feet to the floor. They were bare, completely bare for her stockings had been the first to go but the thought that this stranger had handled her naked flesh mattered little to her. After all, she had been prepared to sell the whole of herself this afternoon for the price of a loaf of bread. She had gambled her last pennies on making herself clean for the new trade she was to go into and it seemed the gamble had paid off.

"Come," he said, "drink the soup while it is still warm."

She was ashamed afterwards for the way in which she devoured the food but starvation does not make for good manners. All she cared about was the delicious spooning of the soup, in which whole pieces of chicken floated, into her eager mouth. In between spoonfuls of soup she crammed chunks of crusty bread, a handful of pork pie, a lump of tasty crumbling cheese, quickly, quickly, her eyes darting about the room as if in fear that it would all be snatched away before she had eaten her fill, if that was possible. Was it? Would she ever have enough to eat again? Would she ever know the day when she would push away a plate with food still on it? She doubted it at the moment for there was scarcely a day in the past months when she had not been hungry.

When there was nothing left on the tray she sat back and sighed.

"Well, I must say, for a young lady of such slender proportions you have a remarkably good appetite." Green eyes gleamed sardonically and a dark eyebrow tilted in amusement.

Instantly she was on the defensive. She stood up and looked about her for her cloak and boots.

"I was hungry and so would you be if you'd eaten what I've eaten in the last few days."

"Oh, and what was that, pray?"

"Nothing, that's why I fainted."

"I do beg your pardon. And now that you have had your fill you are to be on your way, is that it?"

"If I may have my things, yes." She looked about her again, not awfully sure she liked the way he was smiling at her. She was well aware that he probably expected something in return for the exceedingly good meal she had just eaten – in fact, had she not promised him as much? – but now, if she could manage it, she would be off. She was not sure where but she would find something. She always had in the past and she would do so again and the nourishment she had just put inside her would keep her going for a few days.

"And what about the ... things you were to show me?" He lit a cigar and the smoke wreathed about his watchful, smiling face. "I believe that was the phrase you used this afternoon and I must admit to a certain curiosity as to what they may be."

"Things?" She began to edge towards the door.

"That is what you said." The good food had put something in her face that had been missing before. Not roses, certainly, for she had the sort of creamy complexion that would never show much colour, but a flush, a warmth beneath the skin which was a definite improvement. Her eyes, though wary, were alive now, a beautiful clear topaz brown and her mouth had the softness and fullness of a ripe peach. It was not smiling but the corners turned up in quite the most fascinating way. Quite delectable she was, if somewhat skinny, and though he had absolutely no intention of taking what she was so obviously reluctant to give, now that she had a full belly, he was quite diverted by her ... her difference to the other plump and pretty women he had known and, some of them, loved.

"What is your name, my little orphan of the storm?" He drew on his cigar, his mouth still smiling around it. His manner was leisurely, unconcerned, making no movement that might startle her.

"Daisy Brindle."

"Mine is Sam Lassiter. You may call me Sam since it seems we are to be ... friends." He was enjoying himself immensely, enjoying her look of uncertainty since she really had no way of knowing that he was teasing her.

"Thank you," she said politely, still inclined to hang about near the door.

"Tell me about yourself, Daisy."

"There's nothing to tell."

"There must have been something to bring you to the sorry state I found you in. Tell me, was I the first to be ... offered the ... er ... delightful wares you were trying to sell?"

"That's nothing to do with you..."

"Has it not? I was under the impression you were offering them as ... brand new. Never before used so to speak. Come, Daisy, let's have the truth. There must have been something in your past to reduce you to the level of starvation you displayed just now..."

"There's nothing, I tell you, and now I must go." Her voice had become harsh and her face as cold and unyielding as granite. She seemed about to crack and splinter like the icebergs he had seen in the Davis Strait north of Newfoundland. The soft, uncertain vulnerability which he had found so ... so appealing had vanished with the speed of the sun behind a stormcloud. Her full mouth thinned into an ugly white line and her eyes became two brown stones, flat and without expression.

"Dear God, now what have I said? I swear you are the most awkward female I have ever come across. I rescue you from the clutches of some amatory sailor which would certainly have been your fate had I not come along when I did. I catch you when you fall, carry you to my home, let you eat my cupboard bare and when I ask you a civil question you act as though I had made some insulting remark. That is hardly good manners, my pet, but if you wish to keep your past to yourself that is your affair."

"I'm sorry ... really..." The flinty look slowly left her eyes and the grey, tight-lipped line faded from about her mouth. She edged her way back to the sofa and sat down, staring with some great sadness into the fire. He watched its light deepening the red in her hair. She was so serious he was tempted to reach out a hand to her but his instincts told him it would be the wrong thing to do. She could be no more than seventeen or so and yet a moment ago he had seen a hatred, a bitterness, a soul-destroying disillusionment in her which no child, since she was hardly more, should have to suffer. There was something in her, some rancour which had flared up malevolently when he had mentioned her past and yet, battling with it, was a strength and ... yes, a sweetness which showed in the soft droop of her mouth and the slow fall and rise of her childlike lashes, the drawn paleness of her cheek, the defenceless fragility of her slender, work-worn hands. He said nothing more, drawing peacefully on his cigar, and when she fell asleep again in the first warmth and on the first full stomach she had known in a long time, he suspected, he lifted her legs to the sofa and covered her with the rug. He put more coal on the fire and the guard about it and when her soft breathing deepened and slowed he turned down all but one of the lamps and left the room.

He was himself deeply asleep in his own bed when she came to him. She was completely naked, warm and slender, the bones of her sharp and pointed as her body pressed herself against his own. She was weeping desolately and in his sleep-filled, dream-filled awakening he was confused, holding her to him instinctively, soothing her with suddenly trembling, suddenly gentle hands.

"Ssh ... ssh ..." and his mouth, with no thought of her youth now, nor her extreme frailty, moved across hers, licking away the salty tears.

"Don't send me away ... please ... I cannot go back to it ... not to that ..." Her body clutched at his, wrapping itself, long slim legs, twining white arms about him. Her mouth welcomed his, deliciously sweet, and her glorious hair fell about them both in a way which was undoubtedly erotic. He could feel it drift like silk across his upturned face and shoulders and he was surprised to find himself in such a position. She had taken over now, flowing across his hard body in a way which was exquisitely pleasing but incredible. She was kissing him, working from his mouth and face, behind his ears and below his chin, down the long, lean, eager strength of his body to the fine hairs which covered his flat stomach, sliding and undulating in a way she should have known nothing about and his last thought as he raced towards his own explosive orgasm was that someone had taught her well and what a fool he had been to be tricked as he had been tricked. She *was* a whore after all.

He was still awake an hour later, her body pressed lightly against his side, her arm thrown across his chest and her curtain of hair covering them both in a living mantle of warmth as she slept. He smoothed the satin fineness of her narrow back, tracing the weals which striped it, and his thoughts were confused and surprisingly angry. It was like holding a child, light and fine, and had it not been for the wild draining of his body he might have imagined the whole delightful experience. He slept at last and in their sleep they twined themselves closer to one another, their limbs embraced so that when they awoke, clinging fast together, they were both considerably startled.

"Oh . . ." she said, her eyes huge and incredulous in the soft spring light which crept round the curtains, but she was not afraid.

"Yes . . ." he answered, reaching for her and this time it was he who dominated and she who welcomed it. He was amazed at the strength in the small, birdlike frailty of her, her long, slender neck, pointed narrow shoulders, her high, small, tight-nippled breasts in his large hands, yet sweet, filling his mouth, pleasing his lips and his tongue with delicious softness. Her body was lean, boyish, drawn out in a long stretching of pleasure, willing, eager to receive his, no shrinking, no affectation of prudery or modesty, a complete woman, certainly no virgin. They enjoyed one another as men and women do. It was as simple as that with no impediment of emotion or declarations of love and when it was done they smiled, almost as friends might. He held out his arms to her and she seemed to creep with what he thought was thankfulness into their shelter, sighing like a well-pampered cat.

"I'll have the truth now," he said quietly, lying back, one arm behind his head, the other holding her close to him.

"I'm not a whore as you might suppose," she said simply, as though she had read his mind.

"No, I did not seriously believe you were," and in a strange way they both relaxed, their minds and their bodies.

"I had my first man and the scars on my back, when I was ten years old."

"Sweet God . . . !" He raised himself slowly on to his elbow and looked down into her face. It was calm. There was

297

no shame or regret there since what was the use? It was done, her expression said, and had been accepted. Her childhood had been taken from her, if indeed she had known any, along with her virginity and she was not asking for his pity over it. "I worked with my mother and a gang of other women..."

He watched her face during the whole telling of her tale. It was without expression, pale and tranquil, showing no emotion. She spoke of Miles Thornley and her childish love for him which had grown into an obsession, since she knew now that it had been that. She spoke of Cassie and her enduring love for her and even then, even as she told him of what had been done by the man to the child, it was as though it had happened to some other woman, some sad woman who was to be commiserated with but whose plight could never be altered. It was not until she told him about Bess that her expression changed. She had begun to smile by then.

"...and so if it had not been for her I should be dead now." She stared musingly over his shoulder to where a light breeze ruffled the lace at the open window. She could hear the sound of horses' hooves in the street and the cry of a tradesman calling his wares. Someone was whistling and over all there was a feeling of cheerfulness, of coming warmth as spring took a tentative hold, of sunny days ahead, of hope and optimism which she had not known for many months.

"...I had walked all night and worked for sixteen hours before that, you understand, and I was tired and hungry. I was in Denton Green by this time and I knew I could sleep in the shed at the back of the school. It was easy enough to climb the wall and the door was not locked. There were old sacks there so I was soon asleep. I knew no one would come. There is no garden work done in January, you see, but I awoke at some time and I was cold. I'll put on my spare dresses, I thought, the ones Bess had tied in the bundle. They wouldn't fasten up over my black uniform but that wouldn't matter under my cloak and I would be warm. There was a pocket in my woollen dress – I had made it myself . . ." Her eyes were far away, seeing some memory. He touched her cheek softly and she began to speak again. ". . . there was something there. Something wrapped up in a cloth. She must have slipped into the kitchen and taken some bread and cheese. It was the best I had ever tasted but there was something else, something which clinked. She had put in her savings, you see, no more than a few shillings, probably meant for her mother but all she had and it meant all the difference to me. It saw me over those first weeks. Bought me food and shelter . . . of the worst kind I can tell you, but at least it put a roof over my head until I found work. Bess did that for me and I shall never forget her. One day I shall repay her for all she has done for me, just as one day I shall repay Miles Thornley for all he has done *to* me and mine."

"Daisy . . ." He was ready to hold her close, to comfort her as he thought, for he had found her story moving and her strength admirable. He could not bring himself to believe she meant what she said about the bastard who had done this to her. It was the kind of thing all men, and women too, he supposed, said in the heat of the moment when a wrong has been done them. They would have revenge, they cried hotly. The culprit would not be allowed to get away with it. She had reason enough, God knows, but she was not the first housemaid to be seduced by the son of the house and she certainly would not be the last. She was naturally grieving over the death of the girl she called her sister, which was indeed a tragedy, but there again the girl had been fair game for any gentleman who took a fancy to her. Girls like her and Daisy always were. It was a sad fact of life but one which must be faced. He was a product of his age, not heartless as it might seem, but a realist and though he was sorry for the plight of this fragile creature in his arms there was nothing to be done to change what had happened to her in the past. He would keep her with him for a while. Feed her up, make her strong again, buy her pretty things, spoil her since no one else had and make sure she had a new start in life. He would treat her to all the frivolous pleasures she had never known and she would soon put her sadness behind her, and the memory of the man who had damaged her, and her sister, so pitilessly.

He smiled down into her eyes, ready to tell her so, then recoiled sharply for the look of hatred in them was so savage that, if he had been given to such fanciful notions, he might have crossed himself as those who are superstitious do. It was exactly as she had looked last night, a hatred so implacable and cold, so merciless it made him shudder. He was not a man given to the absurd or the ridiculous but he felt a ridiculous and urgent need to take that look away from her for surely it could only damage what was still childlike in her.

He watched as the expression slowly died away, then she smiled and lifted her mouth to be kissed and it was if it had never existed.

"I can stay then?" she said carelessly, an hour or so later, and he grinned as he answered.

"Only if you behave yourself and are willing to do exactly as you're told."

"Of course. Would I dare to do otherwise."

"Starting now?" There was a wicked gleam in his eyes and though she didn't trust him, just as she didn't trust any man on earth and never would again, she grinned at him, perfectly willing to do whatever it was he required of her, for just as long as it suited her.

20

It was the first time in her life that she had ever played. He took her to the Royal Amphitheatre in Christian Street, riding in a hackney carriage from his rooms in Duke Street to the theatre which gave a performance three times a week and was considered the handsomest in the provinces. The front consisted of three storeys, the lower being splendidly rusticated with four Corinthian pilasters supporting the pediment. The interior was spacious and extremely elegant, having a tier of dress boxes, two galleries and a commodious pit. The stage, being movable, was able to contain an arena in which equestrian performances were exhibited and from every part of the theatre a fine view could be had by the four thousand persons it could contain. The roof was high and vaulted, spanning the building without any interior support. Sam directed her attention to all these marvels, at the same time telling her to close her mouth or the surrounding audience would be forced to the conclusion that she had never been inside a theatre before.

Behind the box in which Daisy, bewitched to the point of speechlessness, and Sam were ensconced, there were dainty tables and comfortable chairs set out where they might drink coffee, tea, wine or punch between acts. The dress boxes were three shillings, side boxes two and sixpence, the pits one shilling and the gallery sixpence. They saw performances of *The Corsican Brothers*, *Speed the Plough*, and *The Stranger*, thrilling plays in which such notables as Mr Webster, Madame Celeste, Mr Buckstone, Mrs Fitzwilliam and many other fine artistes performed. Glittering occasions where exquisitely dressed, expensively bejewelled ladies were escorted by faultlessly tailored gentlemen in the black and white of their evening dress. Sam seemed to be on nodding terms with most of the gentlemen, bowing pleasantly through the haze of his fragrant cigar smoke to them, not at all put out, it seemed, by the frosty disregard of their female companions. He held Daisy's arm, guiding her courteously from their dress box through the stylish company to their carriage which was waiting to whisk them off to the Adelphi Hotel at the foot of Mount Pleasant.

The popularity and prestige of the elegant Georgian hotel was immense. It was a recognised stopping-place for members of the Royal Family visiting or passing through Liverpool, Sam told her equably, patient with her constant stream of questions on every facet of this new, quite magical world to which she had been suddenly introduced. Distinguished foreign visitors made it their headquarters. Only a few years since, the celebrated writer Charles Dickens had stayed at the hotel before sailing to America and he had described the dinner served to him on the night before his departure as 'undeniably perfect'.

"Charles Dickens!" Her face was awestruck and her voice reverent, the fairy-tale dining room, the fashionable hotel taking on an even greater prestige at the discovery that the gentleman whose books she herself had read, first at the school and then 'borrowed' from the library at Thornley Green, had possibly dined at the very table where she herself sat.

The small, intimate dining room in which Daisy and Sam ate their late supper was luxurious, softly lit, filled with, or so it seemed to Daisy, the same divine persons they had left behind at the theatre. They drank champagne and ate hors d'oeuvres, Whitebait Carolinas, Medaillon de Boeuf, Grouse Rotie sur Canapés, petits fours with French coffee and liqueurs before he took her back to his own comfortable house, his own spacious bed, and made love to her with a warmth and an expertise which left her physically and delightfully satiated.

They attended the races at Aintree racecourse and grandstand, rubbing shoulders with not only the ordinary inhabitants of Liverpool and the gentry of its vicinity, but the élite of sporting men in the country who came from all parts of it. The course was admitted by these gentlemen, and by those come from several continents, to be the best in the kingdom. Not only for the excellence of the turf at all times and in all weathers, but for its size and the comfort in which the spectators might watch the races. The grandstand was opened in 1829 by Lord Sefton when the first 'Maghull Races' were run. The course was one and a half miles in length and railed on both sides and to the north was the grandstand, a fine and imposing building holding a spacious dining room and several other refreshment rooms. There was a handsome salon, an enormously long room with full-length windows down the whole of one side of it and it was here,

on the gallery which extended along its front, that Daisy
saw her first horse race. Hundreds of spectators, ladies and
gentlemen again so fashionably gowned and suited they
might have been in the presence of the Queen herself,
crowded to see the graceful dash of sleek horses go by,
looking out to the course across a wide, sloping lawn, railed
around its perimeter for the convenience of frequenters of
the stand, and beyond to the sweeping panoramic views of
Walton-on-the-Hill. There was a steeplechase and several
hurdle races on that day and for a dreadful moment, as one
of the beautiful creatures went down, Daisy was taken back
to that moment when Miles Thornley had crashed about
their ears after taking that fatal jump which had killed
Cassie's mother and rendered Cassie herself the sweet,
innocent, childlike creature she was destined always to be.
Then Sam's voice in her ear, shouting on the winner which
she had picked – to his disgust because she liked its pretty
name, which was Summer Breeze – brought her back to the
present and the thrill of her first 'win'.

He took her across the river, going from George's Pierhead to Woodside on the ferryboat *Queen*, the first time she
had been on the water, the journey only five or six minutes
but an enchantment to her from the moment of the ringing
of the bell to summon latecomers, to the small penthouse
on deck which Sam had taken in case of wet weather. They
drank coffee at the Woodside Hotel then took a hackney
coach to Bidston Hill, climbing to the top of the lighthouse
in order to see the splendid sight of Liverpool across the
sliding waters, the skimming graceful dance of three-masted
barques, of frigates and coasters, of fore and aft schooners
and most beautiful and gracious of them all, the tall clipper
ships as they moved up and down the great River Mersey.
There were lush green fields at their backs studded with
sheep and cattle, with red campion and marsh marigold and
beyond them the soft blue outline of the Welsh mountains
They ate ham and eggs and drank apple cider, sitting among
silent, staring farm labourers at a roadside public house
before walking across fields to the water's edge and when
they returned to Duke Street they slept for twelve hours in

one another's arms, only waking when the bell of St Mark's Church at the corner rang out its clangour.

Sam Lassiter was a sea-captain, he told Daisy on that first day, and not only that, he owned his own vessel. He had sailed for the first time as a boy of fourteen, breaking his mother's heart and seriously displeasing his father, being an only son and an only child. His father had been a ship's chandler, making no more than a reasonable living until the day he scraped together a few guineas and bought a block of land in the outlying area of Edgehill in the late 1820s. In 1831 he sold it to the railway companies and with the quite splendid return he earned for himself he was able to extend his business at the bottom end of Water Street which, naturally, he expected his son, then only a boy of six, to take over when he was of an age. He was to be disappointed. The call of the sea sang in the boy's head and throbbed in his veins. His mother's tears and his father's exhortations were gently disregarded since a man must choose his own path to glory or damnation, didn't Daisy agree?

The life of a seaman is one of constant danger and discomfort, he told her, wrapping his arms about her as they lay curled up beneath a fine cashmere rug, come from Asia he said casually, in front of a leaping fire on that second night they spent together. They had not ventured out into the suddenly raw March wind that day, alternating between sleeping, eating and making love in the most surprisingly frequent way. It seemed Daisy Brindle's fine-drawn body delighted Sam Lassiter's, and besides, he felt an inordinate amount of satisfaction to see her make her way steadily and with enormous enjoyment through every morsel of food he put before her. Her appetite was endless. She seemed to put on weight as he watched her, he told her, highly amused, just as though she was some stray he had found on his doorstep and had taken upon himself to rescue.

"Tell me about the world," she commanded through the remains of a crusty steak-and-kidney pie, her eyes glowing in fascinated attention to every word he uttered.

Long hours and low pay was all he got, he continued obligingly, but it had not dissuaded the young Sam Lassiter from battling across decks swept by swirling icy seas as the flimsy clipper ship on her way to China and the tea trade rounded Cape Horn, or from straddling the yards after climbing the creaking masts by the ratlines to secure the sails. In freezing, gale-force winds and turbulent seas this was an heroic task though Sam made no great fuss about it as he recounted his youthful experiences to Daisy. Apprentices were taken on to 'learn the ropes' at a tender age and he was not the only lad to sail on that first journey he took to the other side of the world. But he was the only one to 'get on' since he had, besides ambition and a resolute will to succeed, a magical qualification they had not and that was the ability to read, to cypher and therefore to learn. By the end of three years he had become fourth mate, only, as yet, a very lowly deck officer who still, those above him thought, earned his beatings. He became third mate, second, then first. As a crew member of some importance he was allowed by the captain, with other deck officers, to buy tea, jade and opium in the Eastern ports they visited which they sold in Liverpool on their return, making a decent profit. Sam Lassiter scrupulously put his away for the day when he would buy his own ship.

When he was twenty-five he was given his own command, becoming Captain Sam Lassiter of the clipper *Saucy Jane*, a streamlined square-rigger with a slim hull, a graceful bow and lofty masts and for two years he had sailed the seas of the world, mainly in the tea trade until word reached him that his father had died leaving the chandler's business to his son in a last bid, one presumed, to persuade his feckless lad to settle down.

But Captain Sam Lassiter sold the thriving business, bought his mother a small villa in Everton and with what remained of the capital from the concern his father had painstakingly built up, bought his own sailing ship, the clipper *Golden Lady*. She was beautiful and fast, he told Daisy, and for the most part was used to carry tea and other perishable goods from China although now and again, if the cargo and the returns were to his liking, he might do a shorter run such as the one he had just completed bringing timber from Newfoundland.

"She's the loveliest thing you ever saw, Daisy." His face became soft and his green eyes almost transparent. His mouth curled tenderly and Daisy was made to see that to Sam Lassiter there was nothing so important, so worthy of his devoted care as his *Golden Lady*. "She has the finest lines, with sky-sails and foretopsail studding sails which allow her to ghost along in the lightest of air and yet she handles the big, following seas of the Roaring Forties with ease."

"Can I see it?"

A pained expression crossed his face. "*Her*, if you please."

"Her?"

"Ships are always referred to as *her*, Daisy."

"Her then."

"Perhaps, if you continue to ... please me."

But that was later and before he could take her to see his lovely ship, or indeed anywhere, she must be properly dressed.

"You need some new gowns," he told her the following morning as she strolled unselfconsciously about his rooms wrapped in nothing more than the quilt off his bed. They had breakfasted on hot rolls and creamy butter, fresh strawberry jam and honey, coffee in an enormous pot which he poured into fragile china cups, cream, a bowl of fruit, all mysteriously prepared and laid out on a lace-covered tray.

"I have a man who comes in," he said casually, buttering a morsel of warm bread, spreading it liberally with honey and popping it into her mouth. "Dear God, you're like a fledgling in a nest with its beak forever open. There is no need to eat so quickly, my pet. There is plenty more in the kitchen, I'm sure ..."

"A man?" She spoke through the lovely sweet taste of the orange he had peeled for her which she ate between mouthfuls of bread and honey, the juice running down her chin and on to her small, pointed breasts. He leaned forward to lick it away, the tip of his tongue tracing the tiny pink pearl of her nipples.

"Mmm, he looks after me. Shops, cleans, cooks, does my laundry when I'm ashore, that kind of thing."

"When you're ashore?" She ran her sticky fingers through the thick tumble of his hair, holding his head close to her breasts, arching her back obligingly so that she might be more easily accessible to him. He was no longer listening as he laid her back on the crumpled bed and it was another hour before he answered.

"Yes . . ." just as though no time had elapsed between the question and his reply. "Jack is what you might call in more exalted circles, my 'man'. He goes with me whenever I sail and when I'm in port he comes ashore with me. He lost a leg in an accident. A storm when we were sailing round the Horn, years ago now when I was first mate on a clipper. We took to one another. He watched out for me when I was a lad so I do the same for him now. He can no longer work as he used to but he looks after me like a mother and he does it superbly. He can cook a decent meal and keeps this place shipshape and Bristol fashion, as they say. He is as good, or better than a wife. A wife would need my consideration and time and Jack asks for nothing more than three good meals a day and a place to lay his head at night. He sleeps on the *Golden Lady* but comes back here each day to bring food which he buys at the market on his way up from the berth. He prepares it and leaves it in the kitchen. Very discreet is Jack. He cleans the place when I'm not here though how he knows when that is I've yet to discover."

"And he has been this morning?"

"It seems so."

"And you let me drift about half-naked?"

"Jack wouldn't object, and I seem to recall you were completely naked when you ran into the . . . well, enough of that or I might be tempted to begin again. If we don't get down to the dressmaker that is how you will remain since I refuse to take you anywhere until we have disposed of that hideous black dress I found you in. A visit to the Misses Yeoland first, I think, since they are purported to be the finest dressmakers in Liverpool . . ."

307

"I take it you have some experience in the buying of dresses for ladies then?"

"You ... might say that," he grinned and she grinned back for what Sam Lassiter had done before she met him, or indeed what he was to do in the future, was of no particular concern to Daisy Brindle. She liked him, she wouldn't deny it. He amused her and his lovemaking was not unpleasant to her. He was good-humoured and merry, generous and prepared to be kind providing he got his own way and she was inclined to allow it for, after all, where would she be now if he had not come across her on the Marine Parade? She had been, she was perfectly well aware, at the point where she must find some means, *any* means of feeding herself, or quite simply starve to death. She had tried for nearly three months to find a decent occupation, knocking on the back door of house after house in the respectable Georgian crescents which were laid out in a semicircle from the river, begging for work as a housemaid, a kitchenmaid or even a skivvy. She had been turned away from them all. Bess's few shillings, carefully hoarded and spent at the cheapest stalls in the market, on the barest minimum of food necessary to keep her body alive, had gone within two weeks and the employment she had found, shamefully paid and where she was shamefully treated, had driven her at last to the painful knowledge that there was only one employment left open to her, and here she was, employed in it. She had in a sense fallen on her feet – or on her back, she supposed wryly – in that Sam Lassiter, though not exactly a gentleman since his family had been in trade, was clean, not unattractive and had no inclination for the perverted and often cruel practices she had heard tell some men required of the women they bought, since she was, of course, a bought woman. She was well fed for the first time since leaving Thornley Green. She was bathed, her dress and boots cleaned by the so far invisible Jack and she was prepared, now that she had recovered her strength and been given a breathing space, to give value for money. It might be only for a few days whilst the Captain was in port but she was back on her feet and she must gain what advantage she could from it. Had not life taught her that lesson only too well?

She wore the black dress since she had nothing else and her stout boots, somewhat thin at the sole, which had carried her from Thornley Green to Liverpool and had scarce been off her feet since. When one shares a room and sometimes a bed with a dozen others of like circumstance at the Night Asylum, which provided shelter for the aged, the destitute and distressed, which she herself had certainly been at the time, or at least the last two, one does not remove any particle of clothing since by morning it would have vanished. It was the same at the Magdalen Asylum which, strictly speaking, was an institution to house penitent prostitutes but which would not turn away a woman or a girl who was obviously not fit to be left out on the streets after dark.

"Put your cloak on and can you not do something with your hair? Splendid as it is, you can hardly enter the Misses Yeolands' establishment looking like a gypsy."

Obligingly, indifferently, she swept it up into an enormous coil, tying it with the golden ribbons he had first seen her in. "And must you put those pathetic ribbons in your hair, my pet? I shall buy you some more but in the meanwhile, pretty as they are, they really do not . . ."

She sprang away from his hand like a tiger, her eyes narrowing into a warning, jewel-like glitter. From her came such an air of danger he drew back his hand sharply, then held them both up in a pose of mock alarm. His eyes were keen though and there was a certain cast about his shadowed face which seemed to say that though he might be indulgent of her sharp temper up to a point, beyond that point he himself could be dangerous.

"They have some . . . value to you then, those ribbons?" he asked, his expression of smiling unconcern not quite reaching his eyes. "Perhaps a gift from the Honourable Miles Thornley?"

"No, and I'll thank you to keep your hands off them. They are mine and I'll wear them when and where I please."

"Of course." He shrugged, moving to the door to open it

for her but she could see she had displeased him and she relented grudgingly.

"They were given to me by Cassie." Her voice was husky and her eyes misted with sudden tears and at once he was contrite.

"Sweetheart, why did you not say so? Come, don't look so woebegone. You're like a little wet moorhen which has been left out in the rain in that damned black sack you're wearing but you shall have a decent gown by nightfall. One to match your ribbons, how will that be? and tonight we will dine out and all the other fellows will say, 'My God, who is that beauty with Sam Lassiter? What a lucky dog he is.'"

And he had kissed her laughingly, smoothing away her frowning displeasure with the engaging charm which could appear and disappear, she had discovered, so rapidly.

Every head in the elegant salon turned as the tall, immaculately tailored gentleman ushered the equally tall, but not so fashionably turned-out girl, obviously of the servant class, through the front door of the dressmaking and millinery establishment in Bold Street. The Misses Yeoland, Gladys and Emily, had moved on many years ago from the middle-class trade they had once served to that of the gentry and even, on occasion, to the aristocracy, dressing the well-to-do of Liverpool in their own exquisite and clever designs. They were renowned for their ingenuity with fabrics of the most costly sort; with a scrap of lace, a length of satin ribbon, a flower, a feather and the small dressmaker's and milliner's concern they had begun was now a luxurious salon of soft carpets, bright, gilt-framed mirrors, beautifully draped curtains at each long window, silk-covered walls, comfortable but dainty chairs and sofas, fresh flowers and pretty pictures so that the exclusive clientele might almost believe they were in the comfort of their own home. The sisters catered, of course, only to the very rich. Their splendid establishment in Bold Street was on the route where elegant ladies who drove in velvet-lined carriages attended by footmen and coachmen might easily see it. It was a fine, wide thoroughfare, the most fashionable in town, famous for its stylish shops and the splendour of the socialites who paraded there and it was here that the Misses Yeoland had made their respected name.

A tall, graceful figure in black came towards them, indicating with a long slender hand which had not stitched a hem for a long time now, that the slack-jawed seamstresses and milliners who were in her employ and who had all stopped whatever they were doing to stare, should resume their duties at once. They did so reluctantly but the whispers rustled from group to group where the rich and fashion-conscious of Liverpool congregated to drink coffee and chocolate, or even sparkling white wine if they had a fancy for it, as they restocked their already bulging wardrobes. Miss Gladys Yeoland, simply dressed for it would never do to look more fashionable than one's clients, smiled at the gentleman who had entered her salon, not allowing her expression to show by the merest flicker her surprise at his choice of companion. A girl above medium height, thin, quite plain really, sullen almost, Miss Yeoland would have said, but with a mass of carefully confined hair of the most magnificent shade of autumn red. Automatically Miss Yeoland began to choose the colours and fabrics in which the girl would look her best. Rich shades of amber velvet, of course, a warm burnt almond in gauzy tulle, cream silk, tarlatan in pale coffee, cinnamon merino, gold, a tawny-gold satin with a touch of black lace, rich green velvet, a deep hyacinth brocade, blond taffeta with her hair drawn back from those high cheekbones into an intricate chignon. In the time it took Miss Yeoland to move graciously from the foot of her wide, curved staircase, which led up to even more superb rooms in which her ladies might avail themselves of all the little luxuries she had to offer, she had rid the girl of her cumbersome blue cloak, the plain black dress beneath it, her boots, which, if her slender white ankles were to be believed she wore without stockings, and completely redressed her in her own splendid creations.

"Good morning, Captain Lassiter, what a pleasant surprise." Miss Yeoland smiled, holding out her hand to him since he was, after all, a gentleman who had in the past spent considerable sums of money in her salon. This was not the first young lady he had accompanied in the purchase of the French ribbon and blondes, the Grecian laces and figured tulles, the beads and handkerchiefs, the fans and mother-of-pearl combs, the gold and silver tissue which were part of her trade, not to mention her gowns which ranged from the magnificence of a ballgown to the simplest morning dress.

"Miss Yeoland." With a courtly movement of his head and shoulders Captain Lassiter bowed over her hand, his manners perfect, too perfect for a real gentleman she knew that, as did several ladies who watched, for young bloods of their class did not greet a mere dressmaker as he had done.

"What can I do for you, Captain? Perhaps you and..."

"Miss Brindle." A polite and gracious nod of the head to Miss Brindle. "Perhaps you would care to come upstairs and take a cup of coffee with me? Or perhaps something stronger..."

With Sam's hand at her elbow Daisy drifted through the delicately perfumed air, hardly touching the rich, biscuit-coloured carpet of Miss Yeoland's wide stairs with her scuffed down-at-heel black boots. Miss Yeoland seated them with all the pomp of visiting royalty in the comfort of a small, private sitting room before the warm, crackling coals of a pleasant fire, pressed them to partake of coffee in a fine bone china coffeecup, a wisp of macaroon, whilst all the while discussing with the Captain the merits of muslin and velvet, wool and damask, appliqué work and chenille fringing just as though he himself was a couturier and would know exactly what she meant.

At last Daisy found her voice.

"I want a dress to match these ribbons," she said harshly and if Miss Yeoland was considerably startled by this curious request, though not at all disconcerted, it did not show. Sam Lassiter, however, should anyone have been looking in his direction at that particular moment, had a most strange expression in his usually mocking green eyes.

She went out on his arm like a young queen. Though the Misses Yeoland did not sell boots or slippers or indeed any kind of footwear since *their* ladies only wore the handmade sort and it was a specialised trade, they had an arrangement with a bootmaker several doors along Bold Street. Within minutes of a message being delivered as to Miss Yeoland's requirements, boots and shoes and slippers of every imaginable size, style and colour were sent from the back door of one establishment to the other. The bootmaker did a thriving trade in ready-made footwear as well as his made-to-measure custom, and Daisy Brindle's narrow foot was efficiently and smoothly measured and fitted. The Misses Yeoland, naturally, made their clients' garments to fit each individual, prized lady, but they also kept a quantity of gowns of different styles and sizes for such a person as this friend of the Captain's. Ready-made, like the bootmaker's footwear, and should an emergency arise, such as this one, they were well able to fill its need.

Her gown was of russet Genoa velvet, extremely plain but sculpted to her fine-drawn slenderness within the hour by the clever fingers of Miss Emily Yeoland. The bodice was a short basque with buttons to match its colour from neckline to waist. The sleeve was close-pleated at the armhole then full to the wrist where it was gathered into a wristband and the skirt was wide and enormous, supported on a cage crinoline. There were rows of flounces at the hem, each one edged in satin, the exact shade of the golden hair ribbons.

"A bonnet, I think, Miss Yeoland," the Captain said, his eyes warm with approval as he watched Daisy Brindle being twirled for his scrutiny before the mirror which covered the whole of one wall.

"The 'bavolet' is very fashionable, Captain Lassiter."

It was large and flat, like a pancake, Daisy thought, though stiff, set on top of her head and tipped forward over her eyes. It was the same colour as her dress. It had a wide golden ribbon round the crown which fell down her back and was trimmed beneath the brim with ruched golden tulle. The colour reflected in her creamy skin, putting a warmth into its paleness, and Miss Yeoland began to see what had attracted Captain Lassiter, whose taste had usually been for the pretty and the plump, to this unusual young woman.

"And a shawl..." The Captain's eyes were narrowed and very green.

"Of course."

It was very large and made of cashmere, a French shawl Miss Yeoland called it, and in it were all the colours of autumn. With high-heeled cream kid boots and gloves to match, Daisy was quite indistinguishable from any of the other well-bred young ladies who frequented Miss Yeoland's establishment, indeed Miss Yeoland privately considered Miss Brindle had a style, a certain unique *something*, to which she could put no name. She had seen it on very few but it set them apart from the others, who were merely fashionable.

"And the rest of the gowns will be delivered...?" There was a question in the Captain's voice but also the undoubted belief that Miss Yeoland would make absolutely certain that this order would naturally be put to the front of any other she might have.

"I will set my girls to it at once."

"Miss Brindle and I are to dine at the Adelphi tonight."

"Of course." Captain Lassiter need say no more.

They next visited what was called, or so it said over the door, the 'Emporium for Rich and Elegant Furs'. Mr H. G. Ireland respectfully invited the attention of the nobility of Liverpool and its vicinity to his splendid stock of furs, and splendid indeed they were. Fur coats, fur capes, fur wraps. Full length or short, boleros, jackets of sable which, Mr Ireland informed them, though somewhat expensive, were very chic. Mink, sealskin, chinchilla, camel, astrakhan, Persian lamb, musquash, pony, bear, skunk, Tibetan goat, beaver, otter, miniver and ermine. Captain Lassiter had but to name his choice for the young lady, who he himself was of the opinion would look quite magnificent in a certain pale grey chinchilla wrap he had in mind, and it could be produced at once.

It was probably then, as the incredible beauty and softness of the pale grey chinchilla which Mr Ireland thought so fetching was draped about her shoulders, as the fur smoothed itself about her throat and caressed her chin, that

Daisy Brindle awoke from the dream world in which Sam Lassiter had cocooned her for the past forty-eight hours. Despite his enthusiastic and frequent lovemaking she felt well and rested. Her stomach was filled and already she could sense the wiry return of the strength she had always known, and with it her wits, and her sharp brain asked her what she was doing here in this fairy-tale world of opulent velvets and sumptuous furs, of crystal chandeliers and dainty gilt chairs in which Mr Ireland had seated her. She had sipped a glass of Madeira, quite dazed and dazzled, as Mr Ireland flung rippling furs about his apple-green carpet with the carelessness of an Arabian sheikh and the man who had brought her here lounged indolently on a velvet sofa, his long legs stretched out before him, studying her through the smoke of his cigar just as though she was a doll he was dressing for his own entertainment, which she supposed he was!

Sam Lassiter! Who was he? Who the devil was he? Oh, she knew his background, or at least all he had told her. She knew what he *did*, but she had not the faintest notion of who the man *was*. She knew he had salvaged her from what was known as a fate worse than death – if she had found the courage to go through with it, which she doubted – brought her back to his house in Duke Street and nourished her with good food, with warmth and sleep and the comfort of his own luxurious surroundings for which she had repaid him with the currency of her body. But why had he acted as he had done, as he was doing now? And why had he accepted her as lightly and as effortlessly as he might some kitten he had found on his doorstep? Why did he seem to find her so ... so pleasing, so ... well, the word she sought was not *lovable* since there was no love between them, but perhaps ... enticing? Why was he doing this? She had twisted and turned obediently, when told, for the best part of three hours in the sumptuous salon of the Misses Yeoland whilst they had measured her for so many gowns she had lost count of them. It had seemed like a dream, a dream in which a girl she recognised as herself but who had nothing at all to do with the real Daisy Brindle, was manipulated by a group of strangers, the strangest of them all, Sam Lassiter. She had been clothed in a beautiful dress the likes of which she had never before worn in her young life, carried on light and dreamlike feet from the salon to this splendid emporium and was now hung about in a dead animal whose cost she was perfectly certain would feed a labouring man and his family for the rest of his life.

Why? Why was he doing this? He didn't know her. He didn't love her. Was he such a philanthropist that, from the goodness of his Christian heart, he was prepared to spend a small fortune on a girl who had, only a few months ago, been a housemaid and since then had done menial tasks of such vileness she could barely think of them without a shudder?

"Don't you like it, my pet?" Sam's lazy drawl broke through her reverie and she turned to him in a graceful swirl, the fur moving about her like the living animal from which it had come. She was completely unaware of her pale and quite enchanting beauty.

"Don't be daft, Sam Lassiter," she said tartly, to the consternation of Mr Ireland, "it's lovely and well you know it but don't you think you and me had better have a little chat before you spend any more of your brass on me? About what's happening here and about where all this is leading."

"Daisy, really, you are embarrassing Mr Ireland." Sam's eyes narrowed in pretended reproach but he was not displeased. He was not even offended by her outspoken words. In fact she had the impression he was enjoying himself enormously. What was beneath the engaging good-humoured charm he showed to her and the rest of those with whom they had come in contact today? What did he intend in their future relationship, if indeed they were to have one? She would dearly like to know but from the expression of sardonic amusement in his watchful, hooded eyes, it was unlikely he was about to tell her.

"This is hardly the time or place to discuss my 'brass' as you quaintly call it," he went on, drawing deeply on his cigar, "and if you don't care for the wrap you have only to say so."

Daisy turned to Mr Ireland, slipping the beautiful fur from her shoulders and into his unwilling hands.

"Thank you, Mr Ireland. The fur is quite magnificent, I'm sure, but not what I'm looking for at the moment," and with the hauteur of a great lady, those whom she had just recently served, swept from his shop, the door only just being opened in time by the obsequious assistant who was there for that purpose.

"Have it delivered to my home, Ireland," the Captain said, grinning with delight as he sauntered after her.

21

"You may do exactly as you please, Daisy, you know that. We have no claim on one another and if you should decide to go I won't try to stop you, but really, this is very pleasant, don't you think? We are asking nothing of one another except that we enjoy each other's company. Companions in search of a little diversion..."

"A bit more than that, I would say. I have barely been out of your bed in the last week..."

"But has it not been fun, my pet?"

"Yes, I can't deny it, but..."

"Then why should you want it to end?"

"I don't, but I can't see where it's to go."

"Must it go anywhere, my sweet? Can we not merely carry on like this until we have both had enough of it and when that day comes say goodbye without acrimony?"

"But why me? Why are you doing this for *me*?"

"Why not? You are an extremely attractive woman and becoming lovelier with each day that passes. You are getting positively fat, my pet. Just look at that delightfully rounded

317

breast. Why, last week it was scarcely noticeable and look at it now ... yes, I think I will look at it now, and perhaps a little taste ..."

"Sam! Will you be serious for a moment ..."

"No, I don't think I will. Why don't you put on that splendid fur I bought you and give me a preview of how you will look when we dine out tonight ..."

"... and that's another thing. I told that chap not to send it and when we got home there it was with dozens of boxes and packages and will you look at that gown ..." but she could not keep the note of satisfaction from her voice as she fingered the flowing folds of glowing golden tissue the Misses Yeoland had contrived for her. She lifted the dress gently from the box in which it was packed, then carrying it carefully to the long cheval mirror in the corner of the bedroom held it against her naked figure, eyeing her own reflection with evident pleasure.

"You like it then, Daisy?" he asked softly, lying back among the pillows. He reached for a cigar and lit it and his eyes narrowed as he watched her through the wreath of smoke.

"It's lovely, Sam, really it is. Quite the most beautiful ... but when am I to wear such a lovely thing?" She turned to him in exasperation. "I really don't know what I was thinking of, letting you buy all these things when a couple of sensible day dresses and a decent pair of boots would have been of much more use to me."

"The ladies who are seen about town with me don't wear sensible day dresses, nor decent boots, my dear, so why should you need such things?" His expression was inscrutable.

"Why? Because then I could ... well ... if I was respectably dressed I could find respectable work. I can hardly ask for work at the back door of a house in that lovely velvet ..." pointing to the russet morning gown on the back of the chair where he had carelessly flung it an hour since "... and that too, which is, well, I love it, but it's just not suitable, Sam. Not for me and what I do."

"And what is that, Daisy? Tell me what that is."

"You know what I do, Sam Lassiter. I told you honestly on that first day what I did. What I am."

"And is that what you mean to be again, my pet?"

"I know nothing else." Her voice was tart.

"I see. So you will be content with that, will you? Because you know nothing else you are willing to settle for that?"

"Yes ... no! ... Sam! ... you are confusing me. I don't know what to make of this conversation, nor of you." Her expression was mutinous, uncertain, and he smiled. She was a woman, a complete and exciting woman in his bed, knowing instinctively, it seemed, how best to please him and more than willing to learn his needs and erotic fancies. She was uninhibited, enjoying his enjoyment, finding fulfilment, or so it appeared, in what they did together. She showed no reluctance for the expensive oils he had brought back from the East where such things were understood and with which he required her to massage his sensual body, nor to lie posing on the rug before the fire whilst his eyes and his mouth and his hands explored every silken curve of her, every sweet, moist hollow. And yet out of his bed she was like a child in many ways, a child who has lost its way and so clings to the first friendly hand which is held out to it. He knew she could not understand his motives in taking her in, and neither could he, he admitted to himself, but he was enjoying himself more than he had done in years. It was like taking a little girl into the magical world of a toyshop where she had only, up to then, stood with her face pressed to the window. She was bright and humorous, now that she had recovered somewhat from the hardships she had suffered, not only in the last few months but for most of her life. She had the knack of putting out of her mind what was only lumber and therefore not necessary for survival, throwing it off and lightening the load so that she might more easily get on with life. He admired that. He admired her resolve. She reminded him of himself when he had first gone to sea, taking knocks a less stalwart boy would have been unable to take, and not only that but picking himself up afterwards for more. She was like that and he had taken it into his head over the last few days to see what she would make of herself if she was given a chance, a *real* chance at what life had to offer. He had taken a fancy to giving her that chance. To say, 'Here, dress yourself up in the prettiest gown you have, take this handful of sovereigns, put on your brightest smile and see what you can do with the world.' He had the feeling she would make more of it than most!

She was looking at him now with a frown on her face, her eyes clouded, ready to believe the worst of him for the men she had known in her life had made her that way. But despite that she had survived, she had picked herself up like the young Sam Lassiter had done and grabbed at the coat-tails of the person most likely to take her upwards. Perhaps not intentionally but from what she had told him she had had an instinct for who that might be and she had not backed away from a challenge. She had gone to school when the opportunity came, had learned more in two years than many an 'educated' young lady might in ten and but for her unfortunate passion for the young squire, or whoever it was she had been seduced by, might have risen high in the household of his father. Not employment of a great intellectual standard but for a girl born in her circumstances an achievement worthy of praise.

So what could she do now, given the chance which he had half a mind to hold out to her? He was a wealthy man. He made a splendid profit from the cargoes he carried. On one voyage to the China coast, sailing in waters far beyond the reach of the futuristic steamships, he had made a net profit of £20,000. He had investments in other concerns and some property in the city which he rented out and he could afford to ... shall we say ... invest in this girl if he had the notion to, and he had.

"Daisy, why do you worry so much about the 'whys' and 'wherefores' of this life? Cannot you just enjoy what comes your way ... ?"

"No, I can't, and neither would you if you'd gone hungry and cold like I have."

"Sweet Christ, hungry and cold! What d'you think life at sea was like, my pet? Not a bloody Sunday-school picnic, I can tell you. There were days when we ran before the wind and every man and boy had to man the foresail braces and sheets. Such atrocious weather we were soaked through for days on end, sleeping in wet clothes, when we could, and eating nothing but ship's biscuits. Wild foaming seas submerged the deck so that you couldn't see where the devil you were going, with only a line between you and purgatory but then, you know nothing of that and I can't expect you to understand, but believe me, I know what hardships are, Daisy."

"Perhaps you do but you have got through them. You have this ..." She swept a hand about the comfortable bedroom, indicating the deep pile carpet, the soft patina of lovely furniture, the wide bed, the cheerfully blazing fire. The room was large, simply furnished in muted colours of blue, apple green and cream, the walls hung with a darker blue silk. An elegant room, but not in the least feminine. "You know where your next penny is coming from and all the others to follow, but when you ... when you..."

"What is it, Daisy?"

She flung up her head and her hair tumbled across her shoulders and down her back. She still held the delicate finery of the evening gown to her breast and her eyes were bright and moist as she clung to her composure. It was all very well for him, her defiant expression said, but what was to happen to Daisy Brindle when this enjoyable game he was playing became no longer so diverting?

"When you've had enough of me what will you do with me then?" she demanded to know, not humbly, not even caring really, her expression would have him believe, for what was it to Daisy Brindle who could always look after herself, but her eyes were afraid. She did not want to return to the stews of Liverpool. Her only salvation lay in finding a decent servant's position, at least for the time being, so how long did he intend to play this game he had begun a week ago? her expression asked.

"Come here," he said.

"No, I want to know what you're up to? Why have you

bought me all these ... these things? This fur ... this dress ... ?"

"Put the bloody dress down, Daisy, and come here to me. I haven't much time because I have to go down to the docks. Do you realise that it has been a week and I haven't shown my face there? My crew will begin to think I have jumped ship. There are things I have to see to because I'll be sailing soon ... Dear God, will you come here and listen to me?"

Carefully she replaced the dress in its box, her expression denying her rejection of its splendour, and he smiled as he watched her. When it was folded to her satisfaction, and not before, she sauntered across the room, her manner conveying to him that she came because she wanted to, not because he had ordered her to.

"Yes?" she said imperiously.

He studied her for several moments, letting his eyes roam admiringly about her long, slender loveliness. It was true she had become rounder and softer in the last week and could you wonder at it, he mused, the amount of food she put away. Her firm, healthy flesh was a creamy amber in the fire's glow. Her breasts, high and pert, peaked with the warmth of his glance which caressed her tiny waist, the curve of her narrow hips, her long legs and the glowing copper curls of her pubic hair which protected the sweet core of her womanhood.

"You're a damned lovely woman, my pet. Not in the accepted sense of beauty, I'll admit that, but there is a look about you which is quite original. It will attract men to you and they won't really know why. That hair ... well, if you ever cut it you would have me to answer to and though you are slender there is a womanliness about you ..." His voice was strangely husky. "Take a look in the mirror and you won't have to ask yourself why *any* man should not keep you firmly at his side."

"And is that the only reason you have taken me in?" She tossed her head, moving back to avoid his caressing hand.

"I ... enjoy your company, will that do?"

"It might."

"And you enjoy mine, admit it."

"I might," she said reluctantly, still gliding away from his hand but there was a gleam of warm laughter, a hint of desire matching his own which he was beginning to recognise in her eyes.

"So why don't we just leave it at that for now. I'm to sail for Charleston at the end of next week but I won't be gone for long. No more than three weeks and I would be happy to have you stay here whilst I'm away. I shall leave Jack to look after you . . ."

"I see! You don't trust me to remain alone in your house, is that it?"

"Good God, woman, are you never bloody satisfied? Must you see insult where none is intended?" but she was right, of course, for Sam Lassiter, from hard experience trusted no one, especially on such short acquaintance, guarding fiercely what was his. He had an instinct which told him who could be depended upon and his instinct whispered that Daisy was open-hearted and without guile and could be relied on not to empty his house and make off with the proceeds whilst he was at sea, but best be certain. And Jack was really getting too old for the hard life on board a sailing vessel. This would give him a chance to get the old dog ashore without injuring his delicate pride. They could watch each other, the two of them, both gaining something from it, as he would.

"This is a heavensent opportunity for me, Daisy," he went on seriously, going on to explain about Jack, ". . . so if he thinks he's keeping an eye on you *and* my possessions he'll probably agree to stay ashore. What d'you say?"

"And then what?" She allowed him to lay a hard, exploratory hand against her flat stomach.

"Come here. Lie down beside me . . ." His mouth followed his hand, sliding down to the fine brush of hair between her thighs.

"Not before you tell me . . ." but he pulled her to him roughly, tucking her against his hard, amber body.

"Sweet Jesus, Daisy, if I promise not to turn you out into the cold without prior notice and then with a sum of money to keep you in the style to which I'm sure you will very soon become accustomed, will you ... ?" and the rest became a groan of approval as her arms crept round his neck and clung.

She looked quite stunning that evening as she moved gracefully by his side once again into the restaurant of the Adelphi Hotel. She wore the gown of gold tissue, the tremendous skirt stitched over its wire cage drifting about her like a sun-streaked cloud, the neck so low it clearly showed the tops of her lovely new breasts, a pearl-scattered gold velvet ribbon around her neck. She had pinned up her hair in a tumble of wild curls, slightly and deliberately dishevelled, with her own golden ribbons fastened amongst them, the only thing she retained of her old life since Sam had insisted on burning her black dress, her boots and her good navy cloak. She trailed a shawl of sheer, gold-coloured lace behind her and Sam smiled, most gratified to see every male head in the room turn to stare.

"Did I not tell you," he murmured as the head waiter hurried across to bow them to their table. "They are asking one another who the devil is that beauty with Sam Lassiter, envying me, of course, so smile at me, my darling, and perhaps move a little closer as though you really cannot bear to be more than a whisper away from me. There, is that not splendid? They think you are some great society beauty being wicked with her lover and by this time tomorrow it will be all over Liverpool that Sam Lassiter has done it again."

"Done what again, Sam?" but she obediently did as he told her, gazing up into his face with evident adoration, though her eyes were bright with mischief for really he was like a small boy who has the best toy boat on the pond and was he like this with his *Golden Lady*, she wondered?

Suddenly she realised what he had done and she began to laugh out loud, turning heads towards her again for it seemed to them that not only was Sam Lassiter's companion beautiful but she was highly amused at something into the bargain.

"That's why I'm got up like this, isn't it, Sam?" Her eyes glowed a warm, transparent brown, the colour of her dress putting glints in them like golden stars. "Why you insisted on this colour and this outfit. Because of the *Golden Lady*?"

He chuckled, the aroma of good cigars and good brandy drifting about him, enveloping her in what she would always recognise, though she might not admit it, as his possessive, masculine strength.

"Of course. It does no harm to let others see what you have. I am well known in this city, Daisy. They know me for a shrewd businessman as well as a fine seaman. I make no bones about it and can see no reason for false modesty. I have two 'golden ladies' now and by God, if that's not a sure sign of success then tell me what is," and his eyes were warm and approving as they rested on her creamy shoulders and bosom. "Now then, champagne, I think, and some oysters..." and without asking her what she might care to eat he ordered her whole meal, taking it for granted his choice would be hers.

There was soft laughter from a dozen female throats and the deeper sound of men's voices. The silent, sure-footed service of dozens of waiters, the chink of silver on china, the delicate aroma of expensive French perfume and expensive Havana cigars, the lovely colours of exquisite evening gowns, many of them turned out by the Misses Yeoland. Sam watched Daisy. She ate with great enjoyment, leaving nothing on her plate as well-bred and well-brought-up 'ladies' were supposed to, tasting, he was sure, many of the dishes for the first time in her life. He saw her study what he did, using the correct cutlery as though she had been used all her life to sitting down at a snowy, damask-covered table, to crystal goblets, to out-of-season flowers and fruit, to champagne and caviare and lobster, to French wines and the admiring glances of every gentleman in the room. She smiled at him over the rim of her glass, her eyes warm, inviting, in the candlelight, playing to perfection the part he had devised for her. She listened to whatever he had to say with fascinated interest, quite genuine, he knew, for she sincerely was fascinated. She was not afraid to speak up when she had something to say and was clearly enjoying herself enormously.

"Would you like to do something else?" he asked, lounging back in his chair, caressing her hand which lay on the table.

"I thought we had already done it today, several times in fact," and her eyes gleamed with impish humour.

"Of course, and we will again, my sweet, and very soon. You're a wickedly desirable woman, Daisy Brindle, and quite insatiable which is unusual in ... well, enough of that for it was not what I had in mind, not just at the moment, anyway."

"What then?"

"I feel lucky tonight so shall we go and have a flutter?"

"A flutter?"

"Yes. Gambling. You have heard of gambling, have you not?"

Instantly she was carried back to the servants' hall at Thornley Green. She could hear Lady Thornley's maid, Kitty Green, speaking, her voice acid, her expression gloating with satisfaction to be the one to bear the tittle-tattle about that 'naughty boy', the son of the house. Gambling debts at Baden-Baden, it was said, and his young lordship's attempts to wheedle money from his mother to pay them. The gossip which was bandied about the kitchen, of his lordship's harsh anger, and the belief that he would cut off his own son from his inheritance if he did not give up his wild life and come home to see to the estate which would one day be his. She remembered her own ferocious denial of Miles Thornley's riotous behaviour, her staunch loyalty to him and her belief that the servants were no more than spiteful and jealous. Dear God, what a fool she had been, determined to see only what she wanted to see in a man who was completely wrong, bad to the very marrow of his bones. All of the vices had been his. A drunkard, a lecher, a spendthrift and an obsessive gambler. There had not been a folly or a shortcoming or a mad extravagance Miles Thornley had not taken to with avid ease and she had refused to see it.

Oh yes, she had heard of gambling!

"Daisy, what is the matter? Where have you gone to? You

326

look as though you have come face to face with a ghost, girl. What did I say, for Christ's sake?"

Sam was leaning forward. He had placed his cigar between his teeth and he held her hand in both of his. His face was surprisingly alarmed but at the same time there was a spark of anger there and it echoed in his voice as he spoke.

"It's that bloody Thornley, isn't it? He's the one who puts that look on your face. Well, let me tell you this, Daisy. He's gone, finished with, in the past, and I don't ever again want to see you look as though you had been struck a blow to the heart whenever something from the past reminds you of him, d'you hear? It was the talk of gambling, wasn't it? Well, put him out of your mind, *and* the bloody past, d'you hear? You're with me now and by God, I'll not have any woman of mine peering back over her shoulder to some chap she knew before she met me."

"I'm not peering back into the past, and I'm *not* your woman, Sam Lassiter. I belong to no man and never will."

"Is that so? Well, it seems to me you've given yourself quite without reserve over the last few days." He smiled, a flash of white teeth in his dark face, his good humour quite returned. "And it seems to me that I've paid you well for it and what I pay for is mine, Daisy Brindle."

"Really, well, in that case you'd better have it all back because I'll be beholden to no man."

His hands were hard on her wrists now but he was still smiling, the smoke from the cigar which was clamped between his teeth, narrowing his eyes. Good humour gone again, he looked dangerous.

"Don't you trust me, Daisy?"

"I trust no man, Sam," and she allowed him to see it in her eyes and in the sharp bite of her voice.

"No, of course you don't, and perhaps you're right. We're a selfish breed, Daisy, using women and anything else we can get our hands on for our own ends, as well you know it, but don't let the experiences you have suffered prevent you from enjoying what is offered you. Life can be very

327

pleasant, you know, if you keep your wits and your heart intact."

"As you have done, you mean?"

"Of course." His grip eased on her wrists and he sat back in his chair, retaining one of her hands, caressing it with every sign of good fellowship. "So let me make you a gesture of goodwill to put your mind at rest. I mean to give you only the pleasures of life, Daisy, indeed I do, and what one gives, whether it be good or bad surely comes back in repayment, and you will repay me most pleasurably, make no mistake on that score."

He reached into his pocket and took out his wallet which was crammed with notes. He removed a handful and threw them on the table. "See what you can do with those," he said.

"What d'you mean?" She looked affronted, conscious of the faces turned in their direction, curious, some of them avidly so, for it seemed to them that the woman – surely one of sinister reputation – with the attractive and immaculately dressed gentleman was being paid in the most blatant fashion, and for all to see.

"I'm going to take you to a certain sporting house. A *salle de jeux*, as it is known on the Continent, though not as smart nor as sophisticated as Hamburg or Baden-Baden. I want to test your nerve and your instinct which something tells me will be sharp and true. And something else. I want to test your good sense. You will have your choice of several games and I will guide you in them. Roulette, faro, dice and the chance to come away with more money than you took in. Or perhaps with nothing."

"And what if I should say I'm not interested?" She sipped her champagne, her expression haughty, the banknotes lying unheeded on the white tablecloth between them. Waiters skirted the tables, eyeing the money unbelievingly, and so great was the interest in what seemed some game between the two players that several gentlemen, trying to attract their attention, were ignored.

"Then you're not the ... gambler ... and I mean that without offence, that I thought you to be, nor the woman."

There was a tense silence as they sized one another up. What was it he *really* wanted of her? She could feel the question bubble to her lips but she would not ask it again. Surely it was not just her body since there must be a score of women who knew just as much as she did, or more, in the ways of pleasing a gentleman's appetite, but what did it matter? She felt a tremor of excitement beneath the gauzy bodice of her gown. His eyes were still on her, his mouth curved in that whimsical, enquiring humour she was beginning to know so well as though to dare her to do it. Why not, his expression said. Take it, enjoy it, for that is what life is, Daisy Brindle. A challenge to be seized, to be wrestled with, to be shaped into the size and colour you want it to be.

She grinned and tossed back the glass of champagne. Reaching for the notes she stuffed them, as carelessly as he had thrown them, into her reticule, her eyes still on his, and his registered approval. He held out his hand to her and she put hers in it and it seemed to everyone in the restaurant that night that a vow had been taken, a pact made.

The club, or 'dining house' as it was euphemistically called, stood in Bold Street, a few yards beyond the Rotunda which was a billiard room frequented by the higher classes who, when they wished for a game of a more exciting sort, moved on to the Royale Club House. It was for members only, naturally, since betting or gaming was against the law, as the Suppression of Betting Houses Act of 1853 stated. The entrance was no more than a door between two shopfronts. Once inside the hallway was brightly lit, the lamps showing up the rather shabby air of an establishment which once might have been grand. There was flock velvet on the walls and a crimson-carpeted staircase leading up to the sound of voices and laughter and at the top a chandelier in which several of the prisms were broken. A large man with a somewhat battered face but with shoulders on him like an ox took Sam's cloak, indicating with what was meant to be a cordial smile that they were to go on up.

The large room they entered was filled with people, most of them gentlemen in evening dress but dotted here and there were young 'ladies', no more than girls really, and very pretty. As Daisy's eyes darted about the room, trying to absorb a dozen sensations at once, bright colours, the aroma of good cigars and perfume, movement and laughter, the sound of voices chanting some strange and rhythmic words, the click and rattle of dice, the slap of playing cards, she was aware that a door at the far end of the room was opened and closed from time to time and that through it the gentlemen drifted, always accompanied by one of the pretty girls.

"What's through there?" she asked Sam, inclined, now that she was here, to cling to his arm.

"Nothing to interest you, my sweet," he answered, leading her amongst the tables on which strange wheels spun, on which colourful cards were set out and at which gentlemen sat; where dice fell and were picked up, and thrown again and again. It was a world of gilt and velvet, of bright lights and shaded corners, of elegance and wealth but beneath the surface was a feeling of desperation, of excited, tense desperation and Daisy wondered what generated it. The door which she had noticed opened again and two girls came through it, one of them as black as Sam's evening coat, her skin glossy and smooth, her eyes enormous and heavily lashed. The girls were beautifully dressed, the black girl in white, the white girl in black, and they made a stunning picture. They were arm in arm and as Daisy watched them, her mouth open in amazement since it was the first time she had ever seen a black person, they were approached by a florid-faced, heavy-set gentleman. They smiled and so did he and in a moment all three had vanished through the mysterious doorway.

"Sam." Her voice was no more than a hiss in his ear.

"What is it?" He bent down to her conspiratorial whisper. "Is this . . . ?"

"Yes," he answered tartly, "but that part of the trade is of no concern to you," and she knew from his attitude that when she was not here it probably could be to Sam Lassiter.

For an hour they moved from table to table as dozens of others did, watching the fortunes, and misfortunes, of the players. There were tables where bezique was played, a quiet corner in which two gentlemen bet quietly, the counters and chips used to be settled in cash at the end of the last round. There was hazarde, played with only two dice but with as many players who cared to bet and could stand round the large table. There was euchre with six players and thirty-two playing cards involved, chemin de fer with six packs of cards, and roulette where the wheel, its forty pockets a blur of colour in the gaslight, never seemed to stop spinning.

"What will it be, my pet?" Sam asked lazily. "The *chef de partie* is calling you to *faites vos jeux*!"

"What does that mean?"

"It means to 'make your games'. In other words to place your bets."

She looked about her, carefully studying all the types of play there were. Card games, dice games, the wheels in the game of roulette. She knew nothing of the first, and the second did not appeal to her but that dancing, whirring spin of chance, the click of the ball as the fates chose into which pocket it might fall, the brightly coloured gaming tokens all seemed to draw her, to speak to her, to beckon to her with a magic finger.

"*Faites vos jeux*," the croupier called and without further hesitation she moved towards the table.

22

She had not counted the banknotes Sam had given her, merely piling the gaming chips he had exchanged for them into neat piles in front of her, but as that pile doubled and tripled word got around that someone was making a killing on the roulette table; when a crowd began to gather, to gasp, even to applaud as her success grew, she thought she had never felt so exhilarated in her life. It was like nothing she had experienced before and she said so rapturously to Sam, her eyes glowing a deep copper gold in her white face, turning to him again and again as the numbers she chose went her way, as the pile grew and the sycophants gathered in even greater numbers, and when, for the first time in a long and nerve-racking run her number, incredibly, let her down, she was only momentarily taken aback.

"It will come again," she announced confidently, her eyes sparkling, her fingers clinking the chips together in a fever of impatience as the croupier's now familiar cry rang out and she waited for the wheel to spin.

"Don't worry, I shall have the next one," she said firmly to Sam, whether to reassure him or herself she was not certain, after her third loss and when, at the end of an hour, the only gentleman remaining to see her go down was Sam, her last token gone, though she had not the faintest idea how much she had won and then lost, she felt a sense of loss so great, an emotion so close to bereavement, she could have wept.

"Lend me some more," she said feverishly, her hand held out, barely turning to Sam, her eyes watching that beckoning wheel go round, scarcely able to stand the moments which passed before she could get another bet on it.

"You have yet to pay me back what I gave you the last time, my love," Sam said, drawing deeply, lazily on his cigar, "but as I didn't mean it as a loan but a gift we will forget it. Now collect your wrap and we'll be off."

She turned then, her face unbelieving, her eyes wide and luminous, almost as though she was drugged, surprising an expression on Sam's face which was unreadable.

"What?" she said impatiently.

"I said, my darling, that the time has come to go home."

"But I want to get that money back I've just lost."

"I dare say you do and I cannot stop you, but unless you have something of your own to bet with how are you to do it?" He smiled.

"Sam, please, only a guinea or two. I'll pay you back from my winnings."

"And if you should lose?"

"I won't, Sam. I know I won't."

"Well, my pet, I'm sorry I can't oblige but I have this strange aversion to throwing good money after bad, you see. So be a good girl, collect your wrap since I really do insist on leaving now. I have to be down early tomorrow at the Goree to arrange for my cargo so I would be obliged if you would make your farewells..." nodding at the bored croupier who had seen it all a hundred times before "...and come at once."

"Sam..."

"Daisy." His voice was soft, his face amiable and smiling but there was absolutely no doubt that he meant what he said.

She was sullen all the way home in the carriage, flouncing away from his hand as he would have helped her down, striding ahead of him up the steps to the front door of the house.

He was gone the next morning when she awoke and for several lazy moments she lay in that pleasurable state, half dream-filled, half awake, in which thoughts slipped in and out of the shadows of her mind like silvered fish sliding through watery currents. None were of great importance, still somewhat insubstantial as she stretched and yawned. Suddenly, through the misted workings of her mind she could remember clearly, just as though it was still happening, the sense of acute, explosive intoxication which had gripped her as she sat at the gaming table the night before. Every tingling sensation, every avid, eager, quite uncontrollable emotion in which nothing mattered except the feel of the chips in her hand, the chattering of the wheel as it spun its blurred circle, the hot smell of gaslamps and cigars, the sound of the croupier's voice, all as sharp as crystal. She could feel it still, that hot-blooded, senseless excitement but as her own senses sharpened they were promptly, blindingly, overtaken by a feeling of horror and she sat up

333

abruptly in the bed she had shared with Sam Lassiter for the past week.

Dear God, what a night it had been, and what a fool, what a damned stupid fool she had been. Sam had been right and she had been wrong. He had been testing her and but for his good sense she would have gone on flinging away money as though tomorrow would never dawn. She had failed him. She didn't know how much he had given her, and that was bad enough in itself but to throw it away, simply *throw it away*, for that was what she had done in her madness, was almost more than her practical, thrifty, careful nature could believe. She who had always had to fight for every penny she had ever earned. To work until she was dazed with exhaustion as she had done at the pit-face for a meagre pittance which had scarce been enough to keep her alive. To do without shoes for her feet, or a bit of warm clothing for her undernourished body, to live like an animal with an animal's instinct to survive, and yet last night she had chucked money away as carelessly as one might discard a thoroughly chewed-over bone. Even worse than that, for did not a bone often still have a scrap of nourishment in it and was therefore to be cherished for another hungry moment? She could hardly believe that she had actually done it, nor could she understand why. And yet at the time it had seemed to be the only thing worthwhile in the whole world. Something she *must* do. Something she *must* have. Something she could not do without. It had, for a couple of wild, insane hours, taken her over, changed her whole nature, turned Daisy Brindle who had been known for her level-headed common sense in the servants' hall at Thornley Green into a person unrecognisable even to herself. She had hated Sam because he would not give her any more money. She had hated him for taking her away from the source of that indescribable excitement which had incredibly entered her blood, and her brain, until she had been incapable of coherent thought.

She threw back the covers of the bed and stepped out on to the creamy white sheepskin beside it, luxuriating in the feel of its soft warmth beneath her feet. She was naked but for the knot of golden ribbons in her hair and she moved across the comfortable, firelit room to the full-length mirror in its corner. Pulling the ribbons – not the ones Cassie had bought her since they were wrapped tenderly, safely into a scrap of tissue in a drawer – she reached for her hairbrush and began to brush the long curling sweep of her hair. It was wild and tangled and was not easy to tame, taking her a full five minutes to pull into some semblance of order. As she brushed she studied her own body dispassionately, turning this way and that, seeing the flesh which this time last week had been so thin every bone beneath had threatened to break through its fragility. Scrawny she had been, there was no other word for it but already those sharp pointed shoulders, the cage of her ribs, her hipbones, were softening, smoothed over with firm flesh. Her breasts, though still small were very nice, she decided, watching them lift as she tied back her hair with a length of green ribbon.

She turned away, aware suddenly of her hunger, and moved towards the bedroom door. When she had broken her fast she would have a good look round Sam's house, she promised herself, for during the past week he had kept her so busy she had had no chance to bestow more than a cursory glance about each immaculate and luxurious room.

Wandering out on to the landing she was about to descend the long curving sweep of the wide staircase which led down to the lower floor when she suddenly realised that for all she knew the mysterious Jack might be in the kitchen. As yet she had not seen him and had begun to wonder if he did indeed exist and had teased Sam about it but it was certainly true that *someone* produced fresh food every day, changed the tangled bed, swept the hearth and made the fires, tidied and cleaned their discarded garments and left the rooms as neat and orderly as Mrs Crosby's linen cupboard.

Slipping back into the bedroom she put on one of the gauzy and completely impractical peignoirs – that was what Miss Yeoland had called them – which Sam had bought for her, in a soft apple green with emerald green velvet ribbons

335

to hold it carelessly across her breasts but which shamelessly revealed her slender legs.

Moving slowly down the stairs she peeped hesitantly into each room, leaving the well-equipped kitchen until the last but there was no one there. A tray was set out on the kitchen table. A fragile china plate with a cup and saucer to match. Bread rolls, still warm, neatly wrapped in a napkin of damask, fresh butter, cream, honey and fruit and on the shining kitchen range a pot of hot coffee. In the centre of the tray, placed in a long slim vase of engraved crystal, was one pale pink rosebud. She picked it up and smelled it, wondering where on earth Jack had got such a thing at this time of the year, smiling at the notion of an old, one-legged mariner scouring the market for it. But would he? Or had it been Sam, but then if it was Sam ... how ... and why, for God's sake?

What was this world into which she had so unwittingly stumbled, she asked herself wonderingly as she sat down slowly at the kitchen table and reached for the bread and honey. It was almost the feeling of being whisked into a fairy tale, into a dream state which had no reality and yet Sam was real and substantial enough. A man with wit and yet a cool practical mind. A man not given to the fanciful, to foolishness and folly, so why should she wonder at his judgement in bringing her here? He certainly was not a man to give something for nothing and so he must be well satisfied with the bargain which appeared to have been struck between them. He seemed to find nothing strange in the situation so why should she? He treated her with a curious lack of concern as though it was the most usual thing in the world to take in some starving waif off the street so why should she wonder at it? It might seem strange to her who had known nothing but regularity for the past five or six years but it seemed that to Sam this was nothing out of the way. He was a man of subtlety, of shades of light and dark with a misted area somewhere in between but he was also a man of shrewd intelligence, was he not? He had certainly proved it last night in letting her gamble freely as she had and then, when she had lost everything, dragging her away from it before she really got into trouble. She had felt so ... so reckless, there was no other word for it unless it was insane. She could have got herself into a difficult, not to say dangerous situation without his whimsical but determined intention to get her away from it. He had shown her one side in the exercise of gambling. He had shown her the sheer, unadulterated thrill of it, the heady intoxication of winning, then he had led her quite brutally to see its obverse side. Its blind greed, its desperation, its hazardous, treacherous danger and as she sat at Sam Lassiter's kitchen table, the sweet taste of his bread and honey on her lips, a pale golden shaft of spring sunshine coming through his window to bathe her in its warmth, the implacable ghost of Miles Thornley slid coldly into her mind.

Miles Thornley. She felt the familiar sensation begin in her breast, spreading throughout her entire body, an emptying, a draining away of warmth and goodwill, of humour and compassion, of all the human feelings that are essential to life itself, leaving her without substance before she began to feel again with an emotion which was as cold and dead as marble. Miles Thornley. She did not repeat to herself how much she loathed him. Not any more, for her mind was far beyond the point where words such as hatred or revenge meant a great deal. There was no way to describe the manifestation of feeling which lay sick and rotting inside her since it defied evocation. She simply became another person. Daisy Brindle ceased to exist and in her place sprang fully to life the woman who had taken her place and who had evolved in the blood and sorrow, the devastation and grief of a bedroom where a girl and an infant had died. A woman who had come into being for no other reason than to hate and hate and hate and who would not fade away to oblivion until justice had been done. Justice for the girl Cassie. No one knew this other being since she was buried deep beneath the smiling, good-natured, hard-working, defiant, strong-willed, quick-tempered, flesh, blood and bone of Daisy Brindle. This being did nothing, harmed no one, demanded, as yet, no more than her own existence. She just *was*, and for the space of thirty seconds she showed in the warm golden eyes of the woman at the table, turning them to a brooding, muddy brown.

He was a gambler. What Daisy Brindle had done last night was what he did himself but multiplied a hundredfold and in that weakness, that malady which surely must make him vulnerable, could there not be the weapon which was needed to bring him down, to wound him, not just in a disabling manner, but fatally?

There was no sound, no movement as she considered it, her posture trance-like, stony, hypnotic, then the kitchen clock which stood above the range struck a cheerful note on the quarter-hour and the moment was gone. Daisy felt the ice-cold implacability of her hidden self begin to thaw and her body shivered ever so slightly as the shaft of sunlight laid a warm benison on her back. Just as though Miles Thornley's presence had not invaded her for an incalculable fraction of time, just as though he did not really have a presence, Daisy's mind moved on and her enjoyment of the food, the hot, sweet coffee, the delicious flesh of the peach she ate and which she had never tasted until this week, was the only consideration in her peaceful mind.

When she had eaten her fill she looked about her at the spotless kitchen. It was in the basement of Sam Lassiter's tall Georgian terraced house, with a door which led out into a small area from which steps went up to the street. There was a separate scullery with its own shallow sink, a draining board and a wooden draining rack. There was a pantry away from the warmth of the kitchen range. The floor was stone-flagged and the walls were lime-washed in a sparkling white. There was a pine dresser with what Daisy took to be every-day kind of crockery, perhaps used by the unseen Jack since she and Sam had eaten only off the finest of bone china. There was a large square pine table and hanging above it dozens of burnished copper pans. It was homely, warm and familiar and she could not imagine Sam setting a foot in it even if his life depended on it.

She poured hot water from the kettle on the range into the sink and like the well-trained housemaid she was, despite the gauzy wrapper which drifted about her like pale green mist, washed the cup, saucer, plate, knife and spoon she had used and set them to drain in the wooden rack, then, her instinct for order appeased, climbed the stairs into the hallway which was cool after the warmth of the kitchen. Here there was a restful spaciousness with rich, damask wall-coverings in a warm, thick cream, the floor tiled in large squares of black and white with an enormous fringed rug of oriental design thrown across it. There was an oak hallstand with several cloaks, a quite dashing cap and a huge umbrella hanging from the hooks. A soft, multicoloured light fell through the stained-glass window of the fanlight above the heavy oak front door, creating patterns on the walls against which stood a long, elaborately carved bench where callers would be invited to sit whilst they waited to be received, and a hall cupboard of solidly crafted oak.

Daisy counted four doors leading off the hall, all standing wide open, one leading into the small parlour to which Sam had brought her on the first night, another to what she had heard Sam call his study, the third to a dining room and the fourth to a large and elegant drawing room which, Sam had told her, was rarely used.

From the hallway the curved staircase, carpeted in velvet the colour of oxblood, stretched away up into the sunlit shadows of the upper landing and the three or four bedrooms which were situated on it and from there another staircase led up to another floor of bedrooms in which she supposed the servants, if there had been any besides Jack, would have slept.

She drifted into the dining room which was of splendid proportions, trailing her foaming wrapper behind her, admiring the rich colours and gilt-framed paintings on the deep cinnamon-coloured walls, the graceful candelabra on the polished oval dining table, the plain, honey-coloured carpet, inches deep it seemed to Daisy, the long velvet curtain in the same shade and the glowing rosewood chiffonier on which fine silver stood. It was a plain room, simply furnished, without a woman's touch perhaps, as were all the rooms in Sam's house, but elegant nevertheless.

It was a handsome house, Daisy decided. What had once

been a family house in an area where men of substance had lived, merchants and those who had made their money in shipping. As their fortunes had grown and their social position improved they had moved their families eastwards and southwards to Everton, Aigburth and Toxteth and the lower-middle class, also on the move up the ladder of success, had taken over the tall Georgian houses. They were solid, reliable and graceful in their simplicity, set in a crescent, each one with a small rear garden shaded by a few trees and bright with flowers in the summer. Most, Daisy had been told, were split up into 'rooms', painted and refurbished and let to doctors and other professional men, the families who had once lived there gone for ever. It was so close to the centre of town that one could walk the distance to the busy commercial area and the docks and there were always plenty of hansom cabs to be had at the corner of Duke Street.

Daisy sighed as she moved languidly up the stairs, not knowing quite what to do with herself. All her life, for as long as she could remember she had never had a moment to simply stand and do nothing, except perhaps for an hour at the end of a long summer's day in the fields, and now, with the house empty, every surface of it cleaned and scrubbed and polished, every room except the bedroom she shared with Sam as neat as a new pin, there was nothing for her to do. She could not even bake a batch of scones or a few biscuits, which she had been taught to do at the School of Industry, since there was no food in the house beyond a jar of coffee and one of tea. Not a bit of flour or fat, no milk or cheese, not a biscuit, not a slice of bread, only the remains of what she herself had eaten for her breakfast. It seemed that Jack provided only what was absolutely necessary in his master's household unless ordered otherwise and somehow Daisy did not think Sam would be involved a great deal in entertaining unless it was a girl such as herself.

There was a sound downstairs which Daisy recognised as a key turning in a lock and without a thought that it could be Jack, since he would probably enter by the basement door anyway, she felt the pleasure bubble up in her and she began to smile.

"Sam, where have you been all morning?" she called out as she raced from the bedroom and on to the landing. "I've been moping about for hours not knowing what on earth to do with myself." She was at the head of the stairs now, her robe flowing back from her slim, bare legs and feet, the ribbons carelessly tied at her breast, the shadowed peaks of her nipples and the crest of hair between her thighs deliciously exposed. Her hair swirled about her head, her skin glowed, her eyes were warm and welcoming and she was completely unaware of her new loveliness as she ran down the stairs to the man who was just turning away from the front door he had closed. "I really will have to find some occupation, Sam . . ." she was saying, her eyes snapping with pleasure, her arms lifting to him.

They were both surprised by the warmth of their greeting. His arms crushed her to him, his own eyes bright with admiring pleasure. Their lips met and clung, tongues touching, warm and unhurried, and when they parted both of them were breathing more quickly.

"Well," he said, his eyes running over her scantily clad body, holding her from him so that he might see her better. "What a splendid welcome and what a perfectly delightful outfit, my pet, and as for that occupation you mention shall we see what we can do about it right now? I really must leave you more often if this is what I shall come home to."

He swung her up in his arms, holding her firmly, one might almost call it possessively, to him and began to carry her up the stairs. As he placed her on the bed, already divesting himself of his own clothing, she began to untie the ribbons of her peignoir.

"I'll do that," he said huskily, ". . . and later, when you have been . . . occupied enough, we will talk."

He had been down to check the repairs done on *Golden Lady*, he told her much later as she lay, languid and stretching, in his arms. Her masts, spars and rigging had been damaged in a wild storm off the Irish coast but she had now been passed fit once more for sea. Her hull had been inspected in dry dock and she was ready to sail. Fresh water and food was to be taken on tomorrow for her next voyage.

341

Her cargo of pottery from St Helens, watches and clocks made in Liverpool, salt from Cheshire, coal, again from St Helens, cotton piece goods from the cotton towns of Oldham and Burnley, machinery, chemicals and railway components, was being loaded at this moment. He would be gone no more than three or four weeks, he explained, and in the meanwhile she was to stay here with Jack whom he had persuaded to remain behind to 'protect' her. He would leave her some money...

She sat up slowly and turned about to look at him, her eyes clouded with a strange expression which he could not read. She looked, as she indeed was, a woman who had been well and lustily loved, her skin warm and rich, her mouth ripe and swollen, her hair like a vivid curtain of flame about her. She was quite glorious and would make him a splendid companion, both in and out of bed, for as long as it suited him, he thought, but she had a certain mutinous set to her mouth, a definite tossing back of her rebellious hair which told him even on such short acquaintance that she was not pleased, that she was not at all pleased at being slotted carefully away in some pigeonhole marked 'for later' whilst he sailed away on the morning tide to what seemed to her to be the other side of the world.

"So! I'm to sit at home and embroider or whatever it is ladies of leisure do and wait for your return, is that what you're saying?"

"Unless you have something else in mind, my sweet, in which case you are perfectly at liberty to do it," he said steadily. He reached for his cigars and lit one, studying her through narrowed eyes, his hand lifting to cup her breast but she pushed it away impatiently.

"And what if I don't want to?"

"Want to what? Stay or go?"

"You know what I mean. What if it doesn't suit me to simply hang around here and wait for you to come back?"

"Then you may do as you please, Daisy," and she could see that he meant it. "I said at the beginning of our ... friendship that neither was tied to the other, did I not? And you were aware of my profession from the start. I am a seaman. I go to sea for weeks, sometimes months on end and if you don't care for that you have only to say so and we will part with no hard feelings." He grinned amiably.

Part? That was what she wanted, was it? She had known him for only a short while but in that time she had grown used to him, grown to like his company, his irreverent, sometimes coarse wit. His hard muscled body pleased hers. He asked nothing of her that she could not give and if she was not prepared to give it, his attitude said, he was not the man to take it by force. He was fair, a reasonable man when he had his own way, and generous. He was self-indulgent, true, but what he had, so did she. She could do a lot worse than stay here, at least until he came back, and then see what might turn up. She had this . . . this . . . well, she could not call it an idea, for ideas have some form, some shape, and this whisper which ran through her mind had none. But the whisper was not quite ready to be listened to yet and until it was she needed this time of peace, of shelter, of nourishment for her bruised heart and wounded mind which no one could see but which hurt her badly just the same, so why not do as he said?

"You'll stay then?" he said lightly, watching the changing expressions on her face and reading them correctly, his eyes amused, one dark eyebrow raised sardonically.

"Will you take me to see *her* before you sail?"

"Is that a condition of your staying?" He grinned, replacing his hand on her breast.

"Yes," and this time she did not resist.

She had never before seen so much activity concentrated in one place at one time. Even the brisk tumult and often frantic haste of the kitchen at Thornley Green, where two or three dozen servants from scullerymaids right up to the august presense of Mrs Crosby herself had been on the move, could not match the busy scene of a ship being made ready to sail. The noise, the sheer energy and vitality of the area about the ship, which was repeated all along the length of the docks from Clarence to the Herculaneum wherever a cargo was being loaded or unloaded, was almost more than the human senses could stand. Men shouted indecipherable messages to one another, answering in like tones and all at the tops of their voices in order to be heard above the hubbub. There was the ear-splitting sound of iron striking iron as men with brawny shoulders swung enormous hammers. Shire horses between the shafts of sturdy waggons whinnied and stamped their iron-shod hooves lustily on the hard ground. Men cursed and whistled and over it all some rich tenor voice sang plaintively of his native Ireland. There were anchors seemingly discarded lying on the quayside, bigger than the magnificent horses which were in their turn dwarfed by intricately carved figureheads jutting out over the quay from the prow of each ship. There were women with buckets balanced on their heads, there were dogs, cats, chickens, perhaps escaped from some crate about to be taken aboard, Daisy thought dazedly. Children leapt nimbly across enormous links of chain and neatly coiled ropes thicker than her waist, undaunted by the tumult, by the kaleidoscope of humanity which had been thrown carelessly down amongst the huddle of boxes and crates and barrels which were being loaded, or unloaded, as the case may be. It was a morning of sun-streaked cloud and salt-breezes mixed with the redolent aroma of new timber, of tar, rum, spices, fruit, and all the commodities which came from every corner of the hemisphere where a ship might sail. Ships which were as close to one another and as high in the sky as the tall trees of Caleb's Wood, frigate and brigantine and schooner, and out on the dancing water just beyond them, the dumb vessel of the Mersey lighter carrying freight from ship to shore.

Sam held her arm protectively for it seemed she must be guarded from the hazards which were strewn across her path, or perhaps, though he would not have admitted it, even to herself, it was a certain pride in the possession of a plaything as unusual as this lovely woman. Other men recognised it in her and envied him and Sam Lassiter liked that. She wore a warm woollen gown of the palest silvery grey, the sleeves frothed with a shower of white lace at the wrist. Her velvet mantle was of a darker grey, banded with the same shade as her dress, the high collar framing her face, and her bonnet of pale grey velvet had a dashing white feather which bobbed as she walked and made her look even taller and more willowy. The sun's rays caught the escaping tendrils of hair which lay over her ears and brow, turning them to fire. Her eyes were a golden blaze in her face and everywhere she went men stopped to look at Captain Lassiter's new woman.

"What a stir you are causing, Daisy," he murmured, not at all displeased as he directed her towards the exaggerated thrusting bow of the tall-masted ship alongside which scores of packing cases of all sizes lay. Men swarmed all over her decks and rigging, hurrying up and down the gangplanks, waterside workers who were loading bags of refined sugar into the hold watched by the first mate.

"Is this it?" she breathed, coming to an abrupt halt, bewitched by the proud beauty of the sleek-hulled clipper ship.

"Aye, this is it, as you so charmingly put it," he answered, smiling ruefully at her choice of words but pleased nevertheless by her obvious admiration.

"It's like . . . like a thoroughbred horse," for had she not seen the lovely, clean-limbed, elegant hunters which lived in the stables at Thornley Green and surely this graceful creature could be compared favourably with any of those.

"Daisy, my darling, if you are to be in the company of seamen, and it seems you are, then you must learn to call a ship *she* and not *it*. But you are right, you know. The clippers are amongst the thoroughbreds of the merchant sailing vessels. They have to be fast, you see, to compete with these new steamships. So they are built on long, lean lines, much finer than they used to be for that way they can be made to move faster through the water. And by piling on as much sail as possible, with royals set above upper and lower topgallant sails and the main course on each mast . . ." he broke off and began to laugh ". . . well, you will not know what I'm talking about but believe me, *Golden Lady* is the fastest ship in the river. Look up to the masts . . ."

Daisy craned her neck, staring up into the cobweb of the rigging until she was dizzy, then down until her eyes came to rest on the figurehead supported at the bow by elegant tailboards.

"She's a goddess," Sam said softly, noticing where Daisy's eyes rested. "A golden sea goddess holding out her arms to welcome the sea which she loves. The Golden Lady, the only lady who has been true to ..." He stopped, somewhat abashed as though caught in the soft and tender involvement of a lover, almost ashamed of the emotion his ship seemed to awaken in him, and Daisy wondered what he had been about to say. The only lady who had been true to Sam Lassiter perhaps? Was that it, or was his ship the only lady ever to have captured Sam Lassiter's wayward heart?

She had no time to dwell on the mystery of it before she was hurried up the steep gangway, across a deck littered with ropes and barrels, bales and crates, down some narrow steps which were awkward to negotiate in her wide crinoline, along a narrow passage and into a tiny, but scrupulously neat cabin in which she recognised the fanatical hand of the mysterious Jack, surely? She had heard Sam shout for him as she was ushered along the passage, telling some barefoot lad to find him. She hardly had time to straighten her bonnet which had been dislodged by a brush with the low frame of the doorway when there was a sharp knock, peremptory and not really meant to be polite or anything so foolish as that, and over the threshold stepped a man who could have been any age between fifty and ninety, so brown, dried up and wrinkled was he, and yet so spry. He wore a seaman's knitted cap, a sea-gansey of coarse wool, rough breeches and one well-polished kneeboot on his remaining leg. The other leg, cut off at the knee, was supported by a roughly carved stump of wood.

"We'll have some coffee, Jack," Sam was already busy with maps and papers on the table which stood in the centre of the cabin and did not even look up, "... and then I want you to take Miss Brindle home. We'll be dining in tonight so you and she can decide on the menu."

"Can't be done." No more than that. Jack looked her up and down with the uncomplicated, uncaring gaze of a man who has seen dozens of women come and go in his years of service with Captain Sam Lassiter and expected to see a dozen more before he was gone. His lip curled, quite amused, it appeared. His eyes were so pale a grey as to be almost colourless, bleached that way by the thousand foreign suns he had witnessed, Daisy supposed. Why should he put himself out for the likes of her, his expression conveyed to her very plainly. What had she got that others hadn't and though the Captain had put her in Jack's care – which duty he would perform, as he did everything else for his captain, with all the skill at his command – she'd go the way of all the rest, of that he'd no doubt.

"Why not?" Sam held a paper up to the small window, studying it with great concentration, not caring really about Jack or Daisy, nor how they were to get along whilst he was away.

"I've things to attend to here seeing as how I'm to be marooned ashore."

"Let someone else do them."

Daisy flung up her head, tossing her white feathered bonnet with all the splendour of a queen. She turned towards the doorway, the space so small her crinoline nearly knocked Jack off his one good leg.

"Good God, I can find my own way home and the pair of you can go to the devil. How d'you think I managed to get from one place to another before I met you, Sam Lassiter? On my own two feet and by my own wit, that's how, and as for this . . . this old man, take him with you wherever you're going because I don't need him, nor you!"

When she had gone, leaving them both open-mouthed but ready to smile, Jack turned to Sam Lassiter and in his eyes was the first spark of the respect he was to feel for Daisy Brindle.

"She's right an' all, Captain. That 'un don't need no minder."

"Possibly, but you'll still guard her with your life, you old fool," and in Sam Lassiter's face was a quiet resolution which no longer held any humour.

23

"Call me a cab, Jack, will you, and tell the driver I want to go to the railway station."

Daisy stood at the top of the stairs which led down into the basement kitchen, fastening into her ears the gold loop earrings Sam had brought her back from New Orleans on his last trip home. She was dressed to go out in a simple but very elegant day dress of pale honey-coloured zephyr, fine and light and silky. The bodice was well fitted to her small, neat breasts, the sleeves tight at the shoulder but flaring out to a wide wrist lined with cream ruffled lace which was repeated in a slit at the back of the wide skirt. She wore what was known as a 'round hat' which looked for all the world like a wide shallow dish worn upside down. That too was honey-coloured, straw, trimmed under the brim with the same cream lace as her gown. The hat was dashing, saucy even as it tipped over her forehead. Peeping from beneath the hem of her skirt were high-heeled cream kid boots.

She had gained a startlingly mature beauty during the five months she had been Sam Lassiter's mistress though she was still very slender. Her skin was like a rich dish of cream and she glowed with good health, glossy and quite magnificent. A thoroughbred, Sam called her, like the expensive bloodstock to be found in the stables of his wealthy fox-hunting acquaintances. Her hair, which was brushed back from her face and twisted into a heavy coil, was burnished to the lustre of the copper pans in Jack's kitchen and her eyes were bright and snapping with some inner excitement.

Jack didn't like it. He didn't like it at all. He came up

the stairs with that curious hop-and-a-jump which he had perfected in his time at sea and battling against the unsteady tilt of steep stairways and heaving decks, as nimble as a child despite his many years. How many, no one knew, but he had served in the fleet of twenty-seven ships under the command of Admiral Horatio, Lord Nelson, and had been in that famous battle of Trafalgar in which the Admiral had died.

"Where you off?" he said now, irritable as a nursemaid with a wayward child, suspicious too, for you never knew with this one what she was up to, gallivanting all over Liverpool when the Captain was away, and by herself which he knew the Captain wouldn't like.

Jack's hands were coated with flour and some of it clung to the enormous protective apron he wore over his sea-gansey and pantaloons which, despite his new life ashore, he still resolutely refused to discard. Some of the flour floated in a dancing haze about him as he reached the top step. He was making bread which he did every day for what else was he to do with his time? he demanded to know fretfully. He was a mariner, for God's sake, not a damned housekeeper and should be on the deck of *Golden Lady* making good headway to North America, the West Indies, South America, West Africa, India, China or even Australia with Captain Lassiter and not beached here in this bloody kitchen and this bloody house with the wilful woman the Captain had put in his charge. Sam Lassiter's woman, for she was undeniably that now, belonging to him as surely as his lovely clipper ship, the fine wines and cigars he purchased, or the immaculately tailored and expensive suits he wore. She might not acknowledge it to herself, if she indeed even considered it, but Jack knew his master better than any man living and though he might speak of freedom and the rights of both those concerned to walk away from a relationship which no longer satisfied, where anything which belonged to *him* was concerned, as this woman belonged to him, that was a horse of a different colour entirely. The Captain was well-known in Liverpool, where he found the cargoes he took to so many parts of the world and where he sold those he carried back, and his new mistress who went everywhere with him when he was in port had become a familiar figure. But she was Sam Lassiter's, and they respected that, for Sam Lassiter was not a man to be trifled with, not if you wanted to keep your health, that is. A man handy with his fists, a man with some influence as wealthy men usually are, and so his woman was treated with respect but there was always *one* fool who might be reckless enough, or mad enough, to approach her and if Daisy Brindle came to harm, or was insulted, which was much the same as offering insult to Sam Lassiter, he would want to know how Jack had let it happen.

So Jack must watch her whilst the Captain was away. Make sure no other dog came sniffing round *his* bitch, which was a crude way of putting it and indeed was not what the Captain had actually said but it was what he had meant just the same. Jack implied that the responsibility he had been given was an onerous one, and the domesticated life that went with it, and he told Daisy so at every turn, slamming the superb food he cooked down before her, crashing about the house when she was within earshot as though he would break every stick of furniture he lovingly polished. He was unaware that she had crept down to the kitchen one night and had seen the contented look on his seamed face as he relaxed before what he now thought of as his own fireplace. He would sit in his rocker, his good leg stretched out beside his wooden stump, the latter in danger of catching fire from the crackling heat of the coals. He had acquired a threadbare marmalade cat from some back alley, thin and spiteful, transforming it into a fat and supercilious beauty within weeks and it would curl on his lap, the two of them breathless in the heat, Jack's rum jar beside him. He and the cat seemed to purr in unison and Daisy was well aware that, though he would have denied it strongly, he was relieved to find himself such a snug berth in which to end his days.

"Where I'm off to is no concern of yours," she answered tartly, running lightly up the stairs to fetch her reticule. "Just nip to the corner..."

"I'm nipping nowhere, missy, and neither are you unless you tell me where it is you're going and even then there's no saying you'll get there, not if I don't like the sound of it.

The Captain said most particular that you was to stay away from the docks..."

"Why the devil should I want to go to the docks?"

"... or anywhere that ... well, where rough characters hang about..." meaning other men, naturally, continuing his diatribe just as though she had not spoken. "The dressmaker whenever you want, he said, for he's a generous man, the Captain, and likes to see his ... well ... his lady tricked out proper, and if you had a hankering for some culture I was to accompany you to the Royal Institution, or Permanent Gallery of Art. Sightseeing, the Captain said, and if you was wanting to go I'll take you. They say the Town Hall's very fine and there's not a ballroom in the land to compare with the one there. And banqueting halls..."

"Jack, you can save your breath. I've no wish to see the Town Hall nor its ballroom."

Daisy ran down the stairs again, her huge skirt swaying wildly, rushing past the old seaman who stood in the middle of the hallway with every intention of stopping this self-willed young woman who, though he did his best to restrain her, went wherever she pleased. He had managed to go with her on most of her excursions which so far had been completely innocent. The Misses Yeolands' dressmaking establishment on many occasions, where Jack waited like a soldier on parade just outside the immaculately painted front door. To visit Mrs Girvan at Number 15, Upper Arcade, next door to the Savings Bank in Bold Street, where the wives and daughters of wealthy Liverpool gentlemen purchased their French flowers and feathers, their headdresses and Berlin wools. To Mr Henry Lacy's bookshop from where he carried away for her a great number of books and prints. To Mr Isaac Woodville's Italian warehouse where might be obtained foreign fruit, Gruyère and Parmesan cheese, macaroni and vermicelli of which she had become inordinately fond. He accompanied her to all of these places, sitting truculently beside her in the hackney carriage, the hood down since it had been a warm, dry summer, inviting curious glances wherever they went. The exquisitely dressed and lovely young woman and the old sea-dog, one-legged, who clung to her skirts like a fox terrier.

But sometimes she eluded him. Sometimes he would stump into the small parlour to ask her brusquely if she wanted a cup of tea or a taste of the ratafia biscuits he had just made and she would not be there, simply not there. Shouting for her all over the bloody house, he was, and no one there but the secret, feline presence of the marmalade cat which liked to curl its tail about itself and lie in the middle of the bed the woman shared with the Captain, just where a shaft of sunlight lay on the silk-quilted coverlet. He daren't tell the Captain she went out on her own. Well, it wasn't that he daren't but somehow he didn't think it necessary for he trusted Daisy Brindle and though she wouldn't tell him where she had been, merely tapping her nose and smiling in that daft way women had when they wanted to keep you guessing, he knew she wasn't double-crossing the man who had taken her in. She wasn't that sort of woman, you could tell that. Once she'd got the measure of you and knew you meant her no harm she'd see you through thick and thin. He wasn't a bad judge of character for you meet all sorts on the deck and in the rigging of a sailing vessel where the men were soon sorted out from the boys.

And here she was off again on some bloody jaunt, her eyes a deep amber like he'd seen them go when she was up to something, the very air about her vibrating with the energy she created. She was a rare one right enough and you could understand why the Captain tried to keep her so hedged about. She had that quality few women had, and few women recognise, but by God men did, and it attracted them to her like bees to honey. Not at first, she hadn't, for though she'd not seen him, he'd seen her in that first week the Captain brought her home. She'd been a plain, gawky slip of a thing, all eyes and hair, but a couple of weeks with Sam Lassiter and she'd been transformed into this unique creature the Captain appeared to value like a piece of rare jade, or one of those brilliant and costly little birds which could be brought back from the Orient and which they kept in cages, if they survived that is.

"Now look here, missy." He always called her that. She was not the sort of woman you could call Miss Brindle, or even Miss Daisy, but at the same time he could not quite bring himself to address her as Daisy. So he compromised with 'missy' which suited him because it gave him the feeling of being, if not her better, then her elder and therefore entitled to be peremptory.

"I've no time for argument, Jack, and if you won't call me a cab I shall have to run down to the corner myself."

"You're going nowhere without me, missy, and if you step through that door I shall be forced to tell the Captain and I mean it this time," though they both knew that was not true.

"He'll not be home for another two weeks, Jack, and you'll have forgotten by then."

"That I won't."

"Goodbye, Jack. I'll be home before dark."

"Before dark! Where in hell's name are you going? Jesus, the Captain'll skin me alive..."

"No he won't, Jack, and in any case, why should he? You know and he knows that I'm not interested in ... well, I've enough on my hands with him without going out to look for further trouble."

Jack was struggling with his apron, a token gesture for he knew what she said was the truth. A fine dusting of flour drifted on to the highly polished surface of the hallstand. Let her go, he told himself. She would anyway and he was too old for this kind of caper, chasing about Liverpool protecting a young woman who, though the Captain would give him an argument, was perfectly able to protect herself.

The carriage she had summoned in St Helens, where she had alighted from the train, put her down outside the cottage door which stood in the centre of a straggling row of others and within thirty seconds every child in the village was gathered about it. The driver got down from his high seat and helped her down too, his face conveying his wonder for what the devil did this fashionably dressed lady – well, perhaps not that for a real lady would have her own carriage and would certainly not go about unescorted –

want with this rundown and clearly impoverished part of Lancashire? The road through the village ran from Wigan to St Helens, only a country lane really and scarcely used now that the railway was spreading like an ever-growing spider's-web across the north. The cottages, all occupied by the labourers of the manorial lord, probably Lord Derby, the driver thought, for he was the biggest landowner in these parts were, at this time of year, a riot of colour as wildflowers grew between every slab and step, around every doorway and even up on the thatched rooftops where seeds had blown. Some of the village women took a pride in their homes and the glint of the reflected sunshine winked out cheerfully from well-polished windows but for the most part the paltry sum of six shillings a week which their husbands were paid, despite the low rents they were charged on their tied cottages, was not enough to keep at bay the poverty which afflicted the working class, and many of the cottage women simply couldn't be bothered.

"Get away from that horse, yer little . . ." The cab driver aimed a clout at the nearest head and the children scattered, most of them on bare feet, but they did not go far, hanging about just beyond his reach to watch the incredible sight of a beautiful lady knock at Sarah Miller's cottage door. It was a long time opening and when it did the slatternly woman who stood just inside it might have been going to her own hanging, so hopelessly cast down did she look.

Daisy smiled encouragingly, at the same time trying to keep the hem of her dress clear of the worst of the dried filth on the step, wondering at her own aversion to it. Had she not lived in a hovel a hundred times worse than this in her own childhood? And yet could she be blamed if the years between had given her the sensibilities and the means to be discriminating? Still, the gown would have to be meticulously cleaned, she thought ruefully, when she got home, since God only knew what she would pick up this day. She was quite amazed by what she could see was dirt of long standing for if this woman was indifferent to it, as it seemed she was, her daughter certainly would not be, from what Daisy remembered of her, and would have had this

354

step so clean you could eat off it, and the rest of the cottage as well.

"Good morning," she said brightly, her eyes, now that they had become accustomed to the gloom at the back of the woman, picking out half a dozen figures which she took to be her children and she cursed herself for not bringing a basket of food with her. Had she become so used to her own luxurious and pampered station in life which Sam Lassiter had provided that she had forgotten the ever-present spectre of hunger which haunted people like this woman and her family and which had once haunted Daisy Brindle?

The woman gaped at her for several long minutes, struck dumb by the vision on her doorstep, but she recovered herself quickly and her face closed up.

"It *is* Mrs Miller, isn't it?" Daisy went on, hovering uncertainly, conscious of the cab driver at her back and of the scores of curious village women which every cottage doorway in the street had disgorged.

"It might be," the woman answered with the defensive air of those who expect the worst and usually receive it.

"I'm Daisy Brindle. I wanted to speak to Bess and this being Sunday and her afternoon off I thought she would be here so . . ."

"Well, she's not," followed by a silence which said quite plainly, take it or leave it, it was all the same to her.

"But does she not come home on Sunday?"

"Sometimes."

"What does that mean?"

"It means that since she lost her job as upper housemaid and was put back ter skivvy she do as she's told. If they can't find a floor for her to scrub or a sinkful of greasy pans to scour they let her off for an hour or two but that don't happen every Sunday, nor every other Sunday neither. If she's lucky it's once a month." Her mouth snapped shut angrily. It was evidently a well-chewed bone of resentment and Daisy had the strange feeling that the woman held her at fault. She had suffered so many knocks, her manner said, so many kicks, so many setbacks as the years went by, from which she had found it harder and harder to recover, so was it any wonder she should find life so intolerable and the cause of this last blow, if she was who she said she was, which was hard to believe, was standing on her own doorstep. The name of Daisy Brindle was like sawdust in her mouth and well it might be for had it not been for her their Bess would still be in her grand job, slipping home every Sunday afternoon, scrubbing her mother's kitchen floor, black-leading the kitchen grate since she was never the one to sit on her bum and do nowt. There would still be a screw of tea and one of sugar, other delicacies brought from the kitchen at Thornley Green which had enhanced Sarah Miller's drab existence and to which she had looked forward each week. Not to mention the few bob Bess had slipped into her hand whenever she could. With the legacy of half a dozen young children still alive and at home, the legacy her dead husband had inopportunely left to her, the extra money had made all the difference between being poor and being destitute. She was a widow living in an estate cottage and in deathly fear ever since Bert went that she would be thrown out of it and on to the Parish. Mr Greenhalgh appeared to have turned a blind eye to her continued occupation of it, perhaps because their Bess was an upper housemaid, but would he go on doing so now that she was no more than a skivvy? That was a question which haunted her, which kept her awake when she should have been peacefully sleeping, and the cause of Bess's disgrace was this elegantly gowned lady who was smiling graciously at her cottage door. Not that Bess had said as much, not in so many words, but Sarah had put two and two together and come up with a pretty accurate picture of what had happened at the big house. Not the details, but the bones of it and that was enough to tell her that this girl had done summat wrong and that Bess had been dragged into it. Daisy Brindle had got the sack, Bess had told her shortly, and she had been chucked back to skivvy, at everyone's beck and call, it seemed, and Sarah Miller had lost the only bit of comfort she had ever known in her hard life. But this one had come to no harm, from the look of her, all dolled up like a lady, and wouldn't you know that if anyone was to suffer it was never the one who caused the bloody trouble in the first place.

"Mrs Miller." Daisy's voice brought Bess's mother from her hard-faced trance. "Mrs Miller, I want to get in touch with Bess but for private reasons I can't go up to the house. Now I don't know what's happened to her since I left though she did tell me she was to be demoted for which I'm truly sorry but I'm here to try and set that right and I can't do it if I can't speak to her. So if I was to send a note by one of your children asking her to come home..."

"She'd lose her job, sure as eggs, besides, what use would a note be to our Bess?" Mrs Miller's voice was cold and scornful. "She can't read."

Bess was on her knees, much as usual, when the summons came. Despite the relief of taking her weight off her aching knee-joints which, no matter how often she rubbed the skin with vinegar, said to harden it, were still chafed and raw at the end of the day, her heart sank. What now, she wondered wearily, heaving the bucket to the sink in the scullery and tipping the dirty water away. She replaced her brushes and floor-cloths, putting the hard scouring soap which opened the skin of her hands like a sharp knife, in its correct place for Mrs Crosby didn't like to see things left about unattended, even for five minutes, wiped her hands on a bit of sacking, removed her apron and hung it on a hook behind the scullery door. She adjusted her coarse cap, smoothed down the hard-wearing material of her skirt and moved dispiritedly along the passage leading to the kitchen.

The flesh had fallen from her in the eight months since she had lost her hard-earned and well-deserved post of upper housemaid at Thornley Green and it was not all the fault of the exhausting menial work she was now compelled to do. She had worked hard, long hours as a housemaid, beginning at five thirty in the morning when she got out of her bed and ending often at ten thirty at night when she fell back into it but it had been work which she had found satisfying, rewarding, a position she had gained by her own efforts and she had been proud of it. Upper housemaid at the age of nineteen had been an achievement not gained by many so young. The work had suited her. She liked the methodical routine of her day and she prized the trust which had been put in her to care for and cherish the beautiful things which crammed the equally beautiful rooms of Thornley Green. She had been a servant of some importance, going somewhere, for there was no doubt she had been well thought of. In the hierarchy of the servants' hall, though she had been quite some way from the top of the ladder, she had been a long way from the bottom.

With a cruel stroke which had come at her from nowhere it had all been stripped away from her and for something which was none of her doing. She had been stripped of her importance, her small share of authority over those not as special as she, of her sense of her own worth, of her position of trust, and at twenty she was back where she had begun at the age of twelve.

But at the age of twelve how easy it had been to do exactly as she was told for she had known nothing else then. She had known nothing but obedience to her superiors and hard work and had been only too thankful to have a job at all. And she had had something else which was now lost to her for good. She had had hope. There was not the slightest possibility in her present state that she would ever regain her elevated status for the simple reason that Mrs Crosby no longer trusted her. She had said so at the bitter interview when Daisy had been sacked. She had said so venomously, the girl's own part in the affair – his lordship's words and oh, how they had flagellated her – which should have been noticed, he said, by those in authority in the servants' hall, making her determined to punish someone, and who was left but Bess Miller?

Mrs Crosby was standing by the open kitchen door as Bess entered the room, her hand on the latch, her eyes like frozen grey snow in her face which was a dangerous shade of puce, not just with the ferocious heat of the kitchen, but with her own rage. The sun shone in a hazed golden shaft from the yard and in it, his face beaded with sweat, his expression one of apprehension, his eyes starting out of his head like that of a trapped rabbit, was Bess's youngest brother, a lad of eight years old. Their Eddy.

She felt her heart sink in despair and wanted nothing more than to collapse at the large table which she must pass to get to the door, put her head on her folded arms and weep the hopeless tears of the downtrodden beast of burden she had become. Dear God, had she not had enough, more than enough, without trouble at home since that could be the only reason Eddy was here? Her mother wouldn't send him unless it was a matter of life and death for with six children under the age of ten to be fed and only herself and Bess to do it with the few shillings a week they earned between them she would be too mortally afraid that Bess might lose her job, pitiful as it was.

Her fear made her aggressive.

"What the devil are you doing here?" she hissed, careless of Mrs Crosby's icy disapproval, rushing at the boy in the doorway, making him rear away in fear. "You know you've not to come here asking for me, no matter what. D'you want me to lose my job?" but all the while she spoke she knew it was not the boy's fault, nor even her mother's. She was not awfully sure where the blame lay for the disaster which had overtaken them, but whatever had happened at home must be faced, despite Mrs Crosby's vast and obvious displeasure.

"What is it, Eddy?" Her thin face, sallow and without the slightest claim to any sort of comeliness, did its best to let him know that there was nothing to fear. He had only to pass on their mother's message, tell her which one of their brothers or sisters had died, was fatally ill or injured, for only the direst of calamities would force her mother to action such as this. When he had divulged it, Eddy could set off home again and it would be left to Bess, and Mrs Crosby, to decide if she was to follow.

"You're to come home," he whispered furtively, edging away from the omnipotent figure in black who stood over their Bess.

"Come home?" Bess's voice rose shrilly. "Why?"

"Me Mam said so."

"But why?" Her despair was getting badly out of control and she thought she might hit him.

"I dunno. Most urgent she said I was to say."

"For God's sake, Eddy. You know I can't just leave here and run home without a good reason."

Mrs Crosby tapped her foot, breathing heavily, her hand on the door ready to slam it shut, even though the figure of the disgraced scullerymaid stood in the doorway. Eddy said nothing. He knew as well as any of those who counted themselves as one of the labouring poor how important a job was, and how difficult to keep. Their Bess had one and could not afford to jeopardise it, but she *must* come home, the grand lady had said so. She had told him to say nothing, to tell no one about her visit to their cottage. "Bess must pretend someone is ill at home," she had said but he couldn't say that, not in front of this woman who had their Bess's life in her hand.

He tried to tell his sister this with much comical rolling of his eyes and twitchy tossings of his head but it was no good, she and the woman merely stared at him as if he was mad. Then he had a brainwave, the first and last he was to have in his life though he was not to know it at the time. He had heard the lady say as she sat at his own Mam's kitchen table how their Bess had given her her own savings, only a few bob, she said, but a life-saver to her and it had impressed him since money was hard to come by and a body didn't chuck it away for no good reason, especially someone like their Bess.

"She says to thank you for the present you give her a few months back. She found it right handy, she says. She'd like to return the favour, she says."

He had to repeat it several times before their Bess caught on and though the woman kept saying "What present, what present?" and then "Don't you dare go over that doorstep, Miller, not if you value your job," Bess came anyway, just as she was, clutching his hand, crying and laughing at the same time, making him run all the way home to Primrose Bank and the cottage where the lady waited.

24

The atmosphere in the bedroom was highly charged and the two people who faced each other across the width of the enormous bed appeared to be ready to spring at one another's throats. Indeed, had it not been for the realisation that the woman over whom they argued was no doubt listening to every word they said, having no option, their disagreement would by now have become even more violent.

Sam Lassiter regarded Daisy with the arrogance that was not only part of his masculine nature but which he had perfected in the company of the high-born gentlemen with whom he was on nodding acquaintance whenever he was in port. Those with whom he drank and gambled and played cards, generally winning, and with whom, had he the time which he had not, nor perhaps the inclination for it, he might have become more intimate for they thought him to be one hell of a fine fellow. They were patrician gentlemen whose ancestors had been privileged and powerful, whose education had been expensive and whose conviction that they were vastly superior to the rest of humanity was a matter of some amusement to him, but he admired it all the same. They had been born to greatness and he had earned what he had for himself but he liked their belief in their own infallibility for it accorded so well with his own. He was, like them, quite convinced of his own rightness in all matters, of his own good judgement, but it seemed that for once his ability to evaluate character had let him down and he wondered at his own foolishness.

"You had absolutely no right to bring her here, Daisy. To fetch her from her own environment, from a job which, though it was undoubtedly menial, was at least one of some permanence. You have placed her in a position where she has no guarantee that next month, next week or even tomorrow she will have a roof over her head. This is not a home for waifs and strays, neither is its function that of an hotel where your friends and acquaintances might stay for as long as it pleases them, or you. If you had taken the trouble and had the good manners to ask me I might have been prepared to allow it for a week or two but I would not have agreed to this friend or yours who, it seems, has thrown caution to the wind, thrown up her job and left her home all on the promise of you yourself, who are not in a position to give it, that she will . . ."

"You are saying my friend is not welcome, is that it?" Daisy's eyes were like slits of pure gold, cat's eyes spitting their venom in a face that did not become flushed as her anger mounted but had turned to the bleached white of icy rage.

"That is what I am saying and I would be obliged if you would find her alternative accommodation. If she is short of money I am prepared to advance her a guinea or two but I really feel that her best course of action would be to take a train back to . . . to wherever it is you brought her from and beg to be reinstated in her job. There is no room for her in my house, not in my life nor yours, and you will tell her so."

"There are plenty of rooms, Sam Lassiter. I deliberately put her in one of those at the back of the house so that she would not . . . disturb you . . ."

"That is not what I mean, Daisy, and you know it." His voice was cold and distant. He turned away, indicating that there was no more to be said on the subject. Moving to the table beside the empty fireplace he poured himself a brandy. Sipping it with every evidence of enjoyment and casual unconcern he sat down and crossed his legs, then reached for a cigar which he lit. He smiled but there was no humour in it and through her white-hot rage Daisy recognised that she must be careful not to antagonise him further if she was to have her way on this but it was difficult to control the flood of resentment which flowed through her.

Why was he acting like this over poor Bess, for God's sake? It was not like him to be small-minded. He was the most generous of men. *With you!* the words jumped like two graceful cats into her mind, sinuous and unexpected, and she was astonished but at the same time knew it to be true. He delighted in showering her with presents, buying her costly gowns and all manner of pretty and feminine creations with which to adorn herself. Remember the fur which hung in the wardrobe, but was he not also possessive, so perhaps he regarded what he gave to her, whom he owned because he had purchased her, as belonging to him as well. In that case, what he threw carelessly into her lap still in reality belonged to him. And he was not prepared to allow anyone, not even Bess, her old friend, to take any part of what was Sam Lassiter's.

He had been in the house no more than an hour. She had been at the door to meet him as she always was when he had been away. Four times he had sailed down the River Mersey and across the Atlantic to some part of North America, and four times he had come back and each time she had welcomed him gladly. She would be dressed in one of the lovely gowns he liked to see her in, her blaze of hair coiled into an intricate chignon which the Misses Yeoland had shown her how to do. Delicately perfumed, her arms lifting to receive him, her eyes glowing, her mouth smiling. He would kick the door shut behind him and pull her into his arms and their reunion had always been surprisingly agreeable to them both. Straight up the stairs to their bedroom, of course, for an hour or more since he was a man of great sensual appetite and though he had probably not been exactly faithful to her whilst he was away – in fact, she was sure he had not for she knew Sam Lassiter and he was not a man to deny himself – he was always very eager to make love to her. Then would come the giving and the receiving of the beautiful and costly gifts he had brought home for her, tossed carelessly on to the crumpled bed with an order to "... try this on, my pet. You came to mind when

I saw it and so . . ." An exquisite string of pearls a yard long, lustrous and creamy, set on a fine chain of gold which he wound round and round her neck, drawing her into the ardent embrace they both seemed to find so pleasant. An enamelled jewel-box in the shape of a butterfly, a row of rubies outlining the wings and decorated in natural pearls set in gold. Swinging earrings three inches long in which diamonds sparkled, a richly decorated, hand-painted fan with gilded mother-of-pearl sticks. He was a man of taste and, she had thought, enormously generous, believing that money was meant to give enjoyment, was to be used for the purpose of giving pleasure which he did abundantly. And it appeared it pleased him more than he would admit, even to her who was the recipient, to watch her delight in receiving his presents, the first she had ever received apart from her treasured knot of ribbons.

In the past five months he had become used to seeing her waiting for him in the hallway of his house, or at the top of the stairs ready to swoop down into his arms. Though he was not a man of a domesticated nature and indeed had really given no thought to the house he owned in Duke Street beyond demanding it be clean and warm when he was in it. He now found there was something added which had been missing before she came. He had not noticed its lack until the comparison with how it had become was brought to his attention. There were flowers in all the rooms, which, though he would not have put them there himself, he found he liked. Rugs appeared, and cushions, and furniture was moved to create a more 'homely' feel to a room. Ornaments, many of them somewhat original and exotic, coming from foreign parts, of ivory and ebony, of silver and mother of pearl, of jade and soapstone and which he had a vague recollection of bringing back from many voyages, were placed on cabinets and chests – again from far-flung corners of the globe – in red and black lacquer, heavily gilded. She seemed to have a knack of blending the old with the new, the exotic with the elegant, and creating an atmosphere which pleased him.

Jack was there, of course, but keeping out of the way,

saying nothing beyond a bluff greeting but letting it be seen that the new 'woman' was more to his liking than those before her, ready to take her orders, it appeared, though with his usual under-the-breath grumbling which was allowed an old servant.

For a week, or a fortnight, while he was in port, they would spend their time most pleasantly, going to the theatre, to concerts and charity balls where he danced every dance with her for no other gentleman would dare, to the Royale Club House where Daisy watched him gamble, though she never again showed any inclination to try it herself, to the races, to elegant restaurants and anywhere Sam had a fancy to take her, to show her off for she was now a sleek and beautiful woman and he prized her as he would any of his valuable possessions, aware that there were any number of gentlemen who would be glad to take her from him if they could.

On fine days they ventured out to the Botanical and Zoological Gardens, strolling in the warm sunshine with hundreds of others to admire the rare plants which grew in the handsome conservatory, the caged wild animals who roared obligingly and were all set out among brilliant flower-beds. There were summer fêtes held there with amusements of a breathtaking nature and magnificent displays of fireworks and illuminations. There was a large lake on the furthest bank of which could be viewed an immense pictorial representation of some celebrated event. Sam, though it was not always to his more sophisticated taste, found he enjoyed Daisy's childlike pleasure in it all, remembering that this was a woman who had had nothing of splendour nor joy in her childhood and was therefore greedy for it now.

She was there whenever he wanted her, in his house, in his bed, and he took for granted that as long as he required it, she would remain there. They no longer spoke of the past, nor the future, and he assumed she was as content with the arrangement as he was himself. He did not ask her what she did when he was away. He had no need for he trusted Jack implicitly and, besides, Liverpool was a place where gossip flew and there was none about Sam Lassiter's woman. He would have heard of it if there was. She often visited the Misses Yeolands' dressmaking establishment, though she was not excessively spendthrift, which was surprising considering how many hours she spent there, according to Jack. She had read every book in his house, she told him, and had bought others which she also had read. She spent a lot of the time studying the newspapers and could discuss with him any aspect of national or international news, which included the siege of Sebastopol and the dreadful conditions suffered by the armies in the Crimean peninsula. She was happily and busily continuing to educate herself, to learn not only the talents of a mistress and companion but those of an accomplished hostess though he often wondered wryly when she would use the latter. Naturally the gentlemen with whom he and Daisy mixed at the Royale, and who were quite ready to smile and engage her in conversation on these occasions, would cut her dead should they come face to face with her in the company of their wives. And, of course, not one would 'receive' her, nor visit her in her home, *his* home. Nevertheless it seemed she was prepared to continue the pleasant life they led together, demanding nothing of him in the way of commitment nor anything which smacked of permanence, but satisfying nonetheless. They had become friends, as well as lovers, and he was well pleased with her and what she had become. His instincts had been good ones, he told himself complacently, on the day he had brought her home. She would be a good investment, he had thought, and now, like a bolt from the blue, after months of congenial and easy companionship, of passion, certainly, but with no emotion involved, she had suddenly taken it into her head to shatter the concord in which they had found themselves by introducing to him that wheyfaced, homely old friend, a creature dressed, from what he had seen of her as she skulked in the shadows of the hallway, in the dreary garb of a servant, and whom Daisy proposed to make part of their household.

"Sam," she was saying, doing her best, he could see, to control her desire to take him by the shoulders and shake him into obedience, "won't you listen to what I have to tell you? I am sure you will agree when you have heard..."

"I'm afraid not, my sweet. It is not part of our bargain to put a roof over the head of any friend of yours who finds herself homeless, nor to have her share what we have here. I am perfectly content with things as they are, Daisy. It is how I like it and that, I'm afraid, is all that need concern you. You have a very gracious, one might say luxurious life here as my mistress, don't you agree?"

"Oh yes, indeed but..."

"For which I am perfectly willing to pay because it suits me so you see I am not..."

"But, Sam, you cannot..."

"But I can, Daisy. I can do whatever I please and it pleases me to have your undivided attention to my needs with no third person..."

"We have Jack and he does not interfere..."

"That is a completely different matter and if I may be allowed to finish, I have this to say. You and I have a most delightful arrangement which satisfies us both. But you see, like all men I am completely selfish and I will share you with no one. Besides which I demand value for money and if I am to vie with someone else, even another woman, for your interest I am not receiving it, wouldn't you agree?"

"No, I would not, and if you would allow *me* to speak perhaps I can convince you otherwise."

He inclined his head graciously, giving her, his manner said, a few moments of his time, but his face was grimly drawn and his green eyes were pale and hazardous in his freshly sunburned, freshly wind-burned face. He was like an eagle, oppressive, arbitrary and unyielding, his smiling humour, the insouciant and engaging charm with which he usually pampered her, completely gone. She was bewildered by it. By his absolute and utter rejection of Bess's admittance into his household which was quite unfathomable. She knew she should have waited to ask him before she brought Bess to Liverpool but she had been ready to move ahead with the next stage in her life and she could not do it without Bess. She had completed her training which had been possible in the completely female atmosphere of the Misses Yeolands' establishment and what she was to do next could not be accomplished without another woman beside her, in the absence, that is, of a man.

The idea, drifting a little at a time into her uncertain mind, like fine mist in a breeze, had begun on the day after she and Sam had first visited the Royale Club House. It had been no more than a vague unformulated image, concerned mainly with Miles Thornley and the way in which he found amusement in the gaming houses of Europe. He and his equally wealthy friends gambled huge amounts, winning and losing hundred of guineas on the turn of a card. It was a weakness which many could not control, an affliction from which some would never be cured and one of those was Miles Thornley. And those who were cursed by this malevolent influence were taken advantage of by those who could see, and make capital out of, their weakness. There were thousands upon thousands of men – not just gentlemen – who would gamble, place a bet whether they could afford it or not, on a horse, on a dog, on the outcome of a cockfight, on one man beating another into insensibility. It got into their blood, she had heard – had she not experienced it herself for the space of several hours? – and took a hold of their lives in a way which spelled disaster, destitution, heartbreak and hunger stalking families. Yes, thousands of men indulging each week, each day, in what Sam had called a 'little flutter', the thrill of it enlivening their often drab lives for the length of time it took a horse to run the length of a track, a dog to be torn to a bloody and agonising death by another, a man to fall down in a prizefighting ring and not to get up again.

But out of a thousand men who took no harm from it, who gambled only within the limit of their own pocket, there would be half a dozen who were possessed by it. Miles Thornley was one of them. He was a frequenter of gaming houses which, as she had made it her business to find out, were only for the wealthy. For those who came from great families with great estates. Gentlemen who were known by those whose profession it was, to be rich enough and influential enough to frequent their establishments. There were famous clubs in London, White's, Brooks's, Crockfords, where, it was said, whole estates were lost in one night! Where, in one twenty-four-hour session at the tables, *one hundred thousand guineas* had been cleared! And in any of these, or any gaming house which was grand enough to accommodate the needs – which were many, demanding and sophisticated – of Miles Thornley, there might he be found.

And despite her loathing of him, or perhaps because of it, Daisy Brindle and Miles Thornley were irrevocably linked together and the link would not be shattered until one or the other was destroyed. She knew it. Had known it in the farthest reaches of her heart and mind ever since the night she had stood outside the gates of Thornley Green, still engulfed by the horror into which she had been flung by Cassie's death. She could not move on, not with Miles Thornley's presence dragging her back, nor with the memories, the nightmares, the terror with which his name was connected, and so she must cut him out of her obsessed mind, cauterise the wound he left and allow it to heal, when she would then be able to go forward to whatever life held for her.

The gaming house, the gaming house which she intended to open and run herself was the opportunity, the chance, the stepping-stone which would guide her to what she wanted, what she needed and which was, quite simply, revenge. She said it to herself a dozen times a day, testing herself with it, testing her ability to be strong enough to manage it for revenge is a bitter thing and can destroy. But her heart, which had been torn and bruised almost beyond repair by what had been done to Cassie, was steadfast in its determination. Her mind, often at odds with her emotions, told her how impossible it was for the likes of Daisy Brindle to take on the son of one of the country's oldest and most revered families, but her heart, still grieving silently the loss of the girl she had loved and protected for so long, would not have it. For months she had been moving stealthily, steadily towards the . . . she could not call it a dream, could she, for the word painted a picture of something sweet and lovely, and this ... this dream was neither. It was an objective, a destination she must reach. Journey's end. And she would reach it. Besides, could she go on as she had been ever since she had met Sam Lassiter? Drifting along in this pleasant but aimless manner towards that day when he would inevitably tire of her. When they would tire of each other since their feelings for one another were as insubstantial as the mist which lay on the river at dawn. What then? She must have work to do. A job to perform. Something to occupy her days and this must be it.

"You have some plan for the two of you, then?" he prompted, watching, casually he would have her believe, but in his eyes was a deep and complex expression she could not read and did not attempt to.

"Yes."

"And may I hear it?"

She drew a deep breath and her own eyes were cool and assessing as she studied his reaction.

"I want to open my own gaming house. A club, a sporting house where those with wealth and position may enjoy an evening's pleasure. Gambling, of course, but also high-class entertainment with the very best performers. Luxurious surroundings, superb food and wines, all free to those who gamble, a French chef perhaps, something to draw gentlemen of the highest rank, the peerage, foreign ambassadors who are passing through Liverpool. Elegance of the first order and every game that such men demand. Primero, hazarde, gleek, tick-tack ..."

"You are to be a Madam, you are saying?" His voice cut through hers, as cold as the icicles which formed on the rigging of his own ship as she sailed the frozen waters of the northern seas.

"Yes, if I think it necessary." Her own voice was the same.

"You are to run a house of ill repute?" He gave her a bitter, mocking smile.

"It will have a reputation, yes, but not in the way you imply. I shall make it the most fashionable and popular club in the north of England, renowned not only for the merits

370

I have just mentioned but for honest dealing. Value for money, if you like. Whatever a gentleman wants, providing it is not ... well, peculiar ... I shall provide, but with ..."

"Do I take it you are able to finance this venture which you and your friend are to take up, since I presume she is to go in with you? In what capacity I cannot imagine but that is neither here nor there. It is the commercial aspect of it that fascinates me, and of course your sublime belief that, having had a game or two of roulette, you are qualified to run a gaming house."

"Damn you to hell and beyond. Do you take me for a complete fool? I know you can't do a job without being trained for it. I learned that at the School of Industry. What do you think I've been doing for these past five months whilst you've been away? I told you I couldn't sit about the drawing room stitching a fine seam, or fill my days spending your money. I have to have something to *do*. All my life I have worked, Sam, and bloody hard, and it seems it's become a habit ..."

"And so you intend to ... ?"

"Will you let me finish?" Her voice was cold and resolute. "I was given the idea when you first took me to the Royale but as I knew less than nothing about gaming I could see that unless I could find someone who did, and whom I could trust, it was really pointless to even try. Then I thought, why not learn then? but from whom, and of course the answer was someone who was involved in it. His name is John Elliott and he's a professional gambler. You may have seen him at the Royale. He works for the club, though naturally, the members are not aware of it. To cut a long story short I approached him one night while you were playing cards and I made him a proposition."

"Daisy, my love, this had better be something with which I can cope." His voice was silky smooth but there was a light in his eyes which spelled danger if it was not.

"I would not bring him here, Sam. You know that, even if Jack had allowed it. I had to take him to somewhere that was ... suitable for a lady to go alone and where else but the Misses Yeoland?"

"*Miss Yeoland?* Do you mean to say . . . ?"

"She is a woman who is in sympathy with those of her own sex who wish to . . . get on, I suppose you would call it. When I told her what I planned to do, and which she was quick to see had a future since you will admit there is not a decent gaming house in Liverpool, she was only too happy to lend me one of her rooms upstairs . . ."

"My God, Daisy, if you think I . . ."

"Stop it, Sam. We did no more than play cards. Any game of cards you can name, John taught me. Vingt-et-un, bezique, ombre, chemin de fer, plus games with dice, hazarde and the like. He says I have some skill with the cards. Though we did not have a roulette wheel he went through the layout, the stakes, the moves, its whole character. He used a diagram of the wheel, patterns of runs, alternations and so on, until he felt I had enough knowledge to at least know what I was about so if you would care to sit down to a game, any game of cards of your choice, and put me to the test I think you will find . . ."

"Really, Daisy," his voice was mocking, "I thought you had more sense. I must admit to a certain admiration for your sheer bloody nerve but it is your wits which I find lacking. Have you the slightest notion of what a club of the sort you propose – when you have found the capital needed, that is – needs to be successful? No, then I will tell you. It needs, primarily, a shrewd business head, one that can see exactly what is needed, how much it takes to get it and whether the profit, if there is any, is enough to justify the whole bloody venture. It needs a clear, sharp brain, the strength of Samson and the stamina of a carthorse. It requires a man, a *man* mark you, who knows other men and how to deal with them, who knows gentlemen and how to deal with *them*, and last but certainly not least it needs as its director someone who knows one card from another which, despite your 'training' as you so quaintly put it, I doubt you do." He laughed harshly though he was not at all amused. She could not recognise what he was feeling. Certainly not pleasure at what she knew he thought of as her arrogance, but there was something in his manner which seemed to say that though he considered her mad, he had it in him to marvel at her sheer bloody gall. He surveyed her through the smoke of his cigar, his expression unreadable, but as she opened her mouth to speak again, to tell him more of what she had been doing whilst he was at sea, his face altered, changing shape and texture under the influence of a terrible suspicion and he sat up slowly.

"But perhaps I have the wrong impression here, my sweet. Perhaps you are not about to ask me for a loan as I originally thought. Perhaps you already have the capital to start this new business venture of yours. Perhaps you are merely doing me the courtesy of letting me know that we are about to part company. Tell me, my darling, what else have you been up to whilst I have been away? Perhaps a little fund-raising in quite another direction? Is that it?" His mouth was a thin, ominous line and deep grooves had appeared on either side of it but it was his eyes which startled her the most for in them was a dark and haunted look of ... of loss, just as though he had been torn open and something dear to him had been taken away, then the look was gone, gone and replaced by an icy green rage which bewildered her. She took a step backwards though the bed was still between them.

"What d'you mean?" she asked, ready to frown for surely he was insulting her in some way.

"You know damn well what I mean," he snarled, standing up and moving around the bed. The menace in his face was absolutely plain. "You have found another protector, is that it? Yes, I believe that is the word. Someone to finance this grand scheme of yours. Whilst I have been away you have been bestowing your charms..." His mouth curled in a frightening sneer and his eyes flared into what she could only call hatred. He seemed to realise then what he was saying, to see himself as she must see him, and with a great effort he dragged himself under control. Breathing deeply he turned away, moving to the window, presenting her with his back which gave nothing away of what had appeared to be – surely not – jealousy. Sam Lassiter! How ridiculous, and when he turned back to her he was as she had always known him to be, cool, unconcerned, mocking, even amused, and she knew that it was her imagination which had put that bewildering expression there.

"Perhaps you have been selling your bits of jewellery as well, my pet, and that splendid fur I gave you. I wouldn't put it past you. You really are the most determined young lady, Daisy." He raised a sarcastic eyebrow and grinned.

"Sam! Stop this damn nonsense and listen to me. Another protector? Dear God in heaven, what would I want with another . . . ?" she had been about to say "another bloody problem" but she caught herself in time, ". . . another lover? Do I not have more than enough with you?" She answered his grin with hers, taking the sting out of the words.

But he was not done. "You should know by now that I share nothing of mine, Daisy. You would be wise to remember that. Nothing. No one takes what belongs to me, not until I have done with it." His expression was hawk-faced and keen. He was completely self-possessed now, his strangeness gone. He strode across the room and threw his cigar into the empty fireplace, seriously disarranging the charming bowl of dried flowers she had put there. Immediately he lit another one, in command of himself and of her too, his manner said, so she'd best like it and if she didn't she knew just what to do. "I am inclined to believe you, my love, and so we will forget this . . . this little contretemps. Say no more about it. Now then, come here and give me a kiss. A proper kiss this time. That chaste peck you allowed me under the righteous gaze of your friend might have been given me by my maiden aunt."

She had fallen asleep after his vigorous lovemaking. Bess might not have existed, nor any of the explosive words which had been flung about the bedroom. They might have been alone in the house and as far as Sam Lassiter was concerned they were, since Jack kept to his kitchen and the room next to it which he had made his own. Daisy's last coherent thought before she was drawn into the sighing sensuality which Sam aroused so easily in her was of poor Bess sitting alone in the comfortable but somewhat arid room at the top of the house, then Bess was forgotten as her body took over her mind, disposing of it quite positively in Sam Lassiter's despotic arms.

It was some time later, how long she did not know. The candle had burned out and in the dark, just above her head, she could see the glow of Sam's cigar.

"Can't you sleep?" she murmured, curling her leg across his body and settling herself more comfortably against him. She was barely awake, warm and at peace for the moment before she took up arms once more against him.

"I've been trying to make up my mind whether Paris or Venice would be the most delightful but as it is September and it is at its best at this time of the year I have decided on Paris."

"You are a bastard, Sam Lassiter," she mumbled sleepily, her cheek against the strong, hard curve of his throat. "You've been home no more than three or four hours and you're talking of leaving me already."

"Did I say anything about leaving you, my love? I believe it is usual for a bride to accompany her husband on their wedding journey."

Something within her, too deeply hidden to have a name, awoke and stirred. She lifted her head numbly and tried to pierce the darkness, to see the expression in his eyes but it was too velvety thick. She felt him smile and her own mouth responded incredulously.

"You don't think I'm going to put my money into some scheme over which I have no control, do you, my pet?" he continued smoothly. "You should know me better than that, really you should. So, we will be married – Mr and Mrs Sam Lassiter – and together we will make this club of yours not only the most celebrated in the north but in the whole of the country. A business partnership, Daisy, a family business partnership. What d'you say, my darling?"

And inside her, beneath the blaze of excitement his words had kindled in her, the tiny something curled up again within her and was still.

25

He was to sail to the Mediterranean to fetch a cargo of fruit at the beginning of October. The fruit trade was a seasonal business and by the end of spring when the season finished over 15,000 tons of oranges, lemons and grapes would be brought to Liverpool by the 'fruit' schooners which could do the journey faster than any other ship afloat. *Golden Lady* was ideally suited to such trade and a good profit was guaranteed providing Captain Lassiter, and any other master who carried the cargo, could reach George's Dock with their fast-ripening merchandise before it became overblown.

"I shall be back within the fortnight, or less if I find favourable weather conditions, so the third week in October for the nuptials would suit admirably, wouldn't you agree, my love? Time for you to acquire all those fripperies so dear to a woman's heart on an occasion such as this. But for God's sake don't ask me to accept that creature in the kitchen to be your bridesmaid for I swear I would not have a moment's peace with her sour face hovering at my back whilst we exchange our vows." His ironic gaze met hers. "And no hole-in-the-corner affair neither. I want you to wear the most splendid and costly outfit that money can buy so get you down to the Misses Yeoland and order whatever you need. I leave it to you. Your taste is excellent, thank the Lord. Now who do you think would be willing to give you away?" His tone of voice was musing and the glint of laughter in his eyes told her he was playing some game which he found vastly amusing. "Jack perhaps, or have you someone in mind? No, then if you have no objection to a one-legged sailor . . . ? St Mark's Church, I think, which being on the corner of Duke Street would be particularly convenient. Oh, and perhaps a new gown for what's-her-name as well, that's if you can get her out of that damned black she seems to find so congenial. I'll have no woman in black at my wedding so tell her, will you?"

Daisy smiled. She was getting his measure now, or so she told herself. Though he proclaimed an aversion to Bess and, in the privacy of their bedroom, called her such names as shrew and termagent, Bess's steadfast refusal to become Daisy's 'companion', an idle occupation in Bess's eyes, and her absolute determination to be exactly as she was, a servant with no desire to get 'above herself', as Daisy was doing, a servant working for a wage and earning that wage, had gained Sam Lassiter's admiration. She would not stay if she could not earn her keep, she had told him bluntly at their first confrontation following his homecoming, no, not even to feed her young brothers and sisters, since she believed in an honest wage for an honest day's work. She was a housemaid and no matter what Daisy said to the contrary that was the kind of employment she required. No, she would not interfere with Mr O'Callaghan in his kitchen duties . . .

"Mr O'Callaghan?" Sam had enquired, perplexed, but Mr O'Callaghan turned out to be Jack who, Bess stated, was a cook and she was not. He would continue to see to what he called the 'vittles', whilst she would take over the running of the house. Each would have their separate duties and would, she thought, do quite well together. Mr O'Callaghan had agreed. They would each have their own private sitting room, if Captain Lassiter had no objection, and if the Captain required it of her she was prepared to accompany the future Mrs Lassiter about Liverpool if the necessity arose, and she could spare the time from her household duties. No, a new outfit was not required. A couple of decent black dresses . . . well, perhaps a sensible shade of grey if the Captain insisted and a stout pair of boots and, seeing that winter was coming on, a warm woollen cloak of a suitable colour.

"Black, I suppose?"

"Thank you, sir," bobbing a curtsey before she left the room.

"You'll not change her mind, Sam. She wants nothing but a chance to do a decent job and see her family safe whatever she might say to the contrary, but it must be work she considers proper to her station in life. She would have stayed at that bucket in the scullery at Thornley Green until she dropped dead and fell into it if I'd not gone for her but she'll be a great help to me while you're away. Don't worry, I'll talk to her. Make her see that she is an essential part of my plan and that without her it will fail."

"And will it?"

"Of course not but if she believes it will she'll do it for my sake."

"I'm glad to see that you're taking seriously your new position as the future Mrs Sam Lassiter, my pet." His tone was ironic but there was a touch of steel in it. "I wouldn't like to think of you running hither and thither all over Liverpool without a ... well, shall we say ... a chaperone, for want of a better word. Heaven knows what trouble you might get yourself into and I would not care to have your name ... *my* name ... bandied about amongst the ... well, you will know what I mean." He leaned casually forward and dropped a light kiss on the creamy skin of her shoulder, revealed by her slipping peignoir. He smiled lazily but she knew he meant exactly what he said. Daisy Brindle and Mrs Sam Lassiter were far from being the same woman in Sam Lassiter's eyes. One could have a mistress who was the talk of the town but not a wife. As Daisy Brindle, though she belonged exclusively to him for as long as it pleased him, she was in the long run still free to do whatever she thought best for herself. Of course, should he not like that, whatever it was, he would simply smile and turn her out, politely, amiably, giving her free rein to do it! But Mrs Sam Lassiter, his wife, the woman who had been given his name, must be above reproach. No one, man or woman, would be given the opportunity to point a finger at her no matter what she might have done before she married him. After all, she had done it only with one other man and he was gone from

378

her life for good, there was no doubt of that! His smiling expression, his cool sea-green eyes, told her so.

She could not get used to the idea that within the month she would be married to this enigmatic man who, though he gave every appearance of being carelessly, humorously candid with her, was in reality as deep and complex as the seas over which he sailed. She knew only one thing for certain about him, though she sometimes pretended differently, and that was that she did not know him at all. They were to be married for one reason only and that was to safeguard the investment he was to make, or so he implied, and who was she to deny it since there could be no other explanation for it? He did not love her in the way she knew the meaning of the word. Which was, of course, in the way she had loved Miles Thornley. Oh yes, much as she hated him now, once she had loved him, she admitted it and she could clearly remember how it had felt. Deep and melting, turning her bones, her sinews and muscles to the weakness of a new-born kitten but at the same time strong and durable, as her heart had been. Willing to suffer and capable of surviving the most devastating blow ... except that of betrayal. An eagerness to give, a longing to share, a need to protect, a readiness to forgive. That was love and she had no wish to endure it again. But because she had, she fully believed that she would recognise it in another and she saw no signs of it in Sam. Perhaps this was the best way to enter a marriage, she thought, the well-judged way to make it manageable. In a clear-headed, realistic manner with none of the weakening qualities of what was known as 'love'. It had nearly destroyed her once and she wanted none of it again, nor did she want to be the target of any man's love. Desire, affection, friendship, yes, they were real emotions which did not blur the mind nor shatter the heart. She and Sam would do well with one another, she told herself. A comradeship which they both found enjoyable. A sexual relationship which they both found pleasing with none of the heart-wringing, heart-breaking, desperate yearning, high peaks and deep troughs which afflicted those 'in love'.

She and Bess spent a most enjoyable two weeks whilst

Sam was away, lightheartedly preparing her 'bride's trousseau' which Sam had insisted upon, though try as she might she could not persuade Bess to allow herself to be 'tricked out', as Bess put it, in one of the Misses Yeolands' modish 'outfits'.

"My friend and companion," she introduced her as to Miss Gladys and Miss Emily. "She and I are to work together in the club my ... fiancé and I are to open in the spring. Yes, that is correct, Miss Yeoland. Captain Lassiter and I are to be married before the end of October. Indeed, most exciting and naturally I would like you to design my ... er ... wedding gown. The Captain is determined it should be very grand but you know my taste so perhaps not too grand. Something simple but very elegant. The skirt very wide, of course, over a hooped 'cage', the bodice and skirt separate in the latest fashion. Undersleeves of broderie anglaise. You will know exactly what I want but I would also like you to put your mind to evening gowns, Miss Yeoland, and they must be ... well, I can only think of the word *wicked*. Yes, wicked. Bold colours, stunning lines but at the same time something Captain Lassiter would not object to his wife wearing. You will know what I have in mind? Of course you will. But the wedding outfit first. No, not white but cream perhaps. The colour of buttermilk, and gowns which will certainly let the ladies of Paris know that we in England have our clever couturiers too. Yes, we are to travel to Paris so I know I can leave it all to you. You will know exactly what I need. Now then, will you not try to tempt Miss Miller with one of your delicious creations? She is absolutely convinced that she wants nothing more than a decent black gown, or perhaps two, but as I keep telling her if she is to accompany me about Liverpool she can hardly do so looking like a poor relation. Perhaps that lovely grape purple you have there, yes, the merino, or that rich midnight blue frieze trimmed with ..."

Sometimes, when she listened to herself talk, heard the words she used and the tone of her voice, she felt a great desire to turn away and smile for really, this was Daisy Brindle speaking who had once been a field girl, a pit-brow lassie, a housemaid, and yet she sounded like one of the high-and-mighty ladies who so very obviously drew their skirts aside as she and Bess entered the Misses Yeolands' establishment. They knew who she was, of course they did, and would rather have been struck dumb than address a word to her, or even to be seen glancing in her direction. She was completely beneath their notice, she and her companion, and though it was all over Liverpool by now that Sam Lassiter was to marry his 'doxy', it made no difference to the wives of the commercial gentlemen with whom he dealt. She was, and always would be what she had begun as, the mistress of a seafaring man. Their husbands might do business with the Captain, indeed the ladies had no objection to *him* for it was a common fact of life that men must indulge in that kind of thing and were thought none the worse for indulging in it. He was, after all, in trade like themselves, and also like themselves, very rich and had been included in several dinner parties in the past but as for *her*, his partner in immorality, no decent woman could be expected to receive her, ever!

But Daisy cared naught for them, nor for the social life they themselves found so satisfying and so she continued to argue with Bess, to give orders to Jack which were sometimes obeyed and sometimes not, to prepare for her wedding to Sam, and to make her cunning plans for the future.

They were married on a fine late October day; one of those which still have a lingering memory of summer in it. There was a high, very delicate blue sky with shreds of pale cloud blown this way and that by a gentle wind as she was driven to St Mark's Church – no more than a stone's throw from the house – in the splendid carriage Sam had hired for the occasion. He required that everything should be done in style though there was none to see it besides Jack and Bess and several startled passers-by. Her buttermilk dress was the most exquisite the Misses Yeoland had ever made for her, its enormous skirt filling the velvet-lined carriage, a cascade of lace and silk, and on her head a flower garden of the palest pink and cream silk roses. The path to the old church was a crunching carpet of autumn leaves beneath her high-stepping cream kid boots, the colour of the leaves no more vibrant than the blaze of her hair. The last crisp leaves of the year floated from the trees in the churchyard, two or three settling amongst the roses on her wide hat, making Sam smile as she drifted down the aisle towards him. He kissed her hand after they had exchanged their vows, looking at her as though he had loved her dearly all his life, though one dark eyebrow was raised in wry amusement. She smiled up at him just as mistily and knew they were well matched despite the lack of what she supposed must be 'romantic' love.

They drank champagne, the four of them, back in the warm, well-lit comfort of what was now *her* drawing room since she had become Mrs Sam Lassiter, and Bess thawed a little, the wine loosening the tight-drawn hold she had on this incredible new state she found herself in. From scrubbing floors to the position of housekeeper – and perhaps companion if she could get used to the fine-sounding description – to the wife of Captain Sam Lassiter, with the hiring and firing, should she choose it, of her own scrubbing maids. To the heady station of ordering Mrs Sam Lassiter's household – with the exception, doubtless, of Jack, whilst her mistress, Daisy Brindle, for God's sake, went about her own affairs, and even, when needed, to accompany Mrs Lassiter when she rode in her *own* carriage which, Bess had been told, would not be long in coming. Or so Daisy Brindle said.

Daisy Brindle! Daisy Lassiter now and looking quite radiant in her wedding gown, creamy and glowing with health and what really did seem to Bess to be genuine happiness. She did not love the Captain, Daisy had explained carefully to Bess only last night, before she had hurried upstairs to climb into his bed, and he did not love her. This was to be a partnership, not of the heart but of the head, the mind, the practical common sense and business ability of them both since she wanted none of the anguish which she had suffered in her love for Miles Thornley.

"We shall give to each other only what we want to give, or what we can give, and I'm sure we shall manage well

enough with that, Bess. You remember how it was with ...
with that devil who killed Cassie? Yes, I'm sure you do. I
have nothing left in me of that, Bess, and I would trust no
man who offered it to me. The Captain and I are well suited.
Neither of us are ... romantically inclined. He is past thirty
he tells me and has had his share of amorous escapades. He
would like to settle down though I'm not at all sure I believe
that but if he tells me so I'll pretend that I do. I need a place,
Bess, somewhere of my own, and a purpose in life. I have
found it with Sam."

"Your health and happiness," Bess said to them both now,
quite suddenly, lifting her glass in their direction, not at all
sure she believed *any* of it. Her eyes were soft for she
remembered how this luminous bride had been only a year
ago and though she was no sentimentalist herself, having
had no time for it in her hard life, she found herself to be
quite overcome with the marvel of what Daisy had now.
Who would have thought it? Daisy Brindle. From housemaid
to the mistress of this grand house and with a fine man like
Captain Lassiter to stand by her for no matter what Daisy
said about a marriage of convenience, there was a certain
glow in the hidden depths of his sea-green eyes which suggested to her that there might be more to Captain Lassiter
than was at first apparent.

"Thank you, Bess," he said now, his arm about his wife's
shoulders, his long lashes hiding that glow as he looked
down into her upturned face. He smiled, his wide, strong
mouth curling over his white teeth and Bess thought how
handsome he was though, strictly speaking, when one compared him to the masculine beauty of Miles Thornley he was
no such thing. He was too ... too keen-faced and keen-eyed,
his features slightly irregular, his body lighter and finer. He
was quite unremarkable really and yet the whole added up
to a uniquely personable man. "I'm sure we shall do our
damnedest to find both, shall we not, my love," he continued, smiling at Mrs Lassiter, "and now I think we'd best
be off or we shall miss the train."

They were in Paris no more than a week. Daisy found the
wonder of travel quite overwhelmingly exciting and said so

continuously, reminding Sam of those first few weeks when he had introduced her to the luxury, the comforts, the pleasures which his money could purchase. She was enchanted with the splendid city of Paris. The flowers, lawns, waterfalls and winding streams of the Bois de Boulogne, transformed it was said, by its third and present Emperor, Louis-Napoleon Bonaparte, nephew of France's first Emperor, Napoleon I. The long, straight lines of tree-lined boulevards radiating in splendid symmetry from the Place de l'Etoile; the Louvre; the Grand Hotel facing the Boulevard des Capucines with its eight hundred rooms of unsurpassed luxury where she and Sam stayed. It took her breath away and rendered her speechless which was a refreshing change, Sam said, smiling wryly.

They visited the Champs Elysées, the gardens of the Tuileries, the Palais Royal, the Luxembourg and the Jardin des Plantes, all once the gardens of kings, only recently opened to the public. Daily they watched the *tour de lac*, the afternoon promenade around the lake in the Bois. Gentlemen riders, many of the famous names of France, and their ladies in elegant riding habits. Gleaming carriages with two, sometimes four horses to pull them, a fashionable procession, indeed one of the great pageants of the Second Empire and one which Daisy found endlessly fascinating. Paris was new and fresh and vital, somewhat like herself as she began on this untrodden journey of her life, an enchanting place of beauty, excitement and movement. Dazzling white buildings, gilded iron railings and gaily-striped awnings. The street-criers calling their wares, the sellers of sugar and soap and mussels, egg merchants and oystermen, flower girls and wandering musicians with flutes and violins. Along the Boulevard du Temple there were organ-grinders, street singers, magicians, jugglers and trained rats and dogs. It was a city of noise and it was a city of crowds. It was a city devoted to entertainment, sparkling and profligate, and Daisy hugged it greedily to her like a child who has been offered as many bonbons as she can eat, devouring them every one even if it made her sick.

They dined in restaurants that catered to every taste and

whim and where money was so unimportant to their clientele it was not uncommon for the waiters to add to the bill the number of the private room in which the meal was served. Restaurants with strange-sounding names such as Voison and Brébant, and the Café de Paris where leading courtesans of the day were entertained by the capital's richest financiers and noblemen.

It was said that Paris was emerging as the fashion centre of the world and the luxurious shops catered to many extravagant tastes.

"Buy something, my darling," Sam drawled as Daisy stood with her nose pressed to the window of a glass-fronted edifice in the Rue de la Paix. "There is no need to stare quite so brazenly. One may enter if one wishes."

"But it's the House of Worth, Sam," she whispered reverently, as though it was a cathedral and the need to worship must be recognised.

"My sweet, if we have money even Daisy Lassiter and her adoring husband may spend it here."

It seemed the fashionable ladies of Paris changed their clothes at least six times a day, their wardrobes positively bursting with negligées, 'toilette de Bois' for the afternoon drive around the lake, dinner dresses, morning dresses, afternoon dresses, ballgowns of every description, created from the marvellously rich and heavy fabrics which were available; from the famous Lyons brocade embroidered with damask roses, bluebells and tulips, to the simplest white lawn, and the Englishman, Charles Frederick Worth, provided them with exactly what he thought they should have.

"Do you intend to go in or not?" Sam said, lounging indolently on the stylish walking cane it seemed was the latest fashion in Paris and which Daisy insisted he have. "You cannot come to Paris, especially on your honeymoon, and not buy something from the house of Worth."

"Oh, Sam!" It was Daisy Brindle, housemaid, who whispered, perhaps for the last time, in the awed tone of the trained servant she had once been.

Inside were handsome young men in bright cravats and

tightly-fitting frock-coats waiting to greet them and escort Madame and Monsieur to the Salon de Lumière where the windows were hermetically sealed and the walls mirrored from floor to ceiling and the gas jets burned brightly.

Attracted by the tall and elegant beauty of the slender English lady – one could tell at a glance that she was English from her gown – and by the vivid burnished flame of her hair – so unusual – beneath her dashing lacy bonnet, the great man himself approached Daisy and Sam, paying Daisy the rare compliment of not only noticing her but telling her what she must purchase from him to enhance her unique loveliness, regardless of cost. A dress of golden gauze, the billowing crinoline skirt trimmed with bronze velvet, a scarlet Zouave jacket, wickedly daring, Kashmir shawls of such incredible lightness they were like mist about her shoulders, in pinks, lilacs and yellow ochres. Russian boots in scarlet to match the jacket, pastel-tinted day dresses in delicate creams and near whites, embroidered gloves and garters of gold and silver filigree.

That night, their last in Paris, and wearing nothing but the waist-length Zouave jacket, the garters and the Russian boots, her unbound hair rippling down her back, Daisy Lassiter made love to her husband. Removing the garments one by tantalising one in a fair imitation of the girls at the Bal Mabille until she was completely naked, she revealed and displayed for his pleasure every erotic movement of her boyish body just as he – and Miles Thornley – had taught her. His own body was caressed in so leisurely and minutely a fashion she brought him to shuddering, groaning orgasm time and time again, whipping up his sensual appetites, using her body, every soft and moist inch of it, until he was spent and begging laughingly for mercy.

"I see," she said, somewhat out of breath herself, "so that is the way of it, is it? Now that we are married it is to be different. Having made an honest woman of me I am expected to behave like one and you are to become the staid husband I have heard so much about. I am a wife now and not a mistress so you are no longer my lover and do not care to do to me all the ..."

"What?" he roared, regaining his strength quite miraculously. "Are you saying that I have not pleased you tonight?" He rose up from the nest of pillows she had arranged about him, treating him, she had said, like an Arabian sheikh she had read of, and with strong, almost cruel but decidedly satisfying hands and mouth, and the long hard muscles of his lean body, showed her most delightfully his prowess, not as a husband but as a lover.

They arrived home on a cold early November day, the fine raw drizzle of that time of the year greeting them as they emerged from Lime Street Station. They were chilled and travel-weary, the northern skies comparing unfavourably with the brilliant late-autumn tints of the city they had just left but glad to be home nevertheless. Daisy, much as she loved Paris and the delights she had found there in Sam's good-humoured company, was gripped tight by the expectation, the anticipation of what she was to do next and the grey skies, the wet slimed cobbles, the dispirited, hurrying, drab-garbed passers-by failed to douse the thrill of excitement which coursed through her.

"Well, my love, you had best count the luggage the porter is staggering under for I should not like to misplace any of the expensive trinkets you have brought home. There must be at least two dozen boxes more than we started out with, not taking into account the ones containing the gifts you have bought for Bess. You do promise not to give them to her unless I am there, don't you? I really should hate to miss the expression on her face when she sees the bonnet you have bought her, and that negligée. Do you think she will ever wear it, because I don't."

"Oh, Sam, of course she will. How can she resist it?" Daisy refused to be put out by his banter. She was going home. She was going home to Bess, laden with frivolous presents, useless and decorative, and more than likely Bess would gasp and be no more than polite when presented with them but what did it matter? It was the giving of them that counted. Being able to return to her friend, the only one she had ever had apart from Cassie, what Bess had given to her over the years. Not in material things, but in a somewhat brusque friendship. All Bess had she had given freely and if she was less than overjoyed with what Daisy had bought her they would both understand the meaning of the giving.

"And that fancy silk waistcoat for Jack will look superb over his sea-gansey," Sam continued sardonically, but his eyes had an unusual softness in them as he helped his wife into the hansom cab. They trotted along Lime Street, turning right into Ranelagh Street with the elegant bulk of the Adelphi Hotel on their left, its outline hazed by the fine drizzle which drifted about it. Passed the Lyceum Newsroom and Library at the bottom of Bold Street and into Hanover Street which led to Duke Street.

They were both there to greet them, Jack and Bess, and Daisy was amazed at her own pleasure in seeing them. It was as though they were her own family, the taciturn old man and the sharp-faced young woman. So many years between them and yet surprisingly alike in the expression which was on each face as the cab drew up to the front door.

"Would you look at those two trying to appear as though your homecoming meant nothing to them, the pair of frauds. I swear Jack is about to embrace you and as for that old maid you call friend, it is taking her a great effort not to smile."

"Don't be silly, Sam. They have probably been at each other's throats all week and are simply longing, both of them, to be the first to tell me about it."

"Nonsense. They are like two faithful terriers whose master, or in this case, mistress has been away and has returned. If Jack had a tail he would wag it. You certainly have the ability to arouse great devotion in the breasts of those who love you, my darling," and he grinned engagingly at the very thought, or so it seemed, of the mystery of such an emotion.

The house was shining with the light from dozens of lamps and warm with the glow from fires which were lit in every room. It had been no more than a week and yet Daisy walked into the gracious hallway with a sense of blessed homecoming. She had lived in this house for eight months now and in that time, though she had not fully realised it, it had wrapped its protection around her and loosened the coils of precariousness with which she had always lived ever since she could remember. Even at Thornley Green, where she had thought at times that she was in paradise, she had never felt this warmth, this . . . this comfort. This was where she belonged. This was her home and these were her family. Bess and Jack. Behind her the man who had given it all to her watched as she turned about on the heels of her new, high-buttoned French boots to gaze with pleasure at the simple beauty of it all. Her eyes snapped joyfully and there was almost a flush beneath her creamy skin. Her eyes passed over him without noticing his expression, without noticing him, and she failed entirely to see the sudden tightening of his jaw and the muscles which jumped beneath the smooth well-shaved cheek.

"And what are you to do now, my pet?" He smiled through the smoke of the cigar he had just lit. "Will I find the house about my ears when I come home from Australia . . . ah yes . . . I had meant to tell you but in the . . ." his eyes gleamed between narrowed lids ". . . in the rapturous delights of our . . . er . . . honeymoon I swear it quite slipped my mind. How very remiss of me. Yes, I have decided to carry emigrants, poor souls, to the furthest corner of the globe since the trade is very profitable. *Golden Lady* has been fitted out to carry passengers who are eager to get in on the rush for gold. Over four hundred of them all told, besides a cargo of piece goods and machinery. I shall carry back wool, of course. Can you manage without me for six months, my pet? Will you pine and fade away for want of me or, more likely, will you hardly notice I'm gone as you get your pretty teeth into this scheme I have allowed myself to be talked into?" He grinned wickedly, his cigar clamped between his white teeth, no sign at all in his carelessly lounging figure that he was waiting for her reaction, or even caring if she had any.

He had made his decision and the statement about his intended destination, on the spur of the moment, at that moment when Daisy's eyes had passed unseeingly over him as though he was as valuable to her as the hallstand. Useful, of course, as the hallstand was useful, but easily replaced with another which would give equally good service. And did it mean anything to him, which was more important, and naturally the answer was no since there were women everywhere who could give him just what Daisy did. He ignored the almost soundless voice deep inside him which begged to know that if that was the case, then why was he suddenly to sail across the world's oceans to get away from her? If that was what he was doing. Which he wasn't, of course. It was time he had a long trip, a profitable trip to the Australian colony, he told himself as he drew on his cigar, and it was the truth when he said the *Golden Lady* had been fitted up to carry passengers. For the past year he had sailed no further than North America, Canada, the Mediterranean, European and African ports but now, being a sailor, a man of the sea, he needed to put the endlessly deep waters of the Atlantic Ocean beneath the strong timbered hull and the cracking sails of this ship. To battle his way through the constant winds of the Roaring Forties to the south of the Cape of Good Hope. To beat his way across the turquoise-blue seas of the Indian Ocean to the vast continent of Australia. The great Canadian-built *Marco Polo*, one of the fastest and most seaworthy ships of her time, had already made the round trip to Australia and back in the amazing time of five months and twenty-one days, and he was eager to prove that *Golden Lady* could do the same. Now was as good a time as any to put her to the test.

He did not ask himself why!

Daisy's excited twirl came slowly to a stop. The smile spilled from her face and her eyes became watchful and shadowed, hiding the sudden expression of ... of what ... ? Of disappointment perhaps, regret, or just surprise? She felt her heart miss an astonishing beat, a painful beat which dismayed her. She faced him, her mouth suddenly dry and unable to form the words which she felt she should speak though she had no idea what they should be. 'So soon' or 'but we have been married no more than a week' but that implied that his presence was important to her and they both knew that to be untrue. She needed no man to make her complete and if Sam should decide to sail to the other side of the world, taking six months to do it, what was it to her? She had what she needed in the way of money which was at her disposal in the form of a draft at the bank in which Sam's wealth was deposited. She had the promise of a further loan should it prove not to be sufficient – at the discretion of the manager, who would always be at the call of Mrs Sam Lassiter and would be only too glad to be of assistance, financial that is, to the Captain's wife. She was to turn this gracious and elegant house – and the one next door when the lease fell due at the end of the year – into the most spectacular gaming house in the north of England. Sam had said so, remarking flippantly that as long as he had a bed to come home to, with her in it, set in the comfort and the luxury which he demanded he had no wish to be told of the details of how it was to be done. She was not to be harassed or gloomy when he came home with tales of problems difficult to solve since he had no desire to be told of them, nor was she to make complaints since he would make none himself, providing she showed him a profit. He was to be her friend and lover, witty, easy, charming and imaginative in their bed and she must expect nothing else of him.

His ironic gaze met hers, one dark eyebrow raised.

"That will not inconvenience you, will it, my darling?" he asked, still smiling.

"Not at all, Sam." She smiled too, whirling away towards the curving staircase, her hand reaching out to Bess who stood waiting at its foot. "Bess and I will be too busy to . . ."

"Miss me?" he finished softly.

"Good heavens, Sam, what an idea." Her laughter floated down to him. The silk of her wide crinoline skirt whispered against the stair carpet and when he turned towards the door which he had only minutes before come through, opening it violently, his face was dark with some dangerous emotion neither of them would have recognised.

26

He came home at the end of May for the opening of 'Daisy Lassiter's', or simply, 'Daisy's', the name by which the club was to be known though it was not what Daisy herself had intended. She and Bess had discussed it endlessly whilst Sam was away, thinking up and discarding dozens of suitable, or not so suitable names. Some hilarious, some, when they became hysterical with laughter, quite rude, but none were just right and on the day of the evening it was to open its doors for the first time to the gentlemen who were invited guests, it was still unnamed.

They had lived for the best part of the six months Sam was absent in what seemed to be a state of mindless chaos, one which would never resolve itself, and Daisy was to say time and time again to Bess it was a blessing Sam was not there to suffer it, for suffer it he would not. Jack hid himself in his kitchen, refusing to have anything at all to do with the bedlam until it became apparent to him that his kitchen was to be his no longer and that what had been a cosy, firelit haven where he had created the tasty dishes he and the Captain had once been satisfied with, was to be transformed into a world where a French chef, an artist at his trade, was to take his place.

And what was he to do with himself, he invited Daisy to tell him, since it was obvious they had no further need of him? Any of them. First the Captain when he had told Jack he was superfluous on the deck of his ship and must stay at home to keep an eye on the Captain's woman, who had, in just over a year, turned their lives upside down and left it every which way, in his opinion. Then it had been the turn of the strait-laced, frozen-faced madam who had come to be housekeeper and companion to the Captain's fine new wife, again usurping Jack from his position in the household, though if he were honest with himself she'd turned out to be the sort of person Jack most admired and that was one who kept her mouth shut and herself to herself, interfering hardly at all in Jack's kitchen. Now it was a bloody French chef and not only that but kitchenmaids, housemaids, and even, he had heard, footmen to serve the gentlemen who were to be members of this damned gaming club his master's house was to become.

"Jack," she said quietly, indicating that he was to sit in the spindle-legged chair beside the fire, but making nothing of it when he refused. "Without you and Bess this undertaking of mine is doomed." Her face was serious and her eyes clear and steady.

"Hmmph," he replied, sneering at the very idea.

"It's true. I must have someone I can trust. A person of authority to watch out for my interests. Mine and the Captain's. I cannot be in three, or even two places at once and so I must depend on you and Bess to keep an eye on what I cannot personally supervise. The chef and his staff will be in the kitchen, naturally. Bess will watch the maidservants, see to the linen, the glassware, the silverware, all the aspects of the house which provide for the guests' comfort but I'm afraid I must leave the burden of maintaining order amongst the menservants to you. There will be a great deal of responsibility, Jack, making sure that everything is running smoothly at the front of the house, in the gaming rooms, the security of the house for there will be ruffians, you know the type, who will try to get in. You have more experience than I with men such as these, being a man of the world yourself, and I was counting on you to take charge."

Take charge! That sounded like something he might be talked into doing, something worthy of his years, his experience, his opinion of his own value. He would be useful, he knew that, for though he was not a big man, nor particularly well-muscled, he had in his unsmiling face and cool grey stare something implacable which had been known to frighten off the biggest, meanest seamen who ever raised fists in a brawl.

"Would you be interested, Jack, only I would hate to have to employ a stranger, someone whose loyalty I was not sure of?"

"I might. I suppose it'd be a good idea to have someone with a bit of sense about the place." He grunted and almost smiled and deep in his weather-beaten old heart, which had never once been touched with a softer emotion for a woman than lust, something stirred with what could only be called devotion for Sam Lassiter's woman.

"Thank you, Jack."

"Will I have to wear a uniform?"

"Is it necessary, do you think?"

"No."

And for several months after the opening those who were new to 'Daisy's' were quite astonished to behold an old seaman, one-legged, in sea-breeches and gansey over which he wore a fancy silk waistcoat, keeping a grim eye on the antics of those 'dressed-up jackanapes', as he called them, the footmen who met guests at the door. Just another bit of whimsy to add to the legends which grew and multiplied about the fabulous Daisy Lassiter and her place and which were to make it famous, not only in Liverpool and the rest of the country, but travelled across the sea with the gentlemen who came to do business in the great seaport.

Daisy was determined that the house should continue to look exactly what it originally was. A gentleman's residence. A private home, elegant and comfortable, discreet and tasteful but above all the luxury and refinement to be found within it only what a gentleman was used to in his own home. The havoc was caused by the need to make two houses, one of which had been the home of a family with six children, now moved to a villa in Tuebrook, into one, well-proportioned building without losing any of the style and classic simplicity of their Regency days. Each house in the long, curving crescent of Duke Street was of three storeys, some wider than others. Several had only three flat sash windows at each level across their front facade whilst others had five, each window on the first floor opening through a long French window on to a delicate cast-iron balcony. Daisy's problem was to successfully transform two of these houses into one, two entrance doors into one, two hallways running side by side in each house into one, and two sets of curving staircases, one on either side, drifting up to a central landing. This was achieved by simply knocking out the wall which divided the two houses on the ground floor giving double the space and creating an imposing entrance in which the delicate staircase, with handrails supported by decorative ironwork, rose up in smoothly curved turns, framing the now square hallway. There was an enormous, brilliantly lit chandelier hanging from an ornate central rose, supplemented by extra wall-lamps and candles. There was a marble-topped table against the back wall beneath the curve of the upstairs landing on which stood a jardinière filled with fresh flowers. A beautifully carved grandfather clock ticked sonorously to one side and a dozen comfortable leather chairs were arranged on the magnificently waxed and polished floor so that guests might sit and converse with friends, drink French champagne and smoke their expensive cigars before moving into the gaming rooms.

These were all on the ground floor off the hallway, except for the Salle Privée, a private salon where Daisy intended only games for extremely high stakes would be played, and which was situated on the first floor adjacent to the large and magnificently appointed supper room. The rooms on the ground floor were just as sumptuous, each one given up to whatever game of chance a gentleman might prefer, eight in all and each as stylish and comfortable as the next in its furnishing and decor. Those which had been in Sam's house were almost as they had been before the change, needing nothing to make them as Daisy required them to be for her 'guests', but the house which had been leased to the departed family and which now belonged to Sam was in sad need of her tasteful touch, and Sam's money. Mr James Clements and Son, of Richmond Row, whose collection included screens, ottoman stools, ornamental chairs and any other article of furniture in the Louis Quatorze, Elizabethan or modern style which his customers might require, was visited almost daily by Mrs Sam Lassiter and her modestly dressed companion, as was Mr Henry Lacey, print-seller and picture-frame manufacturer, and who was also able to supply her with the playing cards she needed, made by the famous firm of De La Rue; and Mr John Hodgson of Hodgson's Rooms in Church Street, who could provide anything Mrs Lassiter needed in the way of glassware, china, silverware, of the very finest quality, naturally, rosewood card tables, beds of all sorts – since her household had grown so enormously – four-poster, tent or canopy, and superb carpeting, figured or plain. She was to have 'suites' of rooms, of what sort the plain townsfolk of Liverpool shuddered to think, where 'gentlemen' who required a bed might stay overnight if they so wished, and what was to go on there, and with whom, was open to speculation but they thought the worst, of course.

The kitchens in the basement were the last word in every modern domestic convenience a kitchen and its servants could possibly need. There was a new range which, it was rumoured, had had devoted to it much scientific ingenuity in the development of its flues for coal-burning. A closed range with a flat hotplate and a controlled oven beside it which had been insisted upon by the temperamental French chef and his assistants who were to provide food of a gourmet nature every hour of the day and night if required. Kitchen gadgets of a sort never before seen were to be introduced. A positive plethora of mincers, choppers, slicers and corers and innumerable instruments the use of which could only be imagined but which were vitally necessary to Chef Armande, it was supposed. A 'boiler', whatever that might be, provided constant hot water to the bathroom Daisy had had installed, with several indoor water closets, and only God knew what else but then having been housemaid in the great country home of the Thornley family she presumably knew what was what in the way of comfort and luxury.

But it was in the gaming rooms that the true taste and

excellence of the surroundings in which Daisy's guests were to be pampered, was to be found. No red damask walls, no flamboyant and gilded mirrors, no ostentatious furnishings and showy decor, which was the usual style, she had heard, of the sporting house, but quiet good taste, elegance, the subtle colours and classical restraint which she was convinced the gentlemen – and those 'ladies' who would accompany them – would find pleasing. There would be books about and musical instruments, chairs and tables grouped for informal entertaining. Light and delicate, pastel carpeted, shades of rose and cream and palest green, tall windows framed in curtains to match. Silks and damasks, paintings in gilt frames, white marble fireplaces in which fires would always blaze. Profusions of flowers fresh each day and, opening out from several rooms at the back of the house, French windows which led down stone steps into the garden where on a fine night guests might stroll or sit on white-painted cast-iron finely wrought garden benches whilst sipping champagne which cost them nothing at all and enjoy the lavender-scented night she intended to supply them with.

In the first-floor dining room, served by several modestly gowned housemaids whose plain dove-grey dresses over which they were to wear starched and frilled muslin aprons had been designed by the Misses Yeoland, was a supper table which would be cleared and reset half a dozen times during the evening with an endless display of Chef Armande's finest dishes, or on into the following day if play demanded it. Capon and oysters, lark pudding, crisp curls of smoked salmon, caviare, pheasant and grouse in season, chicken breasts in white wine and mushrooms, salmon pâté, strawberry ices and apricot tartlets, cream and truffles, with the finest claret, port and champagne, all the refinements to which gentlemen were accustomed for they were the 'guests' Daisy was after.

"Bloody hell" were the first words Sam spoke as he entered the new and considerably larger hallway. His eyes were drawn to the high ceiling where the delicate tracery of acanthus leaves was picked out in gold; to the misted colour of the plasterwork copied in the flowery pastels of the rugs which were scattered about the polished floor; to the arched simplicity of the staircase on either side of the hall, and finally to Daisy herself where she stood at the foot waiting for him. He was tired and not a little uneasy at this change in his house which, though he had given her permission to carry it out and provided the money to do so, was still somewhat of a shock to him. It had taken him many hours to get through the formalities of berthing *Golden Lady* and the preparation for the unloading of her cargo of Australian wool. He had been held up at the docks by the distressing sight of the arrival of the steamship *Cambria* from the battlefields of the Crimea, crammed from bow to stern with sick and wounded officers and men. There had been weeping women and bewildered children come to meet those who had fought so bravely and were now returned, though in what condition, after the fall of Sebastopol. He had watched with hundreds of others, silent and sad, as 243 pitiful men who had left Liverpool with the 3rd Regiment of Lancashire Militia on the *Lord Raglan* were brought ashore. Eight hundred of them had gone in July of the previous year amidst loud and hearty cheering, the bands of the artillery, militia and the 3rd Lancashire playing 'Cheer Boys, Cheer' and 'Auld Lang Syne'. They had been armed with old-fashioned musket and bayonet, perhaps the reason they had fared so ill, Sam had thought as he watched the silent cavalcade of stretcher-bearers carry the wounded to a new building which had been added to the workhouse.

The memory, and something he could not name which settled in his breast as he looked at Daisy, made him sharp.

"What in God's name have you done to the place?"

"Don't you like it?" She was equally sharp. They had not seen one another for over six months. He was fine drawn and as sun-browned as a native of Africa, his sea-green eyes meshed in the fine lines drawn there by weeks of squinting into and across sun-dazzled foreign seas. His immaculately tailored jacket seemed to strain at his wide shoulders and yet at the same time the trousers were somewhat slack about his waist and hips.

"You look well," she said, "but thinner."

"You look rather splendid yourself, but then you always do, my pet."

"Thank you. Your trip has been worthwhile?"

"Oh indeed, and needs to be to pay for all this."

"You don't like it?" she asked him again.

"I didn't say that, in fact it looks very grand but it is something of a shock."

They continued to stare somewhat arrogantly at one another, not at all sure how they should be, it seemed, now that they were together again. His eyes were on the exquisite line of her mouth, the familiar upward tilt at each corner though she was not smiling. She looked beautiful, every inch a lady, serene and in complete control of herself and her life and he wondered where the pale waif, the sorrowing young girl who had wept for her sister, the lovely, slightly dishevelled child in golden gauze, the seductive woman in red boots and gold garters had gone, and who this calm woman in her place might be. She wore the softest, palest blue, so pale it was almost white, simple and elegant, tight-waisted and with an enormous skirt relieved only by the layers of frothy white lace which showed beneath the hem. Her hair had been brushed to glowing copper, arranged in an intricate coil low on her neck, and he wondered at its ability to change its glowing autumn colour in different lights. She was poised, polished, surrounded by the French clocks she had purchased from Mr Hodgson, the potpourri vases and Meissen figurines, the white biscuit porcelain, the superb Rococo sofa inlaid with mother of pearl. She had a chef in her kitchen, a parlourmaid to serve tea, housemaids to clean and polish and carry hot water and a scullerymaid to scrub her floors and black-lead her stove. She had a man whom she did not care to call a butler to answer her door and guard it from intruders, a man to see to her wine cellar, polish her boots and who would drive her carriage when she had one. She had a housekeeper to watch over them all for her in the shape of her devoted friend Bess Miller, and everywhere at once, or so it seemed, making sure his captain's interests were guarded, and hers, she had Jack.

"May I order you something to eat, or a drink perhaps?" She had no idea if he had missed her, or was glad to see her, nor, she was honest enough to admit, how she felt about his return.

"Thank you, no, so perhaps now that we have done with the niceties you might give your husband a somewhat warmer welcome. A wifely kiss, perhaps?" He grinned in his old fashion. "Or even something warmer?"

"Well..." responding to his teasing manner "...there have been one or two alterations at the top of the house which might interest you. A bedroom...?"

Their minds might be wary of one another but their bodies were not, coming joyfully together with the passion and sensuality, the explosive pleasure which they both remembered.

"Well, my darling, some things do not change, thank God," he remarked lazily an hour later. His smooth, cologne-scented cheek rested on her breast, his lips still tasting each sweet pink nipple. "I do believe we are well matched in our desire for pleasure and now that I have made sure that matters are the same as they have always been between us and that you still have the talent to please me, which you know is a necessity in my life, you shall tell me how we are to make our fortune with this splendid establishment you have created. I must admit to a certain admiration with what you have achieved. This bedroom is quite charming now that I have a moment to study it."

He looked about him at the honey-gold watered silk walls, the white-frilled muslin at the tall windows which led out on to a tiny wrought-iron balcony overlooking the long back garden, the rich carpet, the tasteful furniture. She had created a whole suite of rooms for them across the combined top floor of the two houses, with its own private staircase and door. A dining room, as lovely as the one he had had on the ground floor, an elegantly furnished sitting room with its original furniture, even a new and completely separate bathroom fed by piped water from the cavernous, constantly steaming boiler in the basement. It was a private world away from the club and the servants' rooms where they could be completely alone. She had done her best to please him and it seemed she had succeeded.

"And when is the grand opening, my love?" he continued as she slipped from the bed and began to dress herself, her mind already busy again with all the dozens of matters to which she must attend. She must speak to John Elliott who was to manage the gaming side of the club whilst she played hostess, making sure once again that he knew exactly how she wanted him to conduct her new endeavour though she had told him at least a dozen times already. She must have a word with Bess regarding the order for fresh fruit, flowers, salmon, caviare and all the expensive delicacies she intended to give to her guests on this important night, and speak to Chef Armande, though he was not at all willing to be spoken to on the subject of his cooking, and really she did not have a great deal of time for Sam at the moment. She would make it up to him when it was all running smoothly, she promised herself; after all, had it not been for him it would not be happening!

"Tomorrow night, Sam, so if you could get up and..."

"And if I don't care to get up, my darling, in fact if I would prefer you to get back into bed with me, what would you say to that? If you will open that box, the one I threw on the chair just before we began to ... yes, that one, undo it and bring what you find there to me. No, don't unwrap the paper, just remove that charming gown you are hurrying into and try this on for me..."

"Sam, I can't. I have so much to do and I've already..."

"Wasted enough time on me, is that what you're saying?" He smiled, his face and body incredibly brown against the white of the bedcovers. She was distracted for a moment by the long, hard strength of him, by the muscles which moved beneath his smooth skin, by the fineness of him, by the strange expression in his narrowed eyes, by the curve of his strong, humorous mouth, the taste and texture of which she could still feel on her own. Her yielding woman's body was eager to submit itself again to the languid, stretching joy of his hands and lips but her sharp, vexed mind had far too much to do and must be off to do it.

"Don't be silly, Sam. You know that's not what I mean," though it was, of course.

"Do I, Daisy? I have been home no more than an hour or two and already your eyes have a vague look about them as though you are a thousand miles away in your thoughts." He stopped suddenly and took a deep breath just as though he was making an effort to control something which had unaccountably got away from him. He lay back on the heaped pillows over which he had recently draped her in one of his inventive and delightful love games and waved his hand carelessly. "But off you go, my sweet, to whatever it is you are so busy with and I shall entertain myself somehow or other. These can wait . . ." indicating the beautifully wrapped boxes which he had spilled upon the bed ". . . until a more convenient moment. Oh, and by the way, I may not be here when you come to bed, that is if you intend to come to bed tonight, but you'll not object to that, will you?"

"Where are you going?" Her voice was surprised and she turned at the door. "I was hoping you'd come and look at . . . well . . ." she smiled almost shyly, like a child who is eager to show off some amazing feat it had mastered ". . . I was hoping to take you through the house and show you what has been done. Surely you are interested in how your money has been spent?"

"Money? Aah yes, money. An interesting topic, money, but not one I feel particularly disposed to discuss, not tonight. I have no doubt at all that whatever you have done with it, it will not be wasted, nor will it fail to multiply itself most satisfactorily. I think you will prove to have a talent for it, my sweet. I suppose I must have known that from the start else why should I have . . . loaned, shall we call it, so much of it so readily? Oh yes, my pet, I know to a penny exactly how much you have spent. I may be a simple sailor but I am not such a fool as to lose track of where my hard-earned cash has gone. The manager at the bank has kept me informed, so no, I think I will just stay here and smoke a cigar and perhaps if you could send up that delightful little housemaid I saw lurking at the back of the hall when I came in, with a bottle of brandy, I shall make my own amusement."

"Sam, you wouldn't...?"

"Daisy! What can you mean?" He grinned hugely. "No, my darling, I have no interest in the housemaid, charming as she appeared to be. Have I not enough with your delightful ... er ... endeavours in my bed without causing any more difficulties than I can honestly, at the moment, be troubled with? If I needed such ... diversions I would hardly take them here under the same roof as my wife, would I, my sweet?" He smiled at her and she felt the familiar sense of confusion wash over her, then she shrugged it off for was he not always the same and would she have him any other way? It was not as if they were the typically devoted man and wife she had heard tell of and which she had as yet to witness. She suspected Robert and Emma Greenhalgh were the nearest to a matched pair that she knew but then her experience of such things was not wide.

"Well then..."

"Well then, Daisy, off you go to make sure everything is running smoothly in your new and exciting enterprise. Don't let me keep you from your duties, my love. Perhaps I shall still be here, who knows, when you return and if not then I will do my best to be at your side for the grand opening."

"Sam ... is everything all right? You seem..."

"Everything is fine, darling. Why shouldn't it be? Don't worry, I shan't let you down. I have business to attend to at the docks tomorrow but I promise to be back in plenty of time."

"I'd like you to be here, Sam."

"Would you, Daisy?" There was a tenseness about his smiling mouth which she didn't notice. "Why?"

"Sam, how would it look if the club was to open without you, as one of its partners, there beside me? All the gentlemen who have accepted my invitation are your friends and friends of theirs and they will expect to see you here. On the first night at least. After that, if you don't feel like it you can ..."

"Go to hell for all you care, is that it, my love?"

"Of course not, Sam. I know you have ... other concerns and we both agreed when we started our ... relationship that we would not interfere with ..." She was obviously perplexed.

"I'm only joking, sweetheart. I know exactly how much I mean to you, and vice versa. We are the perfect complement for one another, are we not, and shall manage very well. Now then, send up the brandy, Daisy, and make sure there is a bottle always on hand up here, will you? Oh, and ask Jack to come up, will you? I want a word with him. And I think I'll try out that splendid new bathtub you have put up here. A good idea, my love. What a pity you are so fully engaged. It might have been diverting to ... ah, well, some other time when you are not so ... occupied."

He turned away from her, reaching for his cigars, dismissing her, it seemed to her, as though she was a servant and for a moment, as the strange confusion came over her again, she was tempted to stop and have it out with him, whatever it was that had put him in such a curious mood. And yet was he? Was this sardonically smiling man not just as he always was, rare and unpredictable, engaging and filled with that unique humour which often bedevilled her but never, never bored her?

They came in their droves, suave and immaculate in the black and white of their perfectly tailored evening dress, businessmen, journalists, financiers, wits and dandies and fashionable idlers, some of them accompanied by women who were not their wives, beautiful young women of dubious morality. She had spent long hours deciding whether to provide what Sam had euphemistically called 'hostesses' to entertain these gentlemen but she had finally acknowledged to herself that if she did, though it made no difference to her, or so she told herself, she would instantly alienate Bess and Jack who would not work, no matter what she paid them, in what both of them would see as no more than a brothel. She remembered the Royale Club House in Bold Street and the slightly sleazy atmosphere which had lain over the place, the pretty, but somewhat tawdry 'girls', the matched pair, one black and one white, whose duties she fully understood now, and she realised she did not want that for her club. It was a sporting house, a gaming house where honest gambling might be found. Of the expensive, the very expensive sort, certainly, providing for the wealthy, for the distinguished and respected visitors who passed through Liverpool and who would not care for anything which smacked of the unsavoury, and if they did would know where to find it. It would not be at 'Daisy Lassiter's'!

"Lassiter, my dear fellow, how good to see you again and how kind of you to invite me to this simply splendid establishment of yours."

"Not mine, Templeton, my wife's," turning, smiling imperturbably, to Daisy. "May I introduce the real owner of 'Daisy Lassiter's'. That is what the club is to be called, is it not, my love? This is Sir John Templeton, Daisy, who I hope will be a frequent guest at your little club."

"Our club, darling," turning to smile brilliantly at Sir John, giving him her hand to bow over and even to lift for an appreciative brush of his lips. His eyes were warm as they dipped into the low neck of her evening gown. Cream gauze over a foundation of cream embroidered silk with no sleeves and no top to speak of, with a skirt as light as a summer breeze. She carried a cream feathered fan and in the intricate coil of her hair she had threaded cream rosebuds. Around her neck were three strands of creamy pearls, velvet textured, one of the expensive gifts Sam had picked up 'somewhere', he said casually, on his last journey and to which she had paid scant attention. She looked breathtaking. She stood beside Sam at the foot of the delicately curved staircase receiving her guests with the air of a great hostess who has been accustomed to entertaining the high and the mighty of the land all her life. Smiling graciously, exchanging a word or two with most of the gentlemen to whom she was introduced by Sam she was – or seemed to be – completely at her ease.

"Daisy, may I present Mr Alfred Burgess. Alfred, this is my wife . . ."

"...Mr Robert Meade..."

"...Sir William Fosdick..."

"...Ben, you old rogue, may I present my..."

And so it went on for almost two hours as those who had been invited to be members of what promised to be the most exclusive club in Liverpool were introduced to their hostess. They were directed by her, or her ironically smiling husband – and could you blame him for looking so pleased with himself, they asked one another after scrutinising the charms of his wife – into the hands of John Elliott who was to run the gaming rooms for her and who placed them courteously at the game of their choice. Champagne was served by attentive footmen and there was an excellent choice of spirits or wine of the expensive sort for those who had a fancy for it. There was to be a full-scale supper served by pretty girls who passed for parlourmaids and had it not been for the gaming tables a gentleman might have thought himself to be relaxing in the luxury and comfort of his own home.

Daisy moved among them, her spirits high, her skin cream-flushed, her eyes such a glowing golden brown not a few gentlemen imagined they had fallen in love with her and it took all her diplomacy to refuse a dozen assignations. There was colour, warm laughter, the fragrance of the pot-pourri jars she had scattered about the rooms, the rich aroma of brandy and cigars, the excited buzz of conversation as a vast amount of money was won and lost. She was called constantly to the entrance hall to greet fresh arrivals, warned by a watchful footman who had been told to let her know the moment a newcomer arrived for on this first night she wished to greet each one personally.

There was a stir as the splendid front door was opened yet again and a large party of dashing young gentlemen and several 'ladies' of their acquaintance erupted noisily from the street into the hallway. Arrogant, overbearing, demanding the immediate attention to which their birth and upbringing had accustomed them, they were in danger of causing a severe disturbance had not Sam, giving the appearance of hardly moving at all, insinuated himself amongst them, humorously chafing those he knew and courteously welcoming those to whom he was introduced. There were several young military men in full dress uniform amongst them who instantly surrounded Daisy with the eagerness of puppies, vying for her attention, flirting, and every one of them intending to make love to her by the end of the evening since she was after all the keeper, or so they had been told, of this house of enjoyment.

"My wife, gentlemen," Sam drawled, drifting amiably between them and her, "wishes to welcome you most warmly to our establishment and would be honoured if you would make your way into the gaming rooms, or perhaps a spot of supper? There is champagne . . . yes, I beg of you to help yourselves," and with endless good humour he defused what might have become an awkward situation.

"Thank you, Sam," she whispered in his ear, whilst smiling brilliantly over her shoulder at Mr Thomas Hemingway who, it was said, was the eldest son of one of the wealthiest shipowners in Liverpool and about to be married to Miss Emily Bradley, the daughter of another richly endowed commercial gentleman and who would not be best pleased to see the attention her fiancé was paying to the pretty girl who hung on his arm.

"Not at all, my darling," Sam answered, as the gentlemen strolled indolently in the direction which he had pointed them, "but I fear you must devise a more efficient method of cooling the ardour of some of our more amorous guests or you will expose yourself to more than a few awkward moments when I am not here. No, the fact that you are my wife will not protect you, my love, for some of these so-called gentlemen, as you should know full well, are no respecters of the wedded state. I see I shall have to let Jack instruct one or two of the footmen on how to subdue the high spirits of those young dandies or they will imagine you are freely available to them along with the champagne. And that bloody dress doesn't help!"

To her amazement she realised he was rigid with anger. He was still smiling, of course, his cigar clamped between his teeth, but there was a line about his mouth and his eyes were a pale and dangerous green.

"Sam, for God's sake, surely you expected this at first. I know I did. Any woman with any pretence to good looks is fair game to these fine young gentlemen but they will soon learn that I am not included in their games of chance. I will teach them."

"As you did a moment ago, you mean? Come on, Daisy, if I hadn't stepped in when I did God knows what commotion they might have caused."

"Let go of my arm, Sam, and do go and have a game of cards, for heaven's sake. I have to move about the rooms and speak to people or they will begin to wonder what is wrong with their hostess. I can't leave it all to John."

"And that is another matter. I'm not sure I care for the idea of having that young gentleman working in such close proximity to my wife. I have no doubt he is a master at his craft but..."

"Stop it, Sam. Can we not have this conversation later when everyone has gone? I swear I will cope with it should it happen again and they will soon come to realise that no one makes free with Daisy Lassiter, not if they want to continue as members. Jack will watch out for me, and as for John, he has a wife and three children living in Everton and has not the slightest interest in me except as an employer. Please be patient, Sam. It's the first night the club has been open, after all."

"See to it then, my love, or I promise you it will close as quickly as it opened."

And all this was spoken with frozen mouths and frozen smiles as Mr and Mrs Sam Lassiter lounged in the doorway of their lovely drawing room where now the click of the roulette wheel could only just be heard above the sound of the laughter of Mr Thomas Hemingway's party. The lamplight glinted on the mother-of-pearl gaming chips and the ivory dice. Around the hazarde table there were a dozen or more gentlemen standing to watch the play. The croupier's voice chanted the rhythmic refrain of the game, like a priest calling the faithful. "*Faites vos jeux*, gentlemen, *faites vos jeux,*" telling them to place their bets. "*Les jeux sont faix,*" and the players who had been deliberating on which number, which colour might be with them tonight, hurried to decide for the game was ready to commence. "*Rien ne va plus.*" No more bets and those to whom gambling was as necessary to their lives as the air they breathed and to whom the uncertainty was a craving which could never be satisfied, carelessly flung down their pretty *plaques*, breathing in the drug of their addiction.

She moved away from Sam to watch, smiling, the spin of the roulette wheel. A footman offered her a glass of chilled white wine and she took it absently. Catching the bold eye of Sir John Templeton who had just put what looked like a hundred guineas on black fourteen, her smile deepened and he winked at her in a way she knew Sam would not care for, though only God knew why. Conscious of the words he had just flung at her she turned slightly to check the arrangement of a bowl of spring flowers and was in time to see him raise an enquiring eyebrow at one of the exceedingly pretty young ladies who had come in with Thomas Hemingway. She watched him stroll across between the tables and bow gallantly over the girl's hand, a wicked smile on his face. The girl preened and displayed the inviting curve of her young neck and shoulders and Daisy was astonished at the pang of quick outrage her whole body suffered, but when Sam turned to stare at her, questioningly she thought, she merely smiled and turned away to talk to Mr Robert Meade.

She drifted through the evening in the sure knowledge that she was a success. They told her so over and over again, congratulating her on the splendour of her club, the fineness of her claret and champagne, the delicious and endless supper she had provided, her own beauty, wit and talent as a hostess. Some had won and some had lost, the latter with good humour. A great deal of money had changed hands but what did it matter when they had been so royally entertained, they told her as they climbed into their carriages just as dawn was beginning to paint a fine apricot patina on the house-tops.

As she climbed the curving staircase there was a smile on her lips, her heart was light and her eyes were deep and glowing with pride. She and John Elliott had just estimated the night's takings and she could not wait to tell Sam of the 'bank's' assets, but when she reached the top of the house and the firelit, lamplit comfort of their bedroom he was not there. The bed, which the chambermaid had turned down, had not been slept in.

27

Bess studied the child who stood before her, pursing her lips and frowning slightly as though she was having some difficulty in making a decision. The child fidgeted nervously, hardly daring to lift her eyes to this great personage who stood in their Mam's kitchen though she knew they were sisters.

"Well, she looks sturdy enough, Mam," Bess said musingly at last, "but then she's had the benefit of good feeding for the last two years. I reckon she'd do me a treat if she shapes herself and does what she's told. She's ten now and there's no reason why she shouldn't work in my kitchen." She preened somewhat as she spoke though it was by no means deliberate but could she be blamed for feeling a sense of deep satisfaction at being able to make such a statement, even if it was only to her own mother? She was twenty-four years old. She had been born in this estate cottage where her mother lived and at the same age as their Nelly, now standing before her, had gone as a scullerymaid in the great kitchens of the ancestral home of Hugh Charles, Lord Thornley, peer of the realm, Fourteenth Baron of that name. And now, fourteen years later, she was housekeeper to Mrs

Sam Lassiter, better known as Daisy Lassiter, owner of 'Daisy's', the most renowned sporting club in the north of England.

"It'll be best all round if I take her, Mam. Things being what they are I don't reckon there's much chance of her getting put on at Thornley Green. Mrs Crosby'll not have forgotten the name of Bess Miller." She smiled grimly though her expression said she was not unduly concerned by the fact. "So you'll only have our Eddy to see to then and I dare say, if he fancied it, the Captain would find him something . . ."

"Eeh no, love, don't you bother the Captain. There'll be something round here, like as not, that'll suit the lad. He's country born and bred, Bess, and I don't reckon I'd sleep sound in me bed at night at the thought of him being flung on one of them there ships so don't you go saying owt to him, promise me now, or like as not he'd go. You know what lads are like. Anything that sounds a bit adventurous and they're off without a thought for anyone, let alone how it'll turn out. No, he'll find work on one of the farms hereabouts, I dare say, or maybe Mr Greenhalgh can get him fixed up on the estate like he did our Willy and Jasper, and glad I was too about that, I can tell you, for it meant I could keep this estate cottage. And both of them are doing well, he tells me."

Mrs Miller puffed up a little, somewhat in the recent manner of her daughter, proud of her sons, it seemed, and the great future which lay ahead of them with the Thornley family. Besides, she was not at all certain she was ready to lose the last of the fifteen children she had borne, particularly to some unknown and therefore frightening world the like of which she could not even imagine, having been no further in her life than the next village.

"You know how our Willy is with horses," she went on, "and Jasper's set up in the garden. Mind, I don't reckon his lordship knows who either of them are or like as not he'd have them both out on their ear afore you could say knife."

"Why?" Bess reared up indignantly. "Just because they're my brothers, for God's sake? D'you think his lordship's bothered about the likes of me leaving his service without giving notice two years ago, or even knows I've gone, for that matter? He doesn't care who works in his kitchen, Mam, or outside neither, as long as he's waited on in the manner he's always been used to. Mr Greenhalgh has the hiring and firing of the outside staff and Mrs Crosby the inside and providing it all runs smoothly he doesn't know the names of them that serve him. You don't think Mrs Crosby goes running to Lord Thornley, or even to her ladyship, every time a maidservant gets out of line, Mam, do you, so you've no need to fret about our Willy and Jasper. They'll be tucked away somewhere and no one the wiser. Anyroad, Eddy's another year or two yet before he needs to find work but promise me you'll make sure he keeps up with the Dame School, won't you? I'd not like to think I'm spending two-pence a week for him to go playing the fool at my expense. The rest of us never learned to read nor write, not even at Sunday School, but our Eddy's been given the chance and I don't want to hear he's been playing truant so keep your eye on him, won't you, Mam?"

Bess moved a chair away from the table and sat down, carefully smoothing the rich folds of her black merino wool skirt. She had not allowed herself to be coaxed into any other colour by Captain Lassiter or her mistress, and would not, except for a change to a sensible shade of grey during the spring and summer months. Then it might be foulard, or grenadine, which were both light materials, and in her opinion, suitable to her station in life. She had never quite overcome her conviction that she had somehow broken the rules of society which were that all humanity was born into the place in life where it was intended to be and that she, Bess Miller, who had not at the time been able to read or write her own name, with her high position in Daisy Lassiter's house, no longer knew her 'place'. She had 'got above herself'. Mind, she was good at what she did. She knew that and was, though she tried not to be, proud of herself and what she had achieved in the smooth running of Captain and Mrs Sam Lassiter's home and business venture. She could read and write a few words now and do 'sums', which was, of course, necessary when one was responsible for the reckoning and paying of the household accounts. Thanks to Daisy who had taught her her letters in the long evenings during the winter the Captain had been away before the club opened, she at least knew how to add up a column of figures and how every penny was spent. Of course she had always hoped to make her way up the chain of maidservants when she had been employed at Thornley Green, perhaps attaining the post of assistant housekeeper one day, when she was much older. That had seemed to be a natural order of progression for a person of her class but to be in charge in one single leap, so to speak, at the age of twenty-four, of a household of servants, with her own rooms, her own splendid income, her decisions the ones which ruled the domestic arrangement of the house, was something of which dreams were made. She was overwhelmed by the wonder of what she could do for her family, too, and looking round the shining cleanliness of her mother's kitchen and at the well-fed condition of her mother herself she could not help but marvel at the changes which had taken place since that moment, two years or more ago, when she had been summoned here by Daisy. God, it had been filthy then, and her Mam as well. Ground down by the rearing of the children who had survived out of the fifteen she had borne in eighteen years – Bess the eldest – by the constant scraping and making do the wages of a farm labourer forced upon her; by the death of Bess's father who, though he had worked as they all did until it killed him, left her with nothing but his children; and finally by the devastating loss of the few shillings Bess herself had managed to send her now and again, Sarah Miller had given up the struggle against the dirt, the confusion, the hunger, the poverty which she and thousands of others like her had fought so steadfastly, and sunk into the apathetic misery of the hopeless poor. All at sixes and sevens, as she used to describe herself apologetically to Bess, tired of slaving and nothing in return for it but hard knocks, but with the advancement of her daughter to the grand new job up Liverpool way the transformation in her was nothing short of miraculous.

"Will you take our Nelly back with you?" she asked, gazing in wonder through her polished window to the carriage which was tied up at the tidy front of her cottage. It was a sight which never failed to impress and amaze her. The driver had gone down to the Last Shift, given permission to do so by *her* daughter, fastening the horses to a large iron weight which was kept specifically for the purpose, leaving the whole contrivance in the charge of a somewhat more responsible-looking lad than the rest of the village children who always came to gawp. For the price of a halfpenny the boy would prevent them from interfering with the fine pair of matched greys and even, as they had done on one occasion, from sitting in the carriage itself. It came once a month bringing Bess Miller to see her Mam and the whole village basked in the glory of one of 'them' reaching the dizzy heights she had. Sarah Miller was accepted almost as though she was 'gentry' now, so miraculous was her prosperity, which, being at heart a good woman, now that she no longer had to fight merely to stay fractionally on the right side of starvation, she was often willing to share with her neighbours.

"I don't see why not. I might as well since she's doing nothing else but hang about here."

"Nay, she helps me a treat," Sarah protested. "She's a grand little worker is our Nelly and what I shall do without her I don't know. She cleaned them brasses this morning and that stove hasn't been black-leaded so good since you did it last, our Bess. Not that I can't do it meself, you understand, and I suppose I'll have to from now on but it'll not look the same."

Her eyes roamed about the mellow, firelit kitchen, taking in the simple pine table and chairs and the dresser, now hung about with crockery of blue and white in a willow pattern. The central fire was heaped with coal, roaring its blessed warmth halfway up the chimney. There was a brick-lined oven on either side of it and on the fire itself was a perpetually steaming iron kettle ready for the innumerable cups of tea to which Sarah treated herself during the day. A wooden mantelpiece sported a selection of souvenir ornaments, cheap and colourful, mementos of the last summer fair to which, now that Bess was so well set up, the whole family had gone. The brown earthenware sink – only lately put in – was filled with water from the handpump in the centre of the village. It gleamed from much scrubbing and above it hung a variety of copper pans, burnished by Nelly but which Sarah would now have to care for herself. On either side of the fire was a rush-seated armchair made from ash. A couple of rag rugs, bright and clean, lay on the stone floor. From the enormous wooden beam above her head hung wicker baskets, dried mushrooms in nets, a ham and a string of onions. Two purring tabby cats curled about each other before the fire.

Sarah sighed woefully though she really bore her eldest daughter no ill will nor did she resent her youngest following the rest and going out into the world to earn her living. She would have been quite happy for their Nelly to stop at home to do the housework now that she herself was getting on in years, she admitted to herself, but the child must go soon. It was the way of their world. A girl child left the shelter of her home to take up employment when she was around ten years old, usually in the kitchen of some middle-class home if she was lucky for domestic service was much sought after. When she was fifteen or sixteen she would most likely be married to a local lad for they were wed young in their class, and breed the next generation of labourers for the service of the manorial lord, or his equivalent. But their Bess, though she could well afford to leave the girl at home with her mother, was a firm believer in making her younger brothers and sisters, now they were of an age for it, stand on their own two feet, as she had done, dependent on no one, and she meant to see that Nelly was well equipped for it. Train her herself, she said she would, in the kitchen of the Lassiters and when she was done with her she'd be qualified to go into domestic service with the best in the land.

"I'm not sure I want our Nelly working in a place like

that," Sarah had suggested at first, apparently overlooking her eldest daughter's involvement with it.

Bess had rounded on her. "A place like what? It's not a brothel and don't you let me hear you say it is, our Mam. The very idea." She was seriously affronted. "D'you think I'd work there if it was, let alone take our Nelly there? The girls that are under my supervision are decent and hard-working, doing just what they'd do at ... well ... at Thornley Green. Better, in fact, for there's no man at Mrs Lassiter's trying to get his hands up their skirts like what goes on up there, I can tell you. Respectable they are, for Mrs Lassiter won't have it any other way. Oh, there's plenty of the gentlemen who are members of the club'd like to get their hands on one of my parlourmaids for Mrs Lassiter insists that only ... well ... good-looking girls serve them. She says a gentleman likes to see pretty girls about him but she allows no liberties and they know it. Bar them from the club, she would, soon as look at them if they did 'owt she didn't like. Why, I've seen her wipe the floor with one chap and him a 'sir'. You'd have thought he were back in the nursery getting a ticking-off from his Nanny, the way she went at him. He'd got Rosie in a corner under the back stairs and was trying to ..."

Suddenly realising that their Nelly was raptly listening to every word, she stopped abruptly. "Anyway, don't you go making remarks like that, our Mam. Nelly'll be safe at our place, safer than she'd be in a dozen others, I can tell you."

Sarah Miller often wondered at the way her daughter spoke about the girl, younger than herself by two or three years, it was said, and for whom she now worked. They had been housemaids together, up at the big house, with their Bess the senior of the two. Daisy Brindle, or plain Brindle as Bess had initially called her, a fragile bit of flotsam thrown up and flung in their Bess's direction with instructions to keep an eye on her, and would you look at the pair of them now? But what was strange was the way Bess always spoke of Daisy as though the past had never been. It was 'Mrs Lassiter' this and 'Mrs Lassiter' that and never 'Daisy' which was funny, considering what good friends they had been.

Mind you, Daisy Brindle had repaid that friendship a hundredfold and Sarah Miller never stopped giving thanks for it. The last two years had been grand, grand, and would continue to be so as long as that there club was as successful as their Bess told her it was. The most fashionable place to be seen in the whole of the North, Bess said, whatever that meant exactly, and Daisy Lassiter, its hostess, the most talked-about woman in all of Liverpool. Eeh, she'd love to get a squint inside, that she would, just to see all the wonderful things their Bess had described to her but still, second-hand was better than nowt and more than others of her acquaintance had. Bess's picture of life there fair lit up every fourth Sunday for Sarah Miller.

"I'll try and fetch her with me when I come, Mam," Bess was saying, continuing their discussion about Nelly who still stood, her eyes cast down shyly, on the spot where she had been put. "That's if Mrs Lassiter can spare her."

"She'd not begrudge a mother seeing her girl now and again, surely?" Sarah wheedled, not from any great desire to see the child who, unlike their Eddy, was not her favourite, but to add support to her own earlier protest at losing her.

"No, but you can't expect our Nelly to come running home every five minutes, Mam, just because of my position in Mrs Lassiter's household." Bess's voice was firm. "There's lots of girls go away to work and don't see their families for months on end but I'm sure Mrs Lassiter'd not object to once a month. She's never had no family of her own except that poor girl what died, you know . . . ?" nodding her head knowingly and indicating that she could not speak of it in front of their Nelly " . . . but she's good-hearted when she thinks on. Well, we'd best be off, Nelly," becoming brisk, " . . . say goodbye to Mam and get your things . . ."

The words died on her lips and she turned her head sharply towards the window as the sound of a great commotion came from the front of the cottage. Excited voices were raised, children's voices, questioning and eager. The door burst open, ready to be flung from its hinges, she was sure, and over the doorstep came their Eddy. His thin face was a sweated pink and his eyes shone in it like two bright stars. His chest heaved and his breath laboured as he tried to speak. Bess felt her own breath catch in her throat and alarm thudded her heart against her ribcage. Her mother put her hand to her breast in a dramatic gesture. "God love us, lad, what on earth's happened? You didn't half give us a fright coming in like that just as though the devil himself were after you. Me heart's going nineteen to the dozen, yer great daft lummox, and wipe yer feet an' all. You look as though you've been tramping through Abe Dixon's pig-pen ..."

Bess put out an imperious hand to stop the flow of words which her mother directed at her youngest son and to her own surprise Sarah Miller found herself obeying it.

"What is it, Eddy?" Bess asked sharply, aware as her mother was not that there was something more than thoughtless boyish high spirits in her brother's manner. "Speak up, lad."

The boy had caught his breath by now and though he was still almost bursting with self-importance, delighted as the young always are with any event, good or bad, which might enliven the boredom of a routine day, his eyes were wide with a certain awed disbelief.

"He's dead," he said. "I heard Mr Greenhalgh say so with me own ears. 'He's dead,' he said, and to run for the doctor though what good it would do he didn't know. Them were the very words he said. I heard him. I was standing as close to him as I am to you, our Nelly ..." turning to his sister, full of himself and wishing to impress upon her his own masculine superiority. The look on her face was blank and uncomprehending and he turned back to the more satisfying audience of his mother and older sister. "I were looking to see if there were any berries in the hedge against Dingle's Field and I saw the whole thing. Just as close as I am to you, I was." He moved nearer to the spellbound pair at the table, his manner one of wonder. "In fact if I'd been any nearer he might have fell ..."

"Dear God, Eddy, what in heaven's name are you talking

418

about, lad? Who's dead? Just tell us and stop babbling on about hedges and berries."

The boy, thrilled to the marrow to be the bearer of this incredible news, longing to tell them of it but at the same time reluctant to part with it since once they had it he would no longer hold their undivided attention, hesitated, but Bess stood up and he knew she would not be averse to cracking him one if he did not get on with it.

"His lordship." His voice broke and he looked from one to the other expectantly as if waiting for praise.

The eyes of the two women met. The two children, even the reason for Bess's visit, were forgotten as they digested the words Eddy had spoken. Digested them, swallowed them painfully, found them unpalatable and would have liked nothing better than to spit them up again.

"Dear God in heaven!" Sarah Miller's face was white and suddenly as hollow-eyed and gaunt as on the day her Bert had died and she had waited to be evicted from the tied labourer's cottage she had shared with him. "Oh dear God in heaven, what's to become of us?"

Her anguished voice brought Bess from the shocked state into which she had fallen and she turned again to her brother. She took him by the shoulders and carefully drew him to the window so that the light from it fell directly on to his face. He was very much like her in appearance. Eyes pale and of no particular colour somewhere between blue and grey, pale-skinned now the flush of excitement had gone, mouse-coloured hair which her mother cut now and again when it grew over his ears, but his expression was sharp and intelligent, as hers was.

"Tell me what happened."

It seemed that the hunt had been led a merry chase that morning by the fox, starting from Turner's Fold where it had first been sighted, across field after field of patient land awaiting the mild coming of spring, frozen now and hard with winter. The wily animal had skirted Lower Colt and Shed Wood, followed by baying hounds and the long-drawn string of glossy-coated hunters and pink-coated huntsmen until it reached Caleb's Wood where it had gone to ground.

"I could hear 'em baying, our Bess, all the way from Broad Lane then someone shouted. 'There he goes,' they said. 'After him before we lose him again,' and just as they said it the creature pushed through the hedge right next to me. Right through the hedge and across the lane to t'other side. Well, they must all have turned then, the lot of 'em, some of 'em beginning to come across the field, you know the way they do, shouting and yelling and right out in front was his young lordship, flogging that great hunter he rides, going like the wind. His lordship was behind him, half a field away and the rest still further back. He looked round then and saw his Pa, his young lordship. 'Come on, Father,' he says. 'What's holding you back? Five years ago you would have led the field.' Well, his lordship sorta shook in his saddle and his face went a funny colour and he began to whip his horse on. Young lord sailed over the hedge, an' me an' all with no more than an inch to spare, laughing his bloody head off, he was. Then up comes his lordship, like a bull at a gate, not right at all and he were that wild I reckon he were about to have a fit. But he weren't set right for jumping, Bess. I could see that right off. Well, I've had enough hunts-men go by me to know when one's not set right for a hedge or a gate. Over he comes, shearing the top of that there hedge and when he come off, d'you know summat?"

His face was no longer filled with boyish excitement but pale and strained.

"What, love?"

"I heard his neck snap, our Bess, and what's more, so did his young lordship. He didn't see me under the hedge and d'you know what he did, just before the others come up?"

"What did he do, lad?"

"He laughed! He sat on his horse and laughed."

She heard Bess come in. Her voice was soft in the hall as she spoke to the parlourmaid who had opened the door to her then it was quiet again. She must have taken her young sister either down to the kitchen, Daisy thought, or up to the small but comfortable room she was to share with Rosie, the young kitchenmaid. Neither Bess nor Daisy believed in making their servants suffer the hardships they themselves had known at Thornley Green, and their rooms were well-furnished and warm. Bess would be up in a minute to tell Daisy all the gossip she had gleaned in her mother's kitchen. Most of it of not much interest to Daisy, about the life in the village, but sometimes it contained news of what was happening in the big house. Daisy would listen quietly, the names of those mentioned, the images Bess's words evoked bringing back painful memories, some of them almost more than she could bear but she made herself listen nevertheless for it was necessary to her plans that she had every scrap of information she could obtain, from any source, about the Thornley family.

It was two and a half years since the club had first opened and there was no doubt of its success, none at all. She was well aware that there was no more talked-about hostess in the whole of Liverpool but she also knew that there was no more respected one than she. The gentlemen who visited 'Daisy's' admired not only her business acumen, which grew with the years, but her beauty which did the same. They admired her cool mind and warm laughter, the way her eyes blazed when she was displeased with one of them. She was renowned for her almost puritanical ideas where her women servants were concerned, having been one herself, it was rumoured, and if she did not care for the insolent manner in which a gentleman treated one, she said so. She was unique. She was glorious and they would go nowhere else in town for their evening's entertainment. Where else could you find a gaming club in which honest dealing was scrupulously insisted upon? Where else could you find food that was better than that served in the finest restaurant in Paris, the wines which were brought by her husband from the best wine-growing countries in the world? Where the comfort and sheer, unadulterated luxury outdid the homes of the wealthiest in the land and where Daisy herself was always there to make a fellow feel he was the best in the world? She had this distinctive way with her without in the least relinquishing her respectability, of listening, of smiling, of flirting a little, of being completely and sincerely interested in even the most uninteresting! She moved about the place like a bright golden star, or so she had heard them say, men's eyes following her as she stopped to speak, or share a joke, the true 'Golden Lady' of the legend which had grown up about her, and it was not until her husband showed up now and again that they remembered that she was a married woman. She belonged to them all, and to no one, and her name was spoken, amongst gentlemen, of course, as far away as New York, New Orleans and many other cities where businessmen who had passed through Liverpool, gathered.

Yes, she was truly a success, in every aspect of her life, even her marriage. Only this morning she and Sam had shared fresh strawberries – brought at great expense from some hothouse – and chilled white wine, in the soft, warm splendour of their silken bed. They had made love in the night and again as dawn broke, taking and giving to one another the joyous and abandoned pleasure they had known from the very beginning and which, surprisingly, had never waned. She was very attached to him, she admitted to herself, to his lean, strong face which, nowadays, showed nothing but good-humoured tolerance for what he still called 'her little venture' though it had made more money in the two years it had been open than any of the cargoes he had carried in his clipper ship. She enjoyed his company when he was home, which was not often since he would leave for America, for Russia, for Canada and Australia, the Far East, at a moment's notice, giving her no exact idea when she might expect to see him again. Suddenly he would be there, smiling, sweeping her into his strong arms, making ardent love to her, tossing expensive presents into her naked lap saying she had earned them, expecting her undivided attention whilst he was home and if it was not freely available taking himself off, she knew quite well, to other more undistracted arms.

"My darling, here I am," he would say, "entertain me. I have a fancy to go to Ascot ... Paris ... to spend a few days in London ... a picnic at Bidston across the river and I want you by my side so are you to come? Let me look at you, no, really look at you, all of you. By God, but you've turned into a beauty, but then you don't need me to tell you that, do you, surrounded as you are by men who desire you from the four corners of the earth. Can you deny it, my sweet? of course you can't. Who would have thought it, years ago, when I rescued that scrawny child from the rough embrace of some lusty sailor . . ." and she knew he did not mind, was pleased in fact that other men wanted what belonged solely to Sam Lassiter. It appealed to the male in him to see it in their eyes and to know that soon, when they had all gone to their respective homes or hotel rooms he could do to her, and with her, what they could only dream about. He knew that she was interested in no man but him, only in what she could take from those who played in her gaming rooms. He knew that while he was away no man sampled what belonged to Sam Lassiter for he trusted her and besides, did not Jack guard with his life what Captain Lassiter had entrusted him with? She was his, when he wanted her, and if he was unfaithful to her on occasions she did not know of it. He shared no more than a fraction of his life with her but it seemed to satisfy them both. He gave her his humour, his audacious charm, his skill as a lover and his friendship and if he did not love her, then could she blame him for it? For she did not love him.

And in all this time, almost four years since she had left Thornley Green, she had not seen Miles Thornley. Though 'Daisy's' had been open for over two years and was known throughout the land by those of the gambling world, he had not once crossed her threshold though in those first months she had expected it nightly. He was a gambler of the most obsessive kind and surely such a man would be expected to try out the North's newest sporting house, or so *she* had gambled but he had never come and she had been at a loss to understand why. She had heard of his escapades – if such a foolish word could be used to describe his excesses – from Bess, who had word of them from her mother who was told of them by one or other of her sons who worked on the Thornley estate. Of his insane extravagances which had broken his poor mother's heart and spirit. Of the debts, the scandals, the promises made to his father – in the presence of Tipping, who had passed it on to the other servants until it had eventually reached the ears of Sarah's Jasper. Promises made to be broken time and time again. Of his insolence and ingratitude and though his lordship, naturally, would not say such a thing to his wife who had suffered enough, he was overheard to say privately to Sir Christopher Faulkner that there was something lacking in his son which would never be resolved whilst he moved in the bad company he kept, the loose women and wild, gambling men.

Surprisingly, eighteen months ago he had married, the very same whey-faced girl who had been present at dinner on the night of Cassie's death, Lady Caroline Woodward, who had given birth to a son herself exactly nine months after their wedding. For a while, it was said, Lord Thornley and Lady Mary had hoped that the marriage, the birth of their first grandchild, a son to inherit what would one day belong to their son, would bring him to his senses, would settle him to his responsibilities but it seemed they had been disappointed. They had, Daisy had heard from Bess, increased his allowance for was he not a married man with a family but it went the way of the rest, swallowed up in a life which no married man should lead.

Daisy sighed and stood up, moving to one of the long windows of the drawing room, staring out sightlessly across the roofs of the houses which ran in a shallow slope all the way to the river. She could see the water of the Mersey from up here, hazed with a pale winter sunshine, and the slight mist which was beginning to form as the short day came to a close. Ships moved through it soundlessly and for a surprising moment she felt her heart stir for somewhere Sam was on a ship sailing across some deep, unknown water, his face no doubt grinning into the sea-wind for there was nowhere he would rather be than on the deck of his clipper *Golden Lady*. She knew that and accepted it so why, for God's sake, should she feel a deep sense of sadness at the thought?

She turned as Bess entered the room, glad somehow to

push Sam and his long absences to the back of her mind. She smiled warmly.

"Bess, there you are. Come in and I'll have some tea sent up. See, get to the fire and lift your feet to the warmth. You must be frozen. Did you fetch Nelly, then? Is she all right? And your mother? How did she take it?"

All the while she was talking she was fussing around Bess, drawing her to the deep velvet sofa which stood at right angles to the fire, plumping up a cushion at her back, bringing her a footstool and personally putting Bess's sensibly black-booted feet upon it. She leaned across her to ring the bell, the exotic aroma of the perfume Sam brought her from across the world drifting lightly on the air. She was beautifully dressed in an afternoon gown of coffee-coloured silk, plain and quite unadorned but for the multiple flounces, each one edged in coffee-coloured velvet, which frothed about the enormous skirt. In her ears were heavy gold ear-bobs and her glossy hair was arranged in a soft but intricate coil at the back of her head. She was about twenty-one now, she reckoned, and though her beauty was not classical for her face was too strong for that, she had a look about her, an expression of vitality, a glow which was more than beauty. Beside her Bess looked like a small brown sparrow put next to a glorious bird of paradise.

"Stop fussing, Daisy, for heaven's sake. Anyone would think I was in me dotage the way you're carryin' on. I *can* put me own feet on a stool, you know," but though Bess's voice was sharp and her manner exasperated there was a fond gleam in her eye as she looked at Daisy.

Unexpectedly she took her hand. "Sit down, love," she said gently, "and never mind the tea."

Daisy looked at her in amazement, then at their clasped hands for the gesture of affection was so unlike Bess. It quite alarmed her and she sat down obediently on the sofa beside her.

"What is it?" she asked, her voice apprehensive. "Is there something wrong? Is it your mother or one of the family? Or is it Nelly? Will she not suit?" though why that should bring the strange expression to Bess's face she couldn't imagine.

"No, it's not me Mam, nor our Nelly. It's the Thornleys."

Daisy stiffened and into her eyes came the ice-cold patina of hatred which always settled there whenever the Thornleys' name was mentioned. Not that she ever did anything to prevent Bess from talking about them whenever she had any news from her mother and which she always passed on to Daisy. Far from it, Bess had found. She was always eager to hear anything she could about them, demanding that Bess tell her everything she had heard, every little detail though Bess was of the opinion that that part of their lives – especially Daisy's – was best forgotten. Still, this must be told her.

"There's been an accident, lass."

"An accident?" Daisy clutched Bess's hand fiercely though her face remained quite without expression.

"Aye. His lordship. Come off his horse this morning and broke his neck."

"Dead?"

"Aye, so they say."

"So . . . *he's* the new Lord Thornley."

"So it seems, and God help all his tenants for they'll need it."

28

It was as though he had been waiting for the harvest of wealth which was now his to spend without stint, without thought since there was so much of it, without anyone to obstruct him for did it not now all belong exclusively to him, before venturing into the relatively new gaming house in Liverpool about which he had heard so much.

He had meant to go whenever he was at Thornley Green but with the disapproval of his father and the reproach of his mother hanging over him each time he came home, he had been inclined to spend as much time as he could away from his ancestral acres, lingering in London, in Leicestershire hunting with his friends, in Baden-Baden and Rome, in Venice and Paris. His wife and son were dutifully cared for by Lord and Lady Thornley and did not need him and if they had it would have been all the same to him. He had only married the plain and witless cow to get his father off his back and to gain for himself a bigger allowance, but now it was all his to squander as he liked.

And there was so much of it, more than he had ever imagined. Vast tracts of land, farming land from which enormous rents were raised, property in London from which untold wealth poured, money that would last his lifetime no matter what extravagances he indulged in.

They buried Hugh Charles Thornley, the Fourteenth Baron of that name, on a hard and frosty morning a week later, his grieving widow leaning heavily on the arm of her son Miles, Lord Thornley, and by nine o'clock that evening, the same young gentleman, Fifteenth Baron of the line, was strolling with all the arrogance of his kind, accompanied by a number of his wild gentleman friends and several 'ladies' of dubious morality, into the magnificent hallway of 'Daisy's' gaming house.

Daisy was at the head of the stairs exchanging a smiling word with Sir John Templeton who, though his advances had been rejected good-humouredly by his hostess on a number of occasions during the past two and a half years, still pretended he would not accept defeat.

"You are a rogue, Sir John, and would break a lady's heart if allowed."

"Would I could break yours, Daisy, but I feel it is made of stone."

"Not really, sir, but given to my husband."

"Lucky dog," and they were both laughing as she turned

away, aware now, both of them, that it was only a pleasant game they played.

She wore a vivid gown of satin, somewhere between blue and green, a smooth sheath absolutely contrary to the fashion of the day which was for enormous sleeves and skirts. From the back of her knees a full fluted train fanned out, requiring a neat kick from her blue satin shoes in order not to trip over it. Her buttermilk shoulders and half-exposed breasts rose from the low neckline and about her throat and in her ears she wore gems of turquoise, Sam's gift to her on their first wedding anniversary and the exact shade of her dress. She was still extremely slender. Her back and neck were long and graceful and beautifully curved, her breasts though small were high and rounded and every male within fifty feet of her was conscious, as she walked down the curving staircase, of his own manhood.

"It's a good thing I'm home, my love, if you are to wear that ... well, I hardly dare call it a dress ... you have on. Every man in the place will be eager to see it slip even further though I must admit the sight of your ... er ... anatomy would delight any man who *is* a man. I had better stay within sight of you so that should you require it I can protect your honour and mine as your husband," and though Daisy smiled as she kissed him before they left their bedroom she was well aware that the words were not spoken lightly.

Her eyes met those of Miles Thornley as she was halfway down the stairs and though she had been waiting for this moment for nearly three years she felt the shock of it punch her in the chest, drawing the breath from her lungs. She was going to faint, she knew she was, as the blood drained from her head and her legs turned as soft and boneless as the apple jelly she had seen carried into the supper room only an hour since. It was not called that, of course, but had some fancy French name dreamed up by Chef Armande. Drenched in some potent sauce, decorated with fruit and cream, laced with nuts, that was what it was, nevertheless, apple jelly, and that was exactly how she felt as she fluttered insubstantially down the stairs towards the man she had loved and now loathed with an obsession which surely must destroy her. She had waited, patient as an exotic spider, for him to come to her and now he was here and she must let no man – and certainly not Sam who had gone down a step or two ahead of her and now stood, arms folded, in the doorway to the supper room, – see how devastated she was.

For the space of half a minute he didn't recognise her and she felt those warmly appreciative, boldly appraising eyes run over her body from the crown of her burnished hair to the tip of her blue satin slippers. They lingered indolently on her breasts before rising lazily for another look at her frozen face and she saw the recognition smash at him and drain the warm amber from beneath his smooth skin. Her own face had turned the colour of pipeclay.

He was the first to recover. "Well, well, if it isn't my mother's kitchenmaid," he drawled. He began to smile, the lazy cynical smile she knew so well. She watched the cruel mouth curve over his white teeth. He raised one eyebrow in a question and the brilliant blue of his eyes gleamed at the prospect of the renewed chase he anticipated and which would end as it always did with the beautiful woman who was his prey, in his bed. Daisy Brindle, despite their past differences would be the same, she could see the certainty in his smiling expression, his arrogant, well-bred assurance, and the advantage he had put in her hands gave her the steadier she needed to walk gracefully towards him, her hand outstretched, her face serene and smiling.

"Good evening, Lord Thornley," she said. "How splendid to meet you again after all these years. May I offer my condolences on the tragic death of your father."

He didn't like that. She was, after all, not of his class. He lifted his handsome head and there was a touch of ice in his vivid blue eyes. Sam Lassiter straightened up slowly, his face expressionless but in his eyes was a curious glow as they studied his wife and the man she seemed to be challenging.

"I see you remember me, Lord Thornley," she continued warmly, "though it is some years since we met. A dinner party at Thornley Green, as I remember. I believe your wife was there as well, though of course you weren't married then. She is in good health, I hope, and your son?"

She was audacious in her courage, in her challenge of this man who could be dangerous should he take offence. Sam felt the constriction tighten about his heart. In his eyes the glow deepened and had she turned to look at him she would have seen the admiration in them but her whole attention was concentrated on Miles Thornley and the desperate need she had to keep a tight control on the delicate balance of the tension between them. She wanted so badly, so frighteningly to spring at him, to hurt him, wound him, *kill* him in any way she could, the hatred she had known the last time they had met not in the least diminished by the years between. It was as though she had just come from the death stench of Cassie's room, from the desolation and despair that had nailed Robert and Emma Greenhalgh, their servants who had loved Cassie, and herself, to a crucifix of sorrow. It was with her still, though she spoke of it to no one, the grief, the torment of knowing that Cassie's death could be laid at no one's door but her own, and at this man's, and now he was here to pay for it. She would discharge *her* debt for the rest of her life.

"How the hell did you . . . ?" It was in his eyes and his arrogantly curling mouth, the amazement he felt at seeing her here, but before he could finish the sentence which might lead to something she could not contain, she took his arm prettily. "Will you not accompany me into the supper room, Lord Thornley?" Her smile was brilliant and irresistible. "I can promise you a splendid claret, or a glass or two of champagne if you prefer, and then you might care for a game of hazarde or roulette? Yes, you are quite right, I am the Daisy Brindle you once knew but it is Daisy Lassiter now . . ." nodding casually in the direction of Sam who had resumed his lounging position beside the doorway through which she led Miles Thornley. She watched the hard planes of her husband's face as they grew rigid. His mouth had thinned and his eyes had turned to a gleaming icy green. He did not like what she was doing, nor the man whose arm she held, and if she did not walk this tightrope she

430

was on with the utmost care she would tumble off quite devastatingly. But she would deal with Sam later. First she must make this bastard believe that she bore him no ill will, that there was nothing in fact to even consider in their past, which would not be hard, she could see that, for it had meant nothing to him.

"...so if you will be patient with me I will explain it all to you..."

"Don't trouble yourself, my dear Daisy, since I'm sure whatever it is you have you are to be applauded for it. You always were ... well ... we shall not go into that here. We shall be friends again, I'm sure. Come, let us drink to it with that fine champagne you promised me," and the man who was Daisy Lassiter's husband moved slowly into the supper room behind them, followed by the shrill chattering laughter of the crowd of ladies and gentlemen who had come in with the new Lord Thornley.

"Perhaps you could tell me what game you were playing this evening, madam?" Sam's voice was more of a snarl. He snatched at her arm, bringing her sharply about to face him, his face strangely menacing and no more than six inches from her own. "I've yet to see a performance as polished as the one you put on for that swaggering libertine and what I should like to know, if it's not too much to ask, is what it was all for? By God, you have no conception of how close you were to having the hiding of your life and that smirking nincompoop his lovely white teeth knocked down his throat and so I'll have some answers now, if you please, and they had better be the truth. I am well aware that you consider that you and your sister were shabbily done by in the past..."

"Shabbily done by! *Shabbily done by!* My God, he *killed* her, for Christ's sake..."

"Don't be melodramatic, Daisy. Oh, I know he seduced her and she became pregnant but it was hardly his fault that she miscarried..."

"You heartless bastard! You supercilious, cold-blooded bastard, but then what could you expect from a *man*? From

431

someone who can see no wrong in helping himself to any woman he has a fancy for whenever the urge takes him. To throwing some poor girl's skirts over her head to stop her protests, to holding her down and ripping his way into her without thought, nor care for the consequences. It is not *he* who has to suffer them, after all. It is not *he* who is violated, made to feel filthy and degraded and ashamed to be in the company of decent folk and it is not *he* who has to carry and bear the child which is more often than not the outcome of his five minutes' pleasure . . ."

"Daisy . . ." He had begun to look unsure, the ferocity of her obvious pain diluting his own rage. He had been ready to savage her with his mixed and shadowy emotions which had got severely out of hand as he had watched her charm Miles Thornley. The man's eyes had roamed about her body with indecent boldness, with the confident knowledge which had reminded Sam that Miles Thornley had once been Daisy's lover and it had taken all his iron self-control to keep from striding across the supper room and smashing his fist into the man's handsome, audaciously smiling face. Only the fact that they were in full view of two dozen members, all of whom wished they could be in the shoes of the lucky fellow who was making Daisy laugh so engagingly, kept him from it. After all, they were doing nothing that could offend even the most devoted husband, and who was he to lay claim to that title? As long as he could keep them within his line of vision, watch them to see that they did not leave the room together, he must pretend unconcern. She was, after all, the hostess of the club, its co-owner, and must be pleasant to its clients.

"Daisy . . ." he repeated.

"I thought you understood," she went on passionately. "You know what he did to me, let alone Cassie. I was a child, a naïve child and he used me, turned me into his whore . . . yes, that's what he did before he grew tired of me. I was no more than a diversion whilst he waited for something more exciting to come along. But I had accepted that. It . . . it broke my heart which, I do appreciate, was that of a young girl, but . . . it was almost more than I could stand, Sam.

Nevertheless, I had to stand it. I had to get on with my life, but Cassie ... aah, dear sweet Jesus ... Cassie..."

Tears rained down her ashen face, falling in a great torrent from her chin to her heaving breasts, staining the lovely shimmering blue of her gown and Sam, appalled now, tried to take her in his arms but she fought him off.

"Don't ... don't touch me or I swear I'll take your eyes out ..."

"Daisy, please ... I really had no idea. I still don't know ..."

"Well, now you *do* know. Now you know how much I loathe him, not for what he did to me for that, as you so kindly remind me, is an old story and one which even you seem to find hardly worth considering. I suppose even the rape of a defenceless fourteen-year-old, though somewhat more unusual, at least in the circle you move in, is not something to make a fuss about. A fourteen-year-old girl is still, after all, merely a female, to be used for men's pleasure and convenience. But, I stray from the point which is that Miles Thornley killed my Cassie, not personally, I agree, but by what he did to her. She had the innocent mind of a child but he found that no stumbling-block when he made use of her young woman's body. I will admit that she ... seemed to take no harm from it, physically or mentally, since none of us saw signs of distress in her. She must have been ... with him on several occasions, trusting, submitting to what he wanted of her since I know she ... loved him. He was ... nice with her but that is not the ... that does not make it ... that only makes it ... that only makes it ... Oh, dear God, can you not see what a perverted fiend he is? He impregnated her with a child and her child's body rejected it and it killed her. So you see, Sam, though I may have given the impression that I found pleasure in the new Lord Thornley's company, my flesh crawled and my stomach heaved and the blood in my veins turned to ice whilst he sat beside me. Even his eyes on me were slugs creeping over my body but I will continue to make myself pleasant to him whenever he comes in here if it means I can do to him what he did to Cassie and me."

"And what is that, Daisy?"

Sam's voice was low but steady now. He stood before her, his hands in his pockets so that she could not see his clenched fists. His face was dark and inscrutable. His mouth was firm, his lips clamped tightly together. His eyes looked dark in the reflection of the lamplight, dark and sombre as the deep swell of the oceans he crossed. His eyebrows were drawn down above them and in the curve of his jaw a muscle jumped. His hair, which he wore long over his collar, had fallen across his forehead and for one moment she felt the surprising urge to put up a hand and brush it back but her mind was too fevered to wonder at it.

"I must make him pay for what he did, Sam. I believe he should be punished as the law will not punish him." Her voice was quiet, steady now, with none of the impassioned wildness of the past half-hour. "I don't expect you to help me. I know you cannot understand the way I feel but can I ask you not to stand in my way?"

"To what, Daisy? What do you intend to do to this man? What *can* you do to this man which is within the law?"

"Oh, I shan't break the law, believe me. I don't intend to hang for him, if that's what you're thinking. No, he's taken enough from me already and I don't mean him to have my life."

"What then?" His eyes bored into hers and his clenched fists moved savagely deep inside his trouser pockets where she could not see.

"He took everything from me four years ago. Everything I held dear. Now I intend to have everything from him. Everything *he* holds dear. His good name, which despite his reputation, is still honoured by his peers for they respected his father. His title, his inheritance. I have the means to do it now, you see, with this club. Do you know how much he lost tonight, Sam? No, of course you don't since you take little interest in the accounts. Well, I will tell you. He lost ten thousand guineas. *Ten thousand guineas!* He was like a man possessed. A man with a deep and bottomless pocket of money which, now that he is Lord Thornley of Thornley Green, he can dip into as often as he pleases for it will never be empty. He scattered promissory notes about like confetti, owing money to all those good friends of his who know they will be honoured, and others besides, those who are not his friends and who were quite willing to let me have them and receive what they were owed. And that does not include what he lost to the 'bank'. So, one day I will have it all, I swear it, not through *my* efforts but through his madness. Someone would have it from him, you can be sure of that, but I intend it to be me. Does that answer your question?"

She turned her back on him then, moving across to the dressing-table. She dropped her earrings carelessly on to the lacy top, her attitude implying that there were plenty more where those came from. In her manner was supreme indifference, to him, to his opinions, to his feelings, whatever they might be, and it was this which broke his containment. With an oath he sprang after her, turning her about to face him. He put his hands one on either side of her head, tearing her hair from its fastenings so that it fell about her, down her back, across her shoulders and breasts and face. She looked wild, a gypsy in her dishevelled beauty, and he held her between his hard hands, gripping her head cruelly.

His mouth came down on hers, moving fiercely, biting her soft, full underlip, forcing her backwards with his strength, dominating her in the only way he knew. She was as strong as he in every way but this. In her mind and heart and resolution she was as strong as he and he knew he would never subdue her will to his but he could master her body which suddenly he desperately needed to do.

His hands crushed her head, then, cruelty flowing from him at the feel of her familiar silken hair beneath them, becoming sensual and tender at the same time. They brushed it from her forehead and his lips went to her hairline, slipping softly to her ear, the line of her resolute jaw which said she would not give in. Under her chin, to the wildly beating hollow at the base of her throat and along the soft white curve of her shoulder. His hands held her beneath her armpits whilst his mouth explored in a leisurely but determined manner the top of her breasts, then, as he increased their pressure, drawing down the bodice of her dress until the breasts were exposed. They gleamed like white silk in the lamplight, the tiny buds of her nipples a rich rosy pink, hard in the centre of the aureole. His hands reached for them, ready to grip her cruelly again should she deny him but she was sighing for him now, whimpering in the back of her throat which arched with her body to more easily accommodate his. He grinned in triumph for she was *his* woman now, without thought, without mind, senseless and drowning in the sea of love they swam in together.

"You're mine," he shouted harshly, backing her on to the bed.

"Oh yes." Her voice was husky and eternally female.

"Then you will have no objection to this, I take it?" and lifting her skirts he threw them over her head so that she was blind and lost and when he entered her, her body exploded into orgasm after orgasm, wave on wave of it as she lay, like any field girl on her back under her man.

Slowly he drew her skirts down and lifted her up into his arms. She was dazed with it, only half aware of him and his warm and gentle embrace. He kissed her softly, smoothing her tangled hair back from her unfocused eyes as though she was a fretful child, crooning some words which she could not distinguish. He was completely in control of her as she floated back from the rapture he had created for her and when he took her gown from her and put her in their bed, divesting himself of his own garments and laying his lean body beside hers, she pressed herself wordlessly against him before falling into a deep and dreamless sleep.

He was there when she awoke and beside the bed were the fresh strawberries, glistening in their ripe perfection, and two glasses of chilled white wine, just as there always was when they celebrated some success one or the other of them had just achieved. A sea-journey in record time bearing rich profits. A contract snatched from a rival ship's captain, a bargain made over a cargo, a storm beaten. A new member whose name was linked with royalty, a night on which the 'bank' overflowed with its winnings. And next morning the champagne and strawberries which had become a ritual, a symbol of their partnership, a shared pleasure known only to the two of them, and Jack!

She smiled and stretched, turning her face into his shoulder, shaking her hair across him in a heavy, silken curtain.

"Does this mean I am forgiven?" Her mouth was soft in the curve beneath his chin and he held her to him, turning his own face away so that she might not notice the emotion written there for anyone, even the most blind, to see. But his voice when he answered was light.

"Oh, I don't know about that. I would have to be more fully convinced that you are completely penitent. Show me," and she did until they were both spent in the warmth of their passion. He held her close afterwards and his voice was soft as he spoke into her tumbled hair.

"Don't do anything foolish, my pet, will you? Don't do anything which both of us might regret. I don't think I fully realised the . . . the extent of your feelings about Cassie and your need for . . . justice . . ." He did not care for the word revenge. His arms tightened about her though he kept his voice cool and light. "Miles Thornley is a bastard of the first order. One of the very worst examples of his class and his upbringing. He has been reared in the belief that, as a member of the ruling classes, he is entitled to anything the expectations of his privileged birth tell him is his due but even after what he did to you and your sister, and the tragedy it caused, I would not like to think you were capable of . . . of shabbiness in your dealings with him. I have always known you to be fair and honest. Promise me you will do nothing to make me change my mind."

She sat up, pushing back her hair with both hands. The light from the window shone in a pale winter hue through the partly drawn curtains, touching her long, graceful back, creating faint, horizontal shadows where the scars from the gangmaster's whip crossed it. He touched them gently for, as nothing else ever could, they reminded him of the horror of her childhood. She was scarred for life from it. Her skin which was smooth and rich as cream on the rest of her body was raised in narrow weals where he had flogged her. And

437

was she as scarred inside as she was on the exterior of her lovely body? he asked himself wordlessly. Was her mind blemished by what had been done to her in her childhood and girlhood by the two men who had used her? He had not thought so. In the years he had known her she had seemed to him to be marvellously blessed with a steadfast good sense, an equanimity and, yes, a sweetness which had not been soured by her vile experiences. Of course she was quick-tempered, hot-headed and self-willed but that was a part of her and in no way detracted from her charm. He wanted nothing to change in her, nothing. She looked at him now, her expression serious, and her eyes were clear and steady.

"I must be honest with you, Sam, since you would soon know it if I was not."

"Yes?" His questioning voice was wary and his hand on her back became still.

"I cannot just forget Cassie and what Miles Thornley did to her."

"I don't expect you to, my love. What I don't want you to do, which seems to me after what you said last night, to be your purpose, is to spend your life fruitlessly trying to . . . to make him pay for it."

"I shan't, Sam. I can promise you that," and she grinned suddenly, then leaned down to kiss him before leaping from the bed. He watched her stride across the room, her movements almost boyish but her white body was long and slender and elegant, completely female in the muted morning light. She flung back the curtains and stood for a moment outlined against the pale winter sky which could be seen above the rooftops of the houses opposite. She seemed to be filled with some gladness, as though a promise had been fulfilled, and he wondered as he watched her why it was that her words, which should have satisfied him, left him with an unease which, though he saw no difference in her for the remainder of his stay in port, he took with him as his *Golden Lady* flew down the Mersey towards the open sea.

Sam had gone when Miles Thornley came again to 'Daisy's' and it took all her ingenuity to keep him at arm's length for he seemed to believe that there was nothing to prevent them from renewing the relationship they had once known. Indeed, now that she was a woman of the world, a sophisticated and beautiful woman whose husband left her at home alone for long periods of time, it made perfect sense! The past was the past, after all, and long gone as far as he was concerned and he was not one to bear a grudge, he told her magnanimously. She had made that dreadful scene, humiliating him in front of his family and friends, but that had long been forgotten by them and by his mother who was content in the company of her daughter-in-law and grandchild. His father was dead and besides, it was all rather a hazed memory in his own mind, which, more often than not when he visited 'Daisy's', was clouded somewhat by the enormous amount of brandy he drank. The trusting face, the wide eyes and sweet trembling body of Cassie Greenhalgh had merged with the dozens of others he had known, before and since, and what had become of her, and them, was no concern of his, and if he remembered that she was the purported sister of the woman he now lusted after, it is doubtful that would have concerned him either.

"Stay with me, Bess," she instructed her friend. "When he comes in I'll send Jacob for you" – one of the footmen – "and you must not leave my side until he sits down to play. While he's at the table he forgets all about me. I've got to keep him pleasant, somehow, and not antagonise him but at the same time, until he finds someone else who takes his fancy I've got to keep him at arm's length. God, I loathe him, Bess. It takes me all my time to be civil to him but this is the only way I can make him pay for what he did. Remember how I told you I would ride in my carriage up to the front door of Thornley Green? Well, I shall, but in the meantime . . ."

"I've other things to do besides wet-nurse you, lady, and well you know it. And you also know I don't agree with this daft idea you've got in your head so you must deal with his lordship's advances yourself and if he persists show him the door like you do the others. You must know you can't do 'owt to harm him, Daisy. He's too powerful, too rich and he's friendly with about every high-born family in the land. What can *you* do? Oh, I know you've a bit of brass yourself now and you're a success in this club. You know some influential people too, I've no doubt, but you have a fine husband so why not forget the past, lass, and get on with your life? Forget what he did to Cassie an' you for it'll bring you nothing but heartache if you persist with this foolishness. You'll not break a man of his position."

But Daisy only smiled. When she was alone she would reach for the box she kept locked in a drawer in the desk where she sat to do what she called her 'bank-keeping'. A box which contained not the accounts of the club but a growing sheaf of notes on which Miles Thornley's signature was scrawled. There were also records of transactions, all bearing the name of Thornley transferred to that of Daisy Lassiter, and as the months and the years passed, the box became two. By the end of 1860 there were three boxes in Daisy Lassiter's desk drawer and all containing the means to bring about the downfall of Lord Thornley, Fifteenth Baron of the line, peer of the realm, the man whom she hated with a cold passion which is the most dangerous of all.

29

Their lives moved on, each day and each week the same, the pattern changing little beyond the recognition that they were becoming, through the success of the gaming house and the profitable voyages made by the *Golden Lady*, rather wealthy.

"Where has this come from, my darling?" Sam would ask

her casually, indicating an increase in their already healthy bank balance, and she would answer just as casually that she had made, through the advice and instigation of Mr Banfield, their bank manager, a rather splendid investment, giving no hint of the true state of affairs which was that she was becoming a shrewd businesswoman who could scent a bargain, a gamble, a chance to make a profit – which she was not slow to take – where many others would not. She could read the financial newspapers as other women would read a light novelette and her sharp mind and daring often staggered the more cautious Mr Banfield.

"What a clever girl you are, my sweet," kissing her in that light and easy way he had, making rather less of it than she sometimes would have wished. He was the same with her as he had been when he had found her on the Marine Parade, ready to sell herself to the first sailor who came ashore. He was a witty, charming and good-humoured friend, an inventive lover, and she no longer wondered why he had married her, since she imagined she knew. She gave him comfort when he was home, luxury even. She was there, *his*, the moment he returned from his journeying, uncomplicated and good-natured, asking no questions of a serious, personal nature. She demanded nothing of him in the way a wife would be expected to and so he was able to live the life of an eligible bachelor without the attendant irritations of hopeful mothers trying to snare him for their daughters, or eager ladies wishing to put a stronger hold on him than he was prepared to endure. She supposed he was shallow and self-centred in his determination to live his life just as he wished it to be but could she blame him for that since she was exactly the same? They suited one another, she told herself, then wondered why she should sometimes feel a strange sensation of lack, of emptiness, when after all she had everything she had ever dreamed of.

Only last week she had purchased some property in London, a row of rather splendid Georgian houses which had come on the market, the deeds of which had gone into her private strongbox to reside with all the other documents which bore the name of Thornley. She had the most exquisite wardrobe of clothes, thanks to the artistry of the Misses Yeoland. Her afternoon dresses in which she often took the bracing sea-air with Bess beside her were the talk of the town, pastel-tinted, creams and whites. Her richly patterned shawls, brought her by Sam from India and China and other exotic places, were the envy of every woman who studied them, and her, as she walked the promenade on Sam's arm when he was home. Her walking dresses, her bonnets, her furs, her jewels, most of them carelessly flung in her lap by Sam and of the most expensive and exquisite kind, sparkled and glowed at her throat, her wrists and ears. She wore strands of pearls, perfectly matched and lustrous, nets of gold chain to hold her heavy hair which her husband would not allow her to cut, military boots with a long skirt slashed at the hem to show them off and with every day that passed she grew richer and more lovely, to the chagrin of those ladies who had been brought up to believe that purity and goodness had its own rich reward. If that was the case why did the brazen Daisy Lassiter, who had neither, continue to thrive?

It was said that she and her indulgent husband were contemplating building themselves a brand-new house on the outskirts of Liverpool, where the rich and influential shipowners and merchants lived. They had no need to 'live over the shop' any more and indeed 'the shop' or rather the sporting house which was making them a fortune, or even two, was to be extended when the house next door to it fell vacant in the spring. There was even talk of a ballroom where a gentleman might dance with the lady of his choosing and what sort would that be? they wondered. Where would it all lead, they asked one another, when a woman with the morals of an alley cat and a man who was unscrupulous in his business dealings, or so the men of Liverpool would have it, could flourish like weeds when better folk had to work so hard just to sustain a decent standard of living, let alone better it?

"I don't care for the situation in America," Sam said one afternoon towards the end of January, turning the page of the newspaper he was reading. "Things seem to be getting somewhat out of hand and if they're not careful they will find themselves with a serious crisis on their hands."

"Oh, and why is that?" Daisy was not really listening. She was recalling the previous evening when, for the fifth night in a row, Miles Thornley had entered her establishment, surrounded as always by the sycophants and hangers-on who nowadays always seemed to accompany him. The gentlemen who had once been his companions had drifted away as they left their wild youth behind them, settling down to the duties which were the obligation of the privileged classes who inherited the great names and great estates left in their care. Freddy Rawstrone, the son of a viscount, Ernest Woodward whose father was a baronet, Thomas Hemingway whose father had no title but whose mother was the niece of an earl and whose name was as old and venerated as any in the land. They had married and settled down to their responsibilities, as they had been destined to do, to the life which even they with their inbred arrogance knew they could not avoid. Tenants, though they owned it, of the land they held in trust for the future generations of their name. Their place at Miles Thornley's side had been taken by a younger and even more wild and swaggering band of gentlemen, bent, it seemed, on killing not only themselves on their mad round of gambling, drinking and womanising, but anyone who got in their way. Nineteen years old, twenty, no more, to his twenty-nine, he was their leader, the man they would all like to be, an artist in the pursuit of pleasure, of debauchery, since there was no doubt there was no man who could outmatch him at it.

"Good evening, Daisy, glorious evening," he drawled as he threw his caped evening coat to a footman. Her wide entrance hall had seemed too small suddenly as it erupted with young lordlings at play, their superb self-command and overbearing arrogance an almost indecent invasion of the lovely, fragile elegance she had created. For a moment she wanted to plant her hands on her hips and glare her displeasure. Ask them who the hell they thought they were disturbing the gracious calm of her house and if they could not keep a civil tongue in their heads and behave themselves they would be shown the door. As she would have done had it not been for *him*. He it was who was always allowed, much to the amazement and annoyance of her other guests, to shatter the peace and set the serving girls on their ears as Lord Thornley's party strode about the place as though they owned it.

"Good evening, Lord Thornley," she answered pleasantly, watching as one of the gentlemen carelessly threw his cigar stub to the floor and crushed it into her lovely carpet beneath his foot. "It is indeed a lovely evening, so clear and frosty. Do come to the fire with your friends and drink a glass of champagne. Or would you prefer mulled wine as it is so cold?" and it was almost more than she could manage to keep the smile on her face good-humoured and professionally warm. If she crossed him, or displeased him, or máde it in any way plain that his destructive young friends were anything other than absolutely welcome he would go elsewhere to chuck his fortune away, which he did with the obsessive compulsion of the dedicated gambler. Week in and week out, here and in London, abroad at the casinos of Baden-Baden and Hamburg, he continued to erode the fortune his father had left in his care, casually gambling away thousands of pounds as though what he had was never-ending. Sometimes, of course, he won, which only encouraged him to continue, often far into the next day and a second night, whether it suited Daisy or not, expecting to be served with delicious, freshly cooked food on demand; to have champagne or claret or brandy constantly at his elbow. And she let him for it was only in this way could she destroy him.

He had, for the moment at least, given up his intention of renewing what he liked to call their 'friendship', no doubt due to the beautiful young woman who had been willing, for a considerable sum of Daisy's money, to 'entertain' him in his depraved sexual proclivities, to divert him from his enthusiastic onslaught on Daisy. The woman, Cécile, had been with him the previous evening, stunningly dressed in a low-cut froth of lace and sequins, her face that of an innocent child but in her eyes the world-weary expression of a woman who has little illusion left. She was a highly paid whore, much sought after by the gentlemen of the city. She might choose her lovers where she pleased and Miles Thornley wore her openly on his arm and what he did to her in his bed Daisy did not care to contemplate. It was enough that he left *her* alone and if she had to pay for it it was well worth the cost.

Sometimes she felt as though the tightrope she walked was none too securely fastened to its supports, stumbling, when Miles was in the club and Sam home from his travels, from one safe corner to another, the rope between threatening to tip her off into an abyss of disaster. She owned a great deal of what had once belonged to the Thornley family now. Property in London and St Helens and only last week a farm, just a tiny portion of the vast Thornley Green estate, had been bought by some anonymous gentleman, through his agent. The deeds to the farm were in her box in the locked drawer of her desk. She had IOUs by the score, from many parts of the country and even abroad for John Elliott had friends in many casinos and sporting houses and knew exactly where his lordship was and to whom he had given them. When the gentleman who was owed the money was willing to sell an IOU, Daisy, through John, bought it. The agents she employed were careful whom they approached since many of the gentlemen, from the same privileged class as Lord Thornley and, as gentlemen, hanging together, might have become suspicious but most, on the whole, were glad to be rid of the debt and have the money Miles Thornley owed them put in their hand. He never paid his debts in cash, handing out scraps of paper to any man who won from him at cards, with his name, the date, the amount and the signature of a witness scrawled across it, casually saying that his bank would settle it if they cared to present it. He had apparently never queried or, she presumed, even knew that these notes had not been cashed, continuing to deplete his estate with the carelessness of a child.

But increasingly, as the vast supply of ready cash dwindled away, he gave orders for some of his property, a coal-mine or two in which he had no interest, some farming land in

Northumberland, since he never saw it anyway, only a fraction here and there when compared to the size of his estate, to be put on the market. After all, a chap must pay his tailor and his wine merchant and have the price of a good hunter in his pocket. He must have the wherewithal to maintain the Thornley hunt and his personal stables expenses. His private kennels cost him upwards of three thousand pounds a year. There were his racing debts to be paid, though there again he found a promissory note was often accepted from Lord Thornley, friend of the nobility and even royalty; there was the upkeep of Thornley Green, the house itself, though he was seldom in it except during the hunting season, having bought himself several smaller but more convenient establishments in London and Liverpool and another to be close to Ascot, plus a splendid villa in the South of France. When he visited his home he liked to entertain on a lavish scale, to give parties and balls during the hunting season, the grouse in August, and there were often upwards of four dozen guests at a Friday to Monday party. They were wild, turning bawdy, it was said, and fewer and fewer ladies, real ladies, were willing to attend. His own wife and mother were two of them for his young friends, sons of gentlemen, true, but flaunting and disorderly, dashing about the house and estate at a furious, hell-bent pace, were not to the liking of Lady Mary and Lady Caroline who, it was rumoured, was pregnant with her second child. There were 'ladies' there nevertheless, ladies with vulgar accents who were inclined to loud and vulgar laughter and the servants whispered of such goings-on along the bedroom corridors and even on the billiard-room tables that there were fears of young housemaids being unsafe in their own beds at night.

When the time came Daisy Lassiter would call in her money and the law, the justice to which she was entitled and which now must uphold her, would be seen to be done.

"... Lincoln elected to President and the slave states are talking of seceding from the free states and forming a Republic of their own ..."

"I'm sorry, Sam, you were saying ...?"

She shifted her clouded gaze from the heart of the fire

which glowed and crackled in the wide fireplace. It was almost four o'clock and time she was going down to the kitchens to check with Bess and Jack, with Chef Armande and Sobey, the man who saw to her wine cellar, on the arrangements which must always be perfect for the comfort and entertainment of her guests. There was a distinct possibility that tonight one of them would be a certain prince of the realm who was passing through Liverpool on his way to some jaunt which would, no doubt, not please his royal Mama, nor her pious husband, but Daisy had been warned that he had discreetly expressed a desire to visit her establishment. A great honour and one which would do no harm to the reputation of the club. But Sam was looking at her, one dark eyebrow raised in quizzical amusement.

"I was saying, my sweet, though I hardly think you heard me that there is to be trouble in America."

"Oh, what kind of trouble?"

"Surely you, with your finger on the pulse of the financial world, must have heard the rumours? You read the newspapers and they have been full of it. The northern and southern states have been growing further and further apart during the past year. Differences of economic policy are partly to blame but the question of slavery..."

"Oh, that?" She dismissed the matter of the American difficulties with a somewhat careless shrug which was not at all like her and he studied her more closely. She was well read, he knew, and vitally interested in all matters of national and even international importance. She could discuss with any gentleman who showed the slightest inclination to do so most topics which were in the news and yet she appeared to be singularly uninformed about the growing unrest in America. Come to think of it she had seemed somewhat vague, and concerned only with her own affairs lately, those that dealt with the running of the club and the proposed extension to the house on the other side of his original home which they had recently acquired. But now, somehow, it seemed to him it was more than that.

He kept his thoughts to himself. "Yes, that," he said instead, telling himself he would watch her more closely from now on. "The abolitionists are calling for the liberation of the slaves. They are Northerners, naturally, since the Southern states rely heavily on slave labour for their prosperity..."

"Yes, yes, I read about it in the *Liverpool Mercury* but I can't see why it should lead to conflict between the states. Can they not settle their differences amicably?"

"It seems not. Last month the state of South Carolina voted itself out of the Union and already Mississippi, Florida, Alabama and half a dozen others are talking of doing the same. So you see..."

"Yes, it is really most interesting but I shall have to stop you, Sam, and continue later. I have so much to do and if it's true what they say about His Royal Highness visiting us at the club this evening everything must be absolutely perfect."

"Of course, my pet, I can quite see you must be extremely anxious to oversee every small detail so off you go and polish the playing cards or whatever it is one does when royalty is about to descend on one. Shall I wear my new ruffled shirt, d'you think, and practise my bow or is that going too far?"

His ironic grin was completely lost on her but she smiled vaguely, her mind very evidently somewhere else and it was not, he was sure, on the possibility of a royal visitor. She would not let even the presence of such a gentleman have her in the trance which held her now. She was still smiling that faraway smile as she left the room.

He felt his pulse quicken as his mind conjured up what to him was always on the edge of his conscious thoughts and that was the chance that she had fallen in love with one of the many gentlemen who frequented the club when he was away. He and Daisy were not the conventional married couple, God knows. He had his small diversions, he was the first to admit, to himself only of course, but they meant nothing to him. They were just what the word implied. A diversion whilst he was in some foreign port and nothing at all to do with Daisy as any gentleman would understand. But the idea that she might be doing the same filled him not with regret or reproach but with a wild rage, a vicious and maddened need to strike out at the nearest person to him and who was that but Daisy? That's if it was so. *That's if it was so!*

Slowly his mind cleared and his heartbeat returned to normal. His shoulders, which he had been holding rigidly though he had not been aware of it, relaxed and he gave a short half-laugh under his breath. Really, he was being a fool just because his wife was usually erupting with vitality and more than willing to discuss current world affairs with him, to share a joke, to exchange gossip or scandal or indeed anything she heard in the gaming rooms and which could be enjoyed with no one else, except perhaps Bess. To listen to his own accounts of his voyages, to make love, to dance attendance on him in the most delightful way, but today she was in a world of her own in which it appeared there was no room for him. It was nothing. Merely anxiety at the thought of the royal personage to whom Daisy Lassiter, one-time field girl, pit-brow lassie and parlourmaid, was tonight to make her curtsey. She must be nervous, that was what was causing this distracted air of being elsewhere and if that was so he would go at once and let her know he would be there beside her, an arm to lean on, though that was not her way, a hand to hold hers, a voice whispering wickedly in her ear telling her that His Royal Highness was merely a man like all others.

He was at the head of the stairs, about to run down and make his way to the kitchens when he heard a sound from behind the closed door of what was now Daisy's 'work' room. The room where she studied accounts, did her 'bank-keeping', interviewed her staff on any arrangement she wished made in her rapidly growing business. It had once been a servants' bedroom beneath the eaves of the house but she had turned it into a comfortable but workmanlike study with a large leather-topped desk, deep armchairs on either side of the fire, shelves and drawers where the records of the business were kept.

She was on her knees at one of these when he opened the door. He had not meant to be secretive but there was thick-piled carpet on the floor and the hinges of the door were well oiled. He smiled, his eyes soft for her since she was at her favourite pastime of gloating over the profits she had made in the almost five years since the club had opened. May 1856 and now it was April 1861 and in that time 'Daisy's' had become what she had prophesied. The most renowned and respected gaming house in the north of England, perhaps in the land.

The name jumped up at him from the paper she held in her hand and that name was Thornley and for an appalled moment he thought his worst fears had come to life. *Thornley!* That bastard who had once been her lover and who had come back into her life was writing love letters to her! That was what she held in her hand. That was what she was dreaming over, her expression gentle and musing, just as though her thoughts were reflecting on something she found immensely pleasing.

He felt the black snarling anger take him over but when she turned sharply, suddenly aware of his presence, his face was quite blank.

"So this is the way of it, my love, and don't try to deny it. It's written clearly on your face, the guilt, and on that paper you have in your hand, I've no doubt, but I'll hear you say it, if you please. It's Thornley again, isn't it . . ."

"No . . . No, Sam . . ." and she fell back, edging away from the terrible blankness of his eyes.

"*No, Sam*, when you hold a love letter in your hand. A note with *his* name on it, no doubt telling you where to meet him and when. It's true, you dirty bitch, I can see it in your eyes so I'll have what's in your hand, and the rest of . . . of what's in that box you hold so reverently." His madness scorched her, terrified her since she had not known he had it in him to be so violent but wordlessly she handed him the note, one of dozens, scores of dozens, she had stored away in her possession ready for the day when she would bring Miles Thornley to his justice, to *her* justice, and Cassie's.

She watched his face change. A whole range of expressions moved across it, from bewildered incomprehension, to a strange relief, to what could have been derisive laughter and finally to what was the worst of all. To contempt. A contempt which was directed at her and under which she felt, curiously, a desperate hurt and shame. The scorn in his eyes, the contemptuous curl of his strong mouth as he threw the note back into her lap was the hardest thing she had had to bear since Cassie's death and she wondered, for a moment, before he spoke, why that should be.

"You won't let it alone, will you, Daisy?" His face was suddenly bleak. "You promised me that you would not continue this vendetta but you had no intention of keeping your word, did you? You are a liar and a cheat and are no better than the man you apparently mean to hound to his destruction."

He leaned across her, taking the box she had open on the floor. Lifting it high he turned it upside down, allowing all the papers inside it to tumble through the air to the floor all about her. Some struck her heavily, those rolled up in a legal fashion and tied with the red ribbon of the law. He took the other boxes, three in all, and did the same with them until she was besieged by a sea of papers and when she made no move to free herself, staring numbly into his cold, sea-green eyes, he reached for one, then another, reading them before tossing them back at her.

"You virtually own him, don't you?" His lips strained against his teeth in a grin of bitterness. "You're contemptible, do you know that? Pitiable and I want nothing more to do with you, and please, don't insult me with tales of how badly done by you and your sister were..."

"Don't preach at me, Sam. You have no idea how his family, not just him..."

"Oh, I'm sure you would be only too willing to tell me all over again, Daisy, but quite frankly I have had enough of it. You had my sympathy once when I realised what had been done to you by that swine but you also had my admiration, my regard for what you had overcome. I was ... proud of you. Proud of the way you picked yourself up out of the gutter, looked life in the face and decided you were going to fight it, to shape it and make it do what you wanted it to do. Even to selling your body if it meant keeping it alive though I'm not awfully sure you would have gone so far. But you would have found a way, of that I've no doubt. You were so brave, so fierce in your determination to succeed and I wanted nothing more than to give you the start you deserved. But had I known you were to do it just for this . . ." kicking the pile of papers contemptuously to one side ". . . I would have walked on by that afternoon on the Marine Parade. I might even have forgiven it if you had told me the truth two years ago when Thornley first came to the club. You promised me you would not spend your life trying to make him pay for what he had done . . ."

"Fruitlessly, you said."

"I beg your pardon?"

She had risen to her feet now, her own eyes narrowing to dangerous slits.

"You made me promise not to *fruitlessly* spend my life bringing Miles Thornley to justice and I have not. All this has been most fruitful, as you can see."

"Dear God in heaven!" He whirled about, striking his own forehead with the flat of his hand. "Is that what this has brought you to, madam? Sophistry? Mere words which mean absolutely nothing. You knew what I meant when you promised me you would end it and so not only do you cheat yourself but you cheat me and I cannot live with it, nor you. You must make your way to hell on your own for that is where this obsession will lead you."

"Nothing you can threaten me with will make me give this up, Sam, be absolutely sure of that . . ."

"I threaten nothing, Daisy." His voice was weary. "What I say is what I mean. You must do as you please but I won't stay here to witness it. I shall move to an hotel tonight and tomorrow morning I will consult with Mr Banfield on the quickest way to dispose of this . . . this venture. I'm sure there will be no problem in finding a buyer . . ."

"No . . . *no* . . ." Her voice rose to a scream and on the next landing Nelly almost dropped the can of hot water she was carrying. She put it carefully on a marble-topped table, her eyes huge in the pale triangle of her face, before scampering down the stairs to consult with their Bess for surely Captain Lassiter must be murdering her lovely mistress.

"I am finished with it, Daisy, and with you. I want nothing more to do with..."

"Then sell it to me."

That stopped him but only for a moment, then he smiled. "I'm afraid that is not possible." His voice was as cool as any business gentleman transacting a deal with another. His hooded eyes were frozen pools of ice and he stepped away from her as though wishing to put as much distance as he could between them. The words cut like a knife through the cold tension.

"Why? Why is it not possible? I have not been unproductive in my financial affairs."

"I don't doubt that for a moment." He almost lost the leashed snarling of his temper again.

"Then you will sell to me." Her own was just as fierce. "You will sell me your share of the club?"

"So that you can carry on this vendetta?"

"Does it matter to you now?"

He turned abruptly, moving across to the fireplace where he kept a box of cigars. He took one and bending down to the fire lifted a glowing coal with the tongs, lighting the cigar, blowing out smoke until it wreathed about his head. He looked cool, undisturbed, as though he had just cast off something which had been a great burden to him and she felt her heart wrench for she knew she would miss him dreadfully. But she would not deviate from the path she had chosen for herself, not by a fraction of an inch. She had promised Cassie. Not even if she lost Sam's companionship, his ... his ... whatever it was he gave her and which she had found so satisfying. That was the word. He had satisfied something in her which had always been cold and lonely, bereft of human contact, of contact between a man and a woman who were *right* together but it made no difference.

She lifted her head and her face was set in cool and resolute lines.

"Name your price, Sam."

"I cannot do that, my pet."

"For God's sake ... it means nothing to you."

"Does it not, Daisy? Are you sure of that? I'm afraid your new-found experience in the world of commerce has left you sadly lacking, particularly concerning the law, and if you were to consult with Mr King you would find that despite your ... your assets, those which you have gleaned from this club and from your other dealings, your request to purchase what you naïvely call *my* share of it is quite out of the question."

His voice was as smooth and sweet as honey and Daisy's skin prickled in the most extraordinary way for she knew without doubt that some appalling apparition was about to creep up and enfold her in its embrace.

"You see ..." he went on, drawing on his half-smoked cigar, his voice cool and temperate just as though he was explaining some quite inconsequential matter which was of no real importance to either of them. "You see, my dear, I do not have a *share* in the club, I *own* the club and not only that but everything you have schemed and worked for, everything over which you have worried that fine brain of yours, all the property and land you have acquired from the Thornley estate which, from what these legal papers tell me, are extensive. It all belongs to me. You have nothing, my love. Not a farthing to your name. You could not buy yourself a new pair of gloves unless I said so, let alone this property. You see, you are my wife and as such anything you might possess belongs automatically to me. Everything you have, or earn, or inherit is not yours but mine and that includes yourself, my pet. I may do what I like with it all, and you. As a married woman you have no legal identity of your own."

Turning on his heel he opened the door and left the room.

She sank slowly into the nearest chair, feeling her way to it with trembling hands. Her teeth began to chatter though her face and body were on fire. She hugged herself and began to rock backwards and forwards as though she was in great pain and a faint moan escaped from between her white lips.

"Sam ... oh, Sam..." she whispered and it was not the loss of all she had strived for which was torturing her.

30

The message came late the next morning. It was from Mr King, her lawyer, saying that he would be grateful if she could call, at her convenience of course, at his office where he had a matter of extreme importance to discuss with her. Some papers to sign, the note said, and though she had not slept, nor ever would again her stricken, stunned and almost senseless mind told her, she dressed with her usual care, called for her carriage, Sam's carriage, she supposed, and was driven to the solicitor's offices.

There *were* papers to sign, her signature, here and here, Mr King said, to be witnessed and processed by the law which was very rigid about such things. Yes, just below that of the Captain, if you please, Mrs Lassiter, and when it was done to his satisfaction and his great seal put upon it, the business, the buildings in which it was housed and all those buildings contained, in fact the gaming club known as 'Daisy Lassiter's', belonged exclusively to Mrs Daisy Lassiter, deeded to her by her husband. It could not be taken away from her, not even by the man to whom she was married, Mr King explained, for the Captain had insisted upon it, ensuring that it was drawn up in all the legal convolutions Mr King could put his clever mind to. *She* owned it to do with as she liked, run it as she had done, sell it, burn it to the ground if she had a mind to, though Mr King did not advise the latter.

"A fair-minded gentleman, the Captain, if I may be so bold, Mrs Lassiter. There are not many so generous," with their wives, who had no need of such things, he almost added. "Of course all the other ... holdings, those transactions you have made in the past and which were held, naturally, by your husband ... you were not aware of that until recently, oh yes, a wife's earnings belong to ... oh, you had been informed of that? indeed ... well, as I was saying, *they* will remain in your husband's keeping but the gaming club and any future income derived from it is yours. There is one stipulation, though, and that Captain Lassiter insisted upon."

She could not speak but merely stared mutely at the lawyer.

"No one is to know of this, Mrs Lassiter. The Captain wishes it to be believed that the business still belongs to him. That you, as his wife, are in charge of it as you have always been, unless you decide to sell, of course, but its true ownership is not to be revealed."

A fair-minded and generous man. Yes, that was Sam Lassiter. Had she not found that out in the years she had known him? Arrogant, hard-headed, possessive, dangerous at times but always just and now, though she was not awfully sure that he wanted to see her ever again, that though in all probability their marriage, their strange but pleasing relationship was over, he had given her this one last gift. She wept in the carriage as it took her to the place she called home and which was now truly hers.

She did not see him again. She heard of him though. Captain Sam Lassiter.

The war between the North and South in America had finally begun in April of that year and though it took many months before the effects of it began to squeeze the people of Lancashire, it was soon apparent that without the raw cotton which came from the Southern states of America, and which was needed for the spinning and weaving of cotton cloth, many of the operatives in the cotton towns to the east of Liverpool would suffer great hardship when their machines ground to a halt. They were not, of course, the only ones to suffer, for the new President, Abraham Lincoln, proclaimed a blockade of the Southern states' seaboard from the River Potomac in Virginia to the Rio Grande in Texas, a distance of some 3,000 miles in length. Patrolling Union ships were placed at the mouth of the great River Mississippi to cut off New Orleans which was the cotton capital. Also affected were Norfolk, Virginia, Beaufort, New Bern and Wilmington in North Carolina, Savannah in Georgia, Pensacola in Florida, Mobile in Alabama and Galveston in Texas. A 'stoneboat' fleet, twenty-five vessels of 335 tons each, heavily laden with stone, were scuttled in strategic points in the channels leading to these seaports, and the people of the Southern states which these ports fed, like the Lancashire folk, began to suffer not only the ravages of war but the hardships the closing of the ports created.

A new word began to be spoken by the people of England and America and to be written about in the newspapers and that word was 'blockade-runner' and the most audacious of these amongst the British shipowners was Captain Sam Lassiter, out of Liverpool, and though some of those involved during the early months of the American Civil War were captured by the Union navy, due no doubt to their own poor seamanship, he was not one of them.

'Scarcely a dark night passes but a vessel goes in or out of these ports,' wrote a correspondent in *The Times*, 'these ports' being Charleston, and Wilmington, Savannah and Mobile and New Orleans. The Federal captains, in hope of fat prizes, chased them far and wide, leaving ports open to more skilful navigators and they did not catch the wily Captain Lassiter. Carrying all the goods the South could not itself manufacture – blankets, shoes, Manchester goods of all sorts, corsets, buttons, threads, stockings, medicines, salt, boiler iron, steel, copper and zinc – his cargo on the return journey, apart from a small amount of tobacco carried as ballast, consisted of one item only. Cotton. A legend he became, as successful at what he did as his beautiful young wife. He bought a second sailing ship early in 1862, engaging a clever and ambitious young seaman of his acquaintance to be her captain, promising him a share in the profit, and it was rumoured that he was to build a brand-new house for himself south of Toxteth close to the bank of the river by Jericho

Shore and that his wife, the infamous and dashing Daisy Lassiter of the gaming house 'Daisy's', was not to go with him.

"Yes, I heard what was said at the roulette wheel last night," Daisy told Bess casually, when it was mentioned by her friend the following morning, Bess having had it from John Elliott, ". . . and it's nothing to do with me. If Sam wants to have a life of his own apart from me, Bess, that is his own affair . . ." remembering the condition of the deed of gift . . . "Our marriage was one of convenience to us both, you know that, and I'm only surprised we stayed together as long as we did. It suited us both, I suppose, but now we have different interests and different futures so the time has come for us to part." Her voice was airy, her manner unconcerned, but Bess was not convinced and inclined to argue.

"Then why did you marry in the first place, tell me that, Daisy Lassiter? There was no need for it."

Daisy, who had often wondered herself, smiled patiently, her attitude that of someone explaining a problem to a particularly obtuse child.

"It was for business reasons, Bess, and well you know it. Sam wished to be completely certain of his investment which you must admit was considerable and so the only way to safeguard it was by marriage. It meant we were both secure but the club has done so well I was able to return to him the money he 'loaned' me, if you like, with a splendid interest and he can now get on with the life which has always been first with him and that is on the sea. He has been able to buy another ship. This blockade running he has taken up is a lucrative trade and if he is able to build himself a house with the proceeds then good luck to him. And you must remember that this was once his home and I suppose he felt the need for another. Now, shall we talk of something else . . ."

"Well, what I want to know is why Jack, who was *his* servant, hasn't gone with him."

"You must ask Jack."

"I have. He told me to mind my own business."

"Then I suggest you do."

"There's no call to get uppity with me, my lass. I asked a civil question, of Jack and of you, and I expect a civil answer."

But Daisy couldn't give her one. She herself could not understand why Jack was still with her and if she had been told the reason she would not have believed it.

"I'd come along of you, Captain," Jack had said to Sam Lassiter on that night the captain had gone down into the small but achingly neat room in which the old seaman had slept for the past six years, "only I don't think I could manage them decks any more." A rare admission for him to make and one which had taken courage, for Jack was a proud man. "Besides, she'll need a bit of watching."

"That's what I came for, Jack, to say goodbye and to make sure you'd keep an eye on her."

"I'll do that."

"And let me know if...?"

"Oh aye..." and that was all that was needed to be said for Jack had never been a man to question another on his actions and he was not going to start now. The captain was slinging his hook, that was apparent, and by the look of him he was taking it badly but that was nowt to do with Jack. If he needed anything he'd only to ask, the captain knew that, just as he knew that Sam Lassiter's woman, for she'd always be that to Jack, would be safe as long as Jack had breath in his body.

Miles Thornley, who had apparently just got word that Daisy's husband no longer lived on the premises began to pester her again, cornering her one night in her sitting room and had it not been for the timely intervention of Jack, who had noticed that Daisy was a long while coming down to the supper room where her smiling presence was expected and come up to see what she was about, it was doubtful whether Daisy would have avoided losing either her temper or her virtue.

She had known she was in danger from the moment he had slipped into her room that night without knocking, without permission and in the arrogant certainty that he would be welcome since when was he not? He had wanted her again ever since they had become reacquainted after the death of his father and though the presence of her husband had seemed to pose something of an obstacle to a renewed liaison he would not have let that prevent him having what he wanted. He had not forgotten that she had been more than a trifle malicious towards him over the question of her sister but she appeared to have forgotten that and had been extremely civil to him whenever he had frequented her club. Besides, she had had a great deal of his money in one game of chance or another over the course of the years he had been gambling here and so surely she owed him something in return. He had, for some time, been enamoured – if that was the right word to describe his feelings – with Cécile, and Daisy had been put aside, for later he had decided. Now with Cécile on the wane and Daisy's husband gone, it seemed as good a time as any to take up again the delightful diversion she had created for him all those years ago, or so he told himself as he stealthily climbed the staircase which he had been told led to her private quarters.

"Miles, what are you doing up here?" was all she could think of to say as he closed the door behind him. The need to tread warily filled her mind. He had planned this in the mistaken knowledge that she would be as willing as she had been when she was his mother's kitchenmaid, seeing no difference between the innocent sixteen-year-old who had worshipped at his feet and the sophisticated woman of the world she now was. So supremely overweening was his pride he could see no reason why she should not welcome his advances as she had then. And the appalling thing was that if she refused him, which she must do somehow, if she lost her cool and calculating grip on her own hatred for him and screamed it out loud to him, everything she had done, everything she still planned to do, would be for nothing. He would continue to gamble but not in her club. She could perhaps still arrange to buy his IOUs from gentlemen in other parts of the country where John Elliott's colleagues watched out for him. She could, now that her financial affairs were somewhat recovered after the transfer of 'Daisy's' into her own name and with the money she had made since, resume her vigilance in buying his property as he put it up for sale to pay his gambling debts, but without him here, in her club where she could watch his every move, it would take considerably more time. And she had found lately that she was beginning to tire of it, to wish that it was over and done with. Not that she would give it up, not for a minute would she consider that, for Cassie's pale and lifeless face would haunt her for the rest of her days but sometimes, when she was tired, and yes, lonely, when she felt she had broken something and had not quite properly healed, she longed to be able to turn her back on it, on the club, on the scheming, the planning, the need to deftly avoid the pitfalls which seemed to open up before her, to close the door behind her and just go. But go where, her shrewd mind begged to know, and there was no answer. None.

"Come, Daisy, you know why I am here so don't play the innocent with me. Can you deny that what we had was very pleasant, years ago and so, now that your husband has taken himself off and you are alone, as I am, why should we not amuse ourselves again?"

An image flashed madly through her brain. An image of herself in this man's arms, naked and trembling and longing, and as the image was replaced by others just as loathsome she felt her stomach heave and it took all her strength not to let him see the sickness in her. If he touched her it would all be over because she couldn't stand it and she would have to tell him so. She would not be able to contain it, the loathing, the stinking, crawling hatred which she kept alive in herself. She felt a moment of confusion as these last thoughts raced once more around the inside of her head, then, as he smiled that particularly charming, boyish smile of his she was herself again.

"Come now, my lord, you know I don't have ... well, shall we say ... friendships with any of my clientele, much as I am tempted at times." There, that should give him the impression that, but for her position in the club, she would be more than willing to allow his advances. "There is a saying that one should not mix business with pleasure, and really, it is true. That is not to say we cannot be friends, as I am friends with many of my guests, but you must see that if it became known that you and I . . ."

"No one will know, Daisy brown-eyes, I promise." He was sickening in his sentimental attempt to seduce her with the name he had once called her. "If that is your only objection then I can assure you it will be our little secret."

His lips stretched across his even white teeth as he came towards her. She had risen from the sofa by the fire when he entered the room. Now she moved to stand behind it, thinking to put a barrier between herself and him but in her agitation she failed to realise that she was now backed into a corner. The words 'Daisy brown-eyes' rang madly in her head and the memories they conjured up made her usually sharp mind woolly and unfocused.

"Please, Miles, I really must ask you to leave. I have guests waiting for me. Things to arrange for the evening and pleasant as it would be I cannot linger up here . . ."

"It would be pleasant, wouldn't it, Daisy? Do you remember how it used to be?" She might not have spoken for all the notice he took. He licked his lips and his eyes darkened lasciviously. He was standing directly in front of her, apparently hearing only the words he wanted to hear, picking them out like fruit from a tree, savouring what appealed to him, discarding what did not. "Those nights in the summerhouse where you and I did such enjoyable things together. You were so pliable, so obedient, so willing to learn and I could teach you other things, things you could not imagine, so come now, don't hover in that corner. I know you have fire in you for it has scorched me . . ."

"Don't . . ."

He had been about to place a finger beneath her chin to lift her mouth to his but she reared back shuddering and his face hardened.

"Don't! *don't*, Daisy? You didn't say that to me then, my darling. Just the opposite. You begged me, begged me to do to you all those things you loved. Didn't you, didn't you, Daisy?"

462

Oh God help her. "Yes," she said sullenly.

"Well then, what has changed? You still find me attractive, don't you?"

"Yes, I do." Her wooden response seemed not to affront him.

"Good, then we understand one another. I want you, Daisy, and now you shall say you want me."

"Miles ... Lord Thornley ... this is not the time nor the place for this. Come back later when the club is closed..." Anything, *anything* to get that hand which was now stroking her bare shoulder, away from her. She could feel her flesh rising in a wash of revulsion and she longed, yearned for Sam to come in and take this bastard by the neck and fling him down the stairs, crushing him until he was no more than a shattered heap of flesh and bones at its foot. Sam ... oh, Sam ... please ...

"There's time now, Daisy. Just five minutes. See, let me show you," and his shadow fell over her and she thought she would lose her senses. Desperately she turned away, even now trying to avoid the confrontation which would let him see how she really felt and send him from her club for ever. Her face was pressed against the wall. He came up behind her, putting one arm about her waist, his other hand going casually down the front of her black lace bodice, taking her bare breast with cruel fingers and she knew she must either allow it, and the rest of what he would have of her, or she must turn on him, shriek into his insolent face her revulsion and horror and lose all that she had schemed for, agonised over in the last six years. The battle between her hatred and her need for revenge surged up in her, bitter and loathsome, as loathsome and degrading as the feel of his hard, savage hand kneading her breast. She couldn't ... Jesus ... Oh dear Lord ... Oh, Cassie ... Cassie ... she couldn't ...

"There's some gentlemen asking for you downstairs, missy."

The voice was flat, expressionless, quiet in the room which was filled with the harsh breathing of Miles Thornley, but loud enough to be heard, nevertheless. The door was open and Jack held the doorknob, his eyes staring some-where into the far corner of the room, his face impassive but there was something about him which said that though it was none of his business he'd not leave without her and Miles Thornley stepped back, his face black and snarling with defeated lust. He turned, giving Daisy time to pull up her bodice and smooth her hair and before he could order Jack from the room, which he had every intention of doing, she moved quickly towards the door.

"Thank you, Jack, I was just coming." She turned to Miles, smiling. "Perhaps we could go down together," satisfied that his anger was directed at Jack and not at her. After all, she had not objected when he put his hands on her, had she?

But what about the next time? Later that night she sat before her bedroom fire, alone and sleepless. They were all in bed, her household, and the doors securely locked and bolted. She was safe from him now but what about the next time? What about tomorrow night and the next night and the next? Was she to pay all over again the high price which seemed might be necessary to have what was her due, not just from Miles but from the Thornley family who had ground her mercilessly down and thrown her unprotected into the black night six years ago? Lord Thornley was dead but his son lived, and his son's son, and the vow she had made that night still burned in her.

"I want you with me all the time, Jack," she said to him the following day. "Either you or Bess, you understand, and should there be any unpleasantness with a ... certain ... gentleman, you are to take your orders only from me."

She felt the need, curiously, to explain to the old man who seemed neither to care about, nor be particularly inter-ested in, the reason for her request. She laughed somewhat shakily.

"It seems Lord Thornley has developed this passion for me which, of course, I don't return and no matter what I say to him he will not take no for an answer."

"Oh aye." Jack sighed languidly.

"Yes, oh, he'll soon get tired of it but in the meanwhile . . ."

"Right, missy. Will that be all?"

"Yes, thank you, Jack."

It was icily cold that night and she shivered as she checked her appearance in her mirror before she went downstairs. She moved slowly across to the window and drew the curtains to one side, looking out at the deep blue darkness of the sky. There was an eyelash of a moon and a dozen brilliant stars about it and though her room was warm with lamplight and firelight she shivered more violently. A fine coating of frost lay on the rooftops and along the delicate fretwork of the balcony and she wished suddenly that the spring would come and then the summer. Her spirit felt frail tonight at the thought of the trouble which certainly lay ahead for if *he* should come in and corner her again, how could she expect Jack, or Bess, to be strong enough to protect her from him? Only she could do that. With a few scathing words, those she would use with any man who interfered with Daisy Lassiter, she could show him up for what he was, reduce him before his peers to the humiliating size of a schoolboy reprimanded for rudeness, but if she did . . . ?

Oh God, it was like a merry-go-round which somehow, though it never stopped, she must get off.

She had just come down the stairs when Sam came in. She was moving across the softly lit hallway to speak to a new member of the club, a Mr Andrew Hale who was a prosperous and well-thought-of businessman in Liverpool. She had noticed lately that a more respectable type of gentleman was beginning to frequent her club, just as though after all these years they had come to realise that 'Daisy's' was not the den of vice so many Liverpool worthies had at first considered it. There was a respectability about it, despite what went on there, that was increasingly attracting gentlemen of repute and certainly the visit of a famous royal son a year or two back had done its reputation no harm.

Sam was with a thickset, broad-shouldered gentleman, red-faced with a look of the open air about him and they were laughing with Nora, the polite and pretty housemaid who had opened the door to them. Jacob, ostensibly a footman but in reality an ex-bare-knuckle fighter who guarded the front door, stood unobtrusively to one side.

"Good evening, Jacob. A fine, cold night on which a brandy would be more than welcome."

"Indeed, Captain Lassiter."

"This is an American friend of mine, Jacob. See that he has everything he wants, will you?"

"Of course, sir."

Dear God, she couldn't get her breath. It was caught somewhere between her chest and her mouth and had not Mr Hale, a pleasant gentleman of forty-five or so, been congratulating her at length on the opulence of her club, giving her a chance to compose herself, she was certain she would have choked.

"You are very kind, Mr Hale. I must admit to a certain pride in it myself." She smiled warmly, then putting her slim white hand which had done no manual labour for a long, long time on his arm, she excused herself saying she must greet another guest. Mr Hale, who though not personally acquainted with Captain Sam Lassiter, naturally had heard of him, was unaware that he had just come into the club and he wondered at the sudden feverish flush which lit his hostess's skin. He returned her smile, admiring in an obvious but most mannerly fashion her polished beauty, then watched her long, swaying back as she moved across the hallway towards the two men who had just entered.

"Good evening, Sam." Her voice was husky and her heart was thudding badly out of control. She chanced a small smile for she was not awfully certain she could draw breath to do more than greet him. She waited for him to answer, to see if he even would, dreading that he might just cut her dead after what had happened between them at their last meeting, but to her astonishment he took her hands and lifted them to his lips, caressing them with both of his, brushing his mouth against her wrist. His eyes were warm and deep, the green in them more evident than usual. His whole attitude seemed to say she was more dear to him than anyone in the world. For a lovely moment she felt something inside her move joyfully. Something came alive which had long been dead and she grasped his hands, not wanting to let them go, to lose their warm and familiar strength. Her own eyes, which had been uncertain and narrowed to the amber nervousness of a wary cat, became soft and warm and she felt herself sway towards him.

"Here I am, my darling," he said, loudly she thought, and several gentlemen who had been about to go up the wide staircase to the private salon she kept for serious gamblers, turned to stare. By God, their expressions said, it's the wandering husband back again and after everyone had thought he and Daisy were no longer on speaking terms. Where the devil had he been this past year, and what the devil had he been up to? And Daisy was pleased to see him, there was no doubt of that, if the expression on her face was anything to go by. The pair of them would be embracing right there in the damned hallway in a minute and the fellow who was with them could not have been more embarrassed if they had.

Sam, as though just remembering his companion, let go of her hands and turned, his smooth, smiling face brown and almost handsome in the lamplight. Daisy watched him, watched the quirky humorous movement of his mouth, the familiar sardonic lift of his dark eyebrows, the fall of his heavy hair and the movement of his hand as he pushed it boyishly back from his forehead. She felt warm inside her, soft, melting, as though something hard and knotted had dissolved. It was a gentle, accepting sensation. A thawing as the lovely warmth spread throughout her body and soon, when this gentleman he was drawing forward to be introduced, had gone to the gaming rooms she would have a moment to identify it. Blissful, that was how she felt, she decided, a wondrous bliss which she had never before known...

"Daisy, this is Captain Lawrence Duggan, an old friend of mine from America. He and I are in the same line of business." He smiled impishly, reaching to take her hand again. "You may have heard what we are up to ... well, of course you have since there are no secrets between husband and wife, are there, my sweet?" His expression conveyed to one and all that everything they might have heard about Daisy and himself and a possible rift in their marriage was nonsense. "Lawrence is a sea-captain. The owner of the *Nancy Duggan*, a two-masted frigate out of Savannah, which, needless to say, cannot hold a candle to my *Golden Lady*. Lawrence, this is my wife and the owner of this fine club, Daisy Lassiter."

"Captain Duggan."

"Mrs Lassiter."

Though she knew she should lead this genial and well-mannered friend of Sam's in polite conversation, as the hostess, she felt a definite inclination to cling to Sam's arm, to have him turn and smile at her again as he had done a moment ago. To have him somewhere warm and quiet and alone where they could ... Dear Lord in heaven, what was the matter with her? She was grinning like a Cheshire cat, she knew she was, as Captain Duggan bowed over her hand, but her heart was fluttering so and her breathing was still somewhat inclined to a feverish gasp. She must pull herself together or those gentlemen who hovered halfway up the stairs would think she had lost her wits. But she felt so happy, so light and breathless, wanting to laugh, wanting to stretch and run and leap and do all the foolish things she had not done since she was a girl in Caleb's Wood with Cassie beside her.

The front door was opened again, Nora standing back to allow in a noisy group of young men who immediately filled the hall with their rowdy and arrogant presence. They threw their capes to Jacob and stated loudly that they positively must have champagne at once since they were as dry as dust after the excitement of the cock-fight they had just witnessed. The hallway was a mass of black-suited gentlemen, of bobbing housemaids and respectful footmen who had come forward to guide the young men towards the gaming rooms but one, it seemed, had no intention of going anywhere he himself had not chosen, and at a time convenient only to himself. A tall gentleman, exquisitely dressed and exquisitely handsome and some ten years older than the roistering, whoring young bloods who accompanied him.

Miles Thornley!

He stood and looked at her and Sam, as still as a rock which is surrounded by the rushing waters of the river, his face almost bewildered for a moment since he had thought her to be his, before the darkness of anger flooded it. His narrowed eyes moved from her to Sam, and in them she could see the spleen of his thwarted lust which, with her husband apparently back to claim what was his, he would no longer be able to satisfy. She saw him fight to control the instinct to move across the hallway and strike out at Sam, to knock him to the ground and treat him as one would any other common fellow who got in his way, but at the last moment, as she held her breath, reason took over for not even Miles Thornley could trample unceremoniously over the husband to get at the wife, not beneath the fascinated gaze of his own peers. Particularly a husband as well-known and respected as Captain Sam Lassiter. Miles Thornley was a gentleman and though perfectly at liberty to purloin the wife of any man he cared to, if the wife was willing, if that husband and wife were as obviously devoted, even *doting*, as Sam and Daisy Lassiter appeared to be, not even the gentlemen of his own class would condone it.

He turned then, his face as hard as granite, his eyes bleak and filled with an expression which she could not read but which she was certain was dangerous. He walked, stiff-backed, across the hallway and disappeared into the gaming room.

"I have heard a lot about your club, Mrs Lassiter," Captain Duggan said in the drawl of the Southern state of America from which he came, sensing some undercurrent between Sam Lassiter, his lovely wife and the tall and arrogant fellow who had just left, and wishing to dispel it. It was nothing to do with him, of course. He had been surprised when Sam had suggested they come to 'Daisy's' tonight, since he, like Sam's other seafaring acquaintances, had been well aware of the strained relationship between Sam and his wife. But it seemed, like the other gentlemen, he had been wrong for the pair of them were moving up the stairs like lovers towards a tryst. Sam smiled at him over his shoulder, then winked, which was noticed by a score of other gentlemen who grinned knowingly and wished they could be in Sam Lassiter's shoes for the next hour, the lucky dog. Within five minutes every man – and servant – in the club knew that Sam and Daisy were together again and they all smiled except one.

"Sam," she said softly, breathlessly, turning to him as he closed the sitting-room door behind them, and the icy shock of the expression on his no longer smiling face and in his sea-green eyes made her gasp painfully.

"There is no need of games up here, Daisy," he said coolly.

"Games . . . ?"

"I will stay for an hour or so to let them all think we are . . . well, I will not need to draw you a picture, will I, my sweet? So why don't you send for some of that splendid champagne I know you keep for special visitors and perhaps it might be as well if you were to remove your lovely gown and put on something more . . . intimate so that the maid will have something to tell them when she gets back to the kitchen." He grinned cynically.

She was still gripped in a state of trance-like confusion, a state which hovered on the edge of the gladness she had known for the past half-hour, and a dreadful anguish which his words implied would come upon her in a moment. Her heart had gone mad again, beating inside her like a thing possessed, and she could feel her flesh become cold with apprehension, but still she could not quite . . .

"I'm not sure . . . Sam . . . what are you . . . ?"

"Please don't delude yourself that I'm here for your benefit, Daisy," he drawled, taking a cigar from the gold cigar case in his pocket. He selected a cigar and lit it, drawing the smoke deeply, sensuously into his lungs. "You don't need *my* protection now, in fact I doubt you ever did but the fact of the matter is, I need yours, or rather the protection of our marriage." He grinned, somewhat sheepishly he would have her believe, and she could feel the madness, the wild tormented rage begin to move through her veins, putting fire in the flesh which had so recently been like ice. "You see ... well, the fact of the matter is there is this certain lady, and I mean a lady, not a ..."

"Not a whore, like me." Her eyes were like a cat's in the dark, the velvet brown of them flecked with gold, a cat about to take on another which has crept up on it, and her voice was a cat's hiss in the back of her throat.

"Daisy, what a thing to say about yourself," but he did not deny it, merely continued to watch her in that ironic way he had. A way which said what did it matter, what did *she* matter any more? "You see, without the cover of our marriage ... well, not to put too fine a point on it, I am hard pressed to shake off this lady. She is married, of course, so nothing can come of it but I thought if word got round, as it always does, that you and I were ... reunited ... you will know what I mean, then she might be persuaded to be less ... demanding." His grin widened. He pushed his hands deep into his pockets in that characteristic way she knew so well, leaning indolently against the doorjamb, the cigar between his teeth, but when she sprang at him he was ready for her. The cigar fell to the carpet at their feet. He held her arms easily, his face close to hers, his lips close to her, and for a moment she could have sworn she saw something there ... something which did not exactly match the story he had just told her, then, with a gesture which was filled with contempt, he forced her back until she fell on to the sofa beside the glowing fire.

"You surely did not think I was here for some other purpose, did you?" His voice cut through her like an icy wind as he took his hands fastidiously from her arms.

"Of course not, you bastard, and if you had it would have come to nothing. I have better things to do with my time than ... than consort with a man with as few scruples as ..."

"Talking of scruples, you are still continuing with your search for vengeance against his lordship, I take it?"

"Naturally! Did you think there was any man on earth who could stop me?"

"Not for a moment, Daisy. I doubt there is any man on earth who can do anything with you, my love. It is too late

471

for that. Now, shall we call for the champagne? We may as well have something pleasant to while away the next hour."

31

She made no attempt to deny the stories which went round like wildfire about her renewed relationship with Sam for if it had done nothing else it had cooled Miles Thornley's ardour. The year sped by and in that time Sam and Lawrence Duggan called several times at 'Daisy's' as though to give credence to the lie which his first visit had perpetrated. His comings and goings were noted by the members of the club who swore they had seen Captain Lassiter climb the stairs with his wife and though there was a rumour about that he had been seen in the company of a certain lady, at a race meeting at Aintree, a member of the aristocracy, it was said, to whom he had been introduced at a weekend party in Cheshire, what did that signify? the gentlemen asked one another. Many of them were unfaithful to their wives and if the wife made no fuss and the gentleman was discreet, it was of no particular importance.

Captain Lassiter was in and out of Liverpool like a shadow, his clipper ship as beautiful and precise as a bird in flight as she moved across the waters of the river, and it was said that between his two ships, the *Golden Lady* and *Lady of the Sea*, he was making a fortune. The American Civil War was two years old now. 'Stonewall' Jackson, the most daring of the Confederate officers, was dead at Chancellorville, a victory for the South but dearly purchased, and at Gettysburg Robert E. Lee suffered a defeat of appalling proportions and the 'goods' Captain Lassiter brought in to Charleston under the very noses of the Federal navy were sorely needed. It seemed that *Golden Lady* and *Lady of the Sea* bore charmed lives, running the blockade time and time again, relying on their speed and the exceptional seamanship of their two captains to avoid detection, or to escape like soaring birds when they were spotted.

A cotton-carrying blockade-runner could usually be identified from a great distance for the massive, brownish-white, box-like bales on deck gave the vessels a distinctive square and top-heavy silhouette. When one was detected and the Union navy ship gave chase, the captain was forced to throw overboard the precious cargo to increase speed. The value of that cargo could be in the region of £40,000 and the reluctance to part with it was obvious. There was a toast drunk in Nassau in that year: "Here's to the Confederates who produce the cotton, the Yankees who maintain the blockade and keep up the price of cotton, and the Britishers who buy the cotton. Here's to all three!"

In July Daisy was surprised to learn from a wealthy ship-builder from Birkenhead who was a member of her club, though he was not aware that it was the first she had heard of it, that Sam was to have a blockade-running ship built exclusively for that purpose. A four-hundred-ton, twin-screw vessel powered by 250-horsepower engines which could achieve a speed of at least fourteen knots.

"Indeed that is so," she managed to answer, pretending she knew all about it and to be not at all amazed though the thought of Sam in command of a steamship was hard to imagine. She could picture his face when he spoke of his *Golden Lady*, the warmth and love and even gentleness which came over it, the passion in his eyes as he spoke of the wind cracking in her sails, the lovely tilt to her as she raced across the waves, scarcely touching the water beneath her bows ... It was less easy to picture him at the wheel or on the deck of one of the iron-clad monsters, squat and ugly and drowned in their own black and filthy smoke, she had seen squaring their bows through the swell of the Mersey.

Her face hardened then for what did she care which ship he was on, whether it was sail or steam, or indeed if he sank to the bottom of the ocean beneath the guns of a Yankee cutter? He could live in hell for all she cared and she hoped he would after the telling blow he had struck her. She didn't know what had come over her, acting the way she had done, simpering like some virgin maiden at the feel of his hand on her arm. God, she turned sick, even now, at the memory of it and it took all her iron self-control, that which life had taught her over the last fifteen years, not to order him from her club when he visited it and it was only the predatory prowling of Miles Thornley that kept her from it. She was the first to admit that it was Sam's presence, his visits which, though infrequent, safeguarded the fallacy of their marriage and kept Miles from attempting a renewal of their past relationship.

And Miles Thornley, in the five years since the death of his father, had gambled away every penny of his inheritance, as it had been prophesied he would, until all that was left was the actual estate of Thornley Green and little by little, a farm here and a farm there, a bit of rough woodland shoot, a stretch of moorland, some pasture on the edge of the deer park, was being sold off to pay the debts which were now, after all these years, beginning to bring him down. Though all that Daisy had secured in the earlier years now belonged to Sam, she had, with the profits she had made since the ownership of the club had become hers exclusively, purchased more of the Thornley holdings. She had bought property in London, in St Helens, in the salt-bearing lands of Cheshire and the coal-bearing lands of Lancashire. Once she had purchased it, when the price was low, she had sold much of it again for a satisfactory profit, keeping only those assets which were part of the actual estate.

She often smiled to herself, wondering what Abel Dixon and Arnold Chadwick would say if they knew that their farms were now owned by the scrawny field girl who had once worked their land. That the fields she had picked for stones, and weeded and hoed, over which she had broken her back and her child's heart, belonged to that same child, now a woman. Or had they forgotten the defiant rebel who had sworn she would escape the life she had been forced into, and who had, though at what cost? Cassie invaded her thoughts a great deal these days, her lovely innocence shining beside the beast who had killed her. But Miles Thornley was slowly being drawn into the trap his own greed had set him and waiting to spring it was Daisy Lassiter. She knew he was being pressed now, for a wolf knows when its prey is weakening, dunned by debt collectors, and he could only pay them by selling his land, and she was ready. She had men in Lancashire, men who knew about such things and who would give her the nod should something of his come on the market, and her agent, the one she now employed full time to deal with such matters, not just Thornley property, but any other which might make her a quick profit, was kept busy, buying and selling and making himself a nice commission for Mrs Lassiter was generous with those who dealt honestly with her.

It was strange really but it was over a year now since the club, despite the enormous profit the 'bank' made, had been as profitable as what she still called her 'sidelines'. She had discovered, quite by chance, as she bought and then sold Miles Thornley's property that she could gain more from one lucrative land deal than she could in a month of profit from 'Daisy's' and though she had no intention of giving up what was her 'baby', her own brainchild and which still gave her immense satisfaction, she was not as nervous as she had been at its inception that, should it fail, she would be left destitute again. Soon she would be able to give it up if she so wished. Buy a mansion perhaps and live like a duchess, transacting her land and property deals from her own drawing room without the need to be pleasant every evening to gentlemen who considered, despite their admiration for her, that she was no better than she should be and certainly not a fit person to associate with any lady of their acquaintance.

The weather had turned very warm, a humid heat which beat down into the long stretch of garden at the back of the club. There was no breeze to stir the heads of the drooping velvet-headed roses which massed against the high stone walls, and the bushes in the shrubbery which stood on either side of the arbour in the centre of the garden were quite motionless. Clematis and honeysuckle crept fiercely over the arbour roof dispensing an aroma so sweet it made the senses swim. For an hour Daisy and Bess sat in the shade whilst Nelly ran backwards and forwards with iced lemonade until even her youthful energy found it all too much and, under Bess's sharp and suspicious gaze since she wanted no one to accuse her of favouring her own sister, she wilted on to the wooden steps. She was fifteen now and considered 'Daisy's' to be almost her own personal creation, so great was her pride in it and her own involvement in its working. She was to be made up to parlourmaid soon since she had done well under Bess's firm direction. She thought the world of Mrs Lassiter and had one dream in life and that was to become her personal maid. Not that Mrs Lassiter had as yet employed a personal maid, seeing no sense in having another woman dress her and do her hair when she was perfectly well able to do it herself, she said firmly, but Nelly knew the day would come when she would change her mind for she was a great lady and great ladies always had a personal maid.

Nelly sipped her lemonade contentedly, hoping that Bess would not notice her there. All the maids would want to sit about and drink lemonade, Bess would say, if she did, and send Nelly off to perform some task in the kitchen, but in the meanwhile her sister lay dozing in the folding chair, the heat giving her usually sallow face a quite pleasing flush.

"Let's go down to the water," a voice said suddenly. "It'll be cooler there with the breeze off the river. We could even have a ride on the ferry to Woodside and back. What d'you say?"

Nelly lit up like the chandelier which hung in the entrance to the club, her face that of an eager child, which she still was, for it seemed Mrs Lassiter meant to include her in this splendid outing. She would wear her new straw bonnet, the one with the pale pink rosebuds around the crown and the pale pink ribbons which tied in a bow beneath her chin. Change from her black dress and crisp white apron into her pink cotton walking-out dress and perhaps if Mrs Lassiter, or their Bess, for she was the one who was likely to argue, agreed, they could get off the ferry at Woodside and take the coach to Bidston Hall, or even, instead of disembarking at Woodside they could sail to Egremont which was a lovely village beside the river. Perhaps the sands at New Brighton. There'd be a grand breeze there since it was right on the point where the River Mersey ran out into the Irish Channel. She held her breath and waited eagerly.

Bess sighed and slid further down into her comfortable chair. She had been up since six this morning, unlike Daisy who could lie in all day if she cared to, and it would be the early hours of tomorrow before Bess saw her bed again. She was accustomed to having a nap about this time each day and the thought of traipsing about in this heat was not at all to her liking. She frowned, her eyes still closed.

"Not today, lass. I've that crystalware to check before I get dressed. You know how those girls skimp things," which was not true for Bess Miller would have no girl working for her who skimped things. "Besides, it's too hot."

"I wouldn't mind, Mrs Lassiter. I quite fancy a ride on the ferry."

Bess's eyes shot open in consternation and Nelly started with nervousness but Daisy only laughed. She had taken a liking to Bess's sister. She was bright and sweet-natured. She had the family colouring of pale skin, pale eyes and hair, but on her the pale skin had the bloom of good health and the three square meals she ate each day. The pale grey eyes were fringed with long fine eyelashes and her hair was the lightness of silver, shining and smooth beneath her white frilled cap. She was fresh and wholesome and if not exactly pretty she had a comeliness which was pleasing.

"Here now, don't you get above yourself, Nelly Miller," Bess snorted. "You're no more than a servant in this house and don't you forget it. Go with Mrs Lassiter, indeed! I never heard such nonsense in my life and what d'you think you're doing, lolling about on that there step like you'd got nothing better to do? There's some silver wants cleaning ready for tonight and when that's done..."

"Oh, leave her alone, Bess," Daisy laughed. "Why shouldn't she come with me for a ride on the ferry? You have dozens of maids to clean the silver or whatever it is that needs doing and every one of them lounging about the kitchens this minute, I'll be bound. And if you won't come, and I can't go alone or Jack would have my hide, or worse still, come with me, why shouldn't I take Nelly?" Nelly waited, scarcely breathing.

"Because she's my sister, that's why, and well you know it, Daisy Lassiter. I can't put her above the others or I'd be accused of favouritism. And it wouldn't be me that suffered, but her. They'd make her life a misery..."

"Fiddlesticks!"

"Never you mind fiddlesticks! It's true and you'd agree if you gave it a bit of thought. She's to get dressed up and go out with you for an hour, just as though her and you were ... well, friends or summat, and then come back, change into her uniform and be a servant again? It won't do, Daisy. She's either one or the other, she can't be both."

"You are! They all know you and I are friends and have been for eleven years." Her eyes grew soft and unfocused. "My God, Bess, eleven years, would you believe it? Where have they gone? I can't believe..."

"Never mind that, Daisy." Bess was brisk, not at all prepared to be drawn into Daisy's sentimental reminiscences. "Now then, you, Nelly, get back to the kitchen..."

"No." Daisy's voice was soft still, but very sure. Both Bess and Nelly turned to look at her incredulously, on their faces the same stunned expression. Daisy stood up and shook out her creased skirt. There was an air about her which Bess knew well. She had seen it a hundred times before in the past, beginning on the day they had first met and Daisy had offered to scrub the storeroom floor. She had seen it on those many nights when Daisy had crept down the back stairs and out of the house to meet Miles Thornley, and over the years when some seemingly insurmountable barrier stood in her way which she was determined to overcome.

"No, Bess. I'm sorry but I shall have my way in this."

When did she not? Bess's tight-lipped expression asked, but she held her tongue as Daisy continued. "If you think Nelly should not work in the kitchen with the other girls then she shan't..."

"I never said that." Bess was aghast. Nelly's face was as white as the perky cap on her head.

"You said she could not work in the kitchens and ... be a friend. You are a friend, a dear friend, and she is your sister. So, she shall no longer work in the kitchen. She shall be my ... my companion, my personal maid if you must give her a title. Often you are too busy now to go about with me so Nelly shall do it instead." She turned to Nelly. "Go and get changed, Nelly. You shall begin your new duties at once."

It was almost like having Cassie back again, but a Cassie who was not just sweet-tempered and trusting, but bright and hungry for knowledge. A Cassie who never stopped asking questions and who, on that very first day, made Daisy forget her loneliness for the child who had been her 'sister'; made her forget her anger at Sam, her vendetta against Miles Thornley and simply enjoy the ordinary pleasure of doing absolutely nothing but have fun. Nelly was enchanted and enchanting. Shy at first and quite speechless in the new 'post' to which she had been promoted, looking like a country mouse in the plain cotton dress Bess had thought suitable for a housemaid, inclined to be hesitant with the grand Mrs Lassiter who, though she had never been anything but kind to Nelly in the five years she had worked for her, was as far above Nelly as the moon in the sky at night.

"We'll call a cab please, Jacob," Mrs Lassiter had said, drawing on her silk gloves which reached to just above her wrist and had been dyed to match her gown. She wore the palest blue that day, in the finest muslin, light and cool, the skirt looped up to reveal not the brilliantly coloured petticoat which was fashionable but row upon row of delicate cream ruffled lace, short enough at the front to show off her ankles in the smartest and highest-heeled white boots Nelly had ever seen, made for her by the bootmaker in Bold Street. She was taller than Nelly by a head. The gown was the very latest style. A 'Princess' dress, it was called, in which the skirt and bodice were cut in one and much gored to fit at the waist. Buttoned down the front there was a short train which must be kicked smartly when she turned. She wore a 'spoon' bonnet decorated with cream satin rosebuds beneath the high brim and carried a cream silk parasol. Nelly thought she was the most beautiful lady she had ever seen.

They were just about to climb into the hired carriage when Daisy hesitated, then stepped back on to the kerb. She turned about and seemed to sniff the warm air, then she grinned and tossing the parasol to Jacob she took Nelly's hand.

"We'll walk, I think, Nelly. Dear God, it's no more than five brisk minutes from here to Strand Street. I used to walk ten miles a day once and think nothing of it so come on, my lass, let's step out."

Hanover Street into which Duke Street ran was a wide, busy thoroughfare hedged on both sides by tall buildings, casting a shade in which they were glad to walk. A deep bluebell sky edged the roof of the Custom House and from the Post Office beside it men in the scarlet cutaway tailcoats of postmen hurried out to start the fourth of the nine deliveries which took place during the day. Street musicians pierced the crowded air with penny whistles, flutes and fiddles and Nelly, her soft rosebud mouth agape, slowed her step to watch a chattering, grinning monkey in a pillbox hat perform its parody of a jig on the top of a street organ. Voices shouted in more than one language for Liverpool was a cosmopolitan seaport and city. There was the clatter of carriage wheels and the ring of iron horseshoes. Hawkers cried their wares and as they approached Canning Dock, enormous waggons pulled by the majesty of shire horses rumbled across the sturdy bridge which separated the loading area from Strand Street. The dock was crammed with Mersey flatboats, of not much interest to Daisy and Nelly, and they sauntered past it and over the same bridge from which the waggons had come, skirting Canning Graving Dock in which vessels of all sizes were being repaired.

They were walking along by the actual riverside now, its bursting life, its busy traffic, its sliding grey waters dappled today with silver and a hint of the blue sky which was reflected in it, on their left. They crossed another bridge and another, all linking the docks, one to its neighbour, bridges which could be raised to allow the great seagoing vessels to move into and out of their berths. Without consulting one another, as though their thoughts were somehow linked as the bridges linked the docks, they walked on beyond the landing-stage where the ferryboats fussed and fumed, beyond the Marine Parade and the bathhouse where years ago Sam and Daisy had first met, around the perimeter of George's Dock until they stood in the churchyard of St Nicholas. The first religious edifice of the town of Liverpool had been erected here, a chapel of Our Lady and St Nicholas, hundreds of years ago and though this church was not the original it was certainly very old. They studied for a moment the inscription on the dial in the churchyard, Nelly picking out hesitantly, since she had only recently learned to read, the words written there.

Our days upon earth are but a shadow, it said. Nelly glanced shyly at Daisy. "What does it mean, Mrs Lassiter?"

"I think it means that the days we are given do not last for ever, Nelly, so we'd best get a move on and enjoy them," and taking the girl's work-roughened hand in her own she drew her through the ancient tower gateway of the church and on towards the northern docks, both of them ready to laugh now at anything, so great was their enjoyment of this unplanned day. Daisy had discarded her gloves and pushed her bonnet back, letting it hang on its ribbons down her back. Her hair turned to fire in the sunlight, drawing men's admiring glances as she and Nelly strolled back down to the water's edge and the stretch of promenade known as Prince's Parade which stood before the spacious Prince's Dock. In it were berthed the largest of the vessels which were given harbourage in Liverpool, coming from and sailing to North America, South America, the Indies, China and Australia. On the quays were a sprawl of sheds and around them laboured men and horses and waggons, loading taking place to the west of the dock, and discharging to the east. It was a scene of grand and exciting bustle, of vital activity, cheerful and exhibiting the commercial and maritime success of the magnificent port and city of Liverpool. Daisy found herself smiling as she strode along beside Nelly, ready to sing, or whistle as many of the rough labouring men were doing, so splendid did she feel. She was twenty-six now, or thereabouts, and a beautiful, mature woman but she felt as young and giddy with life as the girl beside her and she could not decide whether it was due to the day, the exhilarating scene before her or the child whose hand she held.

"Look at it, Nelly." She pointed down the length of the river, in the direction they were taking, towards its mouth, and as far as the eye could see were a forest of masts from which pennants of all colours were moving languidly in the small sea-breeze which came off the river. "Is it not superb?" and Nelly, fraught with excitement and the joy of walking beside Mrs Lassiter, could only nod her head speechlessly.

On they walked, moving strongly along parade after parade lining the river. Daisy thought she had never felt so alive, so full of vigour, not since the days she had stepped out behind the gangmaster almost twenty years ago. Since then it was doubtful she had walked as far as this in a month, let alone in one afternoon, and her legs stretched eagerly to eat up the distance.

On their right hand were large stretches of enclosed water with stirring names such as Waterloo, Victoria and Trafalgar Docks, bursting from their encrusted walls with ships of every age and size and type. Clippers and frigates and barquentines, steamships and paddle-steamers and packets. Clarence Dock was next, and then across the bridge which divided it from the river, continuing until they arrived at the small island between two bridges on which was the structure known as the Salisbury Tower. The breeze blew steadily in their faces, bringing a flush to their cheeks and a vibrant sparkle in eyes of amber and pale, silvery grey.

"I think we'd best turn back here, Nelly, or Bess will have us both over the coals. We can go no further while the bridges are up, anyway. Look, they are bringing in what looks to be a..."

She stopped speaking abruptly, shading her eyes against the sun which was sinking in the west, low in the reddened sky, and outlining the rigging of the sailing ship which was limping slowly towards the opened gates of the Clarence Graving Dock. It was a fine clipper ship, or once had been, top-heavy with torn sail and blackened shrouds, its spars snapped and tangled in the rigging, the ends splintered like the protruding bones of a man's shattered leg. The mast seemed the only undamaged part of the ship for even in its sides were gaping holes just above the waterline, blackened around their torn edges. At the prow was the figurehead of a lady painted in gold.

"Sam ... Dear sweet Lord ... it's Sam, Nelly," and without knowing she had spoken aloud she let go of the young girl's hand, picked up her skirts and ran, fleet as a deer in her high-heeled kid boots, until she reached the edge of the dock where the gates stood open to receive the wounded ship. Her breasts heaved and her escaping hair flew about her head and shoulders and all around her men who had stopped work to watch in silent sympathy the passage of the lovely broken ship, turned to stare at her. She was as pale as death now, her face ashen, her eyes great drowning pools of deep, brown anguish. She wrapped her arms about herself, waiting with scarce a breath the approach of Sam's ship, waiting for it to be close enough to distinguish the figures of the men who moved about the deck and particularly the one who stood at the wheel navigating her skilfully, despite her appalling injuries, towards the safety of the dock.

"Poor old girl," she heard one man say compassionately and found to her surprise that her own face was wet with tears. They blurred her vision so that the *Golden Lady* and all the ships which clustered around her, offering her support and guidance, were hazed about with a fine pink and apricot mist, standing against the orange ball of the sinking sun. She dashed her hand across her eyes, unconscious of the awkward stares of the men about her, and as her gaze cleared she saw him. His face was brown and yet stained with a curious grey tinge and she knew that from whatever moment in time this disaster had befallen his ship he had never left the wheelhouse. In his mouth was clamped the stub of a cigar and his eyes were narrowed as they judged the width of the opening into the graving dock through which he must guide his ship.

She held her breath for him for the clipper's response was sluggish in her wounded state but even in the gaping depths of his weariness and what must be grief he was as skilful as a woman threading a needle, as careful as a mother with a beloved child, as tender as a man with the woman he loved above all others. The *Golden Lady* passed Daisy so closely she could have leapt from the quayside to her deck if she had had springs on her heels. At the last moment he saw her and for a second or two there was the gleam of his white teeth as he grinned around the cigar stub, then the ship moved into the dock and the berth where she was to rest.

Daisy turned then, empty, drained of all thought and emotion, not wishing to examine too closely what she felt at this moment. Nelly was there beside her, her own young face anxious and pale.

"It was Captain Lassiter, ma'am," she said softly and took Daisy's hand in both of hers, meaning to comfort her for whatever Daisy might have in her mind regarding her feelings towards Sam Lassiter, the truth was there in her face for all to see.

She made no enquiries into his welfare, nor that of the *Golden Lady*, and he came nowhere near the club. She had not yet accepted the reason for her own mad flight along the parade which had been precipitated by the sight of the severely damaged clipper ship, nor its implications, and she had no wish to stir up what she had pushed resolutely to the back of her mind. Instead she turned to her new and surprisingly delightful relationship with Nelly Miller.

"Send her up to me tomorrow morning, Bess, about ten o'clock. I mean to see how she shapes as my ... maid."

"Give over, Daisy. Don't put ideas in the girl's head. It's not fair to her, nor to me, to take her up and play with her like a doll and then set her back to housemaid again."

"Bess! I'm amazed and seriously offended by that remark. I thought you knew me better than that. No one knows more than I the joy of getting somewhere, or thinking you are, and then being knocked back again. Do you think I would do that to Nelly?"

Bess looked crestfallen and somewhat ashamed. "No, you wouldn't," she admitted, "but what *do* you want to do with her?"

"Good God, Bess, don't you want to see your sister become something other than a servant?"

"That's what I am and I've taken no harm from it."

"Don't be foolish. You know you're more than a servant in this house so don't pretend otherwise. Be honest, Bess. You run one side of the club and I run the other. In fact I've a good mind to make you my partner for if you took it into your head to leave me the club would close within a month."

"Rubbish!" but Daisy could see Bess was gratified and the next morning when Nelly shyly put her head round Mrs Lassiter's sitting room there was no argument from her sister.

32

It was almost as though she was living again, only in reverse, the days when she had first met Sam and he had taken her in hand, transforming her from the awkward, shabbily dressed girl she had been into the elegantly fashionable woman she had become. She remembered how she had thought herself to have been transported to a magical world where there was nothing but pleasure-filled outings, more to eat than she had ever known in her life, the wonder of dresses which were not only practical but beautiful to look at and now, eight years later, she was the giver and Nelly the recipient.

She took her everywhere with her, despite Bess's dire misgivings that the lass was bound to get above herself and what would become of her then for she'd be neither fish, flesh nor fowl. The worst thing Bess could think of was that one of *their* class might get ideas above her station and it seemed to her that Nelly was to do just that. Bess said so fiercely, particularly on the day when Daisy brought her back from the Misses Yeolands' establishment where the ladies had made for her sister a wardrobe fit for a princess.

That was what she looked like to Bess. A princess! The simple white dress of sheer lawn, backed with silk and inserted with bands of lace about the skirt, the hem of which just brushed her ankle. The white stockings and dainty white kid boots. The sash of primrose velvet which matched the ribbons in her glossily brushed, neatly arranged coil of hair. The white gloves and pretty frilled parasol transforming her from Bess's sister into someone she didn't know, a young lady, slender now she no longer wore the somewhat shape-less servant's uniform, well bred even, that is until she opened her mouth, first to smile, then to speak in the broad vowels of the north-country woman.

"What d'you think, our Bess?" she asked, pleased as punch with herself but in her eyes was a look which told her sister, and Daisy who watched them both, that she was, despite her new finery, still the same. No matter what Mrs Lassiter did for her, no matter how she was dressed or what she was taught, nothing would change her from the good-humoured and sensible young girl she had been brought up to be. How could she be otherwise with Bess as her sister? her smiling expression asked. Though she might give the impression that she was a swan she would always be a duck-ling at heart. She wanted an education. She wanted to 'get on', just as Bess and Mrs Lassiter had got on since she knew they had both started in the same lowly position as herself, and she would accept any help that was offered to her but she would always be Nelly Miller from Primrose Bank until the end of her days!

She had been speechless in the presence of the Misses Yeoland. It was the first place Daisy had taken her on that

486

first day, possibly, she admitted to herself sadly, to escape from the emotions the sight of Sam and his damaged ship had awakened in her. She had no wish to examine them or think of him and so she flung herself into the pleasant task of transforming Nelly from a raw country girl with not the least pretence to refinement, discrimination or good taste, or even much education, into a young lady; into what she dreamed Cassie would have been had she lived, and been undamaged; of making a silk purse from a sow's ear, as Bess said caustically in those first weeks when she was afraid for her sister. Initially Daisy told herself she meant to train the girl to the position of her own personal maid. To teach her how to look after her gowns of which she had a great many, and her jewellery, of which she had even more. To sew and attend to her hair, to tidy her bedroom and arrange her flowers and do all the hundred and one things the sometimes heavy-handed chambermaids now did. But somehow, when the days were long and empty, when Bess was busy and Jack not at all interested, it was so pleasant to take Nelly with her in her pretty new dresses, to move about Liverpool in the hired hackney carriage, seeing the sights, many of which Daisy had never had the time nor the inclination to visit.

Among these was the Royal Institution and Permanent Gallery of Art in Colquitt Street, originally a private house and where, thanks to its founder, the late William Roscoe, one of Liverpool's most famous and respected businessmen, and a gentleman much concerned with art and literature, great works of art, rare specimens of the old masters, particularly of the earlier school, were displayed. She and Nelly walked round it dutifully, going from room to room, scrutinising sculptures and paintings with the greatest care until, catching Nelly's eye which had become somewhat glazed, they collapsed against one another in a positive frenzy of hysterical laughter before running, under the critical and disapproving eye of Liverpool's art-lovers, out into the bustle of Colquitt Street and down the length of Duke Street towards home. They were giggling like schoolgirls as they burst through the door, seriously offending Bess who became, as she grew older, more and more dignified and considered, on occasion, that Daisy was leading her young sister on a shaking road to damnation. The girl should be doing something about Daisy's bedroom, or sitting room, mending or cleaning something, as she had seen Lady Thornley's personal maid do at Thornley Green, that is, if she was to be a lady's maid as Daisy had promised. Here she was, in one of the unsuitable dresses Daisy had bought for her, looking like a fashionable young lady and laughing in the most unladylike way, right out in the street where everyone could see! And Daisy Lassiter was just as bad. Bess had never seen Daisy giggle like that before, as though she was no more than Nelly's age, come to think of it, and as the thought occurred to her she softened, almost smiling as the pair of them made their way up to Daisy's quarters, where, she promised Bess, she would set her new 'maid' to darning her stockings.

"We ought to see the Town Hall," Daisy told Nelly doubtfully the very next day, remembering the time when Jack had offered to take her there, the impression still in her mind that it was somewhere all discriminating persons should visit. They took a cab this time, driving along Duke Street and into Castle Street, passing the familiar structure of the Custom House and St George's Church until they reached the magnificence of the Town Hall. It had been used for many purposes in the past, Daisy told Nelly solemnly, doing her duty as a guide. A gaol, many years ago, as an assembly room for weddings and dances but now for the purpose, she supposed, since she was woefully ignorant of such things, of running the affairs of the city of Liverpool. They stared up at the splendid arches which supported the building, at the embattled roof, the square tower from whose windows a lookout had once been posted for the sighting of vessels in the river. They walked through the hushed apartments, studying the portrait of His Majesty King George III, one of George IV, then Prince of Wales, and of the late Duke of York. The ballroom, the one spoken of by Jack, was admired, and its three superb chandeliers, the banqueting rooms, and at the end of two hours they fled like two prisoners from the Borough Gaol, finding their way almost like homing pigeons to the bustling activity of the docks.

What was it drew her there? she asked herself again and again, and the answer was such that she could not contemplate it, pushing it furiously to some place where she could ignore it, telling herself it was Nelly's pleasure which concerned her.

"I like it here, Mrs Lassiter," Nelly had said to her, her face to the sun, the breeze ruffling the frills on her dainty parasol, then, as though realising that Daisy might have thought her to be unappreciative of the many fine places she had taken her to see, she turned hastily, her face crumpled in concern. "Not that them grand buildings and paintings and such weren't ... weren't lovely to see but ..."

"I know what you mean, Nelly, and I must agree I myself prefer to be out here," indicating with a sweep of her hand the splendid panorama of the river and its far shore. They could see the outline of the Cheshire woods, and beyond them, no more than a smudge in the distance, the Welsh hills. To the north was the river's opening into the Irish Channel and the comforting strength of the Rock Perch lighthouse and fort, a welcome beacon to the returning sailor on a stormy night. "Tell you what, whilst the weather's fine we might as well make the most of it and visit some of the outdoor sights hereabouts," and so, during the next few weeks, they crossed the river by the Woodside ferry, to Bidston Hill where once she had gone with Sam, to Leasowe Castle and the lighthouse, to New Brighton and Liscard where the magazines were situated and where all powder brought by in-bound vessels was deposited for the sake of safety. To the Wallasey Pool, to Monk's Ferry to visit the old priory of Birkenhead where, years ago, a great stone was dislodged revealing three skeletons in a perfect state of preservation. Nelly had pulled a face and drawn back, not at all sure the skeletons were not to be produced and quite positive that she did not want to see them if they were.

They journeyed to Toxteth Park to stare at the beautiful mansions set in grounds as big as parks themselves. It was here that the immensely rich of Liverpool lived and Daisy remembered the rumour which had been whispered about, that Sam was to build a home for himself here. They were en route for Hale Hall to look at the gardens and conservatories where, it was said, many of the rare plants were well worth seeing, amongst them a cork tree, a tea tree and a banana tree. Nelly had gone on ahead, the tea tree of enormous fascination to her for how could those minute tealeaves which she put into the teapot each day, cling to the branches of a tree and Daisy was alone, in the lovely peace of the Hall's gardens.

She sank down on to a wrought-iron seat, her face in repose drawn and sad. The association of ideas caused by the sight of those grand houses she had just seen created a picture of Sam in her mind, his face as clear and vivid as though he stood before her. All of a sudden it seemed she was unable to keep him at bay any longer and a tidal wave of images crowded upon her. It was three months now since the day when she had taken Nelly down to the docks, on an impulse, she admitted, which had been strange in itself though she had not thought so at the time. She had seen the tragedy of Sam's crippled ship, and though he had grinned at her in his usual sardonic way there had been despair in his eyes. The *Golden Lady* was still in the graving dock, she had heard only the other night in the gossip which went about the club. Perhaps it was this which had loosened her hold on the thoughts which were swallowing her sense and reason. For it was not sensible, nor was it reasonable, to let her mind wander back among the memories, the excitement, the wellbeing, the delight and, yes, the lovely rapture Sam had brought into her life. With a lift of his shoulders in an ironic shrug, a grin of pure wickedness about his wide, strong mouth, he had introduced her to new and often giddy pleasures, taken her on a voyage of magic in his inventive search for the special joy only he could give her. He had carried her into a world of laughter, sometimes boisterous and rowdy, even coarse, sometimes kindly, gentle, whimsical. A deep and complex man who allowed no one to see the real Sam Lassiter. A true man, strong, masculine, earthy, with his feet firmly planted in the world of reality, but a sensitive man, a man of good taste and good humour, and her life was hollow without him.

She became still as she acknowledged the truth. Not just her calm and self-possessed exterior which reclined gracefully on the wrought-iron seat, but the turbulent hidden self of her which no one could see and which she had not, until now, admitted to. What was it saying to her, that stillness in which Sam's face was clearly etched? What was she telling herself, what was she allowing herself to confess to? She had sworn years ago that no man would ever own her again. That no man would hold her to him with chains of what was known as love. That she had done with it, and with *them*, and wanted nothing but the security and independence her own efforts brought her. Now she had them. She wanted nothing else but the ruin of Miles Thornley and he was fast heading on the road to his own destruction. She had schemed to achieve it and though, if she was honest, it had not been *her* efforts which had brought it about but his own wild decadence, it was happening nonetheless.

So why did she feel so ... unfinished? She had found great contentment in Nelly's company. She spent hours with the young girl when her business allowed it, teaching her to read and write fluently and to add up a column of figures as well as Daisy did herself, and with an eye to the future, the rudiments of caring for a lady. She had bought a piano and Nelly was learning to play it, to sing, and though Daisy had jibbed at the fine embroidery it was the custom to put young ladies to, she would one day have all their attributes. She might take up employment as a governess if she so chose but Daisy didn't want that for her, nor the superior condescension with which, as a servant in a middle-class home, she would be treated. She pretended to herself, and to Bess, that that was the idea of training Nelly as she was doing but it was not. It was simply that Daisy was lonely, alone and empty, and needed the girl to fill that emptiness which Sam's going had left in her.

Nelly's voice interrupted her thoughts. For a moment Daisy was disorientated, her lovely face pale and bewildered beneath the flower laden splendour of her hat, then she smiled and held out her hand affectionately. Nelly was a demonstrative child now that someone was willing to take what she offered. Her own mother had been too bedevilled and bowed down to do more than see that her children were as warm and as well fed as her husband's meagre wage could manage, all her emotion channelled into that one purpose in life. Bess, though stout-hearted and generous was unable, through her own upbringing, her years of keeping her emotions firmly under control, to show her love and so Nelly bestowed on Daisy all the repressed affection she had stored up for fifteen years. Remembering Cassie, Daisy returned that affection and the growing bond was strong between them.

"That tree don't ... doesn't have any tealeaves on it, Mrs Lassiter," Nelly declared indignantly and Daisy laughed, drawing the young girl's hand through her arm. What a lot of nonsense she had been wallowing in, she told herself firmly as they strolled beneath the trees towards the carriage. What a lot of sentimental nonsense. She would put it all behind her and get on with the good life she had made for herself, and for Nelly, and damnation to the rest.

She was not awfully sure who she meant by 'the rest'.

The American Civil War dragged on. The North was holding the South in a virtual state of siege. The Yankee gunboats had tightened the nets at the seaports and fewer and fewer ships were able to slip past the blockade. The South had always lived by selling cotton and buying the things it did not produce. Plantation owners with crops stored in their cotton sheds knew that if they could just get the raw cotton to Liverpool it would fetch them a vast fortune but little good that would do them now. General William Sherman was marching his army into Georgia and in the Confederate states of the South the hardships caused by the blockade grew. Privation was severe and the British blockade-running ships grew even more daring.

There was not an evening in 'Daisy's' when Captain Sam

Lassiter's name, or that of one of the other enterprising men who took part in the trade, was not mentioned.

"I see your husband has been in the thick of it again, Daisy," Sir John Templeton said to her in the week between Christmas and the New Year.

"Indeed, Sir John, when has he ever been anything else?" pretending a knowledge she did not have. Her face was suddenly strained, the memory of that dreadful day when the *Golden Lady* had been all but destroyed, sliding unwelcome into her mind. "He has a talent for finding trouble, Sir John," she managed to say, turning away to take a glass of champagne from the tray of a passing footman, beginning to sip it feverishly in the hope that Sir John would not notice her suddenly agitated state.

"And one for eluding it, as well, my dear. What a lucky escape and to come through without a scratch. I suppose it was due to that new steamship of his which I heard can do almost nineteen knots, though your husband swears he will not sail her again but will take on another fellow to do it. A sailing-ship man, he declares himself to be, though the steamer is the fastest of her class, so he was telling me when last I saw him."

"I believe she is, Sir John," willing him to continue for how else was she to discover what had happened to Sam and his new ship, "though I must admit to a sad lack of knowledge on such matters. Sam does not talk about his deeds, you know. I do know he has to make a run for it . . ."

She left the sentence hanging in midair, hoping Sir John would finish it for her and she was not disappointed.

"So he said, though I believe it was as he was entering port that he was spotted. Have I the right story?"

"You have, Sir John, but do go on. I will probably hear more from you than Sam ever tells me," smiling somewhat feverishly, Sir John thought.

"Really?" though he was not surprised. The rumours about the dashing Captain and a certain lady who, it was said, pursued him even more strenuously than the gunboats of the Federal navy, were still whispered in the clubs and business houses of Liverpool and though Lassiter had been in port several times in the last six months not once had he been seen in his wife's company so was it any wonder she knew little about his exploits?

"Well," he continued, "apparently he crept so close between a line of Union warships, under cover of dark, of course, his crew could hear a conversation taking place on the deck of one of them. Unfortunately Captain Lassiter's smoke was spotted against the skyline, and he was challenged. A shot across his bows followed and he was ordered to heave-to, which he did, being a sensible fellow. A prize crew was put aboard but he plied them with fine French brandy, so the tale goes, entertaining them he told them, since they were the victors, and they all became drunk. Then, casting off the towline which linked him to the escorting warship, he drifted silently away into the darkness. His 'captors' woke up to find themselves prisoners inside the Confederate harbour. A clever fellow, that husband of yours."

"Indeed he is, Sir John," barely able to answer coherently for the lump in her throat. Pride, and laughter, filled her since it was just the very thing Sam Lassiter would do and get away with.

"A fine ship, that *Country Girl*, by all accounts."

Country Girl! He had called his ship *Country Girl* and this time she had to excuse herself hastily before Sir John Templeton noticed and remarked on her strange manner. She moved, apparently serene as a swan on a lake, smiling and bowing to her guests until she reached the small plain parlour at the back of the house where Jack, and more often than not, Bess, sat to drink a cup of tea, or hot chocolate, and which had become, without anyone being really aware of it, *their* room. It was known as 'Jack's room' or 'Miss Miller's room', a place cosy and warm in winter with no claim to the elegance of the rest of the house, cool in summer with its French windows opening on to the garden.

Jack was there, turning, startled as she came in. He was very old now, having the crumpled, fragile look of a man who is near the end of his span. Thin as a stick and rheumy of eye he pottered about the place, keeping an 'eye' on

494

'things' for Captain Lassiter, going off now and again on mysterious errands into town, saying nothing to anyone about where he had been but Daisy suspected it was to see Sam.

"Well, missy, to what do I owe this honour?" he asked peevishly, just as though his privacy was about all he had left and now she had come to take even that, but his eyes had softened at the sight of her. He knew all there was to know about Daisy Lassiter and though he did not agree with many of the things she got up to, he would defend to the death her right to get up to them. She was a fine courageous woman but he wouldn't have dreamed of telling her so.

"He's called his ship *Country Girl*, Jack," she burst out without preamble. "Why? What does it mean?" She sat down heavily in the chair opposite him, her eyes huge and shocked in her white face.

"Who told you that?"

"Sir John Templeton, and all about the . . . trouble. Jack, why did he call her *Country Girl*? Do *you* know?"

"Nay, missy, I don't," but of course he did though he would not admit it to her.

"Has it . . . is it anything to do with me? I mean I was a country girl when we met."

Jack snorted ungraciously, then threw back his almost bald head in derisive laughter. He slapped his good leg with what he would have her think was ridicule. "You bloody women! I don't know! You think 'owt a chap does must have summat to do with you, don't you? Just because he's named that floating heap of scrap-iron he calls a ship *Country Girl*, you imagine he was thinking on you when he did it. Give over, lass! You and him have made it quite plain to one another, and to me, that there's nowt left between you, if there was ever anything there in the first place except what's always linked a man and a woman. God knows why he married you because I don't but I suppose the pair of you had some good reason. Now, I'm off to me berth if there's nowt else you want me for. You're welcome to sit by the fire though, if you've a mind to," and he stumped off, slamming the door behind him, leaving Daisy to stare wretchedly into the embers of the dying fire.

It was February when he came into the club again, this time in the company of a young man whose sun-browned face and sun-bleached hair proclaimed him to be of the same profession as Sam Lassiter. They were both immaculate in their black evening dress, bringing with them that unmistakable aura of wealth and power men of means have about them. Men who are used to risk, to the danger and excitement and the gamble they take with their own lives and which is irresistible to women. They smoked expensive cigars and at Sam's cuffs there was the flash of diamonds.

"Daisy, my darling, how charming you look tonight," he drawled, "but then you always do. Did I not say she was charming, Rob?" turning to the younger man who had hung back for a moment to allow Captain Lassiter to greet his wife. Sam kissed her dazed cheek, just as though he had seen her only an hour since, then taking her hand placed it in that of his companion. "This is the master of my *Lady of the Sea*, Daisy. Robert Adams is his name and I have promised him a night of honest gambling which, as we know, is always to be found at 'Daisy's' so perhaps one of your ... minions ... could show him the way. What would you care for, Rob? It is all to be had at 'Daisy's', is it not, my sweet? Brag, ombre, baccarat, vingt-et-un, roulette, just name your play. I shall be down in an hour or so. Daisy and I have something we wish to do in private, have we not, my love, and if I'm not you can find your own way back to your club, I'm sure."

His meaning was obvious but by this time Daisy had got over her shock, the shock and enchantment which last time had allowed her to be led obligingly up the stairs to her own bedroom. This time the rage which she had learned to keep firmly tamped down in her dealings with drunken gentlemen, lecherous gentlemen, gambling gentlemen who had lost everything they had and were offensive about it, erupted from her in a great black snarling surge which threatened to unleash the foul language she had once known as a field girl. Her face turned an ugly grey colour and her eyes glowed, brown and hot and hating this man who was about to make use of her again, she was sure.

She lifted both her hands and sprang at him, an incoherent cry shrilling from her stretched mouth with a force which made the hum of voices about them cease suddenly. Swift as a panther Sam had his arms about her and though she struggled madly, trying to bite his cheek, to kick him wherever she could, preferably between his legs, to scream her hate, her rage, her agony of broken pride, he held her so tightly as he drew her towards the small back parlour, she could do nothing but go with him. His face was as white as hers beneath its dark amber, his eyes a deep anxious green, and when they were out of sight of the gentlemen he lifted her against him, carrying her forcibly to Jack and Bess's room.

"Stop it, for God's sake, stop it. They'll hear you and before you know it it'll be all over Liverpool that Sam and Daisy Lassiter have resorted to fisticuffs in the hallway of the club."

"What the hell do I care, you swine. Let go of me, *let go of me* or I'll tear your cheek to the bone. What the devil d'you mean coming here after all this time . . . ?"

"You've missed me then?"

"Damn you to hell, Sam Lassiter. I suppose that . . . that bloody woman is after you again so you must produce your loving wife to hold her off, is that it? Well, I won't be made use of, d'you hear?" She beat on his head and face with her fists. "Put me down or I swear at the first chance I get I'll kill you." She was beyond caring who heard her, beyond anything but the strange and maddened desire to hurt him in any way she could, to see him fall wounded, bleeding, *dying* at her feet. Her words became obscene, dredged up through the layers of the years which stood between her and the filthy brat who had once thought such language commonplace.

"Hell's teeth, Daisy, where did you learn such words? You sound like some foul guttersnipe from the stews of Liverpool," but he was beginning to smile despite himself, inclined to let go of her if she promised to control herself, and through

the curious madness which had taken her over she could feel
a definite tendency in her to giggle. A realisation of the laugh-
ableness of the past few minutes; the humour which somehow always made itself felt when she and Sam had fought in
the past. It was the quite absurd foolishness of the situation
which had her perched in his arms, high against his chest,
their faces no more than two inches apart and glaring at one
another like two prizefighters.

"Will you promise not to strike me if I put you down?"
he said, his voice huskier than it normally was.

"I promise if you promise not to ..."

"What?"

"Well ..." Her hands had gone to his shoulders without
her knowing how they had got there. She sighed, feeling
the last of the madness leave her, its place taken by a strange
languor. He made no attempt to set her on her feet and the
silence between them was heavy, burdened by the weight
of the unexpected warmth between them. His face was very
serious now, stern almost, his eyes steady and watchful.

"Sam ... I am ... I feel that you should know that ..."

"Yes ... ?"

"... I have no intention of ..."

"... neither have I ..."

"I could never ..."

"Never what, my pet?" and his eyes had wandered to her
mouth which parted, her tongue moving between her lips
to moisten them in a way which had always fascinated him.

"Things can never be in any way different between us ..."

"I know that."

He put her down, turning her gently to face him. His
hands cupped her face, warm and strong and infinitely welcome, and when his mouth brushed hers questioningly it
was waiting for him.

"Daisy ..." she heard him murmur "... no one in the
world ..."

"Sam ..." Her hands rose to close over his, pressing them
about her face and then she heard nothing more, knew
nothing more but the inexpressible joy of being with him,
of being loved by him, of having his hard masculine body

against hers. Somehow they had shed the layers of their clothing and the softness of Bess's rug was beneath them. No one came to see where she was and later she slept in his arms before the leaping fire which he kept replenished during the night.

He was gone when she awoke.

He came back three days later and her heart, which had been dazed by his loss, leapt achingly to greet him across the sun-dappled hallway though her words were cool.

"What is it this time, Sam? A written note from my own hand to let the lady know you are well and truly married? Perhaps she would like to see our wedding lines?"

"Don't, Daisy. I didn't come for that, this time, nor the last, nor the time before that."

"What did you come for then? And I will have the truth, Sam, for I'm tired of these games we seem to play, you and I. I have a mind to see the back of you for good."

The muscles of his face spasmed and he turned away for a moment as though at last she had mortally wounded him. When he spoke his voice was low and she had strain to hear him.

"I came because you are my wife. I came to make sure . . . I had to see for myself that you took no harm. Jack . . . he told me . . . watched out for you whilst I was away. I had left instructions . . . there were men who would have protected you should you have needed it . . . from anyone who might have hurt you. Sweet Christ, do you think I would have . . ." He trembled violently and she longed to cross the hall and take him in her arms but she stayed where she was, needing something from him he had not yet given her. He stared blindly into the corner, his back as straight as an arrow. "You seemed . . . did not appear to object when I . . . the other night, Daisy . . . and I took hope from it. You seemed not to find it . . . unpleasing."

"And you, Sam? How did you view what.... took place between us?"

"Dammit, Daisy, this is hard enough without your scorn. I am to be away tomorrow . . . Jesus, can you not see what I am trying to say?" His pain overwhelmed her, the wild pain and unsteady violence of him which was ready to tip him over. He seemed about to shout and bluster that he would have his way; instead he said quietly, "Don't waste what we have, Daisy. Don't throw it away."

Her throat was tight with tears and she put a hand to her mouth.

"I've missed you, Daisy."

"Yes . . ."

"What else do you want me to say?"

"There must be something you can think of?" and her heart was banging joyfully in her breast.

"Will you marry me, Daisy?" He faced her, smiling, and taking her wrist he turned it over, kissing the crazy pulse which beat there with such gentleness she could hardly bear it.

"Sam, we are already married."

"Not really, Daisy."

"No . . ."

"For God's sake, don't you know I love you?"

"Do you, Sam?" and the ice which had hardened her heart, held it in a frozen state for almost nine years, ever since Miles Thornley had done with her, melted, bursting now with the release of her own love.

"I've loved you for a long time, Daisy."

"Really?" She could hardly contain the delight of it and her face broke into a smile of such great love and tenderness, he fell back for a moment, amazed. She looked as she had done years ago. A child being introduced to joys the likes of which she had never before known.

"Do you . . . ?" he hesitated.

"I love you, Sam. I love you."

He had her in his arms then, deep, deep in his strong arms, lifting her up against him, his face buried in the sweet-scented curve of her neck and shoulder.

"Dear God . . . I've wanted this for so long, so long."

"Sam . . ."

"Jesus, if you only knew."

"I do, my darling, I do."

They spent the rest of that day, and the night, wrapped

together in bemused caresses, talking through the hours they had left of the conflicts that had grown between them, of their hopes and dreams of the future they planned together. They made love, not talking but communicating nevertheless, hands speaking, eyes speaking, touches that sighed of their love for one another. He slept and she watched him, studying his face and body in the light from the lamp beside the bed, her hand whispering against his warm brown skin, the deep-chestnut weight of his tumbled hair. She loved him. She slept with her head on his shoulder, her limbs entwined with his, conscious that he was there to guard her, conscious that she had not known she needed guarding, aware even as she slept that he would be there when she awoke. The joy of being loved, the joy of loving was so great she wept and he comforted her in his arms, understanding.

And then it was time for him to go.

"Three weeks, sweetheart. A month, no more."

She was afraid for him. She thought of all those times she had carelessly let him go and of all those times when he had gone without her knowing. Her heart had been light then, without the burden of the love she now carried. It had had in it only the sweet memories of Cassie, the nightmare of her death and the undertaking she had sworn to uphold to bring about the ruin of Miles Thornley.

At that last moment, as he held her in his arms in the hush of dawn, the winter's morning late in breaking, no more than a sliver of daylight shining across the estuary, she clung to him, wordless, since she knew that soon she must tell him that even this, this joyous love which had come upon them, could not alter what she had set out so long ago to accomplish. Even now, with the sweetness of their love like honey in her veins, with Sam's heart beating at last to the same rhythm as her own, Miles Thornley's arrogantly smiling face hovered behind the closed lids of her eyes.

She was weeping as she watched Sam's lean figure climb into the cab.

33

It was, of course, worse now that she knew love, the loneliness, the emptiness, the fear, the dread of hearing from some casual lips that Captain Lassiter had come to a bad end at last and when, four weeks later, he strode into the house, sweeping her off her feet and into his arms, she found it almost impossible to believe that he had returned to her.

"What, tears?" he laughed, peering into her face which she had pressed frantically against his chest, lifting her chin to kiss them away, to reach for his handkerchief and have her blow her nose like a child, then, before the dumbfounded gaze of Nora who had come running to see what all the commotion was about, carried her up the stairs and into their bed.

"My wife and I are not to be disturbed until a week on Tuesday, Nora," he called over his shoulder, sending the maid into a fit of giggles as she hurried back to the kitchen to tell them what Captain Lassiter had said to her.

"There's been no one but you," he said later, much later, to his wife. It was spoken challengingly and she knew that he was telling her that though he might have been unfaithful to her in the past, he had not been so on this last trip. He was telling her that Sam Lassiter had no need of such things now. He brought her gifts, a fan, emerald earrings and a cameo of exquisite delicacy, a bird in flight set in gold and rows of seed pearls.

"It brought you to mind when it was offered me, my sweet. You always gave the impression that you had alighted for no more than a moment or two on my hand and the instant I tried to get a firmer grip on you, you flew away.

This, I was told, is a dove but a dove is a docile creature and you were never that, my darling. A wild seabird, perhaps. One of those fierce gulls which hang on the wind above the river."

Her face was thoughtful as he put the earrings in her ears, grinning wickedly as he looked for some place to put the cameo since she was naked. She sat cross-legged in the middle of the tumbled bed, the early spring sunshine falling across her from between the partly drawn curtains. It was March now and the day was mild. In the garden the primroses starred the greening grass and bold tulips trumpeted between the denuded rose-bushes. Buds were breaking out and a thrush was pouring forth its joy, the notes of its song proclaiming the ending of winter. Sam had made love to her, his face strong and wild as though now, *now* she was really his. His wife, his woman as she had never been before and the cries of her rapture, the sweet passion they had shared, still echoed about the room.

"You say you were 'offered' these gifts, Sam? What d'you mean? Did you not buy them in the usual way from . . . well, wherever it is you would buy such things?"

The humour slipped away from his face and he sighed as he lay down beside her and pulled her to him. His hand smoothed her shoulder and then came to rest on her small, pink-tipped breast, cupping it possessively.

"There is great privation in the American Southern states, Daisy. They are under virtual siege apart from what we take in. As the armies fight across the land the Generals 'commandeer' everything the people in their path own until they are starving. All they have, the women who have been left behind to look after children, farms, even plantations whilst their men fight, is what jewellery they were given in happier times. These . . ." indicating the earrings and the cameo ". . . are some of them. Oh, I gave her a good price, the lady, and she was a lady, Daisy, who stopped me on the sidewalk of Wilmington. I paid her in gold sovereigns since the paper money of the Confederacy is worth nothing. What I paid for these, my darling, would feed that woman and her family for a year, even with the inflated prices the war has caused. You will wear them proudly, will you not, Daisy, knowing they belonged to a brave woman who would be starving but for your husband?"

He grinned whimsically, taking the pomposity from the words, then before she could answer rolled her on top of him, holding her tightly, kissing her slowly, sensuously, and the earrings and the woman to whom they had belonged were forgotten.

The usual practice of the blockade-runner, he told her later, was to sail between the islands in the Gulf of Mexico and the West Indies, which provided a staging post for them, and the nearest Confederate ports of Galveston and Mobile. They carried goods brought in from Europe and returned with cotton. But Sam was against this, saying that with this method there were too many fingers in the rich pie of blockade-running. Too many middlemen and he preferred to carry out the whole operation himself, therefore gaining the whole profit.

"You're married to a rich man, Daisy," he told her, grinning ruefully. "That *Country Girl* of mine which . . . yes, yes, I did name her for you, my love, and I was sure you must have guessed it . . . you did! . . . what a clever girl you are, and lovely as well as clever . . . so warm here . . . so moist and warm here, and here, and I think I shall just have to put . . . yes, just there, and now, if you would turn your hip so . . . yes, just like that, my darling . . . aah, what a clever, clever girl you are . . ."

Later again, he continued his story. "I can call myself a wealthy man now, Daisy, and when this damned war is over I am going to build you the biggest, the most magnificent and luxurious house you have ever seen. No, not in Toxteth park but south of the city on the shore where I can see the ships and the water and our children can smell the sea and run on the beach. I had a man buy me some land, Daisy, whilst I was away. It was purchased with the proceeds of only one trip, *and* there is some left over to start the building of our house. Do you know, two trips bought that steamship of mine and provided the money to have the *Golden Lady* returned to what she was. I shall sail her next time I go out and put a master on the *Country Girl*. There is money in it, Daisy, more money than I could believe. Half-a-crown becomes a sovereign in one trip, did you know that, when you are in the lucrative business of blockade-running. It won't be for much longer though, of that I'm certain and then, when I'm home, they will say we are the most devoted couple Liverpool has ever seen. So unfashionable, in fact downright bad taste to be in love with one's own wife."

He took her about with him, swearing he could not bear her out of his sight, as he purchased the goods with which he would return to America. Cloth for uniforms, medicines, especially quinine, soap, preserved meat, tea, pepper, ham, boots, the list was endless, but where he went so did she, for the first time neglecting her club and her guests, leaving them and it, knowing they were in good hands under the protection of John Elliott and Bess. John had been given a share of 'Daisy's', just five per cent but the incentive to keep it exactly as she had done, to keep its good name and reputation for luxury, fine food and wine, excellent service and honest dealing, were strong in him. She had offered the same to Bess, saying she deserved it for her years of loyalty and hard work, but Bess had been alarmed and not at all sure she understood what it would mean.

"It would mean you owned a small share of 'Daisy's', and any profit it made."

"Eeh, I couldn't take that, Daisy. Not me. I've no business head on me like you. I wouldn't know what to do with it."

"You could put it in the bank, or invest it. Give it to your mother. Set Eddy up in a business, chuck it in the Mersey for all I care, but it would be yours, Bess, to do with as you please. Think what you could do for your Nelly. Pretty clothes . . ."

Bess sniffed. "She's enough of them as it is and needs no more. Why don't you just . . . well, put it in the bank for me and . . . eeh, I don't know, lass. You see to it."

Daisy realised that Bess was afraid of great wealth, or even the modest prosperity Daisy offered her. It was the idea of 'getting above herself' which had been so ruthlessly indoctrinated into her as a child and a young girl and which would not allow her to think of herself as other than a servant. She had a position of great responsibility at 'Daisy's' but she was still, in her own eyes, a servant, so that was all right. She was comfortable with that.

"I'll open an account for you at my bank then and each month I'll put five per cent of the takings into it for you and then when you want some money all you have to do is take a cab to the bank and draw out what you need."

"Righto, lass," Bess said thankfully and proceeded to ignore the enormous amounts which multiplied in her name, spending only what Daisy gave her in wages which, in her opinion, was her due.

Sam took Daisy to all the special places he and she had visited in those first weeks after they had met. To the Adelphi to dine in the same elegant restaurant, treating her like a queen, holding her hand in his for all the world to see and wonder at, his possessive pride in her causing a sensation wherever they went since his fancy for aristocratic ladies was well known. They went to a charity ball at the Town Hall, dancing every dance in one another's arms beneath the glittering chandeliers which Daisy and Nelly had admired only last summer, and to the opera where her beauty, emphasised by the glowing look of love she bestowed on her husband, which he returned, drew the eyes of every gentleman in the audience. They were the talk of the town for it seemed that Captain and Mrs Sam Lassiter had not only renewed their relationship but were *in love*. A husband and a wife so blatantly devoted to one another was something of a novelty and heads turned to get a better view of this phenomenon as they went by.

On the day before he was to sail he took her to the Clarence Graving Dock to see the restored glory of the *Golden Lady*, holding her hand as he guided her proudly across the small bridge which led to the clipper's berth.

"Look," he said softly, tucking her hand in his arm. "Is she not beautiful again?" and she was, her mended spars, the cobweb of rigging, the tall, swaying grace of her masts reaching up to the pale spring sky. Her broken hull was repaired, smooth and freshly painted, even the chains and ropes which held her captive seeming to have a natural symmetry about them. Slim hull, graceful bow, lofty masts. She was as delicately lovely as a woman, as Daisy herself, and Sam Lassiter could not help but swagger somewhat arrogantly as he stood beside his wife and his ship, both of whom he loved more than his own life.

Gulls swooped above them, screaming into the wind, and on the mended decks of the ship seamen moved about making ready for the next day's sailing. Brasswork which was already gleaming was vigorously polished. A touch of paint was applied where none was needed. A last stitch was put in a sail. At the tip of the thrusting, exaggerated bows the sun gleamed on the figurehead of the Golden Lady herself, proud and flaunting and a symbol of the ship's durability.

"She's magnificent, Sam." Daisy hugged his arm to her, smiling up into his eyes, but in hers, though she did her best to conceal it, was the dreadful fear she felt for his safety, and the whole crew were vastly entertained to see their captain take his pretty wife into his arms. They were ready to nudge one another and wink slyly but something in the quiet embrace, the steady declaration of the love shared by the man and woman, was obvious even to the most obtuse and the tenderness with which their dashing captain comforted his wife held them silent and still.

He had been gone three days when Miles Thornley strolled nonchalantly into the club declaring that he was prepared to play cards with anyone who cared to take him on. Bezique, écarté, piquet, it was all the same to him. He felt lucky, he said, and as they all knew the saying 'Unlucky in love, lucky at cards', he was sure they would take his meaning, leering in a nasty way at Daisy.

He was thirty-two years of age, five years younger than Sam but the life he had led for nearly twenty of those years was beginning to show in the altered shape of his face. The flesh had slipped somewhat, its outlines blurred, dissipation showing in the bloodshot blue of his eyes and the looseness of the sensual mouth. It was a cruel mouth, lifted in a perpetual sneer of contempt for those who, in his opinion, were far beneath him. Daisy was one of them.

He had put on weight since last she saw him for, as his obsession with gambling took over his life, he had abandoned the outdoor gentlemanly pursuits of hunting and fishing, of walking in a line of guns across his grouse moor, spending most of his time lounging about in one sporting house or another. He drank to excess and even his pursuit of women, which had been legendary, was no longer as favourable as once it had been since his strange and sometimes cruel partialities had become well known and were to be avoided. His mother, God rest her soul, had lasted no more than two years after her husband's death, dying of a broken heart, those who were close to her said, and his poor wife, the mother of his son and two daughters – proving he had been home to Thornley Green three times at least – never saw him from one month's end to another. His wealth had gone. His vast estate was gone but for the lovely house of Thornley Green and the park surrounding it and what servants remained; the older ones who could find no other employment, had been paid no wages for years. With the loss of the farms and the land which had provided a great deal of money in rent, his railway shares, his mining shares, long gone in payment of his debts, the dozens of other investments and properties which had belonged to the family for generations, he was bankrupt. His family lived in penury, it was said, but for the allowance his wife's father gave her to feed and clothe herself and her children, and Lord Thornley himself owed vasts amounts of money to casinos and sporting houses over most of Europe. Many of their doors were now closed to him, Daisy had heard, permitting him no more credit since what was the sense in throwing good money after bad?

Her heart, for some strange reason since there was nothing unusual in his demeanour, began to beat more quickly as he shrugged out of his cloak but she nodded her head agreeably in his direction before turning to resume her conversation with a foreign ambassador, from Germany he had told her in his heavily-accented English, who was passing through Liverpool on his country's business. He was accompanied by a well-known member of the English peerage and they were both seriously offended by Lord Thornley's unpardonable rudeness to their hostess, she could see.

"And what do you think to our fine city, sir?" she asked of the ambassador, attempting to divert him from the disturbance caused by Miles Thornley. Jacob was at his lordship's elbow, polite, unobtrusive in his attempt to guide him into one of the gaming rooms. "Is this your first visit?" she went on but Lord Thornley shook off Jacob's hand and continued to advance on Daisy where she sat with her guests.

She was simply dressed, plainly even, the gentleman would have said, in a rich cream silk. An elegant gown which clung to her breasts and waist and had nothing about it but two huge cream silk roses in the small of her back. She wore no jewellery but for the cameo Sam had given her and which was pinned on a length of narrow black velvet ribbon about her throat.

"The gallant Captain has deserted you again then, has he, Daisy?" Miles Thornley drawled. "Gone off to younger, more tempting flesh with a bit of fire in it since I believe you to have none."

"*Mein Gott . . .*" the ambassador spluttered and the peer stood up, his face red with outrage.

"I've tried it, you see, gentlemen, and found it sadly lacking." He turned round to those members who had come in behind him, to those who crowded the doorways, the staircase and the hall of the club, having heard of his outrageous conduct, open-mouthed and horrified, every one of them, at this show of ungentlemanly behaviour from one of their own. He was smiling and insolent, his brandy in one hand, his cigar in the other, lifting the cigar to his lips and raising the brandy glass in an arrogant toast to those who watched. "So here's to Daisy's . . ." here he used a word so obscene it froze every man in his seat, or to the spot on which he stood ". . . and to her once masterly use of it which I am sure every one of you is familiar with. Not what it was when she was sixteen and a maid in my mother's kitchen, when I

509

had exclusive use of it, but then good things cannot last for ever, so they say, and Daisy's . . ."

"I believe you mentioned a game of cards, my lord."

Her voice was silky, a cool silkiness which hid the deep black loathing crawling inside her like a venomous snake. She stood up, unperturbed, putting a light hand on the arm of the noble peer who stood like one poleaxed beside her, smiling graciously at him as though she was immensely grateful for his concern but it was not needed. Flicking open her fan which was attached to her wrist with fine silken ribbons, she used it languidly, not a care in the world she would have them believe and certainly not at all put out by this blackguard who had invaded her club, then moved slowly, gracefully across the hallway until she stood before the tall figure of his lordship. She smiled up at him.

"I will play with you, my lord," she said and the gasp which went round the hallway was universal. Not once in all the years since the club had opened had anyone seen Daisy play the games which were there for her guests' amusement. They had observed her as she moved about the rooms, standing behind this or that player, watch a hand or two, congratulate a winner, smile consolingly at a loser, but she had never sat down with them. Never!

His lordship laughed. "Dear God, what pleasure is there in that for me, or gain? I might as well play Snap with my five-year-old son."

"Well, of course, if you have no taste for a gamble . . . ?" She let the words hang for a moment, ". . . then we must leave it at that, though I have heard otherwise. Your prowess, or lack of it, at the gaming tables is well known. But perhaps you would care for something else. Something more lively and less costly. We are aware, at least I am, that your palate, shall we say, is more excited by the flesh of young innocent girls, those who have no defence, nor redress to the law. Those who cannot protect themselves and so are fair game, and what a game, to a man like you. Not that I am speaking of myself, naturally, being no longer young and innocent but someone I knew was and what pleasure and gain you must have had from *her*."

510

His face drained of every scrap of colour. His eyes were suffused with it and they protruded from his flesh in the most frightening way. He lifted his hand and would have knocked her to the ground had Jacob not caught it between both of his, wrenching it backwards and his lordship with it.

"You filthy whore!" He spat at her, the saliva dribbling down the silken folds of her skirt but she did not flinch. She nodded to Jacob who let him go reluctantly. There was not a man in the club now who did not know of the scene in the hallway and as many as could manage it were crowded in doorways, hanging over the banisters and teetering on the stairs. Bess was pressed against the newel post on the landing, hemmed in by a dozen gentlemen, Jack beside her, his face as drawn and wrinkled as an old monkey since he knew there was nothing he could do to protect the wife his captain loved. Not here. Not from this.

"Whore is it, my lord? Your whore, as was my sister who lies in her grave where *you* put her, killed by the child *you* gave her, and she no more than a child herself, but that is not the issue here, is it? You wanted a game of cards, I believe, but I swear there is not a gentleman here who will play with you. You already owe vast sums to gentlemen up and down the country. Your bad luck is legend, and the way in which every sovereign you once owned has slipped through your fingers. But do you know who has those sovereigns, Lord Thornley, do you?"

Her eyes glowed feverishly in the light from the chandelier high above her head. She had never looked more glorious and yet her glory was cruel, as cruel as he was in a way and the gentlemen about her shifted uneasily, strangely disturbed by it. Her head was flung back, her lovely hair glossy and intricately arranged. Her skin was flawless and yet her mouth which every one of them would, five minutes since, have given a year of his life to kiss, curled in a snarl of something they did not care for.

"Cannot you hazard a guess, my lord? Cannot you even chance one guess on the name of the person who for the past five years has stripped you of almost everything you once owned? Yes, that's right, I can see it in your face. Daisy Brindle is her name. Daisy Brindle who once worked, as you have already told these gentlemen, in your mother's kitchen. Daisy Brindle who was disposed of with as little ceremony as one would dispose of an old woollen glove. Do you remember me, as I was then? Sixteen years old and a bloody nuisance to you, and your father who wanted no filth to stick to his revered name so he removed me. Turned me out for the simple crime of telling the truth about his son. Turned me out beyond his fine gates in the cold of a January night and left me to sink or swim. Well, I did not sink, my lord, as you can see. I have managed quite nicely . . ."

"You bitch! I won't let you forget this . . ."

"I don't intend to forget it, and neither will you, I hope. No, I'm going to give you what you and your family never gave me . . ."

"I want nothing of yours, you slut. Your name will be on everyone's lips before I've done with you, you cheating whore. I'll have it all back . . ."

"I don't think so, my lord, for everything I and my husband, naturally, have of yours was obtained within the law, believe me. But come, where is that gambling spirit of which we have all heard so much, indeed which is known the length and breadth of the land and even beyond? No, I won't give it back but I'll give you a chance to win it back!"

There was a hiss of indrawn breath and up on the landing Bess put her face in her hands. From somewhere Nelly had appeared, drawn by the drama which was known of in every corner of the house and she stood beside her sister, her young face pale and bewildered.

Miles Thornley made a great effort to control himself. He studied the lovely face of the woman who stood before him. Her challenge had been flung down and though he would have liked nothing better than to strip her naked and have her flogged through the town at a cart-tail as his grandfather would have had no compunction in doing, indeed would have been entitled to do since she was a cheating whore, he thought it might be just as satisfying to bring her down in another way, to grind her face in her own filth before all these gentlemen who stood about her. They would spread it round the city, in all the places where the name of Daisy Lassiter was respected, across the land and across the seas to where that husband of hers would hear of it and be destroyed by it. He had never seen her play but there was not a woman in the land who could beat Miles Thornley. There was not a woman in the land who could *play* cards for it was a man's game and even the lower classes frowned on what would be thought of as unwomanly.

His eyes gleamed between narrowed lids. She saw it and though the cold expression on her face did not alter, in her heart she gloried in it.

"Very well, but I name the wager."

"Of course, but what have you left to wager *with*?' Her voice was filled with contempt and his grip on his reason slipped. What the bloody hell *did* he have left that would enable him to play honourably? The irony of the last word escaped him. She would not take him on, give him a chance to get back something of what he had lost, give him a chance to go on and play another day if he did not tempt her with something she could not refuse. And there was, of course, only one thing he had left that would do that.

He smiled and Daisy felt an almost reverential awe flood through her. The moment she had waited for had, it seemed, come at last. He was going to fall into the trap she had so neatly set for him. Years and years and now it was here. Oh, Cassie ... Cassie ... at last.

"There is Thornley Green," he said, turning to smile at those about him. "Against everything you have of mine." They gasped in unison. "If I lose..." he grinned at the foolishness of the idea "...then you shall have Thornley Green. If I win..." he licked his lips, "...then you shall return to me everything, every property, every sovereign you have that once was mine. I'm sure you and that bastard husband of yours have a record of it, in view of what has happened here today."

She pretended to hesitate though if he had asked for the

club, for her jewels, the very gown she had on she would have agreed.

"So," he grinned, "now that I propose a serious wager you hold back. See, I will give this note, witnessed by all these gentlemen to ... to His Grace, here ..." turning to the gentleman with whom Daisy had been in conversation when he himself had entered. "I will write it in my own hand, sign it, have His Grace and any other gentleman you care to name sign it as well. You will do the same and we will play a hand or two of ... what? ... écarté? Do you agree, Daisy?"

"Very well, I agree."

They talked of it for many years in Liverpool, even after the two protagonists were dead and buried. There was even a word, a saying, coined which was used whenever someone put one over on another, when one man got the better of another. It was called 'doing a brindle' or 'brindling' and the woman who was the cause of it became a legend in the clubs and casinos where gambling took place.

It was a fair game, those dozens of gentlemen who were privileged to witness it swore to that, an honest game in which she played better than any man they had ever seen, dealing and using the cards dealt her skilfully and with a flair which they could not have believed. Naturally they did not know of the hours and days, the weeks and the months and the years in which she had played every game in her club ready for this moment. Played behind closed doors with only the man who played with her and her loyal friend Bess Miller to see it and neither of them was likely to tell of it. When it was over, when Miles Thornley had staggered from his chair, and from the club, a man who owned nothing but the clothes he stood up in, she had not crowed, nor seemed to glory in her triumph but merely took the paper His Grace, bowing, handed to her stiffly.

"This is yours, madam."

"I believe it is, sir."

"I cannot find it in my heart to admire what you have done."

"I don't suppose you can, Your Grace, since you are of the same class as Miles Thornley."

She walked away from him then, through the silent crowd of awed spectators, across the hallway, up the stairs and into the arms of the plain woman who stood at the top.

"I think I will go straight to bed, Bess," they heard her say as the woman led her away.

The club had never been so crowded in the weeks that followed, every man and his dog, as Bess said fretfully, wanting to see the woman who had ruined the Thornley family. They talked of nothing else in the city, high and low alike. When would she move to the great house of Thornley Green? they asked one another, or would she sell it? that and the parkland, turning out his lordship's wife and children, his young son who would now never inherit what had belonged to the house of Thornley for nearly four centuries. It was as though she and she alone had brought Miles Thornley down, kicked him as he fell, disinherited his young son, made homeless his daughters, no more than babies, taken the very food from their mouths, his lordship's own part in it overlooked.

She bore it steadfastly, clinging to Bess, to Nelly and Jack, moving about the club each evening, seeing the speculation in the eyes of men who had once only admired her. Seeing the greed, the desire to know what Miles Thornley had known, for surely a woman such as she must be special in that area. She waited, she waited for the scandal to die down. She waited. That was all she did. She waited for Sam Lassiter to come home and when he did she was aware before he closed the door behind him that he knew.

34

She stood up slowly, her heart contracting painfully, the hope in it that he would allow her to explain beginning to die even then. He glanced at her briefly, then, his tread heavy, he moved towards the table where the brandy decanter stood. Removing the stopper he poured himself a glass, filling it to the brim, then sat down, looking at it but not drinking.

"Sam..." Her heart thudded in her chest and she could hardly speak. Her mouth was dry and she was desperately afraid but she tried again. "Sam, I'm so glad to see you. I just..."

He looked up at her and something in his eyes silenced the words on her lips. He looked at her steadily. His eyes were dark and heavy with fatigue and there was no sign of the leaping light of love in them which had become so wonderfully familiar during the last few months. His face was drawn, with a sallow tinge beneath the amber, and she noticed with surprise that he had not shaved. His suit was wrinkled and though he did not touch the brandy in the glass she could smell it on his breath, even from where she stood, as though this was not the first he had poured. She had a fierce desire to sink to her knees before him, to cradle his head against her shoulder, to cry "I love you" but something in him stopped her and she waited despairingly for him to speak.

"I heard of it in Wilmington," he said heavily. "Your ... fame ... has reached even the shores of America." His sombre gaze went past her, staring at some memory which was almost too much for him to bear. "Several gentlemen who had left Liverpool after I did made it their business . . . went out of their way, I should say, to tell me of the night when my wife stripped Lord Thornley of the last of his fortune, stripped him of his family home and of his good name . . ."

"*His good name . . .!*"

She might not have spoken. ". . . Shamed him, it seems, since not one of them thought he had done anything to deserve it. Certainly he had gambled but then who amongst us has not? He drank rather heavily and was unfaithful to his wife, but we all do that, don't we, Daisy, so these gentlemen, though they did not say so to my face, did not seem to admire what you had done. They implied, in fact, that they themselves would not care to frequent a club where the owner might not be wholeheartedly concerned with their enjoyment since Miles Thornley certainly did not enjoy the experience and who was to say it could not happen to them? All over the city it was, apparently, and Daisy Lassiter's name was on everyone's lips. They were inclined to gloat about it, their eyes sharp and watchful to see how I would take it, eager to know if I was aware that not only my wife, but her sister, had been his lordship's whore. And could it be true, they certainly asked one another, the story of how he had killed my wife's sister?" His expressionless eyes went over her shoulder, staring again at that memory. "I knocked them down and threw them off my ship."

Daisy shivered. Something dreadful whispered by her skirts, touching her softly with an icy chill. It was like the night she had stood beside Cassie's bed and known that a sweetness, a goodness had gone from her life for ever. As though it was happening again but somehow she could not bring herself to kneel before him, to beg, to plead, to try and explain, to tell him what she meant to do now. He would not believe her. This was not the time because he simply would not believe her.

His eyes came back to her and his voice was light and cool as he spoke.

"I was a fool, Daisy. I thought it was all over, you see, this obsession you had with Thornley. I thought it would fade from your mind, that you would put it from you, bury it decently before it rotted your soul but I was wrong. It was so obvious that we were meant for one another, you and I. We were both shrewd, determined to get what we wanted from life but I liked to think we were ... honest. Now I know I was wrong about you. We could have had a good life ... well, it doesn't matter now."

His voice was calm and tired and instinctively she made a move towards him, not meaning to but drawn to his pain, wanting to comfort him but he put out a hand. "No, thank you, Daisy ..." smiling politely as though she had offered him another glass of brandy "... don't ... don't try to explain or say how sorry you are because I don't want to hear it. I don't care to risk myself again, you see. I can't risk my heart ..." His words faded as he turned away to stare into the fire but he made no move to leave.

"What will we do?" she said at last. Her figure cast a long shadow, stretching to the corner of the darkening room for it was evening and the light had already vanished beyond the rooftops of the houses opposite. It was July but the day had been cold. There had been heavy rain earlier and distant thunder echoing from the peaks of the Pennine Hills to the east. Overcast and gloomy and almost like winter as the wind howled down the chimney. She and Nelly had walked down to the river, braving the wet and the cold, watching the wind lash the waters into rippling miniature waves, each one topped with a frill of cream. Nelly had held her hand companionably, saying nothing, her attitude one of protective concern. All those in the house knew Mrs Lassiter was not herself. Who amongst them had not heard the whispers, seen the nudges as they themselves went past when they were out, for her notoriety was such that even they were tainted by it. Not that they cared about that. She was a generous mistress was Mrs Lassiter, treating them as though they were human beings and not slaves as many employers did. They worked hard certainly, but under the well-ordered supervision of Miss Miller who had been a housemaid herself and knew what it was like. They did not labour beyond endurance as so many did. They were not hedged about with petty regulations. They were warm and well fed and slept comfortably no more than two to a room. The maids did not live in fear of being seduced by the men of the household, nor of being thrown out for the slightest misdemeanour. They had worked in places where they had wept in exhausted pain, degraded and looked down on, but it was not like that at Mrs Lassiter's and if she had done something wrong, which it seemed she had from all the gossip, then they were not the ones to judge her. The club was just as busy so it seemed to them there was little to be concerned about. Those of them who had been present when his lordship and Mrs Lassiter had played that infamous hand of cards had themselves been dumbfounded but, not really understanding, could not see what all the fuss was about.

Nelly and Bess knew though. They were close to Daisy and they were aware that she was dazed and wounded by what had happened. It was as though two bare-knuckle prizefighters had gone thirty rounds in the ring, a not unusual practice in the world of sport, wearing each other down with every blow until at last the stronger had knocked the weaker to the canvas from where he had not got up. The stronger had won, but at what cost? And Daisy Lassiter, after years of fighting, though she had been the winner was terribly weakened by it and only the anticipation of her husband's return kept her on her feet, Nelly and Bess were both well aware.

There was not a lot Nelly did not know about Daisy Lassiter now, absorbing it little by little in the past twelve months. She loved her and if Nelly could do anything, *anything*, to ease her mistress's suffering – though Daisy could not really be called her mistress any longer – she would. She was always there at the beginning and end of each day. She brought Daisy her early-morning tray, pulling back the curtains, plumping up the pillows at her back, placing the tray across her knees, fussing and fretting as she coaxed Daisy to 'eat up'. She worried as she watched her become thinner, fine drawn, her eyes turning constantly towards the river where her husband's clipper ship would surely soon be sighted. She was with her during the day, quiet and calm, smiling, reading, practising her piano exercises, walking beside her on one of Daisy's many restless pacings up and down the Marine Parade. It was Nelly who saw the sly smiles and nudges, the winks and whispers, the appraising stares from men and women, from ladies and gentlemen who watched the two of them go by. She waited up for her at the end of the long evenings, putting her to bed like a child. She was scarcely more than a child herself, sixteen now but with a maturity, a steadiness and compassion which far exceeded her years. Bess and Jack watched, knowing that what Daisy needed until Captain Lassiter came home she was getting from the one person who seemed able to give it to her and that was Nelly.

Now they waited, all of them, in the kitchens and the stillroom and cellars of the tall house in Duke Street, waited with the breathless, hushed expectancy of those who, though they know something extraordinary is in the air, are not awfully sure what it is, and upstairs the woman who was their mistress waited too. Waited for her husband's answer.

"I don't know what you are going to do, Daisy, and I really don't care."

"Sam . . ." Her face had the waxy pallor of death and her cry was a rending of the heart. She swayed as though she would fall, her shadow moving in sympathy on the sitting-room wall, but she did not sit down. She was like a woman on whom a death sentence has been passed but he only sighed sadly, not greatly concerned, it seemed, with her feelings any longer. He continued to speak, his eyes on the glass of brandy with which he still toyed.

"I shall do one more trip to America. I have . . . commitments there and then . . . well . . ." His voice was empty, drained and sad, ". . . I have a fancy for peace, Daisy. I'm thirty-eight years old and for the past twenty of them I've roamed this earth striving for . . . something. It doesn't seem to matter any more so I think I'll probably buy myself a house abroad somewhere, sit in the sunshine and . . . well, who knows?" He smiled ruefully, looking up at her. "I've had a hell of a good time, Daisy, and I don't suppose that 'peace' will satisfy me for the rest of my days but for now I have a mind to try it."

"Take me with you."

"No."

"Sam..."

"No, Daisy."

She threw out her hands to him in heartbreaking appeal and her love was in her face but he turned away from it indifferently, then rose to his feet.

"We cannot pick up the shattered fragments and put them together again. What is broken, for one reason or another, is broken. Trust has gone. Respect has gone and what is left is not enough. I wish I could feel differently but I don't and so..." He shrugged impassively, then, "Goodbye Daisy."

They heard the front door close, those downstairs, looking at one another fearfully for what did it mean? The Captain had been in the house no more than an hour and was that him gone already? Nelly put her hand to her mouth, her eyes huge and frightened in her face. She turned to Bess but her sister was already out of the kitchen door and halfway up the stairs to the hallway.

They reached the door to Daisy Lassiter's room together.

It went round the city like wildfire, leaping from mouth to mouth, from mansion to villa to hovel, from the Custom House where Captain Lassiter was well known, of course, to the cotton warehouses, indeed to all the places where business was done, from ship to ship, those in harbour and which would carry it even beyond the shores of the land, that Captain Sam Lassiter had gone again. What on earth were the Lassiters up to now, those who knew them asked one another wonderingly, for it seemed that no sooner had the pair of them settled down together, close as two leaves on a branch, dewy-eyed and glowing at one another as though they were newlyweds, than she vanished from the gaming rooms and he was off on the high seas again with scarcely time to load up his ship with a fresh cargo. The *Golden Lady* had already sailed, crammed with the usual goods the Captain took to the dying Southern states of

America. Goods that were desperately needed despite the rebel raids into the state of Maryland where the army plundered for horses, cattle and provisions. The South was reeling under defeat from General Sherman's army which was heading towards Atlanta, the newspapers reported, the stronghold of the South, so could it last much longer, this 'brothers' war', as it was being called, they demanded to know.

Bess and Nelly did not much care as they watched Daisy Lassiter move about the world she and they inhabited, like some shadowed ghost, a vague, insubstantial ghost who did not answer when spoken to, who sat for hours in a darkened room listening for a voice which was silent, watching for a man who did not come. Who ate obediently when told to, who bathed in the steaming, scented bath they placed her in, and dressed herself in the gowns they suggested. She was as elegant, as immaculately toiletted, as lovely as she had always been but her dresses hung on her thin figure and her beauty was as fragile and vulnerable as a snowdrop. She did not go out, nor down into the gaming rooms and it was three weeks before she struggled out of the hopeless pit of despair into which Sam Lassiter had so carelessly flung her.

"There's a chap to see you, Daisy. He's downstairs and he says it's urgent." Bess's voice was stern, harsh even for she was at her wits' end what with trying to keep the club running, her and John Elliott between them, with the talk and the whispers and the constant demands from gentlemen who had come to 'gawk' at Daisy herself who was about to slip into a decline from which she would never recover, if Bess was any judge. She'd be glad of anything to whip her out of this trance she was in, Bess told herself, and though she had no idea what the man wanted, she didn't care if it brought Daisy to life again.

"Should she be bothered?" Nelly whispered anxiously. She sat with Daisy all the time, watching her, anticipating, if she could, her every need, hovering palely like a ghost herself in her willingness to ease Daisy's pain. "It might ... upset her."

"Upset her! Dear God, Nelly, just look at her. D'you reckon 'owt else *could* upset her? I only wish someone would, p'raps then she'd show a bit of life. She can't go on like this, lass," speaking to Nelly just as though Daisy wasn't there which was how it seemed to Bess. "We must fetch her out of it and if this chap, who seems polite and well spoken, though not a gentleman if you know what I mean, can do it, then let's give it a try. I'd let a tribe of Hottentots through here, naked as the day they were born an' all, if I thought she'd take any notice." She turned to Daisy who sat, her hands in her lap, her face serene really, Bess was inclined to think, if you didn't see the shadowed grief in her darkened eyes.

"I'll fetch him up, shall I, Daisy?" she said to the inanimate figure who sat in the chair before the fire. Bess wondered if perhaps it might have been better if Daisy could have wept. She'd heard, though she'd not experienced it herself, of course, that a good cry did a woman the world of good when she was deserted by the man she loved, but then Daisy wasn't a woman for crying, nor for whining and pining away like she seemed about to do now. That was what was so frightening.

She waited and was rewarded by a slow turning of Daisy's head in her direction. She waited again but Daisy said nothing. Bess tutted impatiently though her heart contracted in shared pain since deep within herself was a great admiring love for Daisy Lassiter. She put both her hands on Daisy's shoulders and said, directly into her face, "I'm bringing up a chap who wants to see you, Daisy. Will I fetch tea, or would you like to offer him summat stronger?"

Something moved in Daisy's eyes and her lips parted.

"I ... I'm sorry, Bess, I don't think ..."

"Of course you do, Daisy. You think all the time, my lass. The best brain I ever knew, man or woman, is in that damned head of yours so give it a try, will you? Come on, love," she said in a more kindly tone, "sit up and be the Daisy we used to know. This chap'll not harm you. Besides, me and Nelly will be here. Onceover you'd have eaten him for breakfast."

He bowed formally to Daisy when Nora ushered him into her sitting room and on his face Bess could see the bewilderment of a man who expects a tigress and is confronted with a kitten. Who was this lovely but frail creature who sat so quietly by her fire? He had been told to expect a woman of a most attractive appearance, which this one was but with a look about her of shrewdness and intelligence. A woman who would strike a hard bargain, sharp and experienced in the cut and thrust of the commercial world. Look what she had done to Lord Thornley, for God's sake. She was the owner now of Thornley Green and, it was said, of a huge fortune besides, and where had she got it if not from this club and her masterly management of it? There were rumours, though how true they were remained to be seen, of land deals, property deals done in the name of some mysterious woman who may or may not have been Daisy Lassiter but surely they could not be true, not if this was she?

"This is Mr Francis Richardson, Daisy." Bess stood protectively on one side of Daisy's chair and Nelly on the other, both ready, or so it appeared to Mr Richardson, to defend her to the death should he make a move neither of them cared for. "He is from ... where did you say, sir?"

"From Oldham, Mrs Lassiter," he said directly to Daisy. "I have come prepared to make you an offer for your club." He was a blunt-spoken man with no time for the frivolities of polite society, his manner said. A man who came straight to the point when doing business. Time was money, after all, and though he had a great deal of the latter he did not intend to waste it. He was a north-country man with the north-country man's thrift and caution, but he was also a man who could always see where money was to be made.

For the first time in three weeks Daisy's eyes showed some sign of interest. A tiny light shone there and a muscle jumped in her clenched jaw and Bess felt a small prick of hope.

"Won't you sit down, Mr Richardson?" Bess asked since it seemed Daisy was to leave him standing at the door for ever. "Perhaps you would like some tea?"

"Well..." Mr Richardson evidently realised, much as he would have preferred it, that he could not do a brisk deal in five minutes, particularly standing to attention just inside the closed door of this rather dim room. The curtains were partly drawn, against the sun, he supposed, and a fire leapt in the grate which was surprising as the day was warm.

"Perhaps a whisky?"

"No, tea will do nicely," and flicking up his coat-tails he sat down in the chair opposite Daisy. Bess rang the bell and within five minutes a tray of tea and small, evidently French gâteaux and other dainty, mouth-watering flakes of confectionery were placed on a table beside the speechless Mrs Lassiter. Bess did all the talking, helped by the well-dressed and pretty young girl, a relative of some sort, Mr Richardson imagined, though her colouring was very different to Mrs Lassiter and her Lancashire vowels were as broad as the woman he took to be the housekeeper.

"Well then, Mrs Lassiter," he continued, after a sip of tea, having refused a biscuit. "Would you be interested in hearing my offer?"

"I was not aware that I was to sell, Mr ... er ...?"

"Richardson, madam, and I heard you were," since the rumours of Mrs Lassiter's, one could only call it *strange*, manner in the past few weeks and then her sudden disappearance from the club after the Thornley affair, had reached not only Oldham, but everywhere a hand of cards was played.

Bess held her breath, watching the light become more luminous in Daisy's eyes. It was as though a hand was slowly and carefully turning up a lamp, from the merest glimmer in the darkness towards its brightest peak. Colour, or perhaps only the shadow of it, touched Daisy's cheekbones and her hands which carefully held a cup and saucer began to tremble. She put the cup and saucer on the tray, hiding her hands in the folds of her skirt.

"I cannot think where you should hear such a thing, Mr Richardson, I really can't." Her answer was automatic, a reflex left over from the days when she had said it to gain time to think.

525

"I'll be blunt, ma'am. There is talk that you are ... not well. That you have not been seen in the club for almost four weeks and you must know, being a woman of ... business ... that any concern without its ... its master at its head cannot survive for long. Forgive me, I have no wish to pry into your personal affairs but if this is the case and your health is ... Let me make myself plain. Myself and some other businessmen, all manufacturers in the cotton trade – and you must know the state of that industry at the moment – wish to diversify, if you like, invest some of our cash in another enterprise. A healthy, money-making enterprise and yours is just such a one. We would, naturally, keep on the original staff. It would be a mistake to change in any way the smooth running of such a successful business. And that man you have, John Elliott, he is a good man ... yes, you may well look surprised but naturally my partners and I have enquired very thoroughly into every aspect of 'Daisy's' before committing ourselves and you may be sure we know its exact worth."

Daisy could feel the change in herself. She could feel the hard and merciful casing which had protected her ever since Sam had gone away ... oh dear, dear God ... for ever ... begin to ease from her, leaving her appallingly exposed to any blow, and there would be a lot of those, which might fall on her. Her own vulnerability filled her with despair but she knew, if she was to survive, which she must, she had no recourse but to let it come. Only by fighting it and conquering it could she come to terms with her loss. Sam was gone and with him the love which, though she had not recognised it, had supported her for nine long years and she could not simply sit here and give in. It was not her nature. It was not in her to let adversity sweep her away helplessly like a leaf in a torrent, a leaf which has no choice in the matter. She had! She had a resolution which had been bred in the fields and the coal-mines of Lancashire, in the stews of Liverpool and in the long clawing fight she had fought to get to where she had. But she was tired. So very tired of these battles she fought. No sooner had she overcome one, than another came at her. She needed a breathing-space. Time to heal, to come to terms with her final loss. Peace ... yes, she knew what Sam had meant now. Perhaps a garden ... or even a bit of land to tend, to plant and hoe as once she had done as a child. A basic, almost primitive urge to till the soil. To settle herself in some quiet space where nothing could hurt her again.

And where is that, her breaking heart asked her, and Mr Richardson was shocked by the sudden dreadful expression of suffering on Mrs Lassiter's face. Was she ill? In pain perhaps, struck by some creeping disease which was eating away her flesh since she was quite painfully thin, but then she lifted her bowed, dove-like head and he saw for the first time that quality in her which other men had described to him.

" 'Daisy's' may, or may not be on the market, Mr Richardson. I am very attached to my club. I have put a lot of my time and my money into making it what it is." She waited and at her back Bess and Nelly exchanged exultant glances.

"Naturally my partners and I are aware of this and the splendid reputation your club enjoys. Recently, of course, a certain unfortunate ... well, shall we call it notoriety has attached itself to it and this might perhaps reflect in the asking price?"

"Call it what you like, Mr Richardson, but since that ... incident which you are too gentlemanly to mention occurred our membership has gone up by ten per cent and is growing every week. The publicity has done me no harm at all, in fact just the opposite. The takings of the 'bank' have also multiplied. I am, naturally, perfectly willing to allow you and your partners access to my records." She smiled now. "That is if I decide to sell."

Bess could not help but admire Daisy's adroit manoeuvring. Even now, in the midst of her ravaged pain, or perhaps because of it, she allowed Mr Richardson to twist and turn, to duck and parry, and all the time it was she who was in control. Just when he thought he had her she would sidestep neatly, leaving him with the feeling that he held a handful of smoke, elusive and shadowy and really quite nonexistent and when a price was agreed and he had gone,

527

shaking his head over the cunning of Mrs Lassiter who had proved to be as tough as they said she would be, there was no one but Bess and Nelly to hear the desolation of her weeping.

It took her no more than three weeks to find the place she wanted. It was about three miles out of Liverpool, rural and placid with, on a clear day, a view to the east over fields towards the faraway Pennine Hills and to the west to the great winding curve of the River Mersey as it flowed down past Runcorn from the hills which fed it. An almost perfect square of land set between the great Hemingway estate of Silverdale to the north and Highcross which belonged to Mr and Mrs James Osborne, to the south. Twenty or so acres of pasture with a foursquare house upon it and all leading down to the river's edge and a thin strip of shingled beach. There were some cottages, lived in by labourers and their families who found work wherever they could, a ready supply of men and women who would be glad of regular employment, they said. The house, not lived in for some time since the owner had died and his wife had gone to live with a married daughter in Huddersfield, was in a poor state of decoration but sound as a nut, the agent told her, as did the master builder she got in to look it over. The gardens which surrounded it were overgrown but needed only the concentrated effort of several strong men to dig the earth over, clear it and be ready to plant at her direction. She and Bess and Nelly drove over every morning in the smart landau Daisy had bought, to supervise wallpaper being stripped away from the walls of the well-proportioned rooms; to watch a constant procession of craftsmen and tradesmen; the deliveries of furniture and china and velvet carpets as once again Mr James Clements and Son of Richmond Row, Mr Henry Lacey of Bold Street and Mr John Hodgson of Church Street were honoured, they said, with Mrs Lassiter's custom. The installation of new boilers and stoves, the repairs to chimneys and ceilings and window-frames.

A new cook was set in the kitchen and a girl to clean up

after her. A couple of housemaids and a man to drive the landau and see to the stables, and out in the fields the great horses pulled the plough which turned over the land ready for next year's planting.

She called it 'Ladymeadow'.

She looked better. She had put on weight and her face was composed as she walked with Nelly over the ploughed land. Their arms were linked as they turned towards the river, strolling along the boundary of her land, their faces tinted by the light from the ball of the setting sun. Trees lining the edges of the fields were beginning to lose their leaves but in the hedge plum-coloured thistles were still in bloom and blackberries were fully ripened ready for the picking. There were poppies, boldly scarlet in the field not yet ploughed. A snipe flew up from their feet and away across the water seagulls wheeled and dipped as a fishing boat moved down the river.

"I like it here, Mrs Lassiter," Nelly said, her face as tranquil as a child's now that Mrs Lassiter was herself again. She had removed her bonnet, a country bonnet of straw decorated with red silk poppies and ribbons and the sun gilded her pale hair to silver.

Daisy squeezed her arm and sighed deeply. So did she like it here. It was almost three months since Sam had gone and her heart could only just now acknowledge the desperate grief which still invaded it. She still wept for him in the dark of the night when no one could hear and she knew there would be no permanent recovery for her. She would love him and miss him to the end of her days but she could live with it, she had found, getting through this day and only this one until tomorrow. She was at ease out here in the fields she had done her best to escape from years ago but which she had discovered still had the ability to give her peace, and by the river where Sam would have lived, and loved her, if fate had allowed it. She had Bess and Nelly, and even Jack, who had come with them, saying they needed someone to keep an eye on them and to stop them making complete fools of themselves. She didn't really know how she was to spend the rest of her life but she was content at the moment to let one hour pass by into another, taking each day as it came without concerning herself with what the next would bring.

Bess was waiting for them by the gate which led from the spinney. They had walked along the shifting shingle of the beach, Daisy's land on their right, the lowering sun almost directly in their faces, and when they entered the spinney which edged the beach the shadows of the close-packed trees pressed in on them so that they could hardly see. As they came out at the other side it was almost dark and for a moment Daisy was startled by what seemed to be a silvery glint of tears on Bess's face.

She knew then, of course she did, though she did not let the knowing touch her since she really couldn't bear any more.

"Bess ... what is it, Bess?" It was Nelly who cried out, who ran to her sister, her mind at once on their Mam, or even Eddy for what else could make her stalwart sister cry? She had never seen Bess shed tears, ever, and her young heart was terrified. But Bess was looking beyond her to Daisy, the compassion in her so great Nelly knew, then, who it was, and so did Daisy Lassiter and within her something which had borne hope, and life, died.

Jack decayed before her eyes, shrinking from an old but agile spryness into the weak and pathetic ruin of the senile, struck down by the tale told by Captain Robert Adams, the master of the *Lady of the Sea*, and near to tears himself. He had witnessed it, he told them brokenly, and there could be no doubt that Captain Lassiter had ... well ... it had been almost dark ... but the graceful clipper ship broke up, right there in the surf, and though some of the crew had been picked up by a Union warship, the Captain had not been amongst them. Half a dozen had been killed ... yes, when he himself had managed to get back into Wilmington he had seen the bodies brought ashore under a flag of truce by a Federal longboat, to be dealt with by the Confederacy since it was not their job to see to the burial of British blockade-runners, they said. A shell had blown a hole ... Dear God, it was ... it tore her apart ... that beautiful ship. Then they went in with grape and canister and the ... steersman who would be ... it could only have been the Captain, ma'am, turning to stare blindly into the white blankness of the face of the Captain's wife. "... he went down, I saw him. I could do nothing. I was ... fighting for my life. There were other Union vessels and I could do nothing."

"No, Captain Adams, you must not blame yourself." How calm she had been in the face of the young man's grief. He had been shamefaced about it, as though it should be he comforting her but though he was probably about the same age as herself, he seemed no more than a boy. Why was it, she had wondered idly, that men cannot cope with tears? That it is the woman who must be strong, calm and dry-eyed though her heart broke and died in her breast.

He stayed with them that night, and the next, not knowing where to go whilst his own damaged ship was repaired, not even thinking, as Bess thought in her own bewildered mind, that it, and everything else Sam Lassiter had owned, all now belonged to Daisy Lassiter. Bess stayed with her, day and night, with Nelly like a pale spirit of grieving, moving between Daisy and the young captain who had been incapable in those first few days of bearing his loss alone, clinging to the sweetness and comfort of Nelly Miller like a man who has no other lifeline. But he had borne up at last and gone back to Liverpool and *Lady of the Sea*.

"You are to take no more cargoes through the blockade, Captain Adams," Daisy had told him quietly when he came to bid her farewell. "We will find safer, perhaps less lucrative journeys for you and *Lady of the Sea* to embark on. I remember my husband telling me that half-a-crown can become a sovereign in one run alone but if it costs lives it is too big a price to pay. So, in the meanwhile I would be grateful if you would make it your concern to inform Captain Holden who has *Country Girl* in his command what I have said to you. Perhaps he could call on me, and you too, Captain, before you sail."

And now, after the young man had bidden her a respectful goodbye she had one last undertaking to pursue in the name of Daisy and Cassie Brindle.

35

The carriage drew up to the closed gates of Thornley Green and stopped, waiting for the gatekeeper to open them. When he did so, floundering from the gatehouse like some great fat toad, Daisy recognised him at once. She had boasted to Bess at these very gates that she would come driving back in her own carriage pulled by a pair of matched greys and here she was but it gave her no satisfaction, nor did she feel the need to speak to Dewhurst, or to let him know who she was.

"We are expected," her coachman said loftily to Dewhurst.

"Mrs Lassiter?" Dewhurst enquired politely.

"It is, so if you would open the gates we'll get on."

"Right away, sir," Dewhurst said, wishing he could get a glimpse of the woman who sat far back in the carriage since it was rumoured that she had once been a kitchenmaid in the Thornley kitchens, not that he could believe that, daft tale indeed, but still . . .

The drive up to the house took a lot less time than when the young Daisy Brindle had tramped up it as a girl of fifteen going to her first job. Twelve years ago, but she must not think of that now, she told herself urgently, nor of all the things which had happened to her since but somehow her aching mind would not allow the merciful numbness to cloud it and her thoughts were busy and agonised. She had walked away from here a child, she told herself now, despite what Miles Thornley had done to her, with a child's obdurate determination to 'get her own back' on those who had hurt her. Strong and wilful, without thought for who else might be destroyed by her obsession with revenge, she had sworn to take all this from the Thornley family without the least idea of how she was to go about it. She had, though, she *had* done it, but that gloating, triumphant ride she had promised herself and Bess would never take place. True, she was here, Nelly beside her, but it was to do something she had decided on even before the news of the destruction of *Golden Lady* was given her.

Petch opened the door to her and Nelly, ready it seemed in that first moment to order her round to the back door since that was where servants should be. It was obvious that he had heard who she was and she was not surprised, remembering the servants' grapevine which existed in all such households as this. A message had been sent asking if she might call on Lady Thornley and the kitchen would be agog to hear how Daisy Brindle, the notorious Daisy Lassiter now, looked after all these years.

"Good afternoon, Mr Petch." Her voice was perfectly composed, quiet and perhaps somewhat husky. "I am expected so if you would be good enough to inform Lady Thornley I am here I would be obliged."

Obliged. How that word brought back memories. *Obliged.* The first time she had heard it Miles Thornley had said it to her when she had offered to run to this very house to fetch his father when his hunter had fallen and broken his leg. She remembered how she had savoured it on her tongue, a word she had never heard before, nor knew the meaning of though she had guessed, of course. How she had loved that boy. A child herself with no way of judging the nature of him beneath his incredibly handsome exterior, the shallow, greedy, thoughtless youth who would grow into the cold-hearted, arrogant and cruel man he had become. Where was he now, she wondered as she and Nelly sat side by side on the sofa in the drawing room where Petch had put them, the small drawing room where guests of little consequence had been shown in her day as a servant here. Miles Thornley had not been seen, nor heard of as far as she was aware, since that night he had walked out of 'Daisy's', his face grey and empty, his blank eyes staring into the void of his own future. She had expected threats, recriminations, a menacing presence snarling defiance and a care to her own safety but none had come. He was not here, as she had been assured he would not be by the gentlemen who were expected shortly.

She looked about her, studying the blend of luxury and neglect which was so obvious in this room she and Bess had once cleaned. A gradual running-down of the standards set by Mrs Crosby – was she still here? – the laxness of servants who have no one to guide them and the lack of money which was needed to keep a house of this size in the state of splendour it had known when old Lord Thornley had been alive. The fraying of curtains, the brocade exposed carelessly to the sunlight, the wearing of carpets, and stains – claret or brandy? – on the worn velvet of the sofa. Cobwebs hanging from the dimmed crystal droplets of the chandeliers and dust moving in a shaft of sunlight and clinging in a fine film to the smeared marble top of an occasional table. The fire was almost out, spluttering feebly for want of a parlourmaid's attention, and in a vase of exquisite and costly design, dead flowers. The state of the grounds had not escaped her notice as the carriage swept up the drive, the gravel itself unraked, the grass of the park uncut, leaves in untidy heaps where once they would have been neatly raked and burned. Summer flowers, brown and withered in beds which had been unwatered for months, and saddest of all to her, remembering her wonderment on the first day she saw them, the dozens of privet bushes, once clipped to such perfection not a leaf had been out of place. Round and square and cone-shaped, some floating down to the ground like the wide and flounced tiers of a lady's gown, they were now overgrown and unsightly. She had turned her head away sharply, unable to bear the decay of such beauty.

The silence in the parlour was broken only by the steady ticking of the ormolu clock on the mantelshelf above the fire. Nelly's shoulder touched hers and she was aware that the girl was afraid. After all, she was only Nelly Miller from

534

Primrose Bank, the sister of the once gardening labourer, long gone to work elsewhere, and of the kitchenmaid who had left under peculiar circumstances. This was the drawing room of the great Thornley family and her own presumption in daring to sit on the sofa here appalled her. She was delightfully dressed in a gown of pale blue foulard, long-sleeved and high-necked. Her gloves and boots were dyed to match and on her head was a pale blue bonnet decorated with the palest of pink silk roses. She could have been the well-bred daughter of the house, suitably dressed for her age and station in life. Beside her in cream silk shantung, flowing and graceful with a tawny velvet sash the exact colour of her hair, a cream straw bonnet with ribbons to match, cream boots and gloves, Daisy was just as elegant. They were ladies, their appearance said, calling on another and Daisy smiled encouragingly at Nelly to tell her so.

"There is nothing to fear, Nelly," she said softly, reaching for her hand and giving it a squeeze. "We are here quite legitimately. No one will harm us or order us off the premises."

As she spoke the door opened and a woman entered the room. A plain woman nearing forty, Daisy would have said, simply dressed in a gown of some drab grey stuff, unadorned beyond a small brooch at her throat. Her hair appeared to have no particular colour, a mixture of light brown and blended grey, and her tired face was sallow and lined. She was as soft-hued and unexceptional as a grey dove and yet there was that certain quality about her which said she was, quite simply, a lady. A lady with pedigree bred in her bones, from the privileged class which had produced Miles Thornley and his arrogant friends. Sure of herself and yet not overbearing. A lady come to deal with those who were her inferiors and yet must be dealt with courteously for that is the mark of true breeding.

Daisy and Nelly rose to their feet, not humbly but with the politeness one accords an older lady, since surely this could not be the wife of Miles Thornley?

"You are Mrs Lassiter?" she said coolly, moving slowly towards them.

"Yes. I have an appointment to see Lady Caroline Thornley"

"I am she."

Daisy tried not to let the amazement show on her face. She tried to recall that weekend when this woman and her mother had stayed at Thornley Green. A tall, plain girl, awkward, but doing her best to join in the horseplay which Miles Thornley and the merry company he had gathered about him thought so-necessary for a weekend house party. It had been the hunting season and there had been a great deal of wild riding and wild drinking and it had been this woman's mother who had been at the centre of much of it. There had been talk in the kitchen, the usual whispered hints of assignations, of who was – discreetly of course, since Lord Thornley was considered something of a prude – romantically attached to whom and this woman had played a part in it, her mother letting it be known that she was in the marriage market. A decent dowry to go with the plain face, the awkward and shy manner which, despite her mother's efforts, could not be erased. She had been about twenty then, it was said, and heading for spinsterhood if a husband could not be found for her. And one had. Miles Thornley!

"You wanted to see me, Mrs Lassiter?" The words were spoken with a cool distaste which told Daisy that Lady Thornley knew exactly who she was and what she had done to her husband. The quiet dignity, the scornful but well-mannered formality which Lady Thornley directed towards her were only to be expected. Daisy had been surprised when Miles Thornley's wife had agreed to see her. It was three months since Thornley Green had passed into Daisy's hands and yet Lady Thornley was still here, acting as though it was perfectly normal for her to be so. As though Thornley Green still belonged to the Thornley family as it had done for generations.

"If we may be seated, Lady Thornley." Daisy could feel Nelly tremble beside her and though she herself experienced little other than a desperate need to have this done with, to get away from this haunted place and retreat to the sanctuary of Ladymeadow and the peace she hoped to find there, if Nelly did not sit down soon Daisy thought she might crumple at the feet of the woman who was, in Nelly's mind, the wife of her liege lord!

"Please . . ." and with an autocratic wave of her hand Lady Thornley indicated that they might do so. She herself sat on the extreme edge of a green velvet Chippendale chair, no part of her straight back touching the delicately moulded wood, her hands folded serenely in her lap. Her face gave no indication of her thoughts and Daisy was forced to admire this woman who must have suffered as much as she herself had at Miles Thornley's hands. She did not offer them tea.

"You know, I suppose, that I own this house." Daisy had not meant it to be but her voice was abrupt since there was no other way to say the words.

"I had heard, yes." Dear God but she was a cool one, Daisy thought. There really was something in this high-bred endurance that the pedigreed class, the ruling class of this land were purported to have, and it showed in this woman's demeanour. Stiff-backed, stiff-necked, unbending in her belief of who she was and the creed that one did not show one's emotions to one's inferiors no matter what the circumstances.

"You must also have heard how I obtained it?"

"I did, indeed, Mrs Lassiter, but that is my husband's concern and not mine. Now, if you would be good enough to tell me what it is you want with me."

"There are some gentlemen arriving shortly, Lady Thornley. I wished to speak privately with you before they got here. They are legal gentlemen. I have taken the liberty of making out a document which states that your son is to take ownership of this estate. As the next baron he would inherit it from his father so I am returning to him what is rightfully his. The house and the land will be held in trust for him until he is of an age to look after it himself. Until then you are to be trustee, I believe that is the word. There is no way the property can be . . . given . . . to anyone else, nor can it be used as . . . security . . . or credit to obtain a

537

loan ... perhaps in a gambling debt. I trust you understand."

It was a long time before Lady Thornley spoke and when she did she might just have been given some small trinket of little value and even less grace, so cool was her voice.

"You are very kind, Mrs Lassiter. My son and I are grateful."

"You will take it then?"

"I cannot think we ever lost it, Mrs Lassiter," and Daisy was made aware that in her own way Caroline Thornley was telling her that despite the gossip and scandal, the notoriety even which was attached to Mrs Daisy Lassiter's name, there had been no doubt in her mind that her son's inheritance had ever been in danger.

"Why do you say that, Lady Thornley? I won it honestly in a game of cards. It is legally mine at the moment and will be until I put my signature to the document my lawyer has in his possession."

"Indeed, I am aware of that. I am also aware of ... who you are, Mrs Lassiter. Or who you were. Mr Greenhalgh still lives in the little house by the wood. When I had your message asking if you might call I asked him to come and see me." She paused. "He goes regularly to put flowers on the grave of his ... granddaughter, he tells me."

And in the shadowed eyes of Lady Thornley there was a gleam of understanding. Nothing more. No warmth, nor promise of anything but this transaction between herself and the woman who had also suffered at the hands of Miles Thornley. Even so it was undertaken only for the sake of her son, her manner said.

She was speaking of Cassie, of course. She was telling Daisy that she knew of the events which had taken place so long ago. That she knew and perhaps might understand Daisy's motives, and though she, as a lady, could not herself stoop to such actions, she knew why they had been taken.

Daisy stood up and Nelly did the same. "I will wait in the carriage until my lawyer gets here ..."

"May I offer you some tea, Mrs Lassiter, and your ..."

"This is my companion, Nelly Miller."

"Miss Miller," and with a gracious bow in the direction of

the girl whose father had laboured on her father-in-law's land, she reached for the bell to summon her butler.

The days ran into one another now, long and empty and endless. She had done what she had set out to do. It had not merely been a gesture to please the ghost of Sam Lassiter who haunted her days and nights, but because of her own knowledge that all these years in which she had hungered for justice for Cassie had been a lie. Cassie, sweet-natured Cassie whose mind, if it had been capable of reason, would not have considered for a moment the awful vendetta of hate Daisy had conducted in her name. It had been done for Daisy Brindle and no one else and now, with the return of Thornley Green to its rightful owner, Daisy Brindle could rest in peace, even if Daisy Lassiter could not.

But with that accomplished, what was she to do with the rest of her life? She had given Rob Adams, captain of the *Lady of the Sea* a share in the ship, telling him that he must sail her wherever he had a fancy for, carrying whatever cargo he chose as long as he promised that he would not continue to be a blockade-runner and the same offer was repeated to Captain Neil Holden who was master of the *Country Girl*, and who accepted gratefully.

In those early autumn days as she and Nelly walked through the spinney, moving as they always seemed to, towards the shore, the deep September voice of a wood pigeon throbbed in the thinning trees. There was one tree, a chestnut rooted almost on the edge of the spinney, its enormous head leaning away from the prevailing wind off the river, its fruit promising the glossy chestnuts to come later. They would sit with their backs against its rough-barked trunk, watching the gigboats skimming down the river, the little craft often going as far as Holyhead in their quest for inward-bound ships which they assisted into the River Mersey and the docks of Liverpool. Mersey Flats, sailing barges which manoeuvred along the canals leading off the river, their distinctive brownish-red sails bright against the silver-grey waters. The tall masts of deep-sea barques, schooners and fishing trawlers. All were a constant and colourful procession on the broad highway of the river.

Sometimes Bess would come with them, leaving Jack whom she had begun to cosset and pamper as though she was his 'bloody mother', his words, which she ignored. He was frail and empty now, sitting for hours by his window which looked out over the river, watching for something which would surely come one day, though he could not have said what. He had developed sores on the stump of his leg and his wooden peg chafed it. He was too old to use a crutch and hop about like a damned frog, he said peevishly, inclined on the whole to allow himself to be waited on and scolded by Bess, to be read to by Nelly, though he was not comfortable around Daisy since her grief was too like his own.

Nelly had walked to the river's edge that day. She was idly throwing stones into the tiny rippling waves, her bare feet wincing away from the sharp cold of the water. It would be winter soon and the warmth of the sun had a hint in it that summer was gone and autumn was fading.

"What are you going to do wi' yourself, lass?" Bess's voice cut across Daisy's shadowed thoughts in which Sam Lassiter sauntered in the gracefully masculine way he had. In which his whimsical smile rent her heart, and his deep voice, warm and indolent, begged her to make love to him. He was with her in that moment, here on this patch of land here where he himself would have lived, near the river and the ships he loved. He had bought land somewhere along this stretch of river, he had told her, and she supposed that soon, as his widow, she would have to go and see his lawyer who had sent numerous notes begging her permission to call on her and settle Captain Lassiter's affairs.

Bess's voice irritated her, interrupting what was her constant preoccupation now, her reliving of memories of herself and Sam in the few months before he had gone away.

"Must I do something, Bess?"

"I reckon so."

"Oh, and why is that?"

"Because you're not one for sitting about dwelling on

540

what might have been, my lass. And then there's what's to come to be planned for an' all."

"I beg your pardon? What is that supposed to mean?" Her hands had become clenched in a most painful way since she wanted to do no more than ... than ... wait ... for what? ... to sit here in the home she had created at Ladymeadow and ... well, see what the future would bring.

"You can't do it, Daisy." Bess's voice was sharp, just as though she read Daisy's mind.

A spark of anger crackled inside Daisy's head and she turned to glare at Bess.

"Can't do what, for God's sake?"

"Sit about moping, and besides ... well, let me ask you this, Daisy Lassiter, before you start to accuse me of interfering and I reckon it's something you should have asked yourself weeks ago if you weren't so set on sitting in the dark and brooding..."

"*Brooding! In the dark!* I would hardly call this..."

"You know what I mean and will you let me have my say?"

"What is it then?"

Bess's face flamed but she looked directly at Daisy as she spoke. "When did you last see your monthlies?"

"My ...?" Daisy's face turned the colour of tallow for the words brought back those nights when she had crept down to the summerhouse to meet ... Christ, would she never be free of him, that ... that swine who had ... but Bess was ... those were the very words Bess had used then ... what *was* Bess? ... monthlies...?

Her eyes widened and she put her hand to her mouth. The blood rushed madly away from her frozen brain, dragging thought with it, and sense and reason and she swayed back against the trunk of the tree. She continued to stare at Bess who watched her carefully, ready, should she be needed, to put out a steadying hand.

"Did you hear what I said, love?" she went on softly. "You know what I mean, don't you? It's a couple of months since I saw any of your ... well, I've been sorting the laundry since we came to Ladymeadow and..."

"Oh God, Bess..." Her mouth worked in some odd kind of way as though it was not she who had control of it, "...oh sweet God..." Her hands shook and she held them out to Bess who gripped them tightly. "Bess...I hadn't thought...I didn't even notice I was so..."

"Aye, I know, lass, You've had more than any woman should be asked to suffer, what with ... well..." Bess cleared her throat, "...but have you looked at yourself in the mirror lately?"

"No." It was no more than a whisper.

"You've put a bit of weight on, Daisy, in your face and..."

"My gowns fit me well enough."

"Aye, but ... you lost flesh when the ... when Sam left, now, you've filled out again and it can only be..." She left the sentence unfinished.

"Bess..." There was a moment of incredulity, then another of wary concentration as though the suspicious child who had learned from experience to keep her head down still lived within Daisy Lassiter and was calculating what this might mean to her. Bitter blows she had taken during her lifetime, the worst being the loss of the two people she had loved best in all the world. Cassie had been the first to stir her heart and have wrapped around her all the love young Daisy Brindle had stored within her. And then there had been Sam. Sam, the man who, like a thief in the night, had stolen her heart almost without her being aware of it. Given her in return a winging, soaring delight before sailing away on his ship and leaving her with her life frayed and worn and with the certainty that it might never be mended.

And now this. This ... this tiny ... what was she to call it? A final gift from Sam Lassiter? So many he had given her, casually tossing them into her lap with little regard for their value, shining trinkets, playthings, lovely all of them, but surely this was the loveliest of them all? Wasn't it? A child, something she would not even have thought of but for Bess's fearful dread on her behalf when Miles Thornley had made love to her. In all the hours of love, of sensual, compelling, overwhelming passion she and Sam Lassiter had shared, she had taken none of the precautions she had heard existed to prevent pregnancy and in eleven years, first with Miles and then with Sam, she had not conceived. Why then, she asked herself, cautiously allowing the first feather of joy to touch her heart, had she done so now? What was fate's purpose in taking Sam from her and leaving her with his child? Was there a purpose, or was it blind chance that had planted his seed within her and allowed it to take root?

She turned to look at Bess who was watching her carefully and down on the waterline, Nelly, who had been about to saunter back in their direction, hesitated, sensing a tension in the still figures of her sister and Daisy. And yet the tension was not sorrowing but just the opposite. It was a feeling of some inner excitement which longed to break free. It was as though the grief Daisy had endured since the day she had lost the Captain had lifted a little, been replaced by an expectation which lit her eyes and skin with a luminosity Nelly had not seen in her since Sam Lassiter had gone.

"Can it be true, Bess?" she heard her say. "Can it really be true?"

"I'd say so, my lass, for I can't think what else it could be," Bess replied dryly.

"But ... why? Why now when ... ?"

"Nay, Daisy, don't ask me? I'm only surprised it hasn't happened before, the way you and him ... well, you know what I mean ..." her face flaming. "Sam Lassiter was a real man, by all accounts, and I dare say sooner or later ..."

"Not *was*, Bess." Daisy straightened up slowly, wrapping her arms about her bent knees. She put her chin on her crossed arms and stared out across the river, her eyes alive and vital. She narrowed them as she watched the skimming progress of a gigboat, and they shone like amber-tinted candles from between her thick brown lashes. A ferryboat ploughed through the water towards Eastham, heavily laden with passengers bound for the far side of the river.

"Daisy ... ?" Bess leaned forward to look into her face.

"Not *was*, Bess. *Is!* He *is* a real man and somewhere in those damned Southern states of America Sam Lassiter is fighting to stay that way. He's alive, Bess! I know he is, here..." striking her chest with a clenched fist. "Do you think a man like Sam would allow himself to drown on the deck of his sinking vessel? Oh, I know the belief is that a captain goes down with his ship, but not Captain Sam Lassiter. Much as he loved the *Golden Lady* he's not the kind of lunatic who would die with her. He's a realist, Bess, and he knows that whereas he could build another ship, he only has *one* life and he wouldn't throw it away on such foolishness."

"But Captain Adams said he saw him fall."

"Maybe he did, but that doesn't mean he was dead, or even wounded. He'd have his wits about him and if he could see a chance to survive he'd take it. That's what I'd do and he and I are ... we think alike, Bess. If it was me I'd slip ashore under the cover of all the confusion and when the chance came I'd ... well, I'd find a way to come home or let those who are concerned know..."

Her voice trailed away painfully and Nelly began to move more quickly since it appeared the fine flash of joy she had seen in Daisy was gone and the despair returned but Daisy lifted her head defiantly, turning again to look towards the mouth of the river as though fully expecting to see a ship bearing Captain Sam Lassiter dashing across the tossing waters towards her.

"Very well ... we have not heard ... he'd hardly write to me, would he, after what happened, even if he could get a letter out of the country. Besides, if he could get a letter out he'd get himself out, don't you think? And if he got caught up in the fighting ... he was coming out of Wilmington when it happened, Rob Adams said. The Federals had destroyed the rebel fleet, you heard him say so with your own ears. Atlanta fell only last week, the rebels were defeated and Fort Morgan at Mobile was captured. Can you imagine what chaos there must be with two armies fighting ... Oh, Bess, please don't look like that. Let me believe this, please. It's the only way I can ... I *will* believe it, I will. If I am to have his child then it is because he will come home to me. Life, Bess, his life and his child's and knowing Sam Lassiter as I do for the most stubborn and obstinate devil who ever lived..."

"Somewhat like yourself, in other words ..."

"Yes, oh yes, so don't you think he wouldn't move heaven and earth to come home to make sure I was bringing up his child as he thinks that child *should* be brought up?"

"But, lass ... if he is alive ..."

"He is, *he is*, Bess."

"Very well, if he is alive how can he possibly know you're in the family way? You didn't know yourself until half an hour ago."

"Because he's Sam Lassiter, that's how. Don't ask me what I mean, Bess, because I'm not sure myself but believe me when I say that he is alive and will come home as soon as he is able."

36

Savannah fell that winter. General Sherman's great march had brought him and his army of 60,000 men to the capital of Georgia, devastation marking the path of his columns. Columbia, the fall of Charleston including Fort Sumter where it had all begun, and other defences cut off all escape for the Confederates since the blockading army held the ports, and the end of the agony was in sight for the Southern Confederation. And as the two armies prepared for what they knew was the end, the Confederates standing bravely against overwhelming and vigorous assault by the Union forces, Sam and Daisy Lassiter's son was born.

It was a fine March day, soft with the coming of spring. In Daisy's fields early potatoes had been planted, and carrots, the ground which had been levelled by her tenant labourers from the cottages, well frosted in the bitter weather of January and February, rich and ripe with dug-in manure. Cabbages, broccoli, and between the rows of vegetables, radishes sown thinly so as not to waste space. In her fruit orchard the apple and pear trees had been pruned and against the wall of the enclosed garden strawberry beds were uncovered, the beds weeded and the plants trimmed. Only one small paddock had been allowed to lie uncultivated, rough with coarse grass, and it was here that Daisy's carriage horses were let loose to crop and where she intended to put a pony ready for the day when Sam Lassiter's child should be ready to ride it.

"Grand ideas you have, Daisy Lassiter, if you ask me," Bess snorted. "A pony indeed! In my day only the gentry had ponies, the rest of us had to walk. And what are you and Sam Lassiter, tell me that? No more than working folk when all's said and done. What else is this child to have, I'd like to know? A nanny in the nursery and a governess you'd be telling me next. And what on earth are you going to do with all this food you're growing? There'll be enough carrots and potatoes and fruit to feed the whole of Liverpool the rate you're going. All them fields under cultivation ..."

"Only three, Bess," Daisy said placidly, rocking herself and her unborn child in the chair she had placed in a square of sunshine, her expression serene beneath Bess's onslaught. It was only Bess's way of showing how worried she was over everything and everybody who touched Daisy Lassiter's life, lest it bring back the agony of grief she had known last autumn.

She and Daisy were in the small conservatory which was attached to the back of the house, its three sides catching the rays of the sun during most of the day. The house, being on a slight incline, had a view across the gardens and the spinney to the river and it was here that Daisy liked to sit while she waited. Waited for the birth of her child, she told herself and Bess, but Nelly who was more perceptive than her level-headed sister knew she watched the ships which sailed up the river, waiting for news of Sam Lassiter. None had been received. It was as though he had been swallowed up by the sea on which his ship had foundered, or by the devastation of the death throes of the Confederate states of

America, but Daisy still waited, shading her eyes against the sun as she studied the traffic on the river. In a strange way they had known great contentment in the winter months they had spent at Ladymeadow, despite Daisy's often shadowed face and far-seeing, unfocused eyes which reached across the sea to where she told herself her husband was. They had lived an isolated existence, concerned for the first time with things of a domestic nature, with making a home, not only for Daisy and her coming child, for Sam Lassiter when he returned, which Daisy insisted could not be long now, but for Bess and Nelly and Jack who were all the family Daisy had ever had.

They tried their hand at many things they had never done before in those icy winter days when the east wind blew across the Pennines to freeze the marrow of your bones should you show your face out of doors, or so Fred Wainwright said when he brought the logs he had cut to stack against the back kitchen door. Fred lived with his wife and many assorted children in one of the cottages, glad of the work about the place which fed and clothed his family, and willing to do ''owt' the ladies wanted providing this sudden good fortune which had come upon him and the other families continued.

There were mornings of savage white frosts and thick fog coming off the river, mornings in which, when the fog cleared, the trees stood against the pale winter sky in an exquisite tracery of silver and white. Days wild and stormy, filled with sharp pellets of snow which turned to icy sleet and Daisy and Nelly could not get out to tramp the fields and the beach.

Mrs Simpson, newly installed as cook at Ladymeadow, was often vastly surprised, though unperturbed being of an equable nature, when Mrs Lassiter and the young Miss Miller invaded her kitchen, determined to learn how to bake bread and pies, they said, to create apple tarts from the great store of apples they had picked from the trees when they first moved into the house. To preserve pears in brandy, and pickle onions dug up from the overgrown vegetable garden. To make nourishing soups from beef bones for Jack to taste since his appetite was not what it was. To make mincepies and plum pudding at Christmas. To study the art of decorating butter since with the arrival of a cow at Ladymeadow a dairymaid churned their own butter and made their own cheese. They made chestnut sauce from the fruit of the tree by the river's edge and learned how to bake apple dumplings. Their laughter filled the kitchen until the scullerymaid, overcome by the presence of her silk-clad mistress in Mrs Simpson's own voluminous apron, fell into hysterical laughter herself over the potato peelings and then into woebegone tears at her own temerity.

But Nelly, Mrs Simpson and the little maid whose name was Polly were often disconcerted by the sudden falling of Mrs Lassiter into a deep and desolate silence. She would quietly put down her mixing spoon, her soup ladle, or the bowl containing the fruit cake she mixed and simply walk away from them, leaving the merry warmth of the kitchen and going up to her room. It too looked over the river and Bess or Nelly would find her there, sitting crouched in the wide window-bottom, her back to the frame, her sombre gaze turned towards the north and the opening of the river into the sea. Though Bess did not say so, not even to Nelly who was infected with Daisy's belief that Captain Lassiter would come home as soon as the war in America was over, she wished wholeheartedly that Daisy would accept his death and grieve for him properly, as a widow should. It did no good hanging on to this mad conviction that he would be here by and by, just as though he had gone no further than the docks and would turn in at the gate when his business was done ... It would have to be faced one day, and the sorrowing for her husband borne, and the longer it was put off the harder it would be to bear. Even Captain Adams was positive Captain Lassiter was dead, privately enlarging to Bess on the moment he had seen him fall to the deck of his ship, bleeding, he said, from his head and neck.

Whenever the weather permitted Daisy and Nelly walked over Daisy's land, Nelly hovering solicitously at her elbow as Daisy grew more cumbersome in her pregnancy.

Thrushes and blackbirds sang as the winter began to make way for spring and robins flitted about in the topmost boughs of the trees. Rabbits nibbled on the leaves at the edge of the fields, bobbing away at Daisy and Nelly's approach with their white scuts flashing. The men were in the fields by then, preparing the earth for planting, and the women too, in their clogs and sacking aprons. Life was quiet, holding its breath in those last weeks as it awaited the birth of Daisy Lassiter's son.

"I shall work here as soon as I am able, Nelly, just as I once did," she said on that last day. "I remember all the things I used to do when I was a child and though for the life of me I cannot think why, I feel a great need to do them again."

Her labour began that night in the huge four-poster bed she had bought from Mr Hodgson of Church Street, the bed in which one day she would sleep again with Sam Lassiter, she told herself resolutely. She lay for a while, savouring the pain, wanting to keep it to herself, wanting to share this with no one but Sam who should have been here with her.

"Oh, Sam . . . I love you and this child we have made and who will be born soon," she whispered into the darkness. "I'm afraid without you, Sam . . ." and to her surprise her face was wet with tears. It was not the pangs of birth of which she was afraid, nor of death, nor the realisation that she would soon have a baby, since she knew nothing of babies, but she was fearful of a life without the watchful, mocking, vigorous love Sam Lassiter had given her. He would laugh at her if he was here, not cruelly but with that whimsical humour which would banish all her fears. He would not let death touch her, nor the pain go unshared if he was here, she knew that.

She rang the bell for Bess.

Her son was born the following day, arriving without too much fuss, and she lay back amongst her pillows as Bess and Nelly, the doctor and midwife gone, fussed and fretted over him, exclaiming to one another on the perfection of his limbs and the fat creases in his neck, the beauty of his ears and the remarkable strength which was already displayed by the loudness of his shouts. He was no more than a bundle in Bess's arms, white clad and hastily cleaned of the blood of birth. It seemed she could not summon the strength, the inclination or the courage to look at what they marvelled over since all she really wanted on this day of exhaustion and aching muscles was Sam's arms about her.

"Here he is then," Bess said gloatingly, already the infant's willing slave. "Put him to thy breast," reverting in her bemusement to her native northern dialect.

"Must I, Bess? I'm awfully tired."

"Nay, give ower, he'll do all't work."

She saw the thick twist of damp hair first. It was a bright tawny gold, darker at its roots as though its owner had not yet made up his mind to follow his father's or his mother's colouring. There was a nose, a blob no more, above pursed and sucking rosebud lips. Dark eyebrows slanting across a tiny forehead, then, miraculously, one of them rose in an exact duplication of Sam Lassiter's sardonic expression and Daisy's heart lurched frantically in her breast.

"Did you see that, Bess?"

"What, lass?"

"His eyebrows. He's got Sam's eyebrows. What an amazing thing, Bess. Look, Nelly, can you see, and look . . . look at his hands." She drew a small starfish hand from its wrappings. It jerked convulsively against the white flesh of her breast and with a sigh of shared joy Daisy Lassiter and her son were linked as his mouth closed over her nipple.

She could not say exactly at that moment that she loved him since she barely knew him but she knew she would protect him with her own life. Her feelings were of concern for his welfare since he was dependent entirely on her, of amazement that he should look so completely like Sam and, as the days went by, of grief that Sam should not be here to see the miracle of his son's first strong grasp on life.

"I'll take him, Daisy," Bess said to her later on the day he was born since Daisy had been inclined to keep him in the safety of her own bed, guarded by the strength of her own mothering instinct.

Bess spoke with authority. "He's to be bathed properly yet and I promised Jack I'd take him in to see him."

"I'll take him to see Jack."

Bess was scandalised. "Nay, Daisy Lassiter. A full fortnight in bed before you put a foot to the floor ..."

"Don't be daft, Bess. I'll be up tomorrow and then I'll take him in to see Jack," clutching the lolling head of her son against her breast.

"Daisy, don't you trust me with him, love? I've had brothers and sisters younger than me, you know that. Why, I nursed our Nelly when I was no more than a nipper meself, didn't I, Nelly?" just as though Nelly would remember.

"Well, all right, but if he should cry bring him straight back and ... don't let Jack hold him, Bess. You know how frail he is and he might drop him. Wrap him up warm, Bess, it's gone very cold in here ... see, send for Polly to fetch more coal and will you promise to bathe him in here where I can see him ... Oh careful, Bess ... careful ..."

The days went by and she could not bear him out of her sight lest someone should damage him or steal him away just as she was beginning to love him quite devastatingly and she was as ecstatic as Bess and Nelly about his male beauty and strength. The hawthorns were in the hedges when Bryn Lassiter took his first airing with his mother, the red buds tight and unbroken. The misty green of new growth was everywhere. The cones of the cedar tree had landed heavy-side-down and burst open to scatter their winged seeds and at Daisy's feet seedlings made an incredibly bright green forest. New things growing, new life, new hope, and a new spring in Daisy Lassiter's heels as she showed her son the bright new world.

The tall, exceedingly thin gentleman moved slowly down the gangway of the packet ship just come from Charleston, stepping carefully on to the quay beside Coburg Dock. The dock had been deepened recently in order to take North America steamers which carried mail, passengers and light freight to and from the eastern ports of America. Eleven days it took on the homeward passage, a day or two longer out, but the gentleman who stood for a moment looking about him at his surroundings seemed not to care much about that. He drew in a deep breath as though some long-awaited pleasure was on hand which he was about to savour. He narrowed his eyes as he studied the Liverpool skyline, then turned his back on it and allowed his gaze to wander out across the river to the far shore.

He was shabbily dressed in an ill-matched assortment of clothing, not at all suitable for the bite in the end-of-winter wind which blew directly into his face. He shivered and drew his worn, cape-like overcoat about him. He settled his hat more firmly on his head, drew in another deep and satisfied breath then stepped out with a swing in his long stride in the direction of Strand Street which ran beside the dock area. He carried a small carpet bag in his right hand which he changed to his left as he turned a corner, away from the river and into Hanover Place.

He passed by the imposing building of the Custom House, striding out until he reached the corner of Duke Street where he hesitated, then came to a full stop. His thin face was pale, the glowing tint of good health he had once had, faded.

He began to walk again until he reached the elegant front-age of a tall building which had once been two houses, studying the well-polished windows, the freshly washed-down front door and window-frames, the gleaming door-knocker and the brilliance of the recently whitened steps leading up to it. He moved up them and knocked and when the door was opened by a trim maid who, being only recently employed in the house, did not recognise him, his voice was husky when he spoke.

"Mrs ... Mrs Daisy Lassiter? Would she be at home?"

Daisy and Nelly were in the garden and beside them in his cradle was Bryn Lassiter, eight weeks old and the apple of his mother's eye.

"You'll spoil that child, Daisy Lassiter," Bess warned, "picking him up every time he opens his mouth to cry, and before sometimes. He is as strong as a little bull and there's nothing wrong with him. He only cries when he's hungry," but she was the worst offender of them all, unless it was Jack, the pair of them fighting over who was to nurse him next. It had put the sap back into Jack and no mistake, Bess said testily, the birth of Sam Lassiter's son, even curing the sores on his stump, he told her, allowing him to wear his peg leg again and get himself down to the cradle and guard the child.

"Someone's got to teach the lad to ride that pony when it comes," he said querulously, "and it won't be none of you daft twittering women."

"When did you ever ride a horse, Jack O'Callaghan?" Bess mocked him. "Go on, tell me that."

"When I was in Texas, that's when."

"I never even heard of the place."

"Me and the Captain had sailed into Galveston and we decided, whilst t'ship was being loaded up, to have us a look at that wild country they got out there..."

"Oh, go on with you, you great daft lummox."

There was a feeling of happiness to come in the air. The war was over. Only last week, on April the ninth, at a courthouse in a place called Appomattox, General Robert E. Lee had surrendered to General Grant, the capitulation of the army of Virginia signalling the end of the hostilities. General Johnston was to do the same and the armies were to be disbanded. The soldiers were to go home and would Captain Sam Lassiter, last seen in August of the previous year, do the same?

Daisy said so, over and over again, refusing to believe that the vital, stubborn spark of Sam Lassiter had been blown out. That somewhere he was not making his way home to his son who waited for him with his son's mother. She said so again on this day of flowering blossom and budding lilac for spring had come early that year to the coast of Lancashire. A great sweep of trumpet-headed daffodils carpeted the lawn down to the spinney. Primroses clustered thickly about the wide trunks of the trees and three wall butterflies danced together in delirious abandonment. The ash trees and the sycamore trees were in flower and high in the sky, soaring almost out of sight until it was no more than a quivering dot, a skylark sang its heart out. Fred had brought them a puppy from a farm litter somewhere, a cheerful-faced mongrel with a tight-curled coat the colour of wheat and a short stubby tail which never ceased to wag. They called him 'Chump' because he was such a fool but already, although he was no more than three or four months old, he had taken it upon himself to guard the newest and smallest, and presumably in his estimation the most defenceless member of the household. He panted now in the warm sun. The child stirred in the safety of his cradle and above his head the blossom danced for his delight.

"I wonder where Sam is, Nelly, right now at this very moment?" They lay on their backs side by side on a rug Nelly had spread on the newly cut grass, their hands behind their heads in identical positions, gazing up through the blossom to the pale blue arc of the sky. "Now that the war is over he will be looking for a ship to bring him home," she continued, blind, it appeared, to the certainty that Sam Lassiter could have contrived a berth with any number of homeward-bound blockading captains of his acquaintance in the last six months. "D'you know, I've a mind to send Rob Adams over there now that the danger is past of him being blown out of the water. And Captain Holden too. They could call in at all the ports on that coast, beginning where the *Golden Lady* foundered. Have a look round and make a few enquiries about him. He's well known in those parts and someone may have seen him."

"Yes . . ."

"Do you know, if it weren't for Bryn I'd damn well go myself. Rob could take me. I'd spend as long as it takes to . . . to . . ."

Abruptly she turned over on to her stomach, burying her face in her arms. Her hair had been carelessly plaited and hung in a thick twisting cable across her shoulder. The sun turned it to living flame, as fiercely bright as it had been when she was a child and had first washed her hair in the stream she and Cassie had bathed in. Nelly sat up slowly and, putting out a gentle hand, stroked it in perfect understanding.

"Don't give up, Daisy," she whispered, calling the woman who was supposedly her mistress by her given name for the first time. Nelly was no longer a girl and though no one in the house had recognised it, being too taken up with Daisy, with her pregnancy and then her son, the girl had grown up in the last six months. She was almost seventeen now and the bloom of womanhood was upon her. She was quiet and peace-loving with none of Bess's down-to-earth, no-nonsense flow of words which told everyone exactly what *she* considered to be right. Bess was the manager of the household, its running, its financial complications, its domestic arrangements and the supervision of its servants. In the house, in the small dairy and in the yard. She ran it like Mrs Crosby had once run Thornley Green, wisely, fairly, strictly but with a kindness Mrs Crosby had never shown and her voice could be heard laying down *her* law from attic to cellar and from morning until night. But not so Nelly. In the two years since she had become Daisy's companion she had grown to love books, music; she painted watercolours, standing down by the water's edge, sometimes in the very teeth of a howling gale putting on paper the sliding waters, the grey-streaked sky, the scudding ships and the screaming gulls which hung above the river. She was a delightful companion, listening with rapt attention and wide, intent eyes to anyone who cared to address her from Fred Wainwright's youngest who was three years old and had a constantly running nose, to Polly the maid who was twelve and missed her Mam ferociously, to Jack in one of his reminiscing monologues about his adventures on the west coast of Africa, to Daisy when she talked of Sam and what their future would be, to Bess even, who could be sharp and critical, but most of all to Captain Rob Adams when he called.

He had said nothing that could not be overheard by her own sister, believing that young ladies, of which he seemed to think she was one, were to be treated with the deference he, as a young gentleman, had been brought up to believe in. They had walked in the garden and down on the shore, never very far from the house, during the winter months when he was home, no more than three or four times between September and March when Bryn was born. Next week *Lady of the Sea* was expected in port again. Captain Adams would drive up to Ladymeadow to report to his employer, Mrs Daisy Lassiter and ... Nelly's thoughts went no further than that. No further than the certainty, despite his reticence, that ever since the night he had come to tell them of the news of Captain Lassiter's death there had been something between them, some unspoken promise which, when the time was right, would be fulfilled.

Nelly's pale skin flushed to a deep rose at the thought but at the moment Daisy was her concern. She who loved knew the doubts which come to those who suffer the state, and though Daisy was vehement in her determination that Sam Lassiter was not dead, how could she not agonise on his failure to return, if not to her then to his commitments in Liverpool? To his two ships which still sailed the oceans. To the profits which were made on lucrative cargoes. Property he owned here and there on which rents were raised must be managed, decisions made since concerns such as his, or indeed *any* business must move on, or stagnate.

"Where is he?" Daisy's voice was muffled in her arms and she clasped them more fiercely about her bright head. "Where is he, Nelly? Why has he not returned to Liverpool?" speaking the very words Nelly was thinking. "Can I be wrong? Is this conviction I have inside me only the figment of my own folly in refusing to admit he is dead?" Her voice was high and anguished. "I try so hard, Nelly, to hang on to it. I feed it with pictures of him caught somewhere ... perhaps a prisoner but then if that is the case why has he not written? I force myself to hope, to *believe*, and sometimes I do but it is getting harder and harder ..."

"Ssh ... ssh, darling ..." Nelly could feel her own tears gather, the pain in Daisy's despairing voice tearing at her heart. She stroked Daisy's hair tenderly, wishing she could think of words to nourish her hope again, but was that not just as cruel in a way, for if Sam Lassiter *was* dead that hope was false and should be put away.

Daisy lay for a while on her stomach, her cheek pressed to the soft wool of the rug. She was quiet now and though Nelly continued to smooth her hair, somewhat in the manner of a mother soothing a hurt child, it seemed the crisis was over. The baby crowed in the cradle and the dog rose and stretched, then sauntered over to check that all was as it should be with his charge. Chancing a moment to wander off on a call of nature, he returned to flop once more into his position as protector. Nelly watched him, smiling a little, wondering on how perfect life would be if only the Captain would come home to his grieving wife.

Daisy sat up suddenly and the dog cocked an enquiring eye in her direction. "Heavens, Nelly, this is really quite ridiculous, lolling about here feeling sorry for myself. Sam will come when he is good and ready and I must be patient though it's damned hard for someone of my disposition. He always was pig-headed and awkward and if he knew how badly I am taking this he would say I have only myself to blame."

She stood up, reaching out her hands to clasp Nelly's, pulling her to her feet. "Come on, my lass, we have things to do in the fields. Crops won't wait for the likes of you and me to feel in the mood to tend them, will they?" This despite the fact that she had half a dozen willing labourers, male and female, ready to weed and hoe, to pick stones and scare the birds and watch over the tender, growing young plants. She was like a field girl again as she moved amongst them, her head uncovered, her ankles bare, her feet pushed into stout boots to protect them since they were not as tough as they had been when Daisy Brindle was a child. She wore an old cotton skirt, plain and well washed, with a short-sleeved bodice. The plait of hair was tied up with a bright ribbon, the free curling ends twisting over her breast as she bent down to the earth which seemed to nourish her and give her strength. They had planted late potatoes and turnips and cabbages and the cottagers were jubilant for she had told them they could have their pick for their own pots. She had still no idea what she would do with the bountiful crop which would come but there were always hungry mouths to feed among the poor and she had no fears that it would be wasted.

She and Bess had recreated the small kitchen garden to the side of the house, planting parsley, spinach, chervil, Jerusalem and globe artichokes and asparagus, herbs to season the plain, nourishing and tasty meals Mrs Simpson thought suitable for plain folk such as themselves. They were not gentry. Mrs Simpson had known that from the start despite the abundance of luxury with which Mrs Lassiter surrounded herself, and the gourmet cooking of the French chef Mrs Lassiter had employed at that club of hers was not Mrs Simpson's style. Still, she cooked a good meal and they had no reason to complain, she knew that, and the vegetables and herbs Mrs Lassiter provided from the garden would be fresh and very welcome.

They had just checked the tender state of the new asparagus in the kitchen garden, she and Bess, smiling together at the progress of the plants which they had thinned out the previous day.

"That'll be right tasty, Daisy," Bess said, studying the sturdy rows with satisfaction, but somehow Daisy was not beside her any more and when Bess turned to look for her she was moving slowly in the direction of the gate which led out into what was known as Beech Lane. It was no more than a rough track edged on either side by old beech trees, meandering away from the river, past the row of cottages and on to Aigburth Road which led to Liverpool.

"Daisy ... lass ... ?"

Daisy's sun-browned hand was at her throat, then at her mouth as though to keep in the sound which was surely about to erupt. Her face was chalk-white and her eyes had darkened to a brown which was almost black.

She began to move more quickly, flinging open the gate and stepping out into Beech Lane and it was then Bess saw the man. He was tall and thin and shabbily dressed. His head was bent forward and she could not see his face as he put one weary foot in front of the other as though he really could not go another step. She felt her heart, usually so steady and strong, lurch with joy, then something in the abrupt stilling of Daisy's winging figure turned Bess cold and afraid.

The man had stopped too, lifting his smiling face to Daisy's.

It was Miles Thornley.

37

"What do you want?" Her voice was flat and empty, not really concerned with the answer to her question since her whole flowing body was as cold as ice, frozen in a state of shock since he was not Sam as she had thought. The soaring joy, the exultant rush of happiness had turned just as abruptly to a despairing desolation when she saw the man's face. It did not seem to matter that it was Miles Thornley. All that did matter was that it was not Sam and she felt as though her heart had been wrenched violently from her body. She stood where her flying feet had taken her with wild yellow primrose and the blue of speedwell flaunting their beauty and hope about her whilst her own died within her. The wildflowers seemed to mock her with their anticipation of a life to come whilst she had none without Sam and Miles Thornley's presence meant nothing to her. That part of her life was done with. She had suffered for it and so had others but she had paid her dues and it had been put behind her.

"Well, if it isn't the delectable Mrs Daisy Lassiter," he drawled, his arrogantly cruel face sneering, his tall figure falling at once into the insolent and lounging pose she knew so well. His bright blue eyes ran over her, studying with great amusement the plainness of the gown she wore, the stout boots on her feet and the carelessly haphazard confinement of her plaited hair in a length of ribbon. His lip curled and his eyes narrowed with a curious intensity, a spark of awakening and unconcealed desire in them just as though she was still no more than a field girl, or his mother's kitchenmaid, and as such deserving of no man's, certainly no gentleman's, respect. "Your outfit, charming as it is, is somewhat different to the one you wore the last time we met but I must admit it suits you. More fitting, I would say. Back to your beginnings, is that it, Daisy? Back to what you came from?" and again his eyes travelled over her. He licked his lips and a coarse gloating expression came over his dissolute face.

Yet still she really could not find the strength to care. He meant nothing to her now. She felt no emotion, she had no feelings, not of revulsion nor loathing. Merely a great emptiness which she knew would never be filled up again until Sam came back to her. This man was merely an irritant, like a vagrant who must be sent on his way with a lump of bread and cheese and a few pence in his hand which she would give to any vagrant.

She sighed deeply, ready to turn away but he moved quickly, barring the path to the gate through which she had just come, and the kitchen garden where Bess still stood.

"Just a minute, my girl." His voice was soft and menacing and Bess felt her heart begin to thud though Daisy merely looked at him dispassionately, her face smooth and without expression, without fear, or indeed concern of any kind. It seemed to anger Miles Thornley, her indifference to him, and his own face became suffused with savage colour. His eyes were chips of steel, flinty and dangerous as he spoke again.

"Don't look at me like that, madam," he hissed, moving again to cut off her way of escape though she had made no attempt to go. "I don't like it, I don't like it at all, but then you were always somewhat inclined to put on airs and graces above your station, were you not, Daisy, just as though you really were as good as those who are your superiors. But still, it will make it all the more enjoyable when I see you with your face in the filth at my feet. Pride goeth before a fall, I believe the saying is, and I think it is about time you realised..."

"Oh stop it, Miles." Her voice was weary. "This is really quite foolish and I would be glad if we could end it once and for all. We have ... hurt one another and we have ... paid the price, both of us, so can you not go back to wherever it is you have come from and..."

"America, Daisy, that is where I have come from." He smiled triumphantly at the sudden flare of interest in her face. "Yes, I thought that might be of some concern to you. I heard that your husband had had his ship blown out from under him off the coast of Wilmington and that you still looked for him despite a certainty that he was drowned. Oh, news travels fast in this day of steamships and I still have some friends who are willing to keep me up-to-date on what goes on here and there. I had decided to try my luck in the New World, you see. I am well known here and in Europe. Well, I would be, wouldn't I, after what you did, and I was aware that the doors of sporting houses would all be closed to me in this part of the world but I am unknown in America, you see. The land of opportunity, they call it, where any man might get rich if he has luck with him and I was of the opinion that my luck *must* change for the better. My wife had some jewellery, not much since the best pieces had long since been sold." He grinned wolfishly. "I had many debts, Daisy, as you are aware, and many gentlemen wishing to get their hands on me. I had enough to buy a ticket and a few guineas to stake me. Just a couple of good wins, that was all I needed to see me right. Just a small portion of luck, I told myself, nothing too great, and that is exactly what I had. Just that last bit of good fortune which every man deserves and it came to me with the news that Sam Lassiter was dead and that his widow, still refusing to believe it, had borne him a son."

The air about them turned cold somehow, lapping against her like the winter waves of the river. It held her and Miles Thornley in a circle of deathly chill and she could feel the blood in her veins become sluggish and her heart stilled. She was afraid now.

Behind Miles Thornley Bess took a step towards the frozen couple in the sun-filled lane, her face anguished as indecision racked her. Daisy was in danger, immediate and terrible, and with every instinct in her Bess wanted to run through the gateway to help her stand against this devil who had come back to menace them but if he should overcome them both, since men in a rage as savage as his were extraordinarily strong, who would run to fetch help to stop him? And if she ran to bring the men who were two fields away tending the growing crops, could Daisy escape the madness of Miles Thornley who, as Daisy once had been, was bent on revenge?

"My son is no concern of yours," Daisy said, her voice high and desperate.

"Aah, that has touched you, has it not, Daisy? You come to life when your son is mentioned, as I did when my informant told me of the ... gift you had made to mine." His face spasmed, so great was his rage, and spittle from his twisting lips sprayed across the bodice of Daisy's dress. "How dare you? *How dare you*, you low-born, filthy whore? How dare you give what is mine, *mine*, d'you hear, to that pewling brat my wife bore? It was not yours to give and now I can never get it back. No matter what I do, no matter who I am, the law says it belongs to her and to him and if it's the last thing I do I'll ..."

"But it is back in your family, Miles." She put out her hands in the age-old gesture of appeal, thinking to reason with him, not on her own behalf but for her baby son since he was surely in danger, but he was beyond reason. "It belongs again to the Thornley family. All of it ..." she went on "... the deer park and a great deal of land ... farms and an income from the rents to ... Dear God, Miles, will you not listen? I deeded it all to ..."

"I know that, you bitch. Do you think I don't know that?" He lifted his head, breathing deeply, harshly, and Daisy took a step backwards, preparing to dart away from him, to run with the speed of a hare across the kitchen garden, beyond it to the lawn and the cradle where her son lay, to snatch him up and protect him like the spitting she-cat into which Miles Thornley had turned her.

It was in her eyes and he saw it. His hand shot out and grasped her wrist, pulling her to him and twisting it behind her with a strength and cruelty which snapped the bone cleanly at the wrist. They both heard it and he grinned. The agony of it tore a scream from her and in the yard where he had just spent a pleasing half-hour debating with the visiting groom from the Hemingway stables on a suitable pony for Bryn Lassiter, Jack O'Callaghan heard it and raised his bald head sharply. The groom had gone. They had shared a jug of ale in the square of sunlight, almost faded now in the still short days of spring, against the kitchen door and Jack had been about to stump over to the front of the house to check on Sam Lassiter's son.

For a moment the old man hesitated, seeming to have lost his bearings, then, swift as once he had been on the deck and in the rigging of the *Golden Lady*, he darted into the stable.

The crack of the double-barrelled shotgun lifted a flock of crows in the spinney and it was several minutes before they settled again.

The Superintendent of Police and his Inspector had gone, leaving only a constable who, despite the warmth of the room, refused to remove his beaver top hat and swallowtail coat of office. Perhaps the identifying label badge on his collar gave him a feeling of security in this bizarre case in which one of the leading peers of the realm had been shot, since the constable had been accustomed in his twenty miles a day walking his beat to nothing more exciting than a runaway horse or a 'drag-sneak', a petty criminal specialising in removing goods from carts and carriages, and certainly not to a murder such as this.

He sat by the bedside of the old man, the 'prisoner' as his Inspector had called him, the man who, though he was unconscious at the moment, was to be arrested for the murder as soon as he woke up. He himself was to send for his Inspector when this happened. He fingered his pencil and notebook, smartly bound in leather and an object of great satisfaction to him, ready to jot anything down the prisoner might say on waking as his Inspector had ordered.

On the other side of the bed sat the woman. Not the owner of the house but the housekeeper, he had heard, and who would not budge from the old man's side, no matter what the Inspector, nor even the Superintendent said to her.

"I'm not leaving him on his own." Her voice was clipped and cold.

"But the constable will be with him, madam," the Superintendent said sharply. "He will not be alone."

"I'm not leaving him on his own," she repeated, and that was the end of the matter as far as she was concerned. His Inspector had drawn him on one side as he and the Superintendent left, telling him to watch her though he didn't say what he thought she might do. And all she had done since the doctor left was sit quietly, never taking her eyes from the old man.

There was a knock at the door and jumping smartly to his feet he opened it to admit a young maid carrying a tray on which were a pot of tea and a cup and saucer, milk, sugar and a plate of biscuits.

"Mrs Simpson thought you might like these," she said shyly to him, her eyes turning curiously to the bed.

The woman glanced up at her.

"That will be all, Polly," she said. "Get back to the kitchen."

"Yes, Miss Miller," and bobbing a curtsey Polly scurried out.

The constable balanced the tray on his knee then, suddenly realising what he was about, said awkwardly, "Will you not drink a cup of tea, ma'am?"

"No thank you, Constable. I'll ring if I need anything. You drink up."

"Thank you, ma'am," and he did. Good tea and good biscuits they were, he was just thinking to himself when the door opened again, this time without a knock, and a woman he could only describe as an 'apparition' trembled in the doorway. She wore a loose wrapper of some filmy material made of ribbons and lace, and not much else, to his eyes which were used to the modest flannel nightgown his own wife wore and he hastily averted them but not before he had taken in her pale beauty, the length and thickness of her bright curling hair and the awkward strapping of her injured arm to her waist.

He stood up respectfully, his eyes staring into the corner of the room, then remembering who he was and why he was here and knowing he must do his duty whatever else happened, he turned towards her, doing his best not to look too closely at her.

"Ma'am, I'm sorry, but the Inspector never said nothin' about visitors. I must ask you to leave."

It was as though he had not spoken. The woman drifted across the warm room towards the bed, looking down at the old man with such a look of tender love the constable decided they must be related. No one looked like that at a servant, as the old man was supposed to be.

"How is he, Bess?" she said sadly.

"Just the same, lass. Sleeping. But you should be in your bed an' all. Didn't the doctor give you a draught?"

"Ma'am, I must insist that you leave the prisoner's room . . ."

She turned on him like a cat, her great amber-yellow eyes like a tabby he had once seen trapped in an alley by a tom. Almost without colour they were and narrowed with venom.

"How dare you . . ."

"Daisy, leave it be. He meant no harm."

"Did you hear what he called Jack? I won't have it, not in my house, and if he can't keep a civil tongue in his head I'll have him thrown out."

"Now then, ma'am, you mustn't talk that way to a policeman doing his duty," he said gruffly, recognising her distress and sorry he had spoken as he had. "But I really must ask you to go now."

She sighed wearily, bending her head to look closely at the old man, her hair falling like a closing curtain to enfold just the two of them.

"Call me if he wakes," he heard her whisper to the woman by the bed.

He never woke again, the prisoner, and the constable jotted on a clean page in his notebook the exact time of his death. Of course the doctor had to be called to confirm that he was dead but it was no more than a formality. He'd been a policeman for nearly ten years but before that he had been a soldier, serving in the Crimea, and he'd seen enough 'stiffs' to know one when he saw one. The Inspector told him to report back to the station, both of them acutely embarrassed by the storm of weeping which overcame the young and beautiful woman who was clasped in the arms of the other.

"He was an old man, lass," he heard her say. "You mustn't fret since he died doing what he promised the Captain he'd do. Nay love, don't ask me what it was that killed him since I'm no doctor. Some sort of inflammation to his brain, I suppose, but I reckon he went the way he would have wanted. Fighting to the bloody end."

They buried him at sea. Captain Robert Adams conducted the service from the deck of his sailing ship *Lady of the Sea*. Out in the Irish Channel under an April sky in which gulls wheeled and the sun cast ripples of gold on the water as the coffin slipped smoothly into its depths. Bess and Daisy and Nelly stood on the deck, the only mourners but ones who had sincerely loved and would eternally grieve Jack O'Callaghan.

And across the river, across the miles which lay between Liverpool and St Helens, another funeral took place as Lord Thornley, attended by his wife, his son, the Sixteenth Baron of the line, and several hundred ladies and gentlemen who, now that he was dead, had nothing but good to say of him, was laid to rest in the family vault at Thornley Green.

No one, not even his wife, shed a tear for him.

Spring moved on and became summer and in his cradle and on the rug where his mother now placed him, young Bryn Lassiter, named for both his parents, kicked his bare legs and reached for the bright leaves above him. The sun was at its highest, colouring his sturdy legs to the amber tint of his father's skin, and his hair was a rich, deep chestnut. His eyes, busy with so many fascinating things, his mother's brooch, a bird in the tree, the dog's face above him, the flight of a bee across his vision, were a colour somewhere between green and brown with flecks of gold shining in them.

His mother loved him. She often took him down to the water's edge, dipping his ecstatic toes in the rippling water, holding him in her safe lap, his head on her breast. She talked to him, her soft voice lulling him to sleep, the words she spoke meaning nothing to him, nor the pain with which she spoke them. She left him sometimes in the care of Bess who loved him too, taking Nelly with her.

"Order the carriage, will you, Bess? I think Nelly and I will be elegant ladies again and go into town. Perhaps a saunter on the Marine Parade. What d'you say, Nelly? I feel in need of some fresh air," just as though she was not out in the fields or at the water's edge from morning until night, looking like a gypsy in her country clothes of swinging ankle-length skirt and cotton bodice, her bare brown ankles and low-heeled country shoes. Her hair hung down her back in the thick, curling plait she effected now and the fashionable woman who had once been Daisy Lassiter of 'Daisy's' club and sporting house was gone for ever it seemed. Her wardrobe was stuffed with gowns of silk and lace, of velvet and chiffon, with wide hats drooping about the brim with silk roses and lace and ribbons, with kid boots and ruffled parasols and oriental shawls but she wore none of them and the Misses Yeoland had quite given her up and had gone so far as to consider crossing her off their list of valuable clientele since she had not ordered a new gown for a twelvemonth.

Of course they talked about her in Liverpool, but then when had they not? One scandal after another, beginning with her shockingly blatant relationship with Captain Sam Lassiter, ten years ago now; the club she had run with such success, the flagrant and intriguing state of affairs between herself and her husband over the years and the whispers which had followed them about. And then there was that infamous business with Lord Thornley when she had engaged him in a hand of cards which had brought about his downfall. Gone off to America he had, it was said, a broken man thanks to Daisy Lassiter and no sooner had he come back to what was after all his homeland, presumably to try to build a life for himself and his pitiful family, than he was gunned down by none other than that strange fellow Daisy Lassiter had kept in the front hallway of her notorious club. It was all very odd and surely there was more to it than met the eye, though the police did nothing about it. She still walked as free as air with that baby on her hip and who was the father, they asked one another, since Sam Lassiter had not been seen in Liverpool for over a year now.

She and Nelly walked slowly along the parade just as they had been doing for two years, engulfed for a moment at the landing-stage to the front of George's Dock by a multitude of passengers embarking on the ferryboat *Queen* which was about to leave for Woodside. The double wicket gate at the top of the slip was jammed with people for the five-minute warning bell had already been rung. The two ticket collectors sat calmly in their small centre island, quite unmoved by the press of travellers, and when the second bell tolled, signalling the casting-off of the vessel, they were unconcerned, viewing breathless latecomers with supreme detachment.

The two women crossed the bridge to Prince's Dock, moving in a northerly direction. They were both dressed in the elegant fashions of last year though the men who laboured on the quayside and who watched them go by were unaware of it, seeing only the tawny amber silk of Daisy's gown, her flower-laden hat, her straight back and proud bearing, the neatness of her ankles in their soft kid boots and the pink-cheeked comeliness of the girl beside her. They had seen the two of them before, of course, at least once a week they would have said, moving from dock to dock studying every ship which was berthed between George's and Wellington Dock in the north and down to Brunswick Dock in the South, questioning disembarking seamen in a most flaunting manner. Looking for her husband, it was said, the dashing Captain Sam Lassiter who had gone off to America and never come back to her though if you asked them, which nobody ever did, he must have been blind or wrong in the head to leave her behind in the first place. What a beauty with that red hair of hers and though she was a bit on the thin side for many a man's taste, they would gladly tip their old woman out of the marriage bed to make way for her any day of the week!

There was a great commotion ahead as Daisy and Nelly moved beyond the buildings which lined the quayside between Prince's Dock basin and Waterloo Dock. A vast press of people swarmed there and moving amongst them a man's voice could be heard chanting some words Daisy could not catch because of the hubbub of voices, many of them speaking in tongues she did not recognise.

"What is he saying, Nelly?"

"He's asking all those who've not had a medical examination and had their passage tickets stamped to go to the Medical Inspector's office at once or they won't be allowed to board."

"Where are they off to, d'you think?"

"America, I suppose."

"America . . ." Daisy sighed and her footsteps slowed.

Many of those who were to sail on the packet ship *Empress of India* had embarked twenty-four hours earlier and now hung over the rails studying those not yet on board with all the nonchalance of travellers who had sailed the seven seas on numerous occasions though they had not yet even left the dockside. It was as though a great party was taking place. All was bustle, excitement and high laughter. Men and women danced between decks in one another's arms to the accompaniment of a fiddle. One passenger was skilful with an Irish bagpipe and his music vied with that of the fiddle. Fresh arrivals poured down on to the already packed quayside and Nelly and Daisy were forced back until they stood against the very parapet of the parade. Luggage, boxes, packages, crates, pots and pans tied together with string, horses, waggons, babies grizzling and children screaming in play all added to the confusion and as it was made apparent that the sailing of the vessel was imminent those not yet on board pressed forward dangerously towards the gangway.

The music ceased abruptly. There were still passengers arriving in a flushed and panting state of exhaustion, and yet at the same time enjoying the excitement of being within a few minutes of losing their passage. The gangway was about to be removed and they were in danger of having to scramble up the rigging to board the ship and having their luggage flung willy-nilly over the side and on to the deck, or even into the water! Spectators at the dock gates whistled and clapped them on and from the general air of joviality it would seem they were off on a jaunt to New Brighton instead of across a vast ocean to a new life in a country most of them had scarcely heard of in their ignorance.

The steam tugs were round the ship like worker bees about the queen, ready to tow her out. Hats were raised and handkerchiefs lifted to eyes when people suddenly realised that this would be the last time they would look on a loved one's face, the last time they would see the old country, and though in all probability they had known only suffering and starvation here, it was nevertheless the only home they had ever known and therefore familiar. Irish, many of them, come over only days ago from their own native land and now lamenting for a second time the fear and grief they knew at parting.

Daisy watched the ship move slowly away from her berth and out into the river. She had taken Nelly's hand in hers, clutching it to her in a passion she barely understood and now she squeezed it, her eyes still on the departing packet steamer. Several other people hung about, walking slowly along the dock in the same direction as the ship as though they would follow it and their loved ones who sailed in her to the furthest reaches of Liverpool Bay. To the very edge of the land those on board had left for ever. Most were quiet now, stunned by their sorrow, and Daisy felt her own grief join theirs since it came to her at that moment that Sam would never return to her. She might stand on this dock, or any other, until the end of her days, staring out towards the mouth of the estuary, waiting for a ship to come sailing up the waters with Sam Lassiter aboard but it would not happen. She would grow old and their son become a man never knowing his father, and it would not happen. She'd best make her mind up to it, she thought calmly, and get on and do what had to be done.

She turned then, still holding Nelly's hand, her stride long like that of a man, moving so quickly Nelly had almost to run to keep up with her. Her skirt kicked out around her feet and the dockers were treated to more than a glimpse of her slim ankles and elegant feet. The flowers on her hat bounced. Nelly was gasping for breath as she hurried along at the end of Daisy's arm.

"Where . . . are . . . we . . . going, Daisy? Please . . . I can't . . . get my breath . . . can . . . we not walk . . . more slowly . . ."

"I'm in a hurry, Nelly. I've wasted enough of my life on Sam Lassiter as it is and I really cannot squander any more."

Nelly stopped then, her hand jerking sharply away from Daisy's, her face a bright and rosy pink, her mouth open, her eyes wide.

"Daisy . . . Dear God, Daisy . . . I don't understand. What do you mean to do? Where are we going?"

"We're going to . . . well, to wherever it is one buys a passage to America. I mean to fetch Sam Lassiter home . . ."

"But . . . Daisy . . ." Nelly's face became still and it was in her eyes, the question she feared to ask but Daisy knew what it was.

She sighed deeply. "If he should not be there, Nelly, I don't know what I will do but perhaps then . . . I shall at last be able to accept that I need wait no longer."

571

38

The scene was very much like the one she and Nelly had witnessed last month only this time they were on the deck of the ship and Bess stood on the quayside.

She had agonised for days and argued fiercely with Bess for the whole of the three weeks in which she had made her preparations for the journey, on whether she should take Bryn with her, and when her decision was made and Bess was told what Daisy meant to do, the uproar was worse than even she had anticipated.

Bess had simply been appalled, inclined at first, though she should have known better, to think that Daisy was joking, that this was some mad scheme which had formulated in Daisy's poor, overwrought brain but needing only the application of a mind that was not clouded by emotion, as Daisy's was, to show her the lunacy of the idea. But it seemed Daisy's mind had gone over the plans right down to the smallest detail and was quite made up.

"You can't mean it?" Bess put her hand to her mouth, shaking her head in frantic denial. "You can't mean to take that innocent, defenceless child across the ocean to a land where savages roam and heaven knows what else. Wild animals, I shouldn't wonder, like them out at the Zoological Gardens. Dear God, it's only six months since the war ended and you've heard all the tales of hardship, starvation and disease, the bands of marauding rebel soldiers who won't give up the cause..."

"Bess!"

"No! No, Daisy, I won't have it. He's too young to travel so far. If you must go, then go, but that baby stays with me."

Her face was white and set and her mouth shut tight like a trap. Her eyes stared defiantly into Daisy's, ready to fill with weak tears because deep inside her Bess knew that nothing she could say, nor indeed anyone else for that matter, would make Daisy Lassiter change her mind once it was made up but she'd have a damned good try. The idea of that awful journey terrified her since ships *did* sink and that land over there was vast and unknown for the most part, or so she had heard, and would she ever see her darling again? The 'darling' in question curled strong fingers over the sides of his cradle and heaved himself into a sitting position, his eyes wide and enquiring, ready for some fun, a song perhaps, a loving embrace in any of the numerous female arms which were always eager in this household of women to pick up Master Bryn Lassiter from his cradle. He looked from one set face to the other, his rosy lips parted in a delighted smile which slipped away as, young as he was, he sensed the tension. The dog nosed his hand and, distracted, he turned to it at once, reaching for the handful of springing fur he loved to pull. The dog stood patiently.

"I'm sorry, Bess, but my mind is made up. I can't sit here for the remainder of my days waiting for Sam Lassiter to come home..."

"He's dead, girl, dead! Why won't you believe it? Rob Adams told me he saw him fall..."

"I know that, Bess, but I cannot believe..."

"*Bleeding*, Daisy, he was bleeding..." In her distress Bess was telling Daisy more than she meant to.

"What...?"

"I'm sorry, love ... I'm sorry, but ... I didn't want to say 'owt, not then when you were so ... but now, surely it can be told you? Captain Adams said he saw him fall bleeding to the deck of the ... the ship..."

"Don't ... please don't, Bess..." Daisy bowed her head, putting her hands to her face as though to shut out the terrible image Bess's words had conjured up. The child crowed as the dog's rough tongue moved across his hand and arm and in the hallway outside the room Polly sang in a piping treble 'The Last Goodbye' as, thinking herself unheard and unseen, she sauntered from the drawing room to the kitchen with the pan containing the ashes from yesterday's fire.

Daisy lifted her chin and though her face was even whiter, her jaw was set in a line of rigid determination.

"It makes no difference," she said through clenched teeth. "I will not believe he is dead until I see his grave. I must go. I *must go*. He is like a ghost haunting me, Bess, and I must either find him, resurrect him, or lay his ghost for ever. There is something inside me which will not let me believe he is dead, you see. I know you think I'm mad but I cannot get on with my life, whatever it is to be, until I know what became of him."

"You love him so much?"

"Oh yes, and yet at the same time he ..."

"What, Daisy?"

"I can't explain. One half of me is infuriated by him, by his bloody unyielding obstinacy, and if he walked through that door now I should probably fly at him and do my best to remove his eyes. He has that effect on me. He pushed me too far, incenses me and makes my blood boil, but I really ... I don't know how I shall live without him if he should prove to be ... gone, Bess."

Bess sighed sadly, patting Daisy's shoulder with a comforting hand. She was completely mystified by what she saw as Daisy's illogicality but that was really not the issue here. The issue in question wobbled about amongst his pillows, doing his best to pull the unresisting dog into the cradle with him. She watched him fondly as she spoke.

"Very well, lass. I know you won't rest until you've been to see for yourself where he ... where his ship went down and so I'll say no more. You'll have to take our Nelly, I suppose. You can't travel alone, and you're not to fret about the lad. I'll guard him with my life, you know that."

"Bess." Daisy's voice was cool and steady, her emotions well under control now. "Bess, I am taking my son with me to find his father and that is all there is to say on the matter. I could not bear to be apart from him for ... perhaps six months ..."

"Six months! Oh sweet Lord . . ."

". . . and besides, I am nursing him myself and could not . . ."

"He could be weaned."

"Not in three weeks."

"Heaven help us, Daisy, you can't . . ."

"There are hundreds and hundreds of children sail to America and come to no harm."

"Aye, poor mites, and what have they left behind, tell me that? Slums and squalor and starvation. Our Bryn's got a warm cradle and good food . . ."

"In my breast which is going with me."

"Daisy . . . don't, love. Don't leave me . . ."

"Then come with us, Bess. Come with us. There's nothing to keep you here. Mrs Simpson can look after the house . . ."

"Aye, her and Polly and them other two sitting about on their bums all day doing nowt . . ."

"And Fred will take care of the land. The crops are nearly in and he knows what should be planted . . ."

"The place will be in ruins when we come home . . ."

"So you admit there's a possibility we might get home then?"

And so it went on, round and round and round. From morning till night with Bess clutching to her breast the poor little lad who would be bound to fetch up at the bottom of the sea, or be stolen by them Red Indians she'd heard tell of, die of a fever, fall overboard or any one of a hundred dreadful consequences of Daisy's folly.

But she would not be moved and on the eighth of October Daisy, Nelly and Bryn sailed on the Inman Royal Mail steamer *City of Montreal*, bound for New York via Queenstown. They and their luggage had been brought aboard by tender from the landing-stage at the north side of Huskisson Dock and they had settled themselves briefly in their cabin before returning to the deck to wave goodbye to Bess. She stood alone, a still and silent figure in the midst of the mêlée of embarking passengers, of distraught mothers who knew they would never see their sons and daughters again, of luggage still being loaded on to the tender, and the stretch of water between the ship and the dock might have been the great Atlantic Ocean itself, so tragic was her expression.

"I'll write as soon as I get there, Bess," Daisy mouthed but Bess did not move or answer and when the tugs began to draw the steamer out into the river she continued to gaze at Daisy and the child as if she was looking her last on them. At the final moment she turned her pale grey eyes on her sister and tried a tremulous smile as though to say she didn't blame *her*, then her plainly dressed figure was no more than a blur amongst hundreds of others who stood with her.

Daisy had decided on the Royal Mail steamer because of its superior speed over that of a sailing ship though she would have preferred to cross the seas as Sam had once done, under sail, but Captain Adams, and Captain Holden in his steamship were somewhere on the high seas, Captain Adams and *Lady of the Sea* having taken a cargo of manufactured goods to Canada. He was due back within the month with a load of timber. Captain Holden and the *Country Girl* were further afield bringing wool from Australia. She could wait for neither, Daisy had said impatiently to Nelly, not even noticing the dismayed expression on Nelly's face and if she had it is doubtful she would have commented on it since her own face, her whole being was turned in one direction and that was to where she was convinced – she told all and sundry – Sam Lassiter was to be found.

And she was to start her search in New York. The saloon passage had cost her twenty-one guineas for each of the tickets for herself and Nelly and ten guineas for Bryn. A great deal of money to be sure, but in what luxury they were to travel. A cabin of their own, of course, shown there by a courteous and attentive officer. Ten days they were to be aboard, he said politely, and if he could be of any assistance with their portmanteaux, travelling bags or indeed any of the personal gear which they might need on the journey they had only to ask. They must make use of the spacious saloon, he begged them, which was as delightfully decorated and furnished as any first-rate hotel. Might he ask their final destination, he enquired, wondering how the officers and

576

crew of the *City of Montreal* would view these two extremely attractive and unattached young women.

Daisy saw none of his respectfully admiring glances. Indeed her mind was barely able to contemplate the next ten days in which she must control her eagerly winging excitement towards the shores of the United – at last – States of America. She meant to begin with a certain American ambassador who had frequented her club in the past when he had travelled through Liverpool en route from his own country to hers, and who she was hopeful might give her advice on moving about the ravaged Southern states. He had met Sam once or twice when Sam had been in Liverpool; had even played a hand or two of bezique with him and surely, as one on the winning side in the dreadful war, might he not have some ideas on where she should begin to look for her husband?

The young officer still fidgeted at the door. They had parted company with the Liverpool steam tender now and were beginning to pass, at first slowly but with increasing speed, down the widening estuary towards the open sea. A seaman approached the officer, speaking respectfully, saying something to him and the officer rebuked him sternly.

"There is no need to bother these ladies."

"What is it ... er ... Mr ...?"

"Saunders, ma'am. First officer, at your command," bowing.

"Mr Saunders, what is taking place?"

"A search for stowaways, madam. It is always done before we leave the river so that any found can be returned to Liverpool. They try it on, you see."

"Try it on, Mr Saunders?"

"Indeed, ma'am. Those who have not the price of a ticket. They hide in trunks and chests, even making air-holes to prevent them suffocating. Sometimes they are brought on board in barrels, packed up to their chins in salt or biscuits." Mr Saunders was unconcerned about the whole sorry business, his manner said, for what was an Irish peasant or two to him, but Nelly shuddered. She was doing her best to soothe Bryn who was inclined to be fretful, confined not

577

only in the small space the cabin allowed, but in Nelly's clutching arms.

"All the passengers except those like yourselves in state cabins are summoned to the quarter-deck for roll call and must stay there until the search is completed," Mr Saunders continued. "Naturally you will not be expected to attend, ma'am." He saluted them gallantly before striding off about his duties.

It was a fine sunny day when they entered the port of New York, the skies blue and serene. Their eyes, which for the past ten days had had to content themselves with the blues and greys and whites of the Atlantic, in calm and storm, and the pale tints of an ocean sky, were delighted with the soft hues of the New Jersey hills and the lovely islets and wooded slopes of the harbour itself. The ship steamed slowly along the winding channel and through the narrows amidst a great fleet of varied shipping, not unlike that which sailed the River Mersey. Saucy little tugs puffed noisily about the lovely bay. Lines of large ferry boats crossed the river and harbour in all directions, and Daisy, holding her son to her in a clasp of fevered excitement, drew in her breath for surely here, where ships of all nations crowded like bees in the hive, she would find some clue to Sam Lassiter's whereabouts. The ocean journey had been pleasant enough, got through somehow despite Bryn's fractious bewilderment at the absence of all he loved the best in his small world, which included the dog, the spoiling he received from Bess and the servants and the great open stretch of garden where all its wonders were just becoming apparent to him. Despite an overnight storm which had them all topsy-turvy in their cabin and the close confinement of the ship where she and Nelly could go nowhere without some eager young officer engaging them in admiring conversation. She was tart with them, letting them know she had no time for gallantries, carrying her son, despite the costly elegance of her gown, on her hip as though she was one of the peasant women who did the same in steerage. She walked the deck briskly in almost all weathers, just as though she could not keep still her restless limbs, refusing to be drawn into the smallest flirtation, the curiosity and gossip of those ladies who, escorted by their husbands, travelled with her. They were all intrigued, she was well aware, by the strange and unconventional situation created by two women and a child travelling without masculine protection. The small social gatherings, the shipboard acquaintanceships which grow when people are thrown together in enforced confinement, were of no interest to her. She and Nelly dined each evening in the well-appointed dining room exchanging polite nods here and there, but apart from that they kept to their cabin or walked the deck with the boy.

And now they were here at last.

There were no docks in New York harbour such as Liverpool had, all the shipping discharging and taking on cargo and passengers from wharves which jutted out into the Hudson and East Rivers. The Custom House and its necessary formalities were got through, a carriage found and they and their luggage were conveyed through a district which was neither savoury nor pleasing to the eye. There was a public park at the southern extremity of Manhattan Island, known by the curious name of the 'Battery', presumably because an old Dutch fort had once stood there, Daisy remarked, and starting from there, bissecting Manhattan Island through its whole length, ran a wide and handsome thoroughfare called Broadway on which fine houses and hotels stood.

"I shall call on Mr Stamford immediately," Daisy told Nelly, the moment the porter had gone. Nelly looked about her at the luxurious suite of rooms Daisy had reserved for them. There were two bedrooms and a large sitting room with a superb view down Broadway. There was a graceful church opposite the hotel, Trinity Church it was called, they had been told by the driver of the carriage, one of the landmarks of New York, with a tall spire, built only twenty years ago but Nelly was concerned not with that, nor indeed with any of the bewildering and unfamiliar sights they had encountered since leaving Liverpool but with the awful prospect of being left alone in the midst of them. Daisy was strung up to a fine-drawn tension, nervously adjusting her bonnet which she had not even removed, just as though she expected to see Sam Lassiter within the hour, unconcerned with the sprawl of boxes and trunks which were heaped inside the door. A maid would be up at once, the gentleman in a black morning suit had told them grandly, to unpack and arrange the ladies comfortably, but Nelly was not at all comforted. She was here in a foreign land, far from everything she had ever known in her young life, separated from Rob who did not even know where she was and he would be ... well, to say the least, surprised, not to find her at Ladymeadow when he returned to Liverpool. She was young and inexperienced, with no idea of how to speak to these brisk and bustling Americans who were so different to the unobtrusive and respectful servants she knew. She had been one herself once and believed she knew how they should behave. Now, before she had time to draw breath, Daisy was to leave her alone amongst them and what was she to do if one spoke to her?

"Nelly?" Daisy turned to her questioningly. "What is it?"

"Will you ... be long?" was all Nelly could find to say.

"I have no idea but if I should not be back in time see that Bryn is settled comfortably, will you, darling? You may give him some warm milk and soften a biscuit in it, or order some semolina. I'll feed him when I return but in the meanwhile it won't hurt him to have something else. I suppose I shall have to wean him gradually if I am to have the freedom of..."

Her voice died away, her thoughts not on her son but on his father and Nelly was made aware, as she had not been before, that she herself must learn in this new and alarming world not to depend too much on Daisy Lassiter. The thought of ringing casually to some unknown part of the hotel and demanding a bowl of semolina was terrifying enough but suppose it should be unavailable, or the maid was rude, or incompetent? And if Master Bryn decided he did not care for it and cried for his mother's breast and her not here to supply it, what then?

Nelly was to find herself in many such situations in the next few months of her life, and as they passed, so did she from girl to complete and confident womanhood, finally leaving behind the inexperienced, somewhat gauche and hesitant girl, becoming a travelled woman who dealt easily with porters, chambermaids, cab drivers, hotel receptionists and even overbearing managers of the hotels in which they stayed. Daisy relied on her, not only to care for Bryn whilst she herself chased about on what were always will-o'-the-wisp and unrewarded clues in her search for Sam Lassiter, but to make arrangements for travel on the railways, to wire ahead for suitable accommodation, to pay hotel bills, order meals, see to luggage and be the support and comfort which Daisy needed so desperately as the weeks passed and Sam had not been found, alive or dead!

They had travelled from New York after an advertisement, advised by Mr Stamford and placed in *The New York Herald* and *The New York Times*, both widely read newspapers, he assured her, had failed to bring news of Sam's whereabouts. Two weeks they wasted, Daisy fumed, before taking a train to Washington, the Federal capital since the year 1800, where again Daisy spent time calling on gentlemen Mr Stamford had recommended and who might help her, or at least suggest some course of action in finding a man who had been a 'blockader' and, in a way, a recent enemy of theirs. Perhaps he might have been taken prisoner by the Union forces, they said, but then if that was so, why was he not finding his way homewards as so many Confederate prisoners of war were now doing?

From there they took the train to Richmond, a journey of some 116 miles. The railroad followed the course of the Potomac river and then ran across an area in which, during the war, some of its bloodiest battles were fought. Fredericksburg, Chancellorville and other towns which struck chords in Daisy's memory of those days when she had taken scarcely any account of the desperate wounding struggle this great country had suffered. She had read of them and forgotten them, aware only that Sam, and many others were amassing great fortunes and was it not splendid to be so rich? The memory shamed her when she saw the shattered remains of what had once been pleasant townships.

They travelled to Wilmington, North Carolina, where Sam's ship had foundered and where Daisy had pinned most of her hopes. She stood on the banks of the Cape Fear river watching its swift flow out into the Atlantic Ocean and beside her the courteous gentleman who had done business with Sam Lassiter on many occasions shook his head sadly.

"A brave gentleman, Mrs Lassiter, and an honourable one. He took my cotton, when I had some, and paid me fairly and I was distressed to hear of his passing." The soft Southern drawl of the plantation owner fell pleasantly on Daisy's ears but even as he spoke, turning to smile gallantly, his broad-brimmed hat held to his chest, she could tell that his own disasters were of far more importance to him than hers. He had lost not only his sons, he told her, three of them gone in the same battle, but his way of life and his hope for the future.

"Do you think my husband could have got ashore here, Mr Neville? It is possible, surely, to get inland to a place of safety?"

"Why would he not seek help with those of us who knew him, Mrs Lassiter? Wilmington was then still in our hands and had he sought out myself, or indeed any number of gentlemen hereabouts, we would have been only too glad to get him on to a Liverpool-bound ship. You do believe me, don't you?"

Of course she did, and could see the sense to his words. It was but a few miles from the spot where Rob Adams had seen the *Golden Lady* break up, to the town of Wilmington, so why had he not made his way there? *Because he was dead, you fool*, a quiet voice said inside her head, and she turned away from the silent old gentleman who stared, as she did, into an empty future.

"There were Confederate army patrols about here, looking for provisions," he said musingly, and she whirled back to him eagerly. "Sheridan's men had swung about to South Carolina. There were encounters towards Fayetteville . . . or was that later? My memory is not as sharp as once it was, ma'am . . ." He seemed to lose the thread of what he was saying and she longed to tug on his arm, to pry open his mind to see what was locked inside there, then, "... Major Richards was in command of ... he was amongst them. A distant relative of my wife's, God rest her soul. He was wounded later at Fort Steadman and captured. They pushed us back..."

"Major Richards?"

"Yes, ma'am. He has a plantation ... *had* a plantation over in ... I can give you the address if you would care to..."

"Do you think he might know ... perhaps have heard of an Englishman marooned out here ... or ... ?"

"Who knows, Mrs Lassiter? This war has produced many...." Again his voice faded, then, as though aware that the famous gallantry and respect for gentlewomen for which Southern gentlemen were famous was somehow lacking, he turned on her a smile of such sweetness and charm she found herself returning it despite the knot of hopeless pain which grew daily in her chest.

"We planters prided ourselves on our ... care for our people, you know, Mrs Lassiter, and now they have left us, most of them. Run away on the frail promises made by Yankees that they would grow as rich as any white man."

People? His people? For a moment she was confused before she realised he was speaking of his black slaves who, not surprisingly perhaps, had headed off for the nearest towns, eager to enjoy not only this new and marvellous freedom which was now theirs but the wealth which was to go with it.

"I'm sorry, Mr Neville, truly I am. This war has damaged so many lives." She paused delicately, "Now, if I could know the whereabouts of Major Richards?"

The Major and his gaunt wife were as hospitable and welcoming as though their devastated plantation and the shattered house that stood on it, was just as it had been almost five years ago – when the kitchens overflowed with food and a score of servants waited only for their master's command to do his bidding – begging Daisy and her companion, and of course her delightful son to stay for a meal, for the night, a week even if they could persuade her. They had few visitors, they said, but if she would only permit it they and their neighbours would surely like to get together a party, perhaps a barbecue, yes a real Southern barbecue, and entertain her in the way only those of the South knew so well. Eyeing the scanty food on her plate, delightfully cooked and arranged, by Mrs Richards she suspected, but not enough to feed a child let alone a grown man, she declined regretfully, saying she must get on in her search and return to her own country, with or without her husband.

The Major, only just returned from the prison at Rock Island, Illinois, walked with a heavy limp, leaning on a cane. His wife had, single-handedly but for a couple of their faithful 'people', managed to grow a tiny crop of cotton each year, with a few vegetables, chickens and a pig, keeping the plantation barely alive. Daisy, fingering the winging-dove cameo at her throat, was reminded of the woman Sam had told her about who had sold it to him. She wondered how many of her treasures Mrs Richards had parted with to keep herself and her people alive.

No, the Major knew of no Englishman in these parts though he had been in the area on the night Sam's ship was sunk. There had been a sea-battle, he remembered, in which Confederate ships had also been blown out of the water, with many fatalities. Bodies washed up on the shores along the coast and all but one had been identified. No, he had no idea what had happened to the one which was not claimed, looking compassionately at the stricken face of the lovely Mrs Lassiter. Buried in some unknown grave, he presumed sadly. There had been many unidentified men, dead and alive, in those last desperate battles he had fought. Men in his own troop who had come in towards the end, strangers to him and not trained for fighting but welcome nevertheless. Silent, gaunt men knowing they could do no good but also knowing the southland needed every man at this eleventh hour of the struggle.

"I wish I could help you, ma'am. He may have been one of them but I can see no reason why a man such as your husband would fight for our cause, can you? Particularly with such a charming wife as yourself waiting at home for him."

They were clearly mystified, every man and woman she spoke to in the weeks – running into months – when she travelled down the east coast of America moving with increasing weariness and despair, from town to town, from port to port where Sam Lassiter might have been known. The desolation of such places as Charleston, which still lay in the ruins the Union army had reduced it to, and indeed of many of the lovely old Southern towns which had stood in the way of Sheridan's march through Georgia, saddened her and brought home to her how hopeless her mission really was.

It was almost Christmas when she and Nelly reached New Orleans and Daisy was desperately aware that she could not keep the girl from her home and those she loved for much longer. Bryn, with the resilience of a child, had flourished, seeming to thrive on the constant change of places and faces. He was made much of wherever they went, his enchanting, wide-eyed charm and vast capacity for enjoyment drawing admiring glances in every hotel in which they stayed. Within hours of arriving he had a retinue of willing followers amongst the staff, eager to fetch him whatever his mother or Miss Miller ordered and if it was not immediately available in the hotel, obtaining it at whatever cost from elsewhere.

"He's his father all over again," Daisy said wearily to Nelly, "getting whatever he wants with very little trouble to himself."

"He's only a baby, Daisy. Everyone loves a baby."

"He grows so quickly. Soon he will be walking and ... Sam is missing it ... Oh, Nelly, I really think ..."

"What, darling?"

"Am I a fool? Is it time to ... go home and ... try to forget him?"

"I don't know, Daisy. Perhaps here in New Orleans someone may have heard something of ..."

"We have been saying that for months now. How many thousands of miles have we covered? How many men have we spoken to and all of them have looked at me as though I was out of my mind, as indeed I sometimes think I am. I cannot prove he is alive, neither can I prove he is ... dead.

Perhaps he lies in that ... that grave the Major spoke of, or does the sea have him, after all?"

Daisy spent many hours on the levee situated on the mighty Mississippi river, amongst the multitude of ships which were berthed there, speaking to a complex mixture of races – French and Spanish adventurers, English settlers, men who had been slaves and many others. The war had touched them all severely but it seemed the city was recovering and the bustle and feeling of growth was exciting. This was where Sam Lassiter would be if he was alive, she thought, here where there was a guinea to be made, life and adventure to be had and beautiful women of all colours to be made love to. This great river on which New Orleans lay was where life and the future was, it seemed to say. Foreign steamers were already taking away cotton, sugar, rice and tobacco and river steamboats were loaded for their journey of two thousand miles inland.

It was as it had been everywhere she went. No, they had seen no one of Sam Lassiter's description hereabouts, they told her courteously. Besides, Sam Lassiter was dead, or so they'd heard, his ship sunk by the Yankees more than a year ago. All the blockaders were long gone and most returned to whatever it was they had done before the war. The only one still at it was 'Captain Roberts' who had become a legend wherever blockading was carried on. He had become bored with his peace-time service and had hired himself out to break the blockade of the Greek ports by the rebellious Cretans, or so rumour had it.

"Captain Roberts?" she asked warily, a small bud of excitement leaping to life in her breast but her informer's next words extinguished it for ever.

"This was his alias, ma'am. His real name was Augustus Charles Hobart-Hampden. The younger son of an earl, or so they say."

"Really?" and in Daisy Lassiter's heart, though she did not at that precise moment acknowledge it, Sam Lassiter was gently laid to rest.

39

She stood on the deck of the ship, her hands gripping the rail, staring out into the gathering darkness to the last faint smudge on the horizon which was the coast of America. Nelly had gone to their cabin taking the wailing Bryn with her. For once he was not his usual good-natured self, cutting several teeth and irritable with it. His gums were red and swollen, he was restless, twisting about in Nelly's arms, his fist stuffed as far as it would go into his mouth.

"I'll beg a crust from the steward, Daisy, and see if that will ease him, poor mite."

Daisy, barely hearing Nelly's words, nor, if she was honest, the cries of her son, nodded, her eyes still fixed on the land where not only her love was buried but the hope she had kept alive for so long. Somewhere, somewhere in that land his beloved body lay, in its earth or in its waters, what did it matter, he was gone.

Gulls cried mournfully above her head as they followed the ship, the sound no more melancholy than the lament within her as her true grieving for the man she loved began. She knew she could put it off no longer, the tearing sorrow which was to come. Her stubborn insistence that he lived, her absolute certainty that she would know inside herself if he was dead, could be clung to no longer. There was only one possibility which might be considered and that was that he was still alive but did not want to be found. That he did not want her any longer and if that was the case he was just as dead to her as if he mouldered in his grave and her grieving must still be done.

Her tawny eyes were dark and sombre. Even her outfit

echoed the blackness in her heart. A deep grape-purple travelling outfit, plain, almost stark in its simplicity with nothing to relieve it but the dove cameo. Her bonnet was close-fitting to her head, concealing the vivid brightness of her hair and the pale skin of her clear-cut profile as she continued to watch the faint grey coastline of the land she had just left until it had vanished completely below the horizon.

It was almost dark now. The sea heaved about the ship, heavy and promising to be stormy. Lights from the cabins picked out frills of lacy foam as tiny waves tossed themselves up into the air and from the stern of the ship a great trail of white ran back as far as the eye could see before it was devoured by the darkness.

Men moved at her back, going efficiently about their duties, their voices quiet, muffled, as though they knew her thoughts and were doing their best not to disturb them.

What should she do now? How would she occupy her time for the rest of her life? she asked herself despairingly. From the moment she had been capable of standing on her own somewhat insubstantial legs, not a great deal older than Bryn, she had been occupied with some task. Scaring the birds had been the first, running with a clapper to ward off the flocks which had gathered, circling, to avail themselves of Farmer Dixon's growing crops. Picking stones had been another, her tiny figure keeping up with her mother, the other women and their children to fill the buckets from which their wages were reckoned. It had seemed a game at first until she had been made aware in no uncertain way that this 'game' must be continued long after she had grown tired of it. From that moment she had been a field girl and from that moment her life had been filled with the need to labour. First to put food in her own mouth, then to 'get on', to educate herself, to *be* someone in the servants' hall at Thornley Green, and finally to fulfil the insane need she had to revenge herself on Miles Thornley. Always she had had some goal, some objective to strive towards. And now she had nothing. For twelve months and more she had waited, simply waited for Sam to come home to her. Then, tired of waiting, she had gone in search of him, always looking ahead, eager for the next day when, surely, there would be something, some evidence to take her in one direction or another, leading her to where Sam was. She had not considered why, or allowed herself to dwell on why, he had stayed away from her since that would have destroyed the myth that he still lived. She had gone blindly forward to this moment when hope was finally dead.

So what to to do now? her tired mind begged to know. Let me get through this night, her breaking heart answered. Let me get through this next hour and I shall cope somehow with the one which is to follow, and the one after that. Her eyes burned dry in their sockets, still piercing the darkness which separated her from Sam, wherever he was. Her head ached, and her throat and chest, with the need to weep but she could not. She thought wonderingly, is this all there is? Is this all I shall be from now on? A woman who has loved but who now hates the destiny which has lost me that love?

"He's asleep now, Daisy. Come down to the cabin and rest," Nelly said beside her. "It's cold out here. I'll ask the steward to bring you some soup, or a little chicken. There's no need for us to go into the dining room tonight."

"Presently, Nelly."

"Are you all right, darling?" Nelly peered into her face around the brim of the bonnet, her own face anxious and pleading.

"Yes, Nelly, thank you. I'm all right."

But she was not, of course. Her future had been reduced to the level of what she must endure in it and though Nelly was kind, thoughtful, worried about her, she could feel herself drawing away from her since Nelly had hope and anticipation and Daisy Lassiter had not.

"I'll be down shortly, Nelly," she said, her hollow, aching bones leaning for support on the railing, her burning eyes drawn irresistibly to the silky rocking depths of the water below her.

"Well, put your cloak about you then," wrapping the long, hooded cape, warmly lined and serviceable, about Daisy's shoulders, buttoning it up about her throat, anxious as a mother and Daisy smiled before leaning down to drop a kiss on her cheek.

"I shall be all right, you know, Nelly. Not now, and not tomorrow, but one day."

She began to stride along the deck when Nelly had gone, on and on, round and round, the heavy garment about her shoulders growing heavier with moisture. She had no idea how long she walked, her mind with no purpose in it other than to tire her body to exhaustion so that she might sleep.

The ship began to plunge as it ran into fiercer waters and a biting wind shrieked high in the rigging. She was forced to cling to the railing, the elemental turmoil of the sea and the wind matching exactly her own grief and the voice which whispered again and again in her head, asking her, "What now, Daisy, what now?"

She had no idea of the time, nor of the curious glances which were directed towards her as the seamen went about their duties on the deck. The vibration of the ship's engine beneath her feet, the whipping of the wind above her head had no meaning. She was fighting her own battle, gritting her teeth, hollow-eyed, sightless and almost senseless and when the man stepped out into her path, silent and like herself draped in a long wet cloak, she almost collided with him.

He was a ghost, of course, conjured up by her own maddened pain, by her misery, by her savagery since deep inside her anger raged at what had been done to her. He simply stood there, hatless, the lashing rain which had begun without her noticing, falling through his thick hair and across his drawn cheeks. He blinked rapidly to clear the raindrops which tangled in his dark eyelashes and in the vacuum into which this ghost had precipitated her she watched, quite fascinated, the clenching of his strong jaw. Through the loud sea-roaring in her head she thought she heard the sound of her name but she simply stood, waiting politely, for even a ghost must be treated with courtesy, for it to vanish so that she might continue her frantic pacing. A vault of glass like the ones they put over stuffed birds, or dried flowers, had fallen about her and inside it she was calm, untouched, unable to be reached by or to reach out to the ghost of Sam Lassiter which stood before her.

He spoke her name and she saw his lips move this time. Inside her a bird's wing began to flutter. An injured bird which can do no more than lie low, waiting until the danger is passed. It brushed against her heart which began to move in queer, erratic jerks. She put a hand to her breast to protect it, to try to stop its mad beat, and the vision before her took a step towards her. She shook her head feverishly in denial, not at its presence but at the cruelty with which fate was treating her for when the vision left again, as it surely would when her mind cleared, how much more devastating would be her pain.

"Daisy . . ."

She wouldn't answer, of course she wouldn't, for the men who were still working about the deck, squaring away gear against what promised to be a violent storm would think she had lost her mind, as indeed she had, talking to herself on an empty deck.

"I think we should get below, Daisy."

She felt her arm taken and she was turned about. Like a sleepwalker or someone who is trapped in a pit of deep shock, she allowed herself to be led along the deck to the door which led down the companionway to the corridor on which the state cabins were situated.

"You're soaking wet, Daisy. You must let Nelly get you into some dry clothes. Which is your cabin?" and the sea and the rainwater ran from both of them on to the smooth carpet which lined the corridor, forming dark stains where they stood. Did ghosts get wet when it rained? she mused wonderingly, because this one was, its buff-coloured cape which had a somewhat military look about it darkened in patches to the colour of the underside of a mushroom.

Nelly screamed, her face turning to grey putty, damp and quivering, as she opened the door to them and the ghost tutted irritably.

"For God's sake, girl, you'll wake the child, not to mention the whole bloody ship. Pull yourself together and stop jerking about like a marionette. Take Daisy's bonnet and cloak and here, you can get rid of mine while you're at it. Oh, and ring the bell for the steward, will you? A good stiff brandy will do us all good. Now, pull that chair forward and get Daisy into it before she falls down, that's a good lass. It might be as well when the brandy arrives if you made yourself scarce. Is there another room? In there? Is that where ... the boy is...? Well, if I were you I'd get in there and stuff my ears because when Daisy Lassiter come to her senses the language won't be fit for the likes of a young woman such as yourself. Ah, here's the brandy..."

Daisy could hear his voice and on the edge of her vision his hands were strong and sure as they poured brandy into three glasses. "Only a drop for you, Nelly," she heard him say. "Just enough to get you back on your feet and into the other room. A girl like yourself will not be used to it and I don't want to have to deal with two senseless women."

The hands dealt swiftly with decanters and glasses, rearranged chairs, patted Nelly's shoulder and one hovered briefly on the doorknob which opened the door into the adjoining cabin as though its owner was longing to turn it but it was Nelly who did so, closing the door obediently behind her, her face still white and frightened as she turned for one last look at Daisy.

He sat down slowly in front of her, his knees almost touching hers. His hand reached out and put the glass of brandy between her own, guiding it to her lips. She drank obediently, the fiery warmth of the spirits flowing down inside her and igniting some dormant thing which had lain uneasily there ever since the ghost had approached her. She could feel it come to life, slowly, warming her, feeding the flames of her wild rage and by God it felt good. It was growing gradually, second by second, spreading explosively down her numbed legs to her feet which moved in an involuntary jerk as though they longed to be at something which had not yet reached her brain. Her arms and hands twitched and her breast rose on a great convulsive breath. Her bowed head rose slowly and her great golden eyes, hot and savage in her white face, looked directly at Sam Lassiter who was not a ghost at all but the same quirky, infuriatingly grinning man she had known for most of her adult life and she hated him with every muscle, every bone, every fibre and drop of blood in her body.

"You bastard," she hissed. "You unfeeling, callous, evil bastard. You sit there grinning like some bloody monkey just as though you had been away for no more than a fortnight, expecting me to welcome you back with ... Dear God, I can't believe it. Though I can see it with my own eyes, I cannot believe it, even of you, Sam. Have you any idea of what has been happening while you've been junketing about the world pretending, for some unaccountable reason, to be dead? Jesus, I thought Miles Thornley was the lowest crawling thing that ever came out from under a stone but I see I was wrong because you make him look like a saint. All these months ... over a year ... not knowing whether you were alive or dead ... grieving ... *No*, I don't want to know where you've been, or why..."

She was trembling violently now, the brandy sloshing about in the glass she still held and suddenly aware of it she dashed it in his face before standing up. She moved to the door which led on to the corridor, opening it violently. "Get out. Get out of my cabin, and get out of my life. Go back to wherever it is you've been hiding ... *Get out* before I...I cannot bear to look at you..."

He stood up, the brandy dripping from his chin, and moving swiftly across the cabin tried to close the door but she would not let him. One by one he prised her fingers from the doorknob, holding her back as he pushed the door to, then, with infinite patience, he forced her across the cabin to her chair.

"Sit down, Daisy."

"I can't ... Jesus, oh Jesus God, I swear I'll get even with you for what you have made me do. I waited ... month after month carrying your child..."

"I saw him."

"*You saw him!*" She leapt from her chair and her fingers raked at his face but he avoided them, grabbing for her wrists. Her hands were like claws, twisted and terrible and so strong in her rage it took all his strength to hold her.

"Daisy, for Christ's sake, sit down and let me speak..."

"No..." Her voice rose to a thin scream and on the other side of the door Nelly cowered against the berth, crying quietly and longing for the safe comfort of Rob Adams's arms. What were they doing to each other, Daisy and the resurrected Captain Lassiter? Should she run for someone ... one of the officers perhaps, for surely murder was to be done on this ship tonight?

"Daisy, you must sit down, darling. You must let me speak and I cannot do it with you determined to get your hands about my throat. For God's sake don't scream like that or you'll have the crew and half the passengers knocking on the door..."

"You loathsome bastard ... I've spent three months searching for you ... oh God, all those miles I've travelled ... the people I've questioned, and you just walk in here grinning and making jokes ... I thought you were dead. I mourned you ... I wouldn't believe it, not at first, you see, but finally I had to accept it and here you are, unhurt, returned from wherever you have been as though ... as though it meant nothing. I can never forgive you, never..."

She was weeping brokenheartedly now, the rage, the hatred, the tearing despair of what he had made her suffer draining away on a great wave of desolation. He had *let* her suffer so. He had allowed her to be dragged down into the sorrow and pain she had known at his loss. He had watched her as she searched for him, since he admitted to seeing his son, and without a qualm he had returned when it suited him, for some purpose of his own.

"Will you let me speak, Daisy?" His voice was quiet.

She had turned away from him, standing with her face to the panelled wall. Her shoulders were shaking but she made no attempt to reach him again, or to deny him his say.

"Won't you sit down and look at me?" His voice was even gentler now as though he understood and sympathised with her feeling of betrayal. "I would like you to look at me whilst I speak so that you will know what I am about to tell you is the truth."

"Go to hell, Sam."

"Daisy..."

"Go to hell, Sam Lassiter, and don't ever come back. Not again. What you have done to me, and to your son, is unforgivable and believe me I mean it when I say I never want to look into your face again. I want you gone, Sam." Her voice was expressionless and because of it, quite deadly. "You're not worth the ... the tears I've shed, nor the heartbreak, and I'm only sorry I wasted them on such a man as yourself."

"I mean to make you listen, Daisy. I mean to..."

"*You* mean to! You have no rights here. None. You are nothing to me and if you don't leave I shall ring the bell and have you removed. Sam Lassiter is dead ... *dead*..."

"Christ, you don't change, do you, Daisy? You get some damned idea in your head and come what may you stick to it, whatever the consequences. It was your bloody pigheadedness which caused this ... this parting between us in the first place. You and that blind and deaf obsession you had with Miles Thornley. You drove me to the point..."

"So it's my fault then...?"

"*Will you turn round and look at me.*"

"Go to..."

"No, I will not..." and in a moment he was across the room, his tall, lean frame menacing, his hard hands cruel on her arms, turning her forcibly about to face him. He pinned her to the wall an arm's length away from him, their unyielding faces, so alike in their absolute single-minded purpose, glaring at one another.

"Why do you think I went away, Daisy, *why*? God, I don't know why I ask you because we both know the answer. It was *him*. Miles bloody Thornley. He came between us and had done for years. You hated him with a devotion I could not bear. I was jealous, not of your love for him, but your enduring hatred which blinded your eyes so that you couldn't see me, couldn't see my love for you. No, Daisy, don't look away and don't struggle because you are going to hear me out." He leaned more heavily on her arms and when she would have lifted her knee between his spread legs he avoided her adroitly. "But you were too strong for me, Daisy. I thought we had found each other for a while until ... but you know the rest, don't you?"

"Let me go, damn you."

"Not until I've finished, then you may do as you please." He paused for a moment as though gathering his thoughts. "When I left you I thought I could find what I had before we met. There were other women in the world with warmer hearts than yours. I had the *Golden Lady*. I had lost one but I still had the original and so ... but ... well ... I lost her too."

His voice was infinitely sad and he leaned away from her, taking his hands from her forearms but, strangely, now she was free she did not turn away. He passed a lean brown hand across his face and moved away and as he did so she saw the jagged scar on the side of his neck, just below his right ear.

"I got ashore somehow. There was a hell of a fight going on, shells and grape ... men screaming and when I looked back she had gone ... just some debris. She was a lovely thing, Daisy."

His face had become soft and dreaming and in his deep green eyes was a look of such loving sorrow she took an involuntary step towards him. He shook his head as though to clear away images which were too painful to contemplate. "I was a bit knocked about. I had taken a blow to the head otherwise ... I should have gone straight to Wilmington and found a ship back to Liverpool. There were some soldiers ... Confederates. The ... one of them stitched me up ... I lost a lot of blood and somehow, I don't know how it happened, I just ... stayed with them. I didn't want to face what was ... in Liverpool, Daisy, not then ... so I just stayed with them. There were dead men, soldiers ... that's where I got the cape. I fought alongside them ... brave men. They were ... they gave me a purpose so that I didn't have to think about you ... and Miles Thornley. They gave me ... it seems a strange thing to find in the middle of a war ... but a curious ... peace ... to fight beside men who die gladly for what they believe in even though their cause might have been wrong and was certainly doomed. I just

... drifted along with them, not caring much whether I lived or died, so I lived. Ironic, isn't it? I had lost you and the *Golden Lady* and at that moment there seemed nothing to come back for. The war would be ended soon and then I would make some decision, I told myself."

His gaze was sombre, his face brooding over memories best left forgotten and despite herself she felt herself drawn towards him. Only one step and he scarcely noticed, so deep in the past was he.

"I was at Appomattox, did you know? No, of course you didn't." He sighed deeply and sank down in the chair he had drawn up for her, hours ago it seemed now, the memory of that day when General Lee had given up his sword to Grant affecting him deeply.

"Why did you not come home then?" she asked him.

"I don't know, Daisy. I wish I could tell you but I can't. Perhaps I was afraid I might allow you to ... to take something from me I prized. I hated what you did to Miles Thornley and I hated you for doing it ... but I loved you at the same time, and I knew, of course, that if I saw you I might ..."

"I gave it all back, Sam, to the Thornley boy." She sat down opposite him, her face becoming tranquil at the memory.

"Did you, Daisy? I didn't know. I'm glad." His voice was weary but his gaze was clear now. "There are so many things ... I didn't know you were in America or that we had a son. I only knew one thing."

"What was that, Sam?" She leaned forward into the lamp-light and his eyes went to the splendid profusion of her vivid hair.

"That I could not live with the woman who had done what you did to Miles Thornley, no matter how *he* had treated *you*. It made you as he was and I couldn't bear it. You were so ... so fine, Daisy. Bright and brave and true and to see you tarnished ... I tried to cut you ... out of my life. I thought if I stayed away ... I wasn't thinking clearly ..." His eyes brooded on her frail beauty. He was a handsome, powerful man who had been brought low by this foolish emotion which had him in its grip. An emotion he didn't want to feel since it was alien to him, alien to his nature which had always in the past taken exactly what he wanted from life without hurting himself or any of the pretty women he had lightly loved.

"So . . . I did some blockading with Captain Roberts for a while. You've heard of him, I see. Then I drifted back here . . . to New Orleans. But I couldn't settle. I had to . . . You were so much a part of me, a part of my life which had been good . . . I hadn't realised how much. No one in New Orleans knew me, Daisy. I had grown a full beard. They had been told Sam Lassiter was dead so naturally no one had thought to tell a drifting seaman that a woman called Daisy Lassiter was looking for her husband. But I was coming home, Daisy. I don't know whether it was to you, but I was coming home. I had booked a passage on this ship and then, as I was standing on the levee waiting to come aboard, I saw you. You had the child in your arms and I knew then why you were there. I knew what you had been doing. It was written in your face, your sadness, and I was . . . Dear God, Daisy, have you any idea of how I felt? You had been looking for me!"

The tension in him suddenly relaxed and his mouth began to smile a little. "I do believe you love me, Daisy Lassiter, and I am filled with such joy . . . Dear God . . . I am not often lost for words . . ."

He bowed his head, his emotion too much for him, and his words were muffled. "It seems that by some miracle, at the same moment, we have discovered the true depth of our love. Forgive me, I am not usually so . . . but is it not worth considering that as you looked for me I was returning to you?"

There was a long and poignant silence. Into it small noises fell as the ship plunged onwards into stormier waters. The creak and groan of straining metal and wood. The anguished whine of the wind, and out in the corridor footsteps hurrying by on some errand.

"Daisy, can you tell me I am wrong?"

"It has been too . . . painful, Sam. Really, I cannot just . . . there has been so much . . . I'm tired . . ."

"Rest on me, my love." His haggard eyes were on her, seeming to promise her peace, at least for the moment since she was well aware that life with Sam Lassiter would not always be peaceful. The hard, tense mouth, the weary line of his shoulders, the fatigue and hint of sorrow in him aroused her compassion and something else which she thought had died, something she had not yet acknowledged but it had in it hope, joy, life.

"I love you, Daisy. Do you love me?"

Oh yes, was there any question of it? She had loved him and lost him and could she really chance losing it all again? Their son lay sleeping in the cabin beyond the closed door and he must have the chance to know his father. And what of Daisy Lassiter? What was she to have? She felt the racing beat of her heart slow to a steady calm, and another emotion which she was not yet prepared to name.

She smiled and put out her hand. His was warm and strong as he took it. No more than that yet. Two hands clasped but held between them was memory which had nothing to do with the heart, or the mind, but of the flesh.

"I will see my son now, Daisy," he said, standing up and drawing her to him, then with a wry lift of his eyebrows which his son had inherited, ". . . but perhaps he can wait for an hour or so."

BEYOND THE SHINING WATER

Part 1

1

Lily Elliott narrowed her eyes and squinted into the low flaring of the evening sun which lay across the waters of the river. The sky to the east had gone quite mad with brilliant colours, blood red and apricot fighting with gold and lemon, blush pink and the palest green all merging into a delicate shade of lavender above her head where a solitary star kept company with a sliver of moon. Before this glory stood a tall forest of gently swaying masts towering above sheds and warehouses, a great multitude seemingly linked together with miles of rigging, halyards and reefed sails, dark and graceful against the sunset. For as long as Lily could remember the waterfront had been a magical mixture of spices and coffee, tobacco and turpentine, tar and soot, ropes and rigging, sails and smokestacks, horses and carriers, kegs, casks and barrels and ships flying the flags and colours of every nation. Even the new and ugly steamships had a place in her heart, for they were, after all, things of the sea, but, naturally, her true and everlasting devotion was given to the beautiful sailing ships that lined the dock, one of which belonged to her father.

Her ma and pa had walked on a little way and for a moment she was alone in the dusky subdued murmur of the dockland as it settled down for the night. The sound of gulls crying plaintively as they perched along yardarms and the roofs of warehouses. The gentle suck and slap of the moving water as it lifted and fell against the wall of the dock and swirled about the pilings that supported the piers. The sound of men's voices murmuring from decks and galleys as Lily moved along the cobbled roadway of the dock, gazing up in total enchantment at the dozens of bowsprits that jutted out proudly, sharply spearing the falling dusk from each ship's bow over her head. Voices in many languages, for these lovely vessels came from the four corners of the world, bringing grain from North America, nitrates and guano from South America, bales of raw cotton from the southern states of America, beef and mutton from the meat-exporting countries of the world, raw wool from Australia, timber from America and Canada and Newfoundland, tea and spices from the Orient.

She sniffed enthusiastically, inhaling the pungent aroma of cowhides and jute, the sweetness of molasses and sugar and all the sea-fresh tanginess of the river which was part of the lives of those who lived beside the great crossroads of the city that was second only to London in the British Empire. Lily loved it, its great vigour and swaggering life, its bubbling dynamism, its proud boast that there was no place on earth like Liverpool; every seaman who sailed the seven seas said so and Lily believed it implicitly.

Someone was whistling "The Bonny Sailor Boy", a song about a pretty Liverpool lass who fell in love with a handsome young seaman. Lily knew it well since it was a favourite of her father who sang it in a loud, rich baritone whenever he took a bath. Not that Lily had ever seen her pa in the bath, for that was a private affair that took place before a good fire in her parents' bedroom. Pa would hump the hip bath up the narrow stairs and then he and ma, going up and down a dozen times with cans of hot water, would fill it, close the door and after a good deal of splashing and singing, accompanied by much laughter, there would be silence, a silence that Lily would not dream of interrupting. Ma and Pa loved one another deeply, a love that spilled out and wrapped itself about her but there were times, especially when Pa was home, when Lily knew she was excluded from this special time they spent together. Pa said that he and Ma had taken one look at each other eleven years ago and had fallen instantly and permanently in love.

Her ma and pa were beautiful. Yes, that was how she would describe them, even her pa who was as tall and dark and handsome as her ma was tall and silvery and exquisite. A striking couple, she had heard them called and it was true, for wherever the three of them went she noticed that heads turned to gaze after them. She took after her ma in colouring and was already tall for her age, but whereas ma was serene, calm, tranquil as a swan gliding on unruffled waters, her pa was what Ma called a firebrand, hot-tempered, vigorous, noisy and ready to argue with anyone whose opinion he did not agree with – except Ma, who never really argued anyway – and she, Lily, was the same, determined to have her own way but reluctant to hurt Ma while she got it!

A waggon drawn by two gigantic Shire horses pulled away in the growing gloom bound for the transit sheds where the cargo would be sorted and weighed, the load of barrels on it the last to be discharged from a merchantmen, for it was almost dark.

There were neatly stacked piles of boxes and bales lying close to the water's edge waiting to be taken aboard a clipper ship bound for Lily knew not where, though wherever it might be she would dearly have loved to be aboard it. Lily loved the river, the sea and the ships that sailed them with the same passionate intensity as her pa, and when she was old enough and had finished the schooling her ma insisted upon, then she meant to sign her indenture to serve aboard the *Lily-Jane*, her pa's schooner, for however many years her pa would allow, taking over as master when the time came. That wouldn't be for a long time yet, of course, for Pa was only a young man, in his prime, he said, at forty-one, though it seemed very old to Lily. She would be taught the art, trade and business of a mariner or seaman, as it was quoted in the Certificate of Indenture, as her pa had done as a lad. She had not yet disclosed her plans to Pa since she was only ten years old and there was plenty of time yet, and she was not quite sure how all this would come about, or even how Pa would take it; but she had wanted only one thing in her life ever since she had first been taken aboard the *Lily-Jane* as a toddler, and that was to be a seaman like her pa.

A mongrel suddenly darted out from behind a bollard which it had been sniffing and then, as though it were satisfied with what it found, cocked its leg, urinating in a long stream against it. It turned to give her an enquiring look, stopping for a moment and she held out her hand to it, making the sort of encouraging noises one makes to an animal, wondering where it had come from. If it was a stray perhaps she could persuade it to come with her. It was a nice-looking little thing, a bit scruffy with one ear hanging down and the other pricked and she thought Ma might just take to it, for she was fair game for anything lost or helpless. Lily had always wanted a dog but this one was wary, regarding her suspiciously before walking off briskly in the other direction, evidently on some important business of its own.

Lily straightened up. She lifted her neatly bonneted head and again sniffed the salt-laden, spice-laden, tar-laden air, drawing great draughts of it greedily into her lungs, forgetting the dog that had temporarily diverted her, staring into the future with unfocused, dreaming eyes, almost tripping over a thick length of tarred rope that lay in her path. Unconcerned, she dawdled on over the narrow wooden bridge which linked George's Dock and Canning Dock. Each dock had a master all of its own and the master had a gateman under him whose job it was to attend to the hauling in and out of the vessels and to regulate the height of the water according to the tides. The dock entrance was fitted with massive lock gates fashioned from long-lasting tropical timbers such as greenheart. The gates penned the water inside the dock basins as the tide fell in order to keep the level high enough to float the ships. There was a walkway over these gates which parted to allow the entrance and exit of the ships, a narrow path of sturdy wooden planks with iron posts on either side linked with steel chains. She rattled the chains as she went, longing to swing on them over the water as she had seen daring lads do but she knew her parents might look round at any moment and Ma would be horrified, and upset, a state neither Lily nor her pa could bear to see her in.

Decorously she followed them. Ma and Pa had their heads together. Ma laughed, a lovely soft laugh that Pa said was like the tinkling of bells, and Pa, not caring whether anyone was watching or not, kissed Ma on the lips and she laughed again, holding Pa's arm close to her side. Lily was not surprised, for she was used to her parents' show of affection for one another, even in public.

There were high, many-windowed buildings on either side of them now as they passed between two enormous warehouses, then they were out in the dying sunlight again and on the approach to Canning Dock Basin where Pa's ship was tied up. Lily could see it, lamps shining along its length and, excitement suddenly bubbling up inside her, she began to hurry to catch up with Ma and Pa who had stopped to wait for her at the bottom of the short gangway.

"Come on, slowcoach." Pa smiled, holding out his arm and,

when she reached him, cradling her against him. "It's time we had our meal and got you into your bunk or you'll still be in the land of nod when we set sail in the morning. We have to catch the tide, you know."

"Oh, Pa, I'm sorry but there's always something new to see and even the old things are wonderful. Did you notice that four-masted barque from Buenos Aires? She must have just docked on the last tide. The *Santa Maria*, she was called and I could smell her cargo as I went past."

"You would, sweetheart. It was guano." Pa pulled a wry face, wrinkling his nose.

"It really is awful," her mother offered, but Lily, loyal to the sea and ships and indeed anything at all to do with either, frowned.

"Oh, no, Ma, I thought it was quite . . . interesting."

"Interesting! Lily, you'll have nothing said against even a cargo of guano will you, my darling? Thank heavens you don't have to carry it, Richard." Jane Elliott turned to smile at her husband and for a moment Lily was irritated by Ma's lack of understanding, then she sighed and smiled lovingly as though her mother were some small child who could not be expected to grasp what the adults were discussing. Ma would be happy if all cargoes were of silk or spices, China tea or Brazilian coffee, lovely things to look at and delightful things to smell, and the world of cargoes such as cattle or cement, brimstone or pepper, coal or salt which was where the money lay, her pa would agree with that, was beyond her sweet understanding.

"Well, it's time we were getting aboard, dearest, if we're to prepare for the morning tide. I can see Mr Porter looking at us with great misgivings as though already he believes we are doomed to fetch up at the bottom of the Irish Sea by taking women on board. You'd think he'd be used to it by now, wouldn't you?"

The disapproving face of Pa's second-in-command peered over the side of the ship. He was a lanky Yorkshireman with a craggy face which thirty years at sea had turned to the colour of mahogany. He wore the usual seaman's attire of navy blue gansey, a kind of heavy knitted jersey, and sturdy drill trousers tucked into his boots. In bad weather he would don waterproofs. His peaked cap was a badge of his status on board – the others wore woollen headgear which pulled

down over their ears – and Lily had heard Pa say that if he had
to leave his ship in the charge of one man that man would be
Jethro Porter. This was quite amazing really, for Mr Porter's
family had been in the woollen trade far from the sea for many
generations, and where young Jethro had acquired his love
of ships, never having seen one until he arrived in Liverpool,
was a mystery. His piercing blue eyes, surrounded by a web
of wrinkles, surveyed the two females, for that was how he
thought of all women, with great suspicion, but he had to
accept that on this trip they were to be passengers aboard
the *Lily-Jane*.

"Well, come along, Lily, let's go and see if the luggage is
aboard and whether Johnno's made up your bunk. See, the
hatches are battened down and we'll be ready to sail on the
morning tide. Up you go. Mind your step, Jane," handing his
wife solicitously up the short gangway, "and you, Lily, don't
stir from your mother's side while I go and get changed."

"I won't, Pa."

He smiled at this child of his who was in his eyes quite
perfect except for her gender. Her vivid face was aglow with
excitement and her eyes were a brilliant silvery grey. The
thick fan of her eyelashes constantly shadowed her rounded,
childish cheek as she blinked in what seemed to be a transport
of delight, trying to look at everything at once, determined not
to miss one moment of this memorable journey. She loved all
this as much as he did, as much as his own father had done
and he supposed the sea must be in her blood, for they came
from a long line of seamen. For over a century Elliotts had
been carrying small cargoes to and from all the ports around
the Irish Sea and there was even talk of one of them who
had involved himself in the most profitable trade of all: the
triangle of manufactured parts to Africa, slaves from Africa to
the West Indies and southern states of America and sugar and
tobacco from there to Liverpool. Richard could believe it, for
how had his ancestor been able to accumulate enough money
to purchase the schooner in which his great-grandfather had
finally settled to coastal trading? The *Lily-Jane* was the third
ship from that first one called *Seamaid* and his only concern
was what was to happen when he was gone. Jane should have
no more children, the doctor had told him that after Lily's birth.
No son then, just this one child, but still, he was not a man for
worrying about the future when the present was so hopeful

and filled with promise. He was a happy man who loved his family and his chosen trade and he wouldn't change his life with any man. There were many fabulously wealthy men in Liverpool, merchant princes, shipbuilders, men of vision who were making a fortune out of the sea but he, Richard Elliott, was the luckiest of them all, for wasn't he loved by Jane Elliott which none of the others could claim.

Her ma had shoe-horned herself into the tiny cabin she and Pa shared, laughing as she did her best to stow away – is that the expression, Richard? she asked – the small wardrobe she had brought with her. They had eaten a splendid meal of fresh plaice, bought only that morning from one of the boats of the small fishing fleet that operated from Liverpool, tiny new potatoes and newly picked green peas from the market, all prepared by Johnno who could have got a job in the kitchens at the Adelphi, Mrs Elliott told him in that gracious way she had, making him squirm with pleasure. The ladies had then retired for the night. Not that Lily considered herself a lady. When she was on the *Lily-Jane* she was a seaman, pure and simple, longing to do all the things Johnno and Mick, the fourth member of the crew, did. It was most mortifying to be put to bed like a small child, tucked up in the hammock which hung just outside the cabin in which her parents slept. Of course, to sleep in the hammock almost made up for the indignity of being told to go to sleep like a good girl. It swung most delightfully and was really very comfortable and she thought she might ask Pa if she could have one at home in her bedroom but she didn't think Ma would agree so she'd best make the most of this. The *Lily-Jane*, though she was tied up at the dockside by bow and stern, moved up and down with the rise and fall of the water and though Lily had made up her mind that she would not sleep for a moment, wasting precious time that could be spent in other more exciting ways, she was lulled by the lovely swaying movement of the schooner and was quite put out when Pa woke her to say that they were to cast off in ten minutes and was she to lie there all day!

There were dozens of vessels like themselves all racing to catch the tide, many of them with pilot boats to guide them over the treacherous sand bars: small, strongly built sloops painted white with a green stripe round their sides and a number displayed on their flag. Packet ships, built for speed, carrying the Royal Mail and going to New York, the journey there and back an incredible seventeen days. A beautiful clipper ship under full sail, off to China, Pa told Lily, to bring back tea and spices and opium. There were frigates and brigantines and all making for the estuary to catch the tide so that Lily wondered how her pa could possibly steer through so much traffic. Naturally, she knew he would, for he was the best seaman in the world and one day, when she stood beside him at the helm, she would be just as adroit.

She leaned against her pa, looking back to the hazed morning skyline of Liverpool. By now the docks were a seething mass of men and waggons, cargoes of every sort from timber to tea, the gentle patience of Shire horses, cranes and derricks, women and children selling something or other, and all backed by the cliffs of the warehouses, block after block, and the soaring elegance of St Nicholas Church.

She sighed with deep satisfaction, watching Pa's lean brown hands on the wheel, so strong and sure as he moved into the flow of traffic. They were sailing outward so their course lay to the north beyond the influence of the Gulf Stream and did she notice, Pa asked, that the homeward vessels were sailing south so as to avail themselves of the current? Pa was full of wonderful information like that, all the things he himself had learned and which he was passing on to her, which surely meant he intended her to follow in his footsteps. Ma stayed in the tiny cabin, not at all concerned with the steamships in tow of steam tugs, nor the brig *Henrietta* which passed them to starboard, preferring to read Charlotte Brontë's novel, *Villette*, which was incomprehensible to Lily. Not the novel, which she herself had read and enjoyed, but the fact that Ma could calmly sit below with her nose in a book when she might be up here with her and Pa. The wind sang in the rigging and the gulls wheeled and dived and made their usual cries which sounded just like a baby in distress. The slap of the wind made the sails crack menacingly but Lily wasn't afraid, for her pa had them all safe in his hands, with Mr Porter, who stood just to the right of Pa, snapping out orders to Johnno and Mick, ready to take over if he was needed. Lily had on what her ma called her "adventuring" clothes, a warm woollen skirt, quite short so as not to impede her movements on the deck, stout boots and woollen stockings and a gansey just like the ones the

crew wore, knitted for her by her mother. On her head was a
cabin boy's peaked cap into which the plait her ma had done
for her, thick and heavy, was tucked up. She had a line on
her, for Pa was most careful about safety, at least with her,
though the men, in bare feet, ran and climbed without the
least heed of danger, though the decks, as they raced for the
estuary, were steep and slippery with spray. Lily felt the line
was not needed, for she was as sure-footed as a cat, especially
if she had been allowed to remove her boots and stockings
like Johnno and Mick, but Ma said it was not ladylike and so
that was that as far as Pa was concerned. Ma's word was law!
She, Lily, had even offered to climb aloft to help Mick with
the mainsail which had proved awkward but Pa had smiled
at Mr Porter as though to say what could you do with a girl
like her, but Mr Porter merely "hummphed" in his throat and
exchanged a look with Mick as though he knew exactly what
he would do. Mr Porter did not approve of her and Ma being
aboard, for like many sailors he believed a woman on a ship
was bad luck and they had enough to contend with, with
storms and winds, or the lack of them, with the hazardous
journey out of the river where the tide shifted the silt and
sand from day to day, without adding to it by sailing with
females!

At last they passed the rocks on which the New Brighton
Lighthouse was built, moving out into Liverpool Bay and
steering north. It was a glorious day, sunny and warm with
the clear sea reflecting the blue of the sky. They sailed quite
close to the shore, the lovely long golden beach of what was
known as North Shore, backed by rippling sand-dunes which
disappeared around the northern horizon at Formby Point and
lined the coast of Lancashire for twenty miles.

A windmill stood close to the beach, a tall brick mill called
the Wishing Gate Mill and it was at this point that Ma came
out on deck to watch the bathers who were trundled down to
the water in bathing machines. It was August and high water
and the shore and the sea were crowded with visitors from
the manufacturing districts "coom fur t'ha dip in't watter".
The "dowkers" or "dippers", whose job it was to attend the
machines and help the bathers, kept a watchful eye on the
segregated sexes, for some gentlemen had been known to
swim among the ladies which was strictly forbidden though
for the life of her Lily didn't know why.

Mr Porter was mortified when Captain Elliott casually suggested that his daughter, ten years old for God's sake, might like to take a turn at the wheel and Mrs Elliott looked none too pleased, neither.

"Oh, Pa, can I?" Lily gave her father a look of radiant gratitude as she placed her small hands on the wheel with the reverence one reserved for holy occasions. It warmed his heart and yet at the same time squeezed it with anguish, for he was beginning to recognise what was in his child. This was perhaps the eighth or was it the ninth occasion when his wife and daughter had sailed with him on a coastal voyage. The truth of the matter was that he could barely bear to be apart from his lovely wife and every time he was forced to leave her, though it was not for more than a week or ten days, some part of him felt as though it were being cut out of him with a rusty knife. He knew it was ridiculous and he would not have admitted it to anyone, even to her who knew how much he loved her. If he could arrange for her to go with him, perhaps three or four times a year, he made the excuse that it made a little holiday for her and the child, but in reality it was for his own sake. He had been thirty years old and already a ship-owner when he met the eighteen-year-old delicately lovely daughter of a ship's chandler in Water Street, Liverpool, and, as he had told Lily a dozen times, fell instantly and enduringly in love with her. And she with him which was even more wonderful. They were married within the month and for the first year of their marriage she had gone everywhere with him, much to the disgust of Jethro Porter who had loved no woman and never would. Then Lily was born and the event put an end to the voyages, at least until she was old enough to accompany her mother and father. At five years old she had gone to school, a select private school for young ladies in Walton on the Hill where Richard rented a smart, semi-detached little villa, a school chosen by Jane where the pupils were taught by an enlightened staff of teachers. Not just embroidery and music and painting, which Lily thought to be a complete waste of time, for what use would they be to a seaman, but mathematics, geometry, a little algebra, arithmetic, of course, history and geography. Lily lapped all that up like a cat at a saucer of cream, along with current affairs which she knew would be helpful when she became a sea captain like her father. She would have to know what was going on in government, wouldn't she, and indeed everywhere else if she was to be a success in the world of trade and so she applied herself to the lessons which would not have been wasted on a son, if Richard Elliott had had one.

But when the school was closed for the summer holidays, when there was no threat of winter storms or icy squalls, he took his wife and daughter on one of his coastal trips, or sometimes further. They had been to Ireland for a cargo of grain, Cornwall for china clay and to North Wales for stone, but today they were making for Barrow-in-Furness just beyond Morecambe Bay, only a short run this time which, with *them* aboard, suited Mr Porter down to the ground, to deliver machinery for the ironworks and to fetch back a cargo of pig-iron.

The *Lily-Jane* had been built at Runcorn especially for trading to small ports about the Irish Sea. She had little change in her draught fore and aft and had flat floors to take ground and to remain upright at low tide. She responded with great readiness when sailing in narrow waters. She was a wooden sailing ship, a fast schooner of 298 tons, ninety-nine feet in length and twenty-five feet wide. She was rigged as a two-masted vessel with square sails on both masts plus an additional small mast behind the mainmast to carry a large fore and aft sail called a spanker. She was strongly built with a pointed stern with the rudder hung outboard. In fact she was the perfect vessel for Richard Elliott's trade and even his Lily could have handled her with perfect ease, which he was aware she was longing to do.

Together, his strong seaman's hands on top of her small, still childish ones, they steered the *Lily-Jane* through the relatively calm waters that ran up the coast of Lancashire. The wind blew into their faces, both of them rapt with their shared love of this sailing ship, this joyous union of ship and water, the sunlight creating a diamond path ahead of them into which they fearlessly sailed, and for a moment the mother, the wife, was startled, for their expressions were identical. Her daughter was a beautiful child, even she admitted that, like a white rose, a white rosebud, flushed at the edge of its petals with pink, new and fresh, delicate and fragile. But Lily was not fragile at all: Jane Elliott knew that, for she was like her father with a core of steel in her which, when she was older, would allow her to submit to no one, man or woman. Even now she was trying to edge her father's hands away from hers, longing to have full control of the schooner. Mr Porter was beginning to mutter, not quite loud enough for his employer to hear what he said, but loud enough to make it known that he was complaining about something.

"What are you thinking, sweetheart?" Richard bent his head to Lily, for the moment ignoring his second-in-command's muttering, his own words only just audible to Jane.

"That it's just like flying, Pa, or what I think flying would be like. We seem to be gliding above the water just as that gannet is doing, d'you see?" taking her hand momentarily from the wheel and pointing to the long and slender bird just ahead of the *Lily-Jane*.

Mr Porter "tcch-tcched" angrily. He'd never seen the like, letting a small child, and a girl at that, take the wheel of a ship this size, or indeed any size, and to top it all she'd taken her hand *off* the wheel to point at something that had no bearing on the matter at all, which could have caused the *Lily-Jane* to veer most dangerously. Really, what was his master thinking of?

Richard heard the sound of disapproval and knew reluctantly that he had gone too far in allowing Lily to steer the schooner, even for a few minutes.

"You'd best let me have her now, sweetheart," he whispered, putting her gently to the side of him, hearing her vast sigh.

"Can I do it again, Pa, can I? Perhaps tomorrow?" she pleaded.

"We'll see, sweetheart, we'll see."

She put her arms about her pa's waist and buried her face in the sea-smelling wool of his gansey. Her heart was filled with the magic and delight of the last five minutes and with anticipation, too, for surely her pa would see now what a good sailor she would make and would let her sail with him on all his voyages? She loved him so, her pa. Her ma was lovely, special, kind, but Lily had something inside her that belonged to no one but Pa. She loved her pa so much it hurt her at times but she wouldn't have it any other way. There was no girl in the world who had such a wonderful pa as Lily Elliott.

2

"I've decided that I'm going be a sea captain when I grow up," Lily remarked experimentally at breakfast several days later.

She had made up her mind in bed last night that as she would have to tell her parents of her plans one day, that day might as well be now then they would have time to get used to the idea and her pa might even begin to take her on more frequent trips. As his . . . his apprentice, kind of.

"Have you, sweetheart?" her pa answered, his eyes on her mother, smiling in that certain way grown-ups have when they are not really listening. Ma was at the side table where Mrs Quinn had just brought in the toast and she stood in a shaft of hazed sunlight shining through the dining-room window. The sun turned her already silver pale hair, which hung down her back in a profusion of tumbled curls, to a radiant halo of light. Her flawless skin which was usually the colour of buttermilk had a creamy texture, almost honey-coloured and was touched at her cheekbones with a flush of carnation. Her eyes, as she turned to smile that smile she kept solely for Pa, though they were a dove grey in colour, had in them a hint of lavender. She had not yet changed from her morning robe, a drifting garment made from several layers of pearl grey chiffon tied modestly at the neck and waist with peach-coloured satin ribbons. She looked quite glorious; it was evident that Pa thought so, though Mrs Quinn was inclined to look the other way as though even now, after years of seeing to the Elliotts as a general cook, housekeeper, cleaner, laundry maid and dogsbody, she could not quite become used to the way her mistress dressed. She did it to please Captain Elliott, that much Mrs Quinn knew, and it worked, for the master could not keep his eyes, or his hands sometimes, off his wife. Even he was not properly dressed, decently dressed as Mrs Quinn saw it, but had on some sort of floor-length quilted robe. She shook her head as she left them to it and returned to the kitchen.

Lily made a shallow hole in the centre of the bowl of porridge Mrs Quinn had put in front of her five minutes ago. The sides of the hole kept caving in and with infinite patience she scooped them out again with her spoon. With Ma and Pa behaving in that dreamy way they had sometimes, which meant they were aware of nobody but each other, she had high hopes that she might be able to get away with not eating the gooey mess. Pa said, though she was not always sure he meant it, that she should clean her plate at every meal, for there were thousands of poor, starving children in the city who would be glad of it, and as far as she was concerned they were welcome to it.

She sighed gustily. It was very evident that neither had heard her remark about her future and she dithered about whether she should repeat what she had said. Perhaps not. She'd told them and if there was any argument later she would say, indignantly, that she had already told them and if they didn't agree why hadn't they said so at the time?

Pa was tucking into a vast plate of bacon, sausage and tomatoes, having already eaten his porridge, and Ma was nibbling on a sliver of lightly buttered toast. They were chatting now about the ballet at the Theatre Royal which Ma wanted Pa to take her to see before he set sail again.

"Agnes Mitchell tells me it's absolutely wonderful and I really would love to see it, darling." It seemed some famous dancer whose name Lily could not pronounce, let alone spell, was to perform and it was Ma's dearest wish to see her before the ballet company returned to London.

Pa reached tenderly for Ma's hand. "Then you shall, my angel, and this very night. Will Mrs Quinn stay over for a couple of hours, d'you think?"

"Oh, I'm sure she will, Richard. She's always glad of the extra money."

"I don't need Mrs Quinn, Ma," Lily ventured, but with little hope. "I can stay by myself. I *am* ten after all. Besides, I'd rather like to see the ballet myself."

They both turned to look at her then, smiling with great tolerance.

"You wouldn't like it, sweetheart," her pa told her.

"How d'you know I won't, Pa? How d'you know if I've never been? I might absolutely adore it. I've seen a picture in the art gallery of ballet dancers in perfectly sweet little dresses and Mary wants to be a ballerina when she grows up. She takes it at school," in way of explanation.

"Does she, sweetheart? But I still don't believe it's suitable."

"Why, Pa?"

"It's for grown-ups, Lily, not children. Perhaps when I come home next Ma and I will take you to the . . . the . . ." He looked to his wife for inspiration and Lily knew they would suggest some childish thing like the zoo which she'd already been to a million times.

She stirred her porridge slowly, quite pleased with the swirls and circles this made, then reached for the syrup. Sometimes, if Pa was adamant that she eat it, she was allowed to pour in a spoonful of syrup which made it marginally more edible, but not much.

"How about the Polytechnic Exhibition at the Mechanics Institute, then? It's in Mount Street," she went on artlessly.

"I know where it is, my love, but I don't think that would be suitable, either. It's really for gentlemen, you see."

"I know, that's why I'd like to see it. And why is it that everything that's of the faintest interest to anybody is only for gentlemen?"

"Eat your porridge, darling, or you'll be late for school."

Ignoring her mother, Lily tried again. "Well, will you take me to see the whale?"

"The whale?"

"Yes, the one caught in the Mersey the other day. It's twenty-four feet long and twelve feet across and weighs three tons. If I can't go to the ballet or the exhibition can I go and see the whale?"

Her pa sighed and glanced at his wife for help but she was absorbed with her toast, her eyes lowered, her long, curving lashes forming a fan on her slightly flushed cheek. They had made love no more than half an hour ago and the look about her, languid and sensual, told him that she would not be averse to starting again as soon as breakfast was over.

Lily sighed tragically but they took no notice of her and not for the first time she pondered on how this grand passion her ma and pa had for one another could be a definite disadvantage. Sometimes she felt as though she were invisible. Totally excluded from their life, though she knew they did not mean to be like this. She supposed it was because Pa was away such a lot that Ma felt she had to make up for his absences by being . . . being more attentive when he was home. Mary and Grace Watson's pa, who had several stalls at St John's Market and who came home every evening to his wife and children, did not act like her pa did, and neither did Mrs Watson. They put their cheeks together and kissed the air between them when Mr Watson came home, and she supposed they did the same in the morning, though Mr Watson went out so early Lily had never actually seen him go. The Watsons lived next door.

The Elliotts and the Watsons lived on Walton Lane in Walton on the Hill. It was what was known as a "nice" area of Liverpool. In fact it was almost in the country. Decent. Respectable. Not that it was by any means peopled by the wealthy but the families who rented the small, semi-detached villas which stretched along the tree-lined lane from Everton Valley to the vast acreage of the Walton Nurseries were in regular work, tradesmen, craftsmen who had served their time to many of the trades allied to shipbuilding. Bert Meadows who lived several doors down from the Elliotts was a wheelwright with his own small business at the back of Strand Street opposite Canning Dock, and Andrew Hale had his own cooperage in Water Street. Sean Flanagan, come out from Ireland twenty years earlier, was in house construction with an endless supply of Irish labourers from the old country to whom he paid starvation wages but who had helped him to become what was known in Lancashire as a "warm" man. Liverpool was growing fast, spreading out into the rural areas so that any man who could lay a brick or fashion a window frame was guaranteed employment.

Those living in Walton Lane were of the working classes, Lily's pa said so, for didn't they all, including himself, work for a living, but they were poles apart from the "poor" underprivileged working class who lived in the centre of the city and about the dock area. Among them were the dispossessed Irish, the itinerant Welsh, families from Scandinavia and Europe who, unable to raise the money for the fare, had got no further than Liverpool in their search for the "new world". These men were unskilled and without a regular trade, working as porters, lightermen, dung collectors, cess-pool cleaners and rubbish collectors, street sellers, pedlars and street labourers. The worst off poor were, of course, the Irish immigrants who took jobs even the most destitute Englishman would draw the line at if he had the choice. It was accepted that the proper thing to do was to save not only for your old age but for a rainy day, everyone knew that, but even the wages of a skilled man in full work allowed little margin for saving. So what chance had they in Netherfield Road which was in the centre of the northern dock system, in Park Lane, St James Street, Windsor Street, Northumberland Street and the southern dock area which, it was acknowledged, was where the worst of the slums were situated and in whose back-to-back courts the residents lived as close as maggots in cheese. They wallowed, there could be no other word to describe it, in three-storey houses the structures of which rose from a sea of stench and were so rotten they were ready to tumble to the ground with the weight of people they housed. A pitiful mass of humanity which sweated in the tottering tenements and wretched rat-infested cellars, a vast army of indigent poor who lacked all means of a comfortable existence and who had no prospect of ever getting one. Drunkenness, depravity and crime flourished in the festering warrens where it was said there were more people living, if you could call it that, to the square mile than there were fish in the sea.

Not so in Walton Lane. In fact it is doubtful that the children of the families who lived there were even aware that such people and places existed. Certainly not Lily Elliott or Grace and Mary Watson, Evie and Maggie Meadows, although the Flanagans, whose pa had come a long way from the sod cottage in Ireland where he was born, might have had an inkling, for Sean was proud of his success and was never tired of telling his children about it. There were fields, green and sweet and starred with poppy, buttercup and clover, spread out on the other side of the hawthorn hedge that bordered Walton Lane. There were cows standing knee-deep in pasturage, their placid heads turning to look at the children who sometimes stood on the bottom rung of the gate set in the hedge and called to them. There were farms where they were often sent by their mothers to fetch a can of foaming milk or a dozen eggs or a pound of best butter, and the foetid stink of the alleys off Netherfield Road and

Northumberland Street never reached their noses. They were children of the great seaport of Liverpool which gave their fathers a decent living, born and bred in it, used to the noise and vigour of their city through which poured the peoples of the world, the cosmopolitan population bringing its own cultures and language. They were at home in the bustle of the busy pavements where their mothers shopped at Lewis's, Owen Owen's and T.J. Hughes. The singing excitement of the River Mersey, the landing stage and the long esplanade which stretched from Princes Dock northwards and where their families took their Sunday afternoon walk. The teeming dockland and its fragrances, some heady and delightful, others rank and insidious from the cargoes that came from every part of the world.

But they were also children of the countryside, for they played in its fields and meadows and small woodlands where their mothers knew they were as safe as though they were in their own back gardens. They had been born in Liverpool and spoke with the adenoidal accent which was a mixture of Dublin and Cardiff and Glasgow, and the careful articulation of their teachers, since they all attended decent schools, did nothing to eliminate it.

The neat homes they lived in were well built and well kept. They were each set in a short walled garden to the front and a long stretch at the rear which backed on to a bit of spare ground. They all had a bow window each side of the front door and two flat sash windows above and in the roof a tiny dormer window which allowed light into a slip of an attic. The front door opened into a square, white and black tiled hallway off which were three doors, one to the parlour, one to the dining-room and the third to a modern kitchen which in turn led to a scullery. Upstairs were three good-sized bedrooms. Spacious and airy, or so it would be deemed by those who lived in their own filth down by the docks and who hadn't, in the eyes of the residents of Walton Lane, the gumption to get themselves out of it as they had done. Bloody hard work and perseverance, which they'd all shown, was needed, along with a bit of good old Liverpool common sense, for good fortune didn't come to those who sat about on their arses bemoaning their lot, as Sean Flanagan often said to his wife, in private, of course. He and many others had risen above it by gritting their teeth and getting on with it, working by day and spending their evenings at the Mechanics Institute learning to read and write and add up. They had found that it was possible in this growing and increasingly prosperous city, where shipbuilding trades and house construction opened doors to those willing to labour at it, or took a chance on a small business, working all the hours God sends, to make a success of it, which those in Walton Lane had done.

Having eaten enough of her porridge to please her pa, who told her she was a good girl, and her ma, who said it was time she got ready for school, Lily got down from the table and went upstairs to change from her dressing-gown, in which Ma allowed her to eat breakfast, into her school clothes. Her bedroom was at the back, looking out over the bit of rough ground that lay between Walton Lane and Walton Road. She could see Jack and Charlie Meadows with Finn Flanagan, who should by now have been on their way to the school their parents paid good money for, bending over something in the long grass. There was a sort of pathetic whining coming through her open bedroom window and she leaned out in an effort to see what they were up to. Suddenly they stepped back, their hands held up, almost tripping over their own boots in their effort to get away from whatever it was they had been fiddling with. At once what seemed to be a confused bundle of fur began to roll and writhe, going over and over in the rough and stony ground. Lily stared, leaning out even further as she tried to make out what it was and when she did she let out such a scream Mrs Quinn dropped her frying pan which she was just about to put into steep. It was a dog and a cat which the boys had tied tail to tail. The animals were much the same size and at first attempted to fight one another, but in a moment or two they had had enough and wanted to part company. The dog pulled and then the cat, dragging each other in terror backwards and forwards across the ground while the three boys slapped their thighs and howled with laughter.

It took her no more than twenty seconds to fling herself out of her room, down the stairs, through the kitchen past the startled Mrs Quinn, down the length of the garden and over the high wall like a monkey going up a stick. Her ma and pa had come to the door of the dining-room, ready to run upstairs, and as she flew past them they began to follow her, both begging her to tell them what was wrong and why had she screamed. There didn't seem to be much wrong with her by the vigour of her flight, for which they breathed a sigh of relief. Her scream had frightened them both.

"Lily"? her pa queried, but she was on the other side of the wall by then and when he reached it he was just in time to see her throw herself at the dog and cat, her hands scrabbling to untie the knotted twine that fastened the two animals firmly together.

"It's all right, it's all right," she was muttering to them as they bit and scratched at her, and at each other. In a moment she was dripping with blood, her own or the terrified animals' Richard could not tell. He leaped the wall with the same force as his daughter, unconcerned with the rich satin of his quilted bed-robe and as he held the demented animals apart and away from her, Lily managed to separate the tails of the two animals. The cat streaked away, a black, spitting bundle of fury, disappearing over the wall of a garden on Walton Road but the dog, no more than a puppy really, quivered and whimpered and pressed itself against Lily's chest where she held it, as though seeking human comfort.

"Give the dog to me, Lily," her pa said gently, taking the animal from her arms, wanting to get her inside where the extent of her wounds might be ascertained. It might be that Doctor Draper was needed, for his daughter was in a bit of a mess. "I'll deal with you later," he told the three boys savagely, but later was not good enough for Lily.

With a cry of fury she sprang towards Finn Flanagan, who was the biggest and the oldest at twelve and, completely unprepared for the ferocity of her attack, he was forced back, almost measuring his length as he tripped clumsily on the tussocky grass. Her hands reached as though by instinct for his most vulnerable part, his eyes, raking down his forehead and eyebrows and continuing across both cheeks. Blood flowed and when he put up his fists as though she were another boy and he would fight her she clenched hers and landed one just below his belly where his manhood lay.

He howled in agony, bending double, and so great was Lily's anger she even managed another kick at his shins before her father, hastily dropping the puppy, took her by the arms and dragged her off.

"Let me go, Pa," she shrieked. "Did you see what those buggers had done to those animals?" Her pa was shocked and startled by her language, for her mother was bringing her up to be a lady. "That poor cat . . . is it all right, d'you think? And the puppy? Let me go, please let me go. They deserve a thrashing, all of them. Please, why don't you fetch your whip and I'll see they get it."

"Lily, calm down, sweetheart, they'll all be punished, I swear. Anyway, Finn looks as though you've pretty much finished him off so come home, there's a good girl, and let your mother have a look at you. You've blood all over the place and—"

"No, Pa," struggling to be free of her pa's arms. Her hair, which she could sit on when it was free, was free now, hanging about her in a shroud of silvery gold where the sun caught it and her face was as red as a poppy. She glared about her and even though she was firmly held by her pa, Jack and Charlie Meadows put another few feet of space between them and her.

By now there was a row of fascinated heads peering over every wall within hearing distance, including that of Lena Flanagan who, on seeing her son reduced to a blubbering heap by Lily Elliott, God knows why, yelled for her husband to come and sort this bloody lot out, forgetting for a moment her Walton on the Hill manners and reverting to Scotland Road where Sean had married her.

Though Sean could not for the life of him see what all the fuss was about, since they were only a couple of strays, after all, Richard Elliott was probably the most prosperous and well educated among the residents of Walton Lane. He was a perfectly nice chap who always stopped for a chat and certainly put on no airs and graces, knowing where Sean himself came from, but Sean was a little bit in awe of him and if he said the lads had gone too far, which, in the captain's eyes, it seemed they had, then he was perfectly willing to administer the appropriate punishment to his son, and Bert Meadows was the same. The little lass was a bit of a mess, what with scratches across her hands and even a bite on her lip which had swelled up alarmingly, and the doctor had been sent for, so the captain said, and would he like him to come and see to Sean's lad who, he said with a twinkle in his eye, had got a bit of a pasting from the captain's lass.

Lily lay in a state of interesting suffering on the sofa in the parlour. The doctor had applied some stuff that stung like the devil and had deliberated on whether the bite on her lip might need a stitch. She quite liked the idea of that, for it would be something to show off when she went to school the next day.

"Keep her off today, Mrs Elliott," the doctor had told Ma, after deciding against the stitch. Doctor Draper was a believer in the new and radical "germ theory" and he went on to say that the wounds must be kept scrupulously clean to keep out the germs, and the patient should not touch that animal, referring to the puppy which was tied to the back door handle outside, where it could be heard howling dolefully, since Mrs Quinn would not allow it into her clean kitchen until it was properly bathed in a good carbolic soap.

"But it's not our dog, Doctor Draper," Ma said, horrified that the doctor should believe they would own such a filthy-looking animal.

"Well, your daughter seems to think it is, Mrs Elliott, but that is up to you."

Lily cried and howled and even considered fainting a bit when Pa said he'd take the mongrel off to the . . . well, wherever stray animals were taken, which, he knew very well, though he wasn't going to say so in front of Lily, meant it would be destroyed.

"Please, Pa, I can't bear it," she sobbed against her pa's chest. "Poor little beggar. First it's tied by the tail to a cat and now you mean to take it away and probably someone will wring its neck and make it into stew and it's only a baby. How would you like it if—"

"Now then, darling, you must not say such things to your pa. He's only trying to help. The dog is . . . is verminous and couldn't possibly be let into the house in its condition."

"Oh, Ma, I know that, but if Pa was to give it a bath in the washhouse with . . . with carbolic soap like Doctor Draper said, it'd be clean then and could come in here with me. Please, Ma, please. I can't bear it if you take it away." She had turned china white and her eyes, great brilliant pools overflowing with tears and too big for her face, rent her parent's hearts. They loved her. They knew they sometimes excluded their daughter from their own totally selfish love for one another, though they didn't mean to. It was just that whenever they were apart they missed one another so much and when they were together they felt the need to make every day, hour, minute full of loveliness to make up for the loneliness. Really, would it do any harm to let the child have what she wanted, which was a companion for herself alone? They could not give her a sister or brother which would have eased their own sometimes guilty hearts so what harm could come of letting her have a pet? At least have a look at the thing after it was cleaned up?

Lily could see them weakening and, knowing exactly when to strike, the iron being hot, so to speak, began to babble of never letting the puppy be a nuisance. She would feed it and keep it clean and brushed and take it for walks and never let it interfere with her homework and it could sleep in the washhouse – which she knew it wouldn't do and so did they – and it would never get under Mrs Quinn's feet and if she went back on any of these promises she herself would personally take the dog to . . . to . . . wherever it was Pa had intended taking it. She was not sorry she had given Finn Flanagan a good hiding, not seeing her parents' amusement at the very idea of a ten-year-old girl giving a hiding to a big, twelve-year-old lad, though it was true she had, and she'd not apologise to him, though they had not asked her. She did not tell them that when she was up and about she meant to have a go at Jack and Charlie Meadows, since they were equally as bad as that lout Finn Flanagan.

The puppy, a female, as it happened, which Mrs Quinn happily seemed to think made it more acceptable, was quite a nice little thing when she was washed and brushed. They did their best, her parents, but they couldn't keep Lily out of the washhouse while the ablutions took place. She was heaps better, she told them, dragging her old cloak about her nightgown, and she felt the pup would behave better if she were there to supervise. She didn't. She would keep leaping up and trying to lick Pa's face, then turning her attentions on her, her rough tongue everywhere at once in her canine delight. When Pa got her out of the sink she shook herself so vigorously both she and Pa had to get changed. Her coat was a mottled indeterminate brown and her ears seemed too large for her pointed face. The length of her tail was quite ridiculous, Pa said, which was why it had been so easy to tie it to the cat, which upset Lily all over again but when, at last, she was once more ensconsed on the parlour sofa, a mug of creamy cocoa in one hand, the other arm about the wriggling body of her new friend, Lily Elliott thought she had never, except when she was on the deck of her father's schooner, been so happy in her life.

"Villette," she said sleepily, stroking Villette's rough fur.

"What was that, sweetheart?" Pa asked, putting down the *Liverpool Mercury* which he was reading out loud to her mother. Ma paused in her sewing, and looked up smilingly since she knew what her daughter meant.

"I shall call her Villette. Villy for short."

3

Jane Elliott was the only housewife on Walton Lane to have a servant. Her new husband had told her that she needed one, for he could not bear to see her at the sink with her hands in water, on her knees with a bucket at her side, slaving over an oven or doing any of the hundred and one tasks the wives of working men did every day of the week without a thought. Of course, he could afford one, for when he married her he was already in a fair way of business in the coastal shipping trade and so it was that Molly Quinn, who was ten years older than her mistress, and who, despite her name, was not Irish, came to "do" for her.

Though she was married to a comfortably off sea skipper with his own small schooner Jane Elliott was not a lady in the true sense of the word. She was not allied to the gentry, for her father had been a self-made man with his own ship's chandlery business in Liverpool. He and her mother, overwhelmed by the beauty and seeming fragility of their only child, had not allowed her to work in the business though she had been perfectly willing to do so, being a good-natured lass with no conception of her own loveliness. It might have been that with the awed worship of her parents shaping her life she would become spoiled and selfish but she was a simple girl, not simple meaning a bit backward, but simple with an outlook on life that asked for no more than the content and peace she found in her home and the love with which her parents surrounded her.

When she was seven years old she was sent to a small, select school in Breckfield Road where, at a cost of £5 per annum, she was taught English reading, spelling, grammar, arithmetic, drawing, natural philosophy and chemistry, needlework and vocal music. She also learned to speak correctly, though she never lost her Liverpool accent, to walk properly, to sit gracefully and to use the correct cutlery at table.

Her parents were devastated when she fell in love with Captain Richard Elliott though they could not fault him as a husband. They felt he was exactly the right age for their unworldly eighteen-year-old daughter and was well able to support her, but to lose her, even though she was to go from the comfortable rooms above the shop where they lived no further than Walton on the Hill, was a great blow to them. Still, as she told them on her wedding day, they were welcome to come and visit her and Richard any time they pleased, particularly as he would be gone for days on end when he sailed away on his schooner, then called the *Seamaid*, after the first ship owned by the Elliotts.

There were sea captains, sailors, ship's mates, seamen of all kinds in and out of John Mellor's busy ship's chandlers and it was one of these who killed John and Frances Mellor. Not intentionally, of course, but somewhere on a voyage one of them had picked up one of the diseases that were rife in the tropics and it had swept through the small area about John Mellor's shop, taking fifteen people with it. John and Frances were among them.

Richard deliberated on whether to keep on their thriving little business, putting in a manager to run it, but, making one of the mistakes that seemed to dog him at times, he sold it instead, giving the small profit to his wife to spend as she pleased. Which she did, buying silk fans and gauze scarves, silk dresses and stunning little Zouave jackets, cashmere shawls, velvet gilets, dashing bonnets and morning robes that were nothing but a froth of gauze like sea foam.

Her husband was enchanted with her.

Molly Quinn watched it all with a jaundiced eye, for the pair of them were like children at play, she thought, with no conception of the real world, for they had never had to deal with it. Even the captain, though he worked hard when he was at sea and was what Molly called a real man, a real gent, had inherited what he had from his father. He had never had to struggle and neither had his young wife and yet could you condemn them, for they were the loveliest couple, not just in looks but in their dispositions as well. The same could not be said about herself, not that she was unattractive or had a mean nature but that her life had been one long fight to survive. Molly Quinn had had a hard time of it but she often thought if she'd looked like Mrs Elliott and been as sweet-natured and trusting and lucky she would probably have turned out just like her mistress and done just what she did. But she hadn't!

She and Seamus had been married for no more than four years with four babies to bring up when he had fallen from a crane and broken his neck. They had lived in Brooke Alley off Vauxhall Road with a fine view of the coal yards to one side, the Vitriol Works to the other and a stone's throw from the Borough Gaol where the young prostitutes hung about. Not to find customers from the gaol, though several of the gaolers made use of them, but because it was close to the docks. It was an appalling place to bring up children, with a gin-shop every two or three steps and the gutters awash with those who frequented them. Seamus, who had a steady job, and Molly had a basement cellar all to themselves, which was a luxury in an environment where it was quite normal for not one family but two or three to share a room. The alley was a narrow, flagged passage down the middle of which was an open drain in which floated sewage and all manner of nasty debris. The alley led to a close, a square around which tall, back-to-back houses stood and in which well over a hundred people, along with those who lived in the alley, shared one water supply and a couple of privies.

Molly worked hard to keep her growing family clean and decent, making sure every morning that she had enough water for the day, for sometimes the Communal Water Supply was turned off and there was none to be had until the next morning. She was lucky. She had three decent buckets in which to collect her water but it didn't seem to matter to many of the other tenants who, having no utensil in which to boil a potato let alone collect water, didn't bother overmuch with washing or scouring or anything that might take a little effort. In between pregnancies Molly went out to work, putting a bit by for when she was unable to carry on because of her condition. She went scrubbing or worked over a dolly tub in the laundry at the back of the Vitriol Works and they managed, she and Seamus, proud of themselves and their labours which kept them what Molly liked to think of as respectable. She squared her strong shoulders and worked beside Seamus despite the filth, the derelict people with whom she lived cheek by jowl, the men haggard, drunken, careworn, hopeless, the women weighed down by the yearly pregnancies they could not avoid, nursing their babies at dirty breasts as they sat on the steps that led up to the floors above her own basement. They reminded her strangely of the scurrying earwigs and other creeping insects that one finds when a log that has lain a long time on the ground is lifted, and she had no sympathy with them when they gave up. So many just sank into apathy, too overcome to make any further effort, but Molly was an intelligent young woman, bright and cheerful and optimistic. Until Seamus died.

For a while she sank into the same state of muck and muddle they all lived in, for without Seamus's wage how was she to manage? Her home became as dirty, as verminous, as cold and cheerless as all the others in the alley and it was not until her youngest, a sweet little boy of only seven months, died one night in her arms, because of her neglect, she knew that, that she began to haul herself little by little out of the cesspool her life had become since Seamus's death.

With three young children at her skirts, good little children, all girls, who obeyed her orders to stay where they were put, sometimes tied to a table leg for their own safety, she began a long, tortuous grind of scrubbing and scouring, holystoning the steps of better-off housewives in Everton and West Derby, laundry work at the local washhouse and in her own home at nights; of working in soap factories and pickle factories and indeed anywhere they would pay her for her labour. She was sometimes so exhausted she wished she had died with Seamus, despairing that she would ever get herself up out of the mire of poverty-stricken degradation. It would have been so easy to sell her body down at the docks – she was still a young and attractive woman – to get bread to put in her children's mouths and a rag or two on their backs but she savagely refused to consider that since she had loved Seamus and the children he had left in her trust.

It was not until she discovered, or was discovered by, the Society for Bettering the Condition and Increasing the Comfort of the Poor, that she began to get a proper toehold on a new life. As the children grew it became more and more difficult to keep them safe and quiet while she worked. Victoria, Mary and Alice – Molly was a fervent royalist and had called her children after those of the dear Queen – were obedient and well mannered, for she would have them no other way, but they were children, well fed after that first dreadful fall into despair after Seamus's death, healthy and lively and she began to fear that the fine tight rope she trod between managing, just, and not managing at all, was not going to hold her up for much longer.

The Ladies Benevolent Society, which visited distressed women in their homes and whom many of the inhabitants of Brooke Alley called "bloody interfering cows" were the ones to give her fresh hope. They directed her, through the Society for Bettering the Condition and Increasing the Comfort of the Poor, to a small school established twenty years ago and supported by the Anglican Church where her children would be looked after while she was at work, and indeed would be taught to read and write.

Though Molly Quinn had been brought up as a Catholic she let all the Church's teaching fly out of the window, for a fat lot of good it, or the Church, had done her in her desperate struggle to survive. If her children were to be taught by Protestants what did it matter? She was sure that Seamus up in his Catholic heaven wouldn't mind as long as his girls were safe, healthy and happy and the burden he had left on Molly's shoulders was lifted a little. She begged his forgiveness every night for letting his little son die, for he had loved the child, but perhaps the baby was with his daddy and Seamus happy to have him. She comforted herself with this thought and got on with cherishing the rest of his children which was all she could do, after all.

An added bonus was that the three girls went to Sunday School which meant she had extra hours free to do other jobs and by the time her eldest was ten years old and ready to go as scullery maid to a good and respectable family with a promise of promotion if she "shaped", which Molly knew she would, she was firmly in control of her life. It had taken her six years but she had done it.

But the hardships she had endured and overcome had made her intolerant, impatient with those who could not do, through sheer hard work and determination, what she had done. If she could keep herself respectable with three young children to fetch up then why couldn't others, those who lolled about on doorsteps in the alley where she still lived. Not that her room was anything like theirs. She kept it whitewashed: even the bricks on the outside wall above her cellar window and door and about the basement steps that led down to them were got at every six months. Her small home was scrubbed, polished and scoured every night when she got home from work, for it was constant war to keep down the lice, the fleas, the rats and other vermin that lived beside those all about her. Her stove was blackleaded, her brasses polished and her two remaining children set off each day to school with clean aprons and stout boots and a decent meal for their dinner wrapped in a clean checked napkin. She had a handsome clock under a glass dome, bought second-hand from Paddy's Market so that she was never late for any of her jobs. She had four matched glasses with a cut-out design on them. She had a dresser on which she kept her *full* set of English stoneware, cups, saucers, plates, dinner plates and tureens, second-hand, naturally, and in a drawer a well-polished set of cutlery. She had a good kettle, several saucepans, a round frying pan and a round egg roaster. There was a rug on her scrubbed floor and on her mantelshelf several small figurines of what looked like Chinamen, one or two chipped, certainly, but very pretty and proving that she was able to spend money not just on the necessities of life. She had a big double bed modestly hidden behind a shawl hung over a piece of rope in which she and the girls slept, three armchairs and a pine table scrubbed to the colour of rich cream with four chairs about it. She had snowy nets at her window and curtains she had made herself to keep out the rude curiosity of her neighbours who thought she had got above herself. And most important she had a good strong lock on her door and a shutter on her window for when she was not at home.

This, of course, was not until later in her life, after she had begun to work for Captain and Mrs Elliott.

It was at the church where she took her children every Sunday that she was asked if she would ever consider taking a full-time job as a housekeeper, cook, cleaner.

"It's a nice home where you'd be going, Mrs Quinn. Mrs Mellor, who is a member of our congregation, has a daughter who is getting married and her husband-to-be is keen to get a decent, hardworking woman to look after their home. He's a sea captain and will be away at times."

"I couldn't live in, Mrs Cooper. Me kids're still young as yer know, and I couldn't leave 'em alone."

"I don't think they need anyone to live in, Mrs Quinn. The captain, or so I was told by Mrs Mellor, intends taking his bride with him on his boat, for a time at least," meaning until the babies start putting in an appearance. "He is not away for very long," she went on vaguely, not being in any way familiar with the life of a seaman, even if she did live in Liverpool. "And then, when he's home they will need looking after. I believe the future Mrs Elliott has been . . . she's not very domesticated. She has been well educated and can sew but that seems to be her only accomplishment. Can you cook, Mrs Quinn?"

"A plain cook, Mrs Cooper, when I've summat to cook with," remembering those days when it had been nothing but potatoes and oatmeal mixed with water.

"I shouldn't think they will need more than that, my dear," not meaning the potatoes and oatmeal, of course. "They are ordinary people, not of the gentry or anything like that, if you know what I mean. Mrs Mellor is the wife of a ship's chandler but . . . well, think it over and if you're interested let me know. Don't be too long, though, for it will make a very nice job for someone."

They had just come back from their honeymoon a little over three weeks later when Molly Quinn knocked at the newly painted front door of the grand little house in Walton Lane. She'd walked up from Brooke Alley, along Portland Street and into New Scotland Road which led to Everton Valley and Walton Lane. A walk of no more than twenty minutes which was very convenient and would be an added bonus, for once you got the length of New Scotland Road you were in the prettiest countryside Molly had ever seen. That's if she got the job which, the more she saw of Walton Lane, the smart little semi-detached villa and the handsome couple who lived in it, became more and more desirable. God almighty, she could clean through this place in a morning and if they wanted a bit of cooking done, even the better kind, she'd soon learn.

They'd been to Southport, they told her, sitting on the sofa in the pretty parlour, holding hands and smiling at one another in such a way she began to feel somewhat embarrassed. It was very obvious they were made up with each other and were not really very concerned with how a house should be run or what she was to put in their mouths or whether or not she polished the brass every day. When could she start? the captain asked, not his wife who was mistress of this house, which was strange but then they were not what you'd call an ordinary couple at all, despite what Mrs Cooper had told her. They begged her to have another cup of tea, leaving her to pour it out for herself and would she like an almond tart, shop bought, she supposed, not being able to picture the elegant Mrs Elliott with a mixing bowl in her long-fingered white hands. The captain was to be off in a day or two, he didn't say where, and wanted to know that his wife would be looked after while he was away. He would have taken her with him, he explained, as he meant to do whenever it was possible but his cargo was not one he would like his wife to be close to and when he told her what it was, manufactured goods for Ireland which was quite reasonable but bringing back cattle, she understood what he meant. Over the rim of her china cup she considered the slender loveliness of Mrs Elliott, who looked as though she'd never been in close contact with anything other than flowers and butterflies, blue skies and golden sunshine, pretty dresses and fragrant perfume, kittens and satin ribbons, in fact all the beautiful things in life that Molly Quinn had never encountered. She and Seamus had once taken the ferry to New Brighton, walking on the golden sands, looking in wonder at the pretty houses along the esplanade, the lovely municipal gardens, the sparkling jewels scattered on the sun-kissed river. That had been *their* honeymoon and she would never forget that day as long as she lived. They had held hands as these two were doing, for they were eighteen and had been wed only a week and so she understood, for she had known love.

"Well, Mrs Quinn, I think that's about all," the captain said, "unless you've anything else you'd like to ask, my darling."

His darling proved to be not quite as oblivious to sensible matters as her looks seemed to imply.

"There is the question of Mrs Quinn's wage, Richard. And I'm not even sure she has agreed to come to us." She smiled so devastatingly it was then that Molly Quinn began on the long and enduring role of loving protector she was to play for the remainder of their lives, though no one ever knew of her feelings.

"Oh, dear, Mrs Quinn, forgive me? Of course, Mrs Elliott is right." They turned and stared at one another in wonder, momentarily speechless at the sound of her new name on his lips and Molly felt the smile begin inside her, for there was nothing more certain in this life than that these two needed someone sensible to look after them. How in the name of heaven did the captain manage to run a business if he was as feather-brained as it seemed he was, but she was to learn that Richard Elliott the seaman and Richard Elliott the husband were two totally different men.

Molly sat with her back straight as a pencil, as Mrs Elliott was doing, with a look so stern and disapproving they both leaned back a little, then stared at one another in dismay but, again, it was something they were to learn about her as she was to learn many things about them. Whoever Mrs Quinn cherished she chastised. Ask her daughters! Whatever she was asked to do she did it with such grudging reluctance one could be forgiven for thinking she was not at all pleased and it was only against her own better judgement that she would allow it, whatever it happened to be.

"I've two children, girls," she told them firmly, "an' another in service up near Toxteth Park. Nay, don't bother tha' selves, they're well looked after durin't day burr I've ter gerr'ome to 'em at night so I can't sleep in." She did not apologise, for that was not her way. She told the truth and that was that.

"How old are your children, Mrs Quinn?"

"Victoria's eleven now, Mary's ten an'll be goin' inter service 'erself shortly, and our Alice is nine."

"What pretty names, Mrs Quinn." Molly was to discover that whatever the situation or the topic of conversation, Jane Elliott always had something nice to say. "But what a shame they have to go into service."

"Well, ma'am, the devil drives where't needs must, an' bein' a widder all these years I 'ad no choice, but they're decent lasses an' I'm proud of 'em," and that's the end of that, her firm jaw and truculent expression told them. She wanted no sympathy. She was not prepared to tell them of the hardships she had endured nor the sacrifices she had made to keep them all decent. She did not even brag that they could read and write which was not an accomplishment many slum children could boast.

They loved her, they told one another in that extravagant way they had after she had gone, promising to be at Walton Lane at seven o'clock next Monday morning.

"Oh, there's no need to come quite so early, Mrs Quinn," the captain had demurred.

"Oh, yes, sir, there is. I don't like ter waste time lollin' in me bed an' I can see there's a few things what want putting right round 'ere," turning her gaze disapprovingly on what was evidently something that gave her great offence.

"Well, if that's the case you had better have a key, for I'm not sure . . . we'll be up."

"Right you are, sir." She stood up. Her wages had been agreed and her hours, which were to be somewhat loose, for there might be things, said somewhat vaguely, that Mrs Elliott might need her for. She was to come every day except Sunday, even when the Elliotts were at sea and would, of course, be paid her full wage, which, to Molly Quinn who had scraped along on so little for so long, was absolutely magnificent.

That had been eleven years ago and from that day she had bullied and loved and cherished them through thick and thin, though to be honest there was not much thin. The captain came home every ten days or so, staying perhaps three while he discharged his cargo and picked up another and their lives went on serenely. The time while Mrs Elliott was pregnant and then was forced to stayed at home with her new baby had been a tricky one, for she had pined for her husband.

"I don't know what I would do without you, Mrs Quinn; probably kill myself," she would say, drifting to the window as though it might bring her husband home that much quicker if she watched for him.

"Don't talk daft. I've never 'eard such damn nonsense in me life. You need summat ter *reely* bother yer then yer could talk about killin' yerself, my lass. D'yer not think I don't miss my man, even after all this time, so think on—"

She would get no further, for with a soft rustle of lace and chiffon and a waft of lovely perfume Mrs Elliott would be rushing to put her arms about her and hug her in that endearingly childlike way she had and though Molly loved it, and her, she could not allow it.

"Now give over an' let me gerron wi' this apple turnover or there'll be nowt fer yer dinner."

Molly's culinary efforts had come on apace since she had begun work at the Elliotts. On the quiet she practised all sorts of recipes from the *Ladies Journal* Mrs Elliott bought and was hugely gratified when the captain told her he had never tasted anything as good as her pastry and what had she put in the steak and kidney to make it so mouthwateringly delicious?

When the baby, Lily, was about eighteen months old, Mrs Elliott began to go again on the sea journeys her husband took. Sometimes the child went with them, though Molly often had nightmares about her safety on board that dipping, slippery deck which she herself had been persuaded to visit, and that was only tied up to the dock! She could so easily fall overboard, what with them two for ever canoodling, but she had underrated her employer's sense of responsibility when he was aboard his ship and the little mite had a line on her, apparently, and came to no harm. At other times they left her behind in Molly's care, begging her to bring her own two to stay with her in Walton Lane, which she did until they both went into service. They were good like that, the Elliotts. On Victoria's, Mary's or Alice's day off, her daughters would come to visit her there, despite the fact that she had kept on their home in Brooke Alley. They knew that though she was well set up here, in the pink, so to speak, she would never forget that time after their daddy died and Brooke Alley was a sort of bolt-hole, something to fall back on if anything were to go wrong with this grand job she now had. Not that anything would, for the Elliotts were a lovely couple. The girls had been shy at first but the Elliotts made a great fuss of them and really, life was so bloody wonderful she often shed tears of happiness as she whispered in the night of it to Seamus and it was all thanks to the Elliotts and their kindness to her.

And so the years passed and the child grew and was so different to her ma, not in looks but in her resolute determination to submit to no one. She was not disobedient or rude, in fact she was a well-mannered child but you could see that glint in her eye and that thrust of her small chin which said she didn't agree with you and though she might not say so out loud, she damn well would do what she thought best. Swift to anger she was, like him, but never bore a grudge, again like him, but with a will of iron which was a bit worrying in a child of her age. She had courage, too, which Molly admired. Look at the way she was over them big lads and that dratted dog which was for ever under her feet. Villette! Did you ever hear such a name for a dog? What was wrong with Gyp or Scrap or Rover, tell her that? she'd said to Lily.

"She's a lady dog, Mrs Quinn," the child had told her loftily, "that's why I didn't call her Rover." Her tone was scathing. "Besides, I don't like Scrap or Rover, even if she'd been a boy."

Villette, or Villy as she was called more often than not, ate what seemed to be her own weight in food every day, all the scraps from the family's meals and whatever else she could beg or steal from anyone who took pity on her. The child was very attached to her and often sneaked her into her bedroom to sleep at the foot of her bed and though Molly knew about it she never said owt to her ma and pa.

Molly loved her almost as much as she loved her ma. She scolded her and told her she was a handful and she didn't know what she was going to do with her and she would never grow up to be the lady her ma was, which had not the slightest effect on Lily who didn't want to be like her ma but like her pa! She allowed Mrs Quinn to take her to school each day because she had no option, and then bring her home at the end of it, talking nineteen to the dozen, and Molly listened to her going on about China and Australia and Newfoundland and Peru and her determination to visit all these places, wherever they were, and many more besides. Molly was the only one to listen to Lily's plans for the future which seemed to include becoming a sea captain and sailing away on her pa's schooner and though neither of *them* took any notice, that's if they heard her, Molly Quinn often felt a small sense of unease prick her, for if there was ever a child who would have her own way it was her. Tell her how it was possible and Molly wouldn't be able to say but if there was a way, Lily Elliott would find it.

4

Lily was playing hopscotch with Evie Meadows and Grace Watson when the hansom cab came slowly along Walton Lane, the cabbie leaning across his seat as though looking for the number of a house. With a great deal of "whoa-ing" and pulling of reins it stopped outside hers. The cab door swung open somewhat hesitantly and two men got out. She was surprised to see that one of them was Mr Porter. What on earth was he doing here? was her first thought, naturally, especially as the *Lily-Jane* was to dock today and her pa would need all hands to the pump, as he always joked. She didn't know who the other chap was.

It was the beginning of December and the weather had turned cold. It was not really the right time of the year for hopscotch, which usually took place in the summer months, but they had decided, she and Grace and Evie, that it was silly only to do something you really enjoyed doing when someone else told you to, like Easter for whip and top, July for marbles or "ollies" as they were called in Liverpool, and Cherry Wob which was played mostly by the boys in the autumn. The funny thing was that no one seemed to know who started it. Cherry Wob was understandable, for you needed cherry stones which you could obviously only get in season. They were flicked up the side of a house wall and when they came down if they hit a stone already on the pavement the owner claimed the lot. At least that was their version. But whip and top, wooden bowling hoops and skipping games seemed just to start of their own volition. One day it was whip and top, the next skipping ropes without a word being said and they all fell in with it unquestioningly.

Skipping had its own chanted rhythms.

Dip, dip, dip, my blue ship,
Floating on the water
Like a cup and saucer,
Dip, dip, dip, you're not in!

At this, whoever was skipping was then sent out. That was magical and complicated, the rope whirling with a girl at each end and, depending on the length of the rope, two or three, or sometimes four girls leaping in and out, plaits bobbing, skirts flying, cheeks flushed, eyes shining with the exertion.

But hopscotch was the three girls' particular favourite and this morning, a Saturday, they had carefully marked out their squares on the pavement with chalk and had intoned "Eeny, meeny, miny, mo, catch a nigger by the toe," which was their way of choosing who was to go first. Lily, who had won, had done four and had just slid her stone across the squares with the flair and dexterity for which, as a hopscotch player, she was famous among her peers. It landed as neat as you please on number five.

With a triumphant look at Grace and Evie she was about to hop on to the number one square, then place one foot on each of the squares marked two and three, and so on, avoiding the one with the five on it, and, of course, all the chalked lines, which if she had stepped on would have meant she was "out", when she became aware that neither of her friends was watching her. They had turned, along with every other child who was "playing out", to look curiously at the cab and the two men who had alighted. Both were dressed in sombre suits, just as though they were going to church. Dark jackets, neat black neckties, stand-up collars with turned-down points, narrow-legged trousers. The gentleman who was a stranger wore a top hat and Mr Porter, whom Lily scarcely recognised without his gansey and peaked cap, had a bowler. They both removed these as they moved up the short path to Lily's front door and knocked with restraint on the highly polished brass doorknocker which was in the shape of a mermaid. In unison and almost as though they had practised it, they each lifted their right hand and nervously smoothed down their hair, before turning to gaze for a moment into the lane.

The children stood as one, clutching ollies and hoops, staring, open-mouthed, wide-eyed, as though, already, they knew that something unparalleled was about to happen.

Grace nudged Lily. "They're knocking at your door, Lil," she remarked unnecessarily, putting her hand on Lily's arm.

"I can see that, you daft beggar."

"Wonder what they want."

"How the heck do I know?" Watching as Mrs Quinn opened the door which she had just wiped down with a clean cloth as was her habit when she "did" her windows. She even scrubbed the stone window sills along with the front step, the wrought-iron gate and its posts, the step into the lane, finishing with the pail of soapy water being chucked along the path then brushed vigorously into the gutter. The spilled water had caused considerable inconvenience to the three girls, for it had meant they could not get a decent chalk mark outside Lily's gate and had to move further up the pavement.

The men spoke to Mrs Quinn and after a moment of suspicious scrutiny she stepped back inside the house, holding open the door for Mr Porter and the other chap to follow her in.

"What d'you think's wrong, Lil?" Grace speculated anxiously. "I've never seen them before, have you? You don't think it's anything to do with those apples we scrumped at the back end, do you?" Grace was of a nervous disposition and often wondered why bold and fearless Lily Elliott ever bothered with her. "That chap who chased us might've recognised us, you never know. I didn't want to do it in the first place but you and Charlie made me and Charlie's hair would be recognised by a blind man, it's such an awful ginger."

"Don't be daft, Grace Watson, we never made you and besides, if he had they'd have been here long ago and going to Charlie's house, not mine."

"And who are you, calling our Charlie's hair an awful ginger, anyroad?" a furious Evie spluttered. Evie was Charlie's sister and had the same shock of almost orange curls.

"Oh, do stop it, you two. I know one of them, he's Pa's first mate."

She began to walk slowly towards her own gate, watched by her two friends. The other children had lost interest, since it was not really the men who had caught their attention but the hansom cab, something not often seen in Walton Lane, which had driven away. She began to shiver as an inexplicable fear slithered through her. The sun which had shone weakly from the pale wintry sky had been covered by a wisp of gauze-like cloud and the day seemed suddenly dark and ominous. It's going to snow, she told herself, trying to explain the sudden icy greyness that overwhelmed her and when Mrs Quinn opened the door, her face set like the one on the bronze statue of Her Majesty's husband that stood before St George's Hall, she wanted to turn and run and run to escape the awful something that waited for her in her home.

"Come inside, lamb," Mrs Quinn said, which further frightened her, for Mrs Quinn had never called her "lamb" in all the years she had known her, which was since Lily was born.

There was absolute silence in the house. Through the open doorway of the parlour she could see her mother sitting in the most unusual attitude, unusual for her since she was always so graceful. She was stiff, awkward, her head held at a strange angle as though she were listening for something as she perched on the edge of the seat of a coffee-coloured velvet button-back chair. Mr Porter and the other gentleman were standing awkwardly just inside the door as if reluctant to step on Ma's richly swirled carpet, both still clinging to their hats and their composure by the skin of their teeth, though why she should have such an odd thought Lily couldn't imagine. Nobody spoke and but for the awful, awful feeling of terror, of stark and unbelieving terror, that filled the room from wall to wall and ceiling to floor, it might have been the picture of two gentlemen calling on a lady who was just about to invite them to sit down and take tea with her. Mrs Quinn held Lily's hand and she could feel it tremble and when she looked up at her, her face was as white as the apron she wore and it was moving, twitching even, as though she were afflicted by some strange nervous condition.

Her ma's voice, when she spoke, was so normal Lily almost laughed out loud in her relief.

"I'm afraid you've made some dreadful mistake, gentlemen. You see my husband is due home today. His ship docks on the evening tide and he will be home shortly after that. Mrs Quinn is just preparing his favourite meal, aren't you, Mrs Quinn?" turning a bright smile in Mrs Quinn's direction and Mrs Quinn made some indeterminate sound in the back of her throat. She put her free hand to her mouth as though to keep the sound in and Lily's ma watched her, then began to shake her head, denying something, though what it could be Lily didn't know, or perhaps she did and was terrified to acknowledge it.

Why was Ma so frightened? Her face was expressionless, set in a mould of porcelain perfection with no hint of colour anywhere in it, even her eyes seemed to be blank and empty of their normal smoky grey which was so beautiful. They reminded Lily of rain on a window, or the fog that drifted across from the river, without substance, without tone or depth.

"I'm so sorry, Mrs Elliott, I'm so sorry . . ." Mr Porter began, and to Lily's amazement she could hear the break of tears in his voice. Again she was seriously alarmed, for in her childhood world grown-ups didn't cry so it must be something bad to have upset him like this. She held at bay with a stubborn hardening of her will whatever that something might be. "It happened so sudden, like. You know what a good seaman he was but the storm . . . it were blowin' a force eight and when Johnno slipped and was dashed agin the rail the captain . . ."

Again Mr Porter swallowed something that seemed to fill his throat and all the while her ma stared steadily at him, her face totally blank but in her eyes was a glimmer of something, like a tiny light that had come to illuminate her mind and was shining against her will out on the world. Her back was absolutely rigid, her head still cocked in that strange way, but she appeared to be waiting politely for Mr Porter to finish what he was saying and leave her alone. She was not listening, not really listening to his words but Lily was and inside her something tore in agony, spreading throughout her slender childish body which was not really strong enough or mature enough to cope with it.

"Can I offer you some tea, gentlemen?" her ma said defensively, determined to make this just an unexpected social visit. "Mrs Quinn . . ." She turned blindly to the woman to whose hand Lily's seemed glued and it was then that she broke open. Broke open as though her body had been attacked by some monster child, falling apart like a doll whose stuffing is leaking out. Her mouth opened wide so that every tooth was on display and from it came a scream, then another and another, her lips stretched cruelly. The two gentlemen were appalled, for they had never seen in the space of two or three seconds such a transformation from total disbelieving calmness to a mad and uncontrollable frenzy of emotion. Tears poured down her face in a torrent, falling as steadily as rain and still from her mouth, which the tears kept flowing into, came a wail of such despair they both moved instinctively towards her, for she was like an animal that is being tormented beyond endurance.

Mrs Quinn let go of Lily's hand, leaving her stranded in her own unbelieving nightmare and moved hastily to her ma, lifting her to her feet with great tenderness, clucking something incomprehensible as she began to lead her from the pitying gaze of Mr Porter and the other gentleman. Lily still had the stone in her hand that she had thrown on to the number five then picked up on her way back to Evie and Grace. She was holding it so tightly she felt the sharp edge of it break the skin of her palm and the blood flow between her fingers. She could hear Villy whining and scratching in the scullery where Mrs Quinn must have shut her when she went to answer the door and she dwelled on the thought that Mrs Quinn would be hopping mad if Villy scratched the paintwork.

Mrs Quinn took her mother away and Mr Porter told Lily how sorry he was, how terribly sorry, her pa was a brave man to give his life for another; if there was anything he could do, and . . . well, he supposed they had better be off. They'd come in on the morning tide, making good headway to get her pa back. Well, they couldn't . . . they were all so sorry . . .

Not knowing what else to do with the silent child who stood like a dead-eyed statue where the housekeeper had left her, they told her again how sorry they were and having no one to let them out they did it themselves, hurrying in great relief up the path and along Walton Lane towards the city as though pursued by a pack of wolves. It had been worse than they had thought it would be, they told one another, and what would the poor widow do now? It was known she had been devoted to the captain and as for the child, poor little bugger, who was going to see to her now, for it was plain her ma couldn't.

Lily moved through the next few days with little recollection of what went on, though the sight of a coffin coming through the front door with, she supposed, Pa's poor dead body in it, sent her into such a crescendo of screaming Mrs Quinn had to send for the doctor. He had given her something that made her eyes heavy and she could not remember much after that. There were faces which bent over her, mouths opening and closing, saying something to her, she supposed, though she couldn't decipher what it was. She stared at each one in turn as though they were speaking some foreign language, which, if she listened carefully enough, would make sense, but it didn't. Ma was shut in her bedroom from which no sound came, Mrs Quinn in attendance, and had it not been for Rosa Meadows, Evie's ma, Lily might have fared badly.

"I'll take the child," was one remark Lily did make out, though she was not sure who said it, but after finding herself in the same bed as Evie who slept soundly beside her, she decided it must have been Evie's ma.

"She's in shock," another hollow voice said sympathetically, "and can you blame the poor mite. Her ma's gone out of her mind, so Mrs Quinn says, and she's enough to do looking after her, so the child's best out of the house until after the funeral."

"When's it to be, then?"

"There's to be some sort of enquiry, or an inquest or something, but probably the beginning of next week."

"Poor soul."

It was strange really. She was totally numb, feeling nothing at all. She was convinced that if they stuck pins in her she would feel no pain. It was as though she were not there any more, visible, but at the same time invisible to those who moved around her, talked above her head, stared at her with great curiosity, especially the children who had never been close to anyone whose pa had died before. They didn't speak *to* her. They didn't ask her questions, like, "Would you like a piece of cake, Lily?" but said to one another, "D'you think she'd eat a piece of cake if I offered it to her?"

"Eeh, I don't know," would come the answer until she felt like standing up and shrieking, "I'm here! Ask me!" but it was all too much trouble. She simply didn't care enough, though she couldn't fathom why. The very worst thing she could ever imagine happening to her, had happened. Her pa was dead. Mrs Quinn had taken her on her lap and told her so, though if she was honest she had known that the minute she had seen Mr Porter get out of the cab.

And so she sat at Mrs Meadows's table with Mr Meadows, Mrs Meadows, Evie and Jack and Maggie and Charlie, considering nothing at all really except what an amazement it was that they all had exactly the same-coloured hair, bright ginger, bar Mrs Meadows who was dark and handsome, like a gypsy. It was funny, the odd thoughts that wandered so casually into her head, just out of the blue like that, and she wondered why, not realising that she was in deep shock, that nature was shielding her, for the moment, from the agony of her loss. She was washed and dressed with Evie, who was the same age as her and her best friend and when it was discussed whether to send her to school or not with Evie, for perhaps it might be best for her to continue with her normal routine, she docilely allowed herself to be put on Mrs Meadows's parlour sofa with a book in her hand when it was decided it might be best to keep her at home.

"Look at her, poor little thing," she heard Mrs Meadows say to Mrs Watson who had, apparently, popped in to see if there was anything she could do to help.

"She's not a scrap of trouble," Mrs Meadows continued from the parlour doorway where she and Mrs Watson studied her pityingly. "She's not even shed a tear. Poor little thing."

"What'll her ma do without the captain? I've never known a woman who relied on her husband as she did."

"Mmm, I said as much to Bert last night but she'll just have to get on with it like we all would."

"I know, but she's . . . well . . ." They were not quite sure how to describe Jane Elliott, who was as lovely as the day, always smiling serenely and with a kind word for everyone but about as useful in the house as a toddling infant. Good job she had that Mrs Quinn of hers to see to her. She'd no relatives, so it was said, and neither had he but he must have left her comfortable which was something, they supposed.

Lily managed quite nicely in the cocoon of insensibility she had fallen into, going to bed with Evie when she was told, getting up, getting washed and dressed, eating what was put in front of her and spending her day on Mrs Meadows's sofa. She was so quiet and obedient it was quite eerie, Mrs Meadows said, knowing what a wilful little thing she normally was. She sat there like a little ghost but soon they got quite used to it, so much so that the usual domestic upheaval in which the Meadows family lived swirled about her as though she were nothing more than a chair or the piano that stood in the parlour. After the first fascinated awe with which they treated her and her loss, they found themselves quarrelling and singing and carrying on as they always did, her still little figure causing them little discomfort.

The next outburst was when, having been washed and brushed and put into the best dress Mrs Meadows had fetched from Mrs Quinn, she was led by the hand by Mrs Meadows to her own home. She went, compliant as dove and it was not until she was pushed gently towards the parlour door that it became clear to her confused mind that she was not only expected to enter the room and look at her pa in his coffin but to kiss him goodbye. She could see the magnificence of its gleaming woodwork as it lay on a draped table, the handles of what looked like gold, a sort of white frill all around its edge and just showing over the edge of the frill her pa's face on a pillow. Well, not all his face, just his forehead and his nose, and the curl of long, dark lashes of one eye. He looked as though he were asleep and for a moment joy raced through her but then it went again, for what would her pa be doing lying in a box on the parlour table if he was alive.

"Go and kiss your pa goodbye, sweetheart," Mrs Meadows said to her kindly, ready to sniffle, for it was all so sad. A lovely chap like him being cut down in his prime and his wife quite out of her mind, Mrs Quinn, who dared not take her eyes off her, had told her. The neighbours were taking turns to sit with her to give poor Mrs Quinn a chance to rest, but how long was it going to be before she could see to her own daughter? And there was the funeral to be got through yet! She gave Lily a gentle push.

Lily began to struggle, digging her heels into the carpet and pushing backwards against Mrs Meadows's skirt. Her hands flailed like the sails of a windmill and she began to scream, a thin scream like a rabbit in a trap.

"No, no . . . no, I won't. I won't. Pa, please, Pa, don't let them make me. No . . . no." Her body jerked and Mrs Meadows turned to whoever it was who stood supportively in the hall, her face uncertain and working with compassion. Poor little mite, they couldn't make her, could they? it asked. It was the custom for all friends, relatives and indeed anyone who knew the deceased to come and view the body, say goodbye, so to speak, but the child was ready to throw a fit.

"Go and fetch Mrs Quinn," she hissed, since it seemed she was losing control and perhaps the woman who had practically brought up Lily Elliott might be able to calm her.

From that moment it was as though she had re-entered the world, finding it full of such pain and sorrow she could hardly function but knowing she must. She sobbed for hours on Mrs Quinn's knee while one of the neighbours sat with the comatose widow and Mrs Quinn shushed her and petted her and kissed her until she fell asleep when she was undressed and put into her own bed. The easiest part was over now, at least for Lily, Molly Quinn knew that, for hadn't she suffered it when Seamus died. At first there is the numb, senseless lack of anything that could be called grief, then, when the realisation comes that you would never, in this world, see the person you loved again, a despairing pain that tore at you until it was unbearable. That stayed. That moved about with you wherever you went. That slept with you in your bed at night and was there waiting for you when you woke in the morning and this child would feel it, for she had loved her pa more than anyone in the world. But Lily Elliott was stubborn, strong, courageous and she would make it to the other side, as Molly Quinn had done. She was not so sure about Jane Elliott.

The funeral was lovely, they all agreed, since the whole neighbourhood turned out to follow the magnificent hearse to St Mary's Church where the service was to take place. Four black horses pulled it, plumes nodding, their coats with such a polish on them Lily wondered if Mrs Quinn had been out to them with her duster. On the coffin was a wreath of white flowers; Lily didn't know what they were or who had chosen them, for it was certain it had not been her mother. The doctor had been again that morning and Jane Elliott, under the influence of whatever it was he had given her, was as pale and calm as a lily. Mrs Quinn had dressed her in the appropriate black and draped her in a veil that covered her from the crown of her bonnet to her knees. She sat when told, stood when told, walked when told and, when told, climbed serenely into the carriage that followed the hearse. Mrs Quinn sat beside her, holding her hand lest the draught the doctor had given her wore off and God alone knew what she would do if she came to herself. Lily sat on Mrs Quinn's other side and stared numbly at the hearse within which her pa lay in his coffin and wished someone would hold her hand lest she slip away into some black place where no one would ever reach her again.

The Reverend Campbell met the hearse at the tiny arched gateway, watching gravely as the coffin was lifted out on to the shoulders of four men who turned out to be Mr Flanagan, Mr Porter, Johnno, and Mick, the last three crew of the *Lily-Jane*, and for a blessed moment Lily felt a tiny spasm of gladness, for her pa would have liked to think that he was to go to his last resting place carried by the seamen with whom he had sailed the waters. Johnno's face was awash with tears, for it was for him that Captain Elliott had died.

Inside the church Lily heard words spoken and her pa's name but she seemed to exist for the moment in a bubble of merciful silence which allowed her to keep a good grip on the realisation that her pa would soon be gone for ever. She huddled up to Mrs Quinn and though her heart felt as though it had a spear in it she took comfort from the closeness of the woman who had been, she knew it now, her one sure support all her life. Ma and Pa had always loved her, she knew that, but they had loved one another more and it had been only the scraps and crumbs of that love and caring that had been given to her. But Mrs Quinn, though she was not demonstrative and was downright blunt at times, had simply been there whenever some small crisis had turned up that Lily couldn't resolve on her own. She had never let Lily down, it was as simple as that and even now she was paying Lily the compliment of believing that she was strong enough to bear her loss with dignity. And so she would.

Her mother sat on Mrs Quinn's other side, her eyes on her husband's coffin but it was evident she was not really aware of where she was, or who she was, or even who was in the coffin. She rose obediently when Mrs Quinn told her and went with her out into the cold December drizzle that had begun to fall and it was not until she stood beside the open black grave in which her husband's coffin had just been lowered that she began to tremble. A handful of soil had been pressed into her black-gloved palm and Mrs Quinn was doing her best to persuade her to drop it on the coffin and it was then that she began to struggle. Not to get away but to fling herself into the grave. She began to weep loudly, throwing herself about in a frenzy and it was all Mrs Quinn and Bert Meadows, who stood nearby and had been pushed forward by his wife, could do to stop her downward spiral on to the coffin. Her voice pierced the reverent hush as she cursed fluently, loudly, harshly, furiously on the whim of fate that had taken from her the one complete, unchangeable love of her life.

It was over in thirty seconds, then she lapsed into the quiet hushed world where she was to stay for the rest of her life.

Lily watched her dispassionately, knowing with awful certainty that her mother would never be a woman again and that she would never be a child.

5

"Mrs Quinn."

"Yes?"

"D'you happen to know what happened to my pa's schooner?"

Molly Quinn turned to look at the child at the breakfast table, her hands stilled at their task of slicing bread, and for a moment she was startled by the intense expression on Lily's face. Poor little beggar. What in heaven's name was going through her head now? She'd been like a small ghost creeping round the house, saying little to anyone, grieving in silence for her pa who had been dead these six weeks now. Her ma was of no use to her at all, for her grief had sent her into another world where Molly was certain she searched for her husband who, if she couldn't have with her in hers she was eager to join in his. That was why Molly had to keep her under her eye all the time, even at night when she slept in a little truckle bed beside that of Jane Elliott. She hadn't been home to her place in Brooke Alley in all this time except to check that everything was all right but that had been for no more than a hurried hour while Mrs Meadows or Mrs Watson sat with Mrs Elliott. The trouble was, they didn't care for it, and they told her straight. She was no trouble, really, but she was so totally silent, not just speechless but as though she weren't there at all, her breast scarcely rising as she breathed. In fact Mrs Meadows said she gave her a terrible scare since she'd thought she'd stopped altogether. A house of mourning, but not the usual kind of mourning that afflicts a family where the shock wears off and life returns to normal. This was odd, creepy almost and it was the child she felt sorry for. She wondered what she was on about now.

She answered in what she thought was a comforting tone. "Nay, lass, I couldn't say burr I'm sure someone's lookin' after it."

"She."

"Yer what?"

"You always call boats 'she', Mrs Quinn, not 'it'."

"Yer don't say. Well, I still don't know, lass, an' that's a fact."

"Who d'you think could tell me, Mrs Quinn? You see, I'm worried about her."

"Her?"

Lily sighed and tried not to look too exasperated by Mrs Quinn's total lack of understanding of the jargon of the sea. She couldn't be blamed, poor thing, for though she was Liverpool born and bred, like Lily, she hadn't had much to do with the docks and the shipping that sailed in and out on every tide.

"The *Lily-Jane*, Mrs Quinn. My pa's schooner. It won't do her much good being tied up all this time at her berth." A look of excitement crossed her pale little face. "Unless Mr Porter's been taking her out. D'you think he might, Mrs Quinn?"

"Eeh, I don't know, child."

"Who d'you think would be the best person to ask, Mrs Quinn? If I was to go down to the docks, to the berth at Canning where she usually is, d'you think I might find out?"

"I couldn't say, lass. Wharrabout Mr Meadows? Don't 'e work at docks? 'Appen 'e'd know."

"What a good idea, Mrs Quinn. I'll go at once and ask him." Lily slipped down from her chair and immediately Villy stood up, ready to go with her wherever it might be, but Mrs Quinn had other ideas.

"No, yer don't, madam. Yer've ter be at school in 'alf an 'our an' beside, Mr Meadows will have long gone ter work."

The expression of bright alertness, which had been sadly lacking in the weeks since her pa's death, left Lily's face and she sighed deeply. The dog pushed her cold nose sympathetically into her hand, her devoted gaze turned up to say she fully understood, for hadn't they all been sad ever since the master had failed to return but surely it would do no harm to go out and have a game of ball or something to cheer themselves up.

"See, 'ere's a jug of 'ot water. You'd best go an' wash yer

'ands an' face, child, an' don't forget yer neck. Oh, an' say tara ter yer ma while yer up there. She's awake."

Was she though? Lily asked herself, her face screwed up into the worried, unchildlike expression that was becoming more and more habitual as the weeks passed. Carefully carrying the pretty, rose-painted jug, she trudged up the stairs, Villy at her heels, for Mrs Quinn had become much more lenient since Pa's death and even allowed the dog to sleep in Lily's room. Villy sat and watched her as she washed her face and hands in the bowl that matched the jug, pondering on the state of her ma and when she would be herself again. Even when she was not asleep was her ma awake and with them? She didn't think so. It was becoming more and more apparent with every passing day that Ma would never be any different. She and Pa had been the two halves of a whole and when Pa went Ma could not seem to function without that part of her that had been Pa. She sometimes seemed to know who she, Lily, was, and even spoke to her, asking how she was doing at school but Lily knew she was not really listening to the answers. Ma allowed herself to be hugged and kissed, not knowing, not caring really, Lily thought, how much Lily longed to be held on her lap and comforted. Lily wanted to talk about Pa, to ask Ma if she remembered this or that, the trip they had taken to the Clyde in Scotland, the jokes Pa made and his laughter, the puzzles he set them, all the lovely things that had made up the man her pa had been. It would keep him alive in some strange way if she and Ma could share the memories both of them had of him, but she was afraid to mention his name again. She had done it once. She had told Ma she would like to go down to the docks to see Pa's ship and would Ma come with her, at the time not realising how deep was the affliction her ma had suffered. She had been frightened when Ma had turned, very slowly, to stare at her, her eyes so dreadful Lily thought she had completely lost her mind. They were wide and blank, as though Ma didn't know her at all and was wondering what this stranger was doing in her bedroom, then she had opened her mouth wide and out of it had come some appalling sound, like an animal caught in a trap from which there is no escape. Mrs Quinn had come running and she had given Ma some of the medicine the doctor had left for her, indicating with an abrupt toss of her head that Lily was to leave the room. Lily hadn't spoken of Pa since.

She rubbed the slippery, lavender-scented soap between her hands, squeezing small bubbles through her fingers, wondering where these strange thoughts she had came from. She had always known that Ma and Pa were special, to each other and to her, but now, with Pa's death, she had begun to feel that not only was Pa dead, but so was her ma. She had wondered idly whether Ma knew what was to happen to the *Lily-Jane* but it seemed unlikely and, naturally, she could not bring herself to ask her, not after the last episode. There had been no one near them since the funeral except the neighbours, of course, and none of them would know. She supposed she could try Mr Meadows as Mrs Quinn had suggested, but he was a wheelwright. Nothing to do with actual ships though he was involved with the waggons that worked on the dock. He might know, she supposed, reaching for the fluffy towel that was draped on the rail beside the washstand.

"I think I'm going to have to find out for myself, Villy," she told the dog, who cocked her head enquiringly. "If you want a job doing properly, do it yourself, as Mrs Quinn says, and this is important. I want to know who's going to look after the *Lily-Jane* until I'm old enough, you see, though I don't know who's going to teach me now that Pa's gone, do you? Perhaps Mr Porter, or maybe I could persuade Ma to let me go to one of those schools like the Mechanics Institute where they teach navigation, astronomy and naval architecture." She sighed deeply, since she did not hold out much hope of that happening. It was such a long time before she would be considered old enough to go to sea and what was going to happen to Pa's ship until then?

She was allowed to walk to school on her own now. Or rather Mrs Quinn had no option but to let her, for Mrs Elliott couldn't be left, not just yet and the Goodwin School for Young Ladies was only at the bottom end of Walton Lane where it joined Everton Valley.

Grace and Evie were waiting for her at her gate, dressed in the plain brown calf-length dresses and elastic-sided boots, black, of course, their mothers thought suitable for school. Their skirts were fully gathered and calf-length, and beneath them six inches of modestly frilled pantaloon showed. Over this outfit they wore a simple pinafore, fastened at the back, frilled over the shoulders and a warm, hooded cape in a sensible navy blue.

Not so Lily Elliott. Her mother had laughed at the very idea of her daughter, who was so like herself, wearing such hideous garments and Lily was dressed in lavender blue velvet, apple green muslin, blossom pink shantung and primrose voile which was a very fine wool. In winter she wore a scarlet cloak of velvet lined with dove grey wool and a hood of white rabbit fur and in summer a dashing little jacket like the ones soldiers wore. She even had one trimmed with fur. She had a wide straw leghorn hat that tipped over her eyes and had long streamers of ribbons at the back, and pretty poke bonnets, the brims lined with white lace. She wore grey kid boots with stockings to match her dress, or boots made of coloured cloth with shiny leather toecaps and heels, frilled petticoats and pantaloons. All totally unsuitable, of course, for a child of ten, as her headmistress often remarked to the other teachers, but what could she do when Mrs Elliott insisted upon it and was so punctual with the not inconsiderable fees that were demanded. Lily was the envy of every girl in the school, though to tell the truth she would much rather have been wearing a pair of sea boots, a cap and a sailor's gansey! Today she was in her outdoor costume of misty blue, the jacket trimmed with buttons and cross-bands of velvet of a deeper blue. The full, gathered skirt reached the top of her kid boots and as it swung a fraction of lace petticoat showed above her lace-trimmed pantaloons.

When they reached the school gate Grace and Evie were flabbergasted when Lily coolly told them that she was not going to school today and if anyone asked they were to say she was not well.

"We can't do that, Lil," Evie quavered. "You know you have to have a note from your mother," then fell silent, remembering the state of Lily's mother.

"You could say you'd lost it."

"What, tell a lie?" Grace answered primly.

"It wouldn't be the first time, Grace Watson, and I'm sure it won't be the last. Go on. I'll . . . I'll make it worth your while."

"How?"

"Well, what have I got that you want? Whatever it is, you can have it."

"There's your new fur muff and bonnet that you got for Christmas."

Lily's face became stiff and her eyes frosty. "My pa bought me that before he ... died. You know I can't give you that. Besides, your ma would notice," even if mine didn't, her manner implied.

"Well, that's all I want."

"You can want, then, because you're not getting it. I'll do this on my own."

"Do what?" Both girls edged closer to her, their eyes enormous in their fresh pink faces. "Where you going?"

"Never you mind. If you can't help me then you can go to hell for all I care."

"Lily Elliott!" they both gasped, then stood and watched her in awed disbelief as she stepped out in the direction of the town. Her head was high and her back straight and as she walked her long, silvery plait, so thick and heavy it lifted her chin, bounced vigorously between her shoulder blades. To be honest she was alarmed at her own daring, but there seemed to be no other way of easing the worry that had been plaguing her for weeks now. As she had said more than once, if you wanted something doing right, do it yourself, so she was.

It was a long walk down the length of Kirkdale Road, New Scotland Road, Scotland Road, Byrom Street and into Dale Street which led to Water Street and George's Dock. The *Lily-Jane* was usually tied up at Canning Dock Basin and this was where she was headed. It took her a long time to get there, for there was so much to see on the walk that she found herself stopping at every street corner. Naturally she had seen organ grinders before, and street musicians, hawkers, knife sharpeners and dancing bears, monkeys that jigged and dogs that did a polka on their hind legs but always from the hansom cab in which she rode with Ma and Pa, and she found her steps slowing continually as she stared at close quarters at the performers, human and animal. A blind man with a penny whistle pierced the air with a hauntingly sweet tune and round the hurdy-gurdy man, whose music vied with the penny whistler, a dozen ragged children danced in bare, calloused feet. She could have clapped her hands and joined them, it looked such fun but it soon became obvious that she herself was an object of their curiosity and she thought it might be wise to move on.

It was a grey February day, with a raw wind coming off the river but it in no way hindered Lily's enjoyment of this unexpected day out. It was a serious errand she was on, of course, but really, could you fail to have your heart lifted with joyful intoxication when your spirit rushed to meet the energy and vitality and noise which were all her young heart dreamed of? As she always did, and she had been here many times with her pa, she marvelled at the surge of humanity which sang and whistled and sawed and hammered on every spare bit of space on the docks. There were enormous men who carried bundles as big as themselves on their brawny shoulders, tipping them with ease on to waiting waggons. There were men with huge hammers striking blow after blow on some metal object, the sound of which made her head ring and she wondered why they stopped to stare as she went by them. They took off their caps and scratched their heads and muttered to one another.

"Good morning," she called out to them, enjoying herself for the first time since Pa died.

"Mornin'," they answered hesitantly, watching her as she tripped along towards the bridge that would take her into Canning Dock Basin. The river was a crowded highway carrying ships in and out of the estuary and she stood for a while watching them, dwelling on where they were going to and where they were coming from. She drew great breaths of the salty sea air into her lungs, turning her head to catch the sluggish breeze that carried it to her.

Her attention was caught by a great, almost totally silent crowd of people who were patiently waiting on the dockside. A uniformed policeman accompanied by a dock official in a peaked cap surveyed them, as though prepared to subdue any sign of the trouble that sometimes happened among these crowded and emotional farewells. Not that there seemed to be a spark of anything that might be called energy in this crowd. They were a mixed group, ladies and gentlemen, some of them, the ladies in elegant skirts edged with braid and wearing what was known as a "jacket-bodice", over which was worn a velvet-fringed, pelerine mantlet. Their bonnets tipped over their foreheads and were attached to a snood, or net, to hold their hair tidily, presumably for when they got aboard where the wind would be frolicsome. The gentlemen were stern, with long drooping moustaches, a wide-awake hat of felt and long greatcoats. But these passengers were rare, keeping themselves to themselves, for the rest of the crowd were of the working classes, shod in boots and gaiters, rough check trousers, ill-cut jackets, caps and mufflers. The women were in shawls, most of them with an infant tied into it and several poorly clad children at their rough skirts. The children grizzled fretfully and the women looked worn and haggard as though they hadn't had a square meal for a month. These would be steerage passengers, Lily decided, envying them even that; there was nothing she would like more than to be going with them, for she knew nothing of the perils of the high seas, among them disease and shipboard fever which often claimed more lives than accident or shipwreck. They sat about on boxes and crates, waiting to be told where they were to go which, it seemed to Lily, must be on the steamship that was berthed there. It had a name painted on its bow, the SS *Canadian*, and was to go to St John's in Newfoundland and Halifax, Nova Scotia, a passing dock labourer told her, obviously staggered to be accosted by such a pretty, daintily dressed child, looking round him as though to search out where she belonged. Newfoundland! Nova Scotia! The very names were exciting and she envied with all her heart these people who were to steam to these magical places. Mind you, she wouldn't care to go by steam. No, she would take the *Lily-Jane* and let the wind fill her sails, making her fly across the Atlantic Ocean until they came to the great Canadian seaports.

There were orange sellers moving about the crowds, cap merchants, Everton toffee sellers, vendors of ribbons and lace, nuts and gingerbread, ready to swarm all over the deck of the ship until the very last moment of departure. A man began to play a flute and as if it were a signal the women started to weep and, seeing their mothers in tears, the children joined in. It was a haunting little melody, one that Lily did not know and she found her own heart straining with sorrow, thinking of her pa who had gone and was never to return, as these people were going never to return.

She watched it all, unable to drag herself away until every last passenger was aboard and with a sudden lamenting wail from the women, as though they knew this was their last sight of everything that was familiar, the ship shuddered and began to pull away from the dock, edging into the river with a couple of little tugboats to assist her. Lily watched her sliding away into the February chill and mist, moving the silvery grey waters before her until, at last, she disappeared into the murk.

Lily sighed, then, finding to her surprise that her cheeks were wet with tears, she wiped them away and turned to the reason she had come here.

She knew every inch of the way. She had approached the docks down Water Street, walking along the strand until she reached George's Dock, cutting through a narrow passage at the side of the transit sheds and idling along the dock road which was intersected by railway lines. She had studied every ship tied up in George's Dock, all of them sailing ships and had been tempted to walk on into Strand Street to do the same at Canning Dock, but she had wasted enough time and must get to the other side of the bridge. By now it would have been discovered that she was not where she should be at school and Miss Goodwin would no doubt have contacted her ma. Or at least Mrs Quinn. There would be a great flurry of questions and answers, with poor Grace and Evie, who were known to be her particular friends, probably in tears and it was not their fault. She knew she should not be here, not by herself, but then none of them knew she had come. Nevertheless they would still be in a tear wondering what had happened to her. She must find out about the *Lily-Jane*, perhaps have a word with Mr Porter if he was around and then get right home before Mrs Quinn caused a commotion that might upset her ma.

Briskly she walked between the high walls of the warehouses, dodging the wheels of a portable crane which was lifting some heavy articles of machinery on to a berthed schooner. For a joyous moment she thought it might be the *Lily-Jane* but as she drew closer to the water's edge she saw the ship was called *Elvira*.

There were men discharging a cargo with a hand winch, neatly stacking bales of what smelled like coffee beans on to a waggon. The horse pulling it stood patiently between the shafts while from behind two more were being led by a couple of men, one astride the first horse's back, towards another waggon which was being got ready to receive a cargo of packing cases. A dog sat by a stack of crates, yawning and idly scratching itself, giving her a friendly wag of its tangled tail as she passed. A man shouted something, she didn't know what, or to whom but suddenly her arm was clutched savagely and she was lifted clear off the ground and thrown, there could be no other word for it, on to a pile of timber which stood waist-high to her left. Her hat fell over her eyes and her skirts flew up over her head so that she was temporarily blinded which made it worse and when she finally and indignantly disentangled herself she was more than ready to give a piece of her mind to whoever it was who had manhandled her.

Whoever it was spoke first.

"Yer wanner watch where yer walkin', queen, or there'll be a nasty accident. Didn't yer see them 'orses? One crack wi' one o' them feet'd knock yer senseless. I dunno what yer were thinking of, wanderin' around wi' yer 'ead in th'air. Any road, what's a lass like you doin' 'ere? It's norra place fer the likes o' you."

"Excuse me," she interrupted him tartly, "that is nothing to do with you and I'd be much obliged if you would lift me down and let me get on. I really haven't time to stop and talk—"

"Talk! I'm not talkin' ter yer, queen, I'm tellin' yer to go on back ter yer ma. This is no place fer a little lass like you. I can't think what yer pa's thinking on."

"My pa is dead."

"Oh, well, I'm sorry to 'ear that burrit mekks no difference. Yer shouldn't be 'ere. It's dangerous at best o' times but fer a girl like yersen . . ."

"Oh," she said airily, standing up in readiness to be lifted down, "I'm quite used to the docks. I've been here many times."

"Is tha' so?"

The man who had lifted her on to the pile of timber, apparently out of harm's way, or so he seemed to be telling her, had a face the colour of amber and in it his eyes were the palest blue she had ever seen, just as though years in the sun had bleached the colour out of them. He was a big man, heavy in the shoulders and chest, and his hands were quite enormous. He made no attempt to lift her down and their faces were almost on a level, for he was tall. His hair was like the colour of the corn that grew in the field opposite her house. He was dressed in the casual gansey, drill trousers, sea boots and a peaked cap like the one Mr Porter wore and she knew he was a sailor.

"Well," he said. "Are yer gonner tell me what yer up to?"

He smiled into her face, his hands on the stacked timber, one on either side of her so that she could not get down. She was not frightened of him though.

"That's my business," she told him haughtily.

"Is tha' so? Well, yer'd best mekk it *my* business an' all or I'm fetchin' 't nearest copper. If yer up ter no good it'd best be reported." But there was a gleam in his eye that told her he didn't really mean it, not about the copper. With a lithe jump he was up beside her, seating himself and then inviting her to do the same, with their legs dangling over the edge of the stacked timber.

"Yer a lovely little lass, queen, an' them duds yer've gorron . . . well, I've never seen the like, but yer 'adn't oughter be wanderin' round 'ere on yer own. Where yer from?"

"Well . . . you'll promise not to fetch the copper?"

"Right, if yer'll tell me wha' yer doin' 'ere an' then let me tekk yer back ter where yer belong. Me name's Liam, by't way. Liam O'Connor."

Gravely she turned and put out her hand. "How do you do, Mr O'Connor." He smiled and took it, swallowing it up in his own enormous one.

"An' what's your name, child?"

"Lily Elliott."

"Well, I'll call yer Lily if you'll call me Liam."

Lily was intensely gratified. She had never addressed a grownup by their christian name before and somehow it made her feel very grown up herself. Her face glowed into an enchanting smile and her silvery grey eyes turned at once into what was almost lavender. The man caught his breath, for he had never met anyone quite like her. She was as exquisite as a dainty bit of a flower, her name very appropriate, for she was like the wild lily of the valley which grew in the woods around his home in West Derby, or a piece of lace, the sort his grandmother made and which was as fine as gossamer. But what the devil was such a child doing here on these rough docks where men swore and relieved themselves with no thought for any of the niceties a child like this would be used to?

"Right then, Lily, now p'raps yer'll tell me wha' yer up to?"

She sighed deeply, gazing with those astonishing lavender grey eyes, which had become cloudy with some deep-felt emotion, at the dog that had now come to sit at their feet as though hoping for a titbit. She shook her head and her hat, which she had replaced to its correct position, bobbed precariously.

"I'm looking for the *Lily-Jane*. She's a schooner and—"

"Aye, lass, I know 'er. Lovely little ship, she is, an' I'd be glad ter sail in her meself."

"Would you, Liam?" She nearly knocked him off his perch with the brilliance of her smile.

"I would tha', Lily. Tidiest little schooner this side o't channel."

"Oh, isn't she, that's why I must find her. D'you happen to know where she's berthed, Liam? I would be so grateful."

"Eeh, Lily, she's not 'ere any more."

"Not here?" Her face paled dramatically, then cleared as a thought occurred to her. "Has Mr Porter taken her out then?"

"Nay, lass, I don't know owt about a Mr Porter. I only know Mr Crowther took her a few weeks back."

"Who's . . . who's Mr Crowther?"

"He's her owner, lass."

6

Mrs Quinn had been afraid she would hurt herself, or if not herself, her ma, and had it not been for the big man who brought her home, she would not have managed.

The cab had drawn up at the front door just as Mrs Watson was saying she thought Mrs Quinn had better send for the police. Lily had been missing for five hours. God only knew where she might have got to, or into whose hands she had fallen. Mrs Watson shuddered dramatically, for they had nothing to go on but the statements made by her Grace and Evie Meadows. Lily had walked to school with them as usual, the girls told them, then she had calmly announced she wasn't going in and asked them to lie for her to Miss Goodwin. Naturally, they wouldn't, Grace told them self-righteously, and it was not until the register was called and Lily was found to be missing, with no explanation of why, that she had told Miss Goodwin what Lily had told them. They had been brought home, both Grace and Evie, Evie in a flood of tears, for she could not be comforted, nor reassured that Lily was bound to be found soon, and was thought to be better off at home. Naturally, Mrs Elliott could not be consulted, Mrs Quinn made that very plain to Miss Goodwin, since her health had been very delicate ever since Captain Elliott had died, but she would let Miss Goodwin know the moment that Lily came home. Mrs Quinn had a fair idea where she might have gone, of course, particularly after the discussion they had had only this morning about Captain Elliott's boat.

They had a terrible shock when the child burst in on them, closely followed by an enormous man who was a total stranger. Mrs Watson was seated at Mrs Quinn's table in Mrs Quinn's kitchen, which was how they had both come to think of her place in the Elliott household since the captain had gone. Not that Mrs Quinn would presume to take over if Mrs Elliott were any different. If she came downstairs, for instance, or showed some renewed sign of interest in the affairs of her own home, which she didn't. It had become a sort of habit for Mrs Watson to take a cup of tea with Mrs Quinn on most days. Mrs Quinn was glad of her company since it was a bit of a humdrum sort of life with no one to talk to but a mindless woman and a ten-year-old child. Mrs Elliott had once been a sweet-natured lass with a good sense of humour, ready for a bit of a gossip as long as it was not offensive or likely to hurt anyone. And when the captain was home the house had been filled with laughter and music, since Mrs Elliott played the piano, encouraging him and the child to sing. The house had rung with "Are You Going to Scarborough Fair?", "Cockles and Mussels" and "Greensleeves"; noisy, cheerful, a lovely place to work but now it was like a bloody morgue and though she knew it was not quite right to invite Mrs Watson in to a house which was not, strictly speaking, hers, she was right glad of a bit of ordinary conversation. She was not a garrulous woman. She did not fraternise with anyone back at Brooke Alley but she missed the general bustle, the noise, the whistling and even the cursing, and it was not the same when Victoria, Mary or Alice came here to Walton Lane, which they were now forced to do on their days off. It was as though there were someone with a dread, even fatal illness upstairs and the girls felt the need to speak in whispers almost. They drank a cup of tea with her and told her what had been happening in the kitchens of the grand houses in which they were employed, but she noticed they always appeared to be glad to get away and could you blame them? They were young, attractive girls with their daddy's colouring, lively, and on their day off did not really want to sit in what they obviously felt to be a house of mourning, which it was. Well, there was nothing to be done about it, not until Mrs Elliott picked up, and Molly Quinn was sadly aware that that was very unlikely.

When the back door burst open they both gaped at the child as she erupted into the kitchen. Her face was the colour of dough, and her eyes were huge and glittering. Mrs Quinn had been about to put on her coat and slip down to the police station on St Domingo Road to tell them of Lily's disappearance and her belief that she would be found at Canning Dock Basin where her pa's boat was supposed to be moored, leaving Mrs Watson to hold the fort, and for a moment she stood there, her right arm in one sleeve, the other behind her back. The dog, frightened by the sudden clatter, since she had been peacefully sleeping on the mat before the kitchen range, sprang to her feet and began to bark hysterically and when, a second or two later, the big man came through the door, his hat in his hand, his face working with some emotion neither of the women cared to recognise, it was all they could do not to scream out loud.

"Dear God in heaven." Mrs Watson rolled her eyes in the direction of her own home next door, wondering if her Alf was back from work yet and if so could he get here in time to prevent all their throats being cut. She placed her hand on her heart, which threatened to stop beating but the man put out both hands in a placatory manner.

"I'm that sorry, ladies," he gasped. "I thought I 'ad 'er but she slipped out o' me 'ands like she were a little fish. She's that mad wi' 'er ma an'—"

"Oo the 'ell are you?" Mrs Quinn was beginning to say, ready to pick up a handy frying pan, for big as he was she'd clout him one if he proved dangerous, but the child began to yell, incomprehensible words bubbling from between her lips. Her face changed from mushroom white to a fiery red and spittle flew from her mouth in what seemed to be rage so hot and uncontrollable Mrs Watson stepped back out of range of it.

Words began to be recognised. "She's sold Pa's boat. I'll never forgive her . . . how could she? . . . knew how much I loved it . . . mine . . . mine. Pa would have wanted . . . for me . . . knew I loved the sea . . . and now what shall I do? I hate her, hate her . . . never speak to her again as long as I live. I loved the *Lily-Jane* . . . loved her. What shall I do? Oh, what shall I do?" she finished on a wail of torment. She jerked and trembled, her arms flinging about like a puppet whose puppeteer has lost control, her head snapping convulsively on her neck, her teeth beginning to chatter, and to the astonishment of the two women the man stepped forward and, with a sort of tender murmur, lifted her up and drew her into his arms. He held her to him, her arms about his neck, her face tucked beneath his chin, her cries of anguish muffled against his strong brown throat.

"There, lovebud, there, there. Yer mustn't tekk on so. I told yer in't cab there'd be a good reason an' yer've not 'eard yer ma's side yet. There'll be a decent explanation, you'll see. Yer must consider yer ma in this. What use would a schooner be to 'er? She'd 'ave no choice but ter sell 'er."

Without a by your leave, or even a glance at the two frozen-faced women, he sat down in what was considered to be Mrs Quinn's own special chair and, settling her on his lap, held Lily to him, brushing back her dishevelled hair from her flushed face with a big, gentle hand, and even kissing her forehead. She wept inconsolably, and once struggled to get away from him, declaring that she was going upstairs to tell her ma exactly what she thought of her, but the big man shushed her and patted her shoulder, quietening her until she lay still, hiccuping gently on to his chest.

It was then Mrs Quinn found her voice.

"Right then, we'll 'ave an explanation, if yer please, 'ooever yer are, an' I'd be obliged if yer'd 'and tha' there child over ter me. I don't know what the 'ell's bin goin' on 'ere burr I mean ter find out. See, purr 'er down an' get yer bum off my chair. Mrs Watson, run 'ome, if yer please, an' get yer 'usband ter fetch police, and you, Lily, come over 'ere."

The man looked up and smiled and really if she hadn't been a married woman Mrs Watson would have gone weak at the knees. She actually *did* go weak at the knees, for she'd never seen anything like it. His face sort of lit up, the eyes in it turning from the palest blue to an unbelievable violet just like those that grew in the woods on the far side of the front field. From round them fanned out deep creases which were duplicated in a slash down each side of his mouth. His teeth were a startling white against the sun-bronzed tint of his skin but it was the sense of good humour, of patience and yet strength, of easy-going tolerance which she knew would draw both men and women to him, and which was drawing her now, and she a married woman of thirty-five with two children. She had not thought him a handsome man when he had stood so alarmingly enormous in the doorway, but his male attraction was a tangible thing and one she could sense even Mrs Quinn felt. His hair was like corn silk, falling in an untidy tumble of short curls about his head. He continued to smile, a curious whimsical smile as though he knew this was a little out of the ordinary but he had a perfectly reasonable explanation which he was about to give them.

"Me name's Liam O'Connor, ladies, an' I 'ope you'll forgive this intrusion inter yer 'ome but I found this little lass down't by Canning Dock and I brought 'er 'ome. As yer can see, she were right upset an' I couldn't let 'er wander off an 'er own, could I? I reckon she'd be best in bed, wouldn't yer, lovebud," bending his head to Lily's feverish face. "She's 'ad a bad shock but she's calm now."

"I need . . . to ask . . . Ma why she . . . sold Pa's boat, Liam. Please, I need to ask her why she would . . . do such a thing . . . a cruel thing."

"No, yer don't. Yer need ter be in yer bed, that's where, an' this lady," bowing courteously in Mrs Quinn's fascinated direction, "will put yer there. Tomorrer'll do fer questions."

Lily sat up and stared tearfully into Liam's face, calmer now, but still inclined to tremble. He kept his arm about her, just like her pa used to do, Molly Quinn remembered thinking, as the child looked up at him earnestly.

"Will you come tomorrow, Liam, will you?"

"Nay, lass, I'm sure these ladies'll look after yer."

"No . . . no . . ." Her voice rose again dangerously and he shushed her gently, looking up apologetically to Molly Quinn and Lizzie Meadows. He gave a little shrug as though asking them what he should do. Though neither of them could have explained why, they both nodded acquiescently, trusting him. After he had gone they did their best to reason it out with one another but could come to no logical explanation as to why. He was a seafaring man, that was pretty evident, but they knew nothing about seafaring men, only Captain Elliott and this chap was nothing like that, but though they had never clapped eyes on him before, they found themselves agreeing that he should come tomorrow. The child was happy with that. Well, not exactly happy, for her devastation over the loss of her pa's boat so soon after the loss of her pa would be a sorrow she would carry for a long time, you could see that. Her narrow shoulders were slumped and her head bowed most pathetically as though she were being asked to shoulder a burden too heavy for her fragile strength. Poor little blighter. What was to happen to her?

She wanted Liam to carry her upstairs but he was firm with

her, telling her to be a good girl and go with Mrs Quinn, who had by now introduced herself, and promising to come back tomorrow. He didn't know what for, his helpless shrug and wry look told Mrs Quinn, but if it helped the child in her grief how could he refuse? That's if it was all right with Mrs Quinn, Lily must realise that, he told her. He was to sail tomorrow on the evening tide. No . . . no, they could not talk about that now. She must go to her bed this minute and tomorrow he would tell her all about the vessel he was to sail in, where she was to go and . . . yes, all right, when he would be in Liverpool again.

Without another word, she went, good as gold, believing him, trusting him, satisfied that he meant what he said.

She turned on the stairs as he watched her go, her hand in Mrs Quinn's. "What time will you come, Liam?" she asked him, her face tranquil for the moment.

"Well, I'm not sure . . ."

"Please, Liam, then I can look out for you. I shan't go to school, shall I, Mrs Quinn?" looking up resolutely into Mrs Quinn's face.

"Well, I don't know . . ."

She began to twist about on the stairs, the tranquillity gone and at once Liam O'Connor, recognising what was in her as no one else had, even Molly Quinn, smiled reassuringly.

"Will ten o'clock be too early?" looking enquiringly at Mrs Quinn.

Lily answered him. "No, come at nine if you want, Liam. Come for breakfast, if you like. He can, can't he, Mrs Quinn?"

"Well . . ."

"Please, Liam."

"No, lovebud, I can't. I'll be 'ere at ten. Now go on like a good little lass an' do as Mrs Quinn tells yer."

Mrs Quinn, who was not sure this perfect stranger, agreeable as he was, should be calling the captain's daughter "lovebud", frowned, then sighed, for if it helped the child to get over this second dreadful blow, did it matter? Who cared what happened to her now, except herself? And all that about the captain's boat being sold must be sorted out, for she knew for a fact, none better, that there had been no one to this house to discuss it, or even, now she came to think about it, to discuss *anything* to do with money. Surely a . . . a solicitor – was that right? – should have been round to talk about the captain's affairs and all the dozen and one things that needed to be discussed when someone died. Well, someone with property, that is, or money or something like that. It was six weeks now and the tin box on the kitchen mantelpiece, which the captain had called the "housekeeping box" and in which he left enough money to tide them over until he came home, was nearly empty. He had paid all the bills, she knew that, and Mrs Elliott had an allowance from which she bought her clothes and any personal thing she might need. She never went near the housekeeping box since she took no interest in the housekeeping, leaving it all to Molly Quinn who, she had said laughingly, knew far more about that kind of thing than she did.

Lily slept the clock round plus several hours and it was almost eight thirty when she woke. For a while she lay there, burrowing into the warmth of her bed, her eyes on the ceiling where shadows danced, created by the sunlight in the leaves of the beech tree outside the window. Villy slept curled up in a ball at her side and Lily put a hand out of the blankets to smooth her rough fur. The dog lifted her head at once and in her eyes was the look of devoted adoration she kept for her young mistress. It comforted Lily. No one loved her like Villy did. She supposed Ma still had some affection for her, deep down under the layers of suffering Pa's death had encased her in, but somehow, today, though she remembered that the *Lily-Jane* was no longer hers, for that was how she had thought of the schooner since Pa died, hers, she had the feeling that something nice was going to happen today. At once a pair of smiling blue eyes shone through the murk which her life had become and she sat up eagerly and swung her legs out of bed. Ten o'clock! He was to come at ten o'clock and for the first time since Pa died she would be able to talk about ships and all the things that had interested her to do with the docks and cargoes and ports and tides and every other fascinating subject which had been sadly lacking all these weeks. Liam was coming. Liam would be here for ten o'clock and she must be ready. She could hear Mrs Quinn talking to Ma in the next room while she coaxed her to wash and dress and she wondered if perhaps Ma might be persuaded to come downstairs to meet Liam; then, quite surprisingly, she decided she didn't want Ma to come downstairs and meet Liam, though for the life of her she couldn't have said why. Of course Ma wouldn't be interested in all the things that she and Liam would talk about, would she, so she would be much better off where she was.

She was hopping about at the window at nine thirty, driving Mrs Quinn to distraction, she said, and poking her nose against the window glass which Mrs Quinn had just cleaned wouldn't make him come any faster. Molly Quinn was having second thoughts about the advisability of letting a common seaman into the Elliott home, a common seaman they had none of them ever seen before. He might be a rogue or a bully or, worse, a despoiler of women, though he had brought the child home safely enough which many men would not have bothered to do. She had forgotten the effect Liam O'Connor had had on her and Mrs Watson yesterday or if she had not forgotten it she could not believe she had ever experienced it. She had forgotten the pleasing shape of his firm mouth, the brown smoothness of his shaved cheek and his odd, slanting smile that had so mesmerised them, and it was not until she saw him come striding down Walton Lane from the direction of town that it come flooding back to her. Lily was out of the parlour, across the shining black and white squares of the hallway and, flinging open the door, was halfway down the garden path and would, if she, Molly Quinn, not restrained her, have thrown herself into his arms. What on earth was the matter with the child? she asked herself in amazement, then fell, like Lily herself, under his·spell again. But "spell" was not really the right word to describe what he had, she decided, as he wished her a pleasant good morning. He was not a charmer, one of those men who set out coolly to please a woman. Whatever he had it was natural and though she was not a woman to take to strangers in the first moment of meeting, she'd taken to him. Though he was not a gentleman, far from it, he was gentleman*like*. That was the only way she could describe him. He had been polite with her and Mrs Watson, and firm with the child and though he might have taken advantage of what had been a strained and awkward situation, he had not done so. It was not his choice to be here this morning. In fact he had refused at first and it was only Lily's obvious distress that had brought him. A good heart then, and intelligent enough to know that he was out of place here, out of his depth really, with a little girl who had apparently taken him into her heart like a small kitten that needs a loving hand to comfort it.

"Come in, Liam. I've been waiting for you," Lily told him artlessly, her eyes enormous with excitement in her pale face, putting her small hand in his big one and drawing him into the parlour. "Mrs Quinn has made some scones and jam tarts. Won't you take off your coat and sit here by the fire. Mind, Villy, get out from under Liam's feet. She does love to lie almost in the hearth," she explained, "and if we didn't watch her she can get singed. Now I'll sit here," indicating a pouffe at Liam's feet from where she evidently thought she would get the best view of him. She smiled and put her elbows on her knees and her chin in her hands and waited for him to begin.

Liam O'Connor looked down into the lovely, expectant face of the child who apparently was waiting for him to divulge some stupendous news about the *Lily-Jane* and wondered how he was to tell her what he had been told yesterday afternoon. How was he to advise the woman in the kitchen, the housekeeper it seemed she was, and the child's mother, who he had not yet seen, what they should do now, and he wondered why he should feel so protective of this child who, this time yesterday, he had not even known existed.

"Now, Liam," Lily began gravely, "I want to know all about your life as a seaman, like where you are to sail to today, what's the name of your ship and what sort of ship is she? How long have you been at sea and where you learned to be a sailor and did you know that the only thing *I* ever wanted to do is to be a sailor? I meant to go with Pa . . . when I was old enough but now . . ."

She cleared her throat and blinked, determined not to weep, for she wanted him to know that she was not a child who cried for nothing. She must convince him that she was a sort of half-grown-up kind of girl who must be taken seriously.

Mrs Quinn came in with a tray and set it on the round, chenille-covered table, then poured out the tea, handing a cup to the big man and inviting him to try one of her scones. Today he wore a decent grey jacket over a spanking clean white shirt, a neat black tie, a waistcoat, also grey, and a pair of check woollen trousers in a mixture of greys and black. He had taken off his short overcoat and placed it on a chair. She noticed he wore no hat. He looked smart and clean, not exactly fashionable, for gentlemen today, real gentlemen, wore top hats and frock-coats, but he was very presentable. You knew he was a man from the labouring classes who had come up in the world, the way he spoke told her that, and she wondered how he had done it and what his position in life now was.

Liam O'Connor was twenty-one years old and was a self-educated man who could neither read nor write until, at the age of ten, he had made the decision that if he was to get anywhere in this world he could not do it if he was illiterate. He had gone wherever a bit of learning could be found. Mostly Sunday School, and once, when his grandmother, with whom he had then lived, had a few bob to spare, to the village school in West Derby. It didn't matter what it was, an old newspaper, a dog-eared racing journal, a page out of a magazine found wrapped about a piece of fish from the market, he pored over it, deciphering every word even if the word made no sense to him. Within a year he was being loaned books by the teacher at the Sunday School he attended in West Derby, simple, easy-to-read and understand books at first, but as he soaked it all up, everything he was told, and retained it, he was started on *Masterman Ready* by Captain Frederick Marryat, *Waverley* and *Ivanhoe* by Sir Walter Scott, all heady stuff to the young lad who had spent the first ten years of his life in total ignorance of what went on beyond the perimeter of West Derby.

He was employed by then as a dock labourer, since he was as big as a fully grown man and could do a man's job, but the ships, the river, the smell of the cargoes and the seamen's talk on the docks fascinated him as nothing had ever done before and he wanted to be part of it. The same Sunday School teacher, on learning of the boy's wish to go to sea, had enrolled him in evening classes at the Liverpool Mechanics Institute where he was taught the rudiments of navigation and seamanship and on 22 November 1844, at the age of thirteen, he signed an agreement with Captain Oliver Jenkins to become an apprentice seaman for a period of five years. The indenture was crowded with the activities he should not indulge in, which included frequenting taverns, the games of dice or cards or gambling of any kind, and in return Captain Jenkins would teach him the business of being a mariner, would feed him and give him medical or surgical aid should he need it and would pay him the sum of £30 for his five years of apprenticeship.

He was intelligent, shrewd, conscientious, hardworking, ambitious, tough, the latter essential in a world where young boys were thought to be fair game in the absence of women. His size was a great advantage. He learned to fight, dirty at times. He had to if he wanted to survive, and survive he did and at the age of twenty-one he had his Master's Certificate. He was now first mate on the British and North American packet ship *Caledonia* which carried the Royal Mail, sailing from Liverpool to Boston and on to Halifax. The *Caledonia* was a passenger ship sailing on the 3rd and the 18th of every month – unless these dates fell on a Sunday – and in the winter months, December, January, February and March, only one mail, that of the 3rd, was despatched.

It was 3 February today and if he was not on board within the next two hours he would be in trouble.

Lily listened with rapt attention, her eyes like huge saucers filled with floating stars, her rosy pink mouth dropping open in awe as he told her of his life and how he had got to the position he had and all the time he was wondering how he was to get Mrs Quinn on her own to give her the news that Captain Richard Elliott had been so heavily in debt when he died that the chances of his widow having any sort of an income were absolutely nil. Indeed, his informant had told him, she would soon be asked to leave this house if the rent was not immediately paid. Captain Elliott had paid it up to the end of January but there was a distinct possibility that the bailiffs would be in by the end of the week. The schooner had been taken as part of his debt, but it seemed there were others. Liam was aware now that there was something seriously wrong with Lily's mother, for why was she not here when her child needed her?

He sighed deeply and turned to Molly Quinn.

7

She had no choice but to take them to Brooke Alley. She had refused the loan Liam O'Connor had offered her, appalled at the thought of borrowing from a man she barely knew, and though he had begged her to take it, to "tide her over" until he got back from America, she declined so coolly he knew he had offended her. Of course, she had not known what was to happen then. He had been unable to persuade her and, having to get back to the *Caledonia* unless he wanted to lose his job, he had had to leave.

Lily had been white-faced and stunned when he left, though she had understood that he had no choice. For twenty-four hours it had been almost like having Pa back again, bringing with him all the vigour and excitement and the special feeling of rightness that anything to do with the dockland and the ships berthed there gave her. She did not wonder, like Liam O'Connor did, about what had drawn them together, for, with a child's acceptance of matters which might seem curious to an adult, it had not appeared at all strange. After all, he was a seafaring man, like Pa, and it seemed only natural to her that he and she were in accord about so many things pertaining to what was the most important thing in both their lives. Ships! She had his promise that the moment he docked he would come and visit her again and so she settled down to make the best of things until that day.

Mrs Quinn was upstairs with Ma when the front doorknocker rat-tatted noisily the following Saturday morning.

"Answer it, will you, lass?" Mrs Quinn shouted down the stairwell, her voice sounding somewhat strained, for she was having a more than difficult time persuading Jane Elliott to wash herself and dress in the gown Molly had laid out for her. Her mistress was sitting, as usual, in the rocking-chair which was where she spent most of her day, staring out of the window into the lane where children were playing, and not for the first time Molly came to the conclusion that she was still watching for the captain to come home. Not that she said anything. She answered when she was spoken to, questions like would she fancy a bit of fish for her tea, what gown should Molly put out for her, didn't she think it was a lovely day and what about a bit of a walk to the end of the lane? She was vague and slow, deliberating on what the correct answers should be, just as though she were dragging herself painfully back from the world in which she had dwelled in merciful oblivion for weeks now, turning her head with an almost perceptible creak to look at Molly, then, with a polite smile and bowing of her head she would agree with whatever was said. She refused to go out of the house, though, and Molly was inclined to think that it was because she was afraid the captain would come home and not find her there. She did make a bit of an effort when the child came up, agonisingly clearing her mind, doing her best to take an interest in what her daughter said to her but Molly knew she was thankful when Lily left the room and she could drift back to the vacuum in which she existed. Molly had hoped that with the passage of time she might pull herself together, which was how Molly saw it, and wake up to her responsibility for the little girl who, it was beginning to appear, had lost not only her pa, but her ma.

There were two men on the doorstep, big men with expressions on their faces that said they expected trouble wherever they went and were well qualified to deal with it. They seemed somewhat surprised to be faced with a small, beautifully dressed little girl, but, as though it were a routine they had developed, one of them put his foot in the door so that it could not be closed.

"Is yer mam in?" he asked her, his face as blank as an unused sheet of paper.

Lily looked from one stony face to the other and a small frisson of disquiet ran through her. There had been so many bad things happen to her recently that anything a bit out of the ordinary, which these two men were, alarmed her. Villy was at her feet, ready to dart at anything or anybody that might threaten her young mistress and for some reason her snout drew back over her teeth and she gave a warning growl. Lily didn't know what to say, how to answer the question, for though her ma *was* in, she wasn't really, was she?

"She's not well," she answered vaguely, hoping that that would satisfy them and they would go away but apparently it didn't. She didn't know who they were or why they were asking for Ma but she didn't like them.

They exchanged glances, then the one who seemed to be the spokesman spoke again.

"Oo's at 'ome, then?"

"Pardon?"

"Don't tell me yer lookin' after yer ma all on yer own, queen. There must be someone in charge, like."

"Well, Mrs Quinn is—"

"Right then, we'll 'ave a word wi' Mrs Quinn," and before she could even shout up the stairs to Mrs Quinn that there were two men to see her they were inside, pushing past her and the snarling dog with as much concern as though two little birds stood in their path. They looked about them in an assessing sort of way, fingering the velvet curtain that was pulled over the front door at night to keep out the draught, running a hand over her ma's walnut hallstand, even lifting out one of the half-dozen walking sticks that were kept in it. It had a silver handle and the shaft was made of ebonised wood. It was a handsome thing and had been much loved by her pa.

"Don't touch that," she snapped, unable to bear the sight of it in the rough, calloused hands of this big . . . well, she could only call him a lout and what he was doing here she couldn't imagine. "That belonged to my pa and he wouldn't like it if it was broken."

"I'm not about ter break it, queen, believe me. It belongs ter't courts now, or will do soon as we get this lot sorted out." The men smiled at one another in an unpleasant way, then moved on to run a speculative eye over the framed pictures that hung on the wall, the rug that ran down the centre of the hall, the ornaments that stood on a small, rectangular table and the barometer that her pa had tapped every day he was home.

"D'yer mind tellin' me what's goin' on 'ere?"

The voice at the top of the stairs startled them for a moment but they continued with their appraisal of the contents of the hall before answering in a kind of casual way that seemed to say they had every right to be here, which it seemed they had.

"Bailiffs, queen. Appointed by't court ter collect monies owed by a certain Captain Richard Elliott, deceased. Now, if yer can produce what's owin' we'll be on our way an' that's th' end of it. Burrif yer can't then we 'as ter take what's owin' in kind, if yer get me drift. An' then there's rent which is two weeks be'ind, which means yer've ter be out right away, burrif yer can settle up now – see, 'ere's what's owed – then we'll leave yer in peace."

He showed his big yellow teeth in what was supposed to be a smile, and so did his companion, not friendly smiles at all, Lily thought, a bit frightening really, and what he had said about Pa owing money couldn't be right and Mrs Quinn would tell him so.

Molly Quinn came slowly down the stairs and took Lily's hand in hers, holding it protectively against her white apron. She did not speak. What was there to say? She did not even look at the papers the bailiff held out to her, for she hadn't more than a few quid in the whole world and neither had Mrs Elliott. She had nothing but what these men could see and some nice pieces of jewellery which, the moment she had a chance, Molly's stunned but slowly recovering mind told her, she meant to hide in her corset, for there was nothing more certain than the fact that what she had dreaded, what had niggled at the back of her mind for weeks but which she had kept firmly there, was about to happen. She'd known for certain as soon as the big man had told them about the boat. That had been taken and now the home and all its contents which the Captain and Mrs Elliott had gathered about them over the past eleven years were to go too.

"Can yer pay up, Mrs Elliott?" one of the men asked patiently.

"I'm not Mrs Elliott. I'm housekeeper." Her voice was hollow, totally without expression and Lily looked up at her anxiously.

"We'd best see Mrs Elliott then, an' can we 'urry this up? We've other folk ter deal with."

"Other folk ter turn out inter't street, yer mean?"

"Well, yer could purrit like that but we 'ave a job ter do so if yer'd fetch Mrs Elliott I'd be obliged."

"She's . . . not well. She in 'er bed. Anythin' yer want ter say, say it ter me."

"Well, there's nowt ter say. It's the cash in me 'and or yer'd best pack yer bags and bugger off."

Lily gasped, looking from one man to the other, waiting for Mrs Quinn to give them a piece of her mind for swearing. She still could not understand what was going on. These men seemed to be threatening Mrs Quinn and instead of standing up for herself, which she always did if argued with, she was backing away and taking Lily with her.

"I've ter go an' see ter Mrs Elliott," she was saying. "She'll be wonderin' . . ."

"Go wi' 'er, Bert. There's no knowin' what trick she's up to. We know 'em all, lady, an' if yer think yer can put one over on us, then yer can think again. Yer not gerrin outer our sight."

"An' if *you* think I'm allowing two thugs like you inter a lady's bedroom yer sadly mistaken. Mrs Elliott's not yet gorrover the death of 'er 'usband an' is still under the doctor. God knows what might 'appen to 'er if I was to let yer in, so you do wha' yer come ter do an' leave us alone."

"We can't do that, lady. We're 'ere ter see the law's done right, which means recovering the deceased's goods an' chattels an' escortin' yer from't premises an' if yer purrup a fight we'll 'ave ter send for't scuffers."

"Please yerselves but yer not goin' inter Mrs Elliott. Norrif I 'ave ter knock yer down these bloody stairs meself."

All the time she was speaking Molly was moving slowly up the stairs, drawing Lily with her, step by slow step, and following her, still hesitant, for she was like a spitting she-cat, was one of the big men. The other had started in a leisurely fashion to take down the pictures, to roll up the mat, to gather the walking sticks, piling them on top of the hallstand. He had opened the front door preparatory to carrying them out, revealing a small crowd of interested neighbours on the pavement beyond the gate. Behind them was an empty cart pulled by a sturdy horse.

With one hand Lily clung to Mrs Quinn while the other had hold of Villy's collar. It was awkward going up the stairs backwards and she and Mrs Quinn kept catching their heels in the hems of their skirts. The sunlight falling through the coloured glass in the window at the turn of the stairs fell on the menacing face of the man following them, changing it from red to green and blue, but at the same time it seemed to blind him and when he put up his hand to shield his eyes Mrs Quinn whipped up the last few stairs, dragging Lily and the dog with her. Like a flash she was in her ma's bedroom and the door was locked behind her. Ma never even turned round.

"Quick, lamb," Mrs Quinn gasped, calling her again by that name which Lily knew meant she was highly agitated, "open yer ma's jewellery box an' purras much as yer can in the pocket of yer drawers." Lily gaped at her, for surely she had gone off her head, but Mrs Quinn grasped her roughly, spinning her round to her ma's dressing-table where the jewellery box stood. As she was speaking and tossing Lily about like a rag doll she was opening the front of her own modest bodice, pulling it out at the bottom from the band of her skirt. Her apron got in the way and with a muttered oath she tore it off.

"Don't stand there gawpin', lass. Quick . . . fer God's sake, be quick. See, stuff some down 'ere," indicating the top of her corsets which she was loosening with fumbling fingers. Lily had begun to shake in fright, for she had no idea what was wrong with Mrs Quinn. In a daze she did as she was told, thrusting rings and bracelets and a lovely collar of clear red stones into the pocket in her drawers where her handkerchief usually went. Mrs Quinn was doing the same, only into the top of her corsets, but when the jewellery box was empty she sort of had a fit, or so it seemed to Lily.

"Dear God, wharram I doin'?" she moaned. "They'll know if it's empty, that we've took 'em. Put some back, for Christ's sake," and with a swift movement, as the man began to hammer on the door, she flung a handful back into the box. She was muttering to herself as she did up her bodice and fastened her apron about her curiously swollen figure. "If I'd known . . . if I'd just known I could've sorted 'em out. Dear God in 'eaven, go an' sit wi' yer ma an' say nowt . . . *nowt*, d'yer 'ear me, an' shut that bloody dog up, will yer or I'll chuck it outer t' winder."

Lily was past speech she was so terrified but she still had enough strength to pick up the frantically barking dog and go and sit on the bed beside her ma's chair, holding Villy's muzzle in an attempt to quieten her. By now Jane Elliott was turning blankly in her chair, a terrible wariness creasing her smooth face. The hammering continued, and with one last smoothing of her apron and her hair, Mrs Quinn moved in a dignified manner across the bedroom and unlocked the door, opening it so suddenly the man almost fell inside.

"What the 'ell d'yer think you're up to?" He glared about him, his gaze falling on the beautiful woman whose blank eyes, like pools of grey water in a mist, were fixed on his.

"Yer didn't think I'd let yer come in Mrs Elliott's bedroom an' 'er still undressed, did yer?" Mrs Quinn said to him icily. "Fer the sake o' decency I 'ad ter gerrer dressed. Now, if yer don't mind I'd be glad if yer'd gerron wi' it, wharrever it is yer've come ter do, an' lerrus get packed. I presume we can tekk a few clothes wi' us, or 'ave we ter go in our pinnies?"

"Well, I were told ter tekk everything what could be carried but . . . well . . ." He was staring as though mesmerised at the elegantly gowned woman in the chair. Molly had not had time to put up her hair into the neat bun which was all she could manage, for she was not a lady's maid, and it hung about her face and shoulders and down her back in a curtain of pale, silver gold. Her strange and fragile loveliness quietened even his ferocious need to be getting on with his job. You had to be tough doing what he did, not letting sentiment or pity get in the way and for the most part it didn't bother him overmuch. After years of turning out women and children and what little was left of the rubbish most of them had, he had become immune to it, but this woman, who looked like an angel from some far-off heaven he personally did not believe in, gave him the creeps and that was a fact. She didn't look all there, to tell the truth and the quicker this job was finished and done with the better. There were some nice bits in here that he and Bert might secrete on their persons and if that jewel box had anything in it, all the better.

He managed to tear himself away from the woman's blind gaze, striding over to the dressing-table and opening the box. He lifted out the few rings and a brooch or two that were all Molly had been able to get back into it, then grunted in satisfaction.

"Right, missis, pack yer things an' tekk yerselves off. An' yer'd best 'and over't keys afore yer go."

He nodded civilly in Jane Elliott's direction then clomped off downstairs to see how Bert was getting on.

Lily, who had been sitting in stunned silence beside her

mother, felt something begin to come alive and grow in her. The events of the last half-hour had sent her into a shocked state that had taken her speech and even her sharp mind, and she had dragged along at Mrs Quinn's skirt since she had not known what else to do. She had not understood what was happening, and even now it was not clear to her why these men were boldly helping themselves to Ma and Pa's things. She did know she did not like it and that was enough for the moment. Why didn't Mrs Quinn call for a policeman, or Mr Meadows? The man had said that Pa owed money but she wouldn't believe that, not her pa who had been the most honourable man in the world. There was a feeling of great resentment, anger even, welling up inside her when she remembered the way that man had handled Pa's walking stick, but mostly anger at the way her life had changed, had worsened, ever since the day Mr Porter had come to tell them that Pa had died. She didn't want to pack her things and leave the house in which she had been born and had lived all her life. She didn't want to do as Mrs Quinn said and obediently trot downstairs and place her bags by the front door in readiness for the cab that Mrs Quinn said was to take them somewhere else. She didn't *want* to go anywhere else. She liked it here. She wanted to stay where her memories of Pa were, where her friends were and anyway, Mrs Quinn was only the housekeeper and surely had no say in where she and her ma were to live.

She said so as she struggled downstairs with an overflowing basket.

"I don't want to go to live anywhere else, Mrs Quinn, thank you very much. I like it here and this is where Ma and I will stay. I'm sure it's very kind of you to—"

"Don't be daft, child, we've no choice," Mrs Quinn answered flatly, pushing her to one side as she hefted Ma's trunk on to the front step.

"Well, you may have no choice, but we have. I'll look after Ma until she's better but I would prefer to do it here, if it's all the same to you." She lifted her small chin, firmed her rosy lips and stared mutinously into Mrs Quinn's flustered face. Her own was a bright poppy red with her growing temper. For good measure she put her hands on her hips and took a stance in front of Ma's trunk.

Mrs Quinn sighed wearily. "Gerrout o' me way, queen,

there's a good lass. I've enough on me plate wi'out you kickin' up a fuss."

"Well, I'm sorry about that but we're not coming, me and Ma, and nothing you can say will change my mind. This is our home."

"Oh, give over, child, an' go an' fetch the rest o' yer things, an' yer'd best put that there dog on a lead an' fasten 'er ter't door 'andle. I don't want ter be lookin' for 'er at last minute."

"I don't think you heard me, Mrs Quinn." Lily's face had set into the obstinate mask of determination Mrs Quinn had seen before and she was aware that she really couldn't be bothered with it at the moment. She'd more than enough to see to without this little madam throwing tantrums.

"Yer'll do as yer told, lady, or yer'll feel t'back o' me 'and. See, run upstairs an' fetch—"

"I'm not going, Mrs Quinn, and as you are only my mother's housekeeper you can't make me. She's the one to say whether—"

Mrs Quinn had had enough. Really had enough. What with Mrs Elliott having to be forcibly removed from her chair and made to stand up in order to put her coat on, then led, resisting all the way, down the stairs, not to mention all that had gone before, she just felt like sitting down, throwing her apron over her head and having a damn good cry. But, of course, that was not Molly Quinn's way and she'd not let this little tinker – what on earth had got into her? she wondered in amazement – get the better of her. The child'd best learn right from the start who gave the orders, and who took them in the home that was to be theirs for the foreseeable future. God alone knew what was to happen to them but one day at a time she told herself steadfastly. But it was hard to think that she was to start all over again, or so it seemed, just like she had when Seamus died. This woman and this child dependent on Molly Quinn, but she'd done it once and, by God, she'd do it again.

First the child had to learn who was in charge.

"I think there's summat we'd best get straight before we go any further, young lady, an' that's that I'll say what's ter be done, or not ter be done, not yer ma. Until she's well enough ter look after 'erself an' you, then, I'm boss, see, an' you'll do as you're told, or else."

"Or else what?" Lily answered rudely, glaring at Mrs Quinn.

"I'll paddle yer bum, that's what."

"You wouldn't dare."

"An' 'oo's goin' ter stop me? Certainly not yer ma," glancing in the direction of the woman who was drifting about the hall with her head cocked in that way that had become so familiar and which seemed to say she was listening for something.

Lily wanted to kick Mrs Quinn. She wanted to kick and scream her frustration and anger and fear, but something in Mrs Quinn's face made her hesitate and before she had decided what she might do next there was a shout that the cab was here. Mrs Quinn took her arm, whisked her down the path and had her in the corner seat before she had time to say another word.

The worst part, or at the time what seemed the worst part, had been coaxing Jane Elliott to take her arm, walk through the front door, down the path and into the cab which Finn Flanagan had obligingly run to the corner to acquire for them.

"Where'll you go, Mrs Quinn?" her neighbours had asked her in turn as each had come to find out for themselves, not satisfied with second-hand news, what was happening in the Elliott household. They were agog with it, sorry for the widow, naturally, and the silently defiant child who didn't seem to know what time of day it was, let alone what was happening to her. Mrs Watson had helped Mrs Quinn to pack as much as she could into a lady's basket trunk, covered in dull canvas and bound with black leather and belonging to Mrs Elliott, a leather portmanteau belonging to the captain and several sturdy baskets for the child's clothes. The bailiff, or "bum-bailiff" as Bert Meadows contemptuously called him, watched every item of clothing being packed, only objecting when Molly tried to cram in Mrs Elliott's furs, since they would be easy to sell, which was what Molly had intended. The house seemed to be heaving with people, though in fact it was only Mrs Watson, Mrs Meadows and her husband who had offered to heft the luggage on his brawny shoulders from the house to the cab.

Mrs Watson cried as they did their best to persuade Mrs Elliott that she really must get into the cab and it was not until she had somehow got it into her head that she was going to meet Richard, which she had often done in a hansom, that she allowed herself to be tucked in beside her daughter.

How would Mrs Elliott manage, Mrs Meadows begged Mrs Watson to tell her, her the picture of charm and elegance, in the basement cellar from which Mrs Quinn had come ten years ago? Brooke Alley off the Vauxhall Road and they all knew where that was, and though they were perfectly sure Mrs Quinn's place would be like a new pin, what about the rest of the slum-dwellers with whom she would be surrounded? What on earth was to become of them, the lovely woman and child who would be as out of place as fragile violets on a dung heap? And how was Mrs Quinn, who would be called on to support and protect them both, to cope with it? Dear God, it didn't bear thinking about, they told one another as they went sadly up their own garden paths, to their own warm and comfortable kitchens. The captain and his wife had been a bit above them in the way of things but they'd been grand people and lovely neighbours and they'd be sadly missed.

Grace and Evie stood in the lane and watched the hansom cab until it turned the corner and disappeared from view.

"Never mind, Evie," Grace said kindly to her friend, who was crying as she always did at any sadness. "We'll see Lily at school, won't we, Ma?" to her mother's back as she walked up the path.

"I doubt that, chuck. The school fees'll be too much for the likes of Mrs Elliott now, I reckon."

"Well, we can go and play with her, can't we, Ma?"

Mrs Watson turned on her daughter with a force that made the child take a hasty step backwards.

"No, you cannot. I'll not have you going into that part of the town under any circumstances, d'you hear me? Slums, that's what they are in that quarter and no child of mine is going to mix with slum kids, so think on. Lily Elliott's lost to us now. Eeh, chuck, I'm sorry," as Grace began to cry as pitifully as Evie. "I know Lily was your friend but she's going to another world, child, and not one you're ever likely to see."

It *was* another world and even Jane Elliott seemed to become vaguely aware that she was in a place she did not know, or like. The cab ride down Kirkdale Road and into New Scotland Road had not been so bad. It was when the vehicle turned down Portland Street and into Vauxhall Road that Lily shrank back into the corner of the cab, seeing for the first time what she had not even known existed. The place seemed to be swarming with half-naked children, so coated with grey filth it was difficult to determine their sex. Slatternly women lolled on doorsteps watching the cab go by, while the children ran after it, screaming words Lily could not understand, and inside the cab Villy began to bark her head off. There were old women, dressed like mummies, sprawling in the gutter and young girls holding out their hands to every passing male. Dogs quarrelled over bits of rubbish and a crippled youth sat huddled up against a wall holding a painted board on his knees on which was painted a ghastly picture. It seemed to represent a human figure caught up in some appalling, whirling machinery. Next to him was another man, cadaverous as a corpse with a filthy bandage about his brow. His sign read: *I have had no food for three days. My wife and children are dying*.

The arrival of the hansom cab caused a sensation at the end of Brooke Alley and the cab driver almost flung them and their baggage into the overflowing gutter that ran down its centre in his eagerness to be rid of them and get away to more salubrious quarters. It appeared that every dweller in the tall, teeming houses that lined the narrow alley had got wind of their arrival and they were all outside to greet them. Unemployed and apathetic men in caps and mufflers leaning their shoulders on the walls, women in shawls nursing puny babies, whining toddlers, yelling children who were so undernourished they appeared not to have a yell in them, barking dogs and slinking cats. A man came out of small building in the centre of the courtyard ahead of them, casually buttoning his trousers, apparently unaware of the slimy ooze which crept about his feet.

"Come along in, lass," Mrs Quinn told her in mock cheerfulness, appearing not to be at all dismayed by the state of things. "'Old yer ma's 'and while I get this lot in. Afternoon, Mrs Maloney," she called out, nodding to an old woman on the opposite step while Jane and Lily Elliott held their breath so as not to taste the appalling stench that filled the alley, their nostrils, their head and lungs and to which they were to become so accustomed they did not even notice it.

8

The first setback, and there were many, occurred on the day
they arrived at Brooke Alley, when Mrs Quinn slipped down
to the shop on the corner to buy something for their supper.
She had nothing in her cupboard except stuff that would keep,
sugar, flour, tea, candles and things like that, and if they were
to have a meal, which of course they must, though she had
never felt less like eating in her life, she told herself – since
there was no one else interested – the child needed something
inside her.

Their faces were quite blank. She had become used to Mrs
Elliott looking as though the life had been snuffed out of her
but just at that moment the child was an exact miniature of
her mother. The same strange sense that she was somewhere
else and not here in Molly's dim and dusty basement room.
The same fragile beauty, the same massed tumble of pale
silken hair and ivory, rose-tinted skin, the same velvet grey
eyes surrounded by long, drooping lashes, the same softly
tremulous rosy lips, but where, before this devastation had
come upon them, Lily had been bright and lively, with vivid
life in her face and brilliance in her eyes, now she was as
lifeless as her mother. They sat side by side where she had
put them at the table, their hands folded in their laps, their
eyes looking at nothing, both stunned, especially the child,
by the disaster that had overtaken them.

It was searingly cold in the basement room. It was several
weeks since Molly had been home and there had been no
fire lit in the meantime. That was the first thing to be done
and it was clear she would get no help from these two.
Not that she expected it, for neither of them had ever lit
a fire in their lives and even if one of them offered to

help, which was unlikely, it would be quicker to do it herself.

In no time a good fire was crackling cheerfully in the grate, putting a gleam in the slightly dusty surface of the blackleaded oven and casting flickering orange and gold and rose shadows on the white walls and ceiling. It touched their faces to a more healthy-looking hue and Molly saw Lily begin to glance about her with a faint glimmer of that interest anything new evokes in a child.

"Come up t't fire an' gerra warm," she invited them with as much cheerfulness as she could manage. "See, Mrs Elliott, tekk off yer cloak an' come an' set yerself in th' armchair," a rather resplendent piece of furniture which was Molly's pride and joy. It was a wing chair, upholstered in a plain wool fabric in a pretty pattern of flowers and birds and had carved walnut legs. She had picked it up in one of the markets many years ago when her finances had taken a turn for the better and though it had been badly worn, the stuffing hanging out in places, she had patiently patched it with scraps of material bought from the same market. The different shades where the patches had been sewn on in no way detracted from its attractiveness, but rather gave it the appearance of homely comfort, of being a much loved and cared-for part of Molly's home. The one opposite in which she placed the silent child was not as comfortable, the original old rocker she and Seamus had bought for a few pence when they were first married. There were cushions on it and at once Lily sank back in them and began to rock. The bewildered dog crouched at her feet.

Molly studied them for a moment or two. They seemed settled enough, she thought, both of them staring as though hypnotised into the fire, and with a bit of luck she might just be able to slip to Mrs Nelson's at the corner and get a bit of corned beef and a few potatoes for their supper. She'd be back before they noticed she'd gone. She'd need milk too, for the child, and a tin of chocolate, that's if Mrs Nelson stocked such a thing; if not it would have to be cocoa. She chewed her lip and frowned and wished one of her girls was here to keep an eye on things until she got back, but they weren't so that was that and she'd just have to get on with it best she could.

"I'm just goin' t't corner shop," she told them brightly, doing her best to act as though this situation was nothing out of the ordinary. "I'll not be more'n five minutes. I've put kettle on," which was beginning to hum in the centre of the fire, "an' when I get back we'll 'ave us a nice cuppa tea."

Neither of them answered her. She had not removed her own old but decent black cloak, nor her bonnet, and so, with another anxious look at her guests, she opened the door and climbed the steps into the alley.

"Got visitors then, Mrs Quinn?" a voice accosted her and she turned in irritation to the direction from which it had come. It was the old woman to whom she had spoken earlier.

"Aye, I 'ave, Mrs Maloney," she answered shortly, unwilling to elaborate, though she knew Mrs Maloney was longing to know who they were. She turned away, prepared to move on, since she'd no time for gossiping. She could see several slatternly women propping up the door frames of their homes, arms akimbo, their faces worn and old, though in years they were neither, getting ready to challenge her. It was not often something exciting happened in their lives and none of them had missed the arrival of the cab and the two angelic visions who had descended from it. They all knew that Mrs Quinn had a grand job up Walton way but what on earth was she doing here in this sordid world of theirs, bringing with her these creatures, the likes of which they had never before seen. They knew they existed, of course, in some fairytale world beyond their knowledge, for they had heard tell of them being seen in Bold Street where they shopped, so it was said, but they had never actually clapped eyes on one, and they couldn't wait for another sight of these two.

They had not to wait long.

Mrs Quinn was barely out of the door when Lily leaped from her chair and reached for her cloak, swinging it out and about her shoulders where it settled in swinging folds. She could hear some woman address Mrs Quinn but when she stood on a chair and peered out of the small window, the bottom half of which looked out on to the basement steps, the top into the alley, she was just in time to see her hurrying towards the corner.

"Quick, Ma, put your cloak back on and let's escape while we can," she said briskly, while she pulled her mother's mantle about her and buttoned it under her chin. "If Mrs Quinn thinks we're going to stop here she's sadly mistaken. We'll go down to the docks and ask for Liam. He should be in

port any day now and if he's not docked yet we'll go back to
Walton Lane and see if Mrs Watson or Mrs Meadows will take
us in until he comes." Her voice had been filled with optimism
but it dropped to a sad murmur as she twitched her mother's
cloak more warmly about her unresisting shoulders. "I know
we can't go back to our own house because I saw Mrs Quinn
give the keys to those awful men but we'll find somewhere to
live until Liam comes. He'll help us, I know he will. Now just
wait there a minute while I see if the coast is clear."

Jane Elliott stood obediently by the door, automatically
adjusting her bonnet which her daughter had jammed on
her head, while Lily popped her head above the level of the
area steps. The afternoon was almost at an end and though to
the west where the river placidly ran out to the bay the sun
still shone low in the sky, in this deep valley of decaying stone
and brick it was almost dusk. Children still played games but
with none of the energy Lily and her friends employed. Others
sat with their bare feet in the filthy, clogged water that ran in
the central gutter, splashing one another aimlessly. She had
got no more than a glimpse of them as she and Ma stepped
from the cab and were hurried down Mrs Quinn's area steps
and into her home and as Lily took her first good look at
them and the alley they played in, she was shocked by the
litter that lay about, by the dirty, ragged children themselves,
by the unkempt, uncombed appearance of the women who
leaned listlessly in their doorways. And what was that small
building in the centre of the court further up the alley from
which some dreadful noxious slime seemed to be seeping
and what was that appalling stench that made her want to
gag? There was a pile of rotting garbage against the far wall;
at least she thought that's what it was but it seemed to be
moving. She bit back a desire to scream and on top of that
a great need to get back into the warmth and safety of Mrs
Quinn's clean little room but she must be brave. Whatever it
was and whoever these people were they were nothing to do
with her and Ma and the quicker they got away from here the
better. She couldn't understand why Mrs Quinn had brought
them in the first place. She must have known that she and
Ma were not used to such places. Dear Lord, what *was* that
moving among the pile? It . . . it was an animal, a small animal,
a kitten perhaps and when a rat ran across the alley she almost
fell down the steps in her madness to get out of its way.

But they had to go, she and Ma. They couldn't stay here, could they, and if there were nasty things out there in the alley then they would just have to avert their eyes and hurry by. She'd best get Ma to hold her scented handkerchief to her nose until they got out into the better streets of the area. They would ignore the filth, the mud, the pools of stagnant water and what she was pretty certain was a dead cat and, leaving all their stuff since there was no way she could carry it, make for the river, and Liam.

They caused another sensation when they crept slowly up Mrs Quinn's area steps and moved out into the alley. Everyone in it froze and there was a deep and stunned silence. Lily had on her red velvet cloak. She had pulled the hood up in the hope that it might keep out the worst of the stink, and the fur edging it framed her face which peeped out like a pale flower. Her ma had on a deep blue woollen three-quarter-length mantle, shaped to the waist but flowing loose behind and under it her pale grey woollen dress soon had six inches of brown filth about its hem. Their dainty, pale kid boots skidded in the mess and Jane nearly fell and it was perhaps this that brought her momentarily to her senses.

"I want to go home, Lily," she moaned. "I don't like it here." Her already pale face took on the sheen and tint of bleached bone and her eyes widened to an incredible size in her terror. She clutched Lily's arm and when the noise started, the noise of men and women and children calling out in derision, for it is human nature to deride what is beyond their possessing, what is different to them, what they do not understand, she cowered away and began to babble senselessly.

"It's all right, Ma. There's not far to go and then we'll be out of this. We've only to get down to the docks and then Liam will help us," she said through gritted teeth, for by now she had convinced herself that the big man would be there.

Clinging to one another like two shipwrecked mariners in a storm-tossed sea, with Villy's nose almost attached to the heel of Lily's boot, they reached the end of the alley, but to her consternation she found their way was barred by what appeared to be a canal. Across the canal was some spare ground which was strewn with mouldering rubbish and bits of rusted machinery, of what sort she didn't know, and then beyond that was another narrow sheet of water across which a railway line ran. Towering over all this was a forbidding building with turrets and high walls which must be some sort of castle, Lily thought despairingly, not knowing that she was looking at the silhouette of the Borough Gaol. She could smell the sea now, the familiar smell of the river and the ships and their cargoes and see the gulls wheeling against the sky, but how was she get there, for there was no sign of a bridge and besides which, she thought Ma was about to faint. She was dragging Lily down and if she did how were they to get up again? She could feel her heart lurch in panic, for it was getting dark and if they didn't reach some sort of safety soon her instincts told her she and her ma would be in terrible danger. There was nothing for it but to go back and try to find another way out of this maze of horror into which they had descended. Oh, Pa . . . Pa, how are we to manage without you? What am I to do? Where am I to go? she begged in her ten-year-old terror. She could feel the tears gathering in a lump in her throat but she swallowed them resolutely and, lifting the almost dead weight of her mother, retraced her steps along the alley through which she and Ma had just dragged and when Mrs Quinn's voice demanded what the bloody hell she thought she was doing it was almost a relief.

"We're going home," she said defiantly. "If you would just show us the way."

"Home, is it? Well, Lily, you'd best get used ter the idea that fer the time bein' *this* is yer 'ome." There was no way but to be brutal. "Yer pa's gone an' left you an' yer ma in a birrof a pickle an' I'm th'only one yer've got to 'elp you out of it. Yer should just thank God we've a roof over our 'eads an' a bit o' food ter purrin our mouths fer there's many a family what 'asn't." Her face softened as she put her arms round the wilting figure of Jane Elliott and began to guide her feet back to Brooke Alley. "Yer only a lass," she went on, trying to take Lily's hand in hers but it was twitched angrily away, "an' yer don't understand."

"I understand that you are keeping us here against our will, Mrs Quinn. That's called kidnapping and you can go to prison for it." She was very near tears but she held her head high and clenched her jaw.

"Well, think wha' yer like, lass, but yer've no one but me an' yer'd best mekk most of it. What are you lot starin' at?" she demanded savagely of the crowd who had gathered to see the woman and the kid come back to them.

"Is it bloody Queen yer've got there, Mrs Quinn?" one called out mockingly. "Are yer to 'ave a tea party fer 'Er Majesty, cos if y'are I'm right willin' ter be a guest."

They hooted with laughter, those who heard the exchange, and began to crowd in on the trio as they approached Mrs Quinn's basement steps. They had always had a grudge against this neighbour of theirs, a feeling that she thought herself a cut above them, that she looked down on them in their abject misery. She kept herself to herself and was for ever fetching water from the standpipe, water which was just as available to them as it was to her but somehow they resented her use of it. She was for ever scrubbing and polishing and no matter how many times the kids scrawled on her whitewashed outside walls she continued to paint them again, so in the end they had given up and let her alone. Now they were vastly entertained by what she had brought into their world and were going to make the most of it.

"Gerrout o' my way," Mrs Quinn screeched, doing her best to force a way through the press of unwashed, foul-smelling bodies and at the same time trying to protect her two charges. The women meant no actual harm but they sensed a bit of "fun" with these two glorious creatures who, they supposed, were from where Mrs Quinn worked. They didn't know why they were here and didn't care really, but they had lost their usual apathy and listless acceptance of their lot and were intent on brightening up their lives with what promised to be a bit of unusual and welcome entertainment.

But they not reckoned on Lily Elliott who had stood up to Finn Flanagan and Jack and Charlie Meadows in the defence of the dog who pressed against her skirts. Villy was beginning to sense the danger and was prepared to stand up to it, as she was. She had trailed at their heels all the way down to the canal, her eyes following all the darting things that captured her attention, lifting her muzzle and growling in the back of her throat. When Lily stepped forward and elbowed aside a scraggy woman with a bundle which turned out to be a silent baby at her breast, then another who stood in her way, the dog snapped viciously and they stepped back hastily before she sank her teeth into their leg.

"Let my mother through," the beautiful little girl told them imperiously, "and get off Mrs Quinn's steps. This is a private area and if you don't remove yourselves I'll call for the police."

She tossed her head and her hood fell back. Her hair shone like silver gilt in the darkening alley and her eyes were translucent with anger, turning to the lavender grey which, if they had known it, meant trouble. "Come along, Mrs Quinn, take no notice of them," she said loftily. "Come along, Ma, mind the steps. Villy, it's all right now, you can stop snarling like a jungle beast," and while they watched in total disbelief she ushered Mrs Quinn and her ma through Mrs Quinn's door and out of their sight, slamming the door behind them. They were so astounded they let her do it without another word. One of the children threw a lump of something nasty at the window but by that time Mrs Quinn had the curtains drawn and it slid harmlessly off the glass.

They drank the hot milk she put in their hands, both of them shivering uncontrollably with the memory of the experience they had just gone through, even Lily who had seemed unafraid at the time. They changed into their nightgowns without a murmur, then snuggled down together in Mrs Quinn's bed, clutching one another and the stone hot-water bottle she had wrapped in a towel and thrust in between them. Villy lay at their feet, her nose on her paws, her eyes watchful, for it seemed she would need to be on guard in this place her beloved young mistress had brought her to.

Molly Quinn wept after they had fallen asleep, for this escapade – if you could call such a serious thing an escapade – of Lily's had brought home to her as nothing else had done the true reality of what was ahead of her. She wept, indulging herself, she knew that, as she crouched over her fire in her comfortable chair, but it would be for the last time, she told herself, wiping her eyes on the edge of her apron.

She had a cup of tea, washed the mug and was about to empty the teapot when a thought occurred to her and with all the care she had used in the old days when she had been so hard up she put the used tea leaves into a basin and covered them with a bit of cloth. They would stand a second brew, she told herself, knowing that until she had pulled herself together and decided on a course of action they would have to watch every penny and practise many little economies.

She pulled out the truckle bed in which one or other of her girls sometimes slept. Drawing it up to the fire she undressed in its warmth and pulled her voluminous nightgown over her head. Drawing the blankets about her she prepared herself for a sleepless night, but to her surprise she slept well and woke refreshed to start the first day of their new lives.

The next time Lily tried something on, she planned it more carefully. They had been at Mrs Quinn's for a fortnight and in that time had not once been outside the door, though Mrs Quinn made little forays to the corner shop for food. When she did that she locked them in!

"Why don't we have a walk down to the seafront, Mrs Quinn?" she asked artlessly. "We haven't had a breath of fresh air in all this time and I'm sure it would do Ma good," looking across the table to where her mother sat like a pale and lovely statuette. "Put a bit of colour in her cheeks, and perhaps give her an appetite." Jane Elliott picked at the nourishing food Molly prepared for her, not complaining but not eating much of it either. Her clothes hung on her slender figure and she had lost weight she could ill afford to lose. She no longer had the lovely breasts and rounded hips that had once been hers. She looked ethereal, insubstantial, as though the smallest breeze might have her over. Perhaps the child was right. Perhaps a smell of the sea and a saunter along the Marine Parade would do her good. Molly would keep a firm hold on her, for she herself was as strong as a horse and the child was not likely to run away and leave her ma behind, was she?

Jane took a bit of coaxing to get her up the steps and into the alley. Molly had kept an eye on it, waiting until it was empty of the slum-dwellers who lurked about there on a mild day.

"I don't think I care to go out today, Mrs Quinn."

"Now, lamb, it's just the day fer a walk. Only ter't river an' back. It'll do us all a birra good."

"I think I would prefer to stay by the fire and . . ." Jane seemed to cast about as though looking for something that desperately needed her attention but her empty mind could not remember what that might be.

"Nay, we'll wrap up warm an tekk dog fer a good run. She an't bin out fer a decent run fer weeks now," which was true.

There were no catcalls or interference today. It was cold with a bite in the air which kept the inhabitants of Brooke Alley indoors, huddled together under their few pitiful rags, but Molly's two were well wrapped up in the good winter clothes she had thought to pack. They'd come to no harm in the keen wind that blew off the river and even before they had got to the corner of Vauxhall Road and turned into Leeds Street which led down to Bath Street and Princess Dock – Lily memorising every step of the way – there was a faint flush of pink in Jane's cheek.

They were about to turn north in the direction of the Marine Parade when Lily suddenly darted away, the dog at her heels, in the opposite direction.

"I promise I won't be long, Mrs Quinn," she shouted over her shoulder as Mrs Quinn made to run after her. "God's honour, I'll not go far but I must just go and enquire for Liam and you and Ma would hold me up. Why don't you—"

"You come back, yer little divil," Molly screeched after her, afraid to leave go of Mrs Elliott, who might be frightened if Molly's strong arm was removed. "Come back, yer limb o' Satan, or I'll scorch yer drawers for yer." Her tone turned to one of pleading. "Lily, child, don't run off like that. Yer don't know 'oo might gerrold o' yer. Oh, please, child, come back." But she was shouting into the wind as the little, scarlet-cloaked figure disappeared across the lock gate bridge which barred Princes Dock Basin and headed towards the landing stage off Princes Parade. Mrs Elliott was beginning to show signs of distress, as though Mrs Quinn's raised voice of fear was disturbing the dreadfully shattered equilibrium of her mind. She had begun to pull away as though she were in the grip of a stranger and with a muttered oath Molly set her lips in a grim line and began to walk as fast as Jane would go in the direction Lily had taken.

The *Caledonia* had not yet reached port, an astonished gentleman in a uniform and a peaked and braided cap told her. He was obviously an official of the dockyard which was why Lily had picked on him. No, he couldn't say when, though he did admit she was expected on the 11th which was the day after tomorrow. There had been severe storms in the Atlantic which was unusual for this time of the year, he heard himself explaining to his own amazement to the exquisite child with the steady eyes who had accosted him.

"Anyroad, what d'yer want wi' the *Caledonia*, lass?" he asked her. "Is it a relative yer lookin' for?" beginning to glance about him for someone who might be in charge of her.

"No, a friend. Liam O'Connor he's called. He's first mate," she told him proudly, as though Liam's achievement had had something to do with her. "He's been to North America. I forgot to ask him what his cargo was, or what he was bringing back but I'm sure it's something important."

"I'm sure it is, chuck, burr I've gorra gerron, so if yer'll excuse me," for she was the sort of child, earnest and well mannered, who seemed to command his respect.

"Of course. I know how busy anyone who works on the docks must be. I do envy you."

"Oh, 'ow's that then?"

"Working here where the ships are." Her smile was dazzling and he was dazzled.

"Yer like ships then?"

"Oh, yes, my pa was a sea captain, you see."

"Retired, is 'e?"

"No." Her small face seemed to crumple. "He's dead."

"Well, I'm sorry to 'ear that, lass."

"Perhaps you knew him. He was the best sailor who ever sailed the oceans. His name was Captain Richard Elliott of the *Lily-Jane*."

His face broke into a smile and he leaned down to her. "So you're Captain Elliott's little lass, are yer? Aye, I knew Captain Elliott an' yer right, he were a good sailor. 'E knew 'ow ter 'andle a ship better'n any man outer this port."

Lily was enchanted and she looked up into the man's face as though he had just given down the word of God Himself.

"He did, didn't he?" she breathed, waiting for this man to say some other wonderful thing about her pa, but at that moment Mrs Quinn caught up with her and when the man turned at her high-pitched shriek, caused by fear, he was again knocked sideways by the amazing likeness of the child to the pale and lovely woman on her arm.

"It's all right, queen," he told Mrs Quinn soothingly. "She's only asking about some ship she's expectin'."

"God strewth, I'll give 'er lookin' fer ships when I gerr 'er 'ome. Yer frightened me ter death, Lily Elliott, runnin' away like tha'.

Mrs Quinn might not have spoken for all the notice Lily took of her. She was fishing about in the pocket of her cloak and with a triumphant air she produced a pencil and a piece of paper.

"Now, I've written my name and address – my *present* address – on this piece of paper, sir and I'd be obliged if you would do me a great favour and when the *Caledonia* docks . . . You will know, won't you?" she added anxiously and when the official said he would she smiled the smile that would warm any heart as she handed it to him. She curtseyed, showing off her very best manners and the man found himself returning her smile in what he knew was a daft and foolish manner as he watched her walk away with her hand in that of her mother.

"Liam will be here soon, Ma," he heard her say, "and everything will be all right then, you'll see."

9

"I've gorra find a job, chuck. I've sold all t' bits of 'er jewels. Not tha' I got much for 'em. I know nowt about such things an' I reckon that chap at shop did me. I couldn't argue, yer see, knowin' nowt, an' I were afraid if I kicked up a fuss 'e might start askin' me where I gorrem. Yer can see 'ow I'm placed burr unless I put pair of 'em in't work'ouse, wharrem I ter do?"

"Mam, wharrelse *can* yer do? They're not your responsibility. Oh, I know they've bin good to yer, the Elliotts, I mean, but at your age yer don't want ter be saddled wi' . . . well, look at 'em."

Molly and Victoria Quinn both turned to look at Jane Elliott and her daughter who were perched side by side on two chairs at the table. Jane Elliott might have been in the drawing-room of some lady from the gentry class, her simple gown of pale grey broadcloth falling from her tiny waist in symmetrical folds, her hair shining in the neat chignon Mrs Quinn had recently mastered, her face placid and her manners perfection. Her back was straight and yet graceful as she held a saucer in one hand and a cup in the other, sipping her tea in a ladylike manner, her eyes unfocused as she stared into some place no one else could see. A little to the right of her on the scrubbed deal table was a tray covered with a lace cloth on which delicate china was placed, a milk jug, a sugar bowl with silver tongs and a teapot, the china decorated with pale pink rosebuds. The child had a mug of something on the table before her and it steamed in the chilly air but she was not drinking. As she cut out the figures from what looked like a fashion magazine, her mouth opened and closed as the scissors did.

"An' where in 't name o' heaven did that lot come from?" Victoria went on, nodding at the tea tray. "Don't tell me yer fetched it from Walton Lane?"

Mrs Quinn turned a somewhat apologetic look on her daughter. "An' why not?" she said defiantly. "She's used ter nice things. I managed ter tuck it inter't child's little bag."

"Eeh, Mam, yer barmy, that's all I can say," her daughter told her in exasperation. "An' 'ow yer ter manage I don't know."

"Well, if I could get summat, I dunno, p'raps at laundry in Banastre Street, just until we gerron our feet, like, then—"

"Gerron yer feet! Mam, yer'll never earn enough ter keep three o' yer. On yer own yer could likely gerra job livin' in: 'ousekeeper or summat. P'raps doin' cleanin', norr 'eavy, burr enough ter put food in yer mouth. An' yer know me an' Mary an' Alice'll not see yer wi'out but wi' these two round yer neck, well, I know our Mary an' Alice'll not give their 'ard-earned wages ter support *them* an' neither will I. It's not fair, Mam. On you or on us. Yer do see that, don't yer?" Victoria leaned forward and put a hand on her mother's knee.

Molly sighed deeply, studying the pair at the table.

"Drink yer cocoa, child," she admonished Lily absently, "before it gets cold." Lily took no notice.

"Me mam ses yer ter drink yer cocoa, Lily." Victoria's voice was as cold and cutting as an icicle, since she was well aware that her mother had gone out specially to buy the milk and it infuriated her to see it go to waste.

"I don't want it," Lily answered haughtily. "It tastes funny. Not like the milk we get from the farm."

Victoria gasped. "Well, yer ungrateful little beggar. Yer want a good 'idin' an' if yer were mine yer'd gerrit."

"Well, I'm not yours, so there, and I'm glad. My mother and I didn't ask to come here, did we, Ma?" She did not wait for a reply since she did not expect one. "In fact, we want to go home, don't we, Ma?" She glared ferociously at Victoria, drawing down her eyebrows and screwing up her mouth into a tight bud.

"That'll do, Lily," Mrs Quinn said tartly, then turned to resume her conversation with her daughter, speaking quietly so that Lily wouldn't hear her.

"She's bin like tha' fer weeks now. She was expectin' some chap she met down at docks—"

Victoria gasped. "Some chap she met down at docks! Mam, what're yer sayin'?"

"Oh, don't be daft, our Victoria. It were nowt like tha'. 'E were a nice lad, big chap, 'oo brought 'er 'ome when she went lookin' fer 'er pa's ship. Ever since then she's bin expectin' 'im ter come an' . . . well, I dunno what she expects 'im ter do. Tekk 'er an' her ma back ter Walton Lane, I reckon. Anyroad, 'e never came an' she's bin a little bugger ever since. Cheeky, disobedient, and she were once the best-'earted little lass yer could ever wish ter meet. Well, you knew 'er in't th'old days," meaning when Captain Elliott had been alive and Mrs Elliott in her right mind. "Oh, I know she were lively an' liked, 'an got 'er own way but she were never nasty. She keeps wantin' ter go out an' look fer this chap burr I can't lerr 'er wander about, can I? God knows what'd become of 'er. When I go out ter't shops I 'ave ter lock 'em in. Yer can see wharr I mean, can't yer?"

They both turned again to look at Jane and Lily Elliott. The child and her mother were totally out of place in the dim basement cellar, for they both looked as though they had stepped out of the pages of the very fashion magazine from which Lily was cutting out figures. It was early April now and though the sunlight was laying a golden sheen on the river and polishing the windows and wet roofs of the buildings to copper, none of it reached into the chasms of tortuous alleyways and courtyards that laced the poorest parts of the Liverpool slums. The sun had a bit of warmth in it where it reached but here in the deep and rancid back streets it was damp, raw, bleak, even though a small fire burned in the grate of Molly's blackleaded oven. The oven was a handsome affair, the fire held in by iron bars, on one side a full oven and on the other a half-oven on which a kettle stood. Above the mantelpiece and down each side were numerous shining pans. Just below the mantelpiece was a brass rod on which items of underclothing were airing. There was a brass fender on which Molly and her daughter had their feet propped and along the mantelpiece were lined Molly's cheap but attractive ornaments. So far she had not been forced to sell any of *her* stuff but if something didn't change soon, and God knows what she meant by change, she would have to do something drastic, again not quite knowing what that might be. As Victoria said, she was too old now to do the hard, drudging work she had managed eleven years ago. Though she had been busy from morning till night in the house in Walton Lane, she had gone at her own pace. She had had it easy all these years, she admitted it, soft, luxurious even, for she had eaten the same food as the family, had a decent wage – the savings from which were almost gone – and had lived in a fair degree of comfort, there, and here in her own snug little place. She could only thank God she had kept it on, for only He knew where they would have ended up if they hadn't had Brooke Alley to come back to.

So how was she to find work that she could manage that would support her, Mrs Elliott and the child? And if she found it how was she to go off and leave a small girl and a mindless woman by themselves all day? God, she was worn out with the worry of it going round and round in her head, but there was one thing that remained clear and shining and steadfast within her and would always do so and that was that Jane Elliott and her child would not finish up in the poorhouse, no matter what their Victoria had to say about it.

"Is there nowt up at Silverdale ter suit me?" she asked her daughter diffidently. "You know me, I'm norr afraid o' 'ard work, scrubbin' or summat, an' if you was ter vouch fer me they might tekk me on," despite my age, she appeared to be saying. Her daughter worked as parlourmaid at Silverdale, the home of the Hemingways in Garston, a lovely old house set on the shore of the river in several acres of ornamental gardens and lawns sweeping down to the gliding water, the whole set about by a thick stand of trees. There were terraces leading in steps from the house, each one edged with flowers in due season. Molly knew this because one day, several months after their Victoria had been lucky enough to be taken on as skivvy there, Molly, holding their Mary – who was just about to go as scullery maid at High Cross, another grand house on the shore – by the hand, had walked along by the Pottery Shore, past Dingle Point and Jericho Shore, to stand on the little sandy beach that edged both properties. She and Mary had crept up between the trees, having been told all about it by Victoria, and had had a good scen up the slope where the roof of the house was just visible. They couldn't see the house itself, of course, which Victoria said was grand inside with wonders they could not even imagine, but it had given Mary, who was only ten and of a nervous disposition, some idea of what she might expect.

They had been lucky, the two sisters, working so close together, for it meant that if the servants above them gave them an hour off, not long enough to get home, of course, they could have a walk on the shore together which made it more comforting for the two lasses.

Victoria shook her head sadly, looking into the glowing coals of the fire. There was a pan of stew, scrag end of mutton with carrots, turnips, potatoes and barley, bubbling gently in it, the evening meal of the Elliotts and her mam, smelling delicious and making her mouth water. There was no doubt about it, Mam was a decent cook and could make one penny do the job of two. She had been a good housekeeper, as well, though she was sure the Elliotts had not realised it. Oh, she had been well thought of, she was aware of that, trusted and depended upon and what they'd have done without her, Victoria didn't know. And her loyalty to them, to the two at the table, was unbelievable. She was a strong woman, she and her sisters had always known that, for had it not been for her they might have ended up in one of the terrible situations children with their background got caught up in. Probably in the clutches of the workhouse keeper who would have sold them to some unscrupulous middle man who found children to work in the cotton mills of Lancashire. Mam needed work, decent work that was not too demanding, work that was suited to her many and excellent qualifications and where was she to find such a position and see to the pair at the table at the same time?

Her face was screwed up in thought and then, slowly, her face cleared and she turned to her mam. There was a hesitant look about her and she chewed her lip thoughtfully.

"Well . . ."

"What is it, chuck?" Molly leaned forward eagerly.

"We 'eard only yesterday the 'ousekeeper at Oakwood Place, yer know, the place between me an' our Mary's . . ."

"Aye." Molly hitched herself closer to her daughter so that they sat knee to knee.

"Well, she's givin' up. Retirin'. She must be seventy if she's a day, poor old soul, an' 'ow she's kept goin' all these years, I don't know. There bein' no mistress an' all. Mr Crowther's a widderman so 'appen 'e's not fussy. Men aren't, are they? An' the daughter's too young. Anyroad the groom there . . ." For a moment her face turned a rosy pink and she lowered her lashes, a gesture that would normally have set all Molly Quinn's maternal instincts quivering but she was too transfixed by what her daughter was hinting at even to notice.

"Wha' . . . wha'?"

"'E said they was goin' ter advertise fer a new 'ousekeeper. Now whether the old man'd consider yer, seeing as 'ow yer'd 'ave no references, like, I don't know. Well, she's not gonner give yer any, is she?" turning her gaze on Jane Elliott. "Though 'appen if I was ter 'ave a word wi' Mrs Taylor" – who was in charge of the kitchens at Silverdale where Victoria worked – "'oo's friendly wi' Mrs Jackson at Oakwood Place, she might purrin a word for yer. Knowin' yer were my mam, like, yer might 'ave a chance." Her face fell. "But then yer'd 'ave ter live in, so what yer'd do wi' these two, again I don't know. Eeh, Mam, it'd be ideal for yer if yer didn't 'ave them."

"You don't have to bother about me and Ma," a casual voice from the table said. "When Liam comes we'll go home, won't we, Ma? I don't know why we were forced to come to this horrid place at all."

Victoria turned in fury, her face livid, for did this bloody kid not understand what her presence here meant to her mother? Victoria's mother. If it wasn't for them she was pretty sure Mam could get this job at Oakwood Place as easy as falling off a log but there wasn't a hope of it as things were and she didn't really know why she had mentioned it in the first place.

"You shut yer gob, yer little madam. Yer know nowt about it an' why me mam keeps yer on 'ere, I'll never know."

"Me neither and if you'll just unlock that door, Mrs Quinn, we'll be off. You've no right keeping us prisoner here, has she, Ma?" turning for a moment to her mother. "There's no need to call us a cab, we'll walk," she added loftily. "I'm sure I can find the way to Walton Lane."

"Will you shurrup, yer daft little cow. 'Ave yer any idea—"

"Hush, Victoria. The child's bin through a lot an' doesn't know wha' she's sayin'."

"I don't give a damn about tha', Mam. I can't stand ter 'ear 'er talk like tha' after all you've done for 'er an' 'er mam. Listen 'ere, you," spinning round to face Lily who was still unconcernedly clipping away at the page of the magazine.

"This bloody mess me mam's in is your fault. No, I tell a lie, it's that pa o' yours 'oo's at fault. If 'e 'adn't chucked 'is money about like a man wi' no arms none o' this woulda 'appened. Borrowed it like there were no tomorrer, so I 'eard, no doubt buyin' yer mam all the fal-de-lals she tricked—"

"That's enough, our Victoria. Norr another word or I'll crack yer one, old as you are. It's no good shoutin' at lass, she's don't understand."

Lily was standing up by now, her face as red and bursting as a ripe tomato, her eyes glittering with venom, her fists clenched. She swung round the end of the table and stuck her face close to Victoria's.

"Don't you say things like that about my pa. He was a good man who loved us and he was honourable, and . . . and . . . decent and . . ."

"E'd a gone ter gaol if 'e'd lived," Victoria jeered, incensed past the stage where her usual good sense would have told her she was arguing with a child.

"How dare you . . . you . . . liar . . ."

Mrs Quinn stood up swiftly and before Lily could land one on the end of Victoria's nose, which she clearly intended to do, she pulled her into her arms and on to her lap. Lily struggled, her face like bleached bone now, but in her eyes was an appalling expression which said that though she didn't want to, she knew Victoria was telling the truth. Not that she would admit it, not to anyone, but her own common sense told her she and Ma would not be living here with Mrs Quinn if Pa had left them any money. Liam had said that Pa's boat had gone to pay a debt, which was a bit hard to understand but if Liam said it was so then it must be. She didn't know why Liam had not come in answer to her note, for it was long past the time for the *Caledonia*'s docking but he would come and if he didn't then she meant to go down to the docks to try to get to the bottom of it, that's if she could escape Mrs Quinn's vigilant eye. But she couldn't help but feel that . . . well, perhaps this awful Victoria girl might be telling the truth, about Pa, that is.

"I refuse to believe it," she hissed across the rag rug, almost spitting in Victoria's face, but Victoria was sorry now that she had lost her temper and her face had softened.

"I'm sorry, kid, I shouldn'ta said wharr I did about yer pa. My daddy died when I were a little kid burr I know 'e were a good man and anyone 'oo said different would a gorr a smack in't face from me."

"Really? I didn't know that." Lily leaned against Mrs Quinn's soft breast and felt better. It was nice to have someone's arms about her. It was nice to have someone who cared about her, which it seemed Mrs Quinn did, but really, when Victoria had gone she must have a good talk with Mrs Quinn about what was to happen to them. They couldn't go on hanging around here, could they? Somehow she must find the means to get herself and Ma back to Walton Lane and the house where they had all lived so happily. She wasn't sure how it might be accomplished. If they were very careful surely they could manage it, though again she didn't know how. If only Liam would come.

She was only half listening as Mrs Quinn and Victoria talked, making arrangements about something that seemed to concern Mrs Quinn getting a job somewhere. Perhaps she and Ma might do the same. Ma was so pretty and bright . . . well, she had used to be bright and would be again, Lily was sure, when she had recovered from Pa's death. She just needed a bit of time. She was good with her hands. Pa had always said she was good with her hands. She could knit the most beautiful jumpers, remembering the sea gansey which was packed in the straw basket behind the curtain, and her sewing was exquisite. She made all her own and Lily's undergarments, of the finest lawn and trimmed with lace, and her embroidery, done on the finest and most delicate of fabrics such as net and gauze and from her own design, was the most beautiful that Lily had ever seen. She had tried to teach Lily, just the simplest stitches like stem stitch and satin stitch but it had been hopeless. Lily wanted to be a sailor not a seamstress. She'd stitch sails if she had to, which sailors did, but not petticoats and pantaloons.

As though her thoughts, dreaming and insubstantial, had drifted on the cool, quiet air from her mind to her mother's, she suddenly spoke and they all turned, even the dog which lay before the grate, to look at her.

"Where is my sewing, Mrs Quinn?" she asked in what seemed to be a sensible voice. "I seem to have mislaid it. Do you happen to know where I left it?"

For a moment nobody spoke. It was the very first time she had addressed them without being addressed first. At other times she had hesitantly answered questions but this was different. This had come into her mind without prompting from them and Molly Quinn could feel her shoulders lifting and her back straightening as though a load had been lifted from it. There was no sewing, of course. Mrs Elliott had not done any sewing since the day the men came to tell her her husband was dead and whatever it was she had been doing was put away, or lost in the general upheaval of the day they had left Walton Lane.

But Molly Quinn's quick brain leaped to life and without thinking she put Lily from her and stood up.

"'Old on, I'll gerrit for yer, Mrs Elliott. I seen it somewhere . . . aah, yes, I know."

Both Lily and Victoria watched her with fascinated attention as she moved to the chest of drawers where she kept what little bed linen she had, all much patched but clean and still used, of course.

"Ah, yes, 'ere it is, my lamb." The endearment came from somewhere deep inside Molly Quinn, somewhere that was ready to weep with joy that this beloved woman appeared to have come back from the dead, so to speak. It was a start. It might not be much but it was a start and if Molly Quinn could keep it going, then she'd bloody well do it. She was to call her "my lamb", at least in private, for the remainder of their lives together.

She laid a folded sheet on the table. The Lord only knew where it had come from; she couldn't remember, probably the second-hand stall in Paddy's Market, but it was fine linen edged with lace. The lace was torn and the centre of the sheet was so thin you could have spat through it, in Mrs Quinn's parlance.

"Now you gerron with that, my lamb. You'll know better'n me what wants doin'. Middle ter edge, would yer say and then that lace needs a stitch or two."

"Indeed it does, Mrs Quinn. Now, if you'll hand me my sewing box I'll make a start."

Her sewing box! Dear God, what had become of her sewing box? But if Mrs Quinn's mind went cold and blank, Lily's didn't.

"It seems to be mislaid, Ma, but if Mrs Quinn gives you a needle and thread to be going on with, I'll have a look for it for you."

"Thank you, darling, that is kind of you."

Threading a needle with some hastily unearthed thread, Jane Elliott began to sew, her face tranquil.

It was two days later when the note came. It was delivered by a fresh-faced young lad in what could only be called "country" clothes. Well, it was country where he had come from, he told Lily later. He had taken exception to the jeers and whistles that had followed him through all the back streets and alleyways ever since he had left Chapel Street to venture into the maze of the dockland slums. He had been given precise instructions by Miss Quinn on how he was to get to her mother's house – if you could call it that, his freckled nose wrinkling in disgust. Follow the docks along the river, he had been told, along the Cast Iron Shore to Strand Street until he reached St Nicholas Church and he wasn't to stand gawping at the ships but to go straight there. At St Nicholas Church he was to turn right into Chapel Street to Key Street and Leeds Street and Brooke Alley was dead ahead of him. He was to put the note into Mrs Quinn's hand. Mrs Quinn was Miss Quinn's mother and this was a very important task. Very important indeed.

His rosy-cheeked face, his air of being well fed from the moment his infant mouth had fastened on his mam's nipple, his sturdy limbs, his sturdy boots and gaiters and corduroy breeches, his best jacket and peaked cap, come to him from his master's son who was grown up now, all gave him the look of a toff to the children he encountered and had he not been a lad who was handy with his fists, and with his tongue as well which gave as good as he got, he might have fared ill. As it was he was relieved to find the house, terrible though it seemed to his country-bred eyes, where Miss Quinn's mam apparently lived.

"Me name's Dick," he told the old lady who answered the door, "an' I've come from Silverdale. Miss Quinn gi' me this note an' I've ter wait for an answer. I work there," he added importantly.

He was quite flabbergasted when, on being asked to enter and sit himself down and would he fancy a fresh-baked scone, which of course he did, being a healthy lad with a healthy appetite, he found himself face to face with the most exquisite little girl he had ever come across in his life. She was sitting at the table writing on a bit of paper. He was impressed not only with her beauty and the way she was dressed but by the fact that she could write! Next to her, sewing on something, was a lady who was exactly like her, with silver hair and the softest smile just like the angel in Mam's picture which she directed right at him.

The girl didn't smile though. "Haven't you been told that it's rude to stare, boy," she said to him, without appearing even to look up from her writing.

"Now, Lily, haven't you been told it's rude to make personal remarks to people?"

"He's not people, Ma. He's only a boy."

Mrs Quinn, though her daughters could all read and write, thanks to her, could not and it was Lily who read the letter to her. It was from Victoria and in it she wrote that Mrs Jackson of Oakwood Place would be glad if Mrs Quinn would present herself for an interview for the post of cook/housekeeper on the following day.

"And Victoria says you've not to be late, Mrs Quinn."

"No, I realise that, child," Mrs Quinn answered absently, her mind twisting and turning on the problem of how she was to get from here to – where was it? – Oakwood Place, leaving Mrs Elliott and the child all on their own. It was only two days since Mrs Elliott had picked up her sewing again, stitching serenely from morning till night so that Molly wondered how she was going to keep her supplied with all the materials necessary, not to mention something actually to sew! She had finished the first sheet and was doing some fancy lace work round a pillowcase, but at the rate she was going that would soon be finished. All she could think of was that she would have to tear their clothes deliberately in order that Mrs Elliott could then mend them. She had been down to the pawnshop yesterday afternoon to see if there was a sewing box, complete with needles and threads and a thimble and had been in luck, though it had cost her the last of the savings she had put away for a rainy day. Good God, if it wasn't a rainy day now, when would it be!

"I'd best be gerrin back," the boy said uneasily, since he didn't fancy walking through these lurking streets after dark. He'd a long way to go, all the way to Silverdale and Miss Quinn would be waiting for an answer and would give him what for if he was late. He was the boot boy at Silverdale, not much of a job for a lad with his ambition, but he meant to get on and you had to start somewhere. His pa was a groom for Mr Hemingway and his mam helped with the laundry, but with a cottage filled with children of all ages from toddlers to himself who was the eldest at twelve, he was glad to be out of it and allowed to sleep above the stable with the grooms and stable hands.

Lily wrote the answer in her best handwriting, saying that Mrs Molly Quinn would be pleased to attend Mrs Jackson at Oakwood Place at the time stated, and after Dick had darted away down Brooke Alley all Molly had to do was rack her brains on the best way of going about it.

10

She took them with her in the end. Well, what else could she do? Mrs Elliott seemed calm enough, endlessly sewing on anything Molly put in her hands, simply sitting by the fire, or at the table with no thought in her head but putting in one tiny stitch after another, but Molly didn't trust the child and that was the truth of it. She could lock them in, of course, as she did when she went to the corner shop, but she had no idea how long she would be and she wouldn't put it past the little madam to break the window and climb out in her determination to go down to the docks and find that big chap. She appeared to be obsessed with him, positive that in him lay the answer to all the problems that plagued her and her ma. When he got back he would come. It was as certain as that and even the fact that they had been at Brooke Alley for going on eight weeks now and he had not turned up seemed to make no difference to her, and Molly was reluctant to burst the bubble of hope the child carried almost visibly around with her. It was as though he had taken her pa's place in her young mind and would find the perfect solution, as her pa had always done, for the continuation of Lily and her ma's life as it had been. Molly had even considered whether she might perhaps leave the pair of them with Mrs Meadows or Mrs Watson but something held her back. If Lily found herself back in Walton Lane among her friends she would expect to "play out" with them and Molly could not ask either of their previous neighbours to stand guard over her, or Mrs Elliott for that matter, and naturally there was no one in Brooke Alley who was even vaguely capable of watching over them.

"Are we going to Oakwood Place?" Lily asked her as Molly pulled her little jacket round her and fastened the many tiny gilt buttons that marched up the front to the high, military-style neck. It fitted snugly into her waist and was edged with midnight blue braid. With it she wore a full, gathered, midnight blue skirt which just reached the top of her black-buttoned kid boots. Below the hem hung half an inch of her petticoat which was edged with frilled lace. On her head was perched a jaunty pill-box hat, tilted above her forehead and secured beneath her chin with narrow velvet ribbon. Her thick silvery plait was looped under itself and secured with a knot of scarlet ribbons, for if it was left it hung below her waist. Afterwards Mrs Quinn was often to wonder why she had dressed the child, and her ma, in their best finery, for they were only to sit in the cab and wait for her!

"Ask me no questions an' I'll tell yer no lies," she replied tartly.

"Well, that's the silliest answer I've ever heard, and if you don't tell me I'm not going," Lily told her disdainfully, then her imperious expression changed to one of wild hope. "Is it to the docks? Have you heard that the *Caledonia* has moored? Is Liam coming, is he?"

"No, it isn't an' no, I 'aven't 'eard from him an' I wish yer'd give over worryin' about 'im. Chuck, 'e's got more to think about than . . . well, fer all we know 'e might 'ave a family, a wife an' children of 'is own an' e'll norr'ave time ter come 'ere. Yer know wharra seaman's life's like. In port one day an' out again the next nearly. Yer pa . . ."

But Lily didn't want to be reminded about her pa and she twitched herself away from Mrs Quinn's busy hands, her face mutinous, and Molly wondered despairingly what she was going to do with this lovely but increasingly naughty child who only last night had thrown Mrs Elliott's good china teacup at the wall, smashing it to pieces and making the blasted dog bark its silly head off. Lily had howled that she would go out, she would. She didn't care if all those horrid children outside called her names and threw lumps of shit . . . yes, she had screamed, that was what it was called, she had heard one say so. She'd run away and find Liam or Mr Meadows or Mr Watson or . . . or . . . Here she'd run out of people she knew. She had stamped her feet and wept bitter tears, saying she wanted her pa, so distraught she had upset Mrs Elliott who had begun to cry too. Lily had been sorry then and had hugged her ma and kissed her wet cheek but there was nothing her ma could say to comfort her, and neither could Molly, for the situation seemed hopeless. She couldn't keep them locked up here for much longer, even if it was for their own safety. This job would be a life-saver, if she got it, but then, if she did, what was she to do with these two while she was out? It was a huge dilemma; well, more than that, it was a bloody impossibility and she despaired of ever getting round it. It was her wildest hope that she might be able to persuade them at Oakwood Place to let her go home at night, that's if she got the job, though she didn't hold out much expectation of either: getting the job or of being allowed to live out. Housekeepers and cooks were often required to work until late, so she had heard. The gentry did a lot of entertaining, dinner parties and such and it was hardly likely they'd allow her to take off her pinny at six o'clock and tell them she was off home now, was it? Dear God, she'd finish up in an early grave, she knew she would if this thing wasn't resolved soon. In fact she was beginning to believe that their Victoria was right and that she'd have to put the pair of them into some place of safety, perhaps the Ladies of the Society for Bettering the Condition and Increasing the Comfort of the Poor might be able to guide her to the right place but it had better be soon or they'd all three starve.

Refusing to tell Lily or her ma where they were going, she led them through the stinking streets, beseeching them to hold up their skirts out of the filth, until they reached the corner where Vauxhall Road met Tithebarn Street. There was a hansom cab just discharging a passenger and with a fluttering heart and a dry mouth Molly put up her hand to get the cabbie's attention.

"Where to, ma'am?" he asked her politely, for it was very evident in his eyes that at least one of the females was a lady and the child her daughter. The woman who had hailed him must be the child's nanny, he had decided, or the lady's companion, for she was dressed in respectable black, a good quality cloak and bonnet, her boots well polished and her face well scrubbed.

He had seen a great many pretty ladies, real ladies, in his time but the one who climbed gracefully into his cab was a real head-turner. She was dressed in the palest duck egg blue with a skirt so wide she had the greatest difficulty manoeuvring it into the cab. It was flounced, each flounce edged with blue velvet. The bodice was slightly too large for her, he had time to notice as he handed her in, though it in no way detracted from her elegance and fragile beauty. Draped about her shoulders and hanging over her arms was a large cream shawl, fringed and very fine, embroidered with blue to match her dress, and on her incredible silver blonde hair was what was known as a cream straw "round-hat" – though he was not aware of its name – with a wide flexible brim and a low flat crown. It was mushroom-shaped and trimmed with pale duck egg blue ribbon round the crown with floating ends down her back. It was tied to her head with matching ribbons under her chin from beneath its brim. She carried a dainty drawstring reticule.

It was the woman in black who answered him.

"Oakwood Place on Holmes Lane. D'yer know it?"

"Can't say I do, ma'am, burrif yer was ter direct me I reckon I can find it."

"Are we going about the job, Mrs Quinn?" he heard the child say, but the woman hushed her and the child's mother seemed to drift off into some dream world of her own, taking no notice of the child, her companion or the route they were taking.

It was a Wednesday and as it was on any weekday the streets were bursting with pedestrians dodging smart carriages coming from and going to the fine shops in Bold Street where the wives of the wealthy and influential men of Liverpool had their gowns and bonnets and boots created. The sun broke through clouds which had gathered all morning but which were now drifting out to sea on a mild breeze. The golden light shone brightly on the glossy coats of the fine horses that pulled the carriages and on the equally well-groomed backs of the gigantic, patient Shires that plodded beside them, pulling a completely different kind of equipage: waggons loaded with goods for the docks, with barrels of beer from the brewery, with crates and boxes of every shape and size, lumbering in and out of wide gateways, causing hold-ups and tangles of traffic above which could be heard the curses of the drivers as their wheels seemed in great danger of becoming locked. There were boys on every corner, barefoot and as filthy as the streets they cleared of the droppings of the hundreds of horses that passed by. There were other children, not so apathetic as the ones Lily had become used to seeing from Mrs Quinn's basement window, ready to jeer or throw stones, and there was a policeman, resplendent in his dark blue coat, red waistcoat and tall black hat who chased them away. There were dozens of vehicles, drays and milk carts and hansom cabs, horse-drawn trams, all doing their best to push through the press of people and conveyances and get to where they were going no matter what the risk.

Jane Elliott looked impassively out of the window but when the hansom cab reached the southern outskirts of the city and began to pass pleasant terraced houses and small villas Lily, who had watched with great interest the throbbing scene beyond the cab's window, began to show signs of excitement. She didn't know why really, because it was a suburb of Liverpool she didn't know but it was away from that appalling place where they had lived, like pampered prisoners in an underground cell, for the past eight weeks and surely it promised that some change was under way.

"Oh look, the river's just over there," Lily squeaked excitedly, pointing to her right. "Oh, please, please, won't you tell us what is happening? Are we going to enquire after the job Victoria told us about? Are we Mrs Quinn"?

Her head turned constantly from side to side as the cab driver whipped the horse up to a brisk trot round Princes Park, along Belvedere Road and into Aigburth Road. They were well clear of the city now with open fields on either side cut here and there by high walls with fine gates in them, newly greening trees arching over smoothly raked gravelled drives that led away to some great house probably belonging to a ship-owner or a merchant prince, for there were many such in Liverpool and this was where they chose to live.

The fields, those that were not ploughed into pleasing brown furrows, were a living canvas of golden cowslips and primroses, the pale white and lilac of cuckoo-flowers and the delicate green of new grass in which cows stood knee-deep, turning their slow heads to watch the cab go by. There was a little spinney about halfway along the road beneath whose trees was a carpet of golden daffodils trumpeting the arrival of spring, nodding as though in welcome as the breeze moved their glorious heads.

They came to a sign that told them they were entering Holmes Lane and, turning into it, Lily was enraptured at the sight of pale yellow ox-slips growing on the banks side by side with the sweet purple of dog violets and the striking pink of cranesbill, the hedges themselves already in bud for the explosion of pure white of the hawthorn blossom that would come in May. Lily had her head out of the lowered window by now, and she drew in deep breaths of pure country air, which she had missed for so long, craning her neck to watch a formation of swallows flying high. A blackbird sang madly in the hedge and the sky, now that they were away from the smoke pall of Liverpool, was clear, achingly blue and cloudless.

And she could see the river! It was there, just across the fields, the sun sparking ripples of silver off the water. There were ships, dozens of them, small and large, iron ships, full-rigged, topsail schooners, brigs, three-masted barques, trawlers, tugboats and a ferry boat bobbing up and down on the swell as it made its way from Liverpool to Eastham. Coastal ships and deep-sea ships, every kind of ship, and Lily felt her heart, which had been buried in the deep alleyway where Mrs Quinn had taken them, lift with joy and excited anticipation. Something was afoot. Mrs Quinn would not bring them all this way in a hansom cab, which she knew she could ill afford, having heard nothing but how they must economise for weeks now, just for a casual jaunt.

There was a pair of stone pillars set in a high stone wall and between the pillars were two glossily painted wrought-iron gates, both of them closed. On the other side of the wall, which stretched for as far as Lily could see in both directions, was what appeared to be a small woodland. The river could not be seen from here and Lily had the idea that whatever was behind the wall must run down down to the water.

Mrs Quinn rapped on the roof to attract the attention of the cabbie who at once brought the horse and cab to a halt.

"I think this is it," she told him, staring doubtfully at the rather forbidding gates, "though there's no sign ter tell yer."

"Gentry don't purrup signs, ma'am," he told her through the small window in the roof, "but this is 'Olmes Lane so I reckon this could be't place. Shall I go an' open 't gates?"

"No, I'd best gerrout an' see," she told him firmly. He had leaped down from his seat ready to fling back the gates but at her words he turned back and opened the cab door instead, surprised that the ladies were proposing to walk the length of the drive to get to the house instead of letting him take them there.

"Shall I not tekk yer up there, ma'am," he said politely to the lovely woman, since she must be the mistress of the other but she stared at him in dismay and cowered back in her seat.

"She's not comin'," the lady in black told him shortly. "In fact I want yer ter stay 'ere an' wait fer me. I'll not . . . not be long."

"But wharrabout me fare? I can't afford ter 'ang about 'ere . . ."

"Yer'll be paid wharrever goin' rate is an' a bit beside when yer've gorrus 'ome."

"I thought this were—"

"Yer not paid ter think, lad. You just wait 'ere fer me. 'An don't let these two outer yer sight, d'yer 'ear me."

"'Ere, I'm not paid ter be a nursemaid," though he had to admit it would be pleasant to chat to the lady and the little girl for a few minutes while the older one went and did her errand, whatever it was.

Molly reached back into the cab and took Jane's hand in hers. "I won't be long, lamb. If yer want ter gerrout an' stretch yer legs then I reckon it'll be all right, but don't go outer sight o't cab. See, Lily, look after yer ma, there's a good lass. I've a birra business to attend to burr I'll not be long. Now I'm trustin' yer ter look after yer ma, Lily."

"I will, Mrs Quinn, I promise." Lily well knew by this time that her ma needed a lot of looking after, that the smallest thing upset her. She loved her ma and was passionately protective of her which she knew her pa would approve of. This was turning out to be a grand day and she and ma were going to enjoy it so she must behave herself or it would be spoiled, for her and for Ma.

Mrs Quinn cautiously opened the well-oiled gates and stepped inside, then swung them to behind her with the haunted look of a prisoner taking a last look at the world before going to the gallows. With a last nervous wave at the two faces that peeped at her from the cab window she began to walk up the drive, disappearing from view round a bend.

Lily had persuaded her ma to step out of the cab and come and smell the blossoming buds which were spread like icing sugar on the hedge opposite the gates. It was pleasantly warm and as quiet and tranquil as only a deserted country lane can be. There was no sound but birdsong and the hissing whistle of the cabbie who was becoming increasingly impatient with the situation. He had been disappointed when the woman shrank back when he attempted to engage her in conversation and his irritation showed in the way he slapped the reins on the horse's back. He wasn't awfully sure whether or not the woman had abandoned these two and if so what was he to do, marooned out here in the middle of nowhere with no chance of getting a fare back to the city and nothing to show for the journey he had already made. On top of that he'd been sitting on his bum for half an hour now while the lady and her child wandered further and further out of his sight down the lane.

At last he could stand no more. He jumped down from his high seat and began to walk after them. The horse, unhindered now by the reins, moved in a leisurely plod towards the hedge and began to eat the vegetation with great smacking sounds of appreciation.

"Aay," the cabbie shouted. "'Ow much longer am I supposed ter 'ang about 'ere? Is t'other woman comin' back or wha'? I've a livin' ter earn, yer know."

Lily, who was carefully holding her ma's hand, turned back. She had been enjoying herself for only the second time since Pa died, the first being on the day she walked down to the docks, and she knew Ma was too. Ma had picked a little bunch of wild daffodils which were growing on the bank and was sniffing about her as though the fragrance of the fields and hedges and trees, none of which either of them had known for weeks, was a pleasure to her.

"Well, I don't know. She did say she wouldn't be long."

"That were 'alf an 'our ago, queen." He was beginning to look seriously aggrieved and it was then that Lily had the delightful idea that if she was to go up the gravelled path that Mrs Quinn had taken and enquire for her at the house, which she supposed was where Mrs Quinn had gone, she might get a closer look at the river and the ships.

"Well, I suppose I could go and see if I can find her. That's if you don't mind waiting a few more minutes."

The cabbie, who had already wasted a whole morning, or so it was beginning to appear, told her sullenly that a few more minutes would make no difference to him, resisting the temptation to curse and say she'd best look lively or he'd be off back to town.

"Very well, I'll be as quick as I can and I'll tell Mrs Quinn what you said."

"You do that, queen," he told her truculently, watching as she opened the gates and in a way that surprised him coaxed the woman through them.

"Come on, Ma," she was saying, "there's nothing to be afraid of, God's honour. Just look at those daffodils under the trees, aren't they lovely? Yes, I'll hold your hand, dearest," which she had begun to call her ma because that's what Pa had called her. "We'll just go and find Mrs Quinn and then we might have a walk down to the river, would you like that?"

"I think I would, darling," the mother answered, the first words the cab driver had heard her speak since he had picked them up.

It was not going well, she knew it wasn't. For a start the cook/housekeeper at Oakwood Place was a cantankerous old biddy who, Molly decided, would not be satisfied with anyone, even if she had references from the Queen herself. She had ruled this kitchen for twenty years, ever since the master had brought his young bride home; the kitchen *and* the house for ten years ever since that same young bride had died. She had absolute power over everyone in it, except for the master and the family, of course, and she was furious that her age and increasing infirmities were forcing her to give it up. She could barely walk what with her rheumatics and the pain in her joints, which again put her in such vile moods she had all the housemaids in tears at least once a day. It took her half an hour to get on her feet in the morning and stagger to the chair by the fireside where she remained for most of the day, and though she had managed for almost a year now with the help of Maggie, who was head housemaid, to guide her here and there, it had come to the notice of the master and that was that, of course. She would have a snug cottage and enough money to live out her days, the master had told her that, but it wasn't the same, was it.

Mrs Quinn was the sixth woman she had interviewed and not one had suited her, and she told the master so as each one left. Too old, not clean enough for Mrs Jackson's liking, references not good enough, couldn't cook to save her life in

Mrs Jackson's opinion, though how she knew she wouldn't say, too high and mighty, too meek and mild which attitude wouldn't rule the servants in her care, and so on and so on and it looked as though this one was going the same way. For a start, though she was scrupulously clean and respectable-looking, she hadn't the experience needed in a house like this. She'd been cook/housekeeper for a Mrs Elliott for ten years so she must have been suitable, but it turned out there were only three in the family and no other servants so what use was that to anyone? This house had nine indoor servants not including herself and eight outside and though the outside men were in the charge of the head groom and the head gardener, the housemaids had to be supervised by the housekeeper. And this woman had never been in charge of other servants in her life, it appeared.

"What kind of meals can you prepare, Mrs . . . er . . . Quinn?" she asked Molly, who did her best to think of something that might sound difficult. The sort of meal that might be eaten by a family who lived in a house like this. Even the kitchens overwhelmed her in their grandeur, not just one room but several in which it seemed different tasks were performed. If the kitchens were like this, all gleaming and spotless and containing objects and pieces of machinery whose purpose was a mystery to her, what was the rest of the house like? She had been struck speechless when she turned the bend in the drive and saw the house for the first time, a great towering place with turrets and tall chimneys and what seemed like hundreds of windows, all glittering in the sunlight. The front door was enormous with steps leading up to it from beneath a kind of pillared porch and there were men about in the garden, doing things with trowels and hoes and clippers and when one spoke to her she nearly turned round and fled for her life back down the drive.

"Round the back, queen," he said, evidently recognising her as a person of the lower orders, but smiling kindly just the same.

Now she stammered and stuttered as she did her best to answer Mrs Jackson's probing questions and when a bell jangled somewhere on the wall she nearly jumped out of her skin.

"See what the master wants, Maggie," Mrs Jackson told a woman who was polishing something at the table. Mrs

Jackson had her feet propped up on a stool and every now and again she winced as though struck by a sudden pain.

"Right, Mrs Jackson," the woman, one of six all busy at some task, answered submissively, going through a door which led, Molly supposed, into the house.

She was back in two minutes, shaking her head, her white frilled cap bobbing, her face alight with excitement, barely able to get the words out and it was plain that Mrs Jackson was irritated. Mrs Jackson looked the sort of woman who would become irritated often and very easily.

"For God's sake, woman, speak up. There's no need to stand there gibbering like a halfwit. What did the master want?"

"Oh, Mrs Jackson . . ."

"Yes?" The expression on Mrs Jackson's face was becoming more and more treacherous and Molly had time to think that she would rather work in the laundry in Banastre Street than for this woman.

"There's a woman, Mrs Jackson."

"A woman? Where, in God's name? Pull yourself together, Maggie, or I shall be forced to slap you."

"In the garden, Mrs Jackson, and there's a child with her."

"A child?"

"Yes." The whole of the kitchen had come to a jarring halt, hands poised over bowls and dishes and trays and Molly felt her heart begin to bang against her breastbone. Before her eyes flashed a picture of Mrs Elliott and the child, for who else could it be, either being hauled off to gaol for trespassing or being dumped in the poorhouse for want of anyone to look after them, for she certainly couldn't, not the way things were going.

Mrs Jackson seemed somewhat undecided what her part in this drama, if that was what it was, was to be, but Maggie managed finally to tell her.

"Master says she's to be fetched from the garden and shown in."

"Shown in! To him?"

"Aye, that what he said. 'Go and get that lady from the garden and bring her to me,' he says, 'and ask Mrs Jackson to send in tea.'"

"Tea!"

Molly nearly laughed out loud and had she not been so

frightened for Mrs Elliott and the child she might have done so. Mrs Jackson was acting as though the master, and the woman in the garden, whoever she might be, were in conspiracy to put her day totally out of joint and just when she was enjoying herself, probably for what could be the last time, chucking her weight about with Molly and the servants in her charge.

"Well," she said at last. "You'd best do as he says."

11

Lily was not afraid though she knew her ma was.

They hadn't got as far as the river, which was a shame, for she would have liked to stand on the shore and watch the ships skimming the water but Ma kept being distracted by something she spotted in the truly wonderful garden they had entered and wanted to go and have a closer look. Lily hadn't the heart to stop her, though her whole being, her very heart and soul, was crying out to get down to where the ships where.

The drive curved away from the wrought-iron gates which Lily closed carefully behind her, turning to the right, both sides of it shaded by closely packed trees and huge bushes which were coming into bud in glorious colours of flaming pink and purple. The dense woodland thinned out as she and Ma got further from the gate. The grass beneath these trees was starred with golden clumps of wild daffodils, nearly finished now but still vividly bright and graceful. Rough paths of mown grass meandered off into the stand of trees and Lily would have liked to follow one of them to see where it led but she supposed it would be more sensible to find the house and enquire from someone the whereabouts of Mrs Quinn.

The house, when it came into view, took them both by surprise. It was quite enormous, built of mellow, honey-coloured stone with a turret at each corner and a great pillared entrance to which the drive curved. There were wide steps, some from the great stretch of immaculate lawn which sloped up to the porch and others from the porch up to the front door. There were no trees here except for two ancient spreading oaks, one on either side of the house, but there were flowering shrubs and clipped hedges and bushes that looked like animals and birds and other things that Lily could not identify. Edging the drive were neat rows of narcissus and primula and other spring flowers Lily did not know the names of, ribbons of colour which led away along paved walks to a lake half hidden among the trees and on which swam several ducks. Against the house on either side of the porch and beneath the windows were terraces edged with stone pillars and flowering urns and on them were white-painted wooden benches and vast terracotta pots filled with massed bright and colourful flowers, all carefully tended. Though it was only April there was colour and fragrance everywhere and Jane Elliott was enchanted. She drifted from one lovely plant to another, bending her graceful head to sniff their fragrance, her shawl slipping from her shoulders, the hem of her gown trailing on the close-cut grass and it was in this lovely setting and this enchanting pose that Joshua Crowther saw her for the first time.

He had been considering a business deal with another gentleman which he thought might be rewarding to both of them. Joshua Crowther never did business deals that were any other, which was why he was so wealthy but he did not always work *just* to become wealthy. Sometimes it was the challenge of pitting his wits against another man's which speeded him on and the deal he was mulling over was one of these. He was not in any particular line of business. There was no need to be in this thriving port where so much was going on that any man with his wits about him who was prepared to take a risk had as good a chance of making money as the next. There was shipping, manufacturing, exporting and importing, railways, the building of houses as the city spread outwards, the lending of money to speculators at enormous rates of interest and he had a finger in all of them.

He had been sprawled out before his study fire, his long legs stretched out before him, his feet propped on the fender and crossed at the ankle, his chin resting on his steepled fingers, his thoughts clear and concise as always. Feeling the need to move about, which often helped him to crystallise something in his mind, he stood up, pushed his hands into his trouser pockets and strolled across to the window which looked out over the front lawns.

She was the most exquisite thing he had ever seen and his wife had been considered a beauty but this woman was like nothing he had ever known before and what he felt was like nothing he had ever felt before. He stood for several minutes at the window, watching her, her hand in that of a beautifully dressed little girl. The sun glinted on her hair which was the incredible colour and had the polished sheen of a newly minted silver coin. Even from here he could see the bloom of her flawless skin, cream and rose, and the grace of her long neck which seemed to bend like the stalk of a flower. He was stunned and speechless, incapable of thought, or even wonder at who she was. She looked so exactly right there. So totally in the place that was meant for her, that had been made for her and in that moment Joshua knew he must have her. He hadn't the faintest idea who she was or what she was doing in his garden but it didn't matter. It didn't matter if she was the wife of some other man and completely out of his reach, he must have her and with the same direct ruthlessness with which he dealt with everything from the running of his business interests to the bringing up of his children, he took the shortest route to getting what he wanted.

He rang the bell.

Lily was alarmed when the maidservant appeared at the front door, getting ready to run for cover dragging Ma with her. She was doing nothing wrong, though she supposed they were trespassing, but she had come for a good reason and that was the searching out of Mrs Quinn who was somewhere in this house.

"I'm sorry," she began politely. "I know we shouldn't be here but you see—"

"Never mind that, girl, the master wants to see you." The maid had a sharp face, pointed and foxy but her eyes were not unkind and she was smiling.

"We weren't doing anything bad, God's honour, only Ma loves flowers and I couldn't—"

"It doesn't matter, girl. You come along with me and I'll take you to the master."

"Oh, please, he won't frighten Ma, will he?" Lily pleaded, for already her mother was dragging at her hand in an effort to get back to where they had come from, back to the hansom cab at the gate.

"Nay, lass, he won't hurt you or your mother but you'd best hurry up because he doesn't like to be kept waiting."

"Well, I will if I can get Ma moving."

For the first time Maggie noticed the confusion on the face of the beautiful woman. She had wondered why the child did all the talking instead of the woman but it seemed she was not right in the head or else why should she be so frightened, which is what she appeared to be. She was obviously the girl's mother but she looked so disturbed Maggie glanced about her as though searching for someone to help her. She'd have to get a move on or the master himself might come out and he could be a tartar when he was crossed.

"Dearest," the child was saying to the woman, "there's nothing to be afraid of, really. We are to go inside this lovely house and . . . and have a look round. Wouldn't you like that? The gardens are splendid but I'm sure the inside of the house will be just as wonderful and this lady" – indicating the wondering maid – "has invited us . . ."

"To take tea," the servant finished daringly.

"I'm not sure I should, darling," Jane Elliott quavered, for, as usual, anything that was out of step with the tempo she had got used to frightened her.

Lily looked about her in much the same way that the maid-servant had done, then her mind fastened on the one person who would have this little problem sorted out in a trice.

"Is Mrs Quinn about?" she asked the woman on the step hopefully.

"Mrs Quinn?"

"Yes, she came to see someone here but I don't know who or where she might be."

"You mean her in the kitchen with Mrs Jackson?"

Lily looked baffled, beginning also to look somewhat dishevelled as she struggled to hold on to her mother.

"I suppose so."

"Well . . ."

"I'd be obliged if you'd fetch her," she said in her most grown-up manner. "She knows how to handle Ma, you see."

The maid looked bewildered. Handle Ma! What on earth did the child mean? She hadn't the faintest idea but she'd better get a move on or the master'd be out here to find out what was happening to the order he had just given her and he could frighten the wits out of the most courageous!

It took almost fifteen minutes before the order Joshua Crowther had given to his housemaid was executed and the trembling figure of Jane Elliott was led into his drawing-room which he had decided was more appropriate for entertaining a lady. If he was astonished when she came in on the arm of a decently clad woman who was obviously a servant he did not show it. The lovely child trailed behind them, her face a picture of bright interest.

Joshua Crowther could be kind, charming, gentle, gracious when he chose, showing a side of him that none who did business with him would have recognised. He was not a sensitive man but he was intuitive and his intuition told him that he must tread carefully here.

He rose from the chair where he had seated himself after watching the antics on his lawn, a pleasant smile on his handsome face, but he did not move forward to greet Jane Elliott as he would have done with any other lady. Again his instinct was at work.

"Good morning," he said, "or is it good afternoon. Time gets away from you sometimes, doesn't it? Do you find that? Is it a sign that we are happy, or just forgetful? I have been reading and became so engrossed in my book I did not notice the time. Now please, won't you sit down?" indicating a chair near the wide French window from which she would see the garden she had just been exploring. "I've ordered some tea. May I offer you a cup, and your companion, and perhaps the little girl would care for some . . . some lemonade?"

"Yes, I would, please," Lily said, turning to smile at him from a table crammed with the loveliest things which she had been examining.

"And perhaps some biscuits . . . or . . ." What in hell's name did females like on occasions such as this? He hadn't the faintest idea since he had never attended one.

"Cakes would be nice," Lily told him simply, unafraid and supremely confident.

He passed on Lily's order to the hovering maid who couldn't wait to get back to the kitchen to tell them of the extraordinary goings-on in the drawing-room. Mrs Jackson had nearly thrown the teapot at Mrs Quinn when she was summoned to the front of the house. Mrs Quinn was *hers* and had no right to tread the carpeted hallway that led from the servants' quarters to the family's. What on earth was going on when a woman who had no qualifications, no status, no possible need or reason to be there, could go and sit in the master's drawing-room and drink tea, which Mrs Jackson's staff would have to make for her. It was beyond all comprehending and there was one thing for sure, she'd not step into Mary Jackson's shoes when she retired!

The tea was brought and for a dithering moment Maggie didn't know where the trolley should be placed. It was hardly a man's job to pour, was it and yet these two women were visitors and what the protocol was she couldn't fathom. She put it near Mrs Quinn who seemed the most likely, the most sensible of the two and waited deferentially for further orders. Perhaps she was to pour and hand round the teacups. She hoped so, then she could report back to them in the kitchen what was going on. She was to be disappointed.

"That will be all, thank you, Maggie. I'm sure we can manage nicely. I'll ring if I need you."

He waited until the door was closed behind the maid before he spoke.

"Perhaps we should introduce ourselves first," he said gently, smiling at the troubled face of Jane Elliott. He was glad to see she had calmed down somewhat now that she had the hand of the woman in black to cling to. "My name is Joshua Crowther. May I ask yours?"

It was the woman in black who answered. "I'm afraid my mistress 'as been ill, sir. She . . . she lost 'er 'usband a few weeks back an' it's tekkin' 'er a while ter gerrover it. She's very . . . shy."

A widow! He had always considered himself to be a lucky man, though he firmly believed that a man also made his own luck but this was more than he could have hoped for. No man standing between himself and what he wanted. A woman still in the throes, one presumed and didn't her actions verify it, of grieving. Vulnerable, ready to fall like a sweet, ripe peach into the hands of the first man who was kind to her and Joshua Crowther could be very kind when he chose. He wasn't sure how he was going to get her into his bed but he knew he would eventually. Even if he had to marry her. Which was not a bad idea, for she would grace any man's table.

"I'm so sorry. I know what it's like to lose a loved one."

Jane Elliott's eyes, which had been wide and frightened, became clear and soft and she smiled tremulously at him. Incredibly, he felt his heart stir with something he did not recognise but it made him even gentler with her.

"May I know your name?" His voice was as smooth as silk and Jane Elliott was reassured.

"Jane . . . Elliott." It was said in almost a whisper but it was a good start, he thought. At least she had answered him.

"Mrs Elliott, it is a pleasure to meet you. And you, madam?" turning courteously to Mrs Quinn. Joshua knew exactly who it was, in any deal, who should be deferred to.

"Mrs Quinn, sir. I'm 'ouskeeper ter Mrs Elliott. I've bin lookin' after 'er since the captain died."

"The captain?"

"Mrs Elliott's 'usband."

"Not . . . Richard Elliott?"

"Yes, sir."

"I think we should go home now, Mrs Quinn." Jane began to clutch at Mrs Quinn and Lily moved towards her with the instinct of a mother protecting her child. "It's . . . I think . . . it would be better if . . ."

Joshua knew he had made a mistake in mentioning the name of this woman's husband. She was obviously not herself, in fact she was beginning to struggle with her shawl and her reticule, doing her best to get the housekeeper to her feet and lead her from the room and the child was helping her. He was aware that if she went it might be tricky getting her back again. He had to win her trust *now*. It was unfortunate that he should have blurted out the man's name, the man whose ship he had taken to pay back some of the money Richard Elliott owed him. He had known the man had a wife and child and when the bailiffs were called in to see what could be rescued from the mass of debts he had incurred he had given no thought to what would become of these two. It was a fact of life. Men got into debt and women suffered, but now he could put that right. It was not, of course, the reason for doing what he was determined to do.

"Please, Mrs Elliott, I beg your forgiveness. I'm a crass idiot and deserve to be horsewhipped for upsetting you. Please, don't go. Drink your tea – if you would be so good as to pour, Mrs Quinn – and rest before you go home. I saw you in the garden and noticed how much you enjoyed it and perhaps, when you've finished your tea, you and your companion might like to see the plants in my winter garden. It's a glass conservatory and my wife, sadly gone now, I'm afraid, put in cages of birds and . . . well, when you have finished your tea, if you feel up to it, we shall have a look. It's only through those doors."

The room was on a corner, the front overlooking the gardens but on the second outside wall a conservatory had been built. There were wide doors leading into it and from within could be heard the cheerful twitter of birds. Jane Elliott stopped her tussle with Mrs Quinn, with Lily and her reticule, lifting her head to listen intently to the sound and a look of interest passed across her face, smoothing it, erasing the confusion and grief Joshua's word had aroused in her. She stood up and Mrs Quinn stood up with her and without looking again at Joshua she began to walk towards the open doorway. Lily went with her and, rising to his feet, so did Joshua. Mrs Quinn threw him an apologetic glance but he nodded at her to show her it was all right.

Jane hesitated in the doorway, her lovely eyes which Joshua couldn't decide were grey or violet, looking about her. An expression of wondering delight lit her face. The conservatory, or winter garden as it was known, had been built by the previous owner of Oakwood Place and it was very evident that whoever had lived there had loved the cultivation of flowers. It was a very grand affair, built entirely of graceful fretwork and glass, stretching from the drawing-room at least thirty feet along the side of the house and it was entirely filled with exotic plants. There were small palm trees, plants known as birds of paradise in vivid orange, a monkey-puzzle tree, limes and bleeding heart vines in a delicate white and scarlet, hibiscus with frilly petalled crimson flowers, sweet-scented jasmine, passion flowers, magnolia, all growing in pots of every size and colour. From the high glass ceiling hung baskets with trailing ivy and among them half a dozen pretty cages, each one containing a singing bird. Set in groups on the tiled floor were white-painted basket chairs with brightly coloured cushions, round tables with lace cloths thrown over them and beneath the lace another cloth of deep green. All very inviting. Lying in a patch of sunlight was a black and white cat.

"Ooh . . ." Jane put her hands together as though in prayer, her fingers to her lips. She stepped hesitantly through the doors and slowly began a tour of the garden, touching with tender fingers this bloom and that, bending to smell the jasmine, moving slowly as though in a dream, watched by Molly Quinn and Joshua Crowther. For some reason they turned to smile at one another as though in shared triumph. Jane bent to run her hand over the cat's glossy coat then picked it up as it purred rapturously.

"Look, Lily, is she – or is it a he – not handsome? And did you ever see such a glorious room? Listen to the birds sing and the warmth from the sun would make you want to spend all your day here. It's . . . it's heavenly . . . so peaceful and . . . and safe."

"Perhaps we could have our tea here, Mrs Elliott," Joshua suggested, "if Mrs Quinn would like to bring the trolley through."

"Oh, that would be lovely, Mr . . . ?"

"Crowther. Joshua Crowther."

"Mr Crowther. How lucky you are to have such a lovely place. We can appreciate it all the more after . . ." For a second she became confused again and Lily, who was poking her nose into one of the bird cages, trying to decide what kind of bird was in it, for she had certainly never seen its like before, turned to her and began to stroke the cat in her arms which sounded as though it had an engine rumbling inside it.

"What's its name, Mr Crowther?" she asked. "I have a dog named Villette but we usually call her Villy."

"Have you indeed? It seems we have something in common then, Miss Elliott. I have three dogs out in the stables. Two black labradors and a golden retriever. Henry, Wally and Alex after my three favourite authors."

"Really? Who are they, then? I don't know of an author called Wally."

He laughed and thought what a taking child she was. He would have no trouble assimilating her into his household.

"Well, there's Henry Fielding, Sir Walter Scott and Alexandre Dumas. But I must confess that I don't know the cat's name. I think it must have sneaked in from the kitchen."

While he was talking to the child he was watching her mother as she drifted peacefully about his winter garden. She still held the cat in her arms, her long, slender hand smoothing its fur and he could see she was totally herself now, or as he imagined she would be in normal circumstances. Relaxed and . . . yes, at home in this room which some lady who had once lived here had created. The house was Georgian and he had loved it from the first moment he had set eyes on it, knowing it was the perfect setting for himself, who was then an up-and-coming force in the city, his lovely young bride and the many children they would have. To some extent his dream had been fulfilled but now it seemed it was to be made perfect.

Molly Quinn wheeled in the trolley. She had removed her black cloak, though not her bonnet and with a confidence that amazed her, for she had never been in a place like this before, guided Jane to a seat, told Lily to stop messing about with those birds and sit down, poured the tea with an expert hand and passed a cup first to her mistress, then to the extraordinary Mr Crowther. She was astonished at the way he seemed able to draw out her mistress, speaking softly as though she were to be treated with the greatest respect and courtesy, asking her simple questions that did not tax her fragile grasp on this new experience. Lily behaved impeccably, drinking her lemonade and though she ate half a dozen dainty cucumber sandwiches, five of the little fancy cakes which were sent in at the master's command, two freshly buttered scones and a slice of rich pound cake – and could you blame her, the poor food she had been eating these last weeks – she was as dainty as a little cat about it. Molly's mind was in turmoil, for what was to come out of all this? She hadn't a cat in hell's chance of getting the job of housekeeper, that was for sure. She had seen the expression of venom on the old biddy's face in the kitchen when she had been summoned to the front of the house, but really, had you ever seen a man as taken with a woman as Mr Crowther seemed to be with Mrs Elliott and where might that end? She didn't dare hope. She didn't dare even think about it as she sipped her own cup of tea, hot and sweet and strong just as she liked it.

Lily, with her prettiest manners, just as though she knew she must be on her best behaviour, asked to be excused and might she have a look round the drawing-room at all the lovely things Mr Crowther had on display? She was given permission and as she stood up, so did Jane, drifting off vaguely to sniff a blossom, touch a leaf, gaze out of the window at the men who were working in the garden, the cat still cuddled in her arms.

Joshua Crowther turned politely to Molly Quinn.

"Mrs Quinn, I can see you are troubled about something. Won't you tell me your story, and theirs," indicating the woman at the window and the child who had disappeared into the drawing-room.

Molly drew a deep breath. Perhaps there was a chance for her after all, and if for her, then for them.

"Well, sir," she began, "it started when Captain Elliott died in an accident at sea."

"Tell me about it."

So she did, from that first day when they had been told of his death, the dreadful effect it had had on Mrs Elliott, the bailiffs who had turned them out on the street, their flight to Brooke Alley . . .

"Brooke Alley?"

"Aye, tis off Vauxhall Road and norr at all wha' they're used to."

She could see the appalled shock on his face at the idea of the flower-like Mrs Elliott being forced to live in such a terrible area. He knew what it was like. He had property there.

"I 'ad ter keep 'em locked up. Well, I couldn't lerrem roam t'streets, sir. Yer've no idea the sort what live round there."

"And yet you did, Mrs Quinn."

"I 'ad no choice, sir," she answered him grimly. "I were a widder wi' three girls an' it were all I could afford. Burr I brought 'em up decent."

"I'm sure you did, Mrs Quinn. Go on."

"Well, we was runnin' outer money. I 'ad ter get summat ter put food in our mouths, an' fer't rent so I asked about an' . . . well, I come 'ere terday ter see if I could 'ave 'ousekeeper's job . . ."

"What a splendid idea, Mrs Quinn. I think you would make an admirable housekeeper. The job is yours." What a perfect solution, he was thinking, again marvelling on the luck that seemed to be falling once more into his lap. Get the old woman here, fit her up with some job or other, and surely some reason could be found for Jane Elliott to follow. It couldn't be better and with that direct and compelling way that was his it would be all arranged right this very minute.

"There's a snag, Mr Crowther." Molly Quinn's voice was steady and her face composed though inside she was boiling over.

Mr Crowther frowned and his eyes grew flinty and she realised that this man was not one to be crossed, a lesson she was to learn again and again.

"Yes?"

"I can't live in, sir. I've them ter think on. I can't leave 'em."

His face cleared and broke into its most charming smile.

"Of course you can't and until some suitable arrangements are made you must bring them with you."

Molly's jaw dropped. "Bring 'em wi' me?"

"Yes, I shall arrange for you to have your own quarters and Mrs Elliott and her daughter will live there with you. Now I want no argument, Mrs Quinn, since I'm sure it can only be for the best. Look at her," turning to gaze tenderly at the woman who, an hour ago, he had not known existed. "See how she has responded to the atmosphere here. Perhaps you had not considered that the very place where she has lived with you lately might have been holding her back. She needs light and air and beauty in which to recover her spirits. Wouldn't you agree?"

Molly could feel her own spirits beginning to soar. Yes, she would agree. She had never seen Mrs Elliott look so . . . so content, not since before the captain died, and what a wonderful place for the child. She could roam these gardens and be free from the stink and danger of Brooke Alley and perhaps regain that lovely strong sweetness she had known before her pa died. But . . .

"There's just one thing, sir."

His face hardened again. "Yes?"

"I can't cook."

He grinned like a boy as he leaned to take her hand.

"Don't worry about that, Mrs Quinn. Cooks are easy to find," but lovely women like Jane Elliott were unique, though he did not utter this last.

12

How she got through the next few hours she was never to know, she was to tell Victoria later. It was like being in a lunatic asylum with the inmates all determined on their own way and fighting like tigers to get it. And he was the worst, the master, as she was now to call him apparently, for he wanted to ride roughshod over every suggestion made to him. Mind you, it was sheer heaven to know they were safe, not only her in her grand new job, but Mrs Elliott and the child as well, even if it was completely unorthodox.

And it was worth every unquiet thought in her head over the strangeness of it all just to see that old biddy's face when they were taken, by the master, if you please, into the kitchen. It seemed to be crammed with more servants than before, all busy with some task or other and as the four of them, her and Mrs Elliott, the child and Mr Crowther, entered the room every face became slack with shock, especially that of Mrs Jackson who struggled valiantly to get out of her chair.

Molly had hold of Mrs Elliott who had withdrawn again now that she had been removed from the lovely calm of the winter garden and though it was clear that Mr Crowther longed to offer her his arm he restrained himself, allowing her to cling to Molly even though it did look a bit odd. She peered about her, nervous as a cornered animal until she caught sight of the kitchen tabby which was lying on the rag rug before the fire, its tail curled neatly about itself.

"Oh, how lovely, you have another cat and exactly like the one in the other room. What handsome creatures what both are. Hello, puss," she went on, crouching down in so graceful a manner her wide skirts ballooned about her. She scratched the animal behind its ear and at once it stood up and began to rub itself against her. "Oh, look, Lily," she exclaimed delightedly to her daughter, who was staring about her with the same bright interest she had shown in the drawing-room, "I think it likes me."

The maidservants watched her with silent fascination. Their eyes spoke their thoughts though and it was evident what they were. Who in the name of God was this lovely woman, this beautifully dressed woman who had not only invaded the master's garden but was now in his kitchen playing with the bloody cat? What was she to him and what was she doing here? What was he up to? And what about the child? She was obviously the woman's daughter and would you look at the lovely outfit she had on which must have cost a pretty penny. They had seen the other one, of course, the one who had had hopes of taking Mrs Jackson's place but what was her connection with these two fairy-like creatures?

"Of course it does, Ma," the child said. "I think you must be a cat person. I prefer dogs myself, though I wouldn't mind a kitten. Have you any kittens, Mr Crowther?"

Joshua Crowther came to with an almost perceptible start, for he had been as spellbound as the rest.

"I don't know, Lily. Have we? Does anyone know?"

There was a lad in a glassed-off room who had stopped to stare with the rest of them. He was vigorously cleaning his master's riding boots but at this he popped his bright orange head out through the door. For a moment Lily thought he might be one of the Meadows boys and a shaft of home-sickness for Walton Lane stabbed her but when he stood, a brush in one hand, his other arm inside his master's long riding boot she could see it was not.

"There's plenty in't stables, sir. That there ginger tabby what belongs ter Mrs Arnold the groom's wife 'ad a litter only last month."

"There you are, Lily, perhaps Mrs Arnold will give you one of those." Joshua Crowther was eager to get this over and the child's sidetracking had irritated him. He walked over to where Jane was still fondling the cat and with great gentleness lifted her to her feet, but it seemed Lily had not yet done.

"Well, I'd like a kitten, sir, thank you, but you see I'm not sure Villy would. She's never had anything to do with cats, you see."

"Villy?"

"Yes, I told you about my dog, remember."

"But you—"

Suddenly Joshua pulled himself up short for he had just been about to tell her that her dog would be confined to the stable with his, since he did not allow them in the house, when he realised she was not even aware that she was to live here. And neither was Jane.

"Of course, but first I must make an announcement to the servants. We can discuss dogs and kittens later."

"But—"

"Later, Lily." His voice said that was the end of it.

For some reason Lily did as she was told, closing her mouth though it was thinned to a mutinous line. She frowned, took her ma's hand in hers and waited.

Joshua continued. "This lady here, who I believe you have already met," nodding his head in Molly's direction, "is to be our new housekeeper." There was an audible gasp from the maidservants and Mrs Jackson sat down heavily in her chair as though to say to hell with respect for one's betters. "Her name is Mrs Quinn and she is to start at once which I'm sure will be a great relief to Mrs Jackson. Mrs Quinn is not a cook but she has my permission to engage one. I think that's all, so if you, Mrs Jackson, would ask one of the yard men to help you move your stuff to your cottage I would be obliged. I know you were hoping to go as soon as a suitable replacement was found for you. You will, of course, be paid until the end of the month. Oh, and one more thing. Mrs Elliott here," putting a hand on the one that rested quite trustingly in the crook of his arm and which miraculously he had managed to keep there, "and her daughter are to be my guests, so if a room could be got ready for them at once. The best guest-room, Mrs Jackson, if you please. I think that's all except that I shall need the carriage in half an hour. Will you inform Bentley. Mrs Quinn will be back shortly to make herself known to you, I'm sure, but there are one or two matters to be attended to first. Now then, Mrs Elliott, if you would like to come with me . . . yes, my dear, Mrs Quinn is coming too." This last remark was addressed to Jane who was looking confused.

But Joshua Crowther had reckoned without Lily Elliott who was used to speaking her mind and at the moment it was absorbing what Mr Crowther had just said about her and Ma staying with him. Not that she would mind that. It would be grand to be able to walk down to the river and watch the shipping. It would be grand to be able to play with Villy in the woods they had come through on the way up here. It would be grand to be away from Brooke Alley and the confinement of Mrs Quinn's cellar but she did think this should have been discussed with her and Mrs Quinn before a decision was made. For a start Liam wouldn't know where to find them when he came home, which she was sure he would soon. And, if Mrs Quinn was to be housekeeper here . . . oh, yes, she had not missed *that* even if Ma had, then what was to happen to her and Ma, especially Ma, when their visit with Mr Crowther was over? Where would they go then? In fact, why was Mr Crowther inviting them, perfect strangers, to be his guests? These were all questions Lily would like answered, for, after all, with Pa gone she was responsible for Ma, wasn't she?

"What d'you mean, Mr Crowther?" she asked him, her small face serious as though she were considering his offer and found it wanting. "About me and Ma staying here?"

Joshua, who had been just about to lead Jane Elliott from the kitchen, turned impatiently to the child, then looked to Mrs Quinn as though to say this must be dealt with by her. She knew what he was about, or in part she did, and anything to be said must come from her, but Lily stared at him defiantly, waiting for an explanation.

Mrs Quinn took her hand and tried to prise her loose from her mother but short of a tussle before the spellbound gaze of the servants there was no parting the two of them. Still holding on to her mother Lily had swung round to face Mr Crowther, waiting for an answer.

Joshua's face tightened ominously but he kept his voice smooth, for he did not wish to alarm this child's mother.

"Would you not like to have a holiday, Lily?" he asked her. "Do you not think it would do you and your mother, especially your mother, a power of good to come and stay here for a while? The sea air and the rest, the peace here by the river and—"

"But you don't know us, so why are you asking us to stay with you?"

The servants hung on her every word, for that was what they would like to know, too.

Joshua gritted his teeth. "I think that is for your mother

and me to decide, Lily. And Mrs Quinn, of course. Mrs Quinn will be housekeeper at Oakwood Place and since you have been *her* guests for quite a long time and when she starts here will have nowhere to stay, so she tells me, it seems only sensible for you and your mother to come with her for the time being." As he spoke he wondered why in hell's name he was explaining to this persistent child what was essentially none of her bloody business, and in front of the servants too. It was not his custom to explain his actions to anyone and certainly not to a small girl. But he couldn't afford an upheaval at the moment, for God only knew what Jane Elliott, in her present precarious state, might say or do.

"Well, all right, but can we bring Villy?" Lily interrupted him. "I know she might chase the cats but I'd keep her on her leash when we're out," which was a fib, of course.

"Yes, er . . . Villy can come too."

"And then there's Liam."

"Liam?" For a dreadful moment there flashed through his mind the image of another man making free with what Joshua had earmarked for himself and he could feel the angry blood surge through him. As though she sensed it the woman on his arm slipped her hand from his and moved towards Mrs Quinn, her face taking on that strange expression in which doubt and uncertainty were mixed and he could have cheerfully wrung the child's neck. She was staring at him boldly and he wondered why he had thought her such an engaging little thing.

"Oh, please, sir," Mrs Quinn cut in, almost savagely, for if the little madam spoiled their chances of a good home and herself a good job she'd gladly take a whip to her, which sometimes she wished the captain had done. She was far too knowing for her own good and certainly far too talkative. "'E's some lad 'oo brought 'er 'ome one day when she were lost."

"I was not lost."

Mrs Quinn shook her soundly. "Be quiet an' speak when yer spoken to." She turned eagerly back to the master of the house. "'E's a sailor. We 'ardly know 'im."

"I see, well . . ." Conscious of the avid interest of his servants he turned and opened the door for the two women and the child to go through to the front of the house. "We can talk about that later. Now, don't forget the carriage, in half an hour, if you please."

There was total silence in the kitchen after the door swung to behind the child who was the last to leave, for she had loitered for a moment to have another look at the cat. "It's a nice cat," she told them, "but I like dogs better. Mine would chase this one. That's what dogs do, you see. Chase cats."

The hand of Mrs Quinn appeared round the door and dragged her out!

"Well . . ." Maggie let her breath out on an explosive sigh, hardly daring to turn to Mrs Jackson. The old lady had as good as been given her notice and in no uncertain terms and it didn't seem fair, but then when had Mrs Jackson ever been fair to any of them? A cow was what she had often called her under her breath so perhaps this one – Mrs Quinn – might be an improvement. She exchanged a look with Betsy who was the under-parlourmaid and second to Maggie. She could see everyone was waiting for her to make some comment, but while Mrs Jackson was about she thought it prudent to keep her lip buttoned.

"It seems I'm to be chucked out on me ear," Mrs Jackson said, her voice ice cold with rage, "so I'd best go and get me things packed." So great was her bitterness she threw caution out of the window. "You, Dora," who was her kitchen maid, "can come and help me and if he thinks I'm making dinner for that lot he's got another think coming!"

It had been Joshua Crowther's intention to send Mrs Quinn in his carriage back to Brooke Alley to fetch their things, since he didn't want to let the delectable Mrs Elliott out of his sight, but it seemed Mrs Elliott had other ideas. She would not be parted from Mrs Quinn under any circumstances, it seemed. There was no way of keeping her here short of tying her up; no, not even if her daughter remained with her, which was suggested to her. She said so vehemently and it began to dawn on Joshua Crowther that he must be patient with this lovely, damaged woman if he was to bring her back to full health, which he had every intention of doing.

"Very well, Mrs Elliott. Please, don't upset yourself. I couldn't bear you to be upset, really, so instead I'll come with you and help with the . . . the packing. We'll all go, how would that be?" But even that seemed to cause her some anxiety. So much had happened this day that the vacuum in which she had existed since the death of her husband seemed to have been invaded by demons of some sort and yet at the same time, for the first time, she had known a few minutes of pleasure in the loveliness of the winter garden. She understood that Mr Crowther had invited them to be his guests for a while and as long as she had Mrs Quinn, her child and her sewing, in that order, she thought it might be rather nice to spend time in the warm peace of the glassed room. And she had liked the cats, too. Stroking their silky fur had calmed her in some strange way. But in the back of her mind, in some place that had not been used for many weeks, was the thought that she would not care for Mr Crowther to see that dreadful locality which had dimly filtered into her mind recently.

"Oh, no, no, I don't think so." She shook her head emphatically and several silver blonde curls, which had escaped Mrs Quinn's ministration, bobbed enchantingly about her ears.

"Mrs Elliott, I'm sure . . ."

"Oh, no . . . no . . ."

"P'raps it'd be best if we went on our own, sir," Mrs Quinn told him diplomatically. "She's 'ad a lot ter think about terday an' I must say she's done right well. She . . . I think she trusts yer, sir, if yer don't mind me saying so, but if we was ter move slowly, lerrer come 'ome wi' me an' pack 'er things 'erself she'd take to it better. She's made up wi't idea of 'avin' a 'oliday 'ere burrit's gorra be done right. She loves sewin' an' such an' when she's gorrer bits an' pieces about her she'll settle nicely. Well, why shouldn't she in a lovely place like this."

So, to the consternation of the outside men, and the maid-servants who peeped from upstairs windows, the new house-keeper, the lovely woman and her child went off in style in Mr Crowther's splendid carriage, driven by Mr Crowther's splendidly attired coachman. The carriage was a midnight blue with gold engraving, the inside a darker blue buttoned velvet. The coachman wore a jacket to match with gold buttons, a top hat and magnificently polished boots over his beige breeches. He carried a long whip which now and again he flicked over the backs of the beautifully matched chestnut mares which pulled the equipage and which, since it was such a pleasant day, had its hood down. Beside him, similarly dressed, sat a groom.

The cab had long gone. The driver, disgruntled and tired of sitting on his bum waiting for the ladies to come back, had ventured up the long drive to the house, knocking deferentially at the front door and, after explaining to the astonished housemaid, who had gone to inform her master, had been paid and sent about his business.

To say the residents of Brooke Alley were struck dumb by the magnificence of the carriage, the wonder of the glossy horses that pulled it, the two impeccably turned-out men on the box and the sight of their neighbour climbing down from it, was a vast understatement. It was as though an icy hand had come down and frozen each and every one of them to the spot, at least for the space of ten seconds, then the place erupted. They poured from their crumbling doorways. They rose from their recumbent lounging on doorsteps, they pulled themselves away from the greasy walls on which they had been leaning and, accompanied by a horde of screaming children, surrounded the carriage like the hordes of Israel. They jostled the horses, making them rear and fall back in terror, shook the carriage with the force of their excitement and for a moment it looked as though disaster were to strike. Bentley, who was Mr Crowther's coachman, was to say later that had it not been for the big chap the mass would have overturned the coach and stampeded the horses. Even with Jimmy up beside him it was looking decidedly perilous and he wished despairingly that he had brought the pistol he sometimes had about him when Mr Crowther was out at night. The lady in the back began to moan as the elderly lady, who had stepped down without waiting for Jimmy to open the door for her, was swept away into the crowd. Neither he nor Jimmy fancied leaving the comparative safety of the box but it was at that moment that a roar like that of a maddened bull surged down the alley and what seemed to be the bull itself charged through the crowd. They melted back like magic as the figure reached the carriage. The child in the back began to squeak with what seemed like delight, mouthing a name Bentley could not catch but by now, with reinforcements at hand, both he and Jimmy were in command again. Bentley cracked the whip about the thin shoulders of those within reaching distance and they fell back further.

The elderly lady had gone down some steps and was at the door of what appeared to be a cellar, just the top of her black bonnet visible and before you could say "knife" the big chap had the terrified woman out of the carriage, the child tucked under his arm and with no more ado had them down the area steps of the basement, through the door and tucked away safely inside.

"You all right?" he shouted back to them.

"Aye, but don't be bloody long."

"I knew you'd come, I knew you'd come," Lily kept repeating, her face like a little star in the gloom of the cellar. Mrs Quinn was dashing about the place like a whirling dervish, stuffing things in bags and boxes, stopping frequently to check on Jane Elliott, who sat like a graven image, patting her shoulder and reassuring her that they would be away soon, but Lily was not concerned with anything except the wonderful sight of Liam who had promised to come back and here he was. She did not question why she felt as though her world had suddenly become a lovelier place, why her heart felt as though it would burst with joy, it just did and her feelings shone from her brilliant silvery grey eyes as she knelt at his feet with her arms round Villy's neck.

Liam sat in Molly Quinn's old chair and smiled down at the child. What a lovely little creature she was. He had not given her much thought during the weeks he had been away and had not really meant to look her up again since he was perfectly certain she would be settled now and safe in her home in Walton Lane. But after the *Caledonia* had docked and the dock official had passed him the grubby note which had been in his pocket for weeks, Liam had felt a compulsion to make his way to Brooke Alley to find out what had happened to her and her ma. He had been appalled when he had stood in the alley, himself an object of great curiosity in his good suit of clothes and the jaunty wide-awake hat he wore tipped over one eye. What could have brought that lovely child and her equally lovely mother to this? He knew Richard Elliott had been deeply in debt but surely there must have been something, some insurance which a responsible man would take out to look after his widow and fatherless child. It seemed not and this was where they had landed and now it appeared they were to be off again, and into more salubrious surroundings than these by the look of the carriage waiting for them at the end of the alley.

"I'm sorry, lovebud, but we were held up in Halifax. The ship was damaged in a storm, a right bu— er, corker it was, and it took a while ter get repair done so that's why I'm late gettin' back inter Liverpool. As soon as I got yer note I came straight here."

"See, I told you so." Lily shot another look of triumph at Mrs Quinn. "And what a good job you came today, Liam, or you would have missed us." Her expression was one of horror at how close they had come to missing one another.

"An' why's that, Lily?"

"Oh, please, do call me lovebud. I like it."

His smile deepened and into his mind came the thought that what a joy it would be to have a daughter like this one. Bright and beautiful and innocent, intelligent and honest and open. A child who had not been twisted into the shape of many young girls of good family today, though he supposed she was not really what you would call of good stock. Her father had been a working seaman and her mother's people had been in trade. Perhaps because of this she had been allowed to develop into her true and delightful, if somewhat unconventional and outspoken self, brave in the face of adversity, trusting and with a great capacity for loyalty.

"Lovebud," he said, earning a sharp look from Mrs Quinn.

"Well, Mrs Quinn is to go as housekeeper to a gentleman called Mr Crowther," Lily continued, "and we are to go with her. He lives in a lovely house down by the river and I shall be able to watch the ships and take Villy on to the shore and play in the woods. There's a lovely garden for Ma and you should see what Mr Crowther called the winter garden. Ma loved it, and the cats, though I'm not sure how Villy will take to them. She's not used to cats, you see. It's absolutely splendid, Liam, and when you are in port you'll be able to come and see us. I'm sure Mr Crowther won't mind, will he, Mrs Quinn?"

He exchanged a look with Mrs Quinn, who shook her head slightly as though to say take no notice, but on his face was a look that told her he was not awfully sure if he liked the sound of this. A total stranger who employs a housekeeper was all well and good, and Mrs Quinn must be relieved to have found work, but what was he doing taking on the widow of a sea captain and her small daughter as well? Jane Elliott was a beautiful, defenceless woman, vulnerable in her present state, so could he, Liam O'Connor, put any interpretation on it but the worst?

Lily was still speaking, so enthralled with his arrival just in the nick of time she failed to see the quizzical look

Liam gave Mrs Quinn nor the defiant one she gave him back.

She was still babbling on. "I knew it was something like that, Liam. I was sure it must be a storm or even a shipwreck. I told Mrs Quinn, didn't I, Mrs Quinn," turning a rapturous face to Molly who was still galloping round like something gone mad.

"That yer did, child, but I'd be glad if yer'd gerrof yer bum an' 'elp me wi' these things. That there coachman'll not be 'appy sat out there wi' 'alf o' Brooke Alley 'angin' about 'im an' Mr Crowther'll be waitin' on us."

"Oh, he can wait, Mrs Quinn. I've so many things to ask Liam and I might not see him for a while. Now, Liam." She sat back on her haunches, gazing earnestly up into his face. "What was it like in Halifax? That's in Novia Scotia, isn't it? Did you see any polar bears? What was your cargo? Timber, I expect. One day when—"

"Lily, Lily." Liam held up his hands in mock horror, then bent to cup his calloused palms round her small, pointed face. "Stop . . . stop and let me speak."

"Well, go on then."

"Lovebud, this isn't the time nor't place. Can't yer see that? We can't leave them fellers in that carriage fer much longer or they'll have wheels stripped off it an' them lovely horses whipped away an' carved up fer their Sunday dinners. Now, go and help Mrs Quinn while I go an' give them a hand. I promise I'll not go without . . . well . . ." He was not sure what he meant to say to this child whose face had begun to fall into lines of serious distress. She obviously meant them to have a long and interesting talk about the sea, the ships, his life, where he was to go and when she would see him again, so what was he to do? She missed her father, that was very evident and because he was a mariner, as her father had been, she had transferred something of her pa to him. But this was none of his business. Mrs Quinn was an honest, respectable woman and surely would not allow her mistress to get into some situation that would not be right for her, or the child. From what he could gather they were in dire circumstances right now and this job would give her at least a breathing space.

He stood up and drew Lily to her feet. The dog began to prance, obviously expecting some game, or perhaps a walk.

On an impulse, Liam gently pulled Lily to him so that her cheek was resting on his broad chest. Putting his own cheek on her silky hair, watched by the suddenly still figure of Molly Quinn, he put his arms about her. Hers went instantly round his waist and she appeared to nestle, like a homing pigeon, or a small, abandoned kitten, against him.

"Yer must go, lass, an' so must I, but if yer like I'll take a walk on this shore yer talk of an' we can have us a good old chinwag." Though he wanted to he did not tell her that it might not be advisable to inform Mr Crowther about this meeting. He knew of a man called Mr Crowther and if it was the same one, which he thought it might be, he would not like a common seaman meeting any "guests" of his. He felt uneasy and could you blame him? And for some odd reason he felt responsible, though God knows it was *not* his responsibility. He was in port for a week while the ship was checked over, their cargo unloaded and another, with the Royal Mail, taken on. If he could have a few private moments with Lily, make sure that for the time being she and her mother were safe, he would sail away with an easy mind.

"When, Liam?" Her voice was muffled in his waistcoat.

"How about the day after tomorrow?"

"What time?" having no notion of the routine of the big house where she was to be a guest, and neither had he.

"How about two o'clock?"

"You promise to be there?" She pulled away from him for a moment and peered up into his face. He felt a great desire to drop a comforting kiss on her smooth white forehead.

"I promise, lovebud."

13

Lily was never to forget that day. It was a milestone in her life, though she was not to know it then. The beginning of something that was to test her endurance, to challenge her courage, to subject her childish but resolute will to its very limits and it began the moment she stepped for the second time that day into the wide and gracious hallway of Oakwood Place.

Mr Crowther was waiting at the top of the steps as though he had been watching for them. It had begun to drizzle on the way out of the city and the coachman had stopped to put up the hood. As she got out of the carriage Mr Crowther ran down the steps with an umbrella to hold over her ma, urging her up them, holding her arm solicitously as though she were an invalid, which Lily supposed she was really. She had been ill ever since Pa died, hadn't she, at least in her mind. She was not as strong as Lily but she was recovering slowly and it seemed she had taken to Mr Crowther which was good.

"Come in, my dear, come in out of the rain," he was saying. "Let me take your cloak," which he threw carelessly to the hovering figure of the maidservant. "There's a good fire in the drawing-room and Maggie shall bring us some tea. Dinner won't be for a while," unaware that he would be lucky if dinner arrived at all, since Mrs Jackson had already gone stumping off through the stable yard and across the vegetable garden to the cottage that was now her home.

Lily saw Ma hesitate, waiting for Mrs Quinn, who was direct-ing a couple of maids who had appeared from somewhere or other in the unloading of their bags.

"Nay, don't you touch them, Mrs Quinn. We'll see to 'em. Yer rooms'r ready," one of them told her as she took a basket from the groom which Lily was glad of, for Mrs Quinn looked worried, tired, and could you blame her really? It was Liam who had put such a thought in her head, since up to now what Mrs Quinn had done for her and her ma had not been considered much.

"You'll help Mrs Quinn, won't you, lovebud," he'd told her as they had said goodbye. "She's got a lot on 'er plate wi' you an' yer ma. You must try an' see to yer ma, look after her until she's well again. Will yer promise?" And looking into his concerned face, willing to do anything to please him she had said she would.

"We've put yer on't first floor at th'end an' yer next door to one another fer't minute, not being sure what—"

"That'll do, Rosie." A chilling look from the maid who had taken Ma's cloak cut off the flow but Lily turned to smile at her. For some reason the maid, who seemed no older than herself, winked at her and her soaring spirits soared even further. She had a feeling she and Ma were going to enjoy this holiday, wondering, as the thought struck her, how long it would be for and what would happen when it was over. But it didn't really matter now, for Liam was back and that was all that mattered.

"Thanks, lass. If yer'll show us t'way I'd be grateful," she heard Mrs Quinn say. She took Ma's hand in hers, since it seemed to her that it would be best to get her settled somewhere. Somewhere she could begin to feel at home in. She could see that Mr Crowther didn't like it, though. He didn't want Ma to go to her room. He wanted her to go with him into the drawing-room, pour the tea, engage in conversation of some sort and Lily was surprised, since couldn't he see that Ma wasn't up to it? It all looked so lovely and Ma had gasped in pleasure as they had driven up the drive. It was growing dusk and every lamp in the place seemed to be lit, shining from every window like small bursts of sunshine, warm and welcoming. The hallway was the same, with lamps glowing on tables and even fixed to the wall so that there were circles of soft colour and softer shadows filling the hall and illuminating the staircase. But Ma was not easy, you could tell that.

"I'm sure Mrs Elliott would be glad of a cup of tea, Mrs Quinn," Mr Crowther persisted. "You and Lily go up and . . . well, unpack if you wish. Make sure everything is to your liking," meaning to Jane Elliott's liking he was telling them. "Then perhaps you might like to take over in the kitchen."

She was his servant now and as his servant he was dismissing her.

As they had hovered in the hallway waiting for the housemaid to go before them up the wide curving staircase, Lily had wanted to look about her. This was the second time that day she had entered Oakwood Place. She had been too nervous to notice anything the first time but now, especially since seeing Liam this afternoon and having the secret knowledge inside her that the day after tomorrow she was to see him again, she seemed to float in a stream of joy and well-being. She could feel it inside her, warm and comforting, like the hot toddy of honey, glycerine and lemon Ma used to give her when she had a cough. She could tackle anything now, now that she had Liam again. She could look about her in this lovely house and see things that had gone unnoticed before, but if Mr Crowther didn't leave Ma alone, let her rest for a while, there would be ructions. Today had been a big step for her and she'd done wonderfully well, but she needed to be left alone for a while until she had got used to this new place.

She told him so. "I think Ma would be best having an early night, Mr Crowther." She used her very best manners, polite as Ma and Pa had taught her to be, but Mr Crowther didn't like that either.

"I think your mother and I are the best judge of what she should or should not do, Lily. Now, off you go upstairs with Mrs Quinn. Perhaps it might be wise if *you* were the one to have an early night. Maggie will bring you a tray to your room. Oh, and" – turning to the hovering servant – "see to the dog, will you," eyeing Villy with some misgivings. Villy was excited. She was a young dog and as young dogs do she was busily exploring her new surroundings, sniffing energetically at every table and chair leg, poking her sharp little nose into corners and even jumping up for a moment against Mr Crowther's immaculate trouser leg. "Ask that lad in the kitchen to come and get her. Give her a feed and settle her in the stable with—"

"Oh, you can't do that, sir." On to Lily's face had come an expression of horror and she swooped down and lifted the wriggling dog into her arms, closing them protectively about her. "She sleeps with me, you see," and had done ever since her pa died. She and Villy would both be upset if they were separated now and Mr Crowther must be made to see it.

"Well, she must be taught her new place, Lily," as you must be taught yours, his expression said. "I have never allowed my dogs into the house. They are working dogs, retrievers which go with me on a shoot. I'm not quite sure what use . . . your dog will be but I'm willing to allow her to stay if you keep her—"

"Oh, no, I'm afraid not. If Villy can't stay then neither can I." Her young face was red with indignation. Her eyes flashed their message of defiance and her head tilted imperiously. She was not afraid of him her look told him, and for a moment he had it in him to admire her spirit. But it wouldn't do, of course. "We've never been parted," she went on fiercely, "not since I got her. She'd be frightened in the stable all by herself."

"She would be with my dogs, Lily. Dogs will usually settle down together, especially if one is a bitch."

Lily set her chin at a truculent angle. "I'm sorry, Mr Crowther, but it wouldn't work. She'd pine, you see, and cry all night, wouldn't she, Ma?"

It was as though she knew, through her mother, she had the upper hand of Joshua Crowther. He had taken a great shine to Ma and it seemed to her that whatever her ma wanted, Mr Crowther would provide. She hated to upset her mother, to put her in the position where she must . . . well, stand up for her but she could not have Villy howling away the night in a strange stable. Lily had never been in a stable but she knew you kept horses there and Villy was used to a bed, a proper bed, and would not take kindly to sleeping in straw!

Jane Elliott could feel the dreadful tension begin to paralyse her and, still hanging about at the foot of the stairs, Molly Quinn was ready to seize Lily and box her ears. The servants, clutching this and that ready to take it all upstairs, were frozen to the spot, only their eyes moving. No one, *no one* ever argued with the master and here was this slip of a girl, all big eyes in her flower-like face, tall but slender to the point of thinness, telling him that she would have her own way or she and her ma would be off, presumably taking their new housekeeper with them.

"Dearest?" the child asked her mother questioningly.

"Well, she does sleep on your bed, darling, and I'm not sure . . ."

Lily turned triumphantly to Joshua Crowther. "There, you see. I told you so."

It was in his eyes, not that the child could see it, nor her mother, but the servants who knew him watched, coiled tense as springs, for if he struck her as it seemed he longed to do what in heaven and earth would the mother do?

He gave in. It was the very first day. There were weeks, months, years in which to show this impertinent, obstinate child who was the master of this house but tonight it was in his own interest to keep Jane Elliott calm, happy, settled in and at home in what was to be her home if he had anything to do with it. Let them go upstairs to the suite of rooms he himself had inspected. Let them dine up there, the three of them and the bloody dog, but let the time come when the beautiful woman was totally his and things would be different then.

He was charming, gracious, courteous, the soul of consideration, wanting only their comfort, he told them, even the dog, making himself stroke Villy's rough coat and at once he could see the child was satisfied. Not only with her victory but with him. She believed him again. She trusted him again and if she trusted him, so would the mother.

He did not notice the strange look his new housekeeper shot in his direction. Not that it would have concerned him if he had.

"Sleep well," he told them. "Let the servants know if there is anything you require and we will meet again for breakfast when I shall introduce you to my daughter."

Their rooms were so comfortable, luxurious even, so tastefully decorated, so exquisitely appointed, both Jane and Lily gasped with delight as Maggie and Rosie ushered them in. The bed was the focal point, a large four-poster draped with curtains of cream muslin which were tied back with cream satin ribbon. The dressing-table was layered with the same cream muslin and ribbon and the floor was fitted from wall to wall with a delicately patterned Brussels carpet in peach and cream. The fireplace had a plain marble surround and in the heart of it a glowing fire cast dancing shadows of orange and gold on the plain walls and ceiling. The wardrobe and the chest of drawers were simple in design and of the best mahogany, glowing and satinlike in the light from several pretty lamps. There were flowers, a great vase of pink roses mixed with the misty white of gypsophila placed on a shining table where candles in silver candlesticks had been lit. Maggie moved across what seemed to be a vast amount of carpet and drew the curtains, which matched those of the bed, then beckoned to them to follow her through an open doorway to another room which was just as elegantly furnished, just as warm and comfortable, but smaller. Again there were flowers and a leaping fire and when Lily put Villy down the animal went at once to the rug in front of it, turned a couple of times until she had found the right spot, then lay down and closed her eyes in exhausted sleep. They all smiled, even Maggie.

"Well, someone's settled in at any rate," she said, then went on, "Mr Crowther thought yer might like to have yer own sittin'-room, ma'am. Fer when yer want ter be quiet. An' he ses you're ter make free with his library which yer'll see tomorrow. Now the little miss is ter sleep on that little day bed in't bedroom wi' you, an' Mrs Quinn is right next door."

She sniffed, evidently not agreeing with a housekeeper sleeping in the family's quarters but if Mr Crowther said so, then that was that. What he was up to was anybody's guess but time would tell. They did hope he was not going to take advantage of this lovely frail woman, but then who were they to interfere? What he did with himself, and with others, was nothing to do with them. They had decent jobs, a fair wage, good grub and comfortable quarters. What else could a servant ask for?

The next hurdle came when, after unpacking their bags while the child and Mrs Elliott drifted round like two children in a toyshop, exclaiming over this and that, Mrs Quinn told them briskly that she was off to the kitchen to see about something to eat.

"I'll come with you, Mrs Quinn," Mrs Elliott said at once, hurriedly putting down the slender figure of a shepherdess she had been examining.

"I think it'd be best if you was ter stay wi' Lily, Mrs Elliott. Mr Crowther might not like it if we was ter wander round in 'is 'ouse uninvited, like. You settle down 'ere an' I'll fetch yer up a bite ter eat. Now, what d'yer fancy?" having no idea what might be found in the household's pantry. "'Appen a nice coddled egg an' some toast ter be goin' on with. Look, 'ere's yer sewin' an' while I'm down there I'll see if there's owt else wants mendin'. Bound ter be summat in a place this size, wouldn't yer think?"

Distracted, Jane smiled tentatively. "Yes, indeed. Then . . . then you want me and Lily to stay here," looking round the lovely, firelit, lamplit room and, finding nothing to alarm her, sat down in the small sewing chair by the sitting-room fire. She leaned down and smoothed Villy's rough fur. Villy lifted her head and gently licked her hand, then rested her head on her knee. The child sprawled on the rug at her feet, her arms round the dog's neck and they all three stared placidly into the flames.

Letting out her breath on a long sigh of relief and telling them she wouldn't be long, Mrs Quinn slipped from the room.

She quite enjoyed the atmosphere of the enormous kitchens which were as warm as the rest of the house and smelled of the bread Mrs Jackson had baked that morning. The maids scuttled about as she opened the door and walked in, not sure whether she was to be a harridan like old Mrs Jackson, but Mrs Quinn had decided on a slow, undemanding approach to this new challenge in her life, at least until she'd found her feet.

"Now then, ter start with p'raps it'd be as well if you was ter tell me yer names an' wha' yer duties are."

They were Maggie and Rosie, whom she had already met, Betsy who was second-in-command to Maggie, Jenny who was eleven and general skivvy, Dora who was kitchen maid and the one Mrs Quinn thought would be most useful to her, and Maggie number two, called simply "Maggie Two" to distinguish her from Maggie, the head parlourmaid. There was a Mrs Ambler who was the laundry maid but she had gone home for the night, and Jackie, the boot boy who had been so helpful on the question of the kittens.

Which gave her an idea but first things first.

"Now then, lasses, yer may remember Mr Crowther sayin' I were to employ a cook, which I will, but while one's found we'll 'ave ter mekk do wi' me. A plain cook, that's wharr I am burr I reckon this lass 'ere," indicating Dora, "will give us an 'and. 'As owt been prepared fer ternight?" And when a beautiful piece of roast pork was produced, crisp with crackling and seething in its own juices she was triumphant. There was nothing to making a bit of decent gravy, roasting a few potatoes and steaming the fresh cabbage which it seemed the gardener had left at the kitchen door only an hour since. Rice pudding, what did they say to that? she asked them, plain fare but wholesome and well cooked and could the Queen herself ask for more than that. If Dora'd be so good as to begin on the vegetables, potatoes first to roast in the oven, the magnificence of which overwhelmed her, then she'd just slip up with a tray for Mrs Elliott and the child.

But first she'd like a word with Jackie. The lad's face fell when she called him out, for what could he possibly have done wrong in the short time she had been in the kitchen? He'd been carefully scraping the mud off Miss Eloise's boots, for she had been riding that day and they were in a right mess. He was sure she did it on purpose. How could someone get mud on their bloody boots when they were sitting on a bloody horse, he asked no one in particular, and got no answer, for none of the women in the kitchen gave him the time of day.

His face fell into a delighted smile as she whispered in his ear and he scampered off across the kitchen and out of the back door with great enthusiasm.

They were still sitting by the fire when Molly returned. She wore the voluminous white apron she had found in one of the kitchen drawers and looked every inch what she knew she was going to be, an efficient and well-respected housekeeper. The girls in the kitchen had not exactly jumped to do her bidding but there had been no covert mutterings or a reluctance to obey her orders. They had set to with the vegetables, and with setting up the dining-room table for the master. Maggie had taken her through to see it when she and Betsy had finished and it had looked a real treat. Shining cutlery, silver by the look of it, an immaculate white cloth and napkins, flowers, glassware that gave off shafts of reflected light and this was all for one man. Well, that was how many places had been set.

She had a tray in her hands as she entered the sitting-room but the moment she came in the dog sat up and began to get excited.

"Are you hungry, Villy?" the child asked, taking the tray from Mrs Quinn and setting it on the table which was drawn up to the fireside chairs, but Villy was sniffing at Mrs Quinn's apron pocket, not sure whether to growl, and when Mrs Quinn drew out a dainty kitten and placed it in Mrs Elliott's lap they all burst out laughing since Villy looked so bewildered.

Jane Elliott was enchanted. The kitten blinked in the lamplight, disorientated by its bumpy journey from the kitchen in Mrs Quinn's deep apron pocket. It craned its neck and peered about it, flinching back from the interested face of Villy who put her black button nose on Jane's knee. It seemed she had decided that this strange creature was no threat to her, or to her family and might even be the source of a good game.

Jane laughed in delight. She picked up the tiny, pretty animal, cradling it against her own bright face. It had a black and white patchwork body, a pair of transparent, saucily winking green eyes set in a pointed, triangular face and was as soft and smooth as the finest velvet.

"Aah, Mrs Quinn, Mrs Quinn, isn't he lovely?" she exclaimed, like a child who has just been given an unexpected present. "Is he for me?"

"Aye, lamb, 'e's all yours. Or should I say 'she'. That lad downstairs fetched 'er specially for yer."

"I must go and thank him at once." Jane stood up, the kitten on her shoulder but Mrs Quinn sat her down again.

"Nay, my lass, termorrer'll do. Now I only 'ope that dratted dog tekks to 'er," though in Mrs Quinn's sad opinion that dratted dog would soon be relegated to the stable, since Mr Crowther had struck her as a man who got his own way, one way or another, sooner or later. She'd not missed the twist to his mouth nor the gleam in his eyes when he had given in to the child.

"Can I hold her, Ma?" Lily begged, her eyes shining, her face rosy in the firelight. She took the wriggling body from her mother's shoulder who reluctantly let it go. She kissed its face, then, reaching for a small ball of wool from her ma's workbasket, she put the kitten down, rolled the ball of wool across the carpet and watched the small animal chase it. When the kitten caught the ball, it pawed it delicately, then rose to its back legs in a fierce battle with it. Both Jane and Lily, laughing as they had not laughed since Richard Elliott's death, were on their knees now with Villy an interested spectator but ready to join in at some point. They were giddy with the fun of it, even Molly, and did not hear the knock at the door.

Joshua Crowther, getting no reply, opened the door and

came upon a scene which, even in his wildest, most hopeful imagination, he had not expected. Perhaps a hesitant acceptance of the loveliness he had had created for her. A shy bobbing of her exquisite head, an uncertain smile of politeness, but this merry intoxication, this almost childlike glee, this sense of bewitchment and all over a bloody kitten, filled him with deep satisfaction. Nothing had prepared him for it and he was struck dumb for a moment. He was not awfully sure he cared for her undignified sprawling about on the floor, nor her squeal to the child to "Catch her, darling, before she climbs the curtains," but it was infinitely better than downstairs in the hall when she had clung to Mrs Quinn and a vast improvement on the blank-faced creature she had been this morning. Christ, was it only this morning? It seemed as though weeks had gone by since he had first seen her drifting about his garden, burying her face in his spring flowers, holding the hand of the child beside her. His whole life and what he wanted from it, demanded of it, had been refocused at that moment, to his own astonishment, for he had known many beautiful, desirable women before, during his marriage and after the death of his wife. He had had no wish to marry again in those ten years. He had children. He was a sociable man who did a lot of entertaining, managing it very nicely without a hostess, though there had been many who would gladly have taken up the position. He was entertained in his turn by his many business acquaintances and their wives. He had no friends, not close friends, and needed none. He was perfectly satisfied with his life, wanting for nothing.

Until he had seen Jane Elliott wandering in his garden. He was a man who did not act on impulse, though he could make a snap judgement, or decision in business, but all his senses, all his male instincts, as they had never done before, had become concentrated on this one woman and he must have her for his own as soon as possible. It would have to be marriage, of course. She was too closely linked to her child and the old woman, who had risen respectfully to her feet as he entered the room. They had great influence over her and were fiercely protective of her and if he alarmed her in the slightest she would be whisked away out of his reach.

"What have we here?" His voice was soft with a smile in it as he squatted down beside them. It did not do to tower over a group one wished to join.

Jane turned her velvet grey eyes on him. They were warm with emotion and he was bowled over by the luminous quality of radiance that shone there, not at all concerned that it was not directed at, or for him. He had not known her before her husband's death and so had no conception of how she had been then. No conception of the strength of love that had lived in her, of the sweetness of her spirit, the constancy, the humour and sparkle and yet gentleness which she had given to just one man. If he had he might have paused to consider, but he did not and so he moved gently forward, longing to bulldoze, since he was not a man for waiting.

Here, captured by the absurdity of a black and white kitten, the spirit of Jane Elliott had momentarily returned and he was bewitched by it.

"Look, Mr Crowther, look what Mrs Quinn has found for me. Isn't she darling?" She looked anxious for a moment, a frown dipping her delicately arched eyebrows. "I may keep her, mayn't I? I have quite fallen in love with her."

He could quite cheerfully have strangled the damn thing which, he found to his own annoyance, he felt jealous of. As *he* could not have done, the kitten had brought her back to life again, but he smiled, resisting the temptation to push a shining curl that had come adrift from her neat bun behind her ear.

"Of course you may, as long as she and the dog get along."

"Oh, I'm sure they will." Then, as though suddenly conscious of the unseemly sprawl of her position on the floor, she attempted to rise, trapping her feet in the full skirt of her gown. He rose swiftly and held out his hands to her and with no more than a second's hesitation she took them. He was wise enough to let go of her immediately they were both on their feet, and when she sat down in the fireside chair he lowered himself uncomfortably into the one opposite her.

She was grave now but there was still a small residue of laughter in her eyes as she watched the kitten leap dementedly over the back of the bemused dog.

"I just came up to see if you had everything you need," he told her, doing his best not to stare too long or too fiercely at her glowing face.

"Thank you, I'm sure we have. It is most kind . . ." She stopped as though some sense of the strangeness of the circumstances between them had stirred in her mind, but the child laughed and the dog growled in mock ferocity and she turned back to him, the thought gone.

"We are very comfortable, Mr Crowther, thank you."

"You are more than welcome, Mrs Elliott. I . . . I was just about to dine and wondered . . . ?"

"Yes?"

"Whether you would care to join me? There is no need to change."

He could have kicked himself as the look of confusion and self-doubt clouded her face. He had gone too far and too bloody fast again and just when she was doing so well in her acceptance of the situation, which a woman who had her wits about her would have realised at once was not correct. Not even proper in this world where the "look" of the thing was all-important.

"Or perhaps we might leave it for a day or two?" he went on smoothly, making a great effort to be casual about it and was at once rewarded by her look of gratitude.

"Yes . . . thank you, Mr Crowther."

"Well, I'll leave you to your fun. Perhaps you and your daughter will breakfast with me and my daughter in the morning."

She appeared surprised. Evidently his words earlier had gone unnoticed by her, by her child and by his new house-keeper, for it had not been remarked on.

"You have a daughter, Mr Crowther?"

"Indeed I have, Mrs Elliott. And a son."

"Well . . ."

Seeing that she did not know how to reply to his declaration, he went on smoothly, "My son is away at school at present. His name is Nicholas and he is sixteen. My daughter, who is ten years old, is called Eloise."

"What a pretty name. And your wife?"

"My wife passed away ten years ago when Eloise was born, Mrs Elliott," doing his best to arrange his features into a suitable expression of sorrow. Hadn't he told her this earlier? he asked himself but then she placed her hand on his in great sympathy and every thought wheeled from his head like a flock of starlings swooping over a roof, leaving it empty of anything but the determination that this woman would be his by the time summer came or he would know the reason why.

14

Joshua sat at the head of the breakfast table, his daughter on his left hand, Maggie and Betsy standing self-effacingly at the serving table against the wall. He was not aware that he was almost holding his breath as he waited for her.

The breakfast-room faced south and the sunlight, which was a blessing after the drizzle of the previous afternoon, fell through the two tall windows, clear and bright, burnishing the mahogany of the rectangular table to a mirror-like sheen in which the faces of the father and daughter were reflected. Against the third wall was a delicate Georgian sideboard of varied mahogany veneers on which stood a big Chinese vase painted with deer and little fir trees in brown and green on a white background. The walls were painted a delicate green and the velvet curtains, which were pulled back as far as possible to allow in the light, and the carpet were a much darker green. There was a fireplace with a basket grate in which was banked a coal fire though it was not a cold day. The coal was kept in a bright copper scuttle and next to it on the hearth were a substantial poker, tongs and a shovel. Behind the serving table was a curtain of washable silk on a brass rail to prevent the splashing of grease on the wall. Around the wall were a dozen watercolours of rural landscapes.

When she finally came, the one he was waiting for, he had no idea of the time and patient persuasion it had taken Lily and Mrs Quinn to get her there. It seemed that Jane did not want to leave the safe, calm haven of the room and go through the comfortably solid doors which protected her and had begged to be left here with Beauty, the name she had given the kitten. She would prefer to have breakfast here, she had told them tearfully and all the while Mrs Quinn got her into the simple morning dress of the palest apple blossom unwatered moire she had pleaded in such a pitiful manner Mrs Quinn had almost decided to let her have her way.

"Well, I'm going down, Ma," Lily told her stoutly. "I want to explore the gardens for a start and then I mean to walk down to the river. I know Villy would love it and I'm sure you would too."

"D'you think so, darling? It certainly sounds very pleasant." Her mother sounded doubtful.

"And then it would only be manners to be introduced to his daughter. You know how important manners are. You've always said so."

Clever little thing, Mrs Quinn thought admiringly. She had hit on the very thing that would persuade Mrs Elliott that to go downstairs was the only correct and courteous thing to do. A few days ago not even this would have penetrated the barricade of Jane's grief and tearing sense of loss, but this house, this lovely room, the splendid view of the river which Lily was in raptures over, the conservatory, the kitten, they had all served to draw her from her prison, or at least persuaded her to peep through the open door that had been presented to her.

He stood up as she entered the room, her hand clasped tightly in Lily's. He was not to know that she had clung to her daughter all the way down the stairs. He took in every detail of her gown, the colour of which brought a faint pinkness to her cheeks, and the perfect shape of her mouth, a soft rose. His only criticism was her hair which had been dragged back quite severely from her white brow. He would have liked to see a looseness, perhaps a careless tumble of curls, ribbons of apple blossom twined in it, but quite evidently Mrs Quinn was not up to that sort of thing and one of the first things he must do was to get her a lady's maid. Someone to look after her appearance and her clothes, to dress her hair and present her as the lady, the *wife* he meant her to be. Thank God she was not wearing black as widows were expected to do for God knows how long, wondering why for a moment, then forgetting it as he moved towards her.

Joshua was casually dressed in a tweed jacket and sand-coloured breeches. He was to go riding later and his boots were a credit to the lad in the boot-room off the kitchen. His shirt was immaculately laundered and about his neck was an equally faultless cravat. He looked very distinguished, tall and lean, his dark hair with a touch of grey at the temples, his deep blue, almost black eyes searching hers in a way she did not understand.

"Mrs Elliott, and Lily. We're so glad you felt able to join us, aren't we, darling?" He turned to the young girl at the table who stood up politely as her governess had taught her to do when addressing an adult. "This is my daughter, Eloise. Eloise, this is Mrs Elliott and *her* daughter, Lily. As I told you earlier they are to be our guests for a while."

To Lily's great astonishment Eloise curtseyed prettily to Ma.

"Mrs Elliott," she said, then looked at Lily and in her eyes was something cold and slithery which seemed ridiculous since they were a beautiful hyacinth blue and as innocent as the day. She did not speak and neither did Lily, just looked assessingly as though each were measuring the strengths and weaknesses of the other. Joshua watched them for a moment as though he too were measuring something then he turned back to Jane.

"Come and sit here by me, Mrs Elliott," taking her limp hand and leading her gallantly to the chair opposite his daughter, "and perhaps Lily will sit next to Eloise."

Lily did as she was told, seating herself at the table where a place had already been set for her, or at least for someone. Ma looked as though she longed to sit beside her, as near to her as possible, in fact, but Mr Crowther was holding her chair for her and she had no option but to sit in it.

"Now, what would you like, Mrs Elliott? We have . . ." He turned to Maggie enquiringly.

"There's porridge, sir, or fruit. Peaches and melon and grapefruit. Or perhaps a mixture of all of them." She smiled kindly at the frightened-looking lady who appeared to have lost her tongue. "Shall I bring you a small portion of each, madam?" and with great relief Jane nodded.

"And you, Lily?"

"I'll start with porridge, thanks, then I'll have some fruit." Her pa had always told that porridge set you up for the day and so, though she didn't care for it, that's what she'd have. She shook out her napkin and placed it on her lap, turning to beam at Maggie. She needed a good breakfast, since she meant to be off the minute it was over, though she didn't tell them that.

"Would you care for some coffee, madam?" Maggie began, again speaking in a kindly fashion, for you could tell the poor lady was quite bemused. Maggie didn't know why since she seemed to be a person who would be accustomed to the ways and manners of the gentry, but even last night when they had taken her up to her rooms you could tell she wasn't quite . . . quite right. And her so beautiful and fragile somehow. Mrs Quinn, their new housekeeper, was saying nothing, though while she had supervised the breakfasts this morning they had all tried to get her to divulge something about Mrs Elliott and the child. Well, not *all* of them, for Jenny and Jackie, the skivvy and the boot boy counted for nothing and would no more question those above them than they would speak to Mr Crowther.

"Ma doesn't like coffee, do you, Ma? She'll have tea."

"Of course, madam. With milk or lemon?"

"She likes it with milk for breakfast," Lily told them as she spooned her porridge into her mouth. The girl next to her as yet had said nothing and it seemed she was not going to. Stuck-up little beggar in Lily's opinion but she didn't care. She didn't want to make a friend of anyone who might interfere with her plans for the day, and especially tomorrow.

As though he had read her mind Mr Crowther turned to her mother. "And what do you and Lily plan for today, Mrs Elliott? The weather is so lovely it might be pleasant to show you about the gardens and then, if you feel up to it, we could go up to the paddock and have a look at the horses. I'm to ride later and I could introduce you to my hunter whose name is Ebony." He smiled. "You will see why when you meet him."

"He must be black," Lily offered pleasantly enough, doing her best to make up for Ma's silence and the girl next to her sniggered.

"What's funny about that?" she asked, turning to glare at the dark and dainty prettiness of Eloise Crowther.

"Well, I would have thought it very obvious that he must be black with a name like Ebony," Eloise said loftily, smiling at her father as though to ask had he ever come across such ignorance. The smile slipped from her face when he frowned at her.

161

"That is not a kind thing to say, Eloise. In fact it was rude and we are not rude to guests. Apologise at once."

It was plain that Eloise was flabbergasted. "But, Papa, it *is*—"

"That is enough, child. Apologise to Lily."

She mumbled something in Lily's direction and Lily smiled triumphantly as she passed her empty bowl to Maggie and began to tuck into a heaped plate of colourful and deliciously smelling mixed fruit.

"And will yer 'ave bacon ter follow, Miss Lily?" Maggie asked her, pleased to see someone at this table tuck in. "There's tomatoes or eggs or mushrooms or—"

"I'll have all of that, please, Maggie. What about you, Ma?"

"Oh, I think not . . ."

"Perhaps a slice of toast with marmalade, or honey, madam?"

"Yes, that would be lovely." Jane smiled up at Maggie, then turned to Joshua who caught the tail end of it and was again pole-axed by the loveliness of it.

"So, would you like to see the gardens, Mrs Elliott?" he asked her patiently.

"We would, wouldn't we, Lily?" she asked her daughter.

"Aah . . ." Joshua smiled in what he hoped was a reassuring manner. "I thought while she was here Lily might like to join Eloise in her lessons."

"What!" Lily's head came up swiftly and she swallowed a piece of melon, almost choking.

Joshua ignored the interruption. "From what Mrs Quinn told me Lily has missed a great deal of schooling since . . . well, lately, so I was positive you would agree with me that she should attempt to catch up. Miss Kaye is an excellent governess and would be happy to welcome Lily to the schoolroom."

"Ma, please, you can't . . . oh, please, Ma . . ."

"Lily, I'm sure your mother will agree with me."

"This is nothing to do with you . . . sir," Lily added belatedly. "This is to do with me and Ma. I don't want to be shut up in a schoolroom with" – she turned and gave Eloise a scornful look – "with . . . with anyone. This is supposed to be a holiday, you said so."

"Mrs Elliott, what do *you* think? Is Lily's education important to you?" His smile was gentle, soothing, persuasive.

"Oh, yes, most important . . ."

"There, that is settled then."

"No, it isn't," Lily said desperately. The very idea of being shut away in some schoolroom with only this disdainfully smiling girl and her governess for company was appalling. She intended gathering Villy, and Ma, if Ma wanted it, and finding her way down to the river. To explore every inch of the gardens, which appeared to be extensive. From the bedroom window she had caught sight of neat avenues, ornamental ponds, long paths leading, she was sure, to some wild, exciting place in the woods and even, just beyond the woods and outlined against the sky, a peculiar little building with turrets. She meant to investigate every nook and cranny, every clearing and tree in the woods. Even to climb a few. She wanted to know the exact layout of the property so that tomorrow she could find Liam without delay.

There was a deep, implacable sigh from Mr Crowther.

"Really, Lily, you must learn that children—"

Rescue came from an unexpected quarter and it was a measure of Jane Elliott's slow journey to recovery and her frail courage that made her aware that her child, for the first time, needed her support which she knew had been sadly depleted since Richard's death. She would never, never recover from it totally, she knew that, but something in Mr Crowther's manner, his assumption that he could order Richard's child about as though she were his own, put a fragile and unexpected stiffener in her back. It would not last long, for it meant she had to emerge from the quiet place in which she had felt safe for the past few months, but while it did she must give Lily what she needed, what she was appealing for, from her. From her mother.

"I believe Lily is . . . would like a day or two to get used to things, wouldn't you, darling, as I would, before she is included in . . . whatever plans you might have for her, Mr Crowther. If you would be . . . patient with both of us for a while we would be most grateful. You have been so kind . . ."

It was the longest utterance she had made and both the maids held their breath, wondering what the master would say. Not only the child but the mother defying him, and in front of them as well. Not that there was a lot he could do about it, since she was a guest in his house. He had no influence over her, no rights as a member of her family might have, or a husband, for instance. She was perfectly at liberty to pack her bags and leave as spontaneously as she had come. The little lass was splitting her face in a huge smile of loving approval directed at her ma and you could see Miss Eloise was tickled pink by the whole ruckus and was dying to see her papa's enormous temper let fly.

But Joshua Elliott had learned self-control and patience in his years as the astute businessman he was and though he longed to take the child by the arm and haul her off to the schoolroom with instructions that she was to have a good thrashing for her insolent disobedience, he showed nothing of it in his expressionless face. Inside him was the smouldering fire of anger which was lit when he was crossed but he did not show it to the frail creature beside him. Not yet!

"Of course, my dear, you must do just whatever pleases you, and so must Lily. I want you to feel as though you are in your own home. If you wish to wander about, in the house, or the garden, then you shall. But my offer still stands. Perhaps when I go up to the paddock you might like to accompany me, but if not then I will quite understand."

She even went so far as to put a grateful hand on his sleeve, causing his desire for her to leap like a salmon in a river. Dear God, had any woman ever affected him as this one did? And though he racked his brain he could think of none. Not even as a hot-blooded youth.

Eloise Crowther had listened to this exchange between her father and the interloper, which was how she thought of the girl, with total astonishment, not only that she dare argue with him but that she should get away with it. But now she saw that not only was the girl a trespasser on her father's time, which had up to now been exclusively hers, but the woman had a hold on him too. She was ten years old, the same age as the girl, her father had told her, and for the whole of those ten years she had been his pet, spoiled and indulged by him. And he was the centre of her universe. She knew exactly how far she could go with her coaxing and wheedling and her charming little ways that laughingly persuaded him that this or that was something she must have. He did not often refuse her and she supposed that was because all she had wanted from him in the past had been easily granted. But she knew him to be implacable in his passionate certainty that he was always right, turning away any man's challenge of his authority. Her own brother was an example, for Papa did his best to stamp out any defiance shown by Nicky which was why she was amazed that this girl had so easily overcome him. She was too young to know that it was not Lily who had bested her father but Lily's mother.

Though it was sunny there was a nip in the wind which blew straight from the river and both Lily and Jane were well wrapped up. Villy, released from her overnight prison, went mad with delight, chasing her own tail and generally playing silly beggars, as Lily called it. She ran on ahead of them, eager to be off to whatever waited for them in this wonderful dogs' paradise.

Lily linked her arm in Ma's, stepping out from the side door of the house which Maggie had shown them and which led to a small, sheltered but overgrown garden. Across the neglected garden, and let into a high stone wall, was a handsome wrought-iron gate. They opened it with the excited daring of two travellers in a foreign land, peeping out to see what lay beyond, which turned out to be a vast lawn on which an elderly gardener was steering a lawnmower pulled by a small pony. There was a boy with him who was carefully raking up the sprinkling of grass cuttings and putting them in a wheelbarrow. The lawn already looked immaculate, as did the rest of the garden and the neatly clipped hedge that divided it from whatever was on the other side. Villy instantly disappeared from view.

"Good morning," Lily piped up, smiling at the boy's look of total amazement. She supposed they were a bit of a surprise, her and Ma, for neither of them possessed what might be called country clothes. Her scarlet cloak and Ma's elegant town mantle in which she had arrived yesterday looked entirely out of place but it didn't matter. She had had the foresight to make sure they both wore their stoutest and plainest boots.

The gardener turned, for a moment losing the graceful symmetry of the line he was following on the downward slope of the lawn. He whoa-ed the pony to a stop which it did with great willingness, putting its head down to crop the grass not yet cut.

Both the gardener and his lad stared with respectful admiration at the two lovely females who had been the talk of the servants hall last night. After the new housekeeper had gone up, of course. Who were they and what were they doing here were the two questions that were constantly asked and there had been no answers. Now, here they were, walking briskly through his domain and would they stop and speak? Both of them doffed their caps in readiness.

"Mornin', miss, mornin', ma'am," the older gardener answered.

They stopped at once, the child's eyes bright with interest, the woman's a bit shy, he thought, but ready to smile.

"What a lovely place you have here," the child said artlessly, as though it all belonged to him. "Do you and" – she nodded at the boy who was struck dumb – "do all this by yourselves?"

"Bless yer, no, miss. There's me an' Will 'ere, and then there's Mr Roddy an' 'is lad Benjy."

"And what is your name, sir?"

"I'm Mr Diggle, Miss."

"My name's Lily, Mr Diggle, and this is my ma, Mrs Elliott, and that was my dog Villy who's just vanished behind the hedge. We're guests of Mr Crowther's," she added grandly.

"That's nice, Miss Lily," the gardener answered awkwardly, wondering what to add to this, but Mrs Elliott cleared her throat and at once the man and the boy turned to her.

"Mr Diggle, I wonder . . ." she began hesitantly.

"Yes, ma'am?" he said reverently.

"Could you tell me the name of that lovely yellow bush in the . . . the other part of the garden?"

"Yer'll be meanin' the forsythia, I reckon. It's right bonny, int'it?"

"Oh, yes," Jane breathed.

"Trouble is, it don't last long, the blossom, I mean."

"Doesn't it, Mr Diggle?"

"No, ma'am, more's the pity."

"Oh, indeed. And could you . . . I do hope you don't mind my asking but . . . ?"

"Yes, ma'am?" his expression saying she could ask till the cows came home and he wouldn't mind.

"That little garden," turning to point at the high wall and the gate through which they had just come. "Why is it so neglected? You have the rest so beautiful, I wondered . . ."

"Oh, that were Mrs Crowther's garden, Mrs Elliott. She were

a rare one for herbs, was Mrs Crowther. When she died I wanted to keep it up but Mr Crowther said no. I couldn't tell yer why, ma'am." Then, as though he might have said too much, he clamped his lips together tightly.

Both he and Will waited for the heavenly being to speak again but it was the child, obviously her daughter, who chirped up.

"We thought we would just go down to the shore, Mr Diggle, if you could direct us." She was so excited at the thought of getting down to that magical place where her heart had always lain, her cheeks had flamed to poppy and her eyes were diamond stars in her vivid face. Mr Diggle was hard put to decide who was the more lovely of the two. The slender swaying grace of the woman who made him think of the sweet-scented white jasmine in the winter garden, or the vital colour of the bonny child. They both had the same cloud of silver pale hair, for neither wore a bonnet, but really, he was getting daft in the head and him a bloody grandfather!

"Just follow this path, miss," pointing with a gnarled, soil-encrusted finger along the edge of the lawn to a gap in the hedge. "Go right past the kitchen garden and the greenhouses then turn right. There's an orchard. The ground might be a bit rough. Then yer come to a birra woodland. Just keep on an' yer'll hit the shore."

"Well, thank you, Mr Diggle," the child beamed.

"Thank you, Mr Diggle," the mother echoed and for quite a full minute he and Will stood as though transfixed until they had disappeared through the gap in the hedge.

Mr Diggle hummphed. "Well, don't stand there gawpin', lad. Get them clippin's over ter't compost 'eap," he growled, knowing he was being unfair since he had gawped just as much as Will.

Lily and Jane, with Lily in the lead, followed a dim, chequered tunnel through the narrow strip of woodland described by Mr Diggle. The sun shone through the burgeoning branches already shivering with a light burden of leaves. The grass was soft and starred with wood anemones. A finch chattered in a holly bush, only to fall silent as Villy caught up with them, skidding to a stop as she plunged from the stand of trees to the narrow strip of rough grass that edged it and on to the long stretch of golden sand which lazed away in both directions. It was completely empty as far as the eye could see, which was due, of course, to the fact that the men who owned the houses that lined the shore owned the shore itself, right down to where the little waves trilled on to the sand.

And there they were, the ships, plying busily up and down the great highway of the River Mersey. Ships of every shape and size, some with lilting, graceful lines, dipping through the silver grey waters like birds in flight, others as sturdy and ponderous as the elephants at the Zoological Gardens on West Derby Road. They were on their way to Garston Dock, serving the rapidly growing export trade in coal, to Widnes and Runcorn to discharge cargoes and take on others in the never-ending traffic that had made Liverpool the second biggest port in the country.

Lily sat down on the lightly warmed sand and Villy flopped down beside her but her ma wandered off, bending to pick up shells and stones, perfectly content, it seemed, in the total peace and emptiness that surrounded them. Gulls wheeled dizzily, following in the wake of ships that were discharging rubbish. Ships' sirens hooted. The sun shone and the child and the woman breathed deeply of the sudden sweetness that had come into their lives, lives that had been torn apart so savagely when Richard Elliott died. Sweetness mixed with the salt tang of the sea, the river, the tiny fragrances that came on the ships from faraway places and eddied about them, familiar fragrances to them both, for they had both been born and bred in this great seaport.

Lily sat with her knees drawn up and her arms clasped about them. The old spell of the sea worked in her as she dreamed about what it would be like to sail away on the tide, to go to places with exotic names such as Rio de Janeiro, New Orleans, Trinidad as these ships before her were doing. One day it would be her turn. She just knew it. She didn't know how, she only knew with a certainty that settled in her like the soothing touch of her pa who had comforted her babyhood and young childhood that it was her destiny. She did not know where the *Lily-Jane* had gone to. She had disappeared as Pa had disappeared, but one day she would find her and her life would be complete, rounded, perfect.

In the meanwhile, there was Liam!

15

She did not take Villy, since she thought she might interfere with the important discussions she and Liam were to have. It would not do to be constantly interrupted by the dog who liked to have sticks thrown for her, so she had been left with Ma and Beauty in the quiet of the sitting-room. She hadn't liked it.

Lily saw him coming from a long way off and the pulse of excitement and gladness inside her seemed not at all unusual. It was how she had felt when Pa came home. A great surge of happiness, bliss even, and the certainty that for the period she was with him she was understood, protected, wrapped about in a devoted care that would never let her down. She trusted him as she had trusted her pa and it did not occur to her to wonder why. He had given her back what she had lost with Pa, right from that first moment at Canning Dock when she had gone to look for the *Lily-Jane*, and her heart lifted and her mind sang and her sturdy boots took wing as she sprang to her feet and began to race towards him.

He had not seen her. He had his head bent, looking down at his own feet as he trudged through the sand which was soft and fine. He had walked from the Custom House along Wapping Street at the back of Canning Dock, Salthouse Dock, Wapping Dock and Queen's Dock until he reached Sefton Street, then, when he came to the bathing sheds that served the swimmers, dropped down on to Pottery Beach. From there he continued above the high-water mark round Dingle Point to Jericho Shore. It was here that the mansions of the men of wealth and consequence began. Silverdale, Ladymeadow, High Cross and Oakwood Place, none of which could be seen from the beach. There was a strand of trees edging each property which screened those who lived there from the rude stares of trespassers.

It was another soft spring day, the arch of the sky a pale and lovely blue with a feathering of gauzy clouds away across the river above Birkenhead. As he had walked along Sefton Street, on his left he had passed meadows criss-crossed by footpaths and carpeted with cranesbill, a shimmering lilac-blue carpet moving in the slight breeze. There was lady's bedstraw like delicate lace of the palest yellow tangled with the brilliant green of new grass. Sycamore and beech had sprung, almost overnight in the stretches of woodland that lined the shore, into full-leaved grace and beyond the swell of a dune, through the spread of oak and ash, he could see orchards studded with fruit trees, in a froth of pink and white blossom. It was warm and he had removed his jacket and tie, carrying his jacket over one shoulder, letting the sun and wind brown the already amber skin of his strong throat. The sunshine caught in his short curly hair, turning it to gleaming gold. He lifted his head and his pale blue-grey eyes studied the water to his right. There was shipping of every kind in the river, their movement keeping the waters constantly on the swell and sending wavelets of white foam up on to the beach before sinking back into the sun-gilded river. Several oystercatchers were searching for cockles at the water's edge, their black and white plumage and orange beaks distinctive against the pale sand. Their call was loud and strident, frightening away a more timid grey plover.

He looked away and ahead then and saw her and felt his face split into a huge grin of delight, but, unlike Lily, he was surprised by the strength and strangeness of his feelings. She was skimming the sand as lightly as the gulls rode the breeze over the river, the shining silver weight of her plait thudding between her shoulder blades. She wore a white dress of some light material with a strawberry pink sash of satin about her waist and a bow of the same colour and material tied at the end of the plait. She was laughing, her teeth white and perfect between her rosy lips, her eyes narrowed and gleaming like newly minted silver through her dark lashes. He stopped and held out his arms and when she flew into them he swung her round and round until they were both dizzy, losing their balance to fall in a crazy heap on to the sand. It seemed they couldn't stop laughing though neither knew at exactly what.

It was a lovely day. They were both young with life stretching away ahead of them, hidden perhaps for the moment but certain to be exciting, for they were neither of them willing to settle for the blandness of conformity. He wanted his own ship, and, though it struck him as an odd thought to have, so did she. She wanted her own ship, her father's ship which had been stolen from her by some cruel twist of fate and though he could not see how she could possibly do it, he knew she would try her damnedest. He had learned that much about her in the short time he had known her.

As though she had caught a sense of what was in his mind her first words were of the *Lily-Jane*.

"You haven't seen my pa's ship, have you, Liam?" she asked him wistfully. "I know someone has her, *stole* her, more like." Her voice was sad and bitter, strange in one so young. "When I get the chance I'm going to go down to the docks and have a good nosey round." This was one of Mrs Quinn's expressions. "Someone must know who has her. What about the Mersey Docks and Harbour Board? Don't they keep records of ships moving in and out of port?"

"There are records, yes, lovebud, but whether they'd let yer get a look at 'em, I couldn't say. I've not seen her though," which was not a lie.

"She must be trading, mustn't she, Liam? In the coastal trade like my pa did?"

"Aye, I suppose she must."

"One day I'll find her and when I do I'm going to the police and tell them about her being stolen and when they've gone to gaol, whoever pinched her, I'm going to get Mr Porter and Johnno and Mick to sail her for me. Just until I'm old enough to do it myself." Though she was naïve in her belief that as a woman she would become a sea captain, she was also intelligent enough to realise that she must grow up before that could occur. "I'm going to ask Ma if she'll go with me to the Mechanics Institute in Mount Street and enrol me in the navigation class and all the others I'll need to sail a ship. What d'you think, Liam?"

His heart ached for her. Should he tell her not to set her hopes too high? Should he tell her that the boat had not been stolen as she believed but had been taken legally as payment of a debt? Should he warn her that the chances of her becoming a mariner were so slim as to be non-existent or should he let her go on dreaming her childish dreams and hope to God that, as she grew and became a young woman she would turn to more womanly pursuits. Marriage and children, which were really all that a girl of her upbringing could expect? He was that fond of her he couldn't bear to hurt her, for hadn't she been hurt enough by the death of her father? So he remained silent.

They sat for over an hour, their backs to the grassy bank that lined the shore, their knees drawn up, their shoulders touching, talking, talking, neither of them aware that their talk was of nothing but the sea until, at last, he came to the subject that had been worrying him ever since he had seen her and her mother drive off in the splendid carriage that he knew to be Joshua Crowther's.

"How did yer come ter be stoppin' with Mr Crowther?" he asked her cautiously. "Is . . . was he a friend of yer pa's?"

"Oh, no, nothing like that. It was Mrs Quinn really. She needed a job, you see" – which Liam could see she would with the child and the mother to support – "and when Victoria, that's Mrs Quinn's daughter, came to tell her there was a housekeeper needed at Oakwood Place, that's Mr Crowther's house, she decided to try for it. She got it too," she added proudly.

"An' Mr Crowther . . . didn't mind you an' yer ma goin' too?"

"Oh, no, he was very kind to Ma. He's given us two lovely rooms in his house and says we're to stay as long as we want."

Her innocence was frightening, and so was her mother's. He knew she had been out of her mind when her husband was killed and, had it not been for Mrs Quinn and this lovely child beside him, might have chucked herself in the Mersey. But surely she must know that what she was doing was going against the code of ethics that polite society demanded? And if she didn't *he* certainly did, so what was his game? A young widow in the home of a widower with no female chaperone, no relative except a small girl, and when it became known, as it invariably would, would be the talk of Liverpool. Jane Elliott's reputation would be ruined and he could not stomach the idea of her being exploited by some smooth-talking, apparently quixotic philanderer. She was the most beautiful woman Liam had ever seen and he had been in places where women were dusky, exotic, young and ripe and luscious, glorious in their dissimilarity to their northern sisters but she had about her something that was almost not of this world. Ivory and rose and silver. Sweetness, unworldliness and gentleness combined with a look about her of innocent sensuality which no man could resist. She had been protected by her husband, coming straight from her parents' care and now, when she was at her most defenceless, she was the *guest* of a man whose own reputation was far from spotless. In the world of shipping, indeed any business connected with it, Joshua Crowther was highly respected but he was known to be a gambler and a lover of fast horses and faster women. For which no gentleman criticised him in the least. No, any slur would be laid at the feet of the woman he compromised!

"An' yer ma is happy?" He didn't know how to phrase what he really wanted to say, which was, "Does your ma know what in hell's name she's doing or is her mind so wounded she doesn't know the difference?"

"Oh, yes, she's settled in nicely, thanks. It was the winter garden that did it, and the kitten. She loves that kitten. She calls her Beauty and she loves the garden too. The outside garden, I mean. I think she's going to try her hand at growing a few things herself. Mr Diggle said he'd help her. She loves flowers, you see."

"Mr Diggle?"

"Mr Crowther's gardener."

"An' what about you, lovebud? D'you like it?" He did his best to keep his voice neutral. He wanted to warn her, or at least to make her aware without frightening her that it might be best if she and her mother made other arrangements, but where would they go? From what had been discussed back at Mrs Quinn's cellar home the Elliotts were totally dependent on her. She had done her best for them. She had fed and housed them all these weeks so what else was she to do? And what could he do?

"I like the house and the garden and being down here on the seashore and it's lovely having somewhere to take Villy. She hated being cooped up in Mrs Quinn's place, and so did I."

Lily leaned forward and picking up a small twig began to make squiggles in the soft sand. She shaped some initials, two letter Ls, forming a pattern about them of leaves, but Liam was staring out across the estuary and did not notice, and really, neither did she.

"But I don't like the girl," she added.

"What girl?" He leaned back on his elbows, turning to peer into her face. Her plait had become unravelled slightly and a loose fall of hair covered her face, hiding her expression. He sat up again and, leaning forward, gently pushed the hair back, tucking it behind her little pink ear.

"What girl?" he asked again.

"She's his daughter. She's called Eloise," she said scathingly.

"What's wrong with her?"

"Oh, she's a stuck-up little prig and the worst thing is I'm to have lessons with her in the *schoolroom*."

"What's wrong wi' that?" Dear God, it sounded as though Crowther had long-term plans for Jane Elliott and her daughter or was it just a way of keeping Lily out of the picture while he seduced her mother?

"Liam! How can you ask? Of course, you haven't seen her or you'd know what I mean." Her face fell into lines of deep brooding. "I wish I could see Grace and Maggie and Evie. They were my real friends. They were good at hopscotch. I bet this one doesn't know what it is even. We used to have some good games of hopscotch, me and Grace and Maggie and Evie." She sighed deeply and he smiled as he put his arm about her and drew her head to his shoulder. She was like some tragedy queen in a play!

"An' you will again, lovebud. Why don't you ask yer ma if she'll take yer for a visit? I'm sure yer old neighbours'd like to see yer both."

"Oh, I don't know, Liam. She's better'n she was but I don't think she could cope with . . . well, you know, cabs and that sort of thing. And anyway, we've no money," she finished simply.

"Well, that's easily remedied." He took his arm away, though she continued to lean against him. Fiddling in his trouser pocket he withdrew some coins. Selecting one he put it in her hand, closing her fingers about it. She unfurled them. It was a sovereign!

She gasped, staring down at it, then back at him and, since no one had ever told her that you did not accept money from people you barely knew, she clasped it in her hand as though it were more precious than a precious jewel.

"Oh, thank you, Liam, thank you. You're so good to us. This will be a lovely surprise for Ma."

"No, lovebud, don't tell yer ma. Make this our secret."

Her eyes shone, for there was nothing she liked better than the idea of sharing a secret with Liam.

"Of course, our secret."

"An' there's something else I want yer ter promise me."

"Anything, Liam," hoping it would be something tremendous and hazardous and hard to do. Her face gazed up earnestly into his.

"If . . . if yer should . . . I don't know how ter put this . . ."

"What is it, Liam?"

"If you or your ma are ever in . . . trouble . . ."

"Trouble?"

"Aye, in need o' somewhere ter . . . stay, like . . ."

"To stay? But what about Mr Crowther?"

"I know, lovebud, but if . . . well, yer never know . . ."

"Know what, Liam?"

"Will yer be quiet a minute an' let me finish. I've an old granny . . . she brought me up—"

"Did she? What happened to—?"

"Let me finish, Lily." She knew when he called her Lily that it was serious.

"Sorry, Liam."

"She lives in West Derby. She's a cottage in Lower Breck Lane. Her name's Mrs Earnshaw. I stay wi' her when I'm in port. I . . . well, I told her about you an' yer ma so if you were to turn up unexpected like, she'd be right glad ter give yer a bed. Until I'm home, that is. She's a grand lady an' I say that in the proper meanin' of the word. She's working class just like me but she's a lady all the same." His face was soft and his eyes gazed backwards to where he obviously had known much loving care. "If it wasn't fer her I don't know where I'd've fetched up. She made me work at me readin' an' writin' an' me sums. While other lads were driftin' along doin' nowt with their lives she encouraged me to keep me nose in a book so that when I came to be taken on by Captain Jenkins for a five-year indenture I was a fairly well-educated lad. I can pay me granny back now I've me Master's Certificate an' I'm earnin' a better wage an' when I've me own ship, which I hope won't be too long away, I'll—"

"Can I come with you then, Liam?" she begged him eagerly. "When you've your own ship. Like I used to do with Pa?"

"Yer ma might have something ter say about that, lovebud." Again he smoothed the heavy fall of hair back from her forehead, smiling down into her enraptured face.

"No, she wouldn't mind, God's honour. She really likes you, I can tell."

"Well, that's as maybe but I think it's time you were on your way, an' me too. We'll talk about it another day. I sail on the tide tomorrow."

At once her face fell and the mutinous look of a child refused something dear to its heart crossed her features, the look that asked why it was grown-ups always said they would think about it another day, or they would go somewhere another day. It was always tomorrow, never today and she was disappointed that Liam had turned out the same.

He saw it in her. He seemed to be able to see everything there was to see in her, to read her mind and know her heart and he wished he had time to think about it, to wonder at it, to go over this strange feeling he had for her but he must be off and so must she. He had the idea that Joshua Crowther would not take kindly to some stranger, and especially a man, sitting close to the child of the woman who had taken up residence in his home. Liam was nothing more than a common seaman even if he had got his Master's Certificate and if Joshua Crowther was displeased he had it in his power to damage badly the career of any man who offended him.

"But I don't know when I'll see you again." Her strained face was close to his and in her eyes was such a lost look he wanted to hug her to him and tell her everything would be all right. She was to be a good girl and do as her ma or Mrs Quinn told her, not mentioning Joshua Crowther, and to do her lessons because if she didn't she would never be a sea captain. Something held him back. She was a girl child and must be treated with suitable restraint but, God's teeth, she was becoming as dear to him as if she were his own.

He put up a big hand and cupped her chin. She looked so comically pathetic, as though the world, *her* world, were to come to an end, that he smiled. He bent his head so that their foreheads touched and she squinted in an effort to keep his face in her vision.

"Now give over," he told her firmly. "I'll be home in three or four weeks' time, perhaps less an' we'll see each other then."

"But three or four weeks is *for ever*, Liam," she wailed.

"No, it isn't. Now just get this date in your head, 14th May, got it? An' every day after that you come down here an' see if I've arrived. About the same time. Now cheer up an' give us a smile. Oh, an' I'd keep this just to ourselves, lovebud. Not even yer ma or Mrs Quinn must know. They . . . we might be stopped from seein' one another," and I might lose my career if it became known that I'm meeting a ten-year-old girl, no matter how innocent it is.

She put her arms about his waist and buried her face in the middle buttons of his shirt, hugging herself close to him and without thought he stroked her silky hair and murmured some soft endearment before turning away and striding off down the beach.

She watched him go, her childish face wet with tears, for it was like those days when Pa had left them, her and her ma, both of them bereft without him.

She could find no fault with Mr Crowther during the following weeks. He was so kind and careful with Ma, gently guiding her through the days, days in which he scarcely left her side except to go in to town on urgent business. As spring moved slowly towards its summer blooming he could be seen at any hour of the day walking along the neat gravel paths, Ma's hand in the crook of his arm, his head bent to hers, sometimes pointing out a plant of interest, or standing with her to breathe in the heady scent of the lavender bushes which were coming into bloom.

He sauntered with her up through the kitchen gardens, for she had evinced an interest in the growing of herbs and vegetables, through the white-painted gate that led into the orchard, a breathtaking picture of apple and pear blossom at this time of the year. Beyond were the paddocks where the horses, led up there from the stables by Arnold and Jimmy, the grooms, with Mr Bentley, the coachman, were going mad in the soft, warm sunshine. Even the staid carriage horses kicked their heels and frolicked like the skittish young foal that had been born six weeks earlier to a lovely chestnut mare which was intended, when she was tall enough, for Joshua's daughter. There was Ebony, his coal black hunter, and Star, the pony ridden at the moment by Eloise; the paddock alive with expensive and well-bred horseflesh, except for the lawn-mower pony. His name was Tub, and he cropped amicably among the thoroughbred nobility, unaware that he was not of their class. They didn't seem to mind either, flirting and kicking their heels as though they too welcomed the coming of summer and the pleasure of being out of the stable and in the paddock.

The master and Mrs Elliott were reported by the housemaids to having been seen sauntering down by the lake, stopping to admire the swans which were a recent addition since Jane had admitted a fondness for them. The woods were a misted haze of bluebells, so lovely and delicate Jane said she could not bring herself to walk on them, and so ardent was his passion for her and his need to please her he led her along mossy paths through the woodland, solicitous in his understanding of her fragile hold on the realities of life. He even suffered the kitten which often nestled against her breast. His own dogs, big, gentle creatures who padded obediently at his heels, became her friends, even, like their master, tolerating the kitten. It opened its infant mouth in a wide snarl whenever it saw them, its tail lashing furiously from the safety of Jane's shoulder but if it kept her from falling again into the almost mindless state she had been in when she arrived, Joshua Crowther was prepared to put up with it. For now!

Jane Elliott was regaining her grip on life, trusting the man who, it seemed, was so like Richard in his endeavour to bring peace and a measure of content into her life. It did not occur to her to wonder why, as it did not occur to her daughter, but Molly Quinn was not so easily satisfied.

She had settled in to the routine and the intricate pattern of being housekeeper to Joshua Crowther with remarkable ease, bringing with her her own qualities of honesty, industry and vigilance, particularly where Jane Elliott was concerned. She spent as much time as her duties allowed with her, since the master had told her she was to consider herself Mrs Elliott's companion, and she was elated by the great strides "her lamb" made in her recovery from the loss of her husband. She would never fully recover, Molly knew that, for he had been the linchpin of her life and when a linchpin goes the wheel comes off! Jane's wheel was still treacherously frail but it was working again and moving the vehicle onwards. Molly was aware, if Jane was not, that the master was courting her, with what in mind she could not be sure, and with the utmost delicacy and tact, and if she had been a praying sort of a woman – which she was not, for everything she'd ever obtained in life had come not from some distant God, but from her own perseverance and hard work – she would have prayed that it was marriage. She knew, as she was sure he did, that already there was talk of the woman he had tucked away in his home, but he was the soul of circumspection with Jane Elliott and that, for the moment, was all she could hope for. She had a Mrs Kelly now, recommended by the cook at Highcross, where Alice worked, who was a clever cook herself, and between them, consulting one another politely on what was to be served, the food brought to the master's table had improved beyond recognition. The other servants, after an initial skirmish or two, testing her, she was well aware, worked well under her supervision and though she had never dealt with servants before, since all the houses she had worked in had employed only one, herself in fact, had found that she had a way with her that showed them fairness with firmness in equal measure. The house was polished and scrubbed, dusted and brushed to the perfection of cleanliness she herself required and had it not been for the constant nagging anxiety over what was to happen to her mistress, she would have been made up with her new position in life.

Which could not be said of Lily Elliott. Each day after breakfast she and Eloise would be forced into the schoolroom – not that Eloise needed any forcing – where the underpaid and under-qualified Miss Kaye endeavoured to push a little learning into the head of her master's daughter. From the first day Lily became aware that not only was Miss Kaye woefully ill-educated herself, but she was as unconcerned as Joshua Crowther with the academic range of Eloise's accomplishments. As long as she could read, which she did at a painfully slow pace, speak a little French, sing a song and pick out a tune on the piano in the corner of the schoolroom, paint sweet little watercolours and sew a sampler, that was all he required of his daughter. Miss Kaye was a lady come from good stock, the impoverished and plain daughter of a distant cousin of Joshua's. She knew how to dance, and how to hold a simple conversation, which was all that a gentleman required. How to behave in company, how to be a well-bred member of good society, that was all she passed on to her pupil. They liked one another. They liked the simple routine of their day which included pleasant walks in the garden and woods, and the occasional trip into town to look at a picture or two in the art gallery. Miss Kaye believed that if a young lady could mention a book she had read or a picture she admired, that was enough for any gathering where eligible young men might be looking for a wife. Her pupil was only ten years old but it did not do to waste time when many girls were married before their seventeenth birthday.

She knew from the start that this changeling child who had been cast among them was going to be trouble.

16

It was the end of June when Joshua Crowther announced that he and Mrs Elliott were to marry, causing shock waves to reverberate throughout the house. Molly Quinn, who had been called to his study and informed privately by the master yesterday, breathed a silent prayer of thankfulness. It was official then. They were safe. She and her mistress and her mistress's child were safe. Mrs Elliott had said nothing to her last night when they sat placidly sewing together in Mrs Elliott's sitting-room. Well, she wouldn't, would she, she was so childlike in the twilight world she lived in, and Molly wondered if she really knew what was happening to her. Molly thought it best for her lamb to speak of it first and so she herself had said nothing.

"Well, who would've believed it?" When those in the kitchen were told the news Maggie spoke for them all. They were staggered and almost, but not quite, rendered speechless as they begged one another to give an opinion on the wonder of it all. Work came to a halt as they gathered round Maggie who, as head parlourmaid had been informed by the master. Tell the others, he had said, and then tomorrow he and his bride-to-be would speak to them about the future, whatever that might mean. Would they get the sack under the new regime? they asked one another apprehensively. Surely not. Mrs Kelly and Mrs Quinn had only been employed at Oakwood Place a matter of weeks and the new mistress would hardly get rid of them, would she, and the rest of them had worked here for years. No, she wouldn't do that to them, not her.

But a wedding! They could hardly believe it. They had seen, since they weren't blind, were they, that the master was very taken with their lovely guest, and in the privacy of the kitchen, when Mrs Quinn was not about, they had speculated on what he had in mind for her but it had never once occurred to them that it was to be wedding bells. She was the sweetest lady with a shy word for anyone she met, but surely she knew what was being said about her in the mansions up and down the river, and in Mr Crowther's social circle. News got about so quickly and so efficiently on the servants' grapevine and the scandal of it was all over Liverpool and she had only herself to blame, after all. To live in the same house with an unmarried gentleman and no female relative to chaperone her was asking for trouble, but it seemed the master was to do the right thing by her. This would silence the wagging tongues and no mistake. They could not say they were displeased, providing no sweeping changes were made and that was hardly likely, was it? they asked one another anxiously, for she was so pleasant and gracious. Yes, that was the word, gracious, and with Mrs Quinn and Mrs Kelly in the kitchen to look after things for her she need hardly stir from her fireside, doing nothing except work on the endless bits of embroidery and fine sewing she always had in her hands.

Both Lily and Eloise were not only stunned, they were appalled. Mr Crowther had summoned them to the drawing-room to break the news to them and for the space of ten seconds neither spoke.

A small fire flickered in the fireplace though it was a warm evening, still light beyond the windows which faced west over the gardens. The sun was setting across the broad stretch of the silken river, soft as though draped in gauze, the sky orange and red, gold and apricot. Seagulls floated on the slight wind, flushed underneath with rose and in the drawing-room a stray beam of dying light lit Jane Elliott's hair with a halo of pure silver. She was placidly sewing, her back straight, her lovely head bent gracefully and on the arm of her chair the kitten perched precariously. It was scrabbling with a ball of wool from her workbasket. It took a sideways step as though blown by a sudden gust of wind and nearly fell off but Jane rescued it and held it for a moment to her face. It was as though she had no part in this moment of drama and merely happened to be there when it was announced.

The silence stretched on. Lily's face, which had lost every vestige of colour as Mr Crowther spoke, leaving her eyes enormous murky pools of horror, suddenly rioted with a high colour and she exploded into enraged life.

"Marry Mr Crowther! But you can't do that, Ma," she babbled, the words barely decipherable as they fell from between her rosy lips. Her voice was high and frightened. "What about Pa? He's . . . he's only been gone seven months and anyway, how can you consider marrying this . . . this man after being married to Pa? You know how we loved him, and he loved us and he'd not like to think you were . . . were being so disloyal to his memory, and neither do I. You can't do it, Ma. I won't let you. We must leave here at once and find somewhere else to live."

Both she and Eloise were dressed almost identically in dresses of white tarlatan, each with a broad sash of a different colour about their waists. The necklines were high, the sleeves short and puffed and their soft, full skirts came midway between knee and ankle. They wore cream kid boots and white stocking and both looked as pretty as a picture, one so dark the other so fair. The dresses had been made for them by the dressmaker who had been coming to the house to "do" for Miss Eloise ever since she came out of her baby clothes and a new dress for Lily had been thought appropriate. There was constant consternation over the way she seemed to wear out everything she had on, coming home from goodness knows where with tears in her skirt and rips in her drawers, her boots and stockings wet through and her plait unravelled. She had been told time and time again by Miss Kaye that she was to behave as a lady should, as Miss Eloise behaved, but it did no good, she continued to go off on her own without anyone's permission, let alone Miss Kaye's.

She suddenly became unfrozen from the bit of carpet she had occupied when the news exploded over her, darting to her mother's side and kneeling at her feet. She threw the sewing to the floor and took her mother's hand in hers.

"Please, Ma . . . please, don't do this to Pa," she pleaded, looking up into her mother's alarmed face. It was just as though her mother was considering marrying another man while her husband still lived, but by this time Joshua Crowther had had enough. He had expected something like this, for the child was as rebellious as an unbroken colt. He had let her have her say, but this was as far as he was prepared to go. He had been lounging against the fireplace, one hand in his pocket, the other busy with a cigar, but with a muffled oath he threw the cigar into the fire. He was still careful, though. Until they were married he had to be careful.

"Come now, Lily, let's have no more of these histrionics. It will only upset your mother. Do you not want her to be looked after? Do you not want her to live a life of comfort and luxury which, as my wife, she will get? And you will be as another daughter to me."

"No, I will not," Lily shrieked, springing to her feet to face him. "I already have a father, even though he's dead." Her face was passionate in its fury. "I don't know how you persuaded Ma to this . . . dreadful thing but I won't let it happen, I won't. My pa—"

"As you said, Lily, your pa is dead and I think if your mother is willing to . . . let him go, then so should you."

"*Let him go!* We'll never let him go, never, and if you hadn't . . . well, I don't know how you made her do it."

"Made her do it! Lily, your mother agreed to marry me of her own free will, didn't you, my darling?" turning to take her mother's hand and, bending his head, bringing it to his lips with great gentleness.

Jane continued to look somewhat confused. Sometimes the warm chocolate that she and Joshua – as she had been told to call him – drank together two or three times a day did that to her. It made her feel pleasantly drowsy, relaxed and unconcerned with the day-to-day battle she had with her desolate sense of loss. She grieved continually for Richard and always would, but Mr Crowther, Joshua, was so kind, so solicitous of her comfort, so thoughtful, making her feel at ease in his lovely house, making no demands on her except that she be at peace. Somehow, she had found herself agreeing to become his wife, hardly knowing how it had come about. It would be so much better for Lily, he had told her and she had been forced to agree with him, for how could she, a penniless widow, give her the things Richard's daughter was entitled to. She would never love again, she had told Mr Crowther, Joshua, that, but he had smiled and said she was not to worry about it. He would be her friend and she would be his. His daughter would be a sister for her daughter. And of course, she must realise that living under the same roof with an unmarried man was not really respectable, not proper and the only way to put it right was for her to become his wife. Didn't she agree?

She knew he was right, though now and again her soul fought against it, longing to fly free and join Richard, to find again that wonderful sense of totally belonging, of being one half of a whole person, of being in total loving communion with the man whose death had left her only half alive.

She did not say this to him, of course. She did not want to hurt him, for one thing, and for another she felt so muddled at times she would not have known how to put it into words. On their frequent walks about the gardens and woodland, the paddocks and orchards and even on their occasional carriage drives out into the country beyond Old Swan, he had been so persuasive it had seemed to her that it would be only sensible and so much easier to do as he wished. He did not touch her, though now and again he held her hand, the casual clasp of two friends and she had not found it distasteful. It would be such a relief not to have to worry about money, about Lily's education and even about Mrs Quinn who had been so good to them. Mrs Quinn often came to sit of an evening – when Joshua was not about – not saying much but you could tell she was happy here at Oakwood Place, and if all it took to keep them safe was to marry this kindly man, then how could she refuse?

"Lily, dearest, you must not speak to Mr Crowther like that. It is most rude. I know you miss Pa, and so do I but . . . but . . ." She seemed to lose the thread of what she meant to say, her voice trailing away to nothing, like a drift of smoke that vanishes on a breeze. She stroked the kitten's velvet head, her eyes unfocused, and the little creature mewed with pleasure.

Lily turned this way and that, like a trapped animal looking for a way out, her eyes travelling round the elegant and charming room which Joshua's wife had put together so many years ago. A lovely room, a lovely setting for the beautiful, sense-bereft woman who was her mother. It was right for her, this room and this house, but some instinct, a child's instinct that has not been blunted with the years, seemed to be telling her, warning her that it wasn't right, there was danger here though she didn't know in what way.

Still in the same spot where she had received the news about her father and that woman, Eloise Crowther's eyes burned like hot blue coals in her paper white face. For once she and Lily were in total agreement. They had fought like two cats tied together in a bag for the past few weeks, spitting and clawing at each other throughout every lesson, much to Miss Kaye's distress. The schoolroom which had once been so pleasant and peaceful as she and Eloise pottered through bits of this and that, a poem that was suitable for a young lady's ears, one that taxed neither of them, a sum or two, reading aloud from a child's primer, again not too taxing, had blown up in their very faces as Lily Elliott challenged every word that was spoken.

"One, two, buckle my shoe, three, four, knock at the door . . . Lord, I used to say that when I was about four years old." Lily's voice was derisive. She sprawled at the schoolroom table, refusing to sit up straight no matter how many times Miss Kaye beseeched her. "How about 'Christmas at Sea' by Robert Louis Stevenson? It goes like this:

"The sheets were frozen hard, and they cut the naked
    hand;
The decks were like a slide, where a seaman scarce
    could stand,
The wind was a nor'wester—"

"That will do, Lily," Miss Kaye told her icily, badly affronted that a word like "naked" should be spoken in the presence of ladies. "I will decide what we are to read."

"I don't know why you don't report her to my father, Miss Kaye," Eloise said spitefully. "He'd soon make her behave."

"It'd make no difference if she did, clever clogs. He's your father, not mine and I've no need to take any notice of him. Only my ma can order me about."

"Your *ma*! Honestly, did you ever hear anything so ill-bred. Only the underclasses call their mothers *Ma*. Isn't that so, Miss Kaye? In our circle we say Mama, or Mother."

"Well, as you've neither I can hardly see that it matters."

"How dare you, you . . . offensive, vulgar . . ."

"Well, I may be all those things but at least I can read and write. What on earth you call that scribble you do I can't imagine. It looks as though a spider fell into the inkwell and then crawled across the paper."

"You are the rudest, most ignorant—"

"Girls, girls, please, stop it at once."

"And as for the other things you do, well, all I can say is

186

who wants to learn to sew and paint and play the piano? Where I'm going none of these things matters."

"Oh, yes, and where might that be?" Eloise sneered.

"I'm going to go to . . ." It was at this juncture that something always stopped Lily from revealing her dream – no, not her dream, her *intention* – to these two simpering, silly females. She could just imagine Eloise saying casually at breakfast, which was the only meal they shared with Eloise's father, that Lily Elliott was going to be a sea captain and what a furore that would cause. Besides upsetting Ma it would infuriate Mr Crowther, though how she knew that was a puzzle to her. The less anybody knew, except Liam, of course, about her ambitions, her future plans, the better. When Ma was more recovered Lily was going to beg her to go with her to the Mechanics Institute and enrol her there. She had noticed in a newspaper Mr Crowther had left lying about that not only did the institute teach English, writing, mathematics, mechanical philosophy, navigation, astronomy and naval architecture, but drawing, painting, French, German, Spanish, the classics, vocal music, rhetorical delivery, whatever that might be, perhaps something to do with speaking, and dancing, and surely all these last must be for girls as well as boys? What was she doing sitting here in this dreary room listening to Miss Kaye droning on about buckles and shoes when she could be out in the real world, learning real things? She was wasting her time in this sedate schoolroom when she could be going into Liverpool every day to finish her education at the Mechanics Institute. And when her wonderful day at the institute was over, or at the weekend, she would spend her time off up to the meadow, rolling down the grassy banks with Villy, or down on the seashore, her shoes and stockings discarded, her feet in the cold rippling wavelets of the River Mersey, or curled in the fine sand that edged it. She thought it might be rather nice to ride a pony, as Eloise did, then she could gallop away like the wind and go to all kinds of places where no one could find her. She loved the paddock. The larks would be singing, the horses frisking on their lovely fragile legs, Villy would bark that high, excited bark of hers and even Mr Crowther's dogs, so placid and well behaved when they were with him, would be tempted to high jinks when she secretly let them out of the stable and led them down to the beach. There were so many grand spots to explore or simply lie down in at Oakwood Place, the sun on your face, the dogs panting at your side. She had enjoyed their stay here, apart from the schoolroom, and would have been glad to stay for ever, or at least until Liam came for her and took her to sea, but not with Ma married to Mr Crowther.

She had met Liam several times in the last couple of months, down on the empty seashore and it had all poured out of her, all the things she could tell no one else. Sometimes she wondered what she would do without Liam to listen to her. She was like a bottle that was kept tightly corked, which, when the cork was pulled out, erupted in an endless spray of – what was it Mr Crowther drank? – aah, yes, champagne. Or a volcano like the one she had seen in one of Mr Crowther's books she had "borrowed" from his library. Well, there was nothing to read in the schoolroom, was there, unless she fancied *Through a Needle's Eye* which was about clerical life in an English village, or *Sunday School Romances*, which Miss Kaye thought suitable reading for a young girl. In Mr Crowther's book, called an encyclopedia, there were many things of interest to read about and the best thing was that there were a dozen of them from "A" to "Z". She was halfway through the second one already! She and Liam discussed what was in it and he told her he had actually seen a volcano on his travels. Not erupting, of course, like she felt like doing, he had smiled but a wonderful sight just the same. Would he take her to see it, she had begged, one day when he had his own ship and he had turned her face to his and looking deeply into her eyes had said he would. When she was older and with her ma's permission, he had told her and she had believed him as she believed everything Liam told her.

She tried again. "Ma, dearest, please listen to me. You don't have to marry this man." If she had been looking at Joshua Crowther and not her mother the expression that came and went across his face might have alarmed her. "We could . . . I suppose we could go back to Mrs Quinn's place. Now that you're more yourself you and Mrs Quinn could find a job and I could go to the . . . well, to school. You're a lovely sewer, Ma, and Mrs Quinn's very strong and a good cook. Even I could get work . . . somewhere—"

Mr Crowther's silky voice interrupted her.

"Come, Jane, you're looking tired. I'll ring the bell for Mrs Quinn and you shall go and have a rest. I'm sure all these arguments are very upsetting for you and the last thing I want is for you to be upset."

"Please, Ma, think about it for a while. I can't bear to think of . . . of Mr Crowther taking Pa's place." Her face was wet with tears now and it was this that made itself felt in Jane Elliott's bemused mind. She could not bear to see her little girl upset and for a moment she turned a set face of implacability towards Joshua Crowther. It did not last, that feeling that she must listen to Lily, for Joshua's kind face loomed over her, smiling and speaking of a cup of hot chocolate and a rest before luncheon, shutting out Lily's tears, and when he gave her his hand she allowed him to help her from her chair. He rang the bell and then led her into the hall where Mrs Quinn, steadfast, comfortable Mrs Quinn was there to take her to her room.

There were few guests at the wedding. A business acquaintance or two and their wives, carefully picked not only for their discretion but their usefulness to Joshua in business. They would come back to the house for a glass of champagne and a piece of the exquisite wedding cake Mrs Kelly had made for them. All very circumspect and calm. Nothing to alarm his bride nor wake her up from the dreaming state of suspended animation in which she existed. Joshua Crowther had wisely decided that the quieter the event and the fewer people who came to it, the less chance there was of Jane Elliott baulking at the last moment. Perhaps some memory of her first wedding and her first husband might slip into her confused mind and God alone knew what she might say or do. Right up to the last moment the bloody child had been at her, pleading with her not to go through with it until he had begun to think he might have to lock her up until it was all over. He kept them apart as much as he could, or at least spent as much time as he could with Jane but it didn't stop her. Even with him in the room the bloody kid kept on about it, about her pa and how he must feel up in heaven, weeping most distressingly at times. Not that it distressed him, but he had the devil's own job with Jane when the child was sent up to the schoolroom, or the bedroom she shared with her mother. So the sooner they were married the better.

It took place in July in the tiny church of St Anne's on Aigburth Road. A mild sunny day and in the hedges on the short ride to the church were tangles of wildflowers, dog roses and festoons of black bryony and honeysuckle, pale pink blackberry blossom. Climbing up the banks to meet them were the purple splashes of foxglove and the nodding heads of grasses heavy with pollen. On the far side of the hedges were fields of growing wheat and among the gold, vivid splashes of large red poppies. It was all so beautiful, the larks piercing the air with their sweet song, and yet Lily's heart, as she and Eloise, with Ma and Mrs Quinn drew nearer to the church where Mr Crowther waited, was heavy with desolate despair. Pa, oh, Pa, how has this come to be? it asked over and over again. Ma looked simply glorious in a new dress of pearly pink silk, very simple, the bodice fitted to her small breasts and the skirt enormous. She carried a tiny posy of white rosebuds and under the brim of her bonnet, made from the same material as her gown, was a cluster of the same flowers. The Misses Yeoland in Bold Street had been called out to design and make her dress and to fit her and it was a measure of Joshua Crowther's great wealth and influence that they should extend such a service, since they were much in demand among the fashionable of Liverpool. Lily and Eloise had been fitted into demure little dresses, identical, of white muslin, tiny wreaths of pink rosebuds and ivy in their hair, both of them as obstinate as mules about it. They were to walk behind Jane Elliott as she glided up the aisle towards her groom.

Jane seemed to be unaware of anything, even her own devastating beauty as she approached Joshua Crowther, and the wife of one of the guests was of the opinion that she was drugged and told her husband so afterwards.

"Don't you repeat that remark to anyone, d'you hear?" he had thundered, but he had to admit the bride certainly seemed to be of another world.

The wedding feast, if such it could be called, was as simple as the ceremony, and very short, and the gentlemen of the party agreed among themselves that they would be as eager as Joshua to get rid of them all and take his bride to his bed. He and his new wife, the picture of loving domesticity, stood at the top of the steps, he with his arm about her waist, which somehow did not seem to please her, waving them away. They had noticed that he could not keep his hands off her, which was natural enough, and during the afternoon what had seemed to be docile acceptance on her part had slipped imperceptibly into what might be called distaste, even fear.

That evening the two girls were not present at the dinner table. Maggie and Betsy were hard pressed to keep up with the master who was throwing his food down his throat so quickly it was a wonder he did not choke. He drank a lot of champagne, too, toasting his wife again and again, filling her glass and begging her to drink up, for was this not a special occasion. His hand was constantly on her, fondling her bare neck and shoulder, her arm and hand and Maggie felt herself go hot with embarrassment for a dreadful moment when she thought he was about to thrust it down the front of her bodice.

At last he stood up and held out his hand to his wife. She shrank away from him and in her face was the dawning realisation of what she had done, of what was about to be done and she tried to pull away. She had had no cup of chocolate since just before she left for the church.

"Come, my dear, it is getting late," he said to her, ignoring the cringing presence of the two embarrassed parlourmaids.

"No . . . please . . ."

"No, to your husband?"

It was clear Betsy was about to burst into sympathetic tears, so without being given permission Maggie took her hand and pulled her from the room, almost running with her up the hall and into the kitchen where the maidservants waited, among them Mrs Quinn whose heart was beating thick and sluggishly in her bosom.

"They're . . . they're off," Maggie told them faintly, nodding in the direction of the hallway. It was not even dark outside the kitchen window.

"Poor lady," one of them whispered, waiting for God knew what to happen. They had moved all her things while she and the master were at church into the master's bedroom, on his orders, and what would she think to that, they wondered in the depths of their women's hearts which knew she was, or had not been, in her right mind when she agreed to this.

The screaming began ten minutes later and for half an hour Molly Quinn stuck it out, covering her ears and bending her body as though she were suffering her mistress's agony with her. It was intermittent, the crying, the screaming, the agonised calls that none of them could answer, but at last Molly could bear it no longer.

"I'm norr 'avin' this," she screeched, making them all jump. "'E's treatin' her like a bloody animal an' I'm norr 'avin' it."

The furious knocking at his bedroom door interrupted Joshua Crowther's immense satisfaction and enjoyment of the naked woman in his bed. He had stripped her methodically, his eyes slits of reddened lust, thrown her on the bed and raped her. He hadn't hit her. He was a gentleman, after all. She had fought him, which had been a great surprise and had given an added and pleasurable dimension to the whole exercise. He hadn't expected it, neither had he expected any of his servants to have the temerity to interrupt him on his wedding night.

He should have known, of course. It was that woman, the one who had stood over his wife, before she had become his wife, like some protective knight in armour. The one who was where she was in his household simply because it was the only way he could get what he now had in his bed. At the moment his wife was lying senseless and spreadeagled on her face where he had placed her but when he had got rid of this woman he would . . . well, he had many fancies and she would satisfy them all!

Molly Quinn squared up to him like some small farmyard hen facing the fox.

"Sir, please . . . Mrs Elliott . . . we heard . . ."

"You mean Mrs Crowther, don't you, Mrs Quinn?" he asked her smoothly.

"Yes . . . yes . . . Mrs Crowther. Can I . . . ?"

"You can do one thing, Mrs Quinn, and that's get the hell out of here and if you try to interfere in my household again you will find employment elsewhere. My wife and I have retired for the night . . . *for the night*, do you understand? And you'd best go to that brat and shut her up or *both* of you will be out on your ear by morning."

He shut the door in her face and Molly Quinn, her heart broken, and her spirit as well, moved heavily along the passage to the room that Jane and Lily Elliott had shared and where Lily was doing her best to knock the door down. Molly was not surprised to find it locked!

17

Joshua and Jane Crowther had been married a month when Nicholas Crowther came home for the long "vac".

The deep sense of sadness in the house, the misery that pervaded every corner of it, even out into the gardens where Mr Diggle worked silently alongside young Will, oppressed them all. Mr Diggle had not seen the new mistress since her marriage to the master but he knew, as who did not in the Crowther household, of what the master did to her in that locked room, though they did not speak of it, of course. Well, to say they *knew* was not strictly true but they could only come to one conclusion on what went on there, couldn't they, and they were shocked that a man who had always been perfectly decent to them, if somewhat distant as the gentry are, could treat his new wife as he was doing.

It was often a mystery to those involved how these things became known, since not one of them would shame the lovely Mrs Elliott by discussing her sad plight with one another, but hadn't they all heard those anguished screams, even the stable lads and the gardeners, on the night of the wedding. Of course it was a man's right to take his wife to his bed and to do with her there what he wished and Mrs Crowther was not the first to suffer it, nor would she be the last in this world where a woman was her husband's property, just like his horse or his dog, to do with what he liked. It was a crying shame but what could they do?

She had never cried out again.

Lily did not see her mother for nearly a week after the wedding and though she begged and pleaded, almost on her knees, to Mr Crowther, to let her go into her he would not allow it, saying Lily would upset her.

She had lost her temper then. "*Me!* Me upset her! Tell me what you're doing to her and why did she scream like that in your room? And why does she have to sleep in your bed?" Though she knew that married ladies and gentlemen shared a bed, just like her ma had once done with Pa. "I want to know what you do to my mother," she had shouted defiantly, "and why won't you let me see her? Or Mrs Quinn? Why are Maggie or Betsy not allowed in, tell me that? Even her food is left outside the door. I'm going to call the police if you don't let her out. You can't keep someone prisoner like that. It's against the law."

She was too young and ignorant to realise that it titillated Joshua Crowther's sense of powerful male sexuality to know that the lovely creature who was now his wife was in his bed, naked and dead-eyed, waiting for him, at his own leisure, to go and unlock the door and let himself in, to do with her what he liked, when he liked. It was a new game that he would tire of soon, but not yet, not until he was totally satiated with the body he had craved and denied himself all these months. He would let her out then, when she would take up her duties as his wife, in his bed and out of it. He was looking forward to showing her off to his acquaintances. He would dress her in the finest the Misses Yeoland could provide, deck her out in the jewels that had once been his first wife's, and display her like a trophy to the admiring, covetous eyes of other men. In the meanwhile she stayed where she was and if this bloody child didn't bugger off he would do her a serious injury.

But Lily Elliott was not like Mrs Quinn. She was not afraid they would lose their place or that Mr Crowther might do her ma a serious injury. She was not revolted, disgusted, horrified by what was being done to her mother, since she didn't know what it was. The other women in the house did, or could half guess at it, but Lily was a child with no knowledge of the terrors of sexual abuse and she believed if she made enough of a nuisance of herself Mr Crowther would have to release her ma, or at least let her go into the bedroom and see for herself how she was.

"I mean it," she told him stubbornly. "You've no right to lock her up. I'm going to fetch the police constable from the corner of Aigburth Road and he'll make you let her out."

She faced him rebelliously, her hands behind her back, her chin stuck out at a truculent angle, her eyebrows drawn down

in a ferocious scowl and if he had not been so damned fed
up with her he might have laughed. He had it in him to wish
her mother had a fraction of her spirit, for after that bitter
struggle in the first half-hour, his wife was as submissive, as
pliant as a rubber doll. She made no objection to whatever
he did to her, allowing herself to be pulled this way and
that, arranged into the most perverted poses and positions
to please his fancy, but this one would be a tiger when it
was her turn. The thought startled him, for he was not sure
he knew what he meant himself since the girl was only ten.
Or was it eleven? He seemed to remember she had a birthday
recently. He was in a good mood, since all his bodily senses
were deeply satisfied so he was prepared to humour her.

"Your mother is my wife now, Lily, and she and I . . . do
things that as a child you will know nothing about." He smiled
quite roguishly, a smile Lily did not understand.

"What sort of things?" She frowned even more and stuck
her lip out.

"Really, child, the questions you do ask; one day I will
answer them but in the meantime go and . . . and do whatever
it is you should be doing at this time of day. I'm sure Miss
Kaye must be looking for you."

"Miss Kaye and Eloise have gone for a walk and I—"

"You should have gone with them. That is why I employ
Miss Kaye. To look after you and—"

"I'm worried about my mother and if you—"

"There is nothing to be worried about, Lily, so you'd best
go and join—"

"I want to see my mother. You've no right—"

Suddenly he had had enough. He slapped the newspaper
he had been reading when she burst into his study into a
crumpled heap on his lap and glared at her with eyes that
had gone a furious red.

"Will you get out of my sight, or must I lock you up too,"
he snarled at her, shaking out the newspaper in readiness to
resume his reading.

"That's what I mean. You're not allowed to lock people
up."

"Will you get out of my sight."

"Not until you—"

With an oath he sprang to his feet and from him came a
roar of rage that made even Jane, in the comatose state into

which her husband's attentions had flung her, lift her head to listen. The servants in the kitchen stopped as one what they were doing and Molly drifted slowly to the kitchen door to listen. She opened it a crack and was just in time to see the master dragging his step-daughter up the stairs, not by the hair as he would have liked, but by the arm. Lily was doing her best to struggle free, her voice high with indignation as she told him what she would do to him if he didn't let her go, but he continued up the stairs and along the passage, throwing her into the bedroom she and her ma had shared and where, for now, she still slept, locking the door and pocketing the key.

The maidservants all shrank back as he came down again but he went into his study and banged the door.

It was then, or at least the next day, that Lily began to plead with him. She had found that with a bit of effort and a great deal of slipping and catching herself on sharp sticky-out bits of branches, she could climb down the tree that was directly outside the bedroom window, but when she had done it she wondered why since she could go nowhere, could she? She did reconnoitre under the window of Ma's bedroom, or rather *his* and Ma's bedroom but there was no handy tree there, so, reluctantly, she had climbed back to her own room for it he came and found her gone her means of escape, which might come in handy another time, would be discovered.

It was nearly a week later when Mr Crowther summoned Mrs Quinn to his bedroom, telling her casually that his wife would be down for dinner and she was to instruct Cook in the preparing of a splendid meal. And could she make sure there was a suitable wine to serve with the meal, and, as though it were an afterthought, she was to get his wife ready. He was off to the stables in half an hour and would she send a message to Arnold to saddle Ebony. Oh, and he thought the children might be brought down to dinner since this was a celebration. There was just one more thing. Mrs Crowther was in need of a decent lady's maid since Mrs Quinn's job was to be housekeeper and nothing else from now on, so would she ask around for a suitable woman. Servants always knew these things.

With a brisk nod he left the room.

Hardly daring to move her head for what she might see there, Molly Quinn turned to the lifeless figure propped up in a chair by the window. It wasn't looking at her, that figure, but at something beyond the window, not even in the garden but somewhere way on the horizon, further than that even and Molly could only call it eternity. It was Jane, of course. She could not bring herself to call her Mrs Crowther, or even Mrs Elliott, the poor broken woman by the window, and so she called her by the name, and herself by the name, she had always used that were to be theirs with each other to the end of their days.

"It's Molly, me lamb. I've come ter see to yer," she murmured softly, since it appeared to her that the slightest noise or movement might send her lamb spinning off into that eternity she was studying with such longing. "I'll ge' yer a bath and wash yer 'air," for it was obvious her mistress had had no such attention since her wedding day. "Then our Lily'll come an' see yer. She's bin that worried wi' yer bein' so poorly, like."

She was not really aware that she had called the child the possessive "our Lily" which was only used to speak of or to a member of the family. She was concerned only with putting some excuse, some reason into her lamb's mind that might be used to explain the days she had spent locked in this room. She looked unkempt, her hair in a snarl, the flimsy wrapper which Molly had never seen before and through which her nipples and the triangle of hair between her legs could clearly be seen, crumpled and torn. But at the sound of her daughter's name she turned her head and looked at Molly with eyes that had seen and known things no woman should ever have to know or see. There was desolation of her spirit in her eyes, a great tearing shame, a devastation of the soul which had once been clean and loved by Richard Elliott and which the man who was now her husband had done to death in the cruellest way. She moaned low in the back of her throat, like someone who has been tortured beyond endurance and knows it has not yet come to an end. Her face was a travesty of the serene face Molly Quinn had loved for years, gaunt, hollow-cheeked, the eyes fallen into the sockets below her forehead, the mouth bitten and torn.

"Oh, Molly." It was said so forlornly, like that of a child who has been punished for something it does not understand, and yet with a memory in it of an act so shameful it could be told to no decent woman.

With a cry of pain and rage so great it almost choked her,

Molly flung herself across the room and gathered her into her arms.

It was Lily who got her through those dreadful hours and days and weeks, for of them all in the house and in the garden her innocent child was the only one who did not know the truth. And it was perhaps the horror of what had been done to her by Joshua Crowther that brought her back from the precipice on which she had teetered ever since her husband, her *real* husband, had been killed. Though she could not reason the why of it, Lily gave her a small measure of strength to shore up the barricade that protected her and behind which she hid her real self from the man who shared her bed. He shared her bed. He took her body in any way he fancied but he no longer took *her*.

She kept Lily by her side during the day and Joshua, who cared nothing for the child's education, which was doubtful she got from Miss Kaye anyway, allowed it. He was too busy with the grouse-shooting season which had just begun and as long as she was in his bed at night did not seem to care what she did. Jane renewed her interest in the garden, reassured by the quiet kindliness of Mr Diggle, who treated her as though nothing had happened in the space of time since they had last met, nothing that need matter to them, at any rate. Even Will, who was a simple, uneducated lad, and was not sure what ailed her, only that something did, found the words to speak to her, showing her how to dead-head the roses, to plant geraniums on a south border in the sandy soil, how to sow what were known as "ten-week" stock, how to pot those that would be needed for spring planting. She could be seen kneeling on a cushion planting out pinks, double wallflowers and pansies, her ravaged face at peace for the time being as she put her hands in the life-giving soil. Lily sprawled on the grass beside her, her nose in the latest encyclopedia, waiting patiently for her mother, who she knew depended on her at this moment in her life, walking slowly back to the house with her hand in hers, or up to the potting shed, the enormous hothouses, admiring the vegetable garden and the fruit which burgeoned on the apple trees, the plum and pear trees. These growing things, these simple, God-given things seemed to give comfort to Ma and so, though she longed to be away to more exciting pastimes, Lily curbed her impatience.

On fine days Lily took her down to the seashore where they

sat for hours on end in the warm August sunshine, watching the passing ships, not talking much, for what was there to say between the badly damaged woman and her innocent child? But they held hands and it was as though, for that peaceful moment, Pa was back with them in this world that had been his. The world of the river and the oceans beyond, the lovely sailing ships, the rippling highway of dancing, gold-streaked water which he had loved and which had been passed on to his child.

It was there that Lily found the courage to speak of the Mechanics Institute. She bent her head and stroked her mother's hand with the tenderness a mother might show her child. As though their roles were reversed which, in a way, was true.

"Ma, can I tell you something?" she asked her, looking up to meet her mother's gaze, which had become more tranquil during the last few days, especially since her work in the garden.

"Of course, dearest. What is it?"

"I want to go to school, Ma." Her voice was low and hesitant and she bent her head again as though to hide the desperation in her eyes.

"To school? But what about Miss Kaye? She's teaching Eloise."

"No, Ma, she's not. Oh, she can just about read and write and sew a sampler and play the piano but I don't want that." She looked up again, her face passionate in her sudden determination to let her ma see what Lily Elliott needed and it wasn't sewing a bloody sampler. "I want to learn what Pa learned. Dearest, I don't want to hurt you any more than . . . well, I know you're not happy here and neither am I with . . . with *him* and that damned Eloise is a stuck-up little bitch."

"Lily!"

"She is, Ma. All she does is try to get me into trouble with Miss Kaye. Not that that matters, for I don't give a fig for Miss Kaye but one day she'll tell *him* something and that would mean . . . well, if she found out that . . . that . . ."

"Found out what, dearest?" Jane looked troubled, turning to gaze over her shoulder as though her husband might be lurking over the green bank.

"It's a secret, Ma, but God's honour," she added hastily, "it's nothing bad. You see . . . well, it might get someone into trouble if I told anyone or it got back to . . . to Mr Crowther."

She could not forget Liam's tense entreaty that she must tell no one of their meetings.

"Oh, Lily, please don't do anything to make him angry. He can be very . . . very forceful when he's angry." Jane's distress was growing but Lily continued to stroke her hand, doing her best to calm her, beseeching her to believe that it was nothing dreadful and if she could she'd tell her ma but it wasn't her secret, did Ma see?

"But it's about going to school that I want to talk to you, dearest. To learn properly what I need for . . . for the future."

"Do you mean go back to the Goodwin School for Young Ladies, dearest?" Jane looked doubtful. "Oh, I don't think Mr Crowther would agree to that. Not when there is a governess here in the house to teach you."

"But she teaches us nothing, Ma, don't you see? I want to learn what *Pa* knew. I want what he had. I want to find the *Lily-Jane* and become a mariner like Pa was and the only way I can do that is to go to the Mechanics Institute. Look, I've cut this piece out of the newspaper to show you," pulling the crumpled cutting from her pocket. "They teach all kinds of things, see. French and Spanish and singing, not just the art of seamanship. There will be other girls there, probably not learning what I want to learn but that wouldn't matter. I could go into the boys' classes and . . . oh, please, Ma, say yes. Let me go. Talk to him and make him see . . ."

Even as she spoke Lily felt despair creep over her as she watched her mother retreating towards that barricade she hid behind to escape her husband. Her eyes took on a curiously blank stare as though there were nothing remaining of Jane Elliott inside her head. She had gone, retreated to the place of safety which was the only way she could deal with her situation. Her soul did not even attempt to peep out in case he should notice it, and her, and until the danger had passed over she would remain as still as a bird in a bush when the hawk flies over.

"Ma . . . please, Ma . . . I can't do it without you." Tears slid down Lily's face as she saw her only chance of becoming the sea captain her father had been slip away. She had counted on her mother being able to persuade Mr Crowther to allow her to go to the school and yet when she gave it proper thought, which she was forced to do now, she could see what a fool she had been. Her mother had been almost destroyed by the death of Pa and now, when a man with tenderness and sensitivity might have restored her to her self, her true self, she had married a brute like Mr Crowther who cared for nobody but himself. She did not exactly think in these terms, for she was a child of ten years but she knew with a different man her mother would have been a different woman. A man like Liam, for instance. She had no idea what Mr Crowther and Ma did in their bedroom, nor why he had locked her up for nearly a week, but whatever it was it had certainly made her mother even worse. She was not as vague, as lost as she had been, but she certainly was not capable of demanding the education her child needed, of standing up to him, of arguing that Lily was *her* child and would go to the school *she* chose. That was what Lily had hoped for but she knew she had been sadly, badly mistaken.

There was a sound from further up the beach, the sound of footsteps crunching on seashells and they both froze into stillness. They were afraid to turn to see who intruded on their moment of peace and the youth who approached them was startled by the rigid fear that showed plainly in both still figures.

It was Lily who turned towards him, for into her mind had come the wild hope that it might be Liam, but the tall, dark figure who sauntered towards them was not that of her friend but strangely familiar just the same. Jane sat like a flower petrified by time, her gaze fixed and unblinking, her hand like ice in that of her daughter and when Lily struggled to her feet she rose too, incapable of thought except that it might be *him*.

"Good morning," the young man said, lifting his hand to his head as though expecting to find a hat there which he intended to raise politely. "A lovely day, isn't it?" He smiled and made to pass them, wondering, you could see it in his face, what had caused the strange expressions, the strange stillness in the woman and her daughter, then he stopped.

"I do beg your pardon, ma'am, but aren't you . . . ? I know it sounds foolish but I do believe you might be my new stepmother, and, of course, step-sister."

They both looked at him as though he were a cobra about

to strike and he wondered what sort of a woman his father had married. Very beautiful, he could see that, though she looked as though she were recovering from an illness, but the child was an exquisite replica of her, or of how she must have been herself as a girl. She was dainty, tall and slender, nearly as tall as the woman, with silver-streaked hair in which shades of gold could be seen, silken and curly just like her mama's. Her skin was a fine ivory and rose and her eyes a deep unfathomable grey, almost lavender in the reflection from the lapping water.

Lily cleared her throat and Jane, like some old woman near to death, turned her head slowly to look at him, almost as though she were afraid he might do her an injury.

Lily spoke. "This . . . is my mother. Her name is Jane Elliott . . . No, I beg your pardon, Jane Crowther and I am Lily Elliott. Are you . . . ?"

He gave a merry smile and though his likeness to Joshua Crowther was uncanny they could not help but relax a little. "Then it's true. You are my new mother and sister. I'm Nicholas Crowther but my friends call me Nicky."

"Nicky." Lily cleared her throat again and Jane did not speak.

"Yes, I got home no more than an hour ago but the first thing I always do is to come down here. I love it, the river, and one day, whan I go into my father's business I mean to have my own boat."

"Ship."

"Pardon?"

"You should say ship."

"Well, I never, a girl who knows the difference."

Lily bristled. "And what's strange about that? Some girls are interested in things other than . . . than dolls and embroidery, you know."

He looked startled, as though a kitten he had put out a hand to stroke had turned out to be a full-grown and infuriated tabby.

"I'm sorry. I do apologise, but it is so seldom that anything that interests a male, interests a female."

"Well, it does."

"I can see that. Now are we friends again?"

"Well . . ."

"Please . . ."

"Well, all right."

He sighed, satisfied, and sat down on the warm sand and they sat down beside him, though Jane kept a firm hold on Lily's hand. He did not *feel* like Mr Crowther, nor did he *sound* like Mr Crowther, but this was how Mr Crowther must have been when he was a boy, a young man and until he had proved otherwise she would not trust his son.

"I was sorry I could not come to the wedding," he was saying politely, just as though urgent business had kept him away, though the truth of it was he had not been invited. He had known nothing about it until his father had written to him a week or two back informing him that he had a stepmother and sister and he was to behave himself and remember his manners when he came home. That was how his father talked to him, cuttingly, contemptuously, since they were both aware that he was not the son his father would have liked.

For once Lily was at a loss for words. Like her mother she did not trust anyone with the name of Crowther. If he was anything like his sister or his father she was prepared to loathe him, but at the same time it was hard to tell him so when they had only just met. She was usually forthright, she had heard it called rude, saying whatever came into her head but she had her ma to think of now and if what she said was repeated to *him* and hurt her ma she would never forgive herself. She was learning to watch her tongue. Mr Crowther had absolute power over her mother since she was now his wife and though this last week or two he had been amazingly pleasant at the breakfast table, not only to her and Eloise but to Ma, she would not depend on it to last if he was displeased. The maids, their faces set in the blank mask of the well-trained servant, had exchanged glances, when the master wasn't looking, of course, at his aimiability, reporting back to the kitchen that he was like the cat who had swallowed the cream, which they thought was true though they pitied the poor woman who was providing it. Mrs Quinn said nothing. As soon as he had gone, which he did every day now he no longer had to butter up her mistress, she would slip up to the sitting-room attached to the bedroom her lamb shared with Joshua Crowther, and they would enjoy half an hour together in private, drinking a cup of tea and saying little but being a comfort to one another. There was to be a lady's maid starting next week, a nice little thing, sweet-faced and pleasant and very well trained by some titled lady in Yorkshire and who had been hand-picked by Molly herself. She'd have no grim-faced, hard-hearted, stuck-up biddy looking after her lamb!

He walked back with them, Nicky Crowther, talking pleasantly of this and that. What he meant to do in the "vac", the prospect of a bit of shooting and riding. Did she ride? What a pity, and what about Mrs . . . Mrs Crowther, hesitating over what to call her mother. His eyes were the deepest chestnut brown, soft with anxiety as though he knew what was behind her mother's silence. His gaze was clear and steadfast and his expression earnest. He was sixteen, Lily knew that, but he was still a boy. There was a warmth within him and about him that Lily liked but was not sure she could trust, for hadn't Mr Crowther been just like that to begin with? When they reached the gardens and her mother hesitated beside a bed of lavender, he stopped, bending to crush the flowers between his fingers.

"What a glorious smell," he murmured, "and what a glorious sight, that wall of lavender mist. D'you not think so, Mrs Crowther?" He turned courteously to Jane.

She looked into his eyes and, seeing nothing there of his father, smiled.

Part 2

18

He was waiting for her where he had said he would be, on the steps of the Custom House in Strand Street and for a moment she allowed herself the pleasure of just watching him without him being aware of it. He was leaning gracefully against one of the pillars, his arms crossed, looking directly across the street to the backs of the transit sheds that lined Salthouse Dock, and the plantation of gently swaying ships' masts beyond, from which penants of every colour flew. Many of the ships were square-riggers but a three-masted barque had almost finished loading her cargo and on deck work was under way getting ready for sea. The sails had been roused out of the sail locker and sent aloft and he was scrutinising the activity with keen interest, probably comparing what was taking place with that of his own capable crew. Amid the bowsprit rigging the barque had a finely carved figurehead in toga, tunic and sandals, which was not unusual since all the ships, and unique to each one, had a figurehead. Many of the carved figures, executed in the workshops of Liverpool's carvers, came in a variety of forms, human figures that reflected the name of the ship, or the portrait of their master, or masters' wives or daughters, and docks like Salthouse had been likened to colourful outdoor sculpture galleries.

He still had not seen her. The cab had dropped her at the corner of Canning Place and Strand Street and though she attracted many admiring glances herself, she did not see them, for her whole attention was taken up by Liam O'Connor. For some surprising reason it was as though she were looking at him for the first time with another woman's eyes. That's if you could call Lily Elliott a woman at sixteen. She liked to think so. The sun seemed to be captured in his unruly tumble of wheat-coloured hair which, she noted absently, needed cutting again, striking gilded sparks from it which contrasted agreeably with his dark, sunbrowned face and the sharp intensity of his narrowed, hyacinth blue eyes.

He was frowning slightly as though he were critical of the seamen's performances and he shook his head as a rope ran haphazardly through careless hands. He turned away in what seemed to be scorn for their seamanship and saw her and at once his face lit up, opening into a warm, sweet smile, revealing his excellent teeth and he began to stride towards her. Even then she could not help but be aware of his great height, the breadth of his shoulders and the tapering leanness of his hips and long, well-muscled legs. He was dressed in a well-cut frock-coat of dark grey worsted reaching to his knees, with narrow trousers to match and a pale grey waistcoat. It was what the fashionable young gentleman of growing means would wear but, particularly as he was carrying his hat, he managed to make the suit look casual, informal, as though he were off to a country fair instead of a day in town. He had loosened his necktie since it was a warm day, but his boots were polished and his face well shaved and he drew every female eye to him which, again for some strange reason, did not please her.

A strange moment, then it was gone and he was her dear, familiar Liam again, loved, trusted, depended upon for comfort and support and sympathy when circumstances at Oakwood Place overcame her. Her friend who had never let her down and whom she loved dearly. Her face expressed her feelings, and her eyes glowed like a candle just lit in a darkened room.

"You're late," he told her cheerfully, not at all put out, "and if we don't look sharp we'll not get a decent place. She comes in in half an hour and most of Liverpool seems to be making its way down there. Where've you been, anyroad?" He had taken her arm and was hurrying her across the dock road in the direction of Princes Dock which afforded harbourage for the largest class of vessels. The road was a continuous motion of horse-drawn vehicles, carts and team waggons shifting goods to and from quaysides, from warehouses to the holds of ships tied up alongside the low transit sheds and they were in mortal danger of being run down. Drivers cursed, but the patient plodding Shires that pulled the waggons did not even flinch, fully expecting the small scurrying human creatures to get out of their way, which they did, thanks to Liam.

"Well, if you'll let go of my arm and give me a chance to draw breath I'll tell you." Her voice was tart and as she almost ran to keep up with his long-legged stride her feet barely seemed to touch the ground.

"Can't you talk and walk at the same time, lovebud? Or shall I pick you up and carry you?" He grinned down at her. "It wouldn't be the first time. Remember when we walked all the way from Pottery Beach to Canada Dock and then when we turned to go back you said your boots hurt you and I had to sling you over my shoulder."

"Liam O'Connor, you did no such thing and besides, I was only a child then." Her mouth drew into a prim line and she did her best to toss her head but it was hard to do when you were being propelled at great speed along a pavement crowded with people all going to the same place and intent on getting there before anyone else. Liverpool folk did love ships and they were keen to be the first to get a look at the one that was just about to steam into the Mersey.

Strand Street was almost impassable as people from every walk of life headed towards Princes Dock but with the help of Liam's powerful bulk which shouldered aside those who would have stood in his way, and those who would have argued with him over his methods, they came to St Nicholas Church and the walkway that led down to Princes Landing Stage which was so crowded Lily said she knew how a sardine felt in a sardine tin.

"Get behind me and hold on to my coat," he ordered her, "and don't leave go for anybody. I'll see if I can get us down to the landing stage."

Besides the ordinary men and women who had come to see the biggest ship in the world steam into port were dockers leaning upon the handles of hefty sets of wheels which they would use to trundle the ship's cargo to the warehouse, stevedores, tally clerks, porters and casual labourers, for this was a sight never before seen and no one wanted to miss it. Most of them had a pipe gripped between their stained teeth and smoke wreathed about their heads, mingling with the richer aroma of cigars smoked by gentlemen who had come down to see the fun. And mixed with the smell of tobacco was the pungency of the sea, of tar and coffee beans, of rum and raw brown sugar, of linseed and cocoa and every conceivable cargo which was being unloaded, or loaded, along seven miles of dockland.

Lily was enchanted, wondering why it was she never failed to feel like this whenever she was here. The river was beautiful, the sun glinting on its moving waters and the ships standing silently in their own shadows. Ferries beat out towards New Brighton and Birkenhead, for business must go on despite the arrival of such an important vessel. In the far, far distance she could see the mountains of Wales and behind her rose the bustle of the town, and about her was the clang of hammers, the hoots of the sirens greeting the great ship. She leaned against Liam's shoulder, his arm protectively about her, and knew she had never been so happy as she was on this day. Pa had been gone for six years now but in Liam she had found what she had lost when Pa died.

She beamed at her old friend the piermaster, as she now knew him to be, remembering the day, long ago now, when she had entrusted a note for Liam with him which he had faithfully delivered for her. He was in his smart cap and uniform and was an important man, for he controlled the movement of ships in and out of the docks, helped by a team of dock gatemen. His job was an arduous one because he was expected to attend the opening and closing of the gates into the river before and after each high tide. He had his own house right on the waterfront by the Dock Board which Lily envied enormously and, in the early days, when it began to look as though Mr Crowther was not going to let her go to the Mechanics Institute as she had hoped and learn to become a sea captain, she had thought she might like the piermaster's job. She and Liam had even been to take tea with him and his wife and they had become firm friends.

"A fine sight, Lily," he said to her now. "I've seen some ships come and go in this river but I do believe this is going to be the finest."

"Oh, no, sir, we can't agree, can we, Liam? What could be more beautiful than a clipper ship under full sail? Steam will never replace them, never. Great unwieldy things with all that filthy smoke belching out and the noise of the engines."

Liam and the piermaster exchanged amused looks over her head but just then a great shout went up and there she was.

She came upriver like a queen, regal and if not exactly

beautiful, a sight that filled the crowd with awe. The incredible length of her as she glided over the gilded waters, momentarily quietened them all to open-mouthed silence, even Liam who had known of her dimensions. She was painted a sleek black and had a massive side paddle. She had six masts and five funnels and how they were to fit her into her berth was a mystery to the onlookers. The *Great Eastern* had made the passage from New York with a large cargo and 212 passengers – though she was equipped to accommodate four thousand – in the record time of nine days and eleven hours which was a marvel in itself and the sight of her was a bloody marvel, as one old salt said to another in Lily's hearing. She and Liam were crammed together with men and women from all walks of life, hundreds of them, who were in love with the sea and had come to watch the biggest ship in the world make her stately way upriver towards her berth and if Lily's toes were stepped on and her new bonnet knocked askew, what did it matter? They cheered and shouted and Liam threw his brand-new bowler hat into the air and never saw it again, which didn't matter in the least because they had both agreed that it didn't suit him!

It was a lovely day which, of course, it always was with Liam. Now that the *Great Eastern* was safely berthed and after they had gawped with the rest at her tremendous size close to, they made their way arm-in-arm, along with the now relaxed and sauntering crowd, back up the walkway towards St Nicholas Church. They strode up Chapel Street, their strides matching now, for Lily was tall, cutting through the Exchange Flags behind the Town Hall which was a regular meeting place for cotton brokers, merchants and ship-owners to do deals and exchange gossip. It was packed today with a multitude of gentlemen who had been to see the *Great Eastern*, all dressed in what was almost a uniform of top hat and tails. They came out on Castle Street and then turned at St George's Church into Lord Street.

"Now you can tell me why you were late, lovebud. Not that it matters, but you know I worry if you're not on time. I get it into my head that your stepfather has—"

"Don't call him that, Liam. You know I hate it." She turned a mutinous glare on him and he sighed and shrugged his shoulders.

"Well, that's what he is, Lily, and if he were to say you couldn't leave the house you would have to obey him."

"No, I wouldn't. He has no rights over me. And it wasn't him, anyway, it was Ma. You know she's expecting?"

"Yes. Is she ... pleased?" He had nearly said *resigned* to it, since he had the impression the coming child had been a shock. He was not quite sure how to approach the delicate subject of Jane Crowther's pregnancy after six years of marriage, since he was uncertain of Lily's feelings about it. She had not told him until her mother was in her fifth month and he had the distinct feeling she was ashamed, or felt it in some way to be disloyal to her dead father for his wife to be having a child that was not his. Lily was unpredictable and sometimes, when he least expected it, she took up arms on some point or other and argued until he could have put her over his knee and spanked her.

"I don't know, really," she answered him gloomily. "She is thirty-five and I heard Maggie telling Mrs Quinn that it was a great age to be having a child. Mrs Quinn should know, since she's now a grandmother as well as a mother. Her daughter Victoria married Arnold, the groom, did you know?"

"No, lovebud, I didn't. How could I?"

"Of course. Well, they have a couple of children but Mrs Quinn refuses to say anything about Ma being too old to have a baby. Do you know, Liam? Is it right?"

"Lord, don't ask me. I know nothing about children, only you, and you've always been a handful." He grinned down at her and squeezed her hand which rested in the crook of his arm.

"I meant about ... well, Maggie seemed to be saying there might be ... danger, though Mrs Quinn soon saw her off. Mad as Beauty when she fell into the water butt, she was. I thought she was going to hit Maggie and they're best of friends, really. So it was Ma who held me up. I wanted to make sure she'd be all right while I was out, but Mrs Quinn said she'd sit with her until I got back. *He'd* gone off somewhere on business, after having told me I was to stay close to the house, which he has no right to do so I just ignored him as usual."

"It will get you into trouble one day, lovebud, this determination you have to disobey him at every turn."

This was an old argument, and one they had whenever they met. She did her best to convince him and herself that her mother's husband had no claim on her, as a parent would, and that consequently she could do as she liked. For the most part it was true, for the fact was Joshua had not the faintest notion what she got up to half the time. Neither did Miss Kaye who was supposed to have her in her charge. She had long since given up trying to keep Lily in the schoolroom, or on the tedious walks she and Eloise took up and down the garden paths. She had long since given up coaxing her to accompany them to the art gallery or the museum or the Zoological Gardens.

At first it was a regular occurrence to be hauled up before her mother's husband and an explanation demanded as to where she had been all day and when she refused to say, which she *always* did, she was locked up in her room on a diet of bread and water, or threatened with the strap. It had not the slightest effect. Usually she had been no further than the seashore, the paddocks to see the horses and talk to the grooms, the kitchens where she counted the maidservants as her friends, eating Mrs Kelly's marzipan biscuits and angel cakes, helping to mix the batter for her batter pudding, or reading to Jenny, for whom she felt inordinately sorry, while the scullery maid peeled the spuds. She spent hours in the woodlands, where she took the dogs, including Mr Crowther's so that he complained they were getting out of hand, but she didn't care. She derived great pleasure out of crossing him which, if he had not been somewhat indifferent to her and her whereabouts, might have led to trouble.

Sometimes it was a day such as this, one she spent with Liam when he was in port, walking the length of the parades that lay before each dock. Or up to the top of Duke Street to St James Walk where they would sit and talk and look out over the splendid views to the south-west where, on a clear day, Chester could be seen. To the right of Chester was Park Gate on the east bank of the River Dee and in a straight line dead ahead the smooth and beautifully indented chain of the Derbyshire Hills. There was Bidston Lighthouse across the river, like a slim finger of stone pointing into the sunshine, and on the dancing water the wonderful panorama of the ships racing to beat the tide out to sea. The ferries were busy with their passengers like fussy old ladies dressed in black and full of their own importance. In the distance was the dome of St Paul's with the sunlight glinting off it and circled with the endless crying of the seabirds.

These were precious days, days that made those first months of her mother's marriage to Mr Crowther bearable, at least for her, and she did her best not to jeopardise them. Now and again, mostly at Liam's coaxing, and to give the impression that she was learning to settle down, she spent an hour or so in the schoolroom, but it always ended up with her and Eloise having an argument and Eloise threatening to tell her father about some misdemeanour and Lily would swear she wouldn't come again. Both Eloise and Miss Kaye were as relieved about it as she was!

Ma seemed to have settled at last to being the wife of one of Liverpool's wealthiest men, probably because after the first few months of greedily devouring her every night in his bed, the novelty of it wore off and his demands lessened. Not that Lily was aware of this. She only knew Ma was better, in health and in her looks, especially as Mr Crowther insisted that she have her gowns and outfits made by the Misses Yeoland and, having perfect taste and wonderful style, Ma quickly became known as the most fashionable and best-dressed lady in Liverpool, which vastly pleased Mr Crowther. Lily and Eloise were similarly dressed, in garments suitable for their age, of course, and even Eloise didn't mind accompanying her stepmama, as she called her, to be fitted for her new outfits.

Now and again Nicholas Crowther showed his face, but as he and his father did not agree on anything, and in fact Lily was beginning to think the only one who *did* agree with Joshua was Eloise, she was not surprised. Contrary to his father's wishes he had not joined the family firm of shippers and merchants but had somehow managed to buy himself – with money left him by his mother – a commission in a fashionable regiment and had served in South Africa and Ireland. He had done well, promoted to subaltern at the age of twenty and had scarcely been seen since. Lily had been sorry, for of all the Crowthers he had been the best, in her opinion, and she had thought if he had remained at home they might have become friends.

She and Liam strolled up Lord Street, her hand in the crook of his arm, idly looking in shop windows and admiring the goods displayed there. Lord Street was well groomed, alert, brisk with traffic and pedestrians, like the rest of the town thronging with the vast population of peoples of the world who passed through it. Languages of all nations fell on their ears but they were so used to it it excited little interest. They crossed into Brownlow Hill, walking slowly up towards Mount Pleasant and the Adelphi where he was to take her to lunch.

Liam was conscious, if she was not, of the stir she caused as they entered the dining-room of the hotel. It was filled with the elegant and wealthy of Liverpool, most as fashionable and well turned out as she was. The influence of the Misses Yeoland who were considered to be the best and cleverest dressmakers in Liverpool, clearly showed. It was said they catered to the majority of the discerning wives of shippers, of merchant princes, men of cotton, men with influence and property, and it was all on display here in the dazzling array of jewels, silks, hats laden with lace and flowers, fans with mother-of-pearl handles and parasols with ivory or coral sticks which, when opened, would be seen to be made of costly silk and lace, with the very latest black fringes. It was not often that Liam brought her here, for it was very expensive and way beyond the means of a seaman, even if he had his Master's Certificate, but today was a treat, a wonderful ending to a special day.

All the women, many of them very attractive, appeared overdressed and showy, even coarse beside the delicate silver, ivory and rose loveliness of Lily Elliott. Though she was tall, taller than most women, she was slender and graceful as a swan, with a neck that was white and long. Her glorious hair, which had darkened slightly as she matured to a mixture of tawny gold and silver, was parted in the centre and drawn back into an enormous chignon which had no need of the false hair worn by many ladies. A ringlet or two strayed endearingly behind her ears and on to her neck. In her ears were pearl earrings given to her only last month for her sixteenth birthday by her mother. She wore pale cream lawn. Miss Yeoland had insisted on it, saying that there were only so many years when a woman could wear simple cream and that Lily was to take advantage of it. There was plenty of time for the rich poppy colours, the rose, the buttercup and shades of plum which her mother wore and which suited her so well.

The basque bodice was trimmed with honey-coloured satin ribbon about the neck and at the edges of the pagoda sleeves, and her bonnet was tied beneath her chin with the same coloured ribbon. It was very small, no bigger than a cake plate, called a puff-bonnet, just a scrap of lace and cream satin roses that perched precariously just above her forehead.

"You look very elegant, lovebud," Liam said to her, his eyes intent on her every movement, though he was smiling as she tucked in to her second whipped cream meringue. "And there really is no need to lick the spoon like that. I'm sure if you were to ask the waiter nicely he would fetch you another."

"Thanks, I will. They're lovely. Not quite as good as Mrs Kelly's but scrumptious just the same. Won't you try one?"

He shuddered. "Thanks, but no. I have enough difficulty climbing the rigging without adding extra pounds."

"When do you have to climb the rigging, I'd like to know?" she asked him, her eyes on her dish as she scraped her spoon round it, then popped the spoon into her mouth. He watched her, fascinated by the parted rosy lips, the small pink tongue that came out to give added power to the movement, then looked hastily away as she caught him staring at her.

"What?" she said. "Have I got cream on my nose?"

"Would you be surprised if you had, you greedy child?"

"You didn't answer my question. How many times do you climb the rigging?" for Liam O'Connor was the captain of a fine, fore and aft schooner now, a man of some importance and she knew he was looking about him for a ship of his own. "A captain doesn't do that sort of work."

He grinned wryly. "Well, not very often, I admit, but now and again I like to go up to show the men, and myself, that I can."

She sat back in her chair and carefully folded her napkin before placing it beside her empty plate. Her eyes had become misted and her mouth drooped as she fiddled with the spoon in the saucer of her coffee cup. The fine excitement of the day had vanished for the moment and he knew the reason why, of course. He knew what was in her mind as though he could see inside her head, which in a way he could. He had known her for six years now. They had met as often as he could manage, first down on the shore, then, as she grew and was allowed, or took, more freedom, in the city parks, the art galleries and exhibitions, the library and sometimes here where he brought her for afternoon tea. She had shared every aspect of her life with him, though he could not say the same to her since he was a grown man and she was a child. He knew of her stepfather's cruelty to her mother, not physical from what she told him but of the more sinister kind where a stronger will overpowers a weaker. And yet the man was generous to a fault, a generosity that allowed his wife and her daughter to dress like princesses. Lily had a mare of her own and on fine days met him out towards Speke or Hale Hall, pleasant leafy rides southwards to the point of land where the Mersey narrows and the lighthouse called the Dungeon Light stood.

Liam had done well. He had got on. He was ruthless, hardworking and ambitious and he had got on. He had done his share of scrubbing decks, coiling ropes, climbing rigging to reef and unfurl sails and now what he had always wanted was almost in his grasp. He had saved every penny he had earned, investing it wisely, since he had a good head on his shoulders and soon, when he found her, he would have his own ship.

And that was what his little lovebud wanted and had never achieved, nor was she likely to. He had never heard the last of her plans to enter the Mechanics Institute in her early years, when she had been a child who knows no better but, of course, it had not happened. Her mother, who would have died for her, had had the stuffing knocked out of her by her bullying husband, from what Lily told him, and though Lily herself had stood up to him and demanded that she be given a proper education, he had merely laughed at her and told her to get back to the schoolroom. That was when her education had ended.

He put her in a cab at the front entrance to the Adelphi, then set off at a brisk pace along Renshaw Street, Berry Street, turning into Upper Duke Street where smart town houses climbed the hill from the dock area up towards North Toxteth. It took no more than ten minutes. As he approached a house in the centre of a terrace and opposite a pretty garden area, he glanced up to the small, balconied window, tipping his hat to a woman who smiled at him from behind the nets.

The cab dropped Lily at the gate, for it was still ingrained in her to let Mr Crowther know as little as possible about her movements, even though she was aware that he didn't give a damn what she did. Now Eloise, that was different, but the whereabouts of the rebellious daughter of his wife was a matter of complete indifference to him. As long as she brought no scandal to his door, which he knew was unlikely since she loved her mother too much, she was virtually free to do as she pleased.

Her cream kid boots scrunched on the newly raked gravel of the drive. She waved her hand to young Will who was now a strapping lad of twenty and was surprised when he turned away and bowed his head over his spade. He had been digging so furiously it was a wonder he didn't break the damned thing, she had time to think as she mounted the front steps.

Maggie was standing in the doorway, her hand on the doorknob just as though she had been behind the door, which had been flung open the minute she had spied Lily.

"Well, that's what I call service, Maggie. Were you watching out for me?" She scowled. "He's not been asking for me, has he, because if he has . . ."

Her voice trailed away uncertainly as she stepped into the absolute quiet of the hallway.

Maggie's face was blank, white as paper and she held herself rigidly as though she were afraid she might fold up like a concertina.

"Ma . . . ?" Lily croaked, her expression anguished and was not surprised when Maggie began to cry.

19

They were to call the child Abigail and that was the end of it, he ranted at them, and if there was any more arguing he would knock their heads together. It had been his mother's name and it was to be the child's.

The child. That was how he spoke of his new daughter, how he was always to speak of his new daughter, for there was no doubt he considered her a poor exchange for his beautiful wife. He and his elder daughter, his step-daughter and the household servants had just got back from the funeral which had been gratifyingly well attended, though none of those who had come could really say they had known the dead woman. She had sat at the head of Joshua Crowther's dining table on numerous occasions, looking like some exquisitely dressed doll who only spoke when directly spoken to, but she had been gracious and inoffensive and what was wrong with having a speechless wife? They wished they might be so lucky. Pity it had rained so, though the weather certainly matched the absolute devastation of the dead woman's daughter. She looked like some tall, black, stick insect, painfully slender and completely quenched by her grief, standing somewhat apart from Joshua Crowther and his daughter and totally alone. The servants wept unreservedly, even a tall lad and an elderly man who were said to be the gardeners, and a woman, the housekeeper, they were told, who had come with Mrs Crowther to Oakwood Place, almost fainted dead away she was so distressed as the coffin was lowered into the wet black earth.

The daughter had disappeared after the interment and the drive back to Oakwood Place, heading, it was whispered, to where she had been ever since her mother's death which was the nursery where the infant resided. A bit odd, really, they were inclined to think but they had eaten a morsel or two, the kind that is served after a funeral, and drunk Joshua's excellent sherry and claret, and gone on their way.

"My mother didn't want her to be called Abigail, she told Mrs Quinn before she died. She . . . she wanted Celeste if she had a girl and Thomas for a boy." Thomas had been Pa's second name but she couldn't tell *him* that, could she? "She would have hated Abigail and as she's my mother's child, my sister, I absolutely refuse to allow her to be given that name."

"You refuse! By Christ, that's rich. I'll call my child any damn thing I please and with no help from you, miss."

"Doesn't what her mother wanted count for anything?" Lily asked him desperately.

"No, it bloody well doesn't," he snapped, as though Jane had deliberately gone against his wishes by dying and so had forfeited her right to any say in the matter.

Eloise hissed spitefully, "She happens to be *my* sister too, or hadn't you noticed, and Abigail was my grandmother. Besides, if Papa wants her called that it is surely up to him. Tell her, Papa."

They were all in the deepest black, even the nursemaid who cowered in a chair by the fire, the tiny daughter of Jane Crowther, which neither Jane nor Joshua had wanted, sleeping peacefully in her arms. The baby was like a little scrap of lace, or a perfect rosebud with the dew still on it. She was wrapped in a shawl which looked like a spider's web, or a square of gossamer, knitted by her dead mother, and on her head was a little cap of lace. Even so you could see the wisp of silvery curl beneath it and the length of pale brown eyelashes that rested on her creamy cheek. She had just been fed before Mrs Crowther's elder daughter had burst into the nursery and her rosebud mouth still sucked vigorously, even in sleep. She was a month premature but even the doctor had been surprised at her perfection, for that last month, which often made the difference between a sickly child and a healthy one, was sometimes sadly missed.

"I don't give a damn about that at the moment, Eloise. I just would like to enquire, miss," glaring at Lily, "what in hell you think you're doing coming up here and leaving our guests in such an ill-mannered fashion?"

"They're your guests, not mine, and I—"

"It was *your* mother's funeral they were attending, dammit," not noticing, or even caring, as she flinched from his cruel words.

"I saw my mother decently buried, sir, and I did not care to engage in ineffectual chatter with a group of people I didn't know. Now then, to get back to my mother's daughter . . ."

"You mind your tongue, my girl, or you'll find me a somewhat more watchful parent than I have been before. With your mother dead . . ."

"You are not my parent, sir."

"Thank God for that, is all I can say, though I *am* your guardian so just watch your step."

Ignoring this last she resorted to begging. "Please, Mr Crowther, will you not allow the baby to be called Celeste, knowing it was my mother's choice?" Her voice was desperate as though she would do anything to fulfil this last wish of her mother's. She would never, never forgive herself for not being here on the day the baby was born, and had almost convinced herself that had she been Ma would have survived, no matter what Mrs Quinn said to the contrary. It made no difference but if she could persuade Mr Crowther to call the baby as her mother had wanted it would go some way, a small way, to easing her guilt.

"Celeste! Where the bloody hell did that come from?"

"It's French and it means heavenly. Ma liked it."

"I want no child of mine being called some foreign-sounding—"

"What about Eloise, then?" she whipped back quick as a flash. "That's French."

For a second or two he looked confused. He had not named his daughter, his wife had done that before she too died, and he had not cared enough one way or the other, but this bloody girl had done nothing but stand against him ever since he had married her mother and, if only to deny her, he would call the child anything but what she wanted.

"Well, this one's Abigail which comes from the Bible so that should suit your mother wherever she's fetched up."

"I think Marguerite is nice, Papa," Eloise put in, though to tell the truth the baby meant nothing to her, since she did not associate Jane Crowther's child as being related to herself, despite what she had said to Lily.

Her father turned on her. "Don't you start," he snarled. "It's Abigail and that's that."

He opened the door noisily and left the room, banging it to with such force it made the sleeping child jump. The nurse was seen to heave a great sigh of relief, hoping, no doubt, that her charge's father would not be a frequent visitor to the nursery. She herself was new to the household, having been hastily summoned by Mrs Diggle, her mother's sister, who knew she was looking for a good post.

"There," said Eloise, malevolently, "I hope you're satisfied. You've upset my father and the baby's still to be called what he wanted so you've achieved nothing. I don't know what else you expected, really I don't," and she too left, leaving the nurse, whose name was Dorcas, looking at Lily with great sympathy. Dorcas hadn't liked Celeste, she had to admit. Abigail was much more suitable, but she felt so sorry for the dead woman's older daughter. It was as though she didn't know what to do with herself, where she should be, how she should be acting at this time of great grief. She wandered about the house like a willowy black ghost, turning up in the kitchen where she was received with great sympathy, then drifting off again as though what she searched for were not there. The housekeeper, Mrs Quinn, was lovely with her, holding her when she wept and in front of them all as well. In fact they all wept, for it seemed the dead lady was beloved of everybody except her husband and step-daughter. But her own daughter always finished up back here as though in the whole of her life there remained only this tiny scrap carried over from a life she had once known. Her own flesh and blood. Her *only* flesh and blood, and perhaps, if Dorcas could get the baby into her arms she might find a way to recover.

But there was no sign of it yet. Lily was desolate in her grief and when Mrs Quinn came up to the nursery and whispered in her ear that there was someone down on the seashore to see her, she turned and fled, and was still weeping when she flew into Liam's arms ten minutes later.

"I was there, lovebud, though you didn't see me," he murmured into her hair. "I was standing behind that big oak tree but, by God, I'd have given my right arm to be at your side." His voice had become savage and she turned her wet face up to his in surprise.

"What . . . ?"

"Bloody hell, you were all alone with no one but that bastard to stand by you. I wanted more than anything to stride over and put my arm round you and hold you safe and sure, but I couldn't, I bloody well couldn't. I would only have made things worse for you. I couldn't simply walk over and hold you as a friend should and it almost killed me. Lovebud . . . no . . . no, weep if you want to," when she began to stutter an apology. "I'm here now. I took a chance and called over a lad who was hanging about by the water looking as lost as you do so I reckoned he must have loved your ma."

"It would be Will. He and Mr Diggle adored her."

"Well, he promised to put a note in Mrs Quinn's hand without anyone seeing and . . . here you are. And why, in the name of all that's holy, didn't you put a cloak on? It's pouring with rain and cold enough for two pairs of bootlaces. See, come under my cape and let's shelter beneath those trees."

They stood face to face with his cape about them both. They were not exactly face to face, for hers was pressed into the curve of his neck where her tears wet his collar but he hugged her close and let her cry, though it broke his heart to hear her. Poor little bugger. First her pa and then her ma and who had she left now? And as though she had picked up the thread of his thoughts she pressed herself even closer.

"At least I still have you, Liam," she murmured against his throat and to his horror, as her breath caressed his skin and her young body moulded to his, he felt a stirring in the pit of his stomach and his manhood fought to get free of the restriction of his tight breeches. Thank God she was wearing the usual mass of petticoats and skirts that were the fashion and would not be able to feel it but he could and he was ashamed. He knew the bloody thing had no mind of its own. Put it close to any attractive woman's flesh and it would react in just the same way, but this was his lovebud, the child he had loved and sheltered as best he could ever since she was ten years old. She had been his little sister, his daughter even . . . well, not quite that for there were only eleven years between them, but she was still very dear to him.

But she was a child no longer. She was so slender he could feel the bones of her spine under his fingers and the sharpness of her shoulder blades, but in contrast the roundness of her breasts was pressed so tightly against his shirt front he could swear he could feel her nipples.

She had stopped crying and had gone quiet, leaning against him with that trusting innocence she had always shown him. She was warm now, he could feel the heat of her, for though it was raining it was mid-summer. Her heart was beating somewhat rapidly; he could feel it just below his own. She sighed, still disconsolate, but calm, and when she lifted her face to him, without thought, a purely male response to the closeness of a woman, he laid his mouth gently against hers and heard her sigh in what seemed to be great content.

"Liam . . . ?" she murmured questioningly, her lips still close to his.

"Lovebud . . . ?" He was ready to draw away now, confused, distressed even, as though what he had done were somehow shameful.

"Yes . . . ?"

"I'm sorry," he mumbled. "I don't know . . ."

"I'm no longer a child, Liam," she said, her voice trembling with emotion. Whether it was still grief for her mother or something else he could not tell. She huddled closer to him like a young bird looking for protection beneath its mother's wing, then lifted her face again and this time her lips captured his, parting slightly so that he could feel the bewitchment racing through him as her breath whispered into his mouth. He broke away, gasping, drowning in the sweetness of her, yearning to go on but something in him protested, something that had, for the past six years, known her as a child and was trying to tell him that this was wrong.

They stood for perhaps five minutes in a close embrace, her face cradled against his jawline, while his eager male body lashed him on to do more than this to her, and his cringing mind held it back. They did not kiss again and she did not seem to expect it and he thanked the gods for it, since he knew if she turned her face up to his again he would not have been able to resist. He could feel his love for her – what sort of love? his bewildered mind begged to know – welling up inside him, a protective love, strong and welded by the bond they had forged six years ago on the docks when she had been looking for her father's ship. It had never faltered. Many was the time when he had it in him to wish that he did not have to spend some of his precious time ashore with a child of eleven, twelve, thirteen, but he had never forsaken her, never let her down, he didn't know why even now.

Always he had come to this place and there she would be, her face aglow with joy and merriment, flying into his arms as a child will do with a father.

Strangely, even as she grew from a pretty child into a lovely young woman, he had scarcely noticed, for she was Lovebud, always the same: laughing, argumentative, self-willed, head-strong, good-hearted, bloody-minded at times. Though he had given it no thought at the time he had never been bored in her company. She was keenly interested in everything he did; indeed she had a mind that was inquisitive about matters that other young women did not care about. She read a great deal, all the books in Joshua Crowther's library, many of which had never been opened, and the newspapers he left lying about. She had continued her education without knowing it, without the guidance of a teacher and was far more aware of what was going on in the country, indeed the world, than many a man. Only a month or so ago they had exchanged views on the growing conflict in America and what impact it might have on the cotton trade of Lancashire and he had not been particularly surprised by her knowledge. But he had never once, even then, considered her to be anything other than a child. He was a sailor and though he did not boast that he had a girl in every port, he had great success with women and was not a man who lacked sexual gratification. There was a certain lady in Upper Duke Street, a widow somewhat older than himself, whose husband had left her well provided for. They each enjoyed what the other could give but with no romantic ties.

But now he was overwhelmed by this sudden startling revelation, not just of how much she meant to him, but of her loveliness, her femininity and what it had done to him in the last few minutes. Quite simply, he wanted her as a man wants a woman and what the bloody hell was he to do about it? She was sixteen, for Christ's sake. She had just lost her mother and was frail and vulnerable because of it, so how could he go on with this in the way she seemed to be encouraging him to do? Well, not exactly encouraging him, she was too inexperienced for that, but not unwilling just the same. He could not take advantage of it, not and still call himself a man.

He cleared his throat and removed his arms from about her, holding her by the elbows. His cape was draped about her, hiding the sweet lines of her body but her face was turned up to his expectantly and her lips were parted. She was waiting for him to go on, ready to smile, to continue in any way he told her, her expression saying she had liked the kiss and would not be averse to another but he was not ready to commit himself. Not yet. This was much too fast. Totally unexpected and something that must be thought about carefully, for the last thing he wanted, in fact he would cut off his arm to avoid it, was to hurt her now. She was hurt enough already.

"Lovebud . . ."

"Yes, Liam." Her lips quivered and she put out her tongue to moisten them and inside him that darting flick of pleasure struck him again.

"You must go now, and so must I. I sail on the tide . . ."

"Oh, Liam . . ."

"But I'll be back in three weeks," he added hastily, for her face had paled even further and her eyes filled with tears.

"I'm not sure I can manage without you, Liam. You see, I have no one else."

"You have Mrs Quinn, lovebud. She shares your . . . your grief, you know she does, and will comfort you. You will comfort each other."

"But it's not the same, Liam. You're—"

"Lily, you're used to me coming and going and besides, your new sister will need you."

"Oh, her."

"Yes, her. Don't speak of her as if she were nothing to you. I doubt she'll get much affection in that house." His voice was hard. "So you must provide it. Your ma would have wanted you to love her and you have so much love in you to give, lovebud."

She brightened. "Have I, Liam?"

"Yes." It was all he could manage to say, for he could see it there in her eyes. She didn't know, of course, what she was telling him, for she scarcely knew herself, but what he saw there almost made him drag her back into his arms.

At the last moment, as he bent to place a kiss on her cheek, she turned her head and their lips met with a warmth that shook them both. She clung to him for a moment but he gently loosened her hands.

"Goodbye, lovebud. Three weeks. Take care of that baby. Promise?"

"I promise, Liam."

And she did. Dorcas was quite amazed and not a little put out at the attention Miss Lily showered on her baby sister, almost taking over her job, she told her Aunty Mabel Diggle when she went across to her cottage for a cup of tea. On Miss Lily's instructions!

"She baths 'er an' feeds 'er an' wi'out so much as a by yer leave tekks 'er down ter't kitchen ter show 'er off ter't servants an' wha' can I say since she's the master's stepdaughter? She practically lives in't nursery an' what master'd say I don't know. Not that 'e ever comes, like, or t'other 'un, an' it fair beats me 'ow anyone could stop away from that babby. She's that bonny an' thrivin' an' all, even if she do 'ave ter mekk do wi' cow's milk."

"Yer mustn't grudge poor young lass, our Dorcas. She lost 'er pa an' . . . well, she'd norrad much of a life wi' . . . Well, I shouldn't say it, I suppose, an' yer not ter repeat it to a livin' soul, but 'e's norra *lovin'* man, Mr Crowther. 'E's tekken no notice o' that child."

"What child?" It was plain Dorcas was bewildered.

"Miss Lily, I mean. She's bin allowed ter run wild an' 'er poor ma . . . eeh, she were a lovely woman. My Ted thought sun shone out o' 'er backside, I can tell yer, an' if 'e 'adn't bin past such things I mighter felt jealous."

"Give over, Aunty."

"No, I'm tellin' yer. 'Im an' Will worshipped ground she walked on. Well, she loved flowers an' such an' were never outer't garden, but she were a sad lady, fer all 'er wealth. 'Is wealth, I should say. Dressed like a queen she were . . . you never saw 'er, but she 'ad nowt, not really, only Miss Lily an' I believe Mrs Quinn were right fond of 'er. Now there's this babby . . . eeh, I could cry, reely I could an' Miss Lily's got no one burr 'er."

The first Joshua Crowther knew of it was when his step-daughter waylaid him about a perambulator, of all things, and he could not have been more astonished if she had begged him for her own carriage and horses.

The three of them, Joshua, Eloise and Lily always took breakfast together. It was a habit begun when Joshua married Jane and though she was no longer there it was still kept up. There was little said. Joshua might idly question his daughter on where she and Miss Kaye were to go that day and she would tell him. They might discuss the merits of Eloise's new mare which she thought might make a good jumper. A croquet party to be held at the home of one of Joshua's business acquaintances to which Eloise had been invited. The start of the grouse shooting which Eloise had shown an interest in joining, expressing a desire to learn to shoot which was a perfectly respectable pastime now for a young lady. Neither of them once addressed a remark of any kind to Lily who did not care anyway. She would eat a good breakfast, for she had the healthy unfussy appetite of the young, not like Eloise who was inclined to put on weight and so was careful what she ate. Eloise was seventeen in October and was ready for marriage and there had been interest shown by several of her papa's friends with eligible sons.

When Lily had finished she would politely beg to be excused and wish her stepfather and sister good morning, to which they answered with an absent-minded nod, but not this morning, for she had something she wished to say.

"If I might interrupt this . . . this conversation, Mr Crowther, there is something I wish to ask you. That's if you can spare the time." Joshua missed the irony in her voice. They both turned to stare at her and at the serving table Maggie nudged Betsy. She was going to do it then.

"Oh . . ."

"Yes. Abby . . . Abigail is nearly two months old now and it is time she was pushed out in a baby carriage. While the weather is still pleasant. With this in mind I have taken the trouble to obtain a catalogue and would like your permission to order her one. May I show it to you?"

Joshua Crowther noticed that his step-daughter had lost none of her defiance. Her chin was lifted and the set of her head imperious just as though, should he refuse, she were ready to give him a piece of her mind. By God, she was a feisty one, growing up as well, he thought, noticing the soft swell of her breasts which her proud posture showed off. The bloody image of her mother. Not that he had ever seen her mother at sixteen – was she? . . . or seventeen? – but he had often imagined what she must have looked like then and here she was, alive again in her daughter.

He licked his lips. "I beg your pardon?"

"I asked if I might have permission to buy a perambulator

for . . . for your daughter. She needs to be wheeled out in the fresh air."

"Yes, I heard you."

"Well?"

"Don't take that tone with me, young lady. I swear you do it on purpose just to annoy me," which was not true. She did it because she loathed him. He was smiling as he said it, which to Lily was even worse than his black scowls.

She waited, aware that he was looking at her in a quite strange manner but not particularly concerned by it, for he was a very strange man. Abby, as she called her, was eight weeks old and in those eight weeks he had never once been near the nursery and neither had Eloise, but then, did Lily care? All she wanted for the next few years, until Abby was old enough to . . . well, here she stopped since she was not sure what she intended to do when Abby was old enough. She only knew it involved her and Liam and Abby. But Abby was Joshua Crowther's child and though he had not the slightest speck of feeling for her she knew he regarded her as one of his possessions. Just like Ma had been one of his possessions. Just like his dogs and his horses, this house even, were his possessions. She often wondered what he counted *her* as.

"Shall I bring the catalogue?" she asked him as he continued to study her. "The prices are in it." Her bold, unfearing eyes looked coolly into his.

Suddenly he lost interest, or that was how it seemed. Throwing his napkin to the table he stood up and with a nod at Maggie who ran to open the door for him, strode across the room.

"Do as you like," he growled, "but don't let me see you on the front lawn with the contraption. D'you hear?"

20

She could get down to the beach now, though it was bit of a rough ride for Abby. The baby's little face looked out in astonishment from her cocoon of wrappings as Lily struggled over tree roots, heaving and shoving the perambulator through the rough grass, across hummocks and down shallow dips until the shingle of the beach was reached. Even there it was hard going but it was worth it when she saw the tall, casually dressed figure of Liam coming towards them. She wanted to let go of the handle of the baby carriage and fly over the pebbles and shells and the ripples left by the tide into his arms as she had once done but she knew and he knew that it was different now. Not their great attachment for one another but the make-up of it.

She often wondered why it was that no one ever questioned her constant walks down to the beach, nor see who she met there, but she was mistaken in her belief that it was a secret she and Liam shared with no one. They had known for years, all of them, and at first Ted Diggle, who had reported it to Mrs Quinn, was not at all sure it was seemly, or even safe for the mistress's young daughter to be consorting with a man who was obviously not a gentleman. A seaman, in fact, who wore a fisherman's outfit of gansey, waterproof pea jacket and stout drill trousers. Just off to sea by the look of it, Mr Diggle had told Mrs Quinn. A giant of a chap with a steady look about him, not unfriendly, like, if Mrs Quinn caught his drift, but with a resolute jut to his chin that seemed to say he'd stand no nonsense.

Molly Quinn had been frightened at first. If the master heard of it there'd be trouble, not only for Lily and Molly Quinn's lamb, the master's wife, but for all of them. They would have been expected to have watched over his wife's daughter, not because he feared for her safety but because the idea of a common seaman trespassing on his property would be like a red rag to a bull.

"Oh, that'd be an old friend o' Lily's pa, Mr Diggle," she managed to say calmly, looking up from the menus she and Mrs Kelly were going over. The whole kitchen had come to a halt as they all listened to this astonishing bit of news. They were right fond of Miss Lily who was in and out of the kitchen all day long and this was the first they had heard of any old friend. "He were a seaman an' all, Lily's pa, an' this chap often came ter't th'ouse. A lovely chap an' right fond o' Lily. Bu' . . . well, as yer could see, 'e's norra gentleman an' wouldn't be welcome in Mr Crowther's drawin'-room so't child meets 'im down on't beach when 'e comes inter port. Mrs Crowther knows all about it," which wasn't true, "but we'd best not lerron to anyone else. 'E's quite 'armless, Mr Diggle, so would yer ask the outside men ter keep their traps shut. Poor little beggar don't 'ave much an' she'd be 'eartbroken if the master stopped 'er seein' 'im."

Mr Diggle kept a watchful eye on her at first, quite startled when she showed such obvious affection for the chap, running into his arms like a homing pigeon, but gradually they all became used to Lily's "friend" and Lily's wanderings, which often took her out of their sight. Well, they couldn't watch her all the time, could they, particularly when the master bought her that pony, which she called Precious and which Arnold taught her to ride. They had expected her and Miss Eloise to ride together after that but no, the pair of them were, as usual, like cat and dog, scratching and snarling and agreeing over nothing, going off in different directions, Miss Eloise always accompanied by one of the grooms. She was, after all, the master's daughter.

The baby carriage was a grand affair, called a Victoria and though not exactly suitable for a small infant, since it had been designed for a child who could sit up, Lily and Dorcas thought it was wonderful. It was large, high-backed with four big wheels and a deep hood and with the help of several cushions and the ingenious use of blankets she and Dorcas had arranged Abby in it so that she was quite safe, venturing into the garden for the baby's first walk. They had taken turns to push her, both delighted with the freedom they could now enjoy when the weather was fine. Though she herself loved her little sister, doted on her, in fact, and would have liked to spend all day with her, Lily was aware that she must allow Dorcas to share the caring for the baby, which was, after all, what she had been employed for. When Lily went riding, or into town or somewhere she could not take Abby, Dorcas was there and so far it had worked well enough. They never, ever took the baby carriage to the front of the house, bearing in mind Joshua Crowther's parting shot on the day the purchase of it had been discussed. Because of this, which was a good thing in Lily's opinion, he was never to know who was out with his baby daughter and therefore was not aware of how much time Lily actually spent with her.

It was October now and this would be the fourth time she had seen Liam since the day of her ma's funeral. She would not forget that day. The kisses they had exchanged then had been very different to the ones they had given one another in the past. Childish kisses on her part, smacking kisses on the cheek, big hugs and passionate entreaties to be home soon, for she did miss him so.

Now they had become somewhat constrained when alone together. Those kisses had changed everything between them and though she longed to ask him why, since they had both enjoyed them, she held her tongue for the moment, talking quietly of his latest trip which had been to New York and the next which was to Nova Scotia. They met only on the seashore, for she was still in the deep black of mourning for her mother. She was a young woman who would gladly defy any convention she thought foolish, and did, but respect and love for her ma made her honour this one. She was still grieving and for now was no longer the high-spirited, defiant young creature who would have run away to sea with Liam if he let her. It was as though they were shy with one another, only just met, that is until the day she introduced him to Abby who could dissolve any reserve with one of her huge, toothless grins or her slow, baby chuckle.

"She looks just like you," was the first thing he said about her. And "Can I take her out of the carriage?" was the second.

He had done so, cradling her carefully against his broad chest, not the least bit awkward, pushing down her lacy shawl with a strong, brown finger the better to look more closely at her delicate rose cheeks, the curve of her puckered mouth, the arch of her fair brows, the wide-eyed wondering stare of her lavender grey, unblinking eyes.

"She's the loveliest thing I ever saw and the dead spit of you."

"No, she's prettier than me. She looks like Ma," Lily had answered just like a proud mama herself, still peering down at her sister, not seeing that Liam was looking, not at the baby, but at her.

"I didn't know your ma well, lovebud, but this is how you must have looked at the same age."

"D'you think so?" She was pleased, especially when he put his lips to the baby's cheek in a gentle kiss. It was essential that Liam should love this child as she did, since she knew with great certainty that their futures, the three of them, were inextricably linked.

They had walked that day as far as the Pottery Shore with Liam pushing the perambulator across the difficult bits, then up on to the parade which ran beside Egerton Dock and on to Toxteth Dock, crossing bridge after bridge from granite island to granite island until they came to Queen's Basin where they stopped to absorb the quiet, patient presence of the great sailing ships. They strained their necks to look up at the wrangling cranes perched on their high roofs and walked among the long transit sheds ringing with echoes of men and hammers and whistling cheerfulness.

Many heads turned to watch them go by, the beautiful young woman and the tall, protective chap at her side trundling the baby carriage. You didn't often see a father pushing a perambulator, that was women's work, but you could see it in their smiling glances that they thought they were watching a young husband and wife with their newborn child.

"We'd best turn back now, lovebud. I think this is far enough for one day."

"I want her to love it all as much as we do, Liam. I want her to be an Elliott, not a Crowther. If we bring her here whenever you're home I'm sure she will be. I can't bear to think that part of her is . . . from *him*."

"I know, lovebud."

They had been even more quiet on that day walking back across the Pottery Beach and on the days they had met since, for Jane's ghost, the fragile drifting memory of her came to haunt Lily as though to say look after my child. Love my child, for no one else will.

Sometimes they just sat on the shingle looking across the shimmering water to the training ship on the Cheshire side of the river, or watching the flats going up towards Garston to collect salt, not saying much, smiling down at the baby who lay on the rug between them, or Liam would hold her on his lap, talking down into her face which showed great interest. She would watch his mouth intently, then arch her back in a sudden smile while his curved over her in great tenderness. Lily waited. It was as though some great moment, some important crossroads had been reached in their lives and neither knew which way they should go. They were no longer Liam and Lovebud, the man and child who had loved one another for six years but a man and woman; those kisses had confirmed that simple fact and so Lily waited, for she knew, despite her own headlong wish to move on to the next step in their relationship, she must give Liam the time and the freedom to take it with her.

In the privacy of the room which she had once shared with her mother and which no one had thought to move her out of, she would sit in the window seat in the darkness and stare out over the dim shapes of the garden and wonder about men and women. With Villy twitching in sleep at her feet and Beauty curled up on the rug before the fire she would ponder on the strangeness, the *difference* which showed itself in Liam's reluctance to go forward when it was obvious to her, at least, that that was the only way they could go. In her heart was something so beautiful words could not express it. It ached because of it but she knew it for what it was and did wish that Liam would hurry up and accept it too. Oh, she knew he was still struggling with the image of a small girl with her lace pantaloons showing beneath the hem of her short dress, her bonnet hanging on a ribbon down her back and he was fighting what was in him because of it. She did hope it would not be left to her to bring it out into the open. She supposed she could do what she had always done which was run along the beach to meet him and simply fling herself into his arms and kiss him but something held her back from it. She didn't know what it was, for she had always been the sort of person who said what she thought, and acted on whatever was truth to her.

It was a mellow October day, perfect with that soft warmth that sometimes comes between summer and the onset of winter. The trees were fast losing their leaves and the yellow buttons of tansy bobbed their last blooms in the grass. Bright-eyed jackdaws swooped in and out of the almost naked branches. She did not take Abby with her this day and for some reason was disconcerted by her own feeling when he appeared to be disappointed.

"She has a cold," she told him tartly, "and Dorcas thought it best not to bring her out," which was a lie.

"Since when did what Dorcas say matter to you? I thought you were chief factotum in the nursery."

"Well, you thought wrong. Dorcas is her nursemaid and must be listened to."

He hooted with laughter. "Well, God bless my soul, I never thought to hear you admit that, since you know it's not true."

She turned on him, making a hole in the wet sand with her heel. The water was low and great sandbanks were revealed on which multitudes of seabirds had settled. The low water had left a long stretch of mud and wet sand along the shore and the hem of her black gown dragged through a pool.

"Watch where you're walking, you fool," he said, nettled by her attitude, "you'll ruin your dress."

"Don't change the subject and are you calling me a liar?"

"Don't be daft. Of course I'm not but ever since Abby was born you have decided what is right and wrong for her and now you're telling me Dorcas has forbidden you to bring the child out."

"I didn't say that at all."

"Then what did you say, for God's sake, and why the hell are we arguing like this?"

"I'm not arguing and anyway, you started it," which bit of logic made him laugh. He was ready to brush it aside, this strange mood she was in, not recognising it for what it was, but she wouldn't let it go. She was mad about something, though what in hell it was he had no idea. But, Jesus, she was beautiful. Not in the way of the child she had been, but as a woman. Alive, vibrant, overcoming the quenching effect of her black gown. He felt the pain of it spear him in his fierce masculine need to sweep her into his arms and into his heart where she had always been but that uncomfortable feeling of guilt gripped him and he kept his arms firmly pinned to his sides.

"So what is so humorous about that, may I ask?" Her face was a furious pink and her eyes were enormous in it, a deep lavender grey but glittering like the light on the water. The hot flash of her temper surprised them both. Her nostrils flared and her soft pink mouth had thinned out into a hard line, straining to find the words to hurt him as he had hurt her. Dear God, she had time to think. I'm jealous. I'm jealous of a four-month-old baby, but she was on a path that would not let her turn aside. She wanted him to pull her into his arms and kiss her. She had wanted it for months now and he had been hanging about like some shy schoolboy and, by God, she'd had enough of it but the trouble was she didn't know how to change it.

"Now then, lovebud," Liam managed to say mildly, "there's no need for all this and why you're in such a tantrum . . ."

He couldn't have spoken a word more likely to infuriate her. Tantrum! His look of good-natured tolerance changed at once to amazement as she lifted her hand and aimed it at his face. It did not connect, since he was quick on his feet and his own hand came up and caught her wrist.

"What in hell's name is the matter with you?" he was ready to snarl. He had seen Lily in many moods, most of them those of a thwarted child, a grief-stricken child, a frustrated child, a child who is bewildered by life and what it had done to her. But this was different.

"There's nothing the matter with me, Liam O'Connor," she told him imperiously, lifting her chin and turning away disdainfully, "but I can't say the same about you," wondering as she said it how she'd got herself into this foolish situation, and why!

"What the devil's that supposed ter mean?" In the last few years the rough Liverpool accent he had picked up as a child had gradually been erased from his speech. He had not done it purposely but somehow, on the trips he made and with the men from all parts of the country, and the world, he met, it had slipped away. Except when he was angry, as now.

"You know what it means," she told him, all reason gone. "And I'd be obliged if you would get out of my way. I must get back to the nursery to see how Abby is."

"I'm certainly no' keepin' yer, lass. Yer free ter go wherever yer please."

"Well, then . . ."

"Well, then, what?"

"I'll be on my way. I hope you have a good trip." She lifted her small chin even higher.

Liam pushed his hands through the thick crop of his curls in exasperation, then turned abruptly on his heel, walking a little way from her, keeping his back to her. She watched him breathing heavily. She was too young and inexperienced to know that she was trying to force a confrontation. She loved him, that was all she knew. She had always loved him but now it was not the same. It hurt her, this love, for she did not know what to do with it and Liam was no help at all. He should know. He was the man, older than her and therefore wiser in the ways of love. Why hadn't he kissed her again like he had months ago? Why did he continue to treat her like a child when it was very plain she was a woman now? Why . . . why . . . what should she do? How could she make him notice her again? Since that day they had been neither one thing nor the other. It was as though she had lost him, that man who had been her friend for six years and yet he had not moved on to become someone to replace him. God, she was so confused. So lost if she could not be something, *anything* to him. Why was he holding back like this and if he was, how was she to . . . to recover him?

Suddenly she turned and began to walk away from him in the direction of the rough path that led from the beach through the strip of woodland to the house. Her head was held bravely high and she moved like a young queen, holding her full skirts so that she would not trip on them.

Liam watched her go, knowing exactly what was in her mind, for the same thoughts were in his. But he was a man and could analyse them more easily than she could who still, on one level, thought as a child. A child woman who was simple and forthright in her approach and could not bear the shifting emotions, indeed did not even know of them; that worried him. Dear God, why could he not just accept what had happened to them, to him, and love her as he was meant to? For four months now he had been vacillating, running whenever he was in port to the widow in Upper Duke Street in the hope that she would solve his problems with some plain, unthinking, sexual pleasure. Even she had noticed a change in his performance as a lover and had asked him only last night if he was quite well. This child, no, call her what she is . . . this *woman* who was marching so resolutely away from him was the one who stood between him and other women and unless he did something about it, in one way or another, he would never recover from it. Did he want to recover from it? *Could* he recover from it? There was only one way to find out, but if it failed how was she to go on with the rest of her life? She was so bloody alone, so vulnerable. If he found he could not . . . could not possibly treat her as a woman after all these years of seeing her as a child, what could he say to her? The risk was too great, surely. Surely if he left her alone she would get over it . . . What in hell was he talking about? *Get over it* . . . His lovebud . . . his . . . his . . .

Every thought but one left his head as he began to race after her, his feet making no sound in the soft sand and grass. He caught his head on a branch as he ran, cursing under his breath as he felt the blood begin to flow but it did not stop him. He must catch her before she reached the edge of the trees where they thinned ·and the lawn began but she was still in the clearing which was about halfway through. Her arm was bent up against the broad trunk of an oak tree, her face pressed into it and she was weeping. The thick carpet of autumn leaves, wet from the rain that had fallen the day before, muffled his footsteps. The leaves still fell, drifting in spirals down from the branches and one fell on her hair, a brilliant copper against the silver.

His hands reached out and took her shoulders, then turned her towards him and with a combined cry they fell against one another. His mouth searched for hers and it was there. He kissed her so savagely he could taste blood on his lips, and he wondered vaguely whose it was, hers or his. He slid his mouth across her wet face, leaving a tiny smear of crimson. Her eyes were closed and she seemed to be ready to faint but he could feel the strength of her, the woman's strength of her as she pulled at him to hold her closer. They did not speak. He felt he should be appalled by his own behaviour, for he was not treating her with the gentleness her innocence and inexperience demanded, but his body urged him on since *it* knew this was no child in his arms but a woman. He could feel the peaked roundness of her breasts against his chest, with no more between them than the bodice of her mourning gown and his fine cambric shirt. His hands moved to her throat, stroking the soft flesh beneath her chin, cupping her face as his lips travelled across her eyes and cheeks and down again to her jawline.

"Oh, God," he moaned in the back of his throat, wanting her to stop him, begging her to allow him to go on.

"Liam . . . I love you, Liam." Her warm lips were against his chin, moving to his ear where she caught the lobe with her teeth and he groaned as hot desire flowed madly through him. His hands moved of their own accord to find her breasts and the hard nipples swelled into the palms.

"Dear God . . . Lily Elliott, I love you."

"Yes . . . love me, Liam . . . now . . ." She arched her throat, making some noise that spoke plainly of her own longing. His hands went to the buttons of her gown, a couple of dozen of them marching down the front of the bodice and here, as though it had been designed to repel the eager attention of any male, they defeated him. His hands shook with maddened longing and she was the same, doing her best to help him, both of them desperate to have her naked breasts in his hands but even as they struggled Liam's inflamed mind was cooling to reason.

Taking a deep breath he captured her hands which were still busy at her throat, bringing them to his lips in a gesture of loving tenderness.

"Liam . . . Liam," she moaned, "please . . ."

"Lovebud . . . sweetheart . . ."

"Don't stop, Liam, I want . . ." whatever it is that comes next, her anguished, flower-like face told him.

"Dearest heart . . . stop it . . . calm yourself . . . help me."

"No, I want to be yours, Liam. Please, I don't know what to do . . . please . . ."

He drew her fiercely into his arms, pushing her face into the curve of his shoulder, holding her trembling body close to his own which was doing its own share of trembling. Sweet Christ, this was the hardest thing he had ever done. This woman he loved had not learned to be subtle or artful. All her life she had said exactly what she felt or meant. Now she wanted him to make love to her and so she said so, but he couldn't. He bloody well couldn't. Not because he didn't want to, nor did he have any scruples left about their age difference, or the sudden shift in his emotions from loving the child to loving the woman. It was simply not the time. It was simply not the place. He had something to tell her that would shatter her slowly regained peace of mind and it could not be clouded with their bodies' needs. They must be practical and when the time was right, which he hoped to God would not be long, then they would be married.

"Come and sit down, lovebud. We must . . ."

But she would not let him be. "No, Liam. You love me. You said so. I heard you . . . and I love you. Don't turn from me."

"I'm not turning from you, my love. My love, that's what you are. My love, and when the time is right we will . . . go on from here, but I have something to tell you and I can't do it unless you calm yourself, and allow me to calm myself. This is not easy for me. My body is . . . it wants yours, sweetheart. D'yer know what that means? D'yer know what goes on with a man and woman? Did yer ma not tell yer?"

"No . . . but I've read the encyclopedias in the library and I . . . I think I have a rough idea. There was one about . . . human reproduction, you see." Her innocence enchanted him and before he knew what he was about he had kissed her and for several minutes they lost control again. Now that they were sitting down, their backs to the wide tree-trunk, the buttons on her bodice were more accessible but though his hand cupped her breasts, making her sigh with delight, he put her from him, sitting up and clutching himself round the knees, his head bent, his breathing fast.

"I must say this quickly, lovebud, then go."

"Liam . . ."

"No, darlin', let me speak. I have a present for yer. I was not goin' ter tell yer . . . for a while but now . . . I must. I want yer ter understand . . ."

She sat up and turned to look into his face, which was hidden in the curve of his arms.

"What?"

He lifted his head and in his eyes was a look of such joy she let out her breath on a gasp.

"What? Oh, Liam, what?"

"It's the *Lily-Jane*."

She could not speak. Her heart was bounding in her breast and her face felt suddenly cold as the blood drained away from it. He took her hands in his, turning to kneel before her.

"I've found 'er, lovebud. An' nor only that, I've bought 'er. She's mine ... ours ... and she'll be my wedding present to you."

She began to weep then tears of such joy she could not contain them, lifting her face to the pale stretch of blue sky above the autumn trees, her eyes streaming, her face awash.

"There's just one thing, lovebud," he said quietly. "It's taken every penny I've ever earned ter buy her an' ter restore her ... she's in a right old mess, lovebud. I need to earn a lot more. The only way ter do that is ter go ... long distance. I'm ter sail on the clipper ship *Breeze* tomorrow morning. To China."

21

Remember, I may be far away but I'll always be with you, were the last words he said to her, then she watched as he walked away towards the Pottery Shore, listening to those words as they tried desperately to soothe their way round inside her head. He did not turn, not once in the five minutes it took him to reach Dingle Point where he disappeared. Her heart was like a rock inside her breast, heavy with foreboding, for how was she to manage without him for so long, particularly now when they had just found each other? He had been a small part in the days of her life for the past six years, going away for weeks on end, but always there had been that bright light of expectancy illuminating the interval in between, the warm anticipation of the day of his coming back. While he was at sea she had led her own secret life, roaming the woodlands and the seashore, putting in the occasional appearance in the schoolroom to lull Miss Kaye into a belief that she was turning over a new leaf.

And when the day came he was always here waiting for her as he promised. He had never forsaken her, never made a promise he had not kept and though he had told her he would be home again in approximately 110 days, which was the time a fast clipper took to make the round trip to Foochow and back to Liverpool, he might have said 110 years, for that was how it would seem. February at the very latest, he had told her, crushing her to him in an agony of sorrow at their parting and she had been like a doll in his arms, numb with shock. Now he was gone. No longer to be seen and it was tearing her apart. It did not concern her that Pa's lovely little ship had been found and was to be brought back to life again. How could it when it was separating her and Liam for so long?

The dream she had nurtured for all these years was sterile now as she watched another dream, born only a few months ago, that of her and Liam spending the rest of their lives together, drift away with him. She knew in her mind where sense was that she was being foolish. That she was allowing her heart to distort out of all perspective what was happening but just now it felt as though he had gone from her for good. He was coming back, she knew he was, he had told her so, but not for months and she could not bear it.

She didn't sleep that night. She didn't even get into bed but sat on the window seat with Beauty on her lap and Villy at her feet and stared into the darkness towards the river where Liam still was. There was nothing in her head but pain which did not allow for coherent thought but there was one there, nevertheless.

At first light she let herself out of the side door and glided silently across the grass towards the gate. She had left a note for Mrs Quinn, for she and Maggie and the others would be alarmed if they found her bed not slept in. It was an ambiguous little note, saying nothing much about her destination, hinting that she might have gone riding, just in case *he* should see it.

She wore an ankle-length black cloak, lined with a rich wool, with a hood that framed her pale face, drowning her and yet enhancing her delicate beauty. She walked the length of Beech Lane, turning into Holmes Lane. There was a hackney cab just drawing up to the doors of the Aigburth Hotel from which a gentleman in a top hat and evening clothes was alighting. He looked at her in amazement, for it was barely six o'clock and the sight of a woman who was obviously not of the working class was uncommon at this time of the morning.

She ignored his stares, speaking to the driver who looked equally surprised.

"Can you take me to the docks, please. And as—"

"The docks, miss, at this time of the morning?"

She became the haughty Miss Elliott, her face set and cold.

"Is it any of your business where I go or at what time?" she asked him imperiously, while the top-hatted gentleman watched with great interest.

"No, sorry, miss, it's only that a young lady like you ought not to—"

"Please, spare me your lectures and take me as quickly as possible to the docks. I must catch the tide."

"The tide!"

"Dear God, will you please do as I ask and as quickly as possible."

Breeze was just about to set sail. There was a great bustle amidships, and in the rigging, as sails were unfurled, the men who clung precariously in a line along a lofty spar seemed to be in imminent danger of losing their footing and being dashed to the deck. The gangplanks were drawn away from the ship's sides and there was a last-minute flurry as two men, using thin iron bars, battened down a hatch cover. The mainmast swayed gracefully as *Breeze* began to inch her way out into the river, helped by a couple of tugs, a sliver of greasy water appearing between her and the quayside.

She could see Liam in the wheelhouse standing next to the master, a Captain Fletcher of the Hemingway Line. His face was set in lines of intense concentration and he constantly turned his head as though judging the distance between the ship, the tugs and the land they were leaving behind. He wore no hat and the light from the rising sun, which was still hidden behind the transit sheds, struck gold from his ruffled hair. He wore the dark coat and neat white necktie of an officer and his tall frame dwarfed the other man with him in the wheelhouse. It seemed Liam was at the helm since he was to be second-in-command to the captain. He had a Master's Certificate himself and had been master of a couple of ships since he had gained it, but in order to get a berth on a clipper he had been forced to sign on as first mate. It would be worth it, he had explained to her in those last appalling moments before he left her, for officers in the "Flying Fish" trade, as the China run was known, who had cash to spare were allowed to purchase goods on their own behalf and sell them at immensely inflated prices when they arrived back in port, thereby making a handsome profit. He had not much after the purchase of the *Lily-Jane*, but with what he had he meant to do the same. They would need it if they were to restore the *Lily-Jane*, he had told her, frightened of her icy control and hoping to warm her, melt her with hope for their future which included the schooner she had loved since the day she was old enough to understand her significance.

Imagine it, porcelain, silks, paintings, fans, dishes fashioned in delicate silver, ornate ivory, furnishings of polished wood, lacquerware and all manner of *objects d'art* to be brought back to a market hungry for such things. He had seen them himself carried back from the Far East by men serving on the swift and beautiful clipper ships, and now it was a chance for him to do the same. For them. *Breeze* would sail down the Atlantic, round the Cape of Good Hope and across the Indian Ocean to the port of Melbourne in Australia where they would discharge their passengers and cargo and sail on in ballast to Foochow to load up with tea and other profitable goods. Then it would be a race to be home with the first cases of the new crop of tea which was carried in beautiful ornamental chests, one of which would be her bridal chest, he promised her, smoothing her ice cold cheek with his lips, cupping her face and doing his best to take that look of dread from her eyes. And then there was that far more lucrative trade which concerned opium and from which a fortune might be made but he did not mention that!

Breeze was a newly built British clipper belonging to the Hemingway Shipping Line. She had a raked stern and a hollow bow overhanging the counter-stern. She was finer, and had more delicate lines than her American counterparts, with an improved sail plan which enabled the ship to "ghost" in light winds, and yet she was marvellously efficient in a gale and therefore was a much safer vessel. This was what Liam had told her as he had held her in his arms and as she watched the lovely graceful ship move away towards the centre of the river she tried to get comfort from this.

It was a fine morning, a rosy dawn turning the billowing sails of the clipper to shades of washed pink and rose and outlining the rigging against the lightening sky. It was all so beautiful it hurt her to see it and yet this was her element, hers and the ship's, and she must hold the truth to her, which was that in three months she would be standing here again watching *Breeze* bringing Liam back to her.

It took a long time for *Breeze* to fade from sight. The quayside, which had been crowded with hundreds of people, many of them emigrants sailing on her, the rest there to see them off, was almost deserted now. There had been barrels and boxes and bales, tin trunks and leather portmanteaux, all waiting to go on board but now the space they had taken up was empty and Lily was alone in a great echoing expanse which still held the sad notes of their goodbyes. The voices of the officers shouting commands, relayed from the captain who had stood beside Liam in the wheelhouse, had died away and a curious quiet fell as if, no matter how many times they saw it, the partings saddened the onlookers. There were porters and dock labourers about, leaning on the waggons that had brought the cargo of coal, salt and Manchester piece-goods to the ship. There were many waggons pulled by enormous Shires moving back to the transit sheds for their next loads, and, perched on a bollard, an old seaman was doing some intricate thing with a rope. From inside the transit shed dockers whistled and sang, the latter an old ballad which was popular in Liverpool:

> Come all you dry land sailors behold
> And listen to my song,
> There are but forty verses . . .

And standing on the edge of the quay, so close several dockers looked uneasily at her, Lily watched the vessel carrying her love fade slowly into the pink and gold morning mist in the mouth of the river. For an hour she stood there, a silent, slender figure in the graceful folds of her black cloak, her hood revealing nothing but the curve of her pale cheek and a silver glint of a curl which had escaped and blew across the wool of the hood in the lazy breeze which had got up. They watched her, the men who loaded the waggons which were all on the move now, men busy with the work of the great seaport, wondering what she was doing and why she stood so still and so silently gazing out to the mouth of the river and when one, encouraged by his mates, approached her, he was startled by the blank stare she turned on him when he gently touched her arm.

"Are yer all right, miss?" he asked her in the adenoidal tones of a true "Dicky Sam", a man born within a mile of St Nicholas Church. His face was rough and seamed with his years working in all weathers on the dockside, but it was kind and anxious.

"She 'ad a face like an angel," he was to tell his mates when he rejoined them, but she smiled at him and thanked him for his concern.

She began to walk then, past Albert Dock and the tobacco

warehouses, moving steadily southwards beyond Brunswick Dock, where large lengths of timber from North America were being unloaded through openings in the bows of several vessels. Teams of men and horses dragged them ashore, cursing and sweating as she moved steadily through the brisk activity, seemingly unaware of their presence, staring after her in amazement so that confusion reigned in her wake. She continued along the parade until she reached the Pottery Shore, striding on round Dingle Point, her boots wading through several inches of water, for the tide was high and fast. She did not notice, and it was not until she had reached the strip of sand that stood in front of Oakwood Place that she sank to her knees as though in prayer. Her hood fell back and she bent her head, then folded in on herself and wept brokenheartedly.

An hour later she let herself into the house by the same side door through which she had left, moving quietly up the stairs until she reached the privacy of her bedroom. Villy sprang up to meet her, licking her hand then running to fetch one of her soft toys to show her mistress how pleased she was to see her. Beauty arched her back and smoothed herself against her skirt, purring her own pleasure and when Lily had undressed and put on her nightgown, climbing into bed and burrowing under the covers, the dog and the cat came to lie alongside her. When Maggie popped her head round the door an hour later she reported that Miss Lily was back, and fast asleep in her bed, though God knew where she'd been. Not on her mare, that was for sure, since the hem of her gown and her boots, which she'd left lying on the floor in front of the fire, were soaked with what could only be seawater. Did Mrs Quinn reckon she'd been down to the shore to meet that friend of her pa's then?

"Aye, she coulda done," Molly Quinn answered absently.

"Shall I wake her, d'yer think?"

"Nay, lerrer sleep."

"Mebbe she's not well. It's not like her ter stay in 'er bed."

"Well, leave 'er fer a bit then I'll go up an' see 'ow she is. Sleep's a good 'ealer when yer badly."

It seemed Lily was "badly" for several days, only leaving her room to climb the stairs to the nursery to sit with Abby for half an hour or so. The baby greeted her with welcoming smiles which warmed the cold and distant reaches of her heart which had been empty ever since Liam left.

"Is she all right, Dorcas?" she had asked, peering anxiously into Abby's face.

Dorcas was seriously offended, she told her Aunty Mabel. Anyone'd think the poor little beggar was being neglected without Miss Lily to oversee her and, as Aunty Mabel could see, putting the good-natured baby on to her Aunty Mabel's capacious lap, there was absolutely nowt wrong with her. It was Miss Lily who looked to have something wrong with her and no wonder she had kept to her bed. She only hoped it was nothing catching.

"Where is she now, our Dorcas?" her Aunty Mabel asked her, bouncing the baby on her knee and making her laugh with delight.

"She were back in 'er bed when I left."

Which was where Joshua Crowther found her when, for some reason, scarcely recognised even to himself, he knocked on her door and entered her bedroom.

She was asleep. Her hair, which she had tied carelessly back with a ribbon, was spread like a silver and amber shot cape on the pillow about her head, ruffled into tumbled waves that glinted in the firelit room. One arm was flung above her head and the covers, which she'd pushed down, showed the roundness of her breasts and the high peaks of her nipples beneath the fine cambric of her nightgown. Her eyes were closed, her long thick lashes forming a half-moon on her flushed cheeks and her poppy lips were moist and parted, showing a tiny portion of her tongue and white teeth. She was breathing deeply but when Villy, who had lifted her head at the man's entrance, raised her muzzle and began to growl, she woke with a start.

Joshua Crowther, whose hand had been stretched out to touch her, perhaps her hair – or had he intended something more pleasurable? – jumped back as though a wasp had alighted on his flesh and sunk its barb in him. He recovered quickly, smiling urbanely as though to say there was nothing amiss in a man visiting his unwell step-daughter. Lily reared up on her elbows, pulling the covers up to her chin, then flinched away until her head rested on the headboard. Villy huddled up closer to her, her muzzle still raised though no sound came from her, which was somehow more telling.

"What d'you want?" Lily quavered, her eyes wide and barely focused, not frightened, more astonished, for what in hell's name was he doing in her bedroom? For six years he had taken no interest in her, save a threat now and again if she did not settle down to Miss Kaye's rule, but even those had stopped years ago. Since Ma died they had barely exchanged a word, even at breakfast, the only meal they shared. After Ma died Lily had taken her evening meal in her own small sitting-room, eating off a tray in front of the fire, sharing titbits with Villy, but gradually, over the last month or two, she had begun to eat with Mrs Quinn and the rest of the maidservants in the big, cosy, cheerful kitchen. They had been somewhat surprised at first, for she was one of the daughters of the house, but then they had grown used to it, telling one another that the poor little beggar must be lonely now her ma was gone. She was a lively young girl with a good sense of humour, making them laugh, or at least she had done before Mrs Crowther died, and would again, they were sure, when she had become more used to her loss.

"There is no need for alarm, my dear. Can a man not come to see how his daughter is faring?" he asked smoothly, smiling down at her in a way she did not like. "We missed you at breakfast and when I enquired after you was told that you were unwell so I thought I would see if there was anything you wanted."

He had stepped back from the bed when she woke but now he moved closer, his hands in his pockets. They seemed to be scrabbling for something, shifting about in his pockets in a most odd way and she found her eyes hypnotically drawn there, then back to his face which was smiling. His gaze drifted over her and Villy's hackles rose even more.

"Does that dog have to lie on the bed?" he asked, dreamlike, his eyes narrowed to dark slits in the dim light from the fire. "You know my views on animals in the house. I must ask one of the yard men to come and take her to the stable where she belongs."

"You do and I shall go with her. And I am not your daughter."

"Now then, you are being silly. There is no need for that. You *are* my daughter now, or at least my ward and as for the dog, I'm sure we could come to some agreement about it that suits both of us."

What on earth did he mean by that? her confused mind asked as he sat down on the end of the bed, pushing aside the angry cat. It was a dreary day, the rain beating on the window and the tree outside it lashing against the glass, not a day for sailors at sea, she remembered thinking as Mr Crowther's agreeably smiling face loomed more closely over her. She was reminded of the time when he was wooing her mother. This was how he had been then, smiling and speaking in that deceptively gentle voice. Ma had been taken in but Lily Elliott, who had loathed this man ever since he married her mother, was not so easy to deceive. He wanted something, that was why he was like this, and though she still felt weak and lost without Liam, it would not be for long. She would be strong again very soon and she would show this bugger that though she might look like her mother, inside she was vastly different. How dare he come in here. How dare he!

"I also came to say that the moment you feel well enough I hope to see you at the dinner table with Eloise and myself. It has come to my notice that you are eating with the servants and that will not do at all. Perhaps this evening?" He edged a little closer to her.

Her tone was almost conversational as she spoke. "If you come one inch nearer to me I shall scream the bloody place down," she told him and was amused to see the expression of amazement cross his face, amazement and annoyance. "And as for an agreement between you and me I'd sooner make a pact with a rattlesnake which would be easier to trust."

She spoke bravely. She was supremely confident, her blood pulsing hotly through her veins, believing in her innocence that she had nothing to fear from this man. Even when he smiled that slithery smile of his she was still not afraid. What could he do to her in this house full of servants who had only to call to the men outside and there would be a dozen of them cramming the room to defend her.

"Well, you are a fire-eater, aren't you? I only came to enquire after your health, my dear, so why you are taking this attitude I cannot imagine. But since you are unwilling to accept my offer I'd best go."

"And what offer is that, Mr Crowther?"

"For us to be friends, of course, my dear. This constant touchiness on your part is very tedious. So perhaps we may see you at dinner this evening. I'll leave the matter of the dog for the present. So get some sleep and tonight put on your prettiest dress, leave off that mourning since your mother has been dead for four months now, and come down and dine with us. I mean that, Lily."

When he left the room, turning at the door to smile back at her, she began to shake. She wasn't even sure what had happened. Mr Crowther had come to her room to enquire after her health which had never been anything other than rude in all the time she had been at Oakwood Place. On the face of it there was nothing wrong with that, was there, but she knew there was. He was threatening her with something, holding Villy over her as a lever. Dear God, why did this have to happen to her when she was feeling so low, when she felt as though the bottom had dropped out of her world for the moment? She knew, her sensible mind *knew* that she had only three, four months at the most to get through and then Liam would be back. They would be married and go and live in a house of his choice, perhaps even on the *Lily-Jane* while it was being restored to the condition it had known when Pa was alive. Only four months in this house which held so many special and yet so many unhappy memories. Memories of the peaceful times with her and Ma, with Will and Mr Diggle in the gardens, with Villy prancing beside them and Beauty doing her best to make them believe she didn't give a fig for any of them, but hanging about Ma's skirts just the same. Memories of Liam sprawled on the beach beside her watching the ships move along the busy swaggering river, a bustling highway dancing with eager craft, tall frigates swaying graciously out to sea and bursting into white sail bloom as they went. They had shared such joy, such laughter and yet she had known of her ma's deep unhappiness and could not get it out of her head that perhaps Ma was better off dead, for she would be with Pa now and not that monster who had caused her such pain.

She was sixteen and only this week had learned of the loveliness of being close to and cared for by a man. Liam's kisses, Liam's hands on her body had brought her such a feeling of joy, of racing, bubbling aliveness, if there was such a word, she had felt her senses become dizzy with it. She had wanted in some strange way to hold him so close to her it was as if she were doing her best to force herself *inside* him, to *be* him, or part of him and now that part was gone and she must learn to be patient and strong until it came back to her with

Liam. She loved him. *She loved him.* She was a woman who loved her man, for that was what Liam was, *her* man and she must find some way to get through the days and weeks safely until he came back. Now why should she have said that? she wondered. Why had she said *safely?* And when Mr Crowther's arrogant face swam before her eyes, that cruel, smiling face, she knew why.

She got out of bed and dressed herself in her newly sponged and pressed black gown, clicking her fingers to Villy to come with her, going down the back stairs, which she knew he never used, to the kitchen.

"Why, 'ere she is," Mrs Quinn exclaimed, her face lighting up at the sight of the child who now had the love she had once reserved for Jane Elliott. "Are yer feelin' better, queen? See, Mrs Kelly's medd some lemon curd tarlets an' Betsy were purrin' on't kettle. Sit thi' down an' try one."

She waited to see if Lily had anything to say on the matter of her indisposition of the last few days, but her lamb sat down and with the appetite of a child began to tuck into the lemon curd tartlets. The dog sat at her feet, her head cocked, her ears pricked, her mouth watering as she waited hopefully for some to come her way and when it did, throwing it down her throat without it touching the sides.

Lily licked her fingers and sat back in the kitchen chair, looking about her at the friendly faces, the smiles, the general air of approval, for these women were her friends. They had loved her ma and they were fond of her and surely, in an atmosphere such as this she could come to no harm until it was time for her to go to Liam. Mr Crowther was an evil, filthy old man, that was all, who had done his best to besmirch her mother with his filth but he had not succeeded, for the parts of Ma that were special, that had been loved by her father, could not be touched. She had heard the grooms, when they thought themselves to be alone, speak of their master's exploits – though that was not the word they used – with women, before and after Ma's death, but he could not touch her with his ugliness. He liked to play games, she was aware of that, even in her ignorant state of the ways of men, for she had seen him play them with her mother, baiting her with his "teasing" until she was reduced to tears. Well, he would not play the same games with her.

She felt better as she sat and dreamed before the kitchen fire in Mrs Quinn's chair, her stockinged feet tucked up beneath the hem of her skirt. Mrs Kelly was up to her elbows in flour, for she'd a fancy for a steak and kidney pie for their supper, she told them, though the family were to have Crimped Cod in Oyster Sauce followed by Veal *à la Jardinière*, Wild Duck and then Charlotte *à la Vanille*.

Lily had no intention of dining on the latter. She much preferred steak and kidney pie and tomorrow, she promised herself drowsily, feeling better than she had since Liam left, she would go and see her pa's schooner, *Lily-Jane*, where she was at berth in Canning Half Dock. She sighed and stretched and Molly watched her, her previous feeling of apprehension drifting away in the relaxed atmosphere of the kitchen that she had come to think of as hers.

22

He watched her from beneath hooded lids as she glided gracefully across the room, the hem of her full black mourning gown just brushing the carpet. Tall, slender, exquisite in her young loveliness. Even the way she walked and held her head – though Jane's had become disappointingly bowed latterly – the way she seated herself on his right-hand side opposite Eloise and shook out her napkin was so exactly like her mother she might have been her.

"Good morning," she said to no one in particular, looking at no one in particular, then turned to smile at Maggie who was at the serving table alone this morning.

"I'll have some porridge, please, Maggie, if I may. It has turned very cold and porridge is warming on a day like this." Her pa had told her that more than once.

"Yes, Miss Lily." Maggie beamed at her.

Joshua waited until the maidservant had placed the bowl of steaming, creamy porridge in front of her before he spoke.

"Good morning. I trust you are better, my dear? We have been most anxious about you, haven't we, Eloise?" not looking at his daughter who stared at him in astonishment but did not answer.

"Yes, thank you. I am completely well."

"We're glad to hear it, are we not, Eloise? And may I say we missed you at dinner last night. It seems you went against my express wishes and took your meal with the servants again. May I ask why?"

"It is quite simple. I prefer their company."

Maggie gasped then clattered a spoon against a serving dish to cover the sound. Blessed Mother, the child asked for trouble, saucing the master like that and when she got back to the kitchen she would have a word with Mrs Quinn, who should definitely have one with Lily! They all knew the master was as amiable as a babe when he was not crossed but to provoke him deliberately like that was begging for a box on the ears. Not that he had ever hit his step-daughter, as far as Maggie knew anyway, but there was always a first time. She held her breath and waited for the master's response but it was Miss Eloise who spoke.

"Well, I suppose it's understandable for like to prefer like," she sneered. "It must be easier for you to consort with servants rather than ladies and gentlemen since you were never used to the latter."

"If by the latter you mean yourself then you are right. I find the servants in this house, and outside it, are honest, truthful, warm-hearted and unaffected. They are kind. They are pleased to see me which gives me a warm feeling I have not found . . . elsewhere." Except with Liam, of course, though she did not voice this last.

"Is that so? Well, all I can say is that proves my point about your upbringing. Anyone who finds pleasure in associating with the underclasses can only be considered one of them."

Maggie was not at all sure what Miss Eloise was implying about the underclasses, of which she was one, she only knew it was not kind but she could do nothing about it, merely stand against the wall and stare blankly across the room as though she were not only deaf but half-witted.

"I would sooner count Maggie and Betsy, Mr Diggle and Jackie, the boot boy, as my friends than—"

"That is enough, the pair of you," the master roared. Maggie nearly jumped out of her skin, she was to tell the dumb-founded servants later when she recounted what had been said. It promised to be a real battleground this morning. And them usually so quiet, the master reading his newspaper, Miss Eloise dwelling, no doubt, on the outfits she was to have made for the coming season which included the Hunt Ball, several dances and parties to which she had been invited and the approaching pre-Christmas festivities. Miss Lily never opened her mouth except to put food in it since, up to now, neither the master nor the young miss had ever spoken to her.

"I will not have this bickering," Mr Crowther growled, "and I would be obliged if you would remain silent for the moment, Eloise."

Eloise subsided sullenly. Her father turned to Maggie and pointed to his plate. "I'll have some more bacon, if you please, Maggie, that's if you can drag yourself from that trance you appear to have fallen into."

Maggie jumped to obey, so flustered she almost dripped bacon fat in the master's lap.

"Now then, Lily," he continued when his plate was replenished to his satisfaction, spearing a forkful of bacon and mushroom and carrying it to his mouth. "Let us return to this liking you appear to have developed for consorting with your inferiors, rather than your family. I propose—"

"If by my family you mean yourself and your daughter then let me remind you I am not related to you in any way. Just because my mother was witless" – Dear God, she should not have used that word, she remembered thinking in some part of her brain that was still functioning coolly, for that was what Ma had been at the time – "enough to marry you does not mean you have any control over me."

She gave him cool stare for cool stare, but something inside her was beginning to quiver with what she recognised as dread. It was as though some instinct told her there was worse to come.

"Aah, that's where you're mistaken, my dear. When your mother died I made it my business to consult a lawyer with a view to . . . well, shall we say *adopting* you. You are legally my ward, or even my daughter in the eyes of the law. The legal documents arrived last week. So you see, you are as much my . . . my responsibility as Eloise here and the infant in the nursery. I may do with you . . . and *to* you, as I please. You and my other daughters are my property, you might say, and will obey me as a father expects to be obeyed. You have run wild in recent years but that, I'm afraid, is to end. You will—"

She stood up with such an eruption of violence her chair crashed backwards to the floor. Maggie squeaked, she couldn't help it, putting her hand to her mouth in horror, but Eloise smiled, a smile of triumphant satisfaction as though to say she had been waiting for this day for a long, long time.

High colour rushed to Lily's cheeks, a fierce flame of anger and her eyes glittered like grey ice with the sun reflected in it. She clenched her hands then brought them down with such force on to the table everything on it jumped an inch into the air. Eloise was just as flushed as she was but with excitement.

She looked from her father's face to the girl who had been pronounced her sister – which she did not care for – then back to her father, unaware that she was holding her breath. There was something odd about the way her father was acting but she was too young and ignorant to recognise the sexual undertones in his manner.

"You can go to hell," Lily hissed, "and I hope you fry there. I belong to no one, only my ma and pa and they're both dead." And, of course, one other but it would not be prudent to mention him here. "I'd leave this house and find work rather than be beholden to you. You'll never be my father, never, nor this trollop my sister. I have one sister and she is in the nursery."

"Where she will remain, naturally, no matter what course of action you take, my dear." Joshua Crowther sat back, wiped his lips on his napkin and smiled up at her. She was quite magnificent, despite her youth, the exact replication of her mother, but younger, and spirited. A fighter, and how he would enjoy taming that wildness, putting a curb on that defiance, knocking the rebellion out of her one way or the other. It might take a long time, for she had had her own way for years but how pleasureable it would be. The truth was, he was bored. His business ventures flourished, needing the minimum of attention. His social life, which had picked up when Jane died and he became an eligible widower, was the same old round where nothing new ever happened. He needed something to stimulate his jaded palate and forcing this new daughter of his, which legally she now was, to conform to the social manners and customs of his class and of his generation was just what he needed.

Lily took a deep breath as the truth of what Joshua Crowther had said filtered into her enraged mind. It would be a simple matter to pack a bag and run away from Oakwood Place. Find a room and some work to keep her until Liam came home, though she was not certain how easy that would be, since she was trained for nothing. But if she left she would have to leave Abby behind and Abby was her ma's child and how could she desert her? If she did she knew her sister would not be ill-treated, far from it. She would be brought up as Eloise had been brought up. Eloise who had also lost her mother at birth, a mother who might have had a softening influence on her. From infancy Joshua's eldest daughter had been in the custody of nurses and governesses, raised to believe she was a little princess. She had been given everything the child of a wealthy man can be given, everything but his attention. Everything but the special hours spent with a caring parent which are necessary to a developing child. The feeling that she was cherished. Oh, Dorcas was carelessly affectionate with Abby, giving her a cuddle, dandling her on her knee, making sure she was clean and well fed but Dorcas was a nursemaid, probably the first in a line of nursemaids until a governess took over. Exactly the sort of childhood Eloise had known and look how she'd turned out! She'd been given none of the loving warmth Ma and Pa had wrapped about her, Lily, and though Eloise had been moulded into a perfect young lady, fit to be a gentleman's wife, she was deeply flawed, spiteful and small-minded. But then when Lily left to go to Liam would she not have to leave Abby behind? The thought speared her through the heart, going straight for the place her little sister had settled into. In her recent dreams she had visualised herself, Liam and Abby living together in some pleasant place, no doubt a cottage with roses round the door, she supposed bitterly, realising what a foolish child she had been. Abby was this man's child. She belonged to him and what could Lily Elliott, who was sixteen and only Abby's half-sister, do about that?

Of course she had not known about the *Lily-Jane* then! She lowered her eyes so that he could not see the expression in them and he smiled triumphantly.

"I see you believe me, Lily. I see you finally realise that I am the master here and that my word is law. I am the guardian of three daughters who will remain in my care until they leave it to pass into that of a husband. Believe it, Lily. Now, won't you sit down and eat your breakfast. And do please tell us where it is you are to go on this cold morning and why you seem to feel the need to stoke up with porridge?" His voice sharpened. "Oh, do sit down, girl. You're beginning to get on my nerves, and take that petulant look off your face. There, that's better," as Lily slowly sat down again and picked up her spoon. "The sooner you learn who is ruler here and that my orders are to be obeyed, the happier we will all be, particularly you."

"I don't think so, Mr Crowther," she answered him icily. "Not unless you lock me in my room."

"That can be arranged, my dear." His voice was silky and

against the wall Maggie felt the bitter taste of fear in her mouth, for she remembered another locked room.

Joshua Crowther sipped his coffee, lounging indolently in his chair as he regarded Lily with narrowed eyes. His daughter was breathless with delight. "So, shall we begin with where you intended going today?"

Intended! That seemed to say it all, but Lily Elliott was far from routed on this particular battlefield. She almost smiled in her self-confidence. If he thought he could chain her to the house, bind her and bend her to his will, then he was in for a big surprise. She was no child to be told what she should do and where she should go. She had done as she pleased for a long time now and this bastard was not going to stop her. She had four months to get through and if she spent the whole time fighting him, then she would do so.

"I mean to ride Precious over to Small Ends," which was a lie, of course, since she intended walking along the river's edge and the seafront beyond Pottery Shore to the parades that fronted each dock until she reached Canning Dock where Liam had told her the *Lily-Jane* was berthed. She had no money for a hansom, since she had spent what little she had the other day when she went to see *Breeze* sail away on her long journey. Small Ends was on the bend of the river beyond Hale where the waters turned towards Runcorn Gap, a five-mile ride with the river always in sight on her right, a favourite ride of hers and one she had taken many times, but it seemed Joshua Crowther had other ideas.

"I think not, my dear, at least not alone. Arnold is to accompany Eloise and it might be best if you go with them. It would be more fitting."

Lily cast about desperately in her mind for some way out that would satisfy Mr Crowther, but she knew there really wasn't one. Blind defiance was the only weapon she had and it was not one Mr Crowther would bow down to. Still, she could but try.

"I don't think so, Mr Crowther. I'm used to riding alone and I certainly don't care for Eloise's company." By the serving table Maggie felt a great urge to turn her face to the wall. Don't do this, lass, she was begging silently. Don't antagonise him, for it'll do you no good, but, of course, she could do or say no such thing, at least not here. Just wait until they got her in the kitchen though. She and Mrs Quinn'd have something to say to her then.

"Do you know, Lily," Mr Crowther answered her in a casual tone, "what you do or do not care for is a matter of supreme indifference to me. You will ride with Eloise and Arnold or you will remain in your room. The choice is yours."

"Very well." She stood up and moved towards the door. "My room it is."

His smiling face did not alter. "Then I'll be up to see you shortly," he told her. "I like to think I might be able to change your mind."

With his words echoing menacingly round her head Lily walked up the stairs and as there was no one to see her she let her shoulders slump dispiritedly for a moment. She could feel the oppression move in her but she would not be beaten, far from it, she told herself, straightening her back courageously. The next few months in which she had hoped to spend some time on the *Lily-Jane*, for there was surely something she could do towards restoring her to her former glory even if it were only in the living quarters, were going to be tricky. She could always escape from *him*, of course. Already she had ideas teeming in her head, one of which she meant to put into practice this very day. Oh, yes, Lily Elliott could outsmart Joshua Crowther any day of the week. Just let him try . . .

The door to her bedroom stood wide open and inside Rosie was at the fireplace just putting down a scuttle of coal that she had filled and brought up the back stairs. Maggie Two was stripping the bed beside which, on a convenient chair, was a pile of clean bedding.

When they saw her both maidservants immediately stopped what they were doing and stood like a couple of intruders caught in some criminal act, their hands restlessly smoothing and plucking at their aprons as though in mortal dread. They watched her as she hesitated on the threshold, then dropped their eyes and stared dumbly at the carpet.

"What is it?" she asked sharply, their very attitude frightening her. A wave of apprehension turned her blood to ice, for it was very evident that there was something wrong, something out of place, something missing, but it seemed they were afraid to speak. It was very quiet. Where were the usual sounds that greeted her whenever she returned to her room? The joyful prancing and whining of Villy, the purring pretence at indifference with which Beauty greeted her. Oh, dear God . . . where? What had that bastard done while she had been seated at the breakfast table arguing with him?

"Where are they?" she snarled at the housemaids, so that they cowered away from her. It was not their fault, was it, nor the groom who had been given his orders by the master. They were all sorry but what could they do?

It was Maggie Two who spoke up bravely. "Jimmy . . . came an' took 'em."

"Took them where?"

"Nay, I dunno, Miss Lily. "'E'd 'ad 'is orders, 'e said, from't master."

"The devil, the evil devil. How dare he do this to my animals. Honest to God I swear I'll swing for him, see if I don't."

"Oh, Miss Lily, don't . . ." Maggie Two put out her hands as though to draw Lily to her, or perhaps to stop her from doing something she might regret, but she had whirled about and was running along the passage and down the stairs, two at a time, her skirts held up to her knees so that her lace-trimmed drawers were on display for anyone to see. As she leaped down from the bottom step, almost skidding on the polished floor, the breakfast-room door opened and Joshua Crowther came out into the hall. The expression that was becoming familiar to her, but which she did not understand, clouded his eyes. Behind him was his daughter and, behind her, Maggie. Maggie told them later in the kitchen it was a bloody miracle she didn't faint, she was so terrified. Not for herself but for Miss Lily.

"Aah," said the master. "I wondered how long it would be before you came roaring down here again. You really must learn that a lady should restrain herself, my dear, or be taught. A lesson I would gladly—"

"Where's Villy and Beauty?" she screeched, so that even in the kitchen they heard and upstairs Maggie Two and Rosie clutched at one another in dread. "I promise you this, you bastard, if any harm has come to them you will live to regret the day you and I met.. What have you done with them?"

"*I?*" He was vastly entertained, his manner said, while

behind him his daughter smirked her approval. "I have done nothing with them. They have merely been removed by one of the men to their rightful place."

"You devil . . ."

"What a melodramatic child you are . . ." But she did not hear the rest as she whirled away from him and began to run towards the green baize door that led into the kitchen. They watched her go by, the open-mouthed, dumbstruck servants, each one stilled to silence, except Mrs Quinn who whispered her name and made a move to intercept her. As well try to catch the wind!

They saw her come pelting across the stable yard, Jimmy, Arnold and Mr Bentley, her skirt lifted yet again to show the lace on her drawers. Jimmy and Arnold were mucking out and Mr Bentley was polishing the brass on a tangle of harness. Like the indoor servants they all three stopped and stared and, though he had been expecting it, he was so startled Mr Bentley's pipe fell from between his teeth and shattered on the cobbles.

"Where are they? Where have you put them?" but there was no need of an answer. Hearing her voice, Villy began to howl piteously, springing frantically against the bottom half of the tackroom door. Henry, Wally and Alex, Mr Crowther's game dogs, who had lived in the stables ever since they left their mothers, were restlessly padding about inside, disturbed by Villy's agitation, ready to howl themselves in sympathy.

Lily opened the door and was about to lift Villy into her arms, to soothe her and tell her that it was all right now, speaking as though the animal were a child who had been unfairly treated, and at the same time looking about her for a sign of Beauty, when a hand came to rest on her shoulder. She knew at once who it was, for it seemed to fondle her flesh, to caress as well as restrain and her skin crawled with horror but she took no notice. Twitching it away she bent down and picked up the small dog, hugging her to her, kissing her passionately about the ears, overcome for a moment by the rough tongue on her face, and by memories. Villy was her dog but she could never forget that Pa had been with her, indeed had helped to rescue Villy when the big boys in Walton Lane had tied her tail to that of a cat. Pa and Villy would always be inextricably linked, just as Ma and Beauty were. They were hers, these animals and these memories and no one, least of all this loathsome stepfather of hers, was going to part her from them.

"My dear, if you will insist on keeping them in your room I shall be forced—"

"Where's Beauty? Where's my mother's cat?" Her voice was flat and deadly and even Joshua Crowther found himself stepping back, which vastly annoyed him.

"I'm sure I couldn't say and neither do I—"

"She . . . ran off, Miss Lily," Jimmy mumbled, earning a frown from his master. It was difficult to keep a cat where it didn't want to be, surely the master knew that. Put it in a cage, or fasten it in somewhere and you could bet your last farthing the animal would find some way out of it, but he knew where this one had gone though he wasn't going to say in front of the master. Likely he'd drown the poor creature and her such a favourite of the dead mistress. Followed her everywhere, it had, but as though it knew, and they said cats were intelligent, it had settled down in front of Mrs Diggle's fire where, as far as he knew, it had remained.

"I must go and look for her," Lily said distractedly, still hugging Villy to her as though afraid to let her go.

Mr Crowther tried to put a hand on her arm then decided against it. "I don't think that's a good idea, Lily. Cats have a way of surviving in the most dire circumstances, so just put the dog back in the stable and we'll go inside and have that—"

"She is not going back in there. She's always been with me."

"We all have to learn new things, my dear, and the dog is no exception. If she can't learn, or is not *allowed* to, then I shall be forced to make other arrangements."

The men didn't know where to look, for the little lass – she might be as tall as they were but she was a little lass to them – looked as though she had been punched in the stomach by a hard fist. White as the freshly painted whitewash in the tackroom, she was, ready to fall if someone didn't catch her, for it was clear she didn't know what the hell to do. She wanted to defy him, that was obvious, tell him to go to the devil but the dog's life was at stake. There was nothing surer in this world than the fact that if the master was not obeyed someone would pay for it. They wouldn't put it past him to shoot the animal, or at least order one of them to do it. He'd not soil his own hands with an unpleasant task like that, not him, the bastard. They'd seen the way he'd treated his wife and now it seemed he was to grind her daughter down beneath his expensive and well-polished boot, poor little beggar.

It was Mr Bentley who stepped forward and with gentle hands took the small, wriggling animal from her. Her incredible eyes, so big and such an unusual colour, like lavender set in a coating of grey ice, stared into his and he stared back, doing his best to tell her that as long as he was here the dog would come to no harm. But *she* must do as the master said or not only the dog but she would suffer for it.

"She'll be all right in't stable wi't other dogs, Miss Lily," he told her, braving his master's glare. "Yer can come across an' see 'er whenever yer want. Jimmy'll walk 'er when 'e walks t'other 'uns, don't yer fret."

Villy whined as Lily walked docilely back across the yard with Mr Crowther but she did not look back. He had defeated her this time. He had threatened the life of her dog, she was well aware of that, and there would be other punishments if she did not conform to the life he thought a daughter of his should lead. She was to become a second Eloise, sitting in the schoolroom with her and Miss Yates, embroidering, doing fatuous little watercolours, walking along the tediously safe paths of the garden, riding with Arnold always in attendance and never escaping down to the seashore or to any of the loved and familiar places she had made her own along the river. In one day her life had been turned upside down and she didn't know why. She didn't know why he had suddenly decided that she was his daughter. Didn't he recognise that she loathed him, in her ignorance not knowing that her feelings for him were part of her attraction.

Well, she thought, as she walked ahead of him into his study where he wanted to have a little talk with her, he said, he had won this time but what did they say about forewarned is forearmed?

23

It had turned bitterly cold and the youth who stepped out from among the trees was well wrapped up against the keen wind that blew off the river. He wore a pair of well-cut, sand-coloured cord breeches, knee-high riding boots, a tweed shooting jacket with many pockets which was a couple of sizes too big for him, and a muffler of enormous proportions which wrapped round his neck several times and covered the lower half of his face. On his head was a cloth "quartered" cap, popular several decades ago. At his heels was a small, scruffy brown dog.

The young man jumped with the supple grace and buoyancy of healthy youth from the rough grass bank that edged the seashore, followed by the dog, both of them landing lightly in the sand, then began to run northwards, weightless as the birds that rode the wind above the river. The dog ran straight for the water, jumping madly in and out of the tiny, rippling, white-edged waves, turning to look expectantly at the young man, then, when no notice was taken, shook itself vigorously, then ran after him.

The youth kept to just below the high-water mark where the sand was firm, leaping puddles of seawater in which long strands of seaweed made patterns against the wet sand. His long legs pumped, his arms flailed and his face became bright red with his exertions but he did not stop for a breather, forging ahead along Jericho Shore, cutting across the inlet known as Knotty Hole and skimming the wet sand to Dingle Point. A man busy sawing dead branches off an ancient oak tree on the edge of Dingle Bank stopped and stared at him in astonishment, letting the saw slip across a finger. He jumped and cursed and put the finger to his mouth, then turned, following the young man's mad passage round the point to Pottery Shore. The dog was ahead now, its ears flat to its head as it ran, turning every few seconds to make sure the man was still with him and it was not until they reached the Pottery Slip, down which pleasure boats were launched in the summer, that they stopped. Sitting down close together on the cold grey stone of the slip, they gasped and floundered like two fish just landed from the river.

For several minutes they sat, the man's arm about the dog's neck, his head bent, then he stood up and with a click of his fingers to the animal began to walk more sedately in the direction of Brunswick Dock. A long, steady stride with the dog so close to his heel its nose might have been fastened to it until he reached the Albert Dock Parade and the massive structure of Albert Dock. He kept in the shadows thrown by a pale wintering sun which had not yet crept up from behind the buildings on his right. At least two hundred windows looked out on to the parade, for the colonnaded warehouses each had four floors, every one crowded from wall to wall with goods that were either waiting to be loaded on to ships, or had just been discharged. It had been opened by the Prince Consort in 1845 and named after him and a handsome building it was too, a massive square built round the quays that served the sailing ships at berth there.

The youth turned the corner and the low sun shone directly into his eyes which were a silvery grey, glittering like diamonds under water. The place was teeming with waggons and horses, dockers and drays, hansom cabs delivering passengers, and those on foot taking a short cut across the iron bridge that led to the next granite island and then on to the landing stage and the ferry.

His footsteps slowed, then, noticing an old seaman studying him suspiciously, he pulled his cap further down over his brow, put his hands in his pockets and began to whistle tunelessly as he imagined a young man would do. He was sauntering now, though his heart wanted him to hurry, hurry, hurry on to where he was going and yet to slip backwards in time to where he had been.

He came to the bridge that led across the lock gates, moving as though in a dream until he stood on the quay beside Canning Dock. And there she was, what the young man had come to see, pulling gently at her moorings, leaning a little to one side like some slightly tipsy old lady who, though she has had a bit too much to drink, is not totally drunk. She dipped on a small wave created by the movement of a square rigger as it left the dock, almost curtseying in welcome as though she were glad, at last, of the sight of someone who loved her, since she had been sadly neglected.

The young man sat down on one of the iron bollards that edged the dock and to which the ship's mooring ropes were fastened. He seemed to be unaware of the bustle around him, his hand moving gently in the fur of the dog sitting beside him.

"There she is, Villy," he whispered. "There she is. My pa's schooner. *Lily-Jane*, my beautiful, beautiful *Lily-Jane*. Dear God, I've waited for this day a long, long time and at last it's here. It's the *Lily-Jane*, Villy." A long, bewitched sigh drifted from his lungs and into the cold morning air.

She had found the clothing in a sandalwood chest in the attic one day when, since it was raining stair-rods, as Mrs Quinn put it, she had been unable to go out. Left to herself she would have been perfectly happy to put on her stout, high-laced boots and wrap herself in the mackintosh she had found hanging on a hook inside the cupboard beneath the stairs. She had no idea who the mackintosh belonged to, probably Nicholas Crowther since it was the kind of thing a boy might wear. It was fashioned from a sort of waterproof cloth made with India rubber and smelled absolutely horrible but it certainly kept out the rain. She often wore it when she went for a walk with the animals, but today she took notice of Mrs Quinn, knowing that the housekeeper, who was more than a housekeeper to Lily, was afraid of what Mr Crowther might do to her lamb if she disobeyed him, and stayed indoors.

She read for an hour or two, curled up with a book, a great favourite, Trollope's *Barchester Towers*, in Mr Crowther's study, knowing he was out on some business of his own and would not be back until late afternoon. But she was restless and after a turn or two about the study looking at the prints on the wall, mostly of horses, and scenes of men shooting at birds, at the fishing rods and old smoking pipes of which Mr Crowther had a great number, at the skeleton clock on the mantelpiece, at the desktop telescope and the globe of the world set in a brass meridian on a wood stand, all of which she had seen a score of times before, she wandered out into the hall. She peered from the window beside the front door at the rain which seemed to be coming down heavier than ever. She trailed upstairs, her fingers drifting along the banister, wondering whether to go and have a peep at Abby, who was probably having her afternoon nap, or brave the elements and run across the yard to the tackroom and talk to Villy. It was a week now since she had been removed from Lily's bedroom and though Lily meant to get her back, and Beauty as well, as soon as Mr Crowther had forgotten all about the furore of last week, she had thought it wise to give it a few more days before she attempted it.

It was a dark afternoon, November now and the lamps on the upstairs landing had not yet been lit. She moved on up the stairs that led to the nursery and then, instead of going into the nursery, which was quiet except for the faint sound of Dorcas having forty winks, she continued on until she was at the foot of the stairs that led up to the attics. She peered up them but it was so dark she could barely make out the top of the stairs. She stood for several moments, then, on a whim, went back to the table against the wall opposite the nursery on which a number of candles in holders stood. There were matches and, striking one, she lit a candle then crept back up the stairs in its flickering light. The door to the attic had evidently not been opened for a while, since it gave a shriek like a soul in torment and Lily held her breath, for surely it had woken Dorcas from her light snooze but there was no further sound from the nursery.

The place was filled from the high arched roof to the floor with boxes and baskets and wooden chests, with strange shapes shrouded in sheets and vague pictures in frames leaning against the wall. For a while she had poked about, studying this and that, wondering what half the objects were and what they had been used for, but the sandalwood chest, the smell of which reminded her of the docks, drew her to it as though she knew it were to have some importance for her. It had a beautifully carved design on the lid, of birds and exotic flowers and at each side a black enamelled carrying handle.

She lifted the lid with the raptness of a high priest at the altar. Though it had a lock on it, it was not locked and inside, wrapped by some careful hand in tissue paper, were jackets and trousers, shirts and caps, a pair of riding breeches, mufflers and boots and even a long, sleeved cloak made of wool. All good stuff so why had it been relegated to the attic? Then it came to her and with the thought came the plan. These were the discarded clothes of a schoolboy. Garments he had outgrown but which were too good, in somebody's opinion, probably Maggie since she was known for her thriftiness, to be thrown away or given to charity. So here they had sat, probably for years, just waiting for Lily Elliott to come along and make use of them.

Because she was tall they had fitted her perfectly in length, though across the shoulders and in the waist she had to do a bit of careful arranging to make them fit. A good belt was a help and with the jacket fastened none would be the wiser. Since it was winter the cloak would be a godsend, not only because it was warm but because it disguised her very obvious female figure. With her hair dragged up to the top of her head and fastened securely with ribbon and the cap jammed down over it, the cloak collar turned up or the muffler fastened about her neck she knew she could pass for a youth. She would have to keep her face hidden as much as she could but that was easy at this time of the year when everyone was muffled up to the eyebrows because of the cold.

So, here she was, sitting on a bollard, seeing for the first time in six years her Pa's schooner. She wanted to cry, not just because the poor old *Lily-Jane* looked such a pitiful sight, but because she was overwhelmed by the memories that flooded into her mind and heart. She and her pa at the wheel that last time they had gone up the coast to Barrow to pick up a cargo of pig-iron. Oh, yes, she could even remember the cargo it was so clearly etched in her brain. Her ma standing at the rails watching the bathers, her smile radiant as she turned to smile at Pa. Mr Porter – where was he now? – and Johnno, her pa's crew and friends, she liked to think, for who could fail to make a friend of her pa? And now they were both dead, her pa and ma and all that was left of that lovely time was this poor old schooner which looked as though she were about to sink into the waters of the dock where she had been berthed, where she had been deserted by whoever had sold her to Liam.

"Grand ole' ship, tha'," a laconic voice, thick with the tones of Liverpool, said in her ear. "Or she were once."

"She still is, or will be when I've finished with her."

She didn't even turn, for her eyes were still lovingly drifting over the wooden sailing ship, studying her two masts which swayed gracefully with the slight movement of the water. The spanker, a small mast made to carry a large fore and aft sail, moved with them, dipping and swaying, and at the pointed stern the ropes that held her to the quayside slapped impatiently against the cold grey stones.

"Oh, aye, young feller-me-lad, an' 'oo might yer be, then?" the voice said, a strong voice but with a quaver in it as though its owner were getting on a bit.

"She's my schooner, mine and Liam's," she said, carelessly she realised afterwards but at that moment of joy she had allowed her defences to drop.

"Is tha' right, an' 'oo's Liam an' . . ."

Lily swung round then and found herself looking into an ancient, seamed brown face with faded old eyes that had squinted into a thousand suns and across a thousand seas. It was the old sailor who had eyed her suspiciously. He had a neat, snowy white beard. He wore a cap which had obviously been with him since he had gone to sea as a lad, a faded gansey and drill trousers tucked into his boots. He had a pipe clamped between his stained and broken teeth but there was something enduring about him, something permanent and fixed like the very granite from which the quayside was built.

Instinctively Lily lowered her voice in the way she had practised, thanking her mother for the slight huskiness she had inherited from her. She didn't know who this old sailor was and she didn't care, but she didn't want anybody poking their nose too deeply into what she was about.

"The vessel belongs to a friend of mine. He means to renovate her when . . . well, at the moment he's at sea but when he gets home we are . . ."

The old man was studying her, still suspicious it seemed, as though already he knew there was something very strange about this rather girlish young man, this . . . well, you could only call him a *pretty* young man. Fair-skinned and rosy-lipped and if he wasn't careful he could fall into the hands of men who liked that sort of thing. Many seaman did. Not him, of course. He liked his women, or did when he was an age for such foolishness, to be women, with deep bosoms and a bum you could hang on to. He felt in his pocket, never taking his eyes off the lad, fetching out a piece of chewing tobacco. He put his pipe in the same pocket, then cut off a scrap of tobacco, shoved it in his mouth and began to chew.

Suddenly he smiled, a genial smile but one that said he might be old but he wasn't soft in the head.

"Wan' a 'and?"

"Pardon?"

"I'm doin' nowt at present," just as though his services were in great demand normally, "an' I know me way round a ship. Bin at sea fer fifty year so I bloody should."

"Indeed."

"So, what d'yer say? I'm lookin' fer a berth an' could sleep aboard. Keep me eye on 'er, like. Tommy Graham's me name an' yer can ask anyone round 'ere, even the piermaster 'imself 'oo'll tell yer I'm 'onest an' reliable."

"Oh, I'm sure you are, Mr Graham, but you see—"

"Polite young feller, aincher?" The old eyes looked into hers and Lily's heart sank. She'd only been here five minutes, five minutes into this big adventure, this wonderful escape into the new life she and Liam were going to share and already she had attracted attention, with this chap looking at her knowingly as though he were perfectly aware that beneath her men's clothing there was a woman.

She lifted her head in the familar gesture of imperious hauteur she had learned over the years but the old seaman continued to smile.

"But that don't mean owt ter me," he went on. "I don't give a bugger what folks do as long as it don't interfere wi' me. I know a good vessel when I see 'er," then he winked though the expression on his face didn't change, "an' this craft's a good 'un. I'd like ter see 'er set up proper an' I know the very place where it could be done."

Lily stared at him, mesmerised, her eyes wide and frightened but he winked again, then, with a gesture to her which seemed to ask her permission, climbed down the little ladder at the side of the quay and jumped lithely on to the deck of the *Lily-Jane*.

For half an hour he poked about, ducking his head into the cabin, the wheelhouse, the bilges, getting out his penknife and jabbing it into the wood. He stamped on the deck and ran his hands round the rail while Lily trailed round behind him, her heart beating so fast with excitement she thought she might choke. She didn't know why she felt she could trust this old seadog, probably because he *was* old and therefore – she hoped – of no danger to her, as a woman she meant. She had the feeling that he knew and if he knew perhaps others would, but she also had the feeling that this was a very astute old man, shrewd, not easily hoodwinked and if he was prepared to accept her as a male, then perhaps others on the docks would do the same.

"Sound as a bell, lad," he told her, looking her straight in the eye. "Wants a bit doin' to 'er but there's nowt a birra new plankin' an' a lick o' paint won't cure. Burrit needs doin' by someone 'oo knows wharr 'e's about."

"You, Mr Graham?"

"Nay, not me, lad, though I knows me way round more'n some. Bu' there's a boatbuildin' yard at Runcorn could fix 'er up a treat."

"She was built there, Mr Graham."

"Aye, I reckoned so. She's the look about 'er of the firm I were thinkin' on. Sturdy an' built ter last or she'd've not lasted this long. A nice little craft." He stood and looked about him, nodding his head as though agreeing with his own words, then turned to Lily.

"What's yer name, lad?" It was said quietly, with no intent to trick. He would say nothing, he was telling her, but still she hesitated. She had learned in the past weeks to trust no man, except Liam, of course, and how did she know that this old chap might not run straight to Joshua Crowther, who had an office in Water Street, and tell him that a "person" was about to take over the running of the ship that had once been his.

Tommy Graham watched the lad as he dithered over the question of his name, wondering what the bloody hell he was up to. Oh, it was well known that it had recently been sold to some chap, some young chap, but this wasn't him. The movement of every vessel, small or large, in this port was known to all the old seamen, men who had existed in dockland for all their lives and *Lily-Jane* was a familiar sight since she had been in and out of Liverpool for years. Belonged to a Richard Elliott once but he'd died and it had been taken over by Joshua Crowther and now, it seemed, this young lad was claiming ownership, so what was it all about? Not that he gave a fish's tit. All he wanted was a bit of work about the docks, about the ships, about the place he had worked in and loved all his life.

Strangely enough, though Lily thought he had seen through her disguise she was wrong. Tommy Graham was short-sighted and, like many an old man who has once been young and strong, was too proud even to think of wearing spectacles. He sensed there was something odd about this young man but though he had given the impression to Lily that he was aware of her gender, in fact he was not. There were some lads who were prettier than others, more feminine in their ways than others and this youth was one of them.

"Dick," Lily said abruptly. After all, Richard had been her pa.

"Right, Dick, wha' d'yer say? Will yer tekk me on? I'll not let yer down."

"Mr Graham, the thing is—"

"Afore we go any further, Dick, d'yer reckon yer could call me Tommy?"

She nodded her head shyly, a treacherously feminine gesture which, had he not been so eager to be taken on, Tommy Graham might have recognised as one belonging to no youth.

"Very well, Tommy, but you see, I have no money as yet. When my . . . my friend comes home – he's on the China run – we hope to have enough to put the *Lily-Jane* to rights, but until then she must—"

"Nay, lad, yer can't leave 'er 'ere in't wet basin or she'll rot inter't water. She needs ter be in dry dock, yer see."

Lily felt her heart sink but then it lightened again, for surely Liam would not have left the schooner he had just bought in a wet dock if he had thought she might be damaged by it.

She said so to Tommy, willing to trust him a little bit, for it didn't seem to her that it could do any harm.

"When'll 'e be back, this friend o' yourn?"

"February at the latest."

Tommy took off his cap and scratched his head, studying the *Lily-Jane* with a critical eye. He sighed deeply, then walked up and down her length which was exactly ninety-nine feet. He stood and pulled at his bottom lip then turned away to gaze out to the river as though looking for inspiration.

"Well, I dunno, 'appen it'd be all right fer a few weeks. She's bin in't water all this time an' p'raps . . ."

"There is simply nothing else I can do, Tommy. She must stay where she is until we have the money, but . . ."

"Aye, lad?"

"I would be grateful if you would keep an eye on her. You see, I can't get down here every day." She shifted her gaze from his steady one. "I . . . I'm . . ."

"Yer don't 'ave ter explain owt ter me, Dick. I'd be glad of a berth on 'er, even if she's only stoppin' in't dock. I've a few bob."

"Oh, no, I couldn't possibly . . ."

"I meant ter keep meself, lad, that's all. I do odd jobs about docks burr I'll sleep on board and watch out fer 'er an' when yer can yer can come down an' we'll do a birra work on 'er tergether. Will that suit?"

Would that suit? She almost fell on his neck and kissed him on his whiskery cheek but she remembered just in time that she was a young man and that young men were supposed to be controlled and unemotional, so she told him that it would and that she would probably be over next week and she did hope he would be comfortable. He said he would be and he'd just fetch his tack over from the seamen's mission where he had a bed at the moment and with much goodwill on both sides they parted company.

She was surprised at how easy it was. She slipped in at the side door without anyone apparently having even missed her and when she glided in to the dining-room that evening with that grace and style she had inherited from her mother she failed entirely to see the speculative gleam in Joshua Crowther's eye. She had been dining with him and Eloise now ever since the day he had taken Villy to the stables, where she had remained, and it seemed that things were running smoothly, effortlessly and Lily wished it to remain like that. After all, it was November and perhaps in eight or ten weeks Liam would be home so best not rock the boat, so to speak. She was polite. She did as she was told. She even took herself to the schoolroom where Miss Kaye was reading aloud to them the tale of *The Swiss Family Robinson*, which she herself had read as a child of eight, but she pretended to listen as she pretended to sew on a sampler and so far Mr Crowther seemed to be satisfied with her behaviour.

She was startled when, as they stood up at the end of the meal, he turned to her and with a courteous smile asked her if she could spare him a moment or two in his study, since there was something he thought they should discuss.

"What about?" she asked him brusquely, the colour of her eyes turning to a glinted silver, her mouth thinning to a mutinous line. Joshua Crowther saw it and was jubilant. He had been seriously disappointed by her docile acceptance of his ruling that she was his daughter and must therefore act as Eloise did. He had heard of her volte-face and consequent return to the schoolroom, her walks with Eloise and Miss Kaye about the gardens, and her acquiescence over the matter of her dog's relegation to the tackroom. He had not liked her submission, which reminded him too much of her mother. He had expected fireworks, a stormy refusal to fall in with his wishes, total defiance which he had been prepared to enjoy before he quenched it. For quench it he meant to do and, by God, he'd take great pleasure in doing it, however it came about. She was glaring at him now, quite forgetting what seemed to be a definite effort on her part during these past weeks to appear meek and accommodating. And he wondered why. It had not occurred to him before but now it did. Why had she surrendered to his dictatorship? Why was she putting on this act of being his compliant puppet when it was so far from her own nature of stubborn determination to do as she pleased, which had been so very evident for the past six years? For that was what it had been, he could see it now, an act.

Now, with just a word or two, she had reverted to her real self, truculent, self-willed, ready to tell him to go to hell in a handcart. She had let the mask of conciliation slip and he gloried in it, for he was ready to enjoy the battle to come.

"Well, shall we go into my study and see?" He smiled.

She wanted to refuse, he could see it in her clamped jawline, but she merely nodded her head and walked stiffly into his study. He followed her, shutting the door behind him. He was still smiling and Lily felt the apprehension rise to her throat, choking her, though she wouldn't let him see it.

"Well?" she said. "What do you want?"

"This," he answered, stepping forward and putting his hand on her breast. For a second, perhaps two, she was so dumbfounded she stood and allowed him to fondle her, to cup her breast and squeeze it, then with a cry of revulsion she knocked his hand away and sprang back from him. He was still smiling, not at all put out by her obvious repugnance, her rage, her loathing.

"You bastard," she hissed, her face contorted but he continued to smile, his hands busy in his pockets. "You killed my mother, oh, yes, you did, you killed her even if it did take six years for her to die, but I'm made of stronger stuff, Mr Crowther, and you won't defeat me."

"My dear, I do hope not but what a great deal of pleasure I shall have trying."

24

She didn't remember very much about the next few hours except in flashes which kept repeating themselves in her brain, distorted and filthy. Filthy, that's how she felt and as she fled from the study and ran up the stairs she wanted to scrabble at herself as though she were crawling with lice or fleas. She tripped on every stair, the hem of her wide silk skirt caught in the toe of her kid slippers so that she was forced to clutch at the banister. She remembered thinking, close to hysteria and already beginning to weep, that that was all she needed, to fall and break her leg or her neck. She tumbled into her bedroom, slamming the door fiercely behind her, desperate to lock it on the horror that seemed to creep up the stairs after her, but there was no key, nothing to keep it out, to keep *him* out should he take it into his head to follow her.

Where was Villy? She needed someone, something to cling to until she had recovered – would she ever do that? – from the shock and panic and dread which Joshua Crowther's hand on her had released in her. Now she realised fully what her mother had suffered, day after day, week after week, month after month, year after year. She had more awareness now of what men and women did together in the act of love. Liam's body next to hers had told her that, his hands on her breasts, his mouth on hers, the surge of his masculinity against her which had filled her with a rapturous joy and need, but she and Liam loved one another, not just physically but with a love that had grown from friendship over the past six years. But this, this ... greed ... this lust which she had finally recognised and which had glittered in Joshua Crowther's dark eyes was what had dominated Ma's life and at the end, Lily firmly believed, killed her. She had not fought to live when her child was born and her life's blood had poured from her. She had drifted away with a tranquil smile on her ash white face, Mrs Quinn had told her, glad to leave the man who had treated her like a whore, going to the husband she had never ceased to love.

Now, it seemed, Joshua Crowther had transferred his nasty intentions to her daughter. He had made her uneasy for weeks but she had not attached much importance to it, believing that he did it to frighten her into being the young woman he thought she should be now that she was his daughter. But she had been wrong, woefully, terrifyingly wrong and what was she to do? Liam would be home in February and then she would be safe, but until then who could she turn to to protect her from Joshua's evil? She was alone. She had not even Villy to comfort her. Mrs Quinn was there, of course, where she had always been in Lily's life, willing to do all she could to support Jane Elliott's daughter, but Mrs Quinn was six years older, a grandmother now since her Victoria had married Arnold, the Oakwood groom, and had in four years given birth to three little girls whom Mrs Quinn doted on. There was a whisper that her Victoria wanted her to go and live with her and Arnold and the children in the cottage at the edge of the Oakwood estate, which would mean Victoria could go back to work, but so far Mrs Quinn had resisted as though she knew her lamb's daughter still needed her, the only "family" she had.

Lily huddled on the window seat, staring out into the bitter winter's night. There was a wind keening through the trees; she could hear it even though the windows were firmly shut. The bare branches of the tree that stood beyond the window tapped against the glass and in a small way she felt a tiny shred of comfort, for the tree had always been a symbol of escape for her. A way of winning freedom, a secret way that *he* knew nothing of should he lock her in her bedroom. She had never used it, not yet, but if this man's attentions continued, became worse, if she became trapped she might have to.

Lord, she wished Villy was here. She felt the need to put her arms about some warm creature who would make no demands on her, who would sense her despair and offer comfort, give love and devotion without stint, asking nothing in return. Beauty seemed to have settled quite comfortably with Mrs Diggle, her loyalty to her former mistress a frail thing, but then that was what Ma would have wanted. But Villy. She fretted in the confines of the tackroom. She had Henry and Wally and Alex for company but she pined to be with Lily and had grown thin in the last few weeks. She was only a small dog but her heart and courage were big and she would die in an attempt to defend her beloved mistress. It would give Lily some small measure of comfort, a small feeling of security to have her here in this room, the key to which was in Joshua Crowther's possession. It was little enough to ask, to have Villy with her but he, in his spiteful determination to bend her to his will, would not allow it and the thought that he was winning put a stiffener in her spine and dried her tears which she knew were self-pitying. She was alone. She had been alone since Pa died and alone she would stand up to Joshua Crowther. The first act of defiance would be to bring Villy back.

Without even stopping to put on her warm cloak she was across the room and at the door. Opening it a crack she listened intently but there was no sound bar the slight hiss and splutter of the lamps beyond it. Tiptoeing along the carpeted hallway, past closed bedroom doors and shadowy cupboards, she came to the top of the back stairs leading to the narrow passage which in turn led to the side door and into the small herb garden her mother had revived. Silently as a wisp of fog she eased herself down the stairs and out of the door. As she stole through the garden she could smell the pungent aroma of tansy leaves and for a moment her strength faltered as her mother's sad ghost walked beside her, but then Ma was sad no longer and surely she and Pa, wherever they were, would be watching over her?

She slipped quietly through the well-oiled wrought-iron gate and eased herself left round the dark bulk of the house, the many windows of which threw oblongs of golden light across the dark path. She stepped away from the house to avoid passing through them, moving stealthily round another corner and into the yard at the back of the kitchen. Someone had drawn the window blinds and though she could hear a murmur of voices she knew she could not be seen as she passed through the arched gateway and into the stable yard where again there was no sound except a soft whining which she recognised as Villy in the tackroom.

The blast of icy air whipped round her, lifting her skirts and petticoats and tearing her hair from its neat arrangement of curls, done for her earlier that evening by Mary. Mary was the lady's maid who had looked after her mother and her wardrobe for the past six years and who was now in charge of herself and Eloise. She was a pleasant girl who had been kind to Ma and had the added virtue of being able to keep her mouth shut. She was quiet and self-effacing and could turn the wildest tangle of curls into a most pleasing hairstyle, which she had done this evening, first with Eloise, then with Lily, before going down to the kitchen to join the other servants in their evening meal.

The tackroom door was tightly closed but inside Villy began to make strange noises as though she sensed Lily's presence outside in the yard. She was snuffling at the bottom of the door, scratching a little in her effort to get out and Lily felt a small lift in her spirits at the thought of having the animal with her. She could hear men's voices now, soft and murmuring, coming from the sleeping quarters above the stables and tackroom and one of them laughed. At the end of the row of buildings was Mr Diggle's cottage with a neat little garden in front and a path leading to the orchards, the vegetable gardens, the hothouses which were his domain. A light shone across the garden, warm and golden in the darkness of the night and Lily felt her heart constrict, for she would have given anything to be knocking at Mr Diggle's door and entering its safe haven.

She opened the tackroom door, expecting Villy's warm, rough little body to come hurtling out, dancing on her rear legs in her attempt to jump up into Lily's arms in her joy, but though she could still hear her and the sound of the other dogs as they rustled in the straw at the back of the room, none of them moved and it was perhaps then, in the strange atmosphere that enveloped her, that she knew something was not right. Villy was whining piteously in the back of her throat but Lily couldn't see her, for it was as black as pitch, just as though she had fallen into a deep hole, the earth sliding over her and cutting off any light.

The terror held her for a moment in a frozen block of ice, unable to move, unable to speak to the dogs, to breathe or even think and in that moment, as she became aware that she was not alone, when his voice whispered to her from the blackness she was not surprised.

"I wondered how long it would take you to come for the dog, my dear," it said. It had a hint of amusement in it, a feeling that its owner was pleased and not only pleased but excited. From behind a hard arm wound round her waist, dragging her further inside. A hand gripped her viciously about her breasts and his face pressed itself into the nape of her neck beneath her hair. She could smell brandy – or was it whisky? – on his breath, hot and nasty and his mouth was wet against her shrinking flesh. A second hand came to cover her mouth and the scream that might have saved her was cut off before it had time to reach the men above them. The dogs were silent and she had time to wonder why, even Villy's voice dwindling into what seemed to be a strangled snore, but she had no time for conjecture since she was fighting now, fighting not for her life since he did not want that, but for the sum and substance of Lily Elliott, for the intrinsic quality and core that was peculiar to Lily Elliott. She was fighting for her spirit which would be broken if she lost the battle, for her future with Liam, for her sanity which her ma had clung to somehow in the grip of the vile creature who had now transferred his beastliness to her. If she lost *she* would be lost for ever. It would all be in ashes, what she and Liam had planned, their future together, the *Lily-Jane* and what they were to do with her, so she lifted her feet, going with his weight as he dragged her to the rear of the room. His back hit the wall and he grunted with the force of it, expecting resistance, then she kicked him, backwards and upwards, feeling her soft slippers strike him just above his knees. Dear sweet Christ, if only she had taken the time to change into her boots she could have done him some serious damage, she had time to think, then, turning her towards him, he hit her savagely across her face and she felt the consciousness spin about in her head, looking for a way to escape.

She could feel the prickle of it on her back as he laid her down in the straw next to the snoring dogs. Her arms were flung wide on either side of her like a soul on a cross and his hands began to tear at her skirts, lifting them above her waist, his fingers tugging at the ribbons in her drawers. Her head was thudding on the straw-covered setts as he lifted her this way and that and her hand caught on something that was leaning against the wall. She had no thought in her head about what it might be, no thoughts about anything really, for she was almost senseless as she felt the cold air creep across her naked belly and thighs.

Her hand gripped whatever it was and with the powerful and primitive instinct that is bred in the defenceless female, and with an action that was without coherent thought, she lifted it and brought it down across his back. It was heavy and afterwards she was to dwell on how desperation makes giants of us all, gives strength where none should really be. He made a sound in the back of his throat, not loud, as if even now he wished to keep this loathsome act secret.

Joshua Crowther, inflamed by his lust beyond reasonable thought, beyond rational objectivity, beyond his need to consider his own reputation as a man of shrewdness and cunning, believing only in his own arrogant invincibility, had meant to overpower her and when she was senseless carry her to his room by the same route she, and he, had come by. But the feel of her in his arms, the struggling female fear, the squirming, bewitching movement of her young body, the smell of her in his nostrils, had sent a message to his brain, and to that other mindless but potent part of his body telling it that he could not wait. Not another minute. He must take this lovely, defiant child, dominate and violate her and turn her into his creature, as her mother had been his creature.

He collapsed on top of her, his face pressed into her shoulder. She was almost senseless herself, her mind reeling with horror, her body shuddering with repugnance, but slowly she began to regain awareness of what was happening and though he was heavy she slid out from beneath him and struggled to her feet, dragging at her clothing and returning it to some semblance of decency. He was beginning to moan and now that she had become accustomed to the dark she could see his hands scratching in the straw. She was doing a bit of moaning herself though she was not aware of it. Her body was trembling not only with fear but with disgust, humiliation and a need to be sick.

But she must get away before he completely regained his senses. Get to where there were people, bright lights, safety, wondering as she felt about in the straw for Villy what it was she had hit him with. She didn't care. If her hand had come on a knife she would have stuck it in him without the slightest compunction and gloried in it, but for now she must get Villy and run.

She had meant to make for the kitchen, for in her mind was the thought that she must let them know, his servants, his family and indeed all of Liverpool what sort of man this was. In fact she did not know why she was not screaming her bloody head off right this minute. It would bring them all out, the grooms and gardener's lads who lived above the stables, the maidservants in the kitchen, even Miss prim and proper Eloise to see what kind of a man her father was. She would have him arrested for attempted rape. She would see him in gaol, shown up for what he was. Tell the world what a devil her mother had married. That hidden in the respectable, respected man of business was a lecher, a . . . a pervert – yes, that was what he was and by God she'd have his name all over the town before the week was out. She'd see him dragged through the filth with which he had tried to coat her. She'd finish him in Liverpool and when she'd . . .

"Don't even think about it, girl." His voice came at her from the dark corner where he was attempting to stand up. He was creeping up the wall, hand over hand, his voice shaking, but whether it was with pain or malevolence she could not tell. It slithered about her, menacing and dangerous but in it was the absolute certainty that she would denounce him at her peril!

"It would be your word against mine," he went on, his voice harsh and flat, "and who would believe that an upright, *influential* man such as myself would treat a defenceless girl as you might be considering telling them I did. Oh, yes, I know what you are about to do but think twice before you take on Joshua Crowther, girl. I have a great deal of power in this town. Those with wealth do, you know. I would sue you for slander and, believe me, there is not a court in the country that would believe the word of a hysterical sixteen-year-old over that of a man such as myself. Now, I'd advise you to get back to your room and keep your mouth shut and I'll do the same. We'll keep this between you and I, do you understand, girl, or I promise you you'll regret it."

He was completely upright by now, his back to the wall but it was evident he was in some pain for he made no move towards her.

Without taking her eyes off his shadowy figure she leaned down and picked up the twitching form of Villy, holding her to her like a shield between his voice and herself. She wanted to scream her defiance, tell him to go to hell and rot there but though she had known terror during the last minutes when she had believed with despair that she was to be overpowered and defiled by this man, it was nothing to the dread that crept through her now at his words. She could tell her story to the servants and she believed they would recognise that she was telling the truth, for did they not know what had been done to her own mother. They had seen him dominate her, Lily, over the matter of the dog, and she was sure Maggie and Betsy could not be unaware of the nasty overtones of his conversation at the dinner table, the sordid insinuations which in her naïvety she had ignored.

But that was what they were, servants, ignorant of the ways of the law, most of them unable to read and write, the possessers of good jobs with a man who had been a good master. None of them had been threatened by his peculiar sexual proclivities, indeed they probably were unaware of them. He paid them no attention, for in reality they were no more to him than hands that put his meals – on time – in front of him, well cooked and served, laundered his shirts and polished his boots, groomed his horses and looked after his house and garden. They were satisfied with what they had in a town that was heaving with the homeless, the jobless, the deprived, the underprivileged and would they risk that for the sake of a young girl who would not be believed anyway? *He* would see to that.

She backed away from him though he still leaned awkwardly against the wall. He was no threat to her at the moment, for she had hurt him with whatever it was she had hit him with. She could make out the paleness of his face and his shirt front but that was all and though every nerve in her wanted to scream and run wild and shout to the world that she had been badly wronged, some instinct kept her quiet. She didn't know what, at this moment, she meant to do, but it was not run to the servants and blurt out her horror and pain.

Without a sound she turned and, holding Villy awkwardly in her arms, she began to run back the way she had come. He must have drugged the dogs, she remembered thinking, all four of them, while she was dithering in her bedroom, then waited for her to come to the tackroom. How did he know? He was a devil, Satan himself, with some power, some way of divining in which direction people were going to go and something had told him that she would need comfort, warm flesh-and-blood comfort and since he had not as yet done anything beyond touch her, she would hardly run to the servants with that, would she? He knew her too well. He knew of her attachment for her dog and so . . . Oh, God . . . Oh, God, what was she to do? Liam, Liam, where are you? I need you, I need someone . . . somewhere to hide, for there was nothing surer in her mind than the belief that this was far from over. It was no good appealing to Mrs Quinn or Mr Diggle who, though they would be horrified, would not be able to help her, not with real help that would keep her safe until Liam came for her.

She reached her bedroom and just as though the cry to Liam had brought sanity, a calm reason to soothe her inflamed mind, she knew exactly what she should do. Liam's voice came back to her over the years from when she had been a child, an innocent, confident child who had believed that with the death of her father the worst that could happen to her had happened. He had told her then what to do if she was in trouble though she had scarcely listened but he was telling her again now and this time she did. Though she could not believe that Mr Crowther would come for her again, not tonight, she wished she had a key to lock her door, but she hadn't so in the calmness that had come with Liam's voice she propped a chair beneath the handle of the door and began to make her preparations.

Her mind was clear as it considered the future but her heart was already grieving for what she must leave behind. But what could she do? She had made a vow that she would love and cherish her mother's baby daughter, her own half-sister, but the reality that she now confronted was that it had been a childish vow, impossible to fulfil. Should she go up to the nursery and smuggle Abby out, which would be difficult with Dorcas sleeping beside her, how was she to get the child out of the house and to the destination she had chosen for herself? There would be no room for an infant in that future and besides, Mr Crowther, even if he didn't want her for himself, would not allow his daughter to be taken from him. He would move heaven and earth to get her back and where Lily meant to hide until Liam returned would soon be discovered. Oh, Ma, I'm sorry . . . I'm sorry but what else can I do? I must defend myself and this is the only way. Perhaps . . . perhaps later when . . . when . . . She didn't know how to finish the thought, for she could see no answer to it nor to the future, so with her face wet with tears she turned her mind determinedly to what she would need to go forward into it. Her newest gown of silk, the colour of heather. There was a puff bonnet to match with her pale grey kid boots and her plush patelot trimmed with pale grey fur, for who knew when she might need to look the part of a lady. Petticoats and underwear and all crammed hastily into a carpet bag which was strong, light and roomy. It needed to be light, for she had a long way to carry it.

Dragging out the lady's basket trunk that had belonged to her ma, she dug about underneath the pile of her own clothes which she had long outgrown and which had been kept for some reason, though she didn't know why. It seemed that some habit of thriftiness was ingrained in the servants and it had shown itself in an inability to throw things away. She had not questioned it but had merely burrowed under them to hide her other clothing which she had found similarly packed away in the attic. She took them out now and with that same sense of calm that had come upon her at the thought of Liam began to turn herself from a young girl into a young man. She thought that at some moment in the future she would have to cut her hair, for it was very difficult to get such a mass of it under her cap. It drifted and wisped in the most irritating curls about her face and neck, but she certainly hadn't the time now.

At the last moment she was overcome by the memories invoked by her ma's basket trunk. It was with this piece of luggage that she and Ma had accompanied Pa on coastal voyages aboard the *Lily-Jane*. Happy, it was almost more than she could bear to remember how happy, and unthinking they had been, the three of them. It would last for ever, they had thought, that's if they had thought at all, which she didn't think they did. This was their life, Pa and Ma and her with Mrs Quinn waiting at home for their return, but a twist of cruel fate had decreed otherwise and Pa had gone, and though she had still been alive, so had Ma. There was only Mrs Quinn and Villy left and she was to leave Mrs Quinn behind. Mrs Quinn would probably go and live with Victoria and Arnold and there was nothing Mr Crowther could do to her, unless he sacked Arnold which was unlikely. She doubted if Mr Crowther even knew that his groom was married to his housekeeper's daughter. She must leave a little note for Mrs Quinn before she left, she told herself as she patted her ma's trunk for the last time. She smoothed the rough basketwork and ran her hands round the velvet lining, remembering Ma, and it was then that she came across a small bulge in one of the pockets that ran along the inside at the front.

Her hands trembled, she didn't know why, for it had not yet occurred to her that Jane Elliott might have left some message for her, some message she could not pass on while she herself lived.

She drew it out, a little velvet pouch and inside, beside a scrap of paper, was a necklace, one she had never seen before. Mr Crowther had hung her mother with many fine jewels, all of which must have been worth a small fortune, but this one was simple, a fine network of gold chains like a spider's web no thicker than a thread of cotton among which a dozen green stones hung. That was all it was, nothing ostentatious which was probably why Ma had liked it.

She held it against her breast as she read what was on the note.

Dearest, there is nothing I can give you, or do for you now. You will understand why but there may come a day when you need my help and this is all I have for you. It might buy your freedom, Lily. Forgive me. I love you. I always have and I always will.
Your loving Ma

She wept in earnest then, burying her face into Villy's rough fur. Villy, though still inclined to totter a bit, had come round and was in raptures to be back with her mistress. She licked Lily's face dry of tears and whined but, knowing she must be away, Lily got to her feet and put the dog on her lead, sniffing and wiping her nose on the back of her hand as she did so. She placed the pouch carefully in her jacket pocket, her heart swelling with love, for Ma had given her and Liam the means to restore the *Lily-Jane* which had meant so much to Jane Elliott's beloved husband but she had no time to sit and marvel at it.

Shoving her arms into the sleeves of the mackintosh which she wore over the overcoat and jacket and pulling her cap down over her forehead, she propped the note she had left for Mrs Quinn on the mantelpiece where it would be found first thing in the morning. It said little, bar she was going away and would be quite safe and that as soon as she could she would be in touch.

Looking round her for the last time she moved bravely to the door on the first of her steps to freedom, to Liam and their new life. Villy kept close to her heels as though she too knew this was a decisive moment in their lives and when the door refused to open they were both somewhat taken aback. Lily gave it a slight shake, turning the knob quietly, slowly, then with more vigour but it was no good. It was locked. Somehow, without being heard, someone, and there were no prizes for guessing who, had crept upstairs and locked it!

But it didn't matter. She had meant to slip out of the side door which would have been much easier with Villy but if that devil thought he had her prisoner, then he was wrong. It would be difficult but she and Villy would get down the tree and be off into the night as she had planned. The devil take him, she hissed viciously, her young face hard and bitter, but there was no time for recriminations. She turned to the dog.

"Come on, Villy. Now you must be a good girl and lie still against me and not make a noise, for it will be the devil's own job to get you down the tree. I'll take the bag first and then come back for you. Not a sound, there's a good girl. I'll have to tie you to me. It's a good job you aren't a labrador."

The house was in total darkness as the two shadows slipped across the lawn.

25

Eva Earnshaw was sleeping the light, restive sleep of the elderly, not achieving the dreamless depths the young know and take for granted, and yet not awake. Somewhere between the two, and when the light tapping impinged on her semi-dreaming state it brought her at once to full wakefulness. Ginger, her marmalade-coloured tabby who slept on the bed beside her, raised her head in the dark, light from somewhere catching her eyes and turning them to a silver translucency. She stretched and yawned and Eva put out a hand to her as though seeking some support, for Eva lived alone and did not care for unexplained happenings, particularly in the dead of night. She listened, her hand still smoothing the cat's fur and when the sound repeated itself she felt the rhythm of her heart pick up in alarm.

"What's tha', d'yer think, Puss?" she whispered to the cat who, despite being named Ginger as a kitten she always addressed as Puss. "It . . . it sounds like someone knocking on t'door but 'oo on earth could it be at this time o' night?"

Like most people who live alone she talked out loud, particularly to the cat, and though she received no answer she always felt that Ginger knew exactly what was going on in her mind. Picking up the cat and cradling her to her flannelette-covered breast, she cautiously threw back the covers, lifted her old, heavily veined legs, and edged her way out of her warm bed, stepping first on to the rag rug which she herself had made and then on to the icy cold expanse of the oilcloth. Her flesh cringed from the contact as she moved hesitantly across the bedroom to the window which overlooked the front of her cottage and the stretch of Lower Breck Road on which it stood. Pulling back the curtains with an unsteady hand, for callers at this time of night surely meant bad news, she peeped through the misted glass to the square of garden that fronted her home. She had not stopped to put on her spectacles but in the hazy light from a million stars she could just make out what looked like a man and beside him a dog. The man was looking over his shoulder as though in dread of something and the dog huddled close to his leg. Their breath wreathed about their heads, for it was a cold night with a touch of the first of winter's frosts coating the grass and spiking the shrubs in Eva's garden to an ivory stillness.

Well, whoever it was out there, she didn't know him and if he thought she was going to open her door to a perfect stranger then he was a fool. Her cottage stood in a row of others, separated from one another by a bit of garden and a hawthorn hedge but if she was to open her window and scream blue murder one of her neighbours would be over here before you could say "knife". But before she raised the alarm it might be a good idea to find out who the chap was and what he wanted.

Cradling the cat closer to her for comfort, she opened the window and put her head out into the cold night.

"Yes?" she asked sternly as though to tell whoever was there that she would stand no nonsense. At once the man looked up, his face a white mask in the starlight. The dog looked up too and gave a warning yip. The animal was not happy, anyone could see that, its glance everywhere at once as though fully expecting every night creature for miles around to be making for this particular cottage.

"Good evening," a voice quavered from below. "I've been given your address . . ."

"Good evening!" exclaimed Eva, her voice amazed, no longer alarmed though she could not have said why. "Good evening! It's middle o't night, my lad, an' wharr I wanter know is wha' yer doin' knockin' at my door this late. 'Oo are yer an' yer'd best 'ave a proper answer or I'll shout fer Charlie Ainsworth 'oo lives next door. Now, speak up," she added tartly.

"I'm that sorry, ma'am, to disturb you at this time of night but, you see, I had no choice. I simply have nowhere else to go."

A refined voice, not of the working classes, curiously light for a man, and not in the least threatening. A tired voice and yet it seemed to be making an effort to be courteous. Not a voice to be afraid of but then would a man with wickedness in his heart sound as though he had?

"An' why is tha', pray? 'Ave yer no 'ome o' yer own tha' yer must be knockin' on decent folks' door at this ungodly hour?" Though in truth she had no idea what time of night it was.

"No, ma'am. And I'm so sorry but I seem to have forgotten your name. I remembered the address when Liam told—"

"Liam!" Eva Earnshaw's voice was sharp. "What's our Liam ter do wi' you?"

"It was Liam who told me I was to come to you if I was in trouble. And I'm in trouble, ma'am. He said . . ."

Eva Earnshaw's heart was doing more than picking up its rhythm now, it was thumping and thudding in her chest, for the word trouble had set it moving far faster than was safe in a woman of her age. Trouble, and yet her Liam was on the far side of the world and what connection was there between him and this thin lad who was hunched on her doorstep? It was weeks since he had left her, kissing her lovingly and holding her against his broad chest and promising to bring her back some magical thing from China, so why, after all this time was . . .

Heavens above, would you listen to her picking over in her mind what the lad wanted and why Liam had told him to come here. She really must pull herself together if she was to get to the bottom of the mystery. There was only one way to find out, of course, and that was to ask the lad in, though she knew that Liam would give her what for if he knew she was inviting a complete stranger into her home in the dark of a winter's night. Still, she couldn't carry on a conversation with her head hanging out of the window and the bitter frost already freezing the flesh off her, could she?

"Wait there," she ordered the lad, just as though he were going to run off the minute she closed the window.

Lily Elliott waited. She had walked mile after mile in the starlit dark, her heart in her mouth a dozen times as unfamiliar night sounds whispered about her, always going north, keeping the lights of the town on her left but avoiding any streets that might have some life in them. She knew roughly where West Derby was, east of Liverpool, but she had no idea how many miles she must walk to get there. She had the sovereign Liam had given her all those years ago but though she had been tempted she had decided against taking a hansom, for it would be easy to find and she was pretty certain Mr Crowther would try to trace her.

And so she had set off, the carpet bag in one hand and Villy's lead in the other, moving along Aigburth Road making towards Princes Park and Lodge Lane which ran in a direct line due north. She had studied maps in Mr Crowther's library, at the time having the vague thought that it might be a good idea to know how to get from Oakwood Place to Liam's granny's, for who knew what emergency might arise, but that had been years ago, while Ma was still alive and she herself had been no more than a child.

She had crossed the shining tracks of the London and North Western Railway, stepping carefully in the pitch dark, murmuring encouragingly to Villy whose ears were back and whose tail was down and between her legs in her alarm. Like Lily she had never been out at night before, except in the familiar surroundings of the garden and she snarled and twitched at every sound. Once some creature ran across their path, making Lily let out a stifled scream and Villy began to bark furiously, more in terror than defiance. The worst part was as they passed the Zoological Gardens where, catching the scent of the animals there, Villy began to bark madly, setting off what sounded like a lion which roared its displeasure. The noise woke several dogs in the vicinity and they all howled frantically and Villy did the same. Lily had to crouch down beside her and hold her head which she kept trying to jerk away but gradually she quietened, shivering against Lily's breast.

Lily knew she was on West Derby Road by this time, for that was where the zoo was situated but she was so tired she wanted to sink down, anywhere would do, and sleep until it was light but she knew that would be fatal. She must find Lower Breck Road which she knew was off West Derby Road but the trouble was she didn't know in which direction. She was pretty sure it must be away from the town and so she turned in that direction, blundering on in the dark, ready to fall into the frozen ditch and even when she found a turn to the left she was not certain in the dark that this was it.

She took a chance. Already she could sense a sort of lightening in the starlit blackness of the night and her instinct told her she must be off the road, it didn't matter if it was in a barn, if she couldn't find Liam's granny's house before the dawn broke. A tall, well-dressed young man with a dog in tow and carrying a carpet bag would be a sight not many would forget on these country lanes and her terror that Mr Crowther might cast his net even as far as this gave her the strength to go on.

She walked on and on, passing the dark bulk of a house now and then. She could feel the rutted lane beneath her boots and smell the aromas of the countryside, for there were farms in the vicinity, but at last she came to the four cottages on her right and on the end one was a small sign that she could just make out. It said "Ronald Biddle, Carpenter" and underneath in small letters, "Ivy Cottage, Lower Breck Road". She was here.

For a moment she felt the tiredness slip away from her in her elation but then came the perplexity of how she was to know which cottage belonged to Liam's granny. She could knock on any door, except Mr Biddle's, and find some disgruntled stranger staring out at her which wouldn't matter if that stranger turned out to be Liam's granny, but she had three cottages to choose from and two were not the right ones. She had no desire to wake them up, one after the other, and ask for . . . for . . . Lord, she didn't even remember her name, she only knew it wasn't O'Connor, or it would have struck in her mind, but then she couldn't just stand dithering here at the gate, could she? She must just take a chance and if the first one was wrong she would keep her head down, apologise, ask for Liam's granny – Dear God, she wished she could remember her name – and make her escape.

For some reason she chose the end cottage. Well, she had to start somewhere and it seemed logical to make it the first cottage in the row. Well, the last really, for Mr Biddle was the first. It was the right one! She had found Liam's granny.

A light appeared in the bedroom, then vanished, blooming again in the far reaches of the cottage which she could just make out through the small pane of glass in the stout door. It came nearer, then wandered off into a side room where a faint orange glow still showed, where presumably a fire had been banked down for the night. Again it shone through the pane of door glass and at last the door opened a crack and a suspicious face appeared. The candle in the old lady's hand revealed a stern and wrinkled face, a face that was highly coloured as though it were accustomed to being out of doors and from that face shone Liam's eyes.

It was the first thing Lily said and if she had thought carefully and chosen wisely she could not have spoken words more likely to please Eva Earnshaw. Not only to please but to reassure.

"You have Liam's eyes," she said impulsively.

"Who told you that, lad?"

"No one, ma'am. I can see them, even in this light."

Lily stood patiently while Villy wagged her tail eagerly and the cat at Eva's back shot straight in the air and began to hiss angrily. It was clear that Eva was confused, not knowing whether to put the candlestick down on the table that stood to one side of the door, reach for the cat and heave it out of harm's way, or open the door wider to allow her visitor to enter.

She tut-tutted irritably. "Be quiet, Puss, yer've sin a dog before now so stop actin' like a fool. Is that dog house-trained, lad? Yer'd best come in an' get door shut an' wipe yer feet an' all . . . I dunno, knockin' on folks' door at this time o' night, it's not proper that's wharr I say burr if yer say our Liam sent yer then I can't refuse yer. Come in, come in outer't cold, an' see, set yerself by't fire. Yer look 'alf clemmed an' yer'd best tie that there dog to't chair afore it goes for our Ginger."

"She won't do that, ma'am." Lily sank gratefully into the armchair by the fire, a visible look of relief on her face. "She's used to cats. My ma had a cat. She had it from being a kitten and Beauty, that was the cat's name, and Villy," placing a restraining hand on Villy's neck, "got on very well together."

"Tha's as mebbe but our Ginger's not used ter dogs so I'd best purrer in't kitchen fer now. She'll not like it," which Ginger didn't, struggling to get through the rapidly closing crack in the door.

"Poor Ginger," the lad said, surprising Eva. "it doesn't seem fair to banish her in her own home but . . ."

Lily's voice trailed away uncertainly as she realised that Liam's granny was looking at her with a very strange expression on her face. It was clear that something was bothering her, something that filled her with suspicion, a wavering look of doubt narrowing her eyes and firming her lips into a distrustful line.

"Never mind our Ginger," she said, lifting her head and folding her arms across her bosom. She had taken time to throw a colourful shawl about her shoulders, one that looked as though it might have come from some far-flung corner of the globe and she held it defensively about her. There was something strange here, her expression said, not just in this lad's sudden appearance on her doorstep in the middle of the night but in his *appearance*, the way he looked and spoke, for in her bone-weary exhaustion Lily had quite lost control of the deeper, more masculine way she spoke and the masculine manner she had adopted.

But Eva was the sort of woman who could not let a visitor into her cosy parlour without offering that visitor a nice cup of tea, as she always phrased it. She was hospitable and warm-hearted and this . . . this person looked as though a breath of wind might blow . . . well, she would say *him* for the moment . . . might blow him clean away. His face was quite grey and there were deep mushroom-coloured smudges beneath his eyes. He was a handsome lad, she decided. In fact he was not merely handsome, but beautiful if such a word could be used to describe a young man. She studied him from beneath her lowered lids as her hands busied themselves with sturdy mugs, with the teapot and caddy, with a pretty sugar bowl and milk jug to match, placing them on a round table across which a snow white, embroidered cloth was flung. She had carefully placed some nuggets of coal on the fire and it was blazing nicely and the lad, his head on the back of the chair was already beginning to doze.

Moving lightly, for, despite her years, Eva Earnshaw was agile, she stepped across another of her rag rugs and before the lad knew what she was about she had whipped off his cap. Even she, who had had suspicions about it, was taken aback at the waterfall of silvery, silken hair which fell over the back of her chair, reaching almost to the floor in its lively tumble of curls. Lily cowered away as though expecting a blow, perhaps not from Eva but from someone of whom she was afraid and Eva put out her hand and smoothed that glorious fall of hair back from the grey face.

"Nay, lass, tha's nowt' ter fear in this 'ouse. I know 'oo yer are now. Our Liam's told me all about yer. An' me name's Mrs Earnshaw. Liam's mam was my daughter."

That night, with the help of Mrs Earnshaw's old hands,

which were steadier than hers, her boyish clothes were removed and she was put in a clean, lavender-scented night-dress which Mrs Earnshaw said had once belonged to her lass who had died when Liam was born. It was said without asking for pity, just a simple remark to let Lily know why she had such a pretty thing, obviously belonging to a young woman, in her chest of drawers. A clean bed, also scented with lavender, a touch of Mrs Earnshaw's hand on her brow, a reassuring lick of the tongue from Villy who crouched on the rug beside the bed and would not be moved, and that was the last Lily knew.

She remembered, with her last thought, begging Mrs Earnshaw not to tell a soul that she was here, for even yet, in the aching depths of exhaustion and shock she was in, she could still feel Mr Crowther's hard hands on her body.

"Nay, lass, I'll tell no one. Sleep tight." And so she did, safe, she knew, at last.

It was dark again when she awoke, dark and quiet except for what she thought might be the tweet and twitter of a bird. No other sound but homely, comfortable sounds. The sighing of the wind in the trees and the patter of rain against the window which helped to make her feel even more cosy. There was a small fire in the grate which sang merrily and before it, stretched out as though she were totally at home, was Villy, her nose on her paws and almost touching the flickering coals. Lily smiled and stretched and yawned, knowing exactly where she was with no sense of the disorientation that afflicts someone who awakes in a strange bedroom. She was warm and rested and ravenously hungry. And no wonder, for it must be twenty-four hours since she had last eaten anything.

There was a chair beside the bed on which was thrown a warm woollen robe which she put on. Villy raised her head and then sauntered over, herself yawning and stretching first one back leg then the other. She pushed her nose into Lily's hand and seemed to grin in that almost human way dogs have, as though to say she was well satisfied with this place they had fetched up in.

Mrs Earnshaw was sitting comfortably before her fire in what seemed to be the only sitting-room in the house. The stairs from the tiny landing led directly down into it and behind it was a kitchen and beyond that a scullery. For the first time Lily looked about her, conscious of warmth and homely comfort, of shining copper and brass, of polish and deep plush curtains, of the fire's glow winking on gleaming surfaces, of peace and, best of all, safety. The bird she had heard was in a cage, a bright yellow thing with beautiful plumage that trilled its heart out in ecstasy. Mrs Earnshaw had fallen asleep, her head resting on the back of the chair, her mouth partially open and from it tiny bubbling snores emerged. Ginger was curled on her lap but at the sight of Villy she affected to be not only furious but terrified, spitting and clinging with open claws to Mrs Earnshaw's bibbed apron. Mrs Earnshaw awoke with a start and a mutter of irritation.

"Yer daft beast," she scolded the cat. "'Tis only Lily an' 'er dog. Anyone'd think it were a pack o' wolves, way yer carry on. Now 'old yer tongue or I'll shut yer in't kitchen again."

All the while she spoke she was smoothing the cat's pretended alarm and Lily was reminded of Beauty who was just such a consummate actress as Ginger.

She thought she would never stop eating and felt quite guilty that as fast as Mrs Earnshaw put the food in front of her she wolfed it down, as did Villy.

"That there animal o' yourn wouldn't 'ave a bite, lass, not so much as a sip o' water whilst yer were sleepin'. She stood guard over yer like a good 'un."

There was hot broth to start with, thick with barley and vegetables and tasty shin of beef, followed by home-made bread and freshly churned butter come from Newsham Farm which was just the other side of West Derby Road, and a couple of soft-boiled eggs. There was a rich fruit cake, only just come out of the oven, Mrs Earnshaw told her, accompanied by a mug of strong sweet tea and she'd a bit of cheese if she fancied it. Or perhaps an apple come from her own bit of an orchard at the back of the cottage and stored away for the winter.

She talked all the time Lily ate, glad, it seemed, of an interested audience, not aware as yet that anything anybody said to Lily Elliott about Liam O'Connor was fascinating to the young woman who loved him. About his mam's death when he was born and his no-good pa who had run off soon after, not wanting the responsibility of a child, and had never been seen since. About his childhood with Eva, his brightness and longing to make something of himself other than a farm labourer which was the usual employment in these parts.

About his goodness to her who, since he had begun to earn, had never had to work in a dairy again. That was her trade, dairymaid, and a hard trade it was, too, but it had kept her and Liam out of the poorhouse until he left his childhood behind. She did not mention the hours she had spent on her knees scrubbing other women's sculleries and kitchens after her long day in the dairy was ended, the evenings potato picking, or fruit picking to earn a couple of extra shillings a week to get Liam through his schooling and on the road to his Master's Certificate. Her pride and love shone out of her rosy face as she related his slow but steady rise to success, his small triumphs as a boy, his escapades, for he was no angel, his cheerfulness in the face of hardship, his gentleness with those smaller and weaker than himself, which was everyone really since he had always been a big lad, like his feckless Irish father before him.

And now he was off to China to make his fortune, he had laughingly told her, for he meant to be his own master. In fact – here she leaned forward confidentially, glancing round as though to make sure that no one could overhear what she was about to divulge – he had already bought a boat. When he had the wherewithal to restore her he meant to trade across the oceans of the world, or at least, smiling at her own foolishness, to the ports about the Irish Sea. He would be a sea captain who owned his own ship and there was no prouder man in the world of shipping and no prouder woman than his grandmother would be when he achieved it.

There was silence for a long moment as both the women who loved Liam O'Connor contemplated his wonderful future. They gazed into the fire, mesmerised, both of them, by the sheer joy of it, then Lily broke the silence.

"The *Lily-Jane*. She was my pa's ship."

Eva turned to her in surprise. "Yer pa 'ad a ship called *Lily-Jane* an' all?"

"There is only one *Lily-Jane*, Mrs Earnshaw. She was named after my ma and me, and when Pa died she was taken from us. I swore I would get her back one day but it was Liam who did it. Liam found me – I was only ten years old – and we became friends. He . . . was good to me . . ."

"Aye, that'd be our Liam," Eva said solemnly.

"When the *Lily-Jane* was put up for sale Liam bought her."

"Aye, my lass, 'e told me."

"He bought her for me, Mrs Earnshaw. You see . . ."

Eva Earnshaw's face became stern and her mouth firmed. Her eyes grew flinty, the lovely blue turning to grey just like Liam's did when he was disturbed.

"What're yer sayin', my girl? If yer tellin' me our Liam 'as done summat shameful then yer can gerrout o' my 'ouse right this minnit fer I'll not believe it."

"No, no, Mrs Earnshaw. You must know that Liam would never shame anybody, you or me. He knew how I felt about my pa and about *Lily-Jane* and . . . well, I say he bought her for me but she belongs to him." Just as I do, she thought, but she did not say this last. Some intuition, a woman's intuition told her this was not the right time to tell Liam's granny that Lily and he were to be married on his return, and she could tell her of their plans to restore the schooner to her former glory and to become partners in her endeavours.

But first she must recount to Liam's granny what had happened to her over the last six years, to her and to her ma. She must go over it all again, painful as it was, shameful as it was, particularly the events of the last few days, for Mrs Earnshaw must be made to realise how important it was for Lily to go about as a young man. There was so much to do before Liam came home and she could only do it under the guise of a male. Any female moving about the docks would be sure to excite interest and it would soon get back to Mr Crowther that a well-dressed young lady was concerning herself with an old schooner, once owned by him, that had just been purchased by a seaman. He might even now know about Liam, for she was certain that he would already have put his spies about looking for her and there were men, labourers and dockers who worked with the ships who had seen her and Liam together.

"Mrs Earnshaw . . ."

"Yes, lass? 'Ave yer summat ter tell me?"

"Yes, I have . . ." and already, before she had begun her tale tears were slipping across her cheeks. Not tears of self-pity but of relief that at last she could tend to the wounds that had been inflicted on her by the cruelty of the man her mother had married. Apply to them the ointment that the telling to another woman would heal and feel them soothed and begin to fade.

She sat on the rug before the fire. She laid her cheek against Mrs Earnshaw's knee and, with Mrs Earnshaw's hand smoothing the tangle of her hair and Villy's muzzle resting in her lap, she began.

26

The young and elegant salesman behind the counter felt his breath quicken and for a moment he forgot the ritual that one employed with the rich and well bred and simply stared, mouth agape.

The beautiful and beautifully dressed young lady, accompanied by a respectable elderly woman in sober grey, stood just inside the door looking about her enquiringly, the expression on her face revealing nothing of her inner feelings which, if the salesman had been aware of them, might have surprised him. She turned and smiled coolly in his direction in that way the gentry have when faced with an inferior, then gracefully crossed the vast expanse of luxurious carpet towards him, her wide skirts swaying, and it was then that he remembered who and where he was.

He hurried out from behind his counter and bowed. This was no tuppeny-halfpenny establishment catering to the lower middle classes but a well-known jeweller's and silversmith's where the grand and wealthy families of Liverpool were wont to spend an hour or so choosing something that was invariably connected with precious stones. Nevertheless he felt he was in the presence of someone special, perhaps even a member of the aristocracy. He had never seen her before but the patrician lift to her head and her slightly condescending air impressed him immeasurably.

"Good morning, miss," he declared, his manner somewhat obsequious, for though he was sure of his establishment's worth as a superior jeweller's among the high-class shops of Liverpool, he felt the need to be more than polite. He allowed his admiration to show in his eyes for a moment, for it did no harm to flatter a lady a little as long as it was respectful, and his admiration was not only respectful but genuine. "May I be of help to you?"

He bowed again and pulled out a chair, a little gilt and velvet thing with legs so frail it seemed incapable of supporting even the slender weight of the young lady, fussing about her until she was seated, then did the same with the elderly woman though not quite so tenderly.

"I'm not sure. We were admiring one or two pieces in your window, weren't we, Mrs Earnshaw, and decided to come in and have a closer look. By the way, I have left my carriage just beyond the corner. Will it be safe there? My coachman is somewhat nervous of the traffic where his horses are concerned but I assured him that it would be all right."

"Oh, I'm sure it will, miss. There is always a constable on duty along Bold Street keeping an eye on the carriages of the ladies who shop here."

"Well, that is a relief. Now, if we might . . ."

"Of course. If you would just point out the piece of jewellery you wish to look at I will get it for you."

Another gentleman appeared from some back recess of the shop, bowing and smiling and wishing them good morning. It was plain from his manner that he had appraised the quality of the young lady who was sitting as straight-backed as a duchess in the velvet chair, noting the cut of her gown of heather blue silk and the handsome three-quarter-length sleeved cloak she wore over it. It was slightly shaped to her waist, spreading widely over the fashionable, crinoline-supported skirt of her gown and had wide, pagoda-like sleeves. It was made from plush in the same blue as her gown and was much trimmed about its edges with a pale grey fur. Her bonnet, which he knew to be called a puff bonnet, since he made it his business to know the world of fashion, was the very latest, worn with a forward tilt to accommodate her full and shining, silver pale chignon. She was *very* fashionable; expensive, he would have called her. His expert's eye also noticed that though she wore no other jewellery she had a very fine pair of pearls in her ears. She was very evidently come from a good family which did not let its daughters out alone, for she had her chaperone with her.

"Aah, Mr Dismore." The young salesman addressed him deferentially. "This young lady . . ."

"Yes, yes, thank you, Mr Andrews." Mr Dismore was quite

resplendent in his black frock-coat and waistcoat to match. He wore well-fitting dark grey striped trousers with a strap beneath his highly polished black boots. His collar stood up stiffly under his chin, keeping it in a somewhat supercilious position. His large neckcloth was also in black. Mr Andrews was similarly attired but it seemed to Eva Earnshaw, who spoke little but saw all, that the quality was not so good as his employer's. They both wore a neat buttonhole, a white carnation, specially supplied each day from the florist's on the market. It was a touch Mr Dismore thought in keeping with his reputation as one of Liverpool's finest jewellers.

He waved away the young gentleman, who was obviously his underling, with a disdainful gesture. "I will attend to Miss . . . ?" He waited urbanely, enquiringly, for "Miss" to reveal her name but she merely smiled and said nothing.

"I am Thomas Dismore." He had no choice but to go on, since she seemed unwilling to do so. "The proprietor of this establishment. I happened to overhear you telling Mr Andrews that you were interested in something in my window. Now if you would be good enough to point out . . ."

"Having seen the display you have inside your shop, Mr Dismore, I must admit to being spoiled for choice but if it is no trouble to you might I have a look at that beautiful silverwork set with . . . well, I'm not sure what the stones are but, really, I don't think I have ever seen anything quite so exquisite. Have you, Mrs Earnshaw?" turning to her companion.

Wooden-faced, Mrs Earnshaw said she hadn't.

"It is no trouble at all. You have good taste, Miss . . . er, if I might say so. The pieces are Scandinavian and the gems are called peridot. That particular shade of palest green goes so well with the silver, don't you think? Mr Andrews" – he clicked his fingers peremptorily – "be so good as to get the Scandinavian pieces from the window."

Lily was enchanted with the jewellery and had no need to act out the part. There was a fine bracelet, delicate leaves set in links, between each link a peridot surrounded by finely wrought silver which was shaped to look exactly like diamonds. There were earrings, tiny bunches of grapes hanging from silver leaves and a brooch that was fashioned like a newly opening rosebud, in its centre a pale green gem.

"Might I . . . ?" She held the earrings to her ears.

Mr Dismore clicked his fingers for a mirror and at once Mr

Andrews produced one, watching, both of them, with evident pleasure, as the young lady tried them on, turning her head this way and that. Mr Dismore managed to sneak a quick look at the pearls she had removed from her ears, noting their fineness and even the hallmark on the setting of gold.

"Mmm," she said, glancing about her. "I really love them don't you, Mrs Earnshaw, and I'm sure Papa would approve but . . ."

"Perhaps you might care to glance at some other pieces, miss?" Mr Andrews said boldly.

"What a good idea." She stood up. "Might I . . . ?"

"Of course, please look around."

The shop was tastefully appointed as befitted a jeweller's and silversmith's of Mr Thomas Dismore's standing. There were discreet, glass-fronted cases in which, on velvet cushions, were arranged perhaps one small piece, a delicate gold-framed pendant set with diamonds or a white jade necklace comprising five square pendants set with rubies and emeralds in gold. In one case was what was known as a *grande parure*, a complete set of matching jewellery including a tiara, earrings, a necklace, bracelet and a ring glowing with rubies and sparkling with diamonds.

"It belonged to a celebrated European princess," Mr Dismore breathed into her ear. "The stones are of the finest quality so naturally that is reflected in the price."

"Exquisite," Lily murmured, drifting gracefully across the deep pile of the royal blue carpet to study a necklace of dark purple amethysts, each gem surrounded by natural pearls and set in gold.

"Look, Mrs Earnshaw." She turned to smile at her chaperone. "Oh, do look, is this not exactly like the one Aunt Julia has?"

Mrs Earnshaw obediently got to her feet and moved to stand next to her, regal as a queen, looking down into the glass case with her charge.

"Aye, I believe it is, lass," she said, pressing her shoulder against Lily's and Lily began to think Mrs Earnshaw was enjoying this charade as much as she was. The two gentlemen hovered behind them, eager to show her this and that, watching her as she studied a tray of rings, exclaiming over one that held a rose diamond set in leaf-shaped silver on a triple silver shank.

"Oh, look at this, Mrs Earnshaw. I love this one. Perhaps

I could persuade Papa to buy it for me for Christmas. Is it not beautiful?" She slipped it on her finger and the two gentlemen sighed, mesmerised that it not only fitted her, but that she should do them the honour of admiring it. They watched her every movement, their eyes dwelling on her lovely, expressive face, on the exquisite shape of her rosy mouth which curled at the corners as she smiled, at the soft swell of her breasts which peaked delightfully above her tiny waist, at the widening of her incredible eyes as she caught sight of some further wonder. There was a tiara of diamonds and pearls, a necklace of mother of pearl so fine it was transparent, a gold chased locket studded with emeralds, pearl chokers and exquisite hatpins of gold and silver, of ivory and amber.

"Mr Dismore, I really have not seen such lovely things, even in London. Don't you agree, Mrs Earnshaw?" Mr Dismore swelled visibly with pride and Lily was to wonder, in the part of her mind not involved in this play-acting, how easy it was to dupe a man. Smile and simper and flatter and the fool was eating out of your hand, even a businessman like Mr Dismore, but then they had not yet got to the important part, the tricky part and of course that would be the test. If he did not oblige her in that then her plan would fall apart about her ears.

"You are most kind, Miss . . . er . . . most kind." Still she did not supply her name.

Suddenly she whirled about, her skirts dipping to reveal a tantalising froth of lace, her face rosy and smiling.

"Mr Dismore, would it be too much to ask that I bring Papa to . . . well, it is almost Christmas." She dimpled enchantingly, wondering as she did so how she knew how. "There are so many lovely things here and I'm sure my sisters – I have three, Mr Dismore, not to mention two sisters-in-law – would be thrilled to . . . Oh, Mrs Earnshaw, shall we take the carriage back at once? Papa will be back from hunting, I'm sure . . . We are staying at Knowsley, Mr Dismore. Do you know it?"

Did he know it? Was there any man in Liverpool in the world of business and trading who did not wish he could be connected in some way with the greatest estate in the north-west? His elation was such that he was ready to kiss the young lady's hand, for already his head was juggling with figures which, if his calculations were correct, might run into thousands. Three sisters and two sisters-in-law, if you please, and, of course, the added benefit of becoming known to the family who resided at Knowsley. What a feather in his cap that would be.

"I would be honoured to meet your father, Miss . . . I am here at his disposal—"

"Oh, Mr Dismore, there is just one more thing," she interrupted him, putting her small white hand on his sleeve. He resisted the temptation to pat it, in an avuncular manner, naturally.

"Yes?" he enquired, his expression almost fond.

"Papa did ask me if I might do an errand for him."

"Yes."

"It is this . . . this . . ." She reached for her reticule and rummaged about in it, bringing out a velvet pouch. "It belonged to my . . . mama." Her voice broke quite genuinely and Mr Dismore, sensing tragedy, allowed himself this time to pat her hand. "She . . . she died early this year and . . . well, in the aftermath, this necklace was never insured. Papa asked me to have it valued for that purpose. Could I prevail upon you . . . ?"

"My dear young lady. Nothing could be simpler. It is a lovely piece, certainly." Taking an eyeglass from his pocket he scrutinised the stones which, he noted to himself, were particularly fine emeralds. "Might I have a few moments?"

"Of course, but if I may I must just send Mrs Earnshaw to let Thomas – he is the coachman – know we shall be no more than . . . than . . . ?" She raised her eyebrows and smiled enquiringly at Mr Dismore.

"Five minutes, my dear." Mr Dismore felt he might be allowed to call this bewitching young lady that.

"Five minutes, Mrs Earnshaw. Oh, and you may as well wait for me in the carriage. It is not our carriage, you understand, Mr Dismore. Our host insisted on lending it to me this morning. He is kindness itself."

Mr Dismore was so gratified to be allied to the owner of the great estate of Knowsley, even in such a tenuous way, he was ready to do a jig and when he told Lily the value of Ma's necklace, so was she. He bowed her out of the shop, stepping on to the pavement so that for a horrid moment she was afraid he was going to escort her to the non-existent carriage, but she shook his hand and smiled in that way the pedigreed class have when they are dismissing an underling, then sauntered off with the velvet pouch in which was her and Liam's future tucked safely inside her glove.

There were several good-class jewellers along Bold Street, Lord Street, Upper Arcade and Church Street and in each one she and Mrs Earnshaw repeated the performance they had put on for Mr Dismore and in each one it succeeded. By the time they had reached the last one in Upper Arcade Lily knew exactly how much the necklace was worth, having had it confirmed, with a guinea or two difference here and there, by five experts and therefore knew how much she was going to ask for it. Perhaps she might have to come down, ask less than it was worth if only to get rid of it but at least she was aware of its true value and could state a price.

And that is exactly what she did. The last jeweller they called on was somewhat taken aback when she bluntly told him that she wished to sell the necklace and even more taken aback when she told him how much she wanted for it.

"Now then, young lady," he began, smiling. "I cannot possibly give you that much for a piece of jewellery which, for all I know, will be hard to resell," believing that a lady, for that was what she was, surely, would have no idea of the quality of the emeralds and even less what to ask for them. He was nonplussed when she began to gather up her reticule, the velvet pouch and the necklace, standing up with her companion and preparing to leave his shop which was not quite so sumptuous as Mr Dismore's.

"I'll waste no more of your time then, Mr Jenkinson. I might have been prepared to come down a fraction but . . ."

"How much is a fraction?" he asked her bluntly.

From there, over a period of twenty minutes in which Mrs Earnshaw had to sit down she felt so faint and Lily could feel the sweat break out and cool under her clothes, they haggled, but at last, knowing she could do no more, Lily agreed on a price, her only condition being that he paid her in cash and at once.

The jeweller, who knew he had got the best of the deal, sent his man to the bank, since he did not keep such a large sum in his shop, she must understand that, and for a further twenty minutes she and Mrs Earnshaw sat and waited, doing their best to look unconcerned and wondered whether, instead of the cash, the assistant might fetch a constable.

That night, in the safety and warmth of Mrs Earnshaw's

little cottage they sat, one on either side of the fire, their knees up to the blaze and went over every minute, their eyes, even the old lady's, alive with glee. They relived every perilous instant, reminding one another of this moment and that when they had been certain the game was up, laughing now that it was over but telling one another that they would not have missed it for the world. Mrs Earnshaw, who had not known such a vast amount of money existed, was to a certain degree concerned to have it casually left lying about in her cottage, saying that her Joseph had never earned as much in the whole of his life.

"Mrs Earnshaw, dear. No one but you and me know the money exists, except the man who gave it to us and he hasn't the faintest idea where we live. He is hardly likely to go knocking on the door of his lordship's house to find out, is he? He knew he had made a good deal. Besides, it is safely hidden under the floorboards in Liam's room with a chest of drawers over it. How did you know that that hidey-hole was there, by the way?" she asked curiously.

"Oh, when t' lad were a nipper 'e liked to 'ide 'is bits o' treasures, conkers an' such, thinkin' I knew nowt about 'em so I never lerron. I never dreamed it would come in so 'andy one day."

Lily gazed into the fire, absorbing this new picture of Liam as a young boy, a young boy growing up before she was even born. A boy with conkers and old coins and a catapult, and all the other things dear to the heart of a growing lad, things he had kept secret, or so he thought, from his granny. She knew she was sleeping in his room, in the very bed he had slept in then, and all about the room were signs of his occupancy. Books like *Masterman Ready* by Captain Marryat, *The Last of the Mohicans* and *The Three Musketeers*. Pictures framed by himself, his granny told her, of lovely sailing ships on stormy seas, small jade carvings he had brought back from India and China, and his boyhood clothes, which she was to wear on her next trip down to the docks, hanging in his wardrobe and smelling of the lavender his grandmother dried herself.

Eva smiled into the fire then turned to Lily, bringing her from her reverie.

"Lass, I 'aven't 'ad such a good time since our Liam an' me threw a party fer't neighbours when 'e went away. By gum, I'll not forget that chap's face in a 'urry when yer sed that about

Knowsley. 'E nearly curtseyed to yer. Eeh, it were a stroke o' genius an' I'll say this, yer a clever lass an' if anyone can get that there boat back on't watter 'tis you. An' thing is, we did nutten wrong. It might've felt like it but yer never done owt wrong. I wouldn't've 'elped if yer 'ad, yer know that, don't yer? That were yer ma's necklace what she give yer" – for Mrs Earnshaw had been shown Ma's last note to Lily – "an' yer was entitled ter sell it if yer wanted."

"Yes, I know that, Mrs Earnshaw, but if I could have kept it I would have done. It belonged to Ma and I believe Pa must have bought it for her. She would not have left it for me if . . . if *he* had given it to her, but there's just one more thing I want you to do for me. I know you won't like it and I'm sorry myself, but I have no choice. I . . . I must be safe, you see, until Liam comes home when . . . well . . ."

"Wharris it, lass?"

"Will you cut my hair for me?"

Tommy Graham was delighted to see his young friend again and said so a dozen times as they studied what needed to be done to the *Lily-Jane* to get her ready for her sail up to Runcorn. Dick was dressed more suitably today in an old pair of breeches of dun grey and a navy blue knitted gansey which had seen better days, with a pair of rough woollen trousers and sturdy boots. Over it he wore a pea jacket of warm pilot cloth which was too wide in the shoulders but apart from that fitted well enough, and a battered peaked cap of tweed pulled well down over his pale hair. He also had on a pair of wire-rimmed spectacles and smelled strongly of lavender. Tommy made no comment, however, at least about the lavender.

"I'd about give yer up, Dick, 'onest ter God. It's four weeks since yer was 'ere burr I've kept me eye on 'er. Slept on board an' all an' wait 'till yer see wharr I done in't cabin. Well, I thought as 'ow I might as well mekk meself useful an' be gerrin on wi' summat 'til yer come back. I didn't know yer was short-sighted, lad," he added as he led Lily along the deck.

The spectacles belonged to Mrs Earnshaw's dead husband who could not read but liked to pretend he could. He used to study any old newspaper he found lying about in the ale-house he frequented on a Friday night after he had been paid, sitting outside his cottage of a summer evening with it in his hands. He would shake it out and peer at the print through his spectacles just as though he were reading the news but the spectacles were made of plain glass and were for effect only. It was his one weakness and his widow told Lily she believed that if a man had one weakness only, a good man who was a good husband, then where was the harm in it? The spectacles, more than anything else, helped Lily with her disguise. They drew the eye away from her lovely face, making her seem not exactly plain, for that she could never be, but, as Mrs Earnshaw said, it was a well-known fact that anyone, man or woman, who wore spectacles was considered homely.

"Oh, yes, just a little bit," she said in answer to Tommy's remark. "I can manage without them most days but sometimes when I'm tired . . .." Her voice trailed away indecisively but Tommy, who was a man who could keep his own counsel, said nothing more.

The cabin was quite splendid. Tommy had relined the walls with a lovely polished walnut, so pale it was almost the colour of honey. The floor he had relaid with a darker wood, and set against the wall were two new bunks, one above the other and carved most intricately with a pattern of leaves and flowers. The ones her parents had slept in when Ma was aboard and which had been rotten with worm and damp had gone. It smelled of the fresh aroma of new wood and polish and though there was nothing else in the cabin in the way of furniture it seemed to breathe of life and hope and the future.

"Oh, Tommy, how lovely," she whispered. "How on earth . . . ?"

"There were a brig bein' done up in dry dock up yonder so I scouted about a bit ter see what were bein' chucked out an' got this lot cheap."

"You must let me reimburse you."

"Yer wha'?"

"I . . . I have some money now, Tommy, enough to get *Lily-Jane* back to what she was before . . . before" – she had almost said before Pa died but caught herself in time – "she fell into disrepair and whatever you spent I shall pay you, and a wage as well. I want you to be part of the crew, if you are willing, because . . . well, though I love the sea and *Lily-Jane* I'm sadly lacking in seamanship. I need someone to teach me and I was hoping . . ."

She could swear there were tears in the old man's eyes as he gazed in wonder, first from his efforts in the cabin, to her face and then back again. He stumped over to the small porthole and rubbed the glass vigorously as though it were that and not his eyes that were blurred, then, with a hurried wipe with the back of his hand across his face, he turned.

"I don't know 'oo yer are, Dick, or even if that's yer name but I'll tell yer summat. Yer've found a shipmate in old Tommy Graham an' that's a bloody fact. D'yer know, lad, I'd sail wi' yer fer nowt just ter ge' watter under me feet again. An' I'll tell yer this an' all, yer'll be t'finest seaman ter sail from't port o' Liverpool when I've done wi' yer. Shake on it, will yer?"

It caused quite a commotion in the vicinity of Canning Dock when the *Lily-Jane* edged her way from the quayside towards the lock gates where the piermaster supervised her leaving, along with a dozen others, when the tide was right. She had mouldered for months, falling more and more into a state of disrepair and the men who worked the docks had known that if someone didn't take her in hand before long she would be beyond repair. They hated to see it, even those who did not go to sea, for they loved ships and the sea did these Liverpool men. When old Tommy Graham began to take an interest, lovingly doing this and that they could scarcely believe what he told them about her resurrection which was to take place in the near future. But here she was, floundering like some wounded animal but under the guidance of old Tommy, helped by the slender youth who looked as though the first stiff breeze in the river would have him over the side. Nevertheless, under Tommy's shouted commands he was making a fair job of deck-hand and good luck to the pair of them. Off to Runcorn to have her seen to, old Tommy had told them proudly, and as she turned into the river with Tommy at her wheel there was a great cheer and waving of caps just as if a new ship were being launched. Even the piermaster was fired with enthusiasm, wondering as he watched her sail slowly out into the middle of the river why the lad who was working under Tommy Graham's guidance seemed so familiar!

27

Joshua Crowther studied the tall, lounging figure of his son, envying him his youth and vitality, the smart uniform he wore which made him immediately attractive to every woman in the room, and the dashing nonchalance he seemed to have acquired since he left home. He had always been a mother's boy – when his mother was alive, of course – and by the time she was dead it was apparent to Joshua that it was too late to make him into the son he would have liked. A copy of himself, in fact. Nicholas was gentle, kind to those who served him, considerate of ladies, soft-spoken, meticulously polite, and nervous with his father! Of his own father. He seemed to be perfectly at ease with others, with guests who came to the house, with his friends, those he brought home from school, with the young ladies and gentlemen with whom he went riding, shooting, hunting, in the company of others of his own class, but he appeared to shrink within himself the moment he was alone with his father. Personable, popular, but weak, that was how Joshua would have described him, taking after his mother and what man wants a son who takes after his mother?

But he was exactly what all young girls dream of, as the circle about him testified. He was tall and lean, his years in the army slimming him down to the strength and fineness of the sword he carried. He had a narrow waist and the tight soldier's trousers he wore clung to his hips and the contours of his slim buttocks. His legs were long and shapely in exact proportion to his body. His eyes were a deep chocolate brown framed by long, girlish lashes and his well-shaped mouth was inclined to smile, providing he was not in the vicinity of his father. His hair was thick, dark, curling in a most delightful way about his ears and neck and falling over his forehead in an untidy tumble that was the despair of his commanding officer.

He was wearing the uniform of the Liverpool Regiment in which he was an officer: a scarlet tunic with a high, stiff collar and a silk net sash over his left shoulder. His sword belt was of white enamelled leather and his trousers were a dark blue with a narrow red welt down the outside of each leg. Since he was only a second lieutenant he bore no badge of rank. He was laughing at something one of the young ladies had said to him but the moment he became aware that his father was watching him he flushed, like a young girl, Joshua thought contemptuously. He was not the man his father wanted him to be and, therefore, Joshua had not been totally disappointed when Nicholas had stated, boldly for him, that he did not wish to follow a career in Joshua's business but was intent on taking a commission in the army. Joshua realised that it would have been very irksome to work beside this hesitant, irresolute son of his who flinched when his father raised his voice, so he had made no objection, particularly as it cost him nothing. Nicky had money of his own, for his mother had been a wealthy woman in her own right and had left her son well provided for. He was the catch of the county and surely would be irresistible to any young woman, the still, small voice in Joshua Crowther's warped mind whispered.

Nicholas Crowther had joined the 1st Battalion of the King's Regiment (Liverpool) when he was eighteen and now he was almost twenty-two. It seemed army life suited him. He had served in the second Chinese war in Peking and on the North-West Frontier, honourably it was said, though the picture of his son with a sword in his hand was one that did not come easily to his father, and was due another tour of Ireland when his leave was finished. But before that his father wished to discuss a little matter with him which he intended doing the moment the party was over.

He turned to look at his daughter, his eldest daughter that is, for his youngest was a mere babe in arms and was asleep in her nursery.

He was proud of Eloise. She had done well for him, since this evening was an engagement party for her and the young man she was to marry in the spring, John Patrick, the son of

Sir William Patrick who held a hereditary baronetcy and had a vast estate in Derbyshire. His girl would be *Lady* Patrick one day when the old man had gone and though there was little money, which was probably why Eloise's somewhat meagre claim to breeding had been overlooked, what did it matter? He was prepared to part with some of his cash since it could do no harm in business to mention casually his landed son-in-law. He was a complete nincompoop, of course, with a laugh like a horse and a face to match but Eloise was, like himself, a realist, and was well satisfied with the bargain that had been struck for her. She stood beside him now, already practising her gracious role as a baronet's wife, her arm through that of her future husband, looking quite glorious in a dress of cream satin with an enormous skirt. It had a tiny bodice covered in crystal drops with short puff sleeves. Her bosom was quite magnificent, as every man in the room was aware, even her future father-in-law, though her future mother-in-law was none too pleased about it, believing it was not suitable for so young a girl to have on display the charms that should be seen only by her husband in the privacy of their bedroom. Not even then sometimes! Eloise sported a great, old-fashioned sapphire ring which had been in the Patrick family for generations and was well suited as the half-smile she directed at her father informed him. He smiled back. They understood one another, did he and Eloise.

"There's a man to see you, sir," the quiet voice of Maggie, his head parlourmaid whispered in his ear, and he swung round sharply, for surely the stupid woman could see this was no time for callers. He said so, his mouth twisting in the snarl that was becoming more and more familiar to his servants.

"Get rid of him, Maggie."

"Sir, he was most insistent. He said I was to tell you it was about the little matter of . . . of the young lady."

Joshua Crowther's face did not change expression but a gleam lit his eye, a strange gleam which Maggie did not care for and she stepped back hastily.

"Show him into my study, Maggie, and tell him I'll be along directly."

"Yes, sir." Maggie dropped a curtsey and slid from the room. She had been serving drinks at the buffet supper which Mr Crowther had asked Mrs Kelly to arrange to celebrate Miss Eloise's betrothal. Rosie, Betsy and Maggie Two were still in the drawing-room, circulating among the guests with trays filled with glasses of the most expensive champagne money could buy and later would help to serve the buffet laid out in the dining-room. Mrs Kelly had made a wonderful feast and even Mrs Quinn had been roped in to help. Mrs Quinn, ever since the disappearance of Miss Lily, had lived over at her daughter's cottage which stood on Holmes Lane, right on the edge of Mr Crowther's property. She had been devastated, they all had, wondering what had happened to drive the child away like that, though most of them, including herself, had had a fair idea. But Mrs Quinn had whispered in her ear that she had word that Miss Lily was safe and staying with a friend, probably to do with that big chap who used to come along the shore to meet the child.

She didn't like the look of the man who waited for her in the hall. A ferrety-faced sort of chap with small eyes and a big nose and a mass of face hair hiding his mouth. He was polite enough though, thanking her profusely as she led him into the master's study and asked him please to be seated.

She was on her way across the hall in the direction of the kitchen when the master hurried out of the noise-filled drawing-room, in so much of a hurry he almost knocked her down.

"Sorry, sir," she apologised though it was not her fault, but he took no notice, hurrying towards his study door with the strangest look of anticipation on his face, just like a child on its way to a much-looked-for treat.

The guests had all gone. His daughter had retired and those guests who were staying over – her future husband and in-laws included – were safely tucked up in the comfort his money provided. They pretended they were indifferent to it, being used to a draughty old mansion two hundred years old between Buxton and the Peak Forest and he supposed he would be expected to restore it to some sort of habitable state, the kind his daughter was used to. In the meanwhile they wallowed, there was no other word for it, in the warmth and luxury of Oakwood Place. He'd be glad to see the back of them all, though he thought he might miss Eloise, but if his plans came to fruition and by God, he meant to see they did, then he would not be lonely.

The knock on the door interrupted his pleasant reverie.

"Come in," he called, turning to smile at the tall and honourable figure of his son who already looked distinctly uneasy.

"You wanted to see me, sir?"

"Come in, boy, come in. What d'you say to a nightcap?"

"Well, I have had—"

"Nonsense, one more won't hurt," overruling his son as he always did and his son allowed it, as he always did.

"Now, sit down and let's you and I have a little talk, shall we?"

When they were comfortably seated he raised his glass, smiling in his son's direction. "A toast, I think, to your future, my boy, which is what I wished to discuss with you."

He took a deep swallow of his whisky, indicating that Nicky must do the same and though his heartbeat had quickened at his father's words about his future, Nicky obediently took a sip. He shuddered slightly, for he did not care for the taste of whisky. His father noticed it and his lip curled but he said nothing. The last thing he wanted at the moment was to antagonise his son, for he was the linchpin of his plan, a tortuous plan which, if he had divulged it to anyone, would have been considered the work of a madman. And he supposed he was slightly mad on the subject of Lily Elliott but that did not worry him. He had gone through life bulldozing aside anyone or any obstacle that had stood in the way of his achieving whatever it was he wanted. In business and in his private and social life. One way or the other he got his way and he meant to have it in this. He was prepared to wait. He didn't care how long it took but he meant to succeed. He had brooded over it for weeks now and it was as clear and sharp in his mind as any strategy he had ever devised. But first he must persuade – *force* – his son to come round to his way of thinking. Well, that was not exactly it, for, naturally, he would not tell him the way of it all but he meant to make him see, and would not the girl herself do that, what a splendid idea it was.

He had known almost from the start that there was a man involved. He had questioned every one of the servants, indoor and out, and it had not taken long for him to force it out of the half-witted gardener's lad that Miss Lily met a "big chap" down on the seashore. A big chap! Sweet Christ, the thought that some other man might have taken what he himself lusted after was at first enough to turn his mind, which is probably what it had done, he supposed, not at all concerned. The images of some other man tasting that youthfulness, that freshness, that ripe innocence, that sexual attraction of which she was unaware nearly undid him and the gardener's lad had backed away from him, terrified of the blood that suffused his face and eyes, the harshness of his breathing, and when the boy had bolted from the room it had taken Joshua an hour to compose himself to a semblance of his normal self. And tonight the man he had hired had brought him the news he wanted!

He stared into his glass of whisky and said idly, "Have you ever considered marriage, my boy?"

Nicky gaped. He almost dropped his whisky glass, the question was so unexpected. He had thought his father was about to do his best to persuade him to leave the army, which he loved, and join him in the business or . . . or . . . well, he couldn't think of anything else that might be to his father's advantage, for that was what everything in this house was concerned with. His father's advantage. No one else mattered, not even Eloise who had been sold to the highest bidder, the son of a baronet, which would bring prestige to the Crowther family. It was not that Eloise minded, far from it, she loved the idea of becoming *Lady* Patrick but if she hadn't, if she had fallen in love with a man her father did not approve of, it would have been just too bad!

He couldn't answer he was so confounded.

"I see you are surprised, my boy, and I suppose it is because Eloise is to be comfortably settled that it entered my mind. I would like you to be the same."

"But I'm not yet twenty-two, sir," Nicky managed to gasp, "and my career has not yet really begun. I love the army and—"

"I am not asking you to leave the army, Nicholas. Far from it but . . . well, it is the fact that you are in a somewhat dangerous job that makes me think that if anything were to happen to you our name would die out. Oh, I know we are not what is called an old family, but we are an honourable one and I would like to see it continue. If you were to marry some suitable young lady, with you commanding officer's permission, of course, she could remain here while you continue to soldier wherever you were sent. She would bear your children and eventually become mistress of this house. In fact, she *would* be mistress of this house, here waiting for you when you have had enough of soldiering. I know that many wives of soldiers accompany their husbands when they go abroad but it is a custom of which I do not approve. The climate ages them and kills their children, or so I have heard. In my opinion it is far better they remain at home and—"

He stopped speaking abruptly, aware that he was becoming too intense and that his son was staring at him with something like horror on his face. He had gone too far, too quickly, talking as though Nicky were already betrothed, as though the girl in question were already a fact – as she was to him – as though it were more or less settled and only the matter of where the bride was to live while her husband was abroad was all that needed to be decided.

"I'm sorry, my boy." He grinned in that particularly engaging way he could summon at will and was relieved to see his son relax and even smile a little. "I'm carried away, you see, at the idea of grandchildren to continue our name and . . . our business. I know you have no interest in it, which was a sore disappointment to me – no . . . no, say nothing, it is too late now – but the thought of all that I and my father built up crumbling away for the want of a firm hand on the tiller is sometimes . . ." He even managed a break in his voice as he bowed his head and he was jubilant to see his son edge forward in his seat in sympathy. But he had not yet finished!

"I had not told you this, Nicky, but some months ago I saw a . . . a chap in Harley Street; you know, the place in London." He sighed dramatically. "Well, it seems I've been overdoing it a bit and must . . . take it easy, or at least *easier*. Oh, don't fret, lad, I'm far from done for yet and I have some good men working for me, but it would give me no end of a lift to know that one day there would be someone to carry on. Perhaps even yourself when you have had your fill of adventuring."

"Father, I had no idea." Nicky's voice was soft with compassion and his father felt the contempt work in him, wondering how a grown man could be so taken in by a few sad words. But what the hell, if it worked with this boy, for that was what he still was, then that was all to the good. Now, all he had to do was introduce Lily Elliott into the conversation, but he had no need to fret since his son did that for him. Well, not exactly her name, but the subject that they were discussing.

"It need be of no concern to you, my boy. These things happen but you see now why I'm so keen for you to . . . to be settled."

"I do, sir, but I cannot marry without a bride and how can I find such a person when I'm away so much? She would have to be . . . I would have to be . . . attached to her. You understand? I could not marry without . . . love."

Dear sweet God, did you ever hear such balderdash, but wasn't it typical of this soft-headed son of his. Love! As if that mattered when the woman in question was Lily Elliott. He remembered the day he had seen her mother and the way he had been bowled over by her frail beauty. That had been the closest he had ever come to loving a woman. It had come on him like a thunderclap, changing him from one man to another in the fraction of a second but it had not lasted. He had wanted her, her body and her soul, and when he had them both he had lost interest. He had been obsessed by her for months but it had taken the act of physical possession to cure him, for she had been as passive as a dove in their marriage bed. But her daughter would be different, he was convinced of that. What he had wanted from Jane Elliott was multiplied a hundredfold to what he wanted from Lily. If his obsession for Jane had spurred him on until he had her, this with her daughter was different in every way, as different as Lily was to Jane. Jane had bowed her head to him but Lily had defied him, sneered at him, shown her contempt and total lack of fear for him, her hate and loathing and she would fight him to the end. This was far, far more than an obsession. It was driving him to madness, a goad, a spur in his side that would not let him be. He knew he could never, ever get her back in his house, never, but his son could. If Nicholas could be persuaded to take her to wife and she could be persuaded to accept him, be convinced that he, Joshua Crowther, as Nicky's father and her father-in-law, was no threat to her, then he had won. He would win!

"Nicholas, dear boy, I have the very girl for you and since you already know her and, I think, are fond of her, then I can see no need for looking about us any further. Ah, I see you are bewildered."

"Bewildered is hardly the word for it, sir. I am totally amazed and can only say that I think you must be—" He almost said "mad" but something in his father's face stopped him. "I am to sail for Ireland at the end of January and can hardly conduct a courtship in that time. Then there is the girl's family, whoever they are . . ."

"There will be no difficulty there, my boy, since she has none."

"Has none? What do you mean? Who is she? And how do we know she will be willing and how do you know *I* will be willing, sir?" Nicky Crowther's face was set hard in the first defiance he had ever shown his father and Joshua took a deep breath, for this might be tricky. But then when had he ever shirked a challenge? In fact he loved one. It was the stuff of life to him and if this callow youth thought he was going to put a stop to his, Joshua Crowther's carefully conceived plans then he was in for a rude awakening.

"Son, will you do something for me . . ."

"I must warn you I cannot marry unless my heart is in it, sir." Nicky's voice was stern.

"I know that, my boy. You have told me so quite forcibly but will you listen to me for a moment, then decide. You must, of course, visit Lily before—"

"Lily?" Nicky's mouth fell open.

"Yes, our own Lily who has been so ill I have had to . . . well, you must remember her mother who suffered with a nervous complaint but who fully regained her health and even, at the end, gave me another child."

A child he had not seen in the six months since she was born, though Nicky was meant to believe by the way he said it that he cherished her.

"Of course . . ."

"Lily was devastated by her mother's death, as I was, and I'm afraid . . . well, I was forced to put her in the care of a woman in West Derby. Country air and total peace and quiet and I'm happy to say it is doing her the world of good. I could not leave her here with the child since she was unstable. You understand . . ."

"Dear God!"

"Indeed."

"Then . . . ?"

"I propose you go and visit her. Nothing would be more suitable but there is one thing I must add before you do."

"Yes, sir?"

"She . . . it . . . the illness left her with some strange fancies in her head which the doctor assures me will fade in time. She imagines things, poor girl, though in every other respect she is quite normal. I have decided to leave her with Mrs O'Connor for the time being since she is making such a wonderful recovery but I can only impress on you, that's if you take to each other, how happy I would be to know she is . . . safe. Safe with you."

Nicky shook his head in wonderment, not only at the sad tale his father had told him, but at his father's goodness and compassion, two characteristics he would not have believed could thrive in his father's heart. It seemed he was mistaken and he didn't quite know how to answer. He had been home on several occasions when he had had leave, just for a day or two now and again, and had been conscious of his father's wife and her pretty daughter on the periphery of his own life. But that was all. He had never really known either of them. He had been at school and then in the army, spending most of his holidays and leave with relatives or friends, since he was well aware what his father thought of him, and, more to the point, what he thought of his father. But it seemed he had misjudged him, and, besides, he would like to see the delightfully pretty little girl who had lived in this house for the past six years.

"There is just one more thing, Nicky, if you would oblige me."

"Of course, sir." Nicky found he quite enjoyed this comradeship, this warmth, this feeling of being in his father's confidence which he had never known before.

"The servants know nothing about Lily. They believe she has gone to stay with friends and I would like them to remain in the dark. You know what these women are like. They'd be visiting her on their days off, since I know she was a favourite of theirs so . . ."

"Of course, sir, you can rely on me."

"And Nicky . . ."

"Yes, sir?"

"If you don't find Lily to your liking you have only to say so, but if she is anything like her mother she will be a blessing to you, as her mother was to me."

For a second a picture flashed through Nicholas Crowther's mind and he grasped it uneasily. It was of a woman on the seashore, a woman of delicate beauty and yet at the same time of desperate sadness. A woman who carried tragedy about her in an almost tangible aura, like a mist which blurred that same beauty. She had been afraid of him, he had sensed that even though he had been no more than a boy, and he had wondered why. Why should he be a threat to his father's new wife who clung to her young daughter's hand as though to let go would heap all the horrors of hell on her?

He shook his head to clear the vision and at once it had gone, though it seemed to leave an unpleasant taste in his mouth.

"So, Nicky, will you go and see Lily? Will you call on her and tell her . . . well, perhaps it might be better if you took no messages from me."

"Oh, and why is that, sir?"

"She . . . in her illness she took against me, my boy, and I don't wish her to be reminded. Just visit her as though it were the most natural thing in the world for you to do, which it is since you are in a way related. If she asks how you knew where she was, tell her . . . tell her Mrs Quinn gave you her address. You remember Mrs Quinn, don't you? She was housekeeper when your stepmother was alive but she has retired now and gone to live with her daughter. I believe Lily kept in touch with her."

There was nothing Joshua Crowther did not know about his household and all those who lived in it. And all those who had once lived in it. For the past eight weeks he had been gathering information, unbeknown to them, using the clever, ferrety-faced man who had called on him this evening. He had gathered it all in, like a farmer harvesting his crop or a squirrel hoarding nuts against a harsh winter, collecting every whisper and rumour no matter how trivial it might seem. He even had the name of the "big chap". He knew of the *Lily-Jane* which had once been his in lieu of a debt owed him by Richard Elliott, and the identity of the man who had worked on her recently.

And he knew that he and Lily Elliott had sailed on her to Runcorn only a few days ago, delivering her to a shipbuilder to be restored and had returned via the steam ferry which plied between there and Liverpool.

She would be at the cottage in West Derby now.

28

The old lady who answered the door blinked at the sight of him. Her eyes had the vague and unfocused look of the dim-sighted and yet despite their vagueness they were the most vivid blue. With the arrogant ignorance of the young he thought she must be near a hundred, she was so wrinkled and grey-haired, and yet behind her stare of feeble-mindedness he had the feeling her brain was as alert as his own. Her eyes wandered from him to his bay which he had tethered to the gatepost and which was settling down to a good feed of hawthorn hedge.

"Aye?" That was all. Polite enough but letting him know she had neither the time nor the inclination to stand gossiping on the doorstep, even if he was the smartest thing she had ever seen in his soldier's uniform. He was not to know that her heart was thumping so hard she was sure he could see the beat of it under the bib of her apron. Her expression remained impassive.

"Am I speaking to Mrs O'Connor?" he asked her, removing his forage cap gallantly, ready to salute her, she thought, and had she not been so alarmed she might have preened a little. And really, *alarmed* was not the right word, for she was terrified out of her wits since she knew exactly who he was. Had not the child described to her in the minutest detail every single member of the household at Oakwood Place, just to be on the safe side, she had said, and this could only be that devil's sons. A soldier, Lily had said, and this was a soldier and though he was smiling the nicest smile and looked as though he hadn't a mean bone in his body Eva felt the thrill of dread creep along her old veins. How had he found them? How, after such a few short weeks, had Joshua Crowther's son found the secret haven Lily had secured for herself? She had felt safe, or as safe as she could be until Liam came home, she had said earnestly to Liam's grandmother, unaware that her innocent little face gave her away. Liam was her hero, it seemed, her support and comfort and when he came home she would be wholly safe, but until then only Liam's grandmother, herself, in fact, stood between her and the family from whom she had fled.

"Mrs O'Connor?" the soldier repeated, his smile deepening, although he was beginning to believe that perhaps the old lady was a bit simple. The old lady thought it might be advisable to let him continue to think so.

"There's no Mrs O'Connor 'ere, lad, an' I'd be right obliged if yer'd tekk that animal away from me front gate. It's eatin' me 'edge," she snapped at him, ready to shut the door in his face, for hiding behind it was the girl who, presumably, he was looking for. Lily had just come back from her trip to Runcorn and they had been about to sit down and drink a cup of tea while she told Mrs Earnshaw all about the marvels and wonders she had seen and the marvels and wonders that were to take place on her pa's schooner. And not only that, for on the journey Tommy had told her she had the makings of a first-class seaman! It had only been a short trip from Liverpool to Runcorn but she had obeyed all his orders regarding the sails, knowing which one was which and standing ready to adjust one should it be needed. *Lily-Jane* needed a crew of four but somehow they had managed it between them, sailing into the dock at Runcorn quite unscathed. Of course, they had chosen a calm day. Enough wind to drive them smartly along but the river as flat as a pewter plate.

She had been that excited, hopping about from foot to foot like some overgrown child, her face flushed, her eyes ablaze with exhilaration, her sadly shorn hair standing in a silvery halo about her head. It was a mass of tangled curls, blown about by the breeze on the river, for she had taken off her cap on the outward journey and already it was beginning to grow again, falling about her ears and neck in the most endearing way. That was what she was, endearing, this child who loved Liam; oh, yes, she could not hide it from Eva Earnshaw, and whom, she suspected, Liam loved in return. How could he help it? She had a way with her, a warmth and liveliness which had worked itself into Eva's heart and if this soldier thought he was about to come in here and wreck all their lives he was sadly mistaken. They had been so careful, too. Lily never left nor returned by the front door, slipping out from the scullery into the secluded bit of back garden, making sure there was no one about before moving like a breath of wind through the back hedge, the bit of orchard, across the field at the back of Elm House and on to Breck Road which led to Everton Brow, Richmond Row, across Scotland Road and on to the dock area.

It was fortunate that it was winter, they were to tell each other every time she went out, and cold, for it meant she could wrap up well in her layers of young man's clothing, Liam's boyhood clothing which Eva had altered for her, and which totally diguised her femaleness. With her cap pulled well down and her scarf pulled well up, it was hard to see even her lovely eyes which were almost invisible behind her Bert's spectacles.

It might have been easy to hide Lily when one of her neighbours called on her, which they had a habit of doing, for she was a sociable woman and had always welcomed them in the past, but it had been a bit tricky to explain away the dog. Villy barked, as dogs do, at every sound that was not familiar, and when Sadie Ainsworth had called, Eva could hardly shut the door in her face, could she? Sadie and she had been good neighbours for years, a comfort, not only to Eva but to Liam who liked to think someone was keeping an eye on his granny while he was away.

"I'm just mindin' 'er fer a friend." It was all she could think of to say when Sadie stood on the doorstep and stared in surprise at the small furry animal who leaped up to greet her like she had springs in her back legs. She was a friendly little thing who welcomed company and, like her mistress, you couldn't help but take to her, which made Puss very jealous.

"Wha' friends tha', then, Mrs Earnshaw?" Sadie asked, stepping over the threshold as she always did in expectation of a cup of tea and Eva had no choice but to let her, hoping to God Lily was well hidden behind the bedroom door. It had to be faced sometimes, the neighbours' questions, for they must have heard Villy bark. Dear God in heaven, it was hard to remember where she was up to sometimes, but she'd lie her head off for the poor lass who had been

so badly treated and who, it seemed, their Liam loved, and
so she did, hoping the good Lord would forgive her.

"Oh, 'tis one o' my Bert's old drinkin' pals from't Grimshaw
Arms. 'E . . . 'e died, yer see, an' . . . well, 'is lad come up an'
said would I see to 'is dog fer a week o' two, so I said I
would. She's a grand little thing, though our Ginger don't
like 'er."

"No, I don't suppose she would."

If Sadie was surprised, since Mrs Earnshaw's Bert had been
dead these twenty years, she said nothing. Not daft was Sadie,
and if Mrs Earnshaw had some secret, which Sadie had begun
to think was the case, it was nowt to do with her.

The soldier stood his ground though his face showed his
surprise. He was a good-looking lad, dark as the night with
eyes like chocolate and skin the colour of old amber just as
though he'd been in the sun for too long. She remembered
Lily telling her that he was in some God-forsaken place on
the other side of the world so she supposed that was where
he'd got his dark skin.

"Well, I was given this address by a Mrs Quinn," he said,
flushing – she could see it even through his amber colour –
as though he were lying and for some reason she became
even more afraid. He couldn't get past her without becoming
aggressive and if he tried she'd scream her bloody head off
until Ronny Biddle, who lived at the end and had a small
carpentry business in the shed at the back of his cottage,
and was always about, came running.

"I don't know anyone o' that name," she lied politely, her
face inscrutable. At the back of the door she sensed Lily's
sudden start but her hand, which the soldier could not see,
made a gesture that told Lily to keep quiet and to keep still.
The lad had been given the wrong name, a name that was
not hers but was Liam's and it would be wise to keep that
fact from him until she and Lily had a chance to talk. He'd
said Mrs Quinn, who was about Lily's only friend, had given
him this address but, knowing Mrs Quinn by reputation, Eva
was convinced she would not give it to the son of the man
who Lily feared above any other. She was tempted to ask
him, right here and now, if he knew what his father had
attempted with a sixteen-year-old girl, the daughter of his
own wife, but if she did it would give it away that she
knew Lily. And besides, her instinct told her that not only

was Lily in danger but that menace might be directed at Eva's grandson.

"Will that be all?" she asked the soldier, preparing to shut the door but at that moment, as though she caught the scent of something familiar, the blasted dog ran to the door and wagged her tail. She put her head on one side, considering the man at the door, her ears pricked, then, losing interest, she turned away and began to nose at Lily's hand where she stood hidden.

"Why . . . I know that dog," the soldier said. "I can't remember her name but she belonged to my . . . my step-sister. I've seen them together on several occasions. What is she doing here, Mrs . . . ?"

"Wha' she's doin' 'ere is nowt ter do wi' you, young man. That's if she's t' same dog which she's not. She's my dog, give me by . . . anyroad, I'd be glad if yer'd gerrof me doorstep."

"Villy, that was her name. Villy." The soldier looked inordinately pleased with himself, his young face breaking into a smile and at the sound of her name the dog, struggling in Lily's arms and not caring for the restraint on her, gave a heave and ran out from behind the door. She sat down abruptly and scratched her ear, then stood up again and looked at him, waiting to see what he would do.

"I've come to see Lily, madam. I mean her no harm, really I don't. I'm sorry that I told you a lie about Mrs Quinn but I thought . . ."

"There's no Lily 'ere neither, young man," Eva said despairingly. "I dunno, first Mrs . . . whatsername . . . then Lily. Yer'd do well ter get yer facts right afore yer go botherin' decent folks wi' yer nonsense. Me name's . . . well, what me name is is nowt ter do wi' you so you'd best be off. If yer don't I'll shout fer me neighbour an' then yer'll cop it."

She was doing her best to shut the door, dragging at Villy's collar as she did so when Lily stepped quietly out from behind it. Her face was like paper, her eyes enormous, haunted as though by some nightmare, but she squared her shoulders bravely and lifted her shorn head.

He did not recognise her. It was January, mid-winter and though it was not quite three o'clock, already a misty dusk was falling. The candles had not yet been lit and the only light was from the briskly crackling fire.

He was turning away, he was actually turning away, ready to apologise, returning his forage cap to his head, drawing his soldier's grey frock-coat about him when the flames of the fire caught on a fresh piece of wood that Eva had thrown to the back of the fire before the knock came to the door. As it flared up it lit the left side of Lily's face and he gasped, for though this was a young man standing before him he was the reincarnation of his father's second wife.

"Who . . . ?" His voice could barely be heard.

"You'd better come in," the apparition said, then turned away, shoulders that had been so courageously held slumping in what looked like despair.

"She wasn't there, Father. Whoever gave you the information made a mistake. There is no Mrs O'Connor. There is no one living at that address but an old lady whose name I forget and her young grandson who, I suppose, is about twelve years old. They did their best to be helpful, even calling in the woman next door to see if she knew of anyone answering the description of Lily but I'm afraid a blank was drawn."

Joshua Crowther looked into the bland face of his son and knew he was lying. True, the man he had hired to find Lily had not actually seen her at the address in Lower Breck Road but he was a man who had a reputation for reliability and tenacity and if he said Lily Elliott was living there, then she was. So he had got the name of the old woman wrong. Well, that didn't matter, but what did matter was that this son of his, who had gone cantering off on his bay this noon to call on the girl who was his step-sister, to befriend her, and then, if Joshua's plan worked, to court her, was lying to him, which meant that whatever tale Lily had told him he had believed.

And yet his face was as innocent as an infant's. His eyes were steady and clear of all deception and his father wondered what it was that had put backbone in his son at long last. He was not to know that Nicky had fallen, like Lily's father before him when he saw her mother, instantly and enduringly in love. He had followed the old lady, who had shut the door firmly behind him, in a daze of bewilderment into the tiny, firelit parlour. He had been ordered to sit down in an armchair by the side of the fire and he had obeyed silently, all the while staring at the back of the slim youth with the silver-gold curls, thick and swirling in a short cap about his head. The young man had stood with his hand on the frame of the doorway leading into some back recess of the cottage, clinging to it as though for support. The old lady lowered herself into the chair opposite him, folded her hands in her apron and waited.

The boy turned then and was not a boy but Lily Elliott!

"I don't understand," Nicky stammered. "Why are you dressed like that . . . like a boy? I don't understand. My father said . . ."

"So you are here on behalf of your father, are you, Nicholas Crowther? What has he told you to say to me? Are you to coax me to come back to Oakwood and . . . and . . ." She bowed her head, unable to go on, then she raised it again and her eyes were fierce with hatred.

"He killed my mother, did you know?" Her voice had taken on a light, conversational tone as though she were relating some misfortune that had happened to someone else. "My mother was not to have any more children, so I was told by . . . a friend. When I was born the doctor . . . but *he* didn't care. He wanted another son, so it was said, and so he never left her alone. They say that rape cannot take place between husband and wife but he raped her for six long years. But the death of my mother bearing the child he forced on her was not the only thing he did to her, for she was his . . . Once he locked her in their bedroom for a week and Mrs Quinn said he . . . Dear God . . . he did many dreadful things that I knew nothing of then since I was a child but I know now. So, now that my mother is dead it seems he has taken a fancy . . . to me. I am to be his next victim, did you know that, Nicky? He . . . laid hands on me." Her voice became ragged but she forced herself to go on. "He . . . he tried to rape me."

"Please, Lily . . ."

"He didn't say 'please, Lily'. He just threw me down and tore at my clothes and he would have succeeded had I not . . . I hit him with something but even then, when I had freed myself, he threatened me so I had no choice but to run away. He was right, you see. It would have been his word against mine, though I dare say Mrs Quinn might have backed me up. She knew what had been done to my mother, you see. So, there you have it. Your father is an evil man and, it seems, has even persuaded his son to do his filthy work for him. I don't know how you found me but it certainly wasn't Mrs Quinn who told you where I am for she doesn't know."

"He said you had been ill and that he—"

"I could have been ill. It quite makes you feel ill to be mauled by . . ."

The old lady stood up and moved towards the girl who stood, head bowed, by the kitchen door. She put her arm round her shoulders, clucking soothingly as a mother would with a child, but Lily inched away from her comfort as though she would stand on her own, as she had vowed to do when she left Oakwood Place.

"I shall have to find another hiding place now, for I know he will hound me, as he hounded my mother, until he has what he wants."

"No, Lily, believe me, I won't tell him, I promise." As he was speaking he wondered why it was he had been so naïve as to believe his father's tale of compassion and pity for his devasted step-daughter on the death of her mother, for there was no man in Liverpool who had a harder heart than Joshua Crowther. He had heard tales of his ruthlessness in business, his lack of any sort of feeling for those weaker than himself whom he watched go under without a qualm then took what little they had. He had despised his own son because he was not cut from the same cloth as himself. He had sent him away to school as soon as his mother had died and had not encouraged him to come home, even in the holidays. Nicholas had known no affection since the death of his mother and not until he had become an officer in the army had he found what could be called a family. So why had he believed what his father had told him? He didn't know but he knew this, he would not be taken in again. He had lived a carefree life since joining the army, enjoying the freedom and easy camaraderie, the social life to which, as an officer in a smart Liverpool Regiment, he was entitled. He had given little thought to anything much beyond enjoying himself, but his sudden deep flowering love, he could call it nothing else, seemed to turn him, he could feel it in himself, from an easy-going boy with nothing on his mind but pleasure to a man, a man with a great responsibility to this young woman whom his father had done his best to damage.

He would do anything in his power to keep her safe. He

would not let him get his hands on Lily Elliott again. Oh, if he could persuade her to it he would marry her as his father wanted him to do but he would never take her back to Oakwood Place. What a bastard he was, what a clever, conniving bastard he was, using his own son to get his filthy hands on this lovely girl, for Nicholas Crowther believed her story implicitly and if it had not involved a great deal of dreadful publicity for Lily, would have persuaded her to go to the police.

But that wouldn't do so he must protect her.

Joshua Crowther was still dressed in the black of mourning into which the whole country had fallen at the death of the Prince Consort just before Christmas and Nicky wore a black armband on his sleeve. The sad event had irritated Joshua inordinately, for it had been expected that all businesses would put up their shutters until after the funeral and he had lost one or two good deals because of it.

"So," he said disarmingly, drawing on his expensive cigar and reaching for the glass of brandy that stood at his elbow, "you are telling me that Lily no longer resides with the woman who was looking after her."

"That's if she was ever there, sir, which seems unlikely."

"You could be right, my boy. I never actually took her there myself so it seems we have both been made a fool of. Well, she must be somewhere and as I am concerned for her safety I shall make it my business to find out where."

"Oh, is that necessary, sir?" Nicholas said smoothly. "She is probably with relatives. Surely her mother's family would take her in."

"As far as I know she has no family. Her mother was an only child and I know nothing about her father. He died before I met Jane."

"I see, sir, then . . ."

"Then it seems she has . . . run away, my boy, and God only knows where she could be. But can I just say how much I appreciate your trouble. As to marriage, well" – he smiled his engaging smile, his dark eyes twinkling almost roguishly – "we must look elsewhere for a bride, mustn't we? A well-set-up chap like yourself will have no trouble in that quarter, I'm sure. Now, I'm for bed so I'll say goodnight and see you in the morning. Would you care to come hunting with me, perhaps? It starts from old Anstruther's place so . . ."

He noticed the hesitation in his son's voice and he smiled inwardly, for if the boy thought he could get the better of Joshua Crowther he was a worse fool than even he had believed.

"I'm sorry, sir, I have other plans."

"Of course, then perhaps we will meet at dinner. The Patricks are to go tomorrow, thank God, and it will be pleasant to be alone again."

"Are you telling me that there is absolutely no recourse open to me to get my ward back home again, Barker? That a sixteen-year-old child, a young girl, is to be allowed to wander about unprotected, living God knows where."

"You don't know where she is living, Mr Crowther? But I thought—"

Joshua made a sound of extreme irritation. "Of course I know, you fool, but I can hardly go barging in without some legal paper to say I am entitled to bring her home, can I? If she were my daughter . . ."

"But she is not your daughter, Mr Crowther." Mr Barker, of Barker, Barker and Jenkins, Solicitors, did not like to be called a fool, even by such an influential man as Joshua Crowther. "She is not even your ward from what you tell me, since you did not make the necessary legal arrangements. Is that correct?"

"Yes." Joshua shifted in his chair and pushed to the back of his mind the lie he had told Lily to the contrary.

"When her mother died you made no arrangements to become her guardian?"

"No."

"Why not, sir?"

"Because I did not think it would be necessary. I was not to know the silly child would take it into her head to run away, was I? And if—"

"Why *did* she run away, Mr Crowther? Have you any idea? She had a good home, luxury, affection, one presumes, and—"

"Dear God, man, are you implying she was mistreated?"

Joshua's brow was drawn down menacingly over his eyes and they glared into those of the solicitor. He had come to the conclusion after the sorry affair with Nicky had failed so miserably – and he supposed now it had been a daft idea, for could you expect such a fool to do anything right – he had better do what he should have done in the first place and that was to get the law on his side. It would be easy enough. Lily was a minor with no known living relatives. He himself was a family man with an impeccable reputation, so surely all he had to do was tell this blithering idiot to get on with it. To draw up the documents needed and then he could ride over to the cottage in Lower Breck Road and, with the help of the man he had hired, remove her from the protection of that woman, whoever she was, and return her to her rightful place which was in his home.

Albert Barker watched the shift and play of expressions that crossed his client's face and felt the first stirring of alarm. There was something . . . furtive about Joshua Crowther, something that was not quite right. He supposed the man was at liberty to be concerned about his dead wife's daughter but he had the strangest feeling that there was more to it than that. And he didn't really know why. Crowther had always been an arrogant man, even boorish at times, powerful in the town and therefore feared by many of the men with whom he did business. If he was crossed Albert had heard he could be quite terrifying and looking at him now he could quite believe it.

"So, what do you wish me to do, Mr Crowther?" he asked him patiently.

"My dear man, you have just told me there is nothing you can do. If there is no legal document you can draw up to . . . to insist that Lily, as a minor, must return to her home, to her family, then I am wasting my time."

"You could always have her made a ward of court, sir, if you believe she is in moral or physical danger."

Joshua sat forward eagerly. "That sounds just the ticket, Barker. What does it entail?"

"You would have to take your step-daughter to a magistrate's court where it must be proved that—"

"Would *she* have to be there?"

"Oh, yes, indeed."

"Allowed to speak to . . . to the judge or the magistrate or whoever presides over such matters."

"Oh, yes." Mr Barker sat back in his chair and wondered again why it was he felt so damned uneasy. Crowther was biting his thumbnail, frowning, his eyes staring at something only he could see and when, suddenly, he stood up and made for the door, Mr Barker also wondered why he felt no surprise.

"I'll think it over, Barker, and let you know. Who knows, the minx might come home of her own accord."

"I do hope so, Mr Crowther, I really do."

29

They had been in Upper Duke Street for two weeks when Tommy sent word that *Breeze* had been sighted in the mouth of the river. It was the second week in February and the vessel was a fortnight late.

For a moment she and Mrs Earnshaw just stared at one another in stunned, open-mouthed wonder, for though they had been waiting for this day since the beginning of the month, expecting the moment daily, now that it was here they were speechless. Then, as though prodded by the same goad, they were galvanised into action, beginning to rush about in high excitement, even Eva Earnshaw who, though fifty years older, became infected by Lily's intoxication.

"I want to look my best so I must wear my gown, Mrs Earnshaw, even if it will be a shock for Tommy and the other men to realise that I'm a girl and not a boy." Mrs Earnshaw smiled inwardly, for she had the feeling that the old seaman, who had been to their rooms a time or two in the last weeks to report on the progress of the *Lily-Jane*, had already guessed.

"I must be as presentable as possible, you see." Presentable, what a word to use to describe the girl who was as lovely as a spring morning, as exquisite and sweet-smelling as newly bloomed jasmine and yet as unconscious of it as a new-born infant.

"Now that Liam will be home there is no more danger," she chattered on. "Not with him to protect me. I won't have to wear boy's clothing any more, except when we sail on *Lily-Jane* which we will be doing soon. Oh, Lord, what d' you think he'll make of my hair?" with a quick, almost despairing look in the mirror. "He'll be shocked, I know, but I'm sure he'll understand, won't he, Mrs Earnshaw, though truth to tell I think it might be as well not to let on about . . . about what happened to me . . . or *almost* happened to me," shuddering. "Not yet anyway. Of course we'll have to explain why you are here and not in West Derby and why I'm not at Oakwood but . . . well, I'll think of that when the time comes. We can go straight back to the cottage now. You'll like that, won't you, Mrs Earnshaw? Oh, won't he be thrilled when he hears about the *Lily-Jane*. I think I'll take him at once to Runcorn to see how the work's getting on."

"Lerrim gerris legs under't table, lass, afore yer go rattlin' off ter Runcorn. An' yes, it'll be nice ter gerrome," as it had been a great wrench for Eva to leave the cottage to which she had gone as a bride fifty years ago. Naturally she couldn't let the child go to stay in Upper Duke Street on her own, especially with that lad hanging about night and day, but now, with her grandson home, they could all go back.

"Of course, but I'm so excited I don't know what I'm doing or saying."

"I can see tha', queen. Now settle yerself down a minnit while I get me breath."

"Oh, please, Mrs Earnshaw, please don't ask me to calm down, I just can't. I've waited for so long. Nearly four months and now, in a few hours I'm going to see him."

"I know, lass." Mrs Earnshaw's face was calm and under-standing. They had not spoken of it, she and Lily, but Lily gave it away in a hundred ways, the love, the strong, unbreakable bond that existed between her and Eva's grandson. Eva believed that as yet there had been nothing much of a physical nature between them, for in many ways Lily was still a child and her Liam was a full-grown man with a man's appetites. And he was too decent to take advantage of this sweet young girl who loved him. Lily Elliott was strong, brave, loyal and would make Liam a steadfast partner in life. She was seventeen in May and maturity would come.

Not that you'd think so to see her now, whirling about the three small rooms that Second Lieutenant Crowther had rented for them, her face as rosy as an apple, her eyes brilliant, her mouth stretched wide, either in high laughter or in the babble of words she could not seem to control. Villy raced round with her, sure that this was some wondrous new game and Ginger squirmed gracefully round a table leg begging for attention. The two animals were somewhat confused by this new place they lived in and, in a strange way, just as though they felt a trifle insecure, they now seemed prepared to lie down together in a comfortable tangle, friends in adversity.

They had come here in the dead of night, whispering from the cottage and into the hansom cab Nicholas Crowther had hired for them, their scant wardrobe hastily packed in Lily's carpet bag and an old lidded basket of Eva's. Eva had left a note pinned to Sadie's door to say she was going away for a week or two and Sadie was not to worry and she'd be in touch. Lily had written it for her, since Eva could neither read nor write, and neither could Sadie but she knew someone would read it to her.

So when the ferrety-faced man knocked on Sadie's door asking if she knew the whereabouts of the lady next door Sadie could say in all truthfulness that she'd no idea. Not that she'd have told him if she had, she said to Mary Jarvis who lived on her other side. Nasty eyes he had, the man who'd enquired, set close together and you couldn't see his mouth for the wealth of hair on his face. He'd looked none too pleased and had wanted to press her but Charlie had come to the door and he'd soon buggered off.

Lily and Eva had been quite amazed at Nicky Crowther's ingenuity, for the hansom cab had taken them no further than the stand in West Derby – going *away* from town – where they had changed to another cab which took them to the Zoological Gardens. They had walked from there, Nicky, not wearing his uniform, naturally, carrying their bags, Villy trotting on her lead and Ginger telling them all in no uncertain terms exactly what she thought of the adventure, even if she was tucked up snugly in a basket!

When they reached London Road and the cab stand at the end of Falkland Street, they had taken another hansom which this time went all the way to the furnished rooms in Upper Duke Street. If the cab driver was astonished, and he was, to be picking up a respectable elderly lady, a young lad with a dog and a well-dressed toff carrying a carpet bag and a straw basket in the middle of the night he made no mention of it, no doubt satisfied with the large tip the toff gave him.

They had been exhausted and though Mrs Earnshaw would have liked to inspect the beds before they got into them, even she was too tired to bother. Neither of them had heard Nicky let himself out and had slept until the middle of the next morning, causing Mrs Earnshaw to feel quite wicked. She had never before been up later than six thirty in her life!

Nicky Crowther had never enjoyed anything in his life as much as he did those eight days he spent calling at Upper Duke Street. He left Oakwood Place as soon as it was light, cantering off on Jasper, telling no one where he was going, startling the stable lads with his impatience to be away. He dressed in his oldest clothes, a pair of riding breeches he had discarded years ago, a warm tweed jacket and high-buttoned vest and shirt, with a sleeved cloak sporting slits up the back which was draped over his bay's rump. He wore no hat.

On the third day he did not notice a man on an ancient nag, a man who looked as though he were not accustomed to riding, follow discreetly behind him as he took the road to town. He was in love but only Mrs Earnshaw knew it and she said nothing. His love was as beautiful as her mother had been, even with her hair cut into a cap of short curls. It was streaked with gold and silver and swirled, shining in the sunlight or the candlelight, whenever she moved her head and he longed for nothing more, at that moment, than to run his hands through it. Her eyes reminded him of silvered ice in a winter's sunlight, silver and yet with a touch of lavender – or was it violet? – in them that was quite incredible. He would watch the slow rise and fall of her long, fine lashes, quite mesmerised by the unconsciously seductive movement. When she spoke, or even when she didn't, his eyes would drop to her full, poppy mouth, studying the way her tongue would moisten her lips. Her skin was like satin, smooth and fine with a bloom on it like a peach and he wondered what it would feel like to touch. Eva often marvelled that Lily never seemed to notice his close attention.

When they went out he wished that Lily would discard her boy's clothing and dress as a female, since she was safe enough with him, but when he asked her she refused, saying she wished to take no chances at this last moment. He was not even sure what she meant, though he supposed it was something to do with Mrs Earnshaw's grandson who was due home soon and who would take over Nicholas's self-imposed duty of guard while he was in Ireland. He meant to give up his commission in the army as soon as

he and Lily were married, which he hoped would be in the
very near future. She seemed to like him, to enjoy being
with him which gave him great encouragement, laughing at
his jokes, showing great interest when he spoke of his life
abroad, listening most attentively to whatever he had to say,
which he found quite exhilarating. As soon as his regiment
had done its service in Ireland he meant to ask her but until
then he would go slowly, for who knew how her brush, if
one could call such a horrifying experience a "brush", with
his father had affected her feelings for the male sex. She
needed time to recover and as she was so young time was
what he meant to give her. He was finding it very difficult
living with his father, knowing what he had attempted with
Lily but he knew he must keep up the charade, for Lily's
safety was at stake. They met only at the dinner table and
his father and Eloise kept up a light chatter, his father going
out of his way to be amusing. His sister seemed to think that
her forthcoming wedding was as fascinating to everyone as it
was to her, so conversation flowed smoothly with little effort
on his part. It was only for a few more days then he would
be off, he told himself, and when he came back it would
not be to Oakwood Place. He would buy a small house
somewhere and settle down, hopefully with Lily as his wife.
He had no need to work, thanks to his mother. Life stretched
out before him in all its perfection and in the meantime he
saw his love every day. They would take walks along the
Marine Parade, to the casual observer two young men on
their morning constitutional, and stroll beside the docks to
study the ships and watch the cargoes being discharged,
which was her favourite pastime. They would lean on the
railings of the parade and watch the ships running before
the wind up the river, the graceful vigour of the schooner,
My Lady of Plymouth, a dozen small, iron, full-rigged ships,
brigs and three-masted barques, flying clipper ships barely
seeming to touch the water, clumsy foreign coasters come
from Holland and France and Spain, or just watching the
tally man checking off the cargo as it came ashore.

Sometimes she would consent to go up to St James's Walk
at the top of Duke Street. There was a long gravelled terrace
with a seat on it from where you could see across the river
to the hills of Flintshire and Denbighshire. To the right of
the lighthouse there was a break in the hills which gave a

splendid prospect of the sea and the ships in the distance as they came in on the tide and made for the harbour. Further right the eye reached the most northern extremity of the Cheshire shore, called the Rock and it was round this that every vessel passed going in and out of the river mouth.

It was to this that Lily's eyes constantly turned though Nicky did not notice it.

When he left for the steamship that was to take him and his regiment to Ireland she kissed his cheek warmly and told him they didn't know what they would have done without him and the minute he was home he was to come and see them. They would be back in West Derby by then, of course, she told him and her eyes had shone with tears that he thought were for him. Would she write, he begged her, longing to pull her into his arms and if Mrs Earnshaw had not been standing beside them he might have attempted at least a brotherly hug.

So, yesterday he had gone and now, at last, the day had come for which she had waited since last October.

They took a hansom from the bottom end of Upper Duke Street to the cab stand in Castle Street, alighting behind the Custom House and walking down Canning Street to Canning Dock which was where Tommy had told them that *Breeze* would berth. They meant to proceed alongside the Canning Half Tide Basin to the lock gates and see her come in, perhaps with Liam at the wheel, Lily breathed ecstatically to Mrs Earnshaw, and then, when she was inside the basin, run back to the place where she would berth. Well, Lily could run, Mrs Earnshaw told her, while she followed on behind at her own pace, making that the excuse for letting Lily and her grandson have a minute or two to greet each other without her hanging at their backs. Her turn would come, but she had seen the glow in Lily's eyes and the hectic flush on her cheek and she was aware, for had she not once been in love, that she could not wait to run into Liam's arms.

Lily stood, as silently and as still as she had been almost four months ago when she had watched the lovely ship sail away, taking her heart, her strength, her love with it, her whole being concentrating on the quiet approach of the graceful vessel, quite unaware of the bustle around her. The deck and rigging swarmed with seamen all intent on the important task of getting *Breeze* through the gates and into safe harbourage. After the long and often dangerous journey they had just undertaken they did not want any accidents at this last moment.

Tommy was there and the piermaster, who had time to give her a surprised nod as he supervised the opening of the lock gates to allow the ship inside. The thrusting bow of the tall-masted clipper was very close to brushing the lock gate as she entered but it was not at her bow that Lily looked but at the wheelhouse, for it was there that she would catch her first sight of Liam. She felt as though she could not breathe, for her heart was beating so violently it seemed as if it were determined to leap up into her throat and she could feel herself shivering though she was not cold. Her eyes appeared to be misting over, for the figures in the wheelhouse would not sharpen and become clear and she tried to steady herself. Liam, my love . . . my love . . . where are you? I shall die if I don't see your smiling brown face in a moment, your hand raised to let me know you've seen me. Where are you?

The clipper passed beyond the lock gates and began to move slowly between the other sailing ships berthed there, through Canning Half Dock to Canning Dock where a dozen men were waiting with lines and all the paraphernalia needed in the docking of a ship. There was a gentle bump as whoever was at the helm in the wheelhouse guided *Breeze* to her berth and on the dock Lily felt the first thrill of terror grip at her guts, for it had not been Liam. Behind her Tommy exchanged an anxious glance with the man beside him whom Lily had not noticed and might not have recognised as her pa's old shipmate, Johnno, if she had. The glance said that there was something wrong here, for the first mate always stood either at the helm, or beside the captain at the helm when moving in or out of a port. It was a tricky business. There were tides and currents in the river that needed watching and often a pilot boat was used to give a hand. So where was the man whose job it was to be the right-hand man, second-in-command, if you like, of the master of the clipper?

The gangway was thrown out and several seamen moved down it while other men went up, making for the captain, stepping across a deck littered with ropes and lashed barrels.

A hand on Lily's arm made her jump, for she had been

frozen in a world she could not escape. Though her face was impassive and her figure as still as a statue, inside her mind was a writhing, seething coil of fear, none of it making any particular sense except the words, like a litany repeated again and again: Where is Liam? Where is Liam? Where is Liam?

"Come, lass," a stern voice said in her ears. "Let's gerr aboard. See, 'old me 'and an' 'elp me up that there gangway," which was as good a way as any, Eva Earnshaw thought, of fetching the petrified figure of Lily out of her trance.

The men on the gangway moved respectfully aside as the two women approached and the man who watched from behind a stack of barrels was not surprised, for the girl he had been following for weeks now was the sort of woman men could only stand and stare at in sheer disbelief. He had done so himself the first time he had seen her and he could understand the obsession of the man who had hired him. Now that the soldier had gone they were to make some sort of a move, his employer had intimated, but of what sort he had not yet said.

Lily was incapable of speech her mouth was so dry, but Mrs Earnshaw put out a hand to a seaman, telling him she'd be glad of a word with the captain.

"Well, 'e's right busy at moment, missus," looking at her askance and then relenting she was so upset and, anyroad, what did women know about the difficulties entailed in berthing a ship.

"Then . . . 'appen yer could tell me where I can find Liam O'Connor? 'E's first mate."

At once the man's eyes slid away, looking round for someone to take these women off his hands, for he was only a deck-hand and this was nothing to do with him.

"Well . . . I dunno as . . . yer'd best speak ter't captain, missus . . ." His voice trailed away and again so did his eyes, frantically searching for help.

"What's going on down there," a voice bellowed from the wheelhouse, "and what are those two doing on my ship? Don't they know no women are allowed on board? They must wait with the rest on the quayside."

There were indeed several women and some children, evidently waiting for their men, whom they had not seen for four months. Some, who had spotted husbands or fathers, were waving joyously and there was a feeling of great relief and happiness in the air which contrasted sharply with the dread despair that enfolded Eva and Lily. They stood numbly on the deck, waiting for God to tell them that their reason for living was gone for ever. Or perhaps for Liam to appear suddenly and swing them both into his strong arms. For someone to explain why he was not here among the men who, each and every one of them, was busy at some task. For the captain to ... to ...

The man they had accosted was seen to move hastily to the wheelhouse and say a word or two in the captain's ear and the captain, who had been red-faced with anger at the temerity of the two women, became quiet. He studied them uneasily then spoke over his shoulder to another seaman and with a heavy and obviously reluctant step, walked towards them.

They huddled together, Liam's grandmother and the girl who loved him and in those few seconds it took for him to reach them they both felt the life wither away and die inside them. His face was grave and yet his eyes were kind. He had the sort of pitying look assumed when bad news is about to be imparted.

"You were asking for Liam O'Connor, madam?" he asked Eva, since she looked the more composed of the two. The girl, who had been beautiful when she came on his ship but was now as haggard-faced as an old crone, stared into his face with terrible eyes.

"Yes." Eva spoke through clenched teeth.

"And you are?"

"Eva Earnshaw. Liam O'Connor's grandmother. We were told ..."

"Will you come to my cabin, ma'am, you and the young lady. It is not suitable for you to stand here under the gaze of ... Please, come this way."

They went obediently, following the captain down some steps so narrow it was hard to accommodate Lily's full crinoline, along a slip of a passage and into a tiny but neat cabin with a bunk tucked into one corner. In the bunk lay the figure of a man, a man so tall he was forced to bend his knees to lie in it. He was shivering violently, his wasted frame twisting and turning as though to escape something, his head thudding from side to side on the pillow. His eyes were closed. He was moaning softly. His lips were cracked and peeling and from him came a heat and a smell so dreadful both Lily and Eva recoiled away from him.

"I'm so sorry, Mrs Earnshaw," the captain said helplessly and it was only then that they knew that the mumbling, moaning body in the bunk was Liam O'Connor.

Eva put her hand to her mouth and swayed slightly, looking as though she might be about to fall, her small reserve of strength gone and the captain put out a solicitous hand to steady her. With a small agonised cry Lily flung herself at the bunk, kneeling down at the side and with a gesture that almost brought tears to the eyes of the watching man, drew his first mate's head to her breast, folding her arms about it and pressing her lips to his bony face.

"Liam . . . Liam, oh, my love . . . what has been done to you?" she cried softly, looking down at the emaciated caricature of the man she had last seen as an attractive, smiling giant before whom all other men were mere puppets.

"He had a . . . well, I don't know what it was, Mrs Earnshaw," the captain was explaining to Eva. "A fever of some sort when we were in Foochow but he insisted he was all right and I could not leave him in such a place. It must be something he picked up there . . . a pestilential hole if ever I saw one. None of the rest of the crew was affected but as the journey went on he became worse and . . . well, this is my cabin," which, though it was not meant to, revealed what a kind and Christian man Captain Fletcher was. Not many captains would give up their own cabins for a sick seaman.

"The men have been taking it in turns to watch over him, but there was little we could do. He has eaten nothing for days now and cannot keep even a sip of water down. I did not know what else to do, Mrs Earnshaw, having no doctor on board, except try to get him home. I'm surprised he has lasted as long as this."

He faltered to a halt, turning away from Mrs Earnshaw to look at the woman by the bunk who was smoothing the limp hair away from the face of the man who, in his opinion, was dying.

"He's a strong man, Captain, that is why, and because he knew I was waiting for him," she said without turning. "He has lasted this long . . . coming home to me . . . to us and we'll mend him, won't we, Mrs Earnshaw? I can only thank

God. I believed he was dead, you see. I know it's . . . Well, I would rather he was like this than dead." She kissed him passionately, this time on his cracked lips and as she did so his lids rolled back, revealing glazed and unfocused eyes. With a painfulness that was agony to watch he turned them towards the girl and into them came a glint of life.

"Lovebud?" he whispered wonderingly. The captain was amazed, for he had known no one for days.

"Yes, my darling, it's me. Your grandmother and I have come to take you home. Now, we shall need a . . . a . . . something to carry him home in, Captain, if you would see to it," the young lady told him crisply, "so if you would be so good as to get one of your men to fetch a cab and then accompany us to West Derby."

"West Derby? But I have a cargo to discharge, miss. I cannot spare—"

"Then see if there are a couple of men on the quayside who would be willing to help us. They would, of course, be paid, and quickly, please," for the man on the bed had lapsed once more into unconsciousness. "In fact there is an old chap, Tommy Graham, who was there when you docked. Ask him to come to me. Now, I shall want warm blankets, probably hot-water bottles, if you have such a thing. No? Well, warm bricks and . . . and . . ."

Suddenly her control went and she began to weep, but the man on the bunk did not feel her tears on his face, nor the strong arms that lifted him on to a makeshift stretcher. She held his hand for a moment, kissing it with such love the men who held the ends of it shifted uneasily as though they were prying into someone else's grief.

"Please be careful with him," she begged them, which they were, though if she could have seen the way he was tossed about coming round the Horn she wouldn't have bothered.

The man on the quayside watched in some surprise as the stretcher was carried awkwardly down the narrow gangway, the figure lying in it wrapped about like a parcel, the girl, *his* girl, the one he was following, anxiously hovering at his side, giving orders, snapping at the men when the stretcher slipped for a moment. It was quite a little group, what with the captain and his men, two chaps brought from the quayside, one of them as old as Methuselah with a white beard, the girl and the old woman, who seemed not to know what day it was, she was so bemused.

"Come along, dearest," he heard the girl say to her, taking her hand. "You won't mind sitting in the second cab, will you, then Liam will be more comfortable. I know you'd like to be with him but it's only for another half-hour then we'll have him home and in his own bed. We'll nurse him together, you and I. Tommy has the key and will collect Villy and Ginger and our things. Dearest, he's home, Liam's home and between us we'll make him well again."

As the two hansom cabs moved slowly off the man hurried back to his tiny slit of an office in Water Street to write his report to the man who employed him, eager to let him know about this surprising turn of events.

30

It took the cab driver, Tommy Graham's mate Johnno, Ronny Biddle and Lou Jarvis, who lived on the other side of the Ainsworths and happened to be at home, to get him out of the hansom, through the door of the cottage, across the parlour and – the most difficult part of the whole operation – up the stairs to the bedroom where he had been born and where he had slept, on and off, for twenty-seven years.

"Lay 'im 'on't floor, lads," Eva said briskly, herself again now she had recovered from the shock of his appearance and was busy with a task she understood. "Bed'll 'ave ter be aired and fires lit so keep 'im well wrapped up in them blankets. Aye, you stay wi' 'im, Lily," for Lily could not seem able to convince herself that she should let him out of her arms. She knelt on the floor with his head in her lap, his face turned towards her, her arms about his shoulders, never taking her eyes from his ravaged face. As long as she could hold on to him, see and hear his breathing, dreadful as it was, she knew he was still alive and until she'd got him well again she meant never to let him out of her sight. She'd sleep in this room beside him, she didn't care what anyone thought, and when he was recovered she'd sleep in the *bed* beside him, wedding or no, and if anyone objected, meaning, she supposed, Liam's grandmother, then she was sorry but it would make no difference. She was to spend the rest of her life with this man in her arms, the man she had loved as a child and as a woman for six, almost seven long years and she wasn't going to waste another precious minute!

They were all there, the men hanging about with their hands in their pockets, longing to help, for, as they muttered to one another, they'd not have believed it was Liam if they'd not seen him with their own eyes. That giant of a chap who looked as though he'd knock you for six no trouble at all, and was in reality as gentle as a lamb. It had been most unnerving, heaving him about like that even though he must be about six stone lighter than when he left, and that moaning, had Ronny noticed it? Lou muttered. Enough to really put the wind up you, and if you asked him, which nobody had, he'd not last the night.

The women came to see what Mrs Earnshaw wanted them to do, bustling round with kindling for the fires, the first to be lit in Liam's bedroom, the second in the kitchen range, for the oven would be needed for heating the bricks for his bed, and the third in the parlour where they meant to get Mrs Earnshaw to sit down and have a nice cup of tea. It was a waste of time, of course, for was it likely that Eva Earnshaw would sit on her bum drinking tea when her grandson was in urgent need of her attention, she asked them, rude with them, but they understood. Liam was her pride and joy. She had brought him up, got him to where he was today, and it could only be expected that she would be worried out of her mind about him, but what they wanted to know was, their exchanged glances said, who the hell was the young woman who was holding on to Eva's Liam like a limpet? A beautiful, anguished face, she had, and all the while they were moving about the bedroom, stepping over Liam to make up his bed and get out the clean nightshirt Mrs Earnshaw had ordered for him, they were thunderstruck when they observed her showering kisses on his face. Her bonnet, a pretty little thing of heather blue silk and decorated with fragile white silk rosebuds, had fallen off and they could hardly believe it when they saw how short her hair was. A tangled cap of silver pale curls shot through with gold. The loveliest colour they had ever seen and she, when she was herself, must be just as lovely.

It was like Lime Street Station, Sadie Ainsworth was heard to say, for no sooner had the men begun to drift away, leaving the women to their work, when, lo and behold, a splendid carriage drew up at the door with a groom in livery just as splendid at the reins. A respectable, grey-haired lady was helped down and the men drifted back, for it looked as though their day was going to become even more entertaining.

"Ta, Arnold, yer can gerron 'ome now," she said. "I'll find me own way back." She swept into the cottage without so much as a by your leave, pushing past them all, demanding to know where "her lamb" was, and if the women, who were trying to restrain her, didn't get out of her way she'd knock their blocks off.

They had begun to explain to her what was going on, as best they could, for they didn't know what was wrong with Liam O'Connor, when Tommy arrived in a second cab with Villy barking her head off at the commotion and Ginger spitting and scratching at everyone who came near her. A carpet bag and a straw basket were dumped on the parlour floor, then Tommy paid the driver and joined the men in the front garden, ready to run for the doctor, for surely he would be needed. It seemed to Molly that all that needed to be done, was being done. Her lamb was safe and so she sat down by the fire, her bags about her, and waited.

They had Liam warmly tucked up in his clean and aired bed when the doctor arrived and still the men shuffled about outside. The women were busy with kettles and pans of broth, eyeing the stranger and wondering who she was and, more importantly, who "her lamb" might be, shooing out the children who didn't see why they should be excluded from all the excitement.

It was only Lily and Eva who stood by the bed as the doctor examined Liam. Well, Eva moved respectfully away from the bed, standing back like a wooden image, her face carved and expressionless, but Lily hung over Liam, holding his hand, murmuring his name and kissing his cheek and Eva had time to wonder for a moment how strange it was that they were to take turns, she and Lily, in being calm. She had gone to pieces on the ship and Lily had taken over. Now, when they had him safely home Lily didn't seem to know what she was doing.

"Would you stand aside, young lady," the doctor told her irritably.

"Oh, no, please, let me stay here where he can see me when he opens his eyes," she begged him.

"I cannot examine him properly if you remain there. And . . . well" – he turned to Eva – "I shall need to strip him, Mrs Earnshaw and as this young lady is, presumably, not his wife, it would not be proper . . ."

"I'm not leaving the room, Mrs Earnshaw, tell him, will you and if he tries to make me I shall hit him."

"Well!" The doctor was clearly shocked, sensing hysteria which must be nipped in the bud before it spread, for there was nothing worse for a patient than a woman weeping and wailing all over the place. Not that she was doing either of these things but her face was a peculiar colour and her eyes wide and glittering which usually heralded a commotion. He knew Mrs Earnshaw only slightly, her grandson not at all, for the man had been at sea and, as far as he knew, had the constitution of an ox. The young man on the bed did not look as healthy as an ox now and, like the men outside, he privately thought they had called him too late.

"Explain to me the circumstances, madam, if you please. How has this man got into this . . . sad condition?"

" 'E's me grandson, Doctor. 'E's just got back from a sea voyage. China . . . where is it, Lily?"

"Foochow." Lily didn't even lift her head.

"Aah," the doctor said, as though that explained everything. "It seems your grandson might have picked up some eastern disease, a fever of some sort, for I believe they are rife in those parts. They are not as concerned as some of us are about hygiene and . . . well, cholera, typhoid, though I don't think this is either of those."

"Then what the devil is it?" the young woman at the bed hissed, turning a livid face to him. "Tell us what it is and how it is to be cured and we will cure him. He shall have the best of care."

"First I will examine him." The room was warm now and the doctor threw back the covers and draped them over the end of the bed.

"Help me with his nightgown," he said brusquely to no one in particular but expecting to be obeyed. At once, with something positive to do in the nursing of her love, Lily held Liam's head against her breast while Eva and the doctor removed his nightshirt and laid him naked on the bed. Eva was heard to moan, no more than a whisper in her throat, for she had seen her grandson when he was in his prime, a hard, muscular body, broad shoulders, firm flesh on him, his body shaped with that male beauty which is not often seen. Now the flesh was gone, leaving loose skin that lay in folds like that of a very old man over the skeleton of his frame. His closed eyes lay deep in their sockets, the cheekbones protruding, his lips loose and flat against the high ridge of his teeth, his nose arched above them. He had a thick golden stubble on the bony structure of his chin, like the plush of the cloth on Eva's parlour table. Every bone in his body stood proud, from the deep hollows of his collar bone, to his chest and below to where his ribcage stood out like the jutting of a sail. His belly was completely concave so that it seemed that at any moment what was beneath might break through. The bony ring of his pelvis formed a circle from which his stick-like legs appeared to dangle, like those of a puppet without the strength to move for themselves, even while lying down. Between them was the golden brush of thick hair that hid his genitals and though Lily had never before seen a man naked she seemed unsurprised that there was no apparent difference between male and female. Apart from the fine mat golden of hair that ran from his throat to the base of his belly and the absence of breasts, he looked scarcely dissimilar to herself. His feet were long, the fine bones in them vulnerable, fragile-looking, the nails long, horny and curved over the end of his toes.

The heat coming off him was fierce and so was the stink.

The doctor prodded and poked and did what Lily thought to be all manner of strange things. He pressed what he called a stethoscope to his chest, listening to his heart, he said, which had a good strong beat, which was encouraging. He peered into his eyes, rolling back the lids, lifting his arms and pressing in the armpits, then the groin, turning his ankles and wrists, twisting his head on his neck, studying every inch of him, even his back but there were no marks, no rash, nothing to tell him, it seemed, what was causing Liam O'Connor to lie like a dead man, or one soon to be dead.

"I don't know, Mrs Earnshaw, really I don't. Apart from the high fever I can find nothing to indicate what is wrong with your grandson."

"What shall we do, then?" the young woman at the side of his patient rasped. "Tell us what to do."

"There is nothing you can do, young lady, except pray."

"Pray! You call yourself a doctor and all you can tell us to do is pray. Well, I shan't pray so you can go to hell with your advice. Mrs Earnshaw and I will . . . will make him better, won't we, Mrs Earnshaw? He needs warmth and care . . . good food and between us we'll see that he has it, won't we, Mrs Earnshaw? I think a bath first, don't you?"

"Young lady, I know you are upset about your . . . your . . ."

"We are to be married, Doctor," she told him defiantly. "I love him and I intend to walk up the bloody aisle to him when he's better. I'll make him well. I'll make him well and without your damn prayers. When has God ever listened to my prayers, tell me that? What about my mother? Well, that is another story. Now, give him his fee, Mrs Earnshaw, and let us get down to the business of getting Liam back on his feet."

The doctor's voice was suddenly gentle, recognising what was in this young woman. "Get rid of his fever, Miss . . . Miss . . . and you might have a chance."

"How do I do that?"

"Cool him down. This room is far too warm. Cool his body. It is fighting the fever and he is almost dried out. Make him drink or his organs will be irreparably damaged. His body must maintain its normal functions. How long is it since he passed water?"

"Water?"

"Urine," the doctor said irritably.

"We don't know. We have only just brought him from the ship. The captain told us he couldn't keep even a sip of water down."

"He must be made to. Send someone to find some ice and pack it round him. Now, I'll leave you but I'll call again this evening."

Lily bowed her head, resting her cheek in what seemed to the doctor to be an indecent gesture on the man's bare chest but when she turned to him he could see the desolation and yet determination in her young face.

"I'm sorry if I was rude, Doctor," she said simply. "But you see I love him so much my own life will be ended if he does not recover. He is really all I have or care about."

There were enough of them, they told one another, to run the infirmary, let alone take turns in looking after one sick man. They'd form a sort of – what was the word? – a sort of programme so that one of them was always on call to give Mrs Earnshaw and the incredible young woman a break, but it seemed the young woman did not want a break. She would stay here, she said firmly, until Liam was well again, fixed to his side like a leech. If someone would bring her some water she would have a wash and change into . . . Into what? they asked her. And when she produced her shirt and breeches they were dumbfounded.

And so, not caring what she wore providing it was suitable for nursing Liam, she had changed from her lovely silk gown into a plain grey serge skirt and bodice loaned her by Elsie Biddle who was about the same height though much plumper. A belt was found from somewhere which she fastened round her tiny waist and even in the midst of so much drama Elsie was heard to remark that the dress had never looked like that on *her.*

It was not until an hour or so later that the woman who had arrived in the carriage and who had sat waiting patiently by the fire in the parlour stood up forcefully and said she must speak at once with Lily Elliott. Her face was pale and drawn and though she had drunk innumerable cups of the hot, sweet tea they had pressed absentmindedly on her, she was obviously at the end of her tether.

"Eeh, I don't think there's anyone o' that name round about 'ere, queen," Sadie answered her doubtfully. "'Appen yer've got the wrong 'ouse, or even t'street."

"Mrs Earnshaw's place in Lower Breck Road I were told," the woman answered firmly, "an' I believe this is it."

"Aye, but Mrs Earnshaw's norrin a fit state fer visitors . . . well, with 'er grandson poorly she's—"

"It's Lily I've come ter see an' I'm not movin' until I've seen 'er so yer'd best fetch 'er."

"'Ere, don't you go givin' me orders."

"Look, I've bin outer me mind fer weeks now wonderin' where she was."

"Well, she's norrere."

Sadie folded her arms dangerously over her broad bosom but when Elsie tapped her on the arm and whispered in her ear, she turned back uncertainly.

"Well, there's a lass upstairs wi' . . ."

"Fair lass wi' a lovely face?"

"Aye, that's 'er. She's wi' Liam."

"She would be. They've bin courtin' . . ."

"Yer what?"

"You 'eard. Now, if yer'd oblige me by runnin' an' tellin' 'er that Mrs Quinn's 'ere I'd be grateful."

It took but a moment, then Sadie came spinning downstairs again, the doctor behind her.

"She ses yer ter go up,' she hissed in great excitement as she handed the doctor his coat and led him outside, since he had professed a wish to speak to one of the men. Which one? Any would do as long as he was capable of obeying an order. And they were not to forget he wanted ice delivered at once. Where from? He didn't know, he said, but surely one of the inns had an ice house. He'd leave it to them, he told them, expecting to be obeyed.

Lily allowed Mrs Quinn no more than ten seconds of her time. Ten seconds in which they embraced silently, tearfully, then she was back at Liam's side prepared to sponge him down with cool water until the ice was brought.

"Eeh, lamb." Mrs Quinn was clearly horrified, for the lad hadn't a stitch on him and her lamb was as unworldly as the baby in the nursery at Oakwood. "Can someone else not do tha'?" She turned to the quiet figure on the other side of the bed. "You'll be Mrs Earnshaw, I reckon. Me name's Mrs Quinn," she explained. "I 'ope yer'll forgive this . . . this intrusion burr I've known our Lily since she were born, yer see, and 'er bein' a lass . . . if yer know wharr I mean, it's not right she should be . . . well, not wi't lad nekkid like that."

"I thought it were you, Mrs Quinn." Eva Earnshaw bowed her head politely in Mrs Quinn's direction, then rested it on the chair back in a gesture of total exhaustion. "Lily's spoke of yer times, but you try tellin' 'er to let someone else see to 'im. Yer might as well save yer breath ter cool yer porridge."

"Aye." Mrs Quinn sighed gustily. "She were allus like that from being a bairn. Like 'er pa, she were. Liked 'er own way burra sweeter child yer'd never find. Give yer't shirt off 'er back, she would, so yer see, when she run off like that . . . well, she left me a note, like, burr I didn't know where she were, norr until Master Nicky told me. 'Don't breathe a word to me pa, Mrs Quinn,' 'e said, so I knew exactly what 'ad gone on an' why she'd run off. I . . . I looked after 'er ma, yer see." There was no need to elaborate. Mrs Earnshaw knew exactly what Mrs Quinn was getting at.

"Anyroad, soon as I knew where she were I were up 'ere like a shot. Me son-in-law's groom at Oakwood an' a chap ter be trusted so 'e fetched me up 'ere but yer were gone. No one knew where, or wouldn't say, more like. Yer've some good neighbours there, lass."

"I know."

"An' if yer need any 'elp yer've only ter ask. I've nowt ter do all day now 'cept look after me grandchildren an' I reckon our Victoria can cope on 'er own fer a bit."

"That's kind o' yer, Mrs Quinn, an' yer welcome ter come whenever yer want burrit seems lass won't give 'im up to anyone an' if she does I've plenty o' folk what'll tekk over."

"Can I . . . can I stop fer a while then, Mrs Earnshaw? Not that child's gonner tekk any notice o' me at moment burr I . . . well, I've missed 'er an' just ter sit an' watch 'er'd do me a power o' good. 'Ave yer tried borage?" she asked abruptly.

"Pardon?" Mrs Earnshaw was clearly startled and even Lily looked up from her frantic effort to get a sip of water between Liam's cracked lips. She had devised the simple method of holding his nose and when he opened his mouth involuntarily, she poured a teaspoon of the liquid into his mouth. He would retch a little and the water would come back but each time it happened she patiently repeated the process, hoping some of it would stay down.

"Borage. It fetches down a fever. That's if yer can gerrim ter keep it down. Or hawkweed which yer can pick on't roadside. Then there's marigold." She stopped apologetically. "Me granny were a country woman, yer see. From up north somewhere an' she wouldn't 'ave a doctor in th'ouse. She allus said what God sent were good enough fer 'er. 'God always puts cure alongside ill.' I've 'eard 'er say that times. She lived ter be eighty-four," she finished simply.

A deep silence followed as the two women who loved Liam O'Connor digested this astonishing fact, then: "Borage?"

"Aye. It's what's known as a febrifuge. That's what Granny called it. It'd do 'is waterworks good an' all. Funny 'ow yer remember things. Granny used ter send us out ter gather it when we was nippers, then dry it so I suppose—"

"Where would we get it?" Lily interrupted.

"Well, anywhere in't th'edges. It must grow along this lane an' if yer can't find it—"

"What does it look like, Mrs Quinn? If you went with Tommy or one of the other men could you point it out to them?"

Mrs Quinn looked thoughtful. "Well, it's bin a long time burr I reckon I'd know it. Aye, then all I 'ave ter do is remember 'ow Granny did it. An infusion . . . an' if I can't find it I reckon apothecary in't village'd 'ave it in stock. Dried. Now hawkweed, yer 'ave ter infuse it in white wine an' . . . Dear 'eaven, it's bin so long . . ." She wrinkled her brow and Eva and Lily held their breath. "Three or four cupfuls a day."

Lily felt the despair catch her in its iron grip. Three or four cupfuls a day and it was all she could do to get a teaspoonful of water past his lips. He lay like a man laid out for his coffin, his skin stretched, parched, fiery with heat and with no trace of relieving sweat. He was dying before her eyes, she knew he was and there was nothing she could do to stop him. Nothing even the doctor could do to stop him except advise her to pray but she'd be damned if she'd give in. She had known Liam for six years. She had met him on the seashore every few months during those six years, reinforcing their friendship, a child's friendship with a grown man which had not seemed extraordinary to her who was the child. She had loved him with the simple, trusting love of a child but she had not really known him, she realised that. He had had another life running parallel to the one in which she was a part and it was only his kind heart, his sweet nature, his compassion for a lonely child that had kept him coming back to her.

But the child had grown into a woman and the child's love had become a woman's love. Liam had told her before he went to China that he loved her. She had clung to him, a woman's body clinging to a man's and she knew enough now to realise that a man's body is easily aroused. He had kissed her and held her in his arms but how much of that was due to his good heart, his sympathy, indeed to her own firmness of purpose which had always led her to believe that she had only to fight for something long enough and hard enough and she would have it. Like the *Lily-Jane*! Like Liam O'Connor. She was that same woman who had said goodbye to him that day on the quayside but she wasn't that woman any more, which sounded very muddled but it was true. She knew with every instinct in her that she loved Liam, that she would never love another man, ever. It was deep inside her and she knew, as a woman knows, that it was right. And, when he was recovered, for recovered he would be, she thought savagely, if it turned out that what Liam felt was no more than strong affection for the child he had rescued, a sense of responsibility that had grown with the years, then she would fight for him, turn his feelings of affection to desire, to love, to need. She had loved two men in her life, her pa and Liam, and now, if Liam was to survive and she was to survive she must measure her strength, wrestle with the forces that had turned Liam into this twitching, mumbling, stinking hulk on the bed. She had to bring him back if only to find out if Liam, the man, loved Lily the woman, as a woman and not as the child he had been kind to.

While she continued to ease the water, teaspoon by slow teaspoon into his mouth, forcing it open by pinching his nostrils, first Eva, then, when she was ready to faint with exhaustion, Sadie or Mary or Elsie, sponged him down with cool water. They turned his poor, emaciated body with ease, the indignity of it no one's concern, for if they stopped for a moment to consider the poor bugger who they manhandled, young Lily Elliott, as they knew her now, was at them, cutting as a whip. Four of them in turns, all through that day and then the night, not even stopping when the doctor came, and at the head of the bed Lily went on hour after hour, dripping water into Liam's dried-up body, allowing no one to take a turn, for she did not trust anyone but herself not to drift into sleep or generally fall by the wayside. Her face was a ghastly mask and her eyes sunken and haunted.

"Well, he's holding on," the doctor said after he had poked at him again, listened to his heart and asked if he had passed any water, shaking his head when he was told that he hadn't.

He sighed then, pulling at his lip and Lily knew that though he was not totally dissatisfied, he did not believe Liam would make it.

"And you'd best take a rest, young lady," he told her, "or we'll have two patients on our hands." She ignored him, of course, that's if she even heard him.

Tommy and Mrs Quinn had found the hawkweed and

infused the leaves in some white wine which Ronny Biddle had run to fetch from the Rose and Crown on West Derby Road and in between the water Lily forced a teaspoon of the febrifuge between his lips.

He began to hallucinate the next day, shouting for someone called Frank to "get that sail sorted out", throwing himself about so that in the end they had to tie him to the bed with soft rags to stop himself from flinging himself out of bed. It was difficult, almost impossible, in fact, for Lily to get any sort of liquid inside him. They had to hold him down, the women, forcibly restraining his head while in desperation she poured a half-cupful of the infusion down his throat, waiting hopelessly for it to come back. Which it did and in it was the first spotting of blood.

"Mrs Quinn . . . oh God, Mrs Quinn," she moaned to the woman whose turn it was to sit with her. "I'm losing him . . . I'm losing him."

"No, lamb, no . . . don't give up. Never give up. See, let me 'ave a turn while yer rest in the chair for 'alf an 'our. Mrs Biddle'll be 'ere in a minute to 'elp me."

"No, I can't leave him. I'm so afraid that he might . . . go without me here to hold him back. I . . . I feel that's what I'm doing, Mrs Quinn. Though he doesn't know me, or anyone, I have this strange feeling that . . . that it's only because I'm here that he doesn't slip away."

Tears poured unchecked down her face which was a travesty of her lovely one of a few days ago. Her hair was in a snarl of sweat about her head and she smelled almost as bad as the man on the bed. Apart from the necessary few moments when she left the room to relieve herself, she had not left Liam's side since they had brought him home.

Suddenly, without warning, her eyes rolled up and she slid into a boneless, graceful heap beside the bed.

31

She was in Mrs Earnshaw's bed when she came to and for a moment, though she was surprised to find herself where she was, it was just like any other morning. She sighed and stretched and yawned, turning to gaze out of the window at the silky strand of blue sky she could see beyond it. There was a horse chestnut tree, bare now of leaves, and usually found in and around fields to provide shade for farm animals, which had somehow rooted itself in the corner of the small garden where it had been even before Mrs Earnshaw and her new husband had come to live there. A blackbird fluttered from branch to branch, its song a melodious trill rising and falling, its tail raised and fanned and she watched it from the bed. The cottage windows were small, but low, the sills almost on the floor and she could see the tree, the hedge on the other side of the lane, and the fields beyond the hedge where a man was ploughing, plodding along in the straight furrows behind the steady, rhythmic pull of the horse.

She turned and stretched again and beside her Villy raised her head and pricked her ears. Lily smiled, reaching out her hand to her then suddenly remembrance hit her and with a frantic leap she was out of bed and across the tiny landing to the bedroom where Liam lay. Her heart was pounding so fiercely she thought she might faint in sheer terror. She had no idea how long it was since she had . . . well, she supposed she must have fainted, for you don't just fall asleep standing up, do you? She had no idea of time, barely of place, for everywhere was quiet except for the pitter patter of Villy's paws following her across the polished wooden floor.

He was there, just where she had last seen him, lying neatly in the bed and sitting beside him, one on either side of the bed, were Mrs Earnshaw and Mrs Quinn. Mrs Quinn was holding his nose while Mrs Earnshaw dribbled something into his obediently opening mouth. They had established a pattern, it seemed, working in perfect harmony, smiling at one another, exchanging the occasional word as they gazed down at the gaunt, stubbled face on the pillow.

She tiptoed to the door of the room, almost tripping on the hem of the voluminous nightgown which she recognised as Mrs Earnshaw's, wondering why they had not put her in one of her own. She had been bathed, she could sense that, for her skin felt clean for the first time since they had brought Liam from the ship, and she felt refreshed, she realised, but still the anger began to grow in her. They had washed her and put her to bed while she was not herself, just as though she were a child to be bundled off to bed when the grown-ups had something important to do. How dare they! How bloody well dare they, and here they both were, smiling and nodding at one another as though there was absolutely nothing wrong.

"What in hell's name d'you think you're doing?" she hissed venomously from the doorway and they both turned in surprise. Mrs Earnshaw's expression at once became disapproving, but Mrs Quinn's fell into that familiar, long-suffering look which said what else could you expect from a self-willed young woman like her lamb. They'd got her to bed only because she was unconscious and she'd slept the night through and looked much better for it, but Molly knew they were going to get it in the neck for daring to nurse the young man without her being there to watch over it all. She said the only thing that she knew would distract her.

"'E's keepin' it down, lamb. 'E's still unconscious, though I reckon it'll not be long afore he ses summat. Me an' Mrs Earnshaw 'ave tekken it in turns ter see to 'im while yer 'ad a rest burr 'e's—"

"Has the fever broken?" She flung herself at the bed, crouching down beside it, putting her hands on his face and forehead, brushing back his lank hair in an agony of love and remorse for leaving him, almost tipping over the small bowl Mrs Earnshaw was holding and from which she was spooning the infusion.

"No, not yet, lamb, but doctor's 'opeful it'll be terday and then 'e'll be on't mend."

"I'll get dressed then and take over. Where are the things Mrs Biddle lent me?"

"I sponged an' pressed 'em while yer were asleep. They're on't chair. Mrs Earnshaw's gonner mekk over summat of 'ers for yer, then . . . Eeh, Lily Elliott, yer can't do that 'ere. Not wi't lad lyin' in't bed. Wharrif 'e opens 'is eyes?" for Lily had dragged the nightgown over her head, revealing her slim and lovely body in all its nakedness. Both the women stared in horror at the perky lift of her breasts, the nipples pink and bud-like, her waist no more than a handspan, her buttocks tight, her legs long and shapely. It was the figure of a young girl, only just matured but the strangest sight was the thick bush of *dark* hair between the confluence of her legs. They didn't know where to look, really they didn't, for neither woman had seen another female naked and even their husbands' bodies had been a secret thing in the night. Naturally, Mrs Earnshaw had been privy to Liam's body as a child and, though she would never have told him, had caught a glimpse of him in his full manhood when he took a stripped wash in his bedroom. That was why she had been so dreadfully shocked at his present state.

"If he opened his eyes then I should get down on my knees and pray as the good doctor advised; in the meanwhile I shall put on my drawers and shift; see, I'm decent already," she went on, tugging Elsie Biddle's sensible garments over her tangled curls. "I'm ready now so I'll take over, Mrs Earnshaw."

Mrs Earnshaw was elbowed aside and her mouth thinned dangerously. She and Lily had got on well during the weeks they had been alone together, waiting in harmony for Liam's homecoming. She had been appalled at the reason for the child's escape and flight from Oakwood Place and was happy to take her in, but this was her grandson and she didn't like being pushed aside as though she counted for nothing. She was well aware of the child's devotion to Liam and her terrible need to be nursing him back to health, if that was possible, but she resented this total disregard for her own commitment to Liam.

"Wharrabout summat ter eat, lamb?" Mrs Quinn was saying diplomatically. "Yer've 'ad nowt much fer days an' if yer not careful yer'll fade away ter skin an' bone."

"I'm not hungry, Mrs Quinn, really I'm not. Please, hold

his nose for me so that I can get this spoon in his mouth," for in her distress Mrs Quinn had forgotten to continue with her task.

"Then let me bring yer a bite up 'ere. Wharrabout a bacon sandwich wi' porridge ter start with and a nice cuppa tea?"

"I think Lily should go downstairs an' 'ave a proper breakfast," Mrs Earnshaw interrupted brusquely. "Sadie's in't kitchen an' she'll cook it for 'er an' then there's that dog ter be walked. It'd do yer good, lass, ter gerrout a bit."

"I can't leave Liam, Mrs Earnshaw, not for another minute. I've spent enough time away from him as it is. What if he should come to and not find me here?"

"I'll be here, child."

"I know," Lily said patiently, as though speaking to a half-witted child, "but I would rather . . ."

The old lady drew herself up and, leaning over Lily, took the spoon from her hand. "I think it might be as well if summat were established right 'ere an' now, lass. This is my 'ome an' this is my grandson an' I'd be obliged if yer'd give over ordering me about as if I were a housemaid. Now, go an' 'ave summat to eat and then when yer come back yer can tekk over for me. D'yer understand?"

It looked as though Lily were going to argue. Her face, which had been pale and drawn despite the night's sleep she had had, turned turkey red. She looked from Mrs Earnshaw's face to Liam's where it lay so appallingly still on the spotlessly white pillow and she could feel her heart wrench as she was pulled into a whirlpool of terror. He looked just as he had for the past few days and now and again a faint moan escaped him. Even the strongest body cannot endure the ravages of a consumingly high fever for long and it seemed to her that Liam had very little reserve to see him through. She could not bear to leave him but her innate sense of fair-mindedness told her that Mrs Earnshaw was right. Though she wanted to send them all away, take Liam in her arms and hold him, force the breath of life and living into him, her *own* life, her absolute will that would bring him back to her, she knew that she couldn't do it on her own. She had to keep strong. She had to keep her health in order to give Liam's back to him and she couldn't do it if she didn't eat.

With that surprising sweetness that was part of her she bent impulsively and kissed Mrs Earnshaw's cheek.

"I'm sorry," she told her. "I'll go and get something to eat and take Villy up to the orchard but . . . but I won't be long."

"I know that, child," and the two women smiled at one another and began patiently to spoon the infusion once more between Liam's cracked lips.

She was by herself, both Mrs Quinn and Mrs Earnshaw having creaked downstairs to drink a cup of tea with a promise to send up whoever was on duty in the kitchen to help her, when she sensed the difference in him.

She was leaning over him, her elbows on the bed, her chin resting in her cupped hands, her eyes studying every hollow and protruding peak of bone in his face when something ran, like a tear, from just below his hairline. It was slow-moving, thick and viscous. She watched it in fascination, then there was another and another until his whole face was bathed in it. It popped out in greater and greater gobs from his neck and the backs of his skeletal hands which rested on the covers and even as she watched the light sheets were wet with it. She put her hand wonderingly to his face and it came away with a slick film on it. She was puzzled, confused, but as her eyes looked down at him his eyes opened. His face was blank in the thin shaft of sunlight that peeped through the partly opened windows, then his eyes focused and turned, looking straight at her.

"Lovebud . . . ?" he asked questioningly, just as he had on the ship, his voice no more than a breath and the hairs stood up on the back of her neck.

"Liam . . . oh, Liam, my love," she whispered.

"Lovebud . . . is it . . ."

"Yes, yes, it's me," and the bed shook with the force of her weeping.

"I dreamed . . ."

"Dearest, don't talk . . ."

"Put . . . your . . . arms . . . round me, lovebud. Don't let me go . . . again . . ."

She scrubbed at her face with the palms of her hands, then got to her feet and lay down beside him. With infinite care and tenderness she slipped one arm beneath his neck and drew his head to her breast where he settled with a sigh, too weak to do more than let her cling to him. She kissed him, lifting his chin a little with trembling fingers so that her lips could rest on his, all the while the healing sweat pouring from him in such a torrent she knew she must call the others to change the bed, to sponge him down, to send for the doctor and do all the things that would begin the process of healing, but just for this moment she must have him to herself. To savour the feel of him in her arms even if he was scarcely aware of it. To allow herself for a few precious minutes the joy of having and holding this dear man to herself. She was so completely his. She had been for many years, living only for him to come home to her, even as a child. Now he was completely hers and she held him in gentle but strong arms, putting off the moment for a little while when she must share him again with others. His sweat was soaking into her bodice and it was turning cold but for that moment Liam O'Connor belonged absolutely to Lily Elliott.

They all wanted to come in and have a look at him, even the men, believing that this miracle must surely have returned him at once to the giant of a man they had all known. His face was still shadowed with his illness and of course Lily would not hear of it, for she guarded him now like some ferocious little terrier, taking no notice of his grandmother's pleas to see to her grandson, for he was hers, *hers*, Lily Elliott's and she was going to nurse him back to full health. They could help her if they wanted, she told them loftily, take turns while she rested in the chair by the fire in his bedroom but she would not leave his side, no, not if the Queen up in London demanded it.

The doctor had been and gone, quietly optimistic that his patient had turned the corner, praising the nursing he had received, saying his pulse was slow and strong and his heartbeat good, telling them to keep him warm now, build up the fire, but leave the windows open, for clean air was efficacious to a man who has been ill. Light food, milk, eggs, broth, sleep and more sleep.

Liam slept for two days, a deep, natural, healing sleep, waking only to take the nourishment Lily spooned into him. He had begun to recover in the normal fashion of a healthy young male, beginning to look more like himself though still painfully thin. He watched Lily whenever he was awake, his eyes following her round the room and when she came back after a necessary trip to the privy, they would be waiting for her return. She would kneel at once by the bed, leaning over to kiss his healing lips as though they had been parted for days, gently at first, then with growing urgency, for it seemed both their bodies were in the grip of some sort of growing need. His flesh was weak, feeble, laughing ruefully about it, but his mind wasn't, his eyes told her.

When she was not there, even for half an hour while she took a bath in front of the fire in Mrs Earnshaw's room, he became restive, testy, irritable, fractious, demanding to get up, pushing aside the restraining arms of Mrs Quinn or his grandmother and saying he thought he might take a turn round the bedroom at least. He quietened the moment Lily came back, sinking into his pillows, overcome with his exertions but sighing contentedly when he saw her.

It was this that exploded the vast battle of wills between not only Mrs Earnshaw and herself but with Mrs Quinn. They found her on the third day of his recovery sorting out a pile of clean sheets and blankets, and several pillows, folding them and tucking them neatly into the corner of the room. She was wearing the pale grey woollen skirt and bodice that Mrs Quinn and Mrs Earnshaw had contrived between them for her to wear in the sickroom. Well, Mrs Biddle's reeked of Liam's sweat and needed to be scrubbed before being given back to her. She had washed her hair and it stood about her head in a cloud of soft silver, curls tumbling about her neck and ears and drifting across her forehead. Her eyes were clear and shining with happiness and in her cheek had crept a tinge of carnation. She was thin, like a scarecrow, she said, though Liam, on the mend now, denied it, his eyes straying to the soft swell of her breast.

"What's them for, queen?" Mrs Earnshaw queried, her eyes narrowing suspiciously as she placed a glass of milk, in which a tot of whisky and two eggs had been beaten, on the table beside Liam's bed.

"They're for me," Lily answered airily, hoping even now that there would be no argument. She looked at Mrs Earnshaw from the corner of her eye, then sighed, for she knew it was a vain hope. There had been fierce disagreements, carried on in whispers, over the return of Liam's normal bodily functions.

Mrs Earnshaw had said, and Mrs Quinn had agreed with her, that it was not right and proper for a young, unmarried female to be involved in the embarrassing fetching and carrying, not to mention the cleaning of his body, of a young, unmarried male. She had been overruled only because Liam had turned awkward, and could you blame him, Mrs Quinn said, at the idea of Lily performing such an intimate task for him. She had given in over that but she wasn't going to give in over this.

"For you?"

"Yes, I intend to sleep in here next to Liam's bed until he is well enough to get up himself."

"Over my dead body, lady."

"Mrs Earnshaw, I have been sleeping in that chair by the fire ever since Liam came home so what difference—"

"Aye, so yer 'ave, burr 'e were unconscious then, an' me and Mrs Quinn" – who had been sleeping on the sofa in the parlour – "were close at 'and."

"You'll still be close at hand but I can't leave him alone."

" 'E'll not be alone, lass."

"Mrs Earnshaw, will you stop interfering in what is mine and Liam's business. We are to be married, for God's sake."

"Liam 'asn't said so an' until 'e does . . ."

He hadn't said it to her either, not recently, but his eyes had told her what was in his mind and hers had responded, but how could she explain that to his grandmother. They had discussed nothing yet, for he was still too weak to do much at all beyond a nod of his head, a quiet yes or no to a question, but she knew and so did he. The doubts and uncertainties that had plagued her while he was ill had been swept away the moment he had turned his head into her breast when the fever broke, but it was all so recent she was afraid, terrified, to let him out of her sight, even while she slept, even while he slept. He was still so frail, so helpless and until he was strong again, himself again, she meant to sleep beside his bed.

They couldn't move her, saying it was not proper, that it was not suitable, that it was not decent.

"D'you think I gave a damn about that?" she snarled. "I love him, don't you understand, and I need to be with him," which was true. Her need was greater than his in reality and at last they understood and though they were in unison in their disapproval of it, they let it be.

At the beginning of March he could sit up with a heap of pillows behind him. Whenever anyone came to see how he was, which Lily allowed now as long as they did not tire him, and they asked him how he was he always answered "hungry", his grin stretched wide across his gaunt face. They had begun to make plans. Tommy Graham had been to tell them of the progress of *Lily-Jane*, asking hesitantly had "the captain" sorted out a crew yet, believing implicitly what the "lad", now, amazingly, the "lass", had told him about the future enterprise that was to begin as soon as the captain was up and about again.

"Well, I think I have one crew member here, Tommy," Liam told him, taking Lily's hand in his and putting the back of it to his lips, which so embarrassed the old man he nearly fell off his chair. "But I shall need a mate and a deck-hand so . . ."

"Well, sir, there's Johnno, which is why I asked. Miss Lily'll remember 'im. 'E sailed on't *Lily-Jane* wi' 'er pa, 'e ses, so 'e knows the craft like back of 'is 'and."

"Well, there we are then. A full ship's complement before she has her first cargo."

"An' what'll that be, Captain?" Tommy wanted to know, his seamed face showing his eagerness to be on the deck of a ship once more. Old he might be, but he was experienced and as lively as a man twenty years his junior.

"I don't know yet. But Lily and I will come down to the docks as soon as I'm on my feet, won't we, lovebud," and the questions that bubbled in Tommy Graham's practical mind froze on his lips at the strange promise, not of cargoes, he was sure, that lay behind the words.

He had been home three weeks. Mrs Quinn had finally gone back to Victoria's cottage, quite reluctant to leave, for she and Mrs Earnshaw had taken a great fancy to one another. Mrs Earnshaw was in her own bed and across the small landing her gentle snores could be heard. It was midnight and the house was quiet with the peace that comes when great content has entered it. The fire was aglow in the fireplace and the clock ticked sweetly above it. Lily was sprawled in the chair, her feet bare, her nightgown riding slightly up her calf. She was half asleep already. Beside her was the little bed she had made for herself and when she was sure Liam was asleep she would get into it. She slept lightly, waking at the slightest sound, lifting her head to look at Liam, ready to call Mrs Earnshaw if he needed the special "slipper" bedpan made from brown glazed earthenware, or the glass urinal the doctor had provided.

She sighed and turned to look at him, smiling when she saw that he was watching her. There was a spark of something in his eye which suddenly excited her and she sat up slowly.

He held out his hand and she rose and went to him, putting her hand in his. He drew her down to sit bedside him on the bed, then reached up a hand to the back of her head, drawing her mouth down to his. His kiss was gentle but she sensed a compulsion in it, something urgent that he was making a decent effort to control.

"I love you, lovebud," he murmured, smoothing his hand over the tumbled cap of her curls, smiling a little at the absurdity of it. His lips moved to her jaw then dipped to the faint, childish hollow of her collar bone and without conscious thought she wrapped her arms about his head and pressed his face close to her. He murmured something, his hands at her shoulders now and when they pushed aside the neckline of her nightgown, drawing it down to reveal the satin smoothness of her breasts, she did not object. His hand moved to cup one tight, hard-nippled bud, then his mouth followed and she arched her neck and back to accommodate him, moaning softly in the back of her throat.

"You're beautiful . . . so lovely," he told her, his eyes filled with wondering delight. The child was no longer a child but a woman who was ready to flaunt her love and her desire for him with no thought of false modesty or even the shyness that a woman displays when she is beneath a man's ardent gaze for the first time. His hands began a slow, enchanted wandering, exploring the fine bones beneath of her shoulders, her ribs and finally, as the nightgown was disposed of by one of them – did it matter who? – the curving column of her spine, the soft curve of her waist and hips and down to the vibrant centre of her woman's body.

She was breathing hard now and so was he but he knew she must be the dominant one, for though his masculinity was urging him on and on, his slowly recovering body was lagging behind.

"My love . . . lovebud . . . you'll have to help me . . ."

"Tell me . . . tell me what to do," she gasped, ready to fling herself down beside him, or should she sit up; she didn't know, she only knew she wanted something this man could give her and she wanted it at once. Her body, *inside* her body there was a rippling like overlapping flames, hot and ready to burn her and yet her skin was so tender, so sensitive, she thought a touch could . . . could bruise her. Dear Lord, she was so . . . so . . . she didn't know . . . she didn't know.

"Lie here, beside me, face to face. Dear God, I've watched you, wanted this, but . . ."

"Liam, dearest . . . let me . . ."

"Yes," guiding her hand, "but please . . ." He was gasping a little with what seemed to be laughter.

"What?"

"Be gentle with me."

"Oh, Liam, I love you . . . love you."

Some instinct, some intuition that had come to her woman's body told her what she must do. Slow, delicate, her movements fitting to his, hers the stronger but the building pleasure of his body giving him strength. When he entered her it was as it should be, hard and thrusting and she gasped as she bore down to meet him, then she knew no more as a flood of something she had never before experienced carried her up and up and into a world of colour and light and darkness and shadowed wonder, and when she came down from it he held her in trembling arms, his face pressed to hers, his breath harsh.

"Liam . . ." Her voice was high, almost like a child's, and yet with something in it that was not at all childish.

"Yes, my lovebud?"

"Did you . . . did you experience what . . . ?"

"Oh, yes, my darling, but you were so . . . overcome you didn't notice." He was smiling in great satisfaction.

"I'm sorry."

"Don't be sorry, my love. What you had was what every man wants to give to the woman he loves."

"Will it always be . . . like this?"

"I've no doubt of it, lovebud. Now, put your head on my shoulder and go to sleep."

32

"As soon as I can get out of this bed, Gran, Lily and I will be married," he told his grandmother the next morning, just as though he were informing her of an appointment he had made and forgotten to tell her about. He and Lily studiously avoided each other's glance, both of them aware that the flush of remembrance was warming their faces. Lily could actually feel it flood from her hairline right down to her toes. Not that she was ashamed nor even embarrassed, but it had been so startling, so wonderful, so passionately tender, so ... so private, belonging only to herself and Liam she was reluctant even to share a hint of it with Mrs Earnshaw. She wanted to turn away and busy herself at some task, like the folding of the blankets which, last night, had not been used, but she could hardly show indifference when Liam was announcing their intention to marry, could she? She was still floating in some separate space that was not vouchsafed to other women, and until Mrs Earnshaw had entered the bedroom, carrying Liam's breakfast tray, had been kneeling at his bedside, fully dressed by now, naturally, and engaged in the pleasant pastime of telling him of her love and wonder, of kissing him at the back of his ear which he seemed to like and of arching her back as his fingers traced the nipples of her breasts. If Mrs Earnshaw had not been somewhat heavy-footed she might have caught them at it. As it was Lily had only time to leap up and hastily rearrange her clothing before she came into the bedroom.

"Is that so?" Mrs Earnshaw said grimly, as though Lily were the last girl she would have chosen for her Liam.

"Yes, it is so, Gran. Have you any objection?"

"I'm not sayin' I've any objection; wharr I am sayin' is

it's not before time. All these weeks sharin' a bedroom an' what the neighbours must be sayin' I shudder ter think, fer that Sadie, though a more good – 'earted woman I've yet ter meet, she's a sharp one an' misses nowt. Mrs Quinn agrees wi' me, an' all, an' as she's the only one 'oo can claim a kinship o' some sort wi' Lily, then she's entitled to 'er say."

She banged the tray down on the table with great force, slopping the creamy porridge that she insisted on spooning into Liam at least once a day over the side of the bowl, appearing to be deeply offended; then with a gesture that showed her true feelings she turned and dragged Lily into her arms and kissed her soundly.

"Eeh, lady," she said, apropos of nothing, it seemed, but it was as though she were telling her she was completely aware of everything that went on under her own roof. She wasn't born yesterday, nor even the day before!

She turned back to her grandson, a glint of tears in her eyes, holding his head to her breast for a moment of deep emotion. Then, with a sniff, she picked up the tray and set it before him.

"Yer'd best get that down yer then, fer yer'll need all 't strength yer can get. It'll be a few weeks afore yer can gerrout o' that bed so . . ."

"I intend to try this very day, Gran." With his free hand he reached for Lily's, confirming Eva Earnshaw's suspicions, for the child blushed the rosiest red. In her eyes was that look she had seen in her own when she and her Bert had first been wed and it came from something more then being young and healthy.

"Well, lad, yer can fergerrabout that, can't he, Lily? Now, lass, yer must back me up on this," she added anxiously. "'E's not fit enough ter swing 'is legs over 't side o't bed, lerralone walk."

"We'll see, Gran. With Lily helping me . . ."

"Lily! Look at 'er. She couldn't carry our Ginger, she's that thin."

Lily trusted her voice for the first time since Mrs Earnshaw had come into the bedroom. Just the touch of Liam's hand on hers had the power to spin her into this delicious sensation of melting, particularly at her knees, a melting pleasure so strong she wanted to sit down before she fell down. She could feel her insides beginning to flutter, as though a bird were trapped there, and she could sense a gasp of something that might have been a moan similar to the ones she had uttered last night, rising to her throat as she spoke.

She had to clear her throat before the words would come out. "I think he should try, Mrs Earnshaw. Look how much better he is now. Even if it's only across the bedroom. He's . . . he's quite strong."

"Aye, I shouldn't wonder," Mrs Earnshaw said drily. "Now, go and 'ave yer breakfast. There's bacon an' egg in th'oven. Anyroad, I want ter talk ter me grandson, so off yer go."

There was a letter propped up against a jar of primroses set in the middle of the white-clothed table. It had come by the first of the nine daily postal deliveries and was addressed to her. It was from Nicky Crowther, asking her why she had not answered his letters, for this was not the first he had sent. Almost from the first day they had arrived, sometimes two a week, and in each one he begged her to be careful, to be wary of his father, to stay beside Mrs Earnshaw and never go out alone. He missed her so much, he said, and though he had not wanted to say anything just yet, her silence was worrying him and he felt the need to tell her that the feelings he had for her were very strong. Please, please would she write and let him know she was safe, otherwise he would simply desert and come back to England to find her.

The bacon and egg were left to congeal on the plate as she sat back slowly in the chair. During the past weeks she had been vaguely aware of the letters coming from Nicky. She had even read them, though their contents had gone by her, as insubstantial as smoke from a chimney. She had been too concerned with Liam, too preoccupied with wresting him back from the snapping jaws of death to bother about Nicky Crowther's anxiety for her. She would be eternally grateful to him for what he had done for her and Mrs Earnshaw and she would write and tell him so, but she would also tell him she was to marry Liam O'Connor, Mrs Earnshaw's grandson, as soon as possible, and he must not write to her again. Liam wouldn't care to have his wife corresponding with another man, would he, particularly an officer in the army. Besides, she wanted to forget that part of her life now that she was to embark on a new one. Not forget Ma, of course. She could never do that, but forget the family who had wreaked such havoc on hers. She had heard that Eloise was to marry in a week or two. Mrs Quinn had said the servants were all going to watch the ceremony at St Anne's Church on Holmes Lane but that didn't concern her. Nothing the Crowther family did concerned her. She would marry Liam, that was all that mattered to her, and they would take *Lily-Jane* and sail away just like Pa and Ma used to do. The dream she had dreamed as a small girl was about to be fulfilled. She would never be a seaman, not like her pa and Liam were seaman, with a Master's Certificate to prove it, but she would have the next best thing which was Liam teaching her what *he* had learned. She would be part of the schooner's life, she would be part of Liam's life, not just as his wife but as his partner in a business they would build up together.

It was enough. It was all she had ever wanted. Except for one small thing, and as the picture of the baby her mother had given birth to last year came into her mind she leaned forward and, crossing her arms on the table, put her forehead on them. Abby. She would be nine months old now, living with her nursemaid in the nursery, and though Mrs Quinn had told her that the servants made a big fuss of her, spoiled her when they could, for all children need a bit of spoiling, she was a child without family, without a father's or a mother's love and the thought distressed Lily immeasurably. There was nothing to be done about it, but sometimes she felt the pain and guilt of it pierce her heart. She knew about loneliness, for since Pa died, though Ma had done her best, Lily had missed that absolute security, those loving arms to hold her and she felt guilty that she could not provide them for her half-sister.

Mrs Earnshaw bustled into the kitchen, putting the tray down on the table and moving to the oven where Liam's bacon and eggs were keeping warm.

She tutted when she saw Lily's plate. "I told yer ter get that lot down yer, child, unless yer want ter be ill an' all. There's not a pick on yer. An' what's that lad in Ireland said ter upset yer? Oh, aye, I knew t' letter were from 'im, that's why I never mentioned it in front of our Liam." The look on her face implied she'd skin Nicky Crowther alive if he hurt her, or indeed anyone in her family.

Lily sighed and pushed the heavy fringe of her hair off her forehead. "Oh, it's not him, Mrs Earnshaw."

"Granny!"

Lily blinked. "Pardon?"

"Yer'll 'ave ter call me Granny, now that yer ter be me granddaughter-in-law." She smiled complacently, as though the whole affair had been personally contrived by her.

Lily stood up and put her arms about her. She was taller by half a head but somehow she managed to put her forehead on Eva's shoulder.

"It will be lovely to have a family again," she said softly. "So . . . Granny." They stood for a moment smiling at one another in affectionate understanding, then she drew away, beginning to frown again.

"It's . . . I was thinking about my sister. My half-sister. The thought that she is to be brought up by that monster gives me nightmares, but there's nothing I can do about it. This letter from Nicky reminded me and then there are other things that must be spoken of. You understand?"

"Aye, lass, I do."

She would have to tell Liam. So far, he had not even questioned why she was here at his grandmother's cottage, presuming, she supposed, that she had come as soon as Mrs Earnshaw had got word of his arrival in port. That day when *Breeze* had berthed was not in his memory at the moment but it must all be explained to him before they married. The thought terrified her. Not for herself who had been an innocent victim but for Liam who, when he heard what he had attempted and when he was able, would simply tear Joshua Crowther limb from limb. She knew it without a shadow of a doubt. Easy-going, good-hearted, gentle as big men often are, a man who abhorred violence, his rage would be an explosion of such proportions it could scarcely be imagined. He was a man with a man's need to protect his woman, and his woman's reputation, his *wife's* reputation. She was to be his wife, take his name, and the man who had been her mother's husband would be made to pay for what he had done. Liam had walked through the years beside her, seven years now, and had seen, perhaps even known what sort of a man Joshua Crowther was, but it had not been his business then. Now it was!

Eva took her hand in hers. "Let's get lad on 'is feet, child, afore we start worryin' about what's ter come. When 'e's ready we'll tell 'im together." Though she sounded cheerful, optimistic even, Eva shook her head at the thought of it.

Liam continued to improve, eating enormous amounts of his granny's home-made bread thick with fresh butter, piled high with slabs of cheese. Broths thick with meat and vegetables, beefsteak puddings with mashed potatoes and freshly picked cabbage, home-cured ham with eggs, roast chicken with the skin crisp and brown, apple pies and cream, rice pudding and lemon creams and the flesh crept back on his bones almost overnight. He drank the milk that was brought over from the farm and when, at last, he got out of bed and tottered down the stairs, to the accompanied cheers of every inhabitant of the four cottages, including five dogs, six cats and an assortment of kittens who capered about the garden like butterflies on the wing, it was like a party. Villy and Ginger, who were devoted to one another now, watched in astonishment before curling up companionably together in the warm sunshine.

Mrs Earnshaw had whispered in Sadie's ear that Liam was to come downstairs that day and though there was not enough room in the house for everyone, they were all there. The men drank the ale Mrs Earnshaw had had fetched up from the ale-house and the women had a glass, or even two, of her cowslip wine and the merriment was loud and boisterous. It was a Sunday. It was April and winter had finally let go of its hold and allowed spring to take its place and the improvement in Liam's health was a joy to them all. They sat in the deliciously warm sunshine, crowding about the bit of grass, the children spilling out into the road, watching slyly as Liam held Lily's hand, for they all knew by now that they were to be married at the end of the month. The banns had been called at St Mary's Church in West Derby and a dress was being made by Miss Jenny Hardcastle, a clever young seamstress who had just started up a business in the area and was eager to please. There was a rumour that a double bed had been ordered for the young newly weds who were to stay with Liam's granny until the ship, that one he and Lily had bought, was ready, when, presumably, they would sail away together, or so Lily said, though the women smiled, for if Liam was any sort of a man, and he was, his bride would be pregnant before the may was in bloom. They had all been invited to the wedding, every last one of them, and though Lily was, in their opinion, a lady, a lady with a way of talking that was nothing like theirs, they forgave her for it, accepting her into their midst if only for the fact that her love for their Liam, whom they had known since he was a nipper, had saved his life and shone even now like a candle in her eyes.

There had been, to both Liam's and Lily's regret, no resumption of that one night of love they had shared several weeks back in Liam's bed, for Granny had declared that as he was so much better, Lily's bed could now be brought into *her* room. They were to be decently married, she told them tartly, as though she were well aware of what had happened, fixing them with a stern look that made them both blush. Of course, now that he was on his feet again and the weather fine enough for a walk across the stretch of back garden and into the orchard, which was an enchantment of budding apple blossom, they had the opportunity for many a stolen moment and in the days that followed they would both return in a breathless state, flushed and glowing, and Eva was thankful it was only two weeks to the wedding.

Liam's chests containing the artefacts he had bought while he was in China had been stored at a small warehouse at the back of Canning Dock, Tommy told them on one of his visits. Tommy seemed to have taken up the duty of first mate on the *Lily-Jane* before she had even put to sea, trudging up from the docks with messages on the progress of the schooner, which was expected to be ready by the middle of May, expressions of goodwill from the piermaster and from the captain of *Breeze* who had been delighted that Liam had made such a wonderful recovery. As he had said to Tommy, in confidence, of course, and he was not to repeat it, he had not expected to see him reach Liverpool. No, a funeral at sea had been his forecast, he had said, shaking his head gloomily. There was a message from Johnno who was made up at the thought of sailing on the *Lily-Jane* again and, as word got round, and perhaps remembering Richard Elliott's reputation for fair dealing, expert seamanship and trustworthiness, there had been one or two enquiries on the possibility of cargo. A Mr Atkinson, a merchant in a small way of business in Water Street, but growing, wished to have a consignment of salt taken across the Irish Sea, bringing back cattle and would be glad if Captain O'Connor would call when convenient. There were men who needed someone to carry their iron and steel, their machinery, their cotton goods, their woollen goods, their bricks, cement, their timber, stone, manure, china clay and pitwood. There was no shortage of cargoes to be carried to small ports around the Irish Sea and Lily and Liam clasped hands, their heads together, their kisses scarcely interrupted as they planned for their vivid future. Liam had several buyers for his exotic imports from China – fine porcelain, silks, fans, silver dishes and ornate ivory and lacquerware – which were to be sold to help to pay for the renovations to *Lily-Jane*. Several days before the wedding Sadie Ainsworth's lad ran down to the hackney stand at the corner by the Zoological Gardens to fetch a cab to take Liam and Lily to the docks.

Lily was dressed in her heather blue gown and puff bonnet, a parasol of white lace lined with blue silk that Liam had brought back for her held above her just like the lady she was, the neighbours told one another as they watched her and Liam climb into the hackney. Liam, though still somewhat lean, not quite fitting into his good suit as yet but becoming bronzed by the sun that had shone for the past month, was as tender with her as if she were made of spun sugar, which made the women smile. They had seen her perform gargantuan tasks when Liam was at his worst, almost physically lifting him single-handed, going on hour after hour in the wearying task of nursing him back to health. She was beautiful again now, with that ethereal radiance that she had lost when it seemed Liam was not to recover. Her hair, which Liam had insisted she grow again, was beginning to fall about her shoulders and her slenderness, in that strange way of women in love, women who are loved, had begun to fill out. Man feedeth woman, the saying went, and if Lily Elliott was anything to go by, it was true. Not that the plumpness of her own hips and breast was anything to do with her Charlie, Sadie was heard to remark. Mind you, he never left her alone which probably accounted for the seven children she still had at home, *and* her comfortable frame!

They took the excursion steamboat to Runcorn, disembarking there while the remainder of the passengers were to go on to Manchester by the Canal Packet via the Mersey and Irwell Navigation. They would do it one day, they promised one another, for it should be very interesting, but at that precise moment their whole attention was focused on the walk down to the docks and the schooner that awaited them there.

Lily was ready to weep, clinging to Liam's arm, so filled with joy was her heart. It was the happiest day of her life and yet, she sniffed to Liam, the saddest. If only Pa could have seen her as she is now, she said, looking at the sleek lines of her newly painted timber, the polished wood of her deck, the elegant lift of her two new masts, the gleam of her new white sails, furled up neatly to the cross-spar. He had done his best, she knew that now, but *Lily-Jane* had been allowed to slip away into disrepair and now she and Liam had brought her back to life and she did her best to imagine that somewhere, wherever seamen go when they die, he was watching and gloating over his schooner's resurrection. She'd be ready in two weeks, the shipwright told them and did they want him to fetch her up to Liverpool? an eager expression on his face, since she was a lovely ship.

"No," they said in unison, then looked at one another, smiling, their minds attuned so that they each knew that what they wanted was to bring her home themselves. "Let us know when she'll be ready and we'll be over to pick her up."

"What, both of yer?" The man was clearly surprised.

"Yes, my future wife is as keen a seaman as I am."

They were married on a day of pale pearly blue skies and glowing golden sunshine, the last day in April when the swallows went mad with joy as though in celebration of the day, swooping and swirling about the trees surrounding the churchyard and a carpet of newly blooming harebells hazed the grass with azure. They were trampled on by a hundred pairs of feet, for the crowd come to watch the serious bridegroom and his exquisite young bride as they passed out of the church into the sunshine was extensive. Mrs Earnshaw had lived in these parts for fifty years and was well known, and, of course, the recent illness of her handsome grandson, who had not been expected to survive it, had been a miracle. Mind you, they had heard that his bride, a lady, no less, had fought tooth and nail to keep him alive, though to look at her you wouldn't think she could nurse a kitten. All in white and looking as though she were treading on moonbeams with a face on her that would charm the gods. Smile, she was in heaven with it all, you could tell that, and he looked as though he'd been given the moon and the stars all rolled into one. They told one another they had never seen a happier-looking couple, though it was a well-known fact that a girl's wedding day was the happiest day of her life.

Mrs Quinn cried sharply, telling anyone who would listen that the child was the spit of her mother who Mrs Quinn had known at almost the same age. All those from Oakwood Place who could sneak time off had come, even if it was only a quick dash in Mr Crowther's carriage – he didn't know, naturally – driven by Arnold who was Mrs Quinn's son-in-law and would get the sack if he was found out. Jenny, who once Lily had read to while she peeled the spuds, Dorcas, Rosie, Betsy and both Maggies. They waved and threw flower petals and told one another that she deserved it, the dear little thing, and even Mr Diggle, with Will hanging bashfully at his back, had thrown down his spade and come across to see her wed.

They watched her climb into the hired carriage, the big chap, as they had always called him, fussing tenderly about his bride, their erstwhile little mistress, though she had never really been that, and blessed the gods who had sent someone, at last, to protect her. It was the happiest day and well worth the chance they had taken of slipping across to see her.

The rest, neighbours and friends, guests, even Tommy and Johnno and the piermaster, who had been invited to bring his wife, crammed themselves into Granny Earnshaw's small cottage, or sat on the grass in the garden beneath the shade of the massive and beautiful horse chestnut tree which was in full bloom. They toasted the bride and groom, not only with ale and cowslip wine but with, of all things, a sip of champagne purchased for the occasion by the groom. Mrs Earnshaw, with the help of Mrs Quinn, who came over regularly now, had made the bridecake, rich in fruit and brandy and decorated with the most intricate white icing and, at the end of the day, as darkness fell, though some of them, the men particularly, wanted to carry out the old tradition of seeing the new husband and wife to their bed, they left reluctantly, telling one another it had been a wonderful day and wasn't it splendid that after all the drama of the last few months it had all ended so happily.

They slept at last in their new bed, Mr and Mrs Liam O'Connor, the door firmly and legitimately closed against all comers, conscious of Granny across the landing but not minding, for she was slightly deaf after all.

He had made love to her, not with the uncertain frailty of the last time when he had been only just recovering from his illness, but with the full and lusty passion of a healthy young man. Strong, forceful, claiming what was his, with no concern for gallantry or gentleness, hasty in his need to make her his *wife*, his woman, *his*. He took her with a force that nailed them together, his heavy body crushing hers and she answered him fiercely, for there had been weeks in which his hands and his lips had driven her mad with a desire that they could not satisfy. His invasion, when it came, almost split her asunder and again, as it had the last time, waves poured over her, flames devoured her, leaving her drained, docile, submissive, possessed. His!

He sighed with great satisfaction when she lay against him, her sweated body plastered to his, her face in the hollow beneath his chin, his arms possessively about her.

"I love you, you know that, don't you," he told her almost angrily as though still contesting any man's right to take what was his.

"Dear God, I should hope so," she murmured drowsily, her lips against his throat, "after all that."

"You liked it?" He sounded a trifle smug.

"Mmm. I was just wondering when we were going to do it again."

33

They were to sail the day after tomorrow, taking Mr Atkinson's cargo of salt to Londonderry in Northern Ireland, bringing back Irish cattle, a round trip of ten days, allowing for the discharge of the cargo and the loading of another. They had brought back *Lily-Jane* three days ago, the short journey from Runcorn to Liverpool nothing short of a triumphal journey of hopes fulfilled. It had culminated in the schooner's entry into her berth at Canning Dock where men who knew her, and of her new owners, Captain and Mrs Liam O'Connor, cheered her progress. The piermaster was there in person to open the lock gates, serious-faced, for it was a serious business, but winking at the lovely girl who leaned against her new husband as he steered the sailing ship expertly to her berth. They made a handsome couple, she and her new husband, and their happiness and joy, not only in the vessel but in each other shone out like the Rock Ferry Lighthouse on a dark night.

The crew were smart in their new ganseys and drill trousers, Johnno smirking and red-faced with satisfaction, for it was nearly seven years since he had sailed with Mrs O'Connor's pa in this very ship. It seemed strange to call her Mrs O'Connor, for he could still see that small girl, her own face rosy with excitement, standing before her pa with her hands on the wheel, believing that she was steering *Lily-Jane* up the channel towards the mouth of the river. He could remember Mr Porter's face, his expression of deep disapproval, but the new captain did not look disapproving, in fact his eyes shone with something so deep and loving Johnno felt compelled to look away in guilt as though he were prying into something private.

Tommy shouted orders, first to Johnno and then to the men on the dock, bobbing and weaving about the deck as though he were sixteen instead of sixty, everywhere at once in his efforts to bring the vessel in to his captain's satisfaction. He thought he had died and gone to heaven, he told his mates in the ale-house later, for until the child, meaning Mrs O'Connor, had come into his life he had thought he was beached.

Granny Earnshaw said she was going to miss them, since she had had Lily and then Liam with her for almost six months, but her friend Mrs Quinn was going to come over and stay with her for a few days so that would be very pleasant. Mrs Quinn was not at all settled in her daughter's house, for she was used to her own ways, and Victoria, though a good girl and a splendid housekeeper, was not prepared to take advice from her mother. There it was, that was the younger generation for you and, no doubt, when the time came, meaning when the babies came, for come they surely would, Lily would want her own place too. A bride likes to have supreme domestic authority in her own kitchen, not play second fiddle to some other woman no matter how fond.

Lily had given it no thought, looking no further than the day after tomorrow when she would set sail in *Lily-Jane* for the first time, the first of many journeys she and Liam were to take beyond the shining water of the River Mersey, and talk of houses and housekeeping and domestic doings were of no interest to her. She was to be a seaman, not a housewife. She was to be a friend, a lover, a partner to the man she loved. She had a new gansey and pea jacket, just like Tommy and Johnno, and a pair of navy blue woollen trousers made for her by the clever Miss Jenny Hardcastle, who, though astounded by the order, buckled to and designed, fitted and made it up to her customer's needs. They were all packed neatly in her old carpet bag, the one with which she had arrived on Granny's doorstep last year, along with a change of undergarments and a certain gauzy bit of nonsense trimmed with satin ribbons which Liam liked her to wear.

She wandered to the window of the bedroom she shared with Liam, her face serene and dreaming, pulling back the snowy nets and looking out over the garden, beyond the horse chestnut tree, beyond the splash of red and white where Granny's peonies, planted in a sheltered corner, blazed like a fire, where the lavender-mauve of phlox and the yellow of evening primrose rioted, to the barley field splashed by crimson poppies on the other side of the hawthorn hedge. It was all so beautiful, which was a poor word, really, to describe what was inside her, what she looked at and felt, and the day after tomorrow when—

Her dreaming thoughts were interrupted by the sound of Granny's voice coming up the stairs and when she poked her head round the doorway she was standing at the bottom with Ginger in her arms, her face somewhat flushed and querulous.

"That there 'usband o' yours 'as drunk all't milk. I know I said 'e were ter gerras much down 'him as 'e could burr I wish 'e'd tell me. I were just goin' ter give Puss a drink an' then mekk a custard tart an' now . . ."

"Granny, don't worry. Goodness me, what a to-do. I can easily slip down the lane to Newsham Farm and get some. I'll only be a minute. Liam's at Ronny Biddle's on some great and secretive errand which I am not supposed to know about, but as he's been telling me for days that there is no need for me to pack my clothes just yet I have a feeling it might be something to do with our travels."

As she spoke she was running lightly down the stairs. Granny Earnshaw had begun to smile, turning away to hide it, for she knew all about the sea chest Liam was having made for his new wife. Ronny had found a beautiful piece of mahogany which, he had told Liam, would have a finish like satin when he had done with it. There would be a lid, intricately carved with Lily's initials, L.O'C., intertwined with sailing ships and seabirds, and it would be fitted with drawers, each one lined with strong cambric. A lovely and yet eminently practical piece of luggage for any traveller.

"Yer a sharp one, Lily O'Connor, but when yer gerrit pretend ter be surprised, won't yer. 'E's that pleased wi' 'imself."

"I know, Granny, and I shall be the most surprised wife in Liverpool."

They both smiled, highly delighted, the sound of her new name on Granny's lips and the word "wife" giving them both inordinate pleasure.

"I think I'll take Villy. She hasn't had a walk today."

"She's 'ad a good run, though. She were chasin' a rabbit through th' orchard last time I seen 'er."

"Thank goodness she never catches one."

"Aye. I'm right fond of a birra rabbit but not one mangled up by that there dog."

So Villy was left behind.

As Lily passed Ronny Biddle's cottage she stopped for a moment to see if Liam was in sight but it was evident that he and Ronny were deep in consultation in Ronny's workshed. It would have been pleasant to stroll hand in hand down Upper Breck Road in the soft morning sunshine to the farm which was just across the main West Derby Road and along the rough track, but she hated to disturb him, especially as she might surprise and intrude on a moment Liam did not want her to share.

She had not stopped to put on a bonnet, nor a shawl, since it was May now and the air was warm and pleasant. She drew great breaths of it deep into her lungs, catching the fragrance of sorrel and cranesbill, of sweet Cecily and hedge parsley, which was rising in a tide as summer approached, ready to submerge the banks and hedges on the sides of the lane. Chaffinches were rattling in the hedges, searching for food and one flew up, its pinkish underside flashing for a moment in the sunshine.

She sauntered on, the milk pail in her hand, her silver pale hair glinting and gleaming, lighting to streaks of silvery gold as she moved her head from side to side. She had on the plain country dress Granny and Mrs Quinn had made for her, but round her waist she had knotted a broad scarlet ribbon with a bow at the back, the ends of which hung almost to the hem of her skirt.

She met one of the Ainsworths' boys almost at the end of the road, just where it entered West Derby Road, smiling at him with such brilliance he was quite bowled over. Well, he was almost thirteen and all females were a mystery to him, but Liam's wife was the most beautiful woman he had ever seen.

"Mornin'," Mrs O'Connor," he said to her shyly, scarcely daring to raise his eyes.

"Morning . . . Sam, isn't it?"

"Aye," he managed to gasp before dashing off towards the cottages as though the devil were at his heels.

There was a small dog-leg at the junction, turning to the right and then to the left up the farm track and the hansom cab was standing at the corner. The cab driver, perched on the seat behind the enclosed cab looked as though he had dropped off to sleep and so did the horse. It was all so still and when the woman, grey-haired and respectable-looking, opened the door and popped her head out, Lily walked towards her, smiling. It was obvious she was going to ask for directions and though Lily was not particularly conversant with the area or those who lived in it she could only be polite, couldn't she?

He watched her walk innocently towards him. He had been watching for days, patient as a beast of prey waiting for its quarry. He was crouched as far back in the hansom cab as he could get, the woman who leaned out screening him from the approaching girl, but he could still see her, her rosy, smiling face, the long stalk of her slender white neck, the lift and thrust of her young breasts, the swing of her hips, the way she placed her feet as she moved. She walked differently now, her head high and proud as she had always done, but with that sensual, graceful movement of a woman who was no longer a girl. No longer a maiden, a virgin. His heart was doing the most peculiar things, pounding and roaring in his ears, for he had waited for this moment for six long months and now it was here. Now, at last, she was almost in his grasp and though it was not quite the same as it might have been a few weeks ago, before she married that oaf, nevertheless it was a moment of triumph. He was not to be the first, which, initially, had nearly tipped him over the top in his vitriolic anger, but he had got over that since it made no difference to what he meant to do to her. She would probably put up more of a struggle since it appeared her marriage had been a love match and it quite titillated his senses to think he was to take what was another man's, and to take it against her will. He wanted her to fight him, and she would, at least in the beginning, and when she had stopped fighting he would no longer want her. For weeks, months he had watched and waited, receiving reports from the man he had hired, but the trouble was she never went out alone. In the beginning she had completely outwitted them for weeks by wearing boy's clothing and when, finally, the man he hired to follow her had cottoned on, the big chap had returned and been ill, so his man had told him, and for weeks she'd never gone over the doorstep. He was aware that the pair of them were to sail on that schooner they had somehow found the money to purchase and that if he didn't get her before then, he never would. Before long she would be pregnant, there was no doubt of that, for that was what the working classes did. Produce children like rabbits and then it would be over for him. He wanted her, but not when she was the mother of a child. Some lout's child.

No, this was his last chance and he held his breath as she smiled up into the woman's face.

"Can I help?" she asked, something in her voice, something soft and lilting that he had never heard before and it sickened him for *he* had put it there.

"Pardon?" the woman beside him said. "I'm a little hard of hearing, dear."

"I asked if I could help." Lily raised her voice.

"Ah, yes, I'm looking for someone called Huggett. Now I know they live somewhere on West Derby Road but this driver doesn't seem to have an ounce of sense in his head. Now, dear, have you heard of them?"

"Well, unfortunately, I don't know the—"

"Speak up, dear, I can't hear you. See, put your foot up on the step so that you can get a bit closer."

Lily did as she was told. "I said," she began patiently, then, like a devil from the pits of hell, *he* was there, the nightmare figure she had prayed never to see again, leering over the old woman's shoulder, his eyes wide with what she knew was madness. Hands pulled her in over the woman's lap, his hands and the woman's hands, and before she could scream her fear and loathing he had yelled to the cabbie to move on at once. The man urged the horse forward, the cab began to rock and though she fought like a demon, terror lending her strength, a pad was pressed over her face, blinding her, choking her, filling her head with mist. She struggled for a second or two, doing her best to defend herself but the pad was heavily impregnated with ether and she fell, swiftly and with a roaring in her ears that filled her with despair, into an empty, echoing black hole.

* * *

She had been gone for an hour when Granny began to worry. Puss had been twining round her legs, begging for her milk, and in the end Eva had gone next door to beg a saucerful off Sadie, for the dratted animal was a nuisance. Villy came back, a dejected look on her face, for her nose had been on the rabbit's white scut when it disappeared down its hole. She flopped down by the hearth after first looking about her for Lily, morosely staring into the flames of the fire.

"She's norrere so there's no use lookin' for 'er," Eva told her sharply, "an' if she's not back wi' that there milk soon it'll be too late fer't custard. An' after I've told our Liam 'e were to 'ave one, an' all. God knows wharr 'e'll get ter eat on that there boat an' 'e still needs feedin' up. I'll not be 'appy till I see another couple o' stone on 'im, an' that's the truth."

Her face brightened. "I bet she's stopped off at Ronny's, the little minx, an' after I told 'er I needed milk special. I'll box 'er ears fer 'er, see if I don't, worryin' me like this."

Leaving the front door open, she trudged off down the lane until she reached the last, or first, depending on which way you were approaching, cottage in the row. Pushing open the lopsided gate, wondering why it was that whatever his trade might be a man never seemed to be troubled with what needed doing in his own home. Ronny was a carpenter and yet there were loose window frames, doors hanging skew-whiff, this gate which was ready to come off its hinges, so it seemed, and many other jobs that he was just going to get round to, or so he told his Elsie.

The two men had their heads together over the chest lid which was on the bench. They were agreeing amiably that Ronny had never done a finer bit of work and as soon as the lid was on Liam would come and fetch it and bring Ronny's money.

"Look at this, Gran," he said, taking her arm and guiding her towards the bench, but it seemed Gran wasn't interested, not one little bit, and for a moment Ronny looked offended.

"Never mind chest. 'Ave yer seen our Lily?" she asked abruptly, pulling away from Liam and both men gawped.

"Lily?' Liam asked, as though he didn't know who she meant and Granny wondered again on the daftness of the male sex.

"Yes, Lily. Yer wife, yer big lug. 'Ave yer seen 'er?" She did her best to keep the fear out of her voice, and really, should she be surprised by Liam's confusion? He knew nothing of what had happened to his wife before Christmas for the simple reason Lily had been afraid to tell him. She had confided to Eva that when they reached Ireland, putting the Irish Sea between them and Joshua Crowther, she would tell him, for it would mean that it would be a week before Liam could get at him and perhaps in that time he might have calmed down and she would perhaps be able to persuade him to let it go. She was safe and unharmed and it was unlikely the law would look kindly on a man who killed, or at the very least, maimed another because he had made an improper advance, or so she would imply it had been, to the woman who was now his wife. Six months and they would want to know why he had waited until now. Well, Granny knew what she meant, didn't she, and Granny did.

But where was she now? Ten minutes, or perhaps fifteen for the round trip to the farm and here it was an hour later and her not back. She may have stopped to talk to the dairymaid but dairymaids were hard worked and had not the time to stop and gossip with customers, had they? She should have been back here at least half an hour ago.

She said so, her voice high and beginning to crack with terror and Liam rose slowly from where he was leaning on the bench.

"Gran?" he asked her, her fear beginning to reach out to him. He gripped her forearms so tightly she winced, trying to pull away from him and Ronny Biddle was heard to remonstrate, for the old lady was clearly in great distress.

"'E's gorrer. Dear sweet Jesus, that bugger's gorrer an' it were me what sent 'er for't milk."

"Milk? Who's gorrer? Whar yer talkin' about?" he began to stammer, lapsing into his old way of speaking in his alarm. He started to shake her, his face as white as the milk Granny had sent Lily for. Her head flopped about on her neck and she began to weep.

"'Ere, lad, give over," Ronny told him, doing his best to rescue the old lady from her grandson's frantic grasp, but Liam clipped him under the chin with his elbow and he fell back against the bench, biting his tongue.

"Tell me . . . tell me or I'll kill you," he was saying to his own grandmother, spittle spraying her, his face so close to hers their noses were touching.

"Liam, lad . . . I'm sorry . . . I'll never forgive meself if owt . . . Oh, please, dear Lord, keep 'er safe . . . don't lerrim 'urt 'er."

"*Where is she, you stupid old woman?*" Liam was so far gone in his frantic fear – he didn't know what of – that he was saying dreadful things, doing dreadful things, and to an old woman who loved him and whom he loved and who could not defend herself against him. "'Oo is it? 'Oo's gorrer? What's bin goin' on? Wharr 'appened while I was away? Tell me or I'll break yer bloody neck."

He was shouting so loudly that a crowd had begun to gather at Ronny's gate, women mostly, for the men were at work, but a passing carter had stopped, and the postman, who was just making his third delivery of the day, peered over his shoulder.

"Fer Christ's sake, gerrin 'ere," Ronny yelled at them and after a moment's hesitation they came, appalled to see Liam O'Connor apparently trying to strangle his own grandmother.

"Gerrold of 'im," Ronny screeched at the two men, hanging on for dear life to Liam's arm while the woman managed to snatch Eva from her grandson's stranglehold. He fought the three men to get to her again, just as though she were the one who had done something dreadful to the woman he loved, but he was weakening, sense coming back, his mind beginning to shape itself into thought and reason.

"Fer God's sake, Gran . . ." He was almost sobbing. "What the hell is it that's got yer so terrified? Who are yer talking about? What yer sayin? Where's Lily gone? Fer pity's sake . . ."

Eva trembled against Sadie's shoulder, but she was beginning to get a control of the terrible fear that had consumed her, a fear that had communicated itself to Liam. She knew Liam must get over to Oakwood Place – if that was where he'd taken her. How where they to know? Sweet Jesus . . . so she must tell him the story at once, for there was no time to be lost.

"Joshua Crowther." Her voice was like ice and those crowded about them in Ronny Biddle's workshed gasped. "She 'ad ter run away . . . that's why she were 'ere wi' me.

You told 'er if she were in trouble she were ter come ter me, so she did. 'E'd tried ter . . . interfere wi' 'er after 'er mam died."

Liam tossed his head from side to side like an animal tormented beyond endurance and a roar of violent rage echoed about the shed. The postman and the carter, who really should be getting about their business, could not bear to tear themselves away.

"She dressed as a lad ter ge' down ter't docks ter see ter't *Lily-Jane*; there were a chap lookin' for 'er, Crowther's chap, I were told by someone I know but Crowther's lad, 'is son what were a soldier, 'elped 'er, gorrus somewhere safe ter stay until . . . then when you come 'ome she never left th'ouse so . . ."

"Why didn't yer tell me then I could 'ave protected 'er?" he asked her, his voice totally without expression. He had his head in his hands as though he had just been hit by a brick and couldn't, somehow, get coherent thoughts together, and never would, but there was something to be done and only he could do it and if it was too late he would kill him, the man who had tried to violate his little love, perhaps had even succeeded by now. He could not bear it and when he got hold of him, even if . . . oh, please, God . . . please, God, even if she was unhurt he would knock him to the ground and kick him until the blood ran, then pick him up and start all over again.

He looked up and the suffering and anguish on his face had Sadie Ainsworth in tears and even Ronny felt a prickle at the back of his eyes. He'd always been fond of his Elsie and she of him but what this man felt and suffered for his new wife was beyond his comprehension and he was glad, for the pain of it was surely too much for one man to bear.

Liam stood up and without another word strode out of the shed. When he reached the gate, pushing past the curious onlookers, he crossed the road and with no effort leaped the hedge, then began to run across the field, moving in a straight line from Upper Breck Road to Oakwood Place.

"Go wi' 'im, Ronny," Elsie said to her husband. Ronny was a big man, not as big as Liam, nor as fit, but surely a helping hand; even a bit of moral support would not go amiss.

"I'll borrow Ernie Jenkin's mare," he told them, as though it needed explaining. "I can't run all't way ter – where was it?

– Oakwood Place or I'd be no use ter anyone by't time I got there. Tell me 'ow ter get there, Mrs Earnshaw, will yer?"

The hansom cab turned into the gateway between the two stone posts and drove up the gravelled driveway, stopping at the steps that led up to the front door. Ted Diggle, who was by the front flowerbed on his knees, shaded his eyes, for the sun was in them, then sat back. He and Will were putting in the summer bedding plants, a slow, pleasant task in the midday sunshine, and they both wondered who was calling in a hansom cab. Carriages were the order of the day in the society Mr Crowther moved in.

The front door opened, for Maggie was trained to be on hand at once to see to callers, of which this must be one. She nodded pleasantly at Mr Diggle then stood smiling on the top step, waiting to receive the visitor.

She was totally bemused when the master climbed down, for he had his own carriage in the stable yard so what on earth was he doing in a hired conveyance? She watched him in astonishment as he paid the cab driver then reached back inside the cab and with little effort dragged out a limp figure, a tall young woman, arranging her to his liking across his arms. Her own arms dangled lifelessly and her head hung back, her throat arched and Maggie noticed she wore only one boot. She stood, frozen in horror as she recognised the recently married bride whom she herself had seen wed to the big, handsome sailor only a few weeks ago. Lily, their Lily, Lily Elliott who was now Lily O'Connor.

Putting her hand to her mouth she began to back away, her eyes wide with terror, watching as Mr Crowther turned to the cab driver again, baring his teeth in what was meant to be a smile.

"My daughter," he said. "She's been taken ill so I've brought her home to be nursed."

A small moan escaped from between Maggie's lips and both Mr Diggle and Will stood up uncertainly, sensing something was wrong but not quite knowing what it was, or if they did, how to deal with it.

The cab driver watched his passenger climb the steps, the figure of the girl in his arms. She'd not looked ill to him when she'd walked towards his cab. Far from it, for a handsomer young woman he had yet to see. The old woman had been dropped off at the end of West Derby Road and he himself had been paid and given a good tip so this was nowt to do with him. Besides, there was a respectable housemaid at the door so it must be all right. He clucked to his horse and the cab moved off slowly.

Joshua Crowther strode past his maidservant with that arrogant indifference of his class to those beneath it. He held Lily close to his chest, cuddling her, Maggie wildly thought, and if she was not mistaken her clothing was already disarranged so . . . Jesus . . . Oh, sweet God in heaven . . .

She watched him climb the stairs, his face close to Lily's, then, with a soft cry, she leaped down the steps, almost falling in her haste, and across the lawn to where Mr Diggle and Will stood.

Grabbing Will by the shirt she began to shake him. "Run for Mrs Quinn, Will. Run, lad, fetch Mrs Quinn and a couple of the men from the yard. Run like you've never run before . . . run . . ."

Will ran.

34

Unlike his wife who had kept to roads and lanes as she moved through the dark towards his grandmother's cottage six months ago, he ran in as straight a line as he could manage towards the river where Oakwood Place stood. Like a greyhound just left the slips he went past Newsham Farm where the dairymaid, who was carrying churns across the yard, stopped and stared as he flashed by her. Fields of growing hay and corn and oats and barley were churned through, leaving a track where his flight had taken him and where men, mouths open, gaped at him in amazement, for didn't he know he could damage crops flinging himself about like that. One shouted after him and shook his fist but Liam O'Connor saw none of them, for he had one picture in his mind's eye and it was consuming him with terror. His wife, his lovely bride who came to him every night with such passion and tenderness, the love and treasure of his life, the heart and soul of him, beneath the ravaging hands and body of another man, a perverted man, a madman, surely? The image of it was ready to destroy him and he wanted to stop and scream his rage and fear, shaking his fists at whoever it was up there who had allowed this to happen, but he must go on, and on, and on though his heart was bursting in his chest and his breath rasping in his throat so that it was rubbed raw.

Across Edge Lane, almost careering into a slow plodding waggon loaded with barrels. The horses pulling it shied with terror and the driver hauled on the reins and the whole lot of them nearly ended up in the ditch at the side of the lane but it is doubtful Liam even saw them. He was aware that there were obstacles in his path but he couldn't go round them so he would leap them or knock them down to get to his love who was in the worst danger any woman can be.

He fell down time and again, catching his feet in rabbit holes, on rocks and branches from trees rotting at the edge of fields since winter, picking himself up and flinging himself on without a break in the rhythm of his running.

He ran across the lines of the London and North Western Railway almost under the engine of an oncoming train, unaware of the repeated hoot of the whistle the angry engine driver directed at him.

Through a stretch of woodland that edged Wavertree Road, blundering into trees and catching his bare arms on brambles, the blood beginning to flow, for he had gashed his forehead on a sharp branch. It dripped down his face and on to his shirt but he was not concerned, crossing the road and plunging across more fields in which cows grazed. They backed away as he flew past them, turning their anxious gaze after him as he prepared to leap a hedge as high as himself and when it proved impossible, simply tearing through it and into an orchard which was an enchanting haze of apple blossom. His head and shoulders caught branches and the blossom showered down on him and at the far end the farmer's wife, who was hanging out her washing, let out a shriek piercing enough to wake the dead.

He raced passed her and the neat farmhouse like the wind, his legs pumping, his chest labouring, his face on fire, his eyes blank and unfocused and at last he reached Holmes Lane.

Even here he did not continue along it to Beech Lane, at the end of which was Oakwood Place, but ran in a straight line through the extensive and immaculate gardens of Silverdale and Ladymeadow, both houses belonging to prominent men of business in Liverpool. Gardeners shouted after him, one of them threatening to fetch his gun, but like an arrow from a bow, direct and true, he came to the gates of Oakwood Place.

He began to shout her name as he pounded up the drive and Mr Diggle, who, with Will, and, surprisingly, two small children, was hanging about by the front door, caring nothing for niceties, waiting for word, watched him helplessly as he ran straight at the closed door, going through it like a bull charging a gate.

"Lily . . . Lily . . . Dear God . . . dear God, where is she? Where is she? Lily," he was screaming, twisting and turning in the hall like a cornered beast. He was too late, he knew he was. It was so quiet. He had not run fast enough. His strength had not been up to it. His illness had weakened him and Mrs Quinn, coming down the stairs towards him, her face wrenched by some dreadful thing, watched as he looked up at her, then sank hopelessly to his knees.

Mrs Quinn had been just about to rebuke her eldest grandson, a little beggar if ever she saw one and far too cheeky for his own good, when the gardener's lad burst into Victoria's kitchen without even the pretence of a knock, flinging back the door so violently she, young Jimmy and his brother Eddy all cowered back, thinking the hordes of China were at the gates.

He couldn't speak. For several wasted moments he remained bent over with his hands on his knees, his head hanging down as the breath laboured in his lungs and the words tried to get out. He was wet through with sweat, even under his thatch of hair and when at last he managed to lift his head and look at her, the expression in his eyes terrified her.

"Wha'? Wha'? Dear God, lad, wharrisit?" She thrust the two small boys, who had begun to cry, behind her as though it might be Will who was the threat but he gasped and floundered, clutching at the tiny mouthful of breath he had managed to retrieve from somewhere.

"Miss . . . Lily . . ."

"Lily . . . *Our* Lily . . . wha' . . . ?"

"Maggie ses . . . ter come . . ."

"Why . . . why, what's 'appened?"

In her terror she gripped his shirt collar and forced his head up, her face up close to his, shaking him, and he was a big lad, shaking him until she got the truth from him which she could see was going to be horrific.

"Lad, for God's sake, wharrisit . . . please?"

"The master's gorrer . . . Maggie ses ter come an' fetch a couple o' men."

For a moment she couldn't take it in. The master had got her. What sort of nonsense was that? Lily was married now and as safe as houses with her new husband up at his grandmother's cottage and if there was anything dafter than the idea that Liam O'Connor would allow any harm to come to his lovely and adored young wife, then Molly Quinn had yet to hear it. She had been there only yesterday to say goodbye to them and wish them well on their trip, promising to keep an eye on Eva; in fact she and Eva had decided that she should stay there while they were away. But this . . . this . . . what . . . ?

"Will, talk sense, lad."

Will had got his breath back now. "'E come in a cab, Mrs Quinn, an' 'e 'ad Miss Lily in 'is arms. All of a drift, she were."

"Adrift?"

"Aye, senseless wi' 'er 'ead all over 't place an' 'er lovely arms just 'angin' down." He gulped, clearly agonised by what he had witnessed. "Me an' Mr Diggle saw it wi' our own eyes. Oh, please come, Mrs Quinn. T'others're frightened of 'im, burrif yer fetch Arnold an'—"

"Watch them bairns," she shrieked as she lifted her skirts and began to run across the rough grass that stretched between Victoria and Arnold's cottage and the woodland surrounding the house. Beyond were the orchards, the paddocks in which fine horses grazed, the vegetable gardens, the stable, the stable yard, the kitchen yard and the entrance to the kitchen. Her face was mottled quite dangerously with white and red streaks, for Molly Quinn was no longer a young woman, and besides which the rage boiling up inside her threatened to break out of every pore.

She crashed through the kitchen door like some avenging warrior woman, her shield before her, her spear ready to thrust itself into the enemy's wicked heart. Her hair had come loose in her frantic dash and it streamed about her face and down her back, grey and yet writhing with life.

"Where is 'e?" she snarled, so that even the women, who were all weeping, their aprons to their faces, recoiled away from her. She was a terrifying sight and Mrs Kelly had a moment to think the master had better watch out, for he'd met his match in Molly Quinn. Jenny was hiccuping softly in the chimney corner and Rosie was patting her shoulder, telling her it would be all right and she wasn't to upset herself, just as though Jenny were the only one in tears. The rest were grouped together as though there might be safety in numbers. They could none of them speak, it seemed, they were so terrified, even Maggie, who had had the presence of mind to send for the one person who was not afraid of their master. They were not even sure what was to happen. Perhaps the master had found their Miss Lily ill by the roadside and had brought her home for her own good and if that was the truth of it they dare not interfere, for this was his house and they were his servants and what would he do to them if they tried to intervene? They didn't know, but then neither did they really believe that was the case, but Mrs Quinn would be needed either way, wouldn't she and besides, she no longer worked for him. He was a powerful man in Liverpool, with friends in high places and they, his servants, were the underclasses with no powers to speak of, taught to look up to their betters, to wait on them and keep their traps shut.

Maggie pointed towards the door that led to the front of the house with a trembling finger. As Molly turned, ready to race towards it and up the stairs, ready to knock the bloody door down with her own female and elderly strength, Arnold came through the kitchen door behind her with Will at his back. Under each arm Will carried a small, struggling child, the older one shouting that his dad would fight Will if he didn't put him down at once.

"Where?" Arnold asked, his face like a mask, an iron mask, but underneath it was the horror of a decent man who abhors violence against a defenceless woman and from what he'd been told by Will Miss Lily was in great danger. Behind them were Jimmy and Mr Bentley, both of them ready to batter and bruise any man who would harm the child of the mistress they had all loved.

Molly did not speak but flew out of the kitchen door, along the passage to the foot of the stairs and was up them like a whippet after a rabbit, Arnold close on her heels and, behind him, Jimmy and Mr Bentley.

Straight to the closed door of Joshua Crowther's room she led them since, being outdoor men who had no reason to come inside, they did not know the way.

"Knock it down," she hissed, giving Jimmy a clip across his ear when he would have hesitated, for this was his master's bedroom door, or so he presumed, and the habit of obedience to his master's will was strong in him.

He had laid her on the bed and was just pulling her

pretty lace chemise over her head, the one she wore to please her husband whom she loved. Her dress with the glowing red ribbon lay on the floor and so did her three full white cotton petticoats. Her drawers, again edged with lace, had been drawn down to her knees and the centre of her, the full sweet bush that hid the centre of her womanhood, was dark against the whiteness of her belly.

He turned as they all four crashed through the door, jammed for a moment in the opening, then, as Mrs Quinn launched herself at him, he stood up straight, his face twisting in a grimace of amazement.

"What the devil d'you think you're doing?" he snarled, catching her wrists and flinging her back against the three men. "How dare you break in here, and you three, get out, d'you hear? You'll lose your jobs over this," spitting his venom at the three men, who, with the habit of a life's bowing to authority ingrained in them, began to hesitate, despite the almost naked figure of the woman on the bed. His class's supremacy over them and every man in the land like them was so absolute that almost automatically they fell back before him.

"Get out of this room before I send for the law." His arrogance, his absolute belief in his own authority and power to do as he pleased in his own home, his total unconcern for anything beyond his own gratification, made him a formidable figure. He came from generations of privilege and his rage that these servants of his had had the temerity to break into his bedroom was supreme, but Mrs Quinn cared nothing for that. She was beyond the point where reason or thought or fear for her own future or even life might matter and she launched herself at him again, aiming for his eyes, lifting her knee as she had seen women do in Brooke Alley when defending themselves against predatory males.

"Yer filthy beast," she screamed and down in the kitchen the maids cowered against one another and her two grandchildren, recognising her voice, began to cry.

"You'll pay for this, woman," Joshua Crowther screeched, his face flooded with bright red blood, clutching at the spot between his legs where her knee had connected. "You'll be in Walton Gaol by nightfall and I shall personally see that you spend the rest of your life there."

"Yer mad . . . insane. D'yer think yer can . . . can do this

to that girl on't 'ed, like yer did to 'er ma, an' gerraway wi'
it? See, Arnold, gerrold of 'im. Don't just 'ang about, yer daft
lummox, gerrold of 'im."

They came to their senses then, avoiding the pitiful sight
of the girl on the bed, advancing on him with the slitted eyes
and knotted fists of men who have seen enough and do not
like it, and even before they had touched him something
exploded like a live shell inside him, blowing the safety
valves, rushing like a swollen maddened river to his brain
and as they watched in astonishment he dropped to the
floor as if poleaxed.

Mrs Quinn, beside herself, no longer in control of anything
that might be called sense, let alone herself, began to kick at
his lifeless figure where it sprawled by the bed, obscenities
that she had learned in Brooke Alley pouring from her mouth.
In her mindless fury her lamb was, for the moment, forgotten
and it was Mr Bentley who hastily threw a blanket over the
senseless figure of their Lily. After that first appalled look,
unable to believe the evidence of their own eyes, they had
shifted their gaze away, for they were, though not gentlemen,
decent men and the sight of the child – no longer a child,
of course – unconscious and almost naked on the master's
bed was more then they could handle.

"Mrs Quinn, see to the child," Mr Bentley told her sternly.
The words reached her maddened brain and though she was
still breathing heavily, at once she turned away from
Joshua Crowther, herself again and ready to take charge if
anything of a . . . a . . . nasty nature had taken place. He had
been up here with Lily for almost fifteen minutes in which
the worst could have happened, but then she was not to
know of Joshua Crowther's strange proclivities, his dreaming
contemplation of what he had hungered for for nearly a year,
and even before his wife died, if he was honest. She did not
know of the festering plans he had harboured in his mind
for Lily and it did not entail a quick rape but a lingering,
bestial ravaging, lasting hours, days, in fact for as long as it
suited him. As he had done with her mother. He was out of
his mind, of course, quite, quite mad, for how did he think
he could get away with kidnapping another man's wife and
keeping her in his house? A house filled with servants who
knew exactly what was happening and, eventually, when
they regained their courage, would send for the husband

not to mention the police. He was mad. Out of his mind and she'd see him in a lunatic asylum where he belonged, Mrs Quinn was telling herself as she pulled up Lily's drawers – discreetly beneath the blanket, of course – then tucked the blanket about her neck with careful, comforting hands. She loved this girl, just as she had loved her mother and, by God, he'd be made to pay for this.

The strange silence behind her at last caught her attention. She was on her knees beside the bed, smoothing back Lily's hair, thanking God that the child had known nothing about it. She was heavily drugged and one of the men must ride for the doctor at once but there was something wrong, something unusual going on – or not going on – at her back, and when she turned enquiringly, expecting to see Mr Crowther glowering at her as the men pulled him to his feet she was surprised to see him still in exactly the same position into which he had fallen. She didn't know why. No one had laid a finger on him but despite that he was still lolling on the floor, his arms and legs all over the place, his face in the light from the window drawn up into what looked like a mask of agony. The three men were grouped about him, staring down in growing fear and when Mr Bentley turned away and walked slowly to the door she knew at once that Joshua Crowther was dead.

"Ride for't doctor, Arnold, there's a good lad, while I get Lily decent."

The men left the room, Arnold patting her shoulder reassuringly for a moment as though to tell her there were nothing to fear. As if she cared. She'd gladly swing for him if it meant her Lily was safe. In fact for two pins she'd spit on him, on his dead body for all the pain and misery he had brought to both her lambs.

She settled herself in a low chair by the bed to watch over Lily, for the child would be afraid when she woke. She was very pale but her heartbeat was steady. Mrs Quinn had put her ear to her chest to listen to it and she watched the slow rise and fall of her breast, never taking her eyes from the girl who had become more precious to her than her own daughters.

When she heard the crash of the front door, and the loud, harsh voice, though she couldn't think why he was making such a commotion, she moved to the head of the stairs to meet the doctor, beginning to walk down them. She was just in time to see Liam O'Connor sink to his knees.

She came to just as dusk was falling, wondering why her head was thumping like a steam engine and her mouth was so dry but she was not concerned, for she was in her husband's arms and what could be safer and more comforting than that. They were lying on a bed, a strange bed in a strange room and not their comfortable brass-ended bed at home, she knew that, although she had not yet opened her eyes. It didn't matter. As long as Liam was with her, whether in the depths of darkest Africa, the wilds of the tropical jungles, the vast dry wastes of the Sahara, if Liam was with her it was all right.

She must have moved and made a small noise, for at once Liam's arms tightened about her, so tight, in fact, he was hurting her.

"Lovebud," he said. His voice was hoarse as though he had a sore throat and at once she sat up in his arms, for always in the back of her mind was the terror that his illness would return. She peered at him in the gloom, for the room was lit only by a cheerfully crackling fire in the grate.

She put a hand on his forehead. "Are you coming down with a cold?" she asked him accusingly and was seriously frightened when he began to weep. Now that she had got a good look at him she could see blood on his face and shirt and his arms were a mass of bruises and scratches as though he had crawled through a wilderness.

"Liam . . . Liam, dearest, what is it?" she begged him in an agony of love, pulling him to her so that his wet face was pressed into the curve of her neck.

"Jesus . . . Jesus, if I had lost you I would have run mad," he said, amazingly. She stared at him in wonder then looked about her and was further amazed to find that she and Liam were lying on her bed in what had been her room when she had lived at Oakwood Place. A pleasant room, warm, airy, comfortable, elegantly furnished but a room where she had known nothing but worry and dread and fear, first for her mother and then for herself. A room she had left six months ago and had hoped never to see again and now here she was, she and Liam, lying in one another's arms as though it were quite the most normal thing to do.

Suddenly the face of the madman sprang out at her in all

its terror, looming over the shoulder of a woman . . . hands . . . hands pulling at her, holding her and something pressed over her face. She began to twist and turn in an effort to escape it, and him.

"Liam," she began to scream in a high voice, the voice of a child lost with the bogeyman on her heels, but at once Liam's arms closed round her and at once she was safe.

"He's gone, lovebud," he murmured into her hair. "He's finally gone . . . for ever."

She sat up in renewed terror, her hair falling in a tangle about her pale face, her eyes huge and terrified.

"You've . . . not you, Liam. You've not . . . ?"

"No, not me, my darling, though I would have done if . . . It seems he has had some sort of apoplexy. The men were here . . ."

"The men?"

"Aye, Mrs Quinn's Arnold and two others come to help you but not one of them laid a hand on him. The doctor's been and gone."

"And . . ." She could not seem to get the words out, the dreadful words that would reveal what had happened to her while she had been unconscious.

"And . . . me?" She hung her head as though in shame, but he lifted her chin, cupping her face and kissing her, smoothing her cheek with his thumbs as his eyes told her what she wanted to know.

"Not you, lovebud. You . . . you are totally mine."

They left soon after, driven in the carriage by Arnold, her and Liam and Mrs Quinn, who seemed unable to let her lamb out of her sight again. The servants in the kitchen had embraced Lily quite tearfully when she went down, looking, Jenny said, just as she always did, as though attempted rape must surely change a woman for ever. Of course, she had been unconscious, Maggie had told them all, and of them all, had been the least aware of what was happening, which was just as well, for the master was a frightening man. *Had been* a frightening man, for his body was laid out on the bed in his room where he had tried to . . . well, the least said about that the better, Maggie told them firmly, looking at Jenny's big eyes and trembling mouth. None of them knew what was to happen to them now but with Captain Crowther coming home, summoned by the telegram telling him his father was dead, perhaps their positions were safe. They did hope so, for good jobs were hard to come by.

And wasn't it lovely the way the bairn had been with Miss Lily? It was as if she knew who she was, which was a bit fanciful but she'd put her plump little arms round Miss Lily's neck and pressed her rosy mouth to her cheek, just as Dorcas had taught her. An affectionate little thing and though they were not sure what was to become of her she would be all right now. Either with Miss Lily who was her sister or Captain Crowther who was her brother, and as different to his father as chalk to cheese.

Miss Lily and that handsome husband of hers were off to Ireland themselves the day after tomorrow, so she had told them over a cup of tea while he sat beside her holding her hand as though he must touch her and watch over her even in the safety of the kitchen. Lovely chap, he was and he had told them himself that Miss Abby would never want for a . . . well, he had been going to say father, you could tell, and then Miss Lily had turned and kissed him, right in front of them all, before saying goodbye and climbing into the carriage, telling them she'd see them in ten days' time, promise.

The lovely ship, her sails filled with a hatful of wind, raced towards the mouth of the river, taking advantage of the tide, her captain steering her expertly through the dozens of others who were doing the same. There was a clipper ship off to the far east for the exotic things available nowhere else, whose sails had her flying faster than any of them; several schooners like their own, sailing to Furness or North Wales, small, full-bodied merchant sailing ships with complex rigging, paddle-steamers, four-masted barques and all making for the broad mouth of the River Mersey. Frigates and brigantines and for a moment Lily was taken back to that day nearly seven years ago when she had leaned against her pa on this very same ship. Then she had gazed back at the hazed morning skyline of Liverpool, a small child caught up in the excitement of entering an adult's world, dreaming about the day when she would sail this ship, be a seaman like Pa had been.

Now she was a woman and understood that the dream was no more than that, a dream. Today she would sail through the wide estuary at the mouth of the river towards Liverpool Bay, her back against the broad, safe chest of her husband, his left arm about her while the right guided his ship. For as long as she was allowed she would accompany him but she had other responsibilities now and must give up her dream when the time came. She was not sure how long it would last, this freedom of the sea but when it ended this man would always come back to her, wherever she was.

She would always be waiting.